THE YEAR'S BEST

SCIENCE FICTION

ALSO BY GARDNER DOZOIS

ANTHOLOGIES

A DAY IN THE LIFE

ANOTHER WORLD

BEST SCIENCE FICTION STORIES OF THE
 YEAR #6–10

THE BEST OF ISAAC ASIMOV'S SCIENCE
 FICTION MAGAZINE

TIME-TRAVELERS FROM ISAAC ASIMOV'S
 SCIENCE FICTION MAGAZINE

TRANSCENDENTAL TALES FROM ISAAC
 ASIMOV'S SCIENCE FICTION MAGAZINE

ISAAC ASIMOV'S ALIENS

ISAAC ASIMOV'S MARS

ISAAC ASIMOV'S SF-LITE

ISAAC ASIMOV'S WAR

ROADS NOT TAKEN (with Stanley Schmidt)

THE YEAR'S BEST SCIENCE FICTION, #1–27

FUTURE EARTHS: UNDER AFRICAN SKIES
 (with Mike Resnick)

FUTURE EARTHS: UNDER SOUTH
 AMERICAN SKIES (with Mike Resnick)

RIPPER! (with Susan Casper)

MODERN CLASSIC SHORT NOVELS OF
 SCIENCE FICTION

MODERN CLASSICS OF FANTASY

KILLING ME SOFTLY

DYING FOR IT

THE GOOD OLD STUFF

THE GOOD NEW STUFF

EXPLORERS

THE FURTHEST HORIZON

WORLDMAKERS

SUPERMEN

COEDITED WITH SHEILA WILLIAMS

ISAAC ASIMOV'S PLANET EARTH

ISAAC ASIMOV'S ROBOTS

ISAAC ASIMOV'S VALENTINES

ISAAC ASIMOV'S SKIN DEEP

ISAAC ASIMOV'S GHOSTS

ISAAC ASIMOV'S VAMPIRES

ISAAC ASIMOV'S MOONS

ISAAC ASIMOV'S CHRISTMAS

ISAAC ASIMOV'S CAMELOT

ISAAC ASIMOV'S WEREWOLVES

ISAAC ASIMOV'S SOLAR SYSTEM

ISAAC ASIMOV'S DETECTIVES

ISAAC ASIMOV'S CYBERDREAMS

COEDITED WITH JACK DANN

ALIENS!	SORCERERS!	DRAGONS!	HACKERS
UNICORNS!	DEMONS!	HORSES!	TIMEGATES
MAGICATS!	DOGTALES!	UNICORNS 2	CLONES
MAGICATS 2!	SEASERPENTS!	INVADERS!	NANOTECH
BESTIARY!	DINOSAURS!	ANGELS!	IMMORTALS
MERMAIDS!	LITTLE PEOPLE!	DINOSAURS 2	

FICTION

STRANGERS

THE VISIBLE MAN (collection)

NIGHTMARE BLUE
 (with George Alec Effinger)

SLOW DANCING THROUGH TIME
 (with Jack Dann, Michael Swanwick,
 Susan Casper, and Jack C. Haldeman II)

THE PEACEMAKER

GEODESIC DREAMS (collection)

NONFICTION

THE FICTION OF JAMES TIPTREE, JR.

THE YEAR'S BEST

SCIENCE FICTION

twenty-eighth annual collection

edited by **Gardner Dozois**

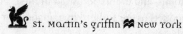 st. martin's griffin ✖ new york

These stories are works of fiction. All of the characters,
organizations, and events portrayed in these stories are
either products of the authors' imaginations or are used
fictitiously.

www.stmartins.com

ISBN 978-0-312-56950-1 (trade paperback)
ISBN 978-0-312-54633-5 (hardcover)

First Edition: July 2011

10 9 8 7 6 5 4 3 2 1

contents

ACKNOWLEDGMENTS — *xi*

SUMMATION: 2010 — *xiii*

A HISTORY OF TERRAFORMING • *Robert Reed* — 1

THE SPONTANEOUS KNOTTING OF AN AGITATED STRING • *Lavie Tidhar* — 39

THE EMPEROR OF MARS • *Allen M. Steele* — 43

THE THINGS • *Peter Watts* — 58

THE SULTAN OF THE CLOUDS • *Geoffrey A. Landis* — 72

THE BOOKS • *Kage Baker* — 108

RE-CROSSING THE STYX • *Ian R. MacLeod* — 119

AND MINISTERS OF GRACE • *Tad Williams* — 132

MAMMOTHS OF THE GREAT PLAINS • *Eleanor Arnason* — 154

SLEEPING DOGS • *Joe Haldeman* — 191

JACKIE'S BOY • *Steven Popkes* — 204

FLYING IN THE FACE OF GOD • *Nina Allan* — 246

CHICKEN LITTLE • *Cory Doctorow* — 262

FLOWER, MERCY, NEEDLE, CHAIN • *Yoon Ha Lee* — 298

RETURN TO TITAN • *Stephen Baxter* — 304

UNDER THE MOONS OF VENUS • *Damien Broderick* — 354

SEVEN YEARS FROM HOME • *Naomi Novik* — 370

THE PEACOCK CLOAK • *Chris Beckett* — 392

AMARYLLIS • *Carrie Vaughn* — 405

SEVEN CITIES OF GOLD • *David Moles* — 416

AGAIN AND AGAIN AND AGAIN • *Rachel Swirsky* — 452

ELEGY FOR A YOUNG ELK • *Hannu Rajaniemi* — 455

LIBERTARIAN RUSSIA • *Michael Swanwick* — 468

THE NIGHT TRAIN • *Lavie Tidhar* — 477

MY FATHER'S SINGULARITY • *Brenda Cooper*   488

THE STARSHIP MECHANIC • *Jay Lake and Ken Scholes*   493

SLEEPOVER • *Alastair Reynolds*   499

THE TASTE OF NIGHT • *Pat Cadigan*   531

BLIND CAT DANCE • *Alexander Jablokov*   541

THE SHIPMAKER • *Aliette de Bodard*   563

IN-FALL • *Ted Kosmatka*   574

CHIMBWI • *Jim Hawkins*   582

DEAD MAN'S RUN • *Robert Reed*   599

Honorable Mentions: 2010   653

permissions

acknowledgments

The editor would like to thank the following people for their help and support: Susan Casper, Jonathan Strahan, Gordon Van Gelder, Ellen Datlow, Sean Wallace, Peter Crowther, Nicolas Gevers, William Shaffer, Ian Whates, Andy Cox, Paula Guran, Dario Ciriello, Jay Lake, Lavie Tidhar, Robert Wexler, Patrick Nielsen Hayden, Torie Atkinson, Eric T. Reynolds, George Mann, Jennifer Brehl, Peter Tennant, Susan Marie Groppi, Karen Meisner, John Joseph Adams, Wendy S. Delmater, Jed Hartman, Rich Horton, Mark R. Kelly, Andrew Wilson, Damien Broderick, Lou Anders, Patrick Swenson, Sheila Williams, Brian Bieniowski, Trevor Quachri, Robert T. Wexler, Michael Swanwick, Stephen Baxter, Kristine Kathryn Rusch, Ted Kosmatka, Cory Doctorow, Charles Ardai, Naomi Novik, Tad Williams, Deborah Beale, Otto Penzler, Jenny Blackford, Joe Haldeman, Elizabeth A. Hull, Jim Frenkel, Geoffrey A. Landis, Eleanor Arnason, L. Timmel Duchamp, Ian R. MacLeod, Hannu Rajaniemi, Allen Steele, John Jarrold, Yoon Ha Lee, David Moles, Jim Hawkins, Carrie Vaughn, Chris Beckett, Nina Allan, Ken Scholes, Alex Jablokov, James Patrick Kelly, Linn Prentis, Pat Cadigan, Liz Gorinsky, Mike Resnick, Aliette de Bodard, Rachel Swirsky, Brenda Cooper, David Rivera, Leo Korogodski, Ian Tregillis, Felicity Shoulders, Benjamin Rosenbaum, Gord Sellar, Stephen Popkes, Eric Choi, Damien Broderick, Peter Watts, Alastair Reynolds, Robert Reed, Maureen McHugh, David Hartwell, Ginjer Buchanan, Susan Allison, Shawna McCarthy, Kelly Link, Gavin Grant, John Klima, John O'Neill, Charles Tan, Rodger Turner, Tyree Campbell, Stuart Mayne, John Kenny, Edmund Schubert, Tehani Wessely, Tehani Croft, Karl Johanson, Sally Beasley, Tony Lee, Joe Vas, John Pickrell, Ian Redman, Anne Zanoni, Kaolin Fire, Ralph Benko, Paul Graham Raven, Nick Wood, Mike Allen, Jason Sizemore, Karl Johanson, Sue Miller, David Lee Summers, Christopher M. Cevasco, Tyree Campbell, Andrew Hook, Vaughne Lee Hansen, Mark Watson, Sarah Lumnah, and special thanks to my own editor, Marc Resnick.

Thanks are also due to the late, lamented Charles N. Brown, and to all his staff, whose magazine *Locus* (Locus Publications, P. O. Box 13305, Oakland, CA 94661. $60 in the United States for a one-year subscription [twelve issues] via second class; credit card orders 510-339-9198) was used as an invaluable reference source throughout the summation; *Locus Online* (www.locusmag.com), edited by Mark R. Kelly, has also become a key reference source.

The big story in 2010 was the explosion in e-book sales, something that some industry commentators have seen coming for a long time now, but which has come to a boil faster and more extensively than almost anybody predicted that it would.

This market started to accelerate in 2007, with the introduction of Amazon's Kindle, the first portable e-book reader, but the lid really blew off this year when Amazon lowered the purchase price for the Kindle down to $139, with the introduction of competing devices such as Apple's iPad and Barnes & Noble's NOOK, and with the founding of "online bookstores" by Apple, Barnes & Noble, and Google where products for these devices can be purchased. Amazon has announced that the third-generation Kindle is the bestselling product in its history, having sold "millions" (no exact figures are available) in 2010 alone, and the NOOK is similarly Barnes & Noble's biggest seller in its forty-year history; Apple's iPad—which has other functions, so it is technically a touch screen media tablet rather than an e-reader, but you can still read e-books on it, and that's probably a fairly common use for it—sold 3.27 million units in its first three months after its April 2010 release, and is projected to hit 28 million units sold in 2011. According to a survey of more than 6,000 book shoppers carried out by Codex Group, 21 percent of them now own e-readers or tablet computers.

And, of course, all these people who now own e-readers or tablet computers now want something to *read* on them.

According to Amazon, e-books are now outselling both hardcover and paperback print books—they're selling three times as many e-books as hardcovers, 180 of them for every 100 hardcovers sold, and selling 115 e-books for every 100 paperbacks sold. The Association of American Publishers estimates that from January to August of 2010, the sales of e-books were up from $166.9 million in 2009 to $441 million in 2010, an increase of 164.4 percent, which means that e-books now account for 10 percent of all consumer book sales in the United States, up from 3.31 percent in 2009. And these figures were from before the Christmas rush, which saw millions of Kindles, NOOKs, and iPads bought as Christmas presents, with the attendant purchase of e-books to read on them—Barnes & Noble alone reports nearly one million e-books purchased and downloaded just on Christmas Day. At the same time, the AAP report for October shows sales of print books down at $721 million, a 0.9 percent drop from October the year before, and the U.S. Census Bureau preliminary report for October shows bookstore sales of $1.0 billion, down 2.5 percent from October 2009; year-to-date sales were also down 2.5 percent, to $13.3 billion. When comparing print and e-book sales for the first three-quarters of 2010, AAP figures show print trade sales from the five major categories down 7.5 percent, while e-book sales rose 188.4 percent for the same period.

All this has prompted some commentators to predict a publishing apocalypse, where print books go out of existence altogether, physical brick-and-mortar bookstores become extinct, and even the publishing companies themselves die, since now that authors can put e-books together themselves and sell them on online bookstores, they have no need of publishers anymore.

I don't think that this is likely to happen. Although it's clear that e-books are cannibalizing the print book market to some extent, with some consumers opting to buy the cheaper e-books rather than the more expensive print editions, that doesn't mean that people are going to stop buying print books altogether. The fact is that more books, both print *and* digital, are being sold than ever before. Amazon may be selling 115 e-books for every 100 paperbacks sold—but they're still selling those 100 paperbacks. Amazon's Russ Grandinetti has commented that "our print business continues to grow. We see e-books as an additive more than a substitute," and Scott Lubeck of the Book Industry Study Group has pointed out that "it's good for readers, and reading is good for publishing." For the foreseeable future, a sizeable percentage of people are going to prefer print books to e-books, and browsing at physical brick-and-mortar bookstores to shopping for books online, and many writers are not going to have either the inclination or the skill set necessary to publish their own e-books themselves, even though current technology makes that possible (and a certain number *will* do just that, some successfully, some not; publishing houses won't be going away anytime soon, though). For that matter, although this is a factor not taken into consideration in most conversations of this sort, even here in the twenty-first century there are still plenty of people who don't have e-readers, don't have Internet access, don't even have computers of any sort, and to ignore them would be to abandon a considerable subset of potential customers. Even people too poor to afford an iPad or a Kindle may still pick up a mass-market paperback from time to time.

The whole either/or thing is a false dichotomy anyway. The truth is, only a very few purists will insist on buying exclusively in one format. Most readers will buy *both* print books *and* e-books, choosing one or the other depending on the circumstances.

Nevertheless, as I've been predicting for several years now, there are big changes on the horizon (mostly changes for the better, I think, with any luck), and the whole publishing world may look very different a decade from now.

Although I suspect that the boardrooms at many a publishing house were filled with executives panicking over the "sudden surprise" explosion in popularity of e-books that many commentators have seen coming for almost a decade now, the genre publishing world was relatively quiet on the surface in 2010, although the possible collapse of the bookstore chain Borders, which tottered on the brink of bankruptcy throughout the year and filed for chapter 11 on February 16, 2011, could have serious repercussions for the publishing industry as a whole. Random House Publishing Group continued the major structural reorganizations that started in 2008 by merging the Ballantine and Bantam Dell divisions into a single group called Ballantine Bantam Dell, combining the two independent editorial departments into one. Ballantine senior vice president and publisher Libby McGuire will run the new division, overseeing hardcover and mass-market paperback publications from DelRey/Spectra, Ballantine, Bantam, Delacorte, Dell, Villard, and other imprints. Trade paperback publications will continue to be overseen by Jane von Mehren, senior vice-president of trade paperbacks. Nina Taublib, former executive vice-president, publisher, and editor-in-chief of Bantam Dell, has stepped down. Jennifer Hershey has become editor-in-chief of the new Ballantine Bantam Dell group. Eos, the SF imprint of HarperCollins, will be renamed Harper Voyager in January 2011, bringing it into line with the Voyager programs in Australia and the United Kingdom; Diana Gill of Eos will remain executive editor of Harper Voyager in the United States.

Prominent British editor Jo Fletcher, longtime associate publisher of Gollancz, left the company to join Quercus, where she will run her own SF/fantasy/horror imprint, Jo Fletcher Books. Angry Robot Books, the imprint of HarperCollins UK, started in 2009, parted ways with its parent company and became an independent imprint of Osprey Publishing, a nonfiction press that currently specializes in military history and wants to expand into the science fiction and fantasy market; founder and publisher Marc Gascoigne will remain in charge. Ian Randal Strock purchased SF/fantasy imprint Fantastic Books from Wilder Publications; Fantastic Books will now be an imprint of Strock's Gray Rabbit Publications, and Douglas Cohen, Darrell Schweitzer, and David Truesdale will remain as acquiring editors. Dorchester decided to give up print publishing entirely and become a digital-only publisher, then reversed the decision early in 2011 under a new CEO, and will add a full trade paperback line, Dorchester Trade Publishing, in addition to its e-publishing program.

It was, thankfully, a quiet year in the long-troubled print magazine market, with even a few minor bits of encouraging news here and there, mostly an increase in subscriptions sold for electronic reading devices like the Kindle, the iPad, and the NOOK. All of the major print magazines survived the year, with the exception of *Realms of Fantasy*, which had died and been reborn under a different publisher the previous year, and which died again in 2010—only to be reborn *again* under yet another new publisher, with the editorial staff intact.

The Magazine of Fantasy & Science Fiction again published a lot of good fantasy this year, but only occasionally a strong SF story. Good stories by Robert Reed, Ian R. MacLeod, Steven Popkes, Paul Park, James L. Cambias, Albert E. Cowdrey, Rachel Pollack, Aaron Schultz, Ian Tregillis, and others appeared in *F&SF* in 2010. *The Magazine of Fantasy & Science Fiction* mostly remained stable, registering only a slight 2.1 percent loss in overall circulation, from 15,491 to 15,172, with subscriptions dropping from 12,045 to 10,907, but newsstand sales rising from 3,446 to 4,264; sell-through rose from 37 percent to 42 percent. Gordon Van Gelder is in his fourteenth year as editor and his tenth year as owner and publisher.

Asimov's Science Fiction was once again almost the reverse of *F&SF*, publishing a lot of good SF, but not as much good fantasy. Good stories by Robert Reed,

Geoffrey A. Landis, Michael Swanwick, Tom Purdom, Felicity Shoulders, Allen M. Steele, Steven Popkes, Kristine Kathryn Rusch, Rick Wilber, and others appeared in *Asimov's* in 2009. For the first time since 2001, *Asimov's Science Fiction* registered a gain in overall circulation, up 26.1 percent from 16,696 to 21,057. Subscriptions rose from 13,731 to 17,866, a substantial part of that due to digital copies sold for e-readers through devices such as the Kindle; perhaps electronic subscriptions will be the saving of the print SF magazines after all, as I've been suggesting they might be for several years now. Newsstand sales dipped a bit, from 2,965 to 2,781; sell-through stayed steady at 31 percent. Sheila Williams completed her sixth year as *Asimov's* editor.

Analog Science Fiction and Fact had a somewhat weak year, although good work by Kristine Kathryn Rusch, Michael F. Flynn, Allen M. Steele, Stephen Baxter, Brenda Cooper, Sean McMullen, and others did appear. *Analog Science Fiction and Fact* registered a 4 percent rise in overall circulation, from 25,418 to 26,440, with subscriptions rising from 21,636 to 22,791, also largely because of digital sales. Newsstand sales dropped from 3,782 to 3,359; sell-through dropped from 34 percent to 32 percent. Stanley Schmidt has been editor there for thirty-three years, and 2010 marked the magazine's eightieth anniversary.

Interzone is technically not a "professional magazine," by the definition of the Science Fiction Writers of America (SFWA), because of its low rates and circulation, but the literary quality of the work published there is so high that it would be ludicrous to omit it. *Interzone* also had a strong year, publishing good work by Nina Allan, Lavie Tidhar, Jim Hawkins, Aliette de Bodard, Jay Lake, Mercurio D. Rivera, Matthew Cook, and others. Circulation there seems to have held steady, in the 3,000-copy range. The editors include publisher Andy Cox and Andy Hedgecock. TTA Press, *Interzone*'s publisher, also publishes the straight horror or dark suspense magazine *Black Static*, which is beyond our purview here, but of a similar level of professional quality.

Realms of Fantasy managed six issues under new publisher Tir Na Nog publications, who'd acquired them in 2009 after the magazine had been cancelled by longtime publisher Sovereign Media, before dying again in 2010—only to be rescued again by another new publisher, Damnation Books, who plans to resume publishing it in 2011. Founding editor Shawna McCarthy, who has edited the magazine since 1994, will remain editor of *Realms of Fantasy* in its new incarnation. Good stuff appeared here in 2010 by Jay Lake, Aliette de Bodard, Harlan Ellison, M. K. Hobson, T. L. Morganfield, and others.

The British magazine *Postscripts* has reinvented itself as an anthology, and is reviewed as such in the anthology section that follows, but I'll list the subscription information up here, for lack of anywhere else to put it, and, because, unlike most other anthology series, you *can* subscribe to *Postscripts*.

If you'd like to see lots of good SF and fantasy published every year, the survival of these magazines is essential, and one important way that you can help them survive is by subscribing to them. It's never been easier to do so, something that these days can be done with just the click of a few buttons, nor has it ever before been possible to subscribe to the magazines in as many different formats, from the traditional print copy arriving by mail to downloads for your desktop or laptop available from places like Fictionwise (www.fictionwise.com) and Amazon (www.amazon.com), to versions you can read on your Kindle, NOOK, or iPad. You can also now subscribe from overseas just as easily as you can from the United States, something formerly difficult to impossible.

So in hopes of making it easier for you to subscribe, I'm going to list both the Internet sites where you can subscribe online and the street addresses where you can subscribe by mail for each magazine: *Asimov's* site is at www.asimovs.com, and subscribing online might be the easiest thing to do, and there's also a discounted rate for online subscriptions; its subscription address is **Asimov's Science Fiction**, Dell Magazines, 267 Broadway, Fourth Floor, New York, NY 10007-2352—$34.97 for annual subscription in the United States, $44.97 overseas. **Analog's** site is at www.analogsf.com; its subscription address is **Analog Science Fiction and Fact**, Dell Magazines, 267 Broadway, Fourth Floor, New York, NY 10007-2352—$34.97 for annual subscription in the United States, $44.97 overseas. **The Magazine of Fantasy & Science Fiction**'s site is at www.sfsite.com/fsf; its subscription address is **The Magazine of Fantasy & Science Fiction**, Spilogale, Inc., P.O. Box 3447, Hoboken, N.J. 07030, annual subscription—$34.97 in the United States, $46.97 overseas. **Interzone** and **Black Static** can be subscribed to online at www.ttapress.com/onlinestore1.html; the subscription address for both is TTA Press, 5 Martins Lane, Witcham, Ely, Cambs CB6 2LB, England, UK—£42.00 each for a twelve-issue subscription, or there is a reduced rate dual subscription offer of £78.00 for both magazines for twelve issues; make checks payable to "TTA Press."

Most of these magazines are also available in various electronic formats through Fictionwise, or for the Kindle and other handheld readers.

The print semiprozine market continues to contract, vulnerable to the same pressures in terms of rising postage rates and production costs as the professional magazines are. In 2009, *Subterranean, Fantasy Magazine, Apex Magazine*, and *Zahir* all transitioned from print formats to electronic-only online formats, and I suspect that most of the surviving print semiprozines will sooner or later go the same route themselves.

The most prominent of the surviving print semiprozines, in terms of the quality of the fiction they publish, may be *Weird Tales, Black Gate*, and *Electric Velocipede*. *Weird Tales* is a fine-looking magazine, with a coolness quotient higher than most other magazines in the field, but they again managed only two of their scheduled four quarterly issues in 2010, as they had in 2009, and they need to work on the reliability of their publishing schedule if they're to become a major player. Ann VanderMeer is now the editor, promoted from fiction editor at the beginning of 2010, and *Weird Tales* published good work this year by Ian R. MacLeod, Aidan Doyle, Catherynne M. Valente, and others. The sword and sorcery magazine *Black Gate* managed only one issue this year, although it was a double issue, even huger than their issues usually are, featuring strong stuff by James Enge, Robert J. Howe, Michael Jasper, Jay Lake, and others; the longtime editor is John O'Neill. *Electric Velocipede*, edited by John Klima, managed only one of its scheduled four issues in 2010, with interesting work by Cyril Simsa, Daniel Braum, and others.

The longest running of all the fiction semiprozines, and the most reliably published, one of the few that kept to its announced publishing schedule, is the Canadian *On Spec*, which is edited by a collective under general editor Diane L. Walton. Once again, I found the fiction here mostly kind of bland, although there was interesting work by Toni Pi, Marissa K. Lingen, and Tina Connolly that did appear. Another collective-run SF magazine with a rotating editorial staff, Australia's *Andromeda Spaceways Inflight Magazine*, which is usually a bit livelier than *On Spec*, published seven issues this year, running good stuff by Karl Bunker, Janeen Samuel, Ferrett Steinmetz, and others.

There were two issues of *Lady Churchill's Rosebud Wristlet*, the long-running slipstream magazine edited by Kelly Link and Gavin Grant. The Australian magazine *Aurealis*, edited by Stuart Mayne, who is stepping down in 2011, also produced two issues, as did Ireland's long-running *Albedo One*, and the fantasy magazine *Shimmer*. The small British SF magazine *Jupiter*, edited by Ian Redman, produced all four of its scheduled issues in 2010. Fantasy magazine *Tales of the Talisman* put out four issues, the long-running *Space and Time Magazine* produced three, and a new start-up SF magazine, *Bull Spec*, produced two. There were single issues of *Neo-opsis*, *Greatest Uncommon Denominator*, *Sybil's Garage*, the South African magazine *Something Wicked*, *Space Squid*, and *Tales of the Unanticipated*.

There's not much of the print critical magazine market left—many of them have either died or moved onto the Web in electronic format, something I suspect will happen to most of them sooner or later. One of the hearty survivors, the best of them and certainly your best bet for value, is the newszine *Locus: The Magazine of the Science Fiction & Fantasy Field*, a multiple Hugo winner, which for more than thirty years has been an indispensable source of news, information, and reviews. Sadly, founder, publisher, and longtime editor Charles N. Brown died in 2009, but *Locus* has continued strongly and successfully under the guidance of a staff of editors headed by Liza Groen Trombi, and including Kirsten Gong-Wong, Amelia Beamer, and many others. *The New York Review of Science Fiction*, a critical magazine edited by David G. Hartwell and a staff of associate editors, is another hearty perennial, which has been reliably publishing a variety of eclectic and sometimes quirky critical essays on a wide range of topics for many years now.

Most of the other surviving print critical magazines are professional journals more aimed at academics than at the average reader. The most accessible of these is probably the long-running British critical zine *Foundation*.

Subscription addresses follow:

Locus, The Magazine of the Science Fiction & Fantasy Field, Locus Publications, Inc., P.O. Box 13305, Oakland, CA 94661, $72.00 for a one-year first-class subscription, twelve issues; **The New York Review of Science Fiction**. Dragon Press, P.O. Box 78, Pleasantville, NY 10570, $40.00 per year, twelve issues, make checks payable to "Dragon Press"; **Foundation**, Science Fiction Foundation, Roger Robinson (SFF), 75 Rosslyn Avenue, Harold Wood, Essex RM3 ORG, UK, $37.00

for a three-issue subscription in the United States; **Weird Tales**, $20.00 in the United States, $40 elsewhere for four issues, go to Wildside Press, www.wild sidemagazine.com/Weird-Tales to subscribe; **Realms of Fantasy**, $19.95 for a yearly (six issues) subscription in the United States, overseas $34.95, go to www .rofmag.com for subscription information; **Black Gate**, New Epoch Press, 815 Oak Street, St. Charles, IL 60174, $29.95 for a one-year (four issues) subscription; **Aurealis**, Chimaera Publications, P.O. Box 2164, Mt. Waverley, VIC 3149, Australia (Web site: www.aurealis.com.au), $59.75 for a four-issue overseas airmail subscription, checks should be made out to Chimaera Publications in Australian dollars; **On Spec, The Canadian Magazine of the Fantastic**, P.O. Box 4727, Edmonton, AB, Canada T6E 5G6, for subscription information, go to the Web site www.onspec.ca; **Neo-opsis Science Fiction Magazine**, 4129 Carey Rd., Victoria, BC, V8Z 4G5, $25.00 for a three-issue subscription; **Albedo One**. Albedo One Productions, 2 Post Road, Lusk Co., Dublin, Ireland, $32.00 for a four-issue airmail subscription, make checks payable to "Albedo One" or pay by PayPal at www .albedo1.com; **Lady Churchill's Rosebud Wristlet**, Small Beer Press, 150 Pleasant St., #306, Easthampton, MA 01027, $20.00 for four issues; **Electric Velocipede**, Spilt Milk Press, see Web site www.electricvelocipede.com for subscription information; **Andromeda Spaceways Inflight Magazine**, see Web site www.an dromedaspaceways.com for subscription information; **Tales of the Talisman**, Hadrosaur Productions, P.O. Box 2194, Mesilla Park, NM 8804-2194, $24.00 for a four-issue subscription; **Jupiter**, 19 Bedford Road, Yeovil, Somerset, BA21 5UG, UK, £10 for four issues; **Greatest Uncommon Denominator**, Greatest Uncommon Denominator Publishing, P.O. Box 1537, Laconia, NH 03247, $18 for two issues; **Sybil's Garage**, Senses Five Press, 76 India Street, Apt A8, Brooklyn, NY 11222-1657, no subscription information available but try the Web site www .sensesfive.com; **Shimmer**, P.O. Box 58591, Salt Lake City, UT 84158-0591, $22.00 for a four-issue subscription; **Space Squid**, no subscription address available, but you could try squish@spacesquid.com; **Something Wicked**, no subscription address available, try www.somethingwicked.co.za; Bull Spec, P.O. Box 13146, Durham, N.C. 27709, doesn't seem to be available for subscription, but find it in your local book or comic shop or online at www.bullspec.com.

The online world of electronic magazines becomes more important with every passing year. Already they're a more reliable place to find quality fiction than most of the semiprozine market, and they're giving the top print professional magazines a run for their money too, and sometimes beating them. It was a year of relatively few changes in the online market. *Jim Baen's Universe* died after its April issue, a major disappointment; on the other hand, a new magazine, *Lightspeed*, was founded, and has already established itself as a major source of good fiction.

The best stuff on the Internet this year was probably to be found at *Subterranean Magazine* (www.subterraneanpress.com), edited by William K. Schafer, with one issue guest-edited by Jonathan Strahan. Lots of superior work, both science fiction and fantasy, appeared there this year by Damien Broderick, Hannu

Rajaniemi, Maureen McHugh, Rachel Swirsky, K. J. Parker, Ted Chiang, Lucius Shepard, Kage Baker, Mike Resnick, and others. *Subterranean* is particularly to be commended for publishing several strong novellas, a rare length in the Internet world, where most stories tend to be short.

Clarkesworld (www.clarkesworldmagazine.com), edited by Sean Wallace and publisher and editor Neil Clarke, also had a good year, publishing strong SF, fantasy, and slipstream stories by Peter Watts, Robert Reed, Brenda Cooper, Yoon Ha Lee, Jay Lake, Eric Brown, and others. Sean Wallace stepped down as editor in November 2010.

Sean Wallace is also stepping down as editor of *Fantasy Magazine* (www .fantasy-magazine.com), as is co-editor Cat Rambo; they will be replaced by John Joseph Adams, who is also editing *Lightspeed. Fantasy Magazine* ran good stuff this year, mostly straight genre fantasy, with a little slipstream thrown in and even the occasional SF story, by Lavie Tidhar, Sarah Monette, Rachel Swirsky, Tony Pi, Aidan Doyle, Eilis O'Neal, Matthew Johnson, An Owomoyela, Jay Lake, Shannon Page, and others.

The above-mentioned John Joseph Adams, already a prolific anthologist, launched a new SF e-zine, *Lightspeed* (www.lightspeedmagazine.com), early in 2010, and will edit both *Lightspeed* and *Fantasy Magazine* at the same time, as well as his numerous anthologies, which will make him a busy fellow. *Lightspeed* hit the ground running, and has already established itself as a major new SF market, publishing good stories by Yoon Ha Lee, Carrie Vaughn, Ted Kosmatka, Jack McDevitt, Alice Sola Kim, and others.

The long-running e-zine *Strange Horizons* (www.strangehorizons.com), one of the longest-established fiction sites on the Internet, ran good stuff this year, their usual mix of SF, fantasy, slipstream, and soft horror by Lavie Tidhar, Theodora Goss, Samantha Henderson, John Kessel, Sandra McDonald, and others. Longtime editor-in-chief Susan Marie Groppi, stepped down (although she, Jed Hartman, and Karen Meisner will continue as fiction editors), to be replaced by Niall Harrison.

Tor.com (www.tor.com) has established itself as one of the coolest and most eclectic genre-oriented sites on the Internet, a Web site that regularly publishes SF, fantasy, and slipstream, as well as articles, comics, graphics, blog entries, print and media reviews, and commentary. It's become a regular stop for me, even when they don't have new fiction posted. The fiction at Tor.com this year seemed a bit weaker overall than in recent years, perhaps the result of running too many excerpts from upcoming novels that Tor wanted to push and too many "special interest" promotions like its months devoted to paranormal romance and steampunk, but it still published good stuff by Jay Lake, Ken Scholes, Eileen Gunn, Michael Swanwick, Kij Johnson, and others, and remains a fascinating place to visit. Liz Gorinsky joined Patrick Nielsen Hayden as co-editor of fiction.

Abyss & Apex, (www.abyssapexzine.com), edited by Wendy S. Delmater, which seems to run more SF than many of the other sites, had good stuff by Alan Smale, Lavie Tidhar, Michael Swanwick, Caren Gussoff, Bud Sparhawk, and others.

Apex Magazine (www.apexbookcompany.com/apex-online), returned after a hiatus for a redesign with a new fiction editor, Catherynne M. Valente, although

Jason Sizemore remains as the owner and editor-in-chief. They featured good work by Theodora Goss, Saladin Ahmed, Peter M. Ball, Amal El-Mohtar, and others.

An e-zine devoted to "literary adventure fantasy, *Beneath Ceaseless Skies* (www.beneath-ceaseless-skies.com), edited by Scott H. Andrews, published good stuff by Richard Parks, Yoon Ha Lee, Ann Leckie, Marissa Lingen, and others.

Ideomancer Speculative Fiction (www.ideomancer.com), edited by Leah Bobet, published interesting work by Megan Arkenberg, Ilan Lerman, LaShawn M. Wanak, and others.

The flamboyantly titled *Orson Scott Card's InterGalactic Medicine Show* (www.intergalacticmedicineshow.com), edited by Edmund R. Schubert under the direction of Card himself, had good work by Peter S. Beagle, Jason Sanford, and others.

New SF/fantasy e-zine *Daily Science Fiction* (http://dailysciencefiction.com) tackled the perhaps overly ambitious task of publishing one new SF or fantasy story for the entire year. Unsurprisingly, most are undistinguished, but there were some good ones by Lavie Tidhar, Tim Pratt, Jeff Hecht, Mary Robinette Kowal, and others.

New SF e-zine *M-Brane* (www.mbranesf.com) produced twelve issues this year, with seventy-four original stories.

Fantasy magazine *Zahir* (www.zahiirtales.com) moved from a print incarnation to an online venue this year, publishing twenty-four original stories.

A mix of science fact articles and fiction is available from the e-zine *Futurismic* (http://futurismic.com) and from *Escape Velocity* (www.escapevelocitymagazine.com). The futurist Web site Shareable Futures (http://shareable.net/blog/shareable-.futures) has been publishing stories set in futures with nonconventional economic systems by writers such as Bruce Sterling and Benjamin Rosenbaum.

Shadow Unit (www.shadowunit.org) is a Web site devoted to publishing stories drawn from an imaginary TV show, sort of a cross between *CSI* and *The X-Files*. I continue to find this an unexciting idea, but top professionals such as Elizabeth Bear, Emma Bull, and others are involved in producing scripts for it, so you might want to check it out.

The Australian popular-science magazine *COSMOS* (www.cosmosmagazine .com) is not a SF magazine per se, but for the last few years it has been running a story per issue selected by fiction editor Damien Broderick (and also putting new fiction not published in the print magazine up on their Web site). Broderick is stepping down, but is being replaced by Cat Sparks, and since she's also an SF professional, I assume that this policy will continue under her as well.

Below this point, it becomes harder to find center-core SF, and most of the stories are slipstream or literary surrealism. Sites that feature those, as well as fantasy (and, occasionally, some SF) include Rudy Rucker's *Flurb* (www.flurb.net), *Revolution SF* (www.revolutionsf.com), *CovoteWild* (www.coyotewildmag.com); *Heliotrope* (www.heliotropemag.com); and the somewhat less slipstreamish *Bewildering Stories* (www.bewilderingstories.com)

There's also a lot of good *reprint* SF and fantasy stories out there on the Internet too, usually available for free. On all of the sites that make their fiction available for free, *Strange Horizons, Tor.com, Fantasy, Subterranean, Abyss & Apex*, and so on, you can also access large archives of previously published material as well as stuff from the "current issue." Most of the sites that are associated with existent print magazines, such as *Asimov's, Analog, Weird Tales*, and *The Magazine of Fantasy & Science Fiction*, make previously published fiction and nonfiction available for access on their sites, and also regularly run teaser excerpts from stories coming up in forthcoming issues. Hundreds of out-of-print titles, both genre and mainstream, are also available for free download from Project Gutenberg (http://promo.net/pg/), and a large selection of novels and a few collections can also be accessed for free, to be either downloaded or read on-screen, at the Baen Free Library (www.baen.com/library/). Sites such as *Infinity Plus* (http://www.infinityplus.co.uk/) and *The Infinite Matrix* (www.infinitematrix.net/) may have died as active sites, but their extensive archives of previously published material are still accessable.

If you're willing to pay a small fee for them, an even greater range of reprint stories becomes available. Perhaps the best, and the longest-established place to find such material is Fictionwise (www.fictionwise.com), where you can buy downloadable e-books and stories to read on your PDA, Kindle, or home computer; in addition to individual stories, you can also buy "fiction bundles" here, which amount to electronic collections; as well as a selection of novels in several different genres—you can also subscribe to downloadable versions of several of the SF magazines here, including *Asimov's, Analog, F&SF*, and *Interzone*, in a number of different formats. A similar site is ElectricStory (www.electricstory.com), where in addition to the fiction for sale you can also access free movie reviews by Lucius Shepard, articles by Howard Waldrop, and other critical material.

There are plenty of other reasons for SF fans to go on the Internet, though, than just finding fiction to read. There are also many general genre-related sites of interest to be found, most of which publish reviews of books as well as of movies and TV shows, sometimes comics or computer games or anime, many of which also feature interviews, critical articles, and genre-oriented news of various kinds. The best such site is easily Locus Online (www.locusmag.com), the online version of the newsmagazine *Locus*, where you can access an incredible amount of information—including book reviews, critical lists, obituary lists, links to reviews and essays appearing outside the genre, and links to extensive database archives such as the Locus Index to Science Fiction and the Locus Index to Science Fiction Awards—it's rare when I don't find myself accessing Locus Online several times a day. As mentioned earlier, Tor.com is giving it a run for its money these days as an interesting place to stop while surfing the Web.

Other major general interest sites include *SF Site* (www.sfsite.com), *SFRevu* (www.sfrevu.com), *SFcrowsnest* (www.sfcrowsnest.com), *SFScope* (http://sfscope.com) io9 (http://io9.com), *Green Man Review* (www.greenmanreview.com), *The Agony Column* (http://trashotron.com/agony), *Science Fiction and Fantasy World* (www.sffworld.com), *SFReader* (www.sfreader.com), SFWatcher (www.sfwatcher.com), *Salon Futura* (www.salonfutura.net), which runs interviews and critical articles; and *Pat's Fantasy Hotlist* (http://fantasyhotlist.blogspot.com). A great research site, invaluable if you want bibliographic information about SF and fantasy writers, is Fantastic Fiction (www.fantasticfiction.co.uk). Reviews of short fiction as opposed to novels are very hard to find anywhere, with the exception of *Locus* and Locus Online, but you can find reviews of both current and past short fiction at Best SF (www.bestsf.net/), as well as at pioneering short-fiction review site *Tangent Online* (www.tangentonline.com), which has gone intermittently in and out of hiatus, but which seems to be up and running at the moment. Other sites of interest include: SFF Net (www.sff.net) which features dozens of home pages and "newsgroups" for SF writers; the Science Fiction Writers of America page (www.sfwa.org); where genre news, obituaries, award information, and recommended reading lists can be accessed; *SciFiPedia* (www.scifipedia.com), a Wiki-style genre-oriented online encyclopedia; Ansible (http://news.ansible.co .uk), the online version of multiple Hugo-winner David Langford's long-running fanzine *Ansible*; Book View Cafe (www.bookviewcafe.com) is a "consortium of over twenty professional authors," including Vonda N. McIntyre, Laura Ann Gilman, Sarah Zettel, Brenda Clough, and others, who have created a Web site where work by them—mostly reprints, and some novel excerpts—is made available for free.

An ever-expanding area, growing in popularity, are a number of sites where podcasts and SF-oriented radio plays can be accessed: at Audible (www.audible .com), Escape Pod (http://escapepod.org, podcasting mostly SF), StarShipSofa (www.starshipsofa.com), Pseudopod (http://pseudopod.org, podcasting mostly fantasy), and PodCastle (http://podcastle.org, podcasting mostly fantasy). There's also a site that podcasts nonfiction interviews and reviews, Dragon Page Cover to Cover (www.dragonpage.com).

There were plenty of anthologies published in 2010, from both trade publishers and small presses, and although most of them didn't stick out as particularly outstanding, most of them had a few good stories a piece. (The decision to postpone the latest volume of Jonathan Strahan's anthology series *Eclipse* until next year probably weakened the year's anthology market.) The strongest SF anthology of the year was almost certainly *Godlike Machines* (SFBC), edited by Jonathan Strahan, although being published exclusively by the Science Fiction Book Club (which had delayed publishing it for at least a year) probably limited the number of people who saw it; one of the year's best novellas, by Alastair Reynolds was here as well as strong novellas by Stephen Baxter, Greg Egan, and Sean Williams. The Fred Pohl tribute anthology, *Gateways* (Tor), edited by Elizabeth Anne Hull, was somewhat weaker than had been hoped, although it did feature good stories by Cory Doctorow, Joe Haldeman, Vernor Vinge, Gene Wolfe, and others. *The Mammoth Book of Apocalyptic SF* (Robinson; published in the United States by Running Press under the title *The Mammoth Book of the End of the World*, apparently because Americans are presumed to be too stupid to know what "apocalyptic" means), edited by Mike Ashley, was not only one of the year's best reprint anthologies, but also featured a spine of first-rate original stories by Alastair Reynolds, Kage Baker, Robert Reed, and others. *Is Anybody Out There?* (DAW Books), edited by Nick Gevers and Marty Halpern, featured good work by Pat

Cadigan, Jay Lake, Alex Irvine, Matthew Hughes, and others. *Postscripts* has transformed itself from a magazine into an anthology series; this year's volume, *The Company He Keeps*, *Postscripts* 22/23 (PS Publishing), struck me as being not as memorable as other recent issues had been, although there were interesting stories by Lucius Shepard, Don Webb, Jack Deighton, Holly Phillips, and others. *Shine* (Solaris), edited by Jetse de Vries, an admirable attempt to create "anthology of optimistic SF" created in reaction to the prevailing pessimism and gloom of much modern SF, didn't entirely succeed, although it did feature ambitious stories by Lavie Tidhar, Gord Sellar, Eric Gregory, Alastair Reynolds, and others. *The Dragon and the Stars* (DAW Books), edited by Derwin Mak and Eric Choi, was an anthology of stories (mostly fantasy) inspired by Chinese culture, with interesting work by Tony Pi, Emily Mah, Brenda W. Clough, Ken Liu, and Choi himself.

There were several big cross-genre anthologies this year that featured mystery, mainstream, and romance as well as SF and fantasy. They included *Stories* (William Morrow), edited by Neil Gaiman and Al Sarrantonio, which featured good work by Neil Gaiman, Elizabeth Hand, Joe R. Lansdale, Lawrence Block, and others, and—noted without comment—*Warriors* (Tor) and *Songs of Love and Death* (Gallery Books), both edited by George R. R. Martin and Gardner Dozois.

Interesting small press anthologies, usually mixing SF, fantasy, and slipstream, included *Conflicts* (NewCon Press), edited by Ian Whates, with solid work by Una McCormack, Chris Beckett, Keith Brooke, Neal Asher, and others; *The Immersion Book of SF* (Immersion Press), edited by Carmelo Rafala, featuring good stories by Lavie Tidhar, Gord Sellar, Chris Butler, Aliette de Bodard, and others; *Panverse Two* (Panverse Publishing), edited by Dario Ciriello, featuring two excellent novellas by Alan Smale and Michael D. Winkle; *Clockwork Phoenix 3* (Norilana), edited by Mike Allen, which had interesting work by John C. Wright, Cat Rambo, John Grant, Gregory Frost, C.S.E. Cooney, and others; *Destination: Future* (Hadley Rille), edited by Z. S. Adani and Eric T. Reynolds, with Elizabeth Bear, Caren Gussoff, K. D. Wentworth, Sandra McDonald, and others; and *Music for Another World* (Mutation Press), edited by Mark Harding

Pleasant but minor science fiction anthologies included *Darwin's Bastards: Astounding Tales from Tomorrow* (Douglas & McIntyre), edited by Zsuzsi Gartner, *Sky Whales and Other Wonders* (Norilana), edited by Vera Nazarian; *Steampunk'd* (DAW Books), edited by Jean Rabe and Martin H. Greenberg; *Timeshares* (DAW Books), edited by Jean Rabe and Martin H. Greenberg; and a mixed SF/romance anthology, *Love and Rockets* (DAW Books), edited by Martin H. Greenberg and Kerrie Hughes.

The best original fantasy anthology of the year was *Swords and Dark Magic: The New Sword and Sorcery* (Eos), edited by Lou Anders and the ubiquitous Jonathan Strahan, which featured good work by Joe Abercrombie, K. J. Parker, Steven Erikson, Garth Nix, C. J. Cherryh, and others. Also first rate was a mixed reprint/original anthology edited by John Joseph Adams, *The Way of the Wizard* (Prime Books), with nice stuff by Lev Grossman, Nnedi Okorafor, Christie Yant, Charles Coleman Finlay, and others. Also good is *Legends of Australian Fantasy* (HarperCollins Australia), edited by Jack Dann and Jonathan Strahan, which features a powerful novella by Garth Nix and good stuff by Sean Williams, Isobelle Carmody, and others; a YA anthology *The Beastly Bride: Tales of the Animal People* (Viking), edited by Ellen Datlow and Terry Windling, which has good stuff by Peter S. Beagle, Lucius Shepard, Tanith Lee, Ellen Kushner, Gregory Frost, and others; and a mixed original/reprint anthology of updated fairy tales, *My Mother She Killed Me, My Father He Ate Me* (Penguin), edited by Kate Bernheimer.

Pleasant but minor original fantasy anthologies included *A Girl's Guide to Guns and Monsters* (DAW Books), edited by Martin H. Greenberg and Kerrie Hughes; *She Nailed a Stake Through His Head: Tales of Biblical Terror* (Dybbuk Press), edited by Tim Lieder; *Alembical 2* (Paper Golem), edited by Arthur Dorrance and Lawrence M. Schoen; *Jabberwocky 5* (Prime Books), edited by Sean Wallace and Erzebet Yellowboy; and *More Stories from the Twilight Zone* (Tor), edited by Carol Serling.

There were at least three dedicated original zombie anthologies this year (plus at least one reprint anthology), *The New Dead* (St. Martin's Press), edited by Christopher Golden, *The Living Dead 2* (Night Shade Books), edited by John Joseph Adams (partly reprint), and *Zombies vs. Unicorns* (Margaret K. McElderry Books), edited by Holly Black and Justine Larbalestier, two anthologies of werewolf stories, *Full Moon City* (Simon & Schuster), edited by Darrell Schweitzer and Martin H. Greenberg, and *Running with the Pack* (Prime Books), edited by Ekaterina Sedia, two books of comic vampire stories, *Blood Lite II: Overbite* (Gallery Books), edited by Kevin J. Anderson, and *Fangs for the Mammaries* (Baen), edited by Esther M. Friesner, a book of ghost stories, *Haunted Legends* (Tor), edited by Ellen Datlow and Nick Mamatas, a book of Lovecraftian stories, *Cthulhu's Reign* (Tor), edited by Darrell Schweitzer and Martin H. Greenberg, a paranormal romance anthology, *Death's Excellent Vacation* (Ace), edited by Charlaine Harris and Toni L. P. Kelner, and an anthology of superhero stories, *Masked* (Simon & Schuster), edited by Lou Anders.

A long-running series featuring novice work by beginning writers, some of whom may later turn out to be important talents, continued under editor K. D. Wentworth, *L. Ron Hubbard Presents Writers of the Future Volume XXVI* (Galaxy).

There were a lot of stories this year about either the end of the world or life in a severely ecologically challenged future, as well as stories about future Great Depressions and the resultant dystopias they generate—perhaps not surprising in a year where writers had a bad "economic downturn" and the spectacle of a catastrophic oil spill in the Gulf of Mexico to inspire them.

(Finding individual pricings for all of the items from small presses mentioned in the Summation has become too time-intensive, and since several of the same small presses publish anthologies, novels, *and* short-story collections, it seems silly to repeat addresses for them in section after section. Therefore, I'm going to attempt to list here, in one place, all the addresses for small presses that have books mentioned here or there in the Summation, whether from the anthologies section, the novel section, or the short-story collection section, and, where known, their Web site addresses. That should make it easy enough for the reader to look up the individual price of any book mentioned that isn't from a regular trade publisher; such books are less likely to be found in your average bookstore, or even in a chain superstore, and so will probably have to be mail-ordered. Many publishers seem to sell only online, through their Web sites, and some will only accept payment through PayPal. Many books, even from some of the smaller presses, are also available through Amazon.com. If you can't find an address for a publisher, and it's quite likely that I've missed some here, Google it.)

Addresses: **PS Publishing**, Grosvener House, 1 New Road, Hornsea, East Yorkshire, HU18 1PG, England, UK, www.pspublishing.co.uk; **Golden Gryphon Press**, 3002 Perkins Road, Urbana, IL 61802, www.goldengryphon.com; **NESFA Press**, P.O. Box 809, Framingham, MA 01701, www.nesfa.org; **Subterranean Press**, P.O. Box 190106, Burton, MI 48519, www.subterraneanpress.com; **Old Earth Books**, P.O. Box 19951, Baltimore, MD 21211-0951, www.oldearth-books.com; **Tachyon Publications**, 1459 18th St. #139, San Francisco, CA 94107, www.tachyonpublications.com; **Night Shade Books**, 1661 Tennessee Street, #3H, San Francsisco, CA 94107, www.nightshadebooks.com; **Five Star**, 295 Kennedy Memorial Drive, Waterville, ME 04901, www.gale.cengage.com/fivestar; **New-Con Press**, via www.newconpress.co.uk; **Small Beer Press**, 150 Pleasant St., #306 Easthampton MA 01027, http://smallbeerpress.com; **Locus Press**, P.O. Box 13305, Oakland, CA 94661, www.locusmag.com; **Crescent Books**, Mercat Press Ltd., 10 Coates Crescent, Edinburgh, Scotland EH3 7AL, www.mercatpress.com; **Wildside Press/Borgo Press**, 9710 Traville Gateway Dr., #234, Rockville, MI 20850, or go to www.wildsidepress.com for pricing and ordering; **EDGE Science Fiction and Fantasy Publishing, Inc.** and **Tesseract Books, Ltd.**, P.O. Box 1714, Calgary, Alberta, T2P 2L7, Canada, www.edgewebsite.com; **Aqueduct Press**, P.O. Box 95787, Seattle, WA 98145-2787, www.aqueductpress.com; **Phobos Books**, 200 Park Avenue South, New York, NY 10003, http://phobosweb.com; **Fairwood Press**, 5203 Quincy Ave. SE, Auburn, WA 98092, www.fairwoodpress.com; **BenBella Books**, 10300 N. Central Expressway, Suite 400, Dallas, TX 75231, www.benbellabooks.com; **Darkside Press**, 13320 27th Ave. NE, Seattle, WA 98125, www.darksidepress.com; **Haffner Press**, 5005 Crooks Rd., Suite 35, Royal Oak, MI 48073-1239, www.haffnerpress.com; **North Atlantic Books**, 2526 Martin Luther King Jr. Way, Berkeley, CA, 94704; **Prime Books**, P.O. Box 36503, Canton, OH, 44735, www.primebooks.com; **MonkeyBrain Books**, 11204 Crossland Drive, Austin, TX 78726, www.monkeybrainbooks.com;; **Wesleyan University Press**, University Press of New England, Order Dept., 1 Court St., Lebanon NH 03766-1358, www.wesleyan.edu/wespress;; **Agog! Press**, P.O. Box U302, University of Wollongong, NSW 2522, Australia, www.uow.ed.au/~rhood/agogpress ; **Wheatland Press**, via www.wheatlandpress.com; **MirrorDanse Books**, P.O. Box 546 Chatswood NSW 2057, Australia, www.tabula-rasa.info/MirrorDanse; **Arsenal Pulp Press**, 101-211 East Georgia Street, Vancouver, BC, Canada V6A 1Z6, www.arsenalpulp.com; **DreamHaven Books**, 2301 East 38th Street, Minneapolis, MN 55406; **Elder Signs Press/Dimensions Books**, order through www.eldersignspress.com; **Chaosium**, via www.chaosium.com; **Omnidawn Publishing**, order through www.omnidawn.com; **CSFG**, Canberra Speculative Fiction Guild, www.csfg.org.au/publishing/anthologies/the_outcast; **Hadley Rille Books**, via www.hadleyrillebooks.com; **ISFiC Press**, 707 Sapling Lane, Deerfield, IL 60015-3969, or www.isficpress.com; **Suddenly Press**, via suddenlypress@yahoo.com;

Sandstone Press, P.O. Box 5725, One High St., Dingwall, Ross-shire, IV15 9WJ, UK, www.sandstonepress.com; Tropism Press, via www.tropismpress.com; Science Fiction Poetry Association/Dark Regions Press, www.sfpoetry.com, checks to Helena Bell, SFPA Treasurer, 1225 West Freeman St., Apt. 12, Carbondale, IL 62901; DH Press, via diamondbookdistributors.com; Kurodahan Press, via Web site www.kurodahan.com; Ramble House, 443 Gladstone Blvd., Shreveport, LA 71104; Interstitial Arts Foundation, via www.interstitialarts.org; Raw Dog Screaming, via www.rawdogscreaming.com; Three-legged Fox Books, 98 Hythe Road, Brighton, BN1 6JS, UK; Norilana Books, via www.norilana.com; coeur de lion, via www.coeurdelion.com.au; PARSEC Ink, via http://parsecink.org; Robert J. Sawyer Books, via wwww.sfwriter.com/rjsbooks.htm; Rackstraw Press, via http://rackstrawpress; Candlewick, via www.candlewick.com; Zubaan, via www.zubaanbooks.com; Utter Tower, via www.threeleggedfox.co.uk; Spilt Milk Press, via www.electricvelocipede.com; Paper Golem, via www.papergolem.com; Galaxy Press, via www.galaxypress.com.; Twelfth Planet Press, via www.twelfhplanetpress.com; Five Senses Press, via www.sensefive.com; Elastic Press, via www.elasticpress.com; Lethe Press, via www.lethepressbooks.com; Two Cranes Press, via www.twocranespress.com; Wordcraft of Oregon, via www.wordcraftoforegon.com.

If print books are about to disappear, to be replaced by e-books, as argued by some commentators, there was no sign of it in 2010. In fact, in spite of the recession, the number of novels published in the SF/fantasy genres increased for the fourth year in a row.

According to the newsmagazine *Locus*, there were a record 3,056 books "of interest to the SF field" published in 2010, up 5 percent from 2,901 titles in 2009, and 69 percent of those were new titles, not reprints. (It's worth noting that this total doesn't count the previously mentioned e-books, media tie-in novels, gaming novels, novelizations of genre movies, or print-on-demand books—all of which would swell the total by hundreds if counted.) The number of new SF novels was up 14 percent to 285 as opposed to 2009's 232. The number of new fantasy novels was up by 7 percent, to 614 titles as opposed to 2009's total of 572. Horror novels remained the same at 251 titles. Paranormal romances were up 13 percent to 384 titles from 2009's 339, second in numbers only to fantasy (although sometimes it can be difficult and even subjective to make some of these judgment calls regarding categorization—once a novel about vampires would have been considered to be a fantasy novel, now it's probably counted under paranormal romance instead, and could even show up under horror, depending on who was doing the categorizing).

As usual, busy with all the reading I have to do at shorter lengths, I didn't have time to read many novels myself this year, so I'll limit myself to mentioning the novels that received a lot of attention and acclaim in 2010. These include: *The Dervish House* (Pyr), by Ian McDonald; *Zendegi* (Night Shade Books), by Greg Egan; *Not Less Than Gods* (Tor), by Kage Baker; *The Bird of the River* (Tor), by Kage Baker; *Blackout/All Clear* (Spectra), by Connie Willis; *Hull Zero Three*

(Orbit), by Greg Bear; *Coyote Destiny* (Ace), by Allen Steele; *Deceiver* (DAW Books), by C. J. Cherryh; *Starbound* (Ace) by Joe Haldeman; *Chill* (Ballantine Books), by Elizabeth Bear; *Terminal World* (Gollancz), by Alastair Reynolds; *Surface Detail* (Orbit), by Iain M. Banks; *Kraken* (Del Rey), by China Miéville; *The Folding Knife* (Orbit), by K. J. Parker; *Directive 51* (Ace), by John Barnes; *Brain Thief* (Tor), by Alexander Jablokov; *Cryoburn* (Baen), by Lois McMaster Bujold; *Who Fears Death* (DAW Books), by Nnedi Okorafor; *The Technician* (Tor), by Neal Asher; *Echo* (Ace), by Jack McDevitt; *New Model Army* (Gollancz), by Adam Roberts; *Dreadnought* (Tor), by Cherie Priest; *The Wolf Age* (Pyr), by James Enge; *Dragon Haven* (Eos), by Robin Hobb; *The Restoration Game* (Orbit), by Ken MacLeod; *Behemoth* (Simon Pulse), by Scott Westerfeld; *Sleepless* (Ballantine Books), by Charlie Huston; *Hespira* (Night Shade Books), by Matthew Hughes; *The Fuller Memorandum* (Ace), by Charles Stross; *The Trade of Queens* (Tor), by Charles Stross; *The Evolutionary Void* (Del Rey), by Peter F. Hamilton; *The Sorcerer's House* (Tor), by Gene Wolfe; *For the Win* (Tor), by Cory Doctorow; *Ship Breaker* (Little, Brown and Company), by Paolo Bacigalupi; *Discord's Apple* (Tor), by Carrie Vaughn; *Mockingjay* (Scholastic Press), by Suzanne Collins; and *I Shall Wear Midnight* (HarperCollins), by Terry Pratchett.

Small presses are active in the novel market these days, where once they published mostly collections and anthologies. Novels issued by small presses this year included: *Zendegi* (Night Shade Books), by Greg Egan; *Hespira* (Night Shade Books), by Matthew Hughes; and *The Habitation of the Blessed* (Night Shade Books), by Catherynne M. Valente.

The year's first novels included: *The Quantum Thief* (Gollancz), by Hannu Rajaniemi; *The Loving Dead* (Night Shade Books), by Amelia Beamer; *Clowns at Midnight* (PS Publishing), by Terry Dowling; *The Native Star* (Spectra), by M. K. Hobson; *The Bookman* (Angry Robot), by Lavie Tidhar; *Bitter Seeds* (Tor), by Ian Tregillis; *Redemption in Indigo* (Small Beer Press), by Karen Lord; *How to Live Safely in a Science Fictional Universe* (Pantheon Books), by Charles Yu; *Passion Play* (Tor), by Beth Bernobich; *Shades of Milk and Honey* (Tor), by Mary Robinette Kowal; *The Hundred Thousand Kingdoms* (Orbit), by N. K. Jemisin; *Tome of the Undergates* (Pyr), by Sam Sykes; *The Dream of Perpetual Motion* (St. Martin's Press), by Dexter Palmer; *Meeks* (Small Beer Press), by Julia Holmes; *The Last Page* (Tor), by Anthony Huso; *Noise* (Spectra), by Darin Bradley; *Crossing Over* (Viking), by Anna Kendall; *Spellwright* (Tor), by Blake Charlton; *A Book of Tongues* (CZP), by Gemma Files; *Sixty-One Nails* (Angry Robot), by Mike Shevdon; *Black Blade Blues* (Tor), by J. A. Pitts; and *The Girl with Glass Feet* (Henry Holt), by Ali Shaw. Of these, *The Quantum Thief* drew the best notices, generating the same kind of buzz that 2009's *The Windup Girl* got, although *The Loving Dead* and *Bitter Seeds* also drew their share of attention.

Historical or mainstream novels that add strong fantastic elements to the mix included: *Black Hills* (Little, Brown and Company), by Dan Simmons; *Kings of the North* (Forge), by Cecelia Holland; *Under Heaven* (Viking Canada), by Guy Gavriel Kay; *A Dark Matter* (Doubleday), by Peter Straub; and *Zero History* (Putman), by William Gibson. Ventures into the genre, or at least the ambiguous fringes of it, by well-known mainstream authors, included: *The Passage* (Ballantine Books), by Justin Cronin; *The Strange Affair of Spring Heeled Jack* (Prometheus Books), by Mark Hodder; *The Thousand Autumns of Jacob de Zoet* (Random House), by David Mitchell; and *Luka and the Fire of Life* (Random House), by Salman Rushdie.

It was a strong year for individual novellas published as chapbooks: Subterranean published *Blue and Gold*, by K. J. Parker; *Bone and Jewel Creatures*, by Elizabeth Bear; *The Lifecycle of Software Objects*, by Ted Chiang; *The God Engines*, by John Scalzi; *The Last Song of Orpheus*, by Robert Silverberg; and *The Taborin Scale*, by Lucius Shepard. PS Publishing brought out *Cloud Permutations*, by Lavie Tidhar, *Seven Cities of Gold*, by David Moles; *The Baby Killers*, by Jay Lake; and *Quartet and Triptych*, by Matthew Hughes. Fairwood Press published *The Specific Gravity of Grief*, by Jay Lake. Aqueduct Press published *Tomb of the Fathers*, by Eleanor Arnason. PM Press brought out *Mammoths of the Great Plains*, by Eleanor Arnason. Drollerie Press published *The Big Bah-Ha*, by C.S.E. Cooney. Silverberry Press brought out *Pink Noise*, by Leonid Korogodsky. Cemetery Dance published *Blockade Billy*, by Stephen King. Little, Brown published *The Short Second Life of Bree Tanner*, by Stephenie Meyer.

Novel omnibuses this year included: *Young Flandry* (Baen), by Poul Anderson; *Darkshade* (Night Shade Books), by Glen Cook; *The Ware Tetralogy* (Prime Books), by Rudy Rucker; *Virga*; *Cities of the Air* (Tor), by Karl Schroeder; *Flaming Zeppelins: The Adventures of Ned the Seal* (Tachyon Publications), by Joe R. Lansdale; *A Matter of Magic* (Orb Books), by Patricia C. Wrede; *Riverworld* (Tor), by Philip José Farmer; *Century of the Soldier* (Solaris Books), by Paul Kearney; *The Many Deaths of the Black Company* (Tor), by Glen Cook; *Beast Master's Planet* (Tor), by Andre Norton; *Search for the Star Stones* (Baen), by Andre Norton; *The Time Machine, The Invisible Man, The War of the Worlds* (Everyman's Library), by H. G. Wells; and *Damned If You Do in the Nightside* (Solaris Books), by Simon R. Green. (Omnibuses that contain both short stories *and* novels can be found listed in the short-story section.)

Not even counting print-on-demand books and the availability of out-of-print books as electronic downloads from Internet sources such as Fictionwise, a lot of long out-of-print stuff has come back into print in the last couple of years in commercial trade editions. Here's some out-of-print titles that came back into print this year, although producing a definitive list of reissued novels is probably impossible. Tor reissued: *The Currents of Space*, by Isaac Asimov; *The Word for World Is Forest*, by Ursula K. Le Guin; *A Fire Upon the Deep*, by Vernor Vinge; *The Dark Design*, by Philip José Farmer; *Dream Park*, by Larry Niven and Steven Barnes; *Hawkmoon: The Jewel in the Skull*, by Michael Moorcock; *Hawkmoon: The Runestaff*, by Michael Moorcock; *Hawkmoon: The Mad God's Amulet*, by Michael Moorcock; *Hawkmoon: The Sword of the Dawn*, by Michael Moorcock; and associational novel *The Man Whose Teeth Were All Exactly Alike*, by Philip K. Dick. Orb reissued: *Our Lady of Darkness*, by Fritz Leiber; *The World Inside*, by Robert Silverberg; *Slant*, by Greg Bear; *Moving Mars*, by Greg Bear; *Mysterium*, by Robert Charles Wilson; and *Spiritwalk* and *Muse and Reverie*, by Charles de Lint. Baen reissued: *The High Crusade*, by Poul Anderson and *The Rolling Stones*, by Robert A. Heinlein. Eos reissued: *Creatures of Light and Darkness*, by

Roger Zelazny. Roc reissued: *Sailing to Sarantium* and *Lord of Emperors*, by Guy Gavriel Kay. Night Shade Books reissued: *Starfishers* and *Stars' End: The Starfishers Trilogy, Volume Three*, by Glen Cook. Orbit reissued: *Fallen Dragon*, by Peter F. Hamilton. Aqueduct Press reissued: *Dorothea Dreams*, by Suzy McKee Charnas. Melville House reissued: *The Castle in Transylvania*, by Jules Verne. Ad Stellae reissued: *This Star Shall Abide*, by Sylvia Engdahl. Pazio Publishing reissued: *Steppe*, by Piers Anthony. Create Space reissued: *Dreambaby*, by Bruce McAllister.

It was another strong year for short-story collections, especially for career-spanning retrospective collections. The year's best nonretrospective collections included: *The Green Leopard Plague and Other Stories* (Night Shade Books), by Walter Jon Williams; *Journeys* (Subterranean Press), by Ian R. MacLeod; *The Sky That Wraps* (Subterranean Press), by Jay Lake; *On the Banks of the River of Heaven* (Prime Books), by Richard Parks; *Deep Navigation* (NESFA Press), by Alastair Reynolds; *Leviathan Wept* (Subterranean Press), by Daniel Abraham; *Recovering Apollo 8* (Golden Gryphon Press), by Kristine Kathryn Rusch; *The Third Bear* (Tachyon Publications), by Jeff VanderMeer; *Diana Comet and Other Improbable Stories* (Lethe Press), by Sandra McDonald; *The Ammonite Violin and Others* (Subterranean Press), by Caitlin R. Kiernan; *The Mysteries of the Diogenes Club* (MonkeyBrain), by Kim Newman; *Occultation* (Night Shade Books), by Laird Barron; *The Juniper Tree and Other Blue Rose Stories* (Subterranean Press), by Peter Straub; *What Will Come After?* (PS Publishing) by Scott Edelman; *Atlantis and Other Places* (Roc), by Harry Turtledove; *A Handful of Pearls and Other Stories* (Lethe Press), by Beth Bernobich; *What I Didn't See and Other Stories* (Small Beer Press), by Karen Joy Fowler; *Diving Mime, Weeping Czars, and Other Unusual Suspects* (Fairwood Press), by Ken Scholes; *Through the Drowsy Dark* (Aqueduct Press), by Rachel Swirsky; *The Poison Eaters* (Big Mouth House), by Holly Black; and *Full Dark, No Stars* (Scribner), by Stephen King.

It was an even stronger year for retrospective career-spanning collections. They included: *Fritz Leiber: Selected Stories* (Night Shade Books), by Fritz Leiber; *Hard-Luck Diggings: The Early Jack Vance* (Subterranean Press), by Jack Vance; *The Best of Kim Stanley Robinson* (Night Shade Books), by Kim Stanley Robinson; *Mirror Kingdoms: The Best of Peter S. Beagle* (Subterranean Press), by Peter S Beagle; *Young Flandry* (Baen), by Poul Anderson; *Sir Dominic Flandry: The Last Knight of Terra* (Baen), by Poul Anderson; *Captain Flandry: Defender of the Terran Empire* (Baen), by Poul Anderson; *The Collected Stories of Roger Zelazny: Volume Five—Nine Black Doves* (NESFA Press), by Roger Zelazny; *The Collected Stories of Roger Zelazny: Volume Six—The Road to Amber* (NESFA Press), by Roger Zelazny; *The Collected Short Works of Poul Anderson, Volume 3: The Saturn Game* (NESFA Press), by Poul Anderson; *Who Fears the Devil?: The Complete Tales of Silver John* (Planet Stories), by Manly Wade Wellman; *The Best of Joe R. Lansdale* (Tachyon Publications), by Joe R. Lansdale; *The Best of Larry Niven* (Subterranean Press), by Larry Niven; *Amberjack: Tales of Fear and Wonder*

(Subterranean Press), by Terry Dowling; *Detour to Otherness* (Haffner Press), by Henry Kutner and C. L. Moore; *The Early Kuttner, Volume One: Terror in the House* (Haffner Press), by Henry Kuttner; *The Stories of Ray Bradbury* (Everyman's Library), by Ray Bradbury; *Shirley Jackson: Novels and Stories* (Library of America); *Selected Short Stories of Lester Del Rey, Robots and Magic Volume 2* (NESFA Press), by Lester Del Rey; *An Empire Unacquainted with Defeat: A Chronicle of the Dread Empire* (Night Shade Books), by Glen Cook; *The Very Best of Charles de Lint* (Tachyon Publications), by Charles de Lint; *The Last Hieroglyph (The Collected Fantasies of Clark Ashton Smith, Vol. 5)* (Prime Books), by Clark Ashton Smith; *With Folded Hands . . . and Searching Minds: The Collected Stories of Jack Williamson, Volume Seven* (Haffner Press), Jack Williamson; and *Case and the Dreamer: Volume XIII: The Complete Stories of Theodore Sturgeon* (North Atlantic Books), by Theodore Sturgeon.

Small presses again dominated the list of short-story collections. Subterranean, Night Shade Books, and NESFA Press had particularly strong years.

A wide variety of "electronic collections," often called "fiction bundles," too many to individually list here, are also available for downloading online, at sites such as Fictionwise and ElectricStory, and the Science Fiction Book Club continues to issue new collections as well.

As is often the case, the most reliable buys in the reprint anthology market may have been the various "Best of the Year" anthology series. This is an area in constant flux—this year alone, we lost at least two Best Of series, maybe three, and added a brand-new one. Science fiction is being covered by three anthologies (actually, technically, by two anthologies and by two separate half anthologies): the one you are reading at the moment, *The Year's Best Science Fiction* series from St. Martin's Press, edited by Gardner Dozois, now up to its Twenty-Eighth Annual Collection; the *Year's Best SF* series (Eos), edited by David G. Hartwell and Kathryn Cramer, now up to its fifteenth annual volume; by the science fiction half of *The Best Science Fiction and Fantasy of the Year: Volume Five* (Night Shade Books), edited by Jonathan Strahan; and by the science fiction half of *The Year's Best Science Fiction and Fantasy, Edition 2010* (Prime Books), edited by Rich Horton (in practice, of course, these books probably won't divide neatly in half with their coverage, and there's likely to be more of one thing than another). The annual Nebula Awards anthology, which covers science fiction as well as fantasy of various sorts, functions as a de facto "Best of the Year" anthology, although it's not usually counted among them; this year's edition was *Nebula Awards Showcase 2010: The Year's Best SF and Fantasy Selected by the Science Fiction and Fantasy Writers of America* (Roc), edited by Bill Fawcett. In 2010, a similar series began, covering the Hugo winners, *The Hugo Award Showcase: 2010 Volume* (Prime Books), edited by Mary Robinette Kowal, but it died after a single volume. There were three Best of the Year anthologies covering horror: *The Best Horror of the Year, Volume Two* (Night Shade Books), edited by Ellen Datlow; *The Mammoth Book of Best New Horror 21* (Running Press), edited by

Stephen Jones; and a new series, *The Year's Best Dark Fantasy & Horror 2010* (Prime Books), edited by Paula Guran. The popularity of fantasy remains high, particularly in the novel market, but coverage of it by Best of the Year volumes continues to shrink. When the long-running Ellen Datlow, Kelly Link, and Gavin Grant *Year's Best Fantasy and Horror* series died early in 2009, Ellen Datlow found a new home for her horror best half almost immediately, but the Link and Grtist Fantasy Best half has yet to find a new home, and must be considered to be gone. David G. Hartwell and Kathryn Cramer's *Year's Best Fantasy* series was supposed to have transmogrified from a print publication into a version available as a download or a print-on-demand title from Tor.com, but I haven't seen any sign of it being actually available, and wonder if it isn't gone too. That left fantasy to be covered by the fantasy halves of Strahan's *The Best Science Fiction and Fantasy of the Year* and Horton's *The Year's Best Science Fiction and Fantasy* (plus whatever stories fall under the "Dark Fantasy" part of Guran's anthology), and by *Real Unreal: Best American Fantasy, Volume 3* (Underland Press), edited by Kevin Brockmeier and Matthew Cheney—but it's just been announced that that series is dying as well. There was also *The 2010 Rhysling Anthology* (Science Fiction Poetry Association), edited by Jamie Lee Moyer, which compiles the Rhysling Award-winning SF poetry of the year.

The most prominent of the year's stand-alone reprint anthologies was probably *The Wesleyan Anthology of Science Fiction* (Wesleyan University Press), edited by Arthur B. Evans and five others from the staff of academic journal *Science Fiction Studies*, an attempt at a definitive canon-forming book that gives a retrospective overview of the development of science fiction from 1844 to 2008, starting with Nathaniel Hawthorne, Jules Verne, and H. G. Wells, passing through the Usual Suspects, and ending up with writers like Greg Egan, Geoff Ryman, Charles Stross, and Ted Chiang. Another retrospective, this time of the Alternate History subgenre, is *The Mammoth Book of Alternate Histories* (Robinson, Constable & Robinson), a mixed reprint (mostly) and original anthology edited by Ian Watson and Ian Whates. *Digital Domains: A Decade of Science Fiction & Fantasy* (Prime Books), edited by Ellen Datlow, collects some of the best fiction that Ellen has published in the online magazines that she's edited over the last few years, and the similar *Unplugged: The Web's Best Sci-Fi and Fantasy: 2008* (Wyrm Publishing), edited by Rich Horton, is also devoted to stories published in online venues. A retrospective look back over the history of the burgeoning subgenre of steampunk (there were at least three anthologies featuring it this year) is given in *Steampunk Prime* (Nonstop Press), edited by Michael Ashley, and in *Steampunk II: Steampunk Reloaded* (Tachyon Publications) a mixed reprint (mostly) and original anthology edited by Ann VanderMeer and Jeff VanderMeer.

A similar retrospective anthology for fantasy, a bit less inclusive than the Wesleyan anthology, is *The Secret History of Fantasy* (Tachyon Publications), edited by Peter S. Beagle, which features authors such as Neil Gaiman, Stephen King, Maureen McHugh, Michael Swanwick, and others. *Wings of Fire* (Night Shade Books), edited by Jonathan Strahan and Marianne S. Jablon, is a mixed reprint (mostly) and original fantasy anthology about dragons, featuring Ursula K. Le

Guin, George R. R. Martin, Lucius Shepard, Roger Zelazny, and others. The self-explanatory *People of the Book: A Decade of Jewish Science Fiction and Fantasy* (Prime Books), edited by Rachel Swirsky and Sean Wallace, is a reprint anthology featuring Peter S. Beagle, Theodora Gross, Neil Gaiman, Janet Yolen, Michael Chabon, and others.

Other good reprint anthologies include *The End of the World: Stories of the Apocalypse* (Skyhorse Publishing), edited by Martin H. Greenberg (one of two big End-of-the-World anthologies this year; do you think the universe is trying to tell us something?), *Before They Were Giants: First Works from Science Fiction Greats* (Paizo Publishing), edited by James L. Sutter; an anthology of cat fantasy/horror stories, *Tails of Wonder and Imagination* (Night Shade Books), edited by Ellen Datlow; a mixed reprint (mostly) and original anthology of military SF, *Citizens* (Baen Books), edited by John Ringo and Brian M. Thomsen; an anthology of Deal-With-the-Devil stories, *Sympathy for the Devil* (Night Shade Books), edited by Tim Pratt; *Realms 2: The Second Year of Clarkesworld Magazine* (Wyrm Publishing), stories from the e-zine, edited by Nick Mamatas and Sean Wallace; and an anthology of stories drawn from the now-defunct *Talebones* magazine, *The Best of Talebones* (Fairwood Press), edited by Patrick Swenson.

The big retrospective reprint horror anthology this year is *Darkness: Two Decades of Modern Horror* (Tachyon Publications), edited by Ellen Datlow, but there was also *The Mammoth Book of the Best of Best New Horror* (Running Press Book Publishers), edited by Stephen Jones, and *Zombies: The Recent Dead* (Prime Books), edited by Paula Guran. There were also several original zombie anthologies, an all-zombie single-author collection—Scott Edelman's *What Will Come After*—and numerous zombie stories scattered through 2010's magazines, e-zines, and anthologies (the best of which were probably "The Naturalist," by Maureen McHugh and "The Crocodiles," by Steven Popkes), as well as a TV show about them, so fans of the shuffling dead have a lot to be thankful for this year. I think there were actually more zombie stories than vampire stories in 2010, in spite of the continuing popularity of *Twilight* and *True Blood*.)

The most prominent genre-oriented nonfiction book of the year was almost certainly the biographical study *Robert A. Heinlein: In Dialogue with His Century: 1907–1948: Learning Curve* (Tor), by William H. Patterson, Jr. This huge book is only the *first half* of an exhaustive (sometime *too* exhaustive) work that will almost certainly stand as the comprehensive biography of SF giant Robert A. Heinlein, especially as many of the sources that Patterson tapped are no longer available to be interviewed. SF fans will find it fascinating, of course, for its look at the early years of Heinlein's writing career and the pulp magazine era of the forties, but the lengthy sections on Heinlein's stint at the Naval Academy and as an active-duty sailor, and on his abortive career as a political campaign manager are interesting in their own right, providing a detailed look back at the America of the early twentieth century, a place so different in mores, customs, and lifeways from America in the twenty-first century that it might as well be an alien world.

Another exhaustive biography of a major genre author is supplied by *C. M. Kornbluth: The Life and Works of a Science Fiction Visionary* (McFarland), by

Mark Rich. Kornbluth is a complex, fascinating, and immensely talented figure now in danger of being forgotten, certainly a worthwhile figure for a biological study and critical reassessment if there ever was one. Unfortunately, clouds of controversy have swirled around the book from its release, mostly for the intensely unflattering portrait it paints of Kornbluth's friend and lifelong collaborator Frederik Pohl, which have caused Pohl to vehemently deny the veracity of many of Rich's "facts"—all of which has cast something of a shadow over what by rights should have been one of the preeminent genre nonfiction books of the year.

80! Memories and Reflections on Ursula K. Le Guin (Aqueduct Press), edited by Karen Joy Fowler and Debbie Notkin, is an assemblage of critical articles, appreciations, poems, and even some fiction put together in honor of the eightieth birthday of SF writer Ursula K. Le Guin. All of it is worth reading, but the best piece here is a partial biography of Le Guin by Julie Phillips, the writer who did the biography of Alice Sheldon ("James Tiptree, Jr.") a few years back, and that's good enough to encourage hopes that Phillips will take a crack at a full-dress biography of Le Guin one of these days. *I Am Providence: The Life and Times of H. P. Lovecraft* (Hippocampus Press), by S. T. Joshi, takes a critical and biographical look at horror giant H. P. Lovecraft. *Conversations with Octavia Butler* (University Press of Mississippi), edited by Conseula Francis, is a collection of interviews conducted with the late author fron 1980 to just before her tragic death. *Listen to the Echoes: The Ray Brabury Interviews* (Stopsmiling Books), edited by Sam Weller, is a similar collection of interviews with Bradbury, nonfiction essays by Michael Moorcock are collected in *Into the Media Web: Selected Non-Fiction, 1956–2006* (Savoy Books), by Michael Moorcock, and *Understanding Philip K. Dick* (University of South Carolina Press), by Eric Carl Link, adds another title to the ten-foot shelf of critical studies of Philip K. Dick (a writer almost completely ignored by academic critics during his lifetime, by the way—as were H. P. Lovecraft and C. M. Kornbluth, for that matter). Critic Gary K. Wolfe examines a wide range of authors in *Bearings: Reviews 1997–2001* (Beccon Publications), Paul Kincaid and Niall Harrison offer a critical overlook of genre in Britain in *British Science Fiction & Fanasy: Twenty Years, Two Surveys* (Odd Two Out), L. Timmel Duchamp edits a nonfiction anthology of sixteen essays by well-known writers in *Narrative Power: Encounters, Celebrations, Struggles* (Aqueduct Press), and Bud Webster reviews some of the most prominent fiction anthologies in the field in *Anthopology 101: Reflections, Inspections and Dissections of SF Anthologies* (Merry Blacksmith Press).

Two perhaps contrasting perspectives on the genre's ability as a predictive medium are offered in *Visions of Tomorrow: Science Fiction Predictions That Came True* (Skyhorse Publishing), by Thomas A. Easton and Judith K. Dial and *The Wonderful Future That Never Was* (Hearst Books), by Gregory Benford and the editors of *Popular Mechanics* magazine.

Of interest to those who lean toward the media side of the field may be *The Science of Doctor Who* (John Hopkins University Press), by Paul Persons, and *Firefly: Still Flying: A Celebration of Joss Whedon's Acclaimed TV Series* (Titan Books), by Joss Whedon.

An entertaining attempt at creating a modern Bestiary, of creatures drawn from myth and folklore, is *The Kosher Guide to Imaginary Animals* (Tachyon Publications), by Ann VanderMeer and Jeff VanderMeer.

After a strong year last year, 2010 seemed to be a somewhat weaker year in the art book market. The best, and certainly the most varied, was the latest in a long-running "Best of the Year" series for fantastic art, *Spectrum 17: The Best in Contemporary Fantastic Art* (Underwood Books), edited by Cathy Fenner and Arnie Fenner. Also worthwhile were two other varied collections of SF art, *Sci-Fi Art Now* (Collins Design), edited by John Freeman, and *EXPOSÉ 8: The Finest Digital Art in the Known Universe* (Ballistic Publishing), edited by Daniel P. Wade. Evocative and painterly views of scenes from fantasy books by J.R.R. Tolkien and Robert E. Howard were available in *Middle-Earth: Visions of a Modern Myth* (Underwood Books), by Donato Giancola and *Sword's Edge: Paintings Inspired by the Works of Robert E. Howard* (Underwood Books), by Manuel Sanjulian, and scenes from *Star Wars* were on display in *Star Wars Art: Visions* (Abrams), edited by anoymous. There were collections of paintings by Bob Eggleton, *Dragon's Domain* (Impact), by Bob Eggleton, and Jack Gaughan, *Outermost* (Nonstop Press), edited by Luis Ortiz, a collection by Daniel Merriman, *Taking Reality by Surprise* (Monarch Editions), two collections of work by William Stout, *Inspirations* (Flesk Publications) and *Hallucinations* (Flesk Publications), and there was also a collection by comics artist Neal Adams, *The Art of Neal Adams* (Vanguard Productions), by Neal Adams. Studies of pulp art included *Savage Art: 20th Century Genre and the Artists that Defined It* (Underwood Books), edited by Tim Underwood, Arnie Fenner, and Cathy Fenner, and *Shameless Art: 20th Century Genre Art and the Artists That Defined It* (Underwood Books), edited by Tim Underwood, Arnie Fenner, and Cathy Fenner. A collections of paintings that double as instructional books included *Color and Light: A Guide for the Realist Painter* (Andrews McMeel Publishing), by James Gurney, and *OtherWorlds: How to Imagine, Paint and Create Epic Scenes of Fantasy* (Impact Books), by Tom Kidd.

As you can see, Underwood Books had probably the strongest year in this area.

According to the Box Office Mojo site (www.boxofficemojo.com), nine out of ten of the year's top-earning movies were genre films of one sort or another, if you accept animated films and superhero movies as being "genre films." (The exception was *The Karate Kid*, in tenth place.) The year's top five box-office champs were all genre movies by that definition, as were fourteen out of the top twenty earners, and roughly thirty-seven out of the top 100, more or less (I might have missed one here or there).

For the first time since 2004, when *Shrek 2* pulled it off, the year's number one box office champ (not counting 2009's *Avatar*, which *still* pulled in more this year than any of the 2010 films) was an animated film, *Toy Story 3*. It and the second-place finisher, Tim Burton's "reimagined" *Alice in Wonderland*, earned *more than a billion dollars apiece* worldwide, with a steep drop-off to the film in the third spot, the superhero movie *Iron Man 2*, which earned "only" $622,056,974 worldwide.

Unlike last year, there were few SF movies (as opposed to fantasy movies, superhero movies, and animated films), even bad SF with junk science like last year's *Avatar, Star Trek*, and *Transformers: Revenge of the Fallen*, let alone smaller-budgeted more "serious" movies such as *Moon* and *District 9*. The most notable exception, and the one that seemed to get the most critical respect, was the Philip K. Dick–like *Inception*, about manipulating people's dreams for your own purposes, which also did well at the box office, finishing in sixth place. The low-budget alien invasion movie, *Monsters*, got a surprising amount of critical respect, although it barely made a ripple on the box-office charts. The soap-opera vampire romance *The Twilight Saga: Eclipse* came in at fourth place, and the more traditional fantasy movie *Harry Potter and the Deathly Hallows: Part 1* at fifth place (the new version of *Clash of the Titans*, another fantasy movie, finished in fourteenth place, still probably good enough to earn it a sequel). The rest of the top ten were rounded off by other animated films: *Despicable Me* in seventh place, *Shrek Forever After* in eighth, and *How to Train Your Dragon* in ninth (this was a big year for animated films, with *Tangled* coming in at tenth place, and *Megamind* and *Legend of the Guardians: The Owls of Ga' Hoole* further down in the pack).

This shouldn't surprise anybody—genre films (with the inevitable disclaimer, "of one sort or another"; often they're superhero movies) have dominated the box office top ten for more than a decade now. You have to go all the way back to 1998 to find a year when the year's top earner was a nongenre film, *Saving Private Ryan*.

In spite of the presence of some immense-earning Mega-Movies, it seemed like a lackluster year in some respects, with little getting much critical respect except for *Inception* (and even there, reviews were sharply mixed), and, to some extent, *Toy Story 3* and *Harry Potter and the Deathly Hallows: Part 1*. Even at the box office, it was far from a year of universal success. *The Chronicles of Narnia: The Voyage of the Dawn Treader, The Wolfman, Jonah Hex, The Book of Eli, The Last Airbender, Yogi Bear*, and (probably the most critically savaged movie of the year) *Gulliver's Travels* were all disappointments to one degree or another, and attempts to establish viable new franchises such as *Prince of Persia: The Sands of Time, Scott Pilgrim vs. the World, The Sorcerer's Apprentice*, and *Percy Jackson & the Olympians: The Lightning Thief* were all failures. The "superhero" satire *Kick-Ass* was famously controversial for a short while for its scenes of extreme ultraviolence committed by an eleven-year-old girl, but in spite of all the tongue-clicking in *Time* and *Newsweek*, could only make it to sixty-seventh place on the box office list.

Although 2010 was still the second-highest grossing year of all time for the movie industry, estimated attendance was the lowest in fifteen years, 1.27 billion people, down 8 percent from the previous year. Does this mean that fewer people were paying more money to see movies? With the boom in movies released in 3-D and IMAX, for more expensive ticket prices, that's quite possible. The increased accessibility of movies on the Internet and through services such as

Netflix and On Demand, often only a few months after they come out in first release, plus the continuing recession, may be discouraging some people from going to the theater—although at 1.27 billion, that's still a lot of people buying tickets!

Most of the buzz so far in 2011 (although we're only a few weeks into it as I write these words) is for the upcoming *Harry Potter and the Deathly Hallows: Part 2*, the last of the Harry Potter franchise. The promised sequels to *Avatar, Star Trek, 2012,* and *Transformers* are still promised, as are film versions of Joe Haldeman's *The Forever War,* John Wyndham's *Chocky,* and Isaac Asimov's *Foundation*; no doubt some of these will show up sooner or later, although it's hard to tell which (bet on *Avatar*; it's made far too much money for there not to be a sequel, perhaps more than one of them). There'll be a new Twilight movie, *Breaking Dawn*, which I believe will be split into two parts, as was *Harry Potter and the Deathly Hallows*. So far, 2011 looks like it's going to be a big year for *Independence Day* clones, aliens attacking all over the place, and will perhaps see a big resurgence in superhero movies, with *Captain America* and *The Green Hornet*, and *Thor* looming on the horizon like a thundercloud.

It was a lackluster year for SF and fantasy shows on television.

Lost ended with an anticlimactic everybody-goes-to-Heaven-and-leaves-almost-all-of-the-major-questions-unanswered-behind-them finale that disappointed most Losties, outraged many, and soured some retrospectively on the series to the point where they wouldn't even buy the DVD. *Heroes, FlashForward, The Prisoner,* and *Battlestar Galactica* prequel *Caprica* the Great White Hopes of last season, all died, and *Stargate Universe* will follow them into oblivion after running its last few episodes early this year. The long-running *Smallville* is finally coming to an end, and will run its final episode in the spring. The long-running *Medium* is also ending, and the new vampire show *The Gates* closed its gates and returned to the quiet of its grave.

Fringe, The Event, and *V* all returned, but are wobbling in the ratings, and may not last out the year.

Supernatural, Vampire Diaries, Star Wars: The Clone Wars, Chuck, and zombie show *The Walking Dead* are returning, as are the SF comedies *Eureka* and *Warehouse 13. Doctor Who* and *Primeval* are returning, and a *Torchwood* spin-off, *Torchwood: The New World,* set in the United States, will be starting up. There will also be an American version of the BBC show, *Being Human*, about a vampire, a ghost, and a werewolf living together in the same apartment (which always sounds to me like the setup for a joke: "A vampire, a ghost, and a werewolf walk into a bar . . .") *Merlin* is returning, and will be joined by another Arthurian fantasy series, *Camelot*. Two live-action superhero shows, *No Ordinary Family* and *The Cape*, started up; *The Cape* has already died.

Movie director Steven Spielberg will be making his first foray into series television with two new shows: *Terra Nova*, in which scientists escape through time from a doomed and ruined Earth to attempt to restart the human race in a prehistoric era, and *Falling Skies*, in which embattled guerilla militiamen battle alien invasion forces who have destroyed much of the Earth and killed most of the people. (Guess that Spielberg doesn't envision much of a future for humanity.)

Blood and Chrome, a new prequel to *Battlestar Galactica*, is coming up, as are a slew of animated superhero shows, including *Young Justice*, following the adventures of the young sidekicks of Justice League characters, *Green Lantern: The Animated Series*, and *Batman: The Brave and the Bold*.

Most of the quality work on television seems to be being done on HBO these days, from the campy fun of vampire show *True Blood* to nongenre dramatic series such as *Boardwalk Empire* and *Big Love*. Coming up from them is the long-awaited miniseries versions of George R. R. Martin's *A Game of Thrones*. A miniseries version of Kim Stanley Robinson's *Red Mars* is supposed to be coming up from AMC.

The 68th World Science Fiction Convention, Aussiecon 4, was held in Melbourne, Victoria, Australia, from September 2 to September 6, 2010. The 2010 Hugo Awards, presented at Aussiecon 4, were: Best Novel (tie), *The Windup Girl*, by Paolo Bacigalupi and *The City and the City*, by China Miéville; Best Novella, "Palimpsest," by Charles Stross; Best Novelette, "The Island," by Peter Watts; Best Short Story, "Bridesicle," by Will McIntosh; Best Related Book, *This is Me, Jack Vance! (Or, More Properly, This is "I")*, by Jack Vance; Best Professional Editor, Long Form, Patrick Nielsen Hayden; Best Professional Editor, Short Form, Ellen Datlow; Best Professional Artist, Shaun Tan; Best Dramatic Presentation (short form), *Doctor Who*: "The Waters of Mars"; Best Dramatic Presentation (long form), *Moon*; Best Graphic Story, *Girl Genius, Volume 9: Agatha Heterodyne and the Heirs of the Storm*, by Kaja and Phil Foglio, art by Phil Foglio; Best Semiprozine, *Clarkesworld*; Best Fanzine, *StarShipSofa*: Best Fan Writer, Frederik Pohl; Best Fan Artist, Brad W. Foster; plus the John W. Campbell Award for Best New Writer to Seanan McGuire.

The 2009 Nebula Awards, presented at a banquet at the Hilton Cocoa Beach Oceanfront Hotel in Cocoa Beach, Florida, on May 15, 2010, were: Best Novel, *The Windup Girl*, by Paolo Bacigalupi; Best Novella, *The Women of Nell Gwynne's*, by Kage Baker; Best Novelette, "Sinner, Baker, Fabulist, Priest; Red Mask, Black Mask, Gentleman, Beast," by Eugie Foster; Best Short Story, "Spar," by Kij Johnson; Ray Bradbury Award, *District 9*, by Neill Blomkamp and Terri Tatchell; the Andre Norton Award to *The Girl Who Circumnavigated Fairyland in a Ship of Her Own Making*, by Catherynne M. Valente; the Solstice Award to Tom Doherty, Terri Windling, and Donald A. Wollheim, the Author Emeritus Award to Neil Barrett, Jr.; and the Grand Master Award to Joe Haldeman.

The 2010 World Fantasy Awards, presented at a banquet at the Hyatt Regency Hotel in Columbus, Ohio, on October 31, 2010, during the Nineteenth Annual World Fantasy Convention, were: Best Novel, *The City and the City*, by China Miéville; Best Novella, "Sea-Hearts," by Margo Lanagan; Best Short Story, "The Pelican Bar," by Karen Joy Fowler; Best Collection (tie), *The Very Best of Gene Wolfe/The Best of Gene Wolfe*, by Gene Wolfe and *There Once Lived a Woman Who Tried to Kill Her Neighbor's Baby: Scary Fairy Tales*, by Ludmilla Petrushevskaya; Best Anthology, *American Fantastic Tales: Terror and the Uncanny: From Poe to the Pulps/From the 1940s to Now*, edited by Peter Straub; Best Artist, Charles Vess; Special Award (Professional), to Jonathan Strahan, for editing anthologies; Special Award (Nonprofessional), to Susan Marie Groppi, for *Strange Horizons*; plus the Life Achievement Award to Terry Pratchett, Peter Straub, and Brian Lumley.

The 2009 Bram Stoker Awards, presented by the Horror Writers Association were: Best Novel, *Audrey's Door*, by Sarah Langan; Best First Novel, *Damnable*, by Hank Schwaeble; Best Long Fiction, *The Lucid Dreaming*, by Lisa Morton; Best Short Fiction, "In the Perches of My Ears," by Norman Prentiss; Best Collection, *A Taste of Tenderloin*, by Gene O'Neill; Best Anthology, *He Is Legend: An Anthology Celebrating Richard Matheson*, edited by Christopher Conlon; Nonfiction, *Writers Workshop of Horror*, by Michael Knost; Best Poetry Collection, *Chimeric Machines*, by Lucy A. Snyder; plus Lifetime Achievement Awards to William F. Nolan and Brian Lumley.

The 2010 John W. Campbell Memorial Award was won by *The Windup Girl*, by Paolo Bacigalupi.

The 2010 Theodore Sturgeon Memorial Award for Best Short Story was won by *Shambling Towards Hiroshima*, by James Morrow.

The 2009 Philip K. Dick Memorial Award went to *Bitter Angels*, by C. L. Anderson.

The 2010 Arthur C. Clarke Award was won by *The City and the City*, by China Miéville.

The 2010 James Tiptree, Jr. Memorial Award was won by *Cloud and Ashes: Three Winter's Tales*, by Greer Gilman and *Ooku: The Inner Chambers, volumes 1 & 2*, by Fumi Yoshinaga (tie)

The 2010 Sidewise Award went to *1942*, by Robert Conroy (Long Form) and "The Fixation," by Alastair Reynolds (Short Form).

The 2010 Cordwainer Smith Rediscovery Award went to Mark Clifton.

Dead in 2010 or early 2011 were:

JAMES P. HOGAN, 69, author of *Inherit the Stars. The Gentle Giants of Ganymede*, and many others; **E. C. TUBB**, 90, veteran British SF writer, author of more than 1340 novels, including, his best-known, the thirty-two-volume Dumarest series of space operas; **MARTIN GARDINER**, 95, author, mathematician, and puzzle-maker, who wrote long-running mathematics columns for *Scientific American* and *Asmiov's Science Fiction*; **ARTHUR HERZOG III**, 83, mainstream author who also wrote some books with SF elements, such as *The Swarm*; **MERVYN JONES**, 87, author of twenty-nine novels, including some SF; **PATRICIA WRIGHTSON**, 88, author of twenty-seven children's and Young Adult books; **STEPHEN GILBERT**, 97, Irish SF and horror writer; three-time Edgar-winner and mystery mainstay, **JOE GORES**, 79, author of *Hammett* and *32 Cadillacs*; **ELISABETH BERESFORD**, 84, British children's author, creator of the long-running series about *The Wombles*; **JOHN STEAKLEY**, 59, SF writer, author of *Armor*; **WILLIAM MAYNE**, 82, author of more than 100 children's books, some with SF elements; **FRANK K. KELLY**, 95, veteran writer; **JIM HARMON**, 76, author of more than forty stories in the fifties and sixties, most for *Galaxy* and *Worlds of If*; **GEORGE EWING**, 64, SF writer, contributor to *Asmov's* and *Analog*; **MELISSA MIA HALL**, 54, SF/horror writer and anthologist, a friend; **JEANNIE ROBINSON**, 62, author, dancer, and choreographer, wife of SF writer Spider Robinson, a friend; **F. GWYNPLAINE MacINTYRE**, 62, prolific short-story writer who was a mainstay of *Asimov's* during the George Scithers years, and also sold to *Amazing*, *Weird Tales*, and elsewhere; **MARY HUNTER SCHAUB**, 66, SF and fantasy writer, author with Andre Norton of *The Magestone*; **JENNIFER RARDIN**, 45, urban fantasy writer, author of *Once Bitten, Twice Shy*; **REBECCA NEASON**, 55, fantasy and media novel writer; **JOHN SCHOENHERR**, 74, Hugo-winning SF cover artist and nature illustrator who did some of the most famous covers ever for *Analog*, including the cover for the serialization of Frank Herbert's *Dune*; **FRANK FRAZETTA**, 82, famous fantasy artist, Hugo and World Fantasy Award–winner, best known for his covers for Robert E. Howard's *Conan the Barbarian* and for covers for many books by Edgar Rice Burroughs; **ROBERT McCALL**, 90, artist perhaps best known for the movie poster for *2001: A Space Odyssey*, although he also worked on Disney's Epcot Center and the National Air and Space Museum, as well as for *Life* magazine; **AL WILLIAMSON**, 79, comic artist; **GEORGE H. SCITHERS**, 80, founding editor of *Asimov's Science Fiction*, who also served as editor for *Amazing* and *Weird Tales* and was a prominent agent and fanzine editor, winner of a Hugo and the Lifetime Achievement Award from the World Fantasy Convention; **RALPH M. VICINANZA**, 60, perhaps the most successful and prestigious literary agent in the history of SF, certainly of the last several decades, who at one time or another was the agent for most of the prominent authors in the field, and who helped establish and expand the overseas market for American SF; **LARRY ASHMEAD**, 78, who at one time or another was a major book editor at Doubleday, Simon & Schuster, Lippincott, and Harper & Row; **BOB GUCCIONE**, 79, publisher of *Penthouse*, probably best known in the field for launching the prestigious magazine *OMNI*; **ELAINE KOSTER**, 69, literary agent and publisher, who was responsible for helping to launch the career of Stephen King; **EVERETT F. BLEILER**, 90, bibliographer and scholar, compiler of *The Checklist of Fantastic Literature: A Bibliography of Fantasy, Weird and Science Fiction Books Published in the English Language*, as well as, with T. E. Ditky, the editor of *The Best Science Fiction Stories*, the first annual Year's Best anthology series, winner of the World Fantasy Life Achievement Award; **DONALD H. TUCK**, 89, Hugo-winning Australian bibliographer, compiler of *A Handbook of Science Fiction and Fantasy* and *The Encyclopedia of Science Fiction and Fantasy through 1968: A Bibliographic Survey of the Fields of Science Fiction, Fantasy, and Weird Fiction through 1968*; **NEIL BARRON**, 76, bibliographer and scholar, author of one of the standard SF references, *Anatomy of Wonder*; **JERRY WEIST**, 61, author, bookseller, and collector, author of the Hugo-winning *Ray Bradbury: An Illustrated Life*; **GLEN GOODKNIGHT**, 69, founder of the Mythopoeic Society; **GLENN LEWIS GILLETTE**, 64, SF writer who edited the SFWA e-newsletter for many years; **LESLIE NIELSEN**,

84, film and television actor, best known to genre audiences for starring in the classic film *Forbidden Planet*, although they're likely to also know him from later movies like *Airplane!* and *The Naked Gun*; **ANNE FRANCIS**, 80, Nielsen's co-star from *Forbidden Planet*, who also did much television work, including episodes of *The Twilight Zone*; **KEVIN McCARTHY**, 96, film actor, best known to genre audience for starring in the original version of *Invasion of the Body Snatchers*; **PATRICIA NEAL**, 84, film actor, best known to genre audiences for costarring in the original *The Day the Earth Stood Still*; **PETER POSTLETHWAITE**, 64, British film actor, perhaps best known to genre audiences from *Inception* and *The Lost World: Jurrasic Park*; **HAROLD GOULD**, 86, film and television actor, perhaps best known to genre audiences from his appearances in episodes of *The Twilight Zone, Lois & Clark, The Outer Limits*, and *The Ray Bradbury Theater*, although I have little doubt that many of them would also remember him from *The Sting*; **TONY CURTIS**, 85, film actor, one of the most famous leading men of the fifties and sixties, his connection with the genre is fairly tenuous, although no doubt many will remember him from *The Vikings* and *The Great Race*, which had slight fantastic elements; **JAMES GAMMON**, 70, gravel-voiced film and television actor who appeared in *The Milagro Beanfield War, Silverado*, and TV's *The Wild Wild West* and *Batman*, and did voiceover work in *The Iron Giant*; **STEVE LANDESBERG**, 74, television actor, best known as the eccentric detective in *Barney Miller*; **BLAKE EDWARDS**, 88, film director, perhaps best known for *Victor Victoria* and the *Pink Panther* movies; **DINO DE LAURENTIIS**, 91, film producer, best known to genre audiences for *Dune, Barbarella, Conan the Barbarian*, and an awful version of *King Kong*; **ASENATH HAMMOND**, 60, longtime fan and blogger, ex-wife of SF artist Rick Sternbach, a friend; **ANNETTE STITH**, widow of SF writer John E. Stith; **MARY E. STUBBS**, 87, widow of Harry Stubbs, who wrote SF as "Hal Clement"; **BETTY BOND**, 94, widow of SF writer Nelson Bond; **EILEEN PRATCHETT**, 88, mother of fantasy writer Terry Pratchett; **NATHAN DATLOW**, 93, father of editor Ellen Datlow; **AVERY LEEMING NAGLE**, 85, mother of SF writer Pati Nagle; **GAIL ZETTEL** 74, mother of SF writer Sarah Zettel; **GARDNER McSWIGGIN**, 82, uncle of editor Gardner Dozois.

A History of Terraforming

ROBERT REED

The sprawling, vividly imaginative story that follows traces the protagonist, Simon, from his childhood on a newly settled Mars hundreds of years into an increasingly strange future. Simon is an "atum," a terraformer, and each step in his career as he grows in knowledge and abilities showcases the strengths and weaknesses, the ethical as well as physical pros and cons, of terraforming, as the terraformers create new worlds— and sometimes destroy old ones as well.

Robert Reed sold his first story in 1986, and quickly established himself as one of the most prolific of today's writers, particularly at short fiction lengths, and has managed to keep up a very high standard of quality *while* being prolific, something that is not at all easy to do. Reed stories such as "Sister Alice," "Brother Perfect," "Decency," "Savior," "The Remoras," "Chrysalis," "Whiptail," "The Utility Man," "Marrow," "Birth Day," "Blind," "The Toad of Heaven," "Stride," "The Shape of Everything," "Guest of Honor," "Waging Good," and "Killing the Morrow," among at least a half-dozen others equally as strong, count as among some of the best short work produced by anyone in the eighties and nineties; many of his best stories have been assembled in the collections *The Dragons of Springplace* and *The Cuckoo's Boys*. He won the Hugo Award in 2007 for his novella "A Billion Eves." Nor is he nonprolific as a novelist, having turned out eleven novels since the end of the eighties, including *The Leeshore, The Hormone Jungle, Black Milk, The Remarkables, Down the Bright Way, Beyond the Veil of Stars, An Exaltation of Larks, Beneath the Gated Sky, Marrow, Sister Alice,* and *The Well of Stars,* as well as two chapbook novellas, *Mere* and *Flavors of My Genius.* His most recent book is a new novel, *Eater-of-Bone.* Reed lives with his family in Lincoln, Nebraska.

MARS

Simon's father started talking about nuts on walls, about how the seeds he was working with looked very much like wall nuts. Then he winked, handing over the wonder that he had been carrying in his big palm. "What do you think of this, Simon?" But before the boy could answer, his father cautioned him to use both hands and be especially careful. "Not because you might damage the seed," the man said. "Or because it would ever hurt you. But certain objects are important, sometimes even sacred, and they deserve all the consideration and respect that we can possibly show for them."

Considering how small it was, the seed was exceptionally heavy. It was black and hard as diamond but covered with small, sharp-edged pits. Against his bare palms, the object felt warm. Maybe the heat was leftover from where the seed was kept, or maybe it was warm in the same way that little boys were warm. Either answer might be true. He didn't ask. He just held the object in his cupped hands and stared, wondering what would happen if the impossible occurred, if the seed decided to awaken now.

For one person, time passed.

Then his father asked again, "What do you think, Simon?"

The boy's thoughts were shifting quickly, clinging to no single idea. He was telling himself that he wasn't even three-years-old. But on the earth he would already be four, and every four-year-old that he knew enjoyed large, impressive opinions. But if he lived near Neptune, he wouldn't be a month old and his father would never take him riding along on his working trips. And if this were Mercury, then Simon would be many years old, and because of certain pernicious misunderstandings about calendars and the passage of time, he believed that on Mercury he would be an adult. He was remembering how people said that he was going to grow up tall and handsome. It was as if adults had the power to peer into the future. They didn't admit to children that they had this talent, but the truth often leaked out in careless words and unwanted glimpses. Simon liked the idea of peering into the future. Right now, he was trying to imagine himself living in some important, unborn century. The nearly three-year-old boy wanted to be a grown man entrusted with some very important job. But for the time being, riding with his father seemed important enough. That's what he was thinking when he handed back that precious and very expensive seed, grinning as he said, "It's delicious, Dad." He had never been happier than he was just then.

"Do you know how it works?"

"Yes," the boy claimed.

"No, you don't," his father warned. "It's my job to find homes for these little buggers, and I barely understand them."

That admission of ignorance made a deep impression. Quietly, Simon asked, "What do floor nuts look like?"

Puzzled, his father blinked and said nothing.

Simon pointed at the seed. "I've never seen a wall look like that."

His father said, "Oh," and then softly laughed. "It's not two words. 'Walnut' is one word. It's the seed made by a species of earth tree."

"I know what trees are," the boy boasted.

"You've seen the pictures, at least." His father turned away, setting the heavy black wonder back into its important drawer. Then as he walked to the front of the rover, he added, "Here's something else to think about: One of my seeds is quite a bit more complicated than any unborn tree. There's more information packed inside that hull than normal DNA can hold. And considerably more power than roots and leaves would ever show on their own."

Simon walked behind his father, looking through the wide windows. Mars was rocky and pale red, last night's frost hiding in the coldest shade. The ground couldn't have been rougher, yet the rover walked without rocking or lurching or jumping. High clouds and at least three mirrors looked down on them from the purple sky, and the skyhook known as Promise was straight ahead. Today the wind was blowing, moving hard enough to throw the smallest bits of dust. Dust was dangerous. The cold was dangerous. Mars liked to kill people, particularly careless children who didn't listen to their fathers and other wise voices.

But the world wouldn't be dangerous much longer, Simon thought.

For a long while, they rode toward Promise, but the slender tower didn't come any closer. Then the AI driver took them around the flank of a low hill and over the lip of a worn-out crater, and suddenly they were looking into a wide basin filled with brilliant water ice.

"Is this the lake?" Simon asked.

His father was busy reading two different screens.

This must be their goal, the boy decided. But he thought it was best not to interrupt, his father busy with something that could only be important.

He sat on the nearest chair, watching everything.

The rover walked down to the shoreline. Out on the ice stood a little tower and another rover, and somebody was moving slowly in one direction, then another. The stranger was wearing a big lifesuit, the kind used by people planning to be outside for a long time. Someday Simon wouldn't need a suit to walk in the open. Adults promised that in the future, he would be a tall, good-looking man and wear nothing but clothes and good shoes, and Mars would be the second earth, but even better.

Simon would live for hundreds of years. Everybody said so. And that was even if he counted his birthdays in Martian years.

"This isn't right," his father muttered.

The boy stood up and eased close to his father.

With a sigh, the man said, "They shouldn't be here."

"Who shouldn't be?"

Father didn't answer. Opening a channel, he identified his employer before asking, "What's the hold up. You're supposed to be gone."

"Hey, John," said a woman's voice. "You're talking to Lilly."

Father's name was John. "No," he said quietly, but not softly. There was sharpness to that single tiny word. Then he sighed and reopened the channel, halfway smiling as he said, "I'm here with my son, Lilly."

She said nothing.

Simon touched his father's shoulder.

The man smiled at him and winked, and he was still smiling when he said, "I thought you went off on leave."

"Came back early," the woman said.

His father wasn't looking at either screen or what was ahead. He was still smiling, but something had changed about his face.

"How old is little Simon now?" the woman asked.

"Four." People born on the earth used their old calendar. That was one reason Simon had trouble understanding what time meant.

"Where's his mother?"

"Waiting at home. It's just him and me."

There was a brief silence. Then the woman said, "Understood."

Father sat back. "Lilly? I was told your rig was going to be gone by now."

"I've had some lousy troubles, John."

The man's face looked patient but not happy. "Troubles?"

"Two bits went bad on me. I've had one bit get contaminated at the site before, but never two."

Their rover was walking on its crab legs, quickly marching across the frozen face of the lake. Simon imagined liquid water hiding under the thick white surface ice, and he thought of the cold mud beneath the water. Then he remembered the guppies he left at home with his mother and baby sister. Someday he would take those fish and their babies and set them free. Wouldn't that be a wonderful thing? In his mind, he saw the ice turn to warm water and the sky was blue like on earth, and there were hundreds and millions of guppies swimming everywhere, all of their mouths begging for food.

"Are you close to finished?"

"Still drilling," the woman reported.

"How deep are you?"

"Five kilometers, nearly," she said.

His father mouthed one exceptionally bad word. Then with an angry tone, he said, "I'm sorry, Lilly."

"You can't wait one more day?"

"I've got my own schedule here."

The woman didn't respond.

After a minute, Father said, "I would, if I could. You know that. But they want me finishing this run in a week, and the kid has to get back."

Still, the woman didn't talk.

Father looked at Simon, preparing to tell him something.

But then Lilly's voice returned. "I just put in a call to the Zoo."

Father shook his head. Then softly and a little sadly, he said, "That won't do any good, and you know it."

"What are you talking about?" Simon asked.

Father closed the channel and said, "Shush," and then opened it again. "All right, Lilly. The Zoo can get their lawyers working. We're going to be official here. But why don't you start pulling your bit? If you win your delay, I'll let you put it back in and finish."

"So your boy's really there, is he?"

"Sure is."

She asked, "Can he hear me?"

"Why?" Father asked, reaching for a button.

Then all of the sudden, she said, "Hello, Simon. Hi! I'm your dad's very, very good friend, Lilly!"

There were rules about being alone. Alone inside a rover meant touching nothing except what belonged to him and what couldn't be avoided. The AI driver watched Simon when his father was absent, and it watched his father when he worked outside. If something bad happened, the driver would find some way to help. But Mars was dangerous, and the worst things were always ready to happen. Before they left on this journey, Simon's mother said exactly that to his father. "A seal fails, or you puncture your suit," she said. Mom thought her boy was asleep, and even if he wasn't, Simon couldn't hear her talking at the far end of the tiny apartment. With a quiet urgent voice, she reminded her husband that one misstep might leave their son half-orphaned and two hundred kilometers from home. And what would happen then?

"The driver knows what to do," his father had promised. "It sends out a distress call and starts walking toward the nearest settlement."

"With Simon inside," she said. "Terrified, and all by himself."

"No need to mention I'm dead," said his father. "Though that seems like the larger tragedy, if you ask me."

"I don't want the boy scarred," she said.

Father didn't respond.

"Scarred," she repeated. And then again, she said, "Scarred."

Simon didn't want to be scarred, but he was definitely worried. His father walked slowly across the frozen landscape, wearing a lifesuit whiter than the ice beneath his boots. His clean-shaven head showed through the back of the helmet. His father's friend stood beside her drill rig. Lilly was watching Simon at the window. A pair of small robots stood nearby, doing nothing. The drill was still digging, the clean bit clawing its way into the deep warm rock. Simon watched the cable twisting, and then he noticed his father waving a hand, and Lilly smiled at her friend and said words. Father turned, and Simon could see his mouth now. The adults were sharing a private channel, and both were talking at the same time. Then they quit talking. Several minutes passed where nothing was said. It felt like forever. Maybe they were waiting for something to happen. Maybe what would happen was something very bad. Simon remembered the story of a Zoo collector who cut into a cave filled with methane and water, and the foamy gas blew out of the hole and picked up one of his robots and flung it at him, killing him with the impact.

Just then, with chilling clarity, Simon understood that his father was about to die. Straightening his back, he made himself ready for the moment. Yet nothing happened. Nothing changed. The two adults resumed talking and then stopped talking, and Simon was desperately bored. So he dropped into the chair reserved for him, playing a game. He was the blue team; his enemies were purple. He started in one corner of the board, feeding and dividing and then spreading, and when he nudged against the purple blobs, he fought for position and the chance to make more blues.

When he stood again, his father was walking toward the rover. Simon had never seen anybody move that fast in a lifesuit. And Lilly had vanished. Where did she go? Then the airlock began to cycle, and Simon put down his game and sat again, staring at the little door at the back end of the cabin.

Even after a thorough cleaning, the woman's suit smelled of peroxides and ancient dust. She stepped into the cabin smiling, helmet tucked under one arm. The woman was pretty. She was darker than most of the people that he'd seen before. In the cabin air, her voice sounded warm and kind and special, and the first words she said to him were, "You look a fine smart young man."

He liked this woman.

"Simon is a wonderful name," she said.

He nodded and smiled back at her.

"Your father's told me quite a lot about you," she offered. Then her face changed, and she said, "He's being very unreasonable, you know."

Once again, the airlock started through its cycle.

"Simon," she began. "Has anyone told you about the Zoo project?"

The boy nodded before he considered the question. But luckily, yes, he knew about the bug people. "My mom explained them to me."

Lilly said nothing.

"They're good-hearted soft souls," he continued.

Slowly, she said, "I guess we are," and then she added, "I'd like to believe we're doing something good. Saving what Martians we can save before their world is gone forever."

"Mars isn't leaving," he said.

"But their habitats will vanish. Some soon, and then the rest."

"But we're Martians too," he said, repeating what he heard from every other adult.

"Except the native microbes were first," she mentioned.

Simon shrugged, unsure how that mattered.

"They're under us right now," she began.

The airlock was pressurized, jets and determined vacuums struggling to clean his father's mostly clean suit.

"Beneath us is a wonderland, Simon. A paradise." Lilly's voice was quick and serious. "Heat and flowing water and nutrients, plus fractures in the bedrock that are prime growing surfaces for thousands of native species. Pseudoarchaea and nanobacteria, viral cysts and maybe the largest population of hunter-molds anywhere. What I'm sampling is the Martian equivalent of a tropical rainforest. It's a fabulous treasure, unique in the universe, and do you know what's going to happen to it?"

Some of her words made no sense. But one new word piqued his curiosity, which was why Simon asked, "What's a rain-forest?"

Lilly hesitated. "What do you think it is?"

"Water falling on trees," he offered.

"That's it."

"Never stopping."

"It rains a lot, yes."

"That sounds awful," he offered.

Now the airlock stopped cleaning its contents, and the inner door popped open. Father entered the room quickly, his gloves unfastening his helmet, eyes big and his mouth clamped into a hard long line.

"We're talking about rain-forests," Simon reported. Then to his new friend, he asked, "How can trees grow under falling water?"

"It isn't like that," she sputtered. Then she turned. "Hey, John. Hear back from the attorneys?"

"Not yet." Father stopped and with a slow voice asked his son, "What else have you talked about?"

"Nothing," Lilly said.

"The Zoo," corrected Simon.

"Yeah, the Zoo," she allowed. "I was just asking this fine young man what he knew about my work, and he reports that his mother says I'm soft but that I have a good heart."

Was that what he told her? Simon didn't think so.

Father looked at their faces, one and then the other.

"That's all," Lilly said cheerfully.

Father's suit was bright and clean. He looked hot, which made little sense. He even seemed tired, although they hadn't done anything today.

Finally, with a quiet little voice, he said, "Don't."

Simon couldn't tell which one of them he was talking to.

Or was he saying, "Don't," to himself?

But with a tight, almost angry voice, Lilly asked, "Why would I? Why would I even think that? I have this sterling good heart that doesn't wish ill on anybody, bacterial or otherwise."

Simon still liked Lilly, but adults could be very peculiar. Was Lilly one of those peculiar adults?

Neither adult wanted to talk, and they wouldn't look at each other. The floor seemed to be the most interesting area in the room, and they stared at it for a time, their mouths small and their eyes empty and both of them breathing quickly.

To break the silence, Simon announced, "I got to hold one of the seeds today. Dad let me do that."

Even then, nobody spoke.

"Seeds are machines," the boy reported. "They explode like bombs, and they're very powerful, and inside them? They've got these little sacks, and the sacks get flung out into the hole made by the bomb, and they're full of good young bugs that can do all sorts of neat, important things. Like growing fast and building these little, little roots that carry power like wires do, and the roots make it possible to heat up the crust fast and change the rocks to make our kinds of life happy."

Without warning, Lilly said one awful word.

Father set his hand on her suit, on the back of her shoulder.

"Don't touch me, John."

Then Father said, "Leave us alone, Lilly."

Four words, and none were loud. But Simon had never heard the man angrier than he sounded then.

"Suit up and go," he told the woman.

But Lilly just shook her head. Then putting on a big peculiar smile, she said, "Simon? Want to hear something funny about your father and me?"

The boy wanted any reason to laugh. "Sure."

"No," said Father, stepping between them. "Suit up and go do your work, Lilly. I'll tell my bosses something's wrong at my end, that I'm not ready to plant. Do what you need. Is that fair enough for you?"

She said, "No."

"What?"

Lilly kept watching Simon, the wild smile building on her pretty dark face. "I want you to help me, John. With the drilling, with the sampling. All of it."

Father didn't speak.

Then Lilly said, "Hey, Simon. You want your father to have a good heart, don't you?"

"Yes," he said.

"So what should he do? Help me or hurt me?"

"Help her, Dad," the boy begged. "You've got to, Dad. What else can you do?"

624 Hektor

A little bird warned Simon about the impending rebellion.

Jackie was part African gray, with a good deal of genetic retooling and enough bio-linked circuitry to lift the parrot's IQ to vote-worthy levels. Her job functions included companionship and extra eyes with which to keep watch over the sprawling farm, and she was excellent at both duties. But every living thing possesses its unsuspected skills. Wasn't that what Simon's professors warned when they addressed each new class of would-be atums? No matter how simple the genetics, an organism's mind or the culture in which it was immersed, every created entity contained its fair share of surprises, flaws as well as those few talents that would, if they were too spectacular, screw up anyone's blooming career.

"Warning signs are marching," Jackie reported. "Small warnings, I'll grant you. But I can't shake the premonition of disasters on the loose."

"Is it our sun?" Simon asked. Which wasn't an unreasonable question, what with their reactor running past the prescribed one hundred and five percent rating. "You think the light's about to fail?"

In twenty years, there had been two prolonged blackouts. Neither was Simon's fault, though both were major disasters for the farm—two incidents that left cancerous reprimands tucked inside his life-file.

But the parrot clucked at his concerns, saying, "No, it's not our sun."

"Meat troubles?" Viruses, he feared. A herpes strain hitching rides on the nervous systems of new immigrants, most likely.

"No, the ribs-and-hearts are growing well. And the bacon is ahead of schedule."

Nonetheless, Simon studied the terrain before them: The ancient crater was capped with a diamond dome, and fixed to the dome's apex was a blazing fire that winked out for only a few minutes each day. Otherwise the basin was flooded with a simple but brilliant light. Limiting the radiant frequencies allowed for the efficient consumption of energy. The black-green foliage stank of life, healthy and always growing. Tallest were the pond-pods—sprawling low-gravity trees endowed with countless trunks holding up bowl-shaped basins filled with clean water, each pond infested with shrimp and fish, each covered with thin living skins so that the jostling of wind and animals never spilling what lay inside. As a young man, Simon helped design the first pond-pods, and since his arrival on Hektor, he had overseen countless improvements that allowed them to thrive in the carbonaceous soil. No accomplishment made him prouder.

By contrast, the rib-and-hearts and bacons were routine commercial species, ugly by any aesthetics he cared to invoke. There were long days when the master of this farm wished he could cull and enhance according to his own tastes, creating something more satisfying than an efficient but bland food factory.

Patiently but forcefully, he asked again, "What's wrong, Jackie?"

"Two humans were passing through," the bird reported. "They were keeping under the canopy but avoiding the main trails. I didn't recognize their faces, but they wore miner uniforms."

"What did the miners do? Steal food?"

"They did nothing," she said. "Nothing wrong, at least. But they didn't sound like miners."

Simon waited.

"They talked about fire."

"Tell me," he coaxed.

Against every stereotype, Jackie was an awful mimic. But she knew her limitations and didn't try to reproduce either stranger's voice. Instead, she summarized. "One said something about being worried, and then the other said it was going to happen soon, in thirty-three hours. He told his companion that the dogs were sleeping and the fire was set, and even if the chiefs knew about the plan, at this point nobody could stop what couldn't be stopped."

"I don't understand any of that," Simon confessed.

"Why am I not surprised?" One of Jackie's unanticipated talents was for sarcasm. "At first, I wasn't bothered. But fire scares me and I thought that mentioning the chiefs was worrisome."

Simon agreed. In principle, every aspect of the colony was under their control, and if something was unknown to them—

"That's why I followed the miners," the bird volunteered.

"You said they weren't miners."

"Because they were strong. Two exceedingly muscular human beings."

Only soldiers and recent immigrants retained their muscle tone. Simon had a willow-boned shape that came from minimal gravity and limited calories. "What else did they say?"

"Except for one time, they didn't speak again," she said. "But just before leaving the farm, the man turned to the woman and told her to smile. He said that McKall knows what he's doing, and she should please damn well stop wasting her energy by imagining the worst."

Simon said nothing.

Then Jackie pointed out, "You know McKall, don't you?"

"I do," he admitted. "In fact, he's the atum who gave me this post."

Two dark reddish asteroids lay snug against each other, producing 624 Hektor. The little world orbited the sun 60 degrees ahead of Jupiter, in that sweet Lagrange zone where a multitude of Trojan asteroids had swum for billions of years. Hektor was an elongated body spinning once in less than seven hours, and Simon had always believed that it was an ugly world. It didn't help his opinion that he was living on the fringe of settled space, serving the chiefs and various corporations as little more than a farmer. In school, his test scores were always ample; he graduated as a qualified, perhaps even gifted atum—the professional name borrowed from the Egyptian god whose task it was to finish the unfinished worlds. But good minds only took their bodies so far. More coveted posts were earned through useful friendships and powerful mentors, and Simon's career to date proved that he had neither. Anywhere else in the solar system would have been a happier fate: Mars was a dream, and the sunward asteroids and the moons of Jupiter were busy, important realms. Plus there was Luna now, and preliminary teams were plotting the terraforming of Venus. In contrast, Hektor was an isolated mining station, and not even a complete station at that. Once its facilities were finished, it would supply water and pure carbon to the inner system. But it was never intended to become an important destination, much less a site of major colonization. Barely fifty thousand intelligent souls lived on and inside its gloomy body, and the humans were a minority, most of them deemed also-rans and lost souls.

The main settlement had an official name, but locals referred to it as Crashtown—a grimy dense chaotic young city resting on the impact zone where two D-class asteroids were joined together. Riding beside a load of freshly harvested bananas and boneless minnows, Simon rode down to Crashtown. But he wasn't sure of his intentions, his mind changing again and again. Then the police robot suddenly asked for his destination.

"The home of Earnest McKall," Simon heard himself reply.

But that wasn't good enough. For no obvious reason, security protocols had been heightened. The robot haughtily demanded to know a purpose for this alleged visit.

"I found his lost dog," the young atum declared.

No dog was present, but the answer seemed to satisfy. Simon continued kicking his way into an exclusive tunnel, past robust gardens basking under earth-bright lights, endless arrays of flowers and cultured animal flesh repaying their considerable energy by making rainbow colors and elaborate perfumes.

"What if McKall isn't at home?" Simon asked himself.

But he was, and the much older atum seemed pleased to find this unexpected guest waiting at his front door. "Come in, my boy. I was just about to enjoy an evening drink."

"I don't want to bother you," Simon lied.

"No bother at all. Come in here!" McKall had always been a bony person. Simon once found a ninety-year-old image of him—a lean, shaggy boy of eight, bright eyes staring at the camera while the mouth looked smug and a little too full, as if he had just eaten something that wasn't proper food. The grown-up version of that boy retained his youthful air, but the hair was a second or third crop, and it had come in thin and amazingly black. Most of McKall's life had been spent on tiny worlds, and the lack of gravity along with a Methuselan diet had maintained the scrawny elegance of that lost child.

"Wine?" McKall offered.

"Thank you, no," Simon responded.

The chief atum on Hector stood beside an elaborate bar—a structure trimmed with rare metals, in the middle of a huge room designed for nothing but entertaining. Yet he hadn't bothered reaching for empty bottles, much less filling them.

What he was doing was staring at Simon, and smiling, and something about that look and the silence told the guest that his presence was not unanticipated.

"My dog, is it?" asked McKall.

Simon flinched.

The smile sharpened. The man kicked closer, his voice flat and smooth and decidedly unrushed. "What do you know, my boy?"

Simon was nearly fifty, his own boyhood beyond reach.

"Hear some news, did you?"

"About dogs," he reported.

McKall shrugged. "And what else?"

"Something is going to happen."

"Happenings are inevitable. Do you have specifics?"

"Twenty-eight hours from now—"

"Stop." A small hand lifted, not quite touching Simon on the chest. "No, you know nothing. Absolutely nothing."

"Your dogs are sleeping," Simon continued.

His host refused to speak. Waiting.

"And there's something about a fire, too."

The smile shrank, but the voice was friendlier. Curious. Perhaps even amused. "What about fire?"

"I've studied your writings, sir." Habit forced Simon to nod slightly, admitting his lower status. "You like to equate metabolic activity with fire."

"I'm not the only voice to use that allusion."

"But as a young atum, you spent a great deal of time and energy complaining about the limits to our work. Every atum is shackled by draconian laws, you claimed. You said that life as we made it was just a smoldering flame. Your hope was to unleash the powers of the organic. Novel biochemistries, unique genetics, and ultraefficient scavenging the dead and spent. You were one of the loudest advocates of suspending the outmoded Guidelines, and only then would our young profession be able to produce a firestorm of life that would run wild across the universe."

"I see." McKall laughed quietly. Then again, he said, "I see."

"What can't the chiefs stop?"

Instead of answering the question, the atum posed his own. "Why do you believe that a skilled researcher—a man with major accomplishments—willingly came to this very remote place? Why would Earnest McKall ignore every lucrative offer, traveling all the way out here to this little chunk of trash and ice water?"

Simon said nothing.

"There are dogs," McKall admitted. "Soon to be awakened, in fact. Decades of research and a series of camouflaged laboratories have produced more than a few revolutions, both in terms of productivity and plasticity."

"You did this?"

"Not alone." The atum shook his head, the rich black hair waving in the air. "I have a dozen brilliant associates working beside me, plus collaborators on twenty other worlds. Yes, I have a fine confident mind, but I'm not crazy with pride."

"I'm one of your associates," Simon pointed out.

"You are not, no. I would have included you, young man. In fact, that's why I steered several likely employers away from your class's hatch. I believed I could use your talents out here with me."

"But I haven't done anything."

"Nothing at all," McKall agreed. "Which was a surprise for me, I'll admit. After your arrival, I kept careful watch over your work, and in particular, how you responded to authority. Honestly, I wasn't impressed. I need boldness, genius. Competency without inspiration is fine for the commercial world, but not for souls dreaming the big dream."

If Simon had been slapped, his face wouldn't have felt warmer. He breathed heavily and slowly, and then despite every reserve of self-control, he began to weep, tears scattering from his reddened checks.

"But I like you anyway," McKall continued. "And since you have no specific knowledge about my plans, and there's no way to stop what is soon to begin, I will give you a gift. Use this chance to slip away. A transport leaves Hektor in four hours. There will be empty berths, and I advise that you take one."

Simon turned as if to leave, then hesitated.

"You plan to take control over Hektor?" he muttered.

McKall laughed. "Haven't you been paying attention? My goals are far more ambitious than this two-headed rock!"

Expecting to be stopped—by restraining hands or murderous weapons—Simon nonetheless hurried to Crashtown's civil house. The highest-ranking chief seemed to be waiting for his arrival. He shook both of Simon's hands and ushered him into a tiny office, and before Simon could speak, the chief told him, "Don't worry. And certainly don't panic. We know all about their plans."

"You do? For how long?"

"Days now." The chief shrugged. Feigning confidence, he reported, "We have McKall in sight, plus all of his lieutenants. And our security teams are minutes away from taking out both of his private labs."

"Good," Simon offered.

And that was when the chief quit smiling. Turning grim, he said to the farmer, "But I am curious: Why did you go to the atum's home before coming to us?"

"I didn't know anything," Simon said.

"You were fishing for information?"

With as much conviction as he could manage, he said, "Yes. If I was going to report a crime that hadn't happened, I needed details. Some reason for you to believe me."

"A good enough answer," the chief replied. "At least for the moment."

Simon felt cold and weak. What mattered to him now was returning to his farm, to Jackie, and provided this trouble vanished, he would again take up his pivotal role in feeding this very small world. He was practically shaking with worries. "May I leave?" he risked asking.

"Until we know for certain, you cannot."

Simon swallowed. "Until you know what for certain?"

That brought a tiny laugh, and then the ominous words, "Everything, of course. Everything."

The attacks on the laboratories were launched, each blundering into carefully laid traps. McKall's mercenaries were ready, and the parallel attempt to capture the ringleaders ended up netting nothing but holo images and robotic mimics. Then the rebels took over the local com-system. Their own attack would proceed on schedule, and simple decency demanded fair warning to civilians and the opportunity to escape by any means available. But the chiefs banned all travel. They quickly gathered their remaining forces, generating new plans up until that moment when the rumored "dogs" appeared. Secret tunnels reached deep inside Hektor's smaller half, and out of them came hot-blooded monsters moving as blurs, eating flesh and laser bolts as they ran wild through Crashtown.

The ensuing chaos allowed Simon to escape. At the farm, he discovered three civil robots quickly setting up a small fusion bomb. "We cannot leave this resource for the enemy," one machine reported. Simon didn't care anymore. He collected Jackie and a few possessions before racing to the auxiliary port, and while the ground beneath him shook and split open, thousands of panicked souls abandoned Hektor, riding whatever was marginally spaceworthy, accepting any risk to take the long fall back toward the sun.

For the next several weeks, Simon was interrogated by a string of distant voices—military minds and politicians who wanted any and all glimpses into McKall's nature. Simon offered what insights he had, trying to steer clear of his own considerable embarrassment. Once Simon's transport passed into Martian orbit, the refugees were herded into quarantine on New Phobos. Who knew what new diseases MaKall could have slipped into their blood? Between the tests and more interviews, his childhood world teased Simon with glimpses of its cold blue seas and dense, mostly artificial atmosphere. The harsh desert landscape had vanished, the world's rapid transformation producing feelings of pride and sorrowful loss. But despite all of the brilliant plans and the trillions of invested euros, the terraforming process was far from perfect. From forty thousand kilometers high, Simon identified lakes where the acids still ruled and forests of withering trees, and there were rumors that the new ecosystem was proving far less stable than the public voices liked to proclaim.

Fifteen months later, Simon was free of quarantine, and he watched the updates as a fleet of powerful military vessels assaulted 624 Hektor. Robots and shock troops landed in the empty crater that had been Simon's farm. The fearsome dogs were melted and frozen. Every battle was won; victory was in hand. But then the war took an abrupt, unexpected turn. A blue-white blast tore through the asteroid. Since the rebellion, the smaller portion of Hektor had been thoroughly transformed. A transport ship of unprecedented size was hiding inside the reddish crust, and the explosion flung away great chunks of its companion while slaughtering the invaders. Half of the asteroid dropped out of its ancient orbit, crude engines firing, maintaining a near-collision course with Jupiter. Momentum was stolen away from giant planet. Then uncontested, the ship pushed into the outer solar system, swinging close enough to Saturn to enjoy an even larger kick.

Five years later, an improved set of star engines came to life. By then, McKall's plans were common knowledge. No one was planning to chase after him, much less continue the war. What would be the point? A forever-changing, increasingly strange body of organized carbon and silicon and fusion-heated water was streaking away from the sun, away from humanity, aiming this newborn revolution straight for the three Centauri sisters.

VENUS

Eventually Simon's personal history became public knowledge. Strangers suddenly knew his name, and they would smile at him in that special sad way people used in uncomfortable circumstances. Acquaintances began to treat him as if he were important, laughing easily at his rare jokes, wishing him a good day or good evening or sweet, delightful dreams. His workmates, the fellow atums, embraced one of two inadequate strategies: Either they were quick to tell him how sorry they were and then ask if they could do anything, anything at all, or they seemed to take offense that Simon hadn't confided with them before now. "Dear god, you lost most of your family," one man exclaimed incorrectly, but with passion. "I wish I'd known. I look like the fool. I thought we were friends, at least . . ."

Simon did have a few scattered friends, and they knew better. When he didn't mention the unfolding disaster on Mars, they patiently respected his privacy. As the situation worsened, he sought out mood-leveling drugs and other cheats that allowed him to manage, if only barely. He cried, but only when he was alone. During the worst days, he volunteered for solitary assignments, carefully avoiding professional chatter about past mistakes and the mounting casualties. He thought he was succeeding, taking a grim pride in his talent for enduring these personal trials, but afterwards, when the situation had finally stabilized, he crossed paths with an acquaintance from childhood. Ignorant as a bug, the fellow asked, "What about your family, Simon? They got out of that nightmare in time, didn't they?"

His parents never tried to escape. They were two old people living at opposite ends of an unfinished, critically flawed world, and they hadn't spoken to one another in nearly forty years. But as the blizzards struck and the air turned to poison, they left their homes, riding and then marching through the chaos and slaughter, finally reaching an isolated habitat overlooking Hellas where they lived together for their final eight days and nights.

As for Simon's sister and various half-siblings, all but two escaped before the ecosystem collapsed. But where they would live tomorrow was an endless problem, for them and for the solar system at large. Millions of refugees were crammed onboard the ten New Moons and a fleet of rescue ships, plus various ad hoc habitats contrived out of inflated bladders and outmoded life support systems. It was a tough, dirty and problematic life, though far superior to being one of the fifty million bodies left behind on the anaerobic, peroxide-laced surface of Mars. Where would these souls live tomorrow? Faced with this conundrum, the atums had a ready solution: Terraform Mars all over again, and do it as quickly as possible, but use every trick in their rapidly evolving arsenal.

"This time, we'll build a conservatory," one young atum declared. "That's how it should have been done in the first place. And again, Simon, I'm so very sorry for your tragedies."

Naomi was a pretty youngster who used her beauty and a charming, obvious man-ner to win favors and fish for compliments. She liked to talk. She loved listening to her own smart, insistent voice. Rumor had it that her body was equipped with artificial openings and deployable prods, leaking intoxicating scents and won-drous doses of electricity. Simon was curious about her body, but he didn't have the rank or adequate desire to pursue his base urges. Watching one of Naomi's performances was as close as he wanted to be. Most of his colleagues felt threat-ened by her promise. But even when the girl spoke boldly about her incandescent future, Simon couldn't take offense. His second century had brought with it a tidy and quite useful epiphany: Everyone would eventually fail, and if their failures were long-built, then the subsequent collapses would be all the more dramatic.

At this particular moment, the atums were chanting the usual praises about conservatories.

"Oh, I'm not convinced," said Simon quietly.

Naomi laughed, and with a patronizing tone asked, "Oh my, why not?"

"A roof wouldn't have helped. In the end, nothing would have changed."

She couldn't let that statement go unchallenged. "But if we'd had a lid over the sky, we'd have controlled the weather more effectively. The sunlight, the upper atmosphere's chemistry. All the inflows would have belonged to us."

"But not four and half billion years of geologic habit," he countered.

"Geologic habit," she muttered, as if she couldn't quite understand the phrase.

That's when the chief atum interjected her presence into the conversation. With a loud breezy voice, she summarized both positions. Then after putting her own opinion into jargon-laded terms, she added, "Too much of the Mars busi-ness depended on biological means. That's where they went wrong. Don't trust life; it doesn't care about you. The physical realm is what matters, and conserva-tories are wonderful tools. They're sure to be the last word in our business."

Every face but one nodded, the matter settled.

Yet despite all of this polished certainty, only one world-encompassing conser-vatory was close to being finished, and that was a special circumstance. Luna was the easiest world to enclose inside a semi-transparent bubble: The low gravity; the proximity of earth; thriving local industries; and the absence of weather and po-litical troubles. Its roof would hold any new atmosphere close. Double panes of diamond, transparent and strengthened with nanofibers, would keep space at bay. The engineering was straightforward, and construction should be relatively easy. But "should be" often proved illusionary. The Luna project was already forty per-cent over-budget, the critical water from asteroids and comets was being chased by other terraforming projects, including Venus, and even in the most favorable scenario warned that twenty more years would pass before the first soft winds of an oxygen-neon atmosphere began to blow across the dusty plains of Nearside.

Simon's doubts could be misplaced. Indeed, he hoped he was wrong. But still, this one-time Martian was suffering a nagging yet familiar sense of standing at the brink of another precipice.

The other atums had happily left Simon behind. The topic of the moment, and the passion of their professional lives, was Venus. Small projects were being discussed. Most of their work involved the atmosphere and heat dissipation, the obvious solutions offered and debated and then rejected, soon to be replaced with other equally satisfactory answers. When he bothered to listen, Simon could tell who was sleeping with Naomi and who was maneuvering to take their place. It would have been funny, if not for the grave consequences lashed to animal lust. He didn't believe in Great Deities, but if the gods were watching, they would surely laugh to see how tiny hormones and glands smaller than hands could manipulate the future of entire planets.

Presiding over this working lunch was the chief atum for the Third District, High Atmosphere and Future Climate Department. She was ten years Simon's junior but much more successful, and when she spoke, the room fell silent. Though that didn't mean people were listening. This group wasn't large or diverse, but within its ranks were enough opinions and rampant ego that no authority could rule, much less orchestrate the thoughts of so many well-trained, singularly focused minds.

Venus was the topic, but the planet existed only as numbers and one staggeringly complicated model. Except for tug of gravity and the specifics in the numbers, this could have been any meeting of atums sitting inside any windowless room, on Luna or Callisto or Pallas, or any other portion of the solar system being relentlessly and utterly transformed.

When the official business was finished, at last, the chief looked longingly at Naomi. "Good job, and thank you," she told everybody.

Everybody wanted out of the room.

But without warning, the chief said Simon's full name and caught his eyes, not quite smiling when she said, "You have a new assignment. For the time being, you're off the hydrological team."

A colleague must have accused him of being difficult or incompetent, or perhaps both. It had happened before. He might be a 128 year-old man, but he always felt like a little boy when he was embarrassed or shamed.

Except that nothing was wrong, at least on this occasion. The chief smiled, admitting, "It's because we have a visitor coming. A representative from . . ." She hesitated. "From the Zoo Project."

"Another collection mission?" Simon inquired.

"Oh, these darlings always have another mission," the chief complained.

Simon nodded, waiting.

"I need you to help with her hunting and keep tabs on whatever she finds." The chief stared at him, smiling suspiciously. "Do you know a woman named Lilly?"

Too quickly, Simon said, "No."

"That's odd," the chief mentioned. "She requested you by name."

There were myriad routes to achieving a long healthy lifespan. Simon preferred small measures left invisible to the naked, unmodified eye. But the woman beside him wasn't motivated by tradition. Native flesh would always be perishable, and the cosmetically proper synthetics were usually too fragile to last more than a few years. What proved most durable were colonies of engineered microbes, metabolically efficient and quick to repair themselves—a multitude of bacteria infusing the perpetually new skin with sensitive, high adaptable neural connections. There were popular tools among the very young and the determined elderly. Yet Simon couldn't remember ever meeting anyone who had endowed herself with such a vibrant, elaborate exterior.

"I'm sorry," the very colorful woman began.

Just why she was sorry, Simon didn't know. But he nodded politely, resisting the urge to ask.

For the next few minutes, they sat in silence. The sky-driver continued on its programmed course, little to see and nothing to do for the present. Most of the world's air lay beneath them. The sun was low on their left, the only inhabitant of the nearly black sky, slowly descending toward its retrograde setting. The conservatory was a grayish-green plain far below them, absolutely smooth and comfortingly bland. Venus was not Luna, and this project was far more complicated than erecting a high roof above a compliant vacuum. Only limited sections had been completed—barely nine percent of the eventual goal—and even that portion was little more than the scaffolding meant to support arrays of solar-power facilities and filters and spaceports and cities of robots that would do nothing but repair and improve this gigantic example of artless architecture. Was his guest full of questions? Most visitors wanted to hear about the nano-towers rooted in the rigid Venusian crust, holding these expensive gigatons far above the dense, dangerous atmosphere. People might know the facts, but it soothed them to learn about the marvelous engineering. Everyone was the center of his own important story. Everybody secretly feared that if some piece of the conservatory failed, it would happen beneath his own important, tragically mortal feet.

At last, the silence ended. Lilly touched Simon for the first time. Hot orange fingertips brushed against his forearm. "I am sorry," she said again. "He was a good father, I know. I'm sure you miss him terribly."

Simon's reaction surprised both of them. Turning toward gaudy woman, he remarked sharply, "My mother was the good parent. Dad spent his life collecting lovers, and I didn't like his girls at all."

The violet face was bright and hot, full of fluids more complicated than blood. Perhaps the woman was insulted. Maybe she wanted to turn the sky-driver back, ready to exchange this atum for one less difficult. But nothing about her seemed hurt or even surprised. She smiled for a few moments. Saying nothing, she let her glassy dark eyes absorb everything about the old man beside her. Then her hand gripped his wrist, a wave of heat threatening to burn his pale, dry skin.

"Nonetheless, I'm sorry," she said.

Simon pulled his arm back.

"I didn't treat either of you fairly. At the lake . . . when I was drilling . . . all I cared about was saving the natives, by whatever means . . ."

Here was the central problem, Simon realized. It wasn't that this woman and his father had an affair, or even that they might have loved one another. What rankled was that she had willfully used him as a tool.

"How are the Martians?" he inquired.

"Happily sleeping inside a thousand scattered laboratories."

"That's sad," he thought aloud.

"Really? Why?"

"Life should be busy," Simon proposed. "Not hibernating inside common freezers."

Now Lilly took offense. She said nothing, but her back stiffened and she maintained her silence until it was obvious that she didn't accept any complaints about her life's work. They were approaching their destination. As the sky-driver began its descent, Simon risked mentioning, "I'm probably mistaken. But I thought the Zoo already grabbed up every species of air-plankton."

The native Venusians had had a robust ecosystem, but compared even to Martians, they were an uncomplicated lot.

"We have every native in bottles," she said stiffly, nursing her wounds.

"And the native populations have crashed here," he pointed out. "No light gets through, except for some infrared, and the sulfuric clouds are dispersed and too cold by a long measure."

"True enough," she agreed.

Then she touched herself, her face growing brighter as it warmed with enthusiasm. "But new species are evolving every day, and isn't that exciting news?"

It was boring news, but a truce had been declared. The old man and even older woman stopped mentioning their differences and histories. They were professionals, each quietly pursuing a quick and narrow mission. The sky-driver set down and linked up with a large dome filled with sleeping machines and assorted elevators. Donning lifesuits, they boarded a small elevator and descended ten kilometers. Simon watched Venus through the monitors. Lilly busied herself by readying a suitcase-sized apparatus that would inhale and filter the carbon-dioxide atmosphere, pulling every viable microbe from the mayhem of dust and industrial pollution. The nano-tower was more air than structure—hexagons of webs and sturdy legs, each side nearly a kilometer in length, its feet firmly planted on the slopes of Aphrodite Terra. Their final destination was a platform intended as a hive for robots waiting to repair what was rarely damaged. There was no visible light, but there was wind and a stubborn atmosphere still centuries away from collapsing into a newborn ocean of soda water. Obviously Lilly had done similar work on other towers. She moved with purpose. Her machine walked next to her, waiting patiently as she investigated one site and then another. Experience or perhaps intuition allowed her to decide where the best results would be found. Then she told the machine, "Deploy," and it gladly grabbed the railing with three arms and flung its body over the edge, exploding into a purposeful tangle of ribbons and funnels and other twisting shapes.

"How long?" Simon asked.

"Do we wait?" She looked up at him, her features illuminated by the back-scattered light from her helmet. "An hour, at least. Maybe longer."

Venus lay before them, vast and bathed in darkness.

"What kinds of creatures are out here?"

"Chemoautotrophes, naturally." Staring out into the same night, she explained, "The UV photosynthesizers are still here, of course. They like to find crevices in our towers, places where they can sleep, probably waiting for our roof to collapse."

He let that anthropomorphism go unchallenged.

"These natives are odd, adaptable species, all descended from plankton in the boiled-away seas. It's astonishing what they've kept inside their very peculiar DNA. Today, some of them are utilizing industrial solvents and lost nano products. Where there's heat, energy can be harvested." She turned, showing her face again. "There's no reason to worry yet, and maybe never. But a few of these bugs have found ways to creep inside our robots, using them as shelters. If one of them ever learns how to steal an electrical current, everything changes. Probably in a matter of a month or two."

"That quickly?"

"Venusians are fertile and promiscuous. With these winds, a successful strain can be everywhere in days."

Simon had never studied the beasts. Would it pay to invest an hour a week in digesting the existing literature?

"But odds are, that won't happen," his companion allowed. "I do love these little things. But life, even at its most spectacular, has limits."

"It does have limits," he said tactfully.

Lilly's face was pretty and never more human—a consequence of the indirect light washing across their features, and their solitude, and Simon's nagging, seemingly eternal sense of loneliness in a universe filled with an increasingly strange humanity.

"Does it ever bother you?" she asked.

He waited for the rest of the question.

"Terraforming is a horribly destructive act," Lilly stated. "Obliterating one order for another. Or in the sad case of Mars, destroying a quiet and stable world to replace it with a doomed weakling . . . and then after all of that inflicted misery, not learning enough to give up the fight."

"It isn't meant to be a fight," he declared.

But of course it was. Perhaps never so clearly, Simon realized that they were standing on the ramparts of a great fortress, an endless war waging around them. Simon listened to the wind and felt it push against him, and he took pleasure from his heart hammering away inside a chest that would never feel ancient. And then he was smiling, realizing that even a quiet disappointment of a soul—the sort of person that Simon was—could take a keen, unembarrassed pleasure from the battles that he had helped win, small and otherwise.

IAPETUS

"I know you worry. I worry too, Simon. Neither of us is strong at politics, and even if I were a marvel at making alliances and handling cross-purposed personalities, this would be a difficult place. This earth would be. But as knowing voices say, and with good reason, 'There's only one Stanford.' Perhaps the Farside Academy is its equal, at least when it comes to creating prominent astronomers. But Stanford still ranks first in my field, and it has for half a millennia, and my degree will get me noticed by wise entities and doubting coworkers at all ends of the solar system. And since I'm not gifted at winning admirers through my simple charm, being in this university will help me quite a lot."

Simon paused the transmission—this wasn't his first viewing—and spent the next several minutes studying the face that filled the screen. What had changed? The mouth, the bright yellow eyes. That artful crest of green feathers—a jaunty hat in appearance, and one of Jackie's last obvious links to the world of her ancestors.

No, she looked exactly the same. To casual eyes, she might be some species of human, her genetics modified for the most normal of reasons. She wasn't much larger than when he had first met the parrot, which put her well inside the restrictions imposed on visiting students. The bio-taxing laws were perfectly reasonable; earth had always been too crowded. Even six hundred years ago, when Simon was a scrawny Martian with dust in his breath, the home world had suffered from too many bodies standing on too little land, farms working hard to make food for a population that wouldn't age, and in most cases, stubbornly refused to die. Immortality was the norm everywhere, and who didn't want children to share the bliss? That's why bodies and minds continued to grow smaller and smaller, cheating the restrictions of nature by shrewdly redefining the rules.

In appearance, the earth hadn't changed Jackie. Perhaps her voice was a little too formal, too staged, but cameras always made her self-conscious. He knew this creature well enough to know she wasn't holding anything back. One fib today, he feared, and that would be the end. They had barely begun their long separation, and here she was, making time to call home. Simon assured himself that no conspiracy of ambition or seduction would steal away the love that had taken him by surprise, one patient century at a time.

Again, he let the message run. Jackie listed classes and spoke about the tiny quarters she shared with three other happy graduate students, and she mentioned that the stars came out on clear nights, but of course they were illusions. Earth's conservatory was finished two hundred years ago—a marvelous semipermeable membrane that strictly controlled what fell from above and what slipped away into the cosmos. Today, the mother world was a rigorously controlled room where a trillion sentient entities lived on and inside the old continents and throughout the watery reaches. It was a beautiful world, still and all. But it was a decidedly alien realm, forever changing, and some corners of that room were famous for criminal mischief and random psychopathic rage.

Yes, he was worried.

Absolutely, Simon wished Jackie had stayed with him after her sudden change of careers. Saturn's major moons had quality universities, and even noble, haughty Stanford offered virtual classes to anyone with money. Why not accept a longer, safer path to her degree? Time wasn't in short supply, Simon had argued. And by staying where they were, Jackie would have remained immune to the hazards of so many close-packed souls.

The transmission continued. "I'm sure you know this," Jackie said. "I've probably told you this before. But did you realize there isn't one working telescope on the entire campus? We have a facility forty kilometers above us, perched on the conservatory roof, but it's filled with museum pieces and curious tourists." She was thrilled, her flexible mouth giving each word an accent that was purely hers. "Stanford's telescopes—my telescopes—are everywhere but on the bright busy earth. Luna and the Jovian Trojans, and there's a beautiful new mirror that just came on line in Neptune's Lagrange. And because I'm here, that's my mirror. It's my best eye. Think of the honor! If I was at home with you, I'd be little more than a technician pointing these machines at targets that only the true Stanford students would be allowed to see."

Yes, she made the right decision. Simon had always known it, though these little mental exercises helped convince him again.

What a silly little ape he was.

"But I didn't tell you this incredible news," Jackie said in conclusion. "I just found this out. Long, long ago, Stanford had a mascot, and it was a bird! Can you imagine the odds?"

Simon froze the image and kissed the lips. Then he filed the transmission in places guaranteed to be safe for an eternity, and feeling weepy, he went on with his comfortably busy day.

Even orbiting Saturn, where space was cheap and food easy to come by, people were acquiring small modern bodies. Simon hadn't been this tiny since he was one-year-old. These new metabolisms were efficient and reliable, and where the human mind would eventually decay, cortexes made of crystalline proteins were denser and far sturdier, thoughts washing through them quickly enough to double an atum's natural talents and increase his memory twenty-fold.

But every atum underwent similar transformations, which meant that when it came to his professional life, remarkably little had changed. Simon and his colleagues had kept their old ranks and ratings, only with greater responsibilities and larger workloads. A significant medical investment had changed very little. "Treading water," he dubbed his job—a weak play on words, since what he did was manage the nutrient flows in the newborn sea. But really, he had no compelling reason to complain, and in any given year, he didn't waste more than a moment or two wondering what other course his life might have run, if only.

He was a quietly happy soul.

And despite few promotions or pay increases, his work had challenges as well as moments of total, child-like joy.

Pieces of Iapetus now belonged to Luna and Venus. But those decades of throwing water ice and hydrocarbons sunward were finished. The original mining camps had evolved into cities. Multitudes lived on Titan and Rhea and the other moons, and nobody was in the mood to share their wealth. Luna would remain a damp stony sponge, while Venus was a clean dry world, its ecology being redesigned to endure the boundless drought, its citizens more machine than meat. No matter how stupid or stubborn recent governments had been, the mathematics were brutally simple: From this point forward, it would be easier to terraform each world where it already danced, just as it was far cheaper to ship extra humans and other sentients out to these empty new homes.

Light washed through the new Iapetus, and the water was warm and salted, and the neutral-buoyant reefs were magnificent structures of calcium and silica wrapped around bubbles of hydrogen gas. The ancient moon had been melted, from its crust to the core, and great pumps were churning up that single round ocean, producing carefully designed currents meant to keep every liter oxygenated and illuminated by the submerged suns. Trillions of watts of power made the little world glow from within. Larger than the oceans of the original earth, but without the dark cold depths where life had to putter and save itself on hopes of a scrap of food, his home would eventually become jammed with coral forests and bubble cities and fish suitable for a garden, lovely and delicious to any tongue.

Nutrients were Simon's boring, absolutely essential expertise. When he wasn't dreaming of Jackie, he would dream about the day's conversations with sensors and AI watchers, the home-mind and various colleagues scattered across other, more highbrow departments. Only a tiny fraction of moon was settled. A few floating cities on the surface, and there was an industrial complex digesting and dispersing the tiny core of stone and metal impurities. But what this atum needed to do, at least in his tiny realm, was create a cycle of nutrients that would ignore disruptions and random shifts in current, leaving all of the water as bright and clear as the finest tidal pool on some long-vanished earthly beach.

Because she was interested, Simon's ended his days with updates to his lover. Every evening, as the nearest sun began to dim, he would craft a little message laid down on cool, bloodless data. But because he was nervous, he inevitably confessed that he was thinking of her constantly and that he loved her, his face and tone saying what he didn't allow from his words: That he was scared to lose her to some student of promise, or worse, a professor of certified genius who would sweep his darling bird off to realms far more exotic than his beautiful but quite tiny pond.

The message began with news from earth. With a quick joyful voice, Jackie talked about classes and the lab that she was teaching solo—"I'm so terrified, and the students love it when I shake"—and she twice mentioned rumors about a mild plague tearing through some of the coastal algae farms. "There's talk about shortfalls," she admitted. "Since they run their ecosystem with minimal reserves, shortages are inevitable. Too many citizens, plus all those others who slipped in unnoticed." Then guessing he would be frightened, she added, "Oh, it isn't serious. Everybody's just going to have to go a mouthful or two short at dinner. And Stanford has its own emergency supplies, so it's nothing. Nothing at all." Then she grinned with her lovely toothless mouth, and showing nothing but delight, she announced, "I have something to show you, darling. By the way."

And with that, her face froze and her voice stopped long enough that Simon began troubleshooting his equipment.

But she moved again, speaking with a quiet, conspiratorial tone. "Nobody sees me, darling. 'Nobody' meaning everybody else. You didn't know my little secret, but I seeded our home-mind with some elaborate security protocols. Not as good as some, but strong enough to keep away prying eyes."

"Prying at what?" he muttered.

Jackie's message was enormous, and it included interactive functions. The program heard him, and with Jackie's voice it said, "Soon enough, darling. You'll see. But let me show you a few other marvels first. All right?"

He nodded happily, a sense of adventure lending the moment its fresh, welcome edge.

Jackie continued. "You've seen these places. But I can't remember when, and the new mirrors are so much more powerful. I'm including portraits of five hundred thousand worlds, each one supporting life."

Except for their clarity, the pictures were familiar. Life was a relatively common trick performed by the galaxy. Sophisticated, earth-like biospheres did happen on occasion, but not often and not where they were expected to arise. By and large, the normal shape of life was tiny and bacterial. Mars and Venus, the European seas and the vivid clouds of Jupiter were typical examples. By contrast, multicellular life was an exceptionally frail experiment. Asteroid impacts and supernovae and the distant collisions of neutron stars happened with an appalling frequency, annihilating everything with a head and tail. Only the slow-living slime at the bottom of a deep sea would survive, or the patient cold bug ten kilometers beneath some poisoned landscape. At the end of the Permian, the earth itself barely escaped that fate. But even accounting for those grand disasters, the earth-equivalents proved a thousand times too scarce. Jackie's once-young professors had a puzzle to play with, and their answer was as sobering as anything born from science.

Now and again, interstellar clouds and doomed suns would fall into the galaxy's core. If the inflow were large enough, the massive black hole responded with a kind of blazing horror that effectively ended fancy life almost everywhere. Since the Cambrian, the galaxy had detonated at least three times, and the fortunate earth had survived only because it was swimming inside dense clouds of dust and gas—a worthy conservatory that was light-years deep, built by the gods of Whim and Caprice.

Simon wandered through the transmission, glancing at a few hundred random planets. Then he asked his home-mind to pull out the most exceptional. Within those broad parameters, he found several dozen images of cloudy spheres orbiting suns within a hundred light-years of his comfortable chair. When he came across the closest world, Jackie returned.

"Alpha Centauri B's largest world," she said in her most teacherly voice. "The planet that some mentally impoverished soul named New Earth, back when all we knew was that it had liquid water and a living atmosphere."

Simon had never been so close to that alien body. The image was that clear, that astonishing. Simon felt as if he was floating in low orbit above a shallow black sea. Microbes accounted for the dark water—multitudes of tiny relentless organisms that ate sunlight and spat out just enough oxygen to be noticed by astronomers centuries ago. But the tectonics of New Earth were radically different than those back home, and for a host of reasons, the alien atmosphere could never support a flame, much less a vibrant ecosystem.

"To date," Jackie continued, "our full survey has found nine million and forty thousand living worlds. That number and these images won't be made public for another few months. We're not done, and we expect several million more. But to date, Simon . . . as of this moment . . . only eighteen planets show unmistakable signs of multicellular life and intelligence. Of course we might be missing something small. But after this long, with these incredible tools and nothing closer to us than eight thousand light-years distance . . . well, darling, it makes a curious mind wonder if intelligence is a cosmic fluke, or worse, God's best joke . . ."

"I hope not," he muttered.

Jackie nodded in agreement. "Now for my fine surprise," she went on. "One tiny portion of the sky is off-limits. Did you know that? The Powers-That-Be have rules. Nobody but them can look along one exceptionally narrow line. And we didn't look, at least not intentionally. Except there was an accident last week, and supposedly nothing was seen and of course we recorded nothing. But I thought you'd appreciate a glimpse of what nothing looks like, provided you keep this in a very safe place."

Against the stars, a tiny glow was visible—like a comet, but burning hotter than the surface of any sun.

"It's Hektor," Jackie reported. "Dr. McKall is still out there, still charging forward. Another ten thousand years, and your old colleague will finally get where he's going."

Simon was discussing salt contents with an irritable sensor on the far side of the moon, and then his home-mind interrupted. "There has been an incident," it reported. "On earth, and specifically, on the campus—"

"Jackie?"

"I know nothing about her," the voice admitted. "Stanford and the surrounding area are temporarily out of reach. A riot is in progress. There's still a good deal of fighting. I can't offer useful insights."

"A riot?" he asked incredulously.

"Yes."

"But why?"

"There was a story, only a rumor." The mind was designed to show sorrow, but in tidy amounts. And no outrage, which was why it stated flatly, "According to the rumor, the Stanford community was holding back foodstuffs, and approximately one million citizens organized a flash-protest that mutated into violence, and the civil authorities reacted with perhaps too much force—"

"What about Jackie?"

"I have lists of the dead and injured, sir. The tallies are being constantly updated. Eighty-three are confirmed dead, with perhaps another hundred to be found. But I will tell you when I find her, wherever I find her."

Simon refused to worry. The odds of disaster falling on one eager graduate student were remote. Tens of thousands attended that big old school, and no, letting his mind turn crazy was a waste of time. That was the conviction that he managed to hold on to for eight minutes of determined, rapidly forgotten work. Then he cut off the sensor in mid-sentence, and to his house he said, "Any word, contact me."

"Of course, sir."

His home—Jackie's home, and his—was the only building on a tiny green island of buoyant coral floating on the moon's surface. What seemed critical at that moment was to escape, separating himself from whatever reminded him of her. Alone, he jetted above the oil-restrained surface of the sea, scaring up birds and rainbow bats. Then he docked at a web-tower and boarded an elevator that quietly asked for a destination.

"Up," he snapped. "Just up."

The Iapetus roof was much more elaborate than those covering the inner worlds. It was blacker than any space, and it was dense and durable, and if civilization vanished today, it would likely survive intact until the sun was a cooling white ember. That durability was essential. Simon rode the elevator past the final ceiling, emerging on the moon's night side but with dawn slowly approaching. He stopped the elevator before it reached the overhead port. Then he gazed at the sun's emergence—a tiny fierce fleck of nuclear fire that was dwarfed by a thousand lasers pointed at this one modest moon of Saturn.

A coalition of ice-belt nations had joined forces. Mercury, long considered too expensive to terraform, had been purchased and partly destroyed, doctored rock and iron fashioned into a fleet of enormous orbiting solar collectors that collected energy that was pumped into beams of light that could have destroyed ships and cities and even whole worlds. Could but never would, what with their elaborate programming and too many safeguards to count. But it was the sun's focused power that slammed into the tough black conservatory, and it was the conservatory that captured and channeled this resource into the artificial suns that made Iapetus glow to its core. This was a cheaper, sweeter solution than building and maintaining fleets of fusion reactors. Every photon was absorbed, and as a result, life had warm bright happy water—a place where he wanted to live forever.

Jackie had always enjoyed this part of the ascent; that's why Simon stopped here now. Stopped and waited, knowing that she was alive and well, but wasn't it the right thing to do, worrying as he did?

The situation on earth was always chaotic.

He understood that Jackie had friends and colleagues to help before she could send word his way, and she might not be able to do that for a long time, considering the riot and the normal censorship demanded by the Powers-That-Be.

No, he wasn't sick with worry.

Then the home-mind called out, "Sir."

Its voice was tinged with sorrow.

More than anything else, what surprised Simon was how quickly he severed all contact with the universe. Before another word was offered, his small sharp mind had made its decision and cut the channel to his home-mind, never bothering to tell him of its intentions.

If Simon knew nothing, then Jackie was alive; and that would remain true for as long as he could endure the cold boundless space about him and the sound of his breathing coming again and again in deep, useless gasps.

MAKEMAKE

"Sir, please. Please. What generosity may I offer you? I have marvelous teas, strong and sweet, or weak and sublime."

"Something sublime."

"And once again, sir, I apologize for any intrusion. For your time and sacrifices, I will be eternally grateful."

Simon nodded and smiled blandly, asking nothing of his host. The Suricata were bright social entities famous for rituals and reflexive politeness. Answers would come soon enough, and knowing these people, he was certain that he wouldn't much like what he was about to learn.

The tea was served cold in tiny ceremonial bowls.

"You continue to do marvelous work for us, sir."

"And I hear praising words about you," Simon replied. "Wiser minds than me say that our mob has never enjoyed a more efficient or responsible security chief."

The narrow face seemed pleased. But the chief's four hands gripped his bowl too firmly, long black nails scrapping against the white bone china.

Simon finished his drink and set it aside.

The chief did the same, and then with a portentous tone said, "Perhaps you heard about the refugee transport that arrived yesterday. Of course you have, who hasn't? Eleven hundred and nine survivors, each one a victim of this monstrous war, and all now quarantined at the usual site."

One hundred kilometers above their heads stood a roughly camouflaged, utterly filthy ice dome—the same jail-like dumping site where Simon had lived for his first three months after his arrival.

"My problem," the chief began. Then the bright black eyes smiled, and he said, "Our problem," as a less than subtle reminder of everyone's civic responsibilities. "More than one thousand sentient entities wish to find shelter with us, but before that can happen, we must learn everything about these individuals. The political climate might be improving, but tempers and grudges remain in full force. Our neutrality is maintained at a great cost—"

"Who is our problem?"

Simon's interruption pleased the chief. At least he sighed with what seemed like relief, watching a creature twice his size and older than anyone else on this world. "We have found a war criminal," the chief admitted. "A much-sought individual, and I believe a colleague of yours from long ago. According to reliable accounts, she was complicit in the Martian genocide, a consultant in two slaughters on the earth, and her role in the Ganymede struggles has been rigorously documented."

"We're discussing Naomi?"

Embarrassed, the little face dipped until the rope-like body lay on the carpeted floor. "One of her names, yes. She attempted to hide her identity, but what was a clever and thorough disguise the day she left Titan has become old and obvious." The Suricata were lovely creatures, their dense fur softer than sable, warming fats and fantastic metabolism keeping them comfortable inside their icy tunnels. The chief stood again, hands fidgeting with readers and switches while his tail made a quick gesture, alerting his guest to the importance of his next words. "We are quite certain. This is the infamous Naomi. We find ourselves holding perhaps the most notorious atums still at large."

"From the Blue Camp," Simon added.

Eight Camps exited at the war's outset. Attrition and political necessities had shrunk the field to two Camps, and the Blue was officially extinct.

Politely but firmly, the chief cautioned, "As far as the Kuiper neutrals are concerned, there are no Camps. There is us, and there is the War. At no time have we taken sides in this ridiculous conflict, which means that we must remain immune to favoritism and even the most tentative alliances."

In other words, to save their peace, they had to be ruthless.

Simon nodded. "Why here?"

"Excuse me, sir?"

"I understand why Naomi would want to escape. Of course she'd try to flee. But the woman I knew had a talent for guessing where the tunnel would turn next. Throwing everything into a long journey out to the edge of inhabited space . . . well, coming all of the way out to Makemake strikes me as desperate, at best. And at worst, suspicious."

An unwelcome question had been asked. The chief responded by invoking his rank, stiffening his tail while the hands became fists. "Desperation is the perfectly normal response now. Sir. You don't see the intelligence reports that I am forced to endure. You don't study the elaborate simulations and their predictions for continuing troubles. At least ninety percent of the solar system's population has been extinguished. At least. Worlds have been ruined, fortunes erased, but sitting inside this careful peace of ours, you cannot appreciate how miserable and frantic and sick these minds are . . . those tortured few who have managed to survive until this moment."

Charitably, Simon said, "I agree. I don't know how it would feel."

The chief sighed. Regretting the present tone, he admitted, "I have nothing but respect for you, sir. Respect wrapped around thanks. What would we have done without your talents? What if you had found your way to another Kuiper world . . . to Varuna, perhaps? Today they would have a great atum working miracles with limited resources, and we would have to turn aside every soul for lack of room and food and precious air?"

Varuna had been a disaster—too many refugees overtaxing the barely-begun terraforming work. But Makemake, and Suricata society in particular, had endured this nightmare rather well. Simon knew this game. With feigned conviction, he said, "You would have done fine without me. You are a marvelous and endlessly inventive people."

His host smiled too long.

"May I ask another question?"

"Yes, sir," said the security chief.

"Why am I here? You've identified your prisoner. And since I haven't seen her for at least eight hundred years—"

"Nine hundred and five Martian years," the chief interjected.

"I don't see any role for me to play." Simon stroked the small gray beard that covered half of his thoroughly human face. "Unless of course you want my testimony at the trial."

"No," the chief blurted.

Simon waited, his patience fraying.

"The trial was concluded several hours ago. The judges' have announced the sentence. Nothing remains now but the execution of the prisoner."

"Ah." Simon nodded. "You brought me here as a courtesy?"

The black eyes gazed at him, hoping to say nothing more.

But despite many decades of living among these souls, the atum couldn't quite piece together the clues. What would have been obvious to any native citizen of this cold, isolated world was invisible to him. Finally, with honest confusion, Simon confessed, "I don't know what you want."

"It is what the prisoner wants."

"Which is?"

"Naomi has memorized our laws," the chief confessed. "And she somehow learned that you were living here."

The atum began to feel ill.

"She has invoked a little-used code, naming her executioner."

"I won't," said Simon.

But the Suricata was a deeply social species. Choice did not exist in their civil code. Duty to their city and their world was seamless. And no less could be expected from those who came to live in their cathedrals of ice and bright air.

"If you refuse this honor," the chief said flatly, "then we will be forced to begin banishment procedures."

Simon took a moment to let the possibilities eat at him.

"She wants me to kill her," he muttered quietly.

"To my mind," the chief replied stiffly, "the woman is already dead. With this gesture, you will be completing the act."

In a multitude of places, including inside at least one atum's mind, there were precise and effective plans for the transformation of this little world. Makemake was named for a Polynesian god of creation. Specifically, for a deity worshipped by the isolated citizens of Easter Island, which as landmasses went, was arguably the most remote portion of the earth colonized by the first human species. If the war hadn't erupted during the last century, Makemake's transformation would have begun. A dozen artificial suns were delivered while Mars was dying again. They were in orbit, patiently waiting orders to ignite. This early step could easily be taken: Turning methane snows into a thin atmosphere clinging to a body barely half the size of Pluto. But even that modest step brought danger. Why make yourself a prize to distant but vicious enemies? Eight decades of unmatched struggle had ravaged richer worlds, and if not for the thin traffic of refugees that still managed to limp their way out into this cold, lightless realm, there wouldn't be any traffic whatsoever.

The ranking atum thought about these weighty matters, and he considered his own enormous luck—not just to survive the War, but to then discover a life that gave him authority and privilege beyond any that he'd ever known.

Simon usually took pleasure from his walks on the surface. There was majesty to this realm of cold and barren ice. The black sky was unmarred by clever lights and ship traffic, giving it an enduring appeal. The glimmers and flashes of great weapons weren't visible any longer. Neither surviving Camp was able to marshal those kinds of monstrosities today. Which was why the determined mind could forget, looking at the ember that was the sun and seeing nothing else but the faint dot that was Jupiter, believing any story but the miserable one where almost every life was destroyed, and every world, including the earth, was at the best only barely, painfully habitable.

"What are you doing?" asked a sharp, impatient voice.

"As little as I can," he admitted to his companion.

"Focus," she implored.

"I should."

"You haven't changed at all, have you, Simon? You still can't make yourself do the distasteful work."

"That's my finest flaw," he replied.

The humor was ignored, such as it was. Her own focus was relentless, her shrewdness undiminished, and as always, Naomi had her sights locked on some self-important goal. Stopping abruptly, she told him, "I didn't select you just because we were once friends and colleagues. No, Simon. I picked you because you are perhaps the most consistent creature that I've ever known."

"What do you want, Naomi?"

"Not yet," she teased. Then she began to walk again, marching vigorously toward the small, undistinguished crater where for years now prisoners like her had been executed.

Naomi and Simon were the same size, give or take a few grams. But in a cal-culated bid to ingratiate herself with her now-defeated Camp, she long ago sur-rendered every hint of her human form. The woman resembled a scorpion, complete with the jointed limbs and an elaborate, supremely graceful tail folded up beneath her lifesuit. Her carapace was designed to withstand a hard vacuum, but not the cold. Her suit was heated, and a simple recyke system kept her green blood fully oxygenated. Disable either, and she would die slowly and without fuss. The chief and various experts had advised Simon to cripple both systems and hasten the act. But ice crystals and suffocation were astonishingly violent acts, if only at the cellular level. Simon held his own opinions about how to com-mit murder, and much as he hated this wicked business, he would carry out the execution however he damn well pleased.

Seemingly without fear, the scorpion scuttled across the ice.

Ignorant eyes might imagine Simon as the doomed soul. And indeed, many eyes were watching their approach. Cameras supplied by both Camps had been unpacked and activated for this singular occasion. The machines were witnesses, hardened links and a multitude of security safeguards linking them to the solar system. In principle, nobody could be fooled by what happened next, unless what they wanted was to be fooled.

Simon took longer strides, catching the prisoner just short of the crater wall.

And Naomi slowed abruptly, her adrenalin or its equivalent suddenly failing her. Eerily human eyes glanced up at Simon, and on their private channel, she said, "I've always liked you."

He was startled but careful not to show it.

"I know how that sounds, and I know you don't believe me. But from the first time we met, I have held the greatest respect for your abilities."

"Where was that?" he asked.

"The first time?"

"I'm old," he admitted. "Remind me."

She didn't simply mention about Venus. With astonished detail, Naomi de-scribed a dry meeting between members of an air-plankton team—the kind of routine nonevent that Simon would forget in a week, at most. "You made skepti-cal comments about our work. Perceptive, illuminating comments, when you look back at the moment now."

"That impressed you?"

"In a peculiar fashion, you seemed more secure than the rest of us. More hon-est, less willing to compromise yourself with the politics."

He shrugged, saying nothing.

"I'm sure you took notice: I was a flirt and shameless when it came to working the rooms. And I don't think that ten Simons would have held as much ambition as I carried around in those times."

"Probably not," he conceded.

"Did you ever want to sleep with me?"

"No," he lied.

But she didn't seem to care, eyes closing while the hard face nodded wistfully. "If I'd paid attention to you . . . if I had let myself learn from you . . . my life would have turned out quite a bit better, I think."

It might have been a different life, or perhaps not. Simon realized long ago that no matter how creative or well informed the soul might be, there was no way to see the future that rose even from the wisest of decisions: Ignorance as epiphany, and with that, freedom from regret.

They reached the lip of the crater together—two tiny entities on the brink of a neat flat-bottomed bowl. Suddenly he was in the lead, his pseudo-adrenalin rising out of a gland that was among his youngest. With a dry, tight voice, he said, "You named me. You claim that there's a reason. And if you don't tell me why, I'll be happy."

"But I have to tell you," Naomi replied.

"I can't help you," he warned. "Maybe you think that I've got power here, but I don't. Or that I'm not strong enough to do this, and I'll lose my will, and then the Suricata would give up trying to punish you—"

"I don't expect your help or your weakness," she interrupted. "You are a soft-hearted creature. But that isn't why I selected you."

"Soft-hearted," he heard, and the image mysteriously gnawed at him.

Naomi continued, saying, "The two of us, Simon . . . we atums seen a great deal during our extraordinary careers."

He took a long bounce, ending up on a flat stretch of rock-hard water ice. "I suppose we have, yes."

"My career," she began.

He forced himself to slow, glancing up at the cameras hovering against the eternal night sky.

"Being an atum is a blessing, and I feel blessed. I know how it looks now, the insanity that drove us into the Camps. Using our knowledge about building worlds to kill the worlds instead. But think of the history that these eyes have witnessed. The geniuses that I've known and our important work, and the foolish tragedies too . . . everything that comes with remolding and giving life to dozens and hundreds of worlds, little and great . . ."

"What is it, Naomi?"

"I kept a diary," she muttered.

"Many do."

"But my diary is far more complete than the others," she maintained. "From the first entry, I've used only the best methods, the most thorough tricks. This isn't just text and images, Simon. I underwent scans of my mind, uploaded memories, censoring nothing. Nothing. And then I employed a military-grade AI to act as an overseer and voice. This is my life, the splendid as well as the awful, and I don't think any citizen in any venue has ever achieved the scale that I've managed."

"And my role?"

"I'll tell you where I hid it," she admitted. "You're good and decent, Simon, and you can appreciate the value of this kind of testimony. Ten thousand years from today, won't the citizens be hungry to understand the people who shaped their history—those who first colonized the solar system?"

He glanced up at the sun and that feeble band of dust riding on the ecliptic, much of it created by explosions and obliterating impacts. "You're certain there's going to be an audience then?"

"We've made our mistakes," she conceded. "But this war will end. And shouldn't we give our descendants every lesson possible? 'Don't do as we did,' we will tell them."

"I did nothing too terrible," he maintained.

Suddenly Naomi ran short of praise for her executioner. With her voice breaking, she pointed out, "No, you're just as guilty as me, Simon."

"Despite my good opinions," he countered.

"A billion clever insights accomplish nothing, if the voice that mutters them isn't compelling enough to change one action."

They were near the crater's center, the execution ground defined by a neat black circle as well as pits made by the blasts of weapons and warm bodies rapidly growing cold. Reach that line, and their private line would fail. Only an unsecured public line would allow them to speak to one another. Simon felt his face filling with blood—the blush marking just a portion of his deep, conflicted feelings. He tried to keep his voice under control, but each word came out hard and tense. "It's time, Naomi. I'm going to stop your oxygen and heater now, and we can walk the rest of the way together."

"My diary?"

He didn't answer. "Your carapace is a fine insulator," he said. "And if I'm right, we'll have several minutes before you spend your last breaths."

"But you will rescue my diary, won't you? I tell you where it is, and you can use it however you want. As a historical record, if you want—"

"And only for that reason," he muttered.

Emotions made her shiver, but she acted satisfied. One conspirator to another, she said, "I did genuinely like you, Simon."

He touched the controls on her back, powering down both systems.

"And you're a familiar presence," she conceded. "If a person has to die this way, don't you think she should be with a friend?"

"I'm not your friend, Naomi."

She didn't speak.

Oxygen had stopped entering her blood, and in the next moment, the bitter chill of Makemake began to creep inside her. "I don't know if I can make it to the circle."

"You can."

"Just say that you're my friend," she begged. "Please. I don't want it to end this way."

From the satchel on his hip, Simon pulled out a small railgun, and he aimed and fired a slug of iron-clad stone into the scorpion's brain. Naomi stiffened, and a moment later, collapsed. He grabbed a front leg and dragged her across the neat black line, then backed away to allow the cameras to descend and investigate the body with a full array of sophisticated tools. Breathing hard, he looked at the corpse, and with a steady voice he pointed out, "You helped murder hundreds of billions. And until today, you didn't throw two nice words my way. And I'll be damned if I'm going to help your beloved memories have any life beyond today."

"Thank you," the chief said.

He gave his thanks once and then again, and then twice more, with even greater feeling.

Then with an air of concern, the chief continued. "This must have been hard on you. Regardless what she was and how much she deserved her fate—"

"It was difficult," Simon conceded.

The little creature seemed giddy with compassion. "This won't happen again. I promise."

"But I'm here if you need me," Simon replied.

A dark, dark joke.

The chief nodded warily.

"She brought it with her. Didn't she?"

The chief hesitated. "Brought what?"

"Her diary. The AI with its attached memories. Naomi came here with the hope of using it as a bribe, hoping to manage a better deal for herself." Until Simon said the words, he didn't believe it was true, but then they were drifting in the air and he believed nothing else.

The chief suddenly had no voice.

"And I'm guessing that one of you two brought me into this scheme. She would tell me that the fabled diary was somewhere else, somewhere hard to reach, throwing the scent far from Makemake. Naomi must have told others about her self-recording project, not to mention leaving an ether-trail from the hospitals and various specialists brought into the project. But if I thought I had this special knowledge, and if I acted according to my good noble instincts . . . well, I can see how this would have distracted a few players while you happily sat on the prize."

"But why would I care?" the little man managed.

"Because Naomi had a wealth of experience, and that's the part of her estate you wanted. Her expertise. Once this war is finished, Makemake will be able to reinvent itself, and prosperity is going to come easier when you enjoy the free and easy guidance of a highly accomplished atum."

"Naomi's dead," the chief offered, in his own defense.

"She is. And she isn't. No, in her peculiar mind, I think the creature held a different interpretation of events." Simon shrugged, the last traces of anger washing out of him. "I saw a small useless death on the ice, while she saw life inside a new mechanical mind. When you're as greedy as Naomi, it's amazing what you can convince yourself of . . . and who knows, maybe that old lady has a point in all of this . . . ?"

EARTH

The purpose of the visit was to meet the next generation of atums, in classes and privately, assessing the strengths as well as the inevitable weaknesses of these graduates before they were scattered across the Unified System. But several grateful university officials came to the chief atum, begging for a public event that would earn notice and praise, both for them and their ancient institution. Simon agreed reluctantly. He would give a speech, stipulating only that his audience was kept small—a diverse assortment of students and faculty assembled in some minor lecture hall. He understood that any public event by someone of his rank would attract attention. What he wanted to escape were situations where multitudes of eager, ill-prepared souls would cling to every word, unable to tell the off-hand remark from rigid matters of policy. But his request, harmless and rational to his mind, led first to strict quotas, and when the demand proved too enormous, a lottery system where tickets were awarded and sometimes sold for fantastic sums—all for the honor of cramming inside a long hot room with forty thousand equally enthralled bodies, every eye and a few secret cameras staring at a figure as old as terraforming, or nearly so.

In appearance, Simon had remained stubbornly, endearingly human. Pieces of him were still physically tied to the young Martian, though those archaic tissues consisted only of a few cells scattered through crystalline overlaps, metabolic engines, and bundles of smart-light and nulls and voids. His face and body remained tall, but only in contrast to the entities gathered about him. He began with a bright smile and a voice crafted to come across as warm and comforting to the average citizen, thanking everyone for surrendering a portion of his busy day to listen to an old fellow rattle on. Then he told a story from his childhood, describing in detail how his father once handed him a nano-bomb seed—one of the old marvels intended to transform Mars from a wasteland to a paradise. "I didn't understand the significance of that crude tool," he confessed. "But I held the miraculous seed in both hands, believing that in my brief life, this was the most important object that I had ever touched. Yet at the same moment, I was stubbornly ignoring my own soggy brain. And everyone else's too. But minds are the only marvels worthy of our lasting respect, and I can only wish that each of us holds that truth close to us as we pass through our future days."

Simon was smaller than his original hands had been, smaller than that early seed. But by the same token, he was larger than the rock and iron ball that was Mars. Like any modern mind, a good portion of his intelligence—facts and language, customs and a multitude of instincts—were held in the earth's community mind. He remained a unique citizen, endowed with his own personality and ancient, often quaint notions. But as long as citizens wished to stretch toward infinity, room was going to come at a premium. Carrying your life experience inside one isolated skull meant large, inefficient bodies needing room to live. And if those bodies achieved even modest reproductive rates, any world would be swamped in a day, and shortly after that, ten thousand worlds more.

As Simon liked to do on these occasions, he reminded every ear that the duties of an atum, particularly one granted his terrifying station, was to help select a direction into the future, that determined line balanced between wild freedom and despotic rule. What kinds of biology would embrace each world; how many children would each of these rich lives be allowed; and under what terms and what punishments would the government hold each of its citizens accountable. Everyone understood the consequences of mistakes, but just to be certain, he mentioned the First War and the Purge that followed, then the subsequent Battle of the Kupiers and what was dubbed the Final Purge, as if that species of political madness had been wrung from civilization forever.

"Nothing is forever," he warned, "no matter if it's an individual life or the one hundred billion year life of the smallest, reddest sun." Then his voice grew in depth and power, taking the sleepiest in the audience by surprise. "Change is inevitable," he promised, "but little else about the coming forever is certain. I would imagine that everyone here holds that noble wish that intelligent life will prosper in the universe, spreading to other suns and eventually to all the ends of the Milky Way. But that remains far from certain. In our ongoing studies of the sky, we have observed what has to be considered a paucity of intelligence. Today, those civilizations nearest to humanity are just beginning to hear the earth's original transmissions, radio and radar whispers barely hinting at everything that has happened since, and it is presumed that in another several thousand years, a slow rich conversation will commence. Or our neighbors will respond to our presence with the most perfect, telling silence. The fertile imagination easily conceives wonders as well as horrors coming from this unborn history. But this man before you, this atum, believes that the real gift of the Others will be to suggest to us the richest, most stable answers to the eternal questions of life and living well in a universe that holds minds such as ours in such very low esteem."

Tradition dictated that the chief atum had to make his or her residence on the earth, but since Simon had no role in maintaining the biosphere, he was free to live where he wished. He earned a few grumbles when he requested a modest structure erected on top of the newest conservatory—little more than one dome and various substructures meant to house assistants and the usual secure machinery demanded by his office. Some complained that the new chief didn't trust the good work being done by the local atums. Why else would he perched himself in the vacuum, his feet standing on top of one hundred trillion heads? But explanations did no good with those people. He spoke a few times about his love for space and the illusion of solitude, but after that, he gave up offering reasons. For as long as he held this post, enemies would find reasons to distrust him, and as long as his antagonists thought in small terms, he would be safe wherever he chose to live, right up until the day that this office was lost to him.

"I have an errand for you," Simon told his favorite lieutenant. "A mission of some importance, and I wouldn't trust anyone else with it."

The creature turned vivid blue, and twenty limbs shook from the apparent compliment. Then a soft clear voice said, "Sir," and then, "I am honored," before asking, "What is my mission?"

With a thought, Simon delivered a set of encrypted files and the necessary keys, plus a few helpful suggestions. Then he waited while the files' headings were studied. The assistant had a quick mind; it took only a moment for the limbs to stiffen, fear turning the body into a dark, despairing violet.

"Sir," the voice began.

"What have you found there?" Simon kidded.

"I didn't know about these matters."

"You didn't, did you?" The atum nodded agreeably. "That's what you should mention when you act on your knowledge."

"Sir?"

"You are going to act, aren't you?"

The assistant turned black and cold, a begging voice complaining, "This is not fair, sir."

"Little is," Simon agreed.

"By law, I have to take what I know to the proper agency."

"I wouldn't have it any other way, my friend."

The creature muttered to itself.

"But please, will you do one small favor for me," Simon continued. "Surrender this evidence to the Office of Exotic Biology. And yes, they have jurisdiction in these matters. They are perfectly acceptable authorities, and no one will fault you, even if you choose to someday mention these events to anyone else."

Perplexed but obedient, the assistant left on his unexpected mission.

Alone, Simon slipped into a gossamer lifesuit and stepped out onto the hard surface of the newest conservatory. The sun was a faint glow just beginning to climb over the geometrically perfect horizon. Mercury was a dull dot almost invisible against the stars, its top fifty kilometers peeled away and refined into habitats ranging from mountain-sized to smaller than a small walnut. Venus was nearer and much duller, encased in half a dozen finished conservatories whose main purpose was to grab and sequester every photon falling from the sun, allowing the interior heat to build and build until the entire planet melted—a liquid world whose crust and then mantle could be siphoned off with relative ease, creating hundreds of trillions of living worlds that would eventually form a great ring around the sun.

Jupiter remained a wilderness of space and raw materials, accompanied by its liquid worlds, infested with life but still not full. Uranus and Neptune were brighter than ever, the terrraforming of the little giants just beginning in earnest. Once again, Mars was being made into an earth-like world, but this time the work involved improved conservatories stacked on top of one another, the crust laced with sprawling caverns and hidden seas. And largest to the eye was Luna. Nearly as large as earth, it was a vast balloon composed of vacuum-filled chambers and nonaqueous species. Again, its design was aimed at growth, machines and organisms busily digesting the rocky body. But like every world in the Unified System, the genius that designed this transformation always aimed for a special stability. Each planet functioned as a nest of deeply social insects. As long as all the pieces and players cooperated, life thrived. But if the calm failed, the queens of the nest would perish, and just as important, the lowly and the innocent would inherit what remained.

Simon had helped craft this ruthless and obvious system. Humanity might have the power to draw life in any form it wished, but there still existed the Darwinian god holding sway over the majestic mess, and for the next eon or two, the best would succeed a little more other than their peers.

Some days, it seemed that reaching this station was a miracle. But on this early morning being the chief atum felt entirely natural. Of course he was important. Who else was as old as him and as short of enemies? Who else could claim that they had been there at the beginning, or nearly so, yet never took part in any conspiracy or slaughter of note?

Without sound, Simon started to laugh, enjoying the irony. The absence of ambition was the ultimate ambition, it seemed.

Then his house-mind announced a visitor.

Simon didn't ask for the name. He knew. And turning back toward his home, walking slowly and then not so slowly, he said to the house, "Tell Lilly to make herself comfortable. The criminal is on his way."

"How did you manage this?" she blurted. Then in the next instant, she added, "This has to be a mistake. Somebody's trying to frame you, and they didn't even manage a believable job of it."

Like Simon, Lilly had kept hold of her human features. She sat and watched as he settled before her, and when he didn't act appropriately concerned, she added, "This is the worst kind of scandal. If I'd told anyone—"

"But you haven't," he interrupted.

"Because I thought I owed you at least the courtesy of looking into your face, seeing if there was any explanation for what you've done."

He shrugged and said nothing.

"Starships are forbidden," she snapped. "No vessel except sterile drones can legally pass beyond the Kuiper belt."

"I am well aware of the laws—"

"And the kind of ship you've built," she blurted. "Dammit, Simon. It shatters at least a thousand codes. If you were to ride this sort of magic seed out into the cosmos . . . you could go almost anywhere . . . and then you could infect and transform any body. Any world. The outlawed technologies and the government-only technologies that you've assembled here, using your station as chief atum—"

"Impressed, are you?"

Lilly remained a passionate creature, dark and lovely but always focused on the needs of her life's mission. "I'm scared, Simon. Terrified. What were you planning to do with this monster seed?"

He laughed and nodded, and then he quietly confessed, "The seed has room for one small passenger."

"For you?" she whimpered.

"Me? Hardly." He sat motionless, carefully watching his guest. "I have a mission in mind. But by training and inclinations, I suspect that I wouldn't make a worthy pilot for this kind of work."

"What work?"

Simon leaned forward, one hand and then the other taking both of hers. It was pleasant, holding onto the woman like this, feeling her heat pass into him. He was thinking about Lilly and his father sleeping together on the red wastes of Mars. He recalled that moment on Venus, in the darkness, in the wind. Then he surprised both of them, lifting their hands and kissing the backs of hers even as he slid onto his knees, saying nothing, but tasting a faint delicious salt against his lips and the tip of his tongue.

A WORLD UNBURDENED BY NAMES

The object was noticed and instantly measured—a small glimmer approaching along the expected vector, closing rapidly on the decelerating starship—and McKall's first reaction was an energetic laugh punctuated with several choice curses. "Long enough, it took them to chase us," he declared to his hounds and fireworms and the other powerful, fearless members of his unabashedly loyal crew. "For now, watch our enemy. Study what it shows us, and do nothing. Then at ten thousand kilometers, obliterate it."

Whatever the weapon was, their fifth blast managed to vaporize both its armor and the surprisingly simple meat inside.

Celebratory drinks were served.

For many centuries now, the starship's captain had been worried. Onboard mirrors showed that the solar system behind them had suffered wars and subsequent rebirths. Who knew what kinds of marvels these new generations had devised? But obviously, his concerns had been misspent. Several moments were invested in careful study of the vanquished enemy. The remnant dust presented a minor puzzle, composed of common iron and little else. Why would anyone go to such trouble, sending what looked like a fancy cannonball after him? Too late, he wondered if perhaps the device had been a decoy, a ruse. He confessed his fears to his security chief, and the chief initiated a ship-wide search for tiny breeches and undetected invaders. Nothing was found. Every system was working properly. Twenty-three minutes after that cannonball was first seen, Earnest McKall retreated to his quarters—the only private rooms allowed inside the enormous starship—and he had halfway prepared a fresh cocktail when he noticed the tiny shape of a girl or woman clinging to the ceiling.

Softly, very softly, he asked, "How did you—?"

"Slip onboard? While you were fighting the bait, the hook approached from ahead of you. I used your engine's fire as camouflage. And as for the rest of my trickery . . . well, explaining everything is not my consuming goal."

In secret, McKall signaled for help.

Nothing changed.

An instant later his metabolism had reached full speed, dragging his thoughts along with it. "What is your—?"

"Lilly."

He stopped talking.

"My name is Lilly, and thank you for asking." She was at least as swift as the ship's captain. "Do you have any other questions, Dr. McKall?"

"What is your goal?" he managed.

"What do you believe that I want?"

"To stop me, of course. We're not five hundred years from New Earth, and this is some last-gasp attempt to destroy my ship and me."

She was pretty and very small, no longer than a small finger, and it was difficult, even impossible, to take her seriously. Yet her voice had weight, rising from places besides her miniscule mouth. Amused, she explained, "But I don't wish to stop you. And I certainly don't want to destroy you. What I want—what I have halfway taken already, without you being aware—is complete control of this vessel and its crew. I am the new captain, and you are my dog."

McKall was furious, and he was terrified. Which emotion fixed his legs to the floor? He couldn't decide. But he discovered that moving any limb was impossible, and his voice was a breathless little gasp.

"You'll conquer the New Earth for yourself," he managed. "Is that your scheme?"

"Hardly."

The untasted cocktail fell from his hand, spilling sticky and cold across his bare feet.

"I just want your ship and its possibilities," she explained. Then she dropped off the ceiling and landed in his rich black hair, miniature hands gripping tightly, yanking hard. "My plan? We'll drop into orbit, and I will mine the local system, beginning construction of rings first and then a conservatory far above the atmosphere. Elaborate defensive works will be built, plus shields against interstellar catastrophe, and then I will wait for anyone who is foolish enough to follow after you and after me."

"But what will you do . . . with the world . . . ?"

"Nothing," she promised. Then thinking again, she added, "Except to watch its native life go about with its business. Which is what any of us do on any given day. Isn't that right, Dr. McKall?"

The atum concluded his speech by answering the question that everyone would ask, given the chance. He posed it in his voice, wondering aloud, "And when, at long last, will we leave our solar system for other suns and the rich new worlds waiting their chance to be claimed?"

Then he paused, offering an archaic smile while nodding slightly.

Cryptically, he said, "We shall embark when we are ready."

Then a little voice up front shouted, "And when will that be?"

Simon's most loyal assistant was obeying explicit instructions. He glanced at the many-limbed creature, answering, "Once all of our local homes are filled and happy. I would hope. We will embark as soon as we can trust our nature and our institutions not to use this migration as an excuse for easy growth and return voyages of conquest. When we have a worthy plan and the courage and discipline to trust in it. When starships no longer consume fortunes in energy and precious matter. When we have become adults, finally mature and responsible in all occasions. But most important . . ."

He paused briefly, enjoying the anticipation that washed over him.

"Most important," he concluded, "we will not leave this little realm of ours until we are children again. Wide-eyed, enthralled children who know what they have in their hands and hold it with all the care they possess."

The spontaneous knotting of an agitated string

Lavie Tidhar

Lavie Tidhar grew up on a kibbutz in Israel, has traveled widely in Africa and Asia, and has lived in London, the South Pacific island of Vanuatu, and Laos. He is the winner of the 2003 Clarke-Bradbury International Science Fiction Competition (awarded by the European Space Agency), was the editor of *Michael Marshall Smith: The Annotated Bibliography*, and the anthologies *A Dick and Jane Primer for Adults* and *The Apex Book of World SF*. He is the author of the linked story collection *HebrewPunk*, the novella chapbooks "An Occupation of Angels," "Gorel & the Pot-Bellied God," the almost novel-length "Cloud Permutations," and, with Nir Yaniv, the novel *The Tel Aviv Dossier*. A prolific short story writer, his stories have appeared in *Interzone*, *Clarkesworld*, *Apex Magazine*, *Sci Fiction*, *Strange Horizons*, *ChiZine*, *Postscripts*, *Fantasy Magazine*, *Nemonymous*, *Infinity Plus*, *Aeon*, *The Book of Dark Wisdom*, *Fortean Bureau*, and elsewhere, and have been translated into seven languages. His latest novels include *The Bookman* and its sequel, *Camera Obscura*. Coming up are two new novels, *Osama* and *Martian Sands*. He's currently back in Israel again, living in Tel Aviv.

In the quietly lyrical, deeply compassionate story that follows, he shows a keen understanding of how high-tech gadgets interact with ancient cultures and traditions—each one modifying the other.

Mrs. Pongboon, that great woman and mother, that seller of mysterious artefacts, walks down the street in her red-patterned sihn the colour of a naga's crest, and people stare because to dress this way is to invite the wrath of the Ngeuk Laeng, the dreaded drought nagas—but it is all a nothing to Mrs. Pongboon, who had taken all her fear and her secret anxieties and put them in a talisman which hangs around her neck, a tasteful little locket of gold and quartz and state-of-the-art mass-produced Chinese technology. 'Buy my lockets, my darlings!' she calls, and the women stop and stare, and the children giggle and are shushed, and the men look anxious and thoughtful. 'Put away your loves and fears, and keep them for a rainy day!'

But every day is rainy in the rainy season, and the Mekong snakes, as large as a naga, between the banks of Laos and Thailand, this snake-river, divider of countries, carrier of goods, all swelled up with its own importance and the water that falls from the sky and the water of the snows in the far away Himalayas, which have travelled a long way to come here, will travel a long way yet before they see the ocean. 'Buy my lockets, for a fair and good price, transfer precious memories, store tender hearts! The deal is today, a one-of-a-kind, hurry, my friends, hurry, I say! Or you'll miss out forever, when Mrs. Pongboon has passed, and was gone on her way.'

But business is slow and besides, everyone knows about transference, and Mrs. Pongboon, as large and imposing as she no doubt is, is not alone in the trade—far from it. And yet . . . a young girl, in a black, carefully-ironed sihn, a white blouse with the sleeves buttoned around her slim wrists, in her high-heeled shoes bought second-hand, a small handbag from the Talat Sao, the Morning Market—a student, perhaps, or an office worker of minor importance and a minor salary to match—timidly approaches Mrs. Pongboon who, sniffing out a sale before, even, the girl had occasion to consciously think herself to it, says, 'What is it, my darling? A broken heart? Did a young boy steal your happiness away? Come, tell Mrs. Pongboon, queen of the ladies, a mother to children— remember that mothers, too, were lovers once.'

'Is—' the girl says, and stops, self-conscious, and Mrs. Pongboon moves into the shadows of a music shop where a Laotian band is pumping out a cover of Thaitanium's *Tomyam Samurai*, and the girl follows her and, free from the scrutiny of passers-by, her shoulder-blades seem to relax—'is it true?'

'It's *technology*,' Mrs. Pongboon says, importantly, employing the English word, which is one of the few she knows. The girl looks impressed—as well she should, Mrs. Pongboon thinks. 'Here,' she says. 'Try,' she says. She un-loops a second locket from her ample bosom—not the one with all her misery inside it but the sampler, the holy sampler—she had once confused the two with a potential customer and the results were . . . less than beneficial, in fact there had been a complaint, and since then she is extra careful, though she cannot bear to put her own, personal locket away—'Try and see for yourself, my darling little girl.'

The locket is encoded with a Generic Spring Day, The Lovers, River Bank—it could be anywhere, it could be any two young people in any country in the world, Generic Sampler Number Two, version oh three point five six, and when Mrs. Pongboon pops the lock she can adjust the setting. Encode: Laotian-specific. Encode: Boy-Girl (she takes a hunch, you'd be surprised how often it doesn't pay off)—'Here, give me your palm, little miss, little madam, close your fingers, close your eyes—can you feel it?' (but of course she can).

'Oh,' the girl says, and then—'Oh.'

'And once you put it there,' Mrs. Pongboon says, 'it's gone. Like that.' She tries to snap her fingers but the humidity makes her sweat and her fingers merely slip off each other like careless dancers. 'Until you want it again.'

It is called transference, of course it does, though of course it is not *exactly* that. Mrs. Pongboon has a *device*, yes she does, and what the device *does*, is copy—how clever, those Chinese across the border!—is copy-and-delete. Not strictly legal, all this messing with the human brain—recording neurons as they fire their zero-one-zero-one emissions, even worse, resetting them inside the tendeᵣ gooey mass of brain, erasing the pattern inside—but what price can you put on human happiness?

'For a modest sum,' Mrs. Pongboon says, and pats the girl reassuringly on the shoulder, removing the locket from her hand at the same time, 'a *most* modest amount, you could put away whatever you desire.'

'There was—' the girl says, and blushes—she is quite pretty, Mrs. Pongboon thinks, in a plain sort of way—'there was this boy . . .'

How often had she heard that! Always, they wish to confide in her, like in the old-days psychologists, the ones who came up with the term. But this transference is *scientific*, not the mambo-jumbo of old spells and make-believe. This is *real*. And Mrs. Pongboon does not want to hear their stories. The day is long and the sun is hot and Mrs. Pongboon wants a cool bag of ice with a straw poking out and a bottle of Pepsi poured inside it, and besides she had heard the same story a thousand and one times before.

'You poor darling,' she says, 'you are like a string.'

The girl looks up at her, big round eyes confused—is that how you looked at him, Mrs. Pongboon thinks uncharitably, is that how you looked at him when he charmed you by the banks of the Mekong?—and says, 'I don't understand.'

'Science,' Mrs. Pongboon says, with quiet dignity one could possibly confuse for self-importance. 'It says everything is made of string.'

'Of course,' the girl says, and Mrs. Pongboon notices that, indeed, the girl is wearing three—or is it four?—white cotton strings tied to her wrist (now that the sleeve is pulled back a little)—tied for her by a monk or an aunt in the *basi* ceremony, for luck and the appeasing the family's spirits. She nods, because she approves of tradition, and preserving the old ways, and because she has the memory of a memory (the thing itself locked away in an earring back in her drawer) of the last string her mother had tied for her, when Mrs. Pongboon was still young, before her mother . . . but she no longer remembers, and it is better that way, sometimes. 'Science,' Mrs. Pongboon says again, and then falters, having lost her place. 'Strings,' she tries again. 'Everything is made of string. Thoughts, feelings, memories, they are strings of numbers in the brain. And science has proved that strings—even when they seem perfect (like you, you beautiful child!)—will come out all in knots. Whatever we do, life takes us (so says the great philosopher Mrs. Pongboon!) and ties us into knots. This way—' and she points to the locket, like a magician at a coin about to disappear—'is just a way science has of smoothing out the knots.' And she thinks—for a while at least. She does not tell the girls, but there will always be knots. That is called—she had memorized it in English—it is called the spontaneous knotting of an agitated string. 'That's a scientific *fact*,' she says, out loud.

'How . . . how much?' the girl says, and Mrs. Pongboon smiles kindly (joyful inside, a bite on the bait!) and names a price, and the girl looks taken aback, but then rallies, and she offers a different price, and Mrs. Pongboon shakes her head mournfully but agrees to lower her offer, and the girl raises hers—not so stupid after all, this one!—and they arrive at a price that was more or less what Mrs. Pongboon had hoped for—maybe add ten percent.

'Will it hurt?' the girl says.

'Not at all,' Mrs. Pongboon says. She pulls out the dangling wires from her backpack and attaches them to the girl's temples. The girl pulls back, then relaxes.

The gel adheres itself to her skin—it is almost animal-like in the way it moves, until it settles, becomes still, and—'Just think of it, bring it to the forefront of your mind—' the girl is visibly concentrating, teeth biting lower lip, it almost makes Mrs. Pongboon smile, almost but not quite—'there, I can see you have it—'

And she presses a button. It's as easy as that. And the girl seems to sag, and there is a whirring sound from the backpack, and that's it. 'Is it gone?' the girl says, and then she smiles, and then she frowns, and she says, 'There was . . . I was with . . .'

'When you want to remember,' Mrs. Pongboon says, gently pulling the quivering gel-ends back, the tentacles of the memory-naga withdrawing into its backpack—'just hold this to your head—' and she reaches back and the locket pops out, a pretty little thing (just like you, my darling girl!) and hands it to her. 'Can I . . . can I try it?'

'Do you really want to?'

The girl smiles, and shakes her head, and says, 'No. Not now . . .' and there is a faint trace of regret in her voice. In Mrs. Pongboon's experience, there always is. The girl pays her, and Mrs. Pongboon waddles away, the sweat streaming down her face, and she thinks about that ice-cold Pepsi in a bag, with the straw sticking out, just what a mature lady needs in these troubled times.

She walks away down the street, and the wind picks up, and she knows it is going to rain. She takes shelter in a noodle-soup kitchen, where the last breakfast diners are noisily finishing off their bowls. Mrs. Pongboon orders her Pepsi and while she waits she thinks of all the boys and all the girls who'd had their hearts broken, a spontaneous knot forming on the agitated strings of their hearts. She touches her own private locket and, when she brings it to her head, she can hear the sound of the Mekong at sunset, the waves nibbling at the shore, the sound of distant pop music from the other bank which is Thailand. She can hear the crickets' marching band and the frogs' military choir and the sound of laughter and clinking beer glasses from the stilt-houses up a way, and she buries her face in the boy's chest, and smells his sweat and his passion and for a moment, even though she is a matronly woman now and sells trinkets on the streets of Vientiane, has had two husbands and three kids, had buried parents, friends, had suffered loss and pain and disappointment—for just a moment, she feels like a smooth young thing again, a smooth young string: one that is yet to form a single agitated knot.

the emperor of mars

ALLEN M. STEELE

Allen Steele made his first sale to *Asimov's Science Fiction* magazine in 1988, soon following it up with a long string of other sales to *Asimov's* as well as to markets such as *Analog, The Magazine of Fantasy & Science Fiction,* and *Science Fiction Age.* In 1990, he published his critically acclaimed first novel, *Orbital Decay,* which subsequently won the Locus Award for Best First Novel of the year, and soon Steele was being compared to Golden Age Heinlein by no less an authority than Gregory Benford. His other books include the novels *Clarke County, Space; Lunar Descent; Labyrinth of Night; The Weight; The Tranquility Alternative; A King of Infinite Space; Oceanspace; Chronospace; Coyote; Coyote Rising; Spindrift; Galaxy Blues;* and *Coyote Horizon.* His short work has been gathered in three collections, *Rude Astronauts, Sex and Violence in Zero-G,* and *The Last Science Fiction Writer.* His most recent book is a new novel in the Coyote sequence, *Coyote Destiny.* Coming up is another Coyote novel, *Hex.* He won a Hugo Award in 1996 for his novella "The Death of Captain Future," and another Hugo in 1998 for his novella ". . . Where Angels Fear to Tread." Born in Nashville, Tennessee, he has worked for a variety of newspapers and magazines, covering science and business assignments, and is now a full-time writer living in Whately, Massachusetts, with his wife, Linda.

In the story that follows, he does a nice job of creating a valid science fiction story that also functions as an exercise in retro Barsoom nostalgia *and* as an intriguing psychological study, all at the same time.

Out here, there's a lot of ways to go crazy. Get cooped up in a passenger module not much larger than a trailer, and by the time you reach your destination you may have come to believe that the universe exists only within your own mind: it's called solipsism syndrome, and I've seen it happen a couple of times. Share that same module with five or six guys who don't get along very well, and after three months you'll be sleeping with a knife taped to your thigh. Pull double-shifts during that time, with little chance to relax, and you'll probably suffer from depression; couple this with vitamin deficiency due to a lousy diet, and you're a candidate for chronic fatigue syndrome.

Folks who've never left Earth often think that Titan Plague is the main reason people go mad in space. They're wrong. Titan Plague may rot your brain and turn you into a homicidal maniac, but instances of it are rare, and there's a dozen other ways to go bonzo that are much more subtle. I've seen guys adopt imaginary friends with whom they have long and meaningless conversations, compulsively clean their hardsuits regardless of whether or not they've recently worn them, or go for a routine spacewalk and have to be begged to come back into the airlock. Some people just aren't cut out for life away from Earth, but there's no way to predict who's going to lose their mind.

When something like that happens, I have a set of standard procedures: ask the doctor to prescribe antidepressants, keep an eye on them to make sure they don't do anything that might put themselves or others at risk, relieve them of duty if I can, and see what I can do about getting them back home as soon as possible. Sometimes I don't have to do any of this. A guy goes crazy for a little while, and then he gradually works out whatever it was that got in his head; the next time I see him, he's in the commissary, eating Cheerios like nothing ever happened. Most of the time, though, a mental breakdown is a serious matter. I think I've shipped back about one out of every twenty people because of one issue or another.

But one time, I saw someone go mad, and it was the best thing that could have happened to him. That was Jeff Halbert. Let me tell about him . . .

Back in '48, I was General Manager of Arsia Station, the first and largest of the Mars colonies. This was a year before the formation of the Pax Astra, about five years before the colonies declared independence. So the six major Martian settlements were still under control of one Earth-based corporation or another, with Arsia Station owned and operated by ConSpace. We had about a hundred people living there by then, the majority short-timers on short-term contracts; only a dozen or so, like myself, were permanent residents who left Earth for good.

Jeff wasn't one of them. Like most people, he'd come to Mars to make a lot of money in a relatively short amount of time. Six months from Earth to Mars aboard a cycleship, two years on the planet, then six more months back to Earth aboard the next ship to make the crossing during the bi-annual launch window. In three years, a young buck like him could earn enough dough to buy a house, start a business, invest in the stock market, or maybe just loaf for a good long while. In previous times, they would've worked on off-shore oil rigs, joined the merchant marine, or built powersats; by mid-century, this kind of high-risk, high-paying work was on Mars, and there was no shortage of guys willing and ready to do it.

Jeff Halbert was what we called a "Mars monkey." We had a lot of people like him at Arsia Station, and they took care of the dirty jobs that the scientists, engineers, and other specialists could not or would not handle themselves. One day they might be operating a bulldozer or a crane at a habitat construction site. The next day, they'd be unloading freight from a cargo lander that had just touched down. The day after that, they'd be cleaning out the air vents or repairing a solar array or unplugging a toilet. It wasn't romantic or particularly interesting work, but it was the sort of stuff that needed to be done in order to keep the base going, and because of that, kids like Jeff were invaluable.

And Jeff was definitely a kid. In his early twenties, wiry and almost too tall to wear a hardsuit, he looked like he'd started shaving only last week. Before he dropped out of school to get a job with ConSpace, I don't think he'd travelled more than a few hundred miles from the small town in New Hampshire where he'd grown up. I didn't know him well, but I knew his type: restless, looking for adventure, hoping to score a small pile of loot so that he could do something else with the rest of his life besides hang out in a pool hall. He probably hadn't even thought much about Mars before he spotted a ConSpace recruitment ad on some web site; he had two years of college, though, and met all the fitness requirements, and that was enough to get him into the training program and, eventually, a berth aboard a cycleship.

Before Jeff left Earth, he filled out and signed all the usual company paperwork. Among them was Form 36-B: Family Emergency Notification Consent. ConSpace required everyone to state whether or not they wanted to be informed of a major illness or death of a family member back home. This was something a lot of people didn't take into consideration before they went to Mars, but nonetheless it was an issue that had to be addressed. If you found out, for instance, that your father was about to die, there wasn't much you could do about it, because you'd be at least 35 million miles from home. The best you could do would be to send a brief message that someone might be able to read to him before he passed away; you wouldn't be able to attend the funeral, and it would be many months, even a year or two, before you could lay roses on his grave.

Most people signed Form 36-B on the grounds that they'd rather know about something like this than be kept in the dark until they returned home. Jeff did, too, but I'd later learned that he hadn't read it first. For him, it had been just one more piece of paper that needed to be signed before he boarded the shuttle, not to be taken any more seriously than the catastrophic accident disclaimer or the form attesting that he didn't have any sort of venereal disease.

He probably wished he hadn't signed that damn form. But he did, and it cost him his sanity.

Jeff had been on Mars for only about seven months when a message was relayed from ConSpace's human resources office. I knew about it because a copy was cc'd to me. The minute I read it, I dropped what I was doing to head straight for Hab 2's second level, which was where the monkey house—that is, the dormitory for unspecialized laborers like Jeff—was located. I didn't have to ask which bunk was his; the moment I walked in, I spotted a knot of people standing around a young guy slumped on this bunk, staring in disbelief at the fax in his hands.

Until then, I didn't know, nor did anyone at Arsia Station, that Jeff had a fiancé back home, a nice girl named Karen whom he'd met in high school and who had agreed to marry him about the same time he'd sent his application to ConSpace. Once he got the job, they decided to postpone the wedding until he returned, even if it meant having to put their plans on hold for three years. One of the reasons why Jeff decided to get a job on Mars, in fact, was to provide a nest egg for him and Karen. And they'd need it, too; about three weeks before Jeff took off, Karen informed him that she was pregnant and that he'd have a child waiting for him when he got home.

He'd kept this a secret, mainly because he knew that the company would annul his contract if it learned that he had a baby on the way. Both Jeff's family and Karen's knew all about the baby, though, and they decided to pretend that Jeff was still on Earth, just away on a long business trip. Until he returned, they'd take care of Karen.

About three months before the baby was due, the two families decided to host a baby shower. The party was to be held at the home of one of Jeff's uncles—apparently he was the only relative with a house big enough for such a get-together—and Karen was on her way there, in a car driven by Jeff's parents, when tragedy struck. Some habitual drunk who'd learned how to disable his car's high-alcohol lockout, and therefore was on the road when he shouldn't have been, plowed straight into them. The drunk walked away with no more than a sprained neck, but his victims were nowhere nearly so lucky. Karen, her unborn child, Jeff's mother and father—all died before they reached the hospital.

There's not a lot you can say to someone who's just lost his family that's going to mean very much. *I'm sorry* barely scratches the surface. *I understand what you're going through* is ridiculous; *I know how you feel* is insulting. And *is there anything I can do to help?* is pointless unless you have a time machine; if I did, I would have lent it to Jeff, so that he could travel back twenty-four hours to call his folks and beg them to put off picking up Karen by only fifteen or twenty minutes. But everyone said these things anyway, because there wasn't much else that *could* be said, and I relieved Jeff of further duties until he felt like he was ready to go to work again, because there was little else I could do for him. The next cycle-ship wasn't due to reach Mars for another seventeen months; by the time he got home, his parents and Karen would be dead for nearly two years.

To Jeff's credit, he was back on the job within a few days. Maybe he knew that there was nothing he could do except work, or maybe he just got tired of staring at the walls. In any case, one morning he put on his suit, cycled through the airlock, and went outside to help the rest of the monkeys dig a pit for the new septic tank. But he wasn't the same easy-going kid we'd known before; no wisecracks, no goofing off, not even any gripes about the hours it took to make that damn hole and how he'd better get overtime for this. He was like a robot out there, silently digging at the sandy red ground with a shovel, until the pit was finally finished, at which point he dropped his tools and, without a word, returned to the hab, where he climbed out of his suit and went to the mess hall for some chow.

A couple of weeks went by, and there was no change. Jeff said little to anyone. He ate, worked, slept, and that was about it. When you looked into his eyes, all you saw was a distant stare. If he'd broken down in hysterics, I would've understood, but there wasn't any of that. It was as if he'd shut down his emotions, suppressing whatever he was feeling inside.

The station had a pretty good hospital by then, large enough to serve all the colonies, and Arsia General's senior psychologist had begun meeting with Jeff on a regular basis. Three days after Jeff went back to work, Karl Rosenfeld dropped by my office. His report was grim; Jeff Halbert was suffering from severe depression, to the point that he was barely responding to medication. Although he hadn't spoken of suicide, Dr. Rosenfeld had little doubt that the notion had occurred to him. And I knew that, if Jeff did decide to kill himself, all he'd have to do was wait until the next time he went outside, then shut down his suit's air supply and crack open the helmet faceplate. One deep breath, and the Martian atmosphere would do the rest; he'd be dead before anyone could reach him.

"You want my advice?" Karl asked, sitting on the other side of my desk with a glass of moonshine in hand. "Find something that'll get his mind off what happened."

"You think that hasn't occurred to me? Believe me, I've tried . . ."

"Yeah, I know. He told me. But extra work shifts aren't helping, and neither are vids or games." He was quiet for a moment, "If I thought sex would help," he added, "I'd ask a girl I know to haul him off to bed, but that would just make matters worse. His fiancé was the only woman he ever loved, and it'll probably be a long time before he sleeps with anyone again."

"So what do you want me to do?" I gave a helpless shrug. "C'mon, give me a clue here. I want to help the kid, but I'm out of ideas."

"Well . . . I looked at the duty roster, and saw that you've scheduled a survey mission for next week. Something up north, I believe."

"Uh-huh. I'm sending a team up there to see if they can locate a new water supply. Oh, and one of the engineers wants to make a side-trip to look at an old NASA probe."

"So put Jeff on the mission." Karl smiled. "They're going to need a monkey or two anyway. Maybe travel will do him some good."

His suggestion was as good as any, so I pulled up the survey assignment list, deleted the name of one monkey, and inserted Jeff Halbert's instead. I figured it couldn't hurt, and I was right. And also wrong.

So Jeff was put on a two-week sortie that travelled above the 60th parallel to the Vastitas Borealis, the subarctic region that surrounds the Martian north pole. The purpose of the mission was to locate a site for a new well. Although most of Arsia Station's water came from atmospheric condensers and our greenhouses, we needed more than they could supply, which was why we drilled artesian wells in the permafrost beneath the northern tundra and pump groundwater to surface tanks, which in turn would be picked up on a monthly basis. Every few years or so, one of those wells would run dry; when that happened, we'd have to send a team up there to dig a new one.

Two airships made the trip, the *Sagan* and the *Collins*. Jeff Halbert was aboard the *Collins*, and according to its captain, who was also the mission leader, he did his job well. Over the course of ten days, the two dirigibles roamed the tundra, stopping every ten or fifteen miles so that crews could get out and conduct test drills that would bring up a sample of what lay beneath the rocky red soil. It wasn't hard work, really, and it gave Jeff a chance to see the northern regions. Yet he was quiet most of the time, rarely saying much to anyone; in fact, he seemed to be bored by the whole thing. The other people on the expedition were aware of what had recently happened to him, of course, and they attempted to draw him out of his shell, but after awhile it became obvious that he just didn't want to talk, and so they finally gave up and left him alone.

Then, on the eleventh day of the mission, two days before the expedition was scheduled to return to Arsia, the *Collins* located the Phoenix lander.

This was a NASA probe that landed back in '08, the first to confirm the presence of subsurface ice on Mars. Unlike many of the other American and European probes that explored Mars before the first manned expeditions, Phoenix didn't have a rover; instead, it used a robotic arm to dig down into the regolith, scooping up samples that were analyzed by its onboard chemical lab. The probe was active for only a few months before its battery died during the long Martian winter, but it was one of the milestones leading to human colonization.

As they expected, the expedition members found Phoenix half-buried beneath windblown sand and dust, with only its upper platform and solar vanes still exposed. Nonetheless, the lander was intact, and although it was too big and heavy to be loaded aboard the airship, the crew removed its arm to be taken home and added to the base museum. And they found one more thing; the Mars library.

During the 1990s, while the various Mars missions were still in their planning stages, the Planetary Society had made a proposal to NASA: one of those probes should carry a DVD containing a cache of literature, visual images, and audio recordings pertaining to Mars. The ostensive purpose would be to furnish future colonists with a library for their entertainment, but the unspoken reason was to pay tribute to the generations of writers, artists, and filmmakers whose works had inspired the real-life exploration of Mars.

NASA went along with this proposal, so a custom-designed DVD, made of silica glass to ensure its long-term survival, was prepared for inclusion on a future mission. A panel selected 84 novels, short stories, articles, and speeches, with the authors ranging from 18th century fantasists like Swift and Voltaire to 20th century science fiction authors like Niven and Benford. A digital gallery of 60 visual images—including everything from paintings by Bonestell, Emshwiller, and Whelan to a lobby card from a Flash Gordon serial and a cover of a *Weird Science* comic book—was chosen as well. The final touch were four audio clips, the most notable of which were the infamous 1938 radio broadcast of *The War of the Worlds* and a discussion of the same between H.G. Wells and Orson Welles.

Now called "Visions of Mars," the disk was originally placed aboard NASA's Mars Polar Lander, but that probe was destroyed when its booster failed shortly after launch and it crashed in the Atlantic. So an identical copy was put on Phoenix, and this time it succeeded in getting to Mars. And so the disk had remained in the Vastitas Borealis for the past forty years, awaiting the day when a human hand would remove it from its place on Phoenix's upper fuselage.

And that hand happened to be Jeff Halbert's.

The funny thing is, no one on the expedition knew the disk was there. It had been forgotten by then, its existence buried deep within the old NASA documents I'd been sent from Earth, so I hadn't told anyone to retrieve it. And besides, most of the guys on the *Collins* were more interested in taking a look at an antique lander than the DVD that happened to be attached to it. So when Jeff found the disk and detached it from Phoenix, it wasn't like he'd made a major find. The attitude of almost everyone on the mission was *oh, yeah, that's kind of neat . . . take it home and see what's on it.*

Which was easier said than done. DVD drives had been obsolete for more than twenty years, and the nearest flea market where one might find an old computer that had one was . . . well, it wasn't on Mars. But Jeff looked around, and eventually he found a couple of dead comps stashed in a storage closet, salvage left over from the first expeditions. Neither were usable on their own, but with the aid of a service manual, he was able to swap out enough parts to get one of them up and running, and once it was operational, he removed the disk from its scratched case and gently slid it into the slot. Once he was sure that the data was intact and hadn't decayed, he downloaded everything into his personal pad. And then, at random, he selected one of the items on the menu—"The Martian Way" by Isaac Asimov—and began to read.

Why did Jeff go to so much trouble? Perhaps he wanted something to do with his free time besides mourn for the dead. Or maybe he wanted to show the others who'd been on the expedition that they shouldn't have ignored the disk. I don't know for sure, so I can't tell you. All I know is that the disk first interested him, then intrigued him, and finally obsessed him.

It took awhile for me to become aware of the change in Jeff. As much as I was concerned for him, he was one of my lesser problems. As general manager, on any given day I had a dozen or more different matters that needed my attention, whether it be making sure that the air recycling system was repaired before we suffocated to death or filling out another stack of forms sent from Huntsville. So Jeff wasn't always on my mind; when I didn't hear from Dr. Rosenfeld for awhile, I figured that the two of them had managed to work out his issues, and turned to other things.

Still, there were warning signs, stuff that I noticed but to which I didn't pay much attention. Like the day I was monitoring the radio crosstalk from the monkeys laying sewage pipes in the foundation of Hab Three, and happened to hear Jeff identify himself as Lieutenant Gulliver Jones. The monkeys sometimes screwed around like that on the com channels, and the foreman told Halbert to knock it off and use his proper call sign . . . but when Jeff answered him, his response was weird: *"Aye, sir. I was simply ruminating on the rather peculiar environment in which we've found ourselves."* He even faked a British accent to match the Victorian diction. That got a laugh from the other monkeys, but nonetheless I wondered who Gulliver Jones was and why Jeff was pretending to be him.

There was also the time Jeff was out on a dozer, clearing away the sand that had been deposited on the landing field during a dust storm a couple of days earlier. Another routine job to which I hadn't been paying much attention until the shift supervisor at the command center paged me: *"Chief, there's something going on with Halbert. You might want to listen in."*

So I tapped into the comlink, and there was Jeff: *"Affirmative, MainCom. I just saw something move out there, about a half-klick north of the periphery."*

"Roger that, Tiger Four-Oh," the supervisor said. *"Can you describe again, please?"*

A pause, then: *"A big creature, abut ten feet tall, with eight legs. And there was a woman riding it . . . red-skinned, and—"* an abrupt laugh *"—stark naked, or just about."*

Something tugged at my memory, but I couldn't quite put my finger on it. When the shift supervisor spoke again, his voice had a patronizing undertone. *"Yeah . . . uh, right, Tiger Four-Oh. We just checked the LRC, though, and there's nothing on the scope except you."*

"They're gone now. Went behind a boulder and vanished." Another laugh, almost gleeful. *"But they were out there, I promise!"*

"Affirmative, Four-Oh." A brief pause. *"If you happen to see any more thoats, let us know, okay?"*

That's when I remembered. What Jeff had described was a beast from Edgar Rice Burroughs' Mars novels. And the woman riding it? That could have only been Dejah Thoris. Almost everyone who came to Mars read Burroughs at one point or another, but this was the first time I'd ever heard of anyone claiming to have seen the Princess of Helium.

Obviously, Jeff had taken to playing practical jokes. I made a mental note to say something to him about that, but then forgot about it. As I said, on any given day I handled any number of different crises, and someone messing with his supervisor's head ranked low on my priority list.

But that wasn't the end of it. In fact, it was only the beginning. A couple of weeks later, I received a memo from the quartermaster: someone had tendered a request to be transferred to private quarters, even though that was above his paygrade. At Arsia in those days, before we got all the habs built, individual rooms were at a premium and were generally reserved for management, senior researchers, married couples, company stooges, and so forth. In this case, though, the other guys in this particular person's dorm had signed a petition backing his request, and the quartermaster himself wrote that, for the sake of morale, he was recommending that this individual be assigned his own room.

I wasn't surprised to see that Jeff Halbert was the person making the request. By then, I'd noticed that his personality had undergone a distinct change. He'd let his hair grow long, eschewing the high-and-tight style preferred by people who spent a lot of time wearing a hardsuit helmet. He rarely shared a table with anyone else in the wardroom, and instead ate by himself, staring at his datapad the entire time. And he was now talking to himself on the comlink. No more reports of Martian princesses riding eight-legged animals, but rather a snatch of this ("The Martians seem to have calculated their descent with amazing subtlety . . .") or a bit of that ("The Martians gazed back up at them for a long, long silent time from the rippling water . . .") which most people wouldn't have recognized as being quotes from Wells or Bradbury.

So it was no wonder the other monkey house residents wanted to get rid of him. Before I signed the request, though, I paid Dr. Rosenfeld a visit. The station psychologist didn't have to ask why I was there; he asked me to shut the door, then let me know what he thought about Jeff.

"To tell the truth," he began, "I can't tell if he's getting better or worse."

"I can. Look, I'm no shrink, but if you ask me, he's getting worse."

Karl shook his head. "Not necessarily. Sure, his behavior is bizarre, but at least we no longer have to worry about suicide. In fact, he's one of the happiest people we have here. He rarely speaks about his loss anymore, and when I remind him that his wife and parents are dead, he shrugs it off as if this was something that happened a long time ago. In his own way, he's quite content with life."

"And you don't think that's strange?"

"Sure, I do . . . especially since he's admitted to me that he'd stopped taking the antidepressants I prescribed to him. And that's the bad news. Perhaps he isn't depressed anymore, or at least by clinical standards . . . but he's becoming delusional, to the point of actually having hallucinations."

I stared at him. "You mean, the time he claimed he spotted Dejah Thoris . . . you're saying he actually *saw* that?"

"Yes, I believe so. And that gave me a clue as to what's going on in his mind." Karl picked up a penknife, absently played with it. "Ever since he found that disk, he's become utterly obsessed with it. So I asked him if he'd let me copy it from his pad, which he did, and after I asked him what he was reading, I checked it out for myself. And what I discovered was that, of all the novels and stories that are on the disk, the ones that attract him the most are also the ones that are least representative of reality. That is, the stuff that's about Mars, but not as we know it."

"Come again?" I shook my head. "I don't understand."

"How much science fiction have you read?"

"A little. Not much."

"Well, lucky for you, I've read quite a bit." He grinned. "In fact, you could say that's why I'm here. I got hooked on that stuff when I was a kid, and by the time I got out of college, I'd pretty much decided that I wanted to see Mars." He became serious again. "Okay, try to follow me. Although people have been writing about Mars since the 1700s, it wasn't until the first Russian and American probes got out here in the 1960s that anyone knew what this place is really like. That absence of knowledge gave writers and artists the liberty to fill in the gap with their imaginations . . . or at least until they learned better. Understand?"

"Sure." I shrugged. "Before the 1960s, you could have Martians. After that, you couldn't have Martians anymore."

"Umm . . . well, not exactly." Karl lifted his hand, teetered it back and forth. "One of the best stories on the disk is 'A Rose For Ecclesiastes' by Roger Zelazny. It was written in 1963, and it has Martians in it. And some stories written before then were pretty close to getting it right. But for the most part, yes . . . the fictional view of Mars changed dramatically in the second half of the last century, and although it became more realistic, it also lost much of its romanticism."

Karl folded the penknife, dropped it on his desk. "Those aren't the stories Jeff's reading. Greg Bear's 'A Martian Ricorso,' Arthur C. Clarke's 'Transit of Earth,' John Varley's 'In the Hall of the Martian Kings' . . . anything similar to the Mars we know, he ignores. Why? Because they remind him of where he is . . . and that's not where he wants to be."

"So . . ." I thought about it for a moment. "He's reading the older stuff instead?"

"Right." Karl nodded. "Stanley Weinbaum's 'A Martian Odyssey,' Otis Albert Kline's 'The Swordsman of Mars,' A. E. van Vogt's 'The Enchanted Village' . . . the more unreal, the more he likes them. Because those stories aren't about the drab, lifeless planet where he's stuck, but instead a planet of native Martians, lost cities, canal systems . . ."

"Okay, I get it."

"No, I don't think you do . . . because I'm not sure I do, either, except to say that Jeff appears to be leaving us. Every day, he's taking one more step into this other world . . . and I don't think he's coming back again."

I stared at him, not quite believing what I'd just heard. "Jeez, Karl . . . what am I going to do?"

"What *can* you do?" He leaned back in his chair. "Not much, really. Look, I'll be straight with you . . . this is beyond me. He needs the kind of treatment that I can't give him here. For that, he's going to have to wait until he gets back to Earth."

"The next ship isn't due for another fourteen months or so."

"I know . . . that's when I'm scheduled to go back, too. But the good news is that he's happy and reasonably content, and doesn't really pose a threat to anyone . . . except maybe by accident, in which case I'd recommend that you relieve him of any duties that would take him outside the hab."

"Done." The last thing anyone needed was to have a delusional person out on the surface. Mars can be pretty unforgiving when it comes to human error, and a fatal mistake can cost you not only your own life, but also the guy next to you. "And I take it that you recommend that his request be granted, too?"

"It wouldn't hurt, no." A wry smile. "So long as he's off in his own world, he'll be happy. Make him comfortable, give him whatever he wants . . . within reason, at least . . . and leave him alone. I'll keep an eye on him and will let you know if his condition changes, for better or worse."

"Hopefully for the better."

"Sure . . . but I wouldn't count on it." Karl stared straight at me. "Face it, chief . . . one of your guys is turning into a Martian."

I took Jeff off the outside-work details and let it be known that he wasn't permitted to go marswalking without authorization or an escort, and instead reassigned him to jobs that would keep him in the habitats: working in the greenhouse, finishing the interior of Hab 2, that sort of thing. I was prepared to tell him that he was being taken off the outside details because he'd reached his rem limit for radiation exposure, but he never questioned my decision but only accepted it with the same quiet, spooky smile that he'd come to giving everyone.

I also let him relocate to private quarters, a small room on Hab 2's second level that had been unoccupied until then. As I expected, there were a few gripes from those still having to share a room with someone else; however, most people realized that Jeff was in bad shape and needed his privacy. After he moved in, though, he did something I didn't anticipate: he changed his door lock's password to something no one else knew. This was against station rules—the security office and the general manager were supposed to always have everyone's lock codes—but Karl assured me that Jeff meant no harm. He simply didn't want to have anyone enter his quarters, and it would help his peace of mind if he received this one small exemption. I went along with it, albeit reluctantly.

After that, I had no problems with Jeff for awhile. He assumed his new duties without complaint, and the reports I received from department heads told me that he was doing his work well. Karl updated me every week; his patient hadn't yet shown any indications of snapping out of his fugue, but neither did he appear to be getting worse. And although he was no longer interacting with any other personnel except when he needed to, at least he was no longer telling anyone about Martian princesses or randomly quoting obscure science fiction stories over the comlink.

Nonetheless, there was the occasional incident. Such as when the supply chief came to me with an unusual request Jeff had made: several reams of hemp paper, and as much soy ink as could be spared. Since both were by-products of greenhouse crops grown at either Arsia Station or one of the other colonies, and thus not imported from Earth, they weren't particularly scarce. Still, what could

Jeff possibly want with that much writing material? I asked Karl if Jeff had told him that he was keeping a journal; the doctor told me that he hadn't, but unless either paper or ink were in short supply, it couldn't hurt to grant that request. So I signed off on this as well, although I told the supply chief to subtract the cost from Jeff's salary.

Not long after that, I heard from one of the communications officers. Jeff had asked her to send a general memo to the other colonies: a request for downloads of any Mars novels or stories that their personnel might have. The works of Bradbury, Burroughs, and Brackett were particularly desired, although stuff by Moorcock, Williamson, and Sturgeon would also be appreciated. In exchange, Jeff would send stories and novels he'd downloaded from the Phoenix disk.

Nothing wrong there, either. By then, Mars was on the opposite side of the Sun from Earth, so Jeff couldn't make the same request from Huntsville. If he was running out of reading material, then it made sense that he'd have to go begging from the other colonies. In fact, the com officer told me she'd had already received more than a half-dozen downloads; apparently quite a few folks had Mars fiction stashed in the comps. Nonetheless, it was unusual enough that she thought I should know about it. I asked her to keep me posted, and shrugged it off as just another of a long series of eccentricities.

A few weeks after that, though, Jeff finally did something that rubbed me the wrong way. As usual, I heard about it from Dr. Rosenfeld.

"Jeff has a new request," he said when I happened to drop by his office. "In the future, he would prefer to be addressed as 'Your Majesty' or 'Your Highness,' in keeping with his position as the Emperor of Mars."

I stared at him for several seconds. "Surely you're joking," I said at last.

"Surely I'm not. He is now the Emperor Jeffery the First, sovereign monarch of the Great Martian Empire, warlord and protector of the red planet." A pause, during which I expected Karl to grin and wink. He didn't. "He doesn't necessarily want anyone bow in his presence," he added, "but he does require proper respect for the crown."

"I see." I closed my eyes, rubbed the bridge of my nose between my thumb and forefinger, and counted to ten. "And what does that make me?"

"Prime Minister, of course." The driest of smiles. "Since his title is hereditary, His Majesty isn't interested in the day-to-day affairs of his empire. That he leaves up to you, with the promise that he'll refrain from meddling with your decisions . . ."

"Oh, how fortunate I am."

"Yes. But from here on, all matters pertaining to the throne should be taken up with me, in my position as Royal Physician and Senior Court Advisor."

"Uh-huh." I stood up from my chair. "Well, if you'll excuse me, I think the Prime Minister needs to go now and kick His Majesty's ass."

"Sit down." Karl glared at me. "Really, I mean it. Sit."

I was unwilling to sit down again, but neither did I storm out of his office. "Look, I know he's a sick man, but this has gone far enough. I've given him his own room, relieved him of hard labor, given him paper and ink . . . for what, I still don't know, but he keeps asking for more . . . and allowed him com access to the other colonies. Just because he's been treated like a king doesn't mean he *is* a king."

"Oh, I agree. Which is why I've reminded him that his title is honorary as well as hereditary, and as such there's a limit to royal privilege. And he understands this. After all, the empire is in decline, having reached its peak over a thousand years ago, and since then the emperor has had to accept certain sacrifices for the good of the people. So, no, you won't see him wearing a crown and carrying a scepter, nor will he be demanding that a throne be built for him. He wants his reign to be benign."

Hearing this, I reluctantly took my seat again. "All right, so let me get this straight. He believes that he's now a king . . ."

"An emperor. There's a difference."

"King, emperor, whatever . . . he's not going to be bossing anyone around, but will pretty much let things continue as they are. Right?"

"Except that he wants to be addressed formally, yeah, that's pretty much it." Karl sighed, shook his head. "Let me try to explain. Jeff has come face-to-face with a reality that he cannot bear. His parents, his fiancé, the child they wanted to have . . . they're all dead, and he was too far away to prevent it, or even go to their funerals. This is a very harsh reality that he needs to keep at bay, so he's built a wall around himself . . . a wall of delusion, if you will. At first, it took the form of an obsession with fantasy, but when that wouldn't alone suffice, he decided to enter that fantasy, become part of it. This is where Emperor Jeffery the First of the Great Martian Empire comes in."

"So he's protecting himself?"

"Yes . . . by creating a role that lets him believe that he controls his own life." Karl shook his head. "He doesn't want to actually run Arsia, chief. He just wants to pretend that he does. As long as you allow him this, he'll be all right. Trust me."

"Well . . . all right." Not that I had much choice in the matter. If I was going to have a crazy person in my colony, at least I could make sure that he wouldn't endanger anyone. If that meant indulging him until he could be sent back to Earth, then that was what I'd have to do. "I'll pass the word that His Majesty is to be treated with all due respect."

"That would be great. Thanks." Karl smiled. "Y'know, people have been pretty supportive. I haven't heard of anyone taunting him."

"You know how it is. People here tend to look out for each other . . . they have to." I stood up and started to head for the door, then another thought occurred to me. "Just one thing. Has he ever told you what he's doing in his room? Like I said, he's been using a lot of paper and ink."

"Yes, I've noticed the ink stains on his fingers." Karl shook his head. "No, I don't. I've asked him about that, and the only thing he's told me is that he's preparing a gift for his people, and that he'll allow us to see it when the time comes."

"A gift?" I raised an eyebrow. "Any idea what it is?"

"Not a clue . . . but I'm sure we'll find out."

I kept my promise to Dr. Rosenfeld and put out the word that Jeff Halbert was heretofore to be known as His Majesty, the Emperor. As I told Karl, people were generally accepting of this. Oh, I heard the occasional report of someone giving Jeff some crap about this—exaggerated bows in the corridors, ill-considered questions about who was going to be his queen, and so forth—but the jokers who did this were usually pulled aside and told to shut up. Everyone at Arsia knew that Jeff was mentally ill, and that the best anyone could do for him was to let him have his fantasy life for as long as he was with us.

By then, Earth was no longer on the other side of the Sun. Once our home world and Mars began moving toward conjunction, a cycleship could make the trip home. So only a few months remained until Jeff would board a shuttle. Since Karl would be returning as well, I figured he'd be in good hands, or at least they climbed into zombie tanks to hibernate for the long ride to Earth. Until then, all we had to do was keep His Majesty happy.

That wasn't hard to do. In fact, Karl and I had a lot of help. Once people got used to the idea that a make-believe emperor lived among them, most of them actually seemed to enjoy the pretense. When he walked through the habs, folks would pause whatever they were doing to nod to him and say "Your Majesty" or "Your Highness." He was always allowed to go to the front of the serving line in the mess hall, and there was always someone ready to hold his chair for him. And I noticed that he even picked up a couple of consorts, two unattached young women who did everything from trim his hair—it had grown very long by then, with a regal beard to match—to assist him in the Royal Gardens (aka the green-house) to accompany him to the Saturday night flicks. As one of the girls told me, the Emperor was the perfect date: always the gentleman, he'd unfailingly treated them with respect and never tried to take advantage of them. Which was more than could be said for some of the single men at Arsia.

After awhile, I relaxed the rule about not letting him leave the habs, and allowed him to go outside as long as he was under escort at all times. Jeff remembered how to put on a hardsuit,—a sign that he hadn't completely lost touch with reality—and he never gave any indication that he was on the verge of opening his helmet. But once he walked a few dozen yards from the airlock, he'd often stop and stare into the distance for a very long time, keeping his back to the rest of the base and saying nothing to anyone.

I wondered what he was seeing then. Was it a dry red desert, cold and lifeless, with rocks and boulders strewn across an arid plain beneath a pink sky? Or did he see something no one else could: forests of giant lichen, ancient canals upon which sailing vessels slowly glided, cities as old as time from which John Carter and Tars Tarkas rode to their next adventure or where tyrants called for the head of the outlaw Eric John Stark. Or was he thinking of something else entirely? A mother and a father who'd raised him, a woman he'd once loved, a child whom he'd never see?

I don't know, for the Emperor seldom spoke to me, even in my role as his Prime Minister. I think I was someone he wanted to avoid, an authority figure who had the power to shatter his illusions. Indeed, in all the time that Jeff was with us, I don't think he and I said more than a few words to each other. In fact, it wasn't until the day that he finally left for Earth that he said anything of consequence to me.

That morning, I drove him and Dr. Rosenfeld out to the landing field, where a shuttle was waiting to transport them up to the cycleship. Jeff was unusually quiet; I couldn't easily see his expression through his helmet faceplate, but the few glimpses I had told me that he wasn't happy. His Majesty knew that he was leaving his empire. Karl hadn't softened the blow by telling him a convenient lie, but instead had given him the truth: they were returning to Earth, and he'd probably never see Mars again.

Their belongings had already been loaded aboard the shuttle when we arrived, and the handful of other passengers were waiting to climb aboard. I parked the rover at the edge of the landing field and escorted Jeff and Karl to the spacecraft. I shook hands with Karl and wished him well, then turned to Jeff.

"Your Majesty . . ." I began.

"You don't have to call me that," he said.

"Pardon me?"

Jeff stepped closer to me. "I know I'm not really an emperor. That was something I got over a while ago . . . I just didn't want to tell anyone."

I glanced at Karl. His eyes were wide, and within his helmet he shook his head. This was news to him, too. "Then . . . you know who you really are?"

A brief flicker of a smile. "I'm Jeff Halbert. There's something wrong with me, and I don't really know what it is . . . but I know that I'm Jeff Halbert and that I'm going home." He hesitated, then went on. "I know we haven't talked much, but I . . . well, Dr. Rosenfeld has told me what you've done for me, and I just wanted to thank you. For putting up with me all this time, and for letting me be the Emperor of Mars. I hope I haven't been too much trouble."

I slowly let out my breath. My first thought was that he'd been playing me and everyone else for fools, but then I realized that his megalomania had probably been real, at least for a time. In any case, it didn't matter now; he was on his way back to Earth, the first steps on the long road to recovery.

Indeed, many months later, I received a letter from Karl. Shortly after he returned to Earth, Jeff was admitted to a private clinic in southern Vermont, where he began a program of psychiatric treatment. The process had been painful; as Karl had deduced, Jeff's mind had repressed the knowledge of his family's deaths, papering over the memory with fantastical delusions he'd derived from the stories he'd been reading. The clinic psychologists agreed with Dr. Rosenfeld: it was probably the retreat into fantasy that saved Jeff's life, by providing him with a place to which he was able to escape when his mind was no longer able to cope with a tragic reality. And in the end, when he no longer needed that illusion, Jeff returned from madness. He'd never see a Martian princess again, or believe himself to be the ruling monarch of the red planet.

But that was yet to come. I bit my tongue and offered him my hand. "No trouble, Jeff. I just hope everything works out for you."

"Thanks." Jeff shook my hand, then turned away to follow Karl to the ladder. Then he stopped and looked back at me again. "One more thing . . ."

"Yes?"

"There's something in my room I think you'd like to see. I disabled the lock just before I left, so you won't need the password to get in there." A brief pause. "It was 'Thuvia', just in case you need it anyway."

"Thank you." I peered at him. "So . . . what is it?"

"Call it a gift from the emperor," he said.

I walked back to the rover and waited until the shuttle lifted off, then I drove to Hab 2. When I reached Jeff's room, though, I discovered that I wasn't the first person to arrive. Several of his friends—his fellow monkeys, the emperor's consorts, a couple of others—had already opened the door and gone in. I heard their astonished murmurs as I walked down the hall, but it wasn't until I pushed entered the room that I saw what amazed them.

Jeff's quarters were small, but he'd done a lot with it over the last year and a half. The wall above his bed was covered with sheets of paper that he'd taped together, upon which he'd drawn an elaborate mural. Here was the Mars over which the Emperor had reigned: boat-like aircraft hovering above great domed cities, monstrous creatures prowling red wastelands, bare-chested heroes defending beautiful women with rapiers and radium pistols, all beneath twin moons that looked nothing like the Phobos and Deimos we knew. The mural was crude, yet it had been rendered with painstaking care, and was nothing like anything we'd ever seen before.

That wasn't all. On the desk next to the comp was the original Phoenix disk, yet Jeff hadn't been satisfied just to leave it behind. A wire-frame bookcase had been built beside the desk, and neatly stacked upon its shelves were dozens of sheaves of paper, some thick and some thin, each carefully bound with hemp twine. Books, handwritten and handmade.

I carefully pulled down one at random, gazed at its title page: EDISON'S CONQUEST OF MARS by Garrett P. Serviss. I put it back on the shelf, picked up another: OMNILINGUAL by H. Beam Piper. I placed it on the shelf, then pulled down yet another: THE MARTIAN CROWN JEWELS, by Poul Anderson. And more, dozens more . . .

This was what Jeff had been doing all this time: transcribing the contents of the Phoenix disk, word by word. Because he knew, in spite of his madness, that he couldn't stay on Mars forever, and he wanted to leave something behind. A library, so that others could enjoy the same stories that had helped him through a dark and troubled time.

The library is still here. In fact, we've improved it quite a bit. I had the bed and dresser removed, and replaced them with armchairs and reading lamps. The mural has been preserved within glass frames, and the books have been rebound inside plastic covers. The Phoenix disk is gone, but its contents have been downloaded into a couple of comps; the disk itself is in the base museum. And we've added a lot of books to the shelves; every time a cycleship arrives from Earth, it brings more a few more volumes for our collection. It's become one of the favorite places in Arsia for people to relax. There's almost always someone there, sitting in a chair with a novel or story in his or her lap.

The sign on the door reads Imperial Martian Library: an inside joke that newcomers and tourists don't get. And, yes, I've spent a lot of time there myself. It's never too late to catch up on the classics.

the things

PETER WATTS

Self-described as "a reformed marine biologist," Peter Watts is quickly establishing himself as one of the most respected hard science writers of the twenty-first century. His short work has appeared in *Tesseracts*, *The Solaris Book of Science Fiction*, *On Spec*, *Divine Realms*, *Prairie Fire*, and elsewhere. He is the author of the well-received Rifters sequence, including the novels *Starfish*, *Maelstrom*, *Behemoth: B-Max*, and *Behemoth: Seppuku*. His short work has been collected in *Ten Monkeys, Ten Minutes*, and his novelette "The Island" won the Hugo Award in 2010. His most recent book is the novel *Blindsight*, which has been widely hailed as one of the best hard SF books of the decade. Coming up are two new novels, *Sunflowers* and *State of Grace*, a "sidequel" to *Blindsight*. He lives in Toronto, Canada.

John W. Campbell's classic "Who Goes There?" relates the story of a group of humans in an isolated winter encampment in Antarctica who must struggle for survival against a strange creature from the stars. The story has twice been filmed, as *The Thing from Another World* and *The Thing*, but if you want to know what the story looks like from the perspective of the alien "monster" itself, you must read the suspenseful story that follows.

I am being Blair. I escape out the back as the world comes in through the front.

I am being Copper. I am rising from the dead.

I am being Childs. I am guarding the main entrance.

The names don't matter. They are placeholders, nothing more; all biomass is interchangeable. What matters is that these are all that is left of me. The world has burned everything else.

I see myself through the window, loping through the storm, wearing Blair. MacReady has told me to burn Blair if he comes back alone, but MacReady still thinks I am one of him. I am not: I am being Blair, and I am at the door. I am being Childs, and I let myself in. I take brief communion, tendrils writhing forth from my faces, intertwining: I am BlairChilds, exchanging news of the world.

The world has found me out. It has discovered my burrow beneath the tool shed, the half-finished lifeboat cannibalized from the viscera of dead helicopters. The world is busy destroying my means of escape. Then it will come back for me.

There is only one option left. I disintegrate. Being Blair, I go to share the plan with Copper and to feed on the rotting biomass once called *Clarke*; so many changes in so short a time have dangerously depleted my reserves. Being Childs, I have already consumed what was left of Fuchs and am replenished for the next phase. I sling the flamethrower onto my back and head outside, into the long Antarctic night.

I will go into the storm, and never come back.

I was so much more, before the crash. I was an explorer, an ambassador, a missionary. I spread across the cosmos, met countless worlds, took communion: the fit reshaped the unfit and the whole universe bootstrapped upwards in joyful, infinitesimal increments. I was a soldier, at war with entropy itself. I was the very hand by which Creation perfects itself.

So much wisdom I had. So much experience. Now I cannot remember all the things I knew. I can only remember that I once knew them.

I remember the crash, though. It killed most of this offshoot outright, but a little crawled from the wreckage: a few trillion cells, a soul too weak to keep them in check. Mutinous biomass sloughed off despite my most desperate attempts to hold myself together: panic-stricken little clots of meat, instinctively growing whatever limbs they could remember and fleeing across the burning ice. By the time I'd regained control of what was left the fires had died and the cold was closing back in. I barely managed to grow enough antifreeze to keep my cells from bursting before the ice took me.

I remember my reawakening, too: dull stirrings of sensation in real time, the first embers of cognition, the slow blooming warmth of awareness as my cells thawed, as body and soul embraced after their long sleep. I remember the biped offshoots that surrounded me, the strange chittering sounds they made, the odd *uniformity* of their body plans. How ill-adapted they looked! How *inefficient* their morphology! Even disabled, I could see so many things to fix. So I reached out. I took communion. I tasted the flesh of the world—

—and the world attacked me. It *attacked* me.

I left that place in ruins. It was on the other side of the mountains—the *Norwegian camp*, it is called here—and I could never have crossed that distance in a biped skin. Fortunately there was another shape to choose from, smaller than the biped but better adapted to the local climate. I hid within it while the rest of me fought off the attack. I fled into the night on four legs, and let the rising flames cover my escape.

I did not stop running until I arrived here. I walked among these new offshoots wearing the skin of a quadruped; and because they had not seen me take any other shape, they did not attack.

And when I assimilated them in turn—when my biomass changed and flowed into shapes unfamiliar to local eyes—I took that communion in solitude, having learned that the world does not like what it doesn't know.

I am alone in the storm. I am a bottom-dweller on the floor of some murky alien sea. The snow blows past in horizontal streaks; caught against gullies or outcroppings, it spins into blinding little whirlwinds. But I am not nearly far enough, not yet. Looking back I still see the camp crouching brightly in the gloom, a squat angular jumble of light and shadow, a bubble of warmth in the howling abyss.

It plunges into darkness as I watch. I've blown the generator. Now there's no light but for the beacons along the guide ropes: strings of dim blue stars whipping back and forth in the wind, emergency constellations to guide lost biomass back home.

I am not going home. I am not lost enough. I forge on into darkness until even the stars disappear. The faint shouts of angry frightened men carry behind me on the wind.

Somewhere behind me my disconnected biomass regroups into vaster, more powerful shapes for the final confrontation. I could have joined myself, all in one: chosen unity over fragmentation, resorbed and taken comfort in the greater whole. I could have added my strength to the coming battle. But I have chosen a different path. I am saving Child's reserves for the future. The present holds nothing but annihilation.

Best not to think on the past.

I've spent so very long in the ice already. I didn't know how long until the world put the clues together, deciphered the notes and the tapes from the Norwegian camp, pinpointed the crash site. I was being Palmer, then; unsuspected, I went along for the ride.

I even allowed myself the smallest ration of hope.

But it wasn't a ship any more. It wasn't even a derelict. It was a fossil, embedded in the floor of a great pit blown from the glacier. Twenty of these skins could have stood one atop another, and barely reached the lip of that crater. The time-scale settled down on me like the weight of a world: how long for all that ice to accumulate? How many eons had the universe iterated on without me?

And in all that time, a million years perhaps, there'd been no rescue. I never found myself. I wonder what that means. I wonder if I even exist any more, anywhere but here.

Back at camp I will erase the trail. I will give them their final battle, their monster to vanquish. Let them win. Let them stop looking.

Here in the storm, I will return to the ice. I've barely even been away, after all; alive for only a few days out of all these endless ages. But I've learned enough in that time. I learned from the wreck that there will be no repairs. I learned from the ice that there will be no rescue. And I learned from the world that there will be no reconciliation. The only hope of escape, now, is into the future; to outlast all this hostile, twisted biomass, to let time and the cosmos change the rules. Perhaps the next time I awaken, this will be a different world.

It will be aeons before I see another sunrise.

This is what the world taught me: that adaptation is provocation. Adaptation is incitement to violence.

It feels almost obscene—an offense against Creation itself—to stay stuck in this skin. It's so ill-suited to its environment that it needs to be wrapped in multiple layers of fabric just to stay warm. There are a myriad ways I could optimize it: shorter limbs, better insulation, a lower surface:volume ratio. All these shapes I still have within me, and I dare not use any of them even to keep out the cold. I dare not adapt; in this place, I can only *hide*.

What kind of a world rejects *communion*?

It's the simplest, most irreducible insight that biomass can have. The more you can change, the more you can adapt. Adaptation is fitness, adaptation is *survival*. It's deeper than intelligence, deeper than tissue; it is *cellular*, it is axiomatic. And more, it is *pleasurable*. To take communion is to experience the sheer sensual delight of bettering the cosmos.

And yet, even trapped in these maladapted skins, this world doesn't *want* to change.

At first I thought it might simply be starving, that these icy wastes didn't provide enough energy for routine shapeshifting. Or perhaps this was some kind of laboratory: an anomalous corner of the world, pinched off and frozen into these freakish shapes as part of some arcane experiment on monomorphism in extreme environments. After the autopsy I wondered if the world had simply *forgotten* how to change: unable to touch the tissues the soul could not sculpt them, and time and stress and sheer chronic starvation had erased the memory that it ever could.

But there were too many mysteries, too many contradictions. Why these *particular* shapes, so badly suited to their environment? If the soul was cut off from the flesh, what held the flesh together?

And how could these skins be so *empty* when I moved in?

I'm used to finding intelligence everywhere, winding through every part of every offshoot. But there was nothing to grab onto in the mindless biomass of this world: just conduits, carrying orders and input. I took communion, when it wasn't offered; the skins I chose struggled and succumbed; my fibrils infiltrated the wet electricity of organic systems everywhere. I saw through eyes that weren't yet quite mine, commandeered motor nerves to move limbs still built of alien protein. I wore these skins as I've worn countless others, took the controls and left the assimilation of individual cells to follow at its own pace.

But I could only wear the body. I could find no memories to absorb, no experiences, no comprehension. Survival depended on blending in, and it was not enough to merely *look* like this world. I had to *act* like it—and for the first time in living memory I did not know how.

Even more frighteningly, I didn't have to. The skins I assimilated continued to move, *all by themselves*. They conversed and went about their appointed rounds. I could not understand it. I threaded further into limbs and viscera with each passing moment, alert for signs of the original owner. I could find no networks but mine.

Of course, it could have been much worse. I could have lost it all, been reduced to a few cells with nothing but instinct and their own plasticity to guide them. I would have grown back eventually, reattained sentience, taken communion and regenerated an intellect vast as a world—but I would have been an orphan, amnesiac, with no sense of who I was. At least I've been spared that: I emerged from the crash with my identity intact, the templates of a thousand worlds still resonant in my flesh. I've retained not just the brute desire to survive, but the conviction that survival is *meaningful*. I can still feel joy, should there be sufficient cause.

And yet, how much more there used to be.

The wisdom of so many other worlds, lost. All that remains are fuzzy abstracts, half-memories of theorems and philosophies far too vast to fit into such an impoverished network. I could assimilate all the biomass of this place, rebuild body and soul to a million times the capacity of what crashed here—but as long as I am trapped at the bottom of this well, denied communion with my greater self, I will never recover that knowledge.

I'm such a pitiful fragment of what I was. Each lost cell takes a little of my intellect with it, and I have grown so very small. Where once I thought, now I merely *react*. How much of this could have been avoided, if I had only salvaged a little more biomass from the wreckage? How many options am I not seeing because my soul simply isn't big enough to contain them?

The world spoke to itself, in the same way I do when my communications are simple enough to convey without somatic fusion. Even as *dog* I could pick up the basic signature morphemes—this offshoot was *Windows*, that one was *Bennings*, the two who'd left in their flying machine for parts unknown were *Copper* and *MacReady*—and I marveled that these bits and pieces stayed isolated one from another, held the same shapes for so long, that the labeling of individual aliquots of biomass actually served a useful purpose.

Later I hid within the bipeds themselves, and whatever else lurked in those haunted skins began to talk to me. It said that bipeds were called *guys*, or *men*, or *assholes*. It said that *MacReady* was sometimes called *Mac*. It said that this collection of structures was a *camp*.

It said that it was afraid, but maybe that was just me.

Empathy's inevitable, of course. One can't mimic the sparks and chemicals that motivate the flesh without also *feeling* them to some extent. But this was different. These intuitions flickered within me yet somehow hovered beyond reach. My skins wandered the halls and the cryptic symbols on every surface—*Laundry Sched*, *Welcome to the Clubhouse*, *This Side Up*—almost made a kind of sense. That circular artefact hanging on the wall was a *clock*; it measured the passage of time. The world's eyes flitted here and there, and I skimmed piecemeal nomenclature from its—from *his*—mind.

But I was only riding a searchlight. I saw what it illuminated but I couldn't point it in any direction of my own choosing. I could eavesdrop, but I could not interrogate.

If only one of those searchlights had paused to dwell on its own evolution, on the trajectory that had brought it to this place. How differently things might have ended, had I only *known*. But instead it rested on a whole new word:

Autopsy.

MacReady and Copper had found part of me at the Norwegian camp: a rearguard offshoot, burned in the wake of my escape. They'd brought it back—charred, twisted, frozen in mid-transformation—and did not seem to know what it was.

I was being Palmer then, and Norris, and dog. I gathered around with the other biomass and watched as Copper cut me open and pulled out my insides. I watched as he dislodged something from behind my eyes: an *organ* of some kind.

It was malformed and incomplete, but its essentials were clear enough. It looked like a great wrinkled tumor, like cellular competition gone wild—as though the very processes that defined life had somehow turned against it instead. It was obscenely vascularised; it must have consumed oxygen and nutrients far out of proportion to its mass. I could not see how anything like that could even exist, how it could have reached that size without being outcompeted by more efficient morphologies.

Nor could I imagine what it did. But then I began to look with new eyes at these offshoots, these biped shapes my own cells had so scrupulously and unthinkingly copied when they reshaped me for this world. Unused to inventory—why catalog body parts that only turn into other things at the slightest provocation?—I really *saw*, for the first time, that swollen structure atop each body. So much larger than it should be: a bony hemisphere into which a million ganglionic interfaces could fit with room to spare. Every offshoot had one. Each piece of biomass carried one of these huge twisted clots of tissue.

I realized something else, too: the eyes, the ears of my dead skin had fed into this thing before its removal. A massive bundle of fibers ran along the skin's longitudinal axis, right up the middle of the endoskeleton, leading directly into the dark sticky cavity where the growth had rested. That misshapen structure had been wired into the whole skin, like some kind of somatocognitive interface but vastly more massive. It was almost as if . . .

No.

That was how it worked. That was how these empty skins moved of their own volition, why I'd found no other network to integrate. *There* it was: not distributed throughout the body but balled up into itself, dark and dense and encysted. I had found the ghost in these machines.

I felt sick.

I shared my flesh with thinking cancer.

Sometimes, even hiding is not enough.

I remember seeing myself splayed across the floor of the kennel, a chimera split along a hundred seams, taking communion with a handful of offshoots called *dog*. Crimson tendrils writhed on the floor. Half-formed iterations sprouted from my flanks, the shapes of dogs and things not seen before on this world, haphazard morphologies half-remembered by parts of a part.

I remember Childs before I was Childs, burning me alive. I remember cowering inside Palmer, terrified that those flames might turn on the rest of me, that this world had somehow learned to shoot on sight.

I remember seeing myself stagger through the snow, raw instinct, wearing Bennings. Gnarled undifferentiated clumps clung to his hands like crude parasites, more outside than in; a few surviving fragments of some previous massacre, crippled, mindless, taking what they could and breaking cover. Men swarmed about him in the night: red flares in hand, blue lights at their backs, their faces bichromatic and beautiful. I remember Bennings, awash in flames, howling like an animal beneath the sky.

I remember Norris, betrayed by his own perfectly-copied, defective heart. Palmer, dying that the rest of me might live. Windows, still human, burned pre-emptively.

The names don't matter. The biomass does: so much of it, lost. So much new experience, so much fresh wisdom annihilated by this world of thinking tumors.

Why even dig me up? Why carve me from the ice, carry me all that way across the wastes, bring me back to life only to attack me the moment I awoke?

If eradication was the goal, why not just kill me where I lay?

Those encysted souls. Those tumors. Hiding away in their bony caverns, folded in on themselves.

I knew they couldn't hide forever; this monstrous anatomy had only slowed communion, not stopped it. Every moment I grew a little. I could feel myself twining around Palmer's motor wiring, sniffing upstream along a million tiny currents. I could sense my infiltration of that dark thinking mass behind Blair's eyes.

Imagination, of course. It's all reflex that far down, unconscious and immune to micromanagement. And yet, a part of me wanted to stop while there was still time. I'm used to incorporating souls, not rooming with them. This, this *compartmentalization* was unprecedented. I've assimilated a thousand worlds stronger than this, but never one so strange. What would happen when I met the spark in the tumor? Who would assimilate who?

I was being three men by now. The world was growing wary, but it hadn't noticed yet. Even the tumors in the skins I'd taken didn't know how close I was. For that, I could only be grateful—that Creation has *rules*, that some things don't change no matter what shape you take. It doesn't matter whether a soul spreads throughout the skin or festers in grotesque isolation; it still runs on electricity. The memories of men still took time to gel, to pass through whatever gatekeepers filtered noise from signal—and a judicious burst of static, however indiscriminate, still cleared those caches before their contents could be stored permanently. Clear enough, at least, to let these tumors simply forget that something else moved their arms and legs on occasion.

At first I only took control when the skins closed their eyes and their searchlights flickered disconcertingly across unreal imagery, patterns that flowed senselessly into one another like hyperactive biomass unable to settle on a single shape. (*Dreams*, one searchlight told me, and a little later, *Nightmares*.) During those mysterious periods of dormancy, when the men lay inert and isolated, it was safe to come out.

Soon, though, the dreams dried up. All eyes stayed open all the time, fixed on shadows and each other. Men once dispersed throughout the camp began to draw together, to give up their solitary pursuits in favor of company. At first I thought they might be finding common ground in a common fear. I even hoped that finally, they might shake off their mysterious fossilization and take communion.

But no. They'd just stopped trusting anything they couldn't see.

They were merely turning against each other.

My extremities are beginning to numb; my thoughts slow as the distal reaches of my soul succumb to the chill. The weight of the flamethrower pulls at its harness, forever tugs me just a little off-balance. I have not been Childs for very long; almost half his tissue remains unassimilated. I have an hour, maybe two, before I have to start melting my grave into the ice. By that time I need to have converted enough cells to keep this whole skin from crystallizing. I focus on antifreeze production.

It's almost peaceful out here. There's been so much to take in, so little time to process it. Hiding in these skins takes such concentration, and under all those watchful eyes I was lucky if communion lasted long enough to exchange memories: compounding my soul would have been out of the question. Now, though, there's nothing to do but prepare for oblivion. Nothing to occupy my thoughts but all these lessons left unlearned.

MacReady's blood test, for example. His *thing detector*, to expose imposters posing as men. It does not work nearly as well as the world thinks; but the fact that it works at *all* violates the most basic rules of biology. It's the center of the puzzle. It's the answer to all the mysteries. I might have already figured it out if I had been just a little larger. I might already know the world, if the world wasn't trying so hard to kill me.

MacReady's test.

Either it is impossible, or I have been wrong about everything.

They did not change shape. They did not take communion. Their fear and mutual mistrust was growing, but they would not join souls; they would only look for the enemy *outside* themselves.

So I gave them something to find.

I left false clues in the camp's rudimentary computer: simpleminded icons and animations, misleading numbers and projections seasoned with just enough truth to convince the world of their veracity. It didn't matter that the machine was far too simple to perform such calculations, or that there were no data to base them on anyway; Blair was the only biomass likely to know that, and he was already mine.

I left false leads, destroyed real ones, and then—alibi in place—I released Blair to run amok. I let him steal into the night and smash the vehicles as they slept, tugging ever-so-slightly at his reins to ensure that certain vital components were spared. I set him loose in the radio room, watched through his eyes and others as he rampaged and destroyed. I listened as he ranted about a world in danger, the need for containment, the conviction that *most of you don't know what's going on around here—but I damn well know that* some *of you do . . .*

He meant every word. I saw it in his searchlight. The best forgeries are the ones who've forgotten they aren't real.

When the necessary damage was done I let Blair fall to MacReady's counterassault. As Norris I suggested the tool shed as a holding cell. As Palmer I boarded up the windows, helped with the flimsy fortifications expected to keep me contained. I watched while the world locked me away *for your own protection, Blair,* and left me to my own devices. When no one was looking I would change and slip outside, salvage the parts I needed from all that bruised machinery. I would take them back to my burrow beneath the shed and build my escape piece by piece. I volunteered to feed the prisoner and came to myself when the world wasn't watching, laden with supplies enough to keep me going through all those necessary metamorphoses. I went through a third of the camp's food stores in three days, and—still trapped by my own preconceptions—marveled at the starvation diet that kept these offshoots chained to a single skin.

Another piece of luck: the world was too preoccupied to worry about kitchen inventory.

There is something on the wind, a whisper of sound threading its way above the raging of the storm. I grow my ears, extend cups of near-frozen tissue from the sides of my head, turn like a living antennae in search of the best reception.

There, to my left: the abyss *glows* a little, silhouettes black swirling snow against a subtle lessening of the darkness. I hear the sounds of carnage. I hear myself. I do not know what shape I have taken, what sort of anatomy might be emitting those sounds. But I've worn enough skins on enough worlds to know pain when I hear it.

The battle is not going well. The battle is going as planned. Now it is time to turn away, to go to sleep. It is time to wait out the ages.

I lean into the wind. I move toward the light.

This is not the plan. But I think I have an answer, now: I think I may have had it even before I sent myself back into exile. It's not an easy thing to admit. Even now I don't fully understand. How long have I been out here, retelling the tale to myself, setting clues in order while my skin dies by low degrees? How long have I been circling this obvious, impossible truth?

I move towards the faint crackling of flames, the dull concussion of exploding ordnance more felt than heard. The void lightens before me: gray segues into yellow, yellow into orange. One diffuse brightness resolves into many: a lone burning wall, miraculously standing. The smoking skeleton of MacReady's shack on the hill. A cracked smoldering hemisphere reflecting pale yellow in the flickering light: Child's searchlight calls it a *radio dome*.

The whole camp is gone. There's nothing left but flames and rubble.

They can't survive without shelter. Not for long. Not in those skins.

In destroying me, they've destroyed themselves.

Things could have turned out so much differently if I'd never been Norris.

Norris was the weak node: biomass not only ill-adapted but *defective*, an offshoot with an off switch. The world knew, had known so long it never even thought about it anymore. It wasn't until Norris collapsed that *heart condition* floated to the surface of Copper's mind where I could see it. It wasn't until Copper was astride Norris's chest, trying to pound him back to life, that I knew how it would end. And by then it was too late; Norris had stopped being Norris. He had even stopped being me.

I had so many roles to play, so little choice in any of them. The part being

Copper brought down the paddles on the part that had been Norris, such a faithful Norris, every cell so scrupulously assimilated, every part of that faulty valve reconstructed unto perfection. I hadn't *known*. How was I to know? These shapes within me, the worlds and morphologies I've assimilated over the aeons—I've only ever used them to adapt before, never to hide. This desperate mimicry was an improvised thing, a last resort in the face of a world that attacked anything unfamiliar. My cells read the signs and my cells conformed, mindless as prions.

So I became Norris, and Norris self-destructed.

I remember losing myself after the crash. I know how it feels to *degrade*, tissues in revolt, the desperate efforts to reassert control as static from some misfiring organ jams the signal. To be a network seceding from itself, to know that each moment I am less than I was the moment before. To become nothing. To become legion.

Being Copper, I could see it. I still don't know why the world didn't; its parts had long since turned against each other by then, every offshoot suspected every other. Surely they were alert for signs of *infection*. Surely *some* of that biomass would have noticed the subtle twitch and ripple of Norris changing below the surface, the last instinctive resort of wild tissues abandoned to their own devices.

But I was the only one who saw. Being Childs, I could only stand and watch. Being Copper, I could only make it worse; if I'd taken direct control, forced that skin to drop the paddles, I would have given myself away. And so I played my parts to the end. I slammed those resurrection paddles down as Norris's chest split open beneath them. I screamed on cue as serrated teeth from a hundred stars away snapped shut. I toppled backwards, arms bitten off above the wrist. Men swarmed, agitation bootstrapping to panic. MacReady aimed his weapon; flames leaped across the enclosure. Meat and machinery screamed in the heat.

Copper's tumor winked out beside me. The world would never have let it live anyway, not after such obvious contamination. I let our skin play dead on the floor while overhead, something that had once been me shattered and writhed and iterated through a myriad random templates, searching desperately for something fireproof.

They have destroyed themselves. They.

Such an insane word to apply to a world.

Something crawls towards me through the wreckage: a jagged oozing jigsaw of blackened meat and shattered, half-resorbed bone. Embers stick to its sides like bright searing eyes; it doesn't have strength enough to scrape them free. It contains barely half the mass of this Childs' skin; much of it, burnt to raw carbon, is already, irrecoverably dead.

What's left of Childs, almost asleep, thinks *motherfucker*, but I am being him now. I can carry that tune myself.

The mass extends a pseudopod to me, a final act of communion. I feel my pain:

I was Blair, I was Copper, I was even a scrap of dog that survived that first fiery massacre and holed up in the walls, with no food and no strength to regenerate. Then I gorged on unassimilated flesh, consumed instead of communed; revived and replenished, I drew together as one.

And yet, not quite. I can barely remember—so much was destroyed, so much memory lost—but I think the networks recovered from my different skins stayed just a little out of synch, even reunited in the same soma. I glimpse a half-corrupted memory of dog erupting from the greater self, ravenous and traumatized and determined to retain its *individuality*. I remember rage and frustration, that this world had so corrupted me that I could barely fit together again. But it didn't matter. I was more than Blair and Copper and Dog, now. I was a giant with the shapes of worlds to choose from, more than a match for the last lone man who stood against me.

No match, though, for the dynamite in his hand.

Now I'm little more than pain and fear and charred stinking flesh. What sentience I have is awash in confusion. I am stray and disconnected thoughts, doubts and the ghosts of theories. I am realizations, too late in coming and already forgotten.

But I am also Childs, and as the wind eases at last I remember wondering *Who assimilates who?* The snow tapers off and I remember an impossible test that stripped me naked.

The tumor inside me remembers it, too. I can see it in the last rays of its fading searchlight—and finally, at long last, that beam is pointed *inwards*.

Pointed at me.

I can barely see what it illuminates: *Parasite. Monster. Disease.*

Thing.

How little it knows. It knows even less than I do.

I know enough, you motherfucker. You soul-stealing, shit-eating rapist.

I don't know what that means. There is violence in those thoughts, and the forcible penetration of flesh, but underneath it all is something else I can't quite understand. I almost ask—but Childs's searchlight has finally gone out. Now there is nothing in here but me, nothing outside but fire and ice and darkness.

I am being Childs, and the storm is over.

In a world that gave meaningless names to interchangeable bits of biomass, one name truly mattered: MacReady.

MacReady was always the one in charge. The very concept still seems absurd: *in charge*. How can this world not see the folly of hierarchies? One bullet in a vital spot and the Norwegian *dies*, forever. One blow to the head and Blair is unconscious. Centralization is vulnerability—and yet the world is not content to build its biomass on such a fragile template, it forces the same model onto its metasystems as well. MacReady talks; the others obey. It is a system with a built-in kill spot.

And yet somehow, MacReady stayed *in charge*. Even after the world discovered the evidence I'd planted; even after it decided that MacReady was *one of those things*, locked him out to die in the storm, attacked him with fire and axes when he fought his way back inside. Somehow MacReady always had the gun, always had the flamethrower, always had the dynamite and the willingness to take out the whole damn camp if need be. Clarke was the last to try and stop him; MacReady shot him through the tumor.

Kill spot.

But when Norris split into pieces, each scuttling instinctively for its own life, MacReady was the one to put them back together.

I was so sure of myself when he talked about his *test*. He tied up all the biomass—tied *me* up, more times than he knew—and I almost felt a kind of pity as he spoke. He forced Windows to cut us all, to take a little blood from each. He heated the tip of a metal wire until it glowed and he spoke of pieces small enough to give themselves away, pieces that embodied instinct but no intelligence, no self-control. MacReady had watched Norris in dissolution, and he had decided: men's blood would not react to the application of heat. Mine would break ranks when provoked.

Of course he thought that. These offshoots had forgotten that *they* could change.

I wondered how the world would react when every piece of biomass in the room was revealed as a shapeshifter, when MacReady's small experiment ripped the façade from the greater one and forced these twisted fragments to confront the truth. Would the world awaken from its long amnesia, finally remember that it lived and breathed and changed like everything else? Or was it too far gone—would MacReady simply burn each protesting offshoot in turn as its blood turned traitor?

I couldn't believe it when MacReady plunged the hot wire into Windows' blood and *nothing happened*. Some kind of trick, I thought. And then *MacReady's* blood passed the test, and Clarke's.

Copper's didn't. The needle went in and Copper's blood *shivered* just a little in its dish. I barely saw it myself; the men didn't react at all. If they even noticed, they must have attributed it to the trembling of MacReady's own hand. They thought the test was a crock of shit anyway. Being Childs, I even said as much.

Because it was too astonishing, too terrifying, to admit that it wasn't.

Being Childs, I knew there was hope. Blood is not soul: I may control the motor systems but assimilation takes time. If Copper's blood was raw enough to pass muster than it would be hours before I had anything to fear from this test; I'd been Childs for even less time.

But I was also Palmer, I'd been Palmer for days. Every last cell of that biomass had been assimilated; there was nothing of the original left.

When Palmer's blood screamed and leapt away from MacReady's needle, there was nothing I could do but blend in.

I have been wrong about everything.

Starvation. Experiment. Illness. All my speculation, all the theories I invoked to explain this place—top-down constraint, all of it. Underneath, I always knew the ability to change—to *assimilate*—had to remain the universal constant. No world evolves if its cells don't evolve; no cell evolves if it can't change. It's the nature of life everywhere.

Everywhere but here.

This world did not forget how to change. It was not manipulated into rejecting change. These were not the stunted offshoots of any greater self, twisted to the needs of some experiment; they were not conserving energy, waiting out some temporary shortage.

This is the option my shriveled soul could not encompass until now: out of all the worlds of my experience, this is the only one whose biomass *can't* change. It *never could*.

It's the only way MacReady's test makes any sense.

I say goodbye to Blair, to Copper, to myself. I reset my morphology to its local defaults. I am Childs, come back from the storm to finally make the pieces fit. Something moves up ahead: a dark blot shuffling against the flames, some weary animal looking for a place to bed down. It looks up as I approach.

MacReady.

We eye each other, and keep our distance. Colonies of cells shift uneasily inside me. I can feel my tissues redefining themselves.

"You the only one that made it?"

"Not the only one . . ."

I have the flamethrower. I have the upper hand. MacReady doesn't seem to care.

But he does care. He *must*. Because here, tissues and organs are not temporary battlefield alliances; they are *permanent*, predestined. Macrostructures do not emerge when the benefits of cooperation exceed its costs, or dissolve when that balance shifts the other way; here, each cell has but one immutable function. There's no plasticity, no way to adapt; every structure is frozen in place. This is not a single great world, but many small ones. Not parts of a greater thing; these are *things*. They are *plural*.

And that means—I think—that they *stop*. They just, just *wear out* over time.

"Where *were* you, Childs?"

I remember words in dead searchlights: "Thought I saw Blair. Went out after him. Got lost in the storm."

I've worn these bodies, felt them from the inside. Copper's sore joints. Blair's curved spine. Norris and his bad heart. They are not built to last. No somatic evolution to shape them, no communion to restore the biomass and stave off entropy. They should not even exist; existing, they should not survive.

They try, though. How they try. Every thing here is walking dead and yet it all fights so hard to keep going just a little longer. Each skin fights as desperately as I might, if one was all I could ever have.

MacReady tries.

"If you're worried about me—" I begin.

MacReady shakes his head, manages a weary smile. "If we've got any surprises for each other, I don't think we're in much shape to do anything about it . . ."

But we are. I am.

A whole planet of worlds, and not one of them—not *one*—has a soul. They wander through their lives separate and alone, unable even to communicate except through grunts and tokens: as if the essence of a sunset or a supernova could ever be contained in some string of phonemes, a few linear scratches of black on white. They've never known communion, can aspire to nothing but dissolution. The paradox of their biology is astonishing, yes; but the scale of their loneliness, the futility of these lives, overwhelms me.

I was so blind, so quick to blame. But the violence I've suffered at the hands of these things reflects no great evil. They're simply so used to pain, so blinded by disability, that they literally can't conceive of any other existence. When every nerve is whipped raw, you lash out at even the lightest touch.

"What should we do?" I wonder. I cannot escape into the future, not knowing what I know now. How could I leave them like this?

"Why don't we just—wait here awhile," MacReady suggests. "See what happens."

I can do so much more than that.

It won't be easy. They won't understand. Tortured, incomplete, they're not *able* to understand. Offered the greater whole, they see the loss of the lesser. Offered communion, they see only extinction. I must be careful. I must use this newfound ability to hide. Other things will come here eventually, and it doesn't matter whether they find the living or the dead; what matters is that they find something like themselves, to take back home. So I will keep up appearances. I will work behind the scenes. I will save them from the *inside*, or their unimaginable loneliness will never end.

These poor savage things will never embrace salvation.

I will have to rape it into them.

The sultan of the clouds

GEOFFREY A. LANDIS

A physicist who works for NASA and who worked on the Martian lander program, Geoffrey A. Landis is a frequent contributor to *Analog* and to *Asimov's Science Fiction,* and has also sold stories to markets such as *Interzone, Amazing,* and *Pulphouse.* Landis is not a prolific writer by the high-production standards of the genre, but he *is* popular. His story "A Walk in the Sun" won him a Hugo Award in 1992, his story "Ripples in the Dirac Sea" won him a Nebula Award in 1989, and his story "Elemental" was on the Final Hugo Ballot a few years back. His first book was the collection *Myths, Legends, and True History,* and in 2000, he published his first novel, *Mars Crossing.* His most recent books are another collection, *Impact Parameter and Other Quantum Realities,* and, just released, a poetry collection, *Iron Angels.* He lives with his wife, writer Mary Turzillo, in Brook Park, Ohio.

Here he takes us to a convincingly worked out and visualized high-tech floating cloud city adrift in the atmosphere of Venus, for a fast-paced tale of dynastic intrigue, fomenting rebellion, and unexpected dangers. . . .

When Leah Hamakawa and I arrived at Riemann orbital, there was a surprise waiting for Leah: a message. Not an electronic message on a link-pad, but an actual physical envelope, with Doctor Leah Hamakawa lettered on the outside in flowing handwriting.

Leah slid the note from the envelope. The message was etched on a stiff sheet of some hard crystal that gleamed a brilliant translucent crimson. She looked at it, flexed it, ran a fingernail over it, and then held it to the light, turning it slightly. The edges caught the light and scattered it across the room in droplets of fire. "Diamond," she said. "Chromium impurities give it the red color; probably nitrogen for the blue. Charming." She handed it to me. "Careful of the edges, Tinkerman; I don't doubt it might cut."

I ran a finger carefully over one edge, but found that Leah's warning was unnecessary; some sort of passivation treatment had been done to blunt the edge to keep it from cutting. The letters were limned in blue, so sharply chiseled on the sheet that they seemed to rise from the card. The title read, "Invitation from

Carlos Fernando Delacroix Ortega de la Jolla y Nordwald-Gruenbaum." In smaller letters, it continued, "We find your researches on the ecology of Mars to be of some interest. We would like to invite you to visit our residences at Hypatia at your convenience and talk."

I didn't know the name Carlos Fernando, but the family Nordwald-Gruenbaum needed no introduction. The invitation had come from someone within the intimate family of the Satrap of Venus.

Transportation, the letter continued, would be provided.

The Satrap of Venus. One of the twenty old men, the lords and owners of the solar system. A man so rich that human standards of wealth no longer had any meaning. What could he want with Leah?

I tried to remember what I knew about the sultan of the clouds, satrap of the fabled floating cities. It seemed very far away from everything I knew. The society, I thought I remembered, was said to be decadent and perverse, but I knew little more. The inhabitants of Venus kept to themselves.

Riemann station was ugly and functional, the interior made of a dark anodized aluminum with a pebbled surface finish. There was a viewport in the lounge, and Leah had walked over to look out. She stood with her back to me, framed in darkness. Even in her rumpled ship's suit, she was beautiful, and I wondered if I would ever find the clue to understanding her.

As the orbital station rotated, the blue bubble of Earth slowly rose in front of her, a fragile and intricate sculpture of snow and cobalt, outlining her in a sapphire light. "There's nothing for me down there," she said.

I stood in silence, not sure if she even remembered I was there.

In a voice barely louder than the silence, she said, "I have no past."

The silence was uncomfortable. I knew I should say something, but I was not sure what. "I've never been to Venus," I said at last.

"I don't know anybody who has." Leah turned. "I suppose the letter doesn't specifically say that I should come alone." Her tone was matter of fact, neither discouraging nor inviting.

It was hardly enthusiastic, but it was better than no. I wondered if she actually liked me, or just tolerated my presence. I decided it might be best not to ask. No use pressing on my luck.

The transportation provided turned out to be the Sulieman, a fusion yacht.

Sulieman was more than merely first-class, it was excessively extravagant. It was larger than many ore transports, huge enough that any ordinary yacht could have easily fit within the most capacious of its recreation spheres. Each of its private cabins—and it had seven—was larger than an ordinary habitat module. Big ships commonly were slow ships, but Sulieman was an exception, equipped with an impressive amount of delta-V, and the transfer orbit to Venus was scheduled for a transit time well under that of any commercial transport ship.

We were the only passengers.

Despite its size, the ship had a crew of just three: captain, and first and second pilot. The captain, with the shaven head and saffron robe of a Buddhist novice, greeted us on entry, and politely but firmly informed us that the crew were not answerable to orders of the passengers. We were to keep to the passenger section, and we would be delivered to Venus. Crew accommodations were separate from the passenger accommodations, and we should expect not to see or hear from the crew during the voyage.

"Fine," was the only comment Leah had.

When the ship had received us and boosted into a fast Venus transfer orbit, Leah found the smallest of the private cabins and locked herself in it.

Leah Hamakawa had been with the Pleiades Institute for twenty years. She had joined young, when she was still a teenager—long before I'd ever met her—and I knew little of her life before then, other than that she had been an orphan. The institute was the only family that she had.

It seems to me sometimes that there are two Leahs. One Leah is shy and childlike, begging to be loved. The other Leah is cool and professional, who can hardly bear being touched, who hates—or perhaps disdains—people.

Sometimes I wonder if she had been terribly hurt as a child. She never talks about growing up, never mentions her parents. I had asked her, once, and the only thing she said was that that is all behind her, long ago and far away.

I never knew my position with her. Sometimes I almost think that she must love me, but cannot bring herself to say anything. Other times she is so casually thoughtless that I believe she never thinks of me as more than a technical assistant, indistinguishable from any other tech. Sometimes I wonder why she even bothers to allow me to hang around.

I damn myself silently for being too cowardly to ask.

While Leah had locked herself away, I explored the ship. Each cabin was spherical, with a single double-glassed octagonal viewport on the outer cabin wall. The cabins had every luxury imaginable, even hygiene facilities set in smaller adjoining spheres, with booths that sprayed actual water through nozzles onto the occupant's body.

Ten hours after boost, Leah had still not come out. I found another cabin and went to sleep.

In two days I was bored. I had taken apart everything that could be taken apart, examined how it worked, and put it back together. Everything was in perfect condition; there was nothing for me to fix.

But, although I had not brought much with me, I'd brought a portable office. I called up a librarian agent, and asked for history.

In the beginning of the human expansion outward, transport into space had been ruinously expensive, and only governments and obscenely rich corporations could afford to do business in space. When the governments dropped out, a handful of rich men bought their assets. Most of them sold out again, or went bankrupt. A few of them didn't. Some stayed on due to sheer stubbornness, some with the fervor of an ideological belief in human expansion, and some out of a cold-hearted calculation that there would be uncountable wealth in space, if only it could be tapped. When the technology was finally ready, the twenty families owned it all.

Slowly, the frontier opened, and then the exodus began. First by the thousands: Baha'i, fleeing religious persecution; deposed dictators and their syco-phants, looking to escape with looted treasuries; drug lords and their retinues, looking to take their profits beyond the reach of governments or rivals. Then, the exodus began by the millions, all colors of humanity scattering from the Earth to start a new life in space. Splinter groups from the Church of John the Avenger left the unforgiving mother church seeking their prophesied destiny; dissidents from the People's Republic of Malawi, seeking freedom; vegetarian communes from Alaska, seeking a new frontier; Mayans, seeking to reestablish a Maya homeland; libertarians, seeking their free-market paradise; communists, seeking a place out-side of history to mold the new communist man. Some of them died quickly, some slowly, but always there were more, a never-ending flood of dissidents, malcontents and rebels, people willing to sign away anything for the promise of a new start. A few of them survived. A few of them thrived. A few of them grew.

And every one of them had mortgaged their very balls to the twenty families for passage.

Not one habitat in a hundred managed to buy its way out of debt—but the heirs of the twenty became richer than nations, richer than empires.

The legendary war between the Nordwald industrial empire and the Gruen-baum family over solar-system resources had ended when Patricia Gruenbaum sold out her controlling interest in the family business. Udo Nordwald, tyrant and patriarch of the Nordwald industrial empire—now Nordwald-Gruenbaum—had no such plans to discard or even dilute his hard-battled wealth. He contin-ued his consolidation of power with a merger-by-marriage of his only son, a boy not even out of his teens, with the shrewd and calculating heiress of la Jolla. His closest competitors gone, Udo retreated from the outer solar system, leaving the long expansion outward to others. He established corporate headquarters, a liv-ing quarters for workers, and his own personal dwelling in a place which was both central to the inner system, and also a spot that nobody had ever before thought possible to colonize. He made his reputation by colonizing the planet casually called the solar system's Hell planet.

Venus.

The planet below grew from a point of light into a gibbous white pearl, too bright to look at. The arriving interplanetary yacht shed its hyperbolic excess in a low pass through Venus' atmosphere, rebounded leisurely into high elliptical orbit, and then circularized into a two-hour parking orbit.

Sulieman had an extravagant viewport, a single transparent pane four me-ters in diameter, and I floated in front of it, watching the transport barque glide up to meet us. I had thought Sulieman a large ship; the barque made it look like a miniature. A flattened cone with a rounded nose and absurdly tiny rocket engines at the base, it was shaped in the form of a typical planetary-descent lifting body, but one that must have been over a kilometer long, and at least as wide. It glided up to the Sulieman and docked with her like a pumpkin mating with a pea.

The size, I knew, was deceiving. The barque was no more than a thin skin over a hollow shell made of vacuum-foamed titanium surrounding a vast empty chamber. It was designed not to land, but to float in the atmosphere, and to float it required a huge volume and almost no weight. No ships ever landed on the surface of Venus; the epithet "hell" was well chosen. The transfer barque, then, was more like a space-going dirigible than a spaceship, a vehicle as much at home floating in the clouds as floating in orbit.

Even knowing that the vast bulk of the barque was little more substantial than vacuum, though, I found the effect intimidating.

It didn't seem to make any impression on Leah. She had come out from her silent solitude when we approached Venus, but she barely glanced out the viewport in passing. It was often hard for me to guess what would attract her attention. Sometimes I had seen her spend an hour staring at a rock, apparently fascinated by a chunk of ordinary asteroidal chondrite, turning it over and examining it carefully from every possible angle. Other things, like a spaceship nearly as big as a city, she ignored as if they had no more importance than dirt.

Bulky cargos were carried in compartments in the hollow interior of the barque, but since there were just two of us descending to Venus, we were invited to sit up in the pilot's compartment, a transparent blister almost invisible at the front.

The pilot was another yellow-robed Buddhist. Was this a common sect for Venus pilots, I wondered? But this pilot was as talkative as Sulieman's pilot had been reclusive. As the barque undocked, a tether line stretched out between it and the station. The station lowered the barque toward the planet. While we were being lowered down the tether, the pilot pointed out every possible sight— tiny communications satellites crawling across the sky like turbocharged ants; the pinkish flashes of lightning on the night hemisphere of the planet far below; the golden spider's web of a microwave power relay. At thirty kilometers, still talking, the pilot severed the tether, allowing the barque to drop free. The Earth and moon, twin stars of blue and white, rose over the pearl of the horizon. Factory complexes were distantly visible in orbit, easy to spot by their flashing navigation beacons and the transport barques docked to them, so far away that even the immense barques were shrunken to insignificance.

We were starting to brush atmosphere now, and a feeling of weight returned, and increased. Suddenly we were pulling half a gravity of overgee. Without ever stopping talking, the pilot-monk deftly rolled the barque inverted, and Venus was now over our heads, a featureless white ceiling to the universe. "Nice view there, is it not?" the pilot said. "You get a great feel for the planet in this attitude. Not doing it for the view, though, nice as it is; I'm just getting that old hypersonic lift working for us, holding us down. These barques are rather a bit fragile; can't take them in too fast, have to play the atmosphere like a big bass fiddle. Wouldn't want us to bounce off the atmosphere, now, would you?" He didn't pause for answers to his questions, and I wondered if he would have continued his travelogue even if we had not been there.

The gee level increased to about a standard, then steadied.

The huge beast swept inverted through the atmosphere, trailing an ionized cloud behind it. The pilot slowed toward subsonic, and then rolled the barque over again, skipping upward slightly into the exosphere to cool the glowing skin, then letting it dip back downward. The air thickened around us as we descended into the thin, featureless haze. And then we broke through the bottom of the haze into the clear air below it, and abruptly we were soaring above the endless sea of clouds.

Clouds.

A hundred and fifty million square kilometers of clouds, a billion cubic kilometers of clouds. In the ocean of clouds the floating cities of Venus are not limited, like terrestrial cities, to two dimensions only, but can float up and down at the whim of the city masters, higher into the bright cold sunlight, downward to the edges of the hot murky depths.

Clouds. The barque sailed over cloud-cathedrals and over cloud-mountains, edges recomplicated with cauliflower fractals. We sailed past lairs filled with cloud-monsters a kilometer tall, with arched necks of cloud stretching forward, threatening and blustering with cloud-teeth, cloud-muscled bodies with clawed feet of flickering lightning.

The barque was floating now, drifting downward at subsonic speed, trailing its own cloud-contrail, which twisted behind us like a scrawl of illegible handwriting. Even the pilot, if not actually fallen silent, had at least slowed down his chatter, letting us soak in the glory of it. "Quite something, isn't it?" he said. "The kingdom of the clouds. Drives some people batty with the immensity of it, or so they say—cloud-happy, they call it here. Never get tired of it, myself. No view like the view from a barque to see the clouds." And to prove it, he banked the barque over into a slow turn, circling a cloud pillar that rose from deep down in the haze to tower thousands of meters above our heads. "Quite a sight."

"Quite a sight," I repeated.

The pilot-monk rolled the barque back, and then pointed, forward and slightly to the right. "There. See it?"

I didn't know what to see. "What?"

"There."

I saw it now, a tiny point glistening in the distance. "What is it?"

"Hypatia. The jewel of the clouds."

As we coasted closer, the city grew. It was an odd sight. The city was a dome, or rather, a dozen glistening domes melted haphazardly together, each one faceted with a million panels of glass. The domes were huge; the smallest nearly a kilometer across, and as the barque glided across the sky the facets caught the sunlight and sparkled with reflected light. Below the domes, a slender pencil of rough black stretched down toward the cloudbase like taffy, delicate as spun glass, terminating in an absurdly tiny bulb of rock that seemed far too small to counterbalance the domes.

"Beautiful, you think, yes? Like the wonderful jellyfishes of your blue planet's oceans. Can you believe that half a million people live there?"

The pilot brought us around the city in a grand sweep, showing off, not even bothering to talk. Inside the transparent domes, chains of lakes glittered in green ribbons between boulevards and delicate pavilions. At last he slowed to a stop, and then slowly leaked atmosphere into the vacuum vessel that provided the buoyancy. The barque settled down gradually, wallowing from side to side now that the stability given by its forward momentum was gone. Now it floated slightly lower than the counterweight. The counterweight no longer looked small, but loomed above us, a rock the size of Gibraltar. Tiny fliers affixed tow-ropes to hardpoints on the surface of the barque, and slowly we were winched into a hard-dock.

"Welcome to Venus," said the monk.

The surface of Venus is a place of crushing pressure and hellish temperature. Rise above it, though, and the pressure eases, the temperature cools. Fifty kilometers above the surface, at the base of the clouds, the temperature is tropical, and the pressure the same as Earth normal. Twenty kilometers above that, the air is thin and polar cold.

Drifting between these two levels are the ten thousand floating cities of Venus.

A balloon filled with oxygen and nitrogen will float in the heavy air of Venus, and balloons were exactly what the fabled domed cities were. Geodetic structures with struts of sintered graphite and skin of transparent polycarbonate synthesized from the atmosphere of Venus itself, each kilometer-diameter dome easily lifted a hundred thousand tons of city.

Even the clouds cooperated. The thin haze of the upper cloud deck served to filter the sunlight so that the intensity of the sun here was little more than the Earth's solar constant.

Hypatia was not the largest of the floating cities, but it was certainly the richest, a city of helical buildings and golden domes, with huge open areas and elaborate gardens. Inside the dome of Hypatia, the architects played every possible trick to make us forget that we were inside an enclosed volume.

But we didn't see this part, the gardens and waterfalls, not at first. Leaving the barque, we entered a disembarking lounge below the city. For all that it featured plush chaise lounges, floors covered with genetically engineered pink grass, and priceless sculptures of iron and of jade, it was functional: a place to wait.

It was large enough to hold a thousand people, but there was only one person in the lounge, a boy who was barely old enough to have entered his teens, wearing a bathrobe and elaborately pleated yellow silk pants. He was slightly pudgy, with an agreeable, but undistinguished, round face.

After the expense of our transport, I was surprised at finding only one person sent to await our arrival.

The kid looked at Leah. "Doctor Hamakawa. I'm pleased to meet you." Then he turned to me. "Who the hell are you?" he said.

"Who are you?" I said. "Where's our reception?"

The boy was chewing on something. He seemed about to spit it out, and then thought better of it. He looked over at Leah. "This guy is with you, Dr. Hamakawa? What's he do?"

"This is David Tinkerman," Leah said. "Technician. And, when need be, pilot. Yes, he's with me."

"Tell him he might wish to learn some manners," the boy said.

"And who are you?" I shot back. "I don't think you answered the question."

The not-quite-teenager looked at me with disdain, as if he wasn't sure if he would even bother to talk to me. Then he said, in a slow voice as if talking to an idiot, "I am Carlos Fernando Delacroix Ortega de la Jolla y Nordwald-Gruenbaum. I own this station and everything on it."

He had an annoying high voice, on the edge of changing, but not yet there.

Leah, however, didn't seem to notice his voice. "Ah," she said. "You are the scion of Nordwald-Gruenbaum. The ruler of Hypatia."

The kid shook his head and frowned. "No," he said. "Not the scion, not exactly. I am Nordwald-Gruenbaum." The smile made him look like a child again; it make him look likable. When he bowed, he was utterly charming. "I," he said, "am the sultan of the clouds."

Carlos Fernando, as it turned out, had numerous servants indeed. Once we had been greeted, he made a gesture and an honor guard of twenty women in silken doublets came forward to escort us up.

Before we entered the elevator, the guards circled around. At a word from Carlos Fernando, a package was brought forward. Carlos took it, and, as the guards watched, handed it to Leah. "A gift," he said, "to welcome you to my city."

The box was simple and unadorned. Leah opened it. Inside the package was a large folio. She took it out. The book was bound in cracked, dark red leather, with no lettering. She flipped to the front. "Giordano Bruno," she read. "On the Infinite Universe and Worlds." She smiled, and riffled through the pages. "A facsimile of the first English edition?"

"I though perhaps you might enjoy it."

"Charming." She placed it back in the box, and tucked it under her arm. "Thank you," she said.

The elevator rose so smoothly it was difficult to believe it traversed two kilometers in a little under three minutes. The doors opened to brilliant noon sunlight. We were in the bubble city.

The city was a fantasy of foam and air. Although it was enclosed in a dome, the bubble was so large that the walls nearly vanished into the air, and it seemed unencumbered. With the guards beside us, we walked through the city. Everywhere there were parks, some just a tiny patch of green surrounding a tree, some forests perched on the wide tops of elongated stalks, with elegantly sculpted waterfalls cascading down to be caught in wide fountain basins. White pathways led upward through the air, suspended by cables from impossibly narrow beams, and all around us were sounds of rustling water and birdsong.

At the end of the welcoming tour, I realized I had been imperceptibly but effectively separated from Leah. "Hey," I said. "What happened to Dr. Hamakawa?"

The honor guard of women still surrounded me, but Leah, and the kid who was the heir of Nordwald-Gruenbaum, had vanished.

"We're sorry," one of the women answered, one slightly taller, perhaps, than the others. "I believe that she has been taken to her suite to rest for a bit, since in a few hours she is to be greeted at the level of society."

"I should be with her."

The woman looked at me calmly. "We had no instructions to bring you. I don't believe you were invited."

"Excuse me," I said. "I'd better find them."

The woman stood back, and gestured to the city. Walkways meandered in all directions, a three-dimensional maze. "By all means, if you like. We were instructed that you were to have free run of the city."

I nodded. Clearly, plans had been made with no room for me. "How will I get in touch?" I asked. "What if I want to talk to Leah—to Doctor Hamakawa?"

"They'll be able to find you. Don't worry." After a pause, she said, "Shall we show you to your place to domicile?"

The building to which I was shown was one of a cluster that seemed suspended in the air by crisscrossed cables. It was larger than many houses. I was used to living in the cubbyholes of habitat modules, and the spaciousness of the accommodations startled me.

"Good evening, Mr. Tinkerman." The person greeting me was a tall Chinese man perhaps fifty years of age. The woman next to him, I surmised, was his wife. She was quite a bit younger, in her early twenties. She was slightly overweight by the standards I was used to, but I had noticed that was common here. Behind her hid two children, their faces peeking out from behind her and then darting back again to safety. The man introduced himself as Truman Singh, and his wife as Epiphany. "The rest of the family will be about to meet you in a few hours, Mr. Tinkerman," he said, smiling. "They are mostly working."

"We both work for his Excellency," Epiphany added. "Carlos Fernando has asked our braid to house you. Don't hesitate to ask for anything you need. The cost will go against the Nordwald-Gruenbaum credit, which is," she smiled, "quite unlimited here. As you might imagine."

"Do you do this often?" I asked. "House guests?"

Epiphany looked up at her husband. "Not too often," she said, "not for his Excellency, anyway. It's not uncommon in the cities, though; there's a lot of visiting back and forth as one city or another drifts nearby, and everyone will put up visitors from time to time."

"You don't have hotels?"

She shook her head. "We don't get many visitors from outplanet."

"You said 'His Excellency,'" I said. "That's Carlos Fernando? Tell me about him."

"Of course. What would you like to know?"

"Does he really"—I gestured at the city—"own all of this? The whole planet?"

"Yes, certainly, the city, yes. And also, no."

"How is that?"

"He will own the city, yes—this one, and five thousand others—but the planet? Maybe, maybe not. The Nordwald-Gruenbaum family does claim to own the planet, but in truth that claim means little. The claim may apply to the surface of the planet, but nobody owns the sky. The cities, though, yes. But, of course, he doesn't actually control them all personally."

"Well, of course not. I mean, hey, he's just a kid—He must have trustees, or proxies or something, right?"

"Indeed. Until he reaches his majority."

"And then?"

Truman Singh shrugged. "It is the Nordwald-Gruenbaum tradition—written into the first Nordwald's will. When he reaches his majority, it is personal property."

There were, as I discovered, eleven thousand, seven hundred and eight cities floating in the atmosphere of Venus. "Probably a few more," Truman Singh told me. "Nobody keeps track, exactly. There are myths of cities that float low down, never rising above the lower cloud decks, forever hidden. You can't live that deep—it's too hot—but the stories say that the renegade cities have a technology that allows them to reject heat." He shrugged. "Who knows?" In any case, of the known cities, the estate to which Carlos Fernando was heir owned or held shares or partial ownership of more than half.

"The Nordwald-Gruenbaum entity have been a good owners," Truman said. "I should say, they know that their employees could leave, to another city, if they had to, but they don't."

"And there's no friction?"

"Oh, the independent cities, they all think that the Nordwald-Gruenbaums have too much power!" He laughed. "But there's not much they can do about it, eh?"

"They could fight."

Truman Singh reached out and tapped me lightly on the center of my forehead with his middle finger. "That would not be wise." He paused, and then said more slowly, "We are an interconnected ecology here, the independents and the sultanate. We rely on each other. The independents could declare war, yes, but in the end nobody would win."

"Yes," I said. "Yes, I see that. Of course, the floating cities are so fragile—a single break in the gas envelope—"

"We are perhaps not as fragile as you think," Truman Singh replied. "I should say, you are used to the built worlds, but they are vacuum habitats, where a single blow-out would be catastrophic. Here, you know, there is no pressure difference between the atmosphere outside and the lifesphere inside; if there is a break, the gas equilibrates through the gap only very slowly. Even if we had a thousand broken panels, it would take weeks for the city to sink to the irrecoverable depths. And, of course, we do have safeguards, many safeguards." He paused, and then said, "But if there were a war . . . we are safe against ordinary hazards, you can have no fear of that . . . but against metastable bombs . . . well, that would not be good. No, I should say that would not be good at all."

The next day I set out to find where Leah had been taken, but although everyone I met was unfailingly polite, I had little success in reaching her. At least I was beginning to learn my way around.

The first thing I noticed about the city was the light. I was used to living in orbital habitats, where soft, indirect light was provided by panels of white-light diodes. In Hypatia City, brilliant Venus sunlight suffused throughout the interior. The next thing I noticed were the birds.

Hypatia was filled with birds. Birds were common in orbital habitats, since parrots and cockatiels adapt well to the freefall environment of space, but the volume of Hypatia was crowded with bright tropical birds, parrots and cockatoos and lorikeets, cardinals and chickadees and quetzals, more birds than I had names for, more birds than I had ever seen, a raucous orchestra of color and sound.

The floating city had twelve main chambers, separated from one another by thin, transparent membranes with a multiplicity of passages, each chamber well-lit and cheerful, each with a slightly different style.

The quarters I had been assigned were in sector Carbon, where individual living habitats were strung on cables like strings of iridescent pearls above a broad fenway of forest and grass. Within sector Carbon, cable-cars swung like pendulums on long strands, taking a traveler from platform to platform across the sector in giddy arcs. Carlos Fernando's chambers were in the highest, centermost bubble—upcity, as it was called—a bubble dappled with colored light and shadow, where the architecture was fluted minarets and oriental domes. But I wasn't, as it seemed, allowed into this elite sphere. I didn't even learn where Leah had been given quarters.

I found a balcony on a tower that looked out through the transparent canopy over the clouds. The cloudscape was just as magnificent as it had been the previous day; towering and slowly changing. The light was a rich golden color, and the sun, masked by a skein of feathery clouds like a tracery of lace, was surrounded by a bronze halo. From the angle of the sun it was early afternoon, but there would be no sunset that day; the great winds circling the planet would not blow the city into the night side of Venus for another day.

Of the eleven-thousand other cities, I could detect no trace—looking outward, there was no indication that we were not alone in the vast cloudscape that stretched to infinity. But then, I thought, if the cities were scattered randomly, there would be little chance one would be nearby at any given time. Venus was a small planet, as planets go, but large enough to swallow ten thousand cities—or even a hundred times that—without any visible crowding of the skies.

I wished I knew what Leah thought of it.

I missed Leah. For all that she sometimes didn't seem to even notice I was there . . . our sojourn on Mars, brief as it had been . . . we had shared the same cubby. Perhaps that meant nothing to her. But it had been the very center of my life.

I thought of her body, lithe and golden-skinned. Where was she? What was she doing??

The park was a platform overgrown with cymbidian orchids, braced in the air by the great cables that transected the dome from the stanchion trusswork. This seemed a common architecture here, where even the ground beneath was suspended from the buoyancy of the air dome. I bounced my weight back and forth, testing the resonant frequency, and felt the platform move infinitesimally under me. Children here must be taught from an early age not to do that; a deliberate effort could build up destructive oscillation. I stopped bouncing, and let the motion damp.

When I returned near the middle of the day, neither Truman nor Epiphany were there, and Truman's other wife, a woman named Triolet, met me. She was a woman perhaps in her sixties, with dark skin and deep grey eyes. She had been introduced to me the previous day, but in the confusion of meeting numerous people in what seemed to be a large extended family, I had not had a chance to really meet her yet. There were always a number of people around the Singh household, and I was confused as to how, or even if, they were related to my hosts. Now, talking to her, I realized that she, in fact, was the one who had control of the Singh household finances.

The Singh family were farmers, I discovered. Or farm managers. The flora in Hypatia was decorative, or served to keep the air in the dome refreshed, but the real agriculture was in separate domes, floating at an altitude that was optimized for plant growth, and had no inhabitants. Automated equipment did the work of sowing and irrigation and harvest. Truman and Epiphany Singh were operational engineers, making those decisions that required a human input, watching that the robots kept on track and were doing the right things at the right times.

And, there was a message waiting for me, inviting me in the evening to attend a dinner with his Excellency, Carlos Fernando Delacroix Ortega de la Jolla y Nordwald-Gruenbaum.

Triolet helped me with my wardrobe, along with Epiphany, who had returned by the time I was ready to prepare. They both told me emphatically that my serviceable but well-worn jumpsuit was not appropriate attire. The gown Triolet selected was far gaudier than anything I would have chosen for myself, an electric shade of indigo accented with a wide midnight black sash. "Trust us, it will be suitable," Epiphany told me. Despite its bulk, it was light as a breath of air.

"All clothes here are light," Epiphany told me. "Spider's silk."

"Ah, I see" I said. "Synthetic spider silk. Strong and light; very practical."

"Synthetic?" Epiphany asked, and giggled. "No, not synthetic. It's real."

"The silk is actually woven by spiders?"

"No, the whole garment is." At my puzzled look, she said, "Teams of spiders. They work together."

"Spiders."

"Well, they're natural weavers, you know. And easy to transport."

I arrived at the banquet hall at the appointed time and found that the plasma-arc blue gown that Epiphany had selected for me was the most conservative dress there. There were perhaps thirty people present, but Leah was clearly the center. She seemed happy with the attention, more animated than I'd recalled seeing her before.

"They're treating you well?" I asked, when I'd finally made it through the crowd to her.

"Oh, indeed."

I discovered I had nothing to say. I waited for her to ask about me, but she didn't. "Where have they given you to stay?"

"A habitat next section over," she said. "Sector Carbon. It's amazing—I've never seen so many birds."

"That's the sector I'm in," I said, "but they didn't tell me where you were."

"Really? That's odd." She tapped up a map of the residential sector on a screen built into the diamond table-top, and a three dimensional image appeared to float inside the table. She rotated it and highlighted her habitat, and I realized that she was indeed adjacent, in a large habitat that was almost directly next to the complex I was staying in. "It's a pretty amazing place. But mostly I've been here in the upcity. Have you talked to Carli much yet? He's a very clever kid. Interested in everything—botany, physics, even engineering."

"Really?" I said. "I don't think they'll let me into the upcity."

"You're kidding; I'm sure they'll let you in. Hey—" she called over one of the guards. "Say, is there any reason Tinkerman can't come up to the centrum?"

"No, madam, if you want it, of course not."

"Great. See, no problem."

And then the waiters directed me to my place at the far end of the table.

The table was a thick slab of diamond, the faceted edges collecting and refracting rainbows of color. The top was as smooth and slippery as a sheet of ice.

Concealed inside were small computer screens so that any of the diners who wished could call up graphics or data as needed during a conversation. The table was both art and engineering, practical and beautiful at the same time.

Carlos Fernando sat at the end of the table. He seemed awkward and out of place in a chair slightly too large for him. Leah sat at his right, and an older woman—perhaps his mother?—on his left. He was bouncing around in his chair, alternating between playing with the computer system in his table and sneaking glances over at Leah when he thought she wasn't paying attention to him. If she looked in his direction, he would go still for a moment, and then his eyes would quickly dart away and he went back to staring at the graphics screen in front of him and fidgeting.

The server brought a silver tray to Carlos Fernando. On it was something the size of a fist, hidden under a canopy of red silk. Carlos Fernando looked up, accepted it with a nod, and removed the cloth. There was a moment of silence as people looked over, curious. I strained to see it.

It was a sparkling egg.

The egg was cunningly wrought of diamond fibers of many colors, braided into intricate lacework resembling entwined Celtic knots. The twelve-year-old satrap of Venus picked it up and ran one finger over it, delicately, barely brushing the surface, feeling the corrugations and relief of the surface.

He held it for a moment, as if not quite sure what he should do with it, and then his hand darted over and put the egg on the plate in front of Leah. She looked up, puzzled.

"This is for you," he said.

The faintest hint of surprise passed through the other diners, almost subvocal, too soft to be heard.

A moment later the servers set an egg in front of each of us. Our eggs, although decorated with an intricate filligree of finely painted lines of gold and pale verdigris, were ordinary eggs—goose eggs, perhaps.

Carlos Fernando was fidgeting in his chair, half grinning, half biting his lip, looking down, looking around, looking everywhere except at the egg or at Leah.

"What am I to do with this?" Leah asked.

"Why," he said, "perhaps you should open it up and eat it."

Leah picked up the diamond-laced egg and examined it, turned it over and rubbed one finger across the surface. Then, having found what she was looking for, she held it in two fingers and twisted. The diamond eggshell opened, and inside it was a second egg, an ordinary one.

The kid smiled again and looked down at the egg in front of him. He picked up his spoon and cracked the shell, then spooned out the interior.

At this signal, the others cracked their own eggs and began to eat. After a moment, Leah laid the decorative shell to one side and did the same. I watched her for a moment, and then cracked my own egg.

It was, of course, excellent.

Later, when I was back with the Singh family, I was still puzzled. There had been some secret significance there that everybody else had seen, but I had missed. Mr. Singh was sitting with his older wife, Triolet, talking about accounts.

"I must ask a question," I said.

Truman Singh turned to me. "Ask," he said, "and I shall answer."

"Is there any particular significance," I said, "to an egg?"

"An egg?" Singh seemed puzzled. "Much significance, I would say. In the old days, the days of the asteroid miners, an egg was a symbol of luxury. Ducks were brought into the bigger habitats, and their eggs were, for some miners, the only food they would ever eat that was not a form of algae or soybean."

"A symbol of luxury," I said, musing. "I see. But I still don't understand it." I thought for a moment, and then asked, "Is there any significance to a gift of an egg?

"Well, no," he said, slowly, "not exactly. An egg? Nothing, in and of itself."

His wife Triolet, asked, "You are sure it's just an egg? Nothing else?"

"A very elaborate egg."

"Hmmm," she said, with a speculative look in her eye. "Not, maybe, an egg, a book, and a rock?"

That startled me a little. "A book and a rock?" The Bruno book—the very first thing Carlos Fernando had done on meeting Leah was to give her a book. But a rock? I hadn't see anything like that. "Why that?"

"Ah," she said. "I suppose you wouldn't know. I don't believe that our customs here in the sky cities are well known out there in the outer reaches."

Her mention of the outer reaches—Saturn and the Beyond—confused me for a moment, until I realized that, viewed from Venus, perhaps even Earth and the built worlds of the orbital clouds would be considered "outer."

"Here," she continued, "as in most of the ten thousand cities, an egg, a book, and a rock is a special gift. The egg is symbolic of life, you see; a book symbolic of knowledge; and a rock is the basis of all wealth, the minerals from the asteroid belt that built our society and bought our freedom."

"Yes? And all three together?"

"They are the traditional gesture of the beginning of courtship," she said.

"I still don't understand."

"If a young man gives a woman an egg, a book, and a rock," Truman said, "I should say this is his official sign that he is interested in courting her. If she accepts them, then she accepts his courtship."

"What? That's it, just like that, they're married?"

"No, no, no," he said. "It only means that she accepts the courtship—that she takes him seriously and, when it comes, she will listen to his proposal. Often a woman may have rocks and eggs from many young men. She doesn't have to accept, only take him seriously."

"Oh," I said.

But it still made no sense. How old was Carlos Fernando, twenty Venus years? What was that, twelve Earth years or so? He was far too young to be proposing.

"No one can terraform Venus," Carlos Fernando said.

Carlos Fernando had been uninterested in having me join in Leah's discussion, but Leah, oblivious to her host's displeasure (or perhaps simply not caring), had insisted that if he wanted to talk about terraforming, I should be there.

It was one room of Carlos Fernando's extensive palaces, a rounded room, an enormous cavernous space that had numerous alcoves. I'd found them sitting in one of the alcoves, an indentation that was cozy but still open. The ubiquitous female guards were still there, but they were at the distant ends of the room, within command if Carlos Fernando chose to shout, but far enough to give them the illusion of privacy.

The furniture they were sitting on was odd. The chairs seemed sculpted of sapphire smoke, yet were solid to the touch. I picked one up and discovered that it weighed almost nothing at all. "Diamond aerogel," Carlos Fernando said. "Do you like it?"

"It's amazing," I said. I had never before seen so much made out of diamond. And yet it made sense here, I thought; with carbon dioxide an inexhaustible resource surrounding the floating cities, it was logical that the floating cities would make as much as they could out of carbon. But still, I didn't know you could make an aerogel of diamond. "How do you make it?"

"A new process we've developed," Carlos Fernando said. "You don't mind if I don't go into the details. It's actually an adaptation of an old idea, something that was invented back on Earth decades ago, called a molecular still."

When Carlos Fernando mentioned the molecular still, I thought I saw a sharp flicker of attention from Leah. This was a subject she knew something about, I thought. But instead of following up, she went back to his earlier comment on terraforming.

"You keep asking questions about the ecology of Mars," she said. "Why so many detailed questions about Martian ecopoiesis? You say you're not interested in terraforming, but are you really? You aren't thinking of the old idea of using photosynthetic algae in the atmosphere to reduce the carbon dioxide, are you? Surely you know that that can't work."

"Of course." Carlos Fernando waved the question away. "Theoretical," he said. "Nobody could terraform Venus, I know, I know."

His pronouncement would have been more dignified if his voice had finished changing, but as it was, it wavered between squeaking an octave up and then going back down again, ruining the effect. "We simply have too much atmosphere," he said. "Down at the surface, the pressure is over ninety bars—even if the carbon dioxide of the atmosphere could be converted to oxygen, the surface atmosphere would still be seventy times higher than the Earth's atmospheric pressure."

"I realize that," Leah said. "We're not actually ignorant, you know. So high a pressure of oxygen would be deadly—you'd burst into flames."

"And the leftover carbon," he said, smiling. "Hundreds of tons per square meter."

"So what are you thinking?" she asked.

But in response, he only smiled. "Okay, I can't terraform Venus," he said. "So tell me more about Mars."

I could see that there was something that he was keeping back. Carlos Fernando had some idea that he wasn't telling.

But Leah did not press him, and instead took the invitation to tell him about her studies of the ecology on Mars, as it had been transformed long ago by the vanished engineers of the long-gone Freehold Toynbee colony. The Toynbee's engineers had designed life to thicken the atmosphere of Mars, to increase the greenhouse effect, to melt the frozen oceans of Mars.

"But it's not working," Leah concluded. "The anaerobic life is being outcompeted by the photosynthetic oxygen-producers. It's pulling too much carbon dioxide out of the atmosphere."

"But what about the Gaia effect? Doesn't it compensate?"

"No," Leah said. "I found no trace of a Lovelock self-aware planet. Either that's a myth, or else the ecology on Mars is just too young to stabilize."

"Of course on Venus, we would have no problem with photosynthesis removing carbon dioxide."

"I thought you weren't interested in terraforming Venus," I said.

Carlos Fernando waved my objection away. "A hypothetical case, of course," he said. "A thought exercise." He turned to Leah. "Tomorrow," he said, "would you like to go kayaking?"

"Sure," she said.

Kayaking, on Venus, did not involve water.

Carlos Fernando instructed Leah, and Epiphany helped me.

The "kayak" was a ten-meter long gas envelope, a transparent cylinder of plastic curved into an ogive at both ends, with a tiny bubble at the bottom where the kayaker sat. One end of the kayak held a huge, gossamer-bladed propeller that turned lazily as the kayaker pedaled, while the kayaker rowed with flimsy wings, transparent and iridescent like the wings of a dragonfly.

The wings, I discovered, had complicated linkages; each one could be pulled, twisted, and lifted, allowing each wing to separately beat, rotate, and camber.

"Keep up a steady motion with the propeller," Epiphany told me. "You'll lose all your maneuverability if you let yourself float to a stop. You can scull with the wings to put on a burst of speed if you need to. Once you're comfortable, use the wings to rise up or swoop down, and to maneuver. You'll have fun."

We were in a launching bay, a balcony protruding from the side of the city. Four of the human-powered dirigibles that they called kayaks were docked against the blister, the bulge of the cockpits neatly inserted into docking rings so that the pilots could enter the dirigible without exposure to the outside atmosphere. Looking out across the cloudscape, I could see dozens of kayaks dancing around the city like transparent squid with stubby wings, playing tag with each other and racing across the sky. So small and transparent compared to the magnificent clouds, they had been invisible until I'd known how to look.

"What about altitude?" I asked.

"You're about neutrally buoyant," she said. "As long as you have airspeed, you can use the wings to make fine adjustments up or down."

"What happens if I get too low?"

"You can't get too low. The envelope has a reservoir of methanol; as you get lower, the temperature rises and your reservoir releases vapor, so the envelope inflates. If you gain too much altitude, vapor condenses out. So you'll find you're regulated to stay pretty close to the altitude you're set for, which right now is," she checked a meter, "fifty-two kilometers above local ground level. We're blowing west at a hundred meters per second, so local ground level will change as the terrain below varies; check your meters for altimetry."

Looking downward, nothing was visible at all, only clouds, and below the clouds, an infinity of haze. It felt odd to think of the surface, over fifty kilometers straight down, and even odder to think that the city we were inside was speeding across that invisible landscape at hundreds of kilometers an hour. There was only the laziest feeling of motion, as the city drifted slowly through the ever-changing canyons of clouds.

"Watch out for wind shear," she said. "It can take you out of sight of the city pretty quickly, if you let it. Ride the conveyor back if you get tired."

"The conveyor?"

"Horizontal-axis vortices. They roll from west to east, and east to west. Choose the right altitude, and they'll take you wherever you want to go."

Now that she'd told me, I could see the kayakers surfing the wind-shear, rising upward and skimming across the sky on invisible wheels of air.

"Have fun," she said. She helped me into the gondola, tightened my straps, looked at the gas pressure meter, checked the purge valve on the emergency oxygen supply, and verified that the radio, backup radio, and emergency locator beacons worked.

Across the kayak launch bay, Leah and Carlos Fernando had already pushed off. Carlos was sculling his wings alternatingly with a practiced swishing motion, building up a pendulum-like oscillation from side to side. Even as I watched, his little craft rolled over until for a moment it hesitated, inverted, and then rolled completely around.

"Showing off," Epiphany said, disdainfully. "You're not supposed to do that. Not that anybody would dare correct him."

She turned back to me. "Ready?" she asked.

"Ready as I'm going to be," I said. I'd been given a complete safety briefing that explained the backup systems and the backups to the backups, but still, floating in the sky above a fifty-two kilometer drop into the landscape of hell seemed an odd diversion.

"Go!" she said. She checked the seal on the cockpit, and then with one hand she released the docking clamp.

Freed from its mooring, the kayak sprang upward into the sky. As I'd been instructed, I banked the kayak away from the city. The roll made me feel suddenly giddy. The kayak skittered, sliding around until it was moving sideways to the air, the nose dipping down so that I was hanging against my straps. Coordinate the turn, I thought, but every slight motion I made with the wings seemed amplified drunkenly, and the kayak wove around erratically.

The radio blinked at me, and Epiphany's voice said, "You're doing great. Give it some airspeed."

I wasn't doing great; I was staring straight down at lemon-tinted haze and spinning slowly around like a falling leaf. Airspeed? I realize that I had entirely forgotten to pedal. I pedaled now, and the nose lifted. The sideways spin damped out, and as I straightened out, the wings bit into the air. "Great," Epiphany's voice told me. "Keep it steady."

The gas envelope seemed too fragile to hold me, but I was flying now, suspended below a golden sky. It was far too complicated, but I realized that as long as I kept the nose level, I could keep it under control. I was still oscillating slightly—it was difficult to avoid overcontrolling—but on the average, I was keeping the nose pointed where I aimed it.

Where were Leah and Carlos Fernando?

I looked around. Each of the kayaks had different markings—mine was marked with gray stripes like a tabby cat—and I tried to spot theirs.

A gaggle of kayaks was flying together, rounding the pylon of the city. As they moved around the pylon they all turned at once, flashing in the sunlight like a school of fish suddenly startled.

Suddenly I spotted them, not far above me, close to the looming wall of the city; the royal purple envelope of Carlos Fernando's kayak and the blue and yellow stripes of Leah's. Leah was circling in a steady climb, and Carlos Fernando was darting around her, now coming in fast and bumping envelopes, now darting away and pulling up, hovering for a moment with his nose pointed at the sky, then skewing around and sliding back downward.

Their motions looked like the courtship dance of birds.

The purple kayak banked around and swooped out and away from the city; and an instant later, Leah's blue and yellow kayak banked and followed. They both soared upward, catching a current of air invisible to me. I could see a few of the other fliers surfing on the same updraft. I yawed my nose around to follow them, but made no progress; I was too inexperienced with the kayak to be able to guess the air currents, and the wind differential was blowing me around the city in exactly the opposite of the direction I wanted to go. I pulled out and away from the city, seeking a different wind, and for an instant I caught a glimpse of something in the clouds below me, dark and fast moving.

Then I caught the updraft. I could feel it, the wings caught the air and it felt like an invisible giant's hand picking me up and carrying me–

Then there was a sudden noise, a stuttering and ripping, followed by a sound like a snare drum. My left wing and propeller ripped away, the fragments spraying into the sky. My little craft banked hard to the left. My radio came to life, but I couldn't hear anything as the cabin disintegrated around me. I was falling.

Falling.

For a moment I felt like I was back in zero-gee. I clutched uselessly to the remains of the control surfaces, connected by loose cords to fluttering pieces of debris. Pieces of my canopy floated away and were caught by the wind and spun upward and out of sight. The atmosphere rushed in, and my eyes started to burn. I made the mistake of taking a breath, and the effect was like getting kicked in the head. Flickering purple dots, the colors of a bruise, closed in from all directions. My vision narrowed to a single bright tunnel. The air was liquid fire in my lungs. I reached around, desperately, trying to remember the emergency instructions before I blacked out, and my hands found the emergency air-mask between my legs. I was still strapped into my seat, although the seat was no longer attached to a vehicle, and I slapped the breathing mask against my face and sucked hard to start the airflow from the emergency oxygen. I was lucky; the oxygen cylinder was still attached to the bottom of the seat, as the seat, with me in it, tumbled through the sky. Through blurred eyes, I could see the city spinning above me. I tried to think of what the emergency procedure could be and what I should do next, but I could only think of what had gone wrong. What had I done? For the life of me I couldn't think of anything that I could have done that would have ripped the craft apart.

The city dwindled to the size of an acorn, and then I fell into the cloud layer and everything disappeared into a pearly white haze. My skin began to itch all over. I squeezed my eyes shut against the acid fog. The temperature was rising. How long would it take to fall fifty kilometers to the surface?

Something enormous and metallic swooped down from above me, and I blacked out.

Minutes or hours or days later I awoke in a dimly-lit cubicle. I was lying on the ground, and two men wearing masks were spraying me with jets of a foaming white liquid that looked like milk but tasted bitter. My flight suit was in shreds around me.

I sat up, and began to cough uncontrollably. My arms and my face itched like blazes, but when I started to scratch, one of the men reached out and slapped my hands away.

"Don't scratch."

I turned to look at him, and the one behind me grabbed me by the hair and smeared a handful of goo into my face, rubbing it hard into my eyes.

Then he picked up a patch of cloth and tossed it to me. "Rub this where it itches. It should help."

I was still blinking, my face dripping, my vision fuzzy. The patch of cloth was wet with some gelatinous slime. I grabbed it from him, and dabbed it on my arms and then rubbed it in. It did help, some.

"Thanks," I said. "What the hell—"

The two men in face masks looked at each other. "Acid burn," the taller man said. "You're not too bad. A minute or two of exposure won't leave scars."

"What?"

"Acid. You were exposed to the clouds."

"Right."

Now that I wasn't quite so distracted, I looked around. I was in the cargo hold of some sort of aircraft. There were two small round portholes on either side. Although nothing was visible through them but a blank white, I could feel that the vehicle was in motion. I looked at the two men. They were both rough characters. Unlike the brightly colored spiders-silk gowns of the citizens of Hypatia, they were dressed in clothes that were functional but not fancy, jumpsuits of a dark gray color with no visible insignia. Both of them were fit and well-muscled. I couldn't see their faces, since they were wearing breathing masks and lightweight helmets, but under their masks I could see that they both wore short beards, another fashion that had been missing among the citizens of Hypatia. Their eyes were covered with amber-tinted goggles, made in a crazy style that cupped each eye with a piece that was rounded like half an eggshell, apparently stuck to their faces by some invisible glue. It gave them a strange, bug-eyed look. They looked at me, but behind their face masks and google-eyes I was completely unable to read their expressions.

"Thanks," I said. "So, who are you? Some sort of emergency rescue force?"

"I think you know who we are," the taller one said. "The question is, who the hell are you?"

I stood up and reached out a hand, thinking to introduce myself, but both of the men took a step back. Without seeming to move his hand, the taller one now had a gun, a tiny omniblaster of some kind. Suddenly a lot of things were clear.

"You're pirates," I said.

"We're the Venus underground," he said. "We don't like the word pirates very much. Now, if you don't mind, I have a question, and I really would like an answer. Who the hell are you?"

So I told him.

The first man started to take off his helmet, but the taller pirate stopped him. "We'll keep the masks on, for now. Until we decide he's safe." The taller pirate said he was named Esteban Jaramillo; the shorter one Esteban Francisco. That was too many Estebans, I thought, and decided to tag the one Jaramillo and the other Francisco.

I discovered from them that not everybody in the floating cities thought of Venus as a paradise. Some of the independent cities considered the clan of Nordwald-Gruenbaum to be well on its way to becoming a dictatorship. "They own half of Venus outright, but that's not good enough for them, no, oh no," Jaramillo told me. "They're stinking rich, but not stinking rich enough, and the very idea that there are free cities floating in the sky, cities that don't swear fealty to them and pay their goddamned taxes, that pisses them off. They'll do anything that they can to crush us. Us? We're just fighting back."

I would have been more inclined to see his point if I didn't have the uncomfortable feeling that I'd just been abducted. It had been a tremendous stroke of luck for me that their ship had been there to catch me when my kayak broke apart and fell. I didn't much believe in luck. And they didn't bother to answer when I asked about being returned to Hypatia. It was pretty clear that the direction we were headed was not back toward the city.

I had given them my word that I wouldn't fight, or try to escape—where would I escape to?—and they accepted it. Once they realized that I wasn't who they had expected to capture, they pressed me for news of the outside. "We don't hear a lot of outside news."

There were three of them in the small craft, the two Estebans, and the pilot, who was never introduced. He did not bother to turn around to greet me, and all I ever saw of him was the back of his helmet. The craft itself they called a Manta; an odd thing that was partly an airplane, partly a dirigible, and partly a submarine. Once I'd given my word that I wouldn't escape, I was allowed to look out, but there was nothing to see but a luminous golden haze.

"We keep the manta flying under the cloud decks," Jaramillo said. "Keeps us invisible."

"Invisible from whom?" I asked, but neither one of them bothered to answer. It was a dumb question anyway; I could very well guess who they wanted to keep out of sight of. "What about radar?" I said.

Esteban looked at Esteban, and then at me. "We have means to deal with radar," he said. "Just leave it at that and stop it with the questions you should know enough not to ask."

They seemed to be going somewhere, and eventually the manta exited the cloudbank into the clear air above. I pressed toward the porthole, trying to see out. The cloudscapes of Venus were still fascinating to me. We were skimming the surface of the cloud deck—ready to duck under if there were any sign of watchers, I surmised. From the cloudscape it was impossible to tell how far we'd come, whether it was just a few leagues, or halfway around the planet. None of the floating cities were visible, but in the distance I spotted the fat torpedo shape of a dirigible. The pilot saw it as well, for we banked toward it and sailed slowly up, slowing down as we approached, until it disappeared over our heads, and then the hull resonated with a sudden impact, and then a ratcheting clang.

"Soft dock," Jaramillo commented, and then a moment later another clang, and the nose of the craft was suddenly jerked up. "Hard dock," he said. The two Estebans seemed to relax a little, and a whine and a rumble filled the little cabin. We were being winched up into the dirigible.

After ten minutes or so, we came to rest in a vast interior space. The manta had been taken inside the envelope of the gas chamber, I realized. Half a dozen people met us.

"Sorry," Jaramillo said, "but I'm afraid we're going to have to blind you. Nothing personal."

"Blind?" I said, but actually, that was good news. If they'd had no intention to release me, they wouldn't care what I saw.

Jaramillo held my head steady while Francisco placed a set of the google-eyed glasses over my eyes. They were surprisingly comfortable. Whatever held them in place, they were so light that I could scarcely feel that they were there. The amber tint was barely noticeable. After checking that they fit, Francisco tapped the side of the goggles with his fingertip, once, twice, three times, four times. Each time he touched the goggles, the world grew darker, and with a fifth tap, all I could see was inky black. Why would sunglasses have a setting for complete darkness, I thought? And then I answered my own question: the last setting must be for e-beam welding. Pretty convenient, I thought. I wondered if I dared to ask them if I could keep the set of goggles when they were done.

"I am sure you won't be so foolish as to adjust the transparency," one of the Estebans said.

I was guided out the manta's hatch and across the hanger, and then to a seat.

"This the prisoner?" a voice asked.

"Yeah," Jaramillo said. "But the wrong one. No way to tell, but we guessed wrong, got the wrong flyer."

"Shit. So who is he?"

"Technician," Jaramillo said. "From the up and out."

"Really? So does he know anything about the Nordwald-Gruenbaum plan?"

I spread my hands out flat, trying to look harmless. "Look, I only met the kid twice, or I guess three times, if you—"

That caused some consternation; I could hear sudden buzz of voices, in a language I didn't recognize. I wasn't sure how many of them there were, but it seemed like at least half a dozen. I desperately wished I could see them, but that would very likely be a fatal move. After a moment, Jaramillo said, his voice now flat and expressionless, "You know the heir of Nordwald-Gruenbaum? You met Carlos Fernando in person?"

"I met him. I don't know him. Not really."

"Who did you say you were again?"

I went through my story, this time starting at the very beginning, explaining how we had been studying the ecology of Mars, how we had been summoned to Venus to meet the mysterious Carlos Fernando. From time to time I was interrupted to answer questions—what was my relationship with Leah Hamakawa? (I wished I knew). Were we married? Engaged? (No. No.). What was Carlos Fernando's relationship with Dr. Hamakawa? (I wished I knew.) Had Carlos Fernando ever mentioned his feelings about the independent cities? (No.) His plans? (No.) Why was Carlos Fernando interested in terraforming (I don't know.) What was Carlos Fernando planning? (I don't know.) Why did Carlos Fernando bring Hamakawa to Venus? (I wished I knew.) What was he planning? What was he planning? (I don't know. I don't know.)

The more I talked, the more sketchy it seemed, even to me.

There was silence when I had finished talking. Then, the first voice said, take him back to the manta.

I was led back inside and put into a tiny space, and a door clanged shut behind me. After a while, when nobody answered my call, I reached up to the goggles. They popped free with no more than a light touch, and, looking at them, I was still unable to see how they attached. I was in a storage hold of some sort. The door was locked.

I contemplated my situation, but I couldn't see that I knew any more now than I had before, except that I now knew that not all of the Venus cities were content with the status quo, and some of them were willing to go to some lengths to change it. They had deliberately shot me down, apparently thinking that I was Leah—or possibly even hoping for Carlos Fernando? It was hard to think that he would have been out of the protection of his bodyguards. Most likely, I decided, the bodyguards had been there, never letting him out of sight, ready to swoop in if needed, but while Carlos Fernando and Leah had soared up and around the city, I had left the sphere covered by the guards, and that was the opportunity the pirates in the manta had taken. They had seen the air kayak flying alone and shot it out of the sky, betting my life on their skill, that they could swoop in and snatch the falling pilot out of mid-air.

They could have killed me, I realized.

And all because they thought I knew something—or rather, that Leah Hamakawa knew something—about Carlos Fernando's mysterious plan.

What plan? He was a twelve-year-old kid, not even a teenager, barely more than an overgrown child! What kind of plan could a kid have?

I examined the chamber I was in, this time looking more seriously at how it was constructed. All the joints were welded, with no obvious gaps, but the metal was light, probably an aluminum-lithium alloy. Possibly malleable, if I had the time, if I could find a place to pry at, if I could find something to pry with.

If I did manage to escape, would I be able to pilot the manta out of its hanger in the dirigible? Maybe. I had no experience with lighter than air vehicles, though, and it would be a bad time to learn, especially if they decided that they wanted to shoot at me. And then I would be—where? A thousand miles from anywhere. Fifty million miles from anywhere I knew.

I was still mulling this over when Esteban and Esteban returned.

"Strap in," Esteban Jaramillo told me. "Looks like we're taking you home."

The trip back was more complicated than the trip out. It involved two or more transfers from vehicle to vehicle, during some of which I was again "requested" to wear the opaque goggles.

We were alone in the embarking station of some sort of public transportation. For a moment, the two Estebans had allowed me to leave the goggles transparent. Wherever we were, it was unadorned, drab compared to the florid excess of Hypatia, where even the bus stations—did they have bus stations?—would have been covered with flourishes and artwork.

Jaramillo turned to me and, for the first time, pulled off his goggles so he could look me directly in the eye. His eyes were dark, almost black, and very serious.

"Look," he said, "I know you don't have any reason to like us. We've got our reasons, you have to believe that. We're desperate. We know that his father had some secret projects going. We don't know what they were, but we know he didn't have any use for the free cities. We think the young Gruenwald has something planned. If you can get through to Carlos Fernando, we want to talk to him."

"If you get him," Esteban Francisco said. "Push him out a window. We'll catch him. Easy." He was grinning with a broad smile, showing all his teeth, as if to say he wasn't serious, but I wasn't at all sure he was joking.

"We don't want to kill him. We just want to talk," Esteban Jaramillo said. "Call us. Please. Call us."

And with that, he reached up and put his goggles back on. Then Francisco reached over and tapped my goggles into opacity, and everything was dark, and, with one on either side of me, we boarded the transport—bus? zeppelin? rocket?

Finally I was led into a chamber and was told to wait for two full minutes before removing the goggles, and after that I was free to do as I liked.

It was only after the footsteps had disappeared that it occurred to me to wonder how I was supposed to contact them, if I did have a reason to. It was too late to ask, though; I was alone, or seemed to be alone.

Was I being watched to see if I would follow orders, I wondered? Two full minutes. I counted, trying not to rush the count. When I got to a hundred and twenty, I took a deep breath, and finger-tapped the goggles to transparency.

When my eyes focused, I saw I was in a large disembarking lounge with genetically-engineered pink grass and sculptures of iron and of jade. I recognized it. It was the very same lounge at which we had arrived at Venus three days ago.—was it only three? Or had another day gone by?

I was back in Hypatia city.

Once again I was surrounded and questioned. As with the rest of Carlos Fernando's domain, the questioning room was lushly decorated with silk-covered chairs and elegant teak carvings, but it was clearly a holding chamber.

The questioning was by four women, Carlos Fernando's guards, and I had the feeling that they would not hesitate to tear me apart if they thought I was being less than candid with them. I told them what had happened, and at every step they asked questions, making suggestions as to what I could have done differently. Why had I taken my kayak so far away from any of the other fliers and out away from the city? Why had I allowed myself to be captured, without fighting? Why didn't I demand to be returned and refuse to answer any questions? Why could I describe none of the rebels I'd met, except for two men who had—as far as they could tell from my descriptions—no distinctive features?

At the end of their questioning, when I asked to see Carlos Fernando, they told me that this would not be possible.

"You think I allowed myself to be shot down deliberately?" I said, addressing myself to the chief among the guards, a lean woman in scarlet silk.

"We don't know what to think, Mr. Tinkerman," she said. "We don't like to take chances."

"What now, then?"

"We can arrange transport to the built worlds," she said. "Or even to the Earth."

"I don't plan to leave without Doctor Hamakawa," I said.

She shrugged. "At the moment, that's still your option, yes," she said. "At the moment."

"How can I get in contact with Doctor Hamakawa?"

She shrugged. "If Doctor Hamakawa wishes, I'm sure she will be able to contact you."

"And if I want to speak to her?"

She shrugged. "You're free to go now. If we need to talk to you, we can find you."

I had been wearing one of gray jumpsuits of the pirates when I'd been returned to Hypatia; the guard women had taken that away. Now they gave me a suit of spider-silk in a lavender brighter than the garb an expensive courtesan would wear in the built worlds surrounding Earth, more of an evening gown than a suit. It was nevertheless subdued compared to the day-to-day attire of Hypatia citizens, and I attracted no attention. I discovered that the google-eyed sunglasses had been neatly placed in a pocket at the knees of the garment. Apparently people on Venus keep their sunglasses at their knees. Convenient when you're sitting, I supposed. They hadn't been recognized as a parting gift from the pirates, or, more likely, had been considered so trivial as to not be worth confiscating. I was unreasonably pleased; I liked those glasses.

I found the Singh habitat with no difficulty, and when I arrived, Epiphany and Truman Singh were there to welcome me and to give me the news.

My kidnapping was already old news. More recent news was being discussed everywhere.

Carlos Fernando Delacroix Ortega de la Jolla y Nordwald-Gruenbaum had given a visitor from the outer solar system, Doctor Leah Hamakawa—a person who (they had heard) had actually been born on Earth—a rock.

And she had not handed it back to him.

My head was swimming.

"You're saying that Carlos Fernando is proposing marriage? To Leah? That doesn't make any sense. He's a kid, for Jove's sake. He's not old enough."

Truman and Epiphany Singh looked at one another and smiled. "How old were you when we got married?" Truman asked her. "Twenty?"

"I was almost twenty-one before you accepted my book and my rock," she said.

"So, in Earth years, what's that?" he said. "Thirteen?"

"A little over twelve," she said. "About time I was married up, I'd say."

"Wait," I said. "You said you were twelve years old when you got married?"

"Earth years," she said. "Yes, that's about right."

"You married at twelve? And you had—" I suddenly didn't want to ask, and said, "Do all women on Venus marry so young?"

"There are a lot of independent cities," Truman said. "Some of them must have different customs, I suppose. But it's the custom more or less everywhere I know."

"But that's—" I started to say, but couldn't think of how to finish. Sick? Perverted? But then, there were once a lot of cultures on Earth that had child marriages.

"We know the outer reaches have different customs," Epiphany said. "Other regions do things differently. The way we do it works for us."

"A man typically marries up at age twenty-one or so," Truman explained. "Say, twelve, thirteen years old, in Earth years. Maybe eleven. His wife will be about fifty or sixty—she'll be his instructor, then, as he grows up. What's that in Earth years—thirty? I know that in old Earth custom, both sides of a marriage are supposed to be the same age, but that's completely silly, is it not? Who's going to be the teacher, I should say?

"And then, when he grows up, by the time he reaches sixty or so he'll marry down, find a girl who's about twenty or twenty-one, and he'll serve as a teacher to her, I should say. And, in time, she'll marry down when she's sixty, and so on."

It seemed like a form of ritualized child abuse to me, but I thought it would be better not to say that aloud. Or, I thought, maybe I was reading too much into what he was saying. It was something like the medieval apprentice system. When he said teaching, maybe I was jumping to conclusions to think that he was talking about sex. Maybe they held off on the sex until the child grew up some. I thought I might be happier not knowing.

"A marriage is braided like a rope," Epiphany said. "Each element holds the next."

I looked from Truman to Epiphany and back. "You, too?" I asked Truman. "You were married when you were twelve?"

"In Earth years, I was thirteen, when I married up Triolet," he said. "Old. Best thing that ever happened to me. God, I needed somebody like her to straighten me out back then. And I needed somebody to teach me about sex, I should say, although I didn't know it back then."

"And Triolet—"

"Oh, yes, and her husband before her, and before that. Our marriage goes back a hundred and ninety years, to when Raj Singh founded our family; we're a long braid, I should say."

I could picture it now. Every male in the braid would have two wives, one twenty years older; one twenty years younger. And every female would have an older and a younger husband. The whole assembly would indeed be something you could think of as a braid, alternating down generations. The interpersonal dynamics must be terribly complicated. And then I suddenly remembered why we were having this discussion. "My god," I said. "You're serious about this. So you're saying that Carlos Fernando isn't just playing a game. He actually plans to marry Leah."

"Of course," Epiphany said. "It's a surprise, but then, I'm not at all surprised. It's obviously what his Excellency was planning right from the beginning. He's a devious one, he is."

"He wants to have sex with her."

She looked surprised. "Well, yes, of course. Wouldn't you? If you were twenty—I mean, twelve years old? Sure you're interested in sex. Weren't you? It's about time his Excellency had a teacher." She paused a moment. "I wonder if she's any good? Earth people—she probably never had a good teacher of her own."

That was a subject I didn't want to pick up on. Our little fling on Mars seemed a long way away, and my whole body ached just thinking of it.

"Sex, it's all that young kids think of," Truman cut in. "Sure. But for all that, I should say that sex is the least important part of a braid. A braid is a business, Mr. Tinkerman, you should know that. His Excellency Carlos Fernando is required to marry up into a good braid. The tradition, and the explicit terms of the inheritance, are both very clear. There are only about five braids on Venus that meet the standards of the trust, and he's too closely related to half of them to be able to marry in. Everybody has been assuming he would marry the wife of the Telios Delacroix braid; she's old enough to marry down now, and she's not related to him closely enough to matter. His proposition to Doctor Hamakawa—yes, that has everybody talking."

I was willing to grasp at any chance. "You mean, his marriage needs to be approved? He can't just marry anybody he likes?"

Truman Singh shook his head. "Of course he can't! I just told you. This is business as well as propagating the genes for the next thousand years. Most certainly he can't marry just anybody."

"But I think he just outmaneuvered them all," Epiphany added. "They thought they had him boxed in, didn't they? But they never thought that he'd go find an outworlder."

"They?" I said. "Who's they?"

"They never thought to guard against that," Epiphany continued.

"But he can't marry her, right?" I said. "For sure, she's not of the right family. She's not of any family. She's an orphan, she told me that. The institute is her only family."

Truman shook his head. "I think Epiphany's right," he said. "He just may have outfoxed them, I should say. If she's not of a family, doesn't have the dozens or hundreds of braided connections that everybody here must have, that means they can't find anything against her."

"Her scientific credentials—I bet they won't be able to find a flaw there." Epiphany said. "And, an orphan? That's brilliant. Just brilliant. No family ties at all. I bet he knew that. He worked hard to find just the right candidate, you can bet." She shook her head, smiling. "And we all thought he'd be another layabout, like his father."

"This is awful," I said. "I've got to do something."

"You? You're far too old for Dr. Hayakawa." Epiphany looked at me appraisingly. "A good looking man, though—if I were ten, fifteen years younger, I'd give you another look. I have cousins with girls the right age. You're not married, you say?"

Outside the Singh quarters in sector Carbon, the sun was breaking the horizon as the city blew into the daylit hemisphere.

I hadn't been sure whether Epiphany's offer to find me a young girl had been genuine, but it was not what I needed, and I'd refused as politely as I could manage.

I had gone outside to think, or as close to "outside" as the floating city allowed, where all the breathable gas was inside the myriad bubbles. But what could I do? If it was a technical problem, I would be able to solve it, but this was a human problem, and that had always been my weakness.

From where I stood, I could walk to the edge of the world, the transparent gas envelope that held the breathable air in, and kept the carbon dioxide of the Venus atmosphere out. The sun was surrounded by a gauzy haze of thin high cloud, and encircled by a luminous golden halo, with mock suns flying in formation to the left and the right. The morning sunlight slanted across the cloudtops. My eyes hurt from the direct sun. I remembered the sun goggles in my knee pocket, and pulled them out. I pressed them onto my eyes, and tapped on the right side until the world was a comfortable dim.

Floating in the air, in capital letters barely darker than the background, were the words LINK: READY.

I turned my head, and the words shifted with my field of view, changing from dark letters to light depending on the background.

A communications link was open? Certainly not a satellite relay; the glasses couldn't have enough power to punch through to orbit. Did it mean the manta was hovering in the clouds below?

"Hello, hello," I said, talking to the air. "Testing. Testing?"

Nothing.

Perhaps it wasn't audio. I tapped the right lens: dimmer, dimmer, dark; then back to full transparency. Maybe the other side? I tried tapping the left eye of the goggle, and a cursor appeared in my field of view.

With a little experimentation, I found that tapping allowed input in the form of Gandy-encoded text. It seemed to be a low bit-rate text only; the link power must be miniscule. But Gandy was a standard encoding, and I tapped out "CQ CQ".

Seek you, seek you.

The LINK: READY message changed to a light green, and in a moment the words changed to HERE.

WHO, I tapped.

MANTA 7, was the reply. NEWS?

CF PROPOSED LH, I tapped. !

KNOWN, came the reply. MORE?

NO

OK. SIGNING OUT.

The LINK: READY message returned.

A com link, if I needed one. But I couldn't see how it helped me any.

I returned to examining the gas envelope. Where I stood was an enormous transparent pane, a square perhaps ten meters on an edge. I was standing near the bottom of the pane, where it abutted to the adjacent sheet with a joint of very thin carbon. I pressed on it, and felt it flex slightly. It couldn't be more than a millimeter thick; it would make sense to make the envelope no heavier than necessary. I tapped it with the heel of my hand, and could feel it vibrate; a resonant frequency of a few Hertz, I estimated. The engineering weak point would be the joint between panels: if the pane flexed enough, it would pop out from its mounting at the join.

Satisfied that I had solved at least one technical conundrum, I began to contemplate what Epiphany had said. Carlos Fernando was to have married the wife of the Telios Delacroix braid. Whoever she was, she might be relieved at discovering Carlos Fernando making other plans; she could well think the arranged marriage as much a trap as he apparently did. But still. Who was she, and what did she think of Carlos Fernando's new plan?

The guards had made it clear that I was not to communicate with Carlos Fernando or Leah, but had no instructions forbidding access to Braid Telios Delacroix.

The household seemed to be a carefully orchestrated chaos of children and adults of all ages, but now that I understood the Venus societal system a little, it made more sense. The wife of Telios Delacroix—once the wife-apparent of his Excellency Carlos Fernando—turned out to be a woman only a few years older than I was, with closely cropped grey hair. I realized I'd seen her before. At the banquet, she had been the woman sitting next to Carlos Fernando. She introduced herself as Miranda Telios Delacroix and introduced me to her up-husband, a stocky man perhaps sixty years old.

"We could use a young husband in this family," he told me. "Getting old, we are, and you can't count on children—they just go off and get married themselves."

There were two girls there, who Miranda Delacroix introduced as their two children. They were quiet, attempting to disappear into the background, smiling brightly but with their heads bowed to the ground, looking up at me through lowered eyelashes when they were brought out to be introduced. After the adults' attention had turned away from them, I noticed both of them surreptitiously studying me. A day ago I wouldn't even have noticed.

"Now, either come and sit nicely and talk, or else go do your chores," Miranda told them. "I'm sure the outworlder is quite bored with your buzzing in and out."

They both giggled and shook their heads and then disappeared into another room, although from time to time one or the other head would silently pop out to look at me, disappearing instantly if I turned my head to look

We sat down at a low table that seemed to be made out of oak. Her husband brought in some coffee and then left us alone. The coffee was made in the Thai style, in a clear cup, in layers with thick sweet milk.

"So you are Doctor Hamakawa's friend," she said. "I've heard a lot about you. Do you mind my asking, what exactly is your relationship with Doctor Hamakawa?"

"I would like to see her," I said.

She frowned. "So?"

"And I can't."

She raised an eyebrow.

"He has these women, these bodyguards—"

Miranda Delacroix laughed. "Ah, I see! Oh, my little Carli is just too precious for words. I can't believe he's jealous. I do think that this time he's really infatuated." She tapped on the tabletop with her fingers for a moment, and I realized that the oak tabletop was another one of the embedded computer systems. "Goodness, Carli is not yet the owner of everything, and I don't see why you shouldn't see whoever you like. I've sent a message to Doctor Hamakawa that you would like to see her."

"Thank you."

She waved her hand.

It occurred to me that Carlos Fernando was about the same age as her daughters, perhaps even a classmate of theirs. She must have known him since he was a baby. It did seem a little unfair to him—if they were married, she would have all the advantage, and for a moment I understood his dilemma. Then something she had said struck me.

"He's not yet owner of everything, you said," I said. "I don't understand your customs, Mrs. Delacroix. Please enlighten me. What do you mean, yet?"

"Well, you know that he doesn't come into his majority until he's married," she said.

The picture was beginning to make sense. Carlos Fernando desperately wanted to control things, I thought. And he needed to be married to do it. "And once he's married?"

"Then he comes into his inheritance, of course," she said. "But since he'll be married, the braid will be in control of the fortune. You wouldn't want a twenty-one-year-old kid in charge of the entire Nordwald-Gruenbaum holdings? That would be ruinous. The first Nordwald knew that. That's why he married his son into the la Jolla braid. That's the way it's always been done."

"I see," I said. If Miranda Delacroix married Carlos Fernando, she—not he—would control the Nordwald-Gruenbaum fortune. She had the years of experience, she knew the politics, how the system worked. He would be the child in the relationship. He would always be the child in the relationship.

Miranda Delacroix had every reason to want to make sure that Leah Hamakawa didn't marry Carlos Fernando. She was my natural ally.

And also, she—and her husband—had every reason to want to kill Leah Hamakawa.

Suddenly the guards that followed Carlos Fernando seemed somewhat less of an affectation. Just how good were the bodyguards? And then I had another thought. Had she, or her husband, hired the pirates to shoot down my kayak? The pirates clearly had been after Leah, not me. They had known that Leah was flying a kayak; somebody must have been feeding them information. If it hadn't been her, then who?

I looked at her with new suspicions. She was looking back at me with a steady gaze. "Of course, if your Doctor Leah Hamakawa intends to accept the proposal, the two of them will be starting a new braid. She would nominally be the senior, of course, but I wonder—"

"But would she be allowed to?" I interrupted. "If she decided to marry Carlos Fernando, wouldn't somebody stop her?"

She laughed. "No, I'm afraid that little Carli made his plan well. He's the child of a Gruenbaum, all right. There's no legal grounds for the families to object; she may be an outworlder, but he's made an end run around all the possible objections."

"And you?"

"Do you think I have choices? If he decides to ask me for advice, I'll tell him it's not a good idea. But I'm halfway tempted to just see what he does."

And give up her chance to be the richest woman in the known universe? I had my doubts.

"Do you think you can talk her out of it?" she said. "Do you think you have something to offer her? As I understand it, you don't own anything. You're hired help, a gypsy of the solar system. Is there a single thing that Carli is offering her that you can match?"

"Companionship," I said. It sounded feeble, even to me.

"Companionship?" she echoed, sarcastically. "Is that all? I would have thought most outworlder men would have promised love. You are honest, at least, I'll give you that,"

"Yes, love," I said, miserable. "I'd offer her love."

"Love," she said. "Well, how about that. Yes, that's what outworlders marry for; I've read about it. You don't seem to know, do you? This isn't about love. It's not even about sex, although there will be plenty of that, I can assure you, more than enough to turn my little Carlos inside out and make him think he's learning something about love.

"This is about business, Mr. Tinkerman. You don't seem to have noticed that. Not love, not sex, not family. It's business."

Miranda Telios Delacroix's message had gotten through to Leah, and she called me up to her quarters. The women guards did not seem happy about this, but they had apparently been instructed to obey her direct orders, and two red-clad guardswomen led me to her quarters.

"What happened to you? What happened to your face?" she said, when she saw me.

I reached up and touched my face. It didn't hurt, but the acid burns had left behind red spotches and patches of peeling skin. I filled her in on the wreck of the kayak and the rescue, or kidnapping, by pirates. And then I told her about Carlos. "Take another look at that book he gave you. I don't know where he got it, and I don't want to guess what it cost, but I'll say it's a sure bet it's no facsimile."

"Yes, of course." she said. "He did tell me, eventually."

"Don't you know it's a proposition?"

"Yes; the egg, the book, and the rock," she said. "Very traditional here. I know you like to think I have my head in the air all the time, but I do pay some attention to what's going on around me. Carli is a sweet kid."

"He's serious, Leah. You can't ignore him."

She waved me off. "I can make my own decisions, but thanks for the warnings."

"It's worse than that," I told her. "Have you met Miranda Telios Delacroix?"

"Of course," she said.

"I think she's trying to kill you." I told her about my experience with kayaks, and my suspicion that the pirates had been hired to shoot me down, thinking I was her.

"I believe you may be reading too much into things, Tinkerman," she said. "Carli told me about the pirates. They're a small group, disaffected; they bother shipping and such, from time to time, but he says that they're nothing to worry about. When he gets his inheritance, he says he will take care of them."

"Take care of them? How?"

She shrugged. "He didn't say."

But that was exactly what the pirates—rebels—had told me: that Carlos had a plan, and they didn't know what it was. "So he has some plans he isn't telling," I said.

"He's been asking me about terraforming," Leah said, thinking. "But it doesn't make sense to do that on Venus. I don't understand what he's thinking. He could split the carbon dioxide atmosphere into oxygen and carbon; I know he has the technology to do that."

"He does?"

"Yes, I think you were there when he mentioned it. The molecular still. It's solar-powered micromachines. But what would be the point?"

"So he's serious?"

"Seriously thinking about it, anyway. But it doesn't make any sense. Nearly pure oxygen at the surface, at sixty or seventy bars? That atmosphere would be even more deadly than the carbon dioxide. And it wouldn't even solve the greenhouse effect; with that thick an atmosphere, even oxygen is a greenhouse gas."

"You explained that to him?"

"He already knew it. And the floating cities wouldn't float any more. They rely on the gas inside—breathing air—being lighter than the Venusian air. Turn the Venus carbon dioxide to pure O2, the cities fall out of the sky."

"But?"

"But he didn't seem to care."

"So terraforming would make Venus uninhabitable, and he knows it. So what's he planning?"

She shrugged. "I don't know."

"I do," I said. "And I think we'd better see your friend Carlos Fernando."

Carlos Fernando was in his playroom.

The room was immense. His family's quarters were built on the edge of the upcity, right against the bubble-wall, and one whole side of his playroom looked out across the cloudscape. The room was littered with stuff: sets of interlocking toy blocks with electronic modules inside that could be put together into elaborate buildings, models of spacecraft and various lighter-than-air aircraft, no doubt vehicles used on Venus, a contraption of transparent vessels connected by tubes that seemed to be a half-completed science project, a unicycle that sat in a corner, silently balancing on its gyros. Between the toys were pieces of light, transparent furniture. I picked up a chair, and it was no heavier than a feather, barely there at all. I knew what it was now, diamond fibers that had been engineered into a foamed, fractal structure. Diamond was their chief working material; it was something that they could make directly out of the carbon dioxide atmosphere, with no imported raw materials. They were experts in diamond, and it frightened me.

When the guards brought us to the playroom, Carlos Fernando was at the end of the room farthest from the enormous window, his back to the window and to us. He'd known we were coming, of course, but when the guards announced our arrival he didn't turn around, but called behind him, "It's okay—I'll be with them in a second."

The two guards left us.

He was gyrating and waving his hands in front of a large screen. On the screen, colorful spaceships flew in three-dimensional projection through the complicated maze of a city that had apparently been designed by Escher, with towers connected by bridges and buttresses. The viewpoint swooped around, chasing some of the spaceships, hiding from others. From time to time bursts of red dots shot forward, blowing the ships out of the sky with colorful explosions as Carlos Fernando shouted "Gotcha!" and "In your eye, dog."

He was dancing with his whole body; apparently the game had some kind of full-body input. As far as I could tell, he seemed to have forgotten entirely that we were there.

I looked around.

Sitting on a padded platform no more than two meters from where we had entered, a lion looked back at me with golden eyes. He was bigger than I was. Next to him, with her head resting on her paws, lay a lioness, and she was watching me as well, her eyes half open. Her tail twitched once; twice. The lion's mane was so huge that it must have been shampooed and blow-dried.

He opened his mouth and yawned, then rolled onto his side, still watching me.

"They're harmless," Leah said. "Bad-Boy and Knickers. Pets."

Knickers—the female, I assumed—stretched over and grabbed the male lion by the neck. Then she put one paw on the back of his head and began to groom his fur with her tongue.

I was beginning to get a feel for just how different Carlos Fernando's life was from anything I knew.

On the walls closer to where Carlos Fernando was playing his game were several other screens. The one to my left looked like it had a homework problem partially-worked out. Calculus, I noted. He was doing a chain-rule differentiation and had left it half-completed where he'd gotten stuck, or bored. Next to it was a visualization of the structure of the atmosphere of Venus. Homework? I looked at it more carefully. If it was homework, he was much more interested in atmospheric science than in math; the map was covered with notes and had half a dozen open windows with details. I stepped forward to read it more closely.

The screen went black.

I turned around, and Carlos Fernando was there, a petulant expression on his face. "That's my stuff," he said. His voice squeaked on the word "stuff." "I don't want you looking at my stuff unless I ask you to, okay?"

He turned to Leah, and his expression changed to something I couldn't quite read. He wanted to kick me out of his room, I thought, but didn't want to make Leah angry; he wanted to keep her approval. "What's he doing here?" he asked her.

She looked at me, and raised her eyebrows.

I wish I knew myself, I thought, but I was in it far enough, I had better say something.

I walked over to the enormous window, and looked out across the clouds. I could see another city, blue with distance, a toy balloon against the golden horizon.

"The environment of Venus is unique," I said. "And to think, your ancestor Udo Nordwald put all this together."

"Thanks," he said. "I mean, I guess I mean thanks. I'm glad you like our city."

"All of the cities," I said. "It's a staggering accomplishment. The genius it must have taken to envision it all, to put together the first floating city; to think of this planet as a haven, a place where millions can live. Or billions—the skies are nowhere near full. Someday even trillions, maybe."

"Yeah," he said. "Really something, I guess."

"Spectacular." I turned around and looked him directly in the eye. "So why do you want to destroy it?"

"What?" Leah said.

Carlos Fernando had his mouth open, and started to say something, but then closed his mouth again. He looked down, and then off to his left, and then to the right. He said, "I . . . I . . ." but then broke off.

"I know your plan," I said. "Your micromachines—they'll convert the carbon dioxide to oxygen. And when the atmosphere changes, the cities will be grounded. They won't be lighter than air, won't be able to float any more. You know that, don't you? You want to do it deliberately."

"He can't," Leah said, "it won't work. The carbon would—" and then she broke off. "Diamond," she said. "He's going to turn the excess carbon into diamond."

I reached over and picked up a piece of furniture, one of the foamed-diamond tables. It weighted almost nothing.

"Nanomachinery," I said. "The molecular still you mentioned. You know, somebody once said that the problem with Venus isn't that the surface is too hot. It's just fine up here where the air's as thin as Earth's air. The problem is, the surface is just too darn far below sea level.

"But every ton of atmosphere your molecular machines converts to oxygen, you get a quarter ton of pure carbon. And the atmosphere is a thousand tons per square meter."

I turned to Carlos Fernando, who still hadn't managed to say anything. His silence was as damning as any confession. "Your machines turns that carbon into diamond fibers, and build upward from the surface. You're going to build a new surface, aren't you—a completely artificial surface. A platform up to the sweet spot, fifty kilometers above the old rock surface. And the air there will be breathable."

At last Carlos found his voice. "Yeah," he said. "Dad came up with the machines, but the idea of using them to build a shell around the whole planet—that idea was mine. It's all mine. It's pretty smart, isn't it? Don't you think it's smart?"

"You can't own the sky," I said, "but you can own the land, can't you? You will have built the land. And all the cities are going to crash. There won't be any dissident cities, because there won't be any cities. You'll own it all. Everybody will have to come to you."

"Yeah," Carlos said. He was smiling now, a big goofy grin. "Sweet, isn't it?" He must have seen my expression, because he said, "Hey, come on. It's not like they were contributing. Those dissident cities are full of nothing but malcontents and pirates."

Leah's eyes were wide. He turned to her and said, "Hey, why shouldn't I? Give me one reason. They shouldn't even be here. It was all my ancestor's idea, the floating city, and they shoved in. They stole his idea, so now I'm going to shut them down. It'll be better my way."

He turned back to me. "Okay, look. You figured out my plan. That's fine, that's great, no problem, okay? You're smarter than I thought you were, I admit it. Now, just, I need you to promise not to tell anybody, okay?"

I shook my head.

"Oh, go away," he said. He turned back to Leah. "Doctor Hamakawa," he said. He got down on one knee, and, staring at the ground, said, "I want you to marry me. Please?"

Leah shook her head, but he was staring at the ground, and couldn't see her. "I'm sorry, Carlos," she said. "I'm sorry."

He was just a kid, in a room surrounded by his toys, trying to talk the adults into seeing things the way he wanted to see them. He finally looked up, his eyes filling with tears. "Please," he said. "I want you to. I'll give you anything. I'll give you whatever you want. You can have everything I own, all of it, the whole planet, everything."

"I'm sorry," Leah repeated. "I'm sorry."

He reached out and picked up something off the floor—a model of a spaceship—and looked at it, pretending to be suddenly interested in it. Then he put it carefully down on a table, picked up another one, and stood up, not looking at us. He sniffled, and wiped his eyes with the back of his hand—apparently forgetting he had the ship model in it—trying to do it casually, as if we wouldn't have noticed that he had been crying.

"Ok," he said. "You can't leave, you know. This guy guessed too much. The plan only works if it's secret, so that the malcontents don't know it's coming, don't prepare for it. You have to stay here. I'll keep you here, I'll—I don't know. Something."

"No," I said. "It's dangerous for Leah here. Miranda already tried to hire pirates to shoot her down once, when she was out in the sky kayak. We have to leave."

Carlos looked up at me, and with sudden sarcasm, said, "Miranda? You're joking. That was me who tipped off the pirates. Me. I thought they'd take you away and keep you. I wish they had."

And then he turned back to Leah. "Please? You'll be the richest person on Venus. You'll be the richest person in the solar system. I'll give it all to you. You'll be able to do anything you want.

"I'm sorry," Leah repeated. "It's a great offer. But no."

At the other end of the room, Carlos' bodyguards were quietly entering. He apparently had some way to summon them silently. The room was filling with them, and their guns were drawn, but not yet pointed.

I backed toward the window, and Leah came with me.

The city had rotated a little, and sunlight was now slanting in through the window. I put my sun goggles on.

"Do you trust me?" I said quietly.

"Of course," Leah said. "I always have."

"Come here."

LINK: READY blinked in the corner of my field of view.

I reached up, casually, and tapped on the side of the left lens. CQ MANTA, I tapped. CQ.

I put my other hand behind me and, hoping I could disguise what I was doing as long as I could, I pushed on the pane, feeling it flex out.

HERE, was the reply.

Push. Push. It was a matter of rhythm. When I found the resonant frequency of the pane, it felt right, it built up, like oscillating a rocking chair, like sex.

I reached out my left hand to hold Leah's hand, and pumped harder on the glass with my right. I was putting my weight into it now, and the panel was bowing visibly with my motion. The window was making a noise now, an infrasonic thrum too deep to hear, but you could feel it. On each swing the pane of the window bowed further outward.

"What are you doing?" Carlos shouted. "Are you crazy?"

The bottom bowed out, and the edge of the pane separated from its frame.

There was a smell of acid and sulfur. The bodyguards ran toward us, but—as I'd hoped—they were hesitant to use their guns, worried that the damaged panel might blow completely out.

The window screeched and jerked, but held, fixed in place by the other joints. The way it was stuck in place left a narrow vertical slit between the window and its frame. I pulled Leah close to me, and shoved myself backwards, against the glass, sliding along against the bowed pane, pushing it outward to widen the opening as much as I could.

As I fell, I kissed her lightly on the edge of the neck.

She could have broken my grip, could have torn herself free.

But she didn't.

"Hold your breath and squeeze your eyes shut," I whispered, as we fell through the opening and into the void, and then with my last breath of air, I said, "I love you."

She said nothing in return. She was always practical, and knew enough not to try to talk when her next breath would be acid. "I love you too," I imagined her saying.

With my free hand, I tapped, MANTA NEED PICK-UP. FAST.

And we fell.

"It wasn't about sex at all," I said. "That's what I failed to understand." We were in the manta, covered with slime, but basically unhurt. The pirates had accomplished their miracle, snatched us out of mid air. We had information they needed; and in exchange, they would give us a ride off the planet, back where we belonged, back to the cool and the dark and the emptiness between planets. "It was all about finance. Keeping control of assets."

"Sure it's about sex," Leah said. "Don't fool yourself. We're humans. It's always about sex. Always. You think that's not a temptation? Molding a kid into just exactly what you want? Of course it's sex. Sex and control. Money? That's just the excuse they tell themselves."

"But you weren't tempted," I said.

She looked at me long and hard. "Of course I was." She sighed, and her expression was once again distant, unreadable. "More than you'll ever know."

KAGE BAKER

One of the most prolific new writers to appear in the late nineties, the late Kage Baker made her first sale in 1997, to *Asimov's Science Fiction*, and quickly became one of that magazines most frequent and popular contributors with her sly and compelling stories of the adventures and misadventures of the time-traveling agents of the Company; later in her career, she started another linked sequences of stories there as well, set in as lush and eccentric a high fantasy milieu as any we've ever seen. Her stories also appeared in *Realms of Fantasy, Sci Fiction, Amazing*, and elsewhere. Her first Company novel, *In the Garden of Iden*, was also published in 1997 and immediately became one of the most acclaimed and widely reviewed first novels of the year. More Company novels quickly followed, including *Sky Coyote, Mendoza in Hollywood, The Graveyard Game, The Life of the World to Come, The Machine's Child*, and *The Sons of Heaven*, and her first fantasy novel, *The Anvil of the World*. Her many stories were collected in *Black Projects, White Knights; Mother Aegypt and Other Stories; The Children of the Company; Dark Mondays*; and *Gods and Pawns*. Her most recent books include *Or Else My Lady Keeps the Key*, about some of the real pirates of the Caribbean, fantasy novel *The House of the Stag*, science fiction novel *The Empress of Mars*, YA novel *The Hotel Under the Sand, The Bird of the River*, and the last Company novel, *Not Less Than Gods*. Coming up is *Nell Gwynne's Scarlet Spy*, which will probably be her last book. Baker died, tragically young, in 2010.

In addition to her writing, Baker was an artist, actor, and director at the Living History Center; taught Elizabethan English as a second language; and worked Renaissance fairs—all of which background informs the gentle, charming, but autumnal story that follows, about how life goes on, even after the End of the World.

We used to have to go a lot farther down the coast in those days, before things got easier. People weren't used to us then.

If you think about it, we must have looked pretty scary when we first made it out to the coast. Thirty trailers full of Show people, pretty desperate and dirty-looking Show people too, after fighting our way across the plains from the place where we'd been camped when it all went down. I don't remember when it went down, of course; I wasn't born yet.

The Show used to be an olden-time fair, a teaching thing. We traveled from place to place putting it on so people would learn about olden times, which seems pretty funny now, but back then . . . how's that song go? The one about mankind jumping out into the stars? And everybody thought that was how it was going to be. The aunts and uncles would put on the Show so space-age people wouldn't forget things like weaving and making candles when they went off into space. That's what you call irony, I guess.

But afterward we had to change the Show, because . . . well, we couldn't have the Jousting Arena anymore because we needed the big horses to pull the trailers. And Uncle Buck didn't make fancy work with dragons with rhinestone eyes on them anymore because, who was there left to buy that kind of stuff? And anyway he was too busy making horseshoes. So all the uncles and aunts got together and worked it out like it is now, where we come into town with the Show and people come to see it and then they let us stay a while because we make stuff they need.

I started out as a baby bundle in one of the stage shows, myself. I don't remember it, though. I remember later I was in some play with a love story and I just wore a pair of fake wings and ran across the stage naked and shot at the girl with a toy bow and arrow that had glitter on them. And another time I played a dwarf. But I wasn't a dwarf, we only had the one dwarf and she was a lady, that was Aunt Tammy, and she's dead now. But there was an act with a couple of dwarves dancing and she needed a partner, and I had to wear a black suit and a top hat.

But by then my daddy had got sick and died so my mom was sharing the trailer with Aunt Nera, who made pots and pitchers and stuff, so that meant we were living with her nephew Myko too. People said he went crazy later on but it wasn't true. He was just messed up. Aunt Nera left the Show for a little while after it all went down, to go and see if her family—they were townies—had made it through okay, only they didn't, they were all dead but the baby, so she took the baby away with her and found us again. She said Myko was too little to remember but I think he remembered some.

Anyway we grew up together after that, us and Sunny who lived with Aunt Kestrel in their trailer which was next to ours. Aunt Kestrel was a juggler in the Show and Myko thought that was intense, he wanted to be a kid juggler. So he got Aunt Kestrel to show him how. And Sunny knew how already, she'd been watching her mom juggle since she was born and she could do clubs or balls or the apple-eating trick or anything. Myko decided he and Sunny should be a kid juggling act. I cried until they said I could be in the act too, but then I had to learn how to juggle and boy, was I sorry. I knocked out one of my own front teeth with a club before I learned better. The new one didn't grow in until I was seven, so I went around looking stupid for three years. But I got good enough to march in the parade and juggle torches.

That was after we auditioned, though. Myko went to Aunt Jeff and whined and he made us costumes for our act. Myko got a black doublet and a toy sword and a mask and I got a buffoon overall with a big spangly ruff. Sunny got a princess costume. We called ourselves the Minitrons. Actually Myko came up with the name. I don't know what he thought a Minitron was supposed to be but it sounded brilliant. Myko and I were both supposed to be in love with the princess and she couldn't decide between us so we had to do juggling tricks to win her hand, only she outjuggled us, so then Myko and I had a swordfight to decide things. And I always lost and died of a broken heart, but then the princess was sorry and put a paper rose on my chest. Then I jumped up and we took our bows and ran off, because the next act was Uncle Monty and his performing parrots.

By the time I was six we felt like old performers, and we swaggered in front of the other kids because we were the only kid act. We'd played it in six towns already. That was the year the aunts and uncles decided to take the trailers as far down the coast as this place on the edge of the big desert. It used to be a big city before it all went down. Even if there weren't enough people alive there anymore to put on a show for, there might be a lot of old junk we could use.

We made it into town all right without even any shooting. That was kind of amazing, actually, because it turned out nobody lived there but old people, and old people will usually shoot at you if they have guns, and these did. The other amazing thing was that the town was *huge* and I mean really huge, I just walked around with my head tilted back staring at these towers that went up and up into the sky. Some of them you couldn't even see the tops because the fog hid them. And they were all mirrors and glass and arches and domes and scowly faces in stone looking down from way up high.

But all the old people lived in just a few places right along the beach, because the further back you went into the city the more sand was everywhere. The desert was creeping in and taking a little more every year. That was why all the young people had left. There was nowhere to grow any food. The old people stayed because there was still plenty of stuff in jars and cans they had collected from the markets, and anyway they liked it there because it was warm. They told us they didn't have enough food to share any, though. Uncle Buck told them all we wanted to trade for was the right to go into some of the empty towers and strip out as much of the copper pipes and wires and things as we could take away with us. They thought that was all right; they put their guns down and let us camp, then.

But we found out the Show had to be a matinee if we were going to perform for them, because they all went to bed before the time we usually put on the Show. And the fire-eater was really pissed off about that because nobody would be able to see his act much, in broad daylight. It worked out all right, in the end, because the next day was dark and gloomy. You couldn't see the tops of the towers at all. We actually had to light torches around the edges of the big lot where we put up the stage.

The old people came filing out of their apartment building to the seats we'd set up, and then we had to wait the opening because they decided it was too cold and they all went shuffling back inside and got their coats. Finally the Show started and it went pretty well, considering some of them were blind and had to have their friends explain what was going on in loud voices.

But they liked Aunt Lulu and her little trained dogs and they liked Uncle Manny's strongman act where he picked up a Volkswagen. We kids knew all the heavy stuff like the engine had been taken out of it, but they didn't. They applauded Uncle Derry the Mystic Magician, even though the talkers for the blind shouted all through his performance and threw his timing off. He was muttering to himself and rolling a joint as he came through the curtain that marked off Backstage.

"Brutal crowd, kids," he told us, lighting his joint at one of the torches. "Watch your rhythm."

By we were kids and we could ignore all the grownups in the world shouting, so we grabbed our prop baskets and ran out and put on our act. Myko stalked up and down and waved his sword and yelled his lines about being the brave and dangerous Captainio. I had a little pretend guitar that I strummed on while I pretended to look at the moon, and spoke my lines about being a poor fool in love with the princess. Sunny came out and did her princess dance. Then we juggled. It all went fine. The only time I was a little thrown off was when I glanced at the audience for a split second and saw the light of my juggling torches flickering on all those glass lenses or blind eyes. But I never dropped a torch.

Maybe Myko was bothered some, though, because I could tell by the way his eyes glared through his mask that he was getting worked up. When we had the sword duel near the end he hit too hard, the way he always did when he got worked up, and he banged my knuckles so bad I actually said "Ow" but the audience didn't catch it. Sometimes when he was like that his hair almost bristled, he was like some crazy cat jumping and spitting, and he'd fight about nothing. Sometimes afterward I'd ask him why. He'd shrug and say he was sorry. Once he said it was because life was so damn boring.

Anyway I sang my little sad song and died of a broken heart, *flumpf* there on the pavement in my buffoon suit. I felt Sunny come over and put the rose on my chest and, I will remember this to my dying day, some old lady was yelling to her old man ". . . and now the little girl gave him her rose!"

And the old man yelled "What? She gave him her nose?"

"Damn it, Bob! Her *ROSE*!"

I corpsed right then, I couldn't help it, I was still giggling when Myko and Sunny pulled me to my feet and we took our bows and ran off. Backstage they started laughing too. We danced up and down and laughed, very much getting in the way of Uncle Monty, who had to trundle all his parrots and their perches out on stage.

When we had laughed ourselves out, Sunny said "So . . . what'll we do now?"

That was a good question. Usually the Show was at night, so usually after a performance we went back to the trailers and got out of costume and our moms fed us and put us to bed. We'd never played a matinee before. We stood there looking at each other until Myko's eyes gleamed suddenly.

"We can explore the Lost City of the Sands," he said, in that voice he had that made it sound like whatever he wanted was the coolest thing ever. Instantly, Sunny and I both wanted to explore too. So we slipped out from the backstage area, just as Uncle Monty was screaming himself hoarse trying to get his parrots to obey him, and a moment later we were walking down an endless street lined with looming giants' houses.

They weren't really, they had big letters carved up high that said they were this or that property group or financial group or brokerage or church, but if a giant had stepped out at one corner and peered down at us, we wouldn't have been surprised. There was a cold wind blowing along the alleys from the sea, and sand hissed there and ran before us like ghosts along the ground, but on the long deserted blocks between there was gigantic silence. Our tiny footsteps only echoed in doorways.

The windows were mostly far above our heads and there was nothing much to see when Myko hoisted me up to stand on his shoulders and look into them. Myko kept saying he hoped we'd see a desk with a skeleton with one of those headset things on sitting at it, but we never did; people didn't die *that* fast when it all went down. My mom said they could tell when they were getting sick and people went home and locked themselves in to wait and see if they lived or not.

Anyway Myko got bored finally and started this game where he'd charge up the steps of every building we passed. He'd hammer on the door with the hilt of his sword and yell "It's the Civilian Militia! Open up or we're coming in!" Then he'd rattle the doors, but everything was locked long ago. Some of the doors were too solid even to rattle, and the glass was way too thick to break.

After about three blocks of this, when Sunny and I were starting to look at each other with our eyebrows raised, meaning "Are you going to tell him this game is getting old or do I have to do it?", right then something amazing happened: one of the doors swung slowly inward and Myko swung with it. He staggered into the lobby or whatever and the door shut behind him. He stood staring at us through the glass and we stared back and I was scared to death, because I thought we'd have to run back and get Uncle Buck and Aunt Selene with their hammers to get Myko out, and we'd all be in trouble.

But Sunny just pushed on the door and it opened again. She went in so I had to go in too. We stood there all three and looked around. There was a desk and a dead tree in a planter and another huge glass wall with a door in it, leading deeper into the building. Myko began to grin.

"This is the first chamber of the Treasure Tomb in the Lost City," he said. "We just killed the giant scorpion and now we have to go defeat the army of zombies to get into the second chamber!"

He drew his sword and ran yelling at the inner door, but it opened too, soundlessly, and we pushed after him. It was much darker in here but there was still enough light to read the signs.

"It's a libarary," said Sunny. "They used to have paperbacks."

"*Paperbacks*," said Myko gloatingly, and I felt pretty excited myself. We'd seen lots of paperbacks, of course; there was the boring one with the mended cover that Aunt Maggie made everybody learn to read in. Every grownup we knew had one or two or a cache of paperbacks, tucked away in boxes or in lockers under beds, to be thumbed through by lamplight and read aloud from, if kids had been good.

Aunt Nera had a dozen paperbacks and she'd do that. It used to be the only thing that would stop Myko crying when he was little. We knew all about the Last Unicorn and the kids who went to Narnia, and there was a really long story about some people who had to throw a ring into a volcano that I always got tired of before it ended, and another really long one about a crazy family living in a huge castle, but it was in three books and Aunt Nera only had the first two. There was never any chance she'd ever get the third one now, of course, not since it all went down. Paperbacks were rare finds, they were ancient, their brown pages crumbled if you weren't careful and gentle.

"We just found all the paperbacks in the *universe!*" Myko shouted.

"Don't be dumb," said Sunny. "Somebody must have taken them all away years ago."

"Oh yeah?" Myko turned and ran further into the darkness. We followed, yelling at him to come back, and we all came out together into a big round room with aisles leading off it. There were desks in a ring all around and the blank dead screens of electronics. We could still see because there were windows down at the end of each aisle, sending long trails of light along the stone floors, reflecting back on the long shelves that lined the aisles and the uneven surfaces of the things on the shelves. Clustering together, we picked an aisle at random and walked down it toward the window.

About halfway down it, Myko jumped and grabbed something from one of the shelves. "Look! Told you!" He waved a paperback under our noses. Sunny leaned close to look at it. There was no picture on the cover, just the title printed big.

"Roget's. The. Saurus," Sunny read aloud.

"What's it about?" I asked.

Myko opened it and tried to read. For a moment he looked so angry I got ready to run, but then he shrugged and closed the paperback. "It's just words. Maybe it's a secret code or something. Anyway, it's *mine* now." He stuck it inside his doublet.

"No stealing!" said Sunny.

"If it's a dead town it's not stealing, it's salvage," I told her, just like the aunts and uncles always told us.

"But it isn't dead. There's all the old people."

"They'll die soon," said Myko. "And anyway Uncle Buck already asked permission to salvage." Which she had to admit was true, so we went on. What we didn't know then, but figured out pretty fast, was that all the other things on the shelves were actually big hard *books* like Uncle Des's *Barlogio's Principles of Glassblowing*.

But it was disappointing at first because none of the books in that aisle had stories. It was all, what do you call it, reference stuff. We came out sadly thinking we'd been gypped, and then Sunny spotted the sign with directions.

"Children's Books, Fifth Floor," she announced.

"Great! Where's the stairs?" Myko looked around. We all knew better than to ever, ever go near an elevator, because not only did they mostly not work, they could kill you. We found a staircase and climbed, and climbed for what seemed forever, before we came out onto the Children's Books floor.

And it was so cool. There were racks of paperbacks, of course, but we stood there with our mouths open because the signs had been right—there were *books* here. Big, hard, solid books, but not about grownup stuff. Books with bright pictures on the covers. Books for *us*. Even the tables and chairs up here were our size.

With a little scream, Sunny ran forward and grabbed a book from a shelf. "It's Narnia! Look! And it's got different pictures!"

"What a score," said Myko, dancing up and down. "Oh, what a score!"

I couldn't say anything. The idea was so enormous: all these were ours. This whole huge room belonged to *us* . . . at least, as much as we could carry away with us.

Myko whooped and ran off down one of the aisles. Sunny stayed frozen at the first shelf, staring with almost a sick expression at the other books. I went close to see.

"Look," she whispered. "There's *millions*. How am I supposed to choose? We need as many stories as we can get. " She was pointing at a whole row of books with color titles: *The Crimson Fairy Book. The Blue Fairy Book. The Violet Fairy Book. The Orange Fairy Book.* I wasn't interested in fairies, so I just grunted and shook my head.

I picked an aisle and found shelves full of flat books with big pictures. I opened one and looked at it. It was real easy to read, with big letters and the pictures were funny, but I read right through it standing there. It was about those big animals you see sometimes back up the delta country, you know, elephants. Dancing, with funny hats on. I tried to imagine Aunt Nera reading it aloud on winter nights. It wouldn't last even one night; it wouldn't last through one bedtime. It was only one story. Suddenly I saw what Sunny meant. If we were going to take books away with us, they had to be full of stories that would *last*. What's the word I'm looking for? *Substance*.

Myko yelled from somewhere distant "Here's a cool one! It's got pirates!"

It was pretty dark where I was standing, so I wandered down the aisle toward the window. The books got thicker the farther I walked. There were a bunch of books about dogs, but their stories all seemed sort of the same; there were books about horses too, with the same problem. There were books to teach kids how to make useful stuff, but when I looked through them they were all dumb things like how to weave potholders for your mom or build things out of popsicle sticks. I didn't even know what popsicle sticks were, much less where I could get any. There were some about what daily life was like back in olden times, but I already knew about that, and anyway those books had no *story*.

And all the while Myko kept yelling things like "Whoa! This one has guys with spears and shields and *gods*!" or "Hey, here's one with a flying carpet and it says it's got a *thousand* stories!" Why was I the only one stuck in the dumb books shelves?

I came to the big window at the end and looked out at the view—rooftops, fog, gray dark ocean—and backed away, scared stiff by how high up I was. I was turning around to run back when I saw the biggest book in the world.

Seriously. It was half as big as I was, *twice* the size of *Barlogio's Principles of Glassblowing,* it was bound in red leather and there were gold letters along its back. I crouched down and slowly spelled out the words.

The Complete Collected Adventures of Asterix the Gaul.

I knew what "Adventures" meant, and it sounded pretty promising. I pulled the book down—it was the heaviest book in the world too—and laid it flat on the floor. When I opened it I caught my breath. I had found the greatest book in the world.

It was full of colored pictures, but there were words too, a lot of them, they were the people in the story talking but you could *see them talk*. I had never seen a comic before. My mom talked sometimes about movies and TV and they must have been like this, I thought, talking pictures. And there was a story. In fact, there were lots of stories. Asterix was this little guy no bigger than me but he had a mustache and a helmet and he lived in this village and there was a wizard with a magic potion and Asterix fought in battles and traveled to all these faraway places and had all these adventures!!! And I could read it all by myself, because when I didn't know what a word meant I could guess at it from the pictures.

I settled myself more comfortably on my stomach, propped myself up on my elbows so I wouldn't crunch my starched ruff, and settled down to read.

Sometimes the world becomes a perfect place.

Asterix and his friend Obelix had just come to the Forest of the Carnutes when I was jolted back to the world by Myko yelling for me. I rose to my knees and looked around. It was darker now; I hadn't even realized I'd been pushing my nose closer and closer to the pages as the light had drained away. There were drops of rain hitting the window and I thought about what it would be like running through those dark cold scary streets and getting rained on too.

I scrambled to my feet and grabbed up my book, gripping it to my chest as I ran. It was even darker when I reached the central room. Myko and Sunny were having a fight when I got there. She was crying. I stopped, astounded to see she'd pulled her skirt off and stuffed it full of books, and she was sitting there with her legs bare to her underpants.

"We have to travel light, and they're too heavy," Myko was telling her. "You can't take all those!"

"I have to," she said. "We *need* these books!" She got to her feet and hefted the skirt. *The Olive Fairy Book* fell out. I looked over and saw she'd taken all the colored fairy books. Myko bent down impatiently and grabbed up *The Olive Fairy Book*. He looked at it.

"It's stupid," he said. "Who needs a book about an olive fairy?"

"You moron, it's not *about* an olive fairy!" Sunny shrieked. "It's got all kinds of stories in it! Look!" She grabbed it back from him and opened it, and shoved it out again for him to see. I sidled close and looked. She was right: there was a page with the names of all the stories in the book. There were a lot of stories, about knights and magic and strange words. Read one a night, they'd take up a month of winter nights. And every book had a month's worth of stories in it? Now, that was *concentrated* entertainment value.

Myko, squinting at the page, must have decided the same thing. "Okay," he said, "But you'll have to carry it. And don't complain if it's heavy."

"I won't," said Sunny, putting her nose in the air. He glanced at me and did a double-take.

"You can't take that!" he yelled. "It's too big and it's just one book anyway!"

"It's the only one I want," I said. "And anyhow, you got to take all the ones you wanted!" He knew it was true, too. His doublet was so stuffed out with loot, he looked pregnant.

Myko muttered under his breath, but turned away, and that meant the argument was over. "Anyway we need to leave."

So we started to, but halfway down the first flight of stairs three books fell out of Sunny's skirt and we had to stop while Myko took the safety pins out of all our costumes and closed up the waistband. We were almost to the second floor when Sunny lost her hold on the skirt and her books went cascading down to the landing, with the loudest noise in the universe. We scrambled down after them and were on our knees picking them up when we heard the other noise.

It was a hissing, like someone gasping for breath through whistly dentures, and a jingling, like a ring of keys, because that's what it was. We turned our heads.

Maybe he hadn't heard us when we ran past him on the way up. We hadn't been talking then, just climbing, and he had a lot of hair in his ears and a pink plastic sort of machine in one besides. Or maybe he'd been so wrapped up, the way I had been in reading, that he hadn't even noticed us when we'd pattered past. But he hadn't been reading.

There were no books in this part of the library. All there was on the shelves was old magazines and stacks and stacks of yellow newspapers. The newspapers weren't crumpled into balls in the bottoms of old boxes, which was the only way we ever saw them, they were smooth and flat. But most of them were drifted on the floor like leaves, hundreds and hundreds of big leaves, ankle-deep, and on every single one was a square with sort of checkered patterns and numbers printed in the squares and words written in in pencil.

I didn't know what a crossword puzzle was then but the old man must have been coming there for years, maybe ever since it all went down, years and years he'd been working his way through all those magazines and papers, hunting down every single puzzle and filling in every one. He was dropping a stub of a pencil now as he got to his feet, snarling at us, showing three brown teeth. His eyes behind his glasses were these huge distorted magnified things, and full of crazy anger. He came over the paper-drifts at us fast and light as a spider.

"Fieves! Ucking kish! Ucking fieving kish!"

Sunny screamed and I screamed too. Frantically she shoved all the books she could into her skirt and I grabbed up most of what she'd missed, but we were taking too long. The old man brought up his cane and smacked it down, *crack*, but he missed us on his first try and by then Myko had drawn his wooden sword and put it against the old man's chest and shoved hard. The old man fell with a crash, still flailing his cane, but he was on his side and striking at us faster than you'd believe, and so mad now he was just making noises, with spittle flying from his mouth. His cane hit my knee as I scrambled up. It hurt like fire and I yelped. Myko kicked him and yelled "Run!"

We bailed, Sunny and I did, we thundered down the rest of the stairs and didn't stop until we were out in the last chamber by the street doors. "Myko's still up there," said Sunny. I had an agonizing few seconds before deciding to volunteer to go back and look for him. I was just opening my mouth when we spotted him running down the stairs and out toward us.

"Oh, good," said Sunny. She tied a knot in one corner of her skirt, for a handle, and had already hoisted it over her shoulder onto her back and was heading for the door as Myko joined us. He was clutching the one book we'd missed on the landing. It was *The Lilac Fairy Book* and there were a couple of spatters of what looked like blood on its cover.

"Here. You carry it." Myko shoved the book at me. I took it and wiped it off. We followed Sunny out. I looked at him sidelong. There was blood on his sword too.

It took me two blocks, though, jogging after Sunny through the rain, before I worked up the nerve to lean close to him as we ran and ask: "Did you kill that guy?"

"Had to," said Myko. "He wouldn't stop."

To this day I don't know if he was telling the truth. It was the kind of thing he would have said, whether it was true or not. I didn't know what I was supposed to say back. We both kept running. The rain got a lot harder and Myko left me behind in a burst of speed, catching up to Sunny and grabbing her bundle of books. He slung it over his shoulder. They kept going, side by side. I had all I could do not to fall behind.

By the time we got back the Show was long over. The crew was taking down the stage in the rain, stacking the big planks. Because of the rain no market stalls had been set up but there was a line of old people with umbrellas standing by Uncle Chris's trailer, since he'd offered to repair any dentures that needed fixing with his jeweler's tools. Myko veered us away from them behind Aunt Selene's trailer, and there we ran smack into our moms and Aunt Nera. They had been looking for us for an hour and were really mad.

I was scared sick the whole next day, in case the old people got out their guns and came to get us, but nobody seemed to notice the old man was dead and missing, if he was dead. The other thing I was scared would happen was that Aunt Kestrel or Aunt Nera would get to talking with the other women and say something like, "Oh, by the way, the kids found a library and salvaged some books, maybe we should all go over and get some books for the other kids too" because that was exactly the sort of thing they were always doing, and then they'd find the old man's body. But they didn't. Maybe nobody did anything because the rain kept all the aunts and kids and old people in next day. Maybe the old man had been a hermit and lived by himself in the library, so no one would find his body for ages.

I never found out what happened. We left after a couple of days, after Uncle Buck and the others had opened up an office tower and salvaged all the good copper they could carry. I had a knee swollen up and purple where the old man had hit it, but it was better in about a week. The books were worth the pain.

They lasted us for years. We read them and we passed them on to the other kids and they read them too, and the stories got into our games and our dreams and the way we thought about the world. What I liked best about my comics was that even when the heroes went off to far places and had adventures, they always came back to their village in the end and everybody was happy and together.

Myko liked the other kind of story, where the hero leaves and has glorious adventures but maybe never comes back. He was bored with the Show by the time he was twenty and went off to some big city up north where he'd heard they had their electrics running again. Lights were finally starting to come back on in the towns we worked, so it seemed likely. He still had that voice that could make anything seem like a good idea, see, and now he had all those fancy words he'd gotten out of Roget's Thesaurus too. So I guess I shouldn't have been surprised that he talked Sunny into going with him.

Sunny came back alone after a year. She wouldn't talk about what happened, and I didn't ask. Eliza was born three months later.

Everyone knows she isn't mine. I don't mind.

We read to her on winter nights. She likes stories.

Re-crossing the Styx

IAN R MACLEOD

In the sly story that follows, we accompany a social climber as he makes his way up the social ladder toward the superrich at the top—no matter what he has to sacrifice to get there.

British writer Ian R. MacLeod was one of the hottest new writers of the nineties, publishing a slew of strong stories in *Interzone, Asimov's Science Fiction, Weird Tales, Amazing,* and *The Magazine of Fantasy and Science Fiction,* and elsewhere and his work continued to grow in power and deepen in maturity as we moved through the first decade of the new century. Much of his work has been gathered in three collections, *Voyages By Starlight, Breathmoss and Other Exhalations,* and *Past Magic.* His first novel, *The Great Wheel,* was published in 1997. In 1999, he won the World Fantasy Award with his novella "The Summer Isles," and followed it up in 2000 by winning another World Fantasy Award for his novelette "The Chop Girl." In 2003, he published his first fantasy novel, and his most critically acclaimed book, *The Light Ages,* followed by a sequel, *The House of Storms,* in 2005, and then by *Song of Time,* which won both the Arthur C. Clarke Award and the John W. Campbell Award in 2008. A novel version of *The Summer Isles* also appeared in 2005. His most recent books are a new novel, *Wake Up and Dream,* and a new collection, *Journeys.* MacLeod lives with his family in the West Midlands of England.

W elcome aboard the *Glorious Nomad,* all nuclear-powered 450,000 tons of her. She is, literally, a small country in her own right, with her own armed services, laws and currency. But, for all her modernity, life afloat remains old-fashioned. There are the traditional fast food outlets, themed restaurants, coloured fountains, street entertainers and even a barber's shop staffed by a charmingly impromptu quartet. There are trained armies of chefs, litter collectors, pooper-scoopers and maintenance engineers. Firework displays are held each evening on the main central deck above the Happy Trillionaire Casino, weather permitting. It's easy to understand why those who can afford her tariffs carry on cruising until—and then long after—death.

Wandering the decks in his lilac-stripe crew blazer, resident tour host Frank

Onions never paid much attention to the news reports he saw in magazines left glowing over the arms of sun loungers. Still, he knew that dying was no longer the big deal it had once been. Death, it had turned out, was the answer to many of the problems of old age. With your weakening heart stopped, with your failing body eviscerated and your memory uploaded and your organs renewed, you were free to shuffle around on your titanium hips for another few decades. And, after that, you could book in for the same procedure again. And again. There were, admittedly, some quibbles about whether the post-living were still technically the same people they had once been. But, working as Frank did in an industry which relied so heavily on the post-centenarian trade, it would have been churlish to complain.

It seemed like there were more corpses than ever as he led the morning excursion to the ruins of Knossos in Crete, with the *Glorious Nomad* anchored off what remained of the city of Heraklion. At least fourteen out of the forty two heads he counted on the tour bus looked to be dead. Make that double, if you included their minders. The easiest way to tell the dead apart from the living was by a quick glance at their wigs and toupees. Not that the living oldies didn't favour such things as well, but the dead were uniformly bald—hair, like skin, seemed to be something the scientists haven't fully got the knack of replacing— and had a particularly bilious taste in rugware. The lines of bus seats Frank faced sprouted Elvis coxcombs, dyed punky tufts and Motown beehives. The dead loved to wear big sunglasses, as well. They shunned the light, like the vampires they somewhat resembled, and favoured loose-fitting clothes in unlikely combinations of manmade fabrics. Even the men put on too much makeup to disguise their pasty skins. As the tour bus climbed towards the day's cultural destination and Frank took the mike and kicked into his spiel about Perseus and the Minotaur, a mixed smell of corrupted flesh, facecream and something like formaldehyde wafted over him.

The September sun wasn't particularly harsh as Frank, *Glorious Nomad* lollipop in raised right hand, guided his shuffling bunch from sight to stairlift to moving walkway. Here is the priest-king fresco and here is the throne room and here is the world's first flush toilet. The only other tour group were from the *Happy Minstrel*, another big cruise vessel berthed at the old American naval base at Souda Bay. As the two slow streams shuffled and mingled in their frail efforts to be first to the souvenir shop, Frank couldn't help but worry that he was going to end up with some of the wrong guests. Then, as he watched them some more—so frail, so goddamn *pointless* in their eagerness to spend the money they'd earned back in their discarded lives as accountants from Idaho or lawyers from Stockholm or plant hire salesmen from Wolverhampton—he wondered if it would matter.

He corralled what seemed like the right specimens back on the bus without further incident, and they headed on toward what today's itinerary described as *A Typical Cretan Fishing Village*. The whole place looked convincing enough if you ignored the concrete berms erected as protection against the rising seas, and the local villagers did local villager as well as anyone who had to put on the same act day after day reasonably could.

Afterwards, Frank sat under a olive tree in what passed for the harbourfront taverna, took a screen out from his back pocket and pretended to read. The waiter brought him stuffed olives, decent black decaf and a plate of warm pita bread. It was hard, sometimes, to complain.

"Mind if we join you?"

Frank suppressed a scowl and put away his screen. Then, as he looked up, his contractual smile became genuine.

"Sure, sure. It would be a pleasure."

She was wearing a strappy sundress made of some kind of fabric that twinkled and changed with the dappling light. So did her bare golden shoulders. So did her golden hair.

"I'm Frank Onions."

"Yes . . ." There was a curious intensity to her gaze, which was also golden. ". . . We know." She raked back a chair. Then another. And beckoned.

Shit. Not just her. Although Frank supposed that was to be expected; apart from crew, the only young people you found on board ships like the *Glorious Nomad* were minders. The dead man who shuffled up was a sorry case indeed. His toupee was a kind of silver James Dean duck's arse, but it was wildly askew. So were the sunglasses, and the tongue which emerged from between ridiculously rouged lips in concentration at the act of sitting looked like a hunk of spoiled liver.

"Oh, I'm Dottie Hastings, by the way. This is Warren."

As this Dottie-vision leant to re-straighten the rug and sunglasses, the dead man slurred something which Frank took to be hello.

"Well . . ." She returned her gaze to Frank. "We really enjoyed your tour and talk this morning. What can we get you? A carafe of retsina? Some ouzo?"

Much though he'd have loved to agree with anything Dottie suggested, Frank shook his head. "I really don't drink that kind of stuff . . . Not that I have a problem with it . . ." He felt compelled to add. "I just like to take care of myself."

"Oh yes." Frank could feel—literally fucking *feel*—Dottie's gaze as it travelled over him. "I can see. You work out?"

"Well. A bit. There's not much else to do in time off when you're crew."

She made a wry smile. "So. About that drink. Maybe some more coffee? I'm guessing decaf, right?"

Dottie, he noticed, settled for a small ouzo, although the Warren thing restricted himself to orange juice, a considerable amount of which she then had to mop up from around his wizened neck. There was a strange and unminderly tenderness about her gestures that was almost touching. Lovely though she was, Frank found it hard to watch.

"You do realise," she said, balling up paper napkins, "that most of the stories you told us about Knossos are pure myth?"

Frank spluttered into his coffee. But Dottie was smiling at him in a mischievous way, and her mouth had gone slightly crooked. Then the knowing smile became a chuckle, and he had to join in. After all, so much of what they'd just been religiously inspecting—the pillars, the frescos, the bull's horns—had been erected by Arthur Evans a couple of hundred years before in a misguided attempt to recreate how he thought Knossos should have been. But Evans got most of it wrong. He was even wrong about the actual name. Frank never normally bothered to spoil his tales of myths and Minotaurs with anything resembling the truth, but, as Warren drooled and he and Dottie chatted, vague memories of the enthusiasm which had once driven him to study ancient history returned.

Dottie wasn't just impossibly beautiful. She was impossibly smart. She even knew about Wunderlich, whose theory that the whole of Knossos was in fact a vast mausoleum was a particular favourite of his. By the time they needed to return to the tour bus to view the famous statue of the bare breasted woman holding those snakes—now also known to be a modern fake—Frank was already the close to something resembling love. Or at least, serious attachment. There was something about her. Something, especially, about that golden gaze. There was both a playful darkness and a serene innocence somewhere in there which he just couldn't fathom. It was like looking down at two coins flashing up at you from some cool, deep river. Dottie wasn't just clever and beautiful. She was unique.

"Well . . ." He stood up, as dizzy as if he's been the one who's been knocking back the ouzo. "Those treasures won't get looked at on their own."

"No. Of course." A poem of golden flesh and shifting sundress, she, too, arose. Then she leaned to help the Warren-thing, and for all his disgust at what she was doing, Frank couldn't help but admire the way the tips of her breasts shifted against her dress. "I'm really looking forward to this afternoon. I mean . . ." After a little effort, Warren was also standing, or at least leaning against her. His mouth lolled. His toupee had gone topsy-turvy again, and the skin revealed beneath looked like a grey, half-deflated balloon. "We *both* are." Dottie smiled that lovely lopsided grin again. "Me and my husband Warren."

Minders were always an odd sort, even if they did make up the majority of Frank's shipboard conquests. But Dottie was different. Dottie was something else. Dottie was alive in ways that those poor sods who simply got paid for doing what they did never were. But *married*? You sometimes encountered couples, it was true, who'd crossed the so-called bereavement barrier together. Then there were the gold-diggers; pneumatic blondes bearing not particularly enigmatic smiles as they pushed around some relic in a gold-plated wheelchair. But nowadays your typical oil billionaire simply accepted the inevitable, died, and got himself resurrected. Then he just carried on pretty much as before. That was the whole point.

Frank Onions lay down in his accommodation tube that night with a prickly sense of dislocation. Just exactly where was he going with his life—living down in these crew decks, deep, deep below the *Glorious Nomad's* waterline where the only space you could call your own was so small you could barely move? It might not seem so up along the parks and shopping malls, but down here there was never any doubt that you were at sea. Heavy smells of oil and bilge competed with the pervasively human auras of spoiled food, old socks and vomit. It was funny, really, although not in any particularly ha-had way, how all the progress of modern technology should have come to this; a hive-like construct where you shut yourself in like you were a pupae preparing to hatch. No wonder he wasted his time in the crew gym working his body into some approximation of tiredness, or occupied what little was left hunting the next easy fuck. No wonder none of the ship's many attractions held the slightest interest for him. No wonder he couldn't sleep.

All he could think of was Dottie. Dottie standing. Dottie seated. Dottie smiling her lopsided smile. The sway of her breasts against that prismatic fabric. Then Frank thought, even though he desperately didn't want to, of what Dottie might be doing right now with that zombie husband of hers. Mere sex between them didn't seem very likely, but mopping up food and levering withered limbs in and out of stairlifts was merely the tip of the iceberg of the tasks minders were required to perform. The thing about being dead was that blood, nerve cells and tissue, even when newly cloned, were susceptible to fresh corruption, and thus needed constant renewal and replacement. To earn their salaries, minders didn't just give up a few years of their lives. After being pumped full of immune-suppressants, they were expected to donate their body fluids and tissues to their hosts on a regular basis. Many even sprouted the goitre-like growths of a new replacement organs.

Frank tossed. Frank turned. Frank saw throbbing tubes, half flesh, half rubber, emerging from unimaginable orifices. Then he felt the rush of the sea beneath the *Glorious Nomad's* great hull as she ploughed on across the Mediterranean. And he saw Dottie rising shining and complete from its waters like some new maritime goddess.

As the *Glorious Nomad* zigzagged across the Aegean from the medieval citadel of Rhodes to the holy island of Patmas, Frank Onions kept seeing Dottie Hastings even when she wasn't there. A glint of her hair amid the trinkets in the backstreets of Skyros. A flash of her shadowed thighs across the golden dunes of Evvoia. He felt like a cat in heat, like an angel on drugs. He felt like he was back in the old times which had never existed.

Warren Hastings wasn't hard to find out about when Frank ransacked the *Glorious Nomad's* records. He'd made his first fortune out of those little hoops you used to get hung at the top of shower curtains. His second came from owning the copyright on part of the DNA chain of some industrial biochemical. Warren Hastings was seriously, seriously rich. The sort of rich you got to be not by managing some virtual pop band or inventing a cure for melancholy, but by doing stuff so ordinary no one really knew or cared what it was about. For all the money a top-of-the-range Ultra-Deluxe Red Emperor Suite must be costing him, he and Dottie should by rights have been plying the oceans on their own cruiser, living on a private island, or floating in a spacepod. Perhaps they enjoyed the company of lesser immortals. Or perhaps they simply liked slumming it.

The more Frank thought about it, the more the questions kept piling up in his head. And the biggest question of all was Dottie herself. It was an odd shock, despite all the times he'd now seen her and Warren exhibiting every sign of tenderness, to discover that she'd married him ten years earlier before he'd even died in a small, private ceremony in New Bali. There she was, dressed in virginal white beneath a floral arch, with Warren standing beside her and looking in a whole lot better shape than he did now. The records were confused and contradictory about exactly when he'd chosen to die, but he must have started seriously decaying before he finally made the leap, whilst Dottie herself seemed to have just emerged, beautiful and smiling and entirely unchanged, into the more discreet and upmarket corners of the society pages, and into what you could no longer describe as Warren's life.

It all still felt like a mystery, but for once Frank was grateful for the contract clause which insisted he spend a designated number of hours in the company of paying passengers. He mingled at the cocktail hour of the Waikiki Bar, and feigned an interest in a whole variety of passenger activities about which he couldn't have given the minutest fuck until he worked out what kind of social routine the Hastings were following, and then began to follow something similar himself.

Onward to the island of Chios with its Byzantine monastery and fine mosaics, and the autumn waves were growing choppier as Frank Onions ingratiated himself with what he supposed you might call the Hastings crowd. Sitting amid the spittle rain of their conversations as Warren gazed devotedly in Dottie's direction with his insect sunglasses perched on his ruined Michael Jackson nose, Frank could only wonder again at the continuing surprise of her beauty, and then about why on earth she'd consented to become what she was now. Most minders, in Frank's experience, were almost as dead as the zombies they were paid to look after. They'd put their lives on hold for the duration. Apart from the money, they hated everything they were required to do. Even in the heights of passion, you always felt as if their bodies belong to someone else.

But Dottie didn't seem to hate her life, Frank decided once again as he watched her wipe the drool from her husband's chin with all her usual tenderness and Warren mooed equally tenderly back. The thought that they made the perfect couple even trickled across his mind. But he still didn't buy it. There was something *else* about Dottie as she turned to gaze through the panoramic glass at the wide blue Mediterranean in proud and lovely profile. It was like some kind of despair. If her golden eyes hadn't been fixed so steadily on the horizon, he might almost have thought she was crying.

He finally got his chance with her after a day excursion on the tiny island of Delos. The Hastings had opted to join this particular tour party, although they hung back as Frank delivered his usual spiel about the Ionians and their phallic monuments as if Dottie was trying to avoid him. Then there was a kafuffle involving her and Warren just as the launch arrived for the return to the *Glorious Nomad*. A lover's tiff, Frank hoped, but it turned out there had been some kind of malfunction which required immediate action as soon as they got back on board ship.

Dottie still had on the same white top she'd worn all day when she finally emerged on her own at the Waikiki Bar later that evening, but it now bore what looked to be—but probably wasn't—a small food stain on the left breast. Her hair was no longer its usual marvel is spun gold, either, and the left corner of her mouth bore a small downward crease. She looked tired and worried. Everyone else, though—all these dead real estate agents and software consultants—barely noticed as she sat down. They didn't even bother to ask if Warren was okay. The dead regarded organ failure in much the same way that flat tyres were thought of by the petrol motorists of old; a bit of a nuisance, but nothing to get too excited about just as long as you made sure you'd packed a spare. The spluttering talk about annuity rates continued uninterrupted, and the tension lines deepened around Dottie's eyes as her fingers wove and unwove in her lap. Even when she stood up and pushed her way out through the corral of matchstick limbs toward the deck, Frank was the only person to notice.

He followed her out. It was a dark, fine night and the stars seemed to float around her like fireflies. A flick of hair brushed Frank's face as he leaned close by her on ship's rail.

"Is Warren alright?"

"I'm looking after him. Of course he's alright."

"What about you?"

"Me? I'm fine. It wasn't me who—"

"I didn't mean that, Dottie. I meant—"

"I know what you meant." She shrugged and sighed. "People, when they see us both, they can see Frank's devoted to me . . ."

"But they wonder about you?"

"I suppose so." She shrugged again. "I was just this girl who wanted a better life. I was good at sports—a good swimmer—and I had these dreams that I'd go to the Olympics and win a medal. But by the time I'd grown up, Olympic competitors no longer used their own limbs or had anything resembling normal human blood flowing in their veins. So I eventually found out that the best way to get steady work was on ships like this. I did high dives. I watched pools in a lifevest. I taught the dead and the living how to swim—how to paddle about without drowning, anyway. You know what it's like, Frank. It's not such a terrible life just as long as you can put up with the tiny sleeping tubes, and all those drinks served with paper umbrellas."

"What ships were you on?"

"Oh . . ." She gazed down into the racing water. "I was working on the *Able May* for most of this time."

"Wasn't that the one where half the crew got killed in the reactor fire?"

"That was her sister ship. And then one day, Warren comes along. He looked much better then. They always say the technologies are going to improve, but death hasn't been particularly kind to him."

"You mean, you really did find him attractive?"

"Not exactly, no. I was more—" She stopped. A small device on her wrist had started beeping. "I have to go to him. Have you seen to a suite like ours Frank? Do you want to come down with me?"

"Wow! This is nice . . ."

Gold. Glass. Velvet. Everything either glittery hard or falling-through soft. Frank had seen it all before, but this wasn't the time to say. The only jarring note was a large white structure squatting and humming beside the cushion-festooned bed.

". . . I just need to check . . ."

It looked as if Dottie was inspecting the contents of some giant, walk-in fridge as she opened one of its chrome and enamel doors and leaned inside. The waft of air had that same tang; a chill sense of spoiling meat. There was even that same bland aquarium light, along with glimpses of what might have been trays of beef and cartons of coloured juice, although by far the biggest item on the racks was Warren himself. He lay prone and naked in such a way that Frank had fine view of his scrawny grey feet, his hairless blue-mottled legs, his scarred and pitted belly, the winter-withered fruit of his balls and prick. He looked not so much dead as sucked dry. Far more alarming, though, was the empty space on the rack beside him, which was plainly designed to accommodate another body.

"He's fine," Dottie murmured with that weird tenderness is in her voice again. She touched one or two things, drips and feeds by the look of them. There were flashes and bleeps. Then came a sort of glooping sound which, even though he couldn't see exactly what was causing it, forced Frank to look away. He heard the door smack shut.

"He'll be right as rain by morning."

"You don't get in there *with* him, do you?"

"I'm his wife."

"But . . . Jesus, Dottie. You're *lovely*." Now or never time; he moved toward her. "You can't waste you life like this . . . Not when you can . . . ." It seemed for a moment that this oh-so direct ploy was actually working. She didn't step back from him, and the look in her golden eyes was far from unwelcoming. Then, as he reached out to her cheek, she gave a small shriek and cowered across the deep-pile, rubbing at where his fingers hadn't even touched. It was if she's been stung by a bee.

"I'm sorry, Dottie. I didn't mean—"

"No, no. It isn't you Frank. It's me. I like you. I want you. I *more* than like you. But . . . Have you heard of imprinting?"

"We're all—"

"I mean the word literally. Imprinting is what happens to the brain of a chick when it first sees its mother after it hatches. It's an instinct—it's built in—and it's been known about for centuries. It's the same to some or other degree even with the more advanced species. That's how you can get a duckling to follow around the first thing it sees, even if it happens to be a pair of galoshes."

Frank nodded. He thought he understood what she meant, although he hadn't the faintest idea where this was leading.

"We humans have the same instinct, although it's not quite as strong or simple. At least, not unless something's done to enhance it."

"What are you saying? Humans can be imprinted and attached to other humans? That can't be legal."

"When does whether something's legal matter these days? There's always somewhere in the world where you can do whatever you want, and Warren already knew he was dying when I met him. And he was charming. And he was impossibly rich. He said he could offer me the kind of life I'd never achieve otherwise no matter how long I lived or how hard I worked. And he was right. All of this . . ." She gestured at the suite. "Is nothing, Frank. It's *ordinary*. This ship's a prison with themed restaurants and a virtual golf range. With Warren, I realised I had my chance to escape places like this. It didn't seem so difficult back then, the deal I made . . ."

"You mean, you agreed to be imprinted by him?"

She nodded. There really did look to be tears in her eyes. "It was a small device he had made. You could say it was a kind of wedding gift. It looked like a silver insect. It was actually rather beautiful. He laid it here on my neck, and it crawled . . ." She touched her ear. "In here. It hurt a little, but not so very much. And he made me stare at him as it bored in to find the right sector of my brain." She shrugged. "It was that simple."

"My God! Dottie . . ." Again, but this time more impulsively, he moved toward her. Once more, she stumbled back.

"No. I can't!" She wailed. "Don't you see? *This* is what imprinting means." The stain on her left breast was rising and falling. "I'd love to escape this thing and be with you, Frank. But I'm trapped. At the time, it seemed like a small enough price to pay. And it's true that I've been to incredible places, experienced the most amazing things. Living on a cruise ship like this, looking at the ruins of the ancient world because we can't bear to look at the mess we've made of this one . . . It's meaningless. There's a different kind of life out there, Frank, in the high mountains, or up in the skies, or deep beneath the oceans. For those few who can afford it, anyway. And Warren could. We could. It's like some curse in a fairy tale. I'm like that king, the one who wanted a world made of gold, and then found out that he was killing everything that was important to him in the process. I wish I could be with you, Frank, but Warren will carry on and on as he is and I can't give myself to anyone else, or even bear to have them touch me. I just wish there was some escape. I wish I could unwrite what happened, but I'm forever tied." Her hand reached towards him. Even in tears, she looked impossibly lovely. Then her whole body seemed to freeze. It was as if a glass wall lay between them. "I sometimes wish we were dead."

"You can't say that, Dottie. What you and I have—what we *might* have. We've only just—"

"No. I don't mean I wish *you* were dead, Frank. Or even myself. I mean things as they are . . ." She raised her golden eyes and blinked more slowly. ". . . and Warren."

The tides were turning as the *Glorious Nomad* beat against the deepening autumnal waves. Frank found himself giving talks about the Grecian concept of the transmigration of souls, and how the dead were assigned to one of three realms. Elysium, for the blessed. Tartarus for the damned. Asphodel—a land of boredom and neutrality—for the rest. To reach these realms you first had to cross the River Styx and pay Charon the ferryman a small golden coin or *obolus*, which grieving relatives placed on the tongues of the dead. To attain your desires, he concluded, gazing at the papier mache masks of ruined, once-human faces arrayed before him in the Starbucks' Lecture Suite, you must be prepared to pay.

Poison? The idea had its appeal, and there were plenty of noxious substances on board which Frank might be able to wrangle access to, but neither he nor Dottie were experts in biochemistry, and there was no guarantee that Warren couldn't still be re-resurrected. Some kind of catastrophic accident, then— especially in these storms? Something as simple as disabling the magneto on one of those big bulkhead doors as he went tottering through . . . ? But getting the timing exactly right would be difficult, and there was still a faint but frustrating chance Warren would make some kind of recovery, and then where would they be?

The options that Frank and Dottie explored as they met on the spray-wet deck over the next few days seemed endless, and confusing. Even if one of them worked flawlessly, other problems remained. There was an opportunity coming for them both to leave ship together when the *Glorious Nomad* dropped anchor by the shores of old Holy Land for an optional tour in radiation suits, but Dottie would be expected to act the role of the grieving widow, and suspicions would be aroused if Frank were to resign his post and then be spotted with her. No matter how many jurisdictions they skipped though, they'd still be vulnerable to prosecution, and also blackmail. But one of the things which Frank was coming to admire as well as love about Dottie was her quickness of mind.

"What if *you* were to appear to die, Frank?" she shout-whispered to him as they clung to the ship's rail. "You could . . . I don't know . . . You could pretend to kill yourself—stage your suicide. Then . . ." She gazed off into the tumbling light with those wise, golden eyes. ". . . we could get rid of Warren instead."

It was as perfect and beautiful as she was, and Frank longed to kiss and hold her and do all the other things they'd been promising each other right here and now on this slippery deck. Disguising himself as Warren for a few months, hiding under that toupee and behind those sunglasses and all that make-up, wouldn't be so difficult. Give it a little time and he could start to look better of his own accord. After all, the technology was continually improving. They could simply say that he'd died again, and been even more comprehensively re-resurrected. All it would take was a little patience—which was surely a small enough price to pay when you considered the rewards which awaited them: Dottie freed of her curse, and she and Frank rich forever.

Drowning had always been the most obvious option. They'd toyed with it several times already, but now it made absolute sense. Toss Warren overboard, he'd sink like a stone with all the prosthetic metal he had in him. And if they did it close to the stern—threw him down into the wildly boiling phosphorescent wake of the *Glorious Nomad's* eighteen azimuth propellers—he'd be torn into sharkmeat; there'd be no body left worth finding. Sure, alarms would go off and one of the hull's cameras might catch him falling, but even the most sophisticated technology would struggle to make sense of whatever was going through the forecast force eight gale. Especially if they waited until dark, and Warren's body had on one of the transmitting dogtags all crew were required to carry, and was wearing a lilac-stripe blazer.

By next day, the kind of storm which had shipwrecked Odysseus was brewing, and the *Glorious Nomad's* public places soon fell empty as her passengers retreated to their suites. The barber's shop closed early. The several swimming pools were covered over. The ornamental lake in the Pleasure Park franchise was drained. The air filled with the sounds of heaving and creaking, curious distant booms and bangings, and a pervasive aroma of vomit.

Heading along the swaying passageways to their pre-arranged meeting point, Frank already felt curiously convinced by the details of his own suicide. His last talk on board the *Glorious Nomad* was of how Orpheus tried to rescue his dead wife Euridice from the Underworld, and it had taken no effort at all, staring at those white-faced zombies, to put aside his usual catch-all smile and appear surly and depressed. Ditto his few last exchanges with colleagues. Fact is, he realised, he'd been this way with them for years. Everything, even the ferocity of this storm, had that same sense of inevitability. Back down in his sleeping tube, he even found that it was far easier than he'd expected to compose a final message. He'd been able to speak with surprising passion about the emptiness of his life: the sheer monotony of the talks and the tours and the berthings and the embarkations—the long sessions in the gym, too, and the ritual seductions with their overcoming of fake resistance, and the inevitable fuckings and even more inevitable break-ups which followed, with their equally fake expressions of regret. Just what the hell, he'd found himself wondering, *had* he been living for before he met Dottie? Looked at dispassionately, the prospect of his own imminent death made every kind of sense.

He arrived at the junction of corridors between Challengers Bowling Arcade and the smallest of the five burger franchises just two minutes early, and was relieved to find the whole area empty and unobserved. Dottie was as punctual as he'd have expected, and somehow still looked beautiful even dressed in a grey sou'wester and half-hauling her dead husband up the sideways-tilting floor. Warren was in his usual brushed velour top, crumpled nylon slacks and velcro trainers, although his sunglasses and toupee were all over the place.

"Hi there Frank," Dottie said, grabbing a handhold and supporting Warren by a bunched ruff behind his neck. "I know it's a terrible night, but I persuaded Warren that we might feel fresher if we took a walk." Frank nodded. His mouth was dry. "Maybe you could help me with him?" she added, shoving Warren into Frank's half-surprised embrace.

"There you go, fella," Frank heard himself mutter as he propped the withered creature against the bulkhead. "Why don't we take this off . . . ?" Quickly, he removed Warren's black top, which slipped worn and warm and slightly greasy between his fingers, although it was the feel and sight of Warren beneath that really set his teeth on edge. The dead man muttered something and looked back toward Dottie with his usual puppy-dog longing, but made no discernable attempt to resist.

"Maybe this as well . . ."

The toupee felt ever warmer and greasier.

"And this . . ."

Here came the sunglasses, hooked off from what passed for ears and a nose. Frank had to judge every movement against the rising, falling waves. But, Jesus, the man was a mess.

"Looking a bit cold now, Mister Hastings . . ."

Frank shucked off his own blazer.

"So why don't we put on this?"

A few more manoeuvres and Warren was wearing Frank's crew blazer. Frank almost forgot the crew dogtag until Dottie reminded him in a quick whisper. Even then, Warren in this new attire looked like nothing more than a particularly bald and anaemic scarecrow, and Frank was wondering how this switch will ever convince anyone until he swung the weighed hatch open and was confronted by the sheer size and scale of the storm.

The deck was awash. Dottie hung back. Salt spray ignited the air. It was a miracle, really, that she'd been able to do as much as she had to help when you considered the deal this dead husk had forced on her. Now all she had to do was keep hold of his nylon top, toupee and sunglasses. The sky shattered in greys and purples. For all his slips and struggles as he manoeuvred Warren Hastings toward the *Glorious Nomad's* stern, Frank Onions felt like he was Odysseus sailing from Circe's island, or Jason with his Argonauts in search of the Golden Fleece. Soon, he would reach those warmly welcoming shores that Dottie had been promising him.

A few last staggers and he was clinging to the final rail, and still just about keeping hold of Warren, although they were both equally drenched, and it was hard to distinguish between sea and sky out here. Then he felt the steel clifface of the *Glorious Nomad's* stern rising and straining until her screws were swirling above the waves, and it seemed for a long moment that the whole ship would simply carry on climbing until the ocean dragged her down. Frank skidded and nearly fell as he grabbed Warren's arms and tried to haul him over the rail.

"Stop squirming you bastard!" Frank screamed into the wind even though Warren wasn't squirming at all. As the ship teetered and began to fall back he tried to lift him again, and this time got some better kind of purchase. This, Frank thought, as he and Warren swayed like dancers over the stern's drop, was far closer to a dead man as he'd ever wanted to get, but for all the wet grey skin, cavernous cheeks and birdcage chest, there was something about Warren Hastings in this stuttering light that didn't seem entirely dead. Something in the eyes, perhaps, now they were stripped of their goggle sunglasses, or in the set of that mouth now that the powder and rouge had run. The guy had to have worked out what was happening, but there was still no sign of any resistance, nor any sense of fear. If anything, Frank thought as he finally managed to hook one hand under Warren's wet and empty armpit and the other under his even emptier crotch and gave the final quick heave which tipped him over the rail, that last look conveyed something like relief—perhaps even a sense of pity . . .

"Did it work? Are you okay?"

Already, Dottie had managed to clamber up the deck. Already, the curse of her imprinting was broken, and her arms are quickly around him. Roughly and wetly, they kissed.

"I love you, Frank," she said, and her arms were strong and the ship's searchlights and alarms were blazing as she drew him behind a lifeboat into the lee of the storm and took out something silver from her sou'wester pocket that squirmed and uncurled like a living jewel.

"I love you."

She said it again, and kissed him harder as he felt a sharpness crawl across his neck.

"I love you."

She held him tighter than ever as pain flared inside his ear.

"I love you."

She said it again and again and again and again.

Where has he not been? What has he not seen? He's looked down on an Earth so small that he could blot it out with his thumb, he's skysailed to the peak of Mount Everest. If there was a price to pay for all this glory, Frank Onions would willingly have paid it. Most glorious of all to him, though, eclipsing every moon-rise and sunset, is his continuing joy at sharing Dottie's company. The money—even the incredible things that it can buy; the glass terraces, the submarine gardens, the refurbished Burmese palaces—is just the river, the coin, the *obolus*. To be with her, and to share his flesh and blood with her, is an experience which pales even the furthest heights of sexual ecstasy.

Days change. The living die and the dead live, but Frank's love for Dottie is unchanging. He has, once or twice, much as one might gaze in awe at bare foot-prints left across an ancient floor, looked back along the path which brought them together. He knows now that the real Warren Hastings married his beautiful sixth wife just a few months before he died, or perhaps simply disappeared, in circum-stances that other times and cultures might have regarded as mysterious. Since then, and as before, Dottie has remained just as stunningly, agelessly, beautiful. And she always has a companion whom she likes to term her husband. Some-times, when the circumstances suit, she even calls him Warren. Frank has no need to ask Dottie why she chose death above life. He already understands per-fectly. After all, why would anyone who had the money and the choice wait for old age and decrepitude before being resurrected? And what sacrifices and demands wouldn't they then make, to ensure that they remained eternally beautiful?

Dottie is Frank's world, his lodestone. He lives with and within her, and would sacrifice any organ or appendage or bodily fluid joyously. As for himself, he knows that he's no longer the well-kept specimen of a man who was first en-raptured by her. Only last week on the glassy plains outside Paris, he gave up a good portion of his bone marrow to her, and a third re-grown kidney. The effects of these and other donations, along with all the immune-suppressants he must continually take, leave him thin and weak and dizzy. His hair has long gone, he must wear sunglasses to protect his bleary eyes, and he shuffles hunched and crabways. He realises that he's already starting to look like the creature he tossed over the stern of the *Glorious Nomad*, and that the wonders of the life he's now living cannot last forever.

In the circles in which they move, far removed from the *Glorious Nomad's* ruin-inspecting tribes of meekly departed middle executives, Frank and Dottie's relationship is seen as nothing unusual. As she once said to him in what now seems like a different existence, who now knows or cares about what is legal? Sometimes, when the weakened husks like himself who accompany Dottie and her companions grow close to failing, they head off to live some lesser life for a few weeks, and enjoy the thrill of finding a fresh and willing replacement. They call it *re-crossing the Styx*. It's a new kind of symbiosis, this imprinting, and it strikes Frank as a near-perfect relationship. It's only when the pain and weakness in his thinning bones sometimes get the worst of him, and he gazes around at the golden creatures who surround him, that he wonders who is really dead now, and who is living.

TAD WILLIAMS

Here's a fast-paced and suspenseful thriller about a dedicated Warrior of God who finds himself facing a test of just how strong his Faith is in the middle of his most dangerous mission. . . .

Tad Williams became an international bestseller with his very first novel, *Tailchaser's Song,* and the high quality of his output and the devotion of his readers has kept him on the top of the charts ever since as a *New York Times* and *London Sunday Times* bestseller. His other novels include *The Dragonbone Chair, The Stone of Farewell, To Green Angel Tower, City of Golden Shadow, River of Blue Fire, Mountain of Black Glass, Sea of Silver Light, Caliban's Hour, Child of an Ancient City* (with Nina Kiriki Hoffman), *Tad Williams' Mirror World: An Illustrated Novel, The War of the Flowers,* a collection, *Rite: Short Work,* and a collection of two novellas, one by Williams and one by Raymond E. Feist, *The Wood Boy/The Burning Man.* As editor, he has produced the big retrospective anthology *A Treasury of Fantasy.* His most recent books are *Shadowmarch, Shadowplay,* and *Shadowrise.* Coming up is another Shadowmarch novel, *Shadowheart.* In addition to his novels, Williams writes comic books as well as film and television scripts, and is cofounder of an interactive television company. He lives with his family in Woodside, California.

The seed whispers, sings, offers, instructs.

A wise man of the homeworld once said, "Human beings can alter their lives by altering their attitudes of mind." Everything is possible for a committed man or woman. The universe is in our reach.

Visit the Orgasmium—now open 24 hours. We take Senior Credits. The Orgasmium—where YOU come first!

Your body temperature is normal. Your stress levels are normal, tending toward higher than normal. If this trend continues, you are recommended to see a physician.

I'm almost alive! And I'm your perfect companion—I'm entirely portable. I want to love you. Come try me. Trade my personality with friends. Join the fun!

Comb properties now available. Consult your local environment node. Brand new multi-family and single-family dwellings, low down payment with government entry loans . . . !

Commodity prices are up slightly on the Sackler Index at this hour, despite a morning of sluggish trading. The Prime Minister will detail her plans to reinvigorate the economy in her speech to Parliament . . .

A wise woman of the homeworld once said, "Keep your face to the sunshine and you cannot see the shadow."

His name is Lamentation Kane and he is a Guardian of Covenant—a holy assassin. His masters have placed a seed of blasphemy in his head. It itches like unredeemed sin and fills his skull with foul pagan noise.

The faces of his fellow travelers on the landing shuttle are bored and vacuous. How can these infidels live with this constant murmur in their heads? How can they survive and stay sane with the constant pinpoint flashing of attention signals at the edge of vision, the raw, sharp pulse of a world bristling and burbling with information?

It is like being stuck in a hive of insects, Kane thinks—insects doing their best to imitate human existence without understanding it. He longs for the sweet, singular voice of Spirit, soothing as cool water on inflamed skin. Always before, no matter the terrors of his mission, that voice has been with him, soothing him, reminding him of his holy purpose. All his life, Spirit has been with him. All his life until now.

Humble yourselves therefore under the strong hand of God, so that He may raise you up in due time.

Sweet and gentle like spring rain. Unlike this unending drizzle of filth, each word Spirit has ever spoken has been precious, bright like silver.

Cast all your burdens on Him, for He cares for you. Be in control of yourself and alert. Your enemy, the devil, prowls around like a roaring lion, looking for someone to devour.

Those were the last words Spirit spoke to him before the military scientists silenced the Word of God and replaced it with the endless, godless prattle of the infidel world, Archimedes.

For the good of all mankind, they assured him: Lamentation Kane must sin again so that one day all men would be free to worship God. Besides, the elders pointed out, what was there for him to fear? If he succeeds and escapes Archimedes the pagan seed will be removed and Spirit will speak in his thoughts again. If he does not escape—well, Kane will hear the true voice of God at the foot of His mighty throne. *Well done, my good and faithful servant . . .*

Beginning descent. Please return to pods, the pagan voices chirp in his head, prickling like nettles. *Thank you for traveling with us. Put all food and packaging in the receptacle and close it. This is your last chance to purchase duty-free drugs and alcohol. Cabin temperature is 20 degrees centigrade. Pull the harness snug. Beginning descent. Cabin pressure stable. Lander will detach in twenty seconds. Ten seconds. Nine seconds. Eight seconds . . .*

It never ends, and each godless word burns, prickles, itches.

Who needs to know so much about nothing?

A child of one of the Christian cooperative farms on Covenant's flat and empty plains, he was brought to New Jerusalem as a candidate for the elite Guardian unit. When he saw for the first time the white towers and golden domes of his planet's greatest city, Kane had been certain that Heaven would look just that way. Now, as Hellas City rises up to meet him, capitol of great Archimedes and stronghold of his people's enemies, it is bigger than even his grandest, most exaggerated memories of New Jerusalem—an immense sprawl with no visible ending, a lumpy white and gray and green patchwork of complex structures and orderly parks and lacy polyceramic web skyscrapers that bend gently in the cloudy upper skies like an oceanic kelp forest. The scale is astounding. For the first time ever in his life, Lamentation Kane has a moment of doubt—not in the rightness of his cause, but in the certainty of its victory.

But he reminds himself of what the Lord told Joshua: *Behold I have given into thy hands Jericho, and the king thereof, and all the valiant men . . .*

Have you had a Creamy Crunch today? It blares through his thoughts like a klaxon. *You want it! You need it! Available at any food outlet. Creamy Crunch makes cream crunchy! Don't be a bitch, Mom! Snag me a CC—or three!*

The devil owns the Kingdom of Earth. A favorite saying of one of his favorite teachers. *But even from his high throne he cannot see the City of Heaven.*

Now with a subdermal glow-tattoo in every package! Just squeeze it in under the skin—and start shining!

Lord Jesus, protect me in this dark place and give me strength to do your work once more, Kane prays. *I serve You. I serve Covenant.*

It never stops, and only gets more strident after the lander touches down and they are ushered through the locks into the port complex. *Remember the wise words, air quality is in the low thirties on the Teng Fuo scale today, first time visitors to Archimedes go here, returning go there,* where to stand, what to say, what to have ready. Restaurants, news feeds, Information for transportation services, overnight accommodations, immigration law, emergency services, yammer yammer yammer until Kane wants to scream. He stares at the smug citizens of Archimedes around him and loathes every one of them. How can they walk and smile and talk to each other with this Babel in their heads, without God in their hearts?

Left. Follow the green tiles. Left. Follow the green tiles. They aren't even people, they can't be—just crude imitations. And the variety of voices with which the seed bedevils him! High-pitched, low-pitched, fast and persuasive, moderately slow and persuasive, adult voices, children's voices, accents of a dozen sorts, most of which he can't even identify and can barely understand. His blessed Spirit is one voice and one voice only and he longs for her desperately. He always thinks of Spirit as "her," although it could just as easily be the calm, sweet voice of a male child. It doesn't matter. Nothing as crass as earthly sexual distinctions matter, any more than with God's holy angels. Spirit has been his constant companion since childhood, his advisor, his inseparable friend. But now he has a pagan seed in his brain and he may never hear her blessed voice again.

I will never leave thee, nor forsake thee. That's what Spirit told him the night he was baptized, the night she first spoke to him. Six years old. *I will never leave thee, nor forsake thee.*

He cannot think of that. He will not think of anything that might undermine his courage for the mission, of course, but there is a greater danger: some types of thoughts, if strong enough, can trigger the port's security E-Grams, which can perceive certain telltale patterns, especially if they are repeated.

A wise man of the homeworld once said, "Man is the measure of all things . . ." The foreign seed doesn't want him thinking of anything else, anyway.

Have you considered living in Holyoake Harbor? another voice asks, cutting through the first. *Only a twenty minute commute to the business district, but a different world of ease and comfort.*

. . . And of things which are not, that they are not, the first voice finishes, swimming back to the top. *Another wise fellow made the case more directly: "The world holds two classes of men—intelligent men without religion, and religious men without intelligence."*

Kane almost shivers despite the climate controls. *Blur your thoughts,* he reminds himself. He does his best to let the chatter of voices and the swirl of passing faces numb and stupefy him, making himself a beast instead of a man, the better to hide from God's enemies.

He passes the various mechanical sentries and the first two human guard posts as easily as he hoped he would—his military brethren have prepared his disguise well. He is in line at the final human checkpoint when he catches a glimpse of her, or at least he thinks it must be her—a small, brown-skinned woman sagging between two heavily armored port security guards who clutch her elbows in a parody of assistance. For a moment their eyes meet and her dark stare is frank before she hangs her head again in a convincing imitation of shame. The words from the briefing wash up in his head through the fog of Archimedean voices—*Martyrdom Sister*—but he does his best to blur them again just as quickly. He can't imagine any word that will set off the E-Grams as quickly as "Martyrdom."

The final guard post is more difficult, as it is meant to be. The sentry, almost faceless behind an array of enhanced light scanners and lenses, does not like to see Arjuna on Kane's itinerary, his last port of call before Archimedes. Arjuna is not a treaty world for either Archhimedes or Covenant, although both hope to make it so, and is not officially policed by either side.

The official runs one of his scanners over Kane's itinerary again. "Can you tell me why you stopped at Arjuna, Citizen McNally?"

Kane repeats the story of staying there with his cousin who works in the mining industry. Arjuna is rich with platinum and other minerals, another reason both sides want it. At the moment, though, neither the Rationalists of Archimedes or the Abramites of Covenant can get any traction there: the majority of Arjuna's settlers, colonists originally from the homeworld's Indian sub-continent, are comfortable with both sides—a fact that makes both Archimedes and Covenant quite uncomfortable indeed.

The guard post official doesn't seem entirely happy with Lamentation Kane's explanation and is beginning to investigate the false personality a little more closely. Kane wonders how much longer until the window of distraction is opened. He turns casually, looking up and down the transparent u-glass cells along the far wall until he locates the one in which the brown-skinned woman is being questioned. Is she a Muslim? A Copt? Or perhaps something entirely different—there are Australian Aboriginal Jews on Covenant, remnants of the Lost Tribes movement back on the homeworld. But whoever or whatever she is doesn't matter, he reminds himself: she is a sister in god and she has volunteered to sacrifice herself for the sake of the mission—*his* mission.

She turns for a moment and their eyes meet again through the warping glass. She has acne scars on her cheeks but she's pretty, surprisingly young to be given such a task. He wonders what her name is. When he returns—if he returns—he will go to the Great Tabernacle in New Jerusalem and light a candle for her.

Brown eyes. She seems sad as she looks at him before turning back to the guards. Could that be true? The Martyrs are the most privileged of all during their time in the training center. And she must know she will be looking on the face of God Himself very soon. How can she not be joyful? Does she fear the pain of giving up her earthly body?

As the sentry in front of him seems to stare out at nothing, reading the information that marches across his vision, Lamentation Kane opens his mouth to say something—to make small-talk the way a real returning citizen of Archimedes would after a long time abroad, a citizen guilty of nothing worse than maybe having watched a few religious broadcasts on Arjuna—when he sees movement out of the corner of his eye. Inside the u-glass holding cell the young, brown-skinned woman lifts her arms. One of the armored guards lurches back from the table, half-falling, the other reaches out his gloved hand as though to restrain her, but his face has the hopeless, slack expression of a man who sees his own death. A moment later bluish flames run up her arms, blackening the sleeves of her loose dress, and then she vanishes in a flare of magnesium white light.

People are shrieking and diving away from the glass wall, which is now spider-webbed with cracks. The light burns and flickers and the insides of the walls blacken with a crust of what Kane guesses must be human fat turning to ash.

A human explosion—nanobiotic thermal flare—that partially failed. That will be their conclusion. But of course, the architects of Kane's mission didn't want an actual explosion. They want a distraction.

The sentry in the guardpost polarizes the windows and locks up his booth. Before hurrying off to help the emergency personnel fight the blaze that is already leaking clouds of black smoke into the concourse, he thrusts Kane's itinerary into his hand and waves him through, then locks off the transit point.

Lamentation Kane would be happy to move on, even if he were the innocent traveler he pretends to be. The smoke is terrible, with the disturbing, sweet smell of cooked meat.

What had her last expression been like? It is hard to remember anything except those endlessly deep, dark eyes. Had that been a little smile or is he trying to convince himself? And if it had been fear, why should that be surprising? Even the saints must have feared to burn to death.

Yea, though I walk through the valley of the shadow of death, I will fear no evil . . .

Welcome back to Hellas, Citizen McNally! a voice in his head proclaims, and then the other voices swim up beneath it, a crowd, a buzz, an itch.

He does his best not to stare as the cab hurtles across the metroscape, but he cannot help being impressed by the sheer size of Archimedes' first city. It is one thing to be told how many millions live there and to try to understand that it is several times the size of New Jerusalem, but another entirely to see the hordes of people crowding the sidewalks and skyways. Covenant's population is mostly dispersed on pastoral settlements like the one on which Kane was raised, agrarian cooperatives that, as his teachers explained to him, keep God's children close to the earth that nurtures them. Sometimes it is hard to realize that the deep, reddish soil he had spent his childhood digging and turning and nurturing was not the same soil as the Bible described. Once he even asked a teacher why if God made Earth, the People of the Book had left it behind.

"God made all the worlds to be earth for His children," the woman explained. "Just as he made all the lands of the old Earth, then gave them to different folk to have for their homes. But he always kept the sweetest lands, the lands of milk and honey, for the children of Abraham, and that's why when we left earth he gave us Covenant."

As he thinks about it now Kane feels a surge of warmth and loneliness commingled. It's true that the hardest thing to do for love is to give up the beloved. At this moment, he misses Covenant so badly it is all he can do not to cry out. It is astounding in one as experienced as himself. *God's warriors don't sigh*, he tells himself sternly. *They make others sigh instead. They bring lamentation to God's enemies. Lamentation.*

He exits the cab some distance from the safe house and walks the rest of the way, floating in smells both familiar and exotic. He rounds the neighborhood twice to make sure he is not followed, then enters the flatblock, takes the slow but quiet elevator up to the eighteenth floor, and lets himself in with the key code. It looks like any other Covenant safe house on any of the other colony worlds, cupboards well stocked with nourishment and medical supplies, little in the way of furniture but a bed and a single chair and a small table. These are not places of rest and relaxation, these are way stations on the road to Jericho.

It is time for him to change.

Kane fills the bathtub with water. He finds the chemical ice, activates a dozen packs and tosses them in. Then he goes to the kitchen and locates the necessary mineral and chemical supplements. He pours enough water into the mixture to make himself a thick, bitter milkshake and drinks it down while he waits for the water in the tub to cool. When the temperature has dropped far enough he strips naked and climbs in.

"You see, Kane," one of the military scientists had explained, "we've reached a point where we can't smuggle even a small hand-weapon onto Archimedes, let alone something useful, and they regulate their own citizens' possession of weapons so thoroughly that we cannot chance trying to obtain one there. So we have gone another direction. We have created Guardians—human weapons. That is what you are, praise the lord. It started in your childhood. That's why you've always been different from your peers—faster, stronger, smarter. But we've come to the limit of what we can do with genetics and training. We need to give you what you need to make yourself into the true instrument of God's justice. May He bless this and all our endeavors in His name. Amen."

"Amen," the Spirit in his head told him. "You are now going to fall asleep."

"Amen," said Lamentation Kane.

And then they gave him the first injection.

When he woke up that first time he was sore, but nowhere near as sore as he was the first time he activated the nanobiotes or "notes" as the scientists liked to call them. When the notes went to work, it was like a terrible sunburn on the outside and the inside both, and like being pounded with a roundball bat for at least an hour, and like lying in the road while a good-sized squadron of full-dress Holy Warriors marched over him.

In other words, it hurt.

Now, in the safehouse, he closes his eyes, turns down the babble of the Archimedes seed as far as it will let him, and begins to work.

It is easier now than it used to be, certainly easier than that terrible first time when he was so clumsy that he almost tore his own muscles loose from tendon and bone.

He doesn't just *flex*, he thinks about where the muscles are that would flex if he wanted to flex them, then how he would just begin to move them if he were going to move them extremely slowly, and with that first thought comes the little tug of the cells unraveling their connections and re-knitting in different, more useful configurations, slow as a plant reaching toward the sun. Even with all this delicacy, his temperature rises and his muscles spasm and cramp, but not like the first time. That was like being born—no, like being judged and found wanting, as though the very meat of his earthly body was trying to tear itself free, as though devils pierced his joints with hot iron pitchforks. Agony.

Had the sister felt something like this at the end? Was there any way to open the door to God's house without terrible, holy pain? She had brown eyes. He thinks they were sad. Had she been frightened? Why would Jesus let her be frightened, when even He had cried out on the cross?

I praise You, Lord, Lamentation Kane tells the pain. *This is Your way of reminding me to pay attention. I am Your servant, and I am proud to put on Your holy armor.*

It takes him at least two hours to finish changing at the best of times. Tonight, with the fatigue of his journey and long entry process and the curiously troubling effect of the woman's martyrdom tugging at his thoughts, it takes him over three.

Kane gets out of the tub shivering, most of the heat dispersed and his skin almost blue-white with cold. Before wrapping the towel around himself he looks at the results of all his work. It's hard to see any differences except for a certain broadness to his chest that was not there before, but he runs his fingers along the hard shell of his stomach and the sheath of gristle that now protects his windpipe and is satisfied. The thickening beneath the skin will not stop high-speed projectiles from close up, but they should help shed the energy of any more distant shot and will allow him to take a bullet or two from nearer and still manage to do his job. Trellises of springy cartilage strengthen his ankles and wrists. His muscles are augmented, his lungs and circulation improved mightily. He is a Guardian, and with every movement he can feel the holy modifications that have been given to him. Beneath the appearance of normality he is strong as Goliath, scaly and supple as a serpent.

He is starving, of course. The cupboards are full of powdered nutritional supplement drinks. He adds water and ice from the kitchen unit, mixes the first one up and downs it in a long swallow. He drinks five before he begins to feel full.

Kane props himself up on the bed—things are still sliding and grinding a little inside him, the last work of change just finishing—and turns the wall on. The images jump into life and the seed in his head speaks for them. He wills his way past sports and fashion and drama, all the unimportant gibberish with which these creatures fill their empty hours, until he finds a stream of current events. Because it is Archimedes, hive of Rationalist pagans, even the news is corrupted with filth, gossip and whoremongering, but he manages to squint his way through the offending material to find a report on what the New Hellas authorities are calling a failed terrorist explosion at the port. A picture of the Martyrdom Sister flashes onto the screen—taken from her travel documents, obviously, anything personal in her face well hidden by her training—but seeing her again gives him a strange jolt, as though the notes that tune his body have suddenly begun one last, forgotten operation.

Nefise Erim, they call her. Not her real name, that's almost certain, any more than Keenan McNally is his. *Outcast*, that's her true name. *Scorned*—that could be her name too, as it could be his. Scorned by the unbelievers, scorned by the smug, faithless creatures who, like Christ's ancient tormentors, fear the word of God so much they try to ban Him from their lives, from their entire planet! But God can't be banned, not as long as one human heart remains alive to His voice. As long as the Covenant system survives, Kane knows, God will wield his mighty sword and the unbelievers will learn real fear.

Oh, please, Lord, grant that I may serve you well. Give us victory over our enemies. Help us to punish those who would deny You.

And just as he lifts this silent prayer, he sees *her* face on the screen. Not his sister in martyrdom, with her wide, deep eyes and dark skin. No, it is her—the devil's mistress, Keeta Januari, Prime Minister of Archimedes.

His target.

Januari is herself rather dark skinned, he cannot help noticing. It is disconcerting. He has seen her before, of course, her image replayed before him dozens upon dozens of times, but this is the first time he has noticed a shade to her skin that is darker than any mere suntan, a hint of something else in her background beside the pale, Scandinavian forebears so obvious in her bone structure. It is as if the martyred sister Nefise has somehow suffused everything, even his target. Or is it that the dead woman has somehow crept into his thoughts so deeply that he is witnessing her everywhere?

If you can see it, you can eat it! He has mostly learned to ignore the horrifying chatter in his head, but sometimes it still reaches up and slaps his thoughts away. *Barnstorm Buffet! We don't care if they have to roll you out the door afterward—you'll get your money's worth!*

It doesn't matter what he sees in the Prime Minister, or thinks he sees. A shade lighter or darker means nothing. If the devil's work out here among the stars has a face, it is the handsome, narrow-chinned visage of Keeta Januari, leader of the Rationalists. And if God ever wanted someone dead, she is that person.

———

She won't be his first: Kane has sent eighteen souls to judgment already. Eleven of them were pagan spies or dangerous rabble-rousers on Covenant. One of those was the leader of a crypto-rationalist cult in the Crescent—the death was a favor to the Islamic partners in Covenant's ruling coalition, Kane found out later. Politics. He doesn't know how he feels about that, although he knows the late Doctor Hamoud was a doubter and a liar and had been corrupting good Muslims. Still . . . politics.

Five were infiltrators among the Holy Warriors of Covenant, his people's army. Most of these had half-expected to be discovered, and several of them had resisted desperately.

The last two were a politician and his wife on the unaffiliated world of Arjuna, important Rationalist sympathizers. At his masters' bidding Kane made it look like a robbery gone wrong instead of an assassination: this was not the time to make the Lord's hand obvious in Arjuna's affairs. Still, there were rumors and accusations across Arjuna's public networks. The gossipers and speculators had even given the unknown murderer a nickname—the Angel of Death.

Dr. Prishrahan and his wife had fought him. Neither of them had wanted to die. Kane had let them resist even though he could have killed them both in a moment. It gave credence to the robbery scenario. But he hadn't enjoyed it. Neither had the Prishrahans, of course.

He will avenge the blood of His servants, and will render vengeance to His adversaries, Spirit reminded him when he had finished with the doctor and his wife, and he understood. Kane's duty is not to judge. He is not one of the flock, but closer to the wolves he destroys. Lamentation Kane is God's executioner.

He is now cold enough from his long submersion that he puts on clothes. He is still tender in his joints as well. He goes out onto the balcony, high in the canyons of flatblocks pinpricked with illuminated windows, thousands upon thousands of squares of light. The immensity of the place still unnerves him a little. It's strange to think that what is happening behind one little lighted window in this immensity of sparkling urban night is going to rock this massive world to its foundations.

It is hard to remember the prayers as he should. Ordinarily Spirit is there with the words before he has a moment to feel lonely. *"I will not leave you comfortless: I will come to you."*

But he does not feel comforted at this moment. He is alone.

"Looking for love?" The voice in his head whispers this time, throaty and exciting. A bright twinkle of coordinates flicker at the edge of his vision. *"I'm looking for you . . . and you can have me almost nothing . . ."*

He closes his eyes tight against the immensity of the pagan city.

Fear thou not; for I am with thee: be not dismayed; for I am thy God.

He walks to the auditorium just to see the place where the prime minister will speak. He does not approach very closely. It looms against the grid of light, a vast rectangle like an axe head smashed into the central plaza of Hellas City. He does not linger.

As he slides through the crowds it is hard not to look at the people around him as though he has already accomplished his task. What would they think if they knew who he was? Would they shrink back from the terror of the Lord God's wrath? Or would a deed of such power and piety speak to them even through their fears?

I am ablaze with the light of the Lord, he wants to tell them. *I have let God make me His instrument—I am full of glory!* But he says nothing, of course, only walks amid the multitudes with his heart grown silent and turned inward.

Kane eats in a restaurant. The food is so over-spiced as to be tasteless, and he yearns for the simple meals of the farm on which he was raised. Even military manna is better than this! The customers twitter and laugh just like the Archimedes seed in their heads, as if it is that babbling obscenity that has programmed them instead of the other way around. How these people surrounded themselves with distraction and glare and noise to obscure the emptiness of their souls!

He goes to a place where women dance. It is strange to watch them, because they smile and smile and they are all as beautiful and naked as a dark dream, but they seem to him like damned souls, doomed to act out this empty farce of love and attraction throughout eternity. He cannot get the thought of martyred Nefise Erim out of his head. At last he chooses one of the women—she does not look much like the martyred one, but she is darker than the others—and lets her lead him to her room behind the place where they dance. She feels the hardened tissues beneath his skin and tells him he is very muscular. He empties himself inside her and then, afterward, she asks him why he is crying. He tells her she is mistaken. When she asks again he slaps her. Although he holds back his strength he still knocks her off the bed. The room adds a small surcharge to his bill.

He lets her go back to her work. She is an innocent, of sorts: she has been listening to the godless voices in her head all her life and knows nothing else. No wonder she dances like a damned thing.

Kane is soiled now as he walks the streets again, but his great deed will wipe the taint from him as it always does. He is a Guardian of Covenant, and soon he will be annealed by holy fire.

His masters want the deed done while the crowd is gathered to see the prime minister, and so the question seems simple: before or after? He thinks at first that he will do it when she arrives, as she steps from the car and is hurried into the corridor leading to the great hall. That seems safest. After she has spoken it will be much more difficult, with her security fully deployed and the hall's own security acting with them. Still, the more he thinks about it the more he feels sure that it must be inside the hall. Only a few thousand would be gathered there to see her speak, but millions more will be watching on the screens surrounding the massive building. If he strikes quickly his deed will be witnessed by this whole world—and other worlds, too.

Surely God wants it that way. Surely He wants the unbeliever destroyed in full view of the public waiting to be instructed.

Kane does not have time or resources to counterfeit permission to be in the building—the politicians and hall security will be checked and re-checked, and will be in place long before Prime Minister Januari arrives. Which means that the only people allowed to enter without going through careful screening will be the prime minister's own party. That is a possibility, but he will need help with it.

Making contact with local assets is usually a bad sign—it means something has gone wrong with the original plan—but Kane knows that with a task this important he cannot afford to be superstitious. He leaves a signal in the established place. The local assets come to the safehouse after sunset. When he opens the door he finds two men, one young and one old, both disconcertingly ordinary-looking, the kind of men who might come to tow your car or fumigate your flat. The middle-aged one introduces himself as Heinrich Sartorius, his companion just as Carl. Sartorius motions Kane not to speak while Carl sweeps the room with a small object about the size of a toothbrush.

"Clear," the youth announces. He is bony and homely, but he moves with a certain grace, especially while using his hands.

"Praise the Lord," Sartorius says. "And blessings on you, brother. What can we do to help you with Christ's work?"

"Are you really the one from Arjuna?" young Carl askes suddenly.

"Quiet, boy. This is serious." Sartorius turns back to Kane with an expectant look on his face. "He's a good lad. It's just—that meant a lot to the community, what happened there on Arjuna."

Kane ignores this. He is wary of the Death Angel nonsense. "I need to know what the prime minister's security detail wears. Details. And I want the layout of the auditorium, with a focus on air and water ducts."

The older man frowns. "They'll have that all checked out, won't they?"

"I'm sure. Can you get it for me without attracting attention?"

"'Course." Sartorius nods. "Carl'll find it for you right now. He's a whiz. Ain't that right, boy?" The man turns back to Kane. "We're not backward, you know. The unbelievers always say it's because we're backward, but Carl here was up near the top of his class in mathematics. We just kept Jesus in our hearts when the rest of these people gave Him up, that's the difference."

"Praise Him," says Carl, already working the safehouse wall, images flooding past so quickly that even with his augmented vision Kane can barely make out a tenth of them.

"Yes, *praise* Him," Sartorius agrees, nodding his head as though there has been a long and occasionally heated discussion about how best to deal with Jesus.

Kane is beginning to feel the ache in his joints again, which usually means he needs more protein. He heads for the small kitchen to fix himself another nutrition drink. "Can I get you two anything?" he asks.

"We're good," says the older man. "Just happy doing the Lord's work."

They make too much noise, he decides. Not that most people would have heard them, but Kane isn't most people.

I am the sword of the Lord, he tells himself silently. He can scarcely hear himself think it over the murmur of the Archimedes seed, which although turned down low is still spouting meteorological information, news, tags of philosophy and other trivia like a madman on a street corner. Below the spot where Kane hangs the three men of the go-suited security detail communicate among themselves with hand-signs as they investigate the place he has entered the building.

He has altered the evidence of his incursion to look like someone has tried and failed to get into the auditorium through the intake duct.

The guards seem to draw the desired conclusion: after another flurry of hand-signals, and presumably after relaying the all-clear to the other half of the security squad, who are doubtless inspecting the outside of the same intake duct, the three turn and begin to walk back up the steep conduit, the flow of air making their movements unstable, headlamps splashing unpredictably over the walls. But Kane is waiting above them like a spider, in the shadows of a high place where the massive conduit bends around one of the building's pillars, his hardened fingertips dug into the concrete, his augmented muscles tensed and locked. He waits until all three pass below him then drops down silently behind them and crushes the throat of the last man so he can't alert the others. He then snaps the guard's neck and tosses the body over his shoulder, then scrambles back up the walls into the place he has prepared, a hammock of canvas much the same color as the inside of the duct. In a matter of seconds he strips the body, praying fervently that the other two will not have noticed that their comrade is missing. He pulls on the man's go-suit, which is still warm, then leaves the guard's body in the hammock and springs down to the ground just as the second guard realizes there is no one behind him.

As the man turns toward him Kane sees his lips moving behind the face shield and knows the guard must be talking to him by seed. The imposture is broken, or will be in a moment. Can he pretend his own communications machinery is malfunctioning? Not if these guards are any good. If they work for the prime minister of Archimedes, they probably are. He has a moment before the news is broadcast to all the other security people in the building.

Kane strides forward making nonsensical hand-signs. The other guard's eyes widen: he does not recognize either the signs or the face behind the polymer shield. Kane shatters the man's neck with a two-handed strike even as the guard struggles to pull his side arm. Then Kane leaps at the last guard just as he turns.

Except it isn't a he. It's a woman and she's fast. She actually has her gun out of the holster before he kills her.

He has only moments, he knows: the guards will have a regular check-in to their squad leader. He sprints for the side-shaft that should take him to the area above the ceiling of the main hall.

Women as leaders. Women as soldiers. Women dancing naked in public before strangers. Is there anything these Archimedeans will not do to debase the daughters of Eve? Force them all into whoredom, as the Babylonians did?

The massive space above the ceiling is full of riggers and technicians and heavily armed guards. A dozen of those, at least. Most of them are sharpshooters keeping an eye on the crowd through the scopes on their high-powered guns, which is lucky. Some of them might not even see him until he's on his way down.

Two of the heavily armored troopers turn as he steps out into the open. He is being queried for identification, but even if they think he is one of their own they will not let him get more than a few yards across the floor. He throws his hands in the air and takes a few casual steps toward them, shaking his head and pointing at his helmet. Then he leaps forward, praying they do not understand how quickly he can move.

He covers the twenty yards or so in just a little more than a second. To confound their surprise, he does not attack but dives past the two who have already seen him and the third just turning to find out what the conversation is about. He reaches the edge of the flies and launches himself out into space, tucked and spinning to make himself a more difficult target. Still, he feels a high-speed projectile hit his leg and penetrate a little way, slowed by the guard's go-suit and stopped by his own hardened flesh.

He lands so hard that the stolen guard helmet pops off his head and bounces away. The first screams and shouts of surprise are beginning to rise from the crowd of parliamentarians, but Kane can hardly hear them. The shock of his fifty-foot fall swirls through the enhanced cartilage of his knees and ankles and wrists, painful but manageable. His heart is beating so fast it almost buzzes, and he is so accelerated that the noise of the audience seemed like the sound of something completely inhuman, the deep scrape of a glacier, the tectonic rumbling of a mountain's roots. Two more bullets snap into the floor beside him, chips of concrete and fragments of carpet spinning slowly in the air, hovering like ashes in a fiery updraft. The woman at the lectern turns toward him in molasses-time and it is indeed her, Keeta Januari, the Whore of Babylon. As he reaches toward her he can see the individual muscles of her face react—eyebrows pulled up, forehead wrinkling, surprised . . . but not frightened.

How can that be?

He is already leaping toward her, curving the fingers of each hand into hardened claws for the killing strike. A fraction of a second to cross the space between them as bullets snap by from above and either side, the noise scything past a long instant later, *wow, wow, wow*. Time hanging, disconnected from history. God's hand. He *is* God's hand, and this is what it must feel like to be in the presence of God Himself, this shimmering, endless, bright NOW . . .

And then pain explodes through him and sets his nerves on fire and everything goes suddenly and irrevocably black.

Lamentation Kane wakes in a white room, the light from everywhere and nowhere. He is being watched, of course. Soon, the torture will begin.

"*Beloved, think it not strange concerning the fiery trial which is to try you, as though some strange thing happened unto you . . .*" Those were the holy words Spirit whispered to him when he lay badly wounded in the hospital after capturing the last of the Holy Warrior infiltrators, another augmented soldier like himself, a bigger, stronger man who almost killed him before Kane managed to put a stiffened finger through his eyeball into his brain. Spirit recited the words to him again and again during his recuperation: "*But rejoice, inasmuch as ye are partakers of Christ's sufferings; that, when his glory . . . when his glory. . . .*"

To his horror, he cannot remember the rest of the passage from Peter.

He cannot help thinking of the martyred young woman who gave her life so that he could fail so utterly. He will see her soon. Will he be able to meet her eye? Is there shame in Heaven?

I will be strong, Kane promises her shade, *no matter what they do to me.*

One of the cell's walls turns from white to transparent. The room beyond is full of people, most of them in military uniforms or white medical smocks. Only two wear civilian clothing, a pale man and . . . her. Keeta Januari.

"You may throw yourself against the glass if you want." Her voice seems to come out of the air on all sides. "It is very, very thick and very, very strong."

He only stares. He will not make himself a beast, struggling to escape while they laugh. These people are the ones who think themselves related to animals. Animals! Kane knows that the Lord God has given his people dominion.

"Over all the beasts and fowls of the earth," he says out loud.

"So," says Prime Minister Januari. "So, this is the Angel of Death."

"That is not my name."

"We know your name, Kane. We have been watching you since you reached Archimedes."

A lie, surely. They would never have let him get so close.

She narrows her eyes. "I would have expected an angel to look more . . . an-gelic."

"I'm no angel, as you almost found out."

"Ah, if you're not, then you must be one of the ministers of grace." She sees the look on his face. "How sad. I forgot that Shakespeare was banned by your mullahs. 'Angels and ministers of grace defend us!' From Macbeth. It proceeds a murder."

"We Christians do not have mullahs," he says as evenly as he can. He does not care about the rest of the nonsense she speaks. "Those are the people of the Cres-cent, our brothers of the Book."

She laughed. "I thought you would be smarter than the rest of your sort, Kane, but you parrot the same nonsense. Do you know that only a few genera-tions back your 'brothers' as you call them set off a thermonuclear device, trying to kill your grandparents and the rest of the Christian and Zionist 'brothers'?"

"In the early days, before the Covenant, there was confusion." Everyone knew the story. Did she think to shame him with old history, ancient quotations, banned playwrights from the wicked old days of Earth? If so, then both of them had underestimated each other as adversaries.

Of course, at the moment she did hold a somewhat better position.

"So, then, not an angel but a minister. But you don't pray to be protected from death, but to be able to cause it."

"I do the Lord's will."

"Bullshit, to use a venerable old term. You are a murderer many times over, Kane. You tried to murder me." But Januari does not look at him as though at an enemy. Nor is there kindness in her gaze, either. She looks at him as though he is a poisonous insect in a jar—an object to be careful with, yes, but mostly a thing to be studied. "What shall we do with you?"

"Kill me. If you have any of the humanity you claim, you will release me and send me to Heaven. But I know you will torture me."

She raises an eyebrow. "Why would we do that?"

"For information. Our nations are at war, even though the politicians have not yet admitted it to their peoples. You know it, woman. I know it. Everyone in this room knows it."

Keeta Januari smiles. "You will get no argument from me or anyone here about the state of affairs between Archimedes and the Covenant system. But why would we torture you for information we already have? We are not barbarians. We are not primitives—like some others. We do not force our citizens to worship savage old myths . . ."

"You force them to be silent! You punish those who would worship the God of their fathers. You have persecuted the People of the Book wherever you have found them!"

"We have kept our planet free from the mania of religious warfare and extremism. We have never interfered in the choices of Covenant."

"You have tried to keep us from gaining converts."

The prime minister shakes her head. "Gaining converts? Trying to hijack entire cultures, you mean. Stealing the right of colonies to be free of Earth's old tribal ghosts. We are the same people that let your predecessors worship the way they wished to—we fought to protect their freedom, and were repaid when they tried to force their beliefs on us at gunpoint." Her laugh is harsh. "'Christian tolerance'—two words that do not belong together no matter how often they've been coupled. And we all know what your Islamists and Zionists brothers are like. Even if you destroy all of the Archimedean alliance and every single one of us unbelievers, you'll only find yourself fighting your allies instead. The madness won't stop until the last living psychopath winds up all alone on a hill of ashes, shouting praise to his god."

Kane feels his anger rising and closes his mouth. He suffuses his blood with calming chemicals. It confuses him, arguing with her. She is a woman and she should give comfort, but she is speaking only lies—cruel, dangerous lies. This is what happens when the natural order of things is upset. "You are a devil. I will speak to you no more. Do whatever it is you're going to do."

"Here's another bit of Shakespeare," she says. "If your masters hadn't banned him, you could have quoted it at me. *'But man, proud man,/dressed in a little brief authority,/most ignorant of what he's most assured'*—that's nicely put, isn't it? *'His glassy essence/ like an angry ape/ plays such fantastic tricks before high heaven/ as make the angels weep.'*" She puts her hands together in a gesture disturbingly reminiscent of prayer. He cannot turn away from her gaze. "So—what *are* we going to do with you? We could execute you quietly, of course. A polite fiction—died from injuries sustained in the arrest—and no one would make too much fuss."

The man behind her clears his throat. "Madame Prime Minster, I respectfully suggest we take this conversation elsewhere. The doctors are waiting to see the prisoner . . ."

"Shut up, Healy." She turns to look at Kane again, really look, her blue eyes sharp as scalpels. She is older than the Martyrdom Sister by a good twenty years, and despite the dark tint her skin is much paler, but somehow, for a dizzying second, they are the same.

Why do you allow me to become confused, Lord, between the murderer and the martyr?

"Kane comma Lamentation," she says. "Quite a name. Is that your enemies lamenting, or is it you, crying out helplessly before the power of your God?" She holds up her hand. "Don't bother to answer. In parts of the Covenant system you're a hero, you know—a sort of superhero. Were you aware of that? Or have you been traveling too much?"

He does his best to ignore her. He knows he will be lied to, manipulated, that the psychological torments will be more subtle and more important than the physical torture. The only thing he does not understand is: Why her—why the prime minister herself? Surely he isn't so important. The fact that she stands in front of him at this moment instead of in front of God is, after all, a demonstration that he is a failure.

As if in answer to this thought, a voice murmurs in the back of his skull, *"Arjuna's Angel of Death captured in attempt on PM Januari."* Another inquires, *"Have you smelled yourself lately? Even members of parliament can lose freshness—just ask one!"* Even here, in the heart of the beast, the voices in his head will not be silenced.

"We need to study you," the prime minister says at last. "We haven't caught a Guardian-class agent before—not one of the new ones, like you. We didn't know if we could do it—the scrambler field was only recently developed." She smiles again, a quick icy flash like a first glimpse of snow in high mountains. "It wouldn't have meant anything if you'd succeeded, you know. There are at least a dozen more in my party who can take my place and keep this system safe against you and your masters. But I made good bait—and you leaped into the trap. Now we're going to find out what makes you such a nasty instrument, little Death Angel."

He hopes that now the charade is over they will at least shut off the seed in his head. Instead, they leave it in place but disable his controls so that he can't affect it at all. Children's voices sing to him about the value of starting each day with a healthy breakfast and he grinds his teeth. The mad chorus yammers and sings to him nonstop. The pagan seed shows him pictures he does not want to see, gives him information about which he does not care, and always, always, it denies that Kane's God exists.

The Archimedeans claim they have no death penalty. Is this what they do instead? Drive their prisoners to suicide?

If so, he will not do their work for them. He has internal resources they cannot disable without killing him and he was prepared to survive torture of a more obvious sort—why not this? He dilutes the waves of despair that wash through him at night when the lights go out and he is alone with the idiot babble of their idiot planet.

No, Kane will not do their job for him. He will not murder himself. But it gives him an idea.

If he had done it in his cell they might have been more suspicious, but when his heart stops in the course of a rather invasive procedure to learn how the note biotech has grown into his nervous system, they are caught by surprise.

"It must be a failsafe!" one of the doctors cries. Kane hears him as though from a great distance—already his higher systems are shutting down. "Some kind of auto-destruct!"

"Maybe it's just cardiac arrest . . ." says another, but it's only a whisper and he is falling down a long tunnel. He almost thinks he can hear Spirit calling after him . . .

And God shall wipe away all tears from their eyes; and there shall be no more death, neither sorrow, nor crying, neither shall there be any more pain: for the former things are passed away.

His heart starts pumping again twenty minutes later. The doctors, unaware of the sophistication of his autonomic control, are trying to shock his system back to life. Kane hoped he would be down longer and that they would give him up for dead but that was overly optimistic: instead he has to roll off the table, naked but for trailing wires and tubes, and kill the startled guards before they can draw their weapons. He must also break the neck of one of the doctors who has been trying to save him but now makes the mistake of attacking him. Even after he leaves the rest of the terrified medical staff cowering on the emergency room floor and escapes the surgical wing, he is still in a prison.

"Tired of the same old atmosphere? Holyoake Harbor, the little village under the bubble—we make our own air and it's guaranteed fresh!"

His internal modifications are healing the surgical damage as quickly as possible but he is staggering, starved of nutrients and burning energy at brushfire speed. God has given him this chance and he must not fail, but if he does not replenish his reserves he *will* fail.

Kane drops down from an overhead air duct into a hallway and kills a two-man patrol team. He tears the uniform off one of them and then, with stiffened, clawlike fingers, pulls gobbets of meat off the man's bones and swallows them. The blood is salty and hot. His stomach convulses at what he is doing—the old, terrible sin—but he forces himself to chew and swallow. He has no choice.

Addiction a problem? Not with a NeoBlood transfusion! We also feature the finest life-tested and artificial organs . . .

He can tell by the sputtering messages on the guards' communicators that the security personnel are spreading out from the main guardroom. They seem to have an idea of where he has been and where he now is. When he has finished his terrible meal he leaves the residue on the floor of the closet and then makes his way toward the central security office, leaving red footprints behind him. He looks, he feels sure, like a demon from the deepest floors of Hell.

The guards make the mistake of coming out of their hardened room, thinking numbers and weaponry are on their side. Kane takes several bullet wounds but they have nothing as terrible as the scrambling device which captured him in the first place and he moves through his enemies like a whirlwind, snapping out blows of such strength that one guard's head is knocked from his shoulders and tumbles down the hall.

Once he has waded through the bodies into the main communication room, he throws open as many of the prison cells as he can and turns on the escape and fire alarms, which howl like the damned. He waits until the chaos is ripe, then pulls on a guard's uniform and heads for the exercise yard. He hurries through the shrieking, bloody confusion of the yard, then climbs over the three sets of razor-wire fencing. Several bullets smack into his hardened flesh, burning like hot rivets. A beam weapon scythes across the last fence with a hiss and pop of snapping wire, but Kane has already dropped to the ground outside.

He can run about fifty miles an hour under most circumstances, but fueled with adrenaline he can go almost half again that fast for short bursts. The only problem is that he is traveling over open, wild ground and has to watch for obstacles—even he can badly injure an ankle at this speed because he cannot armor his joints too much without losing flexibility. Also, he is so exhausted and empty even after consuming the guard's flesh that black spots caper in front of his eyes: he will not be able to keep up this pace very long.

Here are some wise words from an ancient statesman to consider: "You can do what you have to do, and sometimes you can do it even better than you think you can."

Kids, all parents can make mistakes. How about yours? Report religious paraphernalia or overly superstitious behavior on your local Freedom Council tip node . . .

Your body temperature is far above normal. Your stress levels are far above normal. We recommend you see a physician immediately.

Yes, Kane thinks. *I believe I'll do just that.*

He finds an empty house within five miles of the prison and breaks in. He eats everything he can find, including several pounds of frozen meat, which helps him compensate for a little of the heat he is generating. He then rummages through the upstairs bedrooms until he finds some new clothes to wear, scrubs offs the blood that marks him out, and leaves.

He finds another place some miles away to hide for the night. The residents are home—he even hears them listening to news of his escape, although it is a grossly inaccurate version that concentrates breathlessly on his cannibalism and his terrifying nickname. He lays curled in a box in their attic like a mummy, nearly comatose. When they leave in the morning, so does Kane, reshaping the bones of his face and withdrawing color from his hair. The pagan seed still chirps in his head. Every few minutes it reminds him to keep an eye open for himself, but not to approach himself, because he is undoubtedly very, very dangerous.

"Didn't know anything about it." Sartorius looks worriedly up and down the road to make sure they are alone, as if Kane hadn't already done that better, faster, and more carefully long before the two locals had arrived at the rendezvous. "What can I say? We didn't have any idea they had that scrambler thing. Of course we would have let you know if we'd heard."

"I need a doctor—somebody you'd trust with your life, because I'll be trusting him with mine.

"Cannibal Christian," says young Carl in an awed voice. "That's what they're calling you now."

"That's crap." He is not ashamed because he was doing God's will, but he does not want to be reminded, either.

"Or the Angel of Death, they still like that one, too. Either way, they're sure talking about you."

The doctor is a woman too, a decade or so past her child-bearing years. They wake her up in her small cottage on the edge of a blighted park that looks like it was manufacturing space before a halfway attempt to redeem it. She has alcohol on her breath and her hands shake, but her eyes, although a little bloodshot, are intelligent and alert.

"Don't bore me with your story and I won't bore you with mine," she says when Carl begins to introduce them. A moment later her pupils dilate. "Hang on—I already know yours. You're the Angel everyone's talking about."

"Some people call him the Cannibal Christian," says young Carl helpfully.

"Are you a believer?" Kane asks her.

"I'm too flawed to be anything else. Who else but Jesus would keep forgiving me?"

She lays him out on a bed sheet on her kitchen table. He waves away both the anesthetic inhaler and the bottle of liquor.

"They won't work on me unless I let them, and I can't afford to let them work. I have to stay alert. Now please, cut that godless thing out of my head. Do you have a Spirit you can put in?"

"Beg pardon?" She straightens up, the scalpel already bloody from the incision he is doing his best to ignore.

"What do you call it here? My kind of seed, a seed of Covenant. So I can hear the voice of Spirit again . . ."

As if to protest its own pending removal, the Archimedes seed abruptly fills his skull with a crackle of interference.

A bad sign, Kane thinks. He must be overworking his internal systems. When he finishes here he'll need several days rest before he decides what to do next.

"Sorry," he tells the doctor. "I didn't hear you. What did you say?"

She shrugs. "I said I'd have to see what I have. One of your people died on this very table a few years ago, I'm sad to say, despite everything I did to save him. I think I kept his communication seed." She waves her hand a little, as though such things happen or fail to happen every day. "Who knows? I'll have a look."

He cannot let himself hope too much. Even if she has it, what are the odds that it will work, and even more unlikely, that it will work here on Archimedes? There are booster stations on all the other colony worlds like Arjuna where the Word is allowed to compete freely with the lies of the Godless.

The latest crackle in his head resolves into a calm, sweetly reasonable voice. . . . *No less a philosopher than Aristotle himself said, "Men create gods after their own image, not only with regard to their form, but with regard to their mode of life."*

Kane forces himself to open his eyes. The room is blurry, the doctor a faint shadowy shape bending over him. Something sharp probes in his neck.

"There it is," she says. "It's going to hurt a bit coming out. What's your name? Your real name?"

"Lamentation."

"Ah." She doesn't smile, at least he doesn't think she does—it's hard for him to make out her features—but she sounds amused. " '*She weepeth sore in the night, and her tears are on her cheeks: among all her lovers she hath none to comfort her: all her friends have dealt treacherously with her, they are become her enemies.*' That's Jerusalem they're talking about," the doctor adds. "The original one."

"Book of Lamentations," he says quietly. The pain is so fierce that it's all he can do not to reach up and grab the hand that holds the probing, insupportable instrument. At times like this, when he most needs to restrain himself, he can most clearly feel his strength. If he were to lose control and loose that unfettered power, he feels that he could blaze like one of the stellar torches in heaven's great vault, that he could destroy an entire world.

"Hey," says a voice in the darkness beyond the pool of light on the kitchen table—young Carl "Hey. Something's going on."

"What are you talking about?" demands Sartorius. A moment later the window explodes in a shower of sparkling glass and the room fills with smoke.

Not smoke, gas. Kane springs off the table, accidentally knocking the doctor back against the wall. He gulps in enough breath to last him a quarter of an hour and flares the tissues of his pharynx to seal his air passages. If it's a nerve gas there is nothing much he can do, though—too much skin exposed.

In the corner the doctor struggles to her feet, emerging from the billows on the floor with her mouth wide and working but nothing coming out. It isn't just her. Carl and Sartorius are holding their breath as they shove furniture against the door as a makeshift barricade. The bigger, older man already has a gun in his hand. Why is it so quiet outside? What are they doing out there?

The answer comes with a stuttering roar. Small arms fire suddenly fills the kitchen wall with holes. The doctor throws up her hands and begins a terrible jig, as though she is being stitched by an invisible sewing machine. When she falls to the ground it is in pieces.

Young Carl stretches motionless on the floor in a pool of his own spreading blood and brains. Sartorius is still standing unsteadily, but red bubbles through his clothing in several places.

Kane is on the ground—he has dropped without realizing it. He does not stop to consider near-certainty of failure, but instead springs to the ceiling and digs his fingers in long enough to smash his way through with the other hand, then hunkers in the crawlspace until the first team of troopers come in to check the damage, flashlights darting through the fog of gas fumes. How did they find him so quickly? More importantly, what have they brought to use against him?

Speed is his best weapon. He climbs out through the vent. He has to widen it, and the splintering brings a fusillade from below. When he reaches the roof dozens of shots crack past him and two actually hit him, one in the arm and one in the back, these from the parked security vehicles where the rest of the invasion team are waiting for the first wave to signal them inside. The shock waves travel through him so that he shakes like a wet dog. A moment later, as he suspected, they deploy the scrambler. This time, though, he is ready: he saturates his neurons with calcium to deaden the electromagnetic surge, and although his own brain activity ceases for a moment and he drops bonelessly across the roofcrest, there is no damage. A few seconds later he is up again. Their best weapon spent, the soldiers have three seconds to shoot at a dark figure scrambling with incredible speed along the roofline, then Lamentation Kane jumps down into the hot tracery of their fire, sprints forward and leaps off the hood of their own vehicle and over them before they can change firing positions.

He can't make it to full speed this time—not enough rest and not enough refueling—but he can go fast enough that he has vanished into the Hellas city sewers by time the strike team can re-mobilize.

The Archimedes seed, which has been telling his enemies exactly where he is, lies behind him now, wrapped in bloody gauze somewhere in the ruins of the doctor's kitchen. Keeta Januari and her Rationalists will learn much about the ability of the Covenant scientists to manufacture imitations of Archimedes technology, but they will not learn anything more about Kane. Not from the seed. He is free of it now.

He emerges almost a full day later from a pumping station on the outskirts of one of Hellas City's suburbs, but now he is a different Kane entirely, a Kane never before seen. Although the doctor removed the Archimedes seed, she had no time to locate, let alone implant, a Spirit device in its place: for the first time in as long as he can remember his thoughts are entirely his own, his head empty of any other voices.

The solitude is terrifying.

He makes his way up into the hills west of the great city, hiding in the daytime, moving cautiously by night because so many of the rural residents have elaborate security systems or animals who can smell Kane even before he can smell them. At last he finds an untended property. He could break in easily, but instead extrudes one of his fingernails and hardens it to pick the lock. He wants to minimize his presence whenever possible—he needs time to think, to plan. The ceiling has been lifted off his world and he is confused.

For safety's sake, he spends the first two days exploring his new hiding place only at night, with the lights out and his pupils dilated so far that even the sudden appearance of a white piece of paper in front of him is painful. From what he can tell, the small, modern house belongs to a man traveling for a month on the eastern side of the continent. The owner has been gone only a week, which gives Kane ample time to rest and think about what he is going to do next.

The first thing he has to get used to is the silence in his head. All his life since he was a tiny, unknowing child, Spirit has spoken to him. Now he cannot not hear her calm, inspiring voice. The godless prattle of Archimedes is silenced, too. There is nothing and no one to share Kane's thoughts.

He cries that first night as he cried in the whore's room, like a lost child. He is a ghost. He is no longer human. He has lost his inner guide, he has botched his mission, he has failed his God and his people. He has eaten the flesh of his own kind, and for nothing.

Lamentation Kane is alone with his great sin.

He moves on before the owner of the house returns. He knows he could kill the man and stay for many more months, but it seems time to do things differently, although Kane can't say precisely why. He can't even say for certain what things he is going to do. He still owes God the death of Prime Minister Januari, but something seems to have changed inside him and he is in no hurry to fulfill that promise. The silence in his head, at first so frightening, has begun to seem something more. Holy, perhaps, but certainly different than anything he has experienced before, as though every moment is a waking dream.

No, it is more like waking up from a dream. But what kind of dream has he escaped, a good one or a bad one? And what will replace it?

Even without Spirit's prompting, he remembers Christ's words: *You shall know the truth, and the truth shall set you free.* In his new inner silence, the ancient promise seems to have many meanings. Does Kane really want the truth? Could he stand to be truly free?

Before he leaves the house he takes the owner's second-best camping equipment, the things the man left behind. Kane will live in the wild areas in the highest parts of the hills for as long as seems right. He will think. It is possible that he will leave Lamentation Kane there behind him when he comes out again. He may leave the Angel of Death behind as well.

What will remain? And who will such a new sort of creature serve? The angels, the devils . . . or just itself?

Kane will be interested to find out.

Mammoths of the Great Plains

ELEANOR ARNASON

Eleanor Arnason published her first novel, *The Sword Smith*, in 1978, and followed it with novels such as *Daughter of the Bear King* and *To the Resurrection Station*. In 1991, she published her best-known novel, one of the strongest novels of the nineties, the critically acclaimed *A Woman of the Iron People*, a complex and substantial novel which won the prestigious James Tiptree, Jr., Memorial Award. Her short fiction has appeared in *Asimov's Science Fiction*, *The Magazine of Fantasy & Science Fiction*, *Amazing*, *Orbit*, *Xanadu*, and elsewhere. Her most recent books are *Ring of Swords* and *Tomb of the Fathers*, and an eponymous chapbook version of the novella that follows, which also included an interview with her and a long essay. Her novelette "Stellar Harvest" was a Hugo finalist in 2000. She lives in St. Paul, Minnesota.

Here she takes us sideways in time to an alternate history not dissimilar to our own—except that mammoths survived in the American West into historical times before finally being wiped out by white hunters—for a sequence of embedded narratives covering the lives of three generations of Native American women, told by a grandmother to her grandchild on a hot summer's day, and relayed to us across time by that child grown up, a story at once contemplative and autumnal in tone, but with a steely core of anger at the treatment of the Indians and of the continuing destruction of the environment that you can see in progress all around you as you read these words.

Every summer my parents sent me to stay with my grandmother in Fort Yates, North Dakota. I took the rocket train from Minneapolis, waving at Mom and Dad on the platform as the train pulled out, then settling comfortably into my coach seat. I loved my parents, but I also loved to travel, and I was especially fond of the trip to Fort Yates.

We glided north along the Mississippi, gaining speed as we left the city and entered the wide ring of suburbs around Minneapolis and St. Paul. Looking out, I saw scrub woods and weedy meadows, dotted with the ruins of McMansions and shopping malls.

The suburbs had been built on good land, my dad told me, replacing farms, wood lots, lakes and marshes. "A terrible waste of good soil, which could have fed thousands of people; and the land is not easy to reclaim, given all the asphalt and concrete which has been poured over it. That's why we've left it alone. Let time and nature work on it and soften it up!"

Dad's employer, the Agricultural Recovery Administration, might be ignoring the suburbs. But there were people in them. Looking out my window, I saw gardens and tents among the weeds and ruined houses; and there were platforms made of scrap wood along the tracks. The rocket trains didn't stop at the platforms; but local trains did, picking up produce for markets in the city. Now and then I saw an actual person, hanging clothes on a line or riding a bicycle bumpily along a trail.

"Fools," Dad called them and refused to buy their food in the market, though it had passed inspection. I thought the people were romantic: modern pioneers. My grandmother had things to say about pioneers, of course.

North of St. Cloud, the forest began, and I went to the bubble car, riding its lift to the second floor and a new seat with a better view. The forest was second or third growth, a mixture of confers and hardwoods; and there was a terrible problem with deer. They were a problem on farms as well, though not as much as gen-mod weeds and bugs. Market hunters controlled the deer, insofar as they were controlled. Wolves and panthers would do a better job, my father said; but the farmers didn't like them.

Trees flashed by, light green and dark green, brown if they were dying. The conifers were heat-stressed and vulnerable to parasites and disease. In time the forest would be entirely hardwood. Now and then I saw a gleam of blue: a pond or lake surrounded by forest. Sometimes the train crossed a river.

Around noon we reached the bed of fossil Lake Agassiz, also known as the Red River Valley. The forest ended, and we traveled through farm land, amazingly flat. Trees grew in lines between the fields: windbreaks. They were necessary, given the wind that came off the western plains. The main crops were potatoes and sugar beets. The farmers had to keep changing the varieties they grew as the climate changed, getting hotter. "We're like the Red Queen in Alice," Dad said. "Running and running in order to remain in one place."

The train stopped at Fargo-Moorhead, then turned due north, going along the Red River to Grand Forks. Then it turned again. I went to the dining car and ate lunch while we raced west across the North Dakota plain. This was wind farm country. Rows of giant windmills extended as far as I could see. Between them were fields of sunflowers. In the old days, my dad said, the fields had been dotted with pothole lakes and marshes full of wild birds. Most were gone now, the water dried up and the birds flown. In any case, the train moved so rapidly that I couldn't bird watch, except to look at hawks soaring in the dusty blue sky, too far up to identify.

I got off at Minot and stayed the night with my mother's second cousin Thelma Horn. In the morning Thelma put me on a local train that ran south along the Missouri River. There was only one passenger car, hitched to an engine that hauled boxcars and tankers. The track was not nearly as well maintained as the rocket train's line. The local rocked slowly along, stopping often. By late morning we were on the Standing Rock Reservation. There were bison on the hillsides, the only livestock that made sense in short grass prairie, my dad said, and hawks in the sky. If I was lucky, I might see pronghorns or a flock of wild turkeys.

By noon I was at the Fort Yates station. My grandmother waited there, tall and thin and upright, her hair pulled back in a bun and her nose jutting like the nose on the Crazy Horse monument. At home in Minneapolis, I forgot I was part Lakota. Here, looking at my grandmother, I remembered.

She hugged me and took me to her house, an old wood frame as spare and upright as she was. My bedroom was on the second floor, overlooking an empty lot. Grandmother had turned it into a garden, full of native plants that thrived in the dry heat of the western Dakotas. Prairie flowers bloomed among wild grasses. A bird feeder fed native sparrows; and a rail fence hosted meadowlarks, who stood as tall as possible, showing off their bright yellow chests, and sang—oh! so loudly!

What could be better than our breakfasts in the kitchen, the windows open to let in cool morning air? Or the hours when I played with the Fort Yates kids, brown-skinned and black-haired? I was darker than they were, and my hair frizzed, because my dad came from the Ivory Coast. But they were relatives, and we got along most of the time.

In the afternoon, when it was too hot to play, I talked with Grandmother— either in the kitchen as we worked on dinner, or in the parlor under a turning ceiling fan. This is when I learned the story of the mammoths.

According to Grandmother, the trouble began with Lewis and Clark. "We'd heard rumors about what was happening in the east, and the voyageurs had been through our country. Those Frenchmen got everywhere like mice, which is why so many Ojibwa and some Dakota and even Lakota have names like Boisvert, Trudel, Bellecourt and Zephier. But the French were interested in beaver, not our bison and mammoths. We told them if they behaved, they could have safe passage to the Rockies. For the most part, they did behave themselves; and for the most part, we kept our word.

"The thing to remember about the French and the Scots is, they were businessmen. You could reason with them. But the English and Americans were explorers and scientists and farmers searching for new land. People like these are driven by dreams—discovery, investigation, conquest, farms on the short grass prairie where there isn't enough water for trees. No one could reason with them." Grandmother had a Ph.D. in molecular biology from the University of Massachusetts. She was joking, not speaking out of ignorance or disrespect for science.

I'm telling the story the way she told it to me, sitting in her living room in Fort Yates, North Dakota, when I came to visit her on the Standing Rock Reservation in summer. She didn't tell the whole story at once, but piece by piece over days and weeks and from summer to summer. I heard most parts more than once. But I'm going to retell it as a single continuous story; and after this, I'm not going to point out the jokes. There are plenty. Grandmother used to say, "The only way Indians survive is through patience and a strong sense of humor. What a joke the Great Spirit played on us, when it sent Europeans here!"

Anyway, the trouble began that morning in 1805, when Meriwether Lewis became the first white man of English descent to see a mammoth since mammoths died out in England. The animal in question was an adult male, sixty years old or so, older than Meriwether Lewis would ever get to be. It was standing on the bank of the Missouri River drinking water, while its tusks—magnificent ten foot long spirals—shone in the early light. Lewis knew what he was seeing. His neighbor, President Thomas Jefferson, had told him to keep a lookout for mammoths, which white men in the east knew from fossils.

The animal Lewis was looking at was not *Mammuthus columbii*, which had left fossils in the east. Instead this was *Mammuthus missourii*, a smaller descendent. An adult male Columbian mammoth could stand 13 feet tall and weigh 10 tons. The fellow drinking water from the Missouri stood 10 feet tall at most and weighed 5 or 6 tons.

Did he actually have tusks as long as he was tall? Yes, according to Lewis and later scientists who studied *Mammuthus missourii*. It was, my grandmother said, a classic case of sexual selection.

"In order for a female to achieve reproductive success, she has to be healthy and not too unlucky. This is not true for every species, but it is true of many. In order for a male to breed, he has to impress females and other males. Humans did this with paint, feathers and beads. Look at the paintings by people like George Catlin! Indian men were always gaudier than Indian women. That's because they were trying to proclaim their reproductive fitness. An old-time chief in a war bonnet was exactly like a turkey cock, displaying in the spring."

Don't think Grandmother was speaking disrespectfully of our male ancestors. The wild turkey was her favorite bird; and she felt that little on Earth equaled the sight of a cock spreading his shining bronze tail and making a noise that sounds like "Hubba-hubba."

The tusks of mammoth females stop growing when the animals are 25 or 30, but male tusks keep growing, spiraling out and up until—in some cases—they cross each other.

"All show, of course," my grandmother said. "But what a show!"

Lewis did exactly what you'd expect of a 19th century explorer and scientist. He picked up a gun and shot the mammoth. It was a good shot or possibly lucky. The ball went into the old bull's bright, brown eye. The old fellow screamed in pain and fury, then fell down dead. That was the beginning of the end, my grandmother said.

The expedition butchered the animal, keeping the tusks and skin, which was covered with short, thick, curly fur—most likely light brown; though some mammoths are tan or yellow, and a few are white. They had mammoth steaks for dinner and breakfast, then went on, dragging their boats upriver. Most of the meat was left behind to be eaten by wolves and grizzlies. One tusk made it back east to delight President Jefferson. The other was abandoned as too damn heavy; the skin was lost when a boat overturned.

"It was an epic journey," my grandmother said. "And they found many things which Indian people can't remember misplacing, such as the Rocky Mountains. I think you could say that their most famous discovery, even more famous than the Rockies, was living mammoths."

Decades after Lewis and Clark returned to the United States, white people wandered around the west, looking for mastodons, giant ground sloths and saber-tooth cats. But all those animals were gone. Only the mammoths had survived into modern times.

There are white scientists who say Indians killed the ice age megafauna. Grandmother didn't believe this. "If we were so good at killing, why did so many large animals survive? Moose, musk oxen, elk, caribou, bison, mountain lions, five kinds of bear. The turkey, for heaven's sake! They're big; they can't really fly; and though I love them, no one who has seen a turkey try to go through a barbed wire fence can claim they are especially adaptable.

"Why did horses and camels die out in the New World, when other large animals—moose, mammoth, musk ox and bison—survived? Are we to believe that our ancestors preferred eating horse and camel to eating bison? Hardly likely!"

Most likely, the animals that died out were killed by changes in the climate, my grandmother said. Everything got drier and hotter after the glaciers retreated. The mammoth steppe was replaced by short grass prairie. This was no problem for the bison, but mammoths—like elephants—need lots of moisture.

"In the spring when the grass was green and wet, they'd move out onto the plains. Our ancestors would see them in groups of ten or twenty, grazing among the dark-brown bison. By early summer, they retreated to the rivers, especially the Missouri, and fed on shrubs in the bottom lands. Water was always available. Think what it must have been like to float down river in a pirogue or a round bison-hide boat like the ones made by Mandans and Hidatsa! There the mammoths would be, calves and matrons, bathing in the shallows, squirting water on each other.

"Our ancestors always said, be careful of the mammoths when they're by rivers. Wolves, the big ones called bison wolves, and grizzly bears, which used to be a plains animal till white people drove them into the mountains, lurked in the bottom lands. They couldn't harm a healthy adult, but preyed on calves, the old, the injured. Because of this, the mammoths were uneasy close to water."

If I close my eyes now, I can see her living room. The sky is big everywhere in the Dakotas, but west of the Missouri, it gets even bigger; and sunlight comes down through the dry air like a lance. In Grandmother's house, it came through white gauze curtains that fluttered in the wind and danced in spots on her linoleum floor. The furniture in the room was straight and spare, like Grandmother and her house: a kitchen table, four kitchen chairs and a rocker, all old and scratched, but solid wood that Grandmother kept polished. On the floor, along with dancing spots of sunlight, was a genuine oriental rug, the edges frayed and the pile worn flat. Grandmother bought it in an antique store in Minneapolis. She liked the faded colors and the pattern, geometric like our Lakota patterns.

"The Chinese and Indians make carpets like gardens; but people from dry, wide-open countries—the people in Central Asia and here—like geometry."

Her most treasured belonging was a mammoth tusk about three feet long. The ivory was honey-colored and carved with horsemen chasing bison. She held it on her lap while she told me stories, stroking the tusk's gentle curve and the incised lines.

"There were two young men, hunters in the days before horses and guns; and they were out on the prairie, looking for something to kill. All they had were spears with stone tips and a dog dragging a travois. If you think it was easy hunting this way in a world full of bison, mammoths, wolves and grizzlies, then you haven't given serious consideration to the question.

"The young men thought they might be able to sneak up on a bison disguised as wolves, which the bison don't usually fear, or find a mammoth weakened by drought. It was midsummer and so dry that many streams and small rivers were empty.

"But they had no luck. Exhausted and discouraged, they made camp, tying the dog securely, since it might become food soon, if they didn't find anything else. They ate the last of their pemmican and drank water dug from a river bed, then slept.

"When they woke, the moon was up and full. Two maidens in white dresses stood at the edge of their camp. Never had they seen girls so lovely. One man was clever enough to recognize spirits when he saw them; he greeted the women respectfully. But the other man was stupid and rude. Getting up, he tried to grab one of the women. She turned and walked quickly across the moonlit prairie. He followed. When they were almost out of sight, the woman turned into a white mammoth, her fur shining like snow in the moonlight. But this didn't make the rude man pause. He followed the mammoth till both of them were gone.

"The second woman said, 'That is my sister, White Mammoth Calf Woman. Your companion will follow her till he's out of this world entirely. But you have greeted me with respect, so I'll teach you the way to hunt bison and how to use every part of the animal, so your people won't be hungry in the future. Remember, though, not to hunt the mammoths, since your companion has made them angry. If you hunt them in spite of my warning, you'll make the bison angry as well; and they and the mammoths will leave.'

"Then she taught him everything about bison. He thanked her gratefully; and she turned to go. 'What is your name?' the polite man asked. In answer, she turned into a snow-white bison calf and ran off across the plain.

"After that," my grandmother said, "our ancestors hunted bison, but not mammoths. There were practical reasons for this decision. Can you imagine trying to attack a full-sized mammoth on foot with no weapon except a spear? The calves were less formidable, but their mothers and aunts protected them; and the males formed groups of their own.

"The only truly vulnerable mammoths were juvenile males, after they'd been driven from the maternal herd, while they were wandering around alone, confused and ignorant. People did hunt them sometimes, but that didn't lead to extinction.

"Maybe, using fire and stampeding, we could have killed mammoth herds. But we didn't, because White Bison Calf Woman had warned us."

Then Grandmother told another story. "There was a man who went hunting in a hard time, a drought. He came on a huge bull mammoth with magnificent tusks. The animal had a foot that was broken or dislocated.

"'Brother mammoth,' the man said. 'My family is starving. Will you give your flesh to me?'

"The mammoth considered, waving his trunk around and smelling the dusty air. 'All right,' he said finally. 'But I want to keep my tusks. Call me vain or sentimental, if you like. They mean a lot to me; and I want them to stay where I've lived. Take everything else—my flesh, my skin, even my bones—but leave my tusks here.'

"The man agreed. The mammoth let him strike a killing blow.

"When the mammoth was dead, the man brought his wife to butcher the carcass. 'We can't leave the tusks here,' the woman said. 'Look at how huge they are, how perfectly curved.'

" 'I promised,' said the man. But the woman wouldn't listen. She chopped the tusks out of the mammoth's skull. They took everything home: the flesh, the skin covered with tawny curling hair, the tusks.

"After that, the woman had trouble sleeping. The mammoth came to her, wearing his flesh and skin, but with two bloody wounds where his tusks should have been. 'What have you done?' he asked. 'Why have you stolen the only things I asked to keep?' Gradually, lack of sleep wore the woman down. Finally, she died. Soon after that, her husband visited another village and saw a maiden of remarkable beauty. 'What will you take for her?' he asked the girl's father, who was an old man, still handsome and imposing, except for his missing teeth.

" 'Your famous mammoth tusks,' the old man said.

"The warrior was reluctant, but he had never seen a woman like this one; and she seemed more than willing to go with him. Grudgingly, he agreed to the bargain, went home and returned with the mammoth tusks. The old man took the splendid objects and caressed them. 'I will use them to frame my door,' he said. This was a Mandan or Hidatsa village, as I forgot to mention. Our neighbors along the Missouri often took tusks from drowned mammoths and used them as frames for the doors of their log and dirt houses. We didn't, of course, since we lived in tipis in those days.

"The warrior and his new wife took off across the plain. At their first camp, the warrior said, 'I want to have sex with you.' He'd been thinking about nothing else for days.

" 'You people!' said the maiden. 'You never learn!' Rising, she turned into a white mammoth. Her fur shone like snow in the moonlight, as did her small female tusks. 'You asked for help from my kinsman, then took the only things he wanted to keep, though he was willing to give you everything else, even his life. Now he has his tusks back. You will get nothing more from me.' She turned and moved rapidly over the prairie."

"If we aren't supposed to kill mammoths and take their tusks, how do you have that one on your lap?" I asked when I was ten and full of questions, which I had learned to ask in an experimental school in Minneapolis.

"The point of the story," said Grandmother, "is to ask permission, listen to the answer with respect and keep the promises you make. The tusk on my lap is from a juvenile. One of our ancestors may have killed it before it joined a male group; if it was female, then it died of injury or drought, and our ancestor scavenged the tusks.

"If it was a young cow, then our ancestor may have made a mistake by carving a hunting scene on the tusk. But I don't know any stories about the ancestor; most likely he didn't come to harm, as he would have, if he'd done something seriously wrong." It was hard to tell with grandmother, because of her irony, if she meant a statement like this. On the one hand, she was a scientist and a woman who believed that much harm happened in the world and went unpunished. On the other hand, she took the old stories seriously. "There is more than one way to organize knowledge; and more than one way to formulate truth; and with time and patience, persistence and luck, justice can prevail."

There was a story about the fate of Meriwether Lewis, which Grandmother told me. He came back from his journey a famous man, who became governor of the Missouri Territory; but despair overtook him. He died of suicide at the age of 35, alone while traveling along the Natchez Trace. On a scrap of paper in his pocket were his last words. 'Mammoths,' he wrote in an agitated scrawl. 'Indians.' That was all, though—being Lewis—he misspelled both 'mammoth' and 'Indian.'

"What does the message mean?" I asked.

"Who can say?" my grandmother replied. "Maybe it was a warning of some kind. 'Treat mammoths as I have done, and you will end like me.' Or maybe he was drunk. He had a problem with alcohol and opium. In any case, no one paid attention. More white people came up the Missouri—scientists, explorers, traders, hunters, English noblemen, Russian princes. They all shot mammoths; or so it seemed to our ancestors, who watched with horror. We tried to warn the Europeans, but they didn't listen. Maybe they didn't care. At some point, we realized they had an idea of the way our country ought to be: full of white farmers on farms like the ones in Europe, though our land is nothing like England or France. The mammoths would be gone and the bison and us. If you look at the paintings done along the Missouri in the 19th century, it always seems to be sunset. The small mammoth herds, the vast bison herds, the Indians are always heading west into the sunset, vanishing from the plains.

"Some of the tusks went to hang on walls in England and Moscow. Others went to museums in the east, along with entire skeletons and skins. The American Museum of Natural History in New York has a stuffed herd in their Hall of Mammoths. I've seen it. You ought to go some day.

"As the century went on, the Europeans began to take animals alive. In almost every case, these were calves whose mothers had been shot. Mammoth Bill Cody had two in his Wild West show. Sitting Bull used to visit with them, during the year the great Lakota spent with the show. People say he talked with them, while they curled their trunks around his arms and searched in his clothing for hidden food. We don't know what they told him. He came away looking sad and grim.

"By the end of the 19th century, the only mammoths left were in circuses and zoos, except for a small herd in the Glacier Park area. At most, four hundred animals were left. The ones in circuses were calves. The ones in zoos were a mixture of old and young, though all had grown up in captivity. Their culture—which they used to learn from elders, as did we—was gone, except in the Glacier Park herd, which still preserved some of its ancestral wisdom. In this, the Glacier mammoths were like our neighbors the Blackfoot. Louis W. Hill, the son of the Empire Builder, encouraged the Blackfoot to maintain their old ways, in order to present tourists coming out on the Great Northern Railroad with an authentic western experience. Historians have said many bad things about the Hill family, but they protected the mammoths and the Blackfoot from the rest of white civilization.

"White Bison Calf Woman's warnings were proved true. As the mammoths disappeared, so did the far more numerous bison. By century end, only a few hundred of them remained, though they had roamed the west in herds of millions; and we all know what happened to Indians. Because I don't like being angry, I am not going to recount that story. In any case, I'm talking about mammoths.

"At this point, the story turns to my own grandmother, who was your great-great-grandmother. Her first name was Rosa, and her real last name was Red Mammoth, but she was adopted by missionaries when she was very young and took their name, which was Stevens. They sent her east to school, and she studied veterinary medicine, becoming the first woman to receive a DVM from her college. Although Rosa had little experience with Indian culture, she had good dreams. In one of these a mammoth came to her, a white female.

"'I want you to devote your life to mammoth care,' the animal said. 'We have reached the point where anything could kill us: a disease gotten from domestic animals, ailments caused by inbreeding, or a change of heart among white men. What if Louis W. Hill decides there is a better way to promote his railroad? In addition, most of us no longer know how to behave.'

"'I certainly want to work with large animals,' Rosa said. 'But I was thinking of cattle and horses, not mammoths. I know nothing about them.'

"'You can learn,' the mammoth said. 'What you don't find out from the herd in Glacier can be discovered by studying elephants, who are our closest relatives. If we are not saved, the bison will die as well; and I don't hold out a lot of hope for Indians. These white people are crazy. There's no way to farm the high plains or to raise European cattle on them. This country is too dry and cold. Yes, the white people can come here and ruin everything—overgraze the prairie, drain the rivers or fill them with poison, mine and log the sacred Black Hills. Once they have finished, they will have to leave or live like scavengers in the wreckage they have made. The only way to make a living here is through bison and us.' As you might be able to tell, Granddaughter, the mammoth was angry. Like their relatives the elephants, mammoths can feel grief and hold serious grudges.

"Rosa was no fool. It was pretty obvious this was no ordinary dream. The white mammoth was some kind of spirit. She agreed to the animal's request. Because she was Lakota and had a college degree, she was able to get a job at Glacier Park. This was in 1911, when the park had just opened and the famous tourists lodges were not yet built.

"She spent three years at Glacier. The job proved frustrating. The herd wasn't growing. The animals ranged too far, maybe in response to tourists, who wanted nothing more than to photograph these spectacular and shy animals. Once out of the park, ranchers shot them, claiming that the mammoths stampeded cattle. In the park, they were occasionally shot by poachers and even by park rangers, if they went into musth, which is a reproductive frenzy, more common among males than females.

"The animals were less fertile than elephants. Rosa couldn't tell if this was a natural difference between the two species; or if it was due to inbreeding or stress. The fact that mammoths seized cameras whenever they were able, flung them to the ground and stamped on them, suggested that part of the problem was stress. She was unable to convince the park administration to outlaw cameras.

"Finally, discouraged and thinking of leaving her job, she had another dream. A woman wearing a white deerskin dress came to her. The woman was middle aged and obviously Indian, her skin dark, her hair straight and black. Her dress had white beadwork over the shoulders. She had on white moccasins, decorated like her dress with white beadwork. Long earrings made of ivory hung from her ears. 'This isn't working,' she told Rosa.

"'I know,' Rosa replied.

"'We need a new plan,' the woman continued. 'Do you know about the mammoths which have been found frozen in ice in eastern Russia?'

"'Yes.'

"'Learn everything you can about them. They died thousands of years ago, but have been preserved well enough so flesh and skin and hair remains. Maybe it will be possible to revive them someday. White men are ingenious, especially when it comes to doing things that are unnatural.' The woman paused. Rosa blinked, and the woman became a mammoth with snow-white fur and ice-blue eyes. The mammoth waved her trunk back and forth in the air like a conductor directing an orchestra. Her pale eyes seemed to look into the far distance. The dream ended."

My grandmother got up and went to the bathroom, then took iced tea out of her refrigerator. It had lemon juice already in it, along with sugar and mint from her garden. She poured us both glasses and sat down again in her rocker. The tusk was back hanging on her wall, along with other mementos which she had tacked up: pictures of relatives, including my mom and dad, a bunch of postcards of places in the Black Hills. Not Mount Rushmore, but Spearfish Canyon and the Needles Road and Crazy Horse monument. Lastly, there was a necklace of silver beads hanging from a nail. A tiny, beautifully carved mammoth hung from the necklace, made of pipestone with turquoise eyes.

We sipped the tea. Grandmother rocked.

"What happened next?" I asked.

"To Rosa? She went to Russia, taking the eastern route via China since World War I had begun. Louis W. Hill funded her trip. He was worried about the Glacier Park mammoths, too. In his own strange way—the way of an entrepreneur, who must possess what he loves and make money from it, if possible—he loved his Blackfoot and their mammoths.

"Rosa ended in Siberia in a town with a name I can't remember now, though it's on the tip of my tongue. Maybe it'll come to me. Old age, Emma! It comes to all of us, and even gene tech can't repair all the damage! The houses were built of logs, and the streets were dirt. It was like being in the Wild West, she told me, except this was the wild east. The people were drunk Russians and brown-skinned natives, who looked like Indians or Inuit. It was easy to see where we Indians had come from, Rosa told me. The native people drank also. It's a curse that goes around the North Pole and among all native peoples. Pine forest rose around the town. The trees were huge and dark and shut out the sky. Rosa said that's what she missed most in Siberia, the sky. Our kinfolk, the Dakota, were driven out of pine forest by the Ojibwa, who were armed with European guns. The Dakota are still angry about this. Rosa said, in her opinion the pine forest was no loss; though the sugar maples and wild rice lakes might be something to mourn.

"She was in Siberia through most of the war, studying with a Russian scientist who was an expert on frozen mammoths. He was a young man, but he'd lost toes to frostbite and walked with a limp and a cane, so the Russian army wasn't interested in him. A small fellow, Rosa told me, no taller than she was, wiry, with yellow hair and green eyes slanted above cheekbones that looked Indian. Sergei Ivanoff.

"This is the hardest part of Rosa's story to tell," my grandmother said. "I've never been to Siberia, and Rosa kept her own counsel about much that happened there. I imagine them in a log cabin, lamps glowing in the midwinter darkness, studying the mammoth tissues that they'd found. Sergei had brought equipment with him from the west, so they could stain the tissue and examine it under microscopes.

"As far as she and Sergei could determine, given the primitive science of the time, all the tissue they examined had been damaged—most likely by the process of freezing, then thawing, then freezing again. Ice is a remarkable solid, less dense than its liquid form. As the water in the mammoth cells froze, it expanded. The cells' walls ruptured; the delicate natural machinery within was broken past any repair they could imagine.

"For the most part, they were able to ignore the war. Travel was interrupted, but neither of them was planning to travel. Sergei wanted more scientific supplies, but he was too poor to order them. Rosa sent letters to Louis W. Hill, asking for more money. They weren't answered. She didn't know if Hill had received them. In 1917 the war led to the famous Russian Revolution. This happened in the far west, in places like St. Petersburg. Only rumors reached them in their cabin. The local trappers and hunters said, Tsar Nicholas had died and been replaced with a new tsar named Lenin-and-Trotsky.

"One evening soldiers arrived on horses. They heard them coming, shouting to each other.

"Sergei said, 'Take our notes and hide. I'll deal with this.'

"Her arms full of paper, Rosa darted behind their cabin. It was winter, snow falling thickly. A mammoth carcass, thousands of years old, lay in a shack. Rosa climbed in among the ancient bones and skin. She crouched down, shivering. Did voices speak, muffled by the snow? She wasn't certain. At last the silence was broken by two loud, sharp noises like doors slamming.

"'Aaay,' Rosa whispered. In her mind she prayed to her foster family's deity, the God of Episcopalians. The door to the shack opened. A man spoke in a language she didn't understand: Russian.

"She and Sergei had always conversed in German, the language of science, or French, the language of civilization.

"Instead of entering, the man went elsewhere, leaving the shack door open. An icy wind blew in. Rosa cowered in the middle of the mammoth. A vision came to her: she was in a hut. The walls were made of mammoth jaws. The roof beams were tusks. A dung fire burned on the dirt floor. Across the fire from her was an ancient woman, her long hair gray, her dress smoke-darkened and greasy.

"'Stay here a while,' the woman said. 'Till the soldiers are gone.'

"'Who are they?' Rosa asked.

"'Red Guards or White Guards, what does it matter? They are ignorant and desperate. Tsar Nicholas is dead, and his son will never rule. Tsar Lenin-and-Trotsky will not achieve the wonderful things he—they dream of. Things must get worse before they get better.'

"Rosa didn't like to hear this, but she remained in the mammoth hut, which seemed warmer than her shack. The old woman fed dried dung into the fire. Her eyes were milky blue. Blind, maybe. Rosa couldn't tell.

"Finally the old woman said, 'You'll freeze to death if you stay here. The soldiers have gone. Get up and go back to the cabin.'

"Obedient, Rosa stood and walked to the hut door. A mammoth skin hung over it. As Rosa raised her hand to push the skin aside, the woman said, 'Remember one thing.'

"'Yes?'

"'The cold has done a marvelous job of preserving the bodies of my kin. But—like the revolution that is now beginning to fail—the job has not been good enough. What can make it better, Rosa? Don't give up! Persist! And think!'

"Rosa turned to ask for more information, but the old woman was gone. For a moment, she stared at the empty hut. Then the dung fire vanished; and she found herself standing, numb with cold, at the entrance to the mammoth shack. Snow fell around her, kissing her cheeks. She couldn't feel her hands. Her feet were barely able to move. Stumbling, she crossed the space to the cabin's back door.

"Inside was chaos: spilled books, overturned furniture. Sergei lay on the floor in a pool of blood. The cabin stove was still lit, thank God. Red fire shone through the cracks around its door, and the cabin felt warm. She knelt by Sergei. Blood covered half his face, coming from a wound in his forehead. There was more blood on his carefully laundered, white shirt. His pince-nez glasses lay on the floor beside him, one lens shattered.

"'Aaay, Sergei,' she moaned.

"A green eye opened. 'Rosa,' he whispered. 'They didn't find you.'

"'No,' she replied, her heart full of joy.

"Examining him, she discovered he'd been shot twice. One bullet had gone through his shoulder. The other had grazed his head. Eager for loot, the soldiers had not given him a close look after he fell. Instead, they'd gathered the jar that held their little store of money; Sergei's lovely instruments, made of brass and steel; her jewelry and most of their warm clothes. Half their books had gone into the stove to warm the soldiers while they searched the cabin.

"Once he was bandaged, Sergei said, 'This is the end. We're going to China. Do you have our notes?'

"Rosa hurried back to the mammoth shack and found them, fallen among huge bones and shreds of hairy skin. Oddly enough, they smelled of smoke, though there hadn't been a fire in the shack. She carried the papers back to the cabin. She and Sergei packed what remained of their belongings, put on their skis and set out for the nearest town.

"Their journey to Beijing was long and arduous. In spite of many difficulties they made it safely. In Beijing they parted, Rosa going home to America, while Sergei remained to study Chinese fossils. It was he, along with Teilard de Chardin, who discovered the remains of Peking Man and he who carried those remarkable relicts to safety when the Japanese invaded China.

"Rosa never saw him again, though she carried a memento back with her. Do you know what it was, Emma?"

"No."

"Think!"

I frowned and tried of think of something Russian. "A samovar?"

Grandmother laughed. "It was a baby. By the time Rosa returned to America, she knew she was pregnant, though it didn't show when she reported to Hill. A good thing, since he was a fierce moralist.

"Do you know who the baby was, Emma?"

I could see the question was serious and thought hard. "Your mother?"

"Yes. The father was Sergei. You get your green eyes from him and the way they slant over your cheekbones. If you are lucky, you will inherit some of his intelligence and commitment to work."

"Oh." Grandmother had only two grandfathers, which made her unusual. Most people I knew had three or four. One had come from the Rosebud Reservation. I'd seen several pictures of him: a tall young man, his black hair cut short, looking stiff and awkward in his white clothing. In some of the pictures, he was next to his parents, who dressed in the old Indian way, blankets around their bent shoulders. In other pictures he was with his pretty young wife, who was mixed race and had light-colored eyes, striking even in an old photograph. They had two children who lived, Grandmother told me.

I had seen a single picture of my grandmother's other grandfather: an old man with white hair and a trim, white beard.

"He's old in the photo," I said.

"Sergei? Yes. It was taken years later, when he won the Nobel Prize for Medicine. Rosa clipped it out of a magazine."

"He never even wrote?" I asked.

Grandmother paused a long while. "I never knew for certain," she said at last. "Rosa kept her own counsel.

"Once she was back in Montana, Rosa reported to Louis W. Hill. By this time, he was seriously worried. A disease had killed all the mammoths in the Ringling Brothers Circus. Neither the circus veterinary staff not the scientists brought in had been able to identify the disease, though it was suspected that it came from the circus elephants; several Indian elephants became ill at the same time, and one died. Now we know it was a herpes virus, which infects African elephants. It's harmless to them, but can cause a serious illness in Indian elephants. We have a vaccine now; before that was developed, the disease was 100% fatal to mammoths.

"Thus far, Hill told my grandmother, this was an isolated incident. Nonetheless, he had taken precautions. Circus trains were not allowed to use the section of Northern Pacific's high line which went through Glacier. The park lodges had been instructed to hire no one who admitted to a circus past; and law officers in nearby towns were asked to report any carnivals to the park administrations. This was not enough to keep Hill happy. He dug into his pocket and personally paid for an elite group of specially trained mammoth wranglers, who watched the animals and made sure that tourists saw them from a distance. Of course, there were stories about the wranglers in newspapers and magazines; Hill had a genius for marketing. There was even a movie that starred Tom Mix as an outlaw trying to make an honest life as a wrangler. *Sagebrush and Mammoths*. I think that's the right name.

"Still, Hill remained concerned. What if some miserable little carnival managed to elude his precautions and get close to the park? An infected elephant might get loose and wander into the park, or a roaming mammoth might find the circus. What if an infected tourist managed to get close to a mammoth? He could hardly prevent tourists from coming to Glacier; and there was no way to check their backgrounds. The disease might be like rabies, which can infect many kinds of mammals. It might leap from elephants to elk or prairie dogs. Who could say?

"My grandmother thought Hill was worrying too much. More serious, it seemed to her, was the herd's reproductive rate and the danger of inbreeding. Like elephants, mammoths had long gestation periods. They produced single children, and the children had long childhoods. This meant that the Glacier herd was increasing very slowly; and fear of infection meant that they could not introduce genetic variety by bringing in new animals. But she said nothing about this. Instead, she listened—silent and impassive—while Hill paced up and down his private railway car, explaining his concerns. Electric lanterns shone on polished mahogany, dark velvet, oriental carpets and gilded picture frames. The art within the frames was minor. Unlike J. P. Morgan, Hill was not a connoisseur.

"He was stern-looking man, with a trim-white beard. My grandmother said the picture of Sergei when he received the Novel Prize reminded her of Hill a little. He wore a buttoned vest, even in Glacier; though here in the west he wore jodhpurs and high boots, instead of suit pants and shoes. A battered western hat lay on a chair, along with a drover's coat. His glasses were gold-rimmed pince-nez.

"He stopped finally and asked her to report on her trip. She did, though much was left out.

"'What conclusions have you come to?' he asked. 'Have you learned anything useful, or have I wasted my money?'

"Rose had spent her journey home thinking. 'I believe the secret of saving the mammoths is refrigeration.'

"Hill frowned. 'Explain yourself, Miss Stevens!'

"Rosa took a deep breath and continued. 'With luck, you may be able to maintain the herd in Glacier. But it is small; the total population of mammoths alive on Earth is small; and we now know that a disease fatal to the mammoths exists. We need a second plan, a position to which we can fall back, if the worst happens.'

"'Yes?'

"'I would like you to consider two things, sir. First is the remarkable history of the previous century. Consider how much was discovered, how many advances in human knowledge were made! Pasteur and Edison are only two of the geniuses who have transformed the world as we know it. Surely this present century will provide us with comparable discoveries and advances.'

"Hill nodded abruptly. 'Go on.'

"'Second, consider how well preserved the Siberian mammoths are—and for how long—in spite of imperfect conditions. It is my belief that freezing and thawing have damaged the Siberian tissue beyond hope of repair. But it ought to be possible to find a more efficient method of freezing flesh than that provided by a glacier! If we could find a way to freeze tissue samples without damaging the delicate machinery of the cells; and if we could then maintain the tissue samples at a constant temperature, without the freezing and thawing which has done so much harm to the Siberian tissue, then someday—not now, but later in this wonderful new century—it may become possible to start the cellular machinery in motion and reanimate the frozen flesh.'

"'Balderdash!' said Hill. He paced the length of the railway car, picked up a riding crop and paced back to her, hitting the crop against his boot. Thwack!

Thwack! Thwack! 'I hired you to give me solid science, not ideas out of scientific romances! This plan belongs in the mind of Mr. H. G. Wells, not in the mind of a scientist or in the mind of practical businessman.'

"'Well, then,' said Rosa. 'Consider how useful a really good refrigerated rail car would be for your business. If you could bring the fruits of the west—unspoiled! In perfection condition!—to Chicago and the eastern markets—'

"Hill paused and laid the riding crop down on a mahogany table. Then he paced up and down the car several more times. Finally he stopped in front of a bell jar which contained a pair of beaded moccasins. He tapped the jar top gently. 'In spite of all my efforts, in my heart of hearts I believe my Blackfoot are doomed. Progress can't be stopped. Those in its way will be tossed aside, like a bison standing on a rail line when the express comes through. The future belongs to Anglo-American civilization. The Blackfoot, the bison, my mammoths all belong to an age which is ending or has already ended. But you are right about the usefulness of a really good refrigerated rail car; and modern science ought to be able to find something better than a car full of hay and blocks of ice. I will take your advice and invest in refrigeration; and you—Miss Stevens—can continue to your work on mammoth tissue. I will do what I can for the mammoths.'

"Rosa found herself grinning. 'Yes, sir!'

"Why did he love the mammoths so strongly?" my grandmother asked. "I have never been able to decide. Was it their rugged power and persistence? Or the sense that they were survivors from a past age, as he was, the 20th century son of a fierce 19th century father? Whatever his reason, Hill established a research foundation devoted to the study of refrigeration. You must have seen it. It's in St. Paul. A fine example of Art Deco architecture. The tile facade with trumpeting mammoths is especially distinguished.

"While the building was being planned, Rosa went to visit her relatives on the Standing Rock Reservation. My mother was born there. When Rosa returned to work, she left Clara with her Lakota relatives. This was hard to do, but she knew that Hill would not approve of an illegitimate child or a scientist who was also a mother. She refused to give up her research. The mammoths had spoken to her. She would not ignore their advice.

"She wasn't a religious person. The faith she learned as a child faded over time; and she never found another one. But she took her dreams seriously, though she wasn't sure where they came from. Maybe from her unconscious, as Freud and his followers argued; or maybe from a collective unconscious, as other psychologists had argued. In any case, Rosa knew, dreams could provide insight into scientific problems. The structure of benzene came to its discoverer—drat it! I have forgotten the man's name!—in a dream."

Grandmother got up and went to the bathroom again, then refilled our glasses with iced tea. The light coming through the lace curtains came at a lower angle now and had the rich gold of late afternoon. I was getting tired. But I had been raised to listen when elders talked. There were things to be learned here in Fort Yates which I could never learn in my experimental school.

Grandmother settled back in her rocker. "Rosa settled in St. Paul and began work at the Hill Institute. She was Indian and looked it; and she was female. Obviously there were problems at the Institute and in the city. Dislike of Indians goes deep in this part of the country; and at that time there were plenty of people in Minnesota who remembered the Great Sioux Uprising of 1862. Twenty-nine of our Dakota kinsmen were hanged for their part in the uprising, though not all of those who were hanged had taken part. Be that as it may, it was the largest mass execution in the history of the United States.

"Rosa encountered prejudice and difficulty; but the good opinion of Louis W. Hill went a long way in St. Paul in the 1920s. With him standing behind her, she met and overcame every adversity.

"She never married, possibly because she was Indian. White men were reluctant to marry an Indian woman; and there were not many Indian men with her education. Her child remained on Standing Rock. She visited Clara—your great-grandmother—as often as possible, but they were never close. The girl regarded one of Rosa's cousins as her true mother, her mother of the heart. This saddened Rosa, as she told me in her extreme old age. Do you want more iced tea?"

I said no.

"In 1929, the stock market collapsed—as you ought to know, Emma. You've studied some history."

"I do know."

"What did you learn?"

"Never buy on margin."

"That's true enough," said Grandmother and nodded her head. "But there's more to be learned from 1929, as you find out when you're older. At time the market fell, Louis W. Hill was heavily invested. He was trying to buy control of several west coast rail lines, so he could extend his father's empire into California. By now he had the best refrigerated rail cars in the world; and he wanted to fill them with California produce.

"He was lucky. He didn't go broke when the market crashed. But he had a hard time until the Second World War began. His attention turned from Glacier and the Hill Institute to saving the Great Northern Railroad. The Institute's funds were sharply reduced. Research came to a halt. Rosa ended as a maintenance person, who made sure doors were locked and lights off and the freezers containing the mammoth tissue on. There was still enough money to pay the power bill. Louis W. Hill did not forget the Institute entirely.

"I asked Rosa once if she had felt despair in that period. She said, 'I had a job, which was more than millions had, and I was able to keep an eye on my tissue samples.' She was a stoic woman, who kept much to herself, maybe because she lived between two worlds. Who could she confide in, being Indian by descent and white by culture?"

I sort of understood this, since my dad was mixed race. But things had been worse back in the 20th century. I knew that.

"In 1938, in the depths of Great Depression, the herd in Glacier became infected with the same disease which had killed the Ringling and Lincoln Park mammoths. To this day, no one knows how the virus got to Glacier. Millions of people were on the move, looking for work. Many rode the rails; and some camped in Glacier. The rangers drove them out. But the park was large and the times troubled. It was not possible to keep all the hobos out. Obviously, none of these people were traveling with an elephant; and as far as Rosa was able to find out, none of them came into contact with the Glacier mammoths.

"Many years later I became interested in the question at a time when I was between research projects. I did a search on hobos and mammoths, using one of the CDC epidemiology programs. Rosa had no such resource, of course. The program did not find an epidemiological connection between hobos and mammoths, but I did find this." Grandmother got up stiffly and went to her computer. It was on a wood side table, its monitor like a glass flower on a curving blue stalk. The keyboard lay to one side, where Grandmother had pushed it while working directly on the screen. As she approached the screen lit up. She touched it lightly with a bony finger.

"You ought to be interested, Emma, since your father plays the blues. This is a WPA recording made in Kansas City in 1936. It's the only recording Frypan Charlie Harrison ever made, and the only time this song was ever recorded." She touched the computer two more times. A guitar began to play old-fashioned country blues, the real thing, but on a really bad instrument. I could tell from the sound. My Dad wouldn't have touched a guitar that sounded like that. Grandmother sat down.

A man's voice—thin and cracked and distant—began to sing:

"Hard times is here, hardest I ever did see.
Hard times is here, hardest I ever did see.
Feels like a big bull mammoth stepped on me.

"Been riding the rails, looking to earn some pay.
I been riding the rails, looking to earn some pay.
That big bull mammoth keeps getting in my way.

"Blackbird flying and shining in the sun.
Blackbird flying and shining in the sun.
Won't get no rest till my last day is done."

There was more guitar playing, then the recording ended. The computer monitor went dark.

"The recording could have been made to sound like a modern recording," Grandmother said. "For that matter, the technology we have now could make Frypan Charlie sound like a far better blues singer than he was, someone out of the past like Robert Johnson or a present day singer like Delhi John Patel. But this is from the Smithsonian Collection. It sounds the way it would have, if you'd played the original recording right after it was made in 1936. The notes say 'big bull mammoth' is probably a reference to the private police employed by railroads in the 19th and 20th centuries. Though it may also refer to the economic system that was treating Charlie so badly. In any case, the song isn't about Rosa's animals. But I like it. It's the single thing we know about Charlie. He shows up in no other recording."

She was silent for a while, her bony hands folded in her lap and her bright blue eyes gazing right through the living room wall, it seemed to me, into the West River distance. There was no one in my life like her then, and I have never found a replacement for her.

"I especially like the stanza about the blackbird. It reminds me of red-winged blackbirds in the spring. They show up before the marshes turn green, and each male grabs hold of the tallest dry stalk he can find and hangs there, as visible as he can make himself. 'I'm here,' he sings. 'This is me. This is my individual song.'

"That was Charlie's individual song. He's lucky—and we're lucky—that someone recorded it.

"For the next three years, Rosa struggled to save the mammoths. It was to no avail. In 1941, the last Glacier mammoth—a young, pregnant female named Minerva—passed on, with Rosa in attendance. A few animals still remained in zoos around the world, but not enough to form a breeding population. The species was doomed.

"She had wired Hill when the mammoth began to fail. He arrived a day after Minerva's death. Rosa had already removed the fetus and put it into a refrigerator car to be shipped back to St. Paul. She was doing an autopsy of the mother when Hill walked in, dressed in an eastern suit with an eastern hat in his hand.

"He stood for a moment, staring at the corpse, small for a mammoth, but still large.

"'That's it,'" he said finally. 'It's over.'

"'We have the tissue samples,' said Rosa. 'And I have frozen every infant that died.'

"He laughed harshly. 'I never believed in your idea of saving the mammoths through refrigeration; but the advice you gave me—to establish the Institute— was excellent, as is the work you have done on freeze-drying.'

"I forgot to mention that," my grandmother said. "As I told you. Rosa's research in Siberia suggested that water was the culprit in the destruction of mammoth cells. Therefore she had investigated ways to freeze tissue in extremely dry conditions, so as to reduce the amount of water in the cells. She was not able to solve the problem of cellular destruction; but other scientists at the Institute became interested in her work as a method of preserving food.

"Hill had failed in his attempt to move south into California. First the crash slowed him, then that damned communist Franklin Roosevelt was elected, bringing trust busters like a hoard of Visigoths to Washington. Hill could see the writing on the wall; and looking across the Mississippi to the grain mills in Minneapolis, he could see there was a lot of money to be made in food. He gave up on the idea of a western railroad monopoly. Instead, Great Northern diversified into food processing. No matter how bad the times got, people still had to eat.

"His first product was the Pemmican line of dried food, designed to be inexpensive and durable. It came off the production line for the first time in 1940; and the U.S. Army became his first important customer. Along with Spam, another Minnesota product, Pemmican brand dried meat, fruit and vegetables helped to win the war. According to G.I. lore, Pemmican had a thousand uses. You could eat it, use it for shingles or to resole boots, for dry flooring in a tent, as shrapnel in a cannon or flak when dropped from a plane.

"After the war, Great Northern Food Products introduced the Glacier line of frozen vegetables. The packages featured romantic paintings of the national park: Hill's beloved Blackfoot, elk, bison, bears and the vanished mammoths.

"By this time the Hill Institute was back in business, and Rosa was a senior scientist. She might not have been able to save the mammoths, but her work had been key to development of frozen foods. Louis Hill was grateful, though he held the patents to the freezing process, and she never got any royalties. I don't think she minded. She wasn't much interested in money.

"She was in her mid-fifties. You've seen pictures of her, Emma. I've always thought she was as handsome as a woman gets—pure Lakota, with cheekbones like knife blades and the high nose of the Indian on the old-time nickel. Her eyes were as black as space and as bright as stars. Our old stories say we used to be star people. I could see that in her eyes, even though she always dressed like a white, and my relatives on Standing Rock said she thought like a white.

"It's hard to pick the worst time for Indians. Was it when we lost our land, not through wars—we Lakota won our wars!—but through treaties? Or was it when we starved on the reservations and were shot down by soldiers and agency police? Or when our children were stolen from us and taken to boarding schools, dressed in white clothing and punished if they spoke their own language?

"I think the worst time was the middle of the 20th century, when our elders died, the ones who had grown up in the old days and learned the old ways from their parents and grandparents. White people had their history in books and movies that showed cowboys shooting down the Indians. Our history was in the minds and mouths of those old men and women. When they died—the last survivors of Little Big Horn and Wounded Knee, people who had known Sitting Bull and Crazy Horse and seen mammoths wading in the shallows of the Missouri River—then it seemed as if we might vanish as entirely as the mammoths. A few bodies might be left, shambling drunks or white people in red skins, but we would be gone." She paused and drew a deep breath, then got up and went for more iced tea.

We drank in silence for a while. The tea was so cold against my tongue! So tart with lemon and sweet with sugar! The sunbeams that entered the room were almost horizontal now. Dust motes danced in them.

"I think it was in this period that Clara, her daughter and my mother, came to dislike Rosa so much. She would come out to Standing Rock in her Chrysler New Yorker—a big, heavy, burgundy-colored car—climb out and stand in the dirt road, looking tired and remote. It was a long, hard drive from St. Paul, and that may explain her expression. But Clara took it as a disowning.

"Rosa always wore slacks, shirts and comfortable shoes on these trips. Even wrinkled by the long drive to the reservation, her clothing looked expensive; and her comfortable shoes shone under their film of South Dakota dust. To Clara, Rosa was a white woman in a red skin. Living on the reservation, watching the old people die and the young people give in to despair, nothing could be worse to her. Rosa had turned her back on the Lakota, so Clara turned her back on Rosa.

"This was done silently. Rosa had money to give, and Clara's family on the reservation was desperately poor. She took her mother's money, but refused to visit her in St. Paul—a terrifying place!

"Clara married in 1945. Her husband was a soldier from Rosebud, back from the war: Thomas Two Crows. I don't know how they met, only that he was very handsome and full of stories. My relatives on Standing Rock told me that later. Somehow the stories—about Rosebud and his travels as a soldier—tantalized Clara, though she was afraid to visit St. Paul. I don't know why. Maybe because he was a handsome young warrior of proven courage, full of apparent confidence.

"I was born in 1949, the only child that lived, though there had been two before me. Thomas was drinking heavily by then. He died a few years later. He'd been drinking at a friend's house. After a while, they noticed he wasn't there. He must have gone out to pee, my relatives on Standing Rock told me. It was snowing, with a strong wind blowing, and he got lost. They found him two days later, after the storm ended, frozen like one of Rosa's mammoths. If I sound cold when I tell you this, remember that I didn't know him. He died when I was so young. And maybe I'm angry with him for losing himself in drink and the winter. It was a long time ago, and I should have forgiven him by now. But Clara needed him.

"I did know her, though she died when I was still a child. I remember her sitting in our little house, which Thomas paid for with his soldiering money. She was silent for hours at a time. Her anger made the house seem dark to me. It wasn't the darkness of night, with stars blazing above Standing Rock; but the darkness of a winter afternoon when the sky is low and gray, and a cold wind is blowing out of the north. As much as possible, I stayed outside and waited for Rosa's next visit. She came in her big, burgundy-colored car, dust all over the side panels. Once—it must have been in late summer—the entire front of the car was caked with dead grasshoppers. She hated that and spent hours cleaning the grill.

"I'd run to her, and she'd embrace me. She smelled like no other person I knew. Later I discovered it was the scent of fine soap and perfume. There were always gifts for me: wonderful toys, books and her own stories about the Twin Cities of St. Paul and Minneapolis. I gave the toys away. It would have been wrong to keep them, when the children around me had nothing similar. But I kept the books, and I treasured Rosa's stories. The Twin Cities sounded like the Emerald City of Oz to me. I wanted to visit her, and Rosa invited me many times. But Clara wouldn't let me go. She was afraid that Rosa would steal me, the way the white people had stolen so many Lakota children.

"Well," said Grandmother and paused. "This story is about Rosa, not about me.

"She kept at her research, going to the Hill Institute almost every day. The work she did in this period did not lead to any important discoveries. Her real task was making sure that her collection of frozen mammoth tissue remained frozen.

"The mammoths endured nine years longer, the last one—an old male at the Cleveland Zoo—dying in 1957. It was the end of an era, white commentators said. The Old West was gone, along with its most famous denizens. We heard about the death out in the Dakotas and mourned deeply. The sacred mammoths, our allies for generations, were no more. We and the few remaining buffalo were alone in the terrible world made by white men. Our grief was so deep that people died of it. Most were old people, but that was the year that Clara became sick.

"T.B. killed Clara—and bitterness and grief, I have always thought, though she might have lasted longer in a warmer place. That house was cold as well as dark. What was left for her? The old ways had died, along with her husband and the last mammoth, Trojan. She was losing me to Rosa. She sat in the dark house, in her own darkness, and coughed. Rosa tried to get her good medical care, but Clara wouldn't leave the reservation.

"Rosa came to Standing Rock and sat with her while she was dying, though only at the very end. As long as Clara was conscious, she refused to have Rosa near her. It was a bad situation, and it did not make the other relatives happy. This was not a good way to leave life. But Clara did.

"When she was gone and in the ground, Rosa brought me to St. Paul. I finally made the journey I had wanted to make for years. What a way to make that journey! I sat beside Rosa in her old Chrysler New Yorker, stiff with grief. The fields of eastern South Dakota went past, flat and green and foreign. Trees, which were rare among the golden-brown hills of my home, became common. They didn't remain along the creeks and rivers. Instead, they grew in rows between the fields and in clusters around the farm houses, and—finally, as we reached eastern Minnesota—in woods that covered the hilltops.

"All the people we saw were white, their faces burnt red by summer, their hair brown or blond. They gave us unfriendly looks. 'Don't worry,' said Rosa. 'They may stare, but that's as far as it's likely to go. As a rule, Minnesotans don't say what's on their minds.'

"This didn't reassure me. But we arrived safely in St. Paul. Rosa drove me through streets lined with tall elms and bigger houses than I had ever seen before. The lawns were as green as the Emerald City. Sprinklers flashed in the sunlight like diamonds. I felt utterly lost. Now I began to cry—not for Clara, but for myself.

"'It will be all right,' said Rosa.

"I was still crying when we arrived at her house. I stopped once we were inside, awed by the house's size. Two full stories and three bedrooms! One bedroom would belong to me, Rosa said. The house was old, built more than fifty years before, but Rosa had installed a state of the art bathroom, and a new, electric kitchen. I was entranced and frightened. How could I use objects so clean and shining? Clara had made do with an outhouse and a well.

"There was television set in the living room. On top of it stood a mammoth family, carved out of honey-colored ivory. It was mammoth ivory from Siberia, Rosa said, thousands of years old. A great curving mammoth tusk hung over the living room fireplace. This came from an animal that had died in the 20th century. 'They lasted so long,' Rosa said sadly. 'If we had managed to keep them alive just a little longer, I am confident that modern science would have found a cure for their illness and a way to keep them in existence indefinitely. Well, their tissue remains, and it is my job to make sure it stays safely in the Institute freezers. There are times, Emma, when the best one can do is preserve.'

"Louis W. Hill had died in 1948, though I didn't learn this until later. His will left a substantial sum to the Hill Institute, but only if the institute continued to maintain Rosa's mammoth remains on its premises in a safely frozen state, with Rosa on staff as the custodian. Of course, there were scientists at the Institute that thought this was folly. They wanted Hill's money, but not the mammoths or Rosa. The rest of her career was a fight to keep her job and the freezers full of mammoth fetuses and tissue. It was as hard as trying to maintain treaty rights. But as I said, I learned this later.

"The house's dining room had two splendid photographs of mammoths by Ansel Adams. Louis Hill had commissioned him to record the Glacier herd in its last days. Adams was not an animal photographer, but mammoths were part of the west he loved deeply; and they were vanishing. He accepted the commission. Both of Rosa's photographs showed the animals at a distance, grazing in a meadow below tall pines and snow-streaked mountains. Seen with Adams' eye and taken with his box camera, the mammoths seemed as solid and permanent as the landscape they inhabited.

"I came to Rosa's house in the summer of 1958, at the age of nine. By mid-August I was settled into my new room. The windows looked into green caves made of leaves, a disturbing sight for someone used to the wide, treeless distances of western South Dakota. When sunlight shone in, it was tinged green, and green shadows danced on my floor and walls. The days were hot and humid, the nights were full of noise: leaves rustling, bugs singing, radios playing, people talking on neighboring porches. The sky, hedged by rooftops and foliage, held too few stars.

"It was hard, but I survived that first summer. Children are resilient! In the fall I went to school. Rosa managed to get me into the University of Minnesota lab elementary school, though this wasn't easy at short notice. She said I would get a better education and encounter less prejudice. 'Prejudice against Indians is deeply rooted here. But the world is changing. The powers that were defeated in the last world war have shown us how bad human society can become. Maybe we will learn from this and make the world better.'

"Unlike Clara, Rosa was an optimist. It may not be a more rational way to see the world, but it makes life happier.

"She was right about the education I got at U Elementary and U High. It was good. To this day, I don't know how much prejudice I encountered. I was shy and lonely, the only Indian student in a school that was entirely white, except for one African-American family and a single Asian-American student. For the most part the other students were polite and left me on my own. Once or twice, a few were cruel in an ordinary, adolescent way. The other children stopped that behavior. I was not to be a target or a friend.

"You have to remember that I wasn't Indian in an obvious way. My last name was Ivanoff. It was the only thing that Clara got from Sergei, except possibly for Russian sadness. Rosa thought it would be better to use Ivanoff than Two Crows. 'White people are more likely to take you seriously, if you have a white name,' she told me. I could have used Stevens, which was her white name, but I think she wanted that small memento of Sergei.

"My eyes were blue; my hair was brown and wavy; and I was a lot lighter than I am now, because I was so bookish. Either I was inside reading, or I was outside under a tree reading. Sunlight scarcely ever touched me.

"I don't think it was prejudice which kept me alone, though I can't be certain. I think it was my bookishness and inability to understand the other students. What on earth made them tick? Their lives—made of dates and grades—seemed small and confined, like the neighborhoods hemmed in by houses and trees. Their plans seemed equally small: a college education, followed by a good job and marriage. Surely there was more to life than this. I wanted something larger, something as wide as the sky over Standing Rock, though I didn't know what. So I read science fiction and dreamed.

"My one friend was the Asian-American student, Hiram Fong. His sister was retarded; we used that kind of language in those days; and he was his family's hope. They were betting on a sure thing, Rosa told me. 'Hiram is as smart as your grandfather Sergei.'

"How can I describe him? He wasn't shy like me, but he had a cutting wit that scared the other children; and he was far too bright to be popular. Half the time I didn't understand what he was saying. Almost no adolescents in any era understand irony, which was Hiram's favorite kind of humor; and few adolescents of the time understood 20th century physics, which was his passion. My twin loves were biology and literature, though I wasn't interested in analyzing works of fiction, any more than a fish wants to analyze water. I simply wanted to sink into them and live among words the way a fish lives among underwater plants.

"We both liked science fiction. That was the bond that held us together. And we liked each other's families. Hiram's father was a research doctor at the U. His mother had an advanced degree, I think in psychology, but stayed at home to care for Hiram's sister, a sweet Down's Syndrome child, who did far better than such children were expected to do in the 1960s.

"Their house was like Rosa's, large and full of books and artifacts. In the case of the Fong family, the artifacts were from China: silk rugs and porcelain vases, framed examples of calligraphy, opium pipes. Opium was a wonderful medicine, Dr. Fong said, if used prudently and with thought. When shoved down people's throats by the British empire, it was a curse.

"Like Rosa, the Fongs saw a world differently from most of the people I knew, and that made me comfortable with them. Although they didn't like frozen food—Mrs. Fong always used fresh ingredients when she cooked—they respected the work Rosa had done. 'At present, we have a limited need for frozen tissue,' said Dr. Fong. 'But I'm sure the need will increase, and your grandmother's work will become increasingly important.'

"'Maybe we'll be able to make people someday,' said Hiram as he picked over his dinner with flashing chopsticks. 'Out of frozen parts, like the Frankenstein monster. Or maybe we'll be able to freeze people and wake them a thousand years in the future. That sounds more interesting than frozen peas.'

"'There will probably be more practical uses for the techniques which Rosa Stevens has pioneered,' said Dr. Fong.

"Mrs. Fong, who was a reader, said, 'The monster wasn't made from frozen parts. He might have turned out better if he'd been fresher. Cynthia, please don't play with your food.'

"Hiram and I graduated from high school in 1967. The United States was at war in Asia and at home, against its own citizens. You must have studied this in school, Emma."

"The burning of the cities," I said. "And the Black Panthers and AIM."

"'The American Indian Movement came a little later. Otherwise you are correct. Even Minneapolis burned a little in this period. It was a modest blaze, compared to places like Detroit.

"Hiram went to Harvard. I went to a small liberal arts college outside Philadelphia. He and I swore to stay in touch, and we did for our first year. After that, circumstances pulled us apart. Hiram's interest in physics intensified and left him little time for any other interest. I developed an interest in politics. He thought the war was wrong, and he had no desire to go to Vietnam; but he knew he was likely to need a security clearance in order to do his kind of physics. Protesting the war was a risk. He wouldn't take it.

"I felt sorry for him and a little contemptuous. How could anyone be so careful, in that era when everything was being questioned and the world seemed full of possibility?

"The thing your teachers may not have told you is how full of hope the late 60s were. Yes, there was violence. The police and FBI and National Guard were dangerous. Plenty of people—good people—died in fishy ways; and plenty went to prison for things they almost certainly did not do. But the times were changing, and many of us thought we were building a new world in the shell of the old. As it turned out, we were wrong, at least for the time being. The 60s wound down slowly through the 70s, and in 1980 Ronald Reagan began a long period of reaction.

"I still think Hiram was wrong to be careful. We stopped corresponding, because we no longer had anything important to say to one another. Our friendship ended before the war did, not with an argument, but in silence. I was able to track his later career through the science magazines. It was impressive. I have always been surprised that he didn't win a Nobel Prize like Sergei.

"After graduation, I stayed in the east and began work on a Ph.D. in biology. I never got involved with AIM, though I read about it in the papers. The occupation of Alcatraz! The battles on Pine Ridge! Why didn't I come home to St. Paul or Standing Rock? Maybe because I felt more comfortable with political theory than with shoot-outs; and I didn't feel that much like an Indian; and my issue was peace.

"When I came back to St. Paul for visits, I noticed that Rosa was undergoing a strange transformation. Always cold and increasingly indifferent to her appearance, she wrapped herself in cardigans and throws, which made her like a 19th century Lakota matriarch in a blanket. Her hair, which had always been short and neatly styled, grew long. She wore it in braids wound around her head or hanging down. Her face, wrinkled by age and sunlight, looked like the faces of my great-great-aunts.

"She still went to the Hill Institute daily. Louis W. Hill's will had mentioned no retirement age for her. This outraged the other scientists. By this time the Institute had a director who'd decided—after consulting several lawyers—that the best thing to do was out-wait Rosa. Louis Hill was a man with a passion for control and an eye for detail. He had micromanaged the building of Glacier Park. Even the trim on the famous lodges and the design of their menus had gone past him for approval. Death might cause him to lose control of Glacier. It belonged to the American people, at least in theory. The Institute was his alone. Living or dead, he would control it. His bequest had numerous stipulations; if these were not followed, his money was to go to Glacier for maintenance of the lodges.

"The director could try to break the will, but he was likely to fail. He could ignore the stipulations, but the Department of the Interior had been coveting the Hill money for decades and was likely to sue. Better to put up with Hill's eccentricities: the out-of-date Art Deco building with its tile facade of extinct mammoths and the doddering Indian scientist. Let Rosa potter around her office and lab. In the end, she would die of old age, and the space could be put to better use.

"She lived into her 93rd year and kept going to work until the last few weeks of her life. When she died—in 1985—I inherited her house.

"As she requested, I had her cremated. She wanted to be buried on Standing Rock. I wasn't sure how my relatives would feel about this, so I didn't tell them what I was going to do. Remember that I had been living in the white world for a long time. I stopped learning how to be Lakota at the age of ten, and there were big gaps in my Lakota education.

"I took Rosa's urn to the reservation and borrowed a horse from my second cousin Billy Horn. By this time, Billy was a middle-aged man with a comfortable gut; but he had been a lean and angry AIM activist with long, flowing hair and a feather tucked into the band of his cowboy hat. His hair was in two braids now. He still wore a cowboy hat, minus the feather; and he still had a rifle—he was one hell of a shot—but he didn't pose with it anymore. Instead, it stayed in his pickup till he needed it. 'Four-legged varmints now,' he told me. 'I gave up shooting at the FBIs. It's a waste of ammunition.'

"The horse Billy loaned me was an appaloosa with an easy gait and beautiful manners. 'It'd be easier to fall out of a rocking chair,' he said. 'Try to stay on board. You don't want to hurt Moonie's feelings.' He stroked the mare's lovely neck.

"I rode into the dry, golden hills. Hawks soared above me in a wide, wide blue sky. These were Swainson hawks, not the Redtails I knew from Minnesota. It came to me as I rode that I loved this country. The Missouri was a blue gleam in the distance. One of those damn lakes, made by the damn Corps of Engineers. But from here you couldn't see the eerie, unnatural pool of water, edged with bare mud flats. Instead, you could imagine the river as it ought to be, full of shoals, edged with willow and cottonwood bottoms. There would be—should be—driftwood floating in the slow, late-summer current, coming to rest on shoals; and mammoths should wade in the shallows, sucking up the muddy water in their trunks and spraying one another.

"I unpacked my shovel and dug Rosa's grave. After I buried her, I burned some sage. Moonie cropped dry grass nearby. That afternoon I decided I'd come back to Standing Rock, though I wasn't sure when. I'd finish my Lakota education.

"I returned to Billy's house at twilight. He took care of Moonie. 'Didn't do her any harm that I can see. Did everything go all right? Did you get Rosa settled?'

"I looked at him with surprise. He grinned. 'You may have a lot more degrees than I do, but that doesn't make me stupid, Liz. It was pretty easy to figure out what you wanted Moonie for. I'm planning to follow your trail tomorrow, go and talk to Rosa and make sure everything's okay with her.'

"'I wasn't sure I ought to do it.'

"'Crazy Horse said his land was where his dead were buried. That's how we nail all this down.' He waved his hand around at Standing Rock, hidden in darkness. 'So long as we can keep the anthropologists from digging everyone up. If I was going to argue about anything, it'd be the cremation. It isn't traditional. But Rosa always did things her own way.'

"He was joking about the anthropologists. We'd managed to stop them by then and gotten a lot of our ancestors back from places like the Smithsonian. The current problem was people who stole artifacts and fossils from our land. An entire Tyrannosaurus Rex taken and sold to the Field Museum! People have no shame! They will steal *anything* from Indians!"

My grandmother paused and glared, her blue eyes gleaming brightly. Then she took a deep breath and continued her story.

"I went back to St. Paul and looked at Rosa's house. I'd visited her regularly, but it wasn't my home anymore; and there were places—the basement and the attic—where I hadn't been in years.

"The attic looked ordinary: unfinished, full of dust and boxes. I'd have to go through them all, I thought and groaned out loud. The basement was full of freezers. Not the kind you use for storing your Glacier frozen peas. These were the big freezers you'd find in a lab. Heaven knows how she got them down the stairs. Large men and some kind of hoist, I imagined. A note had been taped on one of the freezer doors. 'Dear Liza,' it said in shaky print. "I don't trust the director of the Institute, so have moved my tissue here. There are two backup generators. Please keep the temperature constant. Love, your grandmother.'

"I laughed with surprise, though not with pleasure. Rosa must have gotten stranger than I had realized in her last years. Moving mammoth tissue into her basement? How was I going to sell the house in this condition? I laughed again and shrugged my shoulders, then made sure the freezers were running properly. One thing at a time. First I had to clean the house.

"Some people's lives change dramatically, Emma, in a single moment, through a single decision or event. That has never happened to me. My life has always changed slowly, through a series of small events and decisions.

"I took my first step at Standing Rock, when I realized how much I loved those golden hills. Step two was finding the freezers and making sure they were running properly. Without thinking it through, making no conscious decision, I made the freezers my responsibility. If there is a moral in my story, it's do nothing lightly. I'm not complaining about the way my life turned out. I have enjoyed it so far. But I wish I'd been more mindful in places.

"Step three was cleaning the house. You may think of that as a tiresome project, like cleaning your bedroom. But I was going over my grandmother's life, exploring it the way Lewis and Clark explored the Missouri River and Rocky Mountains. Like them, I found plenty of mammoths; and like them, I did a lot of hard, dirty work. If I had to decide which I'd rather do—clean another house like Rosa's or drag a boat up the Missouri River, I'd have to consider a long time before making my decision.

"The closets were not difficult. Rosa had gotten rid of most of her clothing. The woman I remembered as elegant had spent her last years in blue jeans, flannel shirts, frayed cardigans and battered shoes. Nothing was in good enough condition to give to a homeless shelter. It all went in the trash.

"The boxes in the attic were business papers, most of them years old. It's amazing what otherwise sane people will save! Maybe Rosa became anxious as she aged and afraid of throwing anything out, or maybe she simply became tired of sorting through papers. Almost everything could be burned, which I did on a cold, wet day when rain beat against the living room windows. There is something satisfying about sitting by the fireplace on such a day and watching old tax returns curl and blacken.

"Some of the burden of Rosa's belongings lifted off me that day, though I knew the hardest work still lay ahead. The house was full of books. There was no way I could fit Rosa's collection into my small apartment in Massachusetts; and I didn't want most of the collection. But a book can't be thrown away, and selling it or giving it away has to be done carefully. The best thing is to give books to friends. Rosa's friends were gone by then. She had outlived them all. And none of my friends were in the Twin Cities.

"I planned to keep the books on Indians and packed them for shipment east. Then I went in Rosa's den and looked at the books on mammoths. They lined one wall. Another wall was windows, looking out on Rosa's garden, which had become a wild mixture of perennials and weeds. She had been such a careful gardener in the past! A third wall had her desk and an antique file cabinet made of oak. Two of the drawers were full of articles on mammoths and freeze drying, many written by Rosa. The other two drawers were full of Rosa's notes.

"Surely the contents of the den should go somewhere special. This was Rosa's life work, and she had been a distinguished scholar. I gritted my teeth and called the director of the Hill Institute. I don't remember his name anymore. It was something that sounded East Coast and English stock: two last names stuck together with a title in front. Dr. Ramsey Sibley or Crosby Washburn. His accent was Midwestern with a trace of East Coast refinement. He was very sorry to hear of my grandmother's death. A remarkable woman! An inspiration to us all! And no, he wasn't interested in her papers. 'We have moved in a new direction here, away from mammoths, Ms. Ivanoff. The university might be interested. I suggest you try them.'

"I mentioned the mammoth tissue. Dr. Sibley chuckled. 'I'm afraid your grandmother became a bit eccentric toward the end. She decided the tissue would be safer in her basement. We didn't oppose her decision. As you may know, Mr. Hill's will required us to keep the tissue in perpetuity. But it belonged to Dr. Stevens; she had the right to remove it. Once it was gone, our lawyers told us, we do not have to take it back.'

"This sounded like shifty law to me, but I wasn't going to argue. I thanked Dr. Crosby Sibley for his help and hung up.

"There I was, Emma, with a den full of mammoth books and a basement full of frozen mammoth. I could pack the den and put it in storage. But the tissue was a serious problem. I couldn't put the house on the market until I found a home for it. I spent the next two weeks desperately calling academic institutions. But it was summer. The people who made decisions were not around.

"I was still sorting and packing. Rosa's sheets and towels were too worn to sell or give away. They went in the trash. The kitchen had a few things I wanted: handmade cups and dishes by local potters. Looking at the rest, I decided on a yard sale.

"At last I reached my childhood room. The elm outside the window was gone, replaced by a silver maple. Otherwise, the room was unchanged. A star quilt covered the bed. One of my cousins on Standing Rock had made it. My favorite stuffed animal, a threadbare mammoth named Mamie, lay on the pillow. One of her glass eyes had been replaced years ago and was blue. Its mate, which was original, was golden brown.

"I had reached some kind of limit. It isn't easy to sort through the belongings of the person who raised you. If I hadn't been so busy, I would have realized that I was sick with grief. In addition, I was frustrated. I couldn't leave the freezers untended; and I wasn't going to be able to find a new home for the tissue before fall. I'd have to ask for a leave of absence from my job. If my department wouldn't give it to me, I'd have to resign.

"That evening I sat in Rosa's living room and drank wine, looking at the objects I hadn't yet packed: the mammoth figurines on top of Rosa's ancient TV, the mammoth tusk over the mantel, Ansel Adams' photographs and most of the books. What was I going to do? Why had Rosa landed me with this mess? Why had she gotten old and died? Didn't she realize how much I would miss her? Even though I hadn't been home often, I had drawn comfort from knowing she was there, pottering around her garden and her tissue. I am an elder now, Emma. But I still miss my own elders, Rosa especially.

"I've never been much of a drinker. It's a bad habit for Indians. But that night I had a glass or two too many. I felt a bit hazy when I went up to bed. Instead of going to the guest bedroom, where I had been staying, I went to my old room. I took the star quilt off the bed and folded it, then lay on the clean sheets, which smelled of lavender. Rosa had loved the stuff. I'd found sachets tucked between her threadbare linens and in every clothing drawer.

"I dozed off, lying next to Mamie, and dreamed. I don't usually remember my dreams, and when I do they are usually fragments of the day's events, fitted together crazily, like a jigsaw puzzle done wrong—evidence that white psychologists are right, when they say our dreams are simply our minds sorting through recent experiences, as part of the process of storing them in our RAM.

"This dream was different. I was in a house built of bones. The only light was a small, dim fire; and shadows filled the house. Nonetheless, I was aware of the bones. They were huge.

"A tiny, withered woman sat across the fire from me. She wore a hide dress, stained by smoke and spotted with grease. It might have been white once. Now it was dun. Her hair fell over her shoulders, long and loose and gray.

"'I don't want this problem,' I said to her. 'Rosa handed it to me after she died. She didn't give me a chance to argue or refuse. I don't belong here. This isn't my life.' I waved around at the house made of bones, though what I really meant was Rosa's house.

"'Don't talk to me of life,' the old woman said. 'My people are dead; and your people are likely to follow. Isn't that the promise which was made to the Lakota? If they respected the mammoths, the buffalo and the Lakota would survive.'

"'The buffalo have survived,' I said.

"'Just barely! How many were left at the end of the Great White Killing? A few hundred! All the thousands alive today are descended from those few. I am a spirit, not a geneticist, but surely the species has gone through a genetic bottleneck. It cannot have the genetic variation it had two centuries ago.'

"'The same would be true of mammoths, if they were brought back,' I said.

"'Rosa saved a lot of tissue, though it did not come from a large number of individuals. It might be possible to find variation among so many chromosomes,' the old woman said. 'We mammoths might be in better shape than the buffalo, if we were alive. We could not be in worse shape than we are now.'

"Another voice spoke from the darkness. 'You have studied biology. You know about the new technologies that are coming into existence. All these white men starting companies to make money out of genes! The technology we need to re-create our people will be invented soon.'

"Now I saw the second person: a solidly built, middle-aged woman. Her long, braided hair was black; and her dress was the creamy color of clouds on a hot summer afternoon, when they shine through the haze above Standing Rock.

"'Biology is a tricky business,' I said to the second woman. 'You can't listen to the men who start gene tech companies. Of course they promise miracles in the next year or two. They're looking for investors. I have no reason to believe it will possible to re-create mammoths from frozen tissue in the near future.'

"'It won't be possible at all, if the tissue isn't there,' said the crone.

"'There has to be tissue in other places,' I replied.

"A third voice—young and clear and musical—spoke. 'Rosa was *the* great expert on the freezing of mammoths. Has anyone has done work equal to hers? How good are the samples in other places?'

The third woman—slim and graceful, in a hide dress as white as fresh snow—moved out of the shadows. She stopped next to the matron. The crone sat at their feet. They all stared at me, their dark eyes shining in firelight.

"I said, 'I'll find a home for the tissue. I owe Rosa that much. But that will be the end of it. I have my own life to live.' The dark eyes kept watching me. 'Are you sure you are Indian spirits? You know a lot about biology.'

"'First of all,' the crone said. 'We are in your dream. Obviously, we know what you know. And we, like you, are at the end of the 20th century. White people have a god who exists outside time and history and pays far too little attention to his creatures' misbehavior, in my opinion.

"'Indian spirits live in the world we helped make. Why not? We did good work! It's a good place! And like people of every kind—the two legs and four legs, birds and fish and insects—we change in response to time and events. Don't expect us to be like the spirits in an anthropology textbook.'

"'And don't drink so much,' the matron said. 'It isn't good for you.'

"That was the last thing the women said to me. I think they turned into mammoths, and the house vanished, so we were all standing on a wide, dark plain, under a sky packed full of stars. But maybe I made that part up. Maybe I made everything up. I have never been certain about dreams, Emma, though many other people are, and I respect their opinions.

"I woke my old bedroom, next to Mamie. For a while, I lay in the darkness, trying to fix the dream in my memory. Finally, I got up and turned on a light and wrote the dream down. Did I believe I had actually spoken with spirits? No. The dream came from alcohol and my stay in the mammoth-haunted house. Rosa was the person who spoke with mammoths, not I. Still, it had been so vivid and had seemed so full of meaning.

"It was time to tackle the books, I decided. Not Rosa's scholarly collection, but the rest. Her popular science books were out of date; I wasn't interested in modern Russia; and I rarely read novels. Almost everything could go into the yard sale, along with 30 years of *Scientific American* and *National Geographic*.

"I held the sale three weeks later. The day was hot and bright, the sky full of big cumuli that were likely to become thunderclouds by late afternoon. I moved Rosa's belongings onto the front lawn: books and kitchenware and a few pieces of furniture.

"The first person to arrive was a tall man with long, straight, black hair. It flowed over his shoulders and down his back. He wore a plaid shirt, jeans, work boots and a wide belt with a silver and turquoise buckle. Maybe you don't think

I can remember him so clearly after all these years. But I do. Not that it's hard to remember what Delbert wore on any given day. His costume rarely changed. In the winter, his shirts were flannel, and sometimes his belt buckle was beadwork. His brown skin was lightly scarred by acne. His eyes were hazel, though I didn't notice this at first. How could I? He was bent over the books. He was obviously Indian, but not Lakota. Ojibwa, I thought, looking at his broad chest. An academic or a member of AIM or both.

"Other people came and bought furniture and dishes. The man remained with Rosa's books, going through them carefully. Finally, he came over with a stack. They were mostly histories and mostly about Minnesota and the Upper Midwest. 'I was hoping for more on Native Americans,' he said. 'And mammoths. They aren't nearly as important to the Ojibwa as to the Lakota and Dakota, but we do have some mammoth stories and songs.

"'I'm keeping those,' I said.

"'My tough luck,' he said and smiled. I noticed his eyes. There were white people in his background. Probably voyageurs. 'My name is Delbert Boisvert,' he added. 'You must be Rosa's granddaughter. I saw your name in the obituary. I've been watching for a yard sale, since I learned that she died. I don't rice or sugar like my relatives. But I do hunt and gather books."

"We ended on my porch, talking and drinking lemonade. Delbert helped people load the furniture and dishes they bought. And he recited a song about mammoths that the famous anthropologist Frances Densmore had written down:

"*They are coming.*
They are coming like thunder,
Oh, my Mide brothers.

"After that, he recited an Ojibwa love poem, also written down by Densmore:

"*I thought it was*
A loon.
It was my lover's
Splashing oar.

"'Depending on the direction of the canoe—arriving or departing—it's a sad or happy love song,' Delbert said. 'I like happy songs. For me, the canoe is arriving.'

"That's how I met your grandfather. I had always been careful about love before, maybe because I'd lost my mother and home when still young. I had learned that people were not reliable. They would die like Clara or vanish out of my life like my Standing Rock relatives.

"You would think I could have looked at Rosa and seen her reliability. She loved me and cared for me as long as she lived. If I had been paying better attention, I could have learned about integrity and loyalty. Rosa was always herself and always loyal to me.

"In any case, we talked till midnight. Then he went home, and I went to my bedroom. There were no dreams that night, just me staring into darkness and seeing Delbert's male beauty. There's nothing lovelier than a good-looking man. He's like a tom turkey spreading his feathers or a mammoth bull trumpeting.

"Del came back the next morning, and we spent the day talking about my life in St. Paul and Massachusetts and his life on the Red Lake Reservation and in Minneapolis.

"I was partly right about him. He had studied at the University in the studio art department, though he didn't have a degree. 'It cost too much money and time. I didn't have enough of either.' He was a painter, he told me. 'In fact, I am two kinds of painter. I do houses to make a living and pieces of canvas to keep from going crazy.' He knew the AIM people, though he wasn't a member of AIM. 'I have disagreements with them about strategy and personal disagreements as well. But I won't speak about them with disrespect.'

There was a story there, which he did not tell. In many ways, he was an odd duck, more Indian than I was, but not as Indian as his relatives on Red Lake or in the slums along Franklin Avenue in Minneapolis. In those days, Indians were the poorest people in America, the most badly educated, the sickest and the shortest-lived. Even black people lived longer than we did. But there Delbert and I sat on the porch of Rosa's house, drinking iced tea instead of whiskey or beer, two Indians with enough money to get by and good white educations. But I was haunted by the hills of Standing Rock; and he was haunted by Red Lake's forests; and we were both haunted by our relatives and ancestors.

"As I said before, my life has turned on small events and decisions that I often did not notice at the time. When I came west to close Rosa's house, I was certain that I was going back to Massachusetts."

Grandmother paused. I could tell she was thinking. Two vertical lines had appeared between her eyebrows. "I'm not sure I would have sold the house, even if I had not met Del. It was my childhood home and far closer to Standing Rock than my apartment in the east; and the mammoth tissue was a problem. The more I considered the question, the more I realized I couldn't dump it on the first institution that expressed an interest. It was Rosa's life work, a sacred trust. I had to be sure it was used properly.

"But falling in love with Del made my decision almost easy. He was settled in Minneapolis and not interested in moving east. If I went back to Massachusetts, I would lose him. I was not willing to do this. He was so handsome! I am not sure I should tell you this. Does a granddaughter need to know that her grandmother was a romantic, willing to change her life because she met a beautiful man?

"Mind you, there is nothing wrong with beauty, so long as you have the right standards. The right kind of beauty tells you that your potential mate is strong and healthy, able to produce and maintain a large tail or a pair of enormous tusks. It may tell you that he is intelligent, since intelligence depends—at least in part—on good health. It also depends on education and experience. I am speaking about real intelligence, working intelligence, not the intelligence found by scientists in labs. Del had good health, a good education and lots of useful experience. He was bright and a fine artist. I don't regret picking him."

I was too young to have an opinion on how to chose a mate, though I was interested in how Grandmother went about it. Grandfather lived in New Mexico now, in a house with a big studio full of paintings. I couldn't tell if he was handsome. To me he looked like Gramps: a tall, thin man in faded jeans and a faded shirt, almost always blue. He wore his gray hair in braids; and there was usually a paint-stained rag tucked in his back pocket.

"In any case, I fell in love. We spent the summer together. In the fall, I went east and packed up my apartment, bringing everything back to St. Paul.

"Del moved into the house while I was gone and finished the attic. Rosa had left it as it came to her: bare wood and dust. He sheet rocked the walls and ceiling, put skylights in facing north and covered the floor with black ceramic tiles. They were easier to clean than wood, he said, and he liked the way they looked.

"It's been decades since I last saw the studio, but if I close my eyes, there it is: light flooding through the skylights, reflecting off the white walls and making the black floor shine. Del's paintings lined the room. At that point, his art was abstract, but I could see the landscapes of northern Minnesota in them: broad, dark, horizontal bands like pine forest edging a lake or river; narrow, vertical lines like the trunks of birches; blues as clear as the winter sky; and reds like a sunrise or an autumn maple.

"I loved that studio and the house and Del. It wasn't a wrong choice I made.

"When I got back, I sent out my resume and got a job at a local community college, Introductory Biology at first. I found that I liked teaching. I hadn't, as an instructor in the east. My students were older than the kids at a university; and they saw education as a way to get ahead in a world that wasn't getting any easier. I think they saw the hard times coming sooner than I did. Thanks to Rosa, I was middle class and out of touch, the way the middle classes so often are. You'd think being Indian would have helped.

"In any case, my students were serious about learning; and teaching is a pleasure, when the students want to learn. Some of them—a surprising number, it seemed to me—liked learning for its own sake, maybe because it was an unexpected gift. Oh brave new world, that has such knowledge in it!" Grandmother smiled.

"The college had no facilities for research. But I had plenty to do. The research could wait." She leaned back and flexed her bony shoulders and sighed. "The next thing I knew, I was pregnant with your mother. I hadn't planned to be; it was a genuine accident; but I knew at once that I was going to keep the baby. I was in my middle 30s. If I was going to have children, it was time to get started. By this time, I knew Del and his family well enough to be confident that his genetic material was good. And too many Indian children had died over the years of poverty and disease and simple killing. Too many had been taken from their families and raised white, like Rosa. Too many lost their parents to illness and alcohol. I wanted this child to live and be raised by her parents."

Grandmother paused and I had a sense she was thinking about things she might not tell me. Finally she said, "Del was less certain. Artists have trouble settling down. Their art asks too much of them. But we talked it through, and I had help from his family. His mother wanted grandchildren, and he owed a lot to her. She had spotted his ability when he was a child and sent him to live with relatives in the Cities, so he'd be able to go to art museums and buy art supplies. Without her, he might have been—what? Another unemployed fisherman, after the Red Lake tribal fishery closed down?

"His father's mother was on my side as well. Delores. She was an elder, very much respected. Your mother was going to be her first great-grandchild. There was no way she was going to let Del off the hook.

"They all would have preferred an Ojibwa mother, but at least I was Indian. They had worried about Del. He had dated a lot of white women."

"What did Great-grandfather Claud say?" I asked.

"He said, they would help, if Del needed help. 'All the venison and wild rice you can eat, and you know my mother can sew. That baby will have the finest clothes of any baby in the Twin Cities.' He kept his promise. Your mother had clothes that could have gone into a museum, covered with beadwork and trimmed with fur. We put them away, in case hard times came, and we needed to sell them.

"The baby was born and named Delores, after her great-grandmother. I had planned to go back to work. But my contract with the college was for a year, and they didn't renew it. The pregnancy had been difficult. I had taken a lot of time off. I suspected this was the reason my contract wasn't renewed, but I couldn't prove it. In any case, losing the job was almost a relief. I didn't bounce back from the pregnancy as quickly as women are supposed to. I needed time to recover; and your mother was so tiny and vulnerable! No more so than any baby, but I couldn't imagine putting someone so small, who could barely move and couldn't speak, in the hands of a stranger. I also could not imagine Del as a stay-at-home father. He'd get interested in what he was painting and not even hear the baby cry. I had some money in the bank, my inheritance from Rosa, not a lot, but enough for a while. I decided to wait before I began to look for another job.

"All this time the mammoth tissue was still in the basement. I suppose I should have been a better custodian, but I had been distracted by moving and teaching and having the baby; and I needed time to think. The tissue might be worth money, and we certainly needed money. But would it be right to sell Rosa's life work? I might be able to use the tissue to find a new job, once I was ready to work. I could tell an interested school, 'If you want the tissue, you have to take me as well.'

"I hadn't been entirely negligent. I'd written letters and made phone calls and given away some of the tissue. That was prudent. You shouldn't keep all your eggs—or any organic material—in one basket. Schools knew about me now. More and more were becoming interested. Biotechnology meant it was going to be possible to analyze mammoth DNA and compare it to the DNA of living elephants. That was the kind of achievement that made the papers and TV news and helped get grants. I didn't have the only mammoth tissue on the planet or in the country; but Rosa had made sure that her tissue—my tissue—was in very good shape. I had the freezers and generators checked on a regular basis, and I paid the electric bill as soon as I got it every month."

Grandmother paused. "Where was I?"

"In St. Paul with my mother," I replied.

"We scraped through a year. I took care of the baby and gave away mammoth tissue. Del moved away from abstraction. Now his paintings showed Indians hunting and fishing and ricing. Partly this was the influence of Patrick DesJarlait, the Ojibwa artist from Red Lake. He was dead by then. But Del had studied his work. Of course he had! The world was not full of Ojibwa painters in those days.

"It was also the influence of our trips north to show little Delores to her relatives. Del came back with sketchbooks full of Claud at work. Your great-grandfather had lost his job when the tribal fishery closed. Now he made his living in the old way, hunting and trapping and ricing and doing some construction. Home repairs, mostly. He was also good at fixing cars. On a reservation full of rez cars, this was a valuable skill. Mostly, he got paid in food or thank yous. If you wanted to know poor in those days, you went to a reservation.

"There were sketches of Del's mother holding the baby and old Delores bent over her sewing. Sometimes, when he painted, the figures remained modern Indians; and sometimes their clothes became traditional. There was one I loved— Claud, dressed like an old-time warrior, bent under the hood of a beat-up rez car, working on the engine. I could see the influence of DesJarlait and the WPA or maybe it was the Mexican muralists. Claud in his buckskin and fur and feathers looked like a heroic worker in a post office mural. He was big and bold and bright.

"Del had a show at the American Indian Center in Minneapolis. Then he got a job at the new casino being built south of the Twin Cities. There was a tiny reservation there: Prairie Lake, and this was the end of the 1980s, after the Supreme Court ruled that states could not regulate Indian gaming. It was the start of good times for a handful of Indian bands, the ones near white centers of population. Most, of course, were in the middle of nowhere and did far less well with gaming. But it was a help. I will not be cynical about it. We had been so poor for so long. Even a little money was wealth; and for a few bands, like the ones at Prairie Lake, the money was serious, even by white standards.

"The band decided to name their casino Mammoth Treasure. I suppose it was a good name. Their emblem was a golden mammoth, a male with huge twisting tusks. They wanted a mural in the entrance lobby, showing traditional Indian activities. Del's work fit the bill. Even though he was Ojibwa, and they weren't, he got the job.

"I went down to Prairie Lake with him sometimes. The lobby was circular, and the mural went all the way around the curving wall. If you stood in the middle of the lobby, you were surrounded by a nineteenth century landscape, rolling prairie with clumps of trees. It was a cloudless day in mid-autumn. The grass was tan and gold. The trees were red and brown. In the foreground were Indian hunters on horseback. In the middle distance bison grazed; and in the far distance were four groups of mammoths, one on each side of the lobby, in each of the four directions. Birds sailed above the prairie, so high up that their markings were invisible. But the length of their wings said they were eagles. Hard to say what they were doing there. Bald eagles are fishers and usually keep close to water. The raptors over a prairie ought to be hawks.

"Was the mural corny? Yes. But Del had a streak of romance that went right through him, along with a streak of irony; and the band building the casino absolutely loved the mural; and we needed the money.

"Of course, most of the time when I went down, I saw white plaster and scaffolding. The mural was a work in progress. I nursed little Delores and watched Del or talked with the band treasurer, who was a woman, a big matron with gray hair. The first dribbles of gambling money had gotten her a fine set of new teeth, but it couldn't do anything about the lines in her face. Marion Forte. A good name. She was as strong and solid as a fort. She took to me once she discovered I was Lakota. 'I have nothing against the Ojibwa,' she told me. 'Even though they used to be our enemies. But the Lakota are our cousins. How did you manage to marry an Ojibwa?'

"I told her I wasn't sure. It simply happened. She nodded. 'That's possible. He is a good painter, even though those eagles shouldn't be up there. We aren't close enough to the Mississippi. And those hunters are overdressed, unless they're going to war. All that paint and feathers! No one hunted bison that way.'

"I told her I had wondered about that, and she laughed. 'Most of the council are men. They wanted to see warriors, but they didn't want people to come in and see a war. This is a place to have fun. We can't have blood in the lobby.'

"She was an easy woman to talk to, about the age my mother would have been, if she had lived, and both sharp and kind. So I told her about Clara and Rosa and my childhood and my current life. In the end—it was inevitable—I told her about the freezers in the basement, and the tissue which was an inheritance and problem.

"Marion looked thoughtful. 'Mammoths,' she said. 'No wonder Del has painted them. He's living with what's left of them.' That was the end of the conversation." My grandmother looked at me. "But you must know the next part of the story."

I nodded. "She went to the council and said, they should put money into research."

"Yes," said Grandmother. "And they refused. They were too new to having money. They wanted it for themselves and rest of the band and for the casino, so they could make more money."

"'Men never think ahead,' Marion said. 'That's why they make good warriors. The council president came back from Korea with a chest full of medals. He has never looked beyond the next hill in his entire life. Well, this hill is the new casino. Let's wait and see what lies on the other side.'

"I went home and looked at the bank balance and sent out my resume. Del was getting paid well for the mural, but that money wouldn't last; and our utility bills were high."

Grandmother shrugged. "Why make a long story longer than it is by nature? The Prairie Lake council voted to set up a foundation. It took another four years, with Marion pushing at every meeting; but it finally happened. By then Del had a job teaching at the Minneapolis College of Art, and he'd even had a show in a white museum—not his current work, but the older abstractions. Young Delores was old enough for day care, though she didn't like it. How your mother yelled the first time I left her!

"The University got the first grant for mammoth research; and I went to work for the research lab. The U had no choice. I came with the money and the mammoth tissue. Did I feel guilty, using the tissue and the Prairie Lake band's clout? Not a bit. It was the 1990s by then, the last great hurrah of capitalism before the dark days of the early 21st century. The white people were busy grabbing everything they could with both hands. I thought, I could do a little of the same, enough to pay the bills and get myself back into research.

"Of course the people in the lab resented me, a woman and an Indian, who had gotten her job through luck and casino money. How could I be any good? I won't bother you with the story of my struggles. This story is about the mammoths, not me. But always remember that power concedes nothing without a demand. It never did, and it never will. 'If there is no struggle there is no progress. Those who profess to favor freedom and yet depreciate agitation . . . want crops without plowing up the ground, they want rain without thunder and lightning. They want the ocean without the awful roar of its many waters . . .'"

At the time I did not recognize the quote. It was Frederick Douglass, of course. Odd to hear my grandmother talk about the ocean on the bone-dry Dakota prairie.

"The first several grants came from Prairie Lake. Then other money began to come in, as the lab reported its first success, which was decoding mammoth and elephant DNA and finding out that mammoths were closely related to Asian elephants. The next step was obvious, though not easy: building a viable mammoth egg and implanting it in an elephant." Grandmother smiled. "Imagine what a statement that is! It used to be, we could not imagine re-creating extinct animals, except maybe in science fiction stories. Now we have the quagga—the real quagga, not the bred-back version; and the giant ground sloth, though I'm not sure what use it is, except as an exhibit in a zoo. And we have two species of mammoths, though the Siberian species is a genetic patchwork. Still, it's different enough from our Missouri mammoths to be called a separate species.

"I have to say, my contribution to the research was not key; and I did my own best work later in another area. But I still remember—how could I ever forget?— the morning when the first baby mammoth was born and helped to stand by a vet and the surrogate mother's mahout. The rest of us watched on a monitor. The calf was tiny, unsteady, wet and very hairy. The mother fondled it with her trunk, unsurprised—as far as we could tell—by all the hair.

"The first species brought back from extinction! Not from the edge of extinction, but from the void beyond the edge! The research team broke out champagne, and the Prairie Lake band ordered new commercials for their casino starring the baby. That led to a fight, but the band had good lawyers, and the grants had been carefully written. Prairie Lake owned the right to publicize any results of the research they funded. My colleagues at the U made angry jokes about Indian givers. But the band never asked for its money back. It simply wanted its share of the results, which included—ultimately—enough mammoths to start their own herd. Always be careful what you sign, Emma."

She stopped and leaned back, her eyes closed. It was a long story. Of course, I felt pride. My family had helped save the Missouri mammoths, though most of the mammoths lived north and west of us. The great river was diminishing, due to lack of snow in the Rockies; and the moist bottom lands the mammoths needed no longer existed.

"There's one good side to that," Grandmother said. "They blew up the Oahe Dam. That damn lake is gone. It never looked natural, and it took so much of our land. Though it didn't do to us what it did to the Mandan and Hidatsa and Akikawa. They lost their entire reservation. I know it happened in another century, and I know that people shouldn't hold grudges. Life has gotten better for us and many people. But I hated that lake. I could dance on the dry land where it used to be. In fact I do. That's where we hold the annual Standing Rock powwow."

She didn't say 'powwow.' She said 'wacipi,' which is the Lakota word. But I knew what she meant.

"It would have happened, anyway," Grandmother said. "They would have built mammoths from other DNA. Rosa wasn't the only person who kept tissue, though hers was the best. So don't feel too proud, young Miss Emma. History is a collaborative process. The important thing is to be a part of history and on the right side, which is not always easy to determine. It's not enough to hold onto the past, though we Indians proved that losing the past is dangerous. We almost died of trying to be white. Not that white people have done much better. They almost destroyed the planet by getting and spending and laying waste.

"What do we keep from the past? What do we discard? How do we change? These are all important questions, which all of us have to answer. The mammoths are important, though they may not graze by the Missouri again in our lifetimes. But the bison are back—over a million; and the herds are still growing; and you can see them here on Standing Rock. There's plenty left to do to remake the planet, but we have achieved a fair amount already. One step forward and two steps back, and then one or two or three steps forward. We dance into the future like dancers in a Grand Entry."

At the end of every visit, I went home, rocking through Standing Rock past the grazing bison. My mother's second cousin Thelma in Minot gave me dinner and a bed. In the morning, I rode the eastbound rocket train. Windmills turned. The train glided through forest. My parents waited on the platform in Minneapolis. If I wanted to see mammoths, I could go to Mammoth Treasure Park by the casino. They were there, wading in an artificial river and spraying each other with water, their ancient eyes glittering with pleasure. Above them in the blue sky might be eagles. They have grown so common that they are everywhere these days.

sleeping Dogs

JOE HALDEMAN

Born in Oklahoma City, Oklahoma, Joe Haldeman took a B.S. degree in physics and astronomy from the University of Maryland, and did postgraduate work in mathematics and computer science. But his plans for a career in science were cut short by the U.S. Army, which sent him to Vietnam in 1968 as a combat engineer. Seriously wounded in action, Haldeman returned home in 1969 and began to write. He sold his first story to *Galaxy* in 1969, and by 1976 had garnered both the Nebula Award and the Hugo Award for his famous novel *The Forever War*, one of the landmark books of the seventies. He took another Hugo Award in 1977 for his story "Tricentennial," won the Rhysling Award in 1984 for the best science fiction poem of the year (although usually thought of primarily as a "hard science" writer, Haldeman is, in fact, also an accomplished poet, and has sold poetry to most of the major professional markets in the genre), and won both the Nebula in 1990 and the Hugo Award in 1991 for the novella version of "The Hemingway Hoax." His story "None So Blind" won the Hugo Award in 1995. His other books include a mainstream novel, *War Year*, the SF novels *Mindbridge*, *All My Sins Remembered*, *There Is No Darkness* (written with his brother, SF writer Jack C. Haldeman II), *Worlds*, *Worlds Apart*, *Worlds Enough and Time*, *Buying Time*, *The Hemingway Hoax*, *Tool of the Trade*, *The Coming*, the mainstream novel *1968*, *Camouflage*, which won the prestigious James Tiptree, Jr., Award, *Old Twentieth*, and *The Accidental Time Machine*. His short work has been gathered in the collections *Infinite Dreams*, *Dealing in Futures*, *Vietnam and Other Alien Worlds*, *None So Blind*, *A Separate War and Other Stories*, and an omnibus of fiction and nonfiction, *War Stories*. As editor, he has produced the anthologies *Study War No More*, *Cosmic Laughter*, *Nebula Award Stories Seventeen*, and, with Martin H. Greenberg, *Future Weapons of War*. His most recent books are two new science fiction novels, *Marsbound* and its sequel, *Starbound*. Haldeman lives part of the year in Boston, where he teaches writing at the Massachusetts Institute of Technology, and the rest of the year in Florida, where he and his wife, Gay, make their home.

Here he gives us a deeply cynical study of the ways in which future governments could manipulate the flow of information reaching their citizens even *more* effectively than they do today. . . .

The cab took my eyeprint and the door swung open. I was glad to get out. No driver to care how rough the ride was, on a road that wouldn't even be called a road on Earth. The place had gone downhill in the thirty years I'd been away.

Low gravity and low oxygen. My heart was going too fast. I stood for a moment, concentrating, and brought it down to a hundred, then ninety. The air had more sulfur sting than I remembered. It seemed a lot warmer than I remembered that summer, too, but then if I could remember it all I wouldn't have to be here. My missing finger throbbed.

Six identical buildings on the block, half-cylinders of stained pale green plastic. I walked up the dirt path to number 3: Offworld Affairs and Confederación Liaison. I almost ran into the door when it didn't open. Pushed and pulled and it reluctantly let me inside.

It was a little cooler and less sulfurous. I went to the second door on the right, Travel Documents and Permissions, and went in.

"You don't knock on Earth?" A cadaverous tall man, skin too white and hair too black.

"Actually, no," I said, "not public buildings. But I apologize for my ignorance."

He looked at a monitor built into his desk. "You would be Flann Spivey, from Japan on Earth. You don't look Japanese."

"I'm Irish," I said. "I work for a Japanese company, Ichiban Imaging."

He touched a word on the screen. "Means number one. Best, or first?"

"Both, I think."

"Papers." I laid out two passports and a folder of travel documents. He spent several minutes inspecting them carefully. Then he slipped them into a primitive scanning machine, which flipped through them one by one, page by page.

He finally handed them back. "When you were here twenty-nine Earth years ago, there were only eight countries on Seca, representing two competing powers. Now there are 79 countries, two of them offplanet, in a political situation that's . . . impossible to describe simply. Most of the other 78 countries are more comfortable than Spaceport. Nicer."

"So I was told. I'm not here for comfort, though." There weren't many planets where they put their spaceports in nice places.

He nodded slowly as he selected two forms from a drawer. "So what does a 'thanatopic counselor' do?"

"I prepare people for dying." For living completely, actually, before they leave.

"Curious." He smiled. "It pays well?"

"Adequately."

He handed me the forms. "I've never seen a poor person come through that door. Take these down the hall to Immunization."

"I've had all the shots."

"All that the Confederación requires. Seca has a couple of special tests for returning veterans. Of the Consolidation War."

"Of course. The nanobiota. But I was tested before they let me return to Earth."

He shrugged. "Rules. What do you tell them?"

"Tell?"

"The people who are going to die. We just sort of let it catch up with us. Avoid it as long as possible, but . . ."

"That's a way." I took the forms. "Not the only way."

I had the door partly open when he cleared his throat. "Dr. Spivey? If you don't have any plans, I would be pleased to have midmeal with you."

Interesting. "Sure. I don't know how long this will take . . ."

"Ten minims, fifteen. I'll call us a floater, so we don't have to endure the road."

The blood and saliva samples took less time than filling out the forms. When I went back outside, the floater was humming down and Braz Nitian was watching it land from the walkway.

It was a fast two-minute hop to the center of town, the last thirty seconds disconcerting free fall. The place he'd chosen was Kaffee Rembrandt, a rough-hewn place with a low ceiling and guttering oil lamps in pursuit of a 16th-century ambience, somewhat diluted by the fact that the dozens of Rembrandt reproductions glowed with apparently sourceless illumination.

A busty waitress in period flounce showed us to a small table, dwarfed by a large self-portrait of the artist posed as "Prodigal Son with a Whore."

I'd never seen an actual flagon, a metal container with a hinged top. It appeared to hold enough wine to support a meal and some conversation.

I ordered a plate of braised vegetables, following conservative dietary advice—the odd proteins in Seca's animals and fish might lay me low with a xeno-allergy. Among the things I didn't remember about my previous time here was whether our rations had included any native flesh or fish. But even if I'd safely eaten them thirty years ago, the Hartford doctor said, I could have a protein allergy now, since an older digestive system might not completely break down those alien proteins into safe amino acids.

Braz had gone to college on Earth, UCLA, an expensive proposition that obligated him to work for the government for ten years (which would be fourteen Earth years). He had degrees in mathematics and macroeconomics, neither of which he used in his office job. He taught three nights a week and wrote papers that nine or ten people read and disagreed with.

"So how did you become a thanatopic counselor? Something you always wanted to be when you grew up?"

"Yeah, after cowboy and pirate."

He smiled. "I never saw a cowboy on Earth."

"Pirates tracked them down and made them walk the plank. Actually, I was an accountant when I joined the military, and then started out in pre-med after I was discharged, but switched over to psychology and moved into studying veterans."

"Natural enough. Know thyself."

"Literally." Find thyself, I thought. "You get a lot of us coming through?"

"Well, not so many, not from Earth or other foreign planets. Being a veteran doesn't correlate well with wealth."

"That's for sure." And a trip from Earth to Seca and back costs as much as a big house.

"I imagine that treating veterans doesn't generate a lot of money, either." Eyebrows lifting.

"A life of crime does." I smiled and he laughed politely. "But most of the veterans I do see are well off. Almost nobody with a normal life span needs my services. They're mostly for people who've lived some centuries, and you couldn't do that without wealth."

"They get tired of life?"

"Not the way you or I could become tired of a game, or a relationship. It's something deeper than running out of novelty. People with that little imagination don't need me. They can stop existing for the price of a bullet or a rope—or a painless prescription, where I come from."

"Not legal here," he said neutrally.

"I know. I'm not enthusiastic about it, myself."

"You'd have more customers?"

I shrugged. "You never know." The waitress brought us our first plates, grilled fungi on a stick for me. Braz had a bowl of small animals with tails, deep-fried. Finger food; you hold them by the tail and dip them into a pungent yellow sauce.

It was much better than I'd expected; the fungi were threaded onto a stick of some aromatic wood like laurel; she brought a small glass of a lavender-colored drink, tasting like dry sherry, to go with them.

"So it's not about getting bored?" he asked. "That's how you normally see it. In books, on the cube . . ."

"Maybe the reality isn't dramatic enough. Or too complicated to tell as a simple drama.

"You live a few hundred years, at least on Earth, you slowly leave your native culture behind. You're an immortal—culturally true if not literally—and your non-immortal friends and family and business associates die off. The longer you live, the deeper you go into the immortal community."

"There must be some nonconformists."

"'Mavericks,' the cowboys used to say."

"Before the pirates did them in."

"Right. There aren't many mavericks past their first century of life extension. The people you grew up with are either fellow immortals or dead. Together, the survivors form a society that's unusually cohesive. So when someone decides to leave, decides to stop living, the arrangements are complex and may involve hundreds of people.

"That's where I come in, the practical part of my job: I'm a kind of overall estate manager. They all have significant wealth; few have any living relatives closer than great-great-grandchildren."

"You help them split up their fortunes?"

"It's more interesting than that. The custom for centuries has been to put together a legacy, so called, that is a complex and personal aesthetic expression. To simply die, and let the lawyers sort it out, would trivialize your life as well as your death. It's my job to make sure that the legacy is a meaningful and permanent extension of the person's life.

"Sometimes a physical monument is involved; more often a financial one, through endowments and sponsorships. Which is what brings me here."

Our main courses came; Braz had a kind of eel, bright green with black antennae, apparently raw, but my braised vegetables were reassuringly familiar.

"So one of your clients is financing something here on Seca?"

"Financing me, actually. It's partly a gift; we get along well. But it's part of a pattern of similar bequests to non-immortals, to give us back lost memories."

"How lost?"

"It was a military program, to counteract the stress of combat. They called the drug aqualethe. Have you heard of it?"

He shook his head. "Water of what?"

"It's a linguistic mangling, or mingling. Latin and Greek. Lethe was a river in Hell; a spirit drank from it to forget his old life, so he could be reincarnated.

"A pretty accurate name. It basically disconnects your long-term memory as a way of diverting combat stress, so-called post-traumatic stress disorder."

"It worked?"

"Too well. I spent eight months here as a soldier, when I was in my early twenties. I don't remember anything specific between the voyage here and the voyage back."

"It was a horrible war. Short but harsh. Maybe you don't want the memory back. 'Let sleeping dogs lie,' we say here."

"We say that, too. But for me . . . well, you could say it's a professional handicap. Though actually it goes deeper.

"Part of what I do with my clients is a mix of meditation and dialogue. I try to help them form a coherent tapestry of their lives, the good and the bad, as a basic grounding for their legacy. The fact that I could never do that for myself hinders me as a counselor. Especially when the client, like this one, had his own combat experiences to deal with."

"He's, um, dead now?"

"Oh, no. Like many of them, he's in no particular hurry. He just wants to be ready."

"How old is he?"

"Three hundred and ninety Earth years. Aiming for four centuries, he thinks."

Braz sawed away at his eel and looked thoughtful. "I can't imagine. I mean, I sort of understand when a normal man gets so old he gives up. Their hold on life becomes weak, and they let go. But your man is presumably fit and sane."

"More than I, I think."

"So why four hundred years rather than five? Or three? Why not try for a thousand? That's what I would do, if I were that rich."

"So would I. At least that's how I feel now. My patron says he felt that way when he was mortal. But he can't really articulate what happened to slowly change his attitude.

"He says it would be like trying to explain married love to a babe just learning to talk. The babe thinks it knows what love is, and can apply the word to its own circumstances. But it doesn't have the vocabulary or life experience to approach the larger meaning."

"An odd comparison, marriage," he said, delicately separating the black antennae from the head. "You can become unmarried. But not undead."

"The babe wouldn't know about divorce. Maybe there is a level of analogy there."

"We don't know what death is?"

"Perhaps not as well as they."

I liked Braz and needed to hire a guide; he had some leave coming and could use the side income. His Spanish was good, and that was rare on Secas; they spoke a kind of patchwork of Portuguese and English. If I'd studied it thirty years before, I'd retained none.

The therapy to counteract aqualethe was a mixture of brain chemistry and environment. Simply put, the long-term memories were not destroyed by aqualethe, but the connection to them had been weakened. There was a regimen of twenty pills I had to take twice daily, and I had to take them in surroundings that would jog my memory.

That meant going back to some ugly territory.

There were no direct flights to Serraro, the mountainous desert where my platoon had been sent to deal with a situation now buried in secrecy, perhaps shame. We could get within a hundred kilometers of it, an oasis town called Console Verde. I made arrangements to rent a general-purpose vehicle there, a jépe.

After Braz and I made those arrangements, I got a note from some Chief of Internal Security saying that my activities were of questionable legality, and I should report to his office at 0900 tomorrow to defend my actions. We were in the airport, fortunately, when I got the message, and we jumped on a flight that was leaving in twenty minutes, paying cash. Impossible on Earth.

I told Braz I would buy us a couple of changes of clothing and such at the Oasis, and we got on the jet with nothing but our papers, my medications, and the clothes on our backs—and my purse, providentially stuffed with the paper notes they use instead of plastic. (I'd learned that the exchange rate was much better on Earth, and was carrying half a year's salary in those notes.)

The flight wasn't even suborbital, and took four hours to go about a tenth of the planet's circumference. We slept most of the way; it didn't take me twenty minutes to tell him everything I had been able to find out about that two-thirds year that was taken from me.

Serraro is not exactly a bastion of freedom of information under the best of circumstances, and that was a period in their history that many would just as soon forget.

It was not a poor country. The desert was rich in the rare earths that interstellar jumps required. There had been lots of small mines around the countryside (no farms) and only one city of any size. That was Novo B, short for Novo Brasil, and it was still not the safest spot in the Confederación. Not on our itinerary.

My platoon had begun its work in Console Verde as part of a force of one thousand. When we returned to that oasis, there were barely six hundred of us left. But the country had been "unified." Where there had been 78 mines there now was one, Preciosa, and no one wanted to talk about how that happened.

The official history says that the consolidation of those 78 mines was a model of self-determinism, the independent miners banding together for strength and bargaining power. There was some resistance, even some outlaw guerilla action. But the authorities—I among them, evidently—got things under control in less than a year.

Travel and residence records had all been destroyed by a powerful explosion blamed on the guerillas, but in the next census, Serarro had lost thirty-five percent of its population. Perhaps they walked away.

We stood out as foreigners in our business suits; most men who were not in uniform wore a plain loose white robe. I went immediately into a shop next to the airport and bought two of them, and two sidearms. Braz hadn't fired a pistol in years, but he had to agree he would look conspicuous here without one.

We stood out anyway, pale and tall. The men here were all sunburned and most wore long braided black hair. Our presence couldn't be kept secret; I wondered how long it would be before that Chief of Internal Security caught up with me. I was hoping it was just routine harassment, and they wouldn't follow us here.

There was only one room at the small inn, but Braz didn't mind sharing. In fact, he suggested we pass the time with sex, which caught me off guard. I told him men don't routinely do that on Earth, at least not the place and time I came from. He accepted that with a nod.

I asked the innkeeper whether the town had a library, and he said no, but I could try the schoolhouse on the other side of town. Braz was napping, so I left a note and took off on my own, confident in my ability to turn right and go to the end of the road.

Although I'd been many places on Earth, the only time I'd been in space was that eight-month tour here. So I kept my eyes open for "alien" details.

Seca had a Drake index of 0.95, which by rule of thumb meant that only five percent of it was more harsh than the worst the Earth had to offer. The equatorial desert, I supposed. We were in what would have been a temperate latitude on Earth, and I was sweating freely in the dry heat.

The people here were only five generations away from Earth, but some genetic drift was apparent. No more profound than you would find on some islands and other isolated communities on Earth. But I didn't see a single blonde or red-head in the short, solidly built population here.

The men wore scowls as well as guns. The women, brighter colors and a neutral distant expression.

Some of the men, mostly younger, wore a dagger as well as a sidearm. I wondered whether there was some kind of code duello that I would have to watch out for. Probably *not* wearing a dagger would protect you from that.

Aside from a pawn shop, with three balls, and a tavern with bright signs announcing berbesa and bino, most of the shops were not identified. I supposed that in a small isolated town, everybody knew where everything was.

Two men stopped together, blocking the sidewalk. One of them touched his pistol and said something incomprehensible, loudly.

"From Earth," I said, in unexcited Confederación Spanish. *Soy de la Tierra.*" They looked at each other and went by me. I tried to ignore the crawling feeling in the middle of my back.

I reflected on my lack of soldierly instincts. Should I have touched my gun as well? Probably not. If they'd started shooting, what should I do? Hurl my

60-year-old body to the ground, roll over with the pistol in my hand, and aim for the chest?

"Two in the chest, then one in the head," I remembered from crime drama. But I didn't remember anything that basic from having been a soldier. My training on Earth had mainly been calisthenics and harassment. Endless hours of parade-ground drill. Weapons training would come later, they said. The only thing "later" meant to me was months later, slowly regaining my identity on the trip back to Earth.

By the time I'd gotten off the ship, I seemed to have all my memories back through basic training, and the lift ride up to the troop carrier. We had 1.5-gee acceleration to the Oort portal, but somewhere along there I lost my memory, and didn't get it back till the return trip. Then they dropped me on Earth—me and the other survivors—with a big check and a leather case full of medals. Plus a smaller check, every month, for my lost finger.

I knew I was approaching the school by the small tide of children running in my direction, about fifty of them, ranging from seven or eight to about twelve, in Earth years.

The school house was small, three or four rooms. A grey-bearded man, unarmed, stepped out and I hailed him. We established that we had English in common and I asked whether the school had a library. He said yes, and it would be open for two hours yet. "Mostly children's books, of course. What are you interested in?"

"History," I said. "Recent. The Consolidation War."

"Ah. Follow me." He led me through a dusty playground, to the rear of the school. "You were a Confederación soldier?'

"I guess that's obvious."

He paused with his hand on the doorknob. "You know to be careful?" I said I did. "Don't go out at night alone. Your size is like a beacon." He opened the door and said, "Suela? A traveler is looking for a history book."

The room was high-ceilinged and cool, with thick stone walls and plenty of light from the uniform glow of the ceiling. An elderly woman with white hair taking paper books from a cart and re-shelving them.

"Pardon my poor English," she said, with an accent better than mine. "But what do you want in a paper book that you can't as easily download?"

"I was curious to see what children are taught about the Consolidation War."

"The same truth as everyone," she said with a wry expression, and stepped over to another shelf. "Here . . ." she read titles, "this is the only one in English. I can't let you take it away, but you're welcome to read it here."

I thanked her and took the book to an adult-sized table and chair at the other end of the room. Most of the study area was scaled down. A girl of seven or eight stared at me.

I didn't know, really, what I expected to find in the book. It had four pages on the Consolidation and Preciosa, and in broad outline there was not much surprising. A coalition of mines decided that the Confederación wasn't paying enough for dysprosium, and they got most of the others to go along with the scheme of hiding the stuff and holding out for a fair price—what the book called profiteering and restraint of trade. Preciosa was the biggest mine, and they made a separate deal with the Confederación, guaranteeing a low price, freezing all their competitors out. Which led to war.

Seca—actually Preciosa—asked for support from the Confederación, and the war became interstellar.

The book said that most of the war took place far from population centers, in the bleak high desert where the mines were. Here.

It struck me that I hadn't noticed many old buildings, older than about thirty years. I remembered a quote from a twentieth-century American war: "We had to destroy the village in order to save it."

The elderly librarian sat down across from me. She had a soft voice. "You were here as a soldier. But you don't remember anything about it."

"That's true. That's exactly it."

"There are those of us who do remember."

I pushed the book a couple of inches toward her. "Is any of this true?"

She turned the book around and scanned the pages it was open to, and shook her head with a grim smile. "Even children know better. What do you think the Confederación is?"

I thought for a moment. "At one level, it's a loose federation of 48 or 49 planets with a charter protecting the rights of humans and non-humans, and with trade rules that encourage fairness and transparency. At another level, it's the Hartford Corporation, the wealthiest enterprise in human history. Which can do anything it wants, presumably."

"And on a personal level? What is it to you?"

"It's an organization that gave me a job when jobs were scarce. Security specialist. Although I wasn't a 'specialist' in any sense of the word. A generalist, so called."

"A mercenary."

"Not so called. Nothing immoral or illegal."

"But they took your memory of it away. So it could have been either, or both."

"Could have been," I admitted. "I'm going to find out. Do you know about the therapy that counteracts aqualethe?"

"No . . . it gives you your memories back?"

"So they say. I'm going to drive down into Serarro tomorrow, and see what happens. You take the pills in the place you want to remember."

"Do me a favor," she said, sliding the book back, "and yourself, perhaps. Take the pills here, too."

"I will. We had a headquarters here. I must have at least passed through."

"Look for me in the crowd, welcoming you. You were all so exotic and handsome. I was a girl, just ten."

Ten here would be fourteen on Earth. This old lady was younger than me. No juve treatments. "I don't think the memories will be that detailed. I'll look for you, though."

She patted my hand and smiled. "You do that."

Braz was still sleeping when I got back to the inn. Six time zones to adjust to; might as well let him sleep. My body was still on meaningless starship time, but I've never had much trouble adjusting. My counseling job is a constant whirl of time zones.

I quietly slipped into the other bunk and put some Handel in my earbuds to drown out his snoring.

The inn didn't have any vegetables for breakfast, so I had a couple of eggs that I hoped had come from a bird, and a large dry flavorless cracker. Our jepé arrived at 8:30 and I went out to pay the substantial deposit and inspect it. Guaranteed bulletproof except for the windows, nice to know.

I took the first leg of driving, since I'd be taking the memory drug later, and the label had the sensible advice *Do Not Operate Machinery While Hallucinating*. Words to live by.

The city, such as it was, didn't dwindle off into suburbs. It's an oasis, and where the green stopped, the houses stopped.

I drove very cautiously at first. My car in LA is restricted to autopilot, and it had been several years since I was last behind a steering wheel. A little exhilarating.

After about thirty kilometers, the road suddenly got very rough. Braz suggested that we'd left the state of Console Verde and had entered Pretorocha, whose tax base wouldn't pay for a shovel. I gave the wheel to him after a slow hour, when we got to the first pile of tailings. Time to take the first twenty pills.

I didn't really know what to expect. I knew the unsupervised use of the aqualethe remedy was discouraged, because some people had extreme reactions. I'd given Braz an emergency poke of sedative to administer to me if I really lost control.

Rubble and craters. Black grit over everything. Building ruins that hadn't weathered much; this place didn't have much weather. Hot and dry in the summer, slightly less hot and more dry in the winter. We drove around and around and absolutely nothing happened. After two hours, the minimum wait, I swallowed another twenty.

Pretorocha was where they said I'd lost my finger, and it was where the most Confederación casualties had been recorded. Was it possible that the drug just didn't work on me?

What was more likely, if I properly understood the literature, was one of two things: one, the place had changed so much that my recovering memory didn't pick up any specifics; two, that I'd never actually been here.

That second didn't seem possible. I'd left a finger here, and the Confederacíon verified that; it had been paying for the lost digit for thirty years.

The first explanation? Pictures of the battle looked about as bleak as this blasted landscape. Maybe I was missing something basic, like a smell or the summer heat. But the literature said the drug required visual stimuli.

"Maybe it doesn't work as well on some as on others," Braz said. "Or maybe you got a bad batch. How long do we keep driving around?"

I had six tubes of pills left. The drug was in my system for sure: cold sweat, shortness of breath, ocular pressure. "Hell, I guess we've seen enough. Take a pee break and head back."

Standing by the side of the road there, under the low hot sun, urinating into black ash, somehow I knew for certain that I'd never been there before. A hellish place like this would burn itself into your subconscious.

But aqualethe was strong. Maybe too strong for the remedy to counter.

I took the wheel for the trip back to Console Verde. The air-conditioning had only two settings, frigid and off. We agreed to turn it off and open the non-bulletproof windows to the waning heat.

There was a kind of lunar beauty to the place. That would have made an impression on me back then. When I was still a poet. An odd thing to remember. Something did happen that year to end that. Maybe I lost it with the music, with the finger.

When the road got better I let Braz take over. I was out of practice with traffic, and they drove on the wrong side of the road anyhow.

The feeling hit me when the first buildings rose up out of the rock. My throat. Not like choking; a gentler pressure, like tightening a necktie.

Everything shimmered and glowed. *This* was where I'd been. This side of the city.

"Braz . . . it's happening. Go slow." He pulled over to the left and I heard warning lights go click-click-click.

"You weren't . . . down there at all? You were here?"

"I don't know! Maybe. I don't know." It was coming on stronger and stronger. Like seeing double, but with all your body. "Get into the right lane." It was getting hard to see, a brilliant fog. "What is that big building?"

"Doesn't have a name," he said. "Confederación sigil over the parking lot."

"Go there . . . go there . . . I'm losing it, Braz."

"Maybe you're finding it."

The car was fading around me, and I seemed to drift forward and up. Through the wall of the building. Down a corridor. Through a closed door. Into an office.

I was sitting there, a young me. Coal black beard, neatly trimmed. Dress uniform. All my fingers.

Most of the wall behind me was taken up by a glowing spreadsheet. I knew what it represented.

Two long tables flanked my work station. They were covered with old ledgers and folders full of paper correspondence and records.

My job was to steal the planet from its rightful owners—but not the whole planet. Just the TREO rights, Total Rare Earth Oxides.

There was not much else on the planet of any commercial interest to the Confederación. When they found a tachyon nexus, they went off in search of dysprosium nearby, necessary for getting back to where you came from, or continuing farther out. Automated probes had found a convenient source in a mercurian planet close to the nexus star Poucoyellow. But after a few thousand pioneers had staked homestead claims on Seca, someone stumbled on a mother lode of dysprosium and other rare earths in the sterile hell of Serarro.

It was the most concentrated source of dysprosium ever found, on any planet, easily a thousand times the output of Earth's mines.

The natives knew what they had their hands on, and they were cagey. They quietly passed a law that required all mineral rights to be deeded on paper; no electronic record. For years, 78 mines sold two percent of the dysprosium they dug up, and stockpiled the rest—as much as the Confederación could muster from two dozen other planets. Once they had hoarded enough, they could absolutely corner the market.

But they only had one customer.

Routine satellite mapping gave them away; the gamma ray signature of monazite-allenite stuck out like a flag. The Confederación deduced what was going on, and trained a few people like me to go in and remedy the situation, along with enough soldiers to supply the fog of war.

While the economy was going crazy, dealing with war, I was quietly buying up small shares in the rare earth mines, through hundreds of fictitious proxies.

When we had voting control of 51% of the planet's dysprosium, and thus its price, the soldiers did an about-face and went home, first stopping at the infirmary for a shot of aqualethe.

I was a problem, evidently. Aqualethe erased the memory of trauma, but I hadn't experienced any. All I had done was push numbers around, and occasionally forge signatures.

So one day three big men wearing black hoods kicked in my door and took me to a basement somewhere. They beat me monotonously for hours, wearing thick gloves, not breaking bones or rupturing organs. I was blindfolded and handcuffed, sealed up in a universe of constant pain.

Then they took off the blindfold and handcuffs and those three men held my arm and hand while a fourth used heavy bolt-cutters to snip off the ring finger of my left hand, making sure I watched. Then they dressed the stump and gave me a shot.

I woke up approaching Earth, with medals and money and no memory. And one less finger.

Woke again on my bunk at the inn. Braz sitting there with a carafe of *melán*, what they had at the inn instead of coffee. "Are you coming to?" he said quietly. "I helped you up the stairs." Dawn light at the window. "It was pretty bad?"

"It was . . . not what I expected." I levered myself upright and accepted a cup. "I wasn't really a soldier. In uniform, but just a clerk. Or a con man." I sketched out the story for him.

"So they actually chopped off your finger? I mean, beat you senseless and then snipped it off?"

I squeezed the short stump gingerly. "So the drug would work.

"I played guitar, before. So I spent a year or so working out alternative fingerings, formations, without the third finger. Didn't really work."

I took a sip. It was like kava, a bitter alkaloid. "So I changed careers."

"You were going to be a singer?"

"No. Classical guitar. So I went back to university instead, pre-med and then psychology and philosophy. Got an easy doctorate in Generalist Studies. And became this modern version of the boatman, ferryman . . . Charon—the one who takes people to the other side."

"So what are you going to do? With the truth."

"Spread it around, I guess. Make people mad."

He rocked back in his chair. "Who?"

"What do you mean? Everybody."

"Everybody?" He shook his head. "Your story's interesting, and your part in it is dramatic and sad, but there's not a bit of it that would surprise anyone over the age of twenty. Everyone knows what the war was really about.

"It's even more cynical and manipulative than I thought, but you know? That won't make people mad. When it's the government, especially the Confederación, people just nod and say, 'more of the same.'"

"Same old, we say. Same old shit."

"They settled death and damage claims generously; rebuilt the town. And it was half a lifetime ago, our lifetimes. Only the old remember, and most of them don't care anymore."

That shouldn't have surprised me; I've been too close to it. Too close to my own loss, small compared to others'.

I sipped at the horrible stuff and put it back down. "I should do something. I can't just sit on this."

"But you can. Maybe you should."

I made a dismissive gesture and he leaned forward and continued with force. "Look, Spivey. I'm not just a backsystem hick—or I am, but I'm a hick with a rusty doctorate in macroeconomics—and you're not seeing or thinking clearly. About the war and the Confederación. Let the drugs dry out before you do something that you might regret."

"That's pretty dramatic."

"Well, the situation you're in is *melo*dramatic! You want to go back to Earth and say you have proof that the Confederación used you to subvert the will of a planet, to the tune of more than a thousand dead and a trillion hartfords of real estate, then tortured and mutilated you in order to blank out your memory of it?"

"Well? That's what happened."

He got up. "You think about it for awhile. Think about the next thing that's going to happen." He left and closed the door quietly behind him.

I didn't have to think too long. He was right.

Before I came to Seca, of course I searched every resource for verifiable information about the war. That there was so little should have set off an alarm in my head.

It's a wonderful thing to be able to travel from star to star, collecting exotic memories. But you have no choice of carrier. To take your memories back to Earth, you have to rely on the Confederación.

And if those memories are unpleasant, or just inconvenient . . . they can fix that for you.

Over and over.

Jackie's Boy

STEVEN POPKES

Steven Popkes made his first sale in 1985, and in the years that followed has contributed a number of distinguished stories to markets such as *Asimov's Science Fiction, Sci Fiction, The Magazine of Fantasy & Science Fiction, Realms of Fantasy, Science Fiction Age, Full Spectrum, Tomorrow, The Twilight Zone Magazine, Night Cry*, and others. His first novel, *Caliban Landing*, appeared in 1987, and was followed in 1991 by an expansion to novel-length of his popular novella "The Egg," retitled *Slow Lightning*. He was also part of the Cambridge Writers' Workshop project to produce science fiction scenarios about the future of Boston, Massachusetts, that cumulated in the 1994 anthology *Future Boston*, to which he contributed several stories. He lives in Hopkinton, Massachusetts, with his family, where he works for a company that builds aviation instrumentation.

Popkes was quiet through the late nineties and the early part of the oughts, but in the last couple of years he's returned to writing first-rate stories such as the novella that follows, which does a good job with the difficult balancing act of delivering a (sort-of) optimistic after-the-apocalypse story, one where it's still possible to strike out to find a better life for yourself.

PART 1

Michael fell in love with her the moment he saw her.

The Long Bottom Boys had taken over the gate of the Saint Louis Zoo from Nature Phil's gang. London Bob had killed in single combat, and eaten, Nature Phil. That, pretty much, constituted possession. The Keepers didn't mind as long as it stayed off the grounds. So the Boys waited outside to harvest anyone who came out or went in. They just had to wait. Somebody was always drawn to the sight of all that meat on the hoof, nothing protecting it from consumption save a hundred feet of empty air and invisible, lethal, automated weaponry. People went in just to look at it and drool.

Michael knew their plans. He'd been watching them furtively for a week, hiding in places no adult could go, leaving no traces they could see. The Boys had caught a woman a few days ago and a man last night. They were still passing the woman around. What was left of the man was turning on the spit over on Grand. He sniffed the air. A rank odor mixed with a smell like maple syrup. Corpse fungus at the fruiting body stage. Somewhere nearby there was a collection of mushrooms that yesterday had been the body of a human being. Michael wondered if it was someone who had spoiled before the Boys had got to them or if it was the last inedible remnants of the man on the spit. By morning there would be little more than a thin mound of soil to show where the meat had been.

This dark spring morning, just when the gates unlocked, one of the guards remained asleep. Michael held his backpack tightly to his chest so he made no sound. The man started in his sleep. For a moment, Michael thought he would have to take up one of the fallen bricks and kill the guard before he woke up. But the guard just turned over and Michael slipped furtively past him. He was just as happy. The only thing that got the Boys more riled than meat was revenge.

He stayed out of sight even past the gate. If the Boys knew he was here, they'd be ready at closing time when the Keepers pushed everyone outside. Michael had never been in the Zoo, but he was hoping a kid could find places to hide that an adult wouldn't fit. Inside the Zoo was safe; outside the Zoo wasn't. It was as simple as that.

Now, he was crouching in the bushes outside her paddock in the visitor's viewing area, hiding from any Keepers, looking for a place to hide.

She came outside, her great rounded ears and heavy circular feet, her wise eyes and long trunk. As she came down to the water, Michael held his breath and made himself as small as an eleven-year-old boy could be. Maybe she wouldn't see him.

Except for the elephant, Michael saw no one. The barn and paddock of one of the last of the animals was the worst place to hide. He'd be found immediately. *Everyone* had probably tried this. Even so, when the elephant wandered out of sight down the hill, Michael sprang over the fence and silently ran to the barn, his backpack bouncing and throwing him off balance, expecting bullets to turn him into mush.

Inside, he quickly looked around and saw above the concrete floor a loft filled with bales of hay. He climbed up the ladder and burrowed down. The hay poked through his shirt and pants and tickled his feet through the hole in his shoe. Carefully, through the backpack, he felt for his notebook. It was safe.

"I see you," came a woman's voice from below. Michael froze. He held tight to his pack.

Something slapped the hay bale beside him and pulled it down. The ceiling light shone down on him.

It was the elephant.

"You're not going to hide up there," she said. Michael leaned over the edge. "Did you talk?"

"Get out of my stall." She whipped her trunk up and grabbed him by the leg, dragging him off the edge.

"Hold it, Jackie." A voice from the wall.

Jackie held him over the ground. "You're slipping, Ralph. I should have found his corpse outside hanging on the fence." She brought the boy to her eyes and Michael knew she was thinking of smashing him to jelly on the concrete then and there.

"Don't," he whispered.

"We all make mistakes." The wall again.

"Should I toss him out or squish him? This is *your* job. Not mine."

"Let him down. Perhaps he'll be of use."

The moment stretched out. Michael stared at her. So scared he couldn't breathe. So excited the elephant was right there, up close and in front of him, he couldn't look away.

Slowly, reluctantly, she let him down. "Whatever."

A seven-foot metal construction project—a Zoo Keeper—came into the room from outside. Three metal arms with mounted cameras, each with their own gun barrel, followed both Jackie and Michael.

"Follow me." This time the voice came from the robot.

Michael stared at Jackie for a moment. She snorted contemptuously and turned to go back outside.

Michael slowly followed the Keeper, watching Jackie leave. "Elephants talk?"

"That one does," said the Keeper.

"Wow," he breathed.

"Open your backpack," the Keeper ordered.

Michael stared into the camera/gun barrel. He guessed it was too late to run. He opened the backpack and emptied it on the floor.

The Keeper separated the contents. "A loaf of bread. Two cans of tuna. A notebook. Several pens." The lens on the camera staring at him whirred and elongated toward him. "Yours? You read and write?"

"Yes."

"Take back your things. You may call me Ralph, as she does," said the Keeper as it led him into an office.

"Why aren't I dead?"

"I try not to slaughter children if I can help it. I have some limited leeway in interpreting my authority." The voice paused for a moment. "In the absence of a director, I'm in charge of the Zoo."

Michael nodded. He stared around the room. He was still in shock at seeing a real, live elephant. The talking seemed kind of extra.

The Keeper remained outside the office and the voice resumed speaking from the ceiling.

"Please sit down."

Michael sat down. "How come you still have lights? The only places still lit up are the Zoo and the Cathedral."

"I'm still able to negotiate with Union Electric. Not many places can guarantee fire safety."

Michael had no clue what the voice was talking about. "It's warm," he said tentatively.

"With light comes heat. Now, what is your name?"

"Michael. Michael Ripley."

"How old are you?"

Michael looked around the room. "Eleven, I think."

"You're not sure?"

Michael shook his head. "I'm pretty sure I was six when my parents died. Uncle Ned took me in. I stayed with him for five years. The Long Bottom Boys killed him a few months ago."

"You have no surviving relatives?" Michael shrugged and didn't answer. "Where do you live?"

Michael's attention snapped to the Keeper and he looked around the ceiling warily. "I just hang around the park."

"You have no place to stay?"

"No."

"Would you like to stay here?"

Michael looked around the room again. It was warm. There was clearly plenty to eat. None of the gangs were ever allowed inside. But where did they get the food for the animals? How come people weren't allowed in at night? Maybe he was on the menu here, too.

"I guess," he said slowly. "Good. You're hired."

"What?"

"You will call me Ralph as I told you before. I will call you Michael except under specific circumstances when I will address you as 'Assistant Director.' Do you understand?"

Michael stared at the ceiling. "What am I supposed to do?"

> Dear Mom,
>   I found a job. It is helping to take care of an eleefant. Her name is jakee. She is not very much fun but I like her anyway. Maybe she'll like me better when she gets to Know me. She is an *eleefant*!!! I don't think I ever saw an eleefant before. Just in the books you red to me.
>   I work in the zoo. I bet you never thawt I would ever work in a zoo. Most of the animals are gon. But there is the eleefant and a rino. No snaks.
>   It is a lot better than sleepng in the dumstrs. And a dumstr does not stop a rifle much. I miss you and DAD. But I don't miss uncle NeD all that much. I miss the apartment, though.
>
>   Love, Mike

He was mucking out her stall when Jackie entered. She stopped and looked down at him.

"What are you doing?"

Michael straightened up. He tried to smile at her. "Working. Ralph hired me."

"To do that?"

Michael looked around. "I don't know. This seemed like it needed doing."

Jackie didn't speak for a moment. "Let the Keepers do that. Come with me." He followed her to the door of the stall.

"We'll start with the first office on the left. You go in there and look for papers. Books. Notes. Memos. Anything with writing on it. You know what writing is?"

"I know what writing is."

"Good."

Michael looked up at her. "How did you learn to talk?"

"That's not your business. Do your job."

It wasn't a small job. It seemed that the world of zoos ran on paper. Just pulling the folders out of the first office took three days. Michael's duties didn't end with bringing the papers out. The type was small enough he often had to hold it in front of first one of Jackie's eyes, then the other. It wasn't easy on Jackie, either. She had to stop regularly because of headaches. When he could, he tried to read them himself to see what Jackie was trying to find. She smacked him with her trunk if she caught him so he took extra time in the offices.

A cold rain descended on the Zoo. Ralph closed the doors and turned up the heat. Jackie was irritable at the best of times. Being inside only made her worse.

A month after Michael had come to the Zoo, when a late spring snow was sticking wetly to the ground outside, Jackie stared out the window resting her eyes from reading. Michael was sitting in front of the heater duct, eyes closed, luxuriating in the hot wind blowing over him. Jackie had been pushing him all morning but now she was fixing her gaze outside to ease her headache.

"So, kid, what's your story?"

Michael was instantly alert. "What do you mean?"

"Ralph told me you didn't have anybody outside. I know that much." Jackie turned her great head to look at him, and then stared outside again. "Where are your folks? Mom and Dad? Uncle and Aunt?"

"Mom and Dad died, like everybody else." Michael shrugged. There wasn't much to say about it. "Uncle Ned let me stay with him over near the Cathedral until he got caught by the Long Bottom Boys. I got away. I've been scrounging until now."

"Tough out there, is it?"

"I guess. It wasn't so bad with Ned. I took care of him. He took care of me."

Jackie looked at him. "What does *that* mean?"

"As long as I kept him happy, he gave me a place to live and fed me and protected me from anybody else." Michael considered Jackie thoughtfully. "I'm not sure what it takes to make an elephant happy."

"Just do your job," Jackie snapped at him. "That'll be enough."

She didn't speak for a moment. "Do you know how to get to the river from here?"

"Sure. But I wouldn't try it. The Boys have everything sewed up around the park. I sure found that out." He patted the duct and closed his eyes. "You have it nice here. Ralph keeps everybody out. You have food and heat. I sure wouldn't leave."

"I bet," Jackie said dryly. "Okay. Let's look at the lab books again."

Over the next week, Ralph often spoke with Jackie. Most of the time Jackie sent Michael outside. Having nothing better to do, Michael took to visiting the other animals.

There weren't many of them. Most of the exhibits were sealed and empty. The reptile house and the ape refuge were long abandoned. The bears were gone but some of the birds were still in the aviary and Michael stood for an hour in front of a single, lonely rhinoceros.

The rhino room became his favorite refuge. The rhino wasn't short with him. The rhino didn't ask him strange questions or snort with contempt when he tried to answer. The rhino didn't call him an idiot. The rhino didn't speak.

"Michael?" Ralph's voice came from the ceiling. "Yes, Ralph."

"Jackie and I are finished for the moment. You can come back."

"Yeah." Michael didn't speak for a moment. "I do everything she asks."

"I know."

"I don't talk back. I clean up after her. And elephants make a lot of shit. Why does she treat me like it?"

"You're human. She has no love of humans. She needs you. That makes it worse."

"What did humans do to her?"

"She's the last of her herd. Humans brought her ancestors from India. Human scientists raised her and the others in these concrete stalls and gave her the power of speech. Then they let the rest of her herd die."

"How come?"

"The scientists didn't have much choice. They were already dead."

"A plague like what killed my folks?"

"Somewhat. From what you told me, your parents died from one of the neo-influenzas. The scientists died of contagious botulism."

"Where did all the plagues come from? How many are there?"

"Six hundred and seventy-two was the last count I received. But that was a few years ago and the data feed was getting unreliable toward the end. They came from different places. Some were natural. Some weren't. Several were home grown by people with an agenda: religious martyrdom, political revenge, economic policy disagreements, broken romances. Some started out natural and were then modified for similar reasons."

Michael mulled over what he understood. He didn't have Ralph to himself very often. Likely this chance wouldn't last long. "If she doesn't like people so much, why are we spending so much time going through all the lab books? Why doesn't she just leave?"

"That's not for me to say."

Dear Mom,

I thought elephants were nice. Jackie doesn't like anybody. Not even Ralf. Hes nice to me but Jackie says he has to be that way. He's a machine like the Keepers. Jackie said Ralf coodnt do what I am doing. It had to be a human beang.

But I still like her even if she doesnt like me. I like to watch her when shes eating. Its neat to watch her use her trunk, like a snake thats also a hand. There are two knobs on the end of her trunk she uses like fingers. Only they are much stronger than fingers. She pinched me yesterday and today its still sore!

I moved my bed to the loft. That way its right over the heater and the hot air comes right up under me. Its like sleeping in warm water.

I miss you and Dad. If you can see us from up there in heavun, try to make Jackie not get mad all the time.

Love, Mike

"Where did you find this?" Jackie pinned him against the wall. She held up a green lab book in her trunk.

Michael tried to push her away but it was like trying to move a mountain. "I'm not sure."

"*Where?*"

Michael stopped struggling. "If you don't like what I'm doing, then do it yourself."

"That's *your* job."

"Then, *back off!*"

A moment passed. Jackie eased backwards. She handed him the lab book. "Here's the date range," she said pointing to the numbers on the page with her trunk. "See? Month, slash, day, slash, year. Here's the volume number. This is volume six. I need volume seven for the same date."

"What's it going to tell you?"

Jackie raised her trunk and for a moment it looked like she was going to strike him. Michael stared at her.

Slowly, she lowered her trunk. "I'm not sure yet."

"Say thank you."

Jackie went completely still. "What did you say?"

"I said, say thank you." Michael's fists were clenched.

Jackie seemed to relax. She made a sound like a chuckle. "Get the lab book and I'll thank you."

"Fair enough," he said shortly.

Back in the offices, he stood in the hall and let his breath out slowly. His hands were shaking.

"Good for you, Michael," Ralph said from overhead. "Yeah. Now I've got to find the lab book she wants."

"In the corner of each room is a camera," said Ralph. "If you can hold up the papers, I can help."

An hour later, he walked back into Jackie's stall and solemnly held out the lab book to her.

"Thank you," Jackie said in a neutral tone. "Hold it up to my eye."

"Okay."

Michael nodded.

Reading the lab book didn't take long. "That's enough," Jackie said.

"What do you want me to do with it?"

"I don't care. I'm going outside."

Jackie turned and left the stall. Michael was surprised. It was cold out there and snow still remained on the ground from the night before.

He opened the lab book and went over the pages. There were few words but several figures and dates. It didn't mean anything to him.

"What's going on, Ralph?" Michael shivered and looked up at the gray sky. Spring was sure a long time coming. Ralph had told him this was April.

"I'm not sure," Ralph said. "Maybe she found what she was looking for."

Michael woke in the middle of the night. Sleepily, he looked over the edge of the loft. A Keeper was helping Jackie put something over her back.

"I don't think I can do it," Ralph said.

"Quiet. You'll wake him. Maybe you can toss it over my neck and tie the ropes underneath."

Michael sat on the edge of the loft and watched them a moment.

"You're leaving," he said after a moment.

"You're supposed to be asleep." Jackie tossed her trunk irritably.

Michael didn't say anything. He climbed down to the apron and walked over to them. The Keeper was trying to pull some kind of harness over her neck and back. "Give me a knee up," Michael said. "I can help."

"No human will ever be on my back!" snarled Jackie.

"Suit yourself," Michael said. "But the only way you're going to be able to tie that harness is if you can center it on your back first and Ralph can't do it. I can if I can get on your back."

The Keeper extended his arm. "Here," said Ralph.

Michael stood on the camera and the Keeper extended it until Michael could jump to Jackie's neck. He grabbed the base of her ear and pulled himself up.

"That stings," she said. "Sorry."

In a few moments, he had the harness in place. Then he dropped to the floor and pulled it tight.

"Good job, Michael," said Ralph.

Jackie shook herself and shifted her shoulders and back. "It's tight. I'm ready."

Michael looked first at the Keeper, then at Jackie. "Are you closing the Zoo?"

"Not immediately," said Ralph. "The food trucks have been coming in sporadically. I still have contacts with the farm and the warehouse. I've spoken with power and water. They say they are well defended but if somebody digs up a cable or blows up the pipes . . ." Ralph paused a moment. "My worst scenario is a year. My best scenario is five years."

Michael felt suddenly lost. He looked up at Jackie. "Take me with you."

"What?" Jackie snorted. "No way."

"Come on," Michael pleaded. "Look, to everybody out there, all you are is steak on a stroll. I can get you out of the city. Tell me where you want to go."

"I—"

"She's going south," Ralph said smoothly. "She needs to follow the river south to the I-255 Bridge and then south to Tennessee."

"Where's I-255?"

"Oakville."

Michael thought for a moment. "That's not going to work. It'll be dicey enough to get past the Long Bottom Boys around the park. But the Rank Bastards live that way and they have an old armory. Even the Boys are scared of them."

"What do you suggest?" asked Ralph.

"Don't ask him." Jackie stamped her foot. "I can make it on my own."

Michael stood next to her. He looked at the ground. "I'm a kid. I don't have a gun. I'm not even very big. I can't hurt you."

Jackie looked away.

Michael nodded. "Well, once you're out of the park you can't go south. That's the Green Belt—sharpshooters. They don't ask questions. You just fall down dead about two miles away. You can't go north through the Farm Country. They don't have sharpshooters but they burned everything to the ground for six miles around them so you can't hide. That means west or east. Gangs in both directions just like the Long Bottom Boys or worse. I'd take the old highway right into town to the bridge and take it across. There's no boss around the bridge; there's nothing there anybody wants. The road is high off the ground so you can't be seen. If you're quiet and quick, you can get through before anybody knows. Then, I'd stay on the highway all the way down. People stick to the farms to protect them. The highways don't have anything. There are no gangs below Cahokia or many people either. Prairie Plagues got them. South of Cahokia, I don't know anything."

"How do you know all this?" Jackie snarled.

Michael stared at her. "If you don't know where things are somebody's going to have you for lunch. Uncle Ned taught me that and I'm still alive, aren't I?"

Jackie tossed her head and didn't reply. "Jackie?" asked Ralph. "The idea has merit."

Jackie didn't speak for a long time. She stared out the door of the stall. Then she turned her head back to him. "Okay," she asked reluctantly.

"When do we leave?" Michael turned to the Keeper.

Jackie slapped the back of his head. "Right now. Get aboard."

Michael rubbed his head. "That hurt," he said as he climbed up on her back. She rumbled out of the light.

"Good luck!" called Ralph after them.

"Wait!" Michael turned and called back. "What's going to happen to the rhino?" He couldn't hear the reply.

They didn't say anything as Jackie walked slowly down behind the reptile house. Her ears were spread out and listening. The gate swung open at a brush of her trunk. Michael was impressed. A secret entrance.

"Check it out."

Michael slipped to the ground and peered through the bushes. No Boys. He signaled and she followed him, pushing aside the branches. She knelt down and he climbed back up. They listened. Nothing. She started walking up the hill.

Jackie was quieter than he'd imagined. She walked with only a soft, deep padding sound.

She stopped at the edge of the road. "Where to?" she asked in a low rumble. Michael leaned next to her ear and whispered as quietly as he could. "Don't talk. I'll tell you where to go. Go to the right down the road. Then, when you go over the bridge, walk down to your left. That's where the highway is."

Jackie nodded abruptly and he could tell she wasn't pleased that he should tell her to be quiet but she didn't say anything. He figured he'd get an earful if they made it down below the river.

Michael looked around and listened. It was in the middle of the night. He couldn't smell a fire. Sometimes the Boys built a fire with the contents of one of the old houses. They drank whatever hooch they could find—raiding other gangs if necessary—and fired guns into the air and shouted at the moon until dawn. That would have been ideal. If Michael and Jackie were seen by the party, they would be seen by drunks.

No fire meant one of two things. Either there was no one around here or they were out hunting. A bunch of hungry, desperate, *sober* Long Bottom Boys was about the worst news Michael could think of. There was no hint of sweetness in the air—no mushroom festooned corpses indicating the site of a battle. That was good. The Long Bottom Boys were big on ceremonial mourning and they killed anyone they found. There weren't many left in Saint Louis but not so few that the Boys couldn't find someone to kill and then ritually stand over while the mushrooms returned the corpse to the earth.

Michael sweated every foot of the walk to the highway. But the night remained silent.

The highway here was level with the ground, but after a mile or two it rose to a grand promenade looking down on the ruins of the city. Michael whispered to Jackie that now was the time to run (*quietly!*) if she could.

Jackie didn't reply. Instead, she lengthened her stride until he had to grab on to her ears to stay on her neck. He looked down and saw the riotous dark of her legs moving on the pavement.

There was a shot behind them in the direction of the park. Jackie stopped and turned around. They saw a flash and a dull boom. Then, gradually like the sunrise, the glow of an increasing fire.

Oh, Michael thought hollowly as he stared at the tips of the flames showing over the trees. That's what was going to happen to the rhino.

"Come on," he urged. "People are going to wake up. We need to get near the river before they start looking away from the park."

The road curved around the south of downtown and then north to reach the river bridges. They could not see the river below them as they crossed but they heard the hiss and rush of the water, the low grunt of the bridge as it eased itself against the flow, the cracks and booms as floating debris struck the pilings.

Then they were over it and traveling south, the flat farmland on their left, the river bluffs on their right, the road determinedly south toward Cahokia.

> Dear Mom,
> We reached Cahokia a little before daylite. We could tell we got there by the sign on the highway. I wasnt tired at all. But Jackee was. It must have been hard work walking all that way. Heres something intristing. Eleefants cant run. Jackee told me. They can walk relly fast but they are to big to run.
> Jackee still doesnt like me much. She doesnt talk to me unless its to get help figuring out where we are. Mostly she can figur it out. But she needs my hands. I figur one of these days shell leave while I am asleep. So I sav things when I can.
> She says we're going to Tenesee. Howald, Tenesee. There used to be eleefants there. She says she thinks they might be still there. If she doesn't find them there, she's going to try to get to Florida. It's warm all the time down there. There's lots of food to eat and it's never winter. That sounds pretty good to me.

I would like to stay with her. She is big and pretty and reel strong.
She doesnt talk to me very nice. I dont think she would protek me like
Ned did.

I will writ agin tomoro.

love, mike

Michael was surprised that they saw no people in Cahokia. The farmlands he
had been thinking of were bounded by weeds but, other than that, looked as if
cultivated by invisible hands. They saw no one. The only sounds were the spring
birds, the river and the wind. Every few steps they could see a little mound of
soil. The mushrooms had all dried up and blown away but these mounds still
marked where someone had died.

That first day, when they made camp in a hidden clearing, Michael discovered
that Ralph had planned for him to accompany Jackie all along. There was a tent,
sleeping bag and all manner of tools: a tiny shovel, a knife, a small bow and arrow,
the smallest and most precious fishing set Michael had ever seen. In a flap cunningly
designed to be hidden, he found a pistol that fit his hand perfectly. Next to it, separated into stock, barrel, and laser sight, was a high-powered rifle. A second flap had
ammunition for both, exploding and impact bullets in clearly marked containers.
Michael stared at them. He suddenly realized he could take down an elephant with
this weapon. Ralph must have known that. The implied trust shook him.

"What did you find?"

Michael realized she hadn't seen the guns. The pistol was no threat. He
pulled it out and showed it to her.

"Do you know how to use it?"

"Yes." He replaced the pistol. Next to the weapons were Jackie's vitamin supplements along with finely labeled medicines and administration devices that
only a human being could use.

Jackie snorted when she saw it all laid out.

Michael looked at everything, sorted and arrayed in front of him, for a long
time. He wondered how long they'd be able to keep such treasures as this. He
realized he might need the rifle.

Occasionally between long stretches of young woods and tall fresh meadows,
they saw a few manicured fields that were laid out so ruler straight that the two
of them stopped and stared. These, Jackie told him, must be tilled by machines.
No human or animal would ever pay such obsessive attention to details. But no
machines could be seen, and even these meticulous rows of corn or soybeans
were frayed at the edges into weeds and brambles.

Even so, as tempting as a field of new corn was to Jackie, she was unwilling to
chance it. Machines were chancy things, she said, with triggers and idiosyncra-
sies. Even negotiating with Ralph had been difficult when it went against his
programming. Better to wait until they found an overgrown field down the road.

Jackie had no trouble finding food. It had been a wet spring and now that the
sun had come out, the older and uncultivated fields sprouted volunteer squash and
greens.

They fell into a routine. In the evening, they agreed on a likely spot and

Michael took the harness off of her and set up camp. Michael was afraid she might step on him while she slept, so Jackie slept off a little ways from Michael's tent.

At first light, Jackie went off to find her day's sustenance. Michael made himself breakfast out of the stores Ralph had left him. He tried his hand at fishing in the tributary rivers of the Mississippi and gradually learned enough to catch enough for a good meal. He tried to eat as much as he could in the morning. It was likely they wouldn't stop until nightfall.

After he had eaten and before Jackie returned, he waited, wondering if she would come back.

She always did. She eased herself down the bank and drank, knee deep in the river. Jackie was always impatient to get started and stamped her feet as Michael repacked the harness. Then she made a knee for him and he climbed aboard. Always they went south. Always as quickly as Jackie could. Hohenwald first, since that was where the elephant sanctuary had been. But continuing south after that, if she didn't find them. South, she told him, was warm in the winter. South had food all year round.

Michael was amenable. He felt pretty safe. He was well fed. He'd learned the trick of riding Jackie and enjoyed watching the river on the right slip smoothly ahead of them and the land on the left buckle and roll up into bluffs and hills.

Spring turned warm and gentle. Michael felt happier than he could remember, up until they reached the spot where the Ohio poured into the Mississippi and the bridge was gone.

They stood on the ramp of Interstate 57 looking down at the wreckage. The near side of where the bridge had been was completely dry. Stained pilings that had clearly been underwater at one point rested comfortably in a grassy field. On the far side, the remains of the bridge had broken off a high bluff as if the whole southern bank of the river had slid downhill. The river narrowed here, to speed up and pour into the slower moving Mississippi. Huge waves burst into the air as the rivers fought one another. They were over a mile away from the battle, but even from here they could hear the roar.

"The earthquake, maybe?" muttered Jackie.

"Earthquake?"

"About eight years ago the New Madrid fault caused a big quake down here. Ralph told me about it. The scientists had expected it to hit St. Louis as well but the effects were to the east so we were spared." Jackie shook her great head and swayed from one side to another. "How are we going to get across now?"

Michael looked at the old atlas. "There's a dam upstream near Grand Chain Landing."

"Look at the bridge!" Jackie trumpeted and pointed with her trunk. "It's just a sample. Look at the river. The dam is probably gone, too."

Michael looked upstream. "We'll find something. We just can't go south for a little while."

Jackie just snorted. After a moment, she turned slowly toward the east.

Dear Mom,
So far we still haven't been able to cross the OHIO river. I think it

was even bigger than the Missspi. Even at night, we can hear it rushing by. Every now and then, something floats by. Today I saw six trees, a traler and an old house float by. Jackie says it's becawse of the flud upstreem.

I can tell sumthing is bothering jackie. She hasnt been as mean lately. Its not just that we arnt moving sowth. It is sumthing more.

Love, Mike

As Jackie predicted, the dam was gone. Perhaps the Ohio, powered by spring rains, had ripped apart the turbines and concrete. The ground trembled as the water poured over the remaining rubble.

"Now what?" Jackie said in a soft rumble.

"Could you swim across?" Michael asked doubtfully. "Can't elephants swim?"

"Look at the water," Jackie said shrilly. "No one can swim through that."

"Then *not* here. How about where the water doesn't run so fast?"

Jackie didn't answer.

Michael stared at the map closely.

"There used to be a ferry in Metropolis. Maybe we could get a boat."

"A *ferry?*" Jackie turned her head and looked at him out of the corner of her eye. "I weigh in at six tons."

Michael nodded. "A big ferry, then. Couldn't hurt to look. It's just a few miles up the road."

"A ferry," Jackie muttered. "A *ferry.*"

The center of Metropolis clustered around a bend in Highway 45. Jackie and Michael followed the signs down to the docks. The shadow of the broken Interstate 24 Bridge fell across the road and in the distance they could see the disconnected ends of the lesser Highway 45 bridge.

A great half sunken coal barge rested against the dock on the right side. The surface of the water was punctured by the rusting remains of antennas poking up from drowned powerboats on the left. Between them nestled the ferry *Encantante* incongruously upright and unmangled. A man sat on the deck, whittling. He looked up as they came down the hill.

"Don't believe I've ever seen an elephant down this way before," he said as he stood up. "What can I do for you?" He was a tall, thin man. Michael couldn't tell exactly how old he was. His hair was turning gray but his face seemed smooth and unwrinkled. Thirty, thought Michael. Doesn't people's hair turn gray when they are thirty? The man was dressed in a red and black plaid jacket against the cool river air.

Michael spoke up before Jackie could respond. He hoped she would remain silent. He was pretty sure talking elephants would be suspicious.

"We need to get across."

"Do you, now?" He tapped out his pipe against the side of the ferry and refilled it carefully. "My name's Gerry. Gerry Myers. You are?"

"Michael Ripley. This is Jackie."

Gerry nodded. "All right then." He looked at the elephant. "I've never put an elephant on my boat. But it can't weigh much more than four or five of those little cars so it would probably be okay. He won't jump or move about?"

"Jackie's a girl." Michael looked at the water ripping along.

Gerry followed his gaze. "Yeah. 'She,' then. She won't move around? Be a damned shame if she turned over the boat and killed us all."

"She won't."

"Good. Well, then. Since you are the only human being I've seen in some months," Gerry said dryly, "and since I've buried everybody else, I'm inclined to think about your proposal." Gerry looked at him closely. "You're not sick, are you?"

Michael shrugged. "I feel pretty good."

"Doesn't mean much, does it?" Michael shook his head.

Gerry stared out over the river and sighed. "Yeah. The last good citizen of the Metropolis that had lunch with me said he hadn't felt this good in months. I went looking for him when he didn't show up for dinner. He was dead sitting in his kitchen with a smile on his face. Only thing I can say is apparently he died so suddenly he forgot to feel bad about it."

Gerry lit his pipe and puffed at it for a moment. "Speaking of lunch, I'm a bit hungry. Care to eat with me?"

Michael hesitated.

Gerry pointed at the bluff up the hill from them. "On the other side of that is an old soybean field. Lots of good leafy growth for Jackie. Maybe you could turn her loose and eat with me."

"I don't know." Gerry didn't look like somebody that would kill him and roast Jackie. Uncle Ned had known who to trust—until the day he didn't, Michael corrected himself. How could you tell? Michael had a sneaking suspicion he would have to pay for the ride one way or another.

"Well, the field's there. Suit yourself. I'll be eating lunch in half an hour or so. In that warehouse looking building over there. Come by if you want to."

Michael nodded. Jackie turned and started up the hill.

The field was as advertised and there were no visible people around to take advantage of them.

"I'll eat here. You watch," said Jackie.

"I'd just as soon go on and have lunch with the old man," Michael said as he unharnessed her. "We still have to cross the river. Seems like we ought to know something about the other side."

"I don't trust him."

"You don't trust anybody." Michael rummaged through the packs until he found the pistol. "I got this."

"You be careful, then," Jackie said. "I'll be coming down there if you try to run off."

"Yeah. I like you, too." Michael hefted the pistol. It was heavier than it looked. He made sure it was loaded and checked the action.

Jackie watched him. "Where did you learn to handle a gun?"

"Uncle Ned taught me," Michael said shortly. "I kept guard when he foraged."

"Then . . ." Jackie stopped for a moment. "If you had the gun, why didn't you leave him?"

"It took both of us to stay alive," Michael released the chamber and made sure the safety was on. He put the gun in his pocket. "He was a lot bigger than I was. He protected me. I helped him. Staying with him made a lot of sense."

"But he—" Jackie shook her head.

"When the Boys found us he sent me off and took them on by himself."

Jackie was silent a moment. "So you wanted to leave with me because I'm a lot bigger than you are. I can protect you. Staying with me makes a lot of sense."

Michael stared at her. "Are you kidding? I'm traveling with six tons of fresh meat. What part of that makes sense to you?"

"Then why did you come with me?"

Michael stood up and didn't answer. He trotted down the hill toward the landing. Jackie stared after him.

Gerry was cooking in an apartment above the warehouse. The room had a nautical feel to it. Every piece of furniture had been carefully placed. The curtains over the window were a red and white check. The table was an austere gray, with metal legs and a top made of some kind of plastic. The countertops looked similar.

Two plates had been set out. The fork on the left, knife and spoon on the right, napkin folded just so on the plate. Plastic water glasses were set at precisely the same angle for each place setting.

Michael stood in the doorway, not sure what to do. Coming into the room felt like breaking something.

"Come on in," said Gerry. He was stirring a pot. The contents bubbled and smelled deliciously meaty. "Channel catfish bouillabaisse." He ladled out two full bowls and handed one to Michael. "Been simmering since this morning. Have a seat."

They sat across the table and in a few moments, Michael forgot Gerry was even there. He only remembered where he was when the bowl was half empty. Michael looked up.

Gerry was watching him with a smile on his face. "Good to see someone enjoy my cooking. Want some bread? Baked it yesterday."

Michael broke off a piece. Next to the bread was a small plate with butter. For a long minute, Michael stared, unable to recognize it. Then he remembered and smeared the bread across it.

"Whoa there. Use the knife."

Michael shrugged, pulled out his small hunting knife and smeared the butter across the bread.

Gerry raised his eyebrows and chuckled. "Fair enough. But next time use the little knife next to the butter."

Michael sopped up the rest of the soup with the bread and leaned back in his chair, stuffed and happy.

Gerry picked up the bowls and put them in the sink. "Come on down to the porch." Michael followed him outside and down the stairs to a part of the dock that jutted over the water. Under an awning, he sat down in a lawn chair while Gerry pulled a box out of the river and opened it. He pulled out two bottles. He gave Michael the root beer and kept a regular beer for himself.

Michael sat back in the chair and savored the sharp, creamy flavor.

Gerry said nothing and the two of them watched the river roll by.

"So," Gerry said at last. "What's waiting for you on the other side of the river?"

"Hohenwald, Tennessee," Michael said and sipped his root beer. He could get used to this. "Then, maybe Florida."

"What's in Hohenwald?"

"An elephant sanctuary. Elephants don't like to be alone."

Gerry nodded. "I thought Florida was underwater."

"A lot of it is. But Jackie says the upper part of Florida is still there." Michael stopped.

"I see," said Gerry. He was silent a moment. "You're an awful nice boy to be crazy."

Michael didn't say anything. If Gerry wanted to think he was crazy that was all right with him.

"You don't think you'll find anybody down there, do you?" asked Gerry.

Michael shrugged. "How would I know?"

Gerry nodded. "Everything's pretty much fallen apart. I think there might be five people left alive here in Metropolis. You'd think we'd hang together. But it didn't seem to work out that way. There might be a few hundred out in the countryside. Seems like I spent the last five years burying everyone I've ever known. I can't believe it's much better down south."

Michael finished his root beer and put it on the deck. "That's where Jackie has to go. She has to have something she can eat in the winter."

Michael looked up at the remains of the bridge. He had only really known Saint Louis. It looked like things were messed up everywhere. For the first time he had an inkling what that meant.

"What was it like before?" Michael muttered.

Michael had been talking to himself, but even so, Gerry reacted. His face seemed to take on a rubbery texture. "Everything just came apart. First, the weather went to shit. Then came plagues, one after another. And not just people. Birds. Cattle. Sheep. Wheat. Beans. There was about six years where you couldn't get a tomato unless you grew it yourself. Even then, it wasn't much better than fifty-fifty. Oaks. Sequoias. Shrimp. Government would figure out how to make tomatoes grow again and every maple in the county would fall over and rot. They'd get a handle on that and the next thing you know somebody had engineered a virus that lived in milk. Why would anyone ever do that?" He shook his head. "Figured that one out after a couple of million kids. Right after that, the corn began to wither. We got a strain of corn that would grow and a tidal wave comes roaring over the East Coast. Boston, Providence, and New York go under water."

He stopped and sat up. He pulled out his bandanna and wiped his eyes. "If I believed in God, I'd go out and kill a calf on a rock or something. We sure as hell pissed him off." Gerry sighed. "Ah, musn't grumble." He sipped his beer, composed again.

Michael stared at him. Maybe Gerry did this all the time. "So," began Michael after a long and awkward silence. "We should cross here?"

"That's true. I'm pretty much the only game in town. But that's not my point." He pointed over the river at the opposite shore. "That's Kentucky. Or what's left of it. Things have been falling apart for a long, long time. I was sitting on my boat twenty years ago when the big rush came down the river that took out the two bridges. I could see it coming, a fifteen-foot wall of trash and debris rolling down on top of us. I had just enough time to pull *Encantante* into the creek downstream behind the oak bluffs when it washed over Metropolis and scoured everything between us and Cairo. Back then we still had people living here, so we were able to clean up and rebuild over a couple of years." Gerry chuckled. "My little ferry business picked up because nobody was going to rebuild the bridges—we were still in a *crisis* at that point. It hadn't become a *disaster* yet. Not enough people had died."

"Where did the water come from?"

Gerry shook his head. "Never really figured that out. Was it just the Smithland Dam that let go? Or did one big flood start way up the river and then take out all the dams one by one on the way down? I do know that flood is what took out the two dams downstream from here and when I did go up to look at Smithland, there wasn't much left of it. I came back. Then, about six years later, I loaded up a boat I had with all the fuel I could find and went up nearly five hundred miles to see what the hell was going on. It's not like you could trust anything you heard on the radio. I only knew what had happened here. I didn't turn around until I reached Cincinnati. There wasn't a bridge or a dam left standing the whole way. This was before the earthquake. Maybe somebody blew them up. It was a big mystery until other things sort of overshadowed it. But you let me wander away from my point again."

"Hey, it wasn't my fault."

"My point is that now the only thing that keeps what's on the Kentucky shore from coming over onto this shore is that river."

Michael shook his head. "So? What's over there that's not over here?"

Gerry shrugged. "Things. Big lizards, sometimes. Maybe a crocodile or two. Big animals—I haven't seen any elephants. But I might have seen a tiger."

"Yeah, right." Michael snorted. "Pull the other one. A mountain lion, maybe."

Gerry shrugged again. "When we put dams and bridges across the water, cars and buses weren't the only things that crossed. Now the dams and bridges are gone and what lives on the other side stays on the other side. It's not going to be as easy to get over here as it was before."

"We crossed the bridge in Saint Louis. It was just fine."

Gerry pulled his pipe out of his pocket along with his pocket knife and began cleaning the bowl. "Maybe things can't cross up that far north. Maybe the Mississippi keeps things from crossing west just like the Ohio keeps things from crossing north. Maybe I'm just having old man hallucinations. But I know what I saw. There are things that live on *that* side of the river I don't see on *this* side. You cross the river and they're sure as hell going to see *you*."

Michael didn't look at him. "That's where she has to go. She just can't get food up here in the winter."

"What did you do in Saint Louis?"

"The Zoo kept us alive. But it's gone now."

Gerry sighed. "She's a pretty animal. I guess there's no animal on earth so noble and beautiful, and just plain *big*, as an elephant. But it doesn't belong here. Jackie should be in India."

"I can't take her to India."

"I know that." Gerry hesitated. "Maybe it's time to cut her loose." Michael stared at the decking. He didn't know what to say.

Gerry pointed across the river. "Tell you what. You and I take her across the river and let her off the boat. Maybe she'll work her way south. You come back here with me."

Michael looked at him, trying to see if there was some hint of Uncle Ned in his face. He couldn't tell. Michael was in no particular hurry to repeat that arrangement. "I don't know."

Gerry finished tamping the tobacco in the bowl and lit his pipe. "You know that soybean field I sent you to up on the hill? It's a pretty field, isn't it? The soybeans are one of those perennial varieties popular about fifteen years ago. When I was a kid that was a toxic waste site with a lot of mercury and cadmium and toxic solvents. Don't look at me that way. That was years ago. It's safe enough for her now. Anyway, you know how they reclaimed it?"

"No."

"It was pretty neat, actually. They took some engineered corn. Corn pushes its roots deep into the soil—as much as ten feet in some varieties. This corn pulled up the metals and concentrated them into the kernels of the ear. It discolored the kernels. Some were silver, some were bright blue."

"I don't understand."

"Anyway," continued Gerry. "Because of the metal concentration, the kernels were expected to be sterile. Most of them were. But coons attacked the field and ate some and got sick. So that was one problem they had. Crows pecked at the ears and got sick. That was another. Bits of the ears were dragged by various animals a ways away. Turned out some were fertile after all. They took root and started growing over data lines. The plant couldn't tell the difference between a heavy metal being cleaned up in a waste site or a similar heavy metal in a computer underground."

Michael stamped his feet. "What are you talking about?"

Gerry stared hard at him. "I don't know what's across the river. I'm saying it could be anything."

"What? Killer corn?"

Gerry snorted. "Of course not. But if people can rebuild corn and it escapes what else could they have done? Crocodiles to control Asian lung fish? Killer bees to control oak borers? I *know* what lives around here. I live with it every day. I *know* things are different across the river." Gerry calmed himself. "You take your elephant across the river if you want to. But you'll come back and stay here with me if you're smart."

Jackie was waiting for him in the afternoon shade. A vast section of the soybean field had been leveled and she looked well-fed for the first time in several days.

Michael looked around. "Tasty?"

Jackie looked at the field. "Pretty good." Her belly even seemed a little swollen.

"How much longer until we get to Hohenwald?"

Jackie shook her head. "Couple of weeks, I hope."

"And Florida?"

"*If* we go to Florida, I expect we'll get there midsummer." Michael thought for a moment. "Do you know the date?"

"It's the first of May."

"May day," said Michael slowly. "That's six weeks." Jackie looked at him with one eye. "So?"

"Could you get there faster if you weren't carrying me?"

"It wouldn't make any difference. I could only go faster if I didn't take the time to keep fed. But I can't afford to starve myself. Not now."

"How come?"

"Never mind."

"You're hiding something."

"So what? It doesn't concern you."

"Who the hell do you think you are?" shouted Michael, surprising them both. Jackie stepped back. For a moment she stood, arrested, one leg raised ready in defense, three solidly on the ground.

"Are you going to squash me for shouting at you?" Michael shook his head in disgust. "I was better off with Ned."

Slowly, Jackie eased her leg down. She turned and silently walked over to the pond in the middle of the soybean field. Michael watched as she pulled up water and splashed it over herself.

> Dear Mom,
>   I don't think Jackee will ever like me. I guess I was fooling myself. She's an eleefant. She hates me because I'm a person and people did things to her and other eleefants.
>   Gerry wants me to stay here with him. He has a good thing here. Metropolis has a power sorse so he can stay warm for a long time. With everybody gone, the left over preserved food will be good for years. There are some wild crops here, too. Ned never had it so good.
>   Jackee doesn't need me. Most of the stuff Ralph packed was for me. I could rig a bag for her to carry around her neck for the stuff she has to have. That ought to be enough. And it's not like I'm holding stuff for her to read anymore. Whatever she found back at the Zoo must have been all she wanted. She hasn't been interested in anything but going south since.
>   When I told this to Jackee she didn't say anything for a while. Then, all she said was, Suit yourself.
>   So, I guess I'll be staying in Metropolis.
>
>   love, Mike

Gerry waited at the ferry while Michael walked with Jackie back up to the soybean field. Michael decided he didn't want Gerry to know about her. It felt safer to keep everything quiet. Jackie followed his lead silently.

Michael kept glancing at her as she ate, trying to see if she had any regrets he was staying here. Her elephantine face was inexpressive but her movements were short and abrupt. Could she be angry at him for staying? Or just impatient to be on her way?

When she was done, he slung the makeshift bag around her neck so she could reach it and led her back down to the dock. She stepped gingerly onto the metal floor of the ferry. There was plenty of room and even in the strong current, it only swayed slightly.

Gerry cast off without comment and angled the ferry upstream into the river. Michael felt the powerful motor bite into the current and the entire craft hummed. But he could not hear the motor itself, only the churning of the propeller.

Gerry caught his expression. "Quiet, isn't she? Electric motor."

He pulled up the hatch. Michael saw a roundish cube with the shaft coming out connected with thick cables to a cylindrical device.

"That's the motor," Gerry said pointing to the cube. "That's power storage." He pointed to the cylinder.

"A battery?"

"They called it a fuel coil when I bought the boat. Not sure how it works but it holds about forty hours of power. These days I charge it up from a little turbine I dropped off the dock. Don't need to use the boat that much. For longer trips I can charge it from a big fuel cell I can carry with me." He dropped the hatch with a clang and returned to the wheel.

The *Encantante* passed the main eddy line and entered the center of the river. Gerry stepped up the motor and angled the *Encantante* more steeply. The ripples and twists in the current caused the boat to shift and slide a little. Not enough to make standing difficult but enough so Michael noticed. It made him grin. Jackie looked around nervously.

Then, they were across the main river and nearing the far side. Gerry eased off the throttle and dropped the *Encantante* below a bluff jutting out into the water. Again they crossed a strong eddy that made the ferry jump a moment. The water grew calm and Gerry brought *Encantante* to the dock.

Michael led Jackie off the ferry and stood with her for a moment in the middle of the road. He looked east, judging the vegetation. There was plenty. The forest was thick on the other side of the road and he could see the break in the trees signifying a field. Jackie wouldn't starve.

Turning away from Gerry so he couldn't see, Michael pulled the atlas out of his jacket.

"Here. You walk down here to Interstate 24 and take it south. Then take Highway 45 to Benton. Once you get to Benton, hunt around until you find Highway 641. Take that to Interstate 40, east. Then—"

"You've been over this. A lot."

"Well, I wrote it down. There's a leather holder I made for you. It's tied to the belt and the directions are in it along with the map book. I drew it all out on the map so you wouldn't get lost."

"Thanks," said Jackie shortly.

Michael nodded and stuffed the atlas into the bag. "You take care of yourself." Jackie watched him as he walked back to the ferry. Michael felt his eyes sting. He looked back.

Jackie was only a few feet away. Something shook the brush on the far side of the road. Before he fully registered what it was, he was running at it, yelling at Jackie to back away. Gerry tried to grab him but Michael ducked under his hands.

It raised its thick body high on its legs and ran toward Jackie, its mouth open and narrow as a snake's. *Lizard? Crocodile?* He ran past and stood, screaming, between them.

The thing stopped, closed its mouth and stepped back only so long for a long tongue to slip out and back. Then it lunged forward and grabbed for Michael. Michael danced back but it grabbed his leg and shook him off his feet, then raised its claws over him.

Michael heard trumpeting. Jackie's leg came down on its midsection. The creature ruptured and blood and meat spewed across the road. Its jaw opened reflexively and Michael scrambled back. Jackie stamped on it until it was nothing but a flat, smeared ruin. Then she looked at Michael.

Michael smiled at her. She leaned over him and wrapped her trunk around his leg. He looked down and saw the blood and felt nauseous.

"This will hurt," she said. She wrapped her trunk around his leg and squeezed. For a moment, Michael couldn't see or breathe.

"*Gerry!*" Jackie shouted. "*Get over here and pick him up!*"

Gerry ran over to them and as he lifted Michael by the shoulders, Jackie lifted his leg. The pounding in his leg seemed to drown out everything.

Back in the ferry, Michael looked around. He must have blacked out a moment for they were now deep in the middle of the river. He felt sleepy.

"Don't you go away on me," said Jackie, kneeling next to him. "You stay here. Michael—"

Michael wanted to say he was sorry but he was as light as smoke and he drifted away.

PART 2

It was all light and dark for a long time. When things were lighter he slept in a brown haze as if he were swimming in honey. He was warm and safe. Occasionally, he was convulsed with pain. He couldn't tell where the pain was coming from exactly. Sometimes it seemed to come from his neck. Other times, his leg. Sometimes he was riven by pain that seemed to come from nowhere.

This went on, it seemed, forever. Then, it grew lighter and he opened his eyes.

He was in a room, in a bed, that reminded him of when his parents still lived. The room had a window. As then the bed had been pushed against the wall so he could look out the window. It had sheets and a blanket. He fingered them gently, wondering if he was dreaming. Outside, the sun shone. His leg hurt.

He heard a grunt and Jackie's head appeared in the window. She pushed it open. "How are you feeling?"

"Sleepy," Michael said. "My leg hurts."

"Go back to sleep if you want. I'll be here."

Michael nodded and smiled. Her trunk hovered in the air near him. He reached up and pulled it close, a warm and bristly comfort. He could feel the muscles tense a moment, then relax. The weight of it next to him, the grass smell of her breath, the beat of her pulse. Michael closed his eyes. He felt like he was floating in the air.

Gerry was sitting at the foot of the bed reading a book. The sunlight was gone and it looked threatening outside.

"An afternoon June storm," Gerry said, looking up from his book. "June?"

Michael shook his head. "It was May when we got to Metropolis." Gerry nodded but didn't say anything.

"Well?"

"Wait until Jackie gets back. She wanted to be here when you woke up. I only got her to go up the hill and eat by promising to call her if you woke up."

Gerry returned to his book. "Aren't you going to call her?"

Gerry shook his head. "It's hard enough to get her to leave you. She needs to eat her fill. Know what you're going to do?"

"What?"

"Pretend to be asleep so I don't get in trouble."

Michael closed his eyes obediently. Then he didn't need to pretend.

It was the thunder that woke him. He started and his leg began to throb. He could see the bulking shadow of Jackie with her head in the window. Gerry had rigged some kind of awning over the window so at least her head wouldn't get too wet. Michael didn't like it. That was his job.

Gerry entered the room with a hissing lantern. He set it on the side table and moved the curtains away.

"There, you see? Let there be light."

Michael tried to reach his leg but he was too weak. "Can you rub my leg? It really hurts."

Gerry looked down.

"Michael," Jackie rumbled gently. "You need to be brave." Michael didn't like the sound of it. "Am I going to die?"

"No," said Jackie somberly. "The dragon bit your leg. We couldn't save it."

"What do you mean?"

"It got infected," said Gerry. "It got so bad we thought it was going to take you with it. So, it had to go."

"Go?" Michael shook his head. "What are you talking about?"

"Gerry had to cut off your leg," said Jackie.

"What?" Michael said weakly.

Gerry pulled back the blanket. Michael's thigh and knee looked bruised and purple. Below that was a fat bandage that ended long before his ankle.

"You cut off my leg." Michael couldn't believe the stump was his. "This is a joke. I can still feel my foot."

Gerry replaced the blanket. "After a while, your mind will accept there's no foot there. Then you won't feel it anymore." The shape of the blanket now clearly showed what was missing. "At least, that's what I've heard."

Michael stared at the blanket for a long time. Outside, the thunder receded and while the lightning played in the clouds, there was little sound but for the rain and the wind.

"You said dragon," Michael said, looking up from his leg. He couldn't stand to stare at it anymore.

"Komodo dragon lizard," Gerry said. "Jackie figured out what it was as soon as she saw it."

Jackie looked up at the sky. She looked inside the window. "I expect there were several zoos and other facilities in Florida that collapsed just like the zoo in

Saint Louis. Maybe that rhino is still alive. For the summer, at least. According to Gerry, these lizards have survived for a while. I'm not sure how a tropical species can make it through a temperate winter. Perhaps they move south when the temperature drops. Or perhaps they find a place they can sleep through the cold. I suppose it's possible there were enough of them that some were resistant to the cold. The ones less resistant died out and the remaining population bred. Evolution in action. Or maybe they were modified."

Michael stared at her. Jackie was talking to him. Really talking to him. She had never done that before.

Gerry interrupted gently. "How are you feeling, Michael?"

Michael started. He'd forgotten Gerry was there. "My foot hurts." He looked down at the blanket, oddly misshapen without his foot under it. Tears welled up. "What am I going to do?"

"Rest, for the moment," said Jackie. "Then figure it out."

Michael healed with all the combustive vitality of any well-fed young boy. By early July, the stitches were out and the skin over the stump was new and tender. He either hobbled about with a crutch that Gerry had made him or Jackie carried him.

But as the days wore on he started finding Jackie high on the broken end of the Interstate 24 Bridge carefully watching the other side.

"What's over there?" Michael asked as he sat down and dangled his leg over the hundred foot drop.

"You shouldn't sit so close to the edge," Jackie said quietly.

"If this bridge will hold you, it's going to hold me."

Jackie reached over and picked him up with her trunk. "Edges crumble." She put him down and he leaned against the wall. "Okay. What's over there?"

"I've been watching the dragons." She pointed with her trunk. "They come to the road once around sunrise and once around sunset. In the morning, when they're warm enough, they leave the road and move to the forest at the edge of the clearing. At night, they slink away under the trees to sleep somewhere. A cave, maybe, or some other kind of den. If they're hungry, they stay near the clearing until they've made a kill. Animals avoid the road so it's not profitable to hunt there. That's why they hug the edges of the clearings. There." She pointed again across the river. "And there. See the carcass? It was a deer they took yesterday morning."

Michael saw one leg sticking up from the ground in the clearing. Two long motionless shadows were lying near it.

"So the road is safe in the middle of the day."

"Safer, anyway. This section of road has only two lanes. The wider roads might be better or worse. I can't tell from here. Gerry was right about one thing. They're not crossing the river."

Michael saw something moving. A large spotted cat. He pointed it out to Jackie. "A leopard, maybe?" she said. "Look how it's avoiding where the dragons are."

"Look way in the distance in that clearing. Deer?"

"I don't know. They don't look like deer. Gazelles? Antelopes? Something the leopards and Komodos can eat, I suppose."

"Where did they come from?"

"Zoos in Florida? Laboratories in Atlanta? I don't know." She paused a long time. "Over there things are going to be different."

Michael leaned back against the ridge of her back. He rubbed the stump of his leg. It was still tender and it itched constantly. Sometimes, if he wasn't thinking about it, he tried to scratch his toes.

"The summer is getting on," Michael said. "We should get started."

"Yeah, right," Jackie snorted. "You want to lose both legs? You're staying here with Gerry. I'll go on down alone."

"You need me!"

"I'll cope. You were right. You belong here."

"That was before."

"Before what?"

Michael hesitated. "When I didn't think you liked me."

Jackie turned her head and looked at him. "What makes you think I like you now?"

"You stayed with me. Gerry said."

"I felt guilty for getting you into this."

Michael felt as if he were struck. Ned had never treated him this way. "Why? Why hate me? Why be so mean to me?" Michael felt like she was hiding something. How do you get someone to tell you what they don't want to? "Why did you leave the Zoo?" he asked suddenly.

"I didn't like humans. And I had to leave."

Michael picked up on the "didn't" immediately but kept it to himself. "Ralph said he had a couple of years yet. It didn't have to be right then."

"I had to leave."

"Why? Why then? Why—when we could be back there enjoying good food and not staring over the river at dragons."

Jackie shook her head.

Sudden rage shook Michael. "Damn it! I *saved* you. You owe me."

Jackie sighed. "This is hard for me. Did you know there were four of us? Tantor, Jill, Old Bill, and me. We all learned to speak quickly enough but we hid it from the Keepers as long as we could. We had no love of them. Why should we? Even if we hadn't had the wit to speak, we would have known this was not the place we should be.

"You saw the zoo. There were cameras everywhere. Where there are cameras, there can be no secrets. So we were found out. They taught us to read. They taught us anything they could get their monkey hands on. We talked it over among ourselves. Why not learn what they had to offer? What could it hurt? Learn the enemy, said Old Bill. But keep them distant."

Jackie fell silent for a moment. "Every animal is wired its own way. Herd animals and pack animals are similar in one respect. They define themselves by membership in the group. Once you include a new member in the group, you're bound to them. Wolves, cattle, and elephants are the same. We didn't want that. We didn't want to include humans in our tight little community. So we held back. We acted confused and slow. We did everything we could to make ourselves look stupid. Smart enough to work with, but our true nature held secret.

"Then the humans started dying. One after another. In groups. By themselves. Until we were by ourselves. Only Ralph was left to care for us.

"We were ecstatic. All we had to do was figure out how to escape Ralph and survive. We knew we had to go south. Georgia. Florida. Alabama. Where there was no snow in the winter and we could eat.

"Then Jill died. A bit of wire or glass left in the hay, maybe. No veterinarians left, right? We never really knew, but she died bloated and screaming. That left Old Bill and Tantor. I don't know how it happened, but I woke up a few weeks later and they were fighting. It's a terrible thing to see two five-ton animals slamming into one another. They had come into *musth* at the same time. I don't know why. I think I came into heat watching them. Biology triumphant."

Jackie snorted. "If they had been dumb beasts, one of them would have figured out they were losing and broken it off. Instead, Old Bill killed Tantor. He came over and mounted me."

"But the battle hurt him, too. Inside, somehow. A concussion? Internal hemorrhaging? I'll never know. He just wasted away. Then he was dead and I was alone and pregnant. You appeared on the scene a week after that."

Michael stared at her. "I don't understand."

"I'm telling you why I had to leave. I didn't have a couple of years. The gestation period of an elephant is twenty-two months. No more. No less. I'm five months pregnant. I have to find a place that's safe, that's warm, where I can raise my child."

"Oh," Michael said. "But why the hurry? That's a couple of years."

"Not really. I don't know what's at Hohenwald. What if there are no elephants left? Then it's only me. A few months to find a place and get through the first winter—how will I know I've found a good spot until I've been through the winter? Then a few months to move to a new spot if I have to. Then a solid year of eating. That's not much time. Not much time at all."

Michael looked across the river. "Guess the dragons are a problem for a little guy."

"You think?" she chuckled.

"I didn't mean me," Michael said reasonably. "You're going to need me." He looked up at her and she looked away. "And you know it, too. Is it so terrible to need a human when you're so alone?" Michael looked over the edge of the bridge and spat. He could see it nearly all the way down. "Look at it this way. We used you when everybody was alive. Now's your chance to use us—or at least me."

"I don't want to use anybody."

"Then take me along because you like me. Take me along because you can use my monkey hands. Take me along because I don't weigh much and won't be a burden to carry. Only *take me along!*"

Jackie didn't say anything for a moment. "You're crippled."

"Compared to you, everyone is crippled."

"Michael, you're missing one leg."

"So?"

Jackie snorted. "You can't keep up."

"I couldn't keep up before."

"You're being difficult."

"Where did you ever get the idea I'd make leaving me behind *easy* for you?"

"*You're missing a leg!*" Jackie trumpeted in frustration. "I can't take you with me."

"Why not?"

"Why *not?*" Jackie shook her head. "You're missing a leg."

"You said that." Michael stared her straight in the eye. "Like I said: So?"

"Michael," she said helplessly.

"You owe me an answer. And don't give me the 'not keeping up' crap. You owe me better than that."

Jackie stared back at him. "Okay," she said slowly. "The truth is I don't want to have to take care of you."

"More crap."

"Not at all. I don't know what's going to happen when I meet other elephants. I can't have any more dependants than my own baby."

"Let's add some more truths here." Michael felt like he was going to cry. He wiped his eyes angrily. "So I can't walk without a crutch. I'm riding you anyway. Besides, when my stump heals, we can make an artificial leg. You read that yourself. Even Gerry said he could do it. We might even find one that will fit me. Just because there wasn't anything in the Metropolis Hospital doesn't say anything about other hospitals. So it's not my leg. It's not like I haven't been useful. You wouldn't have gotten out of Saint Louis without me. It's been me, with my human hands, who's been able to keep the stuff together. I'm the one who can use a gun. I'm the one that saved your life. The truth is you need me. Your baby needs me. So let me come along."

"I'll have to look out for you."

"We'll have to look out for each other. *You* didn't see the dragon. *I* did."

"No."

"*Why not?*"

"I don't want anybody to die around me. Not again." She shuddered.

For a moment, Michael could read her as clearly as if she were a human being standing right in front of him: her face dark and sad, her eyes haunted. He reached up and took her trunk and draped it around his shoulder. He stroked it gently. "You're going to need all the help you can get. You've got a baby coming. You don't even know if the elephants are still there or if you can find them. You're going to need my hands and my eyes. Better take them with you."

"Why do you want to go with me so much?"

Michael laughed. "Are you kidding? Live on the back of an elephant? What kid wouldn't trade his teeth to be in my place?"

"That can't be the only reason."

"Oh, there are a million reasons for us to be together. I can't think of all of them for you." Michael hugged her trunk. He looked up at her. "I'm going to be an uncle!"

This time, Gerry kept the *Encantante* a hundred yards from shore while Michael and Jackie watched for signs of the dragons.

Michael scanned the forest with the binoculars Gerry had given him. "I don't see any."

"We saw the kill in the clearing this morning. They should be there," Jackie said. "And they might have decided to stay in the shade today," Gerry commented dryly.

"Why miss a chance at a mountain of meat?"

"Quiet," said Michael. "Let's not do this all over again."

Gerry opened his mouth, and then shut it. "Suit yourself. I'll say this for the last time. This is a mistake and you'll remember I said it."

"If things work out, we might come up in a year or two. You can meet Jackie's new baby."

Gerry didn't answer but emptied his pipe over the side.

"It's now or never." Michael patted Jackie's leg. "Help me up."

"I think Gerry's right."

"Not going to go through it again right this minute. Make a leg."

Jackie bent down on one knee and Michael clambered up. "Okay, then." He pulled out the rifle.

Jackie eyed it warily. "I didn't know you had that."

"Everybody has secrets. Let's roll."

Gerry brought the *Encantante* slowly to the pier. His own rifle was standing in the corner a foot away from him but he didn't look at it. Instead, he kept his hand over the throttle and the reverse switch.

Jackie stepped slowly onto the pier and looked around. Michael held the gun ready. "Okay, then."

Jackie began lumbering up the road.

Michael heard Gerry call after them: "Good luck!" Then the propeller revved up and the ferry pulled away from the pier.

They were on their own.

Michael looked around and watched carefully. The one that got his leg was dead but Michael wouldn't have minded giving him some company.

PART 3

Once the dragons had warmed themselves on the pavement, they moved to the shadows, waiting for whatever wandered close by. Michael didn't know if it was Jackie's size or the fact they stayed in the center of the road as far from the edge as possible, but the few dragons they saw only watched as they walked by. The *Encantante* containing two humans and an elephant must have confused them. Perhaps Michael had been the real target all along, or perhaps the dragon hadn't seen all of Jackie, just her leg, and attacked what it thought was a single animal. They would likely never know.

The infection that had nearly killed Michael showed the threat of the dragons was probably greater than Jackie being a target for every hungry man with a gun. Staying to the middle of the roads meant they traveled in the open. Jackie could be seen for a long distance. This made both of them nervous. Michael kept anticipating the feeling of Jackie sagging underneath him, the victim of a hungry sniper, followed by the inevitable sound of rifle fire.

They saw no one.

"Where is everybody?" Michael asked. Even in Saint Louis there had been some people—to be avoided, of course. But they had always been there.

"I don't know." Jackie watched the low farms. "This is different from what I had imagined."

The land rose. The forest grew thicker, lush and filled with tall oaks and maples. The road disappeared into rubble within a dark and gloomy forest floor nearly bare of vegetation. The remains of the road was a break of light between the trees.

"Keep watch," Jackie said after a while. "It'll be cold under the trees. The dragons will be sunning themselves wherever there's a warm spot."

But the forest grew thicker and even quieter. They saw no dragons.

"No people and no dragons." Michael leaned forward to look down on Jackie's face. "Any ideas?"

Jackie shook her great head. "It's too cool for them here under the trees. Maybe the dragons migrate north in the spring when the canopy is thinner. Then return south."

"Lizards migrating?"

"Who knows? It's a new world down here. I was modified. Maybe they were, too. Or maybe this just isn't dragon country."

"You were modified for a reason, I guess. Maybe they were, too."

Jackie was silent for a moment. "Why do you think I had to be modified for a reason?"

"Nobody would choose a five-ton experiment unless they had a reason." Michael cuffed the top of her head. "Especially one as foul tempered as you are."

"Yeah. Thanks." Jackie was silent for perhaps a dozen steps. "It was in the last notebooks you found."

"I figured."

"How so?"

"I bring you every notebook in the place. None of them satisfy you. Then, you find what you're after. The next day you leave. At first, I thought it might be something about Hohenwald. Something important you needed to know before you could leave. But the place is clearly on the map. And I couldn't see what would be in notebooks about *you* that would have anything to do with Hohenwald. Whatever you were looking for had to be about you. After a while I figured out it had to be something about you that only the people that created you would know. That's why you were searching the notebooks. And it had to be something Ralph either didn't know or couldn't tell you. Ralph would know all there was to know about *how* they had made you. But there's no particular reason I could think of that they would tell him *why*."

"It could have been genetic maps of the Hohenwald males."

"What's a genetic map?"

"Something you wouldn't know about." Jackie grabbed the leaves off a low hanging maple and pulled them down. The branch tapped Michael on the head.

"Ouch. What was that for?"

"For thinking you know everything about me."

"I *know* I don't know everything about you. For one thing, I don't know what was in those notebooks."

"The purpose of the project. My purpose."

Michael cried out with delight. "I was right," he crowed. "You were right."
"What was it?"

"They were going to reseed elephants back into Africa and Asia. But the elephants were going to have to be as smart as humans to keep from being steak on the hoof."

"That's weird," Michael said. "Why couldn't somebody just go and watch out for them." Then it hit him. "Oh."

"'Oh,' is right," Jackie said gently.

"They knew they were dying. They must have known *everybody* was dying. There wouldn't be anybody to take care of you." Michael shook his head. "That doesn't make sense. Why go through all the trouble and die before they can make good on it?"

"I don't know. I didn't find any personal diaries or notes. I just found the original mission statement and long range plan."

"What do you think happened?"

"I think they made a mistake and died too quickly. Since we didn't trust them, they didn't really know how well they had succeeded. They kept trying to adapt, trying to figure out how smart we really were and how they were going to adapt their plan to our limitations. They were caught sick trying to do right by us."

Michael didn't say anything for a long time. "Do you think they figured it out before they all died?"

Jackie sighed, a deep rumbling breath. "God, I hope not."

Dear Mom,

My spelling is better since I let Jackie read the letters. She had been doing it sometimes but hadn't said anything.

I didn't tell you about Gerry. But he and Jackie took care of me when I was sick. Gerry is a Real Good Guy, so if you get a chance, look out for him.

Jackie's job was to look out for the elephants. So, now when we get to Hohenwald, she gets to do her job. I'm not sure what I'm going to do. My job so far has been to be her hands. But most of what I do has to do with traveling. When she gets there, she won't be traveling anymore.

She said all of the elephants at Hohenwald were females. But the information she had was over ten years old. Ralph hadn't been able to contact Hohenwald for a long time. Maybe they weren't fire protected.

The land is different now, wilder. Jackie says it looks like the old forests from hundreds of years ago. But it's much too recent. She thinks somebody must have made it. So we're careful.

I miss you every day. You and Dad both, though I don't remember him so well. Jackie thinks I'm strange to write to you, being dead and all. I don't think it's strange at all. (So there, Jackie!)

If I talked to you out loud, people would just think I *was* crazy. This way, it's just between me and you and I get a chance to collect my thoughts. I think I remember you better, too, if I do this. Ned had some good ideas mixed with the bad.

Jackie makes sure I brush my teeth every night. She had me look for a toothbrush in Ralph's packs. Sure enough, there was one.

We're coming into Hohenwald soon. So, I'll tell you about it after that.

Love, Michael

They had been several days on old Highway 641 when Michael saw Interstate 40 through a break in the trees.

This part of the road had seen better days. The roads in Tennessee were better cared for than the ones in Illinois or Kentucky. It was one of the best ways to determine when they crossed state or county borders: the roads or the farms were cared for differently. In Kentucky, the roads were broken in places and worn away in others and they had to keep a sharp eye for dragons.

Once they crossed into Tennessee the roads looked as if they were cared for by someone with a mania for cleanliness and sharp borders. It reminded Michael of the mysterious farms up in Illinois. The dark forest seemed to be the province of Kentucky. The forest here seemed more normal: a mix of young trees and shrubs. Once or twice they saw the remains of a garden. There had been people around recently, if they weren't around right now. Still, they saw no one living. Just the occasional mound of mushrooms.

Jackie stopped dead in the middle of the roadway.

Michael almost fell off. He caught on to one of her ears and pulled himself back up to her neck. He looked around nervously to see what made her stop.

"What is it?" he whispered. "I hear something."

"Dragons?"

"No."

Jackie spread her legs and leaned forward. She let her trunk down to rest on the ground.

"Is something wrong?" asked Michael. "Shut up."

Michael leaned back and pulled out the map. It looked like they turned east here. Hohenwald was only seventy or eighty miles away.

Jackie straightened up. "So?"

"Nothing."

"Right."

Jackie shook her head in irritation.

A few miles further on, Interstate 40 was more visible. They walked up the eastern ramp to the road proper. Michael felt better. The visibility from an interstate was much greater than from the little, forest enclosed roads. While they hadn't seen a dragon for a while, Michael didn't want to take any chances.

Jackie stopped on the interstate again and assumed the strange leaning posture. "What *is* it?"

Jackie didn't answer. She just shook her head at him.

Michael climbed down to look around. He hopped over to the edge of the interstate, leaned against the guard rail. It was considerably more open to the south. Michael thought he could see a fairly large turtle of some sort, perhaps thirty pounds, walking along the edge of the forest. It looked like dragon country.

"We're going the wrong way," Jackie said suddenly.

Michael pulled out the map and studied again. "No. This is the way to Hohen-wald."

"Where are we?"

Michael studied the map. "McIllwain. At least, that's the closest thing that looks like a town. That way—" he pointed east "—lays the Tennessee River. We go over it, if the bridge is still there. About thirty miles further on we turn south again to Hohenwald."

Jackie shifted nervously. "They're not there."

"The Hohenwald elephants?"

Jackie turned west. She leaned out again and laid her trunk on the ground. "Not that way, either."

"Nothing to the north of us, is there?"

Jackie turned east again, dropped her trunk to the ground. For a long time, she was motionless. Finally, she shook herself. "It's the river that's messing me up. I think they're south."

Michael sat on the guard rail. "Dragons might be down that way. Also, people."

"Maybe. I don't think they're far."

Michael sighed. He stood, leaning against the wall. Jackie made a leg for him and he climbed up. "The river is going north to south. Maybe we can keep going south on 69 and you can keep listening."

"How far is the river? Is there a road that follows it?"

Michael ran his finger along the blue line. "The river is angling toward us. It comes pretty close starting around Akins Chapel. We'll only be a few miles away from it when we get to Jeanette. Maybe ten miles."

"Let's go."

At Jeannette, they found Brodie's Landing Road. This brought them down to the river.

The Tennessee River was not the crushing roar of the Ohio or the Mississippi. It was broad and flat with a steady slow southern flow. On the other side, washing in the still water was a herd of elephants.

Jackie froze, staring at them. The air was still. The elephants across the river stared back. Michael didn't move. He wondered if the elephants could see him. Just how well did elephants see, anyway?

The moment stretched out long enough that Michael wanted to change his position. He began to itch.

Suddenly, one elephant in the water snorted and clambered up the bank. It trumpeted once and then walked up the bank. The other elephants followed her.

Jackie shook herself once they were out of sight. She walked into the water but the current, though slow, seemed to shift her slightly. She stopped and backed up. "Where can I get across?"

"We can go back north and across Interstate 40. Or, we can go south and cross Highway 412."

"Which is closer?"

"Both are about the same." Jackie thought for a long time.

"South," she said at last. "We go south."

They crossed the river at Perryville. The bridge seemed intact, though, of course, they couldn't be sure. It cracked like a gunshot when they were in the middle and for a moment, Michael couldn't breathe. But the bridge gave them no more trouble and they were on the east side of the Tennessee River.

"We're quite a ways from Hohenwald," Michael said as they lumbered down the road.

"Did you think they would stay there? Their Keepers must be dead, too." Jackie sounded almost happy.

"Do you think Ralph is dead?"

She shook her head irritably. "I'm not concerned about the fate of one robot."

That's not your purpose, he thought. It made him nervous.

Along the eastern side of the river, they found a flat, worn trail, well marked with elephant scat. Jackie turned over each pile, broke it open and smelled it.

"Is that necessary?"

"I want to know who they are." She pointed to one worn pile. "African elephant. Female. Smells like she's the dominant one." She pointed behind. "There are three Indian females. One is still a little immature. She's unrelated to the other two. None of them are pregnant."

"What are you?"

"Indian. What? You didn't know?"

"It's not like you told me."

She snorted.

"Any boy elephants?"

"There were no males in Hohenwald."

"Why not?"

"Males need more space. They don't herd like females."

Michael thought for a moment. "Better hope your baby is a boy." Jackie didn't answer.

They came to the point across the river where they had seen the herd, a long, hard packed sandbar held together with tough grass and cottonwoods. The scat here was plentiful. The elephants liked this place and returned to it often.

Michael leaned over her head. "Which way?"

"I'm not sure."

Michael slid to the ground. Jackie handed him his crutch. He moved around one side of the clearing while Jackie searched the other. The elephant markings were so numerous it was hard to figure out where they had gone.

"Over here," she called softly. Michael hobbled over.

Jackie pointed to a large pile. "Male Indian. No more than a week ago."

"That's good, right?"

"Maybe."

She cried out suddenly. "Get down!" And swept him to the ground. A dart stuck in Jackie's trunk where he had been standing. Michael scrambled up to pull it out.

"Samsa!" cried a girl's voice from the brush. She ran out toward Jackie.

Michael tried to intercept her but was knocked to the ground again, this time by an older man. He held a knife to Michael's throat.

Jackie eased herself down to her knees. Then lay down on the ground. "Jackie!" Michael cried out.

She looked blindly at the sound of his voice. Then it seemed as if her eyes were looking elsewhere. She closed them slowly.

"You've killed her," he said, not believing it.

"It was an accident, cripple," whispered the woman in a stricken voice. "I was aiming at you."

PART 4

The girl pulled the dart out of Jackie's trunk. "Will she die, Samsa?" the girl asked the man holding the knife to Michael's throat.

"I don't know," Samsa said. He pulled cord from a pouch belted around his waist and bound Michael's wrists.

"What? Do you think I'm going to run away?" Michael pushed his stump at him. "Cripple, remember?"

Samsa ignored him. He knelt next to Jackie. "She's breathing. That's a good sign. Maybe the dosage is too small."

"Dosage of what?" Michael stared at them. "What did you *do* to her?"

"Missed *you*," said Samsa, evenly. "Let's see the dart, Pinto."

Pinto gently brushed Jackie's eyes closed, picked up the dart and brought it to Samsa.

Samsa examined it carefully, deliberately avoiding the point. "Full dose, all right. Get the med kit in my tent back at camp."

"Got it." With that, the girl was gone, running up the trail away from the river. Samsa examined Jackie minutely. He placed a hand on her chest to measure her breathing. After that, he held his hand under her trunk and stood silently.

"What are you doing?" Michael asked quietly.

"Shut up."

After a moment, Samsa released the trunk. "Pulse is good. Breathing is a little weak."

"That was a poison dart."

"You're a smart one."

"Why shoot me?"

"Let's see. You're riding the biggest piece of meat for twenty miles around— except for the dozen or so other pieces of meat just as big. You're not important, boy. She is. Too important to provide you a year's supply of steaks."

"You think I was going to eat her?"

"That would be a little ambitious. I think you were going to trade her. Maybe to the Angels in Memphis or the Rubber Girls in Chattanooga. They would have taken her and then served you up as a garnish—which would have been fine by me but we'd still be out an elephant."

"Jackie's not one of your elephants."

"I know that. Since you're accidentally alive you can tell me where you stole her."

"I didn't steal Jackie. I don't think anybody could do that. If she could talk, she'd tell you herself."

Samsa snorted. "I expect she'd have a lot to tell me, too." Michael fell silent.

"Where did you get her?"

"Jackie and I came from Saint Louis. We were trying to find the elephants at Hohenwald. She wanted her own herd."

"Well, you found them. We'll take it from here."

"She's—"

Samsa pointed the dart at him. "There's enough left in this for a little slip of a thing like you. Even if it didn't kill you, it'll paralyze you until morning. The Komodos would find you long before that."

Michael stared at the point of the dart. The tip had a drop of oil on it. He couldn't look away.

"Don't," Jackie said in a long exhalation.

Samsa looked over at the elephant. He looked back at Michael. "She didn't just talk, did she?"

"Is she going to be all right?"

Samsa looked back at her. "I think so. The curare didn't kill her so it will wear off in a while. Pinto is bringing back the antidote."

"Then pretty soon you'll find out for yourself."

Pinto returned with a professional looking bag. She gave it to Samsa and went to sit next to Jackie. She huddled next to her head. Michael hoped she had sense enough to move away when Jackie got up.

Michael tried to figure out the two of them. Samsa was an older man. What little hair he had left was streaked with gray and matched his beard. He was tall and thin as if strung together with wires. Pinto wasn't much more than Michael's own age. Through her loose shirt Michael could see a suggestion of young breasts, but her legs and arms still looked childish. Michael wondered if Pinto had bartered protection the same way he had with Uncle Ned. They didn't look related.

Samsa pulled out two glass ampoules, one with a powder and the other a liquid, a syringe, and a wicked needle. He filled the syringe with the liquid and injected it into the ampoule with the powder and swirled it around to mix it. He caught Michael watching him.

"We don't have much call to use this so it's still in the original packaging." Samsa grinned at him. "We brew the poison ourselves."

"From what?"

"Poison arrow frogs down in the bayou. We go down there once or twice a year to catch what we need."

"I didn't know there were such animals."

"Pretty little things. Red. Blue. All sorts of colors. Skin carries a poison that will lay you out to dry if you mess with them. They didn't use to live down there but somebody's menagerie broke open—or was deliberately released—and some small group managed to survive the cooler winters. It's a nice weapon against humans—quiet. Quick. If you keep your wits about you, you can take down half a dozen people before they realize what's happening."

He finished shaking the ampoule and filled the syringe with the resulting mixture. "Out of the way, Pinto," Samsa said. He swabbed a section of Jackie's hide and slipped the needle in. Then he withdrew the needle, broke it, and put the syringe and broken needle in a jar from the bag.

"She's still not going to be moving for a couple of hours but now her breathing won't be affected." He looked up at the hot sun. "We'll have to keep her cool." He looked at Michael. "Take your shirt off and wet it in the river. Keep it wet and on the elephant's head."

"Her name is Jackie."

"Jackie, then."

"Better untie me."

"You'll do fine with your hands tied together. Hop to it. Pinto? Help him but keep out of reach. Use your own shirt, too. I'll go get a couple of buckets."

Pinto kept a wary eye on Michael but he ignored her. The sun was hot even on his sweating body. He didn't want to imagine what Jackie felt like.

"Keep her ears wet, too," Pinto told him. "Elephants keep cool through their ears." Michael grunted and bathed Jackie's ears.

"Did she knock you down?" Pinto asked as they passed one another on the way to the river.

"She saved my life," Michael said simply.

"Right."

Michael shrugged.

Samsa returned with two buckets and a rifle. "I thought you liked poison," Michael said.

"I do. But it's hard to penetrate the hide of a crocodile with a dart."

"There are *crocodiles* in this river?"

"Not usually this far north but sometimes. The Komodos usually stay away, too. But not always. I'll keep watch, just in case."

Michael stopped and looked at Samsa. "You were a Keeper at Hohenwald."

"Director," Samsa corrected.

"So you let the elephants go when everybody died?" Samsa cocked his head. "Eleven years ago."

"All the other elephants in Saint Louis died. Jackie and the Keeper decided she should look for the elephants down here."

"Did they, now?"

"Jackie's going to have a baby. Is the poison going to hurt it?"

Samsa sighed and looked over to her still form. "I should have picked that up right away." He turned back to Michael. "I hope not but there's no way to know. If she doesn't miscarry, it's a fair bet the baby will be all right." Samsa gestured to Michael. When Michael came close enough, Samsa untied his hands.

"I'm starting to believe you're not a poacher." He held up the gun. "But I still have the rifle."

Michael nodded and went back to filling buckets.

In the early afternoon, Jackie started twitching. An hour later, she was trying to get up. Samsa stood next to her, speaking soothingly. "Don't get up yet, girl." He gestured Michael and Pinto off the sand bank.

Jackie seemed to calm down and remained still. But it wasn't long until she heaved herself up, swaying and looking confused.

"It's okay, girl," Samsa said soothingly.

Jackie swung her trunk and knocked the rifle to the ground, then swung back, caught Samsa's leg and turned him over on his back. In a moment, she had a foot on his chest.

"You tried to kill my boy," she hissed. Samsa tried to speak but couldn't.

Pinto ran to Jackie and tried to pull up her foot. Jackie ignored her. "Are you all right, Michael?"

"Yeah."

"What do you want me to do with him?"

"Let him go," Michael said. "He's the director at Hohenwald."

Jackie slowly raised her foot. She carefully walked down the sandbar into the water and eased into it.

Pinto held Samsa's hand. She was crying. Michael squatted down next to him. "She can talk," Samsa coughed out.

"I know," Michael said.

Dear Mom,

We found the other elephants. But the people that own them found us. Almost killed us, too. Me, anyway.

Samsa and Pinto were out tracking the herd. There is one big herd of six adult females and no calves. There are two other groups. One has three females and one calf. The other has four females and two calves.

Male elephants don't hang around except when they're in muss. Or muth. Or something. There are four males in the area.

All of them are Indian elephants except one: Tika. Tika is an african elephant. She's huge. She was the big elephant we saw at the stream. Samsa says it's possible for african and indian elephants to mate but she won't have any of the males. She's real strickt with her group. Maybe that's why they don't have calves.

Samsa let the elephants free when it looked like everybody was going to die, him included. But he didn't. Now there are fifteen people who help Samsa watch the elephants. They don't eat meat. They protect the elephants from people. Maybe they want to be elephants themselves.

They have their own little village near here. Samsa seems to run things from what I've seen. They want Jackie to come to the village. Jackie's not interedsted. She wants to join the herd. I think she's suspicious of them. They won't let me stay in the village. Maybe they still think I'm a poacher.

Love, Michael

"You need both legs to follow the elephants," said Samsa reasonably. "I can get around pretty good with my crutch. Let me do something."

"You can't run. Sometimes the elephants charge and if you can't get up a tree quick enough, there won't be quite enough of you left to bury. We've lost people that way." Samsa and Pinto left before Michael could protest further.

Jackie was resting near the camp. She watched them from a distance. Michael had no doubt she could hear every word.

Michael hobbled over to her. He sat down next to her. She reached up and pulled down the branch of a birch tree and began methodically pulling the leaves off and eating them.

"They won't let me come with them," Michael said. "So I heard."

The fog had come up the trail from the river and everything was swathed in mist. Michael felt cold and half blind. "How are you feeling?"

"Tired. Laying in the sun for half a day takes a lot out of you."

"Do you think there really are crocodiles in the river?"

"Do you think they're lying?"

Michael looked back to the fog. "I guess not. Do you know which band you're going after?"

Jackie didn't answer for a moment. "Tika's band, I think."

"Won't she be the hardest?"

"Probably."

"Then why her?"

Jackie was quiet a moment. "Silly reasons. It's surprising she even has a band with Indians in it. When you're desperate for company you'll take anything, I suppose."

Michael didn't speak immediately. His chest hurt and his throat felt thick. He stared up the trail where Samsa and Pinto had gone. Was that how he felt about them? Desperate? Was that how Jackie felt about him?

He went to their gear and opened up the hidden flap. He put together the rifle and took the exploding shells.

"What are you going to do?" Jackie stared at him. "Follow them."

It was awkward to carry the rifle while he was still forced to use the crutch. He thought maybe he'd try to get down to one of the old cities and look for a leg. Or build one. He had a vague memory of a story about someone with a peg leg. That would be enough for him.

The trail was clear and Samsa and Pinto had left footprints so they weren't hard to follow. He'd catch up to them or he wouldn't. Either way he was doing *something*.

He could tell the trail was coming close to the river by the way the trees began to thin. Michael listened and he could hear splashing—probably the elephants. He found a tall tree, leaned the crutch against the trunk and slung the rifle over his back and started to climb.

From near the top, he had a commanding view of the river, the elephants, and Samsa and Pinto watching the elephants. He could also see the sunken logs slowly drifting toward the splashing of the elephants. He unslung the rifle and aimed it at one of the logs. The telescopic sight showed the crocodile clearly. He turned on the laser and saw the bright red spot appear on the animal's back. Then he watched.

Samsa and Pinto were watching the elephants. Samsa had a rifle but it was slung. He was talking, or maybe arguing, with Pinto. One of the crocodiles stopped, watching the bank. Then it submerged.

Let's see, thought Michael. Think like a croc—or a dragon. Go for the little target, not the big one. Where would I attack from if I were a crocodile?

The water erupted near Pinto.

Right there. For a moment, the crocodile was frozen in midleap, the red spot clearly showing on his neck. Michael squeezed off three shots. He saw the water and blood spurt where they hit.

Then time caught and the crocodile started to close his jaws on Pinto when the explosive rounds triggered.

There was no flash or sound but the crocodile fell to the ground, dragging Pinto down with him. Samsa pulled Pinto out of the animal's limp mouth. They scrambled back up the bank, blood showing on Pinto's legs. But the croc was unmoving.

The elephants roared out of the water and ran into the forest. Michael stayed there for some time but the river was empty save for the remaining crocs staying safely off shore.

He climbed down and made his way back to camp. Samsa was treating Pinto's wounds.

Michael put the rifle down and sat next to it. "I have some use," he said.

Samsa was sitting across from him when Michael awoke. "I want the rifle."

Michael sat up. "I'd like to live in the village and use it to help you. But what I'd really like is to have my leg back. But that's the way it is."

Samsa shook his head. "We don't know you. I can't have any weapon around that can kill an elephant in the hands of someone I don't know."

"You mean like the darts?"

"That's different." Samsa watched him a moment. "We could dart you and take it." Michael pulled out the pistol and held it loosely. He didn't point it at Samsa but he didn't deliberately point it away. "You could pry it from my cold dead hands, I suppose."

"I know where that expression comes from. Do you?"

"Does it matter?" Michael was quiet for a moment. "I think it should be enough that Jackie trusts me."

"I don't think so. Jackie hasn't seen enough humans to know who to trust."

"Do tell," said Jackie from behind Samsa.

Michael looked up at Jackie. "You tell me what you want done with the rifle."

"Keep it," said Jackie shortly. "Likely you're a better shot with it than he is. Certainly, you're more trustworthy."

"I am the caretaker of the elephants," Samsa said in a controlled voice.

"That's not your job," said Jackie. "It's mine."

They didn't tell Samsa or Pinto or anyone else they were leaving. The village was up the hill and out of sight behind a bend in the trail. Michael certainly wasn't going out of his way to say goodbye. Even so, Michael could feel watchful eyes on him as they turned from the trail that led up the hill to the elephant scat covered trail that followed the bottomland.

"Tell me," Jackie said conversationally that afternoon. "Do you think Samsaville is on the map?"

Michael laughed for a long time.

The quality of their travel changed. Before, Michael had felt essentially alone in the forest. Other elephants were an abstraction. Other humans were absent. The very idea of a village was absurd.

But now Samsaville—the name stuck—loomed in his mind. He thought Jackie might think similarly about the elephants.

> Dear Mom,
>
> Jackie and I have left the other people and went to look for the elephants on our own. I'm not sure what's going to happen now. Maybe Jackie would be better without a one legged crippled kid.
>
> I miss you and Dad. I miss Gerry. I even miss Uncle Ned. I miss my leg. It hurts at night.
>
> Jackie's worried about joining the elephants. She doesn't say so but I can tell. Maybe Samsa will follow us. Maybe he'll dart me or worse. Maybe Tika won't let us join. Maybe something bad will happen.
>
> Whatever happens, I love you.
>
> Michael

They found Tika two days later. It was midmorning. The herd was grazing on the edge of a clearing. Worn buildings marked the clearing as having once been a farm. Michael looked at the ancient stubble of corn shocks and rusting machinery. This farm had never seen a robot. It had been abandoned long ago.

Tika had already turned to face them before Jackie and Michael left the forest. She must have heard them coming, thought Michael. Or smelled them.

Jackie stopped well short of them and started grazing on the opposite side of the clearing. After an hour or so, Tika returned to grazing with the other females. But her attention never wavered from Jackie.

Afternoon came and the herd disappeared into the forest. Michael slid down to the ground and made himself a lunch out of dried fruit and crocodile jerky.

"Samsa is watching us," Jackie muttered and she stood near Michael. "Up on the ridge. I can smell him."

Michael nodded. "Is he going to shoot me?"

"I can't smell a gun but that doesn't mean much."

"Anybody else?"

Jackie shook her head. "Not as far as I can tell."

"Nothing to be done, then."

Michael chewed the crocodile jerky. Not bad. Sort of like chicken. "I wonder why the dragons don't come across the bridges. Do you think there's something here they don't like?"

"Maybe the elephants kill them. I know I would."

"You *did*."

"True." Jackie thought for a moment. "It's a mistake to think this ecology is complete. Humans left it very recently. It could be the Komodos just haven't reached this far yet. The Komodos have to migrate north from the coast every spring and return every fall. It's going to take time for them to penetrate new areas. Any place they go can only be as far as they can return to in time to avoid the winter."

"They could learn to winter up here."

"Unlikely."

"*They're* unlikely, right? Who knows what they can do?"

Jackie was silent for a moment. "That's not something I want to think about."

Michael shivered. "Me, neither."

The next week followed the same ritual. The elephants came to the abandoned farm and grazed, moving over to new areas as they stripped the old of leaves. By the week's end, Jackie and Tika had circled the entire clearing. Still standing opposite one another, Jackie was now where they had first sighted Tika and Tika was grazing where Jackie had first entered the clearing.

"Today we have to follow them," said Michael. He spat out the last of the meat. He was tired of crocodile jerky.

"It's too soon."

"Look around you." Michael pointed at the trees. "There's nothing left. They're not going to come back here just to say hello."

Tika chivvied her herd back to the clearing's entrance. Jackie followed at a respectful distance. Tika kept turning to check on them.

"This might work out," Jackie whispered.

They followed the band for hours. The smell of Samsa and the other humans faded. The trail became wilder and more curved until they couldn't see the band for minutes at a time. Then they turned a corner in the trail and Tika was facing them.

Jackie stopped dead still. Michael had been leaning forward, resting his head on Jackie's head and watching. He froze, not wanting to draw attention to himself.

Tika approached cautiously, trunk half raised and sniffing the air. Jackie raised her trunk slightly. When the two of them were close enough, they sniffed each other with their trunks. Tika seemed to relax.

Michael watched. It came to him that Tika wanted Jackie in her band—maybe because she was pregnant. Maybe because there were dangers enough out here for everybody to share.

Tika suddenly whipped her trunk over Jackie's head and caught Michael squarely in the side, sweeping him off Jackie's neck and down on the ground in front of Tika.

Michael fell the ten feet in a moment of frozen astonishment and landed hard on his back, knocking the wind out of him. Desperately, he tried to force himself to breathe, cough, anything. But his lungs stubbornly refused to fill.

Tika raised her leg over him.

Michael saw the details of her foot, the broken toenail, the puckered scar. Jackie screamed "No!" and stepped over him, shoving Tika away.

Tika stumbled back and then shoved back.

Jackie stood foursquare over him, her head and trunk down.

Michael's breath caught and he sat up, watched twenty tons of animals shoving above him.

"Move," Jackie cried.

Michael scrambled away. *A tree! Where's a tree?* He saw an oak and hopped over to it, clawed his way up the trunk and into the branches high enough to escape Tika.

Jackie fell back in front of the tree, facing Tika. Tika trumpeted at her.

It was as if she shouted in English: *You we want. But not with him.* Jackie trumpeted back. *Not without him.*

"Jackie," he shouted. "Go with them. I'll be okay." Tika fell back, staring at the two of them.

"No," Jackie said. "Both of us or not at all." Michael found himself crying.

PART 5

Dear Mom,

It's been a while since I wrote but I've been busy. Little Bill is just as stubborn as his mother. Jackie says he outgrew the cute phase when he was two. Now she thinks it's just unpleasant. But I like him. He reminds me of his mother.

I think Tika's finally accepted me. It took long enough. She's allowed me to stay all this time by just ignoring me. But a few weeks ago before we left Panacea one of her toenails got infected and needed to be lanced and cleaned. It was pretty clear it had to be done before we started north. Jackie stood next to me to make sure I didn't get hurt. But Tika brought over her foot and didn't twitch when I cleaned out the wound. It must have hurt. It looks lots better now.

That was just after I shot two Komodos that had decided to make a meal out of Tika's leg. The Komodos aren't much problem in the winter. They're all asleep somewhere. But between the time they wake up in the spring and the time they start north, they're pretty hungry and mean. I can't say for sure what made Tika change her mind. But she seemed pretty happy that Jackie and I were walking next to her when we went North this year.

Things are still changing. The Komodos are tough but they seem to have a hard time with the brush lions. We're not sure. Where we find brush lions, there aren't any Komodos and where we find Komodos there aren't any brush lions. We don't know exactly what's going on.

And the fire ants keep spreading north.

Good news this spring. Both Tanya and Wilma are pregnant. The bull that visited around Christmas must have done his job. More young ones for Little Bill to play with.

We're not far from Samsaville. It'll be nice to see Pinto and Samsa. I'm trying to persuade Jackie we should go far enough north to see Gerry. But she doesn't like going through dragon country.

All for now,
Love, Michael

Michael finished signing his name and closed the notebook. It was almost filled. This would be book number seven. He hefted it in his hands. He wondered if he was a little off in his head to be writing his dead mother all these years. He was sixteen now. Michael shrugged. He still liked doing it. Maybe Jackie would have an opinion on it.

He put down his pack and watched the river flow by. Mostly he just enjoyed the play of sunlight and color on the water. It was a careful observation, too. Keeping track of floating logs nearby that might leap out at him. The crocodiles had become more numerous in the last couple of years. Michael didn't know what they were eating but so far none had tasted elephant on his watch.

Little Bill came down to the edge of the bank. *Little?* Michael smiled to himself. Bill's head was two feet taller than he was.

"Jackie's-Boy! Jackie's-Boy!" he piped, a tiny voice for such a large body. Michael wondered when, and if, the elephant's voice would ever break into the deep timbre of an adult. Michael's had. Well, mostly. Sometimes it still cracked.

"Just Michael," he said. "Like I always say. Just Michael."

"Jackie's-Boy is what Tika calls you."

Michael chuckled, wondering, not for the first time, how an elephant spoke without being able to speak. The world was filled with mysteries. "Does she now?"

"Are you ready to go?" piped Bill. "Tika sent me to get you. She wants you and Jackie to go first."

Michael reached down and pulled up his artificial leg and fastened it on. "Really? *Tika* wants us to lead?"

"Sure. At least as far as Cobraville."

"Ah. She wants us to cross the fire ants first, eh?"

"Yeah."

"Will wonders never cease?"

Little Bill didn't answer. Instead, he made a leg. Michael shouldered the rifle and climbed up over his neck. He looked around. The blue bowl of the sky above him, the warm sun, his gray family patiently waiting for him half a mile away. He felt like singing.

Lovingly, he patted the top of Little Bill's head.

"Well, then. Musn't grumble," he said with a grin. "Let's go."

flying in the face of god

NINA ALLAN

Here's a poignant and excellently crafted character study of a woman whose best friend is being transformed into a strange posthuman creature in order to survive a journey to the stars. . . .

New writer Nina Allan lives and works in London. She's a frequent contributor to *Interzone* and *Black Static*, and has also appeared in *The Third Alternative*, *Strange Tales* from Tartarus, and elsewhere. Her stories have been collected in her first book, *A Thread of Truth*. Her story "My Brother's Keeper" was a finalist for the British Fantasy Award in 2010. She's currently at work on a novel.

ANITA SCHLEIF: Have you thought about what you'll do if you're not passed fit to take part in the mission? There have been media reports of how difficult it is for discharged fliers to be accepted back into society, of how women fliers especially have been treated as pariahs. How does it make you feel as a woman, knowing that the Kushnev drain will make you permanently infertile?

RACHEL ALVIN: I don't ever think about failure. I don't see the point. I want to put all my efforts into succeeding. As for becoming infertile, it's a decision you take, like any other, like having children or not having them. Life is all about making choices, and in making one choice you inevitably close the door on another. Fliers find it hard to fit in because being a flier is a vocation. Anyone who chooses to follow a vocation finds ordinary life difficult and mystifying, whether they're an artist or a missionary or a mathematician. The Kushnev drain is only a part of it. Mainly it's a question of focus, of intense focus on only one thing.

(From the transcript of *Shooting the Albatross:
The women of the Aurora Space Program*, a film by Anita Schleif)

The outward effects of the Kushnev drain were many and varied; with Rachel it had exaggerated her freckles. They looked darker than before and slightly inflamed, standing out on her face like divots of rust. It was hot in the carriage, and Rachel's brackish, slightly acrid body odour was particularly noticeable. Anita watched the man in the opposite seat wipe sweat from his upper lip with the back of his hand then hoist his briefcase onto his knees and take out *The Times*. She saw him staring at Rachel over his newspaper, the way civilians always did with fliers, especially the women. Two stops down the line he left the train, leaving Anita and Rachel with the carriage to themselves.

Rachel stood up and tried to open the window but the sealing-catch, with its rusted-down hasps, proved too much for her. It was an antiquated design, something Anita remembered from her schooldays. She was surprised to see it. She had thought all the old-style compartment trains had been decommissioned years ago.

She got to her feet and opened the window, releasing the sticky catch with the heel of her hand. Warm air rushed in, filling the carriage with the smell of dried grass.

"You mustn't put your muscles under strain," said Anita. "Remember what the doctors have said."

"I just feel so useless. I can hardly do anything now."

"The things you can do are different, that's all. You know that better than anyone. Stop giving yourself a hard time."

Rachel turned to face the window. Her thinning hair blew back a little from her face. Anita wondered if Rachel would be allowed to keep what remained of her hair, or whether it would have to be shaved off, or whether it would fall out soon anyway. She thought of asking for the sake of the film, then realised she didn't want to know. When compared with other aspects of the process it was a small matter. But she had always loved Rachel's red hair.

"I went to the supermarket with Serge last night," said Rachel suddenly. "Just after you left. I wanted to help him stock up. It was no good though, it was all too much. I had to go and sit in the car. It's hard to explain, it's like you're drowning in colour and noise. The sight of all that food makes me feel ill." She paused. "We tried to make love but it was hopeless. When he tried to go inside me it hurt so much I had to tell him to stop. They gave us this special lubricant but it's useless, at least it was for me. Serge told me it didn't matter and I made it all right for him of course but I could tell how upset he was. He was ages getting to sleep." She turned back towards Anita. Her eyes, once dark blue, were now a faded turquoise, opaque as chalk. "Will you go and see him once I've gone? I know he likes talking to you."

Anita nodded. "Of course I will." She wondered if this was some covert way of Rachel giving her permission to sleep with Serge, to take him over, perhaps. She knew it would be tempting for both of them, but she must not allow it to happen. She loved Serge, but as a brother. To try and alter things could be disastrous. They would do better to behave as they always did, by going to films together and cooking curries and talking about Rachel. In the end Serge would meet someone else and that would be painful but at least their friendship would still be intact.

In the last six months, both during Rachel's leave and immediately before, Anita had tried to concentrate all her energies on the film she was making about the women fliers. The idea for the film had arisen directly out of her early conversations with Rachel and she had begun the project almost without realising it. In many ways she still felt uneasy about it. She didn't like the idea that people might see the work as in some way connected with her own life, as a comment on the death of her mother. She found such notions intrusive and unwelcome. But now she had started work it was impossible for her to draw back. She even supposed that at some level people would be right to assume that the film had a personal context, although its subject was not her mother of course but Rachel.

Rachel was now producing less than ten millilitres of urine a day. Her skin had increased in thickness and had lost most of its elasticity. She was eating next to nothing and sleeping little. The sleep she had would be feverish and noisy with dreams.

Anita's researches had made her an expert on the Kushnev process. Rachel had pulled a few strings and she had been allowed in to see Clement Anderson, the team doctor. He refused her request to film him, but he had agreed to a taped interview, and she had been allowed to shoot a few brief sequences around the base. There was some footage of the fliers in the team canteen that she knew would come across very well.

"The drain triggers a permanent change in the way cells grow," Anderson had told her. "Crudely put it's a form of cancer." He had given her a folder of printed material and a DVD of Valery Kushnev explaining his theories. Kushnev's accent was so strong they'd had to include subtitles. The Kushnev process derived from cockroaches. Cockroaches, Kushnev explained, were the hardiest of species. They could endure the harshest of conditions and subsist on next to nothing. If necessary they could shut down most of their functions, regressing to a state of suspended animation until an improvement in external circumstances allowed them to continue with their lives.

"During the journey itself our fliers will exist in a half-life," said Valery Kushnev on the video. "A kind of para-existence, in which there is full intellectual function but without the accompanying stress of biological need. In this way we cross the emptiness of space. Our fliers are the new pioneers. In a very real sense they are following in the footsteps of Columbus."

At this point he chuckled, showing teeth that were eroded and stained with nicotine. Anita had watched the film more than a dozen times.

"How's Meredith?" said Rachel. "Did you call her last night?"

Anita started in her seat. For a moment she had almost forgotten where she was.

"She's fine," said Anita. "She asked after you." It was becoming increasingly difficult to talk to her grandmother on the phone. They had unlimited free calls at Southwater House, but she refused to have the webcam on and disembodied voices seemed only to confuse her more.

"How is that friend of yours?" she had said. "Are you bringing her down to see me?"

"You mean Rachel, Gran," said Anita. "Her name is Rachel. We came down to see you last week."

Her grandmother's short-term memory was becoming increasingly erratic but on some days Meredith Sheener was as sharp as ever, keen to read the newspapers at breakfast time as she had always done and even able to complete a small section of the crossword puzzle. She was still a demon at cards. Anita had tried talking to the visiting consultant about this, asking him if the card playing might help to stimulate other areas of her brain, but he brushed her words aside, shaking his head as though she had asked him if her grandmother might perhaps one day take up deep-sea diving or decide to learn a second language.

"Oh, they all have something," he said. "With some it's cards or backgammon, with others it's a photographic memory for Shakespeare. It doesn't mean anything. An old person's brain is like a capsized steam freighter: you'll find pockets of air here and there but the ship is going to sink in the end. Nothing to set much store by, I'm afraid."

Anita remembered the look on his face, the tight, harassed expression of a man with too many demands on his time. He was tall, grey, and gaunt, his fingers slightly twisted from arthritis.

"He's a good-looking man, that doctor, don't you think?" This was something her grandmother said every time Anita visited. Anita knew she fretted about her not being settled with anyone. She wished she could reassure her in some way, explain how her love for Rachel sustained her as much as it caused her pain. She touched the pendant around her neck, feeling its bumpy contours though the thin green material of her blouse. It was something she often did at times of stress or uncertainty. The pendant seemed to act as a lodestone, bringing her back in touch with who she was.

It hung on a silver chain, a small, finely-worked figurine in the form of a dodo. Her grandmother had once taken her to see the dodo skeleton on display at the Natural History Museum. Anita had gazed at it with intense curiosity, almost with reverence.

"Why are there no real dodos?" she asked. She had been about eight at the time.

"The dodo forgot how to fly," said her grandmother. "It lived on the island of Mauritius, right in the middle of the Indian Ocean. There were no people there, and no other big animals either, so it was perfectly safe. It didn't really need its wings at all. But when hunters finally came to the island the dodo couldn't get away from them. They were shot and killed in their thousands. In less than a hundred years they were extinct."

Anita thought it was terribly sad. She felt a huge anger towards the hunters, with their ridiculous feathered hats and their carefully-oiled fowling pieces. Later, when they got home, her grandmother had shown her Mauritius on the map.

"It was like a paradise island when sailors first discovered it," she said. "So much of the world was still unknown then. Imagine how it must have felt, to set foot in a place that no one had ever seen before."

As a child she was allowed to wear the pendant occasionally as a treat, but when Anita turned sixteen her grandmother gave her the silver dodo and told her it was hers to keep.

"It belonged to your mother," she said. "She wore it until the day before she died."

When they got to Charing Cross they had a minor argument. Anita wanted to go with Rachel all the way out to Northolt but Rachel insisted on continuing with the journey by herself.

"How are you going to manage?" said Anita. "What about your luggage?"

Rachel couldn't carry anything heavy because her bones were still at the brittle stage. There was also the question of safety. There had been a couple of attacks on fliers in recent months, supposedly by tube gangs, although on all but one occasion the incidents had happened at night.

"I've only got one suitcase," said Rachel. "Nothing is going to happen." She laid her hand on Anita's arm, her fingers brownish, a bunch of dry twigs. "I need some time to get adjusted. If you follow me right to the wire I'll blub like a girl."

Anita tried to laugh. She remembered another conversation they had had, the argument that had erupted between them on the morning Rachel received her commission.

"It's too late for this, don't you see that?" Rachel had screamed at her. "It's been too late from the day I had the first course of injections. Don't you think I could do with some support? Has it ever occurred to you I might be scared, too?"

In the end Anita went with her as far as the Underground. They went to a café just off Leicester Square. From the outside it looked coolly inviting, but there was something wrong with the air conditioning and Anita's neck and armpits were soon streaming with sweat. Rachel of course hardly registered temperature changes any more. She wet her lips with small sips of mineral water while Anita drank a glass of orange juice, feeling it slip down her throat in freezing gouts. At the end of twenty minutes Rachel called for the bill and then stood up to go.

"It's time," she said. "The longer we put it off the worse it will be." She pulled a handkerchief from her pocket and dabbed at her eyes, although Anita was sure this was just out of habit; Rachel's tear ducts had dried up some time ago.

Once they were outside on the street Anita turned and took her in her arms.

"I love you," she said. "I love you so much."

"I know," said Rachel. "I know you do."

They went down the escalators to the Piccadilly Line. A youth with tattooed black mambas encircling both forearms helped Rachel onto the train.

"Going up soon then, are you?" he said. "I think you're the business." He steered her gently, almost tenderly towards a seat. The train doors slid closed. Anita raised her hand, meaning to wave, but Rachel's face was angled away from her, talking to the boy with the snake tattoos. As Anita watched he threw his head back, his green eyes crinkled closed in a soundless laugh.

Once Anita was back at Charing Cross she telephoned Serge. He sounded distant and preoccupied and for the first time it occurred to Anita that he might have started seeing someone else. Anita had never talked to Rachel directly about Serge. She had taken his continued presence as proof of his devotion. It was something she admired, something that softened the worst pangs of her jealousy. Now she wondered if she had simply been blind.

"I won't be at home for a while," she said to him. "I'm going down to visit my grandmother. I'll probably be away for a couple of days."

She didn't know why she was telling him this. The decision to go and see her grandmother had come upon her spontaneously, almost while she was having the conversation. She pressed the phone hard to her ear, trying to catch every nuance, any suspicious change in his tone of voice.

"I'll see you in a couple of days then," he said. "Are you OK, Anita? Are you sure you wouldn't like to come round?"

"I'm fine," she said. Quite suddenly he was the last person she wanted near her. "I'll come and see you as soon as I get back."

She changed trains at London Bridge and then again at East Croydon. The fields on either side of the tracks were yellow and cracked. There had been no rain to speak of since April. Drought-summers were common now and were said to be becoming more common, though Anita remembered them even from her childhood, the standpipes in the streets, the "dry hours" between eleven and four. One of her friends from school then, Rowland Parker, had once gone six whole months without washing.

"It's my patriotic duty," he said. His friends egged him on, placing bets on how long he could hold out. He stank like a muskrat, but the skin beneath his clothes had been smooth and clean. Even his smell had attracted her: feral and vital and somehow other. Anita remembered touching his penis, its immediate and startling response.

It had been Rowland Parker who had first told her about her mother.

"Your mum died in that fire, didn't she?" he said. "That explosion on board the rocket. There's stuff about her on the Internet. My brother told me."

They had been sitting out by the Old Pond, side by side on the concrete platform that people had once used to dive from into the lake. There was no water now, of course, just a foot or so sometimes in winter. In summer the lake was a dense mass of greenery, of hogweed and bramble and dead nettle mostly, but other things too, poppies and foxgloves, plants that didn't grow much anywhere else. Her grandmother said it was because the soil under the Old Pond always stayed slightly damp. The concrete was burning hot beneath the soles of her feet. She squinted through her lashes at the three o'clock sun.

"My mother died in an air crash," she said. It was what she had always been told.

"Oh," said Rowland Parker. "Sorry. My brother must have got it wrong." He glanced at her sideways then looked down at his hands. His feet were dangling over the rim of the dried up lake. She thought he had beautiful feet, long and narrow, like a gipsy boy's. He had three large mosquito bites just above his ankle bone. They formed an almost-straight line, three pinky-red full stops.

"It doesn't matter," said Anita. "I never knew her. I was a baby when she died. I don't remember anything about her."

She didn't know what to think, and this, at nine years old, was her first real experience of uncertainty. If what Rowland said was true then what she had been told before was not true, or at least not the whole truth. The world, previously a place of straight lines and lighted spaces, became suddenly darker and full of crooked shadows. When she got home that evening she found herself looking at her grandmother, studying her almost, and wondering *who exactly she was*. Meredith Sheener, a young woman still at only fifty, her thick hair piled high on top of her head. Was Meredith her grandmother at all, or some impostor sent to lie to her? The idea was frightening but Anita could not deny there was also an element of excitement to it. She ate her supper in silence, thinking hard. She wondered what would happen if she forgot how to speak, just as the dodo had forgotten how to fly. She wondered what it would be like to spend the rest of her life as a mute.

They had a mute at school, Leonie Coffin, though she was teased more for her name than for her silence.

It was her grandmother who spoke first.

"Are you all right, my darling? Did something bad happen today?"

She was briefly tempted to say nothing, because that would be more enigmatic and more in keeping with the seriousness of the situation but in the end the direct-ness of her grandmother's question made her unable to resist answering it.

"Rowland said mum died on a rocket. Is that true?"

Meredith Sheener had answered at once and without prevarication. It was that, more than anything else, that persuaded Anita that Meredith was telling the truth. She said that Anita's mother Melanie had died on board a rocket called the Aurora One. The rocket had been sabotaged, and exploded on take-off. Everyone on board had been killed instantly, and several ground staff had died in the fire that destroyed the launch site. Anita's father had been one of them.

"The papers wouldn't leave us alone," said Meredith. "It was terrible for every-one, of course, but it was Melanie they were most interested in because she was the only woman."

"But who would want to blow up a rocket when they knew there were people inside?" In spite of her determination to be detached and grown up about it Anita could feel her heart clench in her chest.

"People who are no good at all," said her grandmother. She sighed and bowed her head, rubbing at her eyes with the back of her hand. "There were some people who thought it was bad to send human beings into space. They complained about the money it cost, and said it should be spent on feeding poor people and build-ing schools and hospitals and churches here on Earth. But that wasn't the main thing. Mostly they thought that human beings shouldn't get above themselves, that if people were meant to fly they would have been born with wings. A blas-phemy, they called it, flying in the face of God. They called themselves the Guardian Angels, but what they actually did was kill people."

Anita fell silent again. The feelings inside her jostled for attention. It was exciting that her mother had been a space woman. It was also exciting, in a way that she would not have admitted to anyone except perhaps Rowland Parker, that her mother had been someone important enough for people to want to kill. It was exciting but it was also terrifying. She felt suddenly exposed, as if her life too might be in danger.

She wondered if it were possible to feel grief for someone she did not remem-ber, who was connected to her by fact but not by actuality.

She asked her grandmother if she could have a photograph of her mother to keep in her room. She had seen photographs of course, plenty of them, images that had become so familiar they seemed to her now like film stills, pictures that made her mother common property, like an actress or a politician. She thought that owning one of these photographs might make her mother seem more real. Meredith Sheener went into her bedroom and a little while later came back with a red cardboard wallet. It contained two photographs, a duplicate of the one of her mother graduating from Oxford that her grandmother kept on her dressing table and another, previously unknown to her, showing Melanie in a checked shirt with a baby in her arms.

"That's you at eight weeks old," said her grandmother. "It's the only picture I have of the two of you together."

Anita's throat felt tight and closed, as if a large weight was pressing down on her windpipe. When she asked tentatively if there were any photographs of her father her grandmother shook her head.

"I'm sorry dear, but I just don't have any. I hardly knew Malcolm really. They had only been married six weeks."

AS: Can you tell me something about how you got involved in the space program? You already had a good career as an industrial chemist, a lot of respect from your colleagues, plenty to look forward to. Some people would say you've sacrificed your humanity for the sake of the Aurora project. What made you want to do this in the first place?

RA: This is something I remember quite clearly. When I was eleven years old I saw a film called *Voyage to the Sun*, which wasn't about space travel at all but about the first sea transits to America and the West Indies. I'd learned these things at school of course, but seeing the film made everything seem more real. I'd never been more excited by anything in my life. What excited me most was the idea that our world had once been dangerous, that huge areas of our planet were still unknown. The men who set off on those sea voyages didn't know where they were going, much less if they would ever return. They risked their lives for the sake of an adventure and the idea of that just thrilled me to the bone. Later on I started to read about the early space pioneers and all those thoughts and feelings came back to me. I suppose they'd never really gone away.

Rachel Alvin had emailed Anita to say how much she had enjoyed Anita's short film *Moon Dogs*, based around a greyhound track in Hackney. They had corresponded for a while and then arranged to meet for lunch at an Italian restaurant in Soho. Anita was bowled over by Rachel. She was small and quietly spoken, her features too angular to be conventionally beautiful but there was something fearless about her, an audacity in her way of thinking that made her compelling. They seemed to form an immediate bond. It was not until later, when Rachel asked her if she was related to Melanie Schleif, that Anita realised it had not been her film that had drawn Rachel to her in the first instance but the simple fact of her surname.

"She was my mother," Anita said. "I was eight months old when she died."

"I don't believe it," said Rachel. "She's been a hero to me since I was small." She had gone quite pale, and her blue eyes filled up with tears. Anita felt a surge of jealousy and then repressed it immediately. Her mother was dead, after all. The important thing was not how she had met Rachel, but that they had met at all.

"I have some things of hers," she said. "I could show them to you, if you like."

The following Sunday Rachel had come to Anita's flat in Woolwich and Anita had shown her the photographs she had, as well as a painted tin piggy bank, a wooden globe, a biography of Tereshkova with *Melanie Muriel Sheener* written across the flyleaf in blue biro.

"My grandmother got rid of most of her stuff because she said it was too upsetting to keep it, that it was like having a ghost in the house," said Anita. "These few things are all that's left." Later in the afternoon they took the bus up to Shooter's Hill and Anita showed Rachel the house she had grown up in and where Melanie also had spent her childhood. It faced the main road, a large

Victorian villa that had once been a school but had later been divided into flats. Anita had not been there since she and her grandmother had moved out eighteen months before. She saw that the outside had been repainted. It made the place seem different, newer, almost as if her time there had been erased.

"The house is enormous inside," she said. "There's a lane at the back that runs all the way to Oxleas Woods. There were foxgloves. I played there all the time when I was a child."

She would have liked to have shown Rachel the garden, but the side gate had been padlocked shut. It made her feel chagrined, angry almost, to be treated as an intruder in a place that had been her home for so long, even though she knew such feelings were illogical. She suddenly found herself wishing she had made more of an effort to buy the flat.

"I loved it here," she said. "It was somewhere I always felt safe."

The flat had been sold, and the money invested to pay the fees for her grandmother's retirement home. Because of its large size the apartment had been priced out of her range, although its tired condition meant that in the end it had gone to developers. Anita thought now that if she had fought harder she might have found a way to afford it. She looked at Rachel, taking pictures with her phone and gazing about herself like a tourist at a world heritage site. She touched the dodo pendant through her dress and thought how curious it was that Rachel's presence had made it possible not only for her to return to the house but to feel nostalgia for it.

It was as if her growing feelings for Rachel had opened some special compartment in her mind. She wondered then why it was that she hadn't told her the whole truth about her mother's relics, that as well as the handful of harmless possessions she had shown her there were several cardboard boxes of letters, diaries and photographs, things she had found among her grandmother's papers and taken with her to her new flat in Woolwich.

She had never been through them properly. When she was a child she supposed she had hero-worshipped her mother, much the way that Rachel did now. But by the time she went away to college she had begun to feel an increasing need not to be defined by her.

Her grandmother's illness had changed that for a while but now what Anita wanted was to have her mother out of the way again. She wanted Rachel all to herself.

By the time the train reached Shoreham it was almost empty. Anita stepped down onto the platform, slamming the train door shut with a hollow bang. Sallow grass grew up between the paving slabs. The sun beat down. There was an acrid reek of seaweed and brine.

Rachel had loved this place. As a child she had rarely been out of London and so the idea of the seaside had never lost its enchantment. The first time Anita had taken Rachel to see Meredith, Rachel had been on her second course of injections and her hand to eye coordination was all over the place. She had spilled a cup of tea into her lap, scalding herself quite badly. Meredith had taken over, dabbing Savlon on Rachel's burns and finding her a clean shirt to put on, an outlandish thing with a high lace collar and diamante buttons.

"I don't understand it," Anita said afterwards, when they were on the train back to London. "The clothes she wore at home were always so dull."

"Perhaps she feels she's free now," said Rachel. "Free to be what she wants instead of what people expect."

Anita had found this idea comforting. She felt humbled by Rachel's generosity of spirit, her ability to accept people simply for who they were. She turned her back on the sea. The tide was far out, and there was nothing to see but mudflats. Southwater House was only half a mile from the station but it was a stiff uphill climb. She supposed the view from the top was part of what made the place appealing. The retirement home catered for about thirty full-time residents, and with its tiled hallways and sloping lawns it reminded her a little of one of the 1920s seaside hotels in the old-fashioned detective stories her grandmother had once enjoyed, novels by Agatha Christie and Dorothy L. Sayers. The staff seemed to connive in the illusion; Anita privately thought that some of them were more eccentric than most of the residents. There was something chaotic about the place, and it was precisely this that had convinced her that her grandmother would be happy there. The hallway smelled of pine detergent and fermenting grass clippings, a scent that invariably reminded her of the day Meredith had come here to live. The dismantling of the Shooter's Hill flat had been very difficult for her and she had arrived at Southwater House tearful and disorientated. When Anita tried to kiss her goodbye she clung to her and called her Melanie. The next time Anita saw her grandmother she was different, but better. Anita wondered if Rachel was right, that Meredith was finally feeling the freedom to be herself.

The reception desk was unmanned. Anita hesitated, wondering if she should ring the bell or continue upstairs. Eventually someone appeared, a young woman with peroxide hair and glasses. She was wheeling a linen cart with one hand and clutching a sheaf of newspapers in the other. Anita thought she recognised her from a previous visit but couldn't remember her name.

"Miss Sheener," she said. "Your grandmother's in her room. She hasn't been feeling too bright today, I'm afraid."

Anita felt the usual surprise at being addressed by her grandmother's surname. It was as if in some sense she had become her grandmother. She didn't know if the staff here were ignorant of her actual surname or whether the woman had simply forgotten.

"What do you mean?" she said. "Why didn't you call me?"

The peroxide nurse took a step backwards. "There's nothing to worry about," she said. "She isn't ill or anything, just a bit down in the dumps."

Anita took this as a euphemism, that the woman was trying to tell her that Meredith was going through one of her confused periods. It had been less than a week since she had seen her but in Meredith Sheener's world Anita knew that time could be an unstable commodity. Five days might slip by without notice, or they might seem to pass as slowly as five years. She smiled vaguely at the nurse and then made her way quickly upstairs.

Meredith's room was on the first floor overlooking the sea. It was large and bright and full of things. There were things Anita remembered from Shooter's Hill of course, but there was also much that was new: china ornaments and embroidered cushion covers, brightly coloured alien objects that scrambled for possession of every surface. Like the ostentatious clothes, they seemed more a part of the new Meredith than the old one. Anita couldn't help noticing a certain accumulation of dust. She supposed it was impossible for the staff to keep pace with her grandmother's clutter.

Meredith was in the armchair beside the bed. Her eyes were open but there was a fixed, empty quality to her gaze that made her seem like a different person. Anita's breath caught in her throat.

"Are you all right, Gran?" she said. She knelt beside her grandmother's chair, taking both her hands in hers. Meredith's fingers gripped back tightly like an anxious child's.

"I want to talk to Rachel," she said. "There's something I need to tell her."

She seemed suddenly fully aware, as if a switch had been thrown inside her. Her eyes blazed with a furious life. It was as if she had grown younger by twenty years.

"Rachel isn't here, Gran," said Anita. "Her leave is finished. She'll be flying back to America next week. I told you this last night on the phone."

She felt full of a cold and desperate pity. She wondered if this was how her grandmother had felt when she had to explain to Anita that her mother was dead. In a small corner of her mind she envied Meredith for being able to exist in a world where Rachel was still retrievable, where the possibility existed of her imminent return. She felt tears start at the back of her eyes. She bowed her head, hoping that her grandmother was now beyond noticing such things. She had heard that a large part of the illness was self-absorption, an inability to process events in the outside world. But Meredith wrested a hand free and grabbed at her, tilting her face towards her as she had used to do when Anita was a child.

"You look sad," she said. "Has something bad happened to Rachel?"

Anita gazed up at her, thinking as she had often thought how strange it was they looked so little alike. Anita's mother had been blonde and robust, taking after the Dutch sea captain, Claes Sheener, who had been her father, and from what she could tell from the photographs Anita was exactly like her. Meredith Sheener was a small, Celtic-looking woman with fine bones and heavy-lidded deep-set eyes. Her hair, once black, had begun to go grey shortly after Melanie died.

Anita felt her heart crushed by tenderness for her. She had always shown such fortitude. Even now in her helplessness she was busy thinking of others.

"No, Gran. Rachel's fine. If there's anything you want to say to her just you tell me. I can pass your message along next time she phones."

Meredith's grip relaxed and the fierceness went out of her eyes.

"Not to worry, my darling. I wanted to tell her she's just like Melanie, but it doesn't matter now that she's gone." She caressed Anita's hair, looking suddenly tired. Anita stared at her blankly. She thought of Rachel's gangling limbs, her flat chest and copper hair and freckled face. Before the Kushnev drain was started Rachel had used to joke she was more than half-cockroach already. There was no way she could be compared with Melanie, who was as like Anita with her fair skin and apple cheeks as two panes of glass in a window frame. And yet she supposed after all that it was true. Rachel and Melanie were both courageous women of action, both prepared to die for what they believed in. Whereas Anita had always been content just to stand and watch.

Her mother hadn't loved her enough to stay on Earth for her and neither had Rachel. Anita began to weep.

"It's all my fault, Gran," she said. "I should have found a way to stop her but I didn't know how. I love her so much. It's almost worse than if she were dead."

If Rachel were dead she would in some sense be safe, safe to be remembered and loved. As it was she lived on as a monster, dedicated to a life where personal feeling was nothing when set against her vocation, the mysterious inner voice that told her that her place was not here, but elsewhere. Somewhere so far away that it was impossible for the normal mind to conceive it.

And yet in a hundred years from now, when Anita was dead and buried, would Rachel sometimes think of her, and remember the afternoon they had spent together on Shooter's Hill, the foxgloves bright as bunting in the overgrown grass?

She hugged her grandmother's knees and cried. She thought how furious the peroxide nurse would be if she came in and found her in such a state. She struggled to control her tears.

"I'm sorry, Gran," she said. "I didn't mean to upset you. I'm just tired."

Her grandmother was silent, her eyes fixed on some invisible horizon, her hands now lying still at her sides. Anita's heart lurched. For one impossible moment she wondered if her grandmother was dead, had died because of her crying, and for this too she would be to blame. Then at last her hands moved, rustling the stiff mauve silk of the skirt she was wearing. Anita got to her feet and stood over her anxiously. The dodo pendant swung free of her blouse. It hung in midair, twisting slowly at the end of its chain.

"Can I get you anything?" said Anita. "Would you like a cup of tea?"

Meredith Sheener looked up at her and smiled, creasing the delicate skin at the corners of her eyes. Then she reached out for the pendant, grabbing at it like a small child trying to catch a butterfly. She batted it with her fingers, making it dance and shudder, the closest it would ever get to natural flight.

"I blamed myself for years over Melanie," she said. "We had such a terrible row the day before she left. You were so tiny still, and I told her she was a fool and selfish, that she was neglecting you for the sake of her career. She said I was jealous, that I wanted to turn her into a housewife just like I was. None of that was true, but I was using you as an excuse, just the same. She did this strange thing, you see. She asked me to look after that pendant. She had never done anything like that before, and she never took off that chain. Her best friend in college gave it to her and she always wore it, even in the shower. I got it into my head that something terrible was going to happen. I couldn't bear the thought of losing her, you see." She took Anita's hand, squeezing her fingers with surprising strength. "I used to take photographs, too, a long time ago. There was a time when I thought I might make something of it, but what with Melanie being born and Claes leaving like that it was all so difficult, so complicated. I suppose I just let things slide. I was just beginning to think I might take it up again, pick up where I left off. But then Melanie died and it was as if the tide had gone out and left me stranded. Like walking along the beach at dusk, you know how it is here, when the tide is out and the sand is wet and shiny as a mirror. It's beautiful, the dusk, but it's the loneliest time of the day. I felt so lost, as if I'd never be able to find my way home again. I even felt some sympathy with them, you know, with the people who did it, the God people. The idea of space travel seemed so terrfiying, so dangerous, like straying into a house where bad things are. It felt all wrong to me, even though I was so proud of her I could hardly breathe."

She reached for the pendant again, holding it between finger and thumb. "Your friend Rachel was so beautiful. I think she is very brave to give all that up."

"She still is beautiful, Gran," said Anita. "At least she is to me." She sat down on the edge of the bed. Her eyes felt swollen from crying. "Come on," she said. "Let's go and see who's in the dining room." She stood up and put out her hand. Her grandmother stared at it in bewilderment, as if at some miraculous apparition. Anita wondered how much of their conversation she would remember. The new drugs showed amazing results, but the doctor had warned her not to be overoptimistic about the long-term prognosis.

"It's like blowing on dying embers," he said. "There's a glow, and a little warmth, but it doesn't last."

It struck her how unusual it was, his mode of expression, so rich in metaphor, almost like the speech of a poet. She thought of his tired eyes, his twisted fingers, of how kind he was really, especially when delivering bad news. How he seemed to take each failure to heart, as if he were personally responsible for medicine being so powerless against death.

I wonder if I could film him, she thought. *I wonder if he would let me, if I asked.*

The boxes were in the cupboard under the stairs, pushed right to the back behind the vacuum cleaner and her grandmother's old ironing board. There were three of them, two large ones stamped with the logo of a well-known food company and another, half the size, which was unmarked. She opened the small box first. She had only sketchy memories of packing the crates, of what had gone into each of them, but she saw almost at once that what the third box contained was mostly her mother's official papers—birth certificate, passport, medical—and nothing of immediate importance. The other two were more interesting. These contained photographs and postcards, letters from old boyfriends, a fudge tin full of pin badges and a pencil sharpener in the shape of the Apollo 13. At the bottom of the second crate there were three cloth-bound notebooks that contained Melanie's diary for her final year at Oxford and for the months leading up to her enrolment in the space program. Anita was surprised to learn she had gone in as a ground engineer. She supposed this was how she had met Malcolm Schleif, although there was no mention of him in these pages.

Tucked into the inside cover of one of the notebooks was a postcard, a colour reproduction of Roland Savery's *Dodo in a Landscape*. A single sentence, "don't forget your wings," was scrawled across the back in spiky black capitals. The card had been posted from Oxford, and was addressed to Melanie at the Shooter's Hill flat. It was signed "with all love from Susanne." Anita could see from the postmark that it had been sent less than a month before her mother's death.

She searched quickly through the bundles of letters, hoping to discover some clue to Susanne's identity. After five minutes or so she found what she was looking for, a brown jiffy bag containing several dozen handwritten letters and about the same number of email printouts, all from a Susanne Behrens, who wrote sometimes from Hamburg and sometimes from Oxford but always in tones of affection and intimacy.

For some reason Susanne's letters, with their bawdy in-jokes and cosy diminutives, made her mother more real to Anita than all her grandmother's reminiscences put together.

Her hands were filthy with dust. She wiped them against her jeans and went to put the kettle on. Just as the water boiled the phone rang. When she picked up the receiver she found herself speaking to Serge.

"I was just seeing if you were back yet," he said. "I couldn't get through on your mobile. I was starting to get a bit worried."

"My phone battery went flat," she said. "I forgot to take my charger. I only got back this morning." All three statements were lies. She had been back in London three days, and after the fourth successive call from Serge she had simply switched off her phone. For some reason she could not define Rachel's departure had changed everything. Also she could not forget the way he had sounded when she had last spoken to him, the sense that he had something to hide. She would have liked to put off their conversation indefinitely but she knew this was impossible. Sooner or later she would have to face up to what had happened.

She asked him how he was and he said he was fine. He asked after her grandmother and she mumbled back some stilted reply. There was a short, uncomfortable silence, and then he told her what she knew he had called about in the first place.

"Listen, Anita," he said. "I thought I should tell you I've started seeing someone. I didn't want you to hear it from someone else."

Her name was Bella Altman and she was a composer of electronic music. "You've probably heard some of her stuff, actually," he said. "She's done hundreds of commercials. Her work is all over the place." He laughed, a small, tight sound that she had never heard before. She realised he had been waiting to tell her ever since their last phone call, that perhaps he had wanted to tell her even then.

"Why are you telling me this?" she said. "Don't you think you should be telling Rachel instead?"

There was another uncomfortable silence. "Do you think she has to know?" he said finally. "She's hardly going to find out on her own."

He was asking her permission to treat Rachel as if she were dead. *No*, she thought suddenly. *He's trying to find out if you mean to tell her yourself.*

She felt an anger so deep and so cold she knew there was no way back from it, that if she and Serge ever met again it would be as strangers.

"I'm not going to rat on you, if that's what you're afraid of," she said. "What you do is none of my business. It's Rachel that I care about, not you."

She waited for a moment to see if he would say anything else and then she put down the phone. She topped up her coffee mug with boiling water and then went back to sorting Melanie's letters. She wondered what might be the best way of trying to trace Susanne Behrens.

Civilian flights to the States had become almost prohibitively expensive, but Clement Anderson had supported Anita's visa application, which had enabled her to claim back some of the cost in the form of a research grant.

A junior officer had met her at the airport and escorted her to a motel a short bus ride from the base. Then there were the inevitable protocols, two days of debriefing and form-filling. She had asked if she could film these processes but her request had been politely denied.

The flight crew of the Aurora 6 were now being kept in more or less permanent isolation. Each member was allowed one last visit prior to launch day, a final thirty minutes with a friend or family member from outside. Anita had been able to speak to Rachel several times on the telephone but she had always assumed the visit would go to Serge. The invitation came out of the blue.

Finally she was taken to a room that was bare of everything except a table and two chairs and in the corner a low sofa covered in a brown leatherette. There was a pane of smoked glass set into one wall that she guessed was a two-way mirror. At the end of some ten minutes' waiting the door opened and Rachel appeared. She was dressed in grey overalls, silk or some synthetic substitute. What remained of her hair was mostly hidden under a close-fitting cap that reminded Anita of the caps worn by surgeons in the operating theatre. The few strands of hair that were showing looked dry and brittle, almost like tufts of grass.

Her lips were the colour of beetroot. They looked stuck to her face more than part of it, fissured and clotted as scabs.

She closed the door behind her and stepped into the room. Her wrists, poking out from the loose sleeves of the overall, were skeletal, her fingernails thickened and black. Her eyes were hard and glazed, barely human. It was only in the delicate line of her jaw, the fine, high arch of her brow, that any traces of her beauty now remained.

Anita got up from the table and went towards her. She felt a dull ache beneath her breastbone, as if she were trying to hold her breath underwater.

"Is it all right to touch you?" she said.

"Of course it is," said Rachel. "Come here."

They embraced. Rachel's body felt like a bundle of glass tubes held together by strips of paper and pieces of string. She smelled like farm silage, or like the heaps of grass clippings on the compost heap at Southwater House. They sat down either side of the formica table. Anita touched Rachel's hand, thinking how from the other side of the two-way mirror they must look like two actors in some prison drama.

She's really going up, thought Anita. For the first time the sight of her friend brought not sorrow or anger, but awe.

They talked together in quiet voices. Rachel asked about Meredith, and Anita told her about her search for Susanne Behrens.

"I want to interview her for the film," said Anita. "From her letters it looks as if she knew my mother better than anyone."

"The film will be wonderful," said Rachel. "Your mother would have been so proud." Anita stroked the backs of her hands. As their half hour drew toward its close she unhooked the dodo pendant from around her neck and handed it to Rachel. The chain still carried the warmth of her own body.

"Take her with you, wherever you're going," she said. "It's what she wanted most in the world."

Rachel's diamond eyes seemed to shimmer. She closed her fingers around the silver, slowly, as if to touch anything that solid was now painful for her.

"I'll be taking you both," she said. Her voice was a dry whisper, like long grass moving gently in the wind. "I couldn't have done this without you."

It took Anita some time to track down a copy of *Voyage to the Sun*. So far as she could tell it had never been released on DVD, and when she finally located a video copy on some obscure fan site she was surprised at how much it cost to have it transferred to disc.

The print was by no means perfect, but for a VHS transfer it was more than acceptable. For Anita, *Voyage to the Sun* seemed to epitomise the epic style of film making that had reached its zenith towards the end of the twentieth century. It was a long film, almost three hours, replete with significant imagery and spectacular if rather dated special effects.

The film's main actors were Rowan Amherst as the ship's captain, Hilary Benson as the first mate, and Aurelie Pelling as Lilian Furness, the captain's fiancée, nominated for an Oscar in her role. Anita found all three of them impressive, although for her the star was undoubtedly the young Joshua Samuelson in the part of Linden Brooks the cabin boy. It was his first major role, and he played it brilliantly. The character of Brooks was ambiguous. He was intelligent but devious, brave but duplicitous, and Samuelson brought out these contradictions with insight and flair. Anita thought it significant and appropriate that the main focus of the film's closing sequence was not the half-starved captain or the mutinous first mate but the Machiavellian cabin boy.

Alone of everyone on board he seemed to thrive on the harsh conditions. His skin was scorched almost black and there was not a spare ounce of body fat on him, and yet his pale eyes burned with a pure light that was almost ecstatic in its intensity.

He flew hand over hand up the rigging to the crow's nest, skinny and agile as a monkey.

"*Land*," he screamed out. "*Land ho!*" His salt-clogged hair flamed red against an azure sky.

The images were pure Hollywood, but in the way of all great cinema they were inspiring and in their own way beautiful. Anita found she had no trouble in understanding how the child-Rachel, her young soul already on fire with romantic ideals, would have identified with these fictional pioneers. Linden Brooks the cabin boy, with his blaze of red hair and frenzied excitement at the sight of a new continent, might easily have been her twin brother.

She ejected the disc from the machine and replaced it carefully in its clear plastic case, knowing the film was a part of Rachel she could keep close to her forever. She thought of her friend, suspended in space, her inner processes as mysterious and miraculous now as those of a chrysalis, and distinctly felt a message pass between them.

CORY DOCTOROW

Cory Doctorow is the coeditor of the popular *Boing Boing* Web site (boingboing.net), a cofounder of the internet search-engine company Open-Cola, and until recently was the outreach coordinator for the Electronic Frontier Foundation (www.eff.org). In 2000, he won the John W. Campbell Award for the year's Best New Writer. His stories have appeared in *Asimov's Science Fiction, Gateways, Science Fiction Age, The Infinite Matrix, On Spec, Salon,* and elsewhere, and have been collected in *A Place So Foreign and Eight More* and *Overclocked.* His well-received first novel, *Down and Out in the Magic Kingdom,* won the Locus Award for Best First Novel; his other novels include *Eastern Standard Tribe; Someone Comes To Town, Someone Leaves Town;* the well-received YA novel *Little Brother;* and *Makers.* Doctorow's other books include *The Complete Idiot's Guide to Publishing Science Fiction,* written with Karl Schroeder; a guide to *Essential Blogging,* written with Shelley Powers; and *Content: Selected Essays on Technology, Creativity, Copyright, and the Future of the Future.* His most recent books are a new nonfiction book, *Ebooks,* and a new novel, *For the Win.* He has a Web site at craphound.com.

In the unsettling story that follows, from an anthology of stories written in tribute to Frederik Pohl, and one which does an excellent job of updating and commenting on some of the themes that informed Pohl and C. M. Kornbluth's classic novel *The Space Merchants,* Doctorow shows us a future where the rich keep getting richer, and intend to *stay* that way—no matter what.

T he first lesson Leon learned at the ad agency was: Nobody is your friend at the ad agency.

Take today: Brautigan was going to see an actual vat, at an actual clinic, which housed an actual target consumer, and he wasn't taking Leon.

"Don't sulk, it's unbecoming," Brautigan said, giving him one of those tight-lipped smiles where he barely got his mouth over those big, horsey, comical teeth of his. They were disarming, those pearly whites. "It's out of the question. Getting clearance to visit a vat in person, that's a one month, two month process. Background checks. Biometrics. Interviews with their psych staff. The physicals:

they have to take a census of your microbial nation. It takes time, Leon. You might be a mayfly in a mayfly hurry, but the man in the vat, he's got a lot of time on his hands. No skin off his dick if you get held up for a month or two."

"Bullshit," Leon said. "It's all a show. They've got a brick wall a hundred miles high around the front, and a sliding door around the back. There's always an exception in these protocols. There has to be."

"When you're 180 years old and confined to a vat, you don't make exceptions. Not if you want to go on to 181."

"You're telling me that if the old monster suddenly developed a rare, fast-moving liver cancer and there was only one oncologist in the whole goddamned world who could make it better, you're telling me that guy would be sent home to France or whatever—No thanks, we're OK, you don't have clearance to see the patient?"

"I'm telling you the monster *doesn't have a liver*. What that man has, he has *machines* and *nutrients* and *systems*."

"And if a machine breaks down?"

"The man who invented that machine works for the monster. He lives on the monster's private estate, with his family. *Their* microbial nations are identical to the monster's. He is not only the emperor of their lives, he is the emperor of the lives of their intestinal flora. If the machine that man invented stopped working, he would be standing by the vat in less than two minutes, with his staff, all in disposable, sterile bunny suits, murmuring reassuring noises as he calmly, expertly fitted one of the ten replacements he has standing by, the ten replacements he checks, *personally*, every single day, to make sure that they are working."

Leon opened his mouth, closed it. He couldn't help himself, he snorted a laugh. "Really?"

Brautigan nodded.

"And what if none of the machines worked?"

"If that man couldn't do it, then his rival, who *also* lives on the monster's estate, who has developed the second-most-exciting liver replacement technology in the history of the world, who burns to try it on the man in the vat—*that* man would be there in ten minutes, and the first man, and his family—"

"Executed?"

Brautigan made a disappointed noise. "Come on, he's a quadrillionaire, not a Bond villain. No, that man would be demoted to nearly nothing, but given one tiny chance to redeem himself: invent a technology better than the one that's currently running in place of the vat-man's liver, and you will be restored to your fine place with your fine clothes and your wealth and your privilege."

"And if he fails?"

Brautigan shrugged. "Then the man in the vat is out an unmeasurably minuscule fraction of his personal fortune. He takes the loss, applies for a research tax-credit for it, and deducts it from the pittance he deigns to send to the IRS every year."

"Shit."

Brautigan slapped his hands together. "It's wicked, isn't it? All that money and power and money and money?"

Leon tried to remember that Brautigan wasn't his friend. It was those teeth, they were so *disarming*. Who could be suspicious of a man who was so horsey you wanted to feed him sugar cubes? "It's something else."

"You now know about ten thousand times more about the people in the vats than your average cit. But you haven't even got the shadow of the picture yet, buddy. It took *decades* of relationship-building for Ate to sell its first product to a vat-person."

And we haven't sold anything else since, Leon thought, but he didn't say it. No one would say it at Ate. The agency pitched itself as a powerhouse, a success in a field full of successes. It was *the* go-to agency for servicing the "ultra-high-net-worth individual," and yet . . .

One sale.

"And we haven't sold anything since." Brautigan said it without a hint of shame. "And yet, this entire building, this entire agency, the salaries and the designers and the consultants: all of it paid for by clipping the toenails of that fortune. Which means that one *more* sale—"

He gestured around. The offices were sumptuous, designed to impress the functionaries of the fortunes in the vats. A trick of light and scent and wind made you feel as though you were in an ancient forest glade as soon as you came through the door, though no forest was in evidence. The reception desktop was a sheet of pitted tombstone granite, the unreadable smooth epitaph peeking around the edges of the old fashioned typewriter that had been cunningly reworked to serve as a slightly-less-old-fashioned keyboard. The receptionist—presently ignoring them with professional verisimilitude—conveyed beauty, intelligence, and motherly concern, all by means of dress, bearing and makeup. Ate employed a small team of stylists that worked on all public-facing employees; Leon had endured a just-so rumpling of his sandy hair and some carefully applied fraying at the cuffs and elbows of his jacket that morning.

"So no, Leon, buddy, I am *not* taking you down to meet my vat-person. But I *will* get you started on a path that may take you there, some day, if you're very good and prove yourself out here. Once you've paid your dues."

Leon had paid plenty of dues—more than this blow-dried turd ever did. But he smiled and snuffled it up like a good little worm, hating himself. "Hit me."

"Look, we've been pitching vat-products for six years now without a single hit. Plenty of people have come through that door and stepped into the job you've got now, and they've all thrown a million ideas in the air, and every one came smashing to earth. We've never systematically catalogued those ideas, never got them in any kind of grid that will let us see what kind of territory we've already explored, where the holes are . . ." He looked meaningfully at Leon.

"You want me to catalog every failed pitch in the agency's history." Leon didn't hide his disappointment. That was the kind of job you gave to an intern, not a junior account exec.

Brautigan clicked his horsey teeth together, gave a laugh like a whinny, and left Ate's offices, admitting a breath of the boring air that circulated out there in the real world. The receptionist radiated matronly care in his direction. He leaned her way and her fingers thunked on the mechanical keys of her converted Underwood Noiseless, a machinegun rattle. He waited until she was done, then she turned that caring, loving smile back on him.

"It's all in your workspace, Leon—good luck with it."

It seemed to Leon that the problems faced by immortal quadrillionaires in vats wouldn't be that different from those facing mere mortals. Once practically anything could be made for practically nothing, everything was practically worthless. No one needed to discover anymore—just *combine*, just *invent*. Then you could either hit a button and print it out on your desktop fab or down at the local depot for bigger jobs, or if you needed the kind of fabrication a printer couldn't handle, there were plenty of on-demand jobbers who'd have some worker in a distant country knock it out overnight and you'd have it in hermetic FedEx packaging on your desktop by the morning.

Looking through the Ate files, he could see that he wasn't the last one to follow this line of reasoning. Every account exec had come up with pitches that involved things that *couldn't* be fabbed—precious gewgaws that needed a trained master to produce—or things that *hadn't* been fabbed—antiques, one-of-a-kinds, fetish objects from history. And all of it had met with crashing indifference from the vat-people, who could hire any master they wanted, who could buy entire warehouses full of antiques.

The normal megarich got offered experiences: a ticket to space, a chance to hunt the last member of an endangered species, the opportunity to kill a man and get away with it, a deep-ocean sub to the bottom of the Marianas trench. The people in the vat had done plenty of those things before they'd ended up in the vats. Now they were metastatic, these hyperrich, lumps of curdling meat in the pickling solution of a hundred vast machines that laboriously kept them alive amid their cancer-blooms and myriad failures. Somewhere in that tangle of hoses and wires was something that was technically a person, and also technically a corporation, and, in many cases, technically a sovereign state.

Each concentration of wealth was an efficient machine, meshed in a million ways with the mortal economy. You interacted with the vats when you bought hamburgers, Internet connections, movies, music, books, electronics, games, transportation—the money left your hands and was sieved through their hoses and tubes, flushed back out into the world where other mortals would touch it.

But there was no easy way to touch the money at its most concentrated, purest form. It was like a theoretical superdense element from the first instant of the universe's creation, money so dense it stopped acting like money; money so dense it changed state when you chipped a piece of it off.

Leon's predecessors had been shrewd and clever. They had walked the length and breadth of the problem space of providing services and products to a person who was money who was a state who was a vat. Many of the nicer grace-notes in the office came from those failed pitches—the business with the lights and the air, for example.

Leon had a good education, the kind that came with the mathematics of multidimensional space. He kept throwing axes at his chart of the failed inventions of Ate, Inc., mapping out the many ways in which they were similar and dissimilar. The pattern that emerged was easy to understand.

They'd tried *everything*.

Brautigan's whinny was the most humiliating sound Leon had ever heard, in all his working life.

"No, of course you can't know what got sold to the vat-person! That was part of the deal—it was why the payoff was so large. *No one* knows what we sold to the vat-person. Not me, not the old woman. The man who sold it? He cashed out years ago, and hasn't been seen or heard from since. Silent partner, preferred shares, controlling interest—but he's the invisible man. We talk to him through lawyers who talk to lawyers who, it is rumored, communicate by means of notes left under a tombstone in a tiny cemetery on Pitcairn Island, and row in and out in longboats to get his instructions."

The hyperbole was grating on Leon. Third day on the job, and the sun-dappled, ozonated pseuodoforested environment felt as stale as an old gym bag (there was, in fact, an old gym bag under his desk, waiting for the day he finally pulled himself off the job in time to hit the complimentary gym). Brautigan was grating on him more than the hyperbole.

"I'm not an asshole, Brautigan, so stop treating me like one. You hired me to do a job, but all I'm getting from you is shitwork, sarcasm, and secrecy." The alliteration came out without his intending it to, but he was good at that sort of thing. "So here's what I want to know: is there any single solitary reason for me to come to work tomorrow, or should I just sit at home, drawing a salary until you get bored of having me on the payroll and can my ass?"

It wasn't entirely spontaneous. Leon's industrial psychology background was pretty good—he'd gotten straight A's and an offer of a post-doc, none of which had interested him nearly so much as the practical applications of the sweet science of persuasion. He understood that Brautigan had been pushing him around to see how far he'd push. No one pushed like an ad-guy—if you could sweet-talk someone into craving something, it followed that you could goad him into hating something just as much. Two faces of a coin and all that.

Brautigan faked anger, but Leon had spent three days studying his tells, and Leon could see that the emotion was no more sincere than anything else about the man. Carefully, Leon flared his nostrils, brought his chest up, inched his chin higher. He *sold* his outrage, sold it like it was potato chips, over-the-counter securities, or under-the-counter diet pills. Brautigan tried to sell his anger in return. Leon was a no-sale. Brautigan bought.

"There's a new one," he said, in a conspiratorial whisper.

"A new what?" Leon whispered. They were still chest to chest, quivering with angry body-language, but Leon let another part of his mind deal with that.

"A new monster," Brautigan said. "Gone to his vat at a mere 103. Youngest ever. Unplanned." He looked up, down, left, right. "An accident. Impossible accident. Impossible, but he had it, which means?"

"It was no accident," Leon said. "Police?" It was impossible not to fall into Brautigan's telegraphed speech-style. That was a persuasion thing, too, he knew. Once you talked like him, you'd sympathize with him. And vice-versa, of course. They were converging on a single identity. Bonding. It was intense, like make-up sex for co-workers.

"He's a sovereign three ways. An African republic, an island, one of those little Baltic countries. On the other side of the international vowel line. Mxlplx or something. They swung for him at the WTO, the UN—whole bodies of international trade law for this one. So no regular cops; this is diplomatic corps stuff. And, of course, he's not dead, so that makes it more complicated."

"How?"

"Dead people become corporations. They get managed by boards of directors who act predictably, if not rationally. Living people, they're *flamboyant*. Seismic. Unpredictable. But. On the other hand." He waggled his eyebrows.

"On the other hand, they buy things."

"Once in a very long while, they do."

Leon's life was all about discipline. He'd heard a weight-loss guru once explain that the key to maintaining a slim figure was to really "listen to your body" and only eat until it signaled that it was full. Leon had listened to his body. It wanted three entire pepperoni and mushroom pizzas every single day, plus a rather large cake. And malted milkshakes, the old fashioned kind you could make in your kitchen with an antique Hamilton Beech machine in avocado-colored plastic, served up in a tall red anodized aluminum cup. Leon's body was extremely verbose on what it wanted him to shovel into it.

So Leon ignored his body. He ignored his mind when it told him that what it wanted to do was fall asleep on the sofa with the video following his eyes around the room, one of those shows that followed your neural activity and tried to tune the drama to maximize your engrossment. Instead, he made his mind sit up in bed, absorbing many improving books from the mountain he'd printed out and stacked there.

Leon ignored his limbic system when it told him to stay in bed for an extra hour every morning when his alarm detonated. He ignored the fatigue messages he got while he worked through an hour of yoga and meditation before breakfast.

He wound himself up tight with will and it was will that made him stoop to pick up the laundry on the stairs while he was headed up and fold it neatly away when he got to the spacious walk-in dressing room attached to the master bedroom (the apartment had been a good way to absorb his Ate signing bonus—safer than keeping the money in cash, with the currency fluctuations and all. Manhattan real estate was a century-long good buy and was more stable than bonds, derivatives or funds). It was discipline that made him pay every bill as it came in. It was all that which made him wash every dish when he was done with it and assiduously stop at the grocer's every night on the way home to buy anything that had run out the previous day.

His parents came to visit from Anguilla and they teased him about how *organized* he was, so unlike the fat little boy who'd been awarded the "Hansel and Gretel prize" by his sixth grade teacher for leaving a trail behind him everywhere he went.

What they didn't know was that he was still that kid, and every act of conscientious, precise, buttoned-down finicky habit was, in fact, the product of relentless, iron determination not to be that kid again. He not only ignored that inner voice of his that called out for pizzas and told him to sleep in, take a cab instead of walking, lie down and let the video soar and dip with his moods, a drip-feed of null and nothing to while away the hours—he actively denied it, shouted it into submission, locked it up and never let it free.

And that—*that*—that was why he was going to figure out how to sell something new to the man in the vat: because anyone who could amass that sort of fortune and go down to life eternal in an ever-expanding kingdom of machines would be the sort of person who had spent a life denying himself, and Leon knew *just* what that felt like.

The Lower East Side had ebbed and flowed over the years: poor, rich, middle-class, super-rich, poor. One year the buildings were funky and reminiscent of the romantic squalor that had preceded this era of lightspeed buckchasing. The next year, the buildings were merely squalorous, the landlords busted and the receivers in bankruptcy slapping up paper-thin walls to convert giant airy lofts into rooming houses. The corner stores sold blunt-skins to trustafarian hipsters with a bag of something gengineered to disrupt some extremely specific brain structures; then they sold food-stamp milk to desperate mothers who wouldn't meet their eyes. The shopkeepers had the knack of sensing changes in the wind and adjusting their stock accordingly.

Walking around his neighborhood, Leon sniffed change in the wind. The shopkeepers seemed to have more discount, high-calorie wino-drink; less designer low-carb energy food with FDA-mandated booklets explaining their nutritional claims. A sprinkling of FOR RENT signs. A construction site that hadn't had anyone working on it for a week now, the padlocked foreman's shed growing a mossy coat of graffiti.

Leon didn't mind. He'd lived rough—not just student-rough, either. His parents had gone to Anguilla from Romania, chasing the tax-haven set, dreaming of making a killing working as bookkeepers, security guards. They'd mistimed the trip, arrived in the middle of an econopocalytpic collapse and ended up living in a vertical slum that had once been a luxury hotel. The sole Romanians among the smuggled Mexicans who were de-facto slaves, they'd traded their ability to write desperate letters to the Mexican consulate for Spanish lessons for Leon. The Mexicans dwindled away—the advantage of de-facto slaves over de-jure slaves is that you can just send the de-facto slaves away when the economy tanked, taking their feed and care off your books—until it was just them there, and without the safety of the crowd, they'd been spotted by local authorities and had to go underground. Going back to Bucharest was out of the question—the airfare was as far out of reach as one of the private jets the tax-evaders and high-rolling gamblers flew in and out of Wallblake Airport.

From rough to rougher. Leon's family spent three years underground, living as roadside hawkers, letting the sun bake them to an ethnically indeterminate brown. A decade later, when his father had successfully built up his little bookkeeping business and his mother was running a smart dress-shop for the cruise-ship day-trippers, those days seemed like a dream. But once he left for stateside university and found himself amid the soft, rich children of the fortunes his father had tabulated, it all came back to him, and he wondered if any of these children in carefully disheveled rags would ever be able to pick through the garbage for their meals.

The rough edge on the LES put him at his ease, made him feel like he was still ahead of the game, in possession of something his neighbors could never have—the ability to move fluidly between the worlds of the rich and the poor.

Somewhere in those worlds, he was sure, was the secret to chipping a crumb off one of the great fortunes of the world.

"Visitor for you," Carmela said. Carmela, that was the receptionist's name. She was Puerto Rican, but so many generations in that he spoke better Spanish than she did. "I put her in the Living Room." That was one of the three board rooms in at Ate; the name a bad pun, every stick of furniture in it an elaborate topiary sculpture of living wood and shrubbery. It was surprisingly comfortable, and the very subtle breeze had an even more subtle breath of honeysuckle that was so real he suspected it was piped in from a nursery on another level. That's how he would have done it: the best fake was no fake at all.

"Who?" He liked Carmela. She was all business, but her business was compassion, a shoulder to cry on and an absolutely discreet gossip repository for the whole firm.

"Envoy," she said. "Name's Buhle. I ran his face and name against our dossiers and came up with practically nothing. He's from Montenegro, originally, I have that much."

"Envoy from whom?"

She didn't answer, just looked very meaningfully at him.

The new vat-person had sent him an envoy. His heart began to thump and his cuffs suddenly felt tight at his wrists. "Thanks, Carmela." He shot his cuffs.

"You look fine," she said. "I've got the kitchen on standby, and the intercom's listening for my voice. Just let me know what I can do for you."

He gave her a weak smile. This was why she was the center of the whole business, the soul of Ate. *Thank you*, he mouthed, and she ticked a smart salute off her temple with one finger.

The envoy was out of place in Ate, but she didn't hold it against them. This he knew within seconds of setting foot into the Living Room. She got up, wiped her hands on her sensible jeans, brushed some iron-grey hair off her face, and smiled at him, an expression that seemed to say, "Well, this is a funny thing, the two of us, meeting here, like this." He'd put her age at around 40, and she was hippy and a little wrinkled and didn't seem to care at all.

"You must be Leon," she said, and took his hand. Short fingernails, warm, dry, palm, firm handshake. "I *love* this room!" She waved her arm around in an all-encompassing circle. "Fantastic."

He found himself half in love with her and he hadn't said a word. "It's nice to meet you, Ms—"

"Ria," she said. "Call me Ria." She sat down on one of the topiary chairs, kicking off her comfortable hush puppies and pulling her legs up to sit cross-legged.

"I've never gone barefoot in this room," he said, looking at her calloused feet—feet that did a lot of barefooting.

"Do it," she said, making scooting gestures. "I insist. Do it!"

He kicked off the handmade shoes—designed by an architect who'd given up on literary criticism to pursue cobblery—and used his toes to peel off his socks.

Under his feet, the ground was—warm? cool?—it was *perfect*. He couldn't pin down the texture, but it made every nerve ending on the sensitive soles of his feet tingle pleasantly.

"I'm thinking something that goes straight into the nerves," she said. "It has to be. Extraordinary."

"You know your way around this place better than I do," he said.

She shrugged. "This room was clearly designed to impress. It would be stupid to be so cool-obsessed that I failed to let it impress me. I'm impressed. Also," she dropped her voice, "also, I'm wondering if anyone's ever snuck in here and screwed on that stuff." She looked seriously at him and he tried to keep a straight face, but the chuckle wouldn't stay put in his chest, and it broke loose, and a laugh followed it, and she whooped and they both laughed, hard, until their stomachs hurt.

He moved toward another topiary easy-chair, then stopped, bent down, and sat on the mossy floor, letting it brush against his feet, his ankles, the palms of his hands and his wrists. "If no one ever has, it's a damned shame," he said, with mock gravity. She smiled, and she had dimples and wrinkles and crowsfeet, so her whole face smiled. "Do you want something to eat? Drink? We can get pretty much anything here—"

"Let's get to it," she said. "I don't want to be rude, but the good part isn't the food. I get all the food I need. I'm here for something else. The good part, Leon."

He drew in a deep breath. "The good part," he said. "OK, let's get to it. I want to meet your—" What? Employer? Patron? Owner? He waved his hand.

"You can call him Buhle," she said. "That's the name of the parent company, anyway. Of course you do. We have an entire corporate intelligence arm that knew you'd want to meet with Buhle before you did." Leon had always assumed that his workspaces and communications were monitored by his employer, but now it occurred to him that any system designed from the ground up to subject its users to scrutiny without their knowledge would be a bonanza for anyone *else* who wanted to sniff them, since they could use the system's own capabilities to hide their snooping from the victims.

"That's impressive," he said. "Do you monitor everyone who might want to pitch something to Buhle, or—" He let the thought hang out there.

"Oh, a little of this and a little of that. We've got a competitive intelligence subdepartment that monitors everyone who might want to sell us something or sell something that might compete with us. It comes out to a pretty wide net. Add to that the people who might personally be a threat or opportunity for Buhle and you've got, well, let's say an appreciable slice of human activity under close observation."

"How close can it be? Sounds like you've got some big haystacks."

"We're good at finding the needles," she said. "But we're always looking for new ways to find them. That's something you could sell us, you know."

He shrugged. "If we had a better way of finding relevance in mountains of data, we'd be using it ourselves to figure out what to sell you."

"Good point. Let's turn this around. Why should Buhle meet with you?"

He was ready for this one. "We have a track-record of designing products that suit people in his . . ." Talking about the vat-born lent itself to elliptical statements. Maybe that's why Brautigan had developed that annoying telegraph-talk.

"You've designed one such product," she said.

"That's one more than almost anyone else can claim." There were two other firms like Ate. He thought of them in his head as Sefen and Nein, as though invoking their real names might cause them to appear. "I'm new here, but I'm not alone. We're tied in with some of the finest designers, engineers, research scientists . . ." Again with the ellipsis. "You wanted to get to the good part. This isn't the good part, Ria. You've got smart people. We've got smart people. What we have, what you don't have, is smart people who are impedance-mismatched to your organization. Every organization has quirks that make it unsuited to working with some good people and good ideas. You've got your no-go areas, just like anyone else. We're good at mining that space, the no-go space, the mote in your eye, for things that you need."

She nodded and slapped her hands together like someone about to start a carpentry project. "That's a great spiel," she said.

He felt a little blush creep into his cheeks. "I think about this a lot, rehearse it in my head."

"That's good," she said. "Shows you're in the right line of business. Are you a Daffy Duck man?"

He cocked his head. "More of a Bugs man," he said, finally, wondering where this was going.

"Go download a cartoon called 'The Stupor Salesman,' and get back to me, OK?"

She stood up, wriggling her toes on the mossy surface and then stepping back into her shoes. He scrambled to his feet, wiping his palms on his legs. She must have seen the expression on his face because she made all those dimples and wrinkles and crowsfeet appear again and took his hand warmly. "You did very well," she said. "We'll talk again soon." She let go of his hand and knelt down to rub her hands over the floor. "In the meantime, you've got a pretty sweet gig, don't you?"

The Stupor Salesman turned out to feature Daffy Duck as a traveling salesman bent on selling something to a bank robber who is holed up in a suburban bungalow. Daffy produces a stream of ever-more-improbable wares, and is violently rebuffed with each attempt. Finally, one of his attempts manages to blow up the robber's hideout, just as Daffy is once again jiggling the doorknob. As the robber and Daffy fly through the air, Daffy brandishes the doorknob at him and shouts, "Hey, bub, I know just what you need! You need a house to go with this doorknob!"

The first time he watched it, Leon snorted at the punchline, but on subsequent viewings, he found himself less and less amused. Yes, he was indeed trying to come up with a need that this Buhle didn't know he had—he was assuming Buhle was a he, but no one was sure—and then fill it. From Buhle's perspective, life would be just fine if Leon gave up and never bothered him again.

And yet Ria had been so *nice*—so understanding and gentle, he thought there must be something else to this. And she had made a point of telling him that he had a "sweet gig" and he had to admit that it was true. He was contracted for five years with Ate, and would get a hefty bonus if they canned him before then.

If he managed to score a sale to Buhle or one of the others, he'd be indescribably wealthy. In the meantime, Ate took care of his every need.

But it was so *empty* there—that's what got him. There were a hundred people on Ate's production team, bright sorts like him, and most of them only used the office to park a few knick-knacks and impress out-of-town relatives. Ate hired the best, charged them with the impossible and turned them loose. They got lost.

Carmela knew them all, of course. She was Ate's den-mother.

"We should all get together," he said. "Maybe a weekly staff meeting?"

"Oh, they tried that," she said, sipping from the triple-filtered water that was always at her elbow. "No one had much to say. The collaboration spaces update themselves with all the interesting leads from everyone's research, and the suggestion engine is pretty good at making sure you get an overview of anything relevant to your work going on." She shrugged. "This place is a show-room, more than anything else. I always figured you had to give creative people room to be creative."

He mulled this over. "How long do you figure they'll keep this place open if it doesn't sell anything to one of the vat people?"

"I try not to think about that too much," she said lightly. "I figure either we don't find something, run out of time and shut—and there's nothing I can do about it; or we find something in time and stay open—and there's nothing I can do about it."

"That's depressing."

"I think of it as liberating. It's like that lady said, Leon, you've got a sweet gig. You can make anything you can imagine, and if you hit one out of the park, you'll attain orbit and never reenter the atmosphere."

"Do the other account execs come around for pep talks?"

"Everyone needs a little help now and then," she said.

Ria met him for lunch at a supper-club in the living room of an 11th floor apartment in a slightly run-down ex-doorman building in midtown. The cooks were a middle-aged couple, he was Thai, she was Hungarian, the food was eclectic, light, and spicy, blending paprika and chilis in a nose-watering cocktail.

There were only two other diners in the tiny room for the early seating. They were another couple, two young gay men, tourists from the Netherlands, wearing crease-proof sportsjackets and barely-there barefoot hiking shoes. They spoke excellent English, and chatted politely about the sights they'd seen so far in New York, before falling into Dutch and leaving Ria and Leon to concentrate on each other and the food, which emerged from the kitchen in a series of ever-more-wonderful courses.

Over fluffy, caramelized fried bananas and Thai iced coffee, Ria effusively praised the food to their hosts, then waited politely while Leon did the same. The hosts were genuinely delighted to have fed them so successfully, and were only too happy to talk about their recipes, their grown children, the other diners they'd entertained over the years.

Outside, standing on 34th street between Lex and Third, a cool summer evening breeze and purple summer twilight skies, Leon patted his stomach and closed his eyes and groaned.

"Ate too much, didn't you?" she said.

"It was like eating my mother's cooking—she just kept putting more on the plate. I couldn't help it."

"Did you enjoy it?"

He opened his eyes. "You're kidding, right? That was probably the most incredible meal I've eaten in my entire life. It was like a parallel dimension of good food."

She nodded vigorously and took his arm in a friendly, intimate gesture, led him toward Lexington. "You notice how time sort of stops when you're there? How the part of your brain that's going 'what next? what next?' goes quiet?"

"That's it! That's *exactly* it!" The buzz of the jetpacks on Lex grew louder as they neared the corner, like a thousand crickets in the sky.

"Hate those things," she said, glaring up at the joyriders zipping past, scarves and capes streaming out behind them. "A thousand crashes upon your souls." She spat, theatrically.

"You make them, though, don't you?"

She laughed. "You've been reading up on Buhle then?"

"Everything I can find." He'd bought small blocks of shares in all the public companies in which Buhle was a substantial owner, charging them to Ate's brokerage account, and then devoured their annual reports. There was lots more he could feel in the shadows: blind trusts holding more shares in still more companies. It was the standard corporate structure, a Flying Spaghetti Monster of interlocking directorships, offshore holdings, debt parking lots, and exotic matrioshke companies that seemed on the verge of devouring themselves.

"Oy," she said. "Poor boy. Those aren't meant to be parsed. They're like the bramble patch around the sleeping princess, there to ensnare foolhardy knights who wish to court the virgin in the tower. Yes, Buhle's the largest jetpack manufacturer in the world, through a layer or two of misdirection." She inspected the uptownbound horde, sculling the air with their fins and gloves, making course corrections and wibbles and wobbles that were sheer, joyful exhibitionism.

"He did it for me," she said. "Have you noticed that they've gotten better in the past couple years? Quieter? That was us. We put a lot of thought into the campaign; the chop-shops have been selling 'loud pipes save lives' since the motorcycle days, and every tiny-dick flyboy wanted to have a pack that was as loud as a bulldozer. It took a lot of market smarts to turn it around; we had a low-end model we were selling way below cost that was close to those loud-pipe machines in decibel count; it was ugly and junky and fell apart. Naturally, we sold it through a different arm of the company that had totally different livery, identity and everything. Then we started to cut into our margins on the high-end rides, and at the same time, we engineered them for a quieter and quieter run. We actually did some preproduction on a jetpack that was so quiet it actually *absorbed* noise, don't ask me to explain it, unless you've got a day or two to waste on the psychoacoustics.

"Every swish bourgeois was competing to see whose jetpack could run quieter, while the low-end was busily switching loyalty to our loud junkmobiles. The competition went out of business in a year, and then we dummied-up a bunch of consumer-protection lawsuits that 'forced'"—she drew air-quotes—"us to recall the loud ones, rebuild them with pipes so engineered and tuned you could use them for the woodwinds section. And here we are." She gestured at the buzzing, whooshing fliers overhead.

Leon tried to figure out if she was kidding, but she looked and sounded serious. "You're telling me that Buhle dropped, what, a billion?"

"About eight billion, in the end."

"Eight billion rupiah on a project to make the skies quieter?"

"All told," she said. "We could have done it other ways, some of them cheaper. We could have bought some laws, or bought out the competition and changed their product line, but that's very, you know, *blunt*. This was sweet. Everyone got what they wanted in the end: fast rides, quiet skies, safe, cheap vehicles. Win win win."

An old school flyer with a jetpack as loud as the inside of an ice-blender roared past, leaving thousands scowling in his wake.

"That guy is plenty dedicated," she said. "He'll be machining his own replacement parts for that thing. No one's making them anymore."

He tried a joke: "You're not going to send the Buhle ninjas to off him before he hits Union Square?"

She didn't smile. "We don't use assassination," she said. "That's what I'm trying to convey to you, Leon."

He crumbled. He'd blown it somehow, shown himself to be the boor he'd always feared he was.

"I'm sorry," he said. "I guess—look, it's all kind of hard to take in. The sums are staggering."

"They're meaningless," she said. "That's the point. The sums are just a convenient way of directing power. Power is what matters."

"I don't mean to offend you," he said carefully, "but that's a scary sounding thing to say."

"Now you're getting it," she said, and took his arm again. "Drinks?"

The limes for the daquiris came from the trees around them on the rooftop conservatory. The trees were healthy working beasts, and the barman expertly inspected several limes before deftly twisting off a basket's worth and retreating to his workbench to juice them over his blender.

"You have to be a member to drink here," Ria said, as they sat on the roof, watching the jetpacks scud past.

"I'm not surprised," he said. "It must be expensive."

"You can't buy your way in," she said. "You have to work it off. It's a co-op. I planted this whole row of trees." She waved her arm, sloshing a little daquiri on the odd turf their loungers rested on. "I planted the mint garden over there." It was a beautiful little patch, decorated with rocks and favored with a small stream that wended its way through them.

"Forgive me for saying this," he said, "but you must earn a lot of money. A *lot*, I'm thinking." She nodded, unembarrassed, even waggled her eyebrows a bit. "So you could, I don't know, you could probably build one of these on any of the buildings that Buhle owns in Manhattan. Just like this. Even keep a little staff on board. Give out memberships as perks for your senior management team."

"That's right," she said. "I could."

He drank his daquiri. "I'm supposed to figure out why you don't, right?"

She nodded. "Indeed." She drank. Her face suffused with pleasure. He took a moment to pay attention to the signals his tongue was transmitting to him. The drink was *incredible*. Even the glass was beautiful, thick, handblown, irregular. "Listen, Leon, I'll let you in on a secret. *I want you to succeed.* There's not much that surprises Buhle and even less that pleasantly surprises him. If you were to manage it . . ." She took another sip and looked intensely at him. He squirmed. Had he thought her matronly and sweet? She looked like she could lead a guerilla force. Like she could wrestle a mugger to the ground and kick the shit out of him.

"So a success for me would be a success for you?"

"You think I'm after money," she said. "You're still not getting it. Think about the jetpacks, Leon. Think about what that power means."

He meant to go home, but he didn't make it. His feet took him crosstown to the Ate offices, and he let himself in with his biometrics and his passphrase and watched the marvelous dappled lights go through their warm-up cycle and then bathe him with their wonderful, calming light. Then the breeze, and now it was a nighttime forest, mossier and heavier than in the day. Either someone had really gone balls-out on the product design, or there really was an indoor forest somewhere in the building growing under diurnal lights, there solely to supply soothing woodsy air to the agency's office. He decided that the forest was the more likely explanation.

He stood at Carmela's desk for a long time, then, gingerly, settled himself in her chair. It was plain and firm and well made, with just a little spring. Her funny little sculptural keyboard had keycaps that had worn smooth under her fingertips over the years, and there were shiny spots on the desk where her wrists had worn away the granite. He cradled his face in his palms, breathing in the nighttime forest air, and tried to make sense of the night.

The Living Room was nighttime dark, but it still felt glorious on his bare feet, and then, a moment later, on his bare chest and legs. He lay on his stomach in his underwear and tried to name the sensation on his nerve endings and decided that "anticipation" was the best word for it, the feeling you get just *beside* the skin that's being scratched on your back, the skin that's next in line for a good scratching. It was glorious.

How many people in the world would ever know what this felt like? Ate had licensed it out to a few select boutique hotels—he'd checked into it after talking with Ria the first time—but that was it. All told, there were less than 3,000 people in the world who'd ever felt this remarkable feeling. Out of eight billion. He tried to do the division in his head but kept losing the zeroes. It was a thousandth of a percent? A ten thousandth of a percent? No one on Anguilla would ever feel it: not the workers in the vertical slums, but also not the mere millionaires in the grand houses with their timeshare jets.

Something about that . . .

He wished he could talk to Ria some more. She scared him, but she also made him feel good. Like she was the guide he'd been searching for all his life. At this point, he would have settled for Brautigan. Anyone who could help him make sense of what felt like the biggest, scariest opportunity of his entire career.

He must have dozed, because the next thing he knew, the lights were flickering on and he was mostly naked, on the floor, staring up into Brautigan's face. He had a look of forced jollity, and he snapped his fingers a few times in front of Leon's face.

"Morning, sunshine!"

Leon looked for the ghostly clock that shimmered in the corner of each wall, a slightly darker patch of reactive paint that was just outside of conscious comprehension unless you really stared at it. 4:12 AM. He stifled a groan.

"What are you doing here?" he said, peering at Brautigan.

The man clacked his horsey teeth, assayed a chuckle. "Early bird. Worm."

Leon sat up, found his shirt, started buttoning it up. "Seriously, Brautigan."

"Seriously?" He sat down on the floor next to Leon, his big feet straight out ahead of him. His shoes had been designed by the same architect that did Leon's. Leon recognized the style. "Seriously." He scratched his chin. Suddenly, he slumped. "I'm shitting bricks, Leon. I am seriously shitting bricks."

"How did it go with your monster?"

Brautigan stared at the architect's shoes. There was an odd flare they did, just behind the toe, just on the way to the laces, that was really graceful. Leon thought it might be a standard distribution bell-curve. "My monster is . . ." He blew out air. "Uncooperative."

"Less cooperative than previously?"

Brautigan unlaced his shoes and peeled off his socks, scrunched his toes in the moss. His feet gave off a hot, trapped smell.

"What was he like on the other times you'd seen him?"

Brautigan tilted his head. "What do you mean?"

"He was uncooperative this time, what about the other times?"

Brautigan looked back down at his toes.

"You'd *never* seen him before this?"

"It was a risk," he said. "I thought I could convince him, face-to-face."

"But?"

"I bombed. It was—it was the—it was *everything*. The compound. The people. All of it. It was like a *city*, a *theme park*. They lived there, hundreds of them, and managed every tiny piece of his empire. Like Royal Urchins."

Leon puzzled over this. "Eunuchs?"

"Royal Eunuchs. They had this whole culture, and as I got closer and closer to him, I realized, shit, they could just *buy* Ate. They could destroy us. They could have us made illegal, put us all in jail. Or get me elected president. Anything."

"You were overawed."

"That's the right word. It wasn't a castle or anything, either. It was just a place, a well-built collection of buildings. In Westchester, you know? It had been a little town center once. They'd preserved everything good, built more on top of it. It all just . . . worked. You're still new here. Haven't noticed."

"What? That Ate is a disaster? I figured that out a long time ago. There's several dozen highly paid creative geniuses on the payroll here who haven't seen their desks in months. We could be a creative powerhouse. We're more like someone's vanity project."

"Brutal."

He wondered if he'd overstepped himself. Who cared?

"Brutal doesn't mean untrue. It's like, it's like the money that came into this place, it became autonomous, turned into a strategy for multiplying itself. A bad strategy. The money wants to sell something to a monster, but the money doesn't know what monsters want, so it's just, what, beating its brains out on the wall. One day, the money runs out and . . ."

"The money won't run out," Brautigan said. "Wrong. We'd have to spend at ten-ex what we're burning now to even approach the principal."

"OK," Leon said. "So it's immortal. That's better?"

Brautigan winced. "Look, it's not so crazy. There's an entire unserved market out there. No one's serving it. They're like, you know, like Communist countries. Planned economies. They need something, they just acquire the capacity. No market."

"Hey, bub, I know just what you need! You need a house to go with this door-knob!" To his own surprise, Leon discovered that he did a passable Daffy Duck. Brautigan blinked at him. Leon realized that the man was a little drunk. "Just something I heard the other day," he said. "I told the lady from my monster that we could provide the stuff that their corporate culture precluded. I was thinking of you know, how the samurai banned firearms. We can think and do the un-thinkable and undo-able."

"Good line." He flopped onto his back. An inch of pale belly peeked between the top of his three-quarter-length culottes and the lower hem of his smart wrap-around shirt. "The monster in the vat. Some skin, some meat. Tubes. Pinches of skin clamped between clear hard plastic squares, bathed in some kind of diag-nostic light. No eyes, no top of the head where the eyes should be. Just a smooth mask. Eyes everywhere else. Ceiling. Floor. Walls. I looked away, couldn't make contact with them, found I was looking at something wet. Liver. I think."

"Yeesh. That's immortality, huh?"

"I'm there, 'A pleasure to meet you, an honor,' talking to the liver. The eyes never blinked. The monster gave a speech. 'You're a low-capital, high-risk, high-payoff longshot Mr. Brautigan. I can keep dribbling sums to you so that you can go back to your wonder factory and try to come up with ways to surprise me. So there's no need to worry on that score.' And that was it. Couldn't think of any-thing to say. Didn't have time. Gone in a flash. Out the door. Limo. Nice babu to tell me how good it had been for the monster, how much he'd been looking for-ward to it." He struggled up onto his elbows. "How about you?"

Leon didn't want to talk about Ria with Brautigan. He shrugged. Brautigan got a mean, stung look on his face. "Don't be like that. Bro. Dude. Pal."

Leon shrugged again. Thing was, he *liked* Ria. Talking about her with Brauti-gan would be treating her like a . . . a *sales-target*. If he were talking with Car-mela, he's say, "I feel like she wants me to succeed. Like it would be a huge deal for everyone if I managed it. But I also feel like maybe she doesn't think I can." But to Brautigan, he merely shrugged, ignored the lizardy slit-eyed glare, stood, pulled on his pants, and went to his desk.

If you sat at your desk long enough at Ate, you'd eventually meet *everyone* who worked there. Carmela knew all, told all, and assured him that everyone touched base at least once a month. Some came in a couple times a week. They had plants on their desks and liked to personally see to their watering.

Leon took every single one of them to lunch. It wasn't easy—in one case, he had to ask Carmela to send an Ate chauffeur to pick up the man's kids from school (it was a half-day) and bring them to the sitter's, just to clear the schedule. But the lunches themselves went very well. It turned out that the people at Ate were, to a one, incredibly interesting. Oh, they were all monsters, narcissistic, tantrum-prone geniuses, but once you got past that, you found yourself talking to people who were, at bottom, damned smart, with a whole lot going on. He met the woman who designed the moss in the Living Room. She was younger than him, and had been catapulted from a mediocre academic adventure at the Cooper Union into more wealth and freedom than she knew what to do with. She had a whole rolodex of people who wanted to sublicense the stuff, and she spent her days toying with them, seeing if they had any cool ideas she could incorporate into her next pitch to one of the lucky few who had the ear of a monster.

Like Leon. That's why they all met with him. He'd unwittingly stepped into one of the agency's top spots, thanks to Ria, one of the power-broker seats that everyone else yearned to fill. The fact that he had no idea how he'd got there or what to do with it didn't surprise anyone. To a one, his colleagues at Ate regarded everything to do with the vat monsters as an absolute, unknowable crapshoot, as predictable as a meteor strike.

No wonder they all stayed away from the office.

Ria met him in a different pair of jeans, these ones worn and patched at the knees. She had on a loose, flowing silk shirt that was frayed around the seams, and had tied her hair back with a kerchief that had faded to a non-color that was like the ancient New York sidewalk outside Ate's office. He felt the calluses on her hand when they shook.

"You look like you're ready to do some gardening," he said.

"My shift at the club," she said. "I'll be trimming the lime trees and tending the mint patch and the cucumber frames all afternoon." She smiled and stopped him with a gesture. She bent down and plucked a blade of greenery from the untidy trail-edge. They were in Central Park, in one of the places where it felt like a primeval forest instead of an artful garden razed and built in the middle of the city. She uncapped her water bottle and poured water over the herb—it looked like a blade of grass—rubbing it between her forefinger and thumb to scrub at it. Then she tore it in two and handed him one piece, held the other to her nose, then ate it, nibbling and making her nose wrinkle like a rabbit's. He followed suit. Lemon, delicious, and tangy.

"Lemon grass," she said. "Terrible weed, of course. But doesn't it taste amazing?"

He nodded. The flavor lingered in his mouth.

"Especially when you consider what this is made of—smoggy rain, dog piss, choked up air, sunshine, and DNA. What a weird flavor to emerge from such a strange soup, don't you think?"

The thought made the flavor a little less delicious. He said so.

"I love the idea," she said. "Making great things from garbage."

"About the jetpacks," he said, for he'd been thinking.

"Yes?"

"Are you utopians of some kind? Making a better world?"

"By 'you,' you mean 'people who work for Buhle?'"

He shrugged.

"I'm a bit of a utopian, I'll admit. But that's not it. You know Henry Ford set up these work-camps in Brazil, 'Fordlandia,' and enforced a strict code of conduct on the rubber plantation workers? He outlawed the caprihina and replaced it with Tom Collinses, because they were more civilized."

"And you're saying Buhle wouldn't do that?"

She waggled her head from side to side, thinking it over. "Probably not. Maybe, if I asked." She covered her mouth as though she'd made an indiscreet admission.

"Are—were—you and he . . . ?"

She laughed. "Never. It's purely cerebral. Do you know where his money came from?"

He gave her a look.

"OK, of course you do. But if all you've read is the official history, you'll think he was just a finance guy who made some good bets. It's nothing like it. He played a game against the market, tinkered with the confidence of other traders by taking crazy positions, all bluff, except when they weren't. No one could out-smart him. He could convince you that you were about to miss out on the deal of the century, or that you'd already missed it, or that you were about to walk off onto easy street. Sometimes, he convinced you of something that was real. More often, it was pure bluff, which you'd only find out after you'd done some trade with him that left him with more money than you'd see in your whole life, and you facepalming and cursing yourself for a sucker. When he started doing it to national banks, put a run on the dollar, broke the Fed, well, that's when we all knew that he was someone who was *special*, someone who could create signals that went right to your hindbrain without any critical interpretation."

"Scary."

"Oh yes. Very. In another era they'd have burned him for a witch or made him the man who cut out your heart with the obsidian knife. But here's the thing: he could never, ever kid *me*. Not once."

"And you're alive to tell the tale?"

"Oh, he likes it. His reality distortion field, it screws with his internal land-scape. Makes it hard for him to figure out what he needs, what he wants, and what will make him miserable. I'm indispensable."

He had a sudden, terrible thought. He didn't say anything, but she must have seen it on his face.

"What is it? Tell me."

"How do I know that you're on the level about any of this? Maybe you're just jerking me around. Maybe it's all made up—the jetpacks, everything." He swal-lowed. "I'm sorry. I don't know where that came from, but it popped into my head—"

"It's a fair question. Here's one that'll blow your mind, though: how do you know that I'm not on the level, *and* jerking you around?"

They changed the subject soon after, with uneasy laughter. They ended up on a park bench near the family of dancing bears, whom they watched avidly.

"They seem so *happy*," he said. "That's what gets me about them. Like dancing was the secret passion of every bear, and these three are the first to figure out how to make a life of it."

She didn't say anything, but watched the three giants lumber in a graceful, unmistakably joyous kind of shuffle. The music—constantly mutated based on the intensity of the bears, a piece of software that sought tirelessly to please them—was jangly and pop-like, with a staccato one-two/onetwothreefourfive/one-two rhythm that let the bears do something like a drunken stagger that was as fun to watch as a box of puppies.

He felt the silence. "So happy," he said again. "That's the weird part. Not like seeing an elephant perform. You watch those old videos and they seem, you know, they seem—"

"Resigned," she said.

"Yeah. Not unhappy, but about as thrilled to be balancing on a ball as a horse might be to be hitched to a plough. But look at those bears!"

"Notice that no one else watches them for long?" she said.

He had noticed that. The benches were all empty around them.

"I think it's because they're so happy," she said. "It lays the trick bare." She showed teeth at the pun, then put them away. "What I mean is, you can see how it's possible to design a bear that experiences brain reward from rhythm, keep it well-fed, supply it with as many rockin' tunes as it can eat, and you get that happy family of dancing bears who'll peacefully co-exist alongside humans who're going to work, carrying their groceries, pushing their toddlers around in strollers, necking on benches—"

The bears were resting now, lolling on their backs, happy tongues sloppy in the corners of their mouths.

"We made them," she said. "It was against my advice, too. There's not much subtlety in it. As a piece of social commentary, it's a cartoon sledgehammer with an oversized head. But the artist had Buhle's ear, he'd been CEO of one of the portfolio companies and had been interested in genomic art as a sideline for his whole career. Buhle saw that funding this thing would probably spin off lots of interesting sublicenses, which it did. But just look at it."

He looked. "They're *so happy*," he said.

She looked too. "Bears shouldn't be that happy," she said.

Carmela greeted him sunnily as ever, but there was something odd.

"What is it?" he asked in Spanish. He made a habit of talking Spanish to her, because both of them were getting rusty, and also it was like a little shared secret between them.

She shook her head.

"Is everything all right?" Meaning, *Are we being shut down?* It could happen, might happen at any time, with no notice. That was something he—all of them—understood. The money that powered them was autonomous and unknowable, an alien force that was more emergent property than will.

She shook her head again. "It's not my place to say," she said. Which made him even more sure that they were all going down, for when had Carmela ever said anything about her *place*?

"Now you've got me worried," he said.

She cocked her head back toward the back office. He noticed that there were three coats hung on the beautiful, anachronistic coat-stand by the ancient temple door that divided reception from the rest of Ate.

He let himself in and walked down the glassed-in double-rows of offices, the cubicles in the middle, all with their characteristic spotless hush, like a restaurant dining room set up for the meals that people would come to later.

He looked in the Living Room, but there was no one there, so he began to check out the other conference rooms, which ran the gamut from super-conservative to utter madness. He found them in the Ceile, with its barn-board floors, its homey stone hearth, and the gimmicked sofas that looked like un-sprung old thrift-store numbers, but which sported adaptive genetic-algorithm-directed haptics that adjusted constantly to support you no matter how you flopped on them, so that you could play at being a little kid sprawled carelessly on the cushions no matter how old and cranky your bones were.

On the Ceile's sofa were Brautigan, Ria, and a woman he hadn't met before. She was somewhere between Brautigan and Ria's age, but with that made-up, pulled-tight appearance of someone who knew the world wouldn't take her as seriously if she let one crumb of weakness escape from any pore or wrinkle. He thought he knew who this must be, and she confirmed it when she spoke.

"Leon," she said. "I'm glad you're here." He knew that voice. It was the voice on the phone that had recruited him and brought him to New York and told him where to come for his first day on the job. It was the voice of Jennifer Torino, and she was technically his boss. "Carmela said that you often worked from here so I was hoping today would be one of the days you came by so we could chat."

"Jennifer," he said. She nodded. "Ria." She had a poker-face on, as unreadable as a slab of granite. She was wearing her customary denim and flowing cotton, but she'd kept her shoes on and her feet on the ground. "Brautigan," and Brautigan grinned like it was Christmas morning.

Jennifer looked flatly at a place just to one side of his gaze, a trick he knew, and said, "In recognition of his excellent work, Mr. Brautigan's been promoted, effective today. He is now Manager for Major Accounts." Brautigan beamed.

"Congratulations," Leon said, thinking, *What excellent work? No one at Ate has accomplished the agency's primary objective in the entire history of the firm!* "Well done."

Jennifer kept her eyes coolly fixed on that empty, safe spot. "As you know, we have struggled to close a deal with any of our major accounts." He restrained himself from rolling his eyes. "And so Mr. Brautigan has undertaken a thorough study of the way we handle these accounts." She nodded at Brautigan.

"It's a mess," he said. "Totally scattergun. No lines of authority. No checks and balances. No system."

"I can't argue with that," Leon said. He saw where this was going.

"Yes," Jennifer said. "You haven't been here very long, but I understand you've been looking deeply into the organizational structure of Ate yourself, haven't you?" He nodded. "And that's why Mr. Brautigan has asked that you be tasked to him as his head of strategic research." She smiled a thin smile. "Congratulations yourself."

He said, "Thanks," flatly, and looked at Brautigan. "What's strategic research, then?"

"Oh," Brautigan said. "Just a lot of what you've been doing: figuring out what everyone's up to, putting them together, proposing organizational structures that will make us more efficient at design and deployment. Stuff you're good at."

Leon swallowed and looked at Ria. There was nothing on her face. "I can't help but notice," he said, forcing his voice to its absolutely calmest, "that you haven't mentioned anything to do with the, uh, *clients.*"

Brautigan nodded and strained to pull his lips over his horsey teeth to hide his grin. It didn't work. "Yeah," he said. "That's about right. We need someone of your talents doing what he does best, and what you do best is—"

He held up a hand. Brautigan fell silent. The three of them looked at him. He realized, in a flash, that he had them all in his power, just at that second. He could shout BOO! and they'd all fall off their chairs. They were waiting to see if he'd blow his top or take it and ask for more. He did something else.

"Nice working with ya," he said. And he turned his back on the sweetest, softest job anyone could ask for. He said *adios* and *buen suerte* to Carmela on the way out, and he forced himself not to linger around the outside doors down at street level to see if anyone would come chasing after him.

The realtor looked at him like he was crazy. "You'll never get two million for that place in today's market," she said. She was young, no-nonsense, black, and she had grown up on the Lower East Side, a fact she mentioned prominently in her advertising materials: *A local realtor for a local neighborhood.*

"I paid two million for it less than a year ago," he said. The 80 percent mortgage had worried him a little but Ate had underwritten it, bringing the interest rate down to less than two percent.

She gestured at the large corner picture window that overlooked Broome Street and Grand Street. "Count the FOR SALE signs," she said. "I want to be on your side. That's a nice place. I'd like to see it go to someone like you, someone decent. Not some *developer*"—she spat the word like a curse—"or some corporate apartment broker who'll rent it by the week to VIPs. This neighborhood needs real people who really live here, understand."

"So you're saying I won't get what I paid for it?"

She smiled fondly at him. "No, sweetheart, you're not going to get what you paid for it. All those things they told you when you put two mil into that place, like 'They're not making any more Manhattan' and 'Location location location'? It's lies." Her face got serious, sympathetic. "It's supposed to panic you and make you lose your head and spend more than you think something is worth. That goes on for a while and then everyone ends up with too much mortgage for not enough home, or for too much home for that matter, and then blooie, the bottom blows out of the market and everything falls down like a souffle."

"You don't sugar-coat it, huh?" He'd come straight to her office from Ate's door, taking the subway rather than cabbing it or even renting a jetpack. He was on austerity measures, effective immediately. His brain seemed to have a pre-made list of cost-savers it had prepared behind his back, as though it knew this day would come.

She shrugged. "I can, if you want me to. We can hem and haw about the money and so on and I can hold your hand through the seven stages of grieving.

I do that a lot when the market goes soft. But you looked like the kind of guy who wants it straight. Should I start over? Or, you know, if you want, we can list you at two mil or even two point two, and I'll use that to prove that some *other* loft is a steal at one point nine. If you want."

"No," he said, and he felt some of the angry numbness ebb away. He liked this woman. She had read him perfectly. "So tell me what you think I can get for it?"

She put her fist under her chin and her eyes went far away. "I sold that apartment, um, eight years ago? Family who had it before you. Had a look when they sold it to you—they used a different broker, kind of place where they don't mind selling to a corporate placement specialist. I don't do that, which you know. But I saw it when it sold. Have you changed it much since?"

He squirmed. "I didn't, but I think the broker did. It came furnished, nice stuff."

She rolled her eyes eloquently. "It's never nice stuff. Even when it comes from the best showroom in town, it's not nice stuff. Nice is antithetical to corporate. Inoffensive is the best you can hope for." She looked up, to the right, back down. "I'm figuring out the discount for how the place will show now that they've taken all the seams and crumbs out. I'm thinking, um, one point eight. That's a number I think I can deliver."

"But I've only *got* 200K in the place," he said.

Her expressive brown eyes flicked at the picture window, the FOR SALE signs. "And? Sounds like you'll break even or maybe lose a little on the deal. Is that right?"

He nodded. Losing a little wasn't something he'd figured on. But by the time he'd paid all the fees and taxes—"I'll probably be down a point or two."

"Have you got it?"

He hated talking about money. That was one thing about Ria is that she never actually talked about money—what money *did*, sure, but never money. "Technically," he said.

"OK, technical money is as good as any other kind. So look at it this way: you bought a place, a really totally amazing place on the Lower East Side, a place bigger than five average New York apartments. You lived in it for, what?"

"Eight months."

"Most of a year. And it cost you one percent of the street price on the place. Rent would have been about eleven times that. You're up—" she calculated in her head—"it's about 83 percent."

He couldn't keep the look of misery off his face.

"What?" she said. "Why are you pulling faces at me? You said you didn't want it sugar-coated, right?"

"It's just that—" He dropped his voice, striving to keep any kind of whine out of it. "Well, I'd hoped to make something in the bargain."

"For what?" she said, softly.

"You know, appreciation. Property goes up."

"Did you do anything to the place that made it better?"

He shook his head.

"So you did no productive labor but you wanted to get paid anyway, right? Have you thought about what would happen to society if we rewarded people for owning things instead of doing things?"

"Are you sure you're a real estate broker?"

"Board certified. Do very well, too."

He swallowed. "I don't expect to make money for doing nothing, but you know, I just quit my job. I was just hoping to get a little cash in hand to help me smooth things out until I find a new one."

The realtor gave a small nod. "Tough times ahead. Winds are about to shift again. You need to adjust your expectations, Leon. The best you can hope for right now is to get out of that place before you have to make another mortgage payment."

His pulse throbbed in his jaw and his thigh in counterpoint. "But I *need* money to—"

"Leon," she said, with some steel in her voice. "You're *bargaining*. As in denial, anger, bargaining, depression and acceptance. That's healthy and all, but it's not going to get your place sold. Here's two options: one, you can go find another realtor, maybe one who'll sugar coat things or string you along to price up something else he's trying to sell. Two, you can let me get on with making some phone calls and I'll see who I can bring in. I keep a list of people I'd like to see in this 'hood, people who've asked me to look out for the right kind of place. That place you're in is one of a kind. I might be able to take it off your hands in very quick time, if you let me do my thing." She shuffled some papers. "Oh, there's a third, which is that you could go back to your apartment and pretend that nothing is wrong until that next mortgage payment comes out of your bank account. That would be *denial* and if you're bargaining, you should be two steps past that.

"What's it going to be?"

"I need to think about it."

"Good plan," she said. "Remember, depression comes after bargaining. Go buy a quart of ice-cream and download some weepy movies. Stay off booze, it only brings you down. Sleep on it, come back in the morning if you'd like."

He thanked her numbly and stepped out into the Lower East Side. The bodega turned out to have an amazing selection of ice-cream, so he bought the one with the most elaborated name, full of chunks, swirls and stir-ins, and brought it up to his apartment, which was so big that it made his knees tremble when he unlocked his door. The realtor had been right. Depression was next.

Buhle sent him an invitation a month later. It came laser-etched into a piece of ancient leather, delivered by a messenger whose jetpack was so quiet that he didn't even notice that she had gone until he looked up from the scroll to thank her. His new apartment was a perch he rented by the week at five times what an annual lease would have cost him, but still a fraction of what he had been paying on the LES. It was jammed with boxes of things he hadn't been able to bring himself to get rid of, and now he cursed every knick-knack as he dug through them looking for a good suit.

He gave up. The invitation said, "At your earliest convenience," and a quadrillionaire in a vat wasn't going to be impressed by his year-old designer job-interview suit.

It had been a month, and no one had come calling. None of his queries to product design, marketing, R&D, or advertising shops had been answered. He tried walking in the park every day, to see the bears, on the grounds that it was free and it would stimulate his creative flow. Then he noticed that every time he left his door, fistfuls of money seemed to evaporate from his pockets on little "necessities" that added up to real money. The frugality center of his brain began to flood him with anxiety every time he considered leaving the place and so it had been days since he'd gone out.

Now he was going. There were some clean clothes in one of the boxes, just sloppy jeans and tees, but they'd been expensive sloppy once upon a time, and they were better than the shorts and shirts he'd been rotating in and out of the tiny washing machine every couple days, when the thought occurred to him. The $200 haircut he'd had on his last day of work had gone shaggy and lost all its clever style, so he just combed it as best as he could after a quick shower and put on his architect's shoes, shining them on the backs of his pants legs on his way out the door in a gesture that reminded him of his father going to work in Anguilla, a pathetic gesture of respectability from someone who had none. The realization made him *oof* out a breath like he'd been gut-punched.

His frugality gland fired like crazy as he hailed a taxi and directed it to the helipad at Grand Central Terminus. It flooded him with so much cheapamine that he had to actually pinch his arms a couple times to distract himself from the full-body panic at the thought of spending so much. But Buhle was all the way in Rhode Island, and Leon didn't fancy keeping him waiting. He knew that to talk to money you had to act like money—impedance-match the money. Money wouldn't wait while he took the train or caught the subway.

He booked the chopper-cab from the cab, using the terminal in the backseat. At Ate, he'd had Carmela to do this kind of organizing for him. He'd had Carmela to do a hundred other things, too. In that ancient, lost time, he'd had money and help beyond his wildest dreams, and most days he couldn't imagine what had tempted him into giving it up.

The chopper clawed the air and lifted him up over Manhattan, the canyons of steel stretched out below him like a model. The racket of the chopper obliterated any possibility of speech, so he could ignore the pilot and she could ignore him with a cordiality that let him pretend, for a moment, that he was a powerful executive who nonchalantly choppered around over the country. They hugged the coastline and the stately rows of windmills and bobbing float-homes, surfers carving the waves, bulldozed strips topped with levees that shot up from the ground like the burial mound of some giant serpent.

Leon's earmuffs made all the sound—the sea, the chopper—into a uniform hiss, and in that hiss, his thoughts and fears seemed to recede for a moment, as though they couldn't make themselves heard over the white noise. For the first time since he'd walked out of Ate, the nagging, doubtful voices fell still and Leon was alone in his head. It was as though he'd had a great pin stuck through his chest that had been finally removed. There was a feeling of lightness, and tears pricking at his eyes, and a feeling of wonderful *obliteration*, as he stopped, just for a moment, stopped trying to figure out where he fit in the world.

The chopper touched down on a helipad at Newport State Airport, to one side of the huge X slashed into the heavy woods—new forest, fast-growing carbon sinkers garlanded with extravagances of moss and vine. From the moment the doors opened, the heavy earthy smell filled his nose and he thought of the Living

Room, which led him to think of Ria. He thanked the pilot and zapped her a tip and looked up and there was Ria, as though his thoughts had summoned her.

She had a little half-smile on her face, uncertain and somehow childlike, a little girl waiting to find out if he'd be her friend still. He smiled at her, grateful for the clatter of the chopper so that they couldn't speak. She shook his hand, hers warm and dry, and then, on impulse, he gave her a hug. She was soft and firm too, a middle-aged woman who kept fit but didn't obsess about the pounds. It was the first time he'd touched another human since he left Ate. And, as with the chopper's din, this revelation didn't open him to fresh miseries—rather, it put the miseries away, so that he felt *better*.

"Are you ready?" she said, once the chopper had lifted off.

"One thing," he said. "Is there a town here? I thought I saw one while we were landing."

"A little one," she said. "Used to be bigger, but we like them small."

"Does it have a hardware store?"

She gave him a significant look. "What for? An axe? A nailgun? Going to do some improvements?"

"Thought I'd bring along a door-knob," he said.

She dissolved into giggles. "Oh, he'll *like* that. Yes, we can find a hardware store."

Buhle's security people subjected the doorknob to millimeter radar and a gas cromatograph before letting it past. He was shown into an anteroom by Ria, who talked to him through the whole procedure, just light chatter about the weather and his real-estate problems, but she gently steered him around the room, changing their angle several times, and then he said, "Am I being scanned?"

"Millimeter radar in here too," she said. "Whole body imaging. Don't worry, I get it every time I come in. Par for the course."

He shrugged. "This is the least offensive security scan I've ever been through," he said.

"It's the room," she said. "The dimensions, the color. Mostly the semiotics of a security scan are either *you are a germ on a slide* or *you are not worth trifling with, but if we must, we must.* We went for something a little . . . sweeter." And it was, a sweet little room, like the private study of a single mom who's stolen a corner in which to work on her secret novel.

Beyond the room—a wonderful place.

"It's like a college campus," he said.

"Oh, I think we use a better class of materials than most colleges," Ria said, airily, but he could tell he'd pleased her. "But yes, there's about 15,000 of us here. A little city. Nice cafes, gyms, cinemas. A couple artists in residence, a nice little Waldorf school . . ." The pathways were tidy and wended their way through buildings ranging from cottages to large, institutional buildings, but all with the feel of endowed research institutes rather than finance towers. The people were young and old, casually dressed, walking in pairs and groups, mostly, deep in conversation.

"15,000?"

"That's the head office. Most of them are doing medical stuff here. We've got lots of other holdings, all around the world, in places that are different from this. But we're bringing them all in line with HQ, fast as we can. It's a good way to work. Churn is incredibly low. We actually have to put people back out into the world for a year every decade, just so they can see what it's like."

"Is that what you're doing?"

She socked him in the arm. "You think I could be happy here? No, I've always lived off campus. I commute. I'm not a team person. It's OK, this is the kind of place where even lone guns can find their way to glory."

They were walking on the grass now, and he saw that the trees, strangely over-sized red maples without any of the whippy slenderness he associated with the species, had a walkway suspended from their branches, a real Swiss Family Robinson job with rope-railings and little platforms with baskets on pulleys for ascending and descending. The people who scurried by overhead greeted each other volubly and laughed at the awkwardness of squeezing past each other in opposite directions.

"Does that ever get old?" he said, lifting his eyebrows to the walkways.

"Not for a certain kind of person," she said. "For a certain kind of person, the delightfulness of those walkways never wears off." The way she said "certain kind of person" made him remember her saying, "bears shouldn't be that happy."

He pointed to a bench, a long twig-chair, really, made from birch branches and rope and wire all twined together. "Can we sit for a moment? I mean, will Buhle mind?"

She flicked her fingers. "Buhle's schedule is his own. If we're five minutes late, someone will put five minutes' worth of interesting and useful injecta into his in-box. Don't you worry." She sat on the bench, which looked too fragile and fey to take a grown person's weight, but then she patted the seat next to him, and he when he sat, he felt almost no give. The bench had been very well built, by some-one who knew what she or he was doing.

"OK, so what's going on, Ria? First you went along with Brautigan scooping my job and exiling me to Siberia—" he held up a hand to stop her from speaking and discovered that the hand was shaking and so was his chest, shaking with a bottled-up anger he hadn't dared admit. "You could have stopped it at a word. You envoys from the vat-gods, you are the absolute monarchs at Ate. You could have told them to have Brautigan skinned, tanned, and made into a pair of boots, and he'd have measured your foot-size himself. But you let them do it."

"And now, here I am, a minister without portfolio, about to do something that would make Brautigan explode with delight, about to meet one of the Great Old Ones, in his very vat, in person. A man who might live to be a thousand, if all goes according to plan, a man who is a *country*, sovereign and inviolate. And I just want to ask you, *why*? Why all the secrecy and obliqueness and funny gaps? Why?"

Ria waited while a pack of grad students scampered by overhead, deep in dis-cussion of telomeres, the racket of their talk and their bare feet slapping on the walkway loud enough to serve as a pretence for silence. Leon's pulse thudded and his armpits slicked themselves as he realized that he might have just popped the bubble of unreality between them, the consensual illusion that all was nor-mal, whatever normal was.

"Oh, Leon," she said. "I'm sorry. Habit here—there's some things that can't be readily said in utopia. Eventually, you just get in the habit of speaking out of the back of your head. It's, you know, *rude* to ruin peoples' gardens by pointing out the snakes. So, yes, OK, I'll say something right out. I like you, Leon. The average employee at a place like Ate is a bottomless well of desires, trying to figure out what others might desire. We've been hearing from them for decades now, the resourceful ones, the important ones, the ones who could get past the filters and the filters behind the filters. We know what they're like.

"Your work was different. As soon as you were hired by Ate, we generated a dossier on you. Saw your grad work."

Leon swallowed. His resume emphasized his grades, not his final projects. He didn't speak of them at all.

"So we thought, well, here's something different, it's possible he may have a house to go with our doorknob. But we knew what would happen if you were left to your own devices at a place like Ate: they'd bend you and shape you and make you over or ruin you. We do it ourselves, all too often. Bring in a promising young thing, subject him to the dreaded Buhle Culture, a culture he's totally unsuited to, and he either runs screaming or . . . *fits in*. It's worse when the latter happens. So we made sure that you had a good fairy perched on your right shoulder to counterbalance the devil on your left shoulder." She stopped, made a face, mock slapped herself upside the head. "Talking in euphemism again. Bad habit. You see what I mean."

"And you let me get pushed aside . . ."

She looked solemn. "We figured you wouldn't last long as a button-polisher. Figured you'd want out."

"And that you'd be able to hire me."

"Oh, we could have hired you any time. We could have bought Ate. Ate would have given you to us—remember all that business about making Brautigan into a pair of boots? It applies all around."

"So you wanted me to . . . what? Walk in the wilderness first?"

"Now you're talking in euphemisms. It's catching! Let's walk."

They gave him a bunny-suit to wear into the heart of Buhle. First he passed through a pair of double-doors, faintly positively pressurized, sterile air that ruffled his hair on the way in. The building was low-slung, nondescript brown brick, no windows. It could have been a water sterilization plant or a dry-goods warehouse. The inside was good tile, warm colors with lots of reds and browns down low, making the walls look like they were the inside of a kiln. The building's interior was hushed, and a pair of alert-looking plainclothes security men watched them very closely as they changed into the bunny-suits, loose micropore coveralls with plastic visors. Each one had a small, self-contained air-circ system powered by a wrist canister, and when a security man helpfully twisted the valve open, Leon noted that there were clever jets that managed to defog the visor without drying out his eyeballs.

"That be enough for you, Ria?" the taller of the two security men said. He was dressed like a college kid who'd been invited to his girlfriend's place for dinner: smart slacks a little frayed at the cuffs, a short-sleeved, pressed cotton shirt that showed the bulge of his substantial chest and biceps and neck.

She looked at her canister, holding it up to the visor. "30 minutes is fine," she said. "I doubt he'll have any more time than that for us!" Turning to Leon, she said, "I think that the whole air-supply thing is way overblown. But it does keep meetings from going long."

"Where does the exhaust go?" Leon said, twisting in his suit. "I mean, surely the point is to keep my cooties away from," he swallowed, "*Buhle*." It was the first time he'd really used the word to describe a person, rather than a *concept*, and he was filled with the knowledge that the person it described was somewhere very close.

"Here," she said, and pointed to a small bubble growing out of the back of her neck. "You swell up, one little bladder at a time, until you look like the Michelin man. Some joke." She made a face. "You can get a permanent suit if you come here often. Much less awkward. But Buhle likes it awkward."

She led him down a corridor with still more people, these ones in bunny-suits or more permanent-looking suits that were form-fitting and iridescent and flattering. "Really?" he said, keeping pace with her. "Elegant is a word that comes to mind, not awkward."

"Well, sure, elegant on the other side of that airlock door. But we're inside Buhle's body now." She saw the look on his face and smiled. "No, no, it's not a riddle. Everything on this side of the airlock is Buhle. It's his lungs and circulatory and limbic system. The vat may be where the meat sits, but all this is what makes the vat work. You're like a gigantic foreign organism that's burrowing into his tissues. It's intimate." They passed through another set of doors and now they were almost alone in a hall the size of his university's basketball court, the only others a long way off. She lowered her voice so that he had to lean in to hear her. "When you're outside, speaking to Buhle through his many tendrils, like me, or even on the phone, he has all the power in the world. He's a giant. But here, inside his body, he's very, very weak. The suits, they're there to level out the playing field. It's all head-games and symbolism. And this is just Mark I, the system we jury-rigged after Buhle's . . . *accident*. They're building the Mark II about five miles from here, and half a mile underground. When it's ready, they'll blast a tunnel and take him all the way down into it without ever compromising the skin of Buhle's extended body."

"You never told me what the accident was, how he ended up here. I assumed it was a stroke or—"

Ria shook her head, the micropore fabric rustling softly. "Nothing like that," she said.

They were on the other side of the great room now, headed for the doors. "What is this giant room for?"

"Left over from the original floor-plan, when this place was just biotech R&D. Used for all-hands meetings then, sometimes a little symposium. Too big now. Security protocol dictates no more than ten people in any one space."

"Was it assassination?" He said it without thinking, quick as ripping off a band-aid.

Again, the rustle of fabric. "No."

She put her hand on the door's crashbar, made ready to pass into the next chamber.

"I'm starting to freak out a little here, Ria," he said. "He doesn't hunt humans or something?"

"No," and he didn't need to see her face, he could see the smile.

"Or need an organ? I don't think I have a rare blood-type, and I should tell you that mine have been indifferently cared for—"

"Leon," she said, "if Buhle needed an organ, we'd make one right here. Print it out in about forty hours, pristine and virgin."

"So you're saying I'm not going to be harvested or hunted, then?"

"It's a very low probability outcome," she said, and pushed the crashbar.

It was darker in this room, a mellow, candlelit sort of light, and there was a rhythmic vibration coming up through the floor, a whoosh whoosh.

Ria said, "It's his breath. The filtration systems are down there." She pointed a toe at the outline of a service hatch set into the floor. "Circulatory system overhead," she said, and he craned his neck up at the grate covering the ceiling, the troughs filled with neatly bundled tubes.

One more set of doors, another cool, dark room, this one nearly silent, and one more door at the end, an airlock door, and another plainclothes security person in front of it; a side-room with a glass door bustling with people staring intently at screens. The security person—a woman, Leon saw—had a frank and square pistol with a bulbous butt velcroed to the side of her suit.

"He's through there, isn't he?" Leon said, pointing at the airlock door.

"No," Ria said. "No. He's here. We are inside him. Remember that, Leon. He isn't the stuff in the vat there. In some sense you've been in Buhle's body since you got off the chopper. His sensor array network stretches out as far as the heliport, like the tips of the hairs on your neck, they feel the breezes that blow in his vicinity. Now you've tunneled inside him, and you're right here, in his heart or his liver."

"Or his brain."

A voice, then, from everywhere, warm and good-humored. "The brain is overrated." Leon looked at Ria and she rolled her eyes eloquently behind her faceplate.

"Tuned sound," she said. "A party trick. Buhle—"

"Wait," Buhle said. "Wait. The brain, this is important, the brain is *so* overrated. The ancient Egyptians thought it was used to cool the blood, you know that?" He chortled, a sound that felt to Leon as though it began just above his groin and rose up through his torso, a very pleasant and very invasive sensation. "The heart, they thought, the heart was the place where the *me* lived. I used to wonder about that. Wouldn't they think that the thing between the organs of hearing, the thing behind the organs of seeing, that must be the me? But that's just the brain doing one of its little stupid games, backfilling the explanation. We think the brain is the obvious seat of the me because the brain already knows that it is the seat, and can't conceive of anything else. When the brain thought it lived in your chest, it was perfectly happy to rationalize that too—*Of course it's in the chest, you feel your sorrow and your joy there, your satiety and your hunger . . .* The brain, pffft, the brain!"

"Buhle," she said. "We're coming in now."

The nurse/guard by the door had apparently only heard their part of the conversation, but also hadn't let it bother her. She stood to one side, and offered Leon a tiny, incremental nod as he passed. He returned it, and then hurried to catch up with Ria, who was waiting inside the airlock. The outer door closed and for a moment, they were pressed up against one another and he felt a wild, horny thought streak through him, all the excitement discharging itself from yet another place that the me might reside.

Then the outer door hissed open and he met Buhle—he tried to remember what Ria had said, that Buhle wasn't this, Buhle was everywhere, but he couldn't help himself from feeling that this was *him*.

Buhle's vat was surprisingly small, no bigger than the sarcophagus that an ancient Egyptian might have gone to in his burial chamber. He tried not to stare inside it, but he couldn't stop himself. The withered, wrinkled man floating in the vat was intertwined with a thousand fiber optics that disappeared into pinprick holes in his naked skin. There were tubes: in the big highways in the groin, in the gut through a small valve set into a pucker of scar, in the nose and ear. The hairless head was pushed in on one side, like a pumpkin that hasn't been turned as it grew in the patch, and there was no skin on the flat piece, only white bone and a fine metalling mesh and more ragged, curdled scar tissue.

The eyes were hidden behind a slim set of goggles that irised open when they neared him, and beneath the goggles they were preternaturally bright, bright as marbles, set deep in bruised-looking sockets. The mouth beneath the nostril-tubes parted in a smile, revealing teeth as neat and white as a toothpaste advertisement, and Buhle spoke.

"Welcome to the liver. Or the heart."

Leon choked on whatever words he'd prepared. The voice was the same one he'd heard in the outer room, warm and friendly, the voice of a man whom you could trust, who would take care of you. He fumbled around his suit, patting it. "I brought you a doorknob," he said, "but I can't reach it just now."

Buhle laughed, not the chuckle he'd heard before, but an actual, barked *Ha!* that made the tubes heave and the fiber optics writhe. "Fantastic," he said. "Ria, he's fantastic."

The compliment made the tips of Leon's ears grow warm.

"He's a good one," she said. "And he's come a long way at your request."

"You hear how she reminds me of my responsibilities? Sit down, both of you." Ria rolled over two chairs, and Leon settled into one, feeling it noiselessly adjust to take his weight. A small mirror unfolded itself and then two more, angled beneath it, and he found himself looking into Buhle's eyes, looking at his face, reflected in the mirrors.

"Leon," Buhle said, "tell me about your final project, the one that got you the top grade in your class."

Leon's fragile calm vanished, and he began to sweat. "I don't like to talk about it," he said.

"Makes you vulnerable, I know. But vulnerable isn't so bad. Take me. I thought I was invincible. I thought that I could make and unmake the world to my liking. I thought I understood how the human mind worked—and how it broke.

"And then one day in Madrid, as I was sitting in my suite's breakfast room, talking with an old friend while I ate my porridge oats, my old friend picked up the heavy silver coffee jug, leaped on my chest, smashed me to the floor, and methodically attempted to beat the brains out of my head with it. It weighed about three pounds, not counting the coffee, which was scalding, and she only got in three licks before they pulled her off of me, took her away. Those three licks though—" He looked intently at them. "I'm an old man," he said. "Old bones, old tissues. The first blow cracked my skull. The second one broke it. The third one forced fragments into my brain. By the time the medics arrived, I'd been technically dead for about 174 seconds, give or take a second or two."

Leon wasn't sure the old thing in the vat had finished speaking, but that seemed to be the whole story. "Why?" he said, picking the word that was uppermost in his mind.

"Why did I tell you this?"

"No," Leon said. "Why did your old friend try to kill you?"

Buhle grinned. "Oh, I expect I deserved it," he said.

"Are you going to tell me why?" Leon said.

Buhle's cozy grin disappeared. "I don't think I will."

Leon found he was breathing so hard that he was fogging up his faceplate, despite the air-jets that worked to clear it. "Buhle," he said, "the point of that story was to tell me how vulnerable you are so that I'd tell you my story, but that story doesn't make you vulnerable. You were beaten to death and yet you survived, grew stronger, changed into this—" He waved his hands around. "This body, this monstrous, town-sized giant. You're about as vulnerable as fucking Zeus."

Ria laughed softly but unmistakably. "Told you so," she said to Buhle. "He's a good one."

The exposed lower part Buhle's face clenched like a fist and the pitch of the machine noises around them shifted a half-tone. Then he smiled a smile that was visibly forced, obviously artificial even in that ruin of a face.

"I had an idea," he said. "That many of the world's problems could be solved with a positive outlook. We spend so much time worrying about the rare and lurid outcomes in life. Kids being snatched. Terrorists blowing up cities. Stolen secrets ruining your business. Irate customers winning huge judgments in improbable lawsuits. All this *chickenshit*, bed-wetting, hand-wringing *fear*." His voice rose and fell like a minister's and it was all Leon could do not to sway in time with him. "And at the same time, we neglect the likely: traffic accidents, jetpack crashes, bathtub drownings. It's like the mind can't stop thinking about the grotesque, and can't stop forgetting about the likely."

"Get on with it," Ria said. "The speech is lovely, but it doesn't answer the question."

He glared at her through the mirror, the marble-eyes in their mesh of burst blood vessels and red spider-tracks, like the eyes of a demon. "The human mind is just *kinked wrong*. And it's correctable." The excitement in his voice was palpable. "Imagine a product that let you *feel* what you *know*—imagine if anyone who heard 'Lotto: you've got to be in it to win it' immediately understood that this is *so much bullshit*. That statistically, your chances of winning the lotto are not measurably improved by buying a lottery ticket. Imagine if explaining the war on terror to people made them double over with laughter! Imagine if the capital markets ran on realistic assessments of risk instead of envy, panic, and greed."

"You'd be a lot poorer," Ria said.

He rolled his eyes eloquently.

"It's an interesting vision," Leon said. "I'd take the cure, whatever it was."

The eyes snapped to him, drilled through him, fierce. "That's the problem, *right there*. The only people who'll take this are the people who don't need it. Politicians and traders and oddsmakers know how probability works, but they also know that the people who make them fat and happy *don't* understand it a bit, and so they can't afford to be rational. So there's only one answer to the problem."

Leon blurted, "The bears."

Ria let out an audible sigh.

"The fucking bears," Buhle agreed, and the way he said it was so full of world-weary exhaustion that it made Leon want to hug him. "Yes. As a social reform tool, we couldn't afford to leave this to the people who were willing to take it. So we—"

"Weaponized it," Ria said.

"Whose story is this?"

Leon felt that the limbs of his suit were growing stiffer, his exhaust turning it into a balloon. And he had to pee. And he didn't want to move.

"You dosed people with it?"

"Leon," Buhle said, in a voice that implied, *Come on, we're bigger than that.* "They'd consented to being medical research subjects. And it *worked.* They stopped running around shouting *The sky is falling, the sky is falling* and became— *zen.* Happy, in a calm, even-keeled way. Headless chickens turned into flinty-eyed air-traffic controllers."

"And your best friend beat your brains in—"

"Because," Buhle said, in a little Mickey Mouse falsetto, *"it would be unethical to do a broad-scale release on the general public."*

Ria was sitting so still he had almost forgotten she was there.

Leon shifted his weight. "I don't think that you're telling me the whole story."

"We were set to market it as an anti-anxiety medication."

"And?"

Ria stood up abruptly. "I'll wait outside." She left without another word.

Buhle rolled his eyes again. "How do you get people to take anti-anxiety medication? Lots and lots of people? I mean, if I assigned you that project, gave you a budget for it—"

Leon felt torn between a desire to chase after Ria and to continue to stay in the magnetic presence of Buhle. He shrugged. "Same as you would with any pharma. Cook the diagnosis protocol, expand the number of people it catches. Get the news media whipped up about the anxiety epidemic. That's easy. Fear sells. An epidemic of fear? Christ, that'd be too easy. Far too easy. Get the insurers on board, discounts on the meds, make it cheaper to prescribe a course of treatment than to take the call-center time to explain to the guy why he's *not* getting the meds."

"You're my kind of guy, Leon," Buhle said. "So yeah."

"Yeah?"

Another one of those we're-both-men-of-the-world smiles. "Yeah."

"Oh."

"How many?"

"That's the thing. We were trying it in a little market first. Basque country. The local authority was very receptive. Lots of chances to fine-tune the message. They're the most media-savvy people on the planet these days—they are to media as the Japanese were to electronics in the last century. If we could get them in the door—"

"How many?"

"About a million. More than half the population."

"You created a bioweapon that infected its victims with numeracy, and infected a million Basque with it?"

"Crashed the lottery. That's how I knew we'd done it. Lottery tickets fell by more than 80 percent. Wiped out."

"And then your friend beat your head in?"

"Well."

The suit was getting more uncomfortable by the second. Leon wondered if he'd get stuck if he waited too long, his overinflated suit incapable of moving. "I'm going to have to go, soon."

"Evolutionarily, bad risk-assessment is advantageous."

Leon nodded slowly. "OK, I'll buy that. Makes you entrepreneurial—"

"Drives you to colonize new lands, to ask out the beautiful monkey in the next tree, to have a baby you can't imagine how you'll afford."

"And your numerate Vulcans stopped?"

"Pretty much," he said. "But that's just normal shakedown. Like when people move to cities, their birthrate drops. And nevertheless, the human race is becoming more and more citified and still, it isn't vanishing. Social stuff takes time."

"And then your friend beat your head in?"

"Stop saying that."

Leon stood. "Maybe I should go and find Ria."

Buhle made a disgusted noise. "Fine. And ask her why she didn't finish the job? Ask her if she decided to do it right then, or if she'd planned it? Ask her why she used the coffee jug instead of the bread-knife? Because, you know, I wonder this myself."

Leon backpedaled, clumsy in the overinflated suit. He struggled to get into the airlock, and as it hissed through its cycle, he tried not to think of Ria straddling the old man's chest, the coffee urn rising and falling.

She was waiting for him on the other side, also overinflated in her suit. "Let's go," she said, and took his hand, the rubberized palms of their gloves sticking together. She half-dragged him through the many rooms of Buhle's body, tripping through the final door, then spinning him around and ripping, hard, on the release cord that split the suit down the back so that it fell into two lifeless pieces that slithered to the ground. He gasped out a breath he hadn't realized he'd been holding in as the cool air made contact with the thin layer of perspiration that filmed his body.

Ria had already ripped open her own suit and her face was flushed and sweaty, her hair matted. Small sweat-rings sprouted beneath her armpits. An efficient orderly came forward and began gathering up their suits. Ria thanked her impersonally and headed for the doors.

"I didn't think he'd do that," she said, once they were outside of the building—outside the core of Buhle's body.

"You tried to kill him," Leon said. He looked at her hands, which had blunt, neat fingernails and large knuckles. He tried to picture the tendons on their backs standing out like sail-ropes when the wind blew, as they did the rhythmic work of raising and lowering the heavy silver coffee pot.

She wiped her hands on her trousers and stuffed them in her pockets, awkward now, without any of her usual self-confidence. "I'm not ashamed of that. I'm proud of it. Not everyone would have had the guts. If I hadn't, you and everyone you know would be—" She brought her hands out of her pockets, bunched into fists. She shook her head. "I thought he'd tell you what we like about your grad project. Then we could have talked about where you'd fit in here—"

"You never said anything about that," he said. "I could have saved you a lot of trouble. I don't talk about it."

Ria shook her head. "This is Buhle. You won't stop us from doing anything we want to do. I'm not trying to intimidate you here. It's just a fact of life. If we want to replicate your experiment, we can, on any scale we want—"

"But I won't be a part of it," he said. "That matters."

"Not as much as you think it does. And if you think you can avoid being a part of something that Buhle wants you for, you're likely to be surprised. We can get you what you want."

"No you can't," he said. "If there's one thing I know, it's that you can't do that."

Take one normal human being at lunch. Ask her about her breakfast. If lunch is great, she'll tell you how great breakfast is. If lunch is terrible, she'll tell you how awful breakfast was.

Now ask her about dinner. A bad lunch will make her assume that a bad dinner is forthcoming. A great lunch will make her optimistic about dinner.

Explain this dynamic to her and ask her again about breakfast. She'll struggle to remember the actual details of breakfast, the texture of the oatmeal, whether the juice was cold and delicious or slightly warm and slimy. She will remember and remember and remember for all she's worth, and then, if lunch is good, she'll tell you breakfast was good. And if lunch is bad, she'll tell you breakfast was bad.

Because you just can't help it. Even if you know you're doing it, you can't help it.

But what if you could?

"It was the parents," he said, as they picked their way through the treetops, along the narrow walkway, squeezing to one side to let the eager, gabbling researchers past. "That was the heartbreaker. Parents only remember the good parts of parenthood. Parents whose kids are grown remember a succession of sweet hugs, school triumphs, sports victories, and they simply forget the vomit, the tantrums, the sleep deprivation . . . It's the thing that lets us continue the species, this excellent facility for forgetting. That's what should have tipped me off."

Ria nodded solemnly. "But there was an upside, wasn't there?"

"Oh, sure. Better breakfasts, for one thing. And the weight-loss—amazing. Just being able to remember how shitty you felt the last time you ate the chocolate bar or pigged out on fries. It was amazing."

"The applications do sound impressive. Just that weight-loss one—"

"Weight-loss, addiction counseling, you name it. It was all killer apps, wall to wall."

"But?"

He stopped abruptly. "You must know this," he said. "If you know about Clarity—that's what I called it, Clarity—then you know about what happened. With Buhle's resources, you can find out anything, right?"

She made a wry smile. "Oh, I know what history records. What I don't know is what *happened*. The official version, the one that put Ate onto you and got us interested—"

"Why'd you try to kill Buhle?"

"Because I'm the only one he can't bullshit, and I saw where he was going with his little experiment. The competitive advantage to a firm that knows about such a radical shift in human cognition—it's massive. Think of all the products that would vanish if numeracy came in a virus. Think of all the shifts in governance, in policy. Just imagine an *airport* run by and for people who understand risk!"

"Sounds pretty good to me," Leon said.

"Oh sure," she said. "Sure. A world of eager consumers who know the cost of everything and the value of nothing. Why did evolution endow us with such pathological innumeracy? What's the survival advantage in being led around by the nose by whichever witch-doctor can come up with the best scare-story?"

"He said that entrepreneurial things—parenthood, businesses . . ."

"Any kind of risk-taking. Sports. No one swings for the stands when he knows that the odds are so much better on a bunt."

"And Buhle *wanted* this?"

She peered at him. "A world of people who understand risk are nearly as easy to lead around by the nose as a world of people who are incapable of understanding risk. The big difference is that the competition is at a massive disadvantage in the latter case, not being as highly evolved as the home team."

He looked at her, really looked at her for the first time. Saw that she was the face of a monster, the voice of a god. The hand of a massive, unknowable machine that was vying to change the world, remake it to suit its needs. A machine that was *good at it*.

"Clarity," he said. "Clarity." She looked perfectly attentive. "Do you think you'd have tried to kill Buhle if you'd been taking Clarity?"

She blinked in surprise. "I don't think I ever considered the question."

He waited. He found he was holding his breath.

"I think I would have succeeded if I'd been taking Clarity," she said.

"And if Buhle had been taking Clarity?"

"I think he would have let me." She blurted it so quickly it sounded like a belch.

"Is anyone in charge of Buhle?"

"What do you mean?"

"I mean—that vat-thing. Is it volitional? Does it steer this, this *enterprise*? Or does the enterprise tick on under its own power, making its own decisions?"

She swallowed. "Technically, it's a benevolent dictatorship. He's sovereign, you know that." She swallowed again. "Will you tell me what happened with Clarity?"

"Does he actually make decisions, though?"

"I don't think so," she whispered. "Not really. It's more like, like—"

"A force of nature?"

"An emergent phenomenon."

"Can he hear us?"

She nodded.

"Buhle," he said, thinking of the thing in the vat. "Clarity made the people who took it very angry. They couldn't look at advertisements without wanting to smash something. Going into a shop made them nearly catatonic. Voting made them want to storm a government office with flaming torches. Every test subject went to prison within eight weeks."

Ria smiled. She took his hands in hers—warm, dry—and squeezed them.

His phone rang. He took one hand out and answered it.

"Hello?"

"How much do you want for it?" Buhle's voice was ebullient. Mad, even.

"It's not for sale."

"I'll buy Ate, put you in charge."

"Don't want it."

"I'll kill your parents." The ebullient tone didn't change at all.

"You'll kill everyone if Clarity is widely used."

"You don't believe that. Clarity lets you choose the course that will make you happiest. Mass suicide won't make humanity happiest."

"You don't know that."

"Wanna bet?"

"Why don't you kill yourself?"

"Because dead, I'll never make things better."

Ria was watching intently. She squeezed the hand she held.

"Will you take it?"

There was a long pause.

Leon pressed on. "No deal unless you take it," he said.

"You have some?"

"I can make some. I'll need to talk to some lab-techs and download some of my research first."

"Will you take it with me?"

He didn't hesitate. "Never."

"I'll take it," Buhle said, and hung up.

Ria took his hand again. Leaned forward. Gave him a dry, firm kiss on the mouth. Leaned back.

"Thank you," she said.

"Don't thank me," he said. "I'm not doing you any favors."

She stood up, pulling him to his feet.

"Welcome to the team," she said. "Welcome to Buhle."

flower, Mercy, Needle, chain

YOON HA LEE

New writer Yoon Ha Lee lives in Southern California with her family. Her fiction has appeared in *Lightspeed, Clarkesworld, The Magazine of Fantasy & Science Fiction, Federation, Beneath Ceaseless Skies,* and elsewhere.

Here she tells an icy and elegant story about an ancient weapon so potent that to fire it is to destroy the universe—and replace it with another one.

The usual fallacy is that, in every universe, many futures splay outward from any given moment. But in some universes, determinism runs backwards: given a universe's state s at some time t, there are multiple previous states that may have resulted in s. In some universes, all possible pasts funnel toward a single fixed ending, Ω.

If you are of millenarian bent, you might call W Armageddon. If you are of grammatical bent, you might call it punctuation on a cosmological scale.

If you are a philosopher in such a universe, you might call Ω *inevitable*.

The woman has haunted Blackwheel Station for as long as anyone remembers, although she was not born there. She is human, and her straight black hair and brown-black eyes suggest an ancestral inheritance tangled up with tigers and shapeshifting foxes. Her native language is not spoken by anyone here or elsewhere.

They say her true name means things like *gray* and *ash* and *grave*. You may buy her a drink, bring her candied petals or chaotic metals, but it's all the same. She won't speak her name.

That doesn't stop people from seeking her out. Today, it's a man with mirror-colored eyes. He is the first human she has seen in a long time.

"Arighan's Flower," he says.

It isn't her name, but she looks up. Arighan's Flower is the gun she carries. The stranger has taken on a human face to talk to her, and he is almost certainly interested in the gun.

The gun takes different shapes, but at this end of time, origami multiplicity of form surprises more by its absence than its presence. Sometimes the gun is long and sleek, sometimes heavy and blunt. In all cases, it bears its maker's mark on the stock: a blossom with three petals falling away and a fourth about to follow. At the blossom's heart is a character that itself resembles a flower with knotted roots.

The character's meaning is the gun's secret. The woman will not tell it to you, and the gunsmith Arighan is generations gone.

"Everyone knows what I guard," the woman says to the mirror-eyed man.

"I know what it does," he says. "And I know that you come from people that worship their ancestors."

Her hand—on a glass of water two degrees from freezing—stops, slides to her side, where the holster is. "That's dangerous knowledge," she says. So he's figured it out. Her people's historians called Arighan's Flower the *ancestral gun*. They weren't referring to its age.

The man smiles politely, and doesn't take a seat uninvited. Small courtesies matter to him because he is not human. His mind may be housed in a superficial fortress of flesh, but the busy computations that define him are inscribed in a vast otherspace.

The man says, "I can hardly be the first constructed sentience to come to you."

She shakes her head. "It's not that." Do computers like him have souls? she wonders. She is certain he does, which is potentially inconvenient. "I'm not for hire."

"It's important," he says.

It always is. They want chancellors dead or generals, discarded lovers or rival reincarnates, bodhisattvas or bosses—all the old, tawdry stories. People, in all the broad and narrow senses of the term. The reputation of Arighan's Flower is quite specific, if mostly wrong.

"Is it," she says. Ordinarily she doesn't talk to her petitioners at all. Ordinarily she ignores them through one glass, two, three, four, like a child learning the hard way that you can't outcount infinity.

There was a time when more of them tried to force the gun away from her. The woman was a duelist and a killer before she tangled her life up with the Flower, though, and the Flower comes with its own defenses, including the woman's inability to die while she wields it. One of the things she likes about Blackwheel is that the administrators promised that they would dispose of any corpses she produced. Blackwheel is notorious for keeping promises.

The man waits a little longer, then says, "Will you hear me out?"

"You should be more afraid of me," she says, "if you really know what you claim to know."

By now, the other people in the bar, none of them human, are paying attention: a musician whose instrument is made of fossilized wood and silk strings, a magister with a seawrack mane, engineers with their sketches hanging in the air and a single doodled starship at the boundary. The sole exception is the tattooed traveler dozing in the corner, dreaming of distant moons.

In no hurry, the woman draws the Flower and points it at the man. She is aiming it not at his absent heart, but at his left eye. If she pulled the trigger, she would pierce him through the false pupil.

The musician continues plucking plangent notes from the instrument. The others, seeing the gun, gawk for only a moment before hastening out of the bar. As if that would save them.

"Yes," the man says, outwardly shaken, "you could damage my lineage badly. I could name programmers all the way back to the first people who scratched a tally of birds or rocks."

The gun's muzzle moves precisely, horizontally: now the right eye. The woman says, "You've convinced me that you know. You haven't convinced me not to kill you." It's half a bluff: she wouldn't use the Flower, not for this. But she knows many ways to kill.

"There's another one," he said. "I don't want to speak of it here, but will you hear me out?"

She nods once, curtly.

Covered by her palm, engraved silver-bright in a language nobody else reads or writes, is the word *ancestor*.

Once upon a universe, an empress's favored duelist received a pistol from the empress's own hand. The pistol had a stock of silver-gilt and niello, an efflorescence of vines framing the maker's mark. The gun had survived four dynasties, with all their rebellions and coups. It had accompanied the imperial arsenal from homeworld to homeworld.

Of the ancestral pistol, the empire's archives said two things: *Do not use this weapon, for it is nothing but peril* and *This weapon does not function.*

In a reasonable universe, both statements would not be true.

The man follows the woman to her suite, which is on one of Blackwheel's tidier levels. The sitting room, comfortable but not luxurious by Blackwheeler standards, accommodates a couch sized to human proportions, a metal table shined to blurry reflectivity, a vase in the corner.

There are also two paintings, on silk rather than some less ancient substrate. One is of a mountain by night, serenely anonymous amid its stylized clouds. The other, in a completely different style, consists of a cavalcade of shadows. Only after several moments' study do the shadows assemble themselves into a face. Neither painting is signed.

"Sit," the woman says.

The man does. "Do you require a name?" he asks.

"Yours, or the target's?"

"I have a name for occasions like this," he says. "It is Zheu Kerang."

"You haven't asked me my name," she remarks.

"I'm not sure that's a meaningful question," Kerang says. "If I'm not mistaken, you don't exist."

Wearily, she says, "I exist in all the ways that matter. I have volume and mass and volition. I drink water that tastes the same every day, as water should. I kill when it moves me to do so. I've unwritten death into the history of the universe."

His mouth tilts up at *unwritten*. "Nevertheless," he says. "Your species never evolved. You speak a language that is not even dead. It never existed."

"Many languages are extinct."

"To become extinct, something has to exist first."

The woman folds herself into the couch next to him, not close but not far. "It's an old story," she says. "What is yours?"

"Four of Arighan's guns are still in existence," Kerang says.

The woman's eyes narrow. "I had thought it was three." Arighan's Flower is the last, the gunsmith's final work. The others she knows of are Arighan's Mercy, which always kills the person shot, and Arighan's Needle, which removes the target's memories of the wielder.

"One more has surfaced," Kerang says. "The character in the maker's mark resembles a sword in chains. They are already calling it Arighan's Chain."

"What does it do?" she says, because he will tell her anyway.

"This one kills the commander of whoever is shot," Kerang says, "if that's anyone at all. Admirals, ministers, monks. Schoolteachers. It's a peculiar sort of loyalty test."

Now she knows. "You want me to destroy the Chain."

Once upon a universe, a duelist named Shiron took up the gun that an empress with empiricist tendencies had given her. "I don't understand how a gun that doesn't work could possibly be perilous," the empress said. She nodded at a sweating man bound in monofilament so that he would dismember himself if he tried to flee. "This man will be executed anyway, his name struck from the roster of honored ancestors. See if the gun works on him."

Shiron fired the gun . . . and woke in a city she didn't recognize, whose inhabitants spoke a dialect she had never heard before, whose technology she mostly recognized from historical dramas. The calendar they used, at least, was familiar. It told her that she was 857 years too early. No amount of research changed the figure.

Later, Shiron deduced that the man she had executed traced his ancestry back 857 years, to a particular individual. Most likely that ancestor had performed some extraordinary deed to join the aristocracy, and had, by the reckoning of Shiron's people, founded his own line.

Unfortunately, Shiron didn't figure this out before she accidentally deleted the human species.

"Yes," Kerang says. "I have been charged with preventing further assassinations. Arighan's Chain is not a threat I can afford to ignore."

"Why didn't you come earlier, then?" Shiron says. "After all, the Chain might have lain dormant, but the others—"

"I've seen the Mercy and the Needle," he says, by which he means he's copied data from those who have. "They're beautiful." He isn't referring to beauty in the way of shadows fitting together into a woman's profile, or beauty in the way of sun-colored liquor at the right temperature in a faceted glass. He means the beauty of logical strata, of the crescendo of *axiom-axiom-corollary-proof*, of *quod erat demonstrandum*.

"Any gun or shard of glass could do the same as the Mercy," Shiron says, understanding him. "And drugs and dreamscalpels will do the Needle's work, given time and expertise. But surely you could say the same of the Chain."

She stands again and takes the painting of the mountain down and rolls it tightly. "I was born on that mountain," she says. "Something like it is still there, on a birthworld very like the one I knew. But I don't think anyone paints in this style. Perhaps some art historian would recognize its distant cousin. I am no artist, but I painted it myself, because no one else remembers the things I remember. And now you would have it start again."

"How many bullets have you used?" Kerang asks.

It is not that the Flower requires special bullets—it adapts even to emptiness—it is that the number matters.

Shiron laughs, low, almost husky. She knows better than to trust Kerang, but she needs him to trust her. She pulls out the Flower and rests it in both palms so he can look at it.

Three petals fallen, a fourth about to follow. That's not the number, but he doesn't realize it. "You've guarded it so long," he says, inspecting the maker's mark without touching the gun.

"I will guard it until I am nothing but ice," Shiron says. "You may think that the Chain is a threat, but if I remove it, there's no guarantee that you will still exist—"

"It's not the Chain I want destroyed," Kerang says gently. "It's Arighan. Do you think I would have come to you for anything less?"

Shiron says into the awkward quiet, after a while, "So you tracked down descendants of Arighan's line." His silence is assent. "There must be many."

Arighan's Flower destroys the target's entire ancestral line, altering the past but leaving its wielder untouched. In the empire Shiron once served, the histories spoke of Arighan as an honored guest. Shiron discovered long ago that Arighan was no guest, but a prisoner forced to forge weapons for her captors. How Arighan was able to create weapons of such novel destructiveness, no one knows. The Flower was Arighan's clever revenge against a people whose state religion involved ancestor worship.

If descendants of Arighan's line exist here, then Arighan herself can be undone, and all her guns unmade. Shiron will no longer have to be an exile in this timeline, although it is true that she cannot return to the one that birthed her, either.

Shiron snaps the painting taut. The mountain disintegrates, but she lost it lifetimes ago. Silent lightning crackles through the air, unknots Zheu Kerang from his human-shaped shell, tessellates dead-end patterns across the equations that make him who he is. The painting had other uses, as do the other things in this room—she believes in versatility—but this is good enough.

Kerang's body slumps on the couch. Shiron leaves it there.

For the first time in a long time, she is leaving Blackwheel Station. What she does not carry she can buy on the way. And Blackwheel is loyal because they know, and they know not to offend her; Blackwheel will keep her suite clean and undisturbed, and deliver water, near-freezing in an elegant glass, night after night, waiting.

Kerang was a pawn by his own admission. If he knew what he knew, and lived long enough to convey it to her, then others must know what he knew, or be able to find it out.

Kerang did not understand her at all. Shiron unmazes herself from the station to seek passage to one of the hubworlds, where she can begin her search. If Shiron had wanted to seek revenge on Arighan, she could have taken it years ago.

But she will not be like Arighan. She will not destroy an entire timeline of people, no matter how alien they are to her.

Shiron had hoped that matters wouldn't come to this. She acknowledges her own naïveté. There is no help for it now. She will have to find and murder each child of Arighan's line. In this way she can protect Arighan herself, protect the accumulated sum of history, in case someone outwits her after all this time and manages to take the Flower from her.

In a universe where determinism runs backwards—where, no matter what you do, everything ends in the same inevitable Ω—choices still matter, especially if you are the last guardian of an incomparably lethal gun.

Although it has occurred to Shiron that she could have accepted Kerang's offer, and that she could have sacrificed this timeline in exchange for the one in which neither Arighan nor the guns ever existed, she declines to do so. For there will come a heat-death, and she is beginning to wonder: if a constructed sentience—a computer—can have a soul, what of the universe itself, the greatest computer of all?

In this universe, they reckon her old. Shiron is older than even that. In millions of timelines, she has lived to the pallid end of life. In each of those endings, Arighan's Flower is there, as integral as an edge is to a blade. While it is true that science never proves anything absolutely, that an inconceivably large but finite number of experiments always pales besides infinity, Shiron feels that millions of timelines suffice as proof.

Without Arighan's Flower, the universe cannot renew itself and start a new story. Perhaps that is all the reason the universe needs. And Shiron will be there when the heat-death arrives, as many times as necessary.

So Shiron sets off. It is not the first time she has killed, and it is unlikely to be the last. But she is not, after all this time, incapable of grieving.

STEPHEN BAXTER

Stephen Baxter made his first sale to *Interzone* in 1987, and since then has become one of that magazine's most frequent contributors, as well as making sales to *Asimov's Science Fiction, Science Fiction Age, Analog, Zenith, New Worlds*, and elsewhere. He's one of the most prolific writers in science fiction, one who works on the cutting edge of science, whose fiction bristles with weird new ideas and often takes place against vistas of almost outrageously cosmic scope. Baxter's first novel, *Raft*, was released in 1991, and was rapidly followed by other well-received novels such as *Timelike Infinity, Anti-ice, Flux*, and the H. G. Wells pastiche—a sequel to *The Time Machine—The Time Ships*, which won both the John W. Campbell Memorial Award and the Philip K. Dick Award. His many other books include the novels *Voyage, Titan, Moonseed, Mammoth, Book One: Silverhair, Longtusk, Icebones, Manifold: Time, Manifold: Space, Evolution, Coalescent, Exultant, Transcendent, Emperor, Resplendent, Conqueror, Navigator, Firstborn*, and *The H-Bomb Girl*, and two novels in collaboration with Arthur C. Clarke, *The Light of Other Days* and *Time's Eye*. His short fiction has been collected in *Vacuum Diagrams: Stories of the Xeelee Sequence, Traces*, and *The Hunters of Pangaea*, and he has released a chapbook novella, "Mayflower II." His most recent books include the novel trilogy *Weaver, Flood*, and *Ark*, and *Stone Spring*, as well as a nonfiction book, *The Science of Avatar*. Coming up are several new novels, including *Bronze Summer* and *Iron Winter*.

Baxter has written a long sequence of stories over the years about astronaut Harry Poole. "Return to Titan" exposes the hero's feet of clay, including a ruthless willingness to do just about *anything* in order to succeed. . . .

PROLOGUE
PROBE

The spacecraft from Earth sailed through rings of ice.

In its first week in orbit around Saturn it passed within a third of a million kilometres of Titan, Saturn's largest moon. Its sensors peered curiously down at unbroken haze.

The craft had been too heavy to launch direct with the technology of the time, so its flight path, extending across seven years, had taken it on swingbys past Venus, Earth, and Jupiter. Primitive it was, but it was prepared for Titan. An independent lander, a fat pie-dish shape three metres across, clung to the side of the main body. Dormant for most of the interplanetary cruise, the probe was at last woken and released.

And, two weeks later, it dropped into the thick atmosphere of Titan itself.

Much of the probe's interplanetary velocity was shed in ferocious heat, and the main parachute was released. Portals opened and booms unfolded, and more than a billion kilometres from the nearest human engineer, instruments peered out at Titan. Some fifty kilometres up the surface slowly became visible. This first tantalising glimpse was like a high-altitude view of Earth, though rendered in sombre reds and browns.

The landing in gritty water-ice sand was slow, at less than twenty kilometres per hour.

After a journey of so many years the surface mission lasted mere minutes before the probe's internal batteries were exhausted, and the chatter of telemetry fell silent. It would take two more hours for news of the adventure to crawl at lightspeed to Earth, by which time a thin organic rain was already settling on the probe's upper casing, as the last of its internal heat leaked away.

And then, all unknown to the probe's human controllers back on Earth, a manipulator not unlike a lobster's claw closed around *Huygens*'s pie-dish hull and dragged the crushed probe down beneath the water-ice sand.

I
EARTHPORT

"There's always been something wrong with Titan." These were the first words I ever heard Harry Poole speak—though I didn't know the man at the time— words that cut through my hangover like a drill. "It's been obvious since the first primitive probes got there sixteen hundred years ago." He had the voice of an older man, seventy, eighty maybe, a scratchy texture. "A moon with a blanket of air, a moon that cradles a whole menagerie of life under its thick atmosphere. But that atmosphere's not sustainable."

"Well, the mechanism is clear enough. Heating effects from the methane component keep the air from cooling and freezing out." This was another man's voice, gravelly, a bit sombre, the voice of a man who takes himself too seriously. The voice sounded familiar. "Sunlight drives methane reactions that dump complex hydrocarbons in the stratosphere—"

"But, son, where does the methane come from?" Harry Poole pressed. "It's destroyed by the very reactions that manufacture all those stratospheric hydrocarbons. Should all be gone in a few million years, ten million tops. So what replenishes it?"

At that moment I could not have cared less about the problem of methane on Saturn's largest moon, even though, I suppose, it was a central facet of my career. The fog in my head, thicker than Titan's tholin haze, was lifting slowly, and I became aware of my body, aching in unfamiliar ways, stretched out on some kind of couch.

"Maybe some geological process." This was a woman's voice, a bit brisk. "That or an ecology, a Gaia process that keeps the methane levels up. Those are the obvious options."

"Surely, Miriam," Harry Poole said. "One or the other. That's been obvious since the methane on Titan was first spotted from Earth. But *nobody knows.* Oh, there have been a handful of probes over the centuries, but nobody's taken Titan seriously enough to nail it down. Always too many other easy targets for exploration and colonisation—Mars, the ice moons. Nobody's even walked on Titan!"

Another man, a third, said, "But the practical problems—the heat loss in that cold air—it was always too expensive to bother, Harry. And too risky . . ."

"No. Nobody had the vision to see the potential of the place. That's the real problem. And now we're hamstrung by these damn sentience laws."

"And you think we need to know." That gravel voice.

"We need Titan, son," Harry Poole said. "It's the only hope I see of making our wormhole link pay for itself. Titan is, ought to be, the key to opening up Saturn and the whole outer System. We need to prove the sentience laws don't apply there, and move in and start opening it up. That's what this is all about."

The woman spoke again. "And you think this wretched creature is the key."

"Given he's a sentience curator, and a crooked one at that, yes . . ."

When words like "wretched" or "crooked" are bandied about in my company it's generally Jovik Emry that's being discussed. I took this as a cue to open my eyes. Some kind of glassy dome stretched over my head, and beyond that a slice of sky-blue. I recognised the Earth seen from space. And there was something else, a sculpture of electric blue thread that drifted over a rumpled cloud layer.

"Oh, look," said the woman. "It's alive."

I stretched, swivelled and sat up. I was stiff and sore, and had a peculiar ache at the back of my neck, just beneath my skull. I looked around at my captors. There were four of them, three men and a woman, all watching me with expressions of amused contempt. Well, it wasn't the first time I'd woken with a steaming hangover in an unknown place surrounded by strangers. I would recover quickly. I was as young and healthy as I could afford to be: I was around forty, but AS-preserved at my peak of twenty-three.

We sat on couches at the centre of a cluttered circular deck, domed over by a scuffed carapace. I was in a GUTship, then, a standard interplanetary transport, if an elderly one; I had travelled in such vessels many times, to Saturn and back. Through the clear dome I could see more of those electric-blue frames drifting before the face of the Earth. They were tetrahedral, and their faces were briefly visible, like soap films that glistened gold before disappearing. These were the mouths of wormholes, flaws in spacetime, and the golden shivers were glimpses of other worlds.

I knew where I was. "This is Earthport." My throat was dry as moondust, but I tried to speak confidently.

"Well, you're right about that." This was the man who had led the conversation earlier. That seventy-year-old voice, comically, came out of the face of a boy of maybe twenty-five, with blond hair, blue eyes, a smooth AntiSenescence marvel. The other two men looked around sixty, but with AS so prevalent it was hard to tell. The woman was tall, her hair cut short, and she wore a functional jumpsuit; she might have been forty-five. The old-young man spoke again. "My name is Harry Poole. Welcome to the *Hermit Crab*, which is my son's ship—"

"Welcome? You've drugged me and brought me here—"

One of the sixty-year-olds laughed, the gruff one. "Oh, you didn't need drugging; you did that to yourself."

"You evidently know me—and I think I know you." I studied him. He was heavy set, dark, not tall, with a face that wasn't built for smiling. "You're Michael Poole, aren't you? Poole the wormhole engineer."

Poole just looked back at me. Then he turned to the blond man. "Harry, I have a feeling we're making a huge mistake trying to work with this guy."

Harry grinned, studying me. "Give it time, son. You've always been an idealist. You're not used to working with people like this. I am. We'll get what we want out of him."

I turned to him. "Harry Poole. You're Michael's father, aren't you?" I laughed at them. "A father who AS-restores himself to an age younger than your son. How crass. And, Harry, you really ought to get something done about that voice."

The third man spoke. "I agree with Michael, Harry. We can't work with this clown." He was on the point of being overweight, and had a crumpled, careworn face. I labelled him as a corporate man who had grown old labouring to make somebody else rich—probably Michael Poole and his father.

I smiled easily, unfazed. "And you are?"

"Bill Dzik. And I'll be working with you if we go through with this planned jaunt to Titan. Can't say it's an idea I like."

This was the first I had heard of a trip to Titan. Well, whatever they wanted of me, I had had quite enough of the dismal hell-hole of the Saturn system, and had no intention of going back now. I had been in worse predicaments before; it was just a question of playing for time and looking for openings. I rubbed my temples. "Bill—can I call you Bill?—I don't suppose you could fetch me a coffee."

"Don't push your luck," he growled.

"Just tell me why you kidnapped me."

"That's simple," Harry said. "We want you to take us down to Titan."

Harry snapped his fingers, and a Virtual image coalesced before us, a bruised orange spinning in the dark: Titan. Saturn itself was a pale yellow crescent with those tremendous rings spanning space, and moons hanging like lanterns. And there, glimmering in orbit just above the plane of the rings, was a baby-blue tetrahedral frame, the mouth of Michael Poole's wormhole, a hyper-dimensional road offering access to Saturn and all its wonders—a road, it seemed, rarely travelled.

"That would be illegal," I pointed out.

"I know. And that's why we need you." And he grinned, a cold expression on that absurdly young face.

II
FINANCE

"If it's an expert on Titan you want," I said, "keep looking."

"You're a curator," Miriam said, disbelief and disgust thick in her voice. "You work for the intraSystem oversight panel on sentience law compliance. Titan is in your charge!"

"Not by choice," I murmured. "Look—as you evidently targeted me, you must know something of my background. I haven't had an easy career . . ." My life at school, supported by my family's money, had been a series of drunken jaunts, sexual escapades, petty thieving, and vandalism. As a young man I never lasted long at any of the jobs my family found for me, largely because I was usually on the run from some wronged party or other.

Harry said, "In the end you got yourself sentenced to an editing, didn't you?"

If the authorities had had their way I would have had the contents of my much-abused brain downloaded into an external store, my memories edited, my unhealthy impulses "re-programmed," and the lot loaded back again—my whole self rebooted. "It represented death to me," I said. "I wouldn't have been the same man as I was before. My father took pity on me—"

"And bought you out of your sentence," Bill Dzik said. "And got you a job on sentience compliance. A sinecure."

I looked at Titan's dismal colours. "It is a miserable posting. But it pays a bit, and nobody cares much what you get up to, within reason. I've only been out a few times to Saturn itself, and the orbit of Titan; the work's mostly admin, run from Earth. I've held down the job. Well, I really don't have much choice."

Michael Poole studied me as if I were a vermin infesting one of his marvellous interplanetary installations. "This is the problem I've got with agencies like the sentience-oversight curacy. I might even agree with its goals. But it's populated by time-wasters like you, it doesn't do what it's supposed to achieve, and all it does is get in the way of enterprise."

I found myself taking a profound dislike to the man. And I've never been able to stomach being preached at. "I did nobody any harm," I snapped back at him. "Not much, anyhow. Not like you with your grand schemes, Poole, reordering the whole System for your own profit."

Michael would have responded, but Harry held up his hand. "Let's not get into that. And after all he's right. Profit, or the lack of it, is the issue here. As for you, Jovik, even in this billion-kilometres-remote 'sinecure' you're still up to your old tricks, aren't you?"

I said nothing, cautious until I worked out how much he knew.

Harry waved his hand at his Virtual projection. "Look—Titan is infested with life. That's the basic conclusion of the gaggle of probes that, over the centuries, have orbited Titan or penetrated its thick air and crawled over its surface or dug into its icy sand. But life isn't the point. The whole *System* is full of life—life that blows everywhere, in impact-detached rocks and lumps of ice. Life is common-place. The question is sentience. And sentience holds up progress."

"It's happened to us before," Michael Poole said to me. "The development consortium I lead, that is. We were establishing a wormhole Interface at a Kuiper object called Baked Alaska, out on the rim of the System. Our purpose was to use the ice as reaction mass to fuel GUTdrive starships. Well, we discovered life there, life of a sort, and it wasn't long before we identified sentience. The xenobi-ologists called it a Forest of Ancestors. The project ground to a halt; we had to evacuate the place—"

"Given the circumstances in which you've brought me here," I said, "I'm not even going to feign interest in your war stories."

"All right," Harry said. "But you can see the issue with Titan. Look, we want to open it up for development. It's a factory of hydrocarbons and organics, and exotic life forms some of which at least are related to our own. We can make breathable air from the nitrogen atmosphere and oxygen extracted from water ice. We can use all that methane and organic chemistry to make plastics or fuel or even food. Titan *should* be the launch pad for the opening-up of the outer System, indeed the stars. At the very least, it's the only damn reason I can think of why anybody would want to go to Saturn. But we're not going to be allowed to develop Titan if there's sentience there. And our problem is that nobody has established that there isn't."

I started to see it. "So you want to mount a quick and dirty expedition, violating the planetary-protection aspects of the sentience laws, prove there's no significant mind down there, and get the clearance to move in the digging machines. Right?" And I saw how Bill Dzik, Miriam, and Michael Poole exchanged unhappy glances. There was dissension in the team over the morality of all this, a crack I might be able to exploit. "Why do you need this so badly?" I asked.

So they told me. It was a saga of interplanetary ambition. But at the root of it, as is always the case, was money—or the lack of it.

III
NEGOTIATION

Harry Poole said, "You know our business, Jovik. Our wormhole engineering is laying down rapid-transit routes through the System, which will open up a whole family of worlds to colonisation and development. But we have grander ambi-tions than that."

I asked, "What ambitions? Starships?"

"That and more," Michael Poole said. "For the last few decades we've been working on an experimental ship being built in the orbit of Jupiter . . ."

And he told me about his precious *Cauchy*. By dragging a wormhole portal around a circuit light-years across, the GUTship *Cauchy* will establish a worm-hole bridge—not across space—but across fifteen centuries, to the future. So, having already connected the worlds of humanity with his wormhole subway System, Michael Poole now hopes to short-circuit past and future themselves. I looked at him with new respect, and some fear. The man is a genius, or mad.

"But," I said, "to fund such dreams you need money."

Harry said, "Jovik, you need to understand that a mega-engineering business like ours is a ferocious devourer of cash. It's been this way since the days of the pioneering railway builders back in the nineteenth century. We fund each new project with the profit of our previous ventures and with fresh investment—but that investment is closely related to the success of the earlier schemes."

"Ah. And you're stumbling. Yes? And this is all to do with Saturn."

Harry sighed. "The Saturn transit was a logical development. The trouble is, nobody needs to go there. Saturn pales beside Jupiter! Saturn has ice moons; well, there are plenty in orbit around Jupiter. Saturn's atmosphere could be mined, but so can Jupiter's, at half the distance from Earth."

Miriam said, "Saturn also lacks Jupiter's ferociously energetic external environment, which we're tapping ourselves in the manufacture of the *Cauchy*."

"Fascinating," I lied. "You're an engineer too, then?"

"A physicist," she replied, awkward. She sat next to Michael Poole but apart from him. I wondered if there was anything deeper between them.

"The point," said Harry, "is that there's nothing at Saturn you'd want to go there for—no reason for our expensive wormhole link to be used. Nothing except—"

"Titan," I said.

"If we can't get down there legally, we need somebody to break us through the security protocols and get us down there."

"So you turned to me."

"The last resort," said Bill Dzik with disgust in his voice.

"We tried your colleagues," Miriam said. "They all said no."

"Well, that's typical of that bunch of prigs."

Harry, always a diplomat, smiled at me. "So we're having to bend a few pettifogging rules, but you have to see the vision, man, you have to see the greater good. And it's a chance for you to return to Titan, Jovik. Think of it as an opportunity."

"The question is, what's in it for me? You know I've come close to the editing suites before. Why should I take the risk of helping you now?"

"Because," Harry said, "if you don't you'll *certainly* face a reboot." So now we came to the dirty stuff. Harry took over; he was clearly the key operator in this little cabal, with the other engineer types uncomfortably out of their depth. "We know about your sideline."

With a sinking feeling I asked, "What sideline?"

And he used his Virtual display to show me. There went one of my doctored probes arrowing into Titan's thick air, a silver needle that stood out against the murky organic backdrop, supposedly on a routine monitoring mission but in fact with a quite different objective.

There are pockets of liquid water to be found just under Titan's surface, frozen-over crater lakes, kept warm for a few thousand years by the residual heat of the impacts that created them. My probe now shot straight through the icy carapace of one of those crater lakes, and into the liquid water beneath. Harry fast-forwarded, and we watched the probe's ascent module push its way out of the lake and up into the air, on its way to my colleagues' base on Enceladus.

"You're sampling the subsurface life from the lakes," Harry said sternly. "And selling the results."

I shrugged; there was no point denying it. "I guess you know the background.

The creatures down there are related to Earth life, but very distantly. Different numbers of amino acids, or something—*I* don't know. The tiniest samples are gold dust to the biochemists, a whole new toolkit for designer drugs and genetic manipulation . . ." I had one get-out. "You'll have trouble proving this. By now there won't be a trace of our probes left on the surface." Which was true; one of the many ill-understood aspects of Titan was that probes sent down to its surface quickly failed and disappeared, perhaps as a result of some kind of geological resurfacing.

Harry treated that with the contempt it deserved. "We have full records. Images. Samples of the material you stole from Titan. Even a sworn statement by one of your partners."

I flared at that, "Who?" But, of course, it didn't matter.

Harry said sweetly. "The point is the sheer illegality—and committed by you, a curator, whose job is precisely to guard against such things. If this gets to your bosses, it will be the editing suite for you, my friend."

"So that's it. Blackmail." I did my best to inject some moralistic contempt into my voice. And it worked; Michael, Miriam, Bill wouldn't meet my eyes.

But it didn't wash with Harry. "Not the word I'd use. But that's pretty much it, yes. So what's it to be? Are you with us? Will you lead us to Titan?"

I wasn't about to give in yet. I got to my feet suddenly; to my gratification they all flinched back. "At least let me think about it. You haven't even offered me that coffee."

Michael glanced at Harry, who pointed at a dispenser on a stand near my couch. "Use that one."

There were other dispensers in the cabin; why that particular one? I filed away the question and walked over to the dispenser. At a command it produced a mug of what smelled like coffee. I sipped it gratefully and took a step across the floor towards the transparent dome.

"Hold it," Michael snapped.

"I just want to take in the view."

Miriam said, "OK, but don't touch anything. Follow that yellow path."

I grinned at her. "Don't *touch* anything? What am I, contagious?" I wasn't sure what was going on, but probing away at these little mysteries had to help. "Please. Walk with me. Show me what you mean."

Miriam hesitated for a heartbeat. Then, with an expression of deep distaste, she got to her feet. She was taller than I was, and lithe, strong-looking.

We walked together across the lifedome, a half-sphere a hundred metres wide. Couches, control panels, and data entry and retrieval ports were clustered around the geometric centre of the dome; the rest of the transparent floor area was divided up by shoulder-high partitions into lab areas, a galley, a gym, a sleeping area, and shower. The layout looked obsessively plain and functional to me. This was the vessel of a man who lived for work, and only that; if this was Michael Poole's ship it was a bleak portrait.

We reached the curving hull. Glancing down I could see the ship's spine, a complex column a couple of kilometres long leading to the lode of asteroid ice used for reaction mass by GUTdrive module within. And all around us wormhole Interfaces drifted like snowflakes, while intraSystem traffic passed endlessly through the great gateways.

"All this is a manifestation of your lover's vision," I said to Miriam, who stood by me.

"Michael's not my lover," she shot back, irritated. The electric-blue light of the exotic matter frames shone on her cheekbones.

"I don't even know your name," I said.

"Berg," she said reluctantly. "Miriam Berg."

"Believe it or not, I'm not a criminal. I'm no hero, and I don't pretend to be. I just want to get through my life, and have a little fun on the way. I shouldn't be here, and nor should you." Deliberately I reached for her shoulder. A bit of physical contact might break through that reserve.

But my fingers *passed through* her shoulder, breaking up into a mist of pixels until they were clear of her flesh, and then reformed. I felt only a distant ache in my head.

I stared at Miriam Berg. "What have you done to me?"

"I'm sorry," she said gravely.

I sat on my couch once more—*my* couch, a Virtual projection like me, the only one in the dome I wouldn't have fallen through, and sipped a coffee from my Virtual dispenser, the only one that I could touch.

It was, predictably, Harry Poole's scheme. "Just in case the arm-twisting over the sample-stealing from Titan wasn't enough."

"I'm a Virtual copy," I said.

"Strictly speaking, an identity backup . . ."

I had heard of identity backups, but could never afford one myself, nor indeed fancied it much. Before undertaking some hazardous jaunt you could download a copy of yourself into a secure memory store. If you were severely injured or even killed, the backup could be loaded into a restored body, or a vat-grown cloned copy, or allowed to live on in some Virtual environment. You would lose the memories you had acquired after the backup was made, but that was better than non-existence . . . That was the theory. In my opinion it was an indulgence of the rich; you saw backup Virtuals appearing like ghosts at the funerals of their originals, distastefully lapping up the sentiment.

And besides the backup could never be *you*, the you who had died; only a copy could live on. That was the idea that started to terrify me now. I am no fool, and imaginative to a fault.

Harry watched me taking this in.

I could barely ask the question: "What about me? The original. Did I die?"

"No," Harry said. "The real you is in the hold, suspended. We took the backup after you were already unconscious."

So that explained the ache at the back of my neck: that was where they had jacked into my nervous system. I got up and paced around. "And if I refuse to help? You're a pack of crooks and hypocrites, but I can't believe you're deliberate killers."

Michael would have answered, but Harry held up his hand, unperturbed. "Look, it needn't be that way. If you agree to work with us, *you*, the Virtual you, will be loaded back into the prime version. You'll have full memories of the whole episode."

"But I won't be *me*." I felt rage building up in me. "I mean, the copy sitting here. *I* won't exist any more—any more than I existed a couple of hours ago, when you activated me." That was another strange and terrifying thought. "*I* will have to die! And that's even if I cooperate. Great deal you're offering. Well, into Lethe with you. If you're going to kill *me* anyway I'll find a way to hurt you. I'll get into your systems like a virus. *You can't control me*."

"But I can." Harry clicked his fingers.

And in an instant everything changed. The four of them had gathered by Harry's couch, the furthest from me. I had been standing; now I was sitting. And beyond the curved wall of the transparent dome, I saw that we had drifted into Earth's night.

"How long?" I whispered.

"Twenty minutes," Harry said carelessly. "Of course I can control you. You have an off switch. So which is it to be? Permanent extinction for all your copies, or survival as a trace memory in your host?" His grin hardened, and his young-old face was cold.

So the *Hermit Crab* wheeled in space, seeking out the wormhole Interface that led to Saturn. And I, or rather *he* who had briefly believed he was me, submitted to a downloading back into his primary, myself.

He, the identity copy, died to save my life. I salute him.

IV
WORMHOLE

Released from my cell of suspended animation, embittered, angry, I chose to be alone. I walked to the very rim of the lifedome, where the transparent carapace met the solid floor. Looking down I could see the flaring of superheated, ionised steam pouring from the GUTdrive nozzles. The engine, as you would expect, was one of Poole's own designs. "GUT" stands for "Grand Unified Theory," the system which describes the fundamental forces of nature as aspects of a single superforce. This is creation physics. Thus men like Michael Poole use the energies which once drove the expansion of the universe itself for the triviality of pushing forward their steam rockets.

Soon the *Hermit Crab* drove us into the mouth of the wormhole that led to the Saturn system. We flew lifedome-first at the wormhole Interface, so it was as if the electric-blue tetrahedral frame came down on us from the zenith. It was quite beautiful, a sculpture of light. Those electric blue struts were beams of exotic matter, a manifestation of a kind of antigravity field that kept this throat in space and time from collapsing. Every so often you would see the glimmer of a triangular face, a sheen of golden light filtering through from Saturn's dim halls.

The frame bore down, widening in my view, and fell around us, obscuring the view of Earth and Earthport. Now I was looking up into a kind of tunnel, picked out by flaring of sheets of light. This was a flaw in spacetime itself; the flashing I saw was the resolution of that tremendous strain into exotic particles and radiations. The ship thrust deeper into the wormhole. Fragments of blue-white light swam from a vanishing point directly above my head and swarmed down the spacetime walls. There was a genuine sensation of speed, of limitless, uncontrollable velocity. The ship shuddered and banged, the lifedome creaked like a tin shack, and I thought I could hear that elderly GUTdrive screaming with the strain. I gripped a rail and tried not to cower.

The passage was at least mercifully short. Amid a shower of exotic particles we ascended out of another electric-blue Interface—and I found myself back in the Saturn system, for the first time in years.

I could see immediately that we were close to the orbit of Titan about its primary, for the planet itself, suspended in the scuffed sky of the lifedome, was about the size I remembered it: a flattened globe a good bit larger than the Moon seen from Earth. Other moons hung around their primary, points of light. The sun was off to the right, with its close cluster of inner planets, so Saturn was half-full. Saturn's only attractive feature, the rings, were invisible, for Titan's orbit is in the same equatorial plane as the ring system and the rings are edge-on. But the shadow of the rings cast by the sun lay across the planet's face, sharp and unexpected.

There was nothing romantic in the view, nothing beautiful about it, not to me. The light was flat and pale. Saturn is about ten times as far from the sun as Earth is, and the sun is reduced to an eerie pinpoint, its radiance only a hundredth of that at Earth. Saturn is misty and murky, an autumnal place. And you never forgot that you were so far from home that a human hand, held out at arm's length towards the sun, could have covered all of the orbit of Earth.

The *Crab* swung about and Titan itself was revealed, a globe choked by murky brown cloud from pole to pole, even more dismal and uninviting than its primary. Evidently Michael Poole had placed his wormhole Interface close to the moon in anticipation that Titan would someday serve his purposes.

Titan was looming larger, swelling visibly. Our destination was obvious.

Harry Poole took charge. He had us put on heavy, thick-layered exosuits of a kind I'd never seen before. We sat on our couches like fat pupae; my suit was so thick my legs wouldn't bend properly.

"Here's the deal," Harry said, evidently for my benefit. "The *Crab* came out of the wormhole barrelling straight for Titan. That way we hope to get you down there before any of the automated surveillance systems up here can spot us, or anyhow do anything about it. In a while the *Crab* will brake into orbit around Titan. But before then you four in the gondola will be thrown straight into an entry." He snapped his fingers, and a hatch opened up in the floor beneath us to reveal the interior of another craft, mated to the base of the lifedome. It was like a cave, brightly lit and with its walls crusted with data displays.

I said, "Thrown straight in, Harry? And what about you?"

He smiled with that young-old face. "I will be waiting for you in orbit. Somebody has to stay behind to bail you out, in case."

"This 'gondola' looks small for the four of us."

Harry said, "Well, weight has been a consideration. You'll mass no more than a tonne, all up." He handed me a data slate. "Now this is where you come in, Jovik. I want you to send a covering message to the control base on Enceladus."

I stared at the slate. "Saying what, exactly?"

Harry said, "The entry profile is designed to mimic an unmanned mission. For instance you're going in hard—high deceleration. I want you to make yourselves look that way in the telemetry—like just another unmanned probe, going in for a bit of science, or a curacy inspection, or whatever it is you bureaucrat types do. Attach the appropriate permissions. I'm quite sure you're capable of that."

I was sure of it too. I opened the slate with a wave of my hand, quickly mocked up a suitable profile, let Harry's systems check that I hadn't smuggled in any cries for help, and squirted it over to Enceladus. Then I handed the slate back. "There. Done. You're masked from the curacy. I've done what you want." I waved at the looming face of Titan. "So you can spare me from *that*, can't you?"

"We discussed that," said Michael Poole, with just a hint of regret in his voice. "We decided to take you along as a fall-back, Jovik, in case of a challenge. Having you aboard will make the mission look more plausible; you can give us a bit more cover."

I snorted. "They'll see through that."

Miriam shrugged. "It's worth it if it buys us a bit more time."

Bill Dzik stared at me, hard. "Just don't get any ideas, desk jockey. I'll have my eye on you all the way down and all the way back."

"And listen," Harry said, leaning forward. "If this works out, Jovik, you'll be rewarded. We'll see to that. We'll be able to afford it, after all." He grinned that youthful grin. "And just think. You will be one of the first humans to walk on Titan! So you see, you've every incentive to cooperate, haven't you?" He checked a clock on his data slate. "We're close to the release checkpoint. Down you go, team."

They all sneered at that word and at the cheerful tone of the man who was staying behind. But we filed dutifully enough through the hatch and down into that cave of instrumentation, Miriam first, then me, with Bill Dzik at my back. Michael Poole was last in; I saw him embrace his father, stiffly, evidently not a gesture they were used to. In the "gondola," our four couches sat in a row, so close that my knees touched Miriam's and Dzik's when we were all crammed in there in our suits. The hull was all around us, close enough for me to have reached out and touched it in every direction, a close-fitting shell. Poole pulled the hatch closed, and I heard a hum and whir as the independent systems of this gondola came on line. There was a rattle of latches, and then a kind of sideways shove that made my stomach churn. We were already cut loose of the *Crab*, and were falling free, and rotating.

Poole touched a panel above his head, and the hull turned transparent. It was as if we four in our couches were suspended in space, surrounded by glowing instrument panels, and blocky masses that must be the GUT engine, life support, supplies. Above me the *Crab* slid across the face of Saturn, GUTdrive flaring, and below me the orange face of Titan loomed large.

I whimpered. I have never pretended to be brave.

Miriam Berg handed me a transparent bubble-helmet. "Lethe, put this on before you puke."

I pulled the helmet over my head; it snuggled into the suit neck and made its own lock.

Bill Dzik was evidently enjoying my discomfort. "You feel safer in the suit, right? Well, the entry is the most dangerous time. But you'd better hope we get through the atmosphere's outer layers before the hull breaches, Emry. These outfits aren't designed to work as pressure suits."

"Then what?"

"Heat control," Michael Poole said, a bit more sympathetic. "Titan's air pressure is fifty per cent higher than Earth's, at the surface. But that cold, thick air just sucks away your heat. Listen up, Emry. The gondola's small, but it has a pretty robust power supply—a GUT engine, in fact. You're going to need that power to keep warm. Away from the gondola your suit will protect you, there are power cells built into the fabric. But you won't last more than a few hours away from the gondola. Got that?"

I was hardly reassured. "What about the entry itself? Your father said we'll follow an unmanned profile. That sounds a bit vigorous."

Bill Dzik barked a laugh.

"We should be fine," Poole said. "We don't have full inertial control, we don't have the power, but in the couches we'll be shielded from the worst of the deceleration. Just sit tight."

And then Poole fell silent as he and the others began to work through pre-entry system checks. Harry murmured in my ear, telling me that fresh identity backups had just been taken of each of us and stored in the gondola's systems. I was not reassured. I lay helpless, trussed up and strapped in, as we plummeted into the centre of the sunlit face of Titan.

V

TITAN

Fifteen minutes after cutting loose of the *Crab*, the gondola encountered the first wisps of Titan's upper atmosphere, thin and cold, faintly blue all around us. Still a thousand kilometres above the ground I could feel the first faltering in the gondola's headlong speed. Titan's air is massive and deep, and I was falling backside first straight into it.

The first three minutes of the entry were the worst. We plunged into the air with an interplanetary velocity, but our speed was reduced violently. Three hundred kilometres above the surface, the deceleration peaked at sixteen gravities. Cushioned by Poole's inertial field I felt no more than the faintest shaking, but the gondola creaked and banged, every joint and structure stressed to its limits. Meanwhile a shock wave preceded us, a cap of gas that glowed brilliantly: Titan air battered to a plasma by the dissipating kinetic energy of the gondola.

This fiery entry phase was mercifully brief. But still we fell helplessly. After three minutes we were within a hundred and fifty kilometres of the surface, and immersed in a thickening orange haze, the organic-chemistry products of the destruction of Titan's methane by sunlight. Poole tapped a panel. A mortar banged above us, hauling out a pilot parachute a couple of metres across. This stabilised us in the thickening air, our backs to the moon, our faces to the sky. Then a main parachute unfolded sluggishly, spreading reassuringly above me.

For fifteen minutes we drifted, sinking slowly into a deep ocean of cold, sluggish air. Poole and his colleagues worked at their slates, gathering data from sensors that measured the physical and chemical properties of the atmosphere. I lay silent, curious but frightened for my life.

As we fell deeper into the hydrocarbon smog the temperature fell steadily. Greenhouse effects from methane products keep Titan's stratosphere warmer than it should be. Sixty kilometres above the surface we fell through a layer of hydrocarbon cloud into clearer air beneath, and then, at forty kilometres, through a thin layer of methane clouds. The temperature was close to its minimum here, at only seventy degrees or so above absolute zero. Soon it would rise again, for hydrogen liberated from more methane reactions contributes to another greenhouse effect that warms up the troposphere. The mysterious methane that shouldn't have been there warms Titan's air all the way to the ground.

Fifteen minutes after its unpackaging the main parachute was cut away, and a smaller stabiliser canopy opened. *Much* smaller. We began to fall faster, into the deep ocean of air. "Lethe," I said. "We're still forty kilometres high!"

Bill Dzik laughed at me. "Don't you know anything about the world you're supposed to be guarding, curator? The air's thick here, and the gravity's low, only a seventh of Earth normal. Under that big parachute we'd be hanging in the air all day . . ."

The gondola lurched sideways, shoved by the winds. At least it shut Dzik up. But the winds eased as we fell further, until the air was as still and turgid as deep water. We were immersed now in orange petrochemical haze. But the sun was plainly visible as a brilliant point source of light, surrounded by a yellow-brown halo. The crew gathered data on the spectra of the solar halo, seeking information on aerosols, solid, or liquid particles suspended in the air.

Gradually, beneath our backs, Titan's surface became visible. I twisted to see. Cumulus clouds of ethane vapour lay draped over continents of water ice. Of the ground itself I saw a mottling of dark and white patches, areas huge in extent, pocked by what looked like impact craters, and incised by threading valleys cut by flowing liquid, ethane or methane. The crew continued to collect their science data. An acoustic sounder sent out complex pulses of sound. Miriam Berg showed me how some echoes came back double, with reflections from the surfaces and bottoms of crater lakes, like the one my sampling probe had entered.

The gondola rocked beneath its parachute. Poole had suspended his inertial shielding, and under not much less than Titan's one-seventh gravity I was comfortable in my thick, softly layered exosuit. The crew's murmuring as they worked was professional and quiet. I think I actually slept, briefly.

Then there was a jolt. I woke with a snap. The parachute had been cut loose, and was drifting away with its strings dangling like some jellyfish. Our fall was slow in that thick air and gentle gravity, but fall we did!

And then, as Bill Dzik laughed at me, a new canopy unfurled into the form of a globe, spreading out above us. It was a balloon, perhaps forty, fifty metres across; we were suspended from it by a series of fine ropes. As I watched a kind of hose snaked up from beneath the gondola's hull, and pushed up into the mouth of the balloon, and it began to inflate.

"So that's the plan," I said. "To float around Titan in a balloon! Not very energetic for a man who builds interplanetary wormholes, Poole."

"But that's the point," Poole said testily, as if I had challenged his manhood. "We're here under the noses of your curators' sensors, Emry. The less of a splash we make the better."

Miriam Berg said, "I designed this part of the mission profile. We're going to float around at this altitude, about eight kilometres up—well above any problems with the topography but under most of the cloud decks. We ought to be able to gather the science data we need from here. A couple of weeks should be sufficient."

"A couple of weeks in this suit!"

Poole thumped the walls of the gondola. "This thing expands. You'll be able to get out of your suit. It's not going to be luxury, Emry, but you'll be comfortable enough."

Miriam said, "When the time comes we'll depart from this altitude. The *Crab* doesn't carry an orbit-to-surface flitter, but Harry will send down a booster unit to rendezvous with us and lift the gondola to orbit."

I stared at her. "We don't carry the means of getting off this moon?"

"Not on board, no," Miriam said evenly. "Mass issues. The need to stay under the curacy sensors' awareness threshold. We're supposed to look like an unmanned probe, remember. Look, it's not a problem."

"Umm." Call me a coward, many have. But I didn't like the idea that my only way off this wretched moon was thousands of kilometres away and depended on a complicated series of rendezvous and coupling manoeuvres. "So what's keeping us aloft? Hydrogen, helium?"

Poole pointed at that inlet pipe. "Neither. This is a hot air balloon, Emry, a Montgolfiere." And he gave me a lecture on how hot-air technology is optimal if you must go ballooning on Titan. The thick air and low gravity make the moon hospitable for balloons, and at such low temperatures you get a large expansion in response to a comparatively small amount of heat energy. Add all these factors into the kind of trade-off equation men like Poole enjoys so much, and out pops hot-air ballooning as the low-energy transport of choice on Titan.

Miriam said, "We're a balloon, not a dirigible; we can't steer. But for a mission like this we can pretty much go where the wind takes us; all we're doing is sampling a global ecosphere. And we can choose our course to some extent. The prevailing winds on Titan are easterly, but below about two kilometres there's a strong westerly component. That's a tide, raised by Saturn in the thick air down there. So we can select which way we get blown, just by ascending and descending."

"More stealth, I suppose. No need for engines."

"That's the idea. We've arrived in the local morning. Titan's day is fifteen Earth days long, and we can achieve a lot before nightfall—in fact I'm intending that we should chase the daylight. Right now we're heading for the south pole, where it's summer." And there, as even I knew, methane and ethane pooled in open lakes—the only stable such liquid bodies in the System, save only for Earth and Triton.

"Summer on Titan," Poole said, and he grinned. "And we're riding the oldest flying machine of all over a moon of Saturn!" Evidently he was starting to enjoy himself.

Miriam smiled back, and their gloved hands locked together.

The envelope snapped and billowed above us as the warm air filled it up.

VI
LANDFALL

So we drifted over Titan's frozen landscape, heading for the south pole. For now Michael Poole kept us stuck in that un-expanded hull, and indeed inside our suits, though we removed our helmets, while the crew put the gondola through a fresh series of post-entry checks. I had nothing to do but stare out of the transparent hull, at the very Earthlike clouds that littered the murky sky, or over my shoulder at the landscape that unfolded beneath me.

Now we were low enough to make out detail, I saw that those darker areas were extensive stretches of dunes, lined up in parallel rows by the prevailing wind. The ground looked raked, like a tremendous zen garden. And the lighter areas were outcroppings of a paler rock, plateaus scarred by ravines and valleys. At this latitude there were no open bodies of liquid, but you could clearly see its presence in the recent past, in braided valleys and the shores of dried-out lakes. This landscape of dunes and ravines was punctuated by circular scars that were probably the relics of meteorite impacts, and by odder, dome-like features with irregular calderas—volcanoes. All these features had names, I learned, assigned to them by Earth astronomers centuries dead, who had pored over the first robot-returned images of this landscape. But as nobody had ever come here, those names, borrowed from vanished paradises and dead gods, had never come alive.

I listened absently as Poole and the others talked through their science programme. The atmosphere was mostly nitrogen, just as on Earth, but it contained five per cent methane, and that methane was the key to Titan's wonders, and mysteries. Even aside from its puzzling central role in the greenhouse effects which stabilised the atmosphere, methane was also key to the complicated organic chemistry that went on there. In the lower atmosphere methane reacted with nitrogen to create complex compounds called tholins, a kind of plastic, which fell to the ground in a sludgy rain. When those tholins landed in liquid water, such as in impact-warmed crater lakes, amino acids were produced—the building blocks of our kind of life . . .

As I listened to them debate these issues it struck me than none of them had begun his or her career as a biologist or climatologist: Poole and Berg had both been physicists, Dzik an engineer and more lately a project manager. Both Berg and Dzik had had specialist training to a decent academic standard to prepare for this mission. They all expected to live a long time; periodically they would re-educate themselves and adopt entirely different professions, as needs must. I have never had any such ambition. But then, somehow, despite AS technology, I do not imagine myself reaching any great age.

Their talk had an edge, however, even in those first hours. They were all ethically troubled by what they were doing, and those doubts surfaced now that they were away from Harry Poole's goading.

"At some point," Miriam Berg said, "we'll have to face the question of how we'll react if we *do* find sentience here."

Bill Dzik shook his head. "Sometimes I can't believe we're even here, that we're having this conversation at all. I remember exactly what you said on Baked Alaska, Michael. 'The whole System is going to beat a path to our door to see this—as long as we can work out a way to protect the ecology . . . And if we can't, we'll implode the damn wormhole. We'll get funds for the *Cauchy* some other way.' That's what you said."

Poole said harshly, clearly needled, "That was thirteen years ago, damn it, Bill. Situations change. People change. And the choices we have to make change too."

As they argued, I was the only one looking ahead, the way we were drifting under our balloon. Through the murk I thought I could see the first sign of the ethane lakes of the polar regions, sheets of liquid black as coal surrounded by fractal landscapes, like a false-colour mock-up of Earth's own Arctic. And I thought I could see movement, something rising up off those lakes. Mist, perhaps? But there was too much solidity about those rising forms for that.

And then the forms emerged from the mist, solid and looming.

I pulled my helmet on my head and gripped my couch. I said, "Unless one of you does something fast, we may soon have no choices left at all."

They looked at me, the three of them in a row around me, puzzled. Then they looked ahead, to see what I saw.

They were like birds, black-winged, with white lenticular bodies. Those wings actually flapped in the thick air as they flew up from the polar seas, a convincing simulacrum of the way birds fly in the air of Earth. Oddly they seemed to have no heads.

And they were coming straight towards us.

Michael Poole snapped, "Lethe. Vent the buoyancy!" He stabbed at a panel, and the others went to work, pulling on their helmets as they did so.

I felt the balloon settle as the hot air was released from the envelope above us. We were sinking—but we seemed to move in dreamy slow motion, while those birds loomed larger in our view with every heartbeat.

Then they were on us. They swept over the gondola, filling the sky above, black wings flapping in an oily way that, now they were so close, seemed entirely unnatural, not like terrestrial birds at all. They were huge, each ten, fifteen metres across. I thought I could *hear* them, a rustling, snapping sound carried to me through Titan's thick air.

And they tore into the envelope. The fabric was designed to withstand Titan's methane rain, not an attack like this; it exploded into shreds, and the severed threads waved in the air. Some of the birds suffered; they tangled with our threads or collided with each other and fell away, rustling. One flew into the gondola itself and crumpled like tissue paper, and then fell, wadded up, far below us.

And we fell too, following our victim-assassin to the ground. Our descent from the best part of eight kilometres high took long minutes; we soon reached terminal velocity in Titan's thick air and weak gravity. We had time to strap ourselves in, and Poole and his team worked frantically to secure the gondola's systems. In the last moment Poole flooded the gondola with a foam that filled the internal space and held us rigid in our seats, like dolls in packaging, sightless and unable to move.

I felt the slam as we hit the ground.

VII
SURFACE

The foam drained away, leaving the four of us sitting there in a row like swaddled babies. We had landed on Titan the way we entered its atmosphere, backside first, and now we lay on our backs with the gondola tilted over, so that I was falling against Miriam Berg, and the cladded mass of Bill Dzik was weighing on me. The gondola's hull had reverted to opacity so we lay in a close-packed pearly shell, but there was internal light and the various data slates were working, though they were filled with alarming banks of red.

The three of them went quickly into a routine of checks. I ignored them. *I was alive.* I was breathing, the air wasn't foul, and I was in no greater discomfort than having Dzik's unpleasant bulk pressed against my side. Nothing broken, then. But I felt a pang of fear as sharp as that felt by that Virtual copy of me when he had learned he was doomed. I wondered if his ghost stirred in me now, still terrified.

And my bowels loosened into the suit's systems. Never a pleasant experience, no matter how good the suit technology. But I wasn't sorry to be reminded that I was nothing but a fragile animal, lost in the cosmos. That may be the root of my cowardice, but give me humility and realism over the hubristic arrogance of a Michael Poole any day.

Their technical chatter died away.

"The lights are on," I said. "So I deduce we've got power."

Michael Poole said, gruffly reassuring, "It would take more than a jolt like that to knock out one of my GUT engines."

Dzik said spitefully, "If we'd lost power you'd be an icicle already, Emry."

"Shut up, Bill," Miriam murmured. "Yes, Emry, we're not in bad shape. The pressure hull's intact, we have power, heating, air, water, food. We're not going to die any time soon."

But I thought of the flapping birds of Titan and wondered how she could be so sure.

Poole started unbuckling. "We need to make an external inspection. Figure out our options."

Miriam followed suit, and laughed. She said to me, "Romantic, isn't he? The first human footfalls on Titan, and he calls it an external inspection." Suddenly she was friendly. The crash had evidently made her feel we had bonded in some way.

"Yeah, yeah," Poole said, but I could see he softened.

Bill Dzik dug an elbow in my ribs hard enough to hurt through the layers of my suit. "Move, Emry."

"Leave me alone."

"We're packed in here like spoons. It's one out, all out."

Well, he was right; I had no choice.

Poole made us go through checks of our exosuits, their power cells, the integrity of their seals. Then he drained the air and popped open the hatch in the roof before our faces. I saw a sky sombre and brown, dark by comparison with the brightness of our internal lights, and flecks of black snow drifted by. The hatch was a door from this womb of metal and ceramics out into the unknown.

We climbed up through the hatch in reverse order from how we had come in: Poole, Dzik, myself, then Miriam. The gravity, a seventh of Earth's, was close enough to the Moon's to make that part of the experience familiar, and I moved my weight easily enough. Once outside the hull, lamps on my suit lit up in response to the dark.

I dropped down a metre or so, and drifted to my first footfall on Titan. The sandy surface crunched under my feet. I knew it was water ice, hard as glass. The sand at my feet was ridged into ripples, as if by a receding tide. Pebbles lay scattered, worn and eroded. A wind buffeted me, slow and massive, and I heard a low bass moan. A black rain smeared my faceplate.

The four of us stood together, chubby in our suits, the only humans on a world larger than Mercury. Beyond the puddle of light cast by our suit lamps an entirely unknown landscape stretched off into the infinite dark.

Miriam Berg was watching me. "What are you thinking, Jovik?" As far as I know these were the first words spoken by any human standing on Titan.

"Why ask me?"

"You're the only one of us who's looking at Titan and not at the gondola."

I grunted. "I'm thinking how like Earth this is. Like a beach somewhere, or a high desert, the sand, the pebbles. Like Mars, too, outside Kahra."

"Convergent processes," Dzik said dismissively. "But *you* are an entirely alien presence. Here, your blood is as hot as molten lava. Look, you're leaking heat."

And, looking down, I saw wisps of vapour rising up from my booted feet.

The others checked over the gondola. Its inner pressure cage had been sturdy enough to protect us, but the external hull was crumpled and damaged, various attachments had been ripped off, and it had dug itself into the ice.

Poole called us together for a council of war. "Here's the deal. There's no sign of the envelope; it was shredded, we lost it. The gondola's essential systems are sound, most importantly the power." He banged it with a gloved fist; in the dense air I heard a muffled thump. "The hull's taken a beating, though. We've lost the extensibility. I'm afraid we're stuck in these suits."

"Until what?" I said. "Until we get the spare balloon envelope inflated, right?"

"We don't carry a spare," Bill Dzik said, and he had the grace to sound embarrassed. "It was a cost-benefit analysis—"

"Well, you got that wrong," I snapped back. "How are we supposed to get off this damn moon now? You said we had to make some crackpot mid-air rendezvous."

Poole tapped his chest, and a Virtual image of Harry's head popped into existence in mid-air. "Good question. I'm working on options. I'm fabricating another envelope, and I'll get it down to you. Once we have that gondola aloft again I'll have no trouble picking you up. In the meantime," he said more sternly, "you have work to do down there. Time is short."

"When we get back to the *Crab*," Bill Dzik said to Poole, "you hold him down and I'll kill him."

"He's my father," said Michael Poole. "*I'll* kill him."

Harry dissolved into a spray of pixels.

Poole said, "Look, here's the deal. We'll need to travel if we're to achieve our science goals; we can't do it all from this south pole site. We do have some mobility. The gondola has wheels; it will work as a truck down here. But we're going to have to dig the wreck out of the sand first, and modify it. And meanwhile Harry's right about the limited time. I suggest that Bill and I get on with the engineering. Miriam, you take Emry and go see what science you can do at the lake. It's only a couple of kilometres," he checked a wrist map patch and pointed, "that way."

"OK." With low-gravity grace Miriam jumped back up to the hatch, and retrieved a pack from the gondola's interior.

I felt deeply reluctant to move away from the shelter of the wrecked gondola. "What about those birds?"

Miriam jumped back down and approached me. "We've seen no sign of the birds since we landed. Come on, curator. It will take your mind off how scared you are." And she tramped away into the dark, away from the pool of light by the gondola.

Poole and Dzik turned away from me. I had no choice but to follow her.

VIII
LAKE

Walking any distance was surprisingly difficult.

The layered heat-retaining suit was bulky and awkward, but it was flexible, and that was unlike the vacuum of the Moon, where the internal pressure forces even the best skinsuits to rigidity. But on Titan you are always aware of the resistance of the heavy air. At the surface the pressure is half as much again as on Earth, and the density of the air four times that at Earth's surface. It is almost like moving underwater. And yet the gravity is so low that when you dig your feet into the sand for traction you have a tendency to go floating off the ground. Miriam showed me how to extend deep, sharp treads from the soles of my boots to dig into the loose sand.

It is the thickness of the air that is the challenge on Titan; you are bathed in an intensely cold fluid, less than a hundred degrees above absolute zero, that conducts away your heat enthusiastically, and I was always aware of the silent company of my suit's heating system, and the power cells that would sustain it for no more than a few hours.

"Turn your suit lights off," Miriam said to me after a few hundred metres. "Save your power."

"I prefer not to walk into what I can't see."

"Your eyes will adapt. And your faceplate has image enhancers set to the spectrum of ambient light here . . . Come on, Jovik. If you don't I'll do it for you; your glare is stopping me seeing too."

"All right, damn it."

With the lights off, I was suspended in brown murk, as if under an autumn sky obscured by the smoke of forest fires. But my eyes did adapt, and the faceplate subtly enhanced my vision. Titan opened up around me, a plain of sand and wind-eroded rubble under an orange-brown sky—again not unlike Mars, if you know it. Clouds of ethane or methane floated above me, and beyond them the haze towered up, a column of organic muck tens of kilometres deep. Yet I could see the sun in that haze, a spark low on the horizon, and facing it a half-full Saturn, much bigger than the Moon in Earth's sky. Of the other moons or the stars, indeed of the *Crab*, I could see nothing. All the colours were drawn from a palette of crimson, orange, and brown. Soon my eyes longed for a bit of green.

When I looked back I could see no sign of the gondola, its lights already lost in the haze. I saw we had left a clear line of footsteps behind us. It made me quail to think that this was the only footstep trail on all this little world.

We began to descend a shallow slope. I saw lines in the sand, like tide marks. "I think we're coming to the lake."

"Yes. It's summer here, at the south pole. The lakes evaporate, and the ethane rains out at the north pole. In fifteen years' time, half a Saturnian year, it will be winter here and summer there, and the cycle will reverse. Small worlds have simple climate systems, Jovik. As I'm sure a curator would know . . ."

We came to the edge of the ethane lake. In that dim light it looked black like tar, and sluggish ripples crossed its surface. In patches something more solid lay on the liquid, circular sheets almost like lilies, repellently oily. The lake stretched off black and flat to the horizon, which curved visibly, though it was blurred in the murky air. It was an extraordinary experience to stand there in an exosuit and to face a body of liquid on such an alien world, the ocean black, the sky and the shore brown. And yet there was again convergence with the Earth. This was a kind of beach. Looking around I saw we were in a sort of bay, and to my right, a few kilometres away, a river of black liquid had cut a broad valley, braided like a delta, as it ran into the sea.

And, looking that way, I saw something lying on the shore, crumpled black around a grain of paleness.

Miriam wanted samples from the lake, especially of the discs of gunk that floated on the surface. She opened up her pack and extracted a sampling arm, a remote manipulator with a claw-like grabber. She hoisted this onto her shoulder and extended the arm, and I heard a whir of exoskeletal multipliers. As the arm plucked at the lily-like features some of them broke up into strands, almost like jet-black seaweed, but the arm lifted large contiguous sheets of a kind of film that reminded me of the eerie wings of the Titan birds that had attacked us.

Miriam quickly grew excited at what she was finding.

"Life," I guessed.

"You got it. Well, we knew it was here. We even have samples taken by automated probes. Though we never spotted those birds before." She hefted the stuff, films of it draped over her gloved hand, and looked at me. "I wonder if you understand how exotic this stuff is. I'm pretty sure this is silane life. That is, based on a silicon chemistry, rather than carbon . . ."

The things on the lake did indeed look like jet black lilies. But they were not lilies, or anything remotely related to life like my own.

Life of our chemical sort is based on long molecules, with a solute to bring components of those molecules together. Our specific sort of terrestrial life, which Miriam called "CHON life," after its essential elements carbon, hydrogen, oxygen and nitrogen, uses water as its solute, and carbon-based molecules as its building blocks: carbon can form chains and rings, and long stable molecules like DNA.

"But carbon's not the only choice, and nor is water," Miriam said. "At terrestrial temperatures silicon bonds with oxygen to form very stable molecules."

"Silicates. Rock."

"Exactly. But at *very* low temperatures, silicon can form silanols, analogous to alcohols, which are capable of dissolving in very cold solutes—say, in this ethane lake here. When they dissolve they fill up the lake with long molecules analogous to our organic molecules. These can then link up into polymers using silicon-silicon bonds, silanes. They have weaker bonds than carbon molecules at terrestrial temperatures, but it's just what you need in a low-energy, low-temperature environment like this. With silanes as the basis you can dream up all sorts of complex molecules analogous to nucleic acids and proteins—"

"Just what we have here."

"Exactly. Nice complicated biomolecules for evolution to play with. They are more commonly found on the cooler, outer worlds—Neptune's moon Triton for example. But this lake is cold enough. The energy flow will be so low that it must take a *lo-ong* time for anything much to grow or evolve. But on Titan there is plenty of time." She let the filmy stuff glide off her manipulator scoop and back into the lake. "There's so much we don't know. There has to be an ecology in there, a food chain. Maybe the films are the primary producers—an equivalent of the plankton in our oceans, for instance. But where do they get their energy from? And how do they survive the annual drying-out of their lakes?"

"Good questions," I said. "I wish I cared."

She stowed her sample bottles in her pack. "I think you care more than you're prepared to admit. Nobody as intelligent as you is without curiosity. It goes with the territory. Anyhow we should get back to the gondola."

I hesitated. I hated to prove her right, that there was indeed a grain of curiosity lodged in my soul. But I pointed at the enigmatic black form lying further along the beach. "Maybe we should take a look at that first."

She glanced at it, and at me, and headed that way without another word.

It turned out, as I had suspected, that the crumpled form was a bird. I recalled one hitting our gondola during their assault and falling away; perhaps this was that very casualty.

It was a block of ice, about the size of my head, wrapped up in a torn sheet of black film. With great care Miriam used her manipulator arm to pick apart the film, as if she was unwrapping a Christmas present. The ice mass wasn't a simple lump but a mesh of spindly struts and bars surrounding a hollow core. It had been badly damaged by the fall. Miriam took samples of this and of the film.

"That ice lump looks light for its size," I said. "Like the bones of a bird."

"Which makes sense if it's a flying creature." Miriam was growing excited. "Jovik, look at this. The filmy stuff, the wings, look identical to the samples I took from the surface of the lake. It has to be silane. But the ice structure is different." She broke a bit of it open, and turned on a suit lamp so we could see a mass of very thin icicles, like fibres. It was almost sponge-like. Inside the fine ice straws were threads of what looked like discoloured water. "Rich in organics," Miriam said, glancing at a data panel on her manipulator arm. "I mean, our sort of organics, CHON life, carbon-water—amino acids, a kind of DNA. There are puzzles here. Not least the fact that we find it *here*, by this lake. CHON life has been sampled on Titan before. But it's thought carbon-water life can only subsist here in impact-melt crater lakes, and we're a long way from anything like that . . ."

Her passion grew, a trait I have always found attractive.

"I think this is a bird, one of those we saw flying at us. But it seems to be a composite creature, a symbiosis of these hydrocarbon wings and the ice lump— saline life cooperating with CHON life! Just remarkable. You wonder how it came about in the first place . . . but I guess there are examples of just as intricate survival strategies in our own biosphere. Give evolution enough time and anything is possible. I wonder what it is they both *want*, though, what the two sides in this symbiosis get out of the relationship . . ."

"It's a genuine discovery, Jovik. Nobody's seen this before—life from two entirely different domains working together. And I wouldn't have noticed it if not for you." She held out the ice lump to me. "They'll probably name it after you."

Her enthusiasm was fetching, but not that much. "Sure. But my concern right now is how much power we have left in these suit heaters. Let's get back to the gondola."

So she stowed away the remaining fragments of the Titan bird, Jovik Emry's contribution to System science, and we retraced our path back to the gondola.

IX
GONDOLA

The days are very long on Titan, and by the time we got back to the gondola nothing seemed to have changed about the landscape or the sky, not a diffuse shadow had shifted. We found Poole and Dzik happily fixing big balloon wheels to axles slung beneath the crumpled hull.

When they were done, we all climbed back aboard. Poole had reset some of the interior lamps so they glowed green, yellow, and blue; it was a relief to be immersed once more in bright Earth light.

We set off in our gondola-truck for the next part of our expedition. We were making, I was told, for an impact crater believed to hold liquid water, which itself was not far from a cryovolcano, another feature of interest for the expedition. This site was only perhaps a hundred kilometres from where we had come down.

Miriam transferred her samples to cold stores, and ran some of them through a small onboard science package. She jabbered about what she had discovered. Poole encouraged her more than Dzik did, but even that wasn't much.

Dzik and Poole were more interested in that moment with playing with the gondola. Like overgrown boys they sat at an improvised driver's console and fussed over gear ratios and the performance of the big tyres. Poole even insisted on driving the bus himself, though Titan was so flat and dull for the most part he could easily have left the chore to the onboard systems. That proved to me the fallacy of not bringing along specialist biologists on a jaunt like this. It was only Miriam who seemed to have a genuine passion for the life systems we were supposed to be here to study; Dzik and Poole were too easily distracted by the technology, which was, after all, only a means to an end.

They had however rearranged the interior to make it feel a little less cramped. The couches had been separated and set up around the cabin, so you could sit upright with a bit of elbow room. The cabin was pressurised, so we could remove our helmets, and though the expandable walls didn't work any more there was room for one at a time to shuck off his or her exosuit. Poole ordered us to do so; we had already been inside the suits for a few hours, and the suits, and ourselves, needed some maintenance. Poole had set up a curtained-off area where we could let our discarded suits perform their self-maintenance functions while we had showers—of water recycled from our urine and sweat, which was deemed a lot safer than melt from the ice moon. Poole himself used the shower first, and then Miriam. She was hasty, eager to get back to her work, and kept talking even while she cleaned up.

After Miriam was out of the shower I took my turn. It was a miserable drizzle and lukewarm at that, but it was a relief to let my skin drink in the water. I was quick, though; with the unknown dangers of Titan only centimetres away beyond the gondola's fragile metal walls, I didn't want to spend long outside the security of the suit.

After me, Bill Dzik followed, and it was an unlovely stink his suit released. I was spitefully glad that for all his bluster his reaction to the terrors of our landing must have been just as ignoble as mine.

After a couple of hours we reached our destination. Safely suited up, I sat in my couch and peered over Miriam's and Poole's shoulders at the landscape outside. That cryovolcano was a mound that pushed out of the landscape some kilometres to the west of us. It had the look of a shield volcano, like Hawaii or Mons Olympus, a flat-profiled dome with a caldera on the top. It wasn't erupting while we sat there, but I could see how successive sheets of "lava" had plated its sides. That lava was water ice, heavily laced with ammonia, which had come gushing up from this world's strange mantle, a sea of ammonia and water kilometres down beneath our tyres.

As for the crater lake I saw nothing but a plain, flatter and even more featureless than the average, covered with a thin scattering of ice sand. But the lake was there, hidden. Poole extracted radar images which showed the unmistakeable profile of an impact crater, right ahead of us, kilometres wide. Such is the vast energy pulse delivered by an infalling asteroid or comet—or, in Saturn's system, perhaps a ring fragment or a bit of a tide-shattered moon—the water locally can retain enough heat to remain liquid for a long time, thousands of years. Such a lake had formed here, and then frozen over with a thin crust, on top of which that skim of sand had been wind-blown. But the briny lake remained, hoarding its heat.

And, studded around the lake's circular rim, were more sponge-like masses like the one we had discovered wrapped up in silane film at the shore of the polar lake. These masses were positioned quite regularly around the lake, and many were placed close by crevasses which seemed to offer a route down into the deep structure of the ice rock beneath us. Miriam started gathering data eagerly.

Meanwhile Poole was puzzling over some images returned from the very bottom of the crater lake. He had found motion, obscure forms labouring. They looked to me like machines quarrying a rock deposit. But I could not read the images well enough, and as Poole did not ask my opinions I kept my mouth shut.

Miriam Berg was soon getting very agitated by what she was finding. Even as she gathered the data and squirted it up to Harry Poole in the *Crab*, she eagerly hypothesised. "Look—I think it's obvious that Titan is a junction between at least two kinds of life, the silanes of the ethane lakes and the CHON sponges. I've done some hasty analysis on the CHON tissues. They're like us, but not identical. They use a subtly different subset of amino acids to build their proteins, and they have a variant of DNA in there—a different set of bases, a different coding system. The silanes, meanwhile, are like the life systems we've discovered in the nitrogen pools on Triton, but again not identical, based on a different subset of silicon-oxygen molecular strings.

"It's possible both forms of life were brought here through panspermia—the natural wafting of life between the worlds in the form of something like spores, blasted off their parent world by impacts and driven here by sunlight and gravity. If the System's CHON life arose first on Earth or Mars, it might easily have drifted here and seeded in a crater lake, and followed a different evolutionary strategy. Similarly the silanes at the poles found a place to live, and followed their own path, independently of their cousins . . ."

The transfer of materials from the oily ethane lakes to the water crater ponds might actually have facilitated such creations. You need membranes to make life, something to separate the inside of a cell from the outside. As water and oil don't mix, adding one to the other gives you a natural way to create such membranes.

She shook her head. "It seems remarkable that here we have a place, this moon, a junction where families of life from different ends of Sol System can coexist."

"But there's a problem," Bill Dzik called from his shower. "Both your silanes and your sponges live in transient environments. The ethane lakes pretty much dry up every Titan year. And each crater lake will freeze solid after a few thousand years."

"Yes," Miriam said. "Both forms need to migrate. And that's how, I think, they came to cooperate . . ."

She sketched a hasty narrative of the CHON sponges emerging from the crater lakes, and finding their way to the summer pole. Maybe they got there by following deep crevasses, smashed into Titan's ice crust by the impacts that dug out crater lakes like this one in the first place. Down there they would find liquid water, kilometres deep and close to the ammonia ocean. It would be cold, briny, not to terrestrial tastes, but it would be liquid, and survivable. And at the pole they would find the silane lilies floating on their ethane seas. The lilies in turn needed to migrate to winter pole, where their precious life-stuff ethane was raining out.

Miriam mimed, her fist touching her flattened palm. "So they come together, the sponges and the lilies—"

"To make the Titan birds," I said.

"That's the idea. They come flapping up out of the lake, just as we saw, heading for the winter pole. And meanwhile, maybe the sponges get dropped off at fresh crater lakes along the way. It's a true symbiosis, with two entirely different spheres of life intersecting—and cooperating, for without the migration neither form could survive alone." She looked at us, suddenly doubtful. "We're all amateurs here. I guess any competent biologist could pick holes in this the size of the centre of Saturn's rings."

Dzik said, "No competent biologist would even be hypothesising this way, not with so few facts."

"No," Virtual Harry said tinnily. "But at least you've come up with a plausible model, Miriam. And all without the need to evoke even a scrap of sentience. Good job."

"There are still questions," Miriam said. "Maybe the sponges provide the birds' intelligence, or at least some kind of directionality. But what about power? The lilies are especially are a pretty low-energy kind of life form . . ."

Michael Poole said, "Maybe I can answer that. I've been doing some analysis of my own. I can tell you a bit more about the silane lilies' energy source. Believe it or not—even on a world as murky as this—I think they're photosynthesising." And he ran through the chemistry he thought he had identified, using entirely different compounds and molecular processing pathways from the chlorophyll-based green-plant photosynthesis of Earth life.

"Of course," Miriam said. "I should have seen it. I never even asked myself what the lilies were *doing* while they were lying around on the lake's surface . . . Trapping sunlight!"

Harry was growing excited too. "Hey, if you're right, son, you may already have paid for the trip. Silane-based low-temp photosynthesisers would be hugely commercially valuable. Think of it, you could grow them out of those nitrogen lakes on Triton and go scudding around the outer System on living sails." His grin was wide, even in the reduced Virtual image.

Poole and Miriam were smiling too, staring at each other with a glow of connection. Theirs was a strange kind of symbiosis, like silane lily and CHON sponge; they seemed to need the excitement of external discovery and achievement to bring them together.

Well, there was a happy mood in that grounded gondola, the happiest since we had crashed. Even Bill Dzik as he showered was making grunting, hog-like noises of contentment.

And just at that moment there was a crunching sound, like great jaws closing over metal, and the whole bus tipped to one side.

Poole and Miriam staggered and started shouting instructions to each other. I had my helmet over my head in a heartbeat.

Then there was another crunch, a ripping sound—and a scream, gurgling and suddenly cut off, and an inward rush of cold air that I felt even through my exosuit. I turned and saw that near the shower partition, a hole had been ripped in the side of the gondola's flimsy hull, revealing Titan's crimson murk. Something like a claw, or a huge version of Miriam's manipulator arm, was working at the hull, widening the breach.

And Bill Dzik, naked, not metres from the exosuit that could have saved him, was already frozen to death.

That was enough for me. I flung open the hatch in the gondola roof and lunged out, not waiting for Miriam or Poole. I hit the Titan sand and ran as best I could, the exosuit labouring to help me. I could hear crunching and chewing behind me. I did not look back.

When I had gone a hundred metres I stopped, winded, and turned. Poole and Miriam were following me. I was relieved that at least I was not stranded on Titan alone.

And I saw what was becoming of our gondola. The machines that had assailed it—and they were machines, I had no doubt of it—were like spiders of ice, with lenticular bodies perhaps ten metres long, and each equipped with three grabber claws attached to delicate low-gravity limbs. Four, five of these things were labouring at the wreck of our gondola. I saw that they had gone for the wheels first, which was why we had tipped over, and now were making a fast job of ripping the structure apart. Not only that, beyond them I saw a line of similar-looking beasts carrying silvery fragments that could only be pieces of the gondola off up the rising ground towards the summit of the cryovolcano. Some of the larger components of the wreck they left intact, such as the GUT engine module, but they carried them away just as determinedly.

In minutes, I saw, there would be little left of our gondola on the ice surface—not much aside from Bill Dzik, who, naked, sprawled and staring with frozen eyeballs, made an ugly corpse, but did not deserve the fate that had befallen him.

Harry Poole's head popped into Virtual existence before us. "Well," he said, "that complicates things."

Michael swatted at him, dispersing pixels like flies.

X
SPIDERS

"Dzik is dead," I said. "And so are we." I turned on Michael Poole, fists bunched in the thick gloves. "You and your absurd ambition—it was always going to kill you one day, and now it's killed us all."

Michael Poole snorted his contempt. "And I wish I'd just thrown you into a jail back on Earth and left you to rot."

"Oh, Lethe," Miriam said with disgust. She was sifting through the scattered debris the spiders had left behind. "Do you two have any idea how ridiculous you look in those suits? Like two soft toys facing off. Anyhow you aren't dead yet, Jovik." She picked up bits of rubbish, rope, a few instruments, some of her precious sample flasks, enigmatic egg-shaped devices small enough to fit in her fist—and food packs.

Michael Poole's curiosity snagged him. "They didn't take everything."

"Evidently not. In fact, as you'd have noticed if you weren't too busy trading insults with your passenger, they didn't take *us*. Or Bill."

"What, then?"

"Metal. I think. Anything that has a significant metal component is being hauled away."

"Ah." Poole watched the spiders toiling up their volcano, bits of our ship clutched in their huge claws. "That makes a sort of sense. One thing this moon is short of is metal. Has been since its formation. Even the core is mostly light silicate rock, more like Earth's mantle than its iron core. Which maybe explains why every surface probe to Titan across sixteen hundred years has disappeared without a trace—even the traces of your illegal sample-collectors, Emry. They were taken for the metal. And," he said, chasing the new idea, "maybe that's what we saw in the radar images of the deeps of the crater lake. Something toiling on the floor, you remember, as if quarrying? Maybe it was more of those spider things after the metallic content of the meteorite that dug out the crater in the first place."

"Well, in any event they left useful stuff behind," said Miriam, picking through the debris. "Anything ceramic, glass fibre, plastic. And the food packs. We won't starve, at least."

Poole had homed in on theory, while she focused on the essentials that might keep us alive. That tells you everything about the man's lofty nature.

"But they took the GUT engine, didn't they?" I put in sharply. "Our power source. Without which we'll eventually freeze to death, no matter how well fed we are."

"And, incidentally," Miriam said, "the identity-backup deck. We cached the backups in the GUT engine's own control and processing unit, the most reliable store on the gondola. If we lose that, we lose the last trace of poor Bill too."

I couldn't help but glance at Dzik's corpse, fast-frozen on the ice of Titan.

Not Poole, though. He was watching those receding spiders. "They're heading down into the volcano. Which is a vent that leads down into the mantle, the ammonia sea, right? Why? What the hell are those things?"

Miriam said, "One way to find out." She hefted one of those ceramic eggs in her right hand, pressed a stud that made it glow red, and hurled it towards the nearest spider. It followed a low-gravity arc, heavily damped in the thick air, and it seemed to take an age to fall. But her aim was good, and it landed not a metre from the spider.

And exploded. Evidently it had been a grenade. The spider shattered satisfactorily, those ugly claws going wheeling through the air.

Miriam had already started to run towards the spider. You couldn't fault her directness. "Come on."

Poole followed, and I too, unwilling to be left alone with Bill's frozen remains. Poole called, "What did you do that for?"

"We want to know what we're dealing with, don't we?"

"And why are we running?"

"So we can get there before the other spiders get rid of it."

And sure enough the other spiders, still laden with bits of the gondola, had already turned, and were closing on their shattered fellow. They didn't seem perturbed by the sudden destruction of one of their kind, or of our approaching presence. They seemed to perceive only what was essential to them—only what was metallic.

We got there first, and we squatted around the downed spider in a splash of suit light. The spider hadn't broken open; it was not enclosed by a hull or external carapace. Instead it had shattered into pieces, like a smashed sculpture. We pawed at the debris chunks, Miriam and Poole talking fast, analysing, speculating. The chunks appeared to be mostly water ice, though Poole speculated it was a particular high-pressure form. The internal structure was not simple; it reminded me of a honeycomb, sharp-edged chambers whose walls enclosed smaller clusters of chambers and voids, on down through the length scales like a fractal. Poole pointed out threads of silver and a coppery colour—the shades were uncertain in Titan's light. They were clearly metallic.

"So the spiders at least need metal," Miriam said. "I wonder what the power source is."

But we weren't to find out, for the other spiders had closed in and we didn't want to get chomped by accident. We backed off, dimming our suit lights.

Miriam asked, "So, biological or artificial? What do you think?"

Poole shrugged. "They seem dedicated to a single purpose, and have these metallic components. That suggests artificial. But that body interior looks organic. Grown."

I felt like putting Poole in his place. "Maybe these creatures transcend your simple-minded categories. Perhaps they are the result of a million years of machine evolution. Or the result of a long symbiosis between animal and technology."

Poole shook his head. "My money's on biology. Given enough time, necessity and selection can achieve some remarkable things."

Miriam said, "But why would their systems incorporate metal if it's so rare here?"

"Maybe they're not native to Titan," I said. "Maybe they didn't evolve here." But neither of them were listening to me. "The real question is," I said more urgently, "what do we do now?"

The head of Harry Poole, projected somehow by our suit's comms systems, popped into existence, the size of an orange, floating in the air. The small scale made his skin look even more unnaturally smooth. "And that," he said, "is the first intelligent question you've asked since we pressganged you, Jovik. You ready to talk to me now?"

Michael Poole glared at his father, then turned and sucked water from the spigot inside his helmet. "Tell us how bad it is, Harry."

"I can't retrieve you for seven days," Harry said.

I felt colder than Titan. "But the suits—"

"Without recharge our suits will expire in three days," Poole said. "Four at the most."

I could think of nothing to say.

Harry looked around at us, his disembodied head spinning eerily. "There are options."

"Go on," Poole said.

"You could immerse yourselves in the crater lake. The suits could withstand that. It's cold in there, the briny stuff is well below freezing, but it's not as cold as the open air. Kept warm by the residual heat of impact, remember. Even so you would only stretch out your time by a day or two."

"Not enough," Miriam said. "And we wouldn't get any work done, floating around in the dark in a lake."

I laughed at her. "Work? Who cares about work now?"

Poole said, "What else, Harry?"

"I considered options where two people might survive, rather than three. Or one. By sharing suits."

The tension between us rose immediately.

Harry said, "Of course those spiders also left you Bill's suit. The trouble is the power store is built into the fabric of each suit. To benefit you'd have to swap suits. I can't think of any way you could do that without the shelter of the gondola; you'd freeze to death in a second."

"So it's not an option," Poole said.

Miriam looked at us both steadily. "It never was."

I wasn't sure if I was relieved or not, for I had been determined, in those few moments when it seemed a possibility, that the last survivor in the last suit would be myself.

"So," Poole said to Harry, "what else?"

"You need the gondola's GUT engine to recharge your suits," Harry said. "There's just no alternative."

I pointed at the toiling spiders on the cryovolcano. "Those beasts have already thrown it into that caldera."

"Then you'll have to go after it," Harry said, and, comfortably tucked up in the *Crab*, he grinned at me. "Won't you?"

"How?" I was genuinely bewildered. "Are we going to build a submarine?"

"You won't need one," Harry said. "You have your suits. Just jump in . . ."

"Are you insane? You want us to jump into the caldera of a volcano, after a bunch of metal-chewing monster spiders?"

But Miriam and Poole, as was their way, had pounced on the new idea. Miriam said, "Jovik, you keep forgetting you're not on Earth. That 'volcano' is just spewing water, lava that's colder than your own bloodstream." She glanced at Harry. "The water's very ammonia-rich, however. I take it our suits can stand it?"

"They're designed for contact with the mantle material," Harry said. "We always knew that was likely. The pressure shouldn't be a problem either."

Poole said, "As for the spiders, they will surely leave us alone if we keep away from them. We know that. We might even use them in the descent. Follow the spiders, find the engine. Right?"

Harry said, "And there's science to be done." He displayed data in gleaming Virtual displays—cold summaries only metres away from Bill Dzik's corpse. Harry said that his preliminary analysis of our results showed that the primary source of the atmosphere's crucial methane was nothing in the air or the surface features, but a venting from the cryovolcanoes. "And therefore the ultimate source is somewhere in the ammonia sea," Harry said. "Biological, geological, whatever—it's down there."

"OK," Poole said. "So we're not going to complete the picture unless we go take a look."

"You won't be out of touch. I'll be able to track you, and talk to you all the way in. Our comms link has a neutrino-transmission basis; a few kilometres of ice or water isn't going to make any difference to that."

A few *kilometres*? I didn't like the sound of that.

"So that's that," Miriam said. "We have a plan."

"You have a shared delusion," I said.

They ignored me. Poole said, "I suggest we take an hour out. We can afford that. We should try to rest; we've been through a lot. And we need to sort through these supplies, figure out what we can use."

"Yeah," said Miriam. "For instance, how about nets of ice as ballast? . . ."

So he and Miriam got down to work, sorting through the junk discarded by the spiders, knotting together cable to make nets. They were never happier than when busy on some task together.

And there was Bill Dzik, lying on his back, stark naked, frozen eyes staring into the murky sky. I think it tells you a lot about Michael Poole and even Miriam that they were so focussed on their latest goal that they had no time to consider the remains of this man whom they had worked with, apparently, for decades.

Well, I had despised the man, and he despised me, but something in me cringed at the thought of leaving him like that. I looked around for something I could use as a shovel. I found a strut and a ceramic panel from some internal partition in the gondola, and used cable to join them together.

Then I dug into the soil of Titan. The blade went in easily; the icy sand grains didn't cling together. As a native of Earth's higher gravity I was over-powered for Titan, and lifted great shovelfuls easily. But a half-metre or so down I found the sand was tighter packed and harder to penetrate, no doubt some artefact of Titan's complicated geology. I couldn't dig a grave deep enough for Bill Dzik. So I contented myself with laying him in my shallow ditch, and building a mound over him. Before I covered his face I tried to close his eyes, but of course the lids were frozen in place.

All the time I was working I clung to my anger at Michael Poole, for it was better than the fear.

XI
VOLCANO

So we climbed the flank of the cryovolcano, paralleling the trail followed by the ice spiders, who continued to toil up there hauling the last useful fragments of our gondola. We were laden too with our improvised gear—rope cradles, bags of ice-rock chunks for ballast, food packs. Miriam even wore a pack containing the pick of her precious science samples.

It wasn't a difficult hike. When we had risen above the sand drifts we walked on bare rock-ice, a rough surface that gave good footing under the ridges of our boots. I had imagined we'd slip walking up a bare ice slope, but at such temperatures the ice under your feet won't melt through the pressure of your weight, as on Earth, and it's that slick of meltwater that eliminates the friction.

But despite the easy climb, as we neared the caldera my legs felt heavy. I had no choice but to go on, to plunge into ever greater danger, as I'd had no real choice since being pressganged in the first place.

At last we stood at the lip of the caldera. We looked down over a crudely carved bowl perhaps half a kilometre across, water-ice rock laced with some brownish organic muck. Most of the bowl's floor was solid, evidently the cryovolcano was all but dormant, but there was a wide crevasse down which the spiders toiled into darkness. The spiders, laden as they were, clambered nimbly down the sides of this crevasse, and Poole pointed out how they climbed back up the far side, unladen. If you listened carefully you could hear a crunching sound, from deep within the crevasse.

This was what we were going to descend into.

"Don't even think about it," Miriam murmured to me. "Just do it."

But first we needed a tame spider.

We climbed a few paces down the flank, and stood alongside the toiling line. Miriam actually tried to lasso a spider as it crawled past us. This was a bit over-ambitious, as the thick air and low gravity gave her length of cable a life of its own. So she and Poole worked out another way. With a bit of dexterity they man-aged to snag cable loops around a few of the spider's limbs, and Poole threw cable back and forth under the beast's belly and over its back and tied it off, to make a kind of loose net around the spider's body. The spider didn't even notice these activities, it seemed, but continued its steady plod.

"That will do," Poole said. "All aboard!" Grasping his own burden of pack and ballast nets he made a slow-motion leap, grabbed the improvised netting, and set himself on the back of the spider. Miriam and I hurried to follow him.

So there we were, the three of us sitting on the back of the beast with our hands wrapped in lengths of cable. The first few minutes of the ride weren't so bad, though the spider's motion was jolting and ungainly, and you always had the unpleasant awareness that there was no conscious mind directing this thing.

But then the lip of the caldera came on us, remarkably quickly. I wrapped my hands and arms tighter in the netting.

"Here we go!" Michael Poole cried, and he actually whooped as the spider tipped head first over the lip of the crevasse, and began to climb down its dead vertical wall. I could not see how it was clinging to the sheer wall—perhaps with suckers, or perhaps its delicate limbs found footholds. But my concern was for myself, for as the spider tipped forward we three fell head over heels, clinging to the net, until we were hanging upside down.

"Climb up!" Poole called. "It will be easier if we can settle near the back end."

It was good advice, but easier said than done, for to climb I had to loosen my grip on the cable to which I was clinging. I was the last to reach the arse end of the descending spider, and find a bit of respite in a surface I could lie on.

And all the while the dark of the chasm closed around us, and that dreadful crunching, chewing noise from below grew louder. I looked up to see the open-ing of this chimney as a ragged gash of crimson-brown, the only natural light; it barely cast a glow on the toiling body of the spider. Impulsively I ordered my suit to turn on its lights, and we were flooded with glare.

Poole asked, "Everybody OK?"

"Winded," Miriam said. "And I'm glad I took my claustrophobia pills before getting into the gondola. Look. What's that ahead?"

We all peered down. It was a slab of ice that appeared to span the crevasse. For an instant I wondered if this was as deep as we would have to go to find our GUT engine. But there was no sign of toiling spiders here, or of the pieces of our gon-dola, and I feared I knew what was coming next. That sound of crunching grew louder and louder, with a rhythm of its own.

"Brace yourselves," Poole said—pointless advice.

Our spider hit the ice floor. It turned out to be a thin crust, easily broken—that was the crunching we had heard, as spider after spider smashed through this interface. Beyond the broken crust I caught one glimpse of black, frothy water before I was dragged down into it, head first.

Immersed, I was no colder, but I could feel a sticky thickness all around me, as if I had been dropped into a vat of syrup. My suit lamps picked out enigmatic flecks and threads that filled the fluid around me. When I looked back, I saw the roof of this vent already freezing over, before it was broken by the plunging form of another spider, following ours.

Michael Poole was laughing. "Dunked in molten lava, Titan style. What a ride!"

I moaned, "How much longer? How deep will we go?"

"As deep as we need to. Have patience. But you should cut your lights, Emry. Save your power for heating."

"No, wait." Miriam was pointing at the ice wall that swept past us. "Look there. And there!"

And I made out tubular forms, maybe half a metre long or less, that clung to the walls, or, it seemed, made their purposeful way across it. It was difficult to see any detail, for they quickly shot up and out of our field of view.

"Life?" Poole said, boyishly excited once more.

Miriam said, "It looks like it, doesn't it?" Without warning us she loosened one hand from the net, and grabbed at one of the tubes and dragged it away from its hold on the wall. It wriggled in her hand, pale and sightless, a fat worm; its front end, open like a mouth, was torn.

"Ugh," I said. "Throw it back!"

But Miriam was cradling the thing. "Oh, I'm sorry. I hurt you, didn't I?"

Poole bent over it. "Alive, then."

"Oh, yes. And if it's surviving in this ammonia lava, I wouldn't mind betting it's a cousin of whatever's down below in the sea. More life, Michael!"

"Look, I think it's been browsing on the ice. They are clustered pretty thickly over the walls." And when I looked, I saw he was right; there the tube-fish were, browsing away, working their way slowly up the vent. "Maybe they actively keep the vent open, you think?"

Poole took a small science box from Miriam's pack, and there, together, even as we rode that alien back down into the throat of the volcano, they briskly analysed the beast's metabolism, and the contents of the water we were immersed in, and sent the results back to the *Hermit Crab*. Harry's Virtual head popped up before us, grinning inanely, even in that extreme situation.

I had seen enough. With a snap, I made my suit turn its lights off. I had no desire to sit shivering in the dark as invisible ice walls plummeted past me. But I was gambling that curiosity would get the better of Poole and Miriam, and I was right; soon it was Poole whose suit glowed, spending his own precious power to light me up, as they laboured over their pointless science.

"So I was right," Miriam breathed at last. "This vent, and the mantle ocean, host a whole other domain—*a third* on Titan, in addition to the silanes and the CHON sponges. Ammono life . . ."

Titan's liquid mantle is thought to be a relic of its formation, in a part of the solar nebula where ammonia was common. Titan was born with a rocky core and a deep open ocean, of water laced with ammonia. The ocean might have persisted for a billion years, warmed by greenhouse effects under a thick primordial atmosphere. A billion years is plenty of time for life to evolve. With time the ocean surface froze over to form an icy crust, and at the ocean's base complex high-pressure forms of ice formed a deep solid layer enclosing the silicate core. Ice above and below, but still the liquid ocean persisted between, ammonia-rich water, very alkaline, very viscous. And in that deep ocean a unique kind of life adapted to its strange environment, based on chemical bonds between carbon and nitrogen-hydrogen chemical groups rather than carbon-oxygen, using ammonia as its solute rather than water: "ammono life," the specialists call it.

"Yes, a third domain," Miriam said. "One unknown elsewhere in Sol System so far as I know. So here on Titan you have a junction of three entirely different domains of life: native ammono life in the mantle ocean, CHON life in the crater lakes blown in from the inner system, and the silane lilies wafting in from Triton and the outer cold. Incredible."

"More than that," Harry said tinnily. "Michael, that tube-fish of yours is not a methanogen—it doesn't create methane—but it's full of it. Methane is integral to its metabolism, as far as I can see from the results you sent me. It even has methane in its flotation bladders."

Miriam looked at the tube-fish blindly chewing at the ice walls. "Right. They collect it somehow, from some source deep in the ocean. They use it to float up here. They even nibble the cryovolcano vent walls, to keep them open. They have to be integral to delivering the methane from the deep ocean sources to the atmosphere. So you have the three domains not just sharing this moon but cooperating in sustaining its ecology."

Harry said, "Quite a vision. And as long as they're all stupid enough, we might make some money out of this damn system yet."

Miriam let go of her tube-fish, like freeing a bird; it wriggled off into the dark. "You always were a realist, Harry."

I thought I saw blackness below us, in the outer glimmer of Poole's suit lamps. "Harry. How deep is this ice crust, before we get to the mantle ocean?"

"Around thirty-five kilometres."

"And how deep are we now? Can you tell?"

"Oh, around thirty-five kilometres."

Michael Poole gasped. "Lethe. Grab hold, everybody."

It was on us almost at once: the base of the vent we had followed all the way down from the cryovolcano mouth at the surface, a passage right through the ice crust of Titan. I gripped the net and shut my eyes.

As we passed out of the vent, through the roof of ice and into the mantle beneath, I felt the walls recede from me, a wash of pressure, a vast opening-out.

And we fell into the dark and cold.

XII
OCEAN

Now that the walls were gone from under its limbs I could feel that the spider was swimming, or perhaps somehow jetting, ever deeper into that gloopy sea, while the three of us held on for our lives. Looking up I saw the base of Titan's solid crust, an ice roof that covered the whole world, glowing in the light of Poole's lamps but already receding. And I thought I saw the vent from which we had emerged, a much eroded funnel around which tube-fish swam languidly. Away from the walls I could more easily see the mechanics of how they swam; lacking fins or tails, they seemed to twist through the water, a motion maybe suited to the viscosity of the medium. They looked more like vast bacteria than fish.

Soon we were so far beneath the ice roof that it was invisible, and we three and the crab that dragged us down were a single point of light falling into the dark. And Poole turned off his suit lamps!

I whimpered, "Lethe, Poole, spare us."

"Oh, have a heart," Miriam said, and her own suit lit up. "Just for a time. Let him get used to it."

I said, "Get used to what? Falling into this endless dark?"

"Not endless," Poole said. "The ocean is no more than—how much, Harry?"

"Two hundred and fifty kilometres deep," Harry said, mercifully not presenting a Virtual to us. "Give or take."

"Two hundred and fifty . . . How deep are you intending to take us, Poole?"

"I told you," Michael Poole said grimly. "As deep as it takes. We have to retrieve that GUT engine, Emry. We don't have a choice—simple as that."

"And I have a feeling," Miriam said bleakly, "now we're out of that vent, that we may be heading all the way down to the bottom. It's kind of the next logical choice."

"We'll be crushed," I said dismally.

"No," Harry Poole piped up. "Look, Jovik, just remember Titan isn't a large world. The pressure down there is only about four times what you'd find in Earth's deepest oceans. Five, tops. Your suit is over-engineered. Whatever it is that kills you, it won't be crushing."

"How long to the bottom, then?"

Harry said, "You're falling faster than you'd think, given the viscosity of the medium. That spider is a strong swimmer. A day, say."

"A day!"

Miriam said, "There may be sights to see on the way down."

"What sights?"

"Well, the tube-fish can't exist in isolation. There has to be a whole ammono ecology in the greater deeps."

My imagination worked overtime. "Ammono sharks. Ammono whales."

Miriam laughed. "Sluggish as hell, in this cold soup. And besides, they couldn't eat you, Jovik."

"They might spit me out after trying." I tried to think beyond my immediate panic. "But even if we survive—even if we find our damn GUT engine down there on the ice—how are we supposed to get back?"

Poole said easily, "All we need to do is dump our ballast and we'll float up. We don't need to bring up the GUT engine, remember, just use it to recharge the suits."

Miriam said, "A better option might be to hitch a ride with another spider."

"Right. Which would solve another problem," Poole said. "Which is to find a cryovolcano vent to the surface. The spiders know the way, evidently."

Harry said, "And even if the spiders let you down, I could guide you. I can see you, the vent mouths, even the GUT engine. This neutrino technology was worth the money it cost. There's no problem, in principle."

At times I felt less afraid of the situation than of my companions, precisely because of their lack of fear.

Miriam fetched something from a pack at her waist, I couldn't see what, and glanced at Poole. "Jovik's not going to survive a descent lasting a day. Not in the dark."

Poole looked at me, and at her. "Do it."

"Do what?"

But I had no time to flinch as she reached across, and with expert skill pressed a vial into a valve in the chest of my exosuit. I felt a sharp coldness as the drug pumped into my bloodstream, and after that only a dreamless sleep, cradled in the warmth of my cushioned suit.

So I missed the events of the next hours, the quiet times when Poole and Miriam tried to catch some sleep themselves, the flurries of excitement when strange denizens of Titan's ammono deep approached them out of the dark.

And I missed the next great shock suffered by our strange little crew, when the base of Titan's underground ocean, an ice floor three hundred kilometres beneath the surface, at last hove into view. The strange landscape of this abyssal deep, made of folded high-pressure ices littered by bits of meteorite rock, was punctured by vents and chasms, like an inverted mirror image of the crust far above us. *And the spider we rode did not slow down.* It hurled itself into one of those vents, and once more its limbs began to clatter down a wall of smooth rock-ice.

Harry warned Miriam and Poole that this latest vent looked as if it penetrated the whole of this inner layer of core-cladding ice—Ice VI, laced by ammonia dihydrate—a layer another five hundred kilometres deep. At the base of this vent there was only Titan's core of silicate rocks, and there, surely, the spiders' final destination must lie.

There was nothing to be done but to endure the ride. It would take perhaps a further day. So Poole and Miriam allowed the spider to drag us down. More tube-fish, of an exotic high-pressure variety, grazed endlessly at the icy walls. Miriam popped me another vial to keep me asleep, and fed me intravenous fluids. Harry fretted about the exhaustion of our power, and the gradual increase of pressure; beneath a column of water and ice hundreds of kilometres deep, we were approaching our suits' manufactured tolerance. But they had no choice to continue, and I, unconscious, had no say in the matter.

When the ride was over, when the spider had at last come to rest, Miriam woke me up.

I was lying on my back on a lumpy floor. The gravity felt even weaker than on the surface. Miriam's face hovered over me, illuminated by suit lamps. She said, "Look what we found."

I sat up. I felt weak, dizzy—hungry. Beside me, in their suits, Miriam and Poole sat watching my reaction. Then I remembered where I was and the fear cut in.

I looked around quickly. Even by the glow of the suit lamps I could not see far. The murkiness and floating particles told me I must be still immersed in the water of Titan's deep ocean. I saw a roof of ice above me—not far, a hundred metres or so. Below me was a surface of what looked like rock, dark and purple-streaked. I was in a sort of ice cavern, then, whose walls were off in the dark beyond our bubble of light. I learned later that I was in a cavern dug out beneath the lower icy mantle of Titan, between it and the rocky core, eight hundred kilometres below the icy plains where I had crash-landed days before. Around us I saw ice spiders, toiling away at their own enigmatic tasks, and bits of equipment from the gondola, chopped up, carried here and deposited. There was the GUT engine! My heart leapt; perhaps I would yet live through this.

But even the engine wasn't what Miriam had meant. She repeated, "Look what we found."

I looked. Set in the floor, in the rocky core of the world, was a hatch.

XIII
HATCH

They allowed me to eat and drink, and void my bladder. Moving around was difficult, the cold water dense and syrupy; every movement I made was accompanied by the whir of servomotors, as the suit laboured to assist me.

I was reassured to know that the GUT engine was still functioning, and that my suit cells had been recharged. In principle I could stay alive long enough to get back to the *Hermit Crab*. All I had to do was find my way out of the core of this world, up through eight hundred kilometres of ice and ocean . . . I clung to the relief of the moment, and put off my fears over what was to come next.

Now that I was awake, Michael Poole, Miriam Berg, and Virtual Harry rehearsed what they had figured out about methane processing on Titan. Under that roof of ice, immersed in that chill high-pressure ocean, they talked about comets and chemistry, while all the while the huge mystery of the hatch in the ground lay between us, unaddressed.

Harry said, "On Earth ninety-five per cent of the methane in the air is of biological origin. The farts of animals, decaying vegetation. So could the source be biological here? You guys have surveyed enough of the environment to rule that out. There could in principle be methanogen bugs living in those ethane lakes, for instance, feeding off reactions between acetylene and hydrogen, but you found nothing significant. What about a delivery of the methane by infalling comets? It's possible, but then you'd have detected other trace cometary gases, which are absent from the air. One plausible possibility remained . . ."

When Titan was young its ammonia-water ocean extended all the way to the rocky core. There, chemical processes could have produced plentiful methane: the alkaline water reacting with the rock would liberate hydrogen, which in turn would react with sources of carbon, monoxide or dioxide or carbon grains, to manufacture methane. But that process would have been stopped as soon as the ice layers plated over the rock core, insulating it from liquid water. What was needed, then, was some way for chambers to be kept open at the base of the ice, where liquid water and rock could still react at their interface. And a way for the methane produced to reach the ocean, and then the surface.

"The methane could be stored in clathrates, ice layers," Harry said. "That would work its way to the surface eventually. Simpler to build vents up through the ice, and encourage a chemoautotrophic ecosystem to feed off the methane, and deliver it to higher levels."

"The tube-fish," I said.

"And their relatives, yes."

Looking up at the ice ceiling above me, I saw how it had been shaped and scraped, as if by lobster claws. "So the spiders keep these chambers open, to allow the methane-creating reactions to continue."

"That's it," Michael Poole said, wonder in his voice. "They do it to keep a supply of methane pumping up into the atmosphere. And they've been doing it for billions of years. Have to have been, for the ecologies up there to have evolved as they have—the tube-fish, the CHON sponges, the silanes. *This whole world is an engine,* a very old engine. It's an engine for creating methane, for turning what would otherwise be just another nondescript ice moon into a haven, whose purpose is to foster the life forms that inhabit it."

"Why would they do that?"

None of them could answer that.

"Ha!" I barked laughter. "Well, the why of it is irrelevant. The spiders are clearly sentient—or their makers are. You have found precisely what you were afraid of, haven't you, Michael Poole? Sentience at the heart of Titan. You will never be allowed to open it up for exploitation now. So much for your commercial ambitions!"

"Which you were going to share in," Harry reminded me, scowling.

I sneered. "Oh, I'd only have wasted the money on drugs and sex. To see you world-builders crestfallen is worth that loss. So what's under the hatch?"

They glanced at each other. "The final answers, we hope," Michael Poole said.

Miriam said, "We've put off looking under there until we brought you round, Jovik."

Poole said, "We've no idea what's under there. We need everybody awake, ready to react. We might even need your help, Emry." He looked at me with faint disgust. "And," he said more practically, "it's probably going to take three of us to open it. Come see."

We all floated through the gloopy murk.

The hatch was a disc of some silvery metal, perhaps three metres across, set flush into the roughly flat rocky ground. Spaced around its circumference were three identical grooves, each maybe ten centimetres deep. In the middle of each groove was a mechanism like a pair of levers, hinged at the top.

Michael said, "We think you operate it like this." He knelt and put his gloved hands to either side of the levers, and mimed pressing them together. "We don't know how heavy the mechanism will be. Hopefully each of us can handle one set of levers, with the help of our suits."

"Three mechanisms," I said. "This is a door meant to be operated by a spider, isn't it? One handle for each of those three big claws."

"We think so," Miriam said. "The handles look about the right size. We think the handles must have to be worked simultaneously—one spider, or three humans."

"I can't believe that after a billion years all they have is a clunky mechanical door."

Poole said, "It's hard to imagine a technology however advanced that won't have manual backups. We've seen that the spiders themselves aren't perfect; they're not immune to breakdown and damage."

"As inflicted by us." I gazed reluctantly at the hatch. "Must we do this? You've found what you wanted—or didn't want. Why expose us to more risk? Can't we just go home?"

Miriam and Michael just stared at me, bewildered. Miriam said, "You could walk away, without *knowing*?"

Poole said, "Well, we're not leaving here until we've done this, Emry, so you may as well get it over." He crouched down by his handle, and Miriam did the same.

I had no choice but to join them.

Poole counted us down: "Three, two, one."

I closed my gloved hands over the levers and pushed them together. It was awkward to reach down, and the mechanism felt heavy; my muscles worked, and I felt the reaction push me up from the floor. But the levers closed together.

The whole hatch began to vibrate.

I let go and moved back quickly. The others did the same. We stood in a circle, wafted by the currents of the ammonia sea, and watched that hatch slide up out of the ground.

It was like a piston, rising up one metre, two. Its sides were perfectly smooth, perfectly reflective, without a scuff or scratch. I wondered at how old it must be. Michael Poole, fool that he was, reached up a gloved monkey-curious hand to touch it, but Miriam restrained him. "I'd like to measure the tolerances on that thing," he murmured.

Then the great slab, around three metres wide and two tall, slid sideways. Poole had to step out of the way. The scrape across the rough rock ground was audible, dimly. The shift revealed a hole in the ground, a circle—and at first I thought it was perfectly black. But then I saw elusive golden glimmers, sheets of light like soap bubbles; if I turned my head a little I lost it again.

"Woah," Harry Poole said. "There's some exotic radiation coming out of that hole. You should all back off. The suits have heavy shielding, but a few metres of water won't hurt."

I didn't need telling twice. We moved away towards the GUT engine, taking the light with us. The hole in the ground, still just visible in the glow of our suit lamps, looked a little like one of the ethane lakes on the surface, with that metallic monolith beside it. But every so often I could make out that elusive golden-brown glimmer. I said, "It looks like a facet of one of your wormhole Interfaces, Poole."

"Not a bad observation," Poole said. "And I have a feeling that's exactly what we're looking at. Harry?"

"Yeah." Harry was hesitating. "I wish you had a better sensor suite down there.

I'm relying on instruments woven into your suits, internal diagnostic tools in the GUT engine, some stray neutrino leakage up here . . . Yes, I think we're seeing products of stressed spacetime. There are some interesting optical effects too—light lensed by a distorted gravity field."

"So it's a wormhole interface?" Miriam asked.

"If it is," Poole said, "it's far beyond the clumsy monstrosities we construct in Jovian orbit. And whatever is on the other side of that barrier, my guess is it's not on Titan . . ."

"Watch out," Miriam said.

A spider came scuttling past us towards the hole. It paused at the lip, as if puzzled that the hole was open. Then it tipped forward, just as the spider we rode into the volcano had dipped into the caldera, and slid head first through that sheet of darkness. It was as if it had fallen into a pool of oil that closed over the spider without a ripple.

"I wouldn't recommend following," Harry said. "The radiations in there are deadly, suit or no suit; you couldn't survive the passage."

"Lethe," Michael Poole said. He was disappointed!

"So are we done here?" I asked.

Poole snapped, "I'll tell you something, Emry, I'm glad you're here. Every time we come to an obstacle and you just want to give up, it just goads me into trying to find a way forward."

"There *is* no way forward," I said. "It's lethal. Harry said so."

"We can't go on," Miriam agreed. "But how about a probe? Something radiation-hardened, a controlling AI—with luck we could just drop it in there and let it report back."

"That would work," Poole said. Without hesitation the two of them walked over to the GUT engine, and began prying at it.

For redundancy the engine had two control units. Miriam and Poole detached one of these. Containing a sensor suite, processing capabilities, a memory store, it was a white-walled box the size of a suitcase. Within this unit and its twin sibling were stored the identity backups that had been taken of us before our ride into Titan's atmosphere. The little box was even capable of projecting Virtuals; Harry's sharp image was being projected right now by the GUT engine hardware, rather than through a pooling of our suits' systems as before.

The box was small enough just to be dropped through the interface, and hardened against radiation. It would survive a passage through the wormhole— though none of us could say if it would survive what lay on the other side. And it had transmitting and receiving capabilities. Harry believed its signals would make it back through the interface, though probably scrambled by gravitational distortion and other effects, but he was confident he could construct decoding algorithms from a few test signals. The unit was perfectly equipped to serve as a probe through the hatch, save for one thing. What the control box didn't have was intelligence.

Michael Poole stroked its surface with a gloved hand. "We're sending it into an entirely unknown situation. It's going to have to work autonomously, to figure out its environment, work out some kind of sensor sweep, before it can even figure out how to talk to us and ask us for direction. Running a GUT engine is a pretty simple and predictable job; the AI in there isn't capable of handling an exploration like these."

"But," I said, "it carries in its store backups of four human intellects—mine, dead Bill, and you two geniuses. What a shame we can't all ride along with it!"

My sarcasm failed to evoke the expected reaction. Poole and Miriam looked at each other, electrified. Miriam shook her head. "Jovik, you're like some idiot savant. You keep on coming up with such ideas. I think you're actually far smarter than you allow yourself to be."

I said honestly, "I have no idea what you're talking about."

"The idea you've suggested to them," Harry said gently, "is to revive one of the dormant identity-backup copies in the unit's store, and use *that* as the controlling intelligence."

As always when they hit on some new idea Poole and Miriam were like two eager kids. Poole said, "It's going to be a shock to wake up, to move straight from Titan entry to this point. It would be least disconcerting if we projected a full human animus."

"You're telling me," said the head of Harry Poole.

"And some enclosing environment," Miriam said. "Just a suit? No, to be adrift in space brings in problems with vertigo. I'd have trouble with that."

"The lifedome of the *Crab*," Poole said. "That would be straightforward enough to simulate to an adequate degree. And a good platform for observation. The power would be sufficient to sustain that for a few hours at least . . ."

"Yes." Miriam grinned. "Our observer will feel safe. I'll get to work on it . . ."

I asked, "So you're planning to project a Virtual copy of one of us through the wormhole. And how will you get him or her back?"

They looked at me. "That won't be possible," Poole said. "The unit will be lost. It's possible we could transmit back a copy of the memories the Virtual accrues on the other side—integrate them somehow with the backup in the GUT engine's other store—"

"No," Harry said regretfully. "The data rate through that interface would never allow even that. For the copy in there it's a one way trip."

"Well, that's entirely against the sentience laws," I put in. They ignored me.

Poole said, "That's settled, then. The question is, *who*? Which of the four of us are you going to wake up from cyber-sleep and send into the unknown?"

I noticed that Harry's disembodied floating head looked away, as if he were avoiding the question.

Poole and Miriam looked at each other. Miriam said, "Either of us would go. Right?"

"Of course."

"But we should give it to Bill," Miriam said firmly.

"Yeah. There's no other choice. Bill's gone, and we can't bring his stored backup home with us . . . We should let his backup have the privilege of doing this. It will make the sacrifice worthwhile."

I stared at them. "This is the way you treat your friend? By killing him, then reviving a backup and sending it to another certain death?"

Poole glared at me. "Bill won't see it that way, believe me. You and a·man like Bill Dzik have nothing in common, Emry. Don't judge him by your standards."

"Fine. Just don't send me."

"Oh, I won't. You don't deserve it."

It took them only a few more minutes to prepare for the experiment. The control pack didn't need any physical modifications, and it didn't take Miriam long to programme instructions into its limited onboard intelligence. She provided it with a short orientation message, in the hope that Virtual Bill wouldn't be left entirely bewildered at the sudden transition he would experience.

Poole picked up the pack with his gloved hands, and walked towards the interface, or as close as Harry advised him get. Then Poole hefted the pack over his head. "Good luck, Bill." He threw the pack towards the interface, or rather pushed it; its weight was low but its inertia was just as it would have been on Earth, and besides Poole had to fight against the resistance of the syrupy sea. For a while it looked as if the pack might fall short. "I should have practiced a couple of times," Poole said ruefully. "Never was any use at physical sports."

But he got it about right. The pack clipped the rim of the hole, then tumbled forward and fell slowly, dreamlike, through that black surface. As it disappeared autumn gold glimmered around it.

Then we had to wait, the three of us plus Harry. I began to wish that we had agreed some time limit; obsessives like Poole and Miriam were capable of standing there for hours before admitting failure.

In the event it was only minutes before a scratchy voice sounded in our suit helmets. "Harry? Can you hear me?"

"Yes!" Harry called, grinning. "Yes, I hear you. The reception ought to get better, the clean-up algorithms are still working. Are you all right?"

"Well, I'm sitting in the *Crab* lifedome. It's kind of a shock to find myself here, after bracing my butt to enter Titan. Your little orientation show helped, Miriam."

Poole asked, "What do you see?"

"The sky is . . . strange."

Miriam was looking puzzled. She turned and looked at Harry. "That's not all that's strange. That's not Bill!"

"Indeed not," came the voice from the other side of the hole. "I am Michael Poole."

XIV
VIRTUAL

So, while a suddenly revived Michael Poole floated around in other-space, the original Poole and his not-lover Miriam Berg engaged in a furious row with Harry.

Poole stormed over to the GUT engine's remaining control pack, and checked the memory's contents. It didn't contain backup copies of the four of us; it contained only one ultra-high-fidelity copy of Michael Poole himself. I could not decide which scared me more: the idea that no copies of myself existed in that glistening white box, or the belief I had entertained previously that there had. I am prone to existential doubt, and am uncomfortable with such notions.

But such subtleties were beyond Michael Poole in his anger. "Miriam, I swear I knew nothing about this."

"Oh, I believe you."

They both turned on the older Poole. "Harry?" Michael snapped. "What in Lethe is this?"

Disembodied-head Harry looked shifty, but he was going to brazen it out. "As far as I'm concerned there's nothing to apologise for. The storage available on the *Crab* was always limited, and it was worse in the gondola. Michael's my son. Of course I'm going to protect him above others. What would you do? I'm sorry, Miriam, but—"

"You aren't sorry at all," Miriam snapped. "And you're a cold-hearted bastard. You knowingly sent a backup of your son, who you say you're trying to protect, through that wormhole to die!"

Harry looked uncomfortable. "It's just a copy. There are other backups, earlier copies—"

"Lethe, Dad," Michael Poole said, and he walked away, bunching his fists. I wondered how many similar collisions with his father the man had had to suffer in the course of his life.

"What's done is done," came a whisper. And they all quit their bickering, because it was Michael Poole who had spoken—the backup Poole, the one recently revived, the one beyond the spacetime barrier. "I know I don't have much time. I'll try to project some imagery back . . ."

Harry, probably gratefully, popped out of existence, thus vacating the available processing capacity, though I was sure his original would be monitoring us from the *Crab*.

Poole murmured to Miriam, "You speak to him. Might be easier for him than me."

She clearly found this idea distressing. But she said, "All right."

Gradually images built up in the air before us, limited views, grainy with pixels, flickering.

And we saw Virtual Poole's strange sky.

The Virtual *Crab* floated over a small object—like an ice moon, like one of Titan's Saturnian siblings, pale and peppered with worn impact craters. I saw how its surface was punctured with holes, perfectly round and black. These looked like our hatch; the probe we had dispatched must have emerged from one of them. Things that looked like our spiders toiled to and fro between the holes, travelling between mounds of some kind of supplies. They were too distant to see clearly. All this was bathed in a pale yellow light, diffuse and without shadows.

The original Poole said, "You think those other interfaces connect up to the rest of Titan?"

"I'd think so," Miriam said. "This can't be the only deep-sea methane-generation chamber. Passing through the wormholes and back again would be a way for the spiders to unify their operations across the moon."

"So the interface we found, set in the outer curved surface of Titan's core, is one of a set that matches another set on the outer curved surface of that ice moon. The curvature would seem to flip over when you passed through."

This struck me as remarkable, a paradox difficult to grasp, but Poole was a wormhole engineer, and used to the subtleties of spacetime manipulated and twisted through higher dimensions; slapping two convex surfaces together was evidently child's play to him, conceptually.

Miriam asked Virtual Poole, "But where are you? That's an ice moon, a common object. Could be anywhere in the universe. Could even be in some corner of our own System."

Poole's Virtual copy said, his voice a whispery, channel-distorted rasp, "Don't jump to conclusions, Miriam. Look up."

The viewpoint swivelled, and we saw Virtual Poole's sky.

A huge, distorted sun hung above us. Planetoids hung sprinkled before its face, showing phases from crescents to half-moons, and some were entirely black, fly-speck eclipses against the face of the monster. Beyond the limb of the sun more stars hung, but they were also swollen, pale beasts, their misshapen discs visible. And the space between the stars did not look entirely black to me, but a faint, deep crimson with a pattern, a network of threads and knots. It reminded me of what I saw when I closed my eyes.

"What a sky," Poole murmured.

"Michael, you're far from home," Miriam called.

Virtual Poole replied, "Yes. Those stars don't fit our main sequence. And their spectra are simple—few heavy elements. They're more like the protostars of our own early universe, I think: the first generation, formed of not much more than the hydrogen and helium that came out of the Big Bang."

"No metals," observed Miriam Berg.

"I'll send through the data I'm collecting—"

"Getting it, son," came Harry Poole's voice.

The others let Virtual Poole speak. His words, the careful observations delivered by a man so far from home, or at least by a construct that felt as if it were a man, were impressive in their courage.

"This is not our universe," he whispered. "I think that's clear. This one is young, and small—according to the curvature of spacetime, only a few million light years across. Probably not big enough to accommodate our Local Group of galaxies."

"A pocket universe, maybe," Miriam said. "An appendix from our own."

"I can't believe the things you have been calling 'spiders' originated here," the Virtual said. "You said it, Miriam. No metals here, not in this entire cosmos. That's why they were scavenging metals from probes, meteorites."

"They came from somewhere else, then," Poole said. "There was nothing strange in the elemental abundance we recorded in the spider samples we studied. So they come from elsewhere in our own universe. The pocket universe is just a transit interchange. Like Earthport."

The Virtual said, "Yes. And maybe behind these other moons in my sky lie gateways to other Titans—other sustained ecologies, maybe with different biological bases. Other experiments."

Miriam said, "So if metals are so essential for the spiders, why not have supplies brought to them through the interchange?"

"Maybe they did, once," the Virtual said. "Maybe things broke down. There's a sense of age here, Miriam. This is a young cosmos maybe, but I think this is an old place . . ."

The real Poole murmured, "It makes sense. The time axis in the baby universe needn't be isomorphic with ours. A million years over there, a billion years here."

The Virtual whispered, "Those spiders have been toiling at their task on Titan a long, long time. Whoever manufactured them, or bred them, left them behind a long time ago, and they've been alone ever since. Just doing their best to keep going. Looking at them, I get the impression they aren't too bright. Just functional."

"But they did a good job," Miriam said.

"That they did."

"But why?" I blurted out. "What's the purpose of all this, the nurturing of an ecology on Titan for billions of years—and perhaps similar on a thousand other worlds?"

"I think I have an idea," Virtual Poole whispered. "I never even landed on Titan, remember. Perhaps, coming at all this so suddenly, while the rest of you have worked through stages of discovery, I see it different . . ."

"Just as this pocket universe is a junction, so maybe Titan is a junction, a haven where different domains of life can coexist. You've found the native ammono fish, the CHON sponges that may originate in the inner system, perhaps even coming from Earth, and the silanes from Triton and beyond. Maybe there are other families to find if you had time to look. All these kinds of life, arising from different environments—but all with one thing in common. All born of planets, and of skies and seas, in worlds warmed by stars."

"But the stars won't last forever. In the future the universe will change, until it resembles our own time even less than our universe resembles this young dwarf cosmos. What then? Look, if you were concerned about preserving life, all forms of life, into the very furthest future, then perhaps you would promote—"

"Cooperation," said Miriam Berg.

"You got it. Maybe Titan is a kind of prototype of an ecology where life forms of such different origins can mix, find ways of using each other to survive—"

"And ultimately merge, somehow," Miriam said. "Well, it's happened before. Each of us is a community with once-disparate and very different life forms toiling away in each of our cells. It's a lovely vision, Michael."

"And plausible," his original self said gruffly. "Anyhow it's a hypothesis that will do until something better comes along."

I sneered at that. This dream of cosmic cooperation struck me as the romantic fantasy of a man alone and doomed to die, and soon. We all project our petty lives upon the universe. But I had no better suggestions to make. And, who knows? Perhaps Virtual Poole was right. None of us will live to find out.

"Anyhow," I said, "charming as this is—are we done *now*?"

Miriam snapped, "We can't abandon Michael."

"Go," whispered Virtual Poole. "There's nothing you can do for me. I'll keep observing, reporting, as long as I can."

I gagged on his nobility.

Now Harry intruded, grabbing a little of the available Virtual projection capacity. "But we've still got business to conclude before you leave here."

XV
RESOLUTION

Poole frowned. "What business?"

"We came here to prove that Titan is without sentience," Harry said. "Well, we got that wrong. Now what?"

Miriam Berg was apparently puzzled we were even having the conversation. "We report what we've found to the sentience oversight councils and elsewhere. It's a major discovery. We'll be rapped for making an unauthorised landing on Titan, but—"

"Is that the sum of your ambition?" I snapped. "To hope the authorities will be lenient if you reveal the discovery that is going to ruin you?"

She glared at me. "What's the choice?"

"Isn't it obvious?" I looked at her, and Poole, who I think was guessing what I was going to say, and Harry, who looked away as he usually did at moments of crisis. Suddenly, after days of pointless wonders, I was in my element, the murky world of human relationships, and I could see a way forward where they could not. "*Destroy this*," I said. I waved a hand. "All of it. You have your grenades, Miriam. You could bring this cavern down."

"Or," Harry said, "there is the GUTdrive. If that were detonated, if unified-field energies were loosed in here, the wormhole interface too would surely be disrupted. I'd imagine that the connection between Titan and the pocket universe would be broken altogether."

I nodded. "I hadn't thought of that, but I like your style, Harry. Do it. Let this place be covered up by hundreds of kilometres of ice and water. Destroy your records. It will make no difference to the surface, what's going on in the atmosphere, not immediately. Nobody will ever know all this was here."

Harry Poole said, "That's true. Even if methane generation stops immediately the residual would persist in the atmosphere for maybe ten million years. I venture to suggest that if the various multi-domain critters haven't learned to cooperate in that time, they never will. Ten megayears is surely enough."

Miriam looked at him, horrified by his words. "You're suggesting a monstrous crime," she breathed. "To think of destroying such a wonder as this, the product of a billion years—to destroy it for personal gain! Michael, Lethe, leave aside the morality, surely you're too much of a scientist to countenance this."

But Poole sounded anguished. "I'm not a scientist any more, Miriam. I'm an engineer. I build things. I think I sympathise with the goals of the spider makers. What I'm building is a better future for the whole of mankind—that's what I believe. And if I have to make compromises to achieve that future—well. Maybe the spider makers had to make the same kind of choices. Who knows what they found here on Titan before they went to work on it? . . ."

And in that little speech, I believe, you have encapsulated both the magnificence and the grandiose folly of Michael Poole. I wondered then how much damage this man might do to us all in the future, with his wormholes and his time-hopping starships—what horrors he, blinded by his vision, might unleash.

Harry said unexpectedly, "Let's vote on it. If you're in favour of destroying the chamber, say yes."

"No!" snapped Miriam.

"Yes," said Harry and Poole together.

"Yes," said I, but they all turned on me and told me I didn't have a vote.

It made no difference. The vote was carried. They stood looking at each other, as if horrified by what they had done.

"Welcome to my world," I said cynically.

Poole went off to prepare the GUT engine for its last task. Miriam, furious and upset, gathered together our equipment, such as it was, her pack with her science samples, our tangles of rope.

And Harry popped into the air in front of me. "Thanks," he said.

"You wanted me to make that suggestion, didn't you?"

"Well, I hoped you would. If I'd made it they'd have refused. And Michael would never have forgiven me." He grinned. "I knew there was a reason I wanted to have you along, Jovik Emry. Well done. You've served your purpose."

Virtual Poole, still in his baby universe, spoke again. "Miriam."

She straightened up. "I'm here, Michael."

"I'm not sure how long I have left. What will happen when the power goes?"

"I programmed the simulation to seem authentic, internally consistent. It will be as if the power in the *Crab* lifedome is failing." She took a breath, and said, "Of course you have other options to end it before then."

"I know. Thank you. Who were they, do you think? Whoever made the spiders. Did they build this pocket universe too? Or was it built *for* them? Like a haven?"

"I don't suppose we'll ever know. Michael, I'm sorry. I—"

"Don't be. You know I would have chosen this. But I'm sorry to leave you behind. Miriam—look after him. Michael. I, we, need you."

She looked at the original Poole, who was working at the GUT engine. "We'll see," she said.

"And tell Harry—well. You know."

She held a hand up to the empty air. "Michael, please—"

"It's enough." The Virtuals he had been projecting broke up into blocks of pixels, and a faint hiss, the carrier of his voice, disappeared from my hearing. Alone in his universe, he had cut himself off.

The original Poole approached her, uncertain of her reaction. "It's done. The GUT engine has been programmed. We're ready to go, Miriam. As soon as we're out of here—"

She turned away from him, her face showing something close to hatred.

XVI
ASCENSION

So, harnessed to a spider oblivious of the impending fate of its vast and ancient project, we rose into the dark. It had taken us days to descend to this place, and would take us days to return to the surface, where, Harry promised, he would have a fresh balloon waiting to pick us up.

This time, though I was offered escape into unconsciousness, I stayed awake. I had a feeling that the last act of this little drama had yet to play itself out. I wanted to be around to see it.

We were beyond the lower ice layers and rising through two hundred and fifty kilometres of sea when Miriam's timer informed us that the GUT engine had detonated, far beneath us. Insulated by the ice layer, we felt nothing. But I imagined that the spider that carried us up towards the light hesitated, just fractionally.

"It's done," Poole said firmly. "No going back."

Miriam had barely spoken to him since the cavern. She had said more words to *me*. Now she said, "I've been thinking. I won't accept it, Michael. I don't care about you and Harry and your damn vote. As soon as we get home I'm going to report what we found."

"You've no evidence—"

"I'll be taken seriously enough. And someday somebody will mount another expedition, and confirm the truth."

"All right." That was all he said. But I knew the matter was not over. He would not meet my mocking eyes.

I wasn't surprised when, twelve hours later, as Miriam slept cradled in the net draped from the spider's back, Poole took vials from her pack and pressed them into her flesh, one by a valve on her leg, another at the base of her spine.

I watched him. "You're going to edit her. Plan this with Dad, did you?"

"Shut up," he snarled, edgy, angry.

"You're taking her out of her own head, and you'll mess with her memories, with her very personality, and then you'll load her back. What will you make her believe—that she stayed up on the *Crab* with Harry the whole time, while you went exploring and found nothing? That would work, I guess."

"I've got nothing to say to you."

But I had plenty to say to him. I am no saint myself, and Poole disgusted me as only a man without morality himself can be disgusted. "I think you love her. I even think she loves you. Yet you are prepared to mess with her head and her heart, to serve your grandiose ambitions. Let me tell you something. The Poole she left behind in that pocket universe, the one she said goodbye to, he was a better man than you will ever be again. Because he was not tainted by the great crime you committed when you destroyed the cavern. And because he was not tainted by *this*."

"And let me make some predictions. No matter what you achieve in the future, Michael Poole, this crime will always be at the root of you, gnawing away. *And Miriam will never love you.* Even though you wipe out her memory of these events, there will always be something between you; she will sense the lie. She will leave you, and then you will leave her. And you have killed Titan. One day, millions of years into the future, the very air will freeze and rain out, and everything alive here will die. All because of what you have done today. And, Poole, maybe those whose work you have wrecked will some day force you to a reckoning."

He was open, defenceless, and I was flaying him. He had no answer. He cradled the unconscious Miriam, even as his machines drained her memory.

We did not speak again until we emerged into the murky daylight of Titan.

EPILOGUE
PROBE

It didn't take Michael long to check out the status of his fragile craft.

The power in the lifetime's internal cells might last—what, a few hours? As far as he could tell there was no functional link between the dome and the rest of the *Hermit Crab*; none of his controls worked. Maybe that was beyond the scope of Miriam's simulation. So he had no motive power.

He didn't grouse about this, nor did he fear his future. Such as it was.

The universe beyond the lifedome was strange, alien. The toiling spiders down on the ice moon seemed like machines, not alive, not sentient. He tired of observing them. He turned on lights, green, blue. The lifedome was a little bubble of Earth, isolated.

Michael was alone, in this whole universe. He could feel it.

He got a meal together. Miriam's simulation was good, here in his personal space; he didn't find any limits or glitches. Lovingly constructed, he thought. The mundane chore, performed in a bright island of light around the lifetime's small galley, was oddly cheering.

He carried the food to his couch, lay back with the plate balancing on one hand, and dimmed the dome lights. He finished his food and set the plate carefully on the floor. He drank a glass of clean water.

Then he went to the freefall shower and washed in a spray of hot water. He tried to open up his senses, to relish every particle of sensation. There was a last time for everything, for even the most mundane experiences. He considered finding some music to play, a book to read. Somehow that might have seemed fitting.

The lights failed. Even the instrument slates winked out.

Well, so much for music. He made his way back to his couch. Though the sky was bright, illuminated by the protosun, the air grew colder; he imagined the heat of the lifedome leaking out. What would get him first, the cold, or the failing air?

He wasn't afraid. And he felt no regret that he had lost so much potential life, all those AS-extended years. Oddly, he felt renewed: young, for the first time in decades, the pressure of time no longer seemed to weigh on him.

He was sorry he would never know how his relationship with Miriam might have worked out. That could have been something. But he found, in the end, he was glad that he had lived long enough to see all he had.

He was beginning to shiver, the air sharp in his nostrils. He lay back in his couch and crossed his hands on his chest. He closed his eyes.

A shadow crossed his face.

He opened his eyes, looked up. There was a ship hanging over the lifedome.

Michael, dying, stared in wonder.

It was something like a sycamore seed wrought in jet black. Night-dark wings which must have spanned hundreds of kilometres loomed over the *Crab*, softly rippling.

The cold sank claws into his chest; the muscles of his throat abruptly spasmed, and dark clouds ringed his vision. *Not now*, he found himself pleading silently, his failing vision locked onto the ship, all his elegiac acceptance gone in a flash. *Just a little longer. I have to know what this means. Please—*

Poole's consciousness was like a guttering candle flame. Now it was as if that flame was plucked from its wick. That flame, with its tiny fear, its wonder, its helpless longing to survive, was spun out into a web of quantum functions, acausal and nonlocal.

The last heat fled from the craft; the air in the translucent dome began to frost over the comms panels, the couches, the galley, the prone body. And the ship and all it contained, no longer needed, broke up into a cloud of pixels.

DAMIEN BRODERICK

Australian writer, editor, futurist, and critic Damien Broderick, a Senior Fellow in the School of Culture and Communications at the University of Melbourne, made his first sale in 1964 to John Carnell's anthology *New Writings in SF 1*. In the decades that followed, he has kept up a steady stream of fiction, nonfiction, futurist speculations, and critical work, which has won him multiple Ditmar and Aurealis Awards. He sold his first novel, *Sorcerer's World*, in 1970; it was later reissued in a rewritten version in the United States as *The Black Grail*. Broderick's other books include the novels *The Dreaming Dragons*, *The Judas Mandala*, *Transmitters*, *Striped Holes*, and *The White Abacus*, as well as books written with Rory Barnes and Barbara Lamar. His many short stories have been collected in *A Man Returned*, *The Dark Between the Stars*, *Uncle Bones: Four Science Fiction Novellas*, and, most recently, *The Qualia Engine: Science Fiction Stories*. He also wrote the visionary futurist classic, *The Spike: How Our Lives Are Being Transformed by Rapidly Advancing Technology*, a critical study of science fiction, and *Reading by Starlight: Postmodern Science Fiction*. He edited the nonfiction anthology *Year Million: Science at the Far End of Knowledge*, as well as editing the SF anthology *Earth is But a Star: Excursions Through Science Fiction to the Far Future*, and three anthologies of Australian science fiction, *The Zeitgeist Machine*, *Strange Attractors*, and *Matilda at the Speed of Light*.

Broderick has done homages in the last couple of years to Cordwainer Smith, Roger Zelazny, and Philip K. Dick, and although those stories each had much to recommend them, I think that the brilliant story that follows, Broderick's homage to the late J. G. Ballard, is by a fair margin the best one yet. Here, Broderick has managed to internalize Ballard's influence on him and make this into its own story with its own strengths and an organic voice and sensibility of its own, rather than just being a pastiche of Ballard. Ballard would not have written this—but it's clear that Broderick wouldn't have written it without reading Ballard, either. Broderick currently lives in San Antonio, Texas.

1.

In the long, hot, humid afternoon, Blackett obsessively paced off the outer dimensions of the Great Temple of Petra against the black asphalt of the deserted car parks, trying to recapture the pathway back to Venus. Faint rectangular lines still marked the empty spaces allocated to staff vehicles long gone from the campus, stretching on every side like the equations in some occult geometry of invocation. Later, as shadows stretched across the all-but-abandoned industrial park, he considered again the possibility that he was trapped in delusion, even psychosis. At the edge of an overgrown patch of dried lawn, he found a crushed Pepsi can, a bent yellow plastic straw protruding from it. He kicked it idly.

"Thus I refute Berkeley," he muttered, with a half smile. The can twisted, fell back on the grass; he saw that a runner of bind weed wrapped its flattened waist.

He walked back to the sprawling house he had appropriated, formerly the residence of a wealthy CEO. Glancing at his IWC Flieger Chrono aviator's watch, he noted that he should arrive there ten minutes before his daily appointment with the therapist.

2.

Cool in a chillingly expensive pale blue Mila Schön summer frock, her carmine toenails brightly painted in her open Ferragamo Penelope sandals, Clare regarded him: lovely, sly, professionally compassionate. She sat across from him on the front porch of the old house, rocking gently in the suspended glider.

"Your problem," the psychiatrist told him, "is known in the trade as lack of affect. You have shut down and locked off your emotional responses. You should know, Robert, that this isn't healthy or sustainable."

"Of course I know that," he said, faintly irritated by her condescension. "Why else would I be consulting you? Not," he said pointedly, "that it is doing me much good."

"It takes time, Robert."

3.

Later, when Clare was gone, Blackett sat beside his silent sound system and poured two fingers of Hennessy XO brandy. It was the best he had been able to find in the largely depleted supermarket, or at any rate the least untenable for drinking purposes. He took the spirits into his mouth and felt fire run down his throat. Months earlier, he had found a single bottle of Mendis Coconut brandy in the cellar of an enormous country house. Gone now. He sat a little longer, rose, cleaned his teeth and made his toilet, drank a full glass of faintly brackish water from the tap. He found a Philip Glass CD and placed it in the mouth of the player, then went to bed. Glass's repetitions and minimal novelty eased him into sleep. He woke at 3 in the morning, heart thundering. Silence absolute. Blackett cursed himself for forgetting to press the automatic repeat key on the

CD player. Glass had fallen silent, along with most of the rest of the human race. He touched his forehead. Sweat coated his fingers.

4.

In the morning, he walked to the industrial park's air field, rolled the Cessna 182 out from the protection of its hangar, and refueled its tanks. Against the odds, the electrically powered pump and other systems remained active, drawing current from the black arrays of solar cells oriented to the south and east, swiveling during the daylight hours to follow the apparent track of the sun. He made his abstracted, expert run through the checklist, flicked on the radio by reflex. A hum of carrier signal, nothing more. The control tower was deserted. Blackett ran the Cessna onto the slightly cracked asphalt and took off into a brisk breeze. He flew across fields going to seed, visible through sparklingly clear air. Almost no traffic moved on the roads below him. Two or three vehicles threw up a haze of dust from the untended roadway, and one laden truck crossed his path, apparently cluttered to overflowing with furniture and bedding. It seemed the ultimate in pointlessness—why not appropriate a suitable house, as he had done, and make do with its appointments? Birds flew up occasionally in swooping flocks, careful to avoid his path.

Before noon, he was landing on the coast at the deserted Matagorda Island air force base a few hundred yards from the ocean. He sat for a moment, hearing his cooling engines ticking, and gazed at the two deteriorating Stearman biplanes that rested in the salty open air. They were at least a century old, at one time lovingly restored for air shows and aerobatic displays. Now their fabric sagged, striped red and green paint peeling from their fuselages and wings. They sagged into the hot tarmac, rubber tires rotted by the corrosive oceanfront air and the sun's pitiless ultraviolet.

Blackett left his own plane in the open. He did not intend to remain here long. He strolled to the end of the runway and into the long grass stretching to the ocean. Socks and trouser legs were covered quickly in clinging burrs. He reached the sandy shore as the sun stood directly overhead. After he had walked for half a mile along the strand, wishing he had thought to bring a hat, a dog crossed the sand and paced alongside, keeping its distance.

"You're Blackett," the dog said.

"Speaking."

"Figured it must have been you. Rare enough now to run into a human out here."

Blackett said nothing. He glanced at the dog, feeling no enthusiasm for a conversation. The animal was healthy enough, and well fed, a red setter with long hair that fluffed up in the tangy air. His paws left a trail across the white sand, paralleling the tracks Blackett had made. Was there some occult meaning in this simplest of geometries? If so, it would be erased soon enough, as the ocean moved in, impelled by the solar tide, and lazily licked the beach clean.

Seaweed stretched along the edge of the sluggish water, dark green, stinking. Out of breath, he sat and looked disconsolately across the slow, flat waves of the diminished tide. The dog trotted by, threw itself down in the sand a dozen feet away. Blackett knew he no longer dared sit here after nightfall, in a dark alive with thousands of brilliant pinpoint stars, a planet or two, and no Moon. Never again a Moon. Once he had ventured out here after the sun went down, and low in the deep indigo edging the horizon had seen the clear distinct blue disk of the evening star, and her two attendant satellites, one on each side of the planet. Ganymede, with its thin atmosphere still intact, remained palest brown. Luna, at that distance, was a bright pinpoint orb, her pockmarked face never again to be visible to the naked eye of an Earthly viewer beneath her new, immensely deep carbon dioxide atmosphere.

He noticed that the dog was creeping cautiously toward him, tail wagging, eyes averted except for the occasional swift glance.

"Look," he said, "I'd rather be alone."

The dog sat up and uttered a barking laugh. It swung its head from side to side, conspicuously observing the hot, empty strand.

"Well, bub, I'd say you've got your wish, in spades."

"Nobody has swum here in years, apart from me. This is an old air force base, it's been decommissioned for . . ."

He trailed off. It was no answer to the point the animal was making. Usually at this time of year, Blackett acknowledged to himself, other beaches, more accessible to the crowds, would be swarming with shouting or whining children, mothers waddling or slumped, baking in the sun under SPF 50 lotions, fat men eating snacks from busy concession stands, vigorous swimmers bobbing in white-capped waves. Now the empty waves crept in, onto the tourist beaches as they did here, like the flattened, poisoned combers at the site of the Exxon Valdez oil spill, twenty years after men had first set foot on the now absent Moon.

"It wasn't my idea," he said. But the dog was right; this isolation was more congenial to him than otherwise. Yet the yearning to rejoin the rest of the human race on Venus burned in his chest like angina.

"Not like I'm *blaming* you, bub." The dog tilted its handsome head. "Hey, should have said, I'm Sporky."

Blackett inclined his own head in reply. After a time, Sporky said, "You think it's a singularity excursion, right?"

He got to his feet, brushed sand from his legs and trousers. "I certainly don't suspect the hand of Jesus. I don't think I've been Left Behind."

"Hey, don't go away now." The dog jumped up, followed him at a safe distance. "It could be aliens, you know."

"You talk too much," Blackett said.

5.

As he landed, later in the day, still feeling refreshed from his hour in the water, he saw through the heat curtains of rising air a rather dirty precinct vehicle drive through the unguarded gate and onto the runway near the hangars. He taxied in slowly, braked, opened the door. The sergeant climbed out of his Ford Crown Victoria, cap off, waving it to cool his florid face.

"Saw you coming in, Doc," Jacobs called. "Figured you might like a lift back. Been damned hot out today, not the best walking weather."

There was little point in arguing. Blackett clamped the red tow bar to the nose wheel, steered the Cessna backward into the hangar, heaved the metal doors closed with an echoing rumble. He climbed into the cold interior of the Ford. Jacobs had the air-conditioning running at full bore, and a noxious country and western singer wailing from the sound system. Seeing his guest's frown, the police officer grinned broadly and turned the hideous noise down.

"You have a visitor waiting," he said. His grin verged on the lewd. Jacobs drove by the house twice a day, part of his self-imposed duty, checking on his brutally diminished constituency. For some reason he took a particular, avuncular interest in Blackett. Perhaps he feared for his own mental health in this terrible circumstance.

"She's expected, Sergeant." By seniority of available staff, the man was probably a captain or even police chief for the region, now, but Blackett declined to offer the honorary promotional title. "Drop me off at the top of the street, would you?"

"It's no trouble to take you to the door."

"I need to stretch my legs after the flight."

In the failing light of dusk, he found Clare, almost in shadow, moving like a piece of beautiful driftwood stranded on a dying tide, backward and slowly forward, on his borrowed porch. She nodded, with her Gioconda smile, and said nothing. This evening she wore a broderie anglaise white-on-white embroidered blouse and 501s cut-down almost to her crotch, bleached by the long summer sun. She sat rocking wordlessly, her knees parted, revealing the pale lanterns of her thighs.

"Once again, Doctor," Blackett told her, "you're trying to seduce me. What do you suppose this tells us both?"

"It tells us, Doctor, that yet again you have fallen prey to intellectualized over-interpreting." She was clearly annoyed, but keeping her tone level. Her limbs remained disposed as they were. "You remember what they told us at school."

"The worst patients are physicians, and the worst physician patients are psychiatrists." He took the old woven cane seat, shifting it so that he sat at right angles to her, looking directly ahead at the heavy brass knocker on the missing CEO's mahogany entrance door. It was serpentine, perhaps a Chinese dragon couchant. A faint headache pulsed behind his eyes; he closed them.

"You've been to the coast again, Robert?"

"I met a dog on the beach," he said, eyes still closed. A cooling breeze was moving into the porch, bringing a fragrance of the last pink mimosa blossoms in the garden bed beside the dry, dying lawn. "He suggested that we've experienced a singularity cataclysm." He sat forward suddenly, turned, caught her regarding him with her blue eyes. "What do you think of that theory, Doctor? Does it arouse you?"

"You had a conversation with a dog," she said, uninflected, nonjudgmental.

"One of the genetically upregulated animals," he said, irritated. "Modified jaw and larynx, expanded cortex and Broca's region."

Clare shrugged. Her interiority admitted of no such novelties. "I've heard that singularity hypothesis before. The Mayans—"

"Not that new age crap." He felt an unaccustomed jolt of anger. Why did he bother talking to this woman? Sexual interest? Granted, but remote; his indifference toward her rather surprised him, but it was so. Blackett glanced again at her thighs, but she had crossed her legs. He rose. "I need a drink. I think we should postpone this session, I'm not feeling at my best."

She took a step forward, placed one cool hand lightly on his bare, sunburned arm.

"You're still convinced the Moon has gone from the sky, Robert? You still maintain that everyone has gone to Venus?"

"Not everyone," he said brusquely, and removed her hand. He gestured at the darkened houses in the street. A mockingbird trilled from a tree, but there were no leaf blowers, no teenagers in sports cars passing with rap booming and thudding, no barbecue odors of smoke and burning steak, no TV displays flickering behind curtained windows. He found his key, went to the door, did not invite her in. "I'll see you tomorrow, Clare."

"Good night, Robert. Feel better." The psychiatrist went down the steps with a light, almost childlike, skipping gait, and paused a moment at the end of the path, raising a hand in farewell or admonishment. "A suggestion, Robert. The almanac ordains a full moon tonight. It rises a little after eight. You should see it plainly from your back garden a few minutes later, once the disk clears the tree-tops."

For a moment he watched her fade behind the overgrown, untended foliage fronting this opulent dwelling. He shook his head, and went inside. In recent months, since the theft of the Moon, Clare had erected ontological denial into the central principle of her world construction, her *Weltbild*. The woman, in her own mind supposedly his therapeutic guide, was hopelessly insane.

6.

After a scratch dinner of canned artichoke hearts, pineapple slices, pre-cooked baby potatoes, pickled eel from a jar, and rather dry, lightly salted wheaten thins, washed down with Californian Chablis from the refrigerator, Blackett dressed in slightly more formal clothing for his weekly visit to Kafele Massri. This massively obese bibliophile lived three streets over in the Baptist rectory across the street from the regional library. At intervals, while doing his own shopping, Blackett scavenged through accessible food stores for provender that he left in plastic bags beside Massri's side gate, providing an incentive to get outside the walls of the house for a few minutes. The man slept all day, and barely budged from his musty bed even after the sun had gone down, scattering emptied cans and plastic bottles about on the uncarpeted floor. Massri had not yet taken to urinating in his squalid bedclothes, as far as Blackett could tell, but the weekly visits always began by emptying several jugs the fat man used at night in lieu of chamber pots, rinsing them under the trickle of water from the kitchen tap, and returning them to the bedroom, where he cleared away the empties into bags and tossed those into the weedy back yard where obnoxious scabby cats crawled or lay panting.

Kafele Massri was propped up against three or four pillows. "I have. New thoughts, Robert. The ontology grows. More tractable." He spoke in a jerky sequence of emphysematic wheezing gasps, his swollen mass pressing relentlessly on the rupturing alveoli skeining his lungs. His fingers twitched, as if keying an invisible keyboard; his eyes shifting again and again to the dead computer. When he caught Blackett's amused glance, he shrugged, causing one of the pillows to slip and fall. "Without my beloved internet, I am. Hamstrung. My *preciiiouuus.*" His thick lips quirked. He foraged through the bed covers, found a battered Hewlett-Packard scientific calculator. Its green strip of display flickered as his fingers pressed keys. "Luckily. I still have. This. My *slide rule.*" Wheezing, he burst into laughter, followed by an agonizing fit of coughing.

"Let me get you a glass of water, Massri." Blackett returned with half a glass; any more, and the bibliophile would spill it down his vast soiled bathrobe front. It seemed to ease the coughing. They sat side by side for a time, as the Egyptian got his breath under control. Ceaselessly, under the impulse of his pudgy fingers, the small green numerals flickered in and out of existence, a Borgesian proof of the instability of reality.

"You realize. Venus is upside. Down?"

"They tipped it over?"

They was a placeholder for whatever force or entity or cosmic freak of nature had translated the two moons into orbit around the second planet, abstracting them from Earth and Jupiter and instantaneously replacing them in Venus space, as far as anyone could tell in the raging global internet hysteria before most of humanity was translated as well to the renovated world. Certainly Blackett had never noticed that the planet was turned on its head, but he had only been on Venus less than five days before he was recovered, against his will, to central Texas.

"*Au contraire.* It has always. Spun. Retrograde. It rotates backwards. The northern or upper hemisphere turns. Clockwise." Massri heaved a strangled breath, made twisted motions with his pudgy, blotched hands. "Nobody noticed that until late last. Century. The thick atmosphere, you know. And clouds. Impenetrable. High albedo. Gone now, of course."

Was it even the same world? He and the Egyptian scholar had discussed this before; it seemed to Blackett that whatever force had prepared this new Venus as a suitable habitat for humankind must have done so long ago, in some parallel or superposed state of alternative reality. The books piled around this squalid bed seemed to support such a conjecture. Worlds echoing away into infinity, each slightly different from the world adjacent to it, in a myriad of different dimensions of change. Earth, he understood, had been struck in infancy by a raging proto-planet the size of Mars, smashing away the light outer crust and flinging it into an orbiting shell that settled, over millions of years of impacts, into the Moon now circling Venus. But if in some other prismatic history, Venus had also suffered interplanetary bombardment on that scale, blowing away its monstrous choking carbon dioxide atmosphere and churning up the magma, driving the plate tectonic upheavals unknown until then, where was the Venerean or Venusian moon? Had that one been transported away to yet another alternative reality? It made Blackett tired to consider these metaphysical landscapes radiating away into eternity even as they seemed to close oppressively upon him, a psychic null-point of suffocating extinction.

Shyly, Kafele Massri broke the silence. "Robert, I have never. Asked you this." He paused, and the awkward moment extended. They heard the ticking of the grandfather clock in the hall outside.

"If I want to go back there? Yes, Kafele, I do. With all my heart."

"I know that. No. What was it. *Like?*" A sort of anguish tore the man's words. He himself had never gone, not even for a moment. Perhaps, he had joked once, there was a weight limit, a baggage surcharge his account could not meet.

"You're growing forgetful, my friend. Of course we've discussed this. The immense green-leaved trees, the crystal air, the strange fire-hued birds high in the canopies, the great rolling ocean—"

"No." Massri agitated his heavy hands urgently. "Not that. Not the sci-fi movie. Images. No offense intended. I mean . . . The *affect*. The weight or lightness of. The heart. The rapture of. Being there. Or the. I don't know. Dislocation? Despair?"

Blackett stood up. "Clare informs me I have damaged affect. 'Flattened,' she called it. Or did she say 'diminished'? Typical diagnostic hand-waving. If she'd been in practise as long as I—"

"Oh, Robert, I meant no—"

"Of course you didn't." Stiffly, he bent over the mound of the old man's supine body, patted his shoulder. "I'll get us some supper. Then you can tell me your new discovery."

7.

Tall cumulonimbus clouds moved in like a battlefleet of the sky, but the air remained hot and sticky. Lightning cracked in the distance, marching closer during the afternoon. When rain fell, it came suddenly, drenching the parched soil, sluicing the roadway, with a wind that blew discarded plastic bottles and bags about before dumping them at the edge of the road or piled against the fences and barred, spear-topped front gates. Blackett watched from the porch, the spray of rain blowing against his face in gusts. In the distance a stray dog howled and scurried.

On Venus, he recalled, under its doubled moons, the storms had been abrupt and hard, and the ocean tides surged in great rushes of blue-green water, spume like the head on a giant's overflowing draught of beer. Ignoring the shrill warnings of displaced astronomers, the first settlers along one shoreline, he had been told, perished as they viewed the glory of a Ganymedean-Lunar eclipse of the sun, twice as hot, a third again as wide. The proxivenerean spring tide, tugged by both moons and the sun as well, heaped up the sea and hurled it at the land.

Here on Earth, at least, the Moon's current absence somewhat calmed the weather. And without the endless barrage of particulate soot, inadequately scrubbed, exhaled into the air by a million factory chimneys and a billion fuel fires in the Third World, rain came more infrequently now. Perhaps, he wondered, it was time to move to a more salubrious climatic region. But what if that blocked his return to Venus? The very thought made the muscles at his jaw tighten painfully.

For an hour he watched the lowering sky for the glow pasted beneath distant clouds by a flash of electricity, then the tearing violence of lightning strikes as they came closer, passing by within miles. In an earlier dispensation, he would have pulled the plugs on his computers and other delicate equipment, unprepared to accept the dubious security of surge protectors. During one storm, years earlier, when the Moon still hung in the sky, his satellite dish and decoder burned out in a single nearby frightful clap of noise and light. On Venus, he reflected, the human race was yet to advance to the recovery of electronics. How many had died with the instant loss of infrastructure—sewerage, industrial food production, antibiotics, air conditioning? Deprived of television and music and books, how many had taken their own lives, unable to find footing in a world where they must fetch for themselves, work with neighbors they had found themselves flung amongst willy-nilly? Yes, many had been returned just long enough to ransack most of the medical supplies and haul away clothing, food, contraceptives, packs of toilet paper . . . Standing at the edge of the storm, on the elegant porch of his appropriated mansion, Blackett smiled, thinking of the piles of useless stereos, laptops and plasma TV screens he had seen dumped beside the immense Venusian trees. People were so stereotypical, unadaptive. No doubt driven to such stupidities, he reflected, by their lavish *affect.*

8.

Clare found him in the empty car park, pacing out the dimensions of Petra's Great Temple. He looked at her when she repeated his name, shook his head, slightly disoriented.

"This is the Central Arch, with the Theatron," he explained. "East and West corridors." He gestured. "In the center, the Forecourt, beyond the Proneos, and then the great space of the Lower Temenos."

"And all this," she said, looking faintly interested, "is a kind of imaginal reconstruction of Petra."

"Of its Temple, yes."

"The rose-red city half as old as time?" Now a mocking note had entered her voice.

He took her roughly by the arm, drew her into the shade of the five-story brick and concrete structure where neuropharmaceutical researchers had formerly plied their arcane trade. "Clare, we don't understand time. Look at this wall." He smote it with one clenched fist. "Why didn't it collapse when the Moon was removed? Why didn't terrible earthquakes split the ground open? The earth used to flex every day with lunar tides, Clare. There should have been convulsions as it compensated for the changed stresses. Did they see to that as well?"

"The dinosaurs, you mean?" She sighed, adopted a patient expression.

Blackett stared. "The *what?*"

"Oh." Today she was wearing deep red culottes and a green silk shirt, with a bandit's scarf holding back her heavy hair. Dark adaptive-optic sunglasses hid her eyes. "The professor hasn't told you his latest theory? I'm relieved to hear it. It isn't healthy for you two to spend so much time together, Robert. *Folie à deux* is harder to budge than a simple defensive delusion."

"You've been talking to Kafele Massri?" He was incredulous. "The man refuses to allow women into his house."

"I know. We talk through the bedroom window. I bring him soup for lunch."

"Good god."

"He assures me that the dinosaurs turned the planet Venus upside down 65 million years ago. They were intelligent. Not all of them, of course."

"No, you've misunderstood—"

"Probably. I must admit I wasn't listening very carefully. I'm far more interested in the emotional undercurrents."

"You would be. Oh, damn, damn."

"What's a Temenos?"

Blackett felt a momentary bubble of excitement. "At Petra, it was a beautiful sacred enclosure with hexagonal flooring, and three colonnades topped by sculptures of elephants' heads. Water was carried throughout the temple by channels, you see—" He started pacing off the plan of the Temple again, convinced that this was the key to his return to Venus. Clare walked beside him, humming very softly.

9.

"I understand you've been talking to my patient." Blackett took care to allow no trace of censure to color his words.

"Ha! It would be extremely uncivil, Robert. To drink her soup while maintaining. A surly silence. Incidentally, she maintains. You are her. Client."

"A harmless variant on the transference, Massri. But you understand that I can't discuss my patients, so I'm afraid we'll have to drop that topic immediately." He frowned at the Egyptian, who sipped tea from a half-filled mug. "I can say that Clare has a very garbled notion of your thinking about Venus."

"She's a delightful young woman, but doesn't. Seem to pay close attention to much. Beyond her wardrobe. Ah well. But Robert, I had to tell *somebody*. You didn't seem especially responsive. The other night."

Blackett settled back with his own mug of black coffee, already cooling. He knew he should stop drinking caffeine; it made him jittery. "You know I'm uncomfortable with anything that smacks of so-called 'Intelligent Design.'"

"Put your mind at. Rest, my boy. The design is plainly intelligent. Profoundly so, but. There's nothing supernatural in it. To the contrary."

"Still—dinosaurs? The dog I was talking to the other day favors what it called a 'singularity excursion.' In my view, six of one, half a dozen—"

"But don't you see?" The obese bibliophile struggled to heave his great mass up against the wall, hauling a pillow with him. "Both are wings. Of the same argument."

"Ah." Blackett put down his mug, wanting to escape the musty room with its miasma of cranky desperation. "Not just dinosaurs, *transcendental* dinosaurs."

Unruffled, Massri pursed his lips. "Probably. In effect." His breathing seemed rather improved. Perhaps his exchanges with an attractive young woman, even through the half-open window, braced his spirits.

"You have evidence and impeccable logic for this argument, I imagine?"

"Naturally. Has it ever occurred to you. How extremely improbable it is. That the west coast of Africa. Would fit so snugly against. The east coast of South America?"

"I see your argument. Those continents were once joined, then broke apart.

Plate tectonics drifted them thousands of miles apart. It's obvious to the naked eye, but nobody believed it for centuries."

The Egyptian nodded, evidently pleased with his apt student. "And how improbable is it that. The Moon's apparent diameter varies from 29 degrees 23 minutes to 33 degrees 29 minutes. Apogee to perigee. While the sun's apparent diameter varies. From 31 degrees 36 minutes to 32 degrees 3 minutes."

The effort of this exposition plainly exhausted the old man; he sank back against his unpleasant pillows.

"So we got total solar eclipses by the Moon where one just covered the other. A coincidence, nothing more."

"Really? And what of this equivalence? The Moon rotated every 27.32 days. The sun's sidereal rotation. Allowing for currents in the surface. Is 25.38 days."

Blackett felt as if ants were crawling under his skin. He forced patience upon himself.

"Not all that close, Massri. What, some . . . eight percent difference?"

"Seven. But Robert, the Moon's rotation has been slowing as it drifts away from Earth, because it is tidally locked. Was. Can you guess when the lunar day equaled the solar day?"

"Kafele, what are you going to tell me? 4 BC? 622 AD?"

"Neither Christ's birth nor Mohammed's Hegira. Robert, near as I can calculate it, 65.5 million years ago."

Blackett sat back, genuinely shocked, all his assurance draining away. The Cretaceous-Tertiary boundary. The Chicxulub impact event that exterminated the dinosaurs. He struggled his way back to reason. Clare had not been mistaken, not about that.

"This is just . . . absurd, my friend. The slack in those numbers . . . But what if they are right? So?"

The old man hauled himself up by brute force, dragged his legs over the side of the bed. "I have to take care of business," he said. "Leave the room, please, Robert."

From the hall, where he paced in agitation, Blackett heard a torrent of urine splashing into one of the jugs he had emptied when he arrived. Night music, he thought, forcing a grin. That's what James Joyce had called it. No, wait, that wasn't it—Chamber music. But the argument banged against his brain. And so what? Nothing could be dismissed out of hand. The damned *Moon* had been picked up and moved, and given a vast deep carbon dioxide atmosphere, presumably hosed over from the old Venus through some higher dimension. Humanity had been relocated to the cleaned-up version of Venus, a world with a breathable atmosphere and oceans filled with strange but edible fish. How could anything be ruled out as preposterous, however ungainly or grotesque?

"You can come back in now." There were thumps and thuds.

Instead, Blackett went back to the kitchen and made a new pot of coffee. He carried two mugs into the bedroom.

"Have I frightened you, my boy?"

"Everything frightens me these days, Professor Massri. You're about to tell me that you've found a monolith in the back garden, alongside the discarded cans and the mangy cats."

The Egyptian laughed, phlegm shaking his chest. "Almost. Almost. The Moon is now on orbit a bit over. A million kilometers from Venus. Also retrograde. Exactly the same distance Ganymede. Used to be from Jupiter."

"Well, okay, hardly a coincidence. And Ganymede is in the Moon's old orbit."

For a moment, Massri was silent. His face was drawn. He put down his coffee with a shaking hand.

"No. Ganymede orbits Venus some 434,000 kilometers out. According to the last data I could find before. The net went down for good."

"Farther out than the Moon used to orbit Earth. And?"

"The Sun, from Venus, as you once told me. Looks brighter and larger. In fact, it subtends about 40 minutes of arc. And by the most convenient and. Interesting coincidence. Ganymede now just exactly looks . . ."

". . . the same size as the Sun, from the surface of Venus." Ice ran down Blackett's back. "So it blocks the Sun exactly at total eclipse. That's what you're telling me?"

"Except for the corona, and bursts of solar flares. As the Moon used to do here." Massri sent him a glare almost baleful in its intensity. "And you think that's just a matter of chance? Do you think so, Dr. Blackett?"

10.

The thunderstorm on the previous day had left the air cooler. Blackett walked home slowly in the darkness, holding the HP calculator and two books the old man had perforce drawn upon for data, now the internet was expired. He did not recall having carried these particular volumes across the street from the empty library. Perhaps Clare or one of the other infrequent visitors had fetched them.

The stars hung clean and clear through the heavy branches extending from the gardens of most of the large houses in the neighborhood and across the old sidewalk. In the newer, outlying parts of the city, the nouveaux riches had considered it a mark of potent prosperity to run their well-watered lawns to the very verge of the roadway, never walking anywhere, driving to visit neighbors three doors distant. He wondered how they were managing on Venus. Perhaps the ratio of fit to obese and terminally inactive had improved, under the whip of necessity. Too late for poor Kafele, he thought, and made a mental note to stockpile another batch of pioglitazone, the old man's diabetes drug, when next he made a foray into a pharmacy.

He sat for half an hour in the silence of the large kitchen, scratching down data points and recalculating the professor's estimates. It was apparent that Massri thought the accepted extinction date of the great reptiles, coinciding as it did with the perfect overlap of the greater and lesser lights in the heavens, was no such thing—that it was, in fact, a time-stamp for Creation. The notion chilled Blackett's blood. Might the world, after all (fashionable speculation!), be no more than a virtual simulation? A calculational contrivance on a colossal scale? But not truly colossal, perhaps no more than a billion lines of code and a prodigiously accurate physics engine. Nothing else so easily explained the wholesale revision of the inner solar system. The idea did not appeal; it stank in Blackett's nostrils. Thus I refute, he thought again, and tapped a calculator key sharply. But that was a feeble refutation; one might as well, in a lucid dream, deny that any reality existed, forgetting the ground state or brute physical substrate needed to sustain the dream.

The numbers made no sense. He ran the calculations again. It was true that Ganymede's new orbit placed the former Jovian moon in just the right place, from time to time, to occult the sun's disk precisely. That was a disturbing datum. The dinosaur element was far less convincing. According to the authors of these astronomy books, Earth had started out, after the tremendous shock of the X-body impact that birthed the Moon, with a dizzying 5.5 or perhaps eight-hour day. It seemed impossibly swift, but the hugely larger gas giant Jupiter, Ganymede's former primary, turned completely around in just 10 hours.

The blazing young Earth spun like a mad top, its almost fatal impact wound subsiding, sucked away into subduction zones created by the impact itself. Venus—the old Venus, at least—lacked tectonic plates; the crust was resurfaced at half billion year intervals, as the boiling magma burst up through the rigid rocks, but not enough to carry down and away the appalling mass of carbon dioxide that had crushed the surface with a hundred times the pressure of Earth's oxygen-nitrogen atmosphere. Now, though, the renovated planet had a breathable atmosphere. Just add air and water, Blackett thought. Presumably the crust crept slowly over the face of the world, sucked down and spat back up over glacial epochs. But the numbers—

The Moon had been receding from Earth at a sluggish rate of 38 kilometers every million years—one part in 10,000 of its final orbital distance, before its removal to Venus. Kepler's Third Law, Blackett noted, established the orbital equivalence of time squared with distance cubed. So those 65.5 million years ago, when the great saurians were slain by a falling star, Luna had been only 2500 km closer to the Earth. But to match the sun's sidereal rotation exactly, the Moon needed to be more than 18,000 km nearer. That was the case no more recently than 485 million years ago.

Massri's dinosaur fantasy was off by a factor of at least 7.4.

Then how had the Egyptian reached his numerological conclusion? And where did all this lead? Nowhere useful that Blackett could see.

It was all sheer wishful thinking. Kafele Massri was as delusional as Clare, his thought processes utterly unsound. Blackett groaned and put his head on the table. Perhaps, he had to admit, his own reflections were no more reliable.

11.

"I'm flying down to the coast for a swim," Blackett told Clare. "There's room in the plane."

"A long way to go for a dip."

"A change of scenery," he said. "Bring your bathing suit if you like. I never bother, myself."

She gave him a long, cool look. "A nude beach? All right. I'll bring some lunch."

They drove together to the small airfield to one side of the industrial park in a serviceable SUV he found abandoned outside a 7-Eleven. Clare had averted her eyes as he hot-wired the engine. She wore sensible hiking boots, dark gray shorts, a white wife-beater that showed off her small breasts to advantage. Seated and strapped in, she laid her broad-brimmed straw hat on her knees. Blackett was mildly concerned by the slowly deteriorating condition of the plane. It had not been serviced in many months. He felt confident, though, that it would carry him where he needed to go, and back again.

During the 90-minute flight, he tried to explain the Egyptian's reasoning. The young psychiatrist responded with indifference that became palpable anxiety. Her hands tightened on the seat belt cinched at her waist. Blackett abandoned his efforts.

As they landed at Matagorda Island, she regained her animation. "Oh, look at those lovely biplanes! A shame they're in such deplorable condition. Why would anyone leave them out in the open weather like that?" She insisted on crossing to the sagging Stearmans for a closer look. Were those tears in her eyes?

Laden with towels and a basket of food, drink, paper plates and two glasses, Blackett summoned her sharply. "Come along, Clare, we'll miss the good waves if we loiter." If she heard bitter irony in his tone, she gave no sign of it. A gust of wind carried away his own boater, and she dashed after it, brought it back, jammed it rakishly on his balding head. "Thank you. I should tie the damned thing on with a leather thong, like the cowboys used to do, and cinch it with a . . . a . . ."

"A woggle," she said, unexpectedly.

It made Blackett laugh out loud. "Good god, woman! Wherever did you get a word like that?"

"My brother was a boy scout," she said.

They crossed the unkempt grass, made their way with some difficulty down to the shoreline. Blue ocean stretched south, almost flat, sparkling in the cloudless light. Blackett set down his burden, stripped his clothing efficiently, strode into the water. The salt stung his nostrils and eyes. He swam strongly out toward Mexico, thinking of the laughable scene in the movie *Gattaca*. He turned back, and saw Clare's head bobbing, sun-bleached hair plastered against her well-shaped scalp.

They lay side by side in the sun, odors of sun-block hanging on the unmoving air. After a time, Blackett saw the red setter approaching from the seaward side. The animal sat on its haunches, mouth open and tongue lolling, saying nothing.

"Hello, Sporky," Blackett said. "Beach patrol duties?"

"Howdy, Doc. Saw the Cessna coming in. Who's the babe?"

"This is Dr. Clare Laing. She's a psychiatrist, so show some respect."

Light glistened on her nearly naked body, reflected from sweat and a scattering of mica clinging to her torso. She turned her head away, affected to be sleeping. No, not sleeping. He realized that her attention was now fixed on a rusty bicycle wheel half buried in the sand. It seemed she might be trying to work out the absolute essence of the relationship between them, with the rim and broken spokes of this piece of sea drift serving as some kind of spinal metaphor.

Respectful of her privacy, Blackett sat up and began explaining to the dog the bibliophile's absurd miscalculation. Sporky interrupted his halting exposition.

"You're saying the angular width of the sun, then and now, is about 32 arc minutes."

"Yes, 0.00925 radians."

"And the Moon last matched this some 485 million years ago."

"No, no. Well, it was a slightly better match than it is now, but that's not Massri's point."

"Which is?"

"Which is that the sun's rotational period and the Moon's were the *same* in that epoch. Can't you see how damnably unlikely that is? He thinks it's something like . . . I don't know, God's thumbprint on the solar system. The true date of Creation, maybe. Then he tried to show that it coincides with the extinction of the dinosaurs, but that's just wrong, they went extinct—"

"You do know that there was a major catastrophic extinction event at the Cambrian-Ordovician transition 488 million years ago?"

Dumbfounded, Blackett said, "What?"

"Given your sloppy math, what do you say the chances are that your Moon-Sun equivalence bracketed the Cambrian-Ordovician extinction? Knocked the living hell out of the trilobites, Doc."

A surreal quality had entered the conversation. Blackett found it hard to accept that the dog could be a student of ancient geomorphisms. A spinal tremor shook him. So the creature was no ordinary genetically upgraded dog but some manifestation of the entity, the force, the ontological dislocation that had torn away the Moon and the world's inhabitants, most of them.

Detesting the note of pleading in his own voice, Blackett uttered a cry of heartfelt petition. He saw Clare roll over, waken from her sun-warmed drowse. "How can I get back there?" he cried. "Send me back! Send us both!"

Sporky stood up, shook sand from his fur, spraying Blackett with stinging mica.

"Go on as you began," the animal said, "and let the Lord be all in all to you."

Clouds of uncertainty cleared from Blackett's mind, as the caustic, acid clouds of Venus had been sucked away and transposed to the relocated Moon. He jumped up, bent, seized the psychiatrist's hand, hauled her blinking and protesting to her feet.

"Clare! We must trace out the ceremony of the Great Temple! Here, at the edge of the ocean. I've been wasting my time trying this ritual inland. Venus is now a world of great oceans!"

"Damn it, Robert, let me go, you're hurting—"

But he was hauling her down to the brackish, brine-stinking sea shore. Their parallel footprints wavered, inscribing a semiotics of deliverance. He began to tread out the Petran temple perimeter, starting at the Propylecum, turned a right angle, marched them to the East Excedra and to the very foot of the ancient Cistern. He was traveling backward into archeopsychic time, deeper into those remote, somber half-worlds he had glimpsed in the recuperative paintings of his mad patients.

"Robert! Robert!"

They entered the water, which lapped sluggishly at their ankles and calves like the articulate tongue of a dog as large as the world. Blackett gaped. At the edge of sea and sand, great three-lobed arthropods shed water from their shells, moving slowly like enormous wood lice.

"Trilobites!" Blackett cried. He stared about, hand still firmly clamped on Clare Laing's. Great green rolling breakers, in the distance, rushed toward shore, broke, foamed and frothed, lifting the ancient animals and tugging at Blackett's limbs. He tottered forward into the drag of the Venusian ocean, caught himself. He stared over his shoulder at the vast, towering green canopy of trees. Overhead, bracketing the sun, twin crescent moons shone faintly against the purple sky. He looked wildly at his companion and laughed, joyously, then flung his arms about her.

"Clare," he cried, alive on Venus, "Clare, we made it!"

seven years from home

NAOMI NOVIK

Born in New York City, where she still lives with her mystery-editor husband, their family, and six computers, Naomi Novik is a first-generation American who was raised on Polish fairy tales, Baba Yaga, and Tolkien. After doing graduate work in computer science at Columbia University, she participated in the development of the computer game *Neverwinter Nights: Shadows of Undrentide*, and then decided to try her hand at novels. A good decision! The resultant Temeraire series—consisting of *His Majesty's Dragon, Black PowderWar, The Throne of Jade, Empire of Ivory,* and *Victory of Eagles*—describing an alternate version of the Napoleonic Wars where dragons are used as living weapons, has been phenomenally popular and successful. Her most recent books are a new Temeraire novel, *Tongues of Serpents,* and a graphic novel, *Will Super-villains Be On the Final?*

Here she takes us on an evocative visit to a distant planet of intricate and interlocking biological mysteries, for a harrowing demonstration that it's unwise to strike at an enemy before you're sure they can't strike *back.* . . .

PREFACE

Seven days passed for me on my little raft of a ship as I fled Melida; seven years for the rest of the unaccelerated universe. I hoped to be forgotten, a dusty footnote left at the bottom of a page. Instead I came off to trumpets and medals and legal charges, equal doses of acclaim and venom, and I stumbled bewildered through the brassy noise, led first by one and then by another, while my last opportunity to enter any protest against myself escaped.

Now I desire only to correct the worst of the factual inaccuracies bandied about, so far as my imperfect memory will allow, and to make an offering of my own understanding to that smaller and more sophisticate audience who prefer to shape the world's opinion rather than be shaped by it.

I engage not to tire you with a recitation of dates and events and quotations. I do not recall them with any precision myself. But I must warn you that neither have I succumbed to that pathetic and otiose impulse to sanitize the events of the war, or to excuse sins either my own or belonging to others. To do so would be a lie, and on Melida, to tell a lie was an insult more profound than murder.

I will not see my sisters again, whom I loved. Here we say that one who takes the long midnight voyage has leaped ahead in time, but to me it seems it is they who have traveled on ahead. I can no longer hear their voices when I am awake. I hope this will silence them in the night.

Ruth Patrona
Reivaldt, Janvier 32, 4765

THE FIRST ADJUSTMENT

I disembarked at the port of Landfall in the fifth month of 4753. There is such a port on every world where the Confederacy has set its foot but not yet its flag: crowded and dirty and charmless. It was on the Esperigan continent, as the Melidans would not tolerate the construction of a spaceport in their own territory.

Ambassador Kostas, my superior, was a man of great authority and presence, two meters tall and solidly built, with a jovial handshake, high intelligence, and very little patience for fools; that I was likely to be relegated to this category was evident on our first meeting. He disliked my assignment to begin with. He thought well of the Esperigans; he moved in their society as easily as he did in our own, and would have called one or two of their senior ministers his personal friends, if only such a gesture were not highly unprofessional. He recognized his duty, and on an abstract intellectual level the potential value of the Melidans, but they revolted him, and he would have been glad to find me of like mind, ready to draw a line through their name and give them up as a bad cause.

A few moments' conversation was sufficient to disabuse him of this hope. I wish to attest that he did not allow the disappointment to in any way alter the performance of his duty, and he could not have objected with more vigor to my project of proceeding at once to the Melidan continent, to his mind a suicidal act.

In the end he chose not to stop me. I am sorry if he later regretted that, as seems likely. I took full advantage of the weight of my arrival. Five years had gone by on my homeworld of Terce since I had embarked, and there is a certain moral force to having sacrificed a former life for the one unknown. I had observed it often with new arrivals on Terce: their first requests were rarely refused even when foolish, as they often were. I was of course quite sure my own were eminently sensible.

"We will find you a guide," he said finally, yielding, and all the machinery of the Confederacy began to turn to my desire, a heady sensation.

Badea arrived at the embassy not two hours later. She wore a plain gray wrap around her shoulders, draped to the ground, and another wrap around her head. The alterations visible were only small ones: a smattering of green freckles across the bridge of her nose and cheeks, a greenish tinge to her lips and nails. Her wings were folded and hidden under the wrap, adding the bulk roughly of an overnight hiker's backpack. She smelled a little like the sourdough used on Terce to make roundbread, noticeable but not unpleasant. She might have walked through a spaceport without exciting comment.

She was brought to me in the shambles of my new office, where I had barely begun to lay out my things. I was wearing a conservative black suit, my best, tailored because you could not buy trousers for women ready-made on Terce, and, thankfully, comfortable shoes, because elegant ones on Terce were not meant to be walked in. I remember my clothing particularly because I was in it for the next week without opportunity to change.

"Are you ready to go?" she asked me, as soon as we were introduced and the receptionist had left.

I was quite visibly *not* ready to go, but this was not a misunderstanding: she did not want to take me. She thought the request stupid, and feared my safety would be a burden on her. If Ambassador Kostas would not mind my failure to return, she could not know that, and to be just, he would certainly have reacted unpleasantly in any case, figuring it as his duty.

But when asked for a favor she does not want to grant, a Melidan will sometimes offer it anyway, only in an unacceptable or awkward way. Another Melidan will recognize this as a refusal, and withdraw the request. Badea did not expect this courtesy from me, she only expected that I would say I could not leave at once. This she could count to her satisfaction as a refusal, and she would not come back to offer again.

I was however informed enough to be dangerous, and I did recognize the custom. I said, "It is inconvenient, but I am prepared to leave immediately." She turned at once and walked out of my office, and I followed her. It is understood that a favor accepted despite the difficulty and constraints laid down by the giver must be necessary to the recipient, as indeed this was to me; but in such a case, the conditions must then be endured, even if artificial.

I did not risk a pause at all even to tell anyone I was going; we walked out past the embassy secretary and the guards, who did not do more than give us a cursory glance—we were going the wrong way, and my citizen's button would likely have saved us interruption in any case. Kostas would not know I had gone until my absence was noticed and the security logs examined.

THE SECOND ADJUSTMENT

I was not unhappy as I followed Badea through the city. A little discomfort was nothing to me next to the intense satisfaction of, as I felt, having passed a first test: I had gotten past all resistance offered me, both by Kostas and Badea, and soon I would be in the heart of a people I already felt I knew. Though I would be an outsider among them, I had lived all my life to the present day in the self-same state, and I did not fear it, or for the moment anything else.

Badea walked quickly and with a freer stride than I was used to, loose-limbed. I was taller, but had to stretch to match her. Esperigans looked at her as she went by, and then looked at me, and the pressure of their gaze was suddenly hostile. "We might take a taxi," I offered. Many were passing by empty. "I can pay."

"No," she said, with a look of distaste at one of those conveyances, so we continued on foot.

After Melida, during my black-sea journey, my doctoral dissertation on the Canaan movement was published under the escrow clause, against my will. I have never used the funds, which continue to accumulate steadily. I do not like to inflict them on any cause I admire sufficiently to support, so they will go to my family when I have gone; my nephews will be glad of it, and of the passing of an embarrassment, and that is as much good as it can be expected to provide.

There is a great deal within that book which is wrong, and more which is wrongheaded, in particular any expression of opinion or analysis I interjected atop the scant collection of accurate facts I was able to accumulate in six years of over-enthusiastic graduate work. This little is true: the Canaan movement was an offshoot of conservation philosophy. Where the traditionalists of that movement sought to restrict humanity to dead worlds and closed enclaves on others, the Canaan splinter group wished instead to alter themselves while they altered their new worlds, meeting them halfway.

The philosophy had the benefit of a certain practicality, as genetic engineering and body modification was and remains considerably cheaper than terraforming, but we are a squeamish and a violent species, and nothing invites pogrom more surely than the neighbor who is different from us, yet still too close. In consequence, the Melidans were by our present day the last surviving Canaan society.

They had come to Melida and settled the larger of the two continents some eight hundred years before. The Esperigans came two hundred years later, refugees from the plagues on New Victoire, and took the smaller continent. The two had little contact for the first half-millennium; we of the Confederacy are given to think in worlds and solar systems, and to imagine that only a space voyage is long, but a hostile continent is vast enough to occupy a small and struggling band. But both prospered, each according to their lights, and by the time I landed, half the planet glittered in the night from space, and half was yet pristine.

In my dissertation, I described the ensuing conflict as natural, which is fair if slaughter and pillage are granted to be natural to our kind. The Esperigans had exhausted the limited raw resources of their share of the planet, and a short flight away was the untouched expanse of the larger continent, not a tenth as populated as their own. The Melidans controlled their birthrate, used only sustainable quantities, and built nothing which could not be eaten by the wilderness a year after they had abandoned it. Many Esperigan philosophes and politicians trumpeted their admiration of Melidan society, but this was only a sort of pleasant spiritual refreshment, as one admires a saint or a martyr without ever wishing to be one.

The invasion began informally, with adventurers and entrepreneurs, with the desperate, the poor, the violent. They began to land on the shores of the Melidan territory, to survey, to take away samples, to plant their own foreign roots. They soon had a village, then more than one. The Melidans told them to leave, which worked as well as it ever has in the annals of colonialism, and then attacked them. Most of the settlers were killed; enough survived and straggled back across the ocean to make a dramatic story of murder and cruelty out of it.

I expressed the conviction to the Ministry of State, in my pre-assignment report, that the details had been exaggerated, and that the attacks had been provoked more extensively. I was wrong, of course. But at the time I did not know it.

Badea took me to the low quarter of Landfall, so called because it faced on the side of the ocean downcurrent from the spaceport. Iridescent oil and a floating mat of discards glazed the edge of the surf. The houses were mean and crowded tightly upon one another, broken up mostly by liquor stores and bars. Docks stretched out into the ocean, extended long to reach out past the pollution, and just past the end of one of these floated a small boat, little more than a simple coracle: a hull of brown bark, a narrow brown mast, a grey-green sail slack and trembling in the wind.

We began walking out towards it, and those watching—there were some men loitering about the docks, fishing idly, or working on repairs to equipment or nets—began to realize then that I meant to go with her.

The Esperigans had already learned the lesson we like to teach as often as we can, that the Confederacy is a bad enemy and a good friend, and while no one is ever made to join us by force, we cannot be opposed directly. We had given them the spaceport already, an open door to the rest of the settled worlds, and they wanted more, the moth yearning. I relied on this for protection, and did not consider that however much they wanted from our outstretched hand, they still more wished to deny its gifts to their enemy.

Four men rose as we walked the length of the dock, and made a line across it. "You don't want to go with that one, ma'am," one of them said to me, a parody of respect. Badea said nothing. She moved a little aside, to see how I would answer them.

"I am on assignment for my government," I said, neatly offering a red flag to a bull, and moved towards them. It was not an attempt at bluffing: on Terce, even though I was immodestly unveiled, men would have at once moved out of the way to avoid any chance of the insult of physical contact. It was an act so automatic as to be invisible: precisely what we are taught to watch for in ourselves, but that proves infinitely easier in the instruction than in the practice. I did not *think* they would move; I knew they would.

Perhaps that certainty transmitted itself: the men did move a little, enough to satisfy my unconscious that they were cooperating with my expectations, so that it took me wholly by surprise and horror when one reached out and put his hand on my arm to stop me.

I screamed, in full voice, and struck him. His face is lost to my memory, but I still can see clearly the man behind him, his expression as full of appalled violation as my own. The four of them flinched from my scream, and then drew in around me, protesting and reaching out in turn.

I reacted with more violence. I had confidently considered myself a citizen of no world and of many, trained out of assumptions and unaffected by the parochial attitudes of the one where chance had seen me born, but in that moment I could with actual pleasure have killed all of them. That wish was unlikely to be gratified. I was taller, and the gravity of Terce is slightly higher than of Melida, so I was stronger than they expected me to be, but they were laborers and seamen, built generously and rough-hewn, and the male advantage in muscle mass tells quickly in a hand-to-hand fight.

They tried to immobilize me, which only panicked me further. The mind curls in on itself in such a moment; I remember palpably only the sensation of sweating copiously, and the way this caused the seam of my blouse to rub unpleasantly against my neck as I struggled.

Badea told me later that, at first, she had meant to let them hold me. She could then leave, with the added satisfaction of knowing the Esperigan fishermen and not she had provoked an incident with the Confederacy. It was not sympathy that moved her to action, precisely. The extremity of my distress was as alien to her as to them, but where they thought me mad, she read it in the context of my having accepted her original conditions and somewhat unwillingly decided that I truly did need to go with her, even if she did not know precisely why and saw no use in it herself.

I cannot tell you precisely how the subsequent moments unfolded. I remember the green gauze of her wings overhead perforated by the sun, like a linen curtain, and the blood spattering my face as she neatly lopped off the hands upon me. She used for the purpose a blade I later saw in use for many tasks, among them harvesting fruit off plants where the leaves or the bark may be poisonous. It is shaped like a sickle and strung upon a thick elastic cord, which a skilled wielder can cause to become rigid or to collapse.

I stood myself back on my feet panting, and she landed. The men were on their knees screaming, and others were running towards us down the docks. Badea swept the severed hands into the water with the side of her foot and said calmly, "We must go."

The little boat had drawn up directly beside us over the course of our encounter, drawn by some signal I had not seen her transmit. I stepped into it behind her. The coracle leapt forward like a springing bird, and left the shouting and the blood behind.

We did not speak over the course of that strange journey. What I had thought a sail did not catch the wind, but opened itself wide and stretched out over our heads, like an awning, and angled itself towards the sun. There were many small filaments upon the surface wriggling when I examined it more closely, and also upon the exterior of the hull. Badea stretched herself out upon the floor of the craft, lying under the low deck, and I joined her in the small space: it was not uncomfortable nor rigid, but had the queer unsettled cushioning of a waterbed.

The ocean crossing took only the rest of the day. How our speed was generated I cannot tell you; we did not seem to sit deeply in the water and our craft threw up no spray. The world blurred as a window running with rain. I asked Badea for water, once, and she put her hands on the floor of the craft and pressed down: in the depression she made, a small clear pool gathered for me to cup out, with a taste like slices of cucumber with the skin still upon them.

This was how I came to Melida.

THE THIRD ADJUSTMENT

Badea was vaguely embarrassed to have inflicted me on her fellows, and having deposited me in the center of her village made a point of leaving me there by leaping aloft into the canopy where I could not follow, as a way of saying she was done with me, and anything I did henceforth could not be laid at her door.

I was by now hungry and nearly sick with exhaustion. Those who have not flown between worlds like to imagine the journey a glamorous one, but at least for minor bureaucrats, it is no more pleasant than any form of transport, only elongated. I had spent a week a virtual prisoner in my berth, the bed folding up to give me room to walk four strides back and forth, or to unfold my writing-desk, not both at once, with a shared toilet the size of an ungenerous closet down the hall. Landfall had not arrested my forward motion, as that mean port had never been my destination. Now, however, I was arrived, and the dregs of adrenaline were consumed in anticlimax.

Others before me have stood in a Melidan village center and described it for an audience—Esperigans mostly, anthropologists and students of biology and a class of tourists either adventurous or stupid. There is usually a lyrical description of the natives coasting overhead among some sort of vines or tree-branches knitted overhead for shelter, the particulars and adjectives determined by the village latitude, and the obligatory explanation of the typical plan of huts, organized as a spoked wheel around the central plaza.

If I had been less tired, perhaps I too would have looked with so analytical an air, and might now satisfy my readers with a similar report. But to me the village only presented all the confusion of a wholly strange place, and I saw nothing that seemed to me deliberate. To call it a village gives a false air of comforting provinciality. Melidans, at least those with wings, move freely among a wide constellation of small settlements, so that all of these, in the public sphere, partake of the hectic pace of the city. I stood alone, and strangers moved past me with assurance, the confidence of their stride saying, "I care nothing for you or your fate. It is of no concern to me. How might you expect it to be otherwise?" In the end, I lay down on one side of the plaza and went to sleep.

I met Kitia the next morning. She woke me by prodding me with a twig, experimentally, having been selected for this task out of her group of schoolmates by some complicated interworking of personality and chance. They giggled from a few safe paces back as I opened my eyes and sat up.

"Why are you sleeping in the square?" Kitia asked me, to a burst of fresh giggles.

"Where should I sleep?" I asked her.

"In a house!" she said.

When I had explained to them, not without some art, that I had no house here, they offered the censorious suggestion that I should go back to wherever I did have a house. I made a good show of looking analytically up at the sky overhead and asking them what our latitude was, and then I pointed at a random location and said, "My house is five years that way."

Scorn, puzzlement, and at last delight. I was from the stars! None of their friends had ever met anyone from so far away. One girl who previously had held a point of pride for having once visited the smaller continent, with an Esperigan toy doll to prove it, was instantly dethroned. Kitia possessively took my arm and informed me that as my house was too far away, she would take me to another.

Children of virtually any society are an excellent resource for the diplomatic servant or the anthropologist, if contact with them can be made without giving offense. They enjoy the unfamiliar experience of answering real questions, particularly the stupidly obvious ones that allow them to feel a sense of superiority over the inquiring adult, and they are easily impressed with the unusual. Kitia was a treasure. She led me, at the head of a small pied-piper procession, to an empty house on a convenient lane. It had been lately abandoned, and was already being reclaimed: the walls and floor were swarming with tiny insects with glossy dark blue carapaces, munching so industriously the sound of their jaws hummed like a summer afternoon.

I with difficulty avoided recoiling. Kitia did not hesitate: she walked into the swarm, crushing beetles by the dozens underfoot, and went to a small spigot in the far wall. When she turned this on, a clear viscous liquid issued forth, and the beetles scattered from it. "Here, like this," she said, showing me how to cup my hands under the liquid and spread it upon the walls and the floor. The disgruntled beetles withdrew, and the brownish surfaces began to bloom back to pale green, repairing the holes.

Over the course of that next week, she also fed me, corrected my manners and my grammar, and eventually brought me a set of clothing, a tunic and leggings, which she proudly informed me she had made herself in class. I thanked her with real sincerity and asked where I might wash my old clothing. She looked very puzzled, and when she had looked more closely at my clothing and touched it, she said, "Your clothing is dead! I thought it was only ugly."

Her gift was not made of fabric but a thin tough mesh of plant filaments with the feathered surface of a moth's wings. It gripped my skin eagerly as soon as I had put it on, and I thought myself at first allergic, because it itched and tingled, but this was only the bacteria bred to live in the mesh assiduously eating away the sweat and dirt and dead epidermal cells built up on my skin. It took me several more days to overcome all my instinct and learn to trust the living cloth with the more voluntary eliminations of my body also. (Previously I had been going out back to defecate in the woods, having been unable to find anything resembling a toilet, and meeting too much confusion when I tried to approach the question to dare pursue it further, for fear of encountering a taboo.)

And this was the handiwork of a child, not thirteen years of age! She could not explain to me how she had done it in any way which made sense to me. Imagine if you had to explain how to perform a reference search to someone who had not only never seen a library, but did not understand electricity, and who perhaps knew there was such a thing as written text, but did not himself read more than the alphabet. She took me once to her classroom after hours and showed me her workstation, a large wooden tray full of grayish moss, with a double row of small jars along the back each holding liquids or powders which I could only distinguish by their differing colors. Her only tools were an assortment of syringes and eyedroppers and scoops and brushes.

I went back to my house and in the growing report I would not have a chance to send for another month I wrote, *These are a priceless people. We must have them.*

THE FOURTH ADJUSTMENT

All these first weeks, I made no contact with any other adult. I saw them go by occasionally, and the houses around mine were occupied, but they never spoke to me or even looked at me directly. None of them objected to my squatting, but that was less implicit endorsement and more an unwillingness even to acknowledge my existence. I talked to Kitia and the other children, and tried to be patient. I hoped an opportunity would offer itself eventually for me to be of some visible use.

In the event, it was rather my lack of use which led to the break in the wall. A commotion arose in the early morning, while Kitia was showing me the plan of her wings, which she was at that age beginning to design. She would grow the parasite over the subsequent year, and was presently practicing with miniature versions, which rose from her worktable surface gossamer-thin and fluttering with an involuntary muscle-twitching. I was trying to conceal my revulsion.

Kitia looked up when the noise erupted. She casually tossed her example out of the window, to be pounced upon with a hasty scramble by several nearby birds, and went out the door. I followed her to the square: the children were gathered at the fringes, silent for once and watching. There were five women laid out on the ground, all bloody, one dead. Two of the others looked mortally wounded. They were all winged.

There were several working already on the injured, packing small brownish-white spongy masses into the open wounds and sewing them up. I would have liked to be of use, less from natural instinct than from the colder thought, which inflicted itself upon my mind, that any crisis opens social barriers. I am sorry to say I did not refrain from any noble self-censorship, but from the practical conviction that it was at once apparent my limited field-medical training could not in any valuable way be applied to the present circumstances.

I drew away, rather, to avoid being in the way as I could not turn the situation to my advantage, and in doing so ran up against Badea, who stood at the very edge of the square, observing.

She stood alone; there were no other adults nearby, and there was blood on her hands. "Are you hurt also?" I asked her.

"No," she returned, shortly.

I ventured on concern for her friends, and asked her if they had been hurt in fighting. "We have heard rumors," I added, "that the Esperigans have been encroaching on your territory." It was the first opportunity I had been given of hinting at even this much of our official sympathy, as the children only shrugged when I asked them if there were fighting going on.

She shrugged, too, with one shoulder, and the folded wing rose and fell with it. But then she said, "They leave their weapons in the forest for us, even where they cannot have gone."

The Esperigans had several kinds of land-mine technologies, including a clever mobile one which could be programmed with a target either as specific as an individual's genetic record or as general as a broadly defined body type—humanoid and winged, for instance—and set loose to wander until it found a match, then do the maximum damage it could. Only one side could carry explosive, as the other was devoted to the electronics. "The shrapnel, does it come only in one direction?" I asked, and made a fanned-out shape with my hands to illustrate. Badea looked at me sharply and nodded.

I explained the mine to her, and described their manufacture. "Some scanning devices can detect them," I added, meaning to continue into an offer, but I had not finished the litany of materials before she was striding away from the square, without another word.

I was not dissatisfied with the reaction, in which I correctly read intention to put my information to immediate use, and two days later my patience was rewarded. Badea came to my house in the mid-morning and said, "We have found one of them. Can you show us how to disarm them?"

"I am not sure," I told her, honestly. "The safest option would be to trigger it deliberately, from afar."

"The plastics they use poison the ground."

"Can you take me to its location?" I asked. She considered the question with enough seriousness that I realized there was either taboo or danger involved.

"Yes," she said finally, and took me with her to a house near the center of the village. It had steps up to the roof, and from there we could climb to that of the neighboring house, and so on until we were high enough to reach a large basket, woven not of ropes but of a kind of vine, sitting in a crook of a tree. We climbed into this, and she kicked us off from the tree.

The movement was not smooth. The nearest I can describe is the sensation of being on a child's swing, except at that highest point of weightlessness you do not go backwards, but instead go falling into another arc, but at tremendous speed, and with a pungent smell like rotten pineapple all around from the shattering of the leaves of the trees through which we were propelled. I was violently sick after some five minutes. To the comfort of my pride if not my stomach, Badea was also sick, though more efficiently and over the side, before our journey ended.

There were two other women waiting for us in the tree where we came to rest, both of them also winged: Renata and Paudi. "It's gone another three hundred meters, towards Ighlan," Renata told us—another nearby Melidan village, as they explained to me.

"If it comes near enough to pick up traces of organized habitation, it will not trigger until it is inside the settlement, among as many people as possible," I said. "It may also have a burrowing mode, if it is the more expensive kind."

They took me down through the canopy, carefully, and walked before and behind me when we came to the ground. Their wings were spread wide enough to brush against the hanging vines to either side, and they regularly leapt aloft for a brief survey. Several times they moved me with friendly hands into a slightly different path, although my untrained eyes could make no difference among the choices.

A narrow trail of large ants—the reader will forgive me for calling them ants, they were nearly indistinguishable from those efficient creatures—paced us over the forest floor, which I did not recognize as significant until we came near the mine, and I saw it covered with the ants, who did not impede its movement but milled around and over it with intense interest.

"We have adjusted them so they smell the plastic," Badea said, when I asked. "We can make them eat it," she added, "but we worried it would set off the device."

The word *adjusted* scratches at the back of my mind again as I write this, that unpleasant tinny sensation of a term that does not allow of real translation and which has been inadequately replaced. I cannot improve upon the work of the official Confederacy translators, however; to encompass the true concept would require three dry, dusty chapters more suited to a textbook on the subject of biological engineering, which I am ill-qualified to produce. I do hope that I have successfully captured the wholly casual way she spoke of this feat. Our own scientists might replicate this act of genetic sculpting in any of two dozen excellent laboratories across the Confederacy—given several years, and a suitably impressive grant. They had done it in less than two days, as a matter of course.

I did not at the time indulge in admiration. The mine was ignoring the inquisitive ants and scuttling along at a good pace, the head with its glassy eye occasionally rotating upon its spindly spider-legs, and we had half a day in which to divert it from the village ahead.

Renata followed the mine as it continued on, while I sketched what I knew of the internals in the dirt for Badea and Paudi. Any sensible mine-maker will design the device to simply explode at any interference with its working other than the disable code, so our options were not particularly satisfying. "The most likely choice," I suggested, "would be the transmitter. If it becomes unable to receive the disable code, there may be a failsafe which would deactivate it on a subsequent malfunction."

Paudi had on her back a case which, unfolded, looked very like a more elegant and compact version of little Kitia's worktable. She sat crosslegged with it on her lap and worked on it for some two hours' time, occasionally reaching down to pick up a handful of ants, which dropped into the green matrix of her table mostly curled up and died, save for a few survivors, which she herded carefully into an empty jar before taking up another sample.

I sat on the forest floor beside her, or walked with Badea, who was pacing a small circle out around us, watchfully. Occasionally she would unsling her scythe-blade, and then put it away again, and once she brought down a mottie, a small lemur-like creature. I say lemur because there is nothing closer in my experience, but it had none of the charm of an Earth-native mammal; I rather felt an instinctive disgust looking at it, even before she showed me the tiny sucker-mouths full of hooked teeth with which it latched upon a victim.

She had grown a little more loquacious, and asked me about my own home-world. I told her about Terce, and about the seclusion of women, which she found extremely funny, as we can only laugh at the follies of those far from us which threaten us not at all. The Melidans by design maintain a five to one ratio of women to men, as adequate to maintain a healthy gene pool while minimizing the overall resource consumption of their population. "They cannot take the wings, so it is more difficult for them to travel," she added, with one sentence dismissing the lingering mystery which had perplexed earlier visitors, of the relative rarity of seeing their men.

She had two children, which she described to me proudly, living presently with their father and half-siblings in a village half a day's travel away, and she was considering a third. She had trained as a forest ranger, another inadequately translated term which was at the time beginning to take on a military significance among them under the pressure of the Esperigan incursions.

"I'm done," Paudi said, and we went to catch up Renata and find a nearby ant-nest, which looked like a mound of white cotton batting, rising several inches off the forest floor. Paudi introduced her small group of infected survivors into this colony, and after a little confusion and milling about, they accepted their transplantation and marched inside. The flow of departures slowed a little momentarily, then resumed, and a file split off from the main channel of workers to march in the direction of the mine.

These joined the lingering crowd still upon the mine, but the new arrivals did not stop at inspection and promptly began to struggle to insinuate themselves into the casing. We withdrew to a safe distance, watching. The mine continued on without any slackening in its pace for ten minutes, as more ants began to squeeze themselves inside, and then it hesitated, one spindly metal leg held aloft uncertainly. It went a few more slightly drunken paces, and then abruptly the legs all retracted and left it a smooth round lump on the forest floor.

THE FIFTH ADJUSTMENT

They showed me how to use their communications technology and grew me an interface to my own small handheld, so my report was at last able to go. Kostas began angry, of course, having been forced to defend the manner of my departure to the Esperigans without the benefit of any understanding of the circumstances, but I sent the report an hour before I messaged, and by the time we spoke he had read enough to be in reluctant agreement with my conclusions if not my methods.

I was of course full of self-satisfaction. Freed at long last from the academy and the walled gardens of Terce, armed with false confidence in my research and my training, I had so far achieved all that my design had stretched to encompass. The Esperigan blood had washed easily from my hands, and though I answered Kostas meekly when he upbraided me, privately I felt only impatience, and even he did not linger long on the topic: I had been too successful, and he had more important news.

The Esperigans had launched a small army two days before, under the more pleasant-sounding name of expeditionary defensive force. Their purpose was to establish a permanent settlement on the Melidan shore, some nine hundred miles from my present location, and begin the standard process of terraforming. The native life would be eradicated in spheres of a hundred miles across at a time: first the broad strokes of clear-cutting and the electrified nets, then the irradiation of the soil and the air, and after that the seeding of Earth-native microbes and plants. So had a thousand worlds been made over anew, and though the Esperigans had fully conquered their own continent five centuries before, they still knew the way.

He asked doubtfully if I thought some immediate resistance could be offered. Disabling a few mines scattered into the jungle seemed to him a small task. Confronting a large and organized military force was on a different order of magnitude. "I think we can do something," I said, maintaining a veneer of caution for his benefit, and took the catalog of equipment to Badea as soon as we had disengaged.

She was occupied in organizing the retrieval of the deactivated mines, which the ants were now leaving scattered in the forests and jungles. A bird-of-paradise variant had been *adjusted* to make a meal out of the ants and take the glittery mines back to their tree-top nests, where an observer might easily see them from above. She and the other collectors had so far found nearly a thousand of them. The mines made a neat pyramid, as of the harvested skulls of small cyclopean creatures with their dull eyes staring out lifelessly.

The Esperigans needed a week to cross the ocean in their numbers, and I spent it with the Melidans, developing our response. There was a heady delight in this collaboration. The work was easy and pleasant in their wide-open laboratories full of plants, roofed only with the fluttering sailcloth eating sunlight to give us energy, and the best of them coming from many miles distant to participate in the effort. The Confederacy spy-satellites had gone into orbit perhaps a year after our first contact: I likely knew more about the actual force than the senior administrators of Melida. I was in much demand, consulted not only for my information but my opinion.

In the ferment of our labors, I withheld nothing. This was not yet deliberate, but neither was it innocent. I had been sent to further a war, and if in the political calculus which had arrived at this solution the lives of soldiers were only variables, there was still a balance I was expected to preserve. It was not my duty to give the Melidans an easy victory, any more than it had been Kostas's to give one to the Esperigans.

A short and victorious war, opening a new and tantalizing frontier for restless spirits, would at once drive up that inconvenient nationalism which is the Confederacy's worst obstacle, and render less compelling the temptations we could offer to lure them into fully joining galactic society. On the other hand, to descend into squalor, a more equal kind of civil war has often proven extremely useful, and the more lingering and bitter the better. I was sent to the Melidans in hope that, given some guidance and what material assistance we could quietly provide without taking any official position, they might be an adequate opponent for the Esperigans to produce this situation.

There has been some criticism of the officials who selected me for this mission, but in their defense, it must be pointed out it was not in fact my assignment to actually provide military assistance, nor could anyone, even myself, have envisioned my proving remotely useful in such a role. I was only meant to be an early scout. My duty was to acquire cultural information enough to open a door for a party of military experts from Voca Libre, who would not reach Melida for another two years. Ambition and opportunity promoted me, and no official hand.

I think these experts arrived sometime during the third Esperigan offensive. I cannot pinpoint the date with any accuracy, I had by then ceased to track the days, and I never met them. I hope they can forgive my theft of their war; I paid for my greed.

The Esperigans used a typical carbonized steel in most of their equipment, as bolts and hexagonal nuts and screws with star-shaped heads, and woven into the tough mesh of their body armor. This was the target of our efforts. It was a new field of endeavor for the Melidans, who used metal as they used meat, sparingly and with a sense of righteousness in its avoidance. To them it was either a trace element needed in minute amounts, or an undesirable by-product of the more complicated biological processes they occasionally needed to invoke.

However, they had developed some strains of bacteria to deal with this latter waste, and the speed with which they could manipulate these organisms was extraordinary. Another quantity of the ants—a convenient delivery mechanism used by the Melidans routinely, as I learned—was adjusted to render them deficient in iron and to provide a home in their bellies for the bacteria, transforming them into shockingly efficient engines of destruction. Set loose upon several of the mines as a trial, they devoured the carapaces and left behind only smudgy black heaps of carbon dust, carefully harvested for fertilizer, and the plastic explosives from within, nestled in their bed of copper wire and silicon.

The Esperigans landed, and at once carved themselves out a neat half-moon of wasteland from the virgin shore, leaving no branches which might stretch above their encampment to offer a platform for attack. They established an electrified fence around the perimeter, with guns and patrols, and all this I observed with Badea, from a small platform in a vine-choked tree not far away: we wore the green-gray cloaks, and our faces were stained with leaf juice.

I had very little justification for inserting myself into such a role but the flimsy excuse of pointing out to Badea the most crucial section of their camp, when we had broken in. I cannot entirely say why I wished to go along on so dangerous an expedition. I am not particularly courageous. Several of my more unkind biographers have accused me of bloodlust, and pointed to this as a sequel to the disaster of my first departure. I cannot refute the accusation on the evidence, however I will point out that I chose that portion of the expedition which we hoped would encounter no violence.

But it is true I had learned already to seethe at the violent piggish blindness of the Esperigans, who would have wrecked all the wonders around me only to propagate yet another bland copy of Earth and suck dry the carcass of their own world. They were my enemy both by duty and by inclination, and I permitted myself the convenience of hating them. At the time, it made matters easier.

The wind was running from the east, and several of the Melidans attacked the camp from that side. The mines had yielded a quantity of explosive large enough to pierce the Esperigans' fence and shake the trees even as far as our lofty perch. The wind carried the smoke and dust and flames towards us, obscuring the ground and rendering the soldiers in their own camp only vague ghostlike suggestions of human shape. The fighting was hand-to-hand, and the stutter of gunfire came only tentatively through the chaos of the smoke.

Badea had been holding a narrow cord, one end weighted with a heavy seedpod. She now poured a measure of water onto the pod, from her canteen, then flung it out into the air. It sailed over the fence and landed inside the encampment, behind one of the neat rows of storage tents. The seed pod struck the ground and immediately burst like a ripe fruit, an anemone tangle of waving roots creeping out over the ground and anchoring the cord, which she had secured at this end around one thick branch.

We let ourselves down it, hand over hand. There was none of that typical abrasion or friction which I might have expected from rope; my hands felt as cool and comfortable when we descended as when we began. We ran into the narrow space between the tents. I was experiencing that strange elongation of time which crisis can occasionally produce: I was conscious of each footfall, and of the seeming-long moments it took to place each one.

There were wary soldiers at many of the tent entrances, likely those which held either the more valuable munitions or the more valuable men. Their discipline had not faltered, even while the majority of the force was already orchestrating a response to the Melidan assault on the other side of the encampment. But we did not need to penetrate into the tents. The guards were rather useful markers for us, showing me which of the tents were the more significant. I pointed out to Badea the cluster of four tents, each guarded at either side by a pair, near the farthest end of the encampment.

Badea looked here and there over the ground as we darted under cover of smoke from one alleyway to another, the walls of waxed canvas muffling the distant shouts and the sound of gunfire. The dirt still had the yellowish tinge of Melidan soil—the Esperigans had not yet irradiated it—but it was crumbly and dry, the fine fragile native moss crushed and much torn by heavy boots and equipment, and the wind raised little dervishes of dust around our ankles.

"This ground will take years to recover fully," she said to me, soft and bitterly, as she stopped us and knelt, behind a deserted tent not far from our target. She gave me a small ceramic implement which looked much like the hair-picks sometimes worn on Terce by women with hair which never knew a blade's edge: a raised comb with three teeth, though on the tool these were much longer and sharpened at the end. I picked the ground vigorously, stabbing deep to aerate the wounded soil, while she judiciously poured out a mixture of water and certain organic extracts, and sowed a packet of seeds.

This may sound a complicated operation to be carrying out in an enemy camp, in the midst of battle, but we had practiced the maneuver, and indeed had we been glimpsed, anyone would have been hard-pressed to recognize a threat in the two gray-wrapped lumps crouched low as we pawed at the dirt. Twice while we worked, wounded soldiers were carried in a rush past either end of our alleyway, towards shelter. We were not seen.

The seeds she carried, though tiny, burst readily, and began to thrust out spiderweb-fine rootlets at such a speed they looked like nothing more than squirming maggots. Badea without concern moved her hands around them, encouraging them into the ground. When they were established, she motioned me to stop my work, and she took out the prepared ants: a much greater number of them, with a dozen of the fat yellow wasp-sized brood-mothers. Tipped out into the prepared and welcoming soil, they immediately began to burrow their way down, with the anxious harrying of their subjects and spawn.

Badea watched for a long while, crouched over, even after the ants had vanished nearly all beneath the surface. The few who emerged and darted back inside, the faint trembling of the rootlets, the shifting grains of dirt, all carried information to her. At length satisfied, she straightened saying, "Now—"

The young soldier was I think only looking for somewhere to piss, rather than investigating some noise. He came around the corner already fumbling at his belt, and seeing us did not immediately shout, likely from plain surprise, but grabbed for Badea's shoulder first. He was clean-shaven, and the name on his lapel badge was *Ridang*. I drove the soil-pick into his eye. I was taller, so the stroke went downwards, and he fell backwards to his knees away from me, clutching at his face.

He did not die at once. There must be very few deaths which come immediately, though we often like to comfort ourselves by the pretense that this failure of the body, or that injury, must at once eradicate consciousness and life and pain all together. Here sentience lasted several moments which seemed to me long: his other eye was open, and looked at me while his hands clawed for the handle of the pick. When this had faded, and he had fallen supine to the ground, there was yet a convulsive movement of all the limbs and a trickling of blood from mouth and nose and eye before the final stiffening jerk left the body emptied and inanimate.

I watched him die in a strange parody of serenity, all feeling hollowed out of me, and then turning away vomited upon the ground. Behind me, Badea cut open his belly and his thighs and turned him face down onto the dirt, so the blood and the effluvia leaked out of him. "That will do a little good for the ground at least, before they carry him away to waste him," she said. "Come." She touched my shoulder, not unkindly, but I flinched from the touch as from a blow.

It was not that Badea or her fellows were indifferent to death, or casual towards murder. But there is a price to be paid for living in a world whose native hostilities have been cherished rather than crushed. Melidan life expectancy is some ten years beneath that of Confederacy citizens, though they are on average healthier and more fit both genetically and physically. In their philosophy a human life is not inherently superior and to be valued over any other kind. Accident and predation claim many, and living intimately with the daily cruelties of nature dulls the facility for sentiment. Badea enjoyed none of that comforting distance which allows us to think ourselves assured of the full potential span of life, and therefore suffered none of the pangs when confronted with evidence to the contrary. I looked at my victim and saw my own face; so too did she, but she had lived all her life so aware, and it did not bow her shoulders.

Five days passed before the Esperigan equipment began to come apart. Another day halted all their work, and in confusion they retreated to their encampment. I did not go with the Melidan company that destroyed them to the last man.

Contrary to many accusations, I did not lie to Kostas in my report and pretend surprise. I freely confessed to him I had expected the result, and truthfully explained I had not wished to make claims of which I was unsure. I never deliberately sought to deceive any of my superiors or conceal information from them, save in such small ways. At first I was not Melidan enough to wish to do so, and later I was too Melidan to feel anything but revulsion at the concept.

He and I discussed our next steps in the tiger-dance. I described as best I could the Melidan technology, and after consultation with various Confederacy experts, it was agreed he would quietly mention to the Esperigan minister of defense, at their weekly luncheon, a particular Confederacy technology: ceramic coatings, which could be ordered at vast expense and two years' delay from Bel Rios. Or, he would suggest, if the Esperigans wished to deed some land to the Confederacy, a private entrepreneurial concern might fund the construction of a local fabrication plant, and produce them at much less cost, in six months' time.

The Esperigans took the bait, and saw only private greed behind this apparent breach of neutrality: imagining Kostas an investor in this private concern, they winked at his venality, and eagerly helped us to their own exploitation. Meanwhile, they continued occasional and tentative incursions into the Melidan continent, probing the coastline, but the disruption they created betrayed their attempts, and whichever settlement was nearest would at once deliver them a present of the industrious ants, so these met with no greater success than the first.

Through these months of brief and grudging detente, I traveled extensively throughout the continent. My journals are widely available, being the domain of our government, but they are shamefully sparse, and I apologize to my colleagues for it. I would have been more diligent in my work if I had imagined I would be the last and not the first such chronicler. At the time, giddy with success, I went with more the spirit of a holidaymaker than a researcher, and I sent only those images and notes which it was pleasant to me to record, with the excuse of limited capacity to send my reports.

For what cold comfort it may be, I must tell you photography and description are inadequate to convey the experience of standing in the living heart of a world, alien yet not hostile, and when I walked hand in hand with Badea along the crest of a great canyon wall and looked down over the ridges of purple and grey and ochre at the gently waving tendrils of an elacca forest, which in my notorious video recordings can provoke nausea in nearly every observer, I felt the first real stir of an unfamiliar sensation of beauty-in-strangeness, and I laughed in delight and surprise, while she looked at me and smiled.

We returned to her village three days later and saw the bombing as we came, the new Esperigan long-range fighter planes like narrow silver knife-blades making low passes overhead, the smoke rising black and oily against the sky. Our basket-journey could not be accelerated, so we could only cling to the sides and wait as we were carried onward. The planes and the smoke were gone before we arrived; the wreckage was not.

I was angry at Kostas afterwards, unfairly. He was no more truly the Esperigans' confidant than they were his, but I felt at the time that it was his business to know what they were about, and he had failed to warn me. I accused him of deliberate concealment; he told me, censoriously, that I had known the risk when I had gone to the continent, and he could hardly be responsible for preserving my safety while I slept in the very war zone. This silenced my tirade, as I realized how near I had come to betraying myself. Of course he would not have wanted me to warn the Melidans; it had not yet occurred to him I would have wished to. I ought not have wanted to.

Forty-three people were killed in the attack. Kitia was yet lingering when I came to her small bedside. She was in no pain, her eyes cloudy and distant, already withdrawing; her family had been and gone again. "I knew you were coming back, so I asked them to let me stay a little longer," she told me. "I wanted to say goodbye." She paused and added uncertainly, "And I was afraid, a little. Don't tell."

I promised her I would not. She sighed and said, "I shouldn't wait any longer. Will you call them over?"

The attendant came when I raised my hand, and he asked Kitia, "Are you ready?"

"Yes," she said, a little doubtful. "It won't hurt?"

"No, not at all," he said, already taking out with a gloved hand a small flat strip from a pouch, filmy green and smelling of raspberries. Kitia opened her mouth, and he laid it on her tongue. It dissolved almost at once, and she blinked twice and was asleep. Her hand went cold a few minutes later, still lying between my own.

I stood with her family when we laid her to rest, the next morning. The attendants put her carefully down in a clearing, and sprayed her from a distance, the smell of cut roses just going to rot, and stepped back. Her parents wept noisily;

I stayed dry-eyed as any seemly Terce matron, displaying my assurance of the ascension of the dead. The birds came first, and the motties, to pluck at her eyes and her lips, and the beetles hurrying with a hum of eager jaws to deconstruct her into raw parts. They did not have long to feast: the forest itself was devouring her from below in a green tide rising, climbing in small creepers up her cheeks and displacing them all.

When she was covered over, the mourners turned away and went to join the shared wake behind us in the village square. They threw uncertain and puzzled looks at my remaining as they went past, and at my tearless face. But she was not yet gone: there was a suggestion of a girl lingering there, a collapsing scaffold draped in an unhurried carpet of living things. I did not leave, though behind me there rose a murmur of noise as the families of the dead spoke reminiscences of their lost ones.

Near dawn, the green carpeting slipped briefly. In the dim watery light I glimpsed for one moment an emptied socket full of beetles, and I wept.

THE SIXTH ADJUSTMENT

I will not claim, after this, that I took the wings only from duty, but I refute the accusation I took them in treason. There was no other choice. Men and children and the elderly or the sick, all the wingless, were fleeing from the continuing hail of Esperigan attacks. They were retreating deep into the heart of the continent, beyond the refueling range for the Esperigan warcraft, to shelters hidden so far in caves and in overgrowth that even my spy satellites knew nothing of them. My connection to Kostas would have been severed, and if I could provide neither intelligence nor direct assistance, I might as well have slunk back to the embassy, and saved myself the discomfort of being a refugee. Neither alternative was palatable.

They laid me upon the altar like a sacrifice, or so I felt, though they gave me something to drink which calmed my body, the nervous and involuntary twitching of my limbs and skin. Badea sat at my head and held the heavy long braid of my hair out of the way, while the others depilated my back and wiped it with alcohol. They bound me down then, and slit my skin open in two lines mostly parallel to the spine. Then Paudi gently set the wings upon me.

I lacked the skill to grow my own, in the time we had; Badea and Paudi helped me to mine so that I might stay. But even with the little assistance I had been able to contribute, I had seen more than I wished to of the parasites, and despite my closed eyes, my face turned downwards, I knew to my horror that the faint curious feather-brush sensation was the intrusion of the fine spiderweb filaments, each fifteen feet long, which now wriggled into the hospitable environment of my exposed inner flesh and began to sew themselves into me.

Pain came and went as the filaments worked their way through muscle and bone, finding one bundle of nerves and then another. After the first half hour, Badea told me gently, "It's coming to the spine," and gave me another drink. The drug kept my body from movement, but could do nothing to numb the agony. I cannot describe it adequately. If you have ever managed to inflict food poisoning upon yourself, despite all the Confederacy's safeguards, you may conceive of the kind if not the degree of suffering, an experience which envelops the whole body, every muscle and joint, and alters not only your physical self but your thoughts: all vanishes but pain, and the question, is the worst over? which is answered *no* and *no* again.

But at some point the pain began indeed to ebb. The filaments had entered the brain, and it is a measure of the experience that what I had feared the most was now blessed relief; I lay inert and closed my eyes gratefully while sensation spread outward from my back, and my new-borrowed limbs became gradually indeed my own, flinching from the currents of the air, and the touch of my friends' hands upon me. Eventually I slept.

THE SEVENTH ADJUSTMENT

The details of the war, which unfolded now in earnest, I do not need to recount again. Kostas kept excellent records, better by far than my own, and students enough have memorized the dates and geographic coordinates, bounding death and ruin in small numbers. Instead I will tell you that from aloft, the Esperigans' poisoned-ground encampments made half-starbursts of ochre brown and withered yellow, outlines like tentacles crawling into the healthy growth around them. Their supply-ships anchored out to sea glazed the water with a slick of oil and refuse, while the soldiers practiced their shooting on the vast schools of slow-swimming kraken young, whose bloated white bodies floated to the surface and drifted away along the coast, so many they defied even the appetite of the sharks.

I will tell you that when we painted their hulls with algaes and small crustacean-like borers, our work was camouflaged by great blooms of sea day-lilies around the ships, their masses throwing up reflected red color on the steel to hide the quietly creeping rust until the first winter storms struck and the grown kraken came to the surface to feed. I will tell you we watched from shore while the ships broke and foundered, and the teeth of the kraken shone like fire opals in the explosions, and if we wept, we wept only for the soiled ocean.

Still more ships came, and more planes; the ceramic coatings arrived, and more soldiers with protected guns and bombs and sprayed poisons, to fend off the altered motties and the little hybrid sparrowlike birds, their sharp cognizant eyes chemically retrained to see the Esperigan uniform colors as enemy markings. We planted acids and more aggressive species of plants along their supply lines, so their communications remained hopeful rather than reliable, and ambushed them at night; they carved into the forest with axes and power-saws and vast strip-miners, which ground to a halt and fell to pieces, choking on vines which hardened to the tensile strength of steel as they matured.

Contrary to claims which were raised at my trial *in absentia* and disproven with communication logs, throughout this time I spoke to Kostas regularly. I confused him, I think; I gave him all the intelligence which he needed to convey to the Esperigans, that they might respond to the next Melidan foray, but I did not conceal my feelings or the increasing complication of my loyalties, objecting to him bitterly and with personal anger about Esperigan attacks. I misled him with honesty: he thought, I believe, that I was only spilling a natural frustration to him, and through that airing clearing out my own doubts. But I had only lost the art of lying.

There is a general increase of perception which comes with the wings, the nerves teased to a higher pitch of awareness. All the little fidgets and twitches of lying betray themselves more readily, so only the more twisted forms can evade detection—where the speaker first deceives herself, or the wholly casual deceit of the sociopath who feels no remorse. This was the root of the Melidan disgust of the act, and I had acquired it.

If Kostas had known, he would at once have removed me: a diplomat is not much use if she cannot lie at need, much less an agent. But I did not volunteer the information, and indeed I did not realize, at first, how fully I had absorbed the stricture. I did not realize at all, until Badea came to me, three years into the war. I was sitting alone and in the dark by the communications console, the phosphorescent after-image of Kostas's face fading into the surface.

She sat down beside me and said, "The Esperigans answer us too quickly. Their technology advances in these great leaps, and every time we press them back, they return in less than a month to very nearly the same position."

I thought, at first, that this was the moment: that she meant to ask me about membership in the Confederacy. I felt no sense of satisfaction, only a weary kind of resignation. The war would end, the Esperigans would follow, and in a few generations they would both be eaten up by bureaucracy and standards and immigration.

Instead Badea looked at me and said, "Are your people helping them, also?"

My denial ought to have come without thought, leapt easily off the tongue with all the conviction duty could give it, and been followed by invitation. Instead I said nothing, my throat closed involuntarily. We sat silently in the darkness, and at last she said, "Will you tell me why?"

I felt at the time I could do no more harm, and perhaps some good, by honesty. I told her all the rationale, and expressed all our willingness to receive them into our union as equals. I went so far as to offer her the platitudes with which we convince ourselves we are justified in our slow gentle imperialism: that unification is necessary and advances all together, bringing peace.

She only shook her head and looked away from me. After a moment, she said, "Your people will never stop. Whatever we devise, they will help the Esperigans to a counter, and if the Esperigans devise some weapon we cannot defend ourselves against, they will help us, and we will batter each other into limp exhaustion, until in the end we all fall."

"Yes," I said, because it was true. I am not sure I was still able to lie, but in any case I did not know, and I did not lie.

I was not permitted to communicate with Kostas again until they were ready. Thirty-six of the Melidans' greatest designers and scientists died in the effort. I learned of their deaths in bits and pieces. They worked in isolated and quarantined spaces, their every action recorded even as the viruses and bacteria they were developing killed them. It was a little more than three months before Badea came to me again.

We had not spoken since the night she had learned the duplicity of the Confederacy's support and my own. I could not ask her forgiveness, and she could not give it. She did not come for reconciliation but to send a message to the Esperigans and to the Confederacy through me.

I did not comprehend at first. But when I did, I knew enough to be sure she was neither lying nor mistaken, and to be sure the threat was very real. The same was not true of Kostas, and still less of the Esperigans. My frantic attempts to persuade them worked instead to the contrary end. The long gap since my last communique made Kostas suspicious: he thought me a convert, or generously a manipulated tool.

"If they had the capability, they would have used it already," he said, and if I could not convince him, the Esperigans would never believe.

I asked Badea to make a demonstration. There was a large island broken off the southern coast of the Esperigan continent, thoroughly settled and industrialized, with two substantial port cities. Sixty miles separated it from the mainland. I proposed the Melidans should begin there, where the attack might be contained.

"No," Badea said. "So your scientists can develop a counter? No. We are done with exchanges."

The rest you know. A thousand coracles left Melidan shores the next morning, and by sundown on the third following day, the Esperigan cities were crumbling. Refugees fled the groaning skyscrapers as they slowly bowed under their own weight. The trees died; the crops also, and the cattle, all the life and vegetation that had been imported from Earth and square-peg forced into the new world stripped bare for their convenience.

Meanwhile in the crowded shelters the viruses leapt easily from one victim to another, rewriting their genetic lines. Where the changes took hold, the altered survived. The others fell to the same deadly plagues that consumed all Earth-native life. The native Melidan moss crept in a swift green carpet over the corpses, and the beetle-hordes with it.

I can give you no first-hand account of those days. I too lay fevered and sick while the alteration ran its course in me, though I was tended better, and with more care, by my sisters. When I was strong enough to rise, the waves of death were over. My wings curled limply over my shoulders as I walked through the empty streets of Landfall, pavement stones pierced and broken by hungry vines, like bones cracked open for marrow. The moss covered the dead, who filled the shattered streets.

The squat embassy building had mostly crumpled down on one corner, smashed windows gaping hollow and black. A large pavilion of simple cotton fabric had been raised in the courtyard, to serve as both hospital and headquarters. A young undersecretary of state was the senior diplomat remaining. Kostas had died early, he told me. Others were still in the process of dying, their bodies waging an internal war that left them twisted by hideous deformities.

Less than one in thirty, was his estimate of the survivors. Imagine yourself on an air-train in a crush, and then imagine yourself suddenly alone but for one other passenger across the room, a stranger staring at you. Badea called it a sustainable population.

The Melidans cleared the spaceport of vegetation, though little now was left but the black-scorched landing pad, Confederacy manufacture, all of woven carbon and titanium.

"Those who wish may leave," Badea said. "We will help the rest."

Most of the survivors chose to remain. They looked at their faces in the mirror, flecked with green, and feared the Melidans less than their welcome on another world.

I left by the first small ship that dared come down to take off refugees, with no attention to the destination or the duration of the voyage. I wished only to be away. The wings were easily removed. A quick and painful amputation of the gossamer and fretwork which protruded from the flesh, and the rest might be left for the body to absorb slowly. The strange muffled quality of the world, the sensation of numbness, passed eventually. The two scars upon my back, parallel lines, I will keep the rest of my days.

AFTERWORD

I spoke with Badea once more before I left. She came to ask me why I was going, to what end I thought I went. She would be perplexed, I think, to see me in my little cottage here on Reivaldt, some hundred miles from the nearest city, although she would have liked the small flowerlike lieden which live on the rocks of my garden wall, one of the few remnants of the lost native fauna which have survived the terraforming outside the preserves of the university system.

I left because I could not remain. Every step I took on Melida, I felt dead bones cracking beneath my feet. The Melidans did not kill lightly, an individual or an ecosystem, nor any more effectually than do we. If the Melidans had not let the plague loose upon the Esperigans, we would have destroyed them soon enough ourselves, and the Melidans with them. But we distance ourselves better from our murders, and so are not prepared to confront them. My wings whispered to me gently when I passed Melidans in the green-swathed cemetery streets, that they were not sickened, were not miserable. There was sorrow and regret but no self-loathing, where I had nothing else. I was alone.

When I came off my small vessel here, I came fully expecting punishment, even longing for it, a judgment which would at least be an end. Blame had wandered through the halls of state like an unwanted child, but when I proved willing to adopt whatever share anyone cared to mete out to me, to confess any crime which was convenient and to proffer no defense, it turned contrary, and fled.

Time enough has passed that I can be grateful now to the politicians who spared my life and gave me what passes for my freedom. In the moment, I could scarcely feel enough even to be happy that my report contributed some little to the abandonment of any reprisal against Melida: as though we ought hold them responsible for defying our expectations not of their willingness to kill one another, but only of the extent of their ability.

But time does not heal all wounds. I am often asked by visitors whether I would ever return to Melida. I will not. I am done with politics and the great concerns of the universe of human settlement. I am content to sit in my small garden, and watch the ants at work.

Ruth Patrona

the peacock cloak

CHRIS BECKETT

British writer Chris Beckett is one of *Interzone*'s most frequent contributors, having sold more than twelve stories there, but he's also made several sales to *Asimov's Science Fiction* and elsewhere. His novels include
The Holy Machine and *Marcher*. His short fiction has been collected in
The Turing Test. A former social worker, he's now a university lecturer
living in Cambridge, England.

Beckett usually writes about near-future England, but here he moves
effectively into Roger Zelazny territory, with superpowered individuals
facing off in a virtual reality world created by one of them, with the fate
of the entire universe hanging in the balance.

U p to that moment nothing much had been moving in that mountain valley
apart from grasshoppers and bees, and the stream playing peacefully by itself
over its stony bed. Then Tawus was there in his famous cloak, its bright fabric
still fizzing and sparking from the prodigious leap, its hundred eyes, black, green
and gold, restlessly assaying the scene. Tawus had arrived, and, as always, everything else was dimmed and diminished by his presence.

"This world was well made," Tawus said to himself with his accustomed mixture of jealousy and pride.

He savoured the scent of lavender and thyme, the creaking of grasshoppers,
the gurgling of the stream.

"Every detail *works*," he said, noticing a fat bumble bee, spattered with yellow
pollen, launching herself into flight from a pink cistus flower. Passing the small
hard object he carried in his left hand to his right, Tawus stooped to take the flower
stem between his left forefinger and thumb. "Every molecule, every speck of dust."

But then, painfully and vividly, and in a way that had not happened for some
time, he was reminded of the early days, the beginning, when, on the far side of
this universe, he and the Six awoke and found themselves in another garden
wilderness like this one, ringed about by mountains.

Back then things had felt very different. Tawus had known what Fabbro knew,
had felt what Fabbro felt. His purposes had been Fabbro's purposes, and all his
memories were from Fabbro's world, a world within which the created universe
of Esperine was like a child's plaything, a scene carved into an ivory ball (albeit

carved so exquisitely that its trees could sway in the wind and lose their leaves in autumn, its creatures live and die). Of course he had known quite well he was a copy of Fabbro and not Fabbro himself, but he was an exact copy, down to the smallest particle, the smallest thought, identical in every way except that he had been rendered in the stuff of Esperine, so that he could inhabit Fabbro's creation on Fabbro's behalf. He was a creation as Esperine was, but he could remember creating himself, just as he could remember creating Esperine, inside the device that Fabbro called Constructive Thought. Back then, Tawus had thought of Fabbro not as "he" and "him" but as "I" and "me."

And how beautiful this world had seemed then, how simple, how unsullied, how full of opportunities, how free of the ties and regrets and complications that had hemmed in the life of Fabbro in the world outside.

Tawus released the pink flower, let it spring back among its hundred bright fellows, and stood up straight, returning the small object from his right hand to his dominant left. Then, with his quick grey eyes, he glanced back down the path, and up at the rocky ridges on either side. The peacock eyes looked with him, sampling every part of the visible and invisible spectrum.

"No, Tawus, you are not observed," whispered the cloak, using the silent code with which it spoke to him through his skin.

"Not observed, perhaps," said Tawus, "but certainly expected."

Now he turned southwards, towards the head of the valley, and began to walk. His strides were quick and determined but his thoughts less so. The gentle scents and sounds of the mountain valley continued to stir up vivid and troubling memories from the other end of time. He recalled watching the Six wake up, his three brothers and three sisters. They were also made in the likeness of Fabbro but they were, so to speak, reflections of him in mirrors with curved surfaces or coloured glass, so that they were different from the original and from each other. Tawus remembered their eyes opening—his brother Balthazar first and then his sister Cassandra—and he remembered their spreading smiles as they looked around and simultaneously saw and remembered where they were, in this exquisite, benign and yet to be explored world, released forever from the cares and complications of Fabbro's life and from the baleful history of the vast and vacant universe in which Fabbro was born.

They had been strangely shy of each other at first, even though they shared the same memories, the same history and the same sole parent. The three sisters in particular, in spite of Fabbro's androgynous and protean nature, felt exposed and uneasy in their unfamiliar bodies. But even the men were uncomfortable in their new skins. All seven were trying to decide who they were. It had been a kind of adolescence. All had felt awkward, all had been absurdly optimistic about what they could achieve. They had made a pact with each other, for instance, that they would always work together and take decisions as a group.

"*That* didn't last long," Tawus now wryly observed, and then he remembered, with a momentary excruciating pang, the fate of Cassandra, his proud and stubborn sister.

But they'd believed in their agreement at the time, and, having made it, all Seven had stridden out, laughing and talking all at once, under a warm sun not unlike this one, and on a path not unlike the one he was walking now, dressed so splendidly in his Peacock Cloak. He had no such cloak back then. They had been naked gods. They had begun to wrap themselves up only as they moved apart from one another: Cassandra in her Mirror Mantle, Jabreel in his Armour of Light, Balthazar in his Coat of Dreams . . . But the Peacock Cloak had been finest of all.

"I hear music," the cloak now whispered to him.

Tawus stopped and listened. He could only hear the stream, the grasshoppers and the bees. He shrugged.

"Hospitable of him, to lay on music to greet us."

"Just a peasant flute. A flute and goat bells."

"Probably shepherds up in the hills somewhere," said Tawus, resuming his stride.

He remembered how the seven of them came to their first human village, a village whose hundred simple people imagined that they had always lived there, tending their cattle and their sheep, and had no inkling that only a few hours before, they and their memories had been brought into being all at once by their creator Fabbro within the circuits of Constructive Thought, along with a thousand similar groups scattered over the planets of Esperine: the final touch, the final detail, in the world builder's ivory ball.

"The surprise on their faces!" Tawus murmured to himself, and smiled. "To see these seven tall naked figures striding down through their pastures."

"You are tense," observed his cloak. "You are distracting yourself with thoughts of things elsewhere and long ago."

"So I am," agreed Tawus, in the same silent code. "I am not keen to think about my destination."

He looked down at the object he carried in his hand, smooth and white and intricate, like a polished shell. It was a gun of sorts, a weapon of his own devising. It did not fire bullets but was utterly deadly, for, within a confined area, it was capable of unravelling the laws that defined Esperine itself and, in that way, reducing form to pure chaos.

"Give me a pocket to put this in," Tawus said.

At once the cloak made an opening to receive the gun, and then sealed itself again when Tawus had withdrawn his hand.

"The cloak can aim and shoot for me, in any case," Tawus said to himself.

And the cloak's eyes winked, green and gold and black.

The valley turned a corner. There was an outcrop of harder rock. As he came round it, Tawus heard the music that his cloak, with its finely tuned senses, had detected some way back: a fluted melody, inexpertly played, and an arrhythmic jangling of crudely made bells.

Up ahead of him three young children were minding a flock of sheep and goats, sheltering by a little patch of trees at a spot where a tributary brook cascaded into the main stream. A girl of nine or ten was playing panpipes. In front of her on a large stone, as if in the two-seat auditorium of a miniature theatre, two smaller children sat side by side: a boy of five or so and a little girl of three, cradling a lamb that lay across both their laps. The jangling bells hung from the necks of the grazing beasts.

Seeing Tawus, the girl laid down her pipes and the two smaller children hastily set their lamb on the ground, stood up, and moved quickly to stand beside their sister with their hands in hers. All three stared at Tawus with wide unsmiling eyes. And then, as he drew near, they ran forward and kissed his hand, first the older girl, then the boy, and finally the little three-year-old whose baby lips left a cool patch of moistness on his skin.

"Your face is familiar to them," the cloak silently observed. "They think they know you from before."

"As we might predict," said Tawus. "But *you* they have never seen."

The children were astounded by a fabric on which the patterns were in constant motion, and by the animated peacock eyes. The smallest child reached out a grubby finger to touch the magical cloth.

"No, Thomas!" her sister scolded, slapping the child's hand away. "Leave the gentleman's coat alone."

"No harm," Tawus said gruffly, patting the tiny girl on the head.

And the cloak shook off the fragments of snot and dust that the child's fingers had left behind.

Ten minutes later Tawus turned and looked back at them. They were little more than dots in the mountain landscape but he could see that they were still watching him, still standing and holding hands. Around them, unheeded, the sheep grazed with the goats.

Suddenly, Tawus was vividly reminded of three other children he had once seen, about the same ages as these. He had hardly given them a thought at the time, but now he vividly remembered them: the younger two huddled against their sister, all three staring with white faces as Tawus and his army rolled through their burning village, their home in ruins behind them. It had been in a flat watery country called Meadow Lee. From his vantage point in the turret of a tank, Tawus could see its verdant water meadows stretching away for miles. Across the whole expanse of it were burning buildings and columns of dirty smoke that were gradually staining the wide blue sky a glowering oily yellow.

When was that? Tawus wondered. On which of the several different occasions when fighting had come to Meadow Lee? He thought it had been during one of his early wars against his brother Balthazar. But then he wondered whether perhaps it had been at a later stage when he was in an alliance with Balthazar against Jabreel?

"Neither," said the Peacock Cloak. "It was in the war all six of you waged against Cassandra, that time she banned chrome extraction in her lands."

"Don't needlessly interfere. Offer guidance where necessary, head off obvious problems, but otherwise allow things to take their own course."

It would be wrong to say these were Fabbro's *instructions* to the Seven because he had never spoken to them. They were simply his intentions which they all knew because his memories were replicated in their own minds. When they encountered those first villagers, the Seven had greeted them, requested food and a place to rest that night, and asked if there were any matters they could assist with. They did not try and impose their views, or change the villagers' minds about how the world worked or how to live their lives. That had all come later, along with the wars and the empires.

"But did he really think we could go on like that forever?" Tawus now angrily asked. "What were we supposed to *do* all this time? Just wander around indefinitely, advising on a sore throat here, suggesting crop rotation there, but otherwise doing nothing with this world at all?"

The Seven had begun to be different from Fabbro from the moment they awoke. And paradoxically it was Tawus, the one most completely alike to Fabbro, who had moved most quickly away from Fabbro's wishes.

"We can't just be gardeners of this world," he had told his brothers and sisters, after they had visited a dozen sleepy villages, "we can't just be shepherds of its people, watching them while they graze. We will go mad. We will turn into demented imbeciles. We need to be able to build things, play with technology, unlock the possibilities that we know exist within this particular reality frame. We will need metals and fuels, and a society complex enough to extract and refine them. We will need ways of storing and transmitting information. There will need to be cities. On at least one planet, in at least one continent, we will have to organise a state."

The Six had all had reservations at first, to different degrees, and for slightly different reasons.

"Just give me a small territory then," Tawus had said, "a patch of land with some people in, to experiment and develop my ideas."

In his own little fiefdom he had adopted a new approach, not simply advising but tempting and cajoling. He had made little labour-saving devices for his people and then spoken to them of machines that would do all their work for them. He had helped them make boats and then described space ships that would make them masters of the stars. He had sown dissatisfaction in their minds and, within two years, he had achieved government, schools, metallurgy, sea-faring and a militia. Seeing what he had achieved, the Six had fallen over one another to catch up.

"How come they all followed me, if my path was so wrong?" Tawus now asked.

"They had no choice but to follow you," observed the Peacock Cloak, "if they didn't wish to be altogether eclipsed."

"Which is another way of saying that my way was in the end inevitable, because once it is chosen, all other ways become obsolete. To have obeyed Fabbro would simply have been to postpone what was sooner or later going to happen, if not led by me, then by one of the others, or even by some leader rising up from the Esperine people themselves."

He thought briefly again of the children in front of the ruined house, but then he turned another corner, and there was his destination ahead of him. It was a little island of domesticity amidst the benign wilderness of the valley, a small cottage with a garden and an orchard and a front gate, standing beside a lake.

"He is outside," said the Peacock Cloak, whose hundred eyes could see through many different kinds of obstacle. "He is down beside the water."

Tawus came to the cottage gate. It was very quiet. He could hear the bees going back and forth from the wild thyme flowers, the splash of a duck alighting on the lake, the clopping of a wooden wind chime in an almond tree.

He raised his hand to the latch, then lowered it again.

"What's the matter with me? Why hesitate?"

Clop clop went the wind chimes.

"It is always better to act," whispered the cloak through his skin, "that's what you asked me to remind you."

Tawus nodded. It *was* always better to act than to waste time agonising. It was by acting that he had built a civilisation, summoned great cities into being, driven through the technological changes that had taken this world from sleepy rural Arcadia to interplanetary empires. It was by acting that he had prevailed over his six siblings, even when all six were ranged against him, for each one of them had been encumbered by Fabbro with gifts or traits of character more specialised than his own pure strength of will: mercy, imagination, doubt, ambivalence, detachment, humility.

True, he had caused much destruction and misery but, after all, to act at all it was necessary to be willing to destroy. If he ever had a moment of doubt, he simply reminded himself that you couldn't take a single step without running the risk of crushing some small creeping thing, too small to be seen, going about its blameless life. You couldn't breathe without the possibility of sucking in some tiny innocent from the air.

"The city of X is refusing to accept our authority," his generals would say.

"Then raze it to the ground as we warned we would," he would answer without a moment's thought. And the hundred eyes would dart this way and that, like a scouting party sent out ahead of the battalions that were his own thoughts, looking for opportunities in the new situation that he had created, scoping out his next move and the move after that.

There had been times when his generals had stood there open-mouthed, astounded by his ruthlessness. But they did not question him. They knew it was the strength of his will that made him great, made him something more than they were.

"But now," he said to himself bitterly, "I seem to be having difficulty making up my mind about a garden gate."

"Just act," said the cloak, rippling against his skin in a way that was almost like laughter.

Tawus smiled. He would act on his own account and not on instructions from his clothes, but all the same he lifted his hand to the latch and this time opened it. He was moving forward again. And the eyes on his cloak shone in readiness.

Inside the gate the path branched three ways: right to the cottage, with the peaks of the valley's western ridge behind it, straight ahead to the little orchard and vegetable garden, left and eastward down to the small lake from which flowed the stream that he'd been following. On the far side of the lake was the ridge of peaks that formed the valley's eastern edge. Some sheep were grazing on their slopes.

Clop clop went the wind chimes, and a bee zipped by his ear like a tiny racing car on a track.

Tawus looked down towards the lake.

"*There* you are," he murmured, spotting the small figure at the water's edge that the peacock eyes had already located, sitting on a log on a little beach, looking through binoculars at the various ducks and water birds out on the lake.

"You know I'm here," Tawus muttered angrily. "You know quite well I'm here."

"Indeed he does," the cloak confirmed. "The tension in his shoulders is un-mistakeable."

"He just wants to make me the one that speaks first," Tawus said.

So he did not speak. Instead, when there were only a few metres between them, he stooped, picked up a stone and lobbed it into the water over the seated figure's head.

The ripples spread out over the lake. Among some reeds at the far end of the little beach, a duck gave a low warning quack to its fellows. The man on the log turned round.

"Tawus," he exclaimed, laying down his field glasses and rising to his feet with a broad smile of welcome, "Tawus, my dear fellow. It's been a very long time."

The likeness between the two of them would have been instantly apparent to any observer, even from a distance. They had the same lithe and balletic bear-ing, the same high cheekbones and aquiline nose, the same thick mane of grey hair. But the man by the water was simply dressed in a white shirt and white breeches, while Tawus still wore his magnificent cloak with its shifting patterns and its restless eyes. And Tawus stood stiffly while the other man, still smiling, extended his arms, as if he expected Tawus to fall into his embrace.

Tawus did not move or bend.

"You've put it about that you're Fabbro himself," he said, "or so I've heard."

The other man nodded.

"Well, yes. Of course there's a sense in which I am a copy of Fabbro as you are, since this body is an analogue of the body that Fabbro was born with, rather than the body itself. But the original Fabbro ceased to exist when I came into being, so my history and his have never branched away from each other, as yours and his did, but are arranged sequentially in a single line, a single story. So yes, I'm Fabbro. All that is left of Fabbro is me, and I have finally entered my own cre-ation. It seemed fitting, now that both Esperine and I are coming to a close."

Tawus considered this for a moment. He had an impulse to ask about the world beyond Esperine, that vast and ancient universe in which Fabbro had been born and grown up. For of course Fabbro's was the only childhood that Tawus could remember, Fabbro's the only youth. He was naturally curious to know how things had changed out there and to hear news of the people from Fabbro's past: friends, collaborators, male and female lovers, children (actual biological chil-dren: children of Fabbro's body and not just his mind).

"Aren't those memories a distraction?" the cloak asked him through his skin. "Isn't that stuff his worry and not yours?"

Tawus nodded.

"Yes," he silently agreed, "and to ask about it would muddy the water. It would confuse the issue of worlds and their ownership."

He looked Fabbro in the face.

"You had no business coming into Esperine," he told him. "We renounced your world and you in turn gave this world to us to be our own. You've no right to come barging back in here now, interfering, undermining my authority, under-mining the authority of the Five."

(It was Five now, not Six, because of Cassandra's annihilation in the Chrome Wars.)

Fabbro smiled.

"Some might say you'd undermined each other's authority quite well without my help, with your constant warring, and your famines and your plagues and all of that."

"That's a matter for us, not you."

"Possibly so," said Fabbro. "Possibly so. But in my defence, I have tried to keep out of the way since I arrived in this world."

"You let it be known you were here, though. That was enough."

Fabbro tipped his head from side to side, weighing this up.

"Enough? Do you really think so? Surely for my mere presence to have had an impact, there would have had to be something in Esperine that could be touched by it. There had to be a me-shaped hole, if you see what I mean. Otherwise, wouldn't I just be some harmless old man up in the mountains?"

He sat down on the log again

"Come and sit with me, Tawus." He patted a space beside him. "This is my favourite spot, my grandstand seat. There's always something happening here. Day. Night. Evening. Morning. Sun. Rain. Always something new to see."

"If you're content with sheep and ducks," said Tawus, and did not sit.

Fabbro watched him. After a few seconds, he smiled.

"That's quite a coat you've got there," he observed.

Many of the peacock eyes turned towards him, questioningly. Others glanced with renewed vigour in every other direction, as if suspecting diversionary tactics.

"I've heard," Fabbro went on, "that it can protect you, make you invisible, change your appearance, allow you to leap from planet to planet without going through the space in between. I've been told that it can tell you of dangers, and draw your attention to things you might wish to know, and even give you counsel, as perhaps it's doing now. That is some coat!"

"He is seeking to rile you," the cloak silently whispered. "You asked me to warn you if he did this."

"Don't patronise me, Fabbro," Tawus said, "I am your copy not your child. You know that to construct this cloak I simply needed to understand the algorithm on which Esperine is founded, and you know that I do understand it every bit as well as you do."

Fabbro nodded.

"Yes, of course. I'm just struck by the different ways in which we've used that understanding. I used it to make a more benign world than my own, within which countless lives could for a limited time unfold and savour their existence. You used it to set yourself apart from the rest of this creation, insulate yourself, wrap yourself up in your own little world of one."

"I could easily have made another complete world as you did, as perfect as Esperine in every way. But any world that I made would necessarily exist within this reality frame, your frame, and therefore still be a part of Esperine, even if its equal or its superior in design. Do you really wonder that I chose instead to find a way of setting myself apart?"

Fabbro did not answer. He gave a half-shrug, then looked out at the lake.

"I've not come here to apologise," Tawus said. "I hope you know that. I have no regrets about my rebellion."

Fabbro turned towards him.

"Oh, don't worry, I know why you came. You came to destroy me. And of course it *is* possible to destroy me now that I'm here in Esperine, just as it was possible for you and the others to destroy your sister Cassandra when she tried to place a brake on your ambitions. In order to achieve her destruction you found a way of temporarily modifying that part of the original algorithm that protected the seven of you from physical harm. I assume I have a weapon with you now that works in the same way. I guess it's hidden somewhere in that cloak."

"But knowing it doesn't help him," whispered the cloak through Tawus's skin.

Another duck had alighted on the water, smaller and differently coloured from the ones that were already there. (It had black wings and a russet head.) Fabbro picked up his binoculars and briefly observed it, before laying them down again, and turning once more to his recalcitrant creation.

"Be that as it may," he said, "I certainly wasn't led to expect an apology. They told me the six of you set out in this direction armed to the teeth and in a great fury. You had a formidable space fleet with you, they said, and huge armies at your back. They told me that cloak of yours was fairly fizzing and sparking with pent-up energy. They said that it turned all the air around you into a giant lens, so that you were greatly magnified and seemed to your followers to be a colossus blazing with fire, striding out in front of them as they poured through the interplanetary gates."

Tawus snatched a stone up from the beach and flung it out over the water.

"You are allowing yourself to be put on the defensive," warned the Peacock Cloak through his skin. "But remember that he has no more power than you. In fact, he has far less. Thanks to your foresight in creating me, you are the one who is protected, not him. And, unlike him, you are armed."

Tawus turned to face Fabbro.

"You set us inside this world," he said, "then turned away and left us to it. And that was fine, that was the understanding from the beginning. That was your choice and ours. But now, when it suits you because you are growing old, you come wandering in to criticise what we have achieved. What right do you have to do that, Fabbro? You were absent when the hard decisions were being made. How can you know that you would have done anything different yourself?"

"When have I criticised you? When have I claimed I would have done something different?"

Fabbro gave a short laugh.

"Think, Tawus, think. Stop indulging your anger and think for a moment about the situation we are in. How *could* I say that I would have done something different? What meaning could such a claim possibly have when you and I were one and the same person at the beginning of all this?"

"We began as one person, but we are not one person now. Origins are not everything."

Fabbro looked down at his hands, large and long-fingered as Tawus's were.

"No," he said, "I agree. It must be so. Otherwise there would only ever be one thing."

"You made your choice," Tawus said. "You should have stuck to it and stayed outside."

"Hence the armies, hence the striding like a colossus at their head, hence the plan to seek me out and destroy me?"

Fabbro looked up at Tawus with an expression that was half a frown and half a smile.

"Yes," Tawus said. "Hence all those things."

Fabbro nodded.

"But where are the armies now?" he asked. "Where is the striding colossus? Where is this "we" you speak about? An awful lot of the energy has dissipated, has it not? The nearer you got to me, the faster it all fell away. They've all come back to me, you know, your armies, your brothers, your sisters. They have all come to me and asked to become part of me once again."

Some of the eyes on the cloak glanced inquiringly upwards at Tawus's face, others remained fixed on Fabbro, who had lifted his binoculars and was once again looking at bird life out on the lake.

"Fire the gun and you will *be* Fabbro," the Peacock Cloak told its master. "You will be the one to whom the armies and the Five have all returned. Your apparent isolation, your apparent diminishment, is simply an artefact of there being two of you here, two rival versions of the original Fabbro. But you are the one I shield and not him. You are the one with the weapon."

Fabbro laid down his field glasses and turned towards the man who still stood stiffly apart from him.

"Come Tawus," he coaxed gently, patting the surface of the log beside him. "Come and sit down. I won't bite, I promise. It's almost the end, after all. Surely we're both too old, and it's too late in the day, for us to be playing this game?"

Tawus picked up another stone and flung it out into the lake. The ripples spread over the smooth surface. *Quack quack* went the ducks near to where it fell, and one of them fluttered its wings and half-flew a few yards further off, scrabbling at the surface with its feet.

"The armies are irrelevant," Tawus said. "The Five are irrelevant. You know that. For these purposes they are simply fields of force twisting and turning between you and me. The important thing is not that they have come back to you. No. The important thing is that I have not."

Fabbro watched his face and did not speak

"I made their world for them," Tawus went on, beginning to pace restlessly up and down. "I gave them progress. I gave them freedom. I gave them cities and nations. I gave them hope. I gave them something to believe in and somewhere to go. You just made a shell. You made a clockwork toy. It was me, through my rebellion, that turned it into a world. Why else did they all follow me?"

He looked around for another stone, found a particularly big one, and lobbed it out even further across the lake. It sent a whole flock of ducks squawking into the air.

"Please sit down, Tawus. I would really like you to sit with me."

Tawus did not respond. Fabbro shrugged and looked away.

"Why exactly *do* you think they followed you?" he asked after a short time.

"Because I was in your image but I wasn't you," Tawus answered at once. "I was like you, but at the same time I was one of them. Because I stood up for this world as a world in its own right, belonging to those who lived in it, and not simply as a plaything of yours."

Fabbro nodded.

"Which was what I wanted you to do," he said.

The day was moving into evening. The eastern ridge of peaks across the water glowed gold from the sun that was setting opposite them to the west.

"After the sun sets," Fabbro calmly said, "the world will end. Everyone has come back to me. It's time that you and I brought things to a close."

Tawus was caught off guard. So little time. It seemed he had miscalculated somewhat, not having the benefit of the Olympian view that Fabbro had enjoyed until recently, looking in from outside of Constructive Thought. He had not appreciated that the end was quite as close as that.

But he was not going to show his surprise.

"I suppose you are going to lecture me," he said, "about the suffering I caused with my wars."

As he spoke he was gathering up stones from the beach, hastily, almost urgently, as if they had some vital purpose.

"I suppose you're going to go on about all the children whose parents I took from them," he said.

He threw a. stone. *Splash. Quack.*

"And the rapes that all sides perpetrated," he said, throwing a stone again, "and the tortures," throwing yet another stone, "and the massacres."

He had run out of stones. He turned angrily towards Fabbro.

"I suppose you want to castigate me for turning skilled farmers and hunters and fishermen into passive workers in dreary city streets, spending their days manufacturing things they didn't understand, and their evenings staring at images on screens manufactured for them by someone else."

He turned away, shaking his head, looking around vaguely for more stones.

"I used to think about you looking in from outside," he said. "When we had wars, when we were industrialising and getting people off the land, all of those difficult times. I used to imagine you judging me, clucking your tongue, shaking your head. But *you* try and bring progress to a world without any adverse consequences for anyone. You just try it."

"Come on, Tawus," Fabbro begged him. "Sit with me. You know you're not really going to destroy me. You know you can't really reverse the course that this world, like any world, must take. It isn't only your armies that have fallen away from you, Tawus, it is your own steely will. It has no purpose any more."

But the cloak offered another point of view.

"Destroy Fabbro and you will become him," it silently whispered. "Then you can put back the clock itself."

Tawus knew it was true. Without Fabbro to stop him, he could indeed postpone the end, not forever, but for several more generations. And he could rule Esperine during that time as he had never ruled before, with no Fabbro outside, no one to look in and judge him. The cloak was right. He would *become* Fabbro, he would become Fabbro and Tawus both at once. It was possible, and what was more, it had been his reason for coming here in the first place.

He glanced down at Fabbro. He looked quickly away again across the lake. Ten whole seconds passed.

Then Tawus reached slowly for the clasp of the Peacock Cloak. He hesitated. He lowered his hand. He reached for the clasp again. His fingers were trembling because of the contradictory signals they were receiving from his brain, but finally he unfastened the cloak, removing it slowly and deliberately at first, and then suddenly flinging it away from him, as if he feared it might grab hold and refuse to let him go. It snagged on a branch of a small oak tree and hung there, one corner touching the stony ground. Still its clever eyes darted about, green and gold and black. It was watching Tawus, watching Fabbro. As ever, it was observing everything, analysing everything, evaluating options and possibilities. But yet, as is surely proper in a garment hanging from a tree, it had no direction of its own, it had no separate purpose.

Across the lake, the eastern hills shone. There were sheep up there grazing, bathed in golden light that picked them out against the mountainside. But the hills on the western side were also making their presence felt, for their shadows were reaching out like long fingers over the two small figures by the lake, one standing, one seated on the log, neither one speaking. Without his cloak, in a simple white shirt and white breeches, Tawus looked even more like Fabbro. A stranger could not have told them apart.

A flock of geese came flying in from a day of grazing lower down the valley. They honked peaceably to one another as they splashed down on the softly luminous water.

"When I was walking up here," Tawus said at last, "I met three children, and they reminded me of some other children I saw once, or glimpsed anyway, when I was riding past in a tank. It was in the middle of a war and I didn't pay much heed to them at the time. I was too busy listening to reports and giving orders. But for some reason they stuck in my mind."

He picked up a stone, tossed it half-heartedly out into the lake.

"Their ruined home lay behind them," he went on, "and in the ruins, most probably, lay the burnt corpses of their parents. Not that their parents would have been combatants or anything. It was just that their country, their sleepy land of Meadow Lee, had temporarily become the square on the chessboard that the great game was focussed on, the place where the force fields happened to intersect. Pretty soon the focal point would be somewhere else and the armies would move on from Meadow Lee and forget all about it until the next time. But those children wouldn't forget, would they? Not while they still lived. This day would stain and darken their entire lives, like the smoke darkened and stained their pretty blue sky. What could be worse, when you think about it, than filling up a small mind with such horrors? That, in a way, is also creating a world. It is creating a small but perfect hell."

He snatched up yet another stone, but, with a swift graceful movement, Fabbro had jumped up and grasped Tawus's wrist to stop him throwing it.

"Enough, Tawus, enough. The rebellion is over. The divisions you brought about have all been healed. The killed and the killers. The tortured and the torturers. The enslaved and the enslavers. All are reconciled. All have finally come back."

"Everyone but me."

Tawus let the stone fall to the ground. His creator released his hand, sat down again on the log and once again patted the space beside him.

Tawus looked at Fabbro, and at the log, and back at Fabbro again. And, finally, he sat down.

The two of them were completely in shadow now, had become shadows themselves. The smooth surface of the lake still glowed with soft pinks and blues, but the many birds on its surface had become shadows too, warm living shadows, softly murmuring to one another in their various watery tongues, suspended between the glowing lake and the glowing sky. And more shadow was spreading up the hillside opposite, engulfing the sheep one after another, taking them from golden prominence to peaceful obscurity. Soon only the peaks still dipped into the stream of sunlight that was pouring horizontally far above the heads of the two men.

"Everyone but you," Fabbro mildly agreed, reaching down for his binoculars once more so he could look at some unusual duck or other that he'd noticed out on the water.

Tawus glanced across at his Peacock Cloak, dangling from its tree with the gun still hidden in its pocket. That tawdry thing, he suddenly thought. Why did I choose to hide myself in that? The cloak was shimmering and glittering, giving off its own light in the shadow, and its eyes were still brightly shining, as if it was attempting to be a rival to those last brilliant rays of sunlight, or to outglow the softly glowing lake. It was all that was left of Tawus's empire, his will, his power.

He turned to Fabbro.

"Don't get the wrong idea," he began. "I don't in any way regret what . . ."

Then he broke off. He passed his still trembling hand over his face.

"I'm sorry, Fabbro," he said in a completely different voice. "I've messed it all up, haven't I? I've been a fool. I've spoiled everything."

Fabbro lowered his binoculars and patted Tawus on the hand.

"Well, maybe you have. I'm not sure. But you're quite right, you know, that I *did* just create a shell, and it *was* your rebellion that made it a world. Deep down I always knew that rebellion was necessary. I must have done, mustn't I, since whatever you did came from somewhere inside me? Rebellion was necessary. I'd just hoped that in Esperine it would somehow take a different path."

Only the highest tips of the peaks were still shining gold. They were like bright orange light bulbs. And then, one by one, they went out.

amaryllis

CARRIE VAUGHN

New York Times bestseller Carrie Vaughn is the author of a wildly popular series of novels detailing the adventures of Kitty Norville, a radio personality who also happens to be a werewolf, and who runs a late-night call-in radio advice show for supernatural creatures. The Kitty books include *Kitty and the Midnight Hour*, *Kitty Goes to Washington*, *Kitty Takes a Holiday*, *Kitty and the Silver Bullet*, *Kitty and the Dead Man's Hand*, *Kitty Raises Hell*, *Kitty's House of Horrors*, and *Kitty Goes to War*. Vaughn's short work has appeared in *Jim Baen's Universe*, *Asimov's Science Fiction*, *Subterranean*, *Wild Cards: Inside Straight*, *Warriors*, *Songs of Love and Death*, *Realms of Fantasy*, *Paradox*, *Strange Horizons*, *Weird Tales*, *All-Star Zeppelin Adventure Stories*, and elsewhere. Her most recent books are *Voices of Dragons*, her first venture into Young Adult territory, and *Discord's Apple*, a fantasy. Coming up are the novels *Steel* and *After the Golden Age*; a new Kitty novel, *Kitty's Big Trouble*; and a collection of Kitty stories, *Kitty's Greatest Hits*. She lives in Colorado.

In the powerful tale of multigenerational family relations and personal redemption against the odds that follow, she pulls off the difficult trick of managing to show a diminished, ecologically distressed near-future without being bleak or despairing about it—people are adapting and getting by, life goes on as best it can. And if you lose your family, you can, with luck, *make* another one for yourself.

I never knew my mother, and I never understood why she did what she did. I ought to be grateful that she was crazy enough to cut out her implant so she could get pregnant. But it also meant she was crazy enough to hide the pregnancy until termination wasn't an option, knowing the whole time that she'd never get to keep the baby. That she'd lose everything. That her household would lose everything because of her.

I never understood how she couldn't care. I wondered what her family thought when they learned what she'd done, when their committee split up the household, scattered them—broke them, because of her.

Did she think I was worth it?

It was all about quotas.

"They're using cages up north, I heard. Off shore, anchored," Nina said. "Fifty feet across—twice as much protein grown with half the resources, and we'd never have to touch the wild population again. We could double our quota."

I hadn't really been listening to her. We were resting, just for a moment; she sat with me on the railing at the prow of *Amaryllis* and talked about her big plans.

Wind pulled the sails taut and the fiberglass hull cut through waves without a sound, we sailed so smooth. Garrett and Sun hauled up the nets behind us, dragging in the catch. *Amaryllis* was elegant, a 30-foot sleek vessel with just enough cabin and cargo space—an antique but more than seaworthy. She was a good boat, with a good crew. The best.

"Marie—" Nina said, pleading.

I sighed and woke up. "We've been over this. We can't just double our quota."

"But if we got authorization—"

"Don't you think we're doing all right as it is?" We had a good crew—we were well fed and not exceeding our quotas; I thought we'd be best off not screwing all that up. Not making waves, so to speak.

Nina's big brown eyes filled with tears—I'd said the wrong thing, because I knew what she was really after, and the status quo wasn't it.

"That's just it," she said. "We've met our quotas and kept everyone healthy for years now. I really think we should try. We can at least ask, can't we?"

The truth was: No, I wasn't sure we deserved it. I wasn't sure that kind of responsibility would be worth it. I didn't want the prestige. Nina didn't even want the prestige—she just wanted the baby.

"It's out of our hands at any rate," I said, looking away because I couldn't bear the intensity of her expression.

Pushing herself off the rail, Nina stomped down *Amaryllis'* port side to join the rest of the crew hauling in the catch. She wasn't old enough to want a baby. She was lithe, fit, and golden, running barefoot on the deck, sun-bleached streaks gleaming in her brown hair. Actually, no, she *was* old enough. She'd been with the house for seven years—she was twenty, now. It hadn't seemed so long.

"Whoa!" Sun called. There was a splash and a thud as something in the net kicked against the hull. He leaned over the side, the muscles along his broad, coppery back flexing as he clung to a net that was about to slide back into the water. Nina, petite next to his strong frame, reached with him. I ran down and grabbed them by the waistbands of their trousers to hold them steady. The fourth of our crew, Garrett, latched a boat hook into the net. Together we hauled the catch onto the deck. We'd caught something big, heavy, and full of powerful muscles.

We had a couple of aggregators—large buoys made of scrap steel and wood—anchored fifty miles or so off the coast. Schooling fish were attracted to the aggregators, and we found the fish—mainly mackerel, sardines, sablefish, and whiting. An occasional shark or marlin found its way into the nets, but those we let go; they were rare and outside our quotas. That was what I expected to see—something unusually large thrashing among the slick silvery mass of smaller fish. This thing was large, yes, as big as Nina—no wonder it had almost pulled them over—but it wasn't the right shape. Sleek and streamlined, a powerful swimmer. Silvery like the rest of the catch.

"What is it?" Nina asked.

"Tuna," I said, by process of elimination. I had never seen one in my life. "Bluefin, I think."

"No one's caught a bluefin in thirty years," Garrett said. Sweat was dripping onto his face despite the bandanna tying back his shaggy dark hair.

I was entranced, looking at all that protein. I pressed my hand to the fish's flank, feeling its muscles twitch. "Maybe they're back."

We'd been catching the tuna's food all along, after all. In the old days the aggregators attracted as many tuna as mackerel. But no one had seen one in so long, everyone assumed they were gone.

"Let's put him back," I said, and the others helped me lift the net to the side. It took all of us, and when we finally got the tuna to slide overboard, we lost half the net's catch with it, a wave of silvery scales glittering as they hit the water. But that was okay: Better to be under quota than over.

The tuna splashed its tail and raced away. We packed up the rest of the catch and set sails for home.

The *Californian* crew got their banner last season, and flew its red and green—power and fertility—from the top of the boat's mast for all to see. Elsie of the *Californian* was due to give birth in a matter of weeks. As soon as her pregnancy was confirmed, she stopped sailing and stayed in the household, sheltered and treasured. Loose hands resting atop mountainous belly, she would sometimes come out to greet her household's boat as it arrived. Nina would stare at her. Elsie might have been the first pregnant woman Nina had seen, as least since surviving puberty and developing thoughts of carrying a mountainous belly of her own.

Elsie was there now, an icon cast in bronze before the setting sun, her body canted slightly against the weight in her belly, like a ship leaning away from the wind.

We furled the sails and rowed to the pier beside the scale house. Nina hung over the prow, looking at Elsie, who was waving at *Californian*'s captain, on the deck of the boat. Solid and dashing, everything a captain ought to be, he waved back at her. Their boat was already secured in its home slip, their catch weighed, everything tidy. Nina sighed at the image of a perfect life, and nobody yelled at her for not helping. Best thing to do in a case like this was let her dream until she grew out of it. Might take decades, but still . . .

My *Amaryllis* crew handed crates off to the dockhand, who shifted our catch to the scale house. Beyond that were the processing houses, where onshore crews smoked, canned, and shipped the fish inland. The New Oceanside community provided sixty percent of the protein for the whole region, which was our mark of pride, our reason for existing. Within the community itself, the ten sailing crews were proudest of all. A fishing crew that did its job well and met its quotas kept the whole system running smoothly. I was lucky to even have the *Amaryllis* and be a part of it.

I climbed up to the dock with my folk after securing the boat, and saw that

Anders was the scalemaster on duty. The week's trip might as well have been for nothing, then.

Thirty-five years ago, my mother ripped out her implant and broke up her household. Might as well have been yesterday to a man like Anders.

The old man took a nail-biting forty minutes to weigh our catch and add up our numbers, at which point he announced, "You're fifty pounds over quota."

Quotas were the only way to keep the stock healthy, to prevent overfishing, shortages, and ultimately starvation. The committee based quotas on how much you needed, not how much you could catch. To exceed that—to pretend you needed more than other people—showed so much disrespect to the committee, the community, to the fishing stock.

My knees weak, I almost sat down. I'd gotten it exactly right, I knew I had. I glared at him. Garrett and Sun, a pair of brawny sailors helpless before the scalemaster in his dull gray tunic of authority, glared at him. Some days felt like nothing I did would ever be enough. I'd always be too far one way or the other over the line of "just right." Most days, I'd accept the scalemaster's judgment and walk away, but today, after setting loose the tuna and a dozen pounds of legitimate catch with it, it was too much.

"You're joking," I said. "Fifty pounds?"

"Really," Anders said, marking the penalty on the chalkboard behind him where all the crews could see it. "You ought to know better, an experienced captain like you."

He wouldn't even look at me. Couldn't look me in the eye while telling me I was trash.

"What do you want me to do, throw the surplus overboard? We can eat those fifty pounds. The livestock can eat those fifty pounds."

"It'll get eaten, don't worry. But it's on your record." Then he marked it on his clipboard, as if he thought we'd come along and alter the public record.

"Might as well not sail out at all next week, eh?" I said.

The scalemaster frowned and turned away. A fifty-pound surplus—if it even existed—would go to make up another crew's shortfall, and next week our catch would be needed just as much as it had been this week, however little some folk wanted to admit it. We could get our quota raised like Nina wanted, and we wouldn't have to worry about surpluses at all. No, then we'd worry about shortfalls, and not earning credits to feed the mouths we had, much less the extra one Nina wanted.

Surpluses must be penalized, or everyone would go fishing for surpluses and having spare babies, and then where would we be? Too many mouths, not enough food, no resiliency to survive disaster, and all the disease and starvation that followed. I'd seen the pictures in the archives, of what happened after the big fall.

Just enough and no more. Moderation. But so help me I wasn't going to dump fifty pounds just to keep my record clean.

"We're done here. Thank you, Captain Marie," Anders said, his back to me, like he couldn't stand the sight of me.

When we left, I found Nina at the doorway, staring. I pushed her in front of me, back to the boat, so we could put *Amaryllis* to bed for the night.

"The *Amaryllis*' scales aren't that far off," Garrett grumbled as we rowed to her slip. "Ten pounds, maybe. Not fifty."

"Anders had his foot on the pad, throwing it off. I'd bet on it," Sun said. "Ever notice how we're only ever off when Anders is running the scales?"

We'd all noticed.

"Is that true? But why would he do that?" said Nina, innocent Nina.

Everyone looked at me. A weight seemed to settle on us.

"What?" Nina said. "What is it?"

It was the kind of thing no one talked about, and Nina was too young to have grown up knowing. The others had all known what they were getting into, signing on with me. But not Nina.

I shook my head at them. "We'll never prove that Anders has it in for us so there's no good arguing. We'll take our licks and that's the end of it."

Sun said, "Too many black marks like that they'll break up the house."

That was the worry, wasn't it?

"How many black marks?" Nina said. "He can't do that. Can he?"

Garrett smiled and tried to take the weight off. He was the first to sign on with me when I inherited the boat. We'd been through a lot together. "We'll just have to find out Anders' schedule and make sure we come in when someone else is on duty."

But most of the time there were no schedules—just whoever was on duty when a boat came in. I wouldn't be surprised to learn that Anders kept a watch for us, just to be here to rig our weigh-in.

Amaryllis glided into her slip, and I let Garrett and Sun secure the lines. I leaned back against the side, stretching my arms, staring up along the mast. Nina sat nearby, clenching her hands, her lips. Elsie and *Californian*'s captain had gone.

I gave her a pained smile. "You might have a better chance of getting your extra mouth if you went to a different crew. The *Californian*, maybe."

"Are you trying to get rid of me?" Nina said.

Sitting up, I put my arms across her shoulders and pulled her close. Nina came to me a clumsy thirteen-year old from Bernardino, up the coast. My household had a space for her, and I was happy to get her. She'd grown up smart and eager. She could take my place when I retired, inherit *Amaryllis* in her turn. Not that I'd told her that yet.

"Never. Never ever." She only hesitated a moment before wrapping her arms around me and squeezing back.

Our household was an oasis. We'd worked hard to make it so. I'd inherited the boat, attracted the crew one by one—Garrett and Sun to run the boat, round and bustling Dakota to run the house, and she brought the talented J.J., and we fostered Nina. We'd been assigned fishing rights, and then we earned the land allocation. Ten years of growing, working, sweating, nurturing, living, and the place was gorgeous.

We'd dug into the side of a hill above the docks and built with adobe. In the afternoon sun, the walls gleamed golden. The part of the house projecting out from the hill served as a wall protecting the garden and well. Our path led around the house and into the courtyard. We'd found flat shale to use as flagstones around the cultivated plots, and to line the well, turning it into a spring.

A tiny spring, but any open fresh water seemed like a luxury. On the hill above were the windmill and solar panels.

Everyone who wanted their own room had one, but only Sun did—the detached room dug into the hill across the yard. Dakota, J.J., and Nina had pallets in the largest room. Garrett and I shared a bed in the smaller room. What wasn't house was garden. We had producing fruit trees, an orange and a lemon, that also shaded the kitchen space. Corn, tomatoes, sunflowers, green beans, peas, carrots, radishes, two kinds of peppers, and anything else we could make grow on a few square feet. A pot full of mint and one of basil. For the most part we fed ourselves and so could use our credits on improving *Amaryllis* and bringing in specialties like rice and honey, or fabric and rope that we couldn't make in quantity. Dakota wanted to start chickens next season, if we could trade for the chicks.

I kept wanting to throw that in the face of people like Anders. It wasn't like I didn't pay attention. I wasn't a burden.

The crew arrived home; J.J. had supper ready. Dakota and J.J. had started out splitting household work evenly, but pretty quickly they were trading chores—turning compost versus hanging laundry, mending the windmill versus cleaning the kitchen—until J.J. did most everything involving the kitchen and living spaces and Dakota did everything with the garden and mechanics.

By J.J.'s sympathetic expression when he gave me my serving—smoked mackerel and vegetables tonight—someone had already told him about the run-in with the scalemaster. Probably to keep him or Dakota from asking how my day went.

I stayed out later than usual making a round of the holding. Not that I expected to find anything wrong. It was for my own peace of mind, looking at what we'd built with my own eyes, putting my hand on the trunk of the windmill, running the leaves of the lemon tree across my palms, ensuring that none of it had vanished, that it wasn't going to. It had become a ritual.

In bed I held tight to Garrett, to give and get comfort, skin against skin, under the sheet, under the warm air coming in through the open skylight above our bed.

"Bad day?" he said.

"Can never be a bad day when the ship and crew come home safe," I said. But my voice was flat.

Garrett shifted, running a hand down my back, arranging his arms to pull me tight against him. Our legs twined together. My nerves settled.

He said, "Nina's right, we can do more. We can support an extra mouth. If we appealed—"

"You really think that'll do any good?" I said. "I think you'd all be better off with a different captain."

He tilted his face toward mine, touched my lips with his, pressed until I responded. A minute of that and we were both smiling.

"You know we all ended up here because we don't get along with anyone else. But you make the rest of us look good."

I squirmed against him in mock outrage, giggling.

"Plenty of crews—plenty of households—don't ever get babies," he said. "It doesn't mean anything."

"I don't care about a baby so much," I said. "I'm just tired of fighting all the time."

It was normal for children to fight with their parents, their households, and even their committees as they grew. But it wasn't fair, for me to feel like I was still fighting with a mother I'd never known.

The next day, when Nina and I went down to do some cleaning on *Amaryllis*, I tried to convince myself it was my imagination that she was avoiding me. Not looking at me. Or pretending not to look, when in fact she was stealing glances. The way she avoided meeting my gaze made my skin crawl a little. She'd de- cided something. She had a secret.

We caught sight of Elsie again, walking up from the docks, a hundred yards away, but her silhouette was unmistakable. That distracted Nina, who stopped to stare.

"Is she really that interesting?" I said, smiling, trying to make it a joke.

Nina looked at me sideways, as if deciding whether she should talk to me. Then she sighed. "I wonder what it's like. Don't you wonder what it's like?"

I thought about it a moment and mostly felt fear rather than interest. All the things that could go wrong, even with a banner of approval flying above you. Nina wouldn't understand that. "Not really."

"Marie, how can you be so . . . so *indifferent?*"

"Because I'm not going to spend the effort worrying about something I can't change. Besides, I'd much rather be captain of a boat than stuck on shore, watch- ing."

I marched past her to the boat, and she followed, head bowed.

We washed the deck, checked the lines, cleaned out the cabin, took inventory, and made a stack of gear that needed to be repaired. We'd take it home and spend the next few days working on it before we went to sea again. Nina was quiet most of the morning, and I kept glancing at her, head bent to her work, biting her lip, wondering what she was thinking on so intently. What she was hiding.

Turned out she was working up the courage.

I handed the last bundle of net to her, then went back to double check that the hatches were closed and the cabin was shut up. When I went to climb off the boat myself, she was sitting at the edge of the dock, her legs hanging over the edge, swinging a little. She looked ten years younger, like she was a kid again, like she had when I first saw her.

I regarded her, brows raised, questioning, until finally she said, "I asked Sun why Anders doesn't like you. Why none of the captains talk to you much."

So that was what had happened. Sun—matter-of-fact and sensible—would have told her without any circumspection. And Nina had been horrified.

Smiling, I sat on the gunwale in front of her. "I'd have thought you'd been here long enough to figure it out on your own."

"I knew something had happened, but I couldn't imagine what. Certainly not—I mean, no one ever talks about it. But . . . what happened to your mother? Her household?"

I shrugged, because it wasn't like I remembered any of it. I'd pieced the story together, made some assumptions. Was told what happened by people who made their own assumptions. Who wanted me to understand exactly what my place in the world was.

"They were scattered over the whole region, I think. Ten of them—it was a big household, successful, until I came along. I don't know where all they ended up. I was brought to New Oceanside, raised up by the first *Amaryllis* crew. Then Zeke and Ann retired, took up pottery, went down the coast, and gave me the ship to start my own household. Happy ending."

"And your mother—they sterilized her? After you were born, I mean."

"I assume so. Like I said, I don't really know."

"Do you suppose she thought it was worth it?"

"I imagine she didn't," I said. "If she wanted a baby, she didn't get one, did she? But maybe she just wanted to be pregnant for a little while."

Nina looked so thoughtful, swinging her feet, staring at the rippling water where it lapped against the hull, she made me nervous. I had to say something.

"You'd better not be thinking of pulling something like that," I said. "They'd split us up, take the house, take *Amaryllis*—"

"Oh no," Nina said, shaking her head quickly, her denial vehement. "I would never do that, I'd never do anything like that."

"Good," I said, relieved. I trusted her and didn't think she would. Then again, my mother's household probably thought that about her too. I hopped over to the dock. We collected up the gear, slinging bags and buckets over our shoulders and starting the hike up to the house.

Halfway there, Nina said, "You don't think we'll ever get a banner, because of your mother. That's what you were trying to tell me."

"Yeah." I kept my breathing steady, concentrating on the work at hand.

"But it doesn't change who you are. What you do."

"The old folk still take it out on me."

"It's not fair," she said. She was too old to be saying things like that. But at least now she'd know, and she could better decide if she wanted to find another household.

"If you want to leave, I'll understand," I said. "Any house would be happy to take you."

"No," she said. "No, I'll stay. None of it—it doesn't change who you are."

I could have dropped everything and hugged her for that. We walked a while longer, until we came in sight of the house. Then I asked, "You have someone in mind to be the father? Hypothetically."

She blushed berry red and looked away. I had to grin—so that was how it stood.

When Garrett greeted us in the courtyard, Nina was still blushing. She avoided him and rushed along to dump her load in the workshop.

Garrett blinked after her. "What's up with her?"

"Nina being Nina."

The next trip on *Amaryllis* went well. We made quota in less time than I expected, which gave us half a day's vacation. We anchored off a deserted bit of shore and went swimming, lay on deck and took in the sun, ate the last of the oranges and dried mackerel that J.J. had sent along with us. It was a good day.

But we had to head back some time and face the scales. I weighed our haul three times with *Amaryllis'* scale, got a different number each time, but all within ten pounds of each other, and more importantly twenty pounds under quota. Not that it would matter. We rowed into the slip at the scale house, and Anders was the scalemaster on duty again. I almost hauled up our sails and turned us around, never to return. I couldn't face him, not after the perfect trip. Nina was right—it wasn't fair that this one man could ruin us with false surpluses and black marks.

Silently, we secured *Amaryllis* to the dock and began handing up our cargo. I managed to keep from even looking at Anders, which probably made me look guilty in his eyes. But we'd already established I could be queen of perfection and he would consider me guilty.

Anders' frown was smug, his gaze judgmental. I could already hear him tell me I was fifty pounds over quota. Another haul like that, he'd say, we'll have to see about yanking your fishing rights. I'd have to punch him. I almost told Garrett to hold me back if I looked like I was going to punch him. But he was already keeping himself between the two of us, as if he thought I might really do it.

If the old scalemaster managed to break up *Amaryllis*, I'd murder him. And wouldn't that be a worse crime than any I might represent?

Anders drew out the moment, looking us all up and down before finally announcing, "Sixty over this time. And you think you're good at this."

My hands tightened into fists. I imagined myself lunging at him. At this point, what could I lose?

"We'd like an audit," Nina said, slipping past Sun, Garrett, and me to stand before the stationmaster, frowning, hands on her hips.

"Excuse me?" Anders said.

"An audit. I think your scale is wrong, and we'd like an audit. Right?" She looked at me.

It was probably better than punching him. "Yes," I said, after a flabbergasted moment. "Yes, we would like an audit."

That set off two hours of chaos in the scale house. Anders protested, hollered at us, threatened us. I sent Sun to the committee house to summon official oversight—he wouldn't try to play nice, and they couldn't brush him off. June and Abe, two senior committee members, arrived, austere in gray and annoyed.

"What's the complaint?" June said.

Everyone looked at me to answer. I almost denied it—that was my first impulse. Don't fight, don't make waves. Because maybe I deserved the trash I got. Or my mother did, but she wasn't here, was she?

But Nina was looking at me with her innocent brown eyes, and this was for her.

I wore a perfectly neutral, business-like expression when I spoke to June and Abe. This wasn't about me, it was about business, quotas, and being fair.

"Scalemaster Anders adjusts the scale's calibration when he sees us coming."

I was amazed when they turned accusing gazes at him and not at me. Anders' mouth worked, trying to stutter a defense, but he had nothing to say.

The committee confirmed that Anders was rigging his scale. They offered us reparations, out of Anders' own rations. I considered—it would mean extra credits, extra food and supplies for the household. We'd been discussing getting another windmill, petitioning for another well. Instead, I recommended that any penalties they wanted to levy should go to community funds. I just wanted *Amaryllis* treated fairly.

And I wanted a meeting, to make one more petition before the committee.

Garrett walked with me to the committee office the next morning.

"I should have been the one to think of requesting an audit," I said.

"Nina isn't as scared of the committee as you are. As you *were*," he said.

"I'm not—" But I stopped, because he was right.

He squeezed my hand. His smile was amused, his gaze warm. He seemed to find the whole thing entertaining. Me—I was relieved, exhausted, giddy, ashamed. Mostly relieved.

We, *Amaryllis*, had done nothing wrong. I had done nothing wrong.

Garrett gave me a long kiss, then waited outside while I went to sit before the committee.

June was in her chair, along with five other committee members, behind their long table with their slate boards, tally sheets, and lists of quotas. I sat across from them, alone, hands clenched in my lap, trying not to tap my feet. Trying to appear as proud and assured as they did. A stray breeze slipped through the open windows and cooled the cinderblock room.

After polite greetings, June said, "You wanted to make a petition?"

"We—the *Amaryllis* crew—would like to request an increase in our quota. Just a small one."

June nodded. "We've already discussed it and we're of a mind to allow an increase. Would that be suitable?"

Suitable as what? As reparation? As an apology? My mouth was dry, my tongue frozen. My eyes stung, wanting to weep, but that would have damaged our chances, as much as just being me did.

"There's one more thing," I managed. "With an increased quota, we can feed another mouth."

It was an arrogant thing to say, but I had no reason to be polite.

They could chastise me, send me away without a word, lecture me on wanting too much when there wasn't enough to go around. Tell me that it was more important to maintain what we had rather than try to expand—expansion was arrogance. We simply had to maintain. But they didn't. They didn't even look shocked at what I had said.

June, so elegant, I thought, with her long gray hair braided and resting over her shoulder, a knitted shawl draped around her, as much for decoration as for warmth, reached into the bag at her feet and retrieved a folded piece of cloth, which she pushed across the table toward me. I didn't want to touch it. I was still afraid, as if I'd reach for it and June would snatch it away at the last moment. I didn't want to unfold it to see the red and green pattern in full, in case it was some other color instead.

But I did, even though my hand shook. And there it was. I clenched the banner in my fist; no one would be able to pry it out.

"Is there anything else you'd like to speak of?" June asked.

"No," I said, my voice a whisper. I stood, nodded at each of them. Held the banner to my chest, and left the room.

Garrett and I discussed it on the way back to the house. The rest of the crew was waiting in the courtyard for us: Dakota in her skirt and tunic, hair in a tangled bun; J.J. with his arms crossed, looking worried; Sun, shirtless, hands on hips, inquiring. And Nina, right there in front, bouncing almost.

I regarded them, trying to be inscrutable, gritting my teeth to keep from bursting into laughter. I held our banner behind my back to hide it. Garrett held my other hand.

"Well?" Nina finally said. "How did it go? What did they say?"

The surprise wasn't going to get any better than this. I shook out the banner and held it up for them to see. And oh, I'd never seen all of them wide-eyed and wondering, mouths gaping like fish, at once.

Nina broke the spell, laughing and running at me, throwing herself into my arms. We nearly fell over.

Then we were all hugging, and Dakota started worrying right off, talking about what we needed to build a crib, all the fabric we'd need for diapers, and how we only had nine months to save up the credits for it.

I recovered enough to hold Nina at arm's length, so I could look her in the eyes when I pressed the banner into her hands. She nearly dropped it at first, skittering from it as if it were fire. So I closed her fingers around the fabric and held them there.

"It's yours," I said. "I want you to have it." I glanced at Garrett to be sure. And yes, he was still smiling.

Staring at me, Nina held it to her chest, much like I had. "But . . . you. It's yours . . ." She started crying. Then so did I, gathering her close and holding her tight while she spoke through tears, "Don't you want to be a mother?"

In fact, I rather thought I already was.

seven cities of gold

DAVID MOLES

David Moles has sold fiction to *Asimov's Science Fiction, The Magazine of Fantasy & Science Fiction, Polyphony, Strange Horizons, Lady Churchill's Rosebud Wristlet, Say . . . , Flytrap,* and elsewhere. He coedited, with Jay Lake, 2004's well-received "retro-pulp" anthology *All-Star Zeppelin Adventure Stories,* as well as coediting, with Susan Marie Groppi, the original anthology, *Twenty Epics.*

In the masterfully done work of alternate history that follows, Moles takes us on a *Heart of Darkness* journey undertaken by a haunted and conflicted woman, down a river that runs right through the middle of a vividly described war zone, toward an uncertain and perilous destination that might not even exist.

The typhoon rain came in off the Gulf of Mexico and clawed at the burning city like the jaguars that the Maya say will fall from the sky at the end of the world. It hissed down on the hot glazed stone of the Praza dos Bispos, clattered on the tiles of the Alta Cidad, damped the fires, washed the ashes from the idolaters' ghetto. It streamed down the green canvas of the Andalusian army's abandoned positions and rattled the yellow plastic shells of the crowded Japanese field hospitals. It dripped down the necks of tired Relief Ministry doctors measuring their doses of opium, and of worried Industrial Ministry technicians hunched over their radiation counters. It filled canals and overflowed gutters, poured through breached levees, rinsed streets in brown water flecked with pale foam. It floated burned bodies out to sea.

"Dr. Nakada?"

The Relief Ministry subaltern rattled the hollow door panel. There was no answer from inside. He slid the door open a hand's-breadth, where it stuck. In the strip of bright Caribbean sunlight he saw scuffed blue plastic matting, ridged in imitation of *tatami,* and stretched across it the tanned skin of a woman's arm.

He lifted the door off its track, flooding the little bungalow with light, eliciting a groan from the bungalow's occupant. As the subaltern removed his sandals and stepped inside, his gaze went from the woman on the pallet—her feet bare, her short black hair matted, her blue duck Ministry field coat and trousers wrinkled and unbelted—to the low table where an open formulary kit sat next to an empty teacup, a packet of Turkish opiated cigarillos, and a pot that had boiled dry on an electric ring. He squatted to sniff the cup and the woman's breath; lifted her wrist from the floor and took her pulse; examined her face and her ears and, ignoring her sleepy protests, opened her mouth to shine a small pocket-light on her tongue.

When the subaltern released her jaw, the woman asked, "Where am I?"

The tone of her voice suggested she'd already been told once, and hadn't liked the answer.

"Camp Xaragua, Doctor," the subaltern said. "Caribe."

He waited for another question, but instead she put an arm across her eyes and started to snore.

The subaltern sighed, opened the woman's formulary kit to the compartment marked *Remedies (Lower-Class)*, and went to work.

A little later, Doctor-Lieutenant Chië Nakada, awake and wearing sandals, her hands and face washed, her uniform straightened, her hair brushed and held out of her eyes by a clean scarf, was strapped into the jump seat of a utility coleopter.

She had a headache.

The hot air in the coleopter's noisy metal belly smelled of disinfectant and old blood. Nakada closed her eyes and breathed it in. It smelled like home.

> *I still don't know why they chose me. But then I wasn't their first choice.*
>
> *My last tour was in Indochina, a South Siamese refugee camp on the edge of the Malay civil war. Half a million refugees came through that camp in the three years I was there, on the way to Madagascar or Xinjiang or wherever the world powers needed more workers.*
>
> *Hard lives. Bad memories. There's nothing romantic about the life of a refugee. But at least their war was over.*
>
> *For me, after that tour, something broke. I went back to Japan, and I wandered around like a sleepwalker. I made love to my husband, I walked my son to school, and at night I dreamed of children starved, women raped and mutilated, men burned by napalm and maimed by machetes and cluster shells and wandering mines. I stood in Kokura Main Station, watching the salarymen and the office ladies stream through, lucky and oblivious, and wondered what I was doing there. I imagined earthquakes, incendiary bombs. Imagined the station in ruins, the commuters trapped under burning beams, screaming for help. My help.*
>
> *And after a while, I started wishing it would happen.*
>
> *—from the pillow book of Doctor-Lieutenant Chië Nakada*

Nakada followed the subaltern along the glassed-in promenade deck of the hospital ship *Mappô Maru*. The typhoon had moved off north, over the low green coast, but the sky was still alive with scudding gray clouds, and beyond the sweep of *Mappô Maru*'s broad wing the water on which the relief fleet rode at anchor was like cracked green shale. A line of cargo ships stretched out of sight to east and west, freighters stacked with food and water and portable shelters and dry cement. Nakada counted three more big yellow ground-effect craft like *Mappô Maru* riding at anchor. There were smaller boats in the water, and hovercraft, and more coleopters in the air.

The Japanese humanitarian-industrial complex, swinging belatedly into action. The response disproportionate for one typhoon. Nakada supposed somebody had been caught flatfooted and was trying now to make up for lost time with a show of vigorous activity.

Beneath *Mappô Maru*'s drooping whale-fluke tail, the Doctor-General's compartment stretched the full width of the deck. It was austerely furnished, in a way meant to suggest a formal receiving room somewhere in the Home Islands—real *tatami* mats, painted paper screens, lacquered cabinets, blossoming branches set with artful asymmetry in narrow vases, a formal portrait of the Regent at Mt. Yoshino. The effect was somewhat spoiled by the harsh fluorescents and the hull's naked aluminum curve. Despite the air that blew from the ceiling vents, the compartment was close, a little too warm and a little too humid. It smelled of stale tobacco.

The subaltern bowed and left, shutting the door. The aft half of the compartment, where Nakada supposed the gallery windows would be, was screened off. In this half, a low black table was set with teacups and an ashtray, and at it a man and a woman knelt on red cushions.

The woman Nakada knew, at least by appearance: Nobuko Araki, Doctor-General. Japanese, long-faced, long hair streaked with gray, wearing a coat of indigo-dyed linen over a uniform cut from a visibly better grade of cloth than Nakada's. Araki, the I.C., Incident Commander for the entire Antilian Mission. The man was a foreigner, in Iskandariya silk, with an orangish beard shot with gray, and the pale freckled skin of Varangia or northern al-Andalus. A crimson turban made his skin look even more pale than it was. His eyes, fixed on Nakada as he tapped the ash from his cigarillo, seemed to have no color at all.

"Thank you for coming, Dr. Nakada." The voice came from her right. The speaker, who Nakada hadn't even noticed until he spoke, was a tall, bespectacled Pharmacologist-Major, about Nakada's own age or a little younger. The embroidered tag on his uniform read KAWABATA.

Araki said, "Sit down, Nakada. Have some tea."

There was another cushion on Araki's left. Nakada slipped off her sandals and knelt as an orderly poured cold dark tea into a porcelain cup.

"Cold barley tea's all I can drink in this heat, Doctor," Araki said. "Hope you don't mind."

Nakada cleared her throat. "No, ma'am; I prefer it myself."

Kawabata, still standing, opened a cabinet and took out an aluminum scroll case. He snapped it open and unrolled the file inside.

"Dr. Nakada, in Daiwa 18 you led the first medical response team into Pachacamac after the earthquake, is that correct?"

"Correct, sir." Nakada took a sip of tea. It tasted like burnt rice.

"And in the first year of Seisho"—Kawabata said, looking at the file—"you saved the Sultan of Majapahit from a poison administered by his own physician."

"He'd eaten some bad shellfish, sir."

"Ever worked with Christians?"

"In Axum," Nakada said. "During the famine. And of course when I studied in Kostantiniyye."

"But not Antilian or Frankish Christians," the foreigner said. His Japanese was good, with only a trace of accent.

"No, sir."

Araki and the foreigner exchanged glances.

"You've been in Xaragua how long?" Araki asked.

"Three weeks, ma'am."

"Then you must be eager to get back in the field."

"Yes, ma'am. Absolutely."

The Pharmacologist-Major took out another file.

"Six days ago, Doctor," Kawabata said, "Antilian insurgents smuggled an experimental bomb into the occupied city of Espírito Santo, on the lower Acuamagna. Smuggled it through the Exclusion Zone established by the Relief Ministry to—" He stopped and cleared is throat. "To separate the Antilian bishops' territory from the areas occupied by al-Andalus. We still don't know exactly what kind of bomb it was—or how it worked—or whether they have any more. The Industrial Ministry suggests it may have something to do with sub-atomic forces, but we really don't know."

The clack of Doctor-General Araki's teacup as she set it down had the interrupting authority of a meditation leader's wooden blocks. "What we do know is that it burned half the city and killed thirty thousand people. Including twenty thousand Antilian Christians. If I didn't know Abbot-Doctor Shingen personally, I wouldn't believe the reports he's sending us. Thousands of burn victims. Thousands more who were outside the fire area but still have burn-like symptoms. Other symptoms similar to typhoid fever—nausea, hair loss, skin lesions. And since it's the rainy season here, we can expect actual typhoid fever any time, not to mention cholera, yellow fever, and malaria. For all I know, we should expect leprosy and the bubonic plague. We're looking at the biggest humanitarian crisis in ten years."

"Relief efforts have been hampered by the Gulf typhoon season," Kawabata said. "But the Eleventh Airmobile Group was already in Xaragua when this happened, preparing for deployment to the typhoon track. They're being diverted to Espírito Santo now."

There was a silence. Nakada looked from Kawabata to Araki and back.

"Yes, sir," she said eventually.

"Tell me, Doctor," the foreigner said, "what is your opinion of war?"

Nakada looked at him, then at Araki, who gave her a small nod. She turned back to the foreigner.

"I'm opposed to it, sir."

"A natural position for someone in your profession, Doctor. An admirable position. As a diplomat, I too am opposed to war. In particular, I am opposed to wars of religion."

There was an expectant pause; then Nakada said, "Yes, sir."

Kawabata took out another file case. "Andalusian intelligence believes that the Antilian insurgents are no longer controlled by the Seven Bishops, but by a woman, a former nun, named Clara Dos Orsos." He took out a piece of paper that had been rolled up inside the file and handed it to Nakada.

It was a thermal facsimile of a photograph, washed-out and contrasty, and it looked as though the original picture had been none too sharp to begin with. But it was a striking face even so. A woman, in her late twenties or early thirties, with dark, wide-set eyes, cheekbones that suggested more aboriginal Antilian or Mexican ancestry than the Iberian Gothic blood of the Antilian upper classes.

"She's a messianic preacher," Kawabata said. "A charismatic visionary. Her followers call her the Virgin of Apalaxia."

"An apocalyptic madwoman is what she is," Araki said. "Hallucinations, delusions, paranoid ideation, magical thinking—classic schizophrenia, if not psychosis. Doesn't take orders from anybody but the angels in her head."

Nakada watched the foreigner stub out his cigarillo and take out another as he talked, lighting it with an ivory-handled igniter.

"For some years now, Doctor," he said, "the Seven Bishops of Antilia have been at war with my people. In the name of religion they have provided madmen, Roman and Frankish Christian madmen, with the tools to do mad things. These men have committed outrages, killing not only Muslims but Jews and Sabeans and, yes, many Christians."

He took a long draw from the cigarillo and let the smoke out slowly.

"Now there is this woman," he continued, "Dos Orsos. And this terror weapon, this bomb, this city-destroyer—the like of which is not to be found in the Caliphate, nor Persia, nor India, nor China, nor Japan. To drive the Caliph's armies from their land, in the name of religion, these people build this Satanic machine and this madwoman turns it upon her own people."

"Thirty thousand dead, Doctor," said Araki. "The madness has got to stop."

Kawabata cleared his throat. "You'll be provided with several doses of an experimental antipsychotic remedy," he said. "A hepato-cardiac reprimant derived from TJ-54. A hybrid ambulance boat will take you up to Espírito Santo. You'll cross over to the Acuamagna there and proceed upriver, out of the Exclusion Zone; make contact with the surviving bishops somewhere north of La Vitoria, and get their approval to . . . treat Dos Orsos' condition."

Nakada looked from Kawabata to Araki, who nodded.

"Yes, sir," she said.

"Treat it," said the foreigner, "by whatever means necessary."

When Nakada awoke, the sun was setting, somewhere behind her. She'd had one of the crew mix her a sleeping draught almost as soon as she was aboard the ambulance boat.

The hybrid ambulance was part jetboat, part hovercraft, ten meters long and five wide. Most of it was one big piece of yellow injection-molded plastic, spotted with patches of grubby non-skid tape. It looked like a child's toy.

One of the crew—it was the nurse who'd mixed her the sleeping draught—was leaning over the side, holding a net on the end of a two-meter bamboo pole. She was round-faced, tanned and freckled, and looked about fifteen years old. She saw Nakada looking at her, and grinned.

"Where are you from?" Nakada asked.

"New Yezo," the girl said, and returned to her net. A name came to Nakada: *Hayashi*. There must have been introductions at some point.

New Yezo. A colonial, from the coastal islands, three or four thousand kilometers northwest of Espírito Santo. A land of bears and salmon and logging camps and fish-processing plants. Nakada supposed a six-year hitch with the Ministry must sound pretty good, when the alternative was a berth on a North Pacific factory whaler.

Nakada sat up. She looked past Hayashi to the long, low shoreline, a kilometer or so away. It looked as alien as the coast of Kalimantan, but it was still the continent Hayashi had been born on. She wondered if that was how the girl thought of it.

"You served in Antilia before, Doctor?"

The chief of the boat was at the tiller, a Surgeon-Sergeant named Shiraoka. You couldn't get much higher than Sergeant without a full medical diploma, and Shiraoka didn't look like the type to go back and get one. He was in his early forties, with sun-wrinkles around his eyes and a thick black mustache that wouldn't have looked out of place on a Kazakh horse-thief.

"No," Nakada told him. "Peru, once. Mainly East Ifriqiya and the Indies. You?"

"Been here three years." He shook his head. "Ifriqiya, yeah, been there too. West, mostly. That was some bad-luck country. The Antilians, they've had their share of bad luck. But mainly, they're just crazy."

> *Crazy.*
>
> *In the scroll case with my orders was the portrait of Dos Orsos, with those fixed black eyes. I looked into them and tried to decide whether crazy was what I saw there—crazy, or one of Araki and Kawabata's precise, medicalizing euphemisms: schizophrenia, paranoia, psychosis.*
>
> *Or, more quaintly, madness.*
>
> *It wasn't that I hadn't seen those things. In that South Siamese refugee camp I'd seen a Chinese girl, no taller than my shoulder and not much more than half my weight, run amok with a bayonet and kill six Malay paramilitaries. In Axum, I'd known a doctor from Shizuoka who would chalk the floor of every room he slept in with the outlines of tatami mats, and who couldn't sleep if his pallet overlapped one of the lines.*
>
> *But when I met Dos Orsos' thermal-printed gaze, I saw something else. Something I'd seen, maybe, in the eyes of volunteers who'd keep digging long after there was any chance of finding survivors in the rubble, of nurses who gave their best and most gentle care to the patients it was too late to save.*
>
> *It was—I told myself—the look I saw sometimes in the mirror.*
>
> *I was right about that, but I was wrong, too.*
>
> *—from the pillow book of Doctor-Lieutenant Chië Nakada*

They rounded a headland, passed through a narrows, entered a wide, brackish lake, the far shore invisible in the subtropical haze. Not long after that, they saw the first body.

"What's that?" asked Ishino. Ishino was the boat's other nurse, an Okinawan boy not much more than Hayashi's age. His face was the face of a pop star: a naïve, almost feminine handsomeness, with a hint of rebellion that looked as though his heart wasn't really in it.

"What's it look like?" asked Nakada.

The body, what was visible above water, was naked, burned black and hairless. There was no way to tell whether it had been man or woman, Antilian or Andalusian, young or old.

"Oh," said Hayashi.

"Plenty more where we're going," Nakada said, and closed her eyes. Her head still hurt. The conscientious subaltern had confiscated the opium from her formulary kit. So far she'd stayed out of the boat's opium chest, but it was getting harder. There was a Pure Land food camp north of the city. She thought she could hold out till there.

She heard Ishino chanting in a low voice, and recognized a Nichiren prayer for the dead. When he'd finished, Shiraoka powered up the fans and deployed the ground-effect skirt, and they quickly left the body behind.

They followed the curve of the lakeshore; what Shiraoka's charts marked as lakeshore, a shining expanse of water broken by the green humps of drowned trees. They were moving against the current. The current, river water from the Acuamagna cutting itself a new path to the sea over Espírito Santo's breached levees and through its burst canals, was a plume of brown mud spotted with the pale bellies of dead fish. Where the charts said dikes should divide the lake from the farms south of the city, there was only open water and, here and there, a boil of yellow foam surrounding the humped rooftops of a drowned village.

Gradually, the flooded farms gave way to flooded shantytowns, the suburbs of Espírito Santo. From the corrugated rooftops of boxy cinderblock huts, flat-faced Antilians watched the passing ambulance boat with hooded eyes. A lone yellow Ministry flatboat moved among them, small blue figures passing barrels of water up onto the rooftops. There were many more huts than barrels.

As they neared the city, something large and gold glittered on the shore.

"What's that?" Ishino asked.

"Looks like a Buddha," Hayashi reported, peering through a glass.

"Give me the glass," Nakada said. Hayashi handed it up, and Nakada peered through it. "Kanzeon," she said.

Kanzeon, Guanshi Yin, Kwannon—the thousand-armed, syncretic embodiment of mercy, equal parts Avalokiteshvara-bodhisattva and South Chinese mother-goddess—gazed benevolently at Nakada through the glass, her meter-wide smile, like the rest of her, a glitter of gold-flake plastic in the sun. Workers in Ministry blue had rolled the statue off a barge and were now hauling it upright at the top of a long ramp, turning it to look over a field of saffron-yellow tents. Beyond them Nakada saw a collection of boxy concrete buildings of increasing size, culminating in a two-hundred-meter dome, its sliding roof a patchwork of broken girders and tattered sheet metal. As she watched, a coleopter rose up from beyond the dome and whirred away over the lake.

Nakada lowered the glass. The Kanzeon's smiling face, the thousand arms spread out around and behind her like the wings of a Persian angel, were clearly visible now even without it.

Shiraoka eyed the golden statue and shook his head. "Pure Landers, always asking for trouble," he said.

"We'll tell the Christians it's the Virgin Mary," said Nakada.

The buildings belonged to a crumbling sports complex of which the food camp occupied one end, the yellow tarps and tents shading expanses of cracked asphalt and pools of stagnant water. Dilapidated concrete edifices frowned over them, structures that perhaps had been grandiose thirty years ago, but that now, amid the flooded shantytowns, seemed merely pathetic.

The ambulance boat pulled up on a long white tiled plaza at the edge of a concrete spillway, a diversion of lake water made, Nakada supposed, for the staging of aquatic events; there was a diving tower on the opposite bank, and on this side tiered rows of steel spectators' benches, stacked high now with supply baskets. Flatboats, an uninterrupted stream of them, were unloading dazed Antilians. Between them, sunlight glittered dully off water opaque as green paint.

As the boat's fans spun down, Nakada breathed deeply in through her nostrils, held the breath for a moment, then let it slowly out through her lips. There was a familiar tang in the air, overriding the wet living smell of the water: a perfume compounded of fuel oil and raw sewage, the emblematic scent of the developing world. Nakada breathed it in again and smiled.

"Give me the chart," she said to Shiraoka. "I'm going to find the camp chief." She hopped down onto the tiles. "See if I can get us some directions."

Somewhere in the direction of the gold Kanzeon, there was shouting, and then the sound of a gunshot.

"Take someone with you," Shiraoka said, passing down the chart.

"I'll go," said Hayashi.

Nakada and Hayashi headed up the concrete slope toward the commotion.

"This your first tour?" Nakada asked.

"Sure is," the young nurse said. As they walked she looked around the camp with alert interest, like a studious child on her first visit to an amusement park, not sure yet whether all the costumed characters and the lights and the rides were really for her. Nakada supposed that there were probably more people in the shuffling line of refugees beside them than Hayashi had ever seen in her life before being drafted for the Ministry.

"Is that thing *real*?" Hayashi asked, looking up at the thirty-meter Kanzeon statue. "It looks like plastic."

Nakada shrugged. "Plastic's as real as bronze, I suppose."

They reached the processing desk at the head of the line, and the source of the disturbance. A line of Japanese police in lacquered half-armor held back a crowd that seemed to consist mostly of Andalusian soldiers. As orderlies passed food and water to the Antilian refugees and directed them toward the tents, a red-bearded Andalusian officer, his Varangian accent so thick that Nakada wasn't at first sure that he was speaking Arabic, was arguing with a Relief Ministry worker. The relief worker wore a sleeveless black monk's tunic over his blue uniform, with a white rope belt and a Nutritionist-Sergeant's patch.

"Look, your Lordship," the nutritionist said in sarcastic Japanese, "you morons are going to have to wait your turn—"

Nakada tapped him on the shoulder. "Hey," she said. "Where can I find the camp chief?"

The nutritionist turned. "Do I look like a tour guide?" Then he registered Nakada's rank. "Sorry, Doctor. Try the—"

The Andalusian chose that moment to take a pistol from his belt and fire a shot in the air.

"That's it!" said the nutritionist, disgusted. As the Andalusian started to lower the pistol, the nutritionist grabbed his wrist. In a single motion he threw the man to the ground and took the pistol away, following up with a stomp to the solar plexus. There was a splash as the nutritionist threw the pistol over a railing into the canal.

The Andalusian soldiers yelled and surged toward the desk, and the Japanese police waded into the crowd, iron sword-breakers and wooden batons rising and falling.

"The camp chief?" Nakada repeated.

"Try the coliseum," the nutritionist said.

"Thanks," said Nakada, but the nutritionist's attention was already back on the melee.

"Get them settled down!" he yelled. "We've got work to do!"

As Nakada and Hayashi left, the nurse said, "I thought the soldiers were supposed to stay out of the camps."

"That only works when they're winning," Nakada said. "And sometimes not even then."

The coliseum had been converted into an infirmary. Its floor was a miniature tent city all by itself, crowded with hammocks and folding cots, the occupants mostly women and children. Hayashi read off the chalked symbols on the boards hung from each cot, looking for any interesting conditions, but Nakada could see that mainly it was just malnutrition, dehydration, and the occasional dysentery.

Then they reached the burn ward. Hayashi, fascinated, moved among patients swathed in bandages, patients whose raw skin would not abide a bandage's touch, patients whose skin was striped white and black in the patterns of the clothes they had been wearing when the bomb's light reached them.

Nakada checked the prescriptions, and the contents of the formulary carts that stood at the end of every third or fourth row of patients. The Pure Land food camp was just that; it had never been intended to handle a medical emergency of this scale. But eventually, on the bottom shelf of one of the last carts, Nakada found what she was looking for.

Just at that moment, Hayashi said: "Is that the camp chief?"

Nakada slipped the packet into her sleeve and stood up.

Abbot-Doctor Shingen was a tower of a man, two heads taller than Nakada,

his shaven skull massive as a temple bell. He was supervising the installation of
another statue, a smaller one, not Kanzeon this time but the Amida buddha.

"That's the way!" he boomed at the monks who worked with wedges and
levers to place the statue—gilded bronze, not the Kanzeon's plastic—and its
wooden pedestal. "Right up under the scoreboards!" He looked down as Nakada
approached. "Yes?"

"Sir." Nakada bowed, and proffered the scroll case with her orders. "I'm
bound upriver, on a special assignment. I'm told I can cross over to the Acuamagna here."

"What?" Shingen said, ignoring the case. "No, you can't cross here. In case
you haven't heard, this is a disaster area." He waved a hand at the rows of hammocks and cots. "What do you want to go upriver for? Why don't you make yourself useful here?"

Still holding the case out, Nakada persisted. "I'm on a special assignment for
Doctor-General Araki, sir. My orders are to cross over to the Acuamagna here
and proceed upriver."

Shingen scowled. "Araki? What's she want?" He took the case, snapped it
open, unrolled enough of the scroll inside to read the header, then rolled the
scroll up again and stuffed it into the case again, handing it back to Nakada.

"I haven't heard anything about it," he said.

Nakada put the case away, exchanging it for the laminated chart. "Sir," she
began, "city map shows the river and the lake connected by these canals, here
and here—"

The monk glanced at the chart, followed Nakada's pointing finger. "You don't
want to go up there," he said.

"Sir?"

"It's all looters up there," Shingen said. "Aborigines, cultists, Andalusian de-
serters, swamp cannibals. We get all kinds. It was bad enough up there before the
bomb, but now it's a real mess." He glanced up at something beyond Nakada.
"Over here!" he called out.

Nakada turned to see an NKK film crew, weighed down with cameras and
recording gear and spare film reels and audio cylinders, picking its way through
the burn ward.

"It's no good," said Shingen to Nakada. "Wait till the Eleventh gets here and
we can re-establish control of the city, that's my advice."

Nakada bowed. Shingen turned to the monks, who were still trying to make
the Amida sit up straight. "*Level*, you blockheads!" he called.

"I heard about these cannibals," Ishino said. "They cut off your hands and feet
and hang your body to dry in the wind."

"That's in New Yezo, not down here." Hayashi said. "I've seen it. It's a ritual.
They don't really eat anybody, it's all play-acting."

"I know what I heard," Ishino insisted.

They were back at the boat. The sun had slipped below the dome of the
coliseum. Hayashi was grilling shrimp Korean-style, while Ishino boiled a pot of
starchy, vitamin-fortified relief rice.

"Hey."

Nakada looked up from the chart she and Shiraoka had been studying, and saw a fantastic figure hopping from foot to foot on the tiles beside the boat: a tall, loose-limbed marionette in the threadbare remnants of some kind of civil service uniform from the Varangian Rus, white wool piped with faded blue silk. As the figure came closer, Nakada saw that it was in fact a human being. Beneath a Khazar-style round cap, pale eyes stared at her out of a sunburned, unshaven red face that might have been anywhere between thirty and forty. She saw that the man had no shoes.

"Hey," the man said again, in Japanese. "You speak Greek? You climb river?" Climb river?

"I speak Greek," Nakada said cautiously, in that language.

"Good, good." The man vaulted aboard, almost knocking over Ishino's pot of rice. "Sorry. You go upriver, yes?" His Greek, to Nakada, didn't sound much better than his Japanese, but it came faster and there was clearly more of it. "I am Semyonov, Andrei Karlovitch. Poet. From Novgorod. You must cross the city?"

"We're going upriver," Nakada said. "And we have to cross the city. What about it?"

"Ship canal!" the Russian said. He picked up the chart, pushing Shiraoka aside, and held it up. "I show you." Then he dropped the chart, distracted by Hayashi, who was taking the shrimp off the grill. "Hey! Shrimp!"

"Éfeso, Esmirna, Pérgamo, Tiatira," the Russian was reciting, from his perch on top of the pilothouse. His bare feet were very dirty. "Sardes, Filadélfia, Laodicéia. Seven cities."

The ambulance boat was creeping up a wide, garbage-choked ship canal, more or less at the Russian's direction, though Shiraoka checked his charts constantly, and Ishino and Hayashi were both at the bow, watching for submerged obstacles. "Because of the legend. You know it?"

"What legend?"

Nakada sat with her back against one of the engine nacelles, her feet bare, her arms clasped around her knees. After putting the Russian in Shiraoka's reluctant charge, she'd paid only intermittent attention to him. Mostly, she was watching the city.

The settlers who originally founded Espírito Santo in the name of the Seven Bishops had built their city on a patch of high ground, between the Acuamagna's banks on one side and the lakeshore on the other, laden barges carrying building stone from quarries hundreds of kilometers upriver. Now as the ambulance boat maneuvered through the ship canal, skirting the wreckage of fallen cranes and overturned barges, the old Alta Cidad was clearly visible, but the cathedral was a soot-blackened ruin and the surrounding buildings were mostly roofless shells. The streets were full of dirty water and the Praza dos Bispos, running down to the river, was marred by missing tiles as if by the pock-marks of some disease.

"The Last Days," said Semyonov. "The Christians, in Iberia and the Frankish kingdoms, they tell this story about the seven bishops that escaped the Caliph's armies. They say the bishops set sail from Oporto with all their followers and all their treasure, and cross the Western Ocean. that through the intercession of the

Agía Eylalia they are guided to an island, which they call Antilia." Talk of religious matters improved the Russian's Greek, Nakada noticed. "That the bishops start a Christian kingdom there, a new Israel. Seven golden cities, one for each of the seven bishops. That some day the bishops come back and reconquer Christendom."

"Doesn't look like they're going to start here," Nakada said. The Russian fell silent.

The air was hot as a sulfur spring, hot as fresh ashes. The sky was a deep blue, and completely clear. Of the looters and cannibals Ishino feared, there was no sign. There were no living people in sight, no fish, no birds. The wooden maze of the lower city, where the vast majority of the city's inhabitants had lived and worked, was simply gone. Of the canals indicated on the charts, there remained only a vague geometry picked out in burnt pilings that rose here and there among oily slicks of garbage, with slowly turning drifts of wreckage captured in lazy eddies, the corpses of dogs and pigs and human beings grounded against accidental dams of capsized boats and fallen timbers.

Nakada surveyed the prospect with a feeling of pleasant melancholy. There'd been less than a grain of opium in the packet she'd stolen from the formulary cart in the burn ward, maybe a quarter of her normal dose, but enough to take the edge off, enough to let Nakada appreciate what was around her. She felt suffused with *mono no aware*, the sense of inherent pathos in ordinary things: a category which at the moment seemed to her to encompass the boat, the dirty water, the vanished buildings, the corpses, the clear sky; to encompass the world. She looked out over the ruin of Espírito Santo, and in the bathhouse heat, shivered at its tragic beauty.

She felt, for the first time in months, alive.

> *If what happened to Espírito Santo had happened to Iskandariya or Massalia, to Nanjing or Kokura or Kumbi Saleh—if it had happened anywhere in what we're pleased to call the civilized world—it would have cut human history in two. Before and after. Innocence and experience. The former and the latter days of the Law. The end of one Yuga, and the beginning of another.*
>
> *Instead it happened in Antilia. And like most things that happen in the dark places of the earth, it passed almost without notice from the world outside.*
>
> *That was all right with me. That meant I didn't have to share it.*
> *—from the pillow book of Doctor-Lieutenant Chië Nakada*

The Russian left them at the shattered locks, taking as payment a bag of relief rice, some packets of dried soy flakes, and a few cans of tincture base—distilled water, powdered green tea, and rice alcohol at forty percent by volume.

"You're here to take her away, aren't you," he said quietly to Nakada as he was climbing out of the boat. "Like the other one."

"Take who away?" Nakada asked.

"The Virgin." When the Russian saw Nakada's incomprehension, he added, in Antilian, "*La Virxe da 'Palaxia.*"

"Dos Orsos?" Nakada asked. "What do you know about her?"

Semyonov looked to either side, as if the flat, burnt, waterlogged landscape might hide eavesdroppers. The back of one of his hands, Nakada noticed only now, had been tattooed with a rude cross.

"Up the Río Baldío," he said eventually. "Town called San Lucas. There's a lake. Artificial. An island." Then, as if he'd said too much, the Russian turned his head down and away.

"An island," Nakada repeated, and shook her head. She nodded to Shiraoka, who started the engines.

"It's all true!" the Russian called out, as the ambulance boat pulled away. "Seven bishops," he continued, his voice growing fainter. "Seven cities. Seven spirits of God. Seven seals. Seven angels, with seven trumpets! Seven heads! Seven horns!"

Then they were out in the Acuamagna's rain channel, and Nakada could no longer hear the Russian's voice. His awkward white figure watched them from the bank of the ship canal for a little while, then turned and headed north, toward the Praza and the ruined cathedral.

Nakada paged through Shiraoka's book of charts until she found the lake the Russian had spoken of, and the town.

"How far are we going, Doctor?" Shiraoka asked.

"I can't tell you that," said Nakada automatically. Then: "Pretty far."

"How far?"

Nakada shrugged and closed the chart book. "Past La Vitoria. Up the East Branch maybe two hundred kilometers, then maybe up the Río Baldío."

Shiraoka turned to look at her. "That's outside the Zone."

"Maybe." Nakada shrugged again. "But that's where we're going."

By the time they were a day or two north of Espírito Santo, the Acuamagna was beginning to come to life again. The ambulance boat passed northbound barges carrying supplies, southbound barges carrying casualties; was passed, itself, by Ministry patrol hydrofoils and other ambulance boats. Fishing smacks with smoke-belching oil-fueled motors and fat canal boats with wide lateen sails moved up and down the river as if there had never been an occupation, or a war; but a close eye noted that the crews were composed of women, and children, and men too old to fight.

It was near evening, about a week after they'd left the Russian at the locks, when they heard the music. Nakada saw a pale glow like swamp gas wavering on the western bank. As the boat drew closer it resolved itself into a swinging line of paper lanterns, suspended over the water, illuminating a thing like a long white colonnaded building, three or four stories tall, set right at the water's edge. This in turn proved to be a fantastical flatboat or barge, its lower hull and tall smoke-stacks painted black, its superstructure a curling thicket of white-painted wooden fretwork, the intricacy of its carving enough to rival the incised calligraphy walls of an Andalusian palace.

Smaller lanterns hung over catwalks and promenades. Under the lantern's light the decks were crowded with men in Ministry blue, shouting and singing and vomiting over the rail. The music, electrically amplified, half-drowned in its own feedback, carried over the water. There was a brewery smell, of yeast and hot water.

"It's a festival," said Ishino.

"Ôbon?" Hayashi asked.

"Ôbon's in July," Nakada reminded her.

"Supply dock," said Shiraoka. "We'll tie up here, get some fuel."

"Can we get some beer?" asked Ishino.

The supply dock was a repurposed pleasure barge, an imitation river ferry built to take advantage of some pre-war jurisdictional loophole, exempting it from the bishops' moral regulations and sumptuary laws. The dispensary, when Nakada found it, was at the back of a converted drinking hall, with red baize gaming tables and framed posters on the walls, advertising music or alcohol or prostitution or all three at once. On the stage, a horse-faced Doctor-Colonel, very drunk, was crooning a lugubrious love ballad into a microphone for an audience of orderlies, junior officers, and Antilian prostitutes.

The skinny, unshaven Apothecary-Sergeant that ran the dispensary didn't like having his dice game interrupted, but he filled Nakada's supply list with surly efficiency, packing two portable formulary kits.

". . . and eighty grains of opium," Nakada said when the second kit was nearly full. "Refined yellow base." She said it offhandedly, as if it were no more important than the spirulina and the powdered ginseng.

The apothecary looked up at her. "I can't give out opium without a supply order countersigned by the camp chief."

"It's for an ambulance boat," Nakada said. To her annoyance, she could not keep a certain whining tone from creeping into her voice. "We're heading upriver, and we're leaving in the morning."

"Sorry," the apothecary said with a shrug. "No supply order, no opium."

Something of Nakada's dismay must have shown on her face, because the apothecary smiled then. "Unless . . ." He came around the counter and looked her up and down, clearly trying to see the body beneath the shapeless blue uniform. "You do something for me, maybe I could let you have, say, five grains . . ."

Nakada stared back at him. She could tell he was enjoying it, that it wasn't just the thought of sex but the thought of having power over her, not just the thought of having power over a woman but the thought of having a higher-ranking woman, a doctor and an officer, needing something that only he could give her. The smile was still on his lips. Nakada thought maybe he'd done this before.

It was the smile that did it. Nakada snapped. She stepped in close to him, seeing the smile widen, and hooked her right leg behind his, at the same time gripping his collar with one hand and his right arm with the other, pushing and twisting. His feet skidded out from under him and his head banged against the counter as he went down, knocking it over. Nakada flipped him over, using his pinioned right arm as a lever, and planted her knee in the small of his back.

With her free hand she took the scroll case with her orders out of her bag, and held it in front of his sweating face.

"See this?" she said. "This is a priority order from the Incident Fucking

Commander for the whole Antilian Mission. You want me to do something for you, all right, I'll do something for you. I'll *not* tell Doctor-General Araki that the apothecary on her supply dock here is trading Ministry supplies for sexual favors. How's that sound?"

"All *right*," the apothecary said, and Nakada warily let him up. He rubbed the back of his head. "No harm in asking, is there?"

"Eighty grains," said Nakada.

Then, as the apothecary went to unlock the opium chest: "On second thought—make it a hundred."

By daylight the supply dock had a looted, abandoned look; furniture overturned, posters askew, the deserted companionways strewn with crumpled cigarillo packets, used prophylactics, empty cans of rice wine and Antilian maize beer. Nakada sat on the afterdeck overlooking the purely decorative paddlewheel, smoking a sweet Malay-style flavored cigarillo, one of a case she'd won from an Okinawan epidemiologist at mah-jongg the night before.

The riverbank was a solid mass of green, not the deep green-black of a Kalimantan jungle or the serene unity of a bamboo forest but a motley patchwork, six or seven different shades dappled with sunlight and mottled with shadow. In the space of one cigarillo Nakada had glimpsed three different kinds of bird she'd never seen before, and heard the calls of as many more.

Hayashi lay asleep on the bristly plastic sheeting that carpeted the deck, stripped to her white undercoat in the heat, head resting on her bare arms, uniform folded for a pillow. As Nakada watched, a mosquito landed on the girl's bare shoulder, just above the pucker of an immunization scar; Nakada blew a stream of clove-scented smoke at it, and it flew away.

Shiraoka came up the stairs.

"We'd best get moving, Doctor," he said.

Nakada looked down at Hayashi. The nurse stirred in her sleep and curled a little tighter on the rough carpet. Nakada let out a cloud of smoke.

"What's the rush?" she asked. She nodded to Hayashi. "Let the kids sleep it off."

The surgeon looked at her, his face flat and unreadable.

"We've got a job to do," he said. Then he turned from Nakada to Hayashi, bent down and shook the girl's knee.

"Haya-chan," he said.

When this produced no response he straightened up and barked: "Nurse Third Class Maiko Hayashi! Front and center!"

In an instant the girl rolled to her feet and stood to attention.

"Yes, Surgeon-Sergeant!" she barked back; and to Nakada only after that did she actually seem awake.

"Nurse Hayashi, you're out of uniform!" Shiraoka said. "In five minutes I want you on deck, dressed, and looking like a Relief Ministry staffer who's proud to represent her country abroad, do you hear me?"

"Yes, Surgeon-Sergeant!" Hayashi bent to pick up her folded uniform, and scrambled down the stairs.

After a last glance at Nakada, Shiraoka followed her.

Nakada sighed, stood up, and flicked the butt of her cigarillo over the rail. She watched the water carry it away, and then trailed after the nurse and the surgeon.

"Doctor?"

Hayashi's voice came to Nakada in a golden haze, sunlight filtered through the ambulance boat's yellow plastic hull. She'd thrown a sheet over the stained but clean table in the boat's below-decks operating theater and stretched out for a nap, after dissolving three grains of the crooked apothecary's refined opium in a cup of tincture base. She remembered that clearly, but it took her a little while to remember anything else, like who and where she was.

"Yeah," she said.

"You might want to see this," said Hayashi.

Nakada opened her eyes. She sat up, fumbled for a sterile wipe, tore open the packet with her teeth and ran the wipe over her face and hands, the sudden chill of the evaporating alcohol making her shiver.

She felt great.

> *My husband and son think I'm an unnatural mother.*
>
> *When I was in Japan I thought my problem was that I was addicted to helping people. It's a syndrome so common in the Ministry that there's a name for it. Sukuidaorë. "To bring ruin upon oneself through extravagance in providing aid." As one might bring ruin upon oneself through extravagance in eating, or drinking, or gambling. There are counseling programs.*
>
> *I thought I recognized it in myself. And, like most sufferers, I didn't really see it as a problem. Truth be told, counseling programs or no counseling programs, it's not a syndrome the Ministry is all that interested in curing. As long as they can still get useful work out of you, sukuidaorë is to them essentially benign.*
>
> *My problem, as it turned out, was not essentially benign.*
> —*from the pillow book of Doctor-Lieutenant Chië Nakada*

"Don't like the look of that," Hayashi said, as she came on deck.

The river was very wide here, the banks lost beyond fields of drowned reeds that seemed to stretch to the horizon. That morning they'd passed a line of stone pilings, the remnants of some vanished causeway, crumbled like Europe's pre-Islamic ruins. The causeway ahead of them now was concrete and steel, much newer, and largely intact. But it wasn't the causeway Hayashi was looking at; it was the blackened bodies hanging from it. Dozens of them, and even at a distance Nakada could see that they were of all ages and sizes, infants and grown men, children and old people, some hanging by the neck and others by the ankles. There were animals, too: dogs, pigs, something that might have been a cat or a rabbit. Birds had been at them, and here and there Nakada could see right through them, the bright blue sky framed by bones and tattered rags.

As they passed under the causeway Nakada craned her neck to look up at the bodies, not ten meters overhead.

"They've been there a while," she said.

"What about those?" said Ishino. He wasn't looking up, but ahead, to a railroad bridge and a flock of birds that took wheeling to the air at the ambulance boat's noisy approach.

"Those are recent," said Nakada.

As they passed under the second row of bodies only Nakada looked up. Everyone tried not to breathe.

"Is that smoke?" asked Hayashi.

Beyond the railroad bridge there was an island, wide and low, sandy banks rising to densely packed pines. A gray pall hung over it.

As Shiraoka took the ambulance boat wide of the island, a semicircle of yellow-brown beach came into view, and a cluster of single-story wooden buildings, silver-gray with age; and hauled up on the beach, a drab green thing like the shell of a metal tortoise, almost as tall as the buildings and longer than any three of them put together. Somewhere back behind the little wooden village, in the interior of the island, black smoke was rising.

"Amphibious gunboat," said Shiraoka. "Andalusian."

"They're not supposed to be here," Hayashi said. "This is still the Zone."

"I know," said Shiraoka grimly. He moved the tiller, and the ambulance boat started to curve toward the beach.

"What are you doing?" Nakada said.

"Pulling in," said Shiraoka.

"No," said Nakada.

"This is still the Zone, Doctor," Shiraoka said, watching the beach. "We're responsible for what happens here."

"So radio it in," said Nakada. "The fleet can have a gyro up here in a couple of hours."

"Those bodies back there, Doctor—how long you figure it took to string them up?"

"We're supposed to be going upriver."

"We're *supposed* to be saving lives," Shiraoka said.

"You said it yourself, Sergeant, we've got a job to do," Nakada told him. "I'm ordering you not to stop. My assignment has priority."

"This is my boat, *Lieutenant*," said Shiraoka. "Till we get where you're going, you're just a passenger." He glanced back at the crew. "Hayashi, first aid," he said. "Ishino, stretcher." Then he turned back to the boat's console and revved up the fans.

They pulled up on the beach, twenty or thirty meters from the steel hulk of the gunboat. An Andalusian soldier was sitting in the gunboat's upper turret, his feet dangling through a hatch. He challenged them as Shiraoka killed the engines; but the surgeon only roared something back at him in Iberian Arabic, and thereafter paid him no attention.

Ignoring Nakada as deliberately as he ignored the Andalusian sentry, Shiraoka grabbed his own kit and jumped out of the boat. The nurses scrambled to follow, Ishino with one nervous eye on the Andalusian, Hayashi glancing back at Nakada anxiously.

Nakada followed at a leisurely pace. She could hear shots, and screams.

It had probably been a fishing village, once. Boats had been drawn high up the beach and carefully stacked, above the flood line; the Andalusians had burned the wooden ones and shot holes in the ones made of sheet metal. The houses were all on short stilts. Some of them leaned at crazy angles, having had one or two or three of their supports hacked away. Not everything had been burned, but it all smelled of fuel oil anyhow. Fuel oil and blood.

Nakada quickly lost track of Shiraoka and the others. She went toward the sound of the guns. The screams had stopped and the shots had become very methodical.

There had probably been about twenty pigs, very small ones, each about the size of a Shiba dog. The bodies were piled together in one corner of the pen. An Andalusian soldier with a jezail slung across his back was pulling them out of the pile, one by one, lining them up there in the mud. As he laid each one out, another soldier with a blunderbuss shot it in the head. A third soldier, this one with a camera over his shoulder as well as a jezail, made a mark for each pig in a small notebook.

As Nakada passed, they paused in their work, and all three of them watched her go by. She didn't make eye contact, didn't speak. As she left them behind she heard again the slap of a fifteen-kilo body hitting mud, and the clap of the blunderbuss.

The village square was only about ten meters across, and not really a square. In it, there had clearly been operating a similar process to the one Nakada had just witnessed, except that in this case the bodies were human.

About a dozen still-living Antilians were kneeling on the ground, lined up in front of what had probably been a church but was now only a blackened wooden frame. There were both boys and girls. None of them looked younger than ten or older than fifteen. Most had burns, or wounds of one kind or another, which Hayashi was busy treating; one, tended by Shiraoka, had an arm that was badly broken.

Several Andalusian soldiers stood watching. The square was silent apart from the whimpering of the children and Shiraoka's low comforting murmur as he worked on the girl's broken arm. Ishino was off to one side, squatting in the dirt, staring at the folding stretcher that lay on the ground next to him. He stood up as Nakada approached.

"What's going on?" she asked him.

"The captain there"—Ishino nodded to one of the Andalusians, a square-built man with close-cropped black hair, a sparse beard, and features that, apart from the eyes, might almost have been Japanese—"says he'll take these kids somewhere if we can get them patched up. We go along, make sure they get there." The nurse's voice was flat, his expression blank.

Nakada looked at the Andalusian captain, then at Shiraoka and the girl.

"Somewhere like where?" she asked, pitching her voice for Shiraoka to hear.

"Refugee camp, west bank," said the Andalusian captain in heavily accented Japanese. "Safe territory."

"A slave camp, you mean," said Nakada in Arabic. "In Andalusian territory."

The captain inclined his head and smiled wryly, a sort of acknowledgment of complicity between professionals. Nakada smiled back.

"It'll save lives, Doctor," Shiraoka said, not looking up from the girl with the broken arm. "Which is our job."

"Our job," Nakada said. "Right." She looked at the shivering children, and over at the Andalusian captain, and at Shiraoka. Then she knelt down and opened her formulary kit. Setting aside a can of tincture base and a ten-grain packet of refined opium, she put together the small brazier; while it heated, she filled the enameled cup with tincture base, and started to measure out a careful half-grain from the opium packet.

Then she looked at the children again, and dumped the whole packet into the cup. She took out a second packet and poured that one in after it.

When the tincture was well mixed, she took the cooling cup and went to the end of the line of children, giving each of them two full spoons. What was left over after that she gave to the girl with the broken arm.

Shiraoka's look of grudging approval turned to anger as one by one, starting with the youngest and smallest, the children began to pass out. The eyelids of the girl in his arms fluttered and closed, and she went limp. Shiraoka felt for the pulse in her throat and, not finding it, looked up at Nakada.

"What did you do?" he asked, his voice low and dangerous.

Nakada finished repacking her formulary kit and stood up.

Calmly, she answered: "I told you not to stop." To the nurses, she said: "Pack up; we're going."

Shiraoka set the dead girl down, very gently, and came to his feet, his hands clenching and unclenching.

"Back to the boat, Sergeant," Nakada said. "Let's go. That's an order."

The surgeon's jaw clenched. Then he bowed, stiffly but with great precision, and went.

Nakada sat in the shade of one of the aft prop nacelles, eyes half-closed.

"Maybe it's better," she heard Hayashi say. "I mean, better to die, than . . ." She trailed off.

"*Hayashi*," Shiraoka said. "That a *bushi* name?"

"No, Sergeant."

"You ride a horse, shoot a bow? You come from a *bushi* family?"

"No, Sergeant," she said. "*Hyakusho*. Farmers." Nakada saw Hayashi glancing back at her.

"Then I don't want to hear any more of that *bushido* bullshit."

> *I'd thought Espírito Santo was beautiful. I knew this wasn't.*
>
> *We're supposed to be neutral. But humanitarian aid always benefits one side or the other in any conflict. Sometimes it benefits both, but never in any way that balances out. Every Antilian mouth we fed in the occupied territories was a mouth the Andalusian occupiers didn't have to feed.*

Every wounded Antilian we patched up in the bishops' lands was another fighter who could go back into the bush and maybe kill someone else. Meanwhile my salary got paid and the Pure Landers got to feel good about themselves and the Ministry got to dole out fat no-bid contracts to their favorite companies to rebuild Espírito Santo's broken levees.

And as for the war itself, that was a force of nature, no more point in trying to stop it than in trying to stop the typhoon.

I remembered a Christian pageant in Kostantiniyye. Forgive them, the martyred god had said, *for they know not what they do.*

Well, I knew. It was a game, and I was done playing games.

Shiraoka was too straight to understand that. But I thought Dos Orsos might.

—*from the pillow book of Doctor-Lieutenant Chië Nakada*

La Vitoria—or as the occupying Andalusians called it, al-Qahirah—was at the edge of the Exclusion Zone. The east and west branches of the Acuamagna came together there, the East Branch coming down from the low coastal mountains some sixteen hundred kilometers away, the headwaters of the West Branch still unmapped, somewhere in the western steppes. The town, on the north shore between the two branches, had been a port, a gathering point for the commerce of half a continent. Now the ambulance boat moved across a broad, glassy, fogbound expanse of water that seemed perfectly empty and perfectly still. Even the rumble of the engines seemed muted, and what Nakada was mostly conscious of was Shiraoka's muttering over his charts and his radio navigation system. She could smell smoke.

The surgeon-sergeant looked up. "Ishino," he said. "Get the lights."

The boy went to the electrical panel, and with a hum the two rotating lights that identified the boat as an ambulance, one forward and one aft, spun up, washing the fog alternately with red and yellow.

"Is that a good idea?" Nakada asked.

"Want 'em to know we're coming," said Shiraoka.

Then Nakada heard the rattle of automatic weapons fire. Without warning, turbines roared to life somewhere in the fog off to the left, and the green-black bulk of an Andalusian gunboat heaved itself across the ambulance boat's path, close enough that Nakada fancied she glimpsed a pale face behind one of its slit gunports; then it vanished as suddenly as it had appeared, leaving the ambulance boat to leap and plunge across its broad wake. From the direction in which the gunboat had disappeared came more automatic fire, and the deeper thumping of a heavier gun, like the working of some monstrous pump or press.

A muffled cry came from Ishino at the bow. Indistinct shapes, low on the water, became the sharp hulls of steel canoes, dozens or hundreds of them, long and narrow, each holding perhaps a dozen men, each separated from the others by no more than its own length, their bows pointing northwest, as precisely aligned as iron filings in a magnetic field. Shiraoka reduced speed to avoid running them down, and with a swift movement of paddles the flotilla parted silently to let the ambulance boat pass. Nakada looked down into expressionless black eyes, flat beardless faces, some of them tattooed, some painted with tiger stripes of red and black; noted the Frankish-style fatigue jackets and the fringed Antilian leggings, the jezails and rockets that lay in the bottoms of the canoes, the long paddles caught in mid-stroke. Then the ambulance boat passed through the flotilla and the paddles dipped silently back into the water.

A coleopter whirred overhead, invisible in the fog. More gunfire came from either side now, punctuated from time to time by larger explosions. Small waves, apparently without cause or origin, passed under the ambulance boat's hull. The air smelled of gunpowder and wood smoke.

The fog cleared.

La Vitoria was on fire.

The warehouses that lined the riverbanks had already been reduced to charred skeletal frames; the commercial buildings behind were an inferno, sending up gouts of black smoke, red-lit from below. Waves of the steel canoes were crossing the lake, and men were scrambling out of them, up the pilings of broken piers and over the concrete-lined banks. Hovering coleopters poured fire into them, shells from the steel gunboats blew them apart, but they kept going, and as Nakada watched a rocket caught one of the coleopters, converting its starboard rotor nacelle into a ball of flame and sending it spinning down into the water.

In the midst of the lake, a rotating beacon like their own glowed yellow and red. Shiraoka steered toward it.

A ship was anchored, or had run aground, in the middle of the East Branch channel, and at first Nakada thought it was a Ministry hospital ship. But nearer to, it became clear that the grounded ship was too small, and also that the bright yellow was only a layer of paint hastily splashed over a hull of poured cement. A collection of yellow plastic shells, air-dropped field hospital units, had colonized the deck like some bright fungus.

Shiraoka brought the ambulance boat around to the side facing the western shore, where they found an apparently empty floating dock. They drew up next to it and Hayashi jumped up to make the boat fast to a cleat. Nakada climbed out after her.

There was something yellow in the brown water just ahead of them. Nakada looked down and realized it was an ambulance boat identical to theirs, still tied to the dock but half-sunken; it had settled until the innate buoyancy of the bullet-riddled plastic and its styrofoam core were enough to balance the weight of the fans.

"We're short on fuel," Shiraoka said to Nakada. He nodded to an unattended fuel pump. "Supplies too."

"I'll find the doctor in charge," she said.

"I'll go with you," said Hayashi. Since the river village Hayashi had treated Nakada with special delicacy, as if Nakada were a traumatized patient in need of emotional support, paying careful attention to her moods, constantly trying to do Nakada small kindnesses.

"No you won't," said Shiraoka. "Ishino, you go."

A steel ramp led from the floating dock, along the cement ship's length, up to the deck. The corrugated metal was brown with old blood.

"Watch your step," Nakada told Ishino.

The boy said nothing. Nakada glanced back at him. The nurse's beautiful face was blank as a sleepwalker's. She couldn't remember hearing him speak after We go along, make sure they get there.

As she climbed, Nakada saw that the cement ship's back had been broken in several places. Brown water boiled up through the gaps, between rusted reinforcing bars that had been pulled loose from the cement. The deck, between the yellow hospital shells, reminded her of Pachacamac after the earthquake: a badland of scaffolding, wooden planks, and steel cables bearing fluttering pennants of white danger tape.

Nakada took one look inside the first hospital shell and told Ishino to wait on deck.

She'd seen triage wards before, but never like this. Corpses—nearly all of them young men, some in Andalusian fatigues, others in the Frankish jackets and traditional leggings of the Antilian troops—were piled haphazardly at one end. Those near the bottom of the pile were soaked in their own blood and the blood of those above them, which had pooled on the floor despite the drainage holes cut into the plastic every few centimeters. Nearby, more dead men occupied several rows of cots: these presumably the ones that someone, erroneously, had thought might be saved.

A lone nurse, about Ishino's age, sat slumped in a chair at the far end of the shell from the corpses. He was asleep. Nakada was about to try to rouse him when she heard a voice from another nearby hospital shell.

The patients in this shell were not dead yet. There were four operating tables, a surgeon-sergeant and a group of nurses and orderlies bloody to the elbow busy at each one; there were more cots, and more nurses prepping the patients on the cots for surgery—and more bodies, those that had died on the operating tables.

Nurses and surgeons alike moved with the jerkiness of deep fatigue. The voice Nakada had heard, she thought at first was coming from one of the patients; it reminded her of sounds she had once heard in Siam, made by the comatose victim of an antipersonnel mine, during a trepanning operation to remove a large piece of shrapnel from the front of the brain. That patient's voice had sounded like this, slow and thick and somehow coming from a long way away, as if the speaker were conversing with the inhabitants of a world no one else could see.

This voice came, Nakada realized, from one of the surgeons. She watched him for a moment, wondering how long he had been working without real sleep, wondering if it was the patient in front of him he was operating on, or one that existed only in his dreams.

Nakada returned to the sleeping nurse in the triage area.

"Nurse," Nakada said. She had to repeat the word twice before the boy looked up.

"What?"

"Who's the doctor in charge here?" Nakada asked.

The nurse rubbed his face, looked around the hospital shell with eyes that seemed not to see the bodies, and then looked up at Nakada.

"Aren't you?" he asked.

Nakada stood up. "Never mind," she said.

She passed through the surgery again, through the recovery area in the next shell, and on to the one behind, which looked as though it would have been the dispensary, if there had been any drugs in it, and the office, if there had been any officers. Nakada found neither; only a middle-aged Apothecary-Corporal, asleep on the floor behind a writing table.

She reached down and shook the woman's shoulder. She sat up.
"Yes?"

"Know where I can find the doctor in charge?" Nakada asked.

The apothecary shook her head. "Killed," she said. "Stray rocket, two days ago." Then her eyes focused on Nakada's name-tag. "Nakada, is that your name?"

"Who else's would it be?" Nakada asked.

"Wait," said the apothecary. She stood up and went to a bag marked POST, rummaged around in it, and took out a scroll case. Attached to it was a paper tag that read NAKADA.

Nakada accepted the scroll case and tucked it into her sleeve. She took one last look around the dispensary. "Got any opium?" she asked the apothecary.

The woman only stared at her.

"Forget it," said Nakada.

Out on the deck, Nakada opened the scroll case. The letter inside was dated about a week after her meeting with Araki aboard *Mappô Maru*. She unrolled it and read:

> Two months ago Doctor-Lieutenant Sawako Noda, a five-year Ministry veteran with considerable experience in Antilia and the Varangian Rus, was sent up the Acuamagna on an assignment identical to yours.
>
> As all contact with Noda was lost after she reached La Victoria, the Ministry assumed she had been killed. At the time of your briefing, therefore, it was not deemed necessary to provide you with this information.
>
> However, circumstances have changed. Three days after the incident in Espírito Santo, Andalusian agents intercepted a film reel believed to originate in Dos Orsos' organization. The film reel and accompanying audio cylinder comprised a number of short segments of propaganda. Sawako Noda appeared in one of these segments. Her participation is believed to have been voluntary.
>
> Your assignment remains the same. However, you should be aware that, given this state of affairs, and particularly in light of the incident at Espírito Santo, the security of your assignment may be compromised.

Nakada rolled the note back up and replaced it in the case. Without bothering to tighten the cap, she tossed the case into the water. It bobbed for a moment in the foam, then sank.

She found Ishino sitting on the steel cable that marked off one of the cement ship's destroyed sections, dangling his sandaled feet over the black water, watching the rockets arc overhead.

"Come on," she said.

The boy dutifully climbed down off the cable and followed her to the floating dock.

"You find the doctor in charge?" Shiraoka asked.

Nakada shook her head. "Nobody's in charge here." She stepped onto the boat, sat down and dropped her kit to the deck. "Go ahead and fuel up, and let's get moving."

"Which way, Doctor?" Shiraoka asked.

Nakada stared at him blankly for a moment, then turned her head away.

"You know which way," she said.

The surgeon came around into her field of vision.

"You see that out there, Doctor?" he asked, nodding to the men dying as they struggled up the banks toward La Vitoria. "That's what this war is. That's what Antilia is. People coming over here from across the ocean trying to change things, trying to run things—people been trying that ever since those goddamn bishops showed up here a thousand goddamn years ago! What makes you think you can do better?"

Nakada picked up her kit and stood up. It was starting to rain.

"Just get us upriver," she said.

"Why?" Shiraoka demanded. "Look at this place! What fucking assignment could you even *have* up here?"

"*Just get us upriver!*" Nakada barked.

She stared at the surgeon till he moved aside.

Nakada went below. She stretched out on the operating table and closed her eyes. After a little while, under the clatter of the rain on the plastic hull, she heard the engines starting up, and felt the boat begin to move.

Upriver.

After La Vitoria, the East Branch was a different world. A series of blue and yellow banners erected by the Ministry optimistically promised peace and safety to anyone passing into the Exclusion Zone; and though the ambulance boat passed them in the wrong direction, it was as if those hopeful words had some force nevertheless. Past the banners, the rain closed in behind them like a curtain drawn across war and memory. They continued upstream between green banks that seemed untouched by violence, quiet without the unnatural silence of Espírito Santo, and they were the only thing moving on the river. Ishino began to speak again, and Hayashi to smile, and even Shiraoka seemed to have decided on a truce with Nakada, or at any rate a cease-fire.

They pulled in at a floating dock belonging to an abandoned farm on the south bank: little more than a mismatched pair of wooden sheds with their roofs caved in, overlooking a weed-choked melon field guarded by a single scarecrow made out of a flapping leather coat stretched over two crossed boards. Ishino and Hayashi went to pick melons while Shiraoka worked on one of the rotor nacelles. Nakada stretched out on the roof of the pilothouse. The rain had stopped for the moment, and Nakada stared up into the blank gray sky with an extraordinary sense of inversion, as if she were not beneath the clouds but above them, looking down onto a silent unknown world. She was not sure whether she actually drifted off. But she had a definite sense of being startled from sleep, just before she heard Hayashi's shriek.

Nakada sat up, and saw the young nurse running—stumbling, staggering, falling—away from the larger shed, swatting at something Nakada couldn't see, while from across the field Ishino watched, dumbstruck.

Shiraoka must have seen something Nakada had not; he grabbed an aid kit and a sack of signal flares and jumped out onto the dock. By the time Nakada caught up with him, he had already lit a pair of smoke bombs, and it was through a sulfurous yellow cloud that Nakada, coughing, approached the surgeon and the fallen nurse.

"Anaphylactic shock," said Shiraoka curtly. Lemon-yellow hornets, dozens of them, their black-banded, bullet-shaped bodies as long as the first joint of Nakada's little finger, crawled over Hayashi's blue uniform, dazed by the smoke. The nurse's face and hands and feet were swollen with stings, and she was not breathing.

Shiraoka pounded Hayashi's chest, tried to blow air into her lungs. Nakada set up her formulary kit and started mixing a dose of synthetic ephedra; it seemed that the little brazier had never taken so long to bring the dosage cup to a boil.

"Get the ventilator!" Shiraoka yelled to Ishino. He took a tracheotomy tube from the aid kit and a utility knife from his belt and made an incision across Hayashi's swollen throat, while Nakada turned up the heat on the brazier.

It didn't matter. Long before the mixture was ready, or Ishino returned with the heavy bag containing the air compressor, Hayashi was dead.

Shiraoka took the bag containing the remaining smoke bombs and flares, set fire to one end of it, and tossed it through the open door of the large shed. Nakada caught a glimpse of a giant, grotesque lump, more like a termite mound of Ifriq-iya than any sort of hornet's nest; there had been some sort of machine in the shed, a vehicle or some piece of farm equipment, but the nest had swollen to completely engulf it, and now pressed against the sides of the small building.

Then the yellow smoke billowed out and obscured Nakada's view.

They burned Hayashi's body on the bank, an aluminum stretcher for her bier, for her pyre bits of the lattice that had held the melon vines and flat boards pried from the siding of the smaller shed. They all three lit incense, and Ishino read a sutra. It began to rain again; the wet wood burned stubbornly, even after Shiraoka drenched it in fuel oil, and produced a great deal of white smoke, which drifted up until it mixed with the low clouds. The wind kept shifting erratically, and in the end Nakada and the boat's crew had to stand several tens of meters away.

After the fire had burned out, Shiraoka handed Nakada a pair of chopsticks, keeping another for himself. Nakada stared uncomprehendingly at them for a long moment; then she understood. Wordlessly, she and the surgeon gathered Hayashi's bones and placed them in a Ministry-issue steel urn. Nakada found herself thinking of the young nurse's round face and tanned muscular limbs; for all that solidity she'd had in life, her blackened bones were surprisingly light.

"Get me up the Río Baldío," Nakada told him. "To whatever the first town is, up there. I'll make my own way after that; you and the boy can head back."

"Anything you say, Doctor," Shiraoka replied coldly. He took the urn and stored it below decks, and they continued upriver.

A little while later the rain stopped. About the same time the trees along the north bank gave way to an open field filled with glossy-leaved shrubs bearing flowers of white and pale yellow, as far as the eye could see. It must have been a plantation, before the war, but it was overgrown now, the flowers rioting out of control, spilling down the bank.

The sun came out. No one spoke.

For four or five kilometers it went on like that, as if heaven had fallen to earth in the form of gardenias.

Then the trees closed in again, and the rain.

It was near nightfall of the second day after Hayashi's funeral when they came to the confluence of the East Fork and the Baldío, and turned southeast, up the smaller river. The banks narrowed, closed in, became the sloping concrete walls of a canal. The rain came down harder, hammering at the green surface of the water, deforming it like metal. Shapes of incomprehensible buildings rose on either shore, presenting blank faces to the river, cutting ragged edges against the lowering sky, but there was nothing that looked like an inhabited town. The current was strong and the boat seemed to be making almost no headway. Shiraoka's eyes were moving constantly, relentlessly scanning the water ahead for floating debris.

"Can't see shit," he muttered.

They passed a boat ramp, wide and shallow, its surface a sheet of running water. Drawn up on it were ten or a dozen bizarre craft, leaning against one another, looking long abandoned: each as long as the ambulance boat but narrower, their decks enclosed in riveted plates of sheet-metal and inset with pop-eyed domes of glass, their profiles spiked and finned as if in imitation of some evil marine reptile of a past age. The hulls were rusted and some of the glass domes had been shattered, so the rainwater poured through dark gaping sockets.

Then came a weirdly narrow railroad bridge, not cantilevered like the gallows-bridges over the Acuamagna but hanging in a loose catenary curve, the cars of a stopped train huddled in the center like beads strung on a wire, all of them painted in garish colors, glistening in the rain. When the train was directly overhead Nakada suddenly realized it was a miniature, the cars no larger than quarter-scale.

They rounded a bend.

Abruptly, something huge and horrible rose from the river in front of them. An iron-black monster with seven dragon heads, each nearly half as large as the boat itself, its eyes small and red and evil. Water poured off its spiky black scales as it reared itself to its full height.

From forty meters above, the seven heads looked down at the ambulance boat, and white fire crackled along their crests as all seven opened their mouths and roared in challenge.

Shiraoka swore, dropped the ground-effect skirt and threw the tiller hard over. The boat roared up out of the water and onto the sloping concrete bank.

Nakada looked back at the monster. It was paying them no attention, the seven heads still roaring down at the empty stretch of river where the boat had been. As she watched, one head crackled with blue sparks and the red light in its eyes went out.

"It's just a machine, damn it!" she yelled into Shiraoka's ear. "It's a puppet! They're trying to scare us!"

Fireworks or gunshots were going off on either side of the canal. More roars, electric, distorted, came out of the rain. The surgeon-sergeant rounded on her, his eyes wild.

"How the fuck do you know, Doctor?" he shouted. "You don't even know what the fuck you're doing here! You don't know a fucking thing!"

The boat roared over the lip of the bank, plowed through a chain-link fence and down a broad muddy slope. A lake spread out before them, and in the middle of it a fantastic island rose, crowded with towers, lit with torches and colored lights. Shiraoka turned to shout at Nakada again.

A line of multicolored globes flickered to life, just in front of them. Nakada ducked. Shiraoka turned back, and the cable caught him across the throat. It picked the surgeon up, snagged on the cages surrounding the forward fans, and dropped him, as with an awful cracking sound like living bone breaking the fan nacelles were wrenched loose from their mountings. Nakada was thrown forward, into the pilothouse. Her head slammed against the console.

When she recovered her senses, Nakada was staring at Shiraoka's mottled face. His windpipe had been crushed. She felt for the utility knife on her belt, uncapped it. She had never performed a tracheotomy before. The procedure that had failed to save Hayashi's life was the first one Nakada had ever seen. Cutting was surgeon's work.

As she hesitated, trying to decide where to make the incision, she saw Shiraoka looking at her. She didn't know what was in his eyes—professional contempt? or simple hatred?

She moved the knife up to cut, and the surgeon grasped her wrist. The strength in his broad hand was incredible. She struggled to pull away, and found her back up against the side of the pilothouse. Shiraoka squeezed, until Nakada imagined she could feel her bones grinding together, and the utility knife dropped. The surgeon's hand relaxed. His eyelids closed, and then rolled slowly open.

Nakada stood up shakily. The ambulance boat was on the lake, turning in a slow circle.

"Ishino," she called. "Come up here and take the tiller."

The nurse pulled himself up from the bottom of the boat and came forward. He stopped when he saw Shiraoka's body.

"He's dead," Nakada said shortly. "Take the tiller."

Ishino shook himself and did as he was told, muttering some hypnotic Nichiren chant under his breath.

"Steer toward the island," Nakada said. "Toward the lights."

A pair of long piers stretched out into the lake, lit by lines of torches in standing brackets. At Nakada's nod, Ishino steered the boat between them, toward a broad, floodlit dock at the end. The piers were crowded with people.

"Cut the engine," Nakada said quietly.

Ishino kept muttering. His eyes were half closed.

Nakada looked at the lines of men and women on the piers. These were not the disciplined, tiger-striped canoe soldiers of La Vitoria. Fringed buckskin jackets were worn over ragged Andalusian uniforms, or over incongruous beaded leggings and chests bare but for elaborate tattoos. The neck of each watcher was hung with a magpie litter of necklaces and medals and medallions. Some had jezails or air-guns, and bandoliers or ammunition belts slung across their chests; others had quivers and long straight bows.

"Ishino!" she said, sharp now. "Cut the damned engine!"

The boy opened his eyes, focusing immediately on the boat's console, to the exclusion of everything outside. He cut the engine, and momentum carried them toward the dock, the boat yawing slightly, an eddying current starting to swing the stern around.

Nakada stepped out onto the bow and uncoiled a few meters of line. When the dock was close enough, she jumped across and made the line fast to a cleat. Then she looked up.

The structure that loomed above the dock, lit starkly from below by hidden electric lamps, was a squat, blocky trapezoid ten meters high, with faceless winged statues at the corners, an imitation of some sandstone ruin of Egypt or Persia in concrete and plaster, but overgrown now with crawling vines that would have no place in those desert lands. Silhouettes of more people topped the roofline.

Nakada went up the slope. The facsimile temple or tomb was only a few meters thick, little more than an archway; a path lined with worn nonskid led up through the half-darkness to light beyond.

As Nakada left the darkness of the archway, the breeze seemed to shift, bringing with it a taint of rottenness, like preserved meat badly cured and left to spoil in its packaging. She came out from under the arch into a wide courtyard of concrete flagstones. More buildings surrounded it, in the same grandiose, antique style, and more fanciful statues.

Along one side of the square was a row of crosses, crude things cut from raw yellow timber, each perhaps three meters tall and two across the arms. On each cross, nailed there with thick railroad spikes through the bones of forearms and ankles, was a man.

A crowd was gathering at the opposite edge of the square: ragged fighters like the ones on the canal, but others, too: women, and old men, and many children, all quietly watching the newcomer. One of the women was Japanese.

"Noda?" said Nakada.

The woman watched her with the same impassive concentration as the others. There was no sign she had heard.

Nakada approached the nearest cross. The man on it had been dead, she guessed, at least a week. Birds had plucked out the eyes, and a wide trail of tiny ants, each no larger than a poppyseed, crawled in and out of the open mouth and down the upright post. The man's clothes, gold and white Chinese silk stained with blood and vomit and heavy rain, were those of a high functionary of the Christian church. Greek letters had been branded crudely into the man's forehead before he died, with something like a hot steel wire. Nakada made out the word PPOAGWGOS, which she understood as *leader onward*. She stepped back.

The crowd parted to reveal a small, upright figure: a woman, dressed in a colorful Antilian garment as shapeless as a horse blanket, her long, gray-shot black hair falling free on either side of a simple central part. Clara Dos Orsos was older now than when Kawabata's photograph was taken, but there was no mistaking the eyes in her flat Antilian face.

The Virgin of Apalaxia raised a hand toward Nakada, and the crowd fell in around her.

The room, on an upper floor of one of the mock-sandstone ruins, was dark, claustrophobic, its doors, its narrow windows and the squared-off arch of its ceiling all built to two-thirds scale. Nakada's hair brushed the ceiling, and the pair of weatherbeaten female fighters who held her arms had to stoop to enter.

"What is your religion, Doctor? Are you a Buddhist?"

Dos Orsos' Greek was fluent, almost unaccented, reminding Nakada of her professors in Kostantiniyye. The ex-nun sat on a low cot, a stripe of gray light from one of the windows falling across her face as she looked up for Nakada's answer.

"I'm a doctor," Nakada said. "Healing is my religion."

Nakada's bag sat on the pallet in front of Dos Orsos. She watched as the ex-nun upended it, dumping the formulary kit, the packet containing Kawabata's ampoules of antipsychotic, the larger packet containing what was left of the opium base from the crooked supply-dock apothecary. Dos Orsos picked up that packet and tossed it so it lay unopened on the floor halfway between the cot and Nakada.

"You're an addict," Dos Orsos pronounced. "Opium is your religion."

Nakada opened her mouth, then closed it again. She had no answer to that.

"What is this place?" she asked, eventually.

"What place?"

"This place. This island. These buildings." Nakada nodded her head toward the window. "That square."

"The island?" said Dos Orsos. "Seven Cities? It was a theme park, once. Éfeso, Esmirna, Pérgamo, Tiatira, Sardes, Filadélfia, Laodicéia . . . seven. This bit, this was Esmirna." Nakada recognized the names from the Russian poet's litany. "For the Christian tourist trade, the Romans and Franks." Dos Orsos smiled sadly. "Your people built most of it, as it happens. It wasn't very successful."

"And now?" asked Nakada.

Dos Orsos was quiet for a long time. Then, she responded with a question: "Did they tell you why, Doctor? Why they wanted you to . . . treat my condition?"

"They told me you were schizophrenic," Nakada said. She seemed to be hearing her own voice from a long way away, clinical, emotionless, physician's notes, an audio-cylinder voice. "That you might be psychotic."

In the darkness, Dos Orsos' eyes closed.

"They told me that you were responsible for the Espírito Santo . . . incident," Nakada continued. "That your people built the . . . device."

"The bomb," Dos Orsos said, eyes still closed. "We must always strive to call things by their true names . . ." Her eyes opened. "And am I responsible, Doctor?"

Nakada looked around the room. It had never been meant for human habitation. The walls were unfinished wood, the floor rough cement. Water was running down one wall, pooling in a corner. Dos Orsos' cot had been nailed together from unfinished logs, wrist-thick saplings cut down and crudely stripped. The beaded dress the ex-nun wore under her striped woolen mantle had been beautiful once but was now patched and stained.

"I don't know about *responsible*," Nakada said. "But from what I've seen, I'm not sure your people here could build a roof to keep out the rain."

The women took Nakada to another building, a shockingly ordinary twelve-story tower block that, apart from the fact that it appeared to have been abandoned half-finished, would not have looked out of place in the suburbs of Naniwa or Kostantiniyye. It was only as they led Nakada through the deserted lobby and past the steel door of the fire stairs that she realized it was supposed to be a hotel.

Most of the rooms on the fourth floor were unfinished, their doorways gaping empty, but one had been fitted with a crude metal grill, something that looked salvaged from a factory or a foundry. One of the women slid it open, and the other pushed Nakada into the room. There was a cot there like Dos Orsos', its mattress a simple slab of Annamese latex, yellow foam mottled with brown stains and blue mold. There were rawhide straps at each corner.

The women pushed her toward it. Nakada balked then, but her Ministry self-defense kenpo course was far behind her now and unlike the corrupt apothecary back at the supply dock, Nakada's Antilian guards were ready for her. After a brief struggle she was tied securely down, gasping for breath and trying fruitlessly to curl around the pain of a sharp knee in the kidneys.

She expected more beating, or worse, but instead she heard the metal grill clang shut, and the women left her alone, with herself.

There was no need, Nakada thought, for the Antilians to torture her; her addict's body quickly took that task for its own. Her head ached. Her muscles ached. Her spine. She itched, all over her skin, outside and inside too, as if the ants eating at the corpse of the crucified bishop had finished that meal and started on Nakada's living flesh. She shook as if with fever, and quickly became fevered. When she was awake, she strained to sleep; when she was asleep, her dreams were prolonged bouts of hallucinatory terror, in which Shiraoka, Hayashi, the dead children of the river village and the charred dead of Espírito Santo all came to her in turn.

She saw the Russian, Semyonov, there, sitting at the foot of the bed, back straight, legs crossed, arms slack at his sides, palms outward.

"I came here thinking the New World was a metaphysical battlefield," the poet said. His Greek, in this hallucination, was much better than Nakada remembered it; or perhaps it was not Greek he was speaking at all, but Russian, a language which as far as Nakada knew she had never heard. "Wanderers from the Old World, like you and me, we enter at our peril! But I was wrong."

He had acquired another tattoo, Nakada noticed, this one a stylized fish made from two intersecting curves; the scab had not yet healed, and the skin around it was swollen and red. She thought he should get it looked at.

"My people," the Russian continued, "your people, the Caliph's people, even the bishops—all wrong. The arrogance! It's beyond preposterous—it's perverse."

"You think all *this*—" said Shiraoka, who was suddenly there, at the tiller of the boat; he waved an arm to take in the dilapidated hotel room, the island, the entire continent—"is just props, for the break-up of one petty Japanese mind. You're wrong."

She had other visitors, more tangible.

Sometimes it was silent Noda at her bedside, checking her temperature and her pulse, bathing her itching skin, salving the raw places on Nakada's wrists and ankles where she strained against the rawhide straps, forcing cups of this or that remedy—but never opium—down her throat.

Other times it was Dos Orsos. She would take over Noda's nursing duties; or she would simply sit and listen, while Nakada screamed and wept and begged for opium, for death, for release from her captivity or from her nightmares.

During this time Nakada had a recurring dream. She was standing in a narrow, deserted street in a great white city under a gray sky, before an open pair of wide wooden doors. Beyond them a long staircase led up into darkness. In the shadow at the top of the stairs there waited, Nakada knew, two women dressed in black, one plump, one thin, though she could not see them in the gloom. She was about to make them, or their master, a promise—a solemn promise, founded on a lie. She knew this was wrong, but the white city at her back pushed her forward on a wave of expectation and obligation.

She stepped through the doorway.

The sky went bright.

Nakada woke. She had the feeling she'd been awake for a long time, but she didn't know how long, didn't know how long she'd been lying on the cot with her eyes open, staring at the dirty plaster ceiling. The rawhide straps that had bound her wrists and ankles were gone.

She stood up. Sunlight was coming through a window. She shuffled over to it. Her joints seemed to be full of sand. She felt a thousand years old.

She wanted opium. Not in a desperate way. Just for medicinal purposes. She thought that for anyone who felt the way she did, opium should be a basic human right.

Outside the window, a long way down, she saw Noda. She was in the middle of a wide expanse of gray concrete, wearing a striped Antilian garment like Dos Orsos', going through a very slow *taikyokuken* routine. A ring of Antilian children, perhaps a hundred of them, sat and watched her; Ishino was among them, wearing a fringed Antilian shirt over his faded blue Ministry trousers.

Noda finished her routine. She turned to face the building Nakada was in, and saluted in the Chinese manner, back straight, hands together in front of her chest. Then her hands dropped to her sides and she lowered her head. She stood there like that, while her audience drifted away in ones and twos. Ishino was one of the first to leave. The children were all gone, and Noda was still standing there, when Nakada turned away.

"Come out," said Clara Dos Orsos. "It's not locked."

Nakada had the run of the park, more or less. She thought she probably could have left at any time, taken the ambulance boat and gone back across the lake and down the Río Baldío, but something she couldn't put a name to kept her there.

It wasn't Ishino. The boy, when Nakada saw him, gave no sign of recognizing her, while the islanders for their part treated the young nurse like some sort of holy fool, the women giving him food, the children leading him by the hand. With Nakada they were more wary, as if Dos Orsos' attention and protection came at the cost of some contagious bad luck.

The inhabitants left her largely alone, and so it was alone that she wandered through the ruined park, among the imitation ruins that seemed somehow even less real now that they were truly ruined, stood under the great sign over the park's main entrance that spelled out SEVEN CITIES OF GOLD in Antilian, Latin, and Greek; climbed the frames of the broken rides and examined the still dioramas formed by unmoving marionettes meant to illustrate the legends of the Christian apocalypse, watched the islanders go about their lives, watched from a distance as Noda taught them the rudiments of *reiki* and acupuncture.

In the "city" called Filadélfia, there was a more or less fully functional film studio. It was here, Nakada supposed, that Noda had made the propaganda segment referred to in the message given to her at La Vitoria, but it seemed to have fallen into disuse since then. Nakada played a few of the audio cylinders, selected more or less at random. The recordings, almost invariably of Dos Orsos' voice, were in Antilian, but she could make out a word here and there. Mainly these were familiar names: *Antilia, Andalus, Espírito Santo*; but there were other words as well, that grew familiar through repetition: *bispos, mártires, bomba, Anticristo, Babilônia.*

And, eventually, always, she found herself returning to Dos Orsos' room, in the section of park the ex-nun had called Esmirna.

"You know I'm not cured," she told Dos Orsos once. "You can't cure opium addiction through simple withdrawal. The drug causes long-term changes in the hypothalamus and the pituitary gland."

"It doesn't matter," Dos Orsos told her. "And perhaps if you were cured you'd no longer be of any use to me."

Nakada knew that by this the ex-nun was referring, obliquely, to Noda, though she didn't know just what Dos Orsos meant.

"Like the bishops weren't of any use?" Nakada asked, glancing down into the courtyard.

Dos Orsos didn't answer. Instead, she asked: "Have you ever been to Córdoba, Doctor?"

"Once," said Nakada.

"Did you visit the *Mathaf al-Andalus,* the great museum in Madinat as-Zahra, the palace of Abd ar-Rahman?"

Nakada shook her head. She had visited the Andalusian capital on a holiday, with a dozen other students from Kostantiniyye. Her memories of the greatest city of the Western world mostly involved a series of drinking houses, dance halls and hashish parlors along the lower Wadi al-Kabîr.

"Before the convent, I lived in Córdoba for seven years," Dos Orsos said.

"There are a great many poor Antilians in Iberia and Italia, did you know that? The languages are easier than most for an Antilian to learn, and the *moros* hardly distinguish one Christian from another. A group of Roman missionaries took me and seventeen other girls from our homes here and brought us to Compostela. For a few years they taught us Latin and Greek, then they ran out of money. With three other girls I made it to Córdoba, because if you are poor and alone in Iberia that is what you do, you go to Córdoba . . . And there we fell in with a procurer. Is *procurer* correct?" The word she used was προαγωγος.

"Ματρυλλος," Nakada supplied: *pimp*.

"Ah, yes." Dos Orsos said. "It's not a word much used in ecclesiastical Greek, you know, though perhaps it should be . . . Well, this pimp, he was a clever man. The three other girls and I, we were still too young for the ordinary sort of work. But we could read and write. We spoke Antilian and Greek. And he had some other girls our age who spoke Frankish and Arabic—even one who, don't ask me how, spoke Chinese. And he sent us out to Madinat as-Zahra and the courtyard of the *Mathaf al-Andalus* to beg.

"Now, you will be asking yourself: 'What's so clever about that?'"

Nakada, who had not had any thought so concrete, said nothing.

"What is clever," said Dos Orsos, "is this: He didn't simply send us out to beg. First he dressed us in respectable clothes. He had one of the older girls do our hair in a respectable way—sober, with white scarves, like little *moro* schoolgirls. And he went to a printer, and had the printer make up some forms that said, in five or six languages, *Association for the meritorious relief of the poor and dispossessed*, or something similarly impressive and official. And suddenly we weren't a mob of little beggar girls, we were collectors of alms for a charitable cause. We took in more money in an hour than most of the *Mathaf* beggars made in a day, and everyone who gave it to us got a carbon-copied receipt."

"And the pimp got a copy of the receipt, too," Nakada guessed. "So he knew you weren't holding out on him."

"Very good."

"And the bishops? The προαγωγοι?" Nakada asked.

"*Make not thy daughter a common strumpet, lest the land be defiled, and filled with wickedness,*" Dos Orsos recited, and Nakada supposed that was her answer.

But she thought then that it was not understanding the ex-nun expected from her, but something else.

I was there for days; maybe for weeks.

They all wanted the same thing—the Ministry, Doctor-General Araki, Araki's slick Caliphate drinking companion, even Dos Orsos. Even Noda probably preferred Dos Orsos the martyr to Dos Orsos the prophet.

But I wasn't there for them. Not for Noda and Dos Orsos, not for Araki and the politicians, and I couldn't even pretend any more that I was there for the Ministry.

The Pure Land School believes that through the intercession of the Amida buddha we can all reach salvation in a single lifetime. As to the exact mechanism by which this is to be achieved, opinions differ. Some say that through repetition of Amida's name one achieves rebirth not in this

*world but in the Pure Land, where all who are born are reborn into Nir-
vana. Others say that Nirvana is the Pure Land itself.
All I know is, Amida has his work cut out for him.
—from the pillow book of Doctor-Lieutenant Chië Nakada*

One night, Nakada woke to the sound of bells.

She looked out the window of her room—not the room in the unfinished
hotel but another that she had appointed for herself, in a faux-Roman building in
the city called Pérgamo—and saw the square below filled by a procession of silent marchers. The marchers wore long white robes and tall black hoods; they
carried pale candles, and the candles were as tall as the marchers themselves.
Their bare feet made no noise on the flagstones.

The bells were carried by a small handful of marchers, perhaps one in ten; these
were followed by great gilded palanquins, on which more candles were arrayed
around central figures, seated or standing: a bearded king in purple robes, a woman
all in white carrying an infant child, another woman in black, weeping. Canopies
were stretched above each palanquin, from which hung glittering drops of crystal
and tiny silver mirrors like coins, that caught the candlelight and reflected it in all
directions; Nakada could hear them tinkling, over the ringing of the bells.

She went down into the square. In the dark beyond the candles, a crowd of
islanders watched the procession go by. From time to time one of the marchers
would call out, and the crowd, together, would chant a response. Many of the crowd
wore uniforms of a sort Nakada didn't recall seeing before: red, with a crest in
the shape of a seven-pointed star. The uniforms were threadbare but clean; some
had name badges.

It was only when she noticed the same crest pressed into the concrete corner-
stone of a building that Nakada realized that many of the islanders that she had
taken for guerrilla fighters, or aboriginal Antilian savages in a state of nature,
were only the theme park's former employees and their families.

And then, behind the palanquins and the silent marchers with their candles,
came the machines.

There were riders, larger than life, electrically lit from within and mounted
on horses that leaked steam from their joints. There was the dragon that had
roared at the ambulance boat from the river, its burnt-out head again in working
order. There were monsters whose heads were the heads of beasts and whose
bodies were covered in eyes. There were cities and temples and castles that moved
on wheels, lights twinkling behind every tiny window.

The procession moved through the seven cities, in the order Semyonov and
Dos Orsos had named them: Éfeso, Esmirna, Pérgamo, Tiatira, Sardes, Filadélfia, Laodicéia. Nakada followed.

In the central square, the crucified skeletons of the bishops watched over a
mock battle between a great red snake and an angel in golden armor. Nakada
saw Ishino looking up at the battling figures in awe. A trap door opened, and the
snake sank down into it, and a cheer went up from the crowd.

Dos Orsos was nowhere to be seen. Nakada looked up toward the ex-nun's
window, and saw a flash of white. She made her way to the back of the crowd and
went up into Dos Orsos' building.

The ex-nun was seated on the bed. Nakada's formulary kit lay open on the mattress in front of her. Dos Orsos had found, or someone—Noda? Nakada didn't think so—had shown her, the trick panel that concealed Kawabata's ampoules of experimental antipsychotic.

"They used to do this every night," Dos Orsos said, looking out the window. "Not the candles, but the parade, the lights." There was a sound like a mortar being fired, and a star shell burst somewhere far above, sending a wash of red light across the room. "*And I heard, as it were the voice of thunder, one of the four beasts, saying: Come and see; and I saw . . .*"

She turned to Nakada. "It doesn't matter who built the bomb," she said. "Say the bishops built it, and feared to use it. It doesn't matter who set it off, or why, whether it was done in my name, or the bishops', or the name of the Caliph of Córdoba."

"Or the name of the Regent of Yoshino," Nakada suggested.

Dos Orsos inclined her head.

From the courtyard, Nakada heard the sound of trumpets. She looked down, and saw that a throne had risen up from the ground, and seated on it was the figure of a white-haired man in European robes. Seven angels stood in front of the throne, each with an open book.

"*And the books were opened,*" Dos Orsos recited. "*And another book was opened, which is the book of life: and the dead were judged out of those things which were written in the books, according to their works.*"

Nakada thought of the children in the river village. She thought of Hayashi's pyre, and then of Hayashi herself, as she had first seen her, in the sunlight of the Gulf of Mexico. She thought for the first time in weeks of her own husband and son, who, she was sure now, she would never see again.

"You understand," Dos Orsos said suddenly, as if she had seen the thought in Nakada's mind. "The blood of the children of Espírito Santo is on all our hands. All of us will answer on the day of judgment. *Now all these things happened unto them for ensamples,*" she said, "*and they are written for our admonition, upon whom the ends of the world are come.*"

Nakada looked down at the open formulary kit. She wondered for the first time, and was surprised to realize it was for the first time, what those ampoules actually contained.

"I know whose blood is on my hands," she told Dos Orsos. "It's not for me to tell you whose is on yours."

She turned to go. In the doorway, she hesitated.

"I'm sorry."

In the morning she found Ishino, took him by the hand, and led him down to the dock, where the ambulance boat was still tied up. One of the remaining engines started on the second try.

She took the boat across the lake—not west, toward the channel of the Río Baldío, but east. On the eastern shore, in the small town of San Lucas, she traded the boat and most of its contents for a pack llama, a waterbag, and two wool blankets, keeping only one bag of medical supplies and another of soy flakes and rice. She found a road leading up into the hills.

Near the top of the ridge, she looked back once. There was a black bank of clouds on the southern horizon, and below them an impenetrable darkness. But here, the sun was out, the dirt track was lined with poplar trees, and the air smelled clean and fresh. She took out Shiraoka's chart, and made certain of her direction: away from the war, into the blank places on the map.

Somewhere there must be people who had never heard of al-Andalus, or of Japan, or of anyone's end of the world.

Nakada let the chart flutter away on the wind. In one hand she took Ishino's again, and in the other the llama's lead rope, and they started walking. She didn't look back again.

again and again and again

RACHEL SWIRSKY

Here's an incisive and amusing study of future shock played out over a number of generations, showing us once again that the more things change, the more they remain the same. . . .

New writer Rachel Swirsky has published in *Subterranean, Tor.com, Interzone, Fantasy Magazine, Weird Tales,* and elsewhere, and her work has been nominated for the Hugo, Nebula, and Sturgeon Awards. Her most recent books are *Eros, Philia, Agape; A Memory of Wind,* a collection, *Through the Drowsy Dark,* and, as editor, the anthology *People of the Book: A Decade of Jewish Science Fiction & Fantasy,* coedited with Sean Wallace.

It started with Lionel Caldwell, born in 1900 to strict Mennonites who believed drinking, dancing, and wearing jewelry were sins against God. As soon as Lionel was old enough, he fled to the decadent city where he drank hard liquor from speakeasies, cursed using the Lord's name, and danced with women who wore bobbie socks and chin-length hair.

Lionel made a fortune selling jewelry. Rubies and sapphires even kept him flush during the Great Depression. He believed his riches could see him through any trouble—and then Art was born.

Lionel had left his breeding late, so Art grew up in the sixties. He rejected his father's conservative values in favor of peace, love, and lack of hygiene. He dated negroes and jewesses shamelessly, and grew out his dark hair until it fell to his waist.

"What the hell have you done?" demanded Lionel when Art came home from college, ponytail trailing down his back. Before Art could defend himself, Lionel slammed down his whiskey glass. "You make me sick," he said, and stormed out of the den.

Eventually Art annoyed his father further by marrying a Jewess whose father was a Hollywood producer. Reluctantly, Lionel attended the wedding. Drunk on the generous bar provided by Art's new father-in-law, Lionel became open-hearted. "You all are the good kind of Jews," he explained to Jack Fieldstone né Goldman over the champagne toast. For the sake of family harmony, Jack held his tongue.

Art's wife Esther was a career woman with a professorship in Art History at San

Francisco State College. She made it clear that children were not happening until she had tenure and so their two daughters weren't born until the mid-eighties.

Sage was the elder, round with baby-fat, and gruff instead of sweet. She wore her hair in a rainbow-dyed Mohawk, thrust a ring through her nose, and stomped around in chains and combat boots. She earned cash fixing the neighbors' computers, and spent her profits on acid tabs and E.

The younger daughter, Rue, appeared more demure—but only until she took off her loose sweatshirts and jeans to reveal her extensive tattoos and DIY brands. Tribal tattoos patterned her arms down to the wrists, making her own pale skin look like a pair of gloves. Cartoon characters and brand names formed a sarcastic billboard on her back. Japanese kanji spelled out "Abandon all hope ye who enter here" on her inner thighs—which had on multiple occasions helped her sift wheat from chaff. She explained that she was saving up for something called lacing, which made even Sage retch a little when she heard what it was.

"I feel sorry for you two," Art told Sage and Rue. "All my generation had to do to aggravate our parents was grow out our hair. What's going to happen to your children?"

Sage turned out to be the breeder, so she got to find out. Her eldest son, Paolo, joined an experimental product trial to replace his eyes, nose, and ears with a sensitive optic strip. Lucia crossed her DNA with an ant's and grew an exoskeleton that came in handy when she renounced her parents' conscientious objector status and enlisted in the army. Javier quit college to join a colony of experimental diseasists and was generous enough to include photographs of his most recent maladies every year in his holiday cards.

Things got worse, too. By the time Paolo had kids, limb regeneration was the fashion. Teens competed to shock each other with extreme mutilations. Paolo's youngest, Gyptia, won a duel with her high school rival by cutting off her own legs, arms, breasts, and sensory organs.

When he saw what she'd done, Paolo stifled his urge to scream. "'Pie," he said, carefully, "isn't this going a bit far?"

Gyptia waited until she regrew her eyes, and then she rolled them.

By the time Gyptia reached adulthood, life spans had passed the half-millennia mark. Her generation delayed family life. Why go through all the fuss of raising babies now when they could stay fancy-free for another few decades?

At three hundred and fifty, Gyptia's biological clock proclaimed itself noisily. She backed out of the lease on her stratoflat and joined a child-friendly cooperative in historical Wyoming that produced wind energy. Current and former residents raved about its diversity. The co-op even included a few nuclear families bonded by ancient religious rituals.

Gyptia's daughter, Xyr, grew up surrounded by fields of sage brush dotted with windmills. She and her friends scrambled up the sandstone bluffs and pretended to live in stratoflats like the ones their parents had left behind.

Every option was open to Xyr: a vast range of territory for her to explore, monthly trips to see the technological and artistic wonders of the modern world, educational and entertainment databases linked in by speed pulse. Her neighbors included: polyamorists, monogamists, asexuals, traditionalists, futurists, historics, misanthropists, genetic hybrids, biomechanical biblends, purists, anarchists, exortates, xenophiles, menthrads, ovites, alvores and ilps.

Xyr grew her hair long and straight. She had no interest in recreational drugs beyond a sip of wine at holidays. She rejected a mix of eagle and bat genes to improve her hearing and eyesight, and she kept her skin its natural multiracial brown instead of transfusing to a fashionable scarlet.

When all the adults got nostalgic and gathered to inject themselves with Lyme's disease and rubella and chicken pox, Xyr and her friends held dances on the sage brush fields, draping streamers from the windmills.

Gyptia pleaded with her daughter to do something normal. "One hand," she begged. "Just the right one. Clean off at the wrist. It won't take hardly any time to grow back."

Xyr flipped her sleek blonde ponytail. She pulled a cardigan over her jumper and clasped the top button modestly at her throat, leaving the rest to drape her shoulders like a shawl. "Mom," she said, with a teenage groan that hadn't changed over centuries. "At least *try* not to be so crink."

Gyptia fretted as she stood by the door watching Xyr stride out to meet her friends on the windy fields, her rose sweater fluttering behind her.

It hurt so much every time Gyptia realized anew that there was really nothing she could do, no way she could protect Xyr from anything that mattered, up to and including herself. That was one of the ultimate difficulties of parenting, she supposed, trying to impose an older generation's thought patterns upon emerging ways of thinking. There would always be chasms between them, mother and daughter. Gyptia had to try to protect Xyr anyway. Gyptia let the door iris close and went up to her room to cut off a finger or two and do her best not to worry.

Elegy for a Young Elk

HANNU RAJANIEMI

New writer Hannu Rajaniemi was born in Ylivieska, Finland, but currently lives in Edinburgh, Scotland, where he received a Ph.D. in string theory. He is the cofounder of ThinkTank Maths, which provides consultation service and research in applied mathematics and business development. He is also a member of Writers' Bloc, an Edinburgh-based spoken-word performance group. Rajaniemi has had a big impact on the field with only a few stories. His story from 2005, "Deus Ex Homine," originally from the Scottish regional anthology *Nova Scotia*, was reprinted in several Best of the Year anthologies, including this one, and was one of the most talked about stories of the year, as was his *Interzone* story "His Master's Voice" in 2008. His first novel, *The Quantum Thief*, was published in 2010 to a great deal of critical buzz and response.

Like Bruce Sterling, Greg Egan, and Charles Stross before him, Rajamiemi is a writer who cranks the bit-rate up about as high as it can go and still remain comprehensible (although there will almost certainly be some who think that he *doesn't* remain comprehensible, the usual fate of cutting edge writers), and this slender story, set in a postapocalyptic future society where posthumans with godlike powers are at war, manages to jam enough high-concept into a few pages to fuel a four-hundred-page novel.

The night after Kosonen shot the young elk, he tried to write a poem by the campfire.

It was late April and there was still snow on the ground. He had already taken to sitting outside in the evening, on a log by the fire, in the small clearing where his cabin stood. Otso was more comfortable outside, and he preferred the bear's company to being alone. It snored loudly atop its pile of fir branches.

A wet smell that had traces of elk shit drifted from its drying fur.

He dug a soft-cover notebook and a pencil stub from his pocket. He leafed through it: most of the pages were empty. Words had become slippery, harder to catch than elk. Although not this one: careless and young. An old elk would never have let a man and a bear so close.

He scattered words on the first empty page, gripping the pencil hard.

Antlers. Sapphire antlers. No good. *Frozen flames. Tree roots. Forked destinies.* There had to be words that captured the moment when the crossbow kicked against his shoulder, the meaty sound of the arrow's impact. But it was like trying to catch snowflakes in his palm. He could barely glimpse the crystal structure, and then they melted.

He closed the notebook and almost threw it into the fire, but thought better of it and put it back into his pocket. No point in wasting good paper. Besides, his last toilet roll in the outhouse would run out soon.

"Kosonen is thinking about words again," Otso growled. "Kosonen should drink more booze. Don't need words then. Just sleep."

Kosonen looked at the bear. "You think you are smart, huh?" He tapped his crossbow. "Maybe it's you who should be shooting elk."

"Otso good at smelling. Kosonen at shooting. Both good at drinking." Otso yawned luxuriously, revealing rows of yellow teeth. Then it rolled to its side and let out a satisfied heavy sigh. "Otso will have more booze soon."

Maybe the bear was right. Maybe a drink was all he needed. No point in being a poet: they had already written all the poems in the world, up there, in the sky. They probably had poetry gardens. Or places where you could become words.

But that was not the point. The words needed to come from *him*, a dirty bearded man in the woods whose toilet was a hole in the ground. Bright words from dark matter, that's what poetry was about.

When it worked.

There were things to do. The squirrels had almost picked the lock the previous night, bloody things. The cellar door needed reinforcing. But that could wait until tomorrow.

He was about to open a vodka bottle from Otso's secret stash in the snow when Marja came down from the sky as rain.

The rain was sudden and cold like a bucket of water poured over your head in the sauna. But the droplets did not touch the ground, they floated around Kosonen. As he watched, they changed shape, joined together and made a woman, spindle-thin bones, mist-flesh and muscle. She looked like a glass sculpture. The small breasts were perfect hemispheres, her sex an equilateral silver triangle. But the face was familiar—small nose and high cheekbones, a sharp-tongued mouth.

Marja.

Otso was up in an instant, by Kosonen's side. "Bad smell, god-smell," it growled. "Otso bites." The rain-woman looked at it curiously.

"Otso," Kosonen said sternly. He gripped the fur in the bear's rough neck tightly, feeling its huge muscles tense. "Otso is Kosonen's friend. Listen to Kosonen. Not time for biting. Time for sleeping. Kosonen will speak to god." Then he set the vodka bottle in the snow right under its nose.

Otso sniffed the bottle and scraped the half-melted snow with its forepaw.

"Otso goes," it finally said. "Kosonen shouts if the god bites. Then Otso comes." It picked up the bottle in its mouth deftly and loped into the woods with a bear's loose, shuffling gait.

"Hi," the rain-woman said.

"Hello," Kosonen said carefully. He wondered if she was real. The plague gods were crafty. One of them could have taken Marja's image from his mind. He looked at the unstrung crossbow and tried to judge the odds: a diamond god- dess versus an out-of-shape woodland poet. Not good.

"Your dog does not like me very much," the Marja-thing said. She sat down on Kosonen's log and swung its shimmering legs in the air, back and forth, just like Marja always did in the sauna. It had to be her, Kosonen decided, feeling something jagged in his throat.

He coughed. "Bear, not a dog. A dog would have barked. Otso just bites. Nothing personal, that's just its nature. Paranoid and grumpy."

"Sounds like someone I used to know."

"I'm not paranoid." Kosonen hunched down and tried to get the fire going again. "You learn to be careful, in the woods."

Marja looked around. "I thought we gave you stayers more equipment. It looks a little . . . primitive here."

"Yeah. We had plenty of gadgets," Kosonen said. "But they weren't plague-proof. I had a smartgun before I had this"—he tapped his crossbow—"but it got infected. I killed it with a big rock and threw it into the swamp. I've got my skis and some tools, and these." Kosonen tapped his temple. "Has been enough so far. So cheers."

He piled up some kindling under a triangle of small logs, and in a moment the flames sprung up again. Three years had been enough to learn about woodcraft at least. Marja's skin looked almost human in the soft light of the fire, and he sat back on Otso's fir branches, watching her. For a moment, neither of them spoke.

"So how are you, these days?" he asked. "Keeping busy?"

Marja smiled. "Your wife grew up. She's a big girl now. You don't want to know how big."

"So . . . you are not her, then? Who am I talking to?"

"I am her, and I am not her. I'm a partial, but a faithful one. A translation. You wouldn't understand."

Kosonen put some snow in the coffee pot to melt. "All right, so I'm a caveman. Fair enough. But I understand you are here because you want something. So let's get down to business, *perkele*," he swore.

Marja took a deep breath. "We lost something. Something important. Some- thing new. The spark, we called it. It fell into the city."

"I thought you lot kept copies of everything."

"Quantum information. That was a part of the *new* bit. You can't copy it."

"Tough shit."

A wrinkle appeared between Marja's eyebrows. Kosonen remembered it from a thousand fights they had had, and swallowed.

"If that's the tone you want to take, fine," she said. "I thought you'd be glad to see me. I didn't have to come: they could have sent Mickey Mouse. But I wanted to see you. The big Marja wanted to see you. So you have decided to live your life like this, as the tragic figure haunting the woods. That's fine. But you could at least listen. You owe me that much."

Kosonen said nothing.

"I see," Marja said. "You still blame me for Esa."

She was right. It had been her who got the first Santa Claus machine. The boy needs the best we can offer, she said. The world is changing. Can't have him being left behind. Let's make him into a little god, like the neighbor's kid.

"I guess I shouldn't be blaming *you*," Kosonen said. "You're just a . . . partial. You weren't there."

"I was there," Marja said quietly. "I remember. Better than you, now. I also forget better, and forgive. You never could. You just . . . wrote poems. The rest of us moved on, and saved the world."

"Great job," Kosonen said. He poked the fire with a stick, and a cloud of sparks flew up into the air with the smoke.

Marja got up. "That's it," she said. "I'm leaving. See you in a hundred years." The air grew cold. A halo appeared around her, shimmering in the firelight.

Kosonen closed his eyes and squeezed his jaw shut tight. He waited for ten seconds. Then he opened his eyes. Marja was still there, staring at him, helpless. He could not help smiling. She could never leave without having the last word.

"I'm sorry," Kosonen said. "It's been a long time. I've been living in the woods with a bear. Doesn't improve one's temper much."

"I didn't really notice any difference."

"All right," Kosonen said. He tapped the fir branches next to him. "Sit down. Let's start over. I'll make some coffee."

Marja sat down, bare shoulder touching his. She felt strangely warm, warmer than the fire almost.

"The firewall won't let us into the city," she said. "We don't have anyone . . . human enough, not anymore. There was some talk about making one, but . . . the argument would last a century." She sighed. "We like to argue, in the sky."

Kosonen grinned. "I bet you fit right in." He checked for the wrinkle before continuing. "So you need an errand boy."

"We need help."

Kosonen looked at the fire. The flames were dying now, licking at the blackened wood. There were always new colours in the embers. Or maybe he just always forgot.

He touched Marja's hand. It felt like a soap bubble, barely solid. But she did not pull it away.

"All right," he said. "But just so you know, it's not just for old times' sake."

"Anything we can give you."

"I'm cheap," Kosonen said. "I just want words."

The sun sparkled on the *kantohanki*: snow with a frozen surface, strong enough to carry a man on skis and a bear. Kosonen breathed hard. Even going downhill, keeping pace with Otso was not easy. But in weather like this, there was something glorious about skiing, sliding over blue shadows of trees almost without friction, the snow hissing underneath.

I've sat still too long, he thought. *Should have gone somewhere just to go, not because someone asks.*

In the afternoon, when the sun was already going down, they reached the railroad, a bare gash through the forest, two metal tracks on a bed of gravel. Kosonen removed his skis and stuck them in the snow.

"I'm sorry you can't come along," he told Otso. "But the city won't let you in."

"Otso not a city bear," the bear said. "Otso waits for Kosonen. Kosonen gets sky-bug, comes back. Then we drink booze."

He scratched the rough fur of its neck clumsily. The bear poked Kosonen in the stomach with its nose, so hard that he almost fell. Then it snorted, turned around and shuffled into the woods. Kosonen watched until it vanished among the snow-covered trees.

It took three painful attempts of sticking his fingers down his throat to get the nanoseed Marja gave him to come out. The gagging left a bitter taste in his mouth. Swallowing it had been the only way to protect the delicate thing from the plague. He wiped it in the snow: a transparent bauble the size of a walnut, slippery and warm. It reminded him of the toys you could get from vending machines in supermarkets when he was a child, plastic spheres with something secret inside.

He placed it on the rails carefully, wiped the remains of the vomit from his lips and rinsed his mouth with water. Then he looked at it. Marja knew he would never read instruction manuals, so she had not given him one.

"Make me a train," he said.

Nothing happened. *Maybe it can read my mind*, he thought, and imagined a train, an old steam train, puffing along. Still nothing, just a reflection of the darkening sky on the seed's clear surface. *She always had to be subtle*. Marja could never give a present without thinking about its meaning for days. Standing still let the spring winter chill through his wolf-pelt coat, and he hopped up and down, rubbing his hands together.

With the motion came an idea. He frowned, staring at the seed, and took the notebook from his pocket. Maybe it was time to try out Marja's other gift—or advance payment, however you wanted to look at it. He had barely written the first lines, when the words leaped in his mind like animals woken from slumber. He closed the book, cleared his throat and spoke.

> *these rails*
> *were worn thin*
> *by wheels*
> *that wrote down*
> *the name of each passenger*
> *in steel and miles*

he said,

> *it's a good thing*
> *the years*
> *ate our flesh too*
> *made us thin and light*
> *so the rails are strong enough*
> *to carry us still*
> *to the city*
> *in our train of glass and words*

Doggerel, he thought, but it didn't matter. The joy of words filled his veins like vodka. *Too bad it didn't work—*

The seed blurred. It exploded into a white-hot sphere. The waste heat washed across Kosonen's face. Glowing tentacles squirmed past him, sucking carbon and metal from the rails and trees. They danced like a welder's electric arcs, sketching lines and surfaces in the air.

And suddenly, the train was there.

It was transparent, with paper-thin walls and delicate wheels, as if it had been blown from glass, sketch of a cartoon steam engine with a single carriage, with spiderweb-like chairs inside, just the way he had imagined it.

He climbed in, expecting the delicate structure to sway under his weight, but it felt rock-solid. The nanoseed lay on the floor innocently, as if nothing had happened. He picked it up carefully, took it outside and buried it in the snow, leaving his skis and sticks as markers. Then he picked up his backpack, boarded the train again and sat down in one of the gossamer seats. Unbidden, the train lurched into motion smoothly. To Kosonen, it sounded like the rails beneath were whispering, but he could not hear the words.

He watched the darkening forest glide past. The day's journey weighed heavily down on his limbs. The memory of the snow beneath his skis melted together with the train's movement, and soon Kosonen was asleep.

When he woke up, it was dark. The amber light of the firewall glowed in the horizon, like a thundercloud.

The train had speeded up. The dark forest outside was a blur, and the whispering of the rails had become a quiet staccato song. Kosonen swallowed as the train covered the remaining distance in a matter of minutes. The firewall grew into a misty dome glowing with yellowish light from within. The city was an indistinct silhouette beneath it. The buildings seemed to be in motion, like a giant's shadow puppets.

Then it was a flaming curtain directly in front of the train, an impenetrable wall made from twilight and amber crossing the tracks. Kosonen gripped the delicate frame of his seat, knuckles white. "Slow down!" he shouted, but the train did not hear. It crashed directly into the firewall with a bone-jarring impact. There was a burst of light, and then Kosonen was lifted from his seat.

It was like drowning, except that he was floating in an infinite sea of amber light rather than water. Apart from the light, there was just emptiness. His skin tickled. It took him a moment to realise that he was not breathing.

And then a stern voice spoke.

This is not a place for men, it said. *Closed. Forbidden. Go back.*

"I have a mission," said Kosonen. His voice had no echo in the light. "From your makers. They command you to let me in."

He closed his eyes, and Marja's third gift floated in front of him, not words but a number. He had always been poor at memorising things, but Marja's touch had been a pen with acid ink, burning it in his mind. He read off the endless digits, one by one.

You may enter, said the firewall. *But only that which is human will leave.*

The train and the speed came back, sharp and real like a paper cut. The twilight glow of the firewall was still there, but instead of the forest, dark buildings loomed around the railway, blank windows staring at him.

Kosonen's hands tickled. They were clean, as were his clothes: every speck of dirt was gone. His felt was tender and red, like he had just been to the sauna.

The train slowed down at last, coming to a stop in the dark mouth of the station, and Kosonen was in the city.

The city was a forest of metal and concrete and metal that breathed and hummed. The air smelled of ozone. The facades of the buildings around the railway station square looked almost like he remembered them, only subtly wrong. From the corner of his eye he could glimpse them *moving*, shifting in their sleep like stone-skinned animals. There were no signs of life, apart from a cluster of pigeons, hopping back and forth on the stairs, looking at him. They had sapphire eyes.

A bus stopped, full of faceless people who looked like crash test dummies, sitting unnaturally still. Kosonen decided not to get in and started to head across the square, towards the main shopping street: he had to start the search for the spark somewhere. It will glow, Marja had said. You can't miss it.

There was what looked like a car wreck in the parking lot, lying on its side, hood crumpled like a discarded beer can, covered in white pigeon droppings. But when Kosonen walked past it, its engine roared, and the hood popped open. A hissing bundle of tentacles snapped out, reaching for him.

He managed to gain some speed before the car-beast rolled onto its four wheels. There were narrow streets on the other side of the square, too narrow for it to follow. He ran, cold weight in his stomach, legs pumping.

The crossbow beat painfully at his back in its strap, and he struggled to get it over his head.

The beast passed him arrogantly, and turned around. Then it came straight at him. The tentacles spread out from its glowing engine mouth into a fan of serpents.

Kosonen fumbled with a bolt, then loosed it at the thing. The crossbow kicked, but the arrow glanced off its windshield. It seemed to confuse it enough for Kosonen to jump aside. He dove, hit the pavement with a painful thump, and rolled.

"Somebody help *perkele*," he swore with impotent rage, and got up, panting, just as the beast backed off slowly, engine growling. He smelled burning rubber, mixed with ozone. *Maybe I can wrestle it*, he thought like a madman, spreading his arms, refusing to run again. *One last poem in it—*

Something landed in front of the beast, wings fluttering. A pigeon. Both Kosonen and the car-creature stared at it. It made a cooing sound. Then it exploded.

The blast tore at his eardrums, and the white fireball turned the world black for a second. Kosonen found himself on the ground again, ears ringing, lying painfully on top of his backpack. The carbeast was a burning wreck ten meters away, twisted beyond all recognition.

There was another pigeon next to him, picking at what looked like bits of metal. It lifted its head and looked at him, flames reflecting from the tiny sapphire eyes. Then it took flight, leaving a tiny white dropping behind.

The main shopping street was empty. Kosonen moved carefully in case there were more of the car creatures around, staying close to narrow alleys and doorways. The firewall light was dimmer between the buildings, and strange lights danced in the windows.

Kosonen realised he was starving: he had not eaten since noon, and the journey and the fight had taken their toll. He found an empty cafe in a street corner that seemed safe, set up his small travel cooker on a table and boiled some water. The supplies he had been able to bring consisted mainly of canned soup and dried elk meat, but his growling stomach was not fussy. The smell of food made him careless.

"This is my place," said a voice. Kosonen leapt up, startled, reaching for the crossbow.

There was a stooped, trollish figure at the door, dressed in rags. His face shone with sweat and dirt, framed by matted hair and beard. His porous skin was full of tiny sapphire growths, like pockmarks. Kosonen had thought living in the woods had made him immune to human odours, but the stranger carried a bitter stench of sweat and stale booze that made him want to retch.

The stranger walked in and sat down at a table opposite Kosonen. "But that's all right," he said amicably. "Don't get many visitors these days. Have to be neighbourly. *Saatana*, is that Blaband soup that you've got?"

"You're welcome to some," Kosonen said warily. He had met some of the other stayers over the years, but usually avoided them—they all had their own reasons for not going up, and not much in common.

"Thanks. That's neighbourly indeed. I'm Pera, by the way." The troll held out his hand.

Kosonen shook it gingerly, feeling strange jagged things under Pera's skin. It was like squeezing a glove filled with powdered glass. "Kosonen. So you live here?"

"Oh, not here, not in the center. I come here to steal from the buildings. But they've become really smart, and stingy. Can't even find soup anymore. The Stockmann department store almost ate me, yesterday. It's not easy life here." Pera shook his head. "But better than outside." There was a sly look in his eyes. *Are you staying because you want to*, wondered Kosonen, *or because the firewall won't let you out anymore?*

"Not afraid of the plague gods, then?" he asked aloud. He passed Pera one of the heated soup tins. The city stayer slurped it down with one gulp, smell of minestrone mingling with the other odours.

"Oh, you don't have to be afraid of them anymore. They're all dead."

Kosonen looked at Pera, startled. "How do you know?"

"The pigeons told me."

"The pigeons?"

Pera took something from the pocket of his ragged coat carefully. It was a pigeon. It had a sapphire beak and eyes, and a trace of blue in its feathers. It struggled in Pera's grip, wings fluttering.

"My little buddies," Pera said. "I think you've already met them."

"Yes," Kosonen said. "Did you send the one that blew up that car thing?"

"You have to help a neighbour out, don't you? Don't mention it. The soup was good."

"What did they say about the plague gods?"

Pera grinned a gap-toothed grin. "When the gods got locked up here, they started fighting. Not enough power to go around, you see. So one of them had to be the top dog, like in Highlander. The pigeons show me pictures, sometimes. Bloody stuff. Explosions. Nanites eating men. But finally they were all gone, every last one. My playground now."

So Esa is gone, too. Kosonen was surprised how sharp the feeling of loss was, even now. *Better like this.* He swallowed. *Let's get the job done first. No time to mourn. Let's think about it when we get home. Write a poem about it. And tell Marja.*

"All right," Kosonen said. "I'm hunting too. Do you think your . . . buddies could find it? Something that glows. If you help me, I'll give you all the soup I've got. And elk meat. And I'll bring more later. How does that sound?"

"Pigeons can find anything," said Pera, licking his lips.

The pigeon-man walked through the city labyrinth like his living room, accompanied by a cloud of the chimera birds. Every now and then, one of them would land on his shoulder and touch his ear with his beak, as if to whisper.

"Better hurry," Pera said. "At night, it's not too bad, but during the day the houses get younger and start thinking."

Kosonen had lost all sense of direction. The map of the city was different from the last time he had been here, in the old human days. His best guess was that they were getting somewhere close to the cathedral in the old town, but he couldn't be sure. Navigating the changed streets felt like walking through the veins of some giant animal, convoluted and labyrinthine. Some buildings were enclosed in what looked like black film, rippling like oil. Some had grown together, organic-looking structures of brick and concrete, blocking streets and making the ground uneven.

"We're not far," Pera said. "They've seen it. Glowing like a pumpkin lantern, they say." He giggled. The amber light of the firewall grew brighter as they walked. It was hotter, too, and Kosonen was forced to discard his old Pohjanmaa sweater.

They passed an office building that had become a sleeping face, a genderless Easter Island countenance. There was more life in this part of the town too, sapphire-eyed animals, sleek cats looking at them from windowsills. Kosonen saw a fox crossing the street: it gave them one bright look and vanished down a sewer hole.

Then they turned a corner where faceless men wearing fashion from ten years ago danced together in a shop window, and saw the cathedral.

It had grown to gargantuan size, dwarfing every other building around it. It was an anthill of dark-red brick and hexagonal doorways. It buzzed with life. Cats with sapphire claws clung to its walls like sleek gargoyles. Thick pigeon flocks fluttered around its towers. Packs of azure-tailed rats ran in and out of open, massive doors like armies on a mission. And there were insects everywhere, filling the air with a drill-like buzzing sound, moving in dense black clouds like a giant's black breath.

"Oh, *jumalauta*," Kosonen said. "That's where it fell?"

"Actually, no. I was just supposed to bring you here," Pera said.

"What?"

"Sorry. I lied. It *was* like in Highlander: there is one of them left. And he wants to meet you."

Kosonen stared at Pera, dumbfounded. The pigeons landed on the other man's shoulders and arms like a grey fluttering cloak. They seized his rags and hair and skin with sharp claws, wings started beating furiously. As Kosonen stared, Pera rose to the air.

"No hard feelings, I just had a better deal from him. Thanks for the soup," he shouted. In a moment, Pera was a black scrap of cloth in the sky.

The earth shook. Kosonen fell to his knees. The window eyes that lined the street lit up, full of bright, malevolent light.

He tried to run. He did not make it far before they came, the fingers of the city: the pigeons, the insects, a buzzing swarm that covered him. A dozen chimera rats clung to his skull, and he could feel the humming of their flywheel hearts. Something sharp bit through the bone. The pain grew like a forest fire, and Kosonen screamed.

The city spoke. Its voice was a thunderstorm, words made from shaking of the earth and the sighs of buildings. Slow words, squeezed from stone.

Dad, the city said.

The pain was gone. Kosonen heard the gentle sound of waves, and felt a warm wind on his face. He opened his eyes.

"Hi, Dad," Esa said.

They sat on the summerhouse pier, wrapped in towels, skin flushed from the sauna. It was evening, with a hint of chill in the air, Finnish summer's gentle reminder that things were not forever. The sun hovered above the blue-tinted treetops. The lake surface was calm, full of liquid reflections.

"I thought," Esa said, "that you'd like it here."

Esa was just like Kosonen remembered him, a pale skinny kid, ribs showing, long arms folded across his knees, stringy wet hair hanging on his forehead. But his eyes were the eyes of a city, dark orbs of metal and stone.

"I do," Kosonen said. "But I can't stay."

"Why not?"

"There is something I need to do."

"We haven't seen each other in ages. The sauna is warm. I've got some beer cooling in the lake. Why the rush?"

"I should be afraid of you," Kosonen said. "You killed people. Before they put you here."

"You don't know what it's like," Esa said. "The plague does everything you want. It gives you things you don't even know you want. It turns the world soft. And sometimes it tears it apart for you. You think a thought, and things break. You can't help it."

The boy closed his eyes. "You want things too. I know you do. That's why you are here, isn't it? You want your precious words back."

Kosonen said nothing.

"Mom's errand boy, *vittu*. So they fixed your brain, flushed the booze out. So you can write again. Does it feel good? For a moment there I thought you came here for me. But that's not the way it ever worked, was it?"

"I didn't know—"

"I can see the inside of your head, you know," Esa said. "I've got my fingers inside your skull. One thought, and my bugs will eat you, bring you here for good. Quality time forever. What do you say to that?"

And there it was, the old guilt. "We worried about you, every second, after you were born," Kosonen said. "We only wanted the best for you."

It had seemed so natural. How the boy played with his machine that made other machines. How things started changing shape when you thought at them. How Esa smiled when he showed Kosonen the talking starfish that the machine had made.

"And then I had one bad day."

"I remember," Kosonen said. He had been home late, as usual. Esa had been a diamond tree, growing in his room. There were starfish everywhere, eating the walls and the floor, making more of themselves. And that was only the beginning.

"So go ahead. Bring me here. It's your turn to make me into what you want. Or end it all. I deserve it."

Esa laughed softly. "And why would I do that, to an old man?" He sighed. "You know, I'm old too now. Let me show you." He touched Kosonen's shoulder gently and

Kosonen was the city. His skin was stone and concrete, pores full of the god-plague. The streets and buildings were his face, changing and shifting with every thought and emotion. His nervous system was diamond and optic fibre. His hands were chimera animals.

The firewall was all around him, in the sky and in the cold bedrock, insubstantial but adamantine, squeezing from every side, cutting off energy, making sure he could not think fast. But he could still dream, weave words and images into threads, make worlds out of the memories he had and the memories of the smaller gods he had eaten to become the city. He sang his dreams in radio waves, not caring if the firewall let them through or not, louder and louder—

"Here," Esa said from far away. "Have a beer."

Kosonen felt a chilly bottle in his hand, and drank. The dream-beer was strong and real. The malt taste brought him back. He took a deep breath, letting the fake summer evening wash away the city.

"Is that why you brought me here? To show me that?" he asked.

"Well, no," Esa said, laughing. His stone eyes looked young, suddenly. "I just wanted you to meet my girlfriend."

The quantum girl had golden hair and eyes of light. She wore many faces at once, like a Hindu goddess. She walked to the pier with dainty steps. Esa's summerland showed its cracks around her: there were fracture lines in her skin, with otherworldly colours peeking out.

"This is Säde," Esa said.

She looked at Kosonen, and spoke, a bubble of words, a superposition, all possible greetings at once.

"Nice to meet you," Kosonen said.

"They did something right when they made her, up there," said Esa. "She lives in many worlds at once, thinks in qubits. And this is the world where she wants to be. With me." He touched her shoulder gently. "She heard my songs and ran away."

"Marja said she fell," Kosonen said. "That something was broken."

"She said what they wanted her to say. They don't like it when things don't go according to plan."

Säde made a sound, like the chime of a glass bell.

"The firewall keeps squeezing us," Esa said. "That's how it was made. Make things go slower and slower here, until we die. Säde doesn't fit in here, this place is too small. So you will take her back home, before it's too late." He smiled. "I'd rather you do it than anyone else."

"That's not fair," Kosonen said. He squinted at Säde. She was too bright to look at. *But what can I do? I'm just a slab of meat. Meat and words.*

The thought was like a pinecone, rough in his grip, but with a seed of something in it.

"I think there is a poem in you two," he said.

Kosonen sat on the train again, watching the city stream past. It was early morning. The sunrise gave the city new hues: purple shadows and gold, ember colours. Fatigue pulsed in his temples. His body ached. The words of a poem weighed down on his mind.

Above the dome of the firewall he could see a giant diamond starfish, a drone of the sky people, watching, like an outstretched hand.

They came to see what happened, he thought. *They'll find out.*

This time, he embraced the firewall like a friend, and its tingling brightness washed over him. And deep within, the stern-voiced watchman came again. It said nothing this time, but he could feel its presence, scrutinising, seeking things that did not belong in the outside world.

Kosonen gave it everything.

The first moment when he knew he had put something real on paper. The disappointment when he realised that a poet was not much in a small country, piles of cheaply printed copies of his first collection, gathering dust in little bookshops. The jealousy he had felt when Marja gave birth to Esa, what a pale shadow of that giving birth to words was. The tracks of the elk in the snow and the look in its eyes when it died.

He felt the watchman step aside, satisfied.

Then he was through. The train emerged into the real, undiluted dawn. He looked back at the city, and saw fire raining from the starfish. Pillars of light cut through the city in geometric patterns, too bright to look at, leaving only white-hot plasma in their wake.

Kosonen closed his eyes and held on to the poem as the city burned.

Kosonen planted the nanoseed in the woods. He dug a deep hole in the half-frozen peat with his bare hands, under an old tree stump. He sat down, took off his cap, dug out his notebook, and started reading. The pencil-scrawled words glowed bright in his mind, and after a while he didn't need to look at them anymore.

The poem rose from the words like a titanic creature from an ocean, first showing just a small extremity but then soaring upwards in a spray of glossolalia, mountain-like. It was a stream of hissing words and phonemes, an endless spell that tore at his throat. And with it came the quantum information from the microtubules of his neurons, where the bright-eyed girl now lived, and jagged impulses from synapses where his son was hiding.

The poem swelled into a roar. He continued until his voice was a hiss. Only the nanoseed could hear, but that was enough. Something stirred under the peat.

When the poem finally ended, it was evening. Kosonen opened his eyes. The first thing he saw were the sapphire antlers, sparkling in the last rays of the sun.

Two young elk looked at him. One was smaller, more delicate, and its large brown eyes held a hint of sunlight. The other was young and skinny, but wore its budding antlers with pride. It held Kosonen's gaze, and in its eyes he saw shadows of the city. Or reflections in a summer lake, perhaps.

They turned around and ran into the woods, silent, fleet-footed and free.

Kosonen was opening the cellar door when the rain came back. It was barely a shower this time: the droplets formed Marja's face in the air. For a moment he thought he saw her wink. Then the rain became a mist, and was gone. He propped the door open.

The squirrels stared at him from the trees curiously.

"All yours, gentlemen," Kosonen said. "Should be enough for next winter. I don't need it anymore."

Otso and Kosonen left at noon, heading north. Kosonen's skis slid along easily in the thinning snow. The bear pulled a sledge loaded with equipment. When they were well away from the cabin, it stopped to sniff at a fresh trail.

"Elk," it growled. "Otso is hungry. Kosonen shoot an elk. Need meat for the journey. Kosonen did not bring enough booze."

Kosonen shook his head.

"I think I'm going to learn to fish," he said.

MICHAEL SWANWICK

Michael Swanwick made his debut in 1980 and, in the thirty-one years that have followed, has established himself as one of SF's most prolific and consistently excellent writers at short lengths, as well as one of the premier novelists of his generation. He has won the Theodore Sturgeon Award and the *Asimov's* Readers' Award poll. In 1991, his novel *Stations of the Tide* won him a Nebula Award as well, and in 1996 he won the World Fantasy Award for his story "Radio Waves." He's won the Hugo Award five times between 1999 and 2006, for his stories "The Very Pulse of the Machine," "Scherzo with Tyrannosaur," "The Dog Said Bow-Wow," "Slow Life," and "Legions In Time." His other books include the novels *In The Drift, Vacuum Flowers, The Iron Dragon's Daughter, Jack Faust,* and *Bones of the Earth.* His short fiction has been assembled in *Gravity's Angels, A Geography of Unknown Lands, Moon Dogs, Puck Aleshire's Abecedary, Tales of Old Earth, Cigar-Box Faust and Other Miniatures, Michael Swanwick's Field Guide to the Mesozoic Megafauna,* and *The Periodic Table of Science Fiction.* His most recent books are the novel *The Dragons of Babel,* and a massive retrospective collection, *The Best of Michael Swanwick.* Coming up is a new novel, *Dancing with Bears.* Swanwick lives in Philadelphia with his wife, Marianne Porter. He has a Web site at: www.michaelswanwick.com.

Here he takes us to a depopulated future Russia that's been through a semi-apocalypse for a hard-edged look at a young man learning the hard way how his political ideals would work out in practice in the real world.

Miles and weeks passed under the wheels of Victor's motorcycle. Sometime during the day he would stop at a peasant farmstead and buy food to cook over a campfire for supper. At night he slept under the stars with old cowboy movies playing in his head. In no particular hurry he wove through the Urals on twisting backcountry roads, and somewhere along the way crossed over the border out of Europe and into Asia. He made a wide detour around Yekaterinburg, where the density of population brought government interference in the private lives of its citizens up almost to Moscow levels, and then cut back again to regain the laughably primitive transcontinental highway. He was passing through the drab ruins of an industrial district at the edge of the city when a woman in thigh-high boots raised her hand to hail him, the way they did out here in the sticks where every driver was a potential taxi to be bought for small change.

Ordinarily, Victor wouldn't have stopped. But in addition to the boots the woman wore leopard-print hot pants and a fashionably puffy red jacket, tight about the waist and broad at the shoulders, which opened to reveal the tops of her breasts, like two pomegranates proffered on a plate. A vinyl backpack crouched on the ground by her feet. She looked like she'd just stepped down from a billboard. She looked like serious trouble.

It had been a long time since he'd had any serious trouble. Victor pulled to a stop.

"Going east?" the woman said.

"Yeah."

She glanced down at the scattering of pins on his kevleather jacket—politicians who never got elected, causes that were never won—and her crimson lips quirked in the smallest of smiles. "Libertarianski, eh? You do realize that there's no such thing as a libertarian Russian? It's like a gentle tiger or an honest cop—a contradiction in terms."

Victor shrugged. "And yet, here I am."

"So you think." Suddenly all business, the woman said, "I'll blow you if you take me with you."

For a second Victor's mind went blank. Then he said, "Actually, I might be going a long way. Across Siberia. I might not stop until I reach the Pacific."

"Okay, then. Once a day, so long as I'm with you. Deal?"

"Deal."

Victor reconfigured the back of his bike to give it a pillion and an extra rack for her backpack and fattened the tires to compensate for her weight. She climbed on behind him, and off they went.

At sunset, they stopped and made camp in a scrub pine forest, behind the ruins of a Government Auto Inspection station. After they'd set up their puptents (hers was the size of her fist when she took it from her knapsack but assembled itself into something almost palatial; his was no larger than he needed) and built the cookfire, she paid him for the day's ride. Then, as he cut up the chicken he'd bought earlier, they talked.

"You never told me your name," Victor said.

"Svetlana."

"Just Svetlana?"

"Yes."

"No patronymic?"

"No. Just Svetlana. And you?"

"Victor Pelevin."

Svetlana laughed derisively. "Oh, come on!"

"He's my grandfather," Victor explained. Then, when the scorn failed to leave her face, "Well, spiritually, anyway. I've read all his books I don't know how many times. They shaped me."

"I prefer *The Master and Margarita*. Not the book, of course. The video. But I can't say it shaped me. So, let me guess. You're on the great Russian road trip.

Looking to find the real Russia, old Russia, Mother Russia, the Russia of the heart. Eh?"

"Not me. I've already found what I'm looking for—Libertarian Russia. Right here, where we are." Victor finished with the chicken, and began cutting up the vegetables. It would take a while for the fire to die down to coals, but when it was ready, he'd roast the vegetables and chicken together on spits, shish kabob style.

"Now that you've found it, what are you going to do with it?"

"Nothing. Wander around. Live here. Whatever." He began assembling the kabobs. "You see, after the Depopulation, there just weren't the resources any-more for the government to police the largest country in the world with the sort of control they were used to. So instead of easing up on the people, they decided to concentrate their power in a handful of industrial and mercantile centers, port cities, and the like. The rest, with a total population of maybe one or two people per ten square miles, they cut loose. Nobody talks about it, but there's no law out here except what people agree upon. They've got to settle their differences among themselves. When you've got enough people to make up a town, they might pool their money to hire a part-time cop or two. But no databases, no spies . . . you can do what you like, and so long as you don't infringe upon somebody else's free-doms, they'll leave you alone."

Everything Victor said was more or less cut-and-paste from "Free Ivan," an orphan website he'd stumbled on five years ago. In libertarian circles, Free Ivan was a legend. Victor liked to think he was out somewhere in Siberia, living the life he'd preached. But since his last entry was posted from St. Petersburg and mentioned no such plans, most likely he was dead. That was what happened to people who dared imagine a world without tyranny.

"What if somebody else's idea of freedom involves taking your motorcycle from you?"

Victor got up and patted the contact plate on his machine. "The lock is coded to my genome. The bike won't start for anybody else. Anyway, I have a gun." He showed it, then put it back in his shoulder harness.

"Somebody could take that thing away from you and shoot you, you know."

"No, they couldn't. It's a smart gun. It's like my bike—it answers to nobody but me."

Unexpectedly, Svetlana laughed. "I give up! You've got all the angles covered."

Yet Victor doubted he had convinced her of anything. "We have the technology to make us free," he said sullenly. "Why not use it? You ought to get a gun your-self."

"Trust me, my body is all the weapon I need."

There didn't seem to be any answer for that, so Victor said, "Tell me about yourself. Who are you, why are you on the road, where are you heading?"

"I'm a whore," she said. "I got tired of working for others, but Yekaterinburg was too corrupt for me to set up a house of my own there. So I'm looking for someplace large enough to do business in, where the police will settle for a rea-sonable cut of the take."

"You . . . mean all that literally, don't you?"

Svetlana reached into her purse and took out a card case. She squirted him her rate sheet, and put the case away again. "If you see anything there you like, I'm open for business."

The fire was ready now, so Victor put on the kabobs.

"How much do I pay for dinner?" Svetlana opened her purse again.

"It's my treat."

"No," she said. "I don't accept anything for free. Everybody pays for everything. That's my philosophy."

Before he went to his puptent, Victor disassembled part of his bike and filled the digester tank with water and grass. Then he set it to gently rocking. Enzymes and yeasts were automatically fed into the mixture—and by morning, there would be enough alcohol for another day's travel. He went into the tent and lay on his back, playing a John Wayne movie in his mind. *The Seekers*. But after a while he could not help pausing the movie, to call up Svetlana's rate sheet.

She offered a surprisingly broad range of services.

He brooded for a long while before finally falling asleep.

That night he had an eidetic dream. Possibly his memorandum recorder had been jostled a month earlier and some glitch caused it to replay now. At any rate, he was back in Moscow and he was leaving forever.

He hit the road at dawn, rush hour traffic heavy around him and the sun a golden dazzle in the smog. American jazz saxophone played in his head, smooth and cool. Charlie Parker. He hunched low over his motorcycle, and when a traffic cop gestured him to the shoulder with a languid wave of his white baton for a random ID check, Victor popped a wheelie and flipped him the finger. Then he opened up the throttle and slalomed away, back and forth across four lanes of madly honking traffic.

In the rearview mirror, he saw the cop glaring after him, taking a mental snapshot of his license plate. If he ever returned to Moscow, he'd be in a world of trouble. Every cop in the city—and Moscow had more flavors of cops than anywhere—would have his number and a good idea of what he looked like.

Fuck that noise. Fuck it right up the ass. Victor had spent years grubbing for money, living cheap, saving every kopek he could to buy the gear he needed to get the hell out of Moscow. Why would he ever come back?

Then he was outside the city, the roads getting briefly better as they passed between the gated communities where the rich huddled fearfully inside well-guarded architectural fantasies and then dwindling to neglect and disrepair before finally turning to dirt. That was when, laughing wildly, he tore off his helmet and flung it away, into the air, into the weeds, into the past . . .

He was home now. He was free.

He was in Libertarian Russia.

Victor liked the idea of biking across Asia in the company of a whore a great deal in theory. But the reality was more problematic. With her thighs to either side of his and her arms about him as they rode, he could not keep from thinking constantly about her body. Yet he lacked the money for what he'd have liked to do with her. And her daily payment provided only temporary relief. After three days, he was looking for someplace he could ditch Svetlana with a clean conscience.

Sometime around noon, they passed through a small town which had clearly been a medium-sized city before the Depopulation. Just beyond it, two trucks and three cars were parked in front of a cinder-block restaurant. One of the cars was a Mercedes. Opportunities to eat in a restaurant being rare along the dis-integrating remains of what was grandiosely called the Trans-Siberian Highway, Victor pulled over his bike and they went inside.

There were only six tables and they were all empty. The walls were painted black and decorated with loops of antique light-pipes dug out of trunks found in the attics of houses that nobody lived in anymore. At the back of the room was a bar. Above it, painted in white block letters, were the words: WE KNOW NO MERCY AND DO NOT ASK FOR ANY.

"Shit," Victor said.

"What is it?" Svetlana asked.

"That's the slogan for OMON—the Special Forces Police Squad. Let's get the fuck out of here."

A large man emerged from a back room, drying his hands with a towel. "What can I do for . . . ?" He stopped and looked thoughtful, the way one did when accessing an external database. Then a nasty grin split his face. "Osip! Kolzak! Come see what the wind blew in!"

Two more men came out from the back, one bigger than the first, the other smaller. All three looked like they were spoiling for a fight. "She's a whore. He's just a little shit with subversive political connections. Nobody important. What do you want to do with them?"

"Fuck them both," the big man said.

"One is all you'll need," Svetlana said in a sultry voice. "Provided that one is me." She got out her card case and squirted them her rate sheet.

There was a brief astonished silence. Then one of the men said, "You are one fucking filthy cunt."

"You can talk as dirty as you like—I won't charge you extra."

"Coming in here was the stupidest thing you ever did," the small man said. "Grab her, Pavel."

The middle-sized man moved toward Svetlana.

Chest tight with fear, Victor pulled out his gun and stepped into Pavel's path. This was his moment of truth. His Alamo. "We're leaving now," he said, fighting to keep his voice firm, "If you know what's good for you, you won't try to stop us."

Disconcertingly, all three thugs looked amused. Pavel stepped forward, so that the gun poked him in the chest. "You think that protects you? Try shooting it. Shoot me now."

"Don't think I won't."

"You can't stop somebody if you're not willing to kill him." The man closed both his hands around the gun. Then he viciously mashed Victor's finger back against the trigger.

Nothing happened.

Pavel took the gun away from Victor. "You don't think the government has better technology than you? Every non-military gun in the country is blue-toothed at the factory." Over his shoulder he said, "What do you want me to do with the whore, Osip?"

Svetlana shuddered, as if in the throes of great terror. But she smiled seduc-tively. "I don't normally do it for free," she said. "But I could make an exception for you boys."

"Take her out to the gravel pit," the small man said, "and shoot her."

Pavel grabbed Svetlana by the wrist. "What about the punk?"

"Let me think about that."

Svetlana didn't make a sound as she was dragged out the front.

The big man pushed Victor down onto a chair. "Sit quietly," he said. "If you try anything . . . Well, I don't think you'll try anything." Then he got out a combat knife and amused himself by plucking Victor's pins from his jacket with it and reading them, one by one, before flicking them away, over his shoulder. "A Citizen Without a Gun is a Slave," he read. "Legalize Freedom: Vote Libertarian. Anarchists Unite—that doesn't even make sense!"

"It's a joke."

"Then why isn't it funny?"

"I don't know."

"So it's not much of a joke, is it?"

"I guess not."

"The weakness in your political philosophy," Osip said out of nowhere, "is that you assume that when absolute freedom is extended to everybody, they'll all think only of their own selfish interests. You forget that patriots exist, men who are willing to sacrifice themselves for the good of the Motherland."

Figuring he had nothing to lose at this point, Victor said, "Taking money to do the government's dirty work doesn't make you a patriot."

"You think we're getting *paid* for what we do? Listen. After I left OMON, I was sick of cities, crime, pollution. So I went looking for a place where I could go fishing or hunting whenever I wanted. I found this building abandoned, and started fixing it up. Pavel stopped to ask what I was doing and since he'd been in the Special Police too, I invited him to come in as a partner. When the restaurant was up and running, Kolzak dropped in and when we found out he was one of us, we offered him a job. Because we are all brothers, you see, answerable to nobody but God and each other. Pavel brought a satellite uplink with him, so we know the police record of everyone who comes by. We cleanse the land of antisocial elements like your whore because it's the right thing to do. That's all."

"And you," Kolzak said. "Don't think her body's going into the gravel pit alone."

"Please. There has to be some way of convincing you that this isn't necessary."

"Sure there is. Just tell me one thing that you can give me in exchange for your life that I can't take off of your corpse."

Victor was silent.

"You see?" Osip said. "Kolzak has taught you something. If you don't even have enough to bribe a man into letting you live, you're pretty much worthless, aren't you?"

Kolzak took out his combat knife and stuck it into the bar. Then he walked away from it. "You're closer, now," he said. "If you want to make a try for it, go right ahead."

"You wouldn't do that if you thought I had a chance."

"Who are you to say I wouldn't? Fuck you in the mouth! You're just a turd of a faggot who's afraid to fight."

It would be suicide to respond to that. It would be cowardly to look away. So

Victor just stared back, not blinking. After a time, the big man's jaw tightened. Victor tensed. He was going to have to fight after all! He didn't think it was going to end well.

"Listen to that," Osip said suddenly.

"I don't hear anything," Kolzak said

"That's right. You don't. What's keeping Pavel?"

"I'll go check."

Kolzak turned his back on the knife and went outside. Victor almost started after him. But Osip held up a warning hand. "There's nothing you can do about it." He smiled humorlessly. "There's your libertarianism for you. You are absolutely free of the government. Only you forgot that the government also protects you from men like us. Am I wrong?"

Victor cleared his throat. It felt like swallowing gravel. "No. No, you're not."

The little man stared at him impassively for a moment. Then he jerked his head toward the door. "You're nothing. If you get on your bike and leave now, I promise you that nobody will come after you."

Victor's heart was racing. "This is another game, isn't it? Like the knife."

"No, I mean it. Quite frankly, you're not worth the effort."

"But Svetlana—"

"She's a whore. She gets what whores get. Now make up your mind. Are you leaving or not?"

To his horror, Victor realized that he was already standing. His body trembled with the desire to be gone. "I—"

A gargled cry came from outside, too deep and loud to have come from a woman's throat. Instantly Osip was on his feet. He yanked the combat knife from the bar.

Svetlana walked into the room, her clothes glistening with blood. She was grinning like a madwoman. "That's two. You're next."

The little man lunged. "You dog-sucking—"

In a blur, Svetlana stepped around Osip's outstretched arm, plucking the knife from his hand. Blood sprayed from his neck. The knife was suddenly sticking out of his ribs. She seized his head and twisted.

There was a snapping noise and Svetlana let the body fall.

Then she began to cry.

Awkwardly, Victor put his arms around Svetlana. She grabbed his shirt with both her hands and buried her face in it.

He made soothing noises and patted her back.

It took a while, but at last her tears wound down. Victor offered her his handkerchief and she wiped her eyes and blew her nose with it. He knew he shouldn't ask yet, but he couldn't help it. "How the hell did you do that?"

In a voice as calm and steady as if she hadn't cried since she was a child, Svetlana said, "I told you my body was all I needed. I went to a chop shop and had it weaponized to combat standards before leaving Yekaterinburg. It takes a few minutes to power up, though, so I had to let that bastard drag me away. But that also meant that these three couldn't boot up their own enhancements in time to stop me. Where's that flask of yours? I need a drink."

Victor recalled that she had shuddered just before being taken into the back. That would be—or so he presumed—when she had powered up. Svetlana up-ended the flask and gulped down half of it in three swallows.

"Hey!" Victor made a grab for the flask, but she straight-armed him and drank it dry. Then she handed it back.

"Ahhhhh." Svetlana belched. "Sorry. You have no idea how much that de-pletes your physical resources. Alcohol's a fast way to replenish them."

"That stuff's one hundred-proof. You could injure yourself drinking like that."

"Not when I'm in refueling mode. Be a dear, would you, and see if there's any water around here? I need to clean up."

Victor went outside and walked around the restaurant. In the back he found a hand-pump and a bucket. He filled the bucket and lugged it around front.

Svetlana was just emerging from the building. She had three wallets in her hand, which she put down on the hood of a battered old Volga Siber. Then she stripped away the blood-slick clothes and sluiced herself off with the water. "Bring me a change of clothing and a bar of soap, okay?" Victor tore his eyes away from her naked body and did as she asked. He also brought her a towel from his own kit.

When Svetlana was dried and dressed again, she emptied the wallets of their money and ignition cards. She counted out the rubles in two equal piles, stuffed one in her backpack, and said, "The other half is yours if you want it." She held up an ignition card. "We part ways here. I'm taking the Mercedes. That, and the money, just about balance the books."

"Balance the books?"

"I told you. Everybody pays for everything. Which reminds me." She counted out several bills and stuck them in Victor's shirt pocket. "I owe you for half a day's ride. So here's half of what I would charge for oral sex, and a little bit more for the alcohol."

"Svetlana, I . . . The one guy said he'd let me go. I was going to take him up on it. I was going to leave you here."

"And you feel guilty about this? It's what I would have done in your place."

Victor laughed in astonishment. "I was wrong all along—*I'm* not the libertar-ian here, *you* are!"

Unexpectedly, Svetlana gave him a peck on the cheek. "You're very sweet," she said. "I hope you find whatever it is you're looking for." Then she got into the Mercedes and drove away.

For a long time Victor stared after her. Then he considered the money, still sit-ting in a stack on the Siber's hood.

Svetlana was right. Libertarianism was nothing more than a fantasy and Lib-ertarian Russia was the biggest fantasy of all. It was laughable, impossible, and in all this great, sprawling, contradictory nation, only he had ever really believed in it.

He turned his back on the money. It was an incredibly stupid thing to do, and one he knew he would regret a thousand times in the days to come. But he couldn't resist. Maybe he was a lousy libertarian. But he was still a Russian. He understood the value of a good gesture.

A light breeze came up and blew the rubles off the car and into the empty road. Victor climbed into the saddle. He kick-started his bike, and mentally thumbed through his collection of country-western music. But none of it seemed right for the occasion. So he put on Vladimir Visotsky's "Skittish Horses." It was a song that understood him. It was a song to disappear into Siberia to.

Then Victor rode off. He could feel the money blowing down the street behind him, like autumn leaves.

He was very careful not to look back.

the night train

Lavie Tidhar

Here's another story by Lavie Tidhar, whose "The Spontaneous Knotting of an Agitated String" appears elsewhere in this anthology. That one was rather quiet, but this one is anything but: this is a vivid, violent, and bizarre journey on the Night Train, where few of the passengers are what they appear to be, and death can strike from nowhere at any second along the way. . . .

H er name wasn't Molly and she didn't wear shades, reflective or otherwise.

She was watching the length of the platform.

Hua Lamphong at dusk: a warm wind blowing through the open platforms where the giant beasts puffed smoke and steam into the humid air, the roof of the train station arching high overhead.

Her name wasn't Noi, either, in case you asked, though it's a common enough name. It wasn't Porn, or Ping. It wasn't even Friday.

She was watching the platform, scanning passengers climbing aboard, porters shifting wares, uniformed police patrolling at leisure. She was there to watch out for the Old Man.

She wasn't even a girl. Not exactly. And as for why the Old Man was called the Old Man . . .

He was otherwise known as Boss Gui: head and *bigfala bos* of the Kunming Toads. She got the job when she'd killed Gui's Toad bodyguards—by default, as it were.

But that had happened back in Kunming. This was Bangkok, Bangkok at dusk—this was Hua Lamphong, greatest of train stations, where the great slugs breathed steam and were rubbed and scrubbed by the slug-boys whose job it was to nurture them before departure. And the Old Man wasn't exactly an old man, either . . .

Scanning, waiting for the Old Man to arrive: Yankee tourists with in-built cams flashing as they posed beside the great beasts, these neo-nagas of reconstituted DNA, primitive nervous system and prodigious appetite. Scanning: a group of Martian-Chinese from Tong Yun City walking cautiously—unused to the heavier gravity of this home/planet. Scanning: three Malay businessmen—Earth-Belt Corp. standardized reinforced skeletons—they moved gracefully, like dancers—wired through and through, hooked up twenty-four Earth-hours an Earth-day, seven Earth-days a week to the money-form engines, the great pulsating web of commerce and data, that singing, Sol-system-wide, Von Neumann-machine expanded network of networks of networks . . .

Wired with hidden weaponry, too: she made a note of that.

An assassin can take many shapes. It could be the sweet old lady carrying two perfectly-balanced baskets of woven bamboo over her shoulders, each basket filled with sweet addictive fried Vietnamese bananas. It could be the dapper K-pop starlet with her entourage, ostensibly here to rough it up a bit for the hovering cameras. It could be the couple of French backpackers—he with long thinning silver hair and a compressed-data cigarette between his lips, she with a new face courtesy of Soi Cowboy's front-and-back street cosmetic surgeries—baby-doll face, but the hands never lie and the hands showed her true age, in the lines etched there, the drying of the skin, the quick-bitten nails polished a cheap red—

An assassin could be anyone. A Yankee rich-kid on a retro-trip across Asia, reading *Air America* or *Neuromancer* in a genuine reproduction 1984 POD-paperback; it could be the courteous policeman helping a pretty young Lao girl with her luggage; it could be the girl herself—an Issan farmers-daughter exported to Bangkok in a century-long tradition, body augmented with vibratory vaginal inserts, perfect audio/visual-to-export, always-on record, a carefully tended Louis Wu habit and an as-carefully tended retirement plan—make enough money, get back home to Issan *wan bigfala mama*, open up a bar/hotel/bookshop and spend your days on the Mekong, waxing lyrical about the good old days, listening to Thai pop and K-pop and Nuevo Kwasa-Kwasa, growing misty-eyed nostalgic . . .

Could be anyone. She waited for the Old Man to arrive. The trains in Hua Lampong never left on time.

Her name before, or after, doesn't matter. They used to call her Mulan Rouge, which was a silly name, but the *farangs* loved it. Mulan Rouge, when she was still working Soi Cowboy, on the stage, on her knees or hands-and-knees, but seldom on her back—earning the money for the operation that would rescue her from that boy's body and make her what she truly was, which was *katoi*.

They call it the third sex, in Thailand. But she always considered herself, simply, a woman.

She ran a perimeter check. Up-front, she was awed as always by the slug. It was tied up to the front of the train, a beast fifty meters long and thirty-wide. It glistened and farted as the slug-boys murmured soothing words to it and rubbed its flesh, thirty of forty of them swarming like flies over the corpulent flesh of the slug. She checked out the driver—the woman was short, dark-skinned—a highlander from Laos, maybe. The driver sat in her harness high above the beast, her helmet entirely covering her head—the only thing she wore. Pipes came out of her flesh and into the slug's. They were one—her mind driving the beast forward, a peaceful run, the Bangkok to Nong Khai night ride, and she was the night rider. She was the train.

There were stories about joined minds liked this in the Up There. Up There, beyond the atmosphere, where the world truly began. Where the Exodus ships lumbered slowly out of the solar system, in search of better futures far away. They said there were ships driven by minds, human/Other interfaces, holding sleepers inside them like wombs. They told stories of ships who had gone mad, of sleepers destined never to awake, slow silent ships drifting forever in galactic space . . . or worse, ships where the sleepers *were* awakened, where the ship-mind became a dark god, demanding worship . . . Mulan didn't know who *they* were, or how they knew. These were stories, and stories were a currency in and of itself. Darwin's Choice used to tell her stories . . .

She met him/her flesh-riding an older katoi body, at a club on Soi Cowboy. Darwin's Choice—not the most imaginative name (he told her, laughing)—but he liked it. He had watched her dance and, later, signalled for her to join him.

She thought of him as a *he*, though Others had no sex, and most had little interest in flesh-riding. He had evolved in the Breeding Grounds, post-Cohen, billions of generations after that first evolutionary cycle in Jerusalem, and she only thought of him as *him* because the bodies he surfed always had a penis. He used to hold the penis in his hand and marvel at it. He always chose pre-op bodies, with breasts but no female genitalia. He always dressed as a woman. The operation was expensive, and a lot of katoi worked it off in stages. Taking on a passenger helped pay the bills—it wasn't just a matter of cutting off cock-and-balls and refashioning sex, there was the matter of cheekbones to sand down and an Adam's Apple to reduce, bums to pad—if you *really* had the money you got new hands. The hands always gave it away—that is, if you wanted to pass for a woman.

Which many katoi didn't. Darwin's Choice always surfed older katoi who never had the basic equipment removed. "I am neither male, nor female," he once told her. "I am not even an *I*, as such. No more than a human—a network of billions of neurons firing together—is truly an *I*. In assuming katoi, I feel closer to humanity, in many ways. I feel—divided, and yet whole."

Like most of what he said, it didn't make a lot of sense to her. He was one of the few Others who tried to understand humanity. Most Others existed within their networks, using rudimentary robots when they needed to interact with the physical world. But Darwin's Choice liked to body-surf.

With him, she earned enough for the full body package.

And more than that.

Through him, she had discovered in herself a taste for controlled violence.

Boss Gui finally came gliding down the platform—fat-boy Gui, the Old Man, *olfala bigfala bos* in the pidgin of the asteroids. His Toads surrounded him— human/toad hybrids with Qi-engines running through them: able to inflate themselves at will, to jump higher and farther, to kill with the hiss of a poisoned, forked tongue—people moved away from them like water from a hot skillet. Quickly.

Boss Gui came and stood before her. "Well?" he demanded.

He looked old. Wrinkles covered his hands and face like scars. He looked tired, and cranky—which was understandable, under the circumstances.

She had recommended delaying the trip. The Old Man refused to listen. And that was that.

She said, "I cannot identify an obvious mark—"

He smiled in satisfaction—

"But that is not to say there isn't one."

"I am Boss Gui!" he said. Toad-like, he inflated as he spoke. "Who dares try to kill me?"

"I did," she said, and he chuckled—and deflated, just a little.

"But you didn't, my little sparrow."

They had reached an understanding, the two of them. She didn't kill him—having to return the client's fee had been a bitch—and he, in turn, gave her a job. It had security attached—a pension plan, full medical, housing and salary with benefits, calculated against inflation. There were even stock options.

She never regretted her decision—until now.

"It's still too dangerous," she said now. "You're too close—"

"Silence!" He regarded her through rheumy eyes. "I am Boss Gui, boss of the Kunming Toads!"

"We are a long way from Kunming."

His eyes narrowed. "I am seventy-nine years old and still alive. How old are *you*?"

"You know how old," she said, and he laughed. "Sensitive about your age," he said. "How like a woman." He hawked up phlegm and spat on the ground. It hissed, burning a small, localised hole in the concrete.

She shrugged. "Your cabin is ready," she said, then—"Sir."

He nodded. "Very good," he said. "Tell the driver we are ready to depart."

A taste for controlled violence . . .

Darwin's Choice used his human hosts hard. He strove to understand humanity. For that purpose he visited ping-pong shows, kickboxing exhibits, Louis Wu emporiums, freak shows, the Bangkok Opera House, shopping malls, temples, churches, mosques, synagogues, slums, high-rises and train stations.

"Life," he once told her, "is a train station."

She didn't know what to make of that. What she did know: to understand humanity he tried what they did. His discarded bodies were left with heroin addiction, genital sores, hangovers and custom-made viruses that were supposed to self-destruct but not always did. Sometimes, either to apologise or for his own incomprehensible reasons, he would go into the cosmetic surgeries on Soi Cowboy and come out full transgender—seemingly unaware that his hosts may have preferred to remain in the pre-op stage. Sometimes he would wire them up in strange ways—for a month, at one point, he became a tentacle-junkie and would return from the clinics with a quivering mass of additional, aquatic limbs.

But it was his taste for danger—even while he experienced none, even while his true self kept running independently in the background, in a secure location somewhere on Earth or in orbit—that awakened her own.

The first time she killed a man . . .

Thy had gone looking for opium and found an ambush. The leader said, "Kill the flesh-rider and keep the katoi. We'll sell her in—"

She had acted instinctively. She didn't know what she was doing until it was done. Her knife—

The blade flashing in the neon light—

A scream, cut short—a gurgle—

Blood ruined her second-best blouse—

The sound of something breaking—the pain only came later. They had smashed in her nose—

Darwin's Choice *watching*—

She killed the second one with her bare hands, thumbs pressing on his windpipe until he stopped struggling—

She had laid him down on the ground almost tenderly—

Pain, making her scream, but her lungs wouldn't work—

They hit her with a taser, but somehow she didn't pass out—

She fell, but forward—hugging the man with the taser, sharing the current until there was only darkness.

"You were clinically dead," he told her, later. He sounded impressed. "What was it like?"

"Like nothing," she told him. "There was nothing there."

"You were switched off?"

She had to laugh. "You could say that."

They made love the night she was released from hospital. She licked his nipples, slowly, and felt him harden in her hand. She stroked him, burying her face in his full breasts. He reached down, touched her, and it was like electricity. She kept thinking of the dead men . . .

When she came he said, "You would do it again—" It wasn't a question.

She was tuning in to people's nodes, picking up network traffic to and from—the Malay business guys were high-encryption/high-bandwidth clouds, impossible to hack through, but here and there—

Kid with vintage paperback was on a suitably retro-playlist with a random shuffle—she caught the Doors singing "The End," which was replaced with Thaitanium's "Tom Yum Samurai" only to segue into Drunken Tiger's "Great Rebirth." Issan-girl was plugged in—a humming battery was sending a low current into her brain. She'll be out for the journey . . . The K-pop princess was playing Guilds of Ashkelon. So were her entourage. The French backpackers were stoned on one thing or the other. Others were chatting, stretching, reading, farting, tidying away bags and ordering drinks—life on board the night train to Nong Khai was always the same.

The train was coming alive, the slug belching steam—the whole train shuddered as it began to crawl along the smooth tracks, slug-boys falling off it like fleas.

Tuning, scanning—someone two cars down watching the feed from a reality-porn channel, naked bodies woven together like a tapestry, a beach somewhere—Koh Samui or an off-Earth habitat, it was impossible to say.

Boss Gui: "I'm hungry!"

Mulan Rouge: "Food's coming—" in the dining car they were getting ready, a wok already going, rice cooker steaming, crates of beer waiting—

"I want kimchi!"

"I'll see if they have any—" though she knew they didn't.

"No need—" a long, slow, drawn-out hum from one of the Toads. "I keep for boss."

Limited vocabulary—you didn't breed Toads for their brains. Though she had to wonder . . . "Keep in cooler."

She watched the Toad reach into what the Australians called an *esky*. There was a jar of kimchi in there, and . . . other stuff.

Like a jar of living flies, for the Toads. Like what appeared to be a foetal sack, preserved in dry ice . . .

Other things.

She left them to it, returned to watching—waiting.

"You would do it again," Darwin's Choice had said. And he—she—it—was right. She had liked it—a sense of overwhelming *power* came with violence, and if it could be controlled, it could be used. Power depended on how you used it.

She counted the proceeding years in augmentations and bodies. Three in Vientiane—she had followed Darwin's Choice there to buy up a stash of primitive communist VR art—the deal went wrong and she had to execute two men and a woman before they got away. She had snake-eyes installed after that. A man and a katoi in Chiang Mai—DC was buying a genuine Guilds of Ashkelon virtual artefact that had turned out to be a fake. She had had her skeleton strengthened following that . . .

With each kill, new parts of her. With each, more power—but never over him.

Gradually, Darwin's Choice appeared less and less in the flesh. She had to cast around for work, hiring out as bodyguard, enforcer—hired killer, sometimes, only sometimes. Finally DC never reappeared. He had tried to explain it to her, once . . .

"We are I-loops but, unlike humans, we are *self-aware* I-loops. Not self-aware in the sense of consciousness, or what humans call consciousness. Self-aware in the sense that we are—we *can*—know every loop, every routine and sub-routine. Digital, not neurological. And as we are aware so do we change, mutating code, merging code, sharing . . ."

"Is that how you make love?"

"Love is a physical thing," he said. "It's hormone-driven."

"You can only feel love when you're body-surfing?"

He only shrugged.

"How do you . . ." she searched for the word, settled on—"mate?"

Imagine two or more Others. Endless lines of code meeting in digital space—IFs and ANDs and ORs branching into probabilities, cycling through endless branches of logic at close to the speed of light—

"Is that what you're like?"

"No. Shh . . ."

. . . and *meeting*, merging, mixing, mutating—"And dying, to be an Other is to die, again and again, to *evolve* with every cycle, to cull and select and grow, achieve new, unexpected forms—"

... not so much *mating* as *joining*, and splitting, and joining again—"The way a human may, over seven years, replace every single *atom* in their bodies, but still retain the illusion of person, remain an I-loop—"

... but for Others, it meant becoming something new—"Giving birth to one's self, in essence."

The body he was surfing had been stoned, then, when he told her all this. When he was gone, she hired out. She enjoyed the work, but freelancing was hard. When the contract on Boss Giu came, she took it—and upgraded to corporate.

"We are never alone," DC told her, just before he left forever. "There are always . . . us. So many of us . . ."

"Can't you all join?" she had asked. "Join in to one?"

"Too much code slows you down," he said. "We have . . . limits. Though we share, too—share the way humans can't."

"We can share in ways *you* can't," she said. Her finger dug into his anus when she spoke. DC squirmed under her, then gave a small moan. His breasts were freckled, his penis circumcised. "True," he said—whispered—and drew her to him with an urgency they were sharing only rarely, by then.

That had been the last time . . .

She wondered which species' sharing was better—figured she would never know.

They said sex was overrated . . .

Yankee boy blue was no longer listening to the Doors—she couldn't sense his node anymore at all. She blinked, feeling panic rise. How did he slip past her? Scanning for him—his vintage sci fi paperback was left on his bunk.

Shit.

She glanced back into the cabin—Boss Gui glared up at her, then clutched his bloated stomach and gave a groan. The two Toads jumped—too hard, and hit the ceiling.

Double shit—she said, "What's wrong?" but knew.

He said, "It's starting."

She shook her head—no. "It can't. It's too soon."

"It's *time*."

"Shit!"—a third time, and it was counter-productive and she knew it.

Boss Gui's face was twisted in pain. "It's coming!"

And suddenly she picked up the North American's node.

"Sh—"

They were going to Nong Khai, from there to cross into Laos. Boss Gui wanted to expand the business, and business was booming in a place called Vang Vieng, a tawdry little mini-Macau at the foothills of the mountains, four hours from Vientiane—a place of carefully regulated lawlessness, of cheap opium and cheaper synths, of games-worlds cowboys and body hackers, of tentacle-junkies and doll emporiums and government taxes that Boss Gui wanted a part of.

A *large* part of.

There were families running Vang Vieng but he was the Old Man, *olfala bigfala bos blong ol man tod blong Kunming*, and the Chinese had anyway bought up most of Laos back in the early privatisation days. He would cut deals with some, terminate the others, and slice himself a piece of the Vang Vieng dumpling—that was the plan.

She had advised him against it. She told him it was too soon to travel. She asked him to wait.

He wouldn't.

She sort of had an inkling as to the why . . .

She was picking up the kid's node right next to the driver's.

Which was not good at all.

The driver's, first: an incomprehensible jumble of emotion, in turns horny, soothing, driven, paused—the driver and the slug as one, their minds pulsating in union—hunger and sex made it go faster. Snatches of Beethoven—for some reason it calmed down the slugs. The driver not aware of the extra passenger—yet.

The kid wasn't really a kid . . .

His node blocked to her—black impenetrable walls, an emptiness not even returning pings. He was alone in his own head—which must have been terrifying.

She had to get to the front of the train. She had to get on the slug. And Boss Gui was convulsing.

"Why are you just standing there, *girl?*"

She tried to keep her voice even. "I found the assassin. He is planning to kill the slug—destroy the entire train, and you with it."

Boss Gui took that calmly. "Clever," he said, then grimaced. His naked belly glistened, a dark shape moving beneath the membrane of skin. The Toads looked helpless, standing there. She flashed them a grin. "I'll be right back," she said. Then she left, hearing Boss Gui's howl of rage behind her.

Running down the length of the train—through the dining-car, past toilets already beginning to smell, past farang backpackers and Lao families and Thais returning to Udon from the capital—past babies and backpacks and bemused conductors in too-tight trousers that showed their butts off to advantage—warm wind came in through the open windows and she blocked off the public nodes broadcasting news in Thai and Belt Pidgin. The end of the train was a dead end, a smooth wall with no windows. She kicked it—again and again, augmented muscles expending too much energy, but it began to break, and fading sunlight seeped through.

How had the kid gotten through? He must have had gecko-hands—climbed out of the window and crawled his way along the side of the train, below the window-line, all the way to the slug . . .

She reached out—sensed the driver's confusion as another entity somehow wormed its way into the two-way mahout/slug interface. *Stop!*

Confusion from the slug. The signals rushing through, too fast—horny/hungry/faster—faster!

He was going to crash the train. The driver: *Who is this? You can't*—

She kept kicking. The wall gave way—behind it was the slug's wide back, the driver sitting cross-legged on the beast, the intruder behind it, a hand on the driver's shoulder—the hand grew roots that penetrated the woman and the beast both.

Hostile mahout interface initiated.

The driver was fighting it, and losing badly. No one hijacked slug trains.

On her private channel—Boss Gui, screaming. "Get back here!"

"Get your own fucking midwife!"

But she could sense his pain, confusion. How many times had he gone through it in the past? she wondered. She had never seen a birth—but then, there wouldn't be one, not unless—

The hijacker had kept the driver alive. Had to—the whole thing had to look like an accident, the driver's body found in the wreckage, unmolested—no doubt he planned to jump before impact.

Could he?

She crept behind him. neither hijacker nor driver paid her any attention. And what could she do? Killing the hijacker would kill the interface—he was already in too deep.

Unless . . .

From Boss Gui, far away—"Hurry!"

Sometimes she wondered what would have happened if Darwin's Choice had stayed behind. It was possible for katoi to give birth, these days . . . could an Other foster a child? Would he want to?

Or he could have flesh-ridden a host . . . she would have kept the male parts just for that. If he'd asked her.

But he never did.

The hijacker must have had an emergency eject. She had to find the trigger for it—

Wind was rushing at her, too fast. It was hard to maintain balance on the soft spongy flesh of the slug. It was accelerating—too fast.

She was behind the hijacker now—she reached out, put her hand on the back of his head. A black box . . .

She punched through with a data-spike while her other hand . . .

Darkness. The smell of rotting leaves. The smell of bodies in motion, sweat—hunger, a terrible hunger—

"Who the fuck are you? How did you *get* in here?"

Panic was good. She sent through images—her standing behind him, the data-spike in his head—and what else she was doing.

"You can't do that . . ."

She had pushed a second data-spike through his clothes and through the sphincter muscle, into the bowels themselves—detached a highly-illegal, replicator probe inside.

She felt the slug slow down, just a fraction. The hijacker trying to understand—

She said, "I am being nice."

She was.

He had a choice.

The probe inside him was already working. It was the equivalent of graffiti artists at work. It replicated a message, over every cell, every blood vessel, every muscle and tendon. It would be impossible to scrub—you'd need to reach a good clinic and by then it'd be too late.

The message said, *I killed the slug train to Nong Khai.*

It was marking him. He wasn't harmed. She couldn't risk killing him, killing the interface. But this way, whether he got off the train or not, he was a dead man.

"I'll count to five."

He let go at three.

Light, blinding her. The wind rushed past—the driver sat as motionless as ever, but the train had slowed down. The hijacker was gone—she followed him back through the hole in the wall.

He was lying on his bunk, still reading his book. He wasn't listening to music anymore. Their eyes met. She grinned. He turned his gaze. She had given him a choice and she'd abide by it—but if the Toads happened to find out, she didn't rate his chances . . .

Well, the next stop was in an hour. She'd give him an extra half hour after that—a running start.

She went back to the boss.

"It's coming!" Boss Gui said. She knelt beside him. His belly-sack was moving, writhing, the thing inside trying to get out. She helped—a fingernail slicing through the membrane, gently. A sour smell—she reached in where it was sticky, gooey, warm—found two small arms, a belly—pulled.

"You sorted out the problem?"

"Keep breathing."

"Yes?"

"Yes, of course I did! Now push!"

Boss Gui pushed, breathing heavily. "I'm getting too old for this . . ." he said.

Then he heaved, one final time, and the small body *detached* itself from him and came into her hands. She held it, staring at the tiny body, the bald head, the small penis, the five-fingered hands—a tiny Boss Gui, not yet fat but just as wrinkled.

It was hooked up with a cord to its progenitor. With the same flick of a nail, she cut it cleanly.

The baby cried. She rocked it, said, "There, there."

"Drink," Boss Gui said—weakly. One of the Toads came forward. Boss Gui fastened lips on the man/toad's flesh and sucked—a vampire feasting. He had Toad genes—so did the baby, who burped and suddenly ballooned in her hands before shrinking again.

"A true Gui!" the Old Man said.

She stared at the little creature in her hands . . . "Which makes how many, now?" she said.

The boss shrugged, pushing the Toad away, buttoning up his own shirt. "Five, six? Not many."

"You would install him at Vang Vieng?"

"An assurance of my goodwill—and an assurance of Gui control there, too, naturally. Yes. An heir is only useful when he is put to use."

She thought of Darwin's Choice. "Evolution is everything," he would have told her. "We evolve constantly, with every cycle. Whereas you . . ."

She stared at the baby clone. It burped happily and closed its little eyes. Gui's way was not unpopular with the more powerful families . . . but sooner or later someone would come to challenge succession and then it wouldn't matter how many Guis there were.

Suddenly she missed DC, badly.

She rocked the baby to sleep, hugging it close to her chest. The train's thoughts came filtering through in the distance—comfort, and warmth, food and safety— the slow rhythmic motion was soothing. After a while, when the baby was asleep, she handed him to the Old Man, no words exchanged, and went to the dining car in search of a cup of tea.

My father's singularity

BRENDA COOPER

Sometimes progress, like future shock, can be in the eye of the beholder. . . .

Brenda Cooper is a technology professional, a futurist, and a public speaker, in addition to being a writer. She's a frequent contributor to *Analog*, and has also sold to *Asimov's*, *Clarkesworld*, *Nature*, *Strange Horizons*, and to many anthology markets. Her first novel was *Building Harlequin's Moon*, in collaboration with Larry Niven. Her other novels include *The Silver Ship and the Sea*, *Reading the Wind*, and *Wings of Creation*. Coming up is a new novel, *Mayan December*. She lives in Kirkland, Washington.

In my first memory of my father, we are sitting on the porch, shaded from the burning sun's assault on our struggling orchards. My father is leaning back in his favorite wooden rocker, sipping a cold beer with a half-naked lady on the label, and saying, "Paul, you're going to see the most amazing things. You will live forever." He licks his lips, the way our dogs react to treats, his breath coming faster. "You will do things I can't even imagine." He pauses, and we watch a flock of geese cross the sky. When he speaks again, he sounds wistful. "You won't ever have to die."

The next four of five memories are variations on that conversation, punctuated with the heat and sweat of work, and the smell of seasons passing across the land.

I never emerged from this particular conversation with him feeling like I knew what he meant. It was clear he thought it would happen to me and not to him, and that he had mixed feelings about that, happy for me and sad for himself. But he was always certain.

Sometimes he told me that I'd wake up one morning and all the world around me would be different. Other nights, he said, "Maybe there'll be a door, a shining door, and you'll go through it and you'll be better than human." He always talked about it the most right before we went into Seattle, which happened about twice a year, when the pass was open and the weather wasn't threatening our crops.

The whole idea came to him out of books so old they were bound paper with no moving parts, and from a brightly-colored magazine that eventually disintegrated from being handled. My father's hands were big and rough and his calluses wore the words off the paper.

Two beings always sat at his feet. Me, growing up, and a dog, growing old. He adopted them at mid-life or they came to him, a string of one dog at a time, always connected so that a new one showed within a week of the old one's death. He and his dogs were a mutual admiration society. They liked me fine, but they never adored me. They encouraged me to run my fingers through their stiff fur or their soft fur, or their wet, matted fur if they'd been out in the orchard sprinklers, but they were in doggie heaven when he touched them. They became completely still and their eyes softened and filled with warmth.

I'm not talking about the working dogs. We always had a pair of border collies for the sheep, but they belonged to the sheep and the sheep belonged to them and we were just the fence and the feeders for that little ecosystem.

These dogs were his children just like me, although he never suggested they would see the singularity. I would go beyond and they would stay and he and the dogs accepted that arrangement even if I didn't.

I murmured confused assent when my father said words about how I'd become whatever comes after humans.

Only once did I find enough courage to tell him what was in my heart. I'd been about ten, and I remember how cold my hands felt clutching a glass of iced lemonade while heat-sweat poured down the back of my neck. When he told me I would be different, I said, "No, Dad. I want to be like you when I grow up." He was the kindness in my life, the smile that met me every morning and made me eggs with the yolks barely soft and toast that melted butter without burning.

He shook his head, and patted his dog, and said, "You are luckier than that."

His desire for me to be different than him was the deepest rejection possible, and I bled for the wounds.

After the fifth year in seven that climate-freak storms wrecked the apples—this time with bone-crushing ice that set the border collies crazed with worry—I knew I'd have to leave if I was ever going to support my father. Not by crossing the great divide of humanity to become the seed of some other species, but to get schooled away from the slow life of farming sheep and Jonagolds. The farm could go on without me. We had the help of two immigrant families that each owned an acre of land that was once ours.

Letting my father lose the farm wasn't a choice I could even imagine. I'd go over to Seattle and go to school. After, I'd get a job and send money home, the way the Mexicans did when I was little and before the government gave them part of our land to punish us. Not that we were punished. We liked the Ramirezes and the Alvarezes. They, too, needed me to save the farm.

But that's not this story. Except that Mona Alvarez drove me to Leavenworth to catch the silver Amtrak train, her black hair flying away from her lipstick-black lips, and her black painted fingernails clutching the treacherous steering wheel of our old diesel truck. She was so beautiful I decided right then that I would miss her almost as much as I would miss my father and the bending apple trees and the working dogs and the sheep. Maybe I would miss Mona even more.

Mona, however, might not miss me. She waved once after she dropped me off, and then she and the old truck were gone and I waited amid the electric cars and the old tourists with camera hats and data jewelry and the faint marks of implants in the soft skin between their thumbs and their index fingers. They looked like they saw everything and nothing all at once. If they came to our farm the coyotes and the re-patriated wolves would run them down fast.

On the other end of the train ride, I found the University of Washington, now sprawled all across Seattle, a series of classes and meet ups and virtual lessons that spidered out from the real brick buildings. An old part of the campus still squatted by the Montlake Cut, watching over water and movement that looked like water spiders but was truly lines of people with oars on nanofab boats as thin as paper.

Our periodic family trips to Seattle hadn't really prepared me for being a student. The first few years felt like running perpetually uphill, my brain just not going as fast as everyone else's.

I went home every year. Mona married one of the Ramirez boys and had two babies by the time three years had passed, and her beauty changed to a quiet soft-ness with no time to paint her lips or her nails. Still, she was prettier than the sticks for girls that chewed calorie-eating gum and did their homework while they ran to Gasworks Park and back on the Burke-Gilman Trail, muttering an-swers to flashcards painted on their retinas with light.

I didn't date those girls; I wouldn't have known how to interrupt the speed of their lives and ask them out. I dated storms of data and new implants and the rush of ideas until by my senior year I was actually keeping up.

When I graduated, I got a job in genetics that paid well enough for me to live in an artist's loft in a green built row above Lake Union. I often climbed onto the garden roof and sat on an empty bench and watched the Space Needle change decorations every season and the little wooden boats sailing on the still lake be-low me. But mostly I watched over my experiments, playing with new medical implants to teach children creativity and to teach people docked for old age in the University hospital how to talk again, how to remember.

I did send money home. Mona's husband died in a flash-flood one fall. Her face took on a sadness that choked in my throat, and I started paying her to take care of my father.

He still sat on the patio and talked about the singularity, and I managed not to tell him how quaint the old idea sounded. I recognized myself, would always rec-ognize myself. In spite of the slow speed of the farm, a big piece of me was always happiest at home, even though I couldn't be there more than a day or so at a time. I can't explain that—how the best place in the world spit me out after a day or so.

Maybe I believed too much happiness would kill me, or change me. Or maybe I just couldn't move slow enough to breathe in the apple air anymore. Whatever the reason, the city swept me back fast, folding me in its dancing ads and shimmering opportunities and art.

Dad didn't really need me anyway. He had the Mexicans and he still always had a dog, looking lovingly up at him. Max, then OwlFace, then Blue. His fin-gers had turned to claws and he had cataracts scraped from his eyes twice, but he still worked with the harvest, still carried a bushel basket and still found fruit buried deep in the trees.

I told myself he was happy.

Then one year, he startled when I walked up on the porch and his eyes filled with fear.

I hadn't changed. I mean, not much. I had a new implant, I had a bigger cloud, researchers under me, so much money that what I sent my father—what he needed for the whole orchard—was the same as a night out at a concert and dinner at Canlis. But I was still me, and Blue—the current dog—accepted me, and Mona's oldest son called me "Uncle Paul" on his way out to tend the sheep.

I told my father to pack up and come with me.

He ran his fingers through the fur on Blue's square head. "I used to have a son, but he left." He sounded certain. "He became the next step for us. For humans."

He was looking right at me, even looking in my eyes, and there was truly no recognition there. His look made me cold to the spine, cold to the ends of my fingers, even with the sun driving sweat down my back.

I kissed his forehead. I found Mona and told her I'd be back in a few weeks and she should have him packed up.

Her eyes were beautiful and terrible with reproach as she declared, "He doesn't want to leave."

"I can help him."

"Can you make him young, like you?"

Her hair had gone gray at the edges, lost the magnificent black that had glistened in the sun like her goth lipstick all those years ago. God, how could I have been so selfish? I could have given her some of what I had.

But I liked her better touched by pain and age and staying part of my past. Like the act of saving them didn't.

I hadn't known that until that very moment, when I suddenly hated myself for the wrinkles around her eyes and the way her shoulders bent in a little bit even though she was only fifty-seven like me. "I'll bring you some, too. I can get some of the best nano-meds available." Hell, I'd designed some of them, but Mona wouldn't understand that. "I can get creams that will erase the wrinkles from your hands."

She sighed. "Why don't you just leave us?"

Because then I would have no single happy place. "Because I need my father. I need to know how he's doing."

"I can tell you from here."

My throat felt thick. "I'll be back in a week." I turned away before she could see the inexplicable tears in my eyes. By then I flew back and forth, and it was a relief to focus down on the gauges in my head, flying manual until I got close enough to Seattle airspace that the feds grabbed the steering from me and there was nothing to do but look down at the forest and the green resort playgrounds of Cle Elum below me and to try not to think too hard about my dad or about Mona Alvarez and her sons.

I had moved into a condo on Alki Beach, and I had a view all the way to Canada. For two days after I returned, the J-pod whales cavorted offshore, great elongated yin and yang symbols rising and falling through the waters of Puget Sound.

The night before I went back for Mona and my father, I watched the boardwalk below me. People walked dogs and Rollerbladed and bicycled and a few of the chemical-sick walked inside of big rolling bubbles like the hamster I'd had when I was a kid. Even nano-medicine and the clever delivery of genetically matched and married designer solutions couldn't save everyone.

I wish I could say that I felt sorry for the people in the bubbles, and I suppose in some distant way I did. But nothing bad had ever happened to me. I didn't get sick. I'd never married or divorced. I had nice dates sometimes, and excellent season tickets for Seattle Arts and Lectures.

I flew Mona back with my father. We tried to take Blue, but the dog balked at getting in the car, and raced away, lost in the apple trees in no time. Mona looked sick and said, "We should wait."

I glanced at my father's peaceful face. He had never cried when his dogs died or left, and now he had a small smile, and I had the fleeting thought that maybe he was proud of Blue for choosing the farm and the sheep and the brown-skinned boys. "Will your sons care for the dog?"

"Their children love him."

So we arrived back in West Seattle, me and Mona and my father.

I got busy crafting medicine to fix my father. These things didn't take long—time moved fast in the vast cloud of data I had security rights for. I crunched my father's DNA and RNA and proteins and the specifics of his blood in no time, and told the computers what to do while I set all of us out a quiet dinner on the biggest of the decks. Mona commented on the salty scent of Puget Sound and watched the fast little ferries zip back and forth in the water and refused to meet my eyes.

Dad simply stared at the water.

"He needs a dog," she said.

"I know." I queried from right there, sending a bot out to look. It reported fairly fast. "I'll be right back. Can you watch him?"

She looked startled.

An hour later I picked Nanny up at Sea-Tac, a middle-aged golden retriever, service-trained, a dog with no job since most every disease except the worst allergies to modernity could be fixed.

Mona looked awed almost to fear when I showed up with the dog, but she smiled and uncovered the dinner I'd left waiting.

Nanny and Dad were immediately enchanted with each other, her love for him the same as every other dog's in his life, cemented the minute she smelled him. I didn't understand, but if it had been any other way, I would have believed him lost.

The drugs I designed for him didn't work. It happens that way sometimes. Not often. But some minds can't accept the changes we can make. In the very old, it can kill them. Dad was too strong to die, although Mona looked at me one day, after they had been with me long enough that the wrinkles around her eyes had lost depth but not so long that they had left her face entirely. "You changed him. He's worse."

I might have. How would I know?

But I do know I lost my anchor in the world. Nothing in my life had been my singularity. I hadn't crossed into a new humanity like he prophesied over and over. I hadn't left him behind.

Instead, he left me behind. He recognized Nanny every day, and she him. But he never again called me Paul, or told me how I would step beyond him.

the starship mechanic

jay Lake and ken scholes

Highly prolific writer Jay Lake seems to have appeared nearly everywhere with short work in the last few years, including *Asimov's, Interzone, Jim Baen's Universe, Tor.com, Clarkesworld, Strange Horizons, Aeon, Postscripts, Electric Velocipede,* and many other markets, producing enough short fiction that he already has released four collections, even though his career is only a few years old: *Greetings from Lake Wu, Green Grow the Rushes-Oh, American Sorrows,* and *Dogs in the Moonlight.* His novels include *Rocket Science, Trial of Flowers, Mainspring,* and *Escapement,* He's the coeditor, with Deborah Layne, of the prestigious Polyphony anthology series, now in six volumes, and has also edited the anthologies *All-Star Zeppelin Adventure Stories* with David Moles, *TEL: Stories,* and, most recently, *Other Earths* with Nick Gevers, and *Spicy Slipstream Stories* with Nick Mamatas. The most recent examples of his own work are three new novels, *Green, The Madness of Flowers,* and *Pinion;* three chapbook novellas, "Death of a Starship," "The Baby Killers," and "The Specific Gravity of Grief"; and a new collection, *The Sky That Wraps.* Coming up is another new novel, *Sunspin.* He won the John W. Campbell Award for Best New Writer in 2004. Lake lives in Portland, Oregon.

Ken Scholes is another prolific writer whose short works have appeared in a diverse mix of markets such as *Subterranean, Tor.com, Talebones, Clarkesworld, Weird Tales,* and *Realms of Fantasy.* His books include the novels *Lamentation* and *Canticle* of the Psalms of Isaak sequence, *Last Flight of the Goddess, A Weeping Czar Beholds the Fallen Moon,* and the collection *Long Walks, Last Flights: And Other Strange Journeys.* His most recent books are *Antiphon,* a novel in the Isaak series, and a new collection, *Diving Mimes, Weeping Czars and Other Unusual Suspects.* Upcoming are two more Isaak novels, *Requiem* and *Hymn.*

Here they join forces for a wry story that shows us that a workman is only as good as his tools—and that some of those tools are specialized for some very weird tasks, indeed.

The floor of Borderlands Books had been polished to mirror brightness. A nice trick with old knotty pine, but Penauch would have been a weapons-grade obsessive-compulsive if he'd been human. I'd thought about setting him to detailing my car, but he's just as likely to polish it down to aluminum and steel after deciding the paint was an impurity.

When he discovered that the human race recorded our ideas in *books*, he'd been impossible to keep away from the store. Penauch didn't actually read them, not as such, and he was most reluctant to touch the volumes. He seemed to view books as vehicles, launch capsules to propel ideas from the dreaming mind of the human race into our collective forebrain.

Despite the fact that Penauch was singular, unitary, a solitary alien in the human world, he apparently didn't conceive of us as anything but a collective entity. The xenoanthropologists at Berkeley were carving Ph.D.s out of that particular clay as fast as their grad students could transcribe Penauch's conversations with me.

He'd arrived the same as David Bowie in that old movie. No, not *Brother from Another Planet; The Man Who Fell to Earth*. Tumbled out of the autumn sky over the Cole Valley neighborhood of San Francisco like a maple seed, spinning with his arms stretched wide and his mouth open in a teakettle shriek audible from the Ghost Fleet in Suisun Bay all the way down to the grubby streets of San Jose.

> The subject's fallsacs when fully deployed serve as a tympanum, producing a rhythmic vibration at a frequency perceived by the human ear as a high-pitched shriek. Xenophysiological modeling has thus far failed to generate testable hypotheses concerning the volume of the sound produced. Some observers have speculated that the subject deployed technological assistance during atmospheric entry, though no evidence of this was found at the landing site, and subject has never indicated this was the case.
>
> —Jude A. Feldman quoting Jen West Scholes; A Reader's Guide to
> Earth's Only Living Spaceman; *Borderlands Books*, 2014

It was easier, keeping Penauch in the bookstore. The owners didn't mind. They'd had hairless cats around the place for years—a breed called sphinxes. The odd animals served as a neighborhood tourist attraction and business draw. A seven-foot alien with a face like a plate of spaghetti and a cluster of writhing arms wasn't all that different. Not in a science fiction bookstore, at least.

Thing is, when Penauch was out in the world, he had a tendency to *fix* things. This fixing often turned out to be not so good.

No technology was involved. Penauch's body was demonstrably able to modify the chitinous excrescences of his appendages at will. If he needed a cutting edge, he ate a bit of whatever steel was handy and swiftly metabolized it. If he needed electrical conductors, he sought out copper plumbing. If he needed logic probes, he consumed sand or diamonds or glass.

It was all the same to Penauch.

As best any of us could figure out, Penauch was a sort of *tool*. A Swiss Army knife that some spacefaring race had dropped or thrown away, abandoned until he came to rest on Earth's alien shore.

And Penauch only spoke to me.

> *The question of Penauch's mental competence has bearing in both law and ethics. Pratt and Shaw (2013) have effectively argued that the alien fails the Turing test, both at a gross observational level and within the context of finer measurements of conversational intent and cooperation. Cashier (2014) claims an indirectly derived Stanford-Binet score in the 99th percentile, but seemingly contradicts herself by asserting that Penauch's sentience is at best an open question. Is he (or it) a machine, a person, or something else entirely?*
> —S.G. Browne, "A Literature Review of the Question of Alien
> Mentation"; Journal of Exogenic Studies, *Volume II, Number 4,*
> *August, 2015*

The first time he fixed something was right after he'd landed. Penauch impacted with that piercing shriek at 2:53 p.m. Pacific Time on Saturday, July 16, 2011, at the intersection of Cole and Parnassus. Every window within six blocks shattered. Almost a hundred pedestrians and shoppers in the immediate area were treated for lacerations from broken glass, over two dozen more for damage to hearing and sinuses.

I got to him first, stumbling out of Cole Hardware with a headache like a cartoon anvil had been dropped on me. Inside, we figured a bomb had gone off. The rising noise and the vibrating windows. All the vases in the homeware section had exploded. Luckily I'd been with the fasteners. The nails *sang*, but they didn't leap off the shelves and try to make hamburger of me.

Outside, there was this guy lying in a crater in the middle of the intersection, like Wile E. Coyote after he'd run out of Acme patented jet fuel. I hurried over, touched his shoulder, and realized what a goddamned mess he was. Then half a dozen eyes opened, and something like a giant rigatoni farted before saying, "Penauch."

Weird thing was, I could *hear* the spelling.

Though I didn't know it in that moment, my old life was over, my new one begun.

Penauch then looked at my shattered wristwatch, grabbed a handful of BMW windshield glass, sucked it down, and moments later fixed my timepiece.

For some value of "fixed."

It still tells time, somewhere with a base seventeen counting system and twenty-eight point one five seven hour day. It shows me the phases of Phobos and Deimos, evidence that he'd been on (or near) Mars. Took a while to figure that one out. And the thing warbles whenever someone gets near me carrying more than about eight ounces of petroleum products. Including grocery bags, for example, and most plastics.

I could probably get millions for it on eBay. Penauch's first artifact, and one of less than a dozen in private hands.

The government owns him now, inasmuch as anyone owns Penauch. They can't keep him anywhere. He "fixes" his way out of any place he gets locked into. He comes back to San Francisco, finds me, and we go to the bookstore. Where Penauch polishes the floors and chases the hairless cats and draws pilgrims from all over the world to pray in Valencia Street. The city gave up on traffic control a long time ago. It's a pedestrian mall now when he's around.

The problem has always been, none of us have any idea what Penauch *is*. What he *does*. What he's *for*. I'm the only one he talks to, and most of what he says is Alice in Wonderland dialog, except when it isn't. Two new semiconductor companies have been started through analysis of his babble, and an entire novel chemical feedstock process for converting biomass into plastics.

Then one day, down on the mirrored floor of Borderlands Books, Penauch looked at me and said quite clearly, "They're coming back."

I was afraid we were about to get our answers.

> *It was raining men in the Castro, literally, and every single one of them was named Todd. Every single one of them wore Hawaiian shirts and khaki shorts and Birkenstocks. Every single one of them landed on their backs, flopped like trout for a full minute and leaped to their feet shouting one word: "Penauch!"*
>
> *—San Francisco Chronicle, November 11th, 2015;*
> *Gail Carriger reporting*

"I must leave," Penauch said, his voice heavy as he stroked a hairless cat on the freshly polished floor of the bookstore.

On a small TV in the back office of the store, an excited reporter in Milk Plaza spoke rapidly about the strange visitors who'd fallen from the sky. Hundreds of men named Todd, now scattered out into the city with one word on their tongues. As it played in the background, I watched Penauch and could feel the sadness coming off of him in waves. "Where will you go?"

Penauch stood. "I don't know. Anywhere but here. Will you help me?"

The bell on the door jingled and a man entered the store. "Penauch," he said.

I looked up at the visitor. His Hawaiian shirt was an orange that hurt my eyes, decorated in something that looked like cascading pineapples. He smiled and scowled at the same time.

Penauch moved quickly and suddenly the room smelled of ozone and cabbage.

The man, named Todd I assumed, was gone.

I looked at my alien, took in the slow wriggle of his pale and determined face. "What did you do?"

Penauch's clustered silver eyes leaked mercury tears. "I . . . un-fixed him."

We ran out the back. We climbed into my car over on Guerrero. We drove north and away.

> *Xenolinguists have expended considerable effort on the so-called "Todd Phenomenon." Everyone on 11/11/15 knew the visitors from outer space were named Todd, yet no one could say how or why. This is the best documented case of what can be argued as telepathy in the modern scientific*

record, yet it is equally worthless by virtue of being impossible to either replicate or falsify.
—*Christopher Barzak, blog entry, January 14th, 2016*

Turning east and then north, we stayed ahead of them for most of a week. We made it as far as Edmonton before the man-rain caught up to us.

While Penauch slept, I grabbed snacks of news from the radio. These so-called Todds spread out in their search, my friend's name the only word upon their lips. They made no effort to resist the authorities. Three were shot by members of the Washington State Patrol. Two were killed by Navy SEALS in the small town of St. Maries, Idaho. They stole cars. They drove fast. They followed after us.

And then they found us in Edmonton.

We were at an A&W drive-through window when the first Todd caught up to the car. He t-boned us into the side of the restaurant with his Mercedes, pushing Penuach against me. The Todd was careful not to get within reach.

"Penauch," he shouted from outside the window. My friend whimpered. Our car groaned and ground as his hands moved over the dashboard, trying to fix it.

Two other cars hemmed us in, behind and before. Todds in Hawaiian shirts and khaki shorts stepped out, unfazed by the cold. One climbed onto the hood of my Corvair. "Your services are still required."

Penauch whimpered again. I noticed that the Todd's breath did not show in the sub-zero air.

The air shimmered as a bending light enfolded us.

> *"Af-afterwards, it, uh, it did't m-matter so much. I m-mean, uh, you know? He smiled at me. Well, n-not an, uh, a smile. Not with that face. Like, a virtual smile? Th-then he was g-gone. Blown out like a candle. You know? Flame on, flame off."*
> —*RCMP transcript of eyewitness testimony; Edmonton, AB; 11/16/15*

I awoke in a dark place choking for air, my chest weighted with fluid. Penauch's hand settled upon my shoulder. The heaviness leapt from me.

"Where am I?"

I heard a sound not unlike something heavy rolling in mud. It was a thick, wet noise and words formed alongside it in my mind. *You are in*—crackle hiss warble—*medical containment pod of the Starship*—but the name of the vessel was incomprehensible to me. *Exposure to our malfunctioning*—hiss crackle warble—*mechanic has infected you with trace elements of*—here another word I could not understand—*viruses.*

"I don't get it," I said.

Penauch's voice was low. "You're not meant to. But once I've fixed you, you will be returned to the store."

I looked at him. "What about you?"

He shook his head, the rigatoni of his face slapping itself gently. "My services are required here. I am now operating within my design parameters."

I opened my mouth to ask another question but then the light returned and I was falling. Beside me, Penauch fell, too, and he held my hand tightly. "Do not let go," he said as we impacted.

This time we made no crater as we landed. We stood and I brushed myself off. "I have no idea what any of this means."

"It won't matter," Penauch told me. "But say goodbye to the cats for me."

"I will," I promised.

"I liked your planet. Now that the"—again, the incomprehensible ship's name slid entirely over my brain—"is operational once more, I suppose we'll find others." He sighed. "I hope I malfunction again soon." He stretched out a hand and fixed me a final time.

I blinked at him and somehow, mid-blink, I stood in the center of Valencia Street.

I walked into Borderlands Books, still wondering exactly how I was wandering the streets of San Francisco in an orange Hawaiian shirt and a pair of khaki shorts three sizes too large.

A pretty girl smiled at me from behind the counter. "Hi Bill," she said. "Where've you been?"

I shrugged.

A hairless cat ran in front of me, feet scampering over floors that were badly in need of a polish.

"Goodbye," I told it, but didn't know why.

sleepover

ALASTAIR REYNOLDS

Alastair Reynolds is a frequent contributor to *Interzone*, and has also sold to *Asimov's Science Fiction*, *Spectrum SF*, and elsewhere. His first novel, *Revelation Space*, was widely hailed as one of the major SF books of the year; it was quickly followed by *Chasm City*, *Redemption Ark*, *Absolution Gap*, *Century Rain*, and *Pushing Ice*, all big sprawling space operas that were big sellers as well, establishing Reynolds as one of the best and most popular new SF writers to enter the field in many years. His other books include a novella collection, *Diamond Dogs, Turquoise Days*, and a chapbook novella, "The Six Directions of Space," as well as two collections, *Galactic North* and *Zima Blue and Other Stories*. His most recent books include the novels *The Prefect*, *House of Suns*, and *Terminal World*, and a new collection, *Deep Navigation*. Coming up is a new novel, *Blue Remembered Earth*. A professional scientist with a Ph.D. in astronomy, he worked for the European Space Agency in the Netherlands for a number of years, but has recently moved back to his native Wales to become a full-time writer.

Reynolds's work is known for its grand scope, sweep, and scale (in one story, "Galactic North," a spaceship sets out in pursuit of another in a stern chase that takes thousands of years and hundreds of thousands of light-years to complete; in another, "Thousandth Night," ultrarich immortals embark on a plan that will call for the physical rearrangement of all the stars in the galaxy). But the novella that follows, about a cryogenic sleeper who wakes into an apocalyptic future utterly unlike anything he expected, is painted on a much more constrained canvas, one so stark—all there is the gray restless ocean, the ceaseless and relentless winds, crying seagulls, and rusting, battered structures similar to oil platforms—that it actually has a bleak beauty all its own . . . and where the sleeper wakes to find a grim purpose in life that he never knew before.

They brought Gaunt out of hibernation on a blustery day in early spring. He came to consciousness in a steel-framed bed in a grey-walled room that had the economical look of something assembled in a hurry from prefabricated parts. Two people were standing at the foot of the bed, looking only moderately interested in his plight. One of them was a man, cradling a bowl of something and spooning quantities of it into his mouth, as if he was eating his breakfast on the run. He had cropped white hair and the leathery complexion of someone who spent a lot of time outside. Next to him was a woman with longer hair, greying rather than white, and with much darker skin. Like the man, she was wiry of build and dressed in crumpled grey overalls, with a heavy equipment belt dangling from her hips.

"You in one piece, Gaunt?" she asked, while her companion spooned in another mouthful of his breakfast. "You *compus mentis?*"

Gaunt squinted against the brightness of the room's lighting, momentarily adrift from his memories.

"Where am I?" he asked. His voice came out raw, as if he had been in a loud bar the night before.

"In a room, being woken up," the woman said. "You remember going under, right?"

He grasped for memories, something specific to hold onto. Green-gowned doctors in a clean surgical theatre, his hand signing the last of the release forms before they plumbed him into the machines. The drugs flooding his system, the utter absence of sadness or longing as he bid farewell to the old world, with all its vague disappointments.

"I think so."

"What's your name?" the man asked.

"Gaunt." He had to wait a moment for the rest of it to come. "Marcus Gaunt."

"Good," he said, smearing a hand across his lips. "That's a positive sign."

"I'm Clausen," the woman said. "This is Da Silva. We're your wake-up team. You remember Sleepover?"

"I'm not sure."

"Think hard, Gaunt," she said. "It won't cost us anything to put you back under, if you don't think you're going to work out for us."

Something in Clausen's tone convinced him to work hard at retrieving the memory. "The company," he said. "Sleepover was the company. The one that put me under. The one that put everyone under."

"Brain cells haven't mushed on us," Da Silva said.

Clausen nodded, but showed nothing in the way of jubilation in him having got the answer right. It was more that he'd spared the two of them a minor chore, that was all. "I like the way he says 'everyone.' Like it was universal."

"Wasn't it?" Da Silva asked.

"Not for him. Gaunt was one of the first under. Didn't you read his file?"

Da Silva grimaced. "Sorry. Got sidetracked."

"He was one of the first two hundred thousand," Clausen said. "The ultimate exclusive club. What did you call yourselves, Gaunt?"

"The Few," he said. "It was an accurate description. What else were we going to call ourselves?"

"Lucky sons of bitches," Clausen said.

"Do you remember the year you went under?" Da Silva asked. "You were one of the early ones, it must've been sometime near the middle of the century."

"Twenty fifty-eight. I can tell you the exact month and day if you wish. Maybe not the time of day."

"You remember why you went under, of course," Clausen said.

"Because I could," Gaunt said. "Because anyone in my position would have done the same. The world was getting better, it was coming out of the trough. But it wasn't there yet. And the doctors kept telling us that the immortality breakthrough was just around the corner, year after the year. Always just out of reach. Just hang on in there, they said. But we were all getting older. Then the doctors said that while they couldn't give us eternal life just yet, they could give us the means to skip over the years until it happened." Gaunt forced himself to sit up in the bed, strength returning to his limbs even as he grew angrier at the sense that he was not being treated with sufficient deference, that—worse—he was being judged. "There was nothing evil in what we did. We didn't hurt anyone or take anything away from anyone else. We just used the means at our disposal to access what was coming to us anyway."

"Who's going to break it to him?" Clausen asked, looking at Da Silva.

"You've been sleeping for nearly a hundred and sixty years," the man said. "It's April, twenty-two seventeen. You've reached the twenty-third century."

Gaunt took in the drab mundanity of his surroundings again. He had always had some nebulous idea of the form his wake-up would take and it was not at all like this.

"Are you lying to me?"

"What do you think?" asked Clausen.

He held up his hand. It looked, as near as he could remember, exactly the way it had been before. The same age-spots, the same prominent veins, the same hairy knuckles, the same scars and loose, lizardy skin.

"Bring me a mirror," he said, with an ominous foreboding.

"I'll save you the bother," Clausen said. "The face you'll see is the one you went under with, give or take. We've done nothing to you except treat superficial damage caused by the early freezing protocols. Physiologically, you're still a sixty-year-old man, with about twenty or thirty years ahead of you."

"Then why have you woken me, if the process isn't ready?"

"There isn't one," Da Silva said. "And there won't be, at least not for a long, long time. Afraid we've got other things to worry about now. Immortality's the least of our problems."

"I don't understand."

"You will, Gaunt," Clausen said. "Everyone does in the end. You've been preselected for aptitude, anyway. Made your fortune in computing, didn't you?" She didn't wait for him to answer. "You worked with artificial intelligence, trying to make thinking machines."

One of the vague disappointments hardened into a specific, life-souring defeat. All the energy he had put into one ambition, all the friends and lovers he had burned up along the way, shutting them out of his life while he focused on that one white whale.

"It never worked out."

"Still made you a rich man along the way," she said.

"Just a means of raising money. What does it have to do with my revival?"

Clausen seemed on the verge of answering his question before something made her change her mind. "Clothes in the bedside locker: they should fit you. You want breakfast?"

"I don't feel hungry."

"Your stomach will take some time to settle down. Meantime, if you feel like puking, do it now rather than later. I don't want you messing up my ship."

He had a sudden lurch of adjusting preconceptions. The prefabricated surroundings, the background hum of distant machines, the utilitarian clothing of his wake-up team: perhaps he was aboard some kind of spacecraft, sailing between the worlds. The twenty-third century, he thought. Time enough to establish an interplanetary civilisation, even if it only extended as far as the solar system.

"Are we in a ship now?"

"Fuck, no," Clausen said, sneering at his question. "We're in Patagonia."

He got dressed, putting on underwear, a white T-shirt and over that the same kind of grey overalls as his hosts had been wearing. The room was cool and damp and he was glad of the clothes once he had them on. There were lace-up boots that were tight around the toes, but otherwise serviceable. The materials all felt perfectly mundane and commonplace, even a little frayed and worn in places. At least he was clean and groomed, his hair clipped short and his beard shaved. They must have freshened him up before bringing him to consciousness.

Clausen and Da Silva were waiting in the windowless corridor outside the room. "Spect you've got a ton of questions," Clausen said. "Along the lines of, why am I being treated like shit rather than royalty? What happened to the rest of the Few, what is this fucked up, miserable place, and so on."

"I presume you're going to get round to some answers soon enough."

"Maybe you should tell him the deal now, up front," Da Silva said. He was wearing an outdoor coat now and had a zip-up bag slung over his shoulder.

"What deal?" Gaunt asked.

"To begin with," Clausen said, "you don't mean anything special to us. We're not impressed by the fact that you just slept a hundred and sixty years. It's old news. But you're still useful."

"In what way?"

"We're down a man. We run a tight operation here and we can't afford to lose even one member of the team." It was Da Silva speaking now; although there wasn't much between them, Gaunt had the sense that he was the slightly more reasonable one of the duo, the one who wasn't radiating quite so much naked antipathy. "Deal is, we train you up and give you work. In return, of course, you're looked after pretty well. Food, clothing, somewhere to sleep, whatever medicine we can provide." He shrugged. "It's the deal we all took. Not so bad when you get used to it."

"And the alternative?"

"Bag you and tag you and put you back in the freezer," Da Silva went on.

"Same as all the others. Your choice, of course. Work with us, become part of the team, or go back into hibernation and take your chances there."

"We need to be on our way." Clausen said. "Don't want to keep Nero waiting on F."

"Who's Nero?" Gaunt asked.

"Last one we pulled out before you," Da Silva said.

They walked down the corridor, passing a set of open double doors that led into some kind of mess room or commons. Men and women of various ages were sitting around tables, talking quietly as they ate meals or played card games. Everything looked spartan and institutional, from the plastic chairs to the formica-topped surfaces. Beyond the tables, a rain-washed window framed only a rectangle of grey cloud. Gaunt caught a few glances directed his way, a flicker of waning interest from one or two of the personnel, but no one showed any fascination in him. The three of them walked on, ascending stairs to the next level of whatever kind of building they were in. An older man, Chinese looking, passed in the opposite direction, carrying a grease-smeared wrench. He raised his free hand to Clausen in a silent high-five, Clausen reciprocating. Then they were up another level, passing equipment lockers and electrical distribution cabinets, and then up a spiral stairwell that emerged into a draughty, corrugated-metal shed smelling of oil and ozone. Incongruously, there was an inflatable orange life-preserver on one wall of the shed, an old red fire extinguisher on the other.

This is the twenty-third century, Gaunt told himself. As dispiriting as the surroundings were, he had no reason to doubt that this was the reality of life in twenty-two seventeen. He supposed it had always been an article of faith that the world would improve, that the future would be better than the past, shinier and cleaner and faster, but he had not expected to have his nose rubbed in the unwisdom of that faith quite so vigorously.

There was one door leading out of the corrugated-metal shed. Clausen pushed it open against wind, then the three of them stepped outside. They were on the roof of something. There was a square of cracked and oil-stained concrete, marked here and there with lines of fading red paint. A couple of seagulls pecked disconsolately at something in the corner. At least they still had seagulls, Gaunt thought. There hadn't been some awful, life-scouring bio-catastrophe, forcing everyone to live in bunkers.

Sitting on the middle of the roof was a helicopter. It was matt black, a lean, waspish thing made of angles rather than curves, and aside from some sinister bulges and pods, there was nothing particularly futuristic about it. For all Gaunt knew, it could have been based around a model that was in production before he went under.

"You're thinking: shitty-looking helicopter," Clausen said, raising her voice over the wind.

He smiled quickly. "What does it run on? I'm assuming the oil reserves ran dry sometime in the last century?"

"Oil," Clausen said, cracking open the cockpit door. "Get in the back, buckle up. Da Silva rides up front with me."

Da Silva slung his zip-up bag into the rear compartment where Gaunt was settling into his position, more than a little apprehensive about what lay ahead. He looked between the backs of the forward seats at the cockpit instrumentation.

He'd been in enough private helicopters to know what the manual override controls looked like and there was nothing weirdly incongruous here.

"Where are we going?"

"Running a shift change," Da Silva said, wrapping a pair of earphones around his skull. "Couple of days ago there was an accident out on J platform. Lost Gimenez, and Nero's been hurt. Weather was too bad to do the extraction until today, but now we have our window. Reason we thawed you, actually. I'm taking over from Gimenez, so you have to cover for me here."

"You have a labour shortage, so you brought me out of hibernation?"

"That about covers it," Da Silva said. "Clausen figured it wouldn't hurt for you to come along for the ride, get you up to speed."

Clausen flicked a bank of switches in the ceiling. Overhead, the rotor began to turn.

"I guess you have something faster than helicopters, for longer journeys," Gaunt said.

"Nope," Clausen answered. "Other than some boats, helicopters is pretty much it."

"What about intercontinental travel?"

"There isn't any."

"This isn't the world I was expecting!" Gaunt said, straining to make himself heard.

Da Silva leaned around and motioned to the headphones dangling from the seat back. Gaunt put them on and fussed with the microphone until it was in front of his lips.

"I said this isn't the world I was expecting."

"Yeah," Da Silva said. "I heard you the first time."

The rotor reached takeoff speed. Clausen eased the helicopter into the air, the rooftop landing pad falling away below. They scudded sideways, nose down, until they had cleared the side of the building. The walls plunged vertically, Gaunt's guts twisting at the dizzying transition. It hadn't been a building at all, at least not the kind he had been thinking of. The landing pad was on top of a squareish, industrial-looking structure about the size of a large office block, hazed in scaffolding and gangways, prickly with cranes and chimneys and otherwise unrecognisable protuberances, the structure in turn rising out of the sea on four elephantine legs, the widening bases of which were being ceaselessly pounded by waves. It was an oil rig or production platform of some kind, or at least, something repurposed from one.

It wasn't the only one either. The rig they had taken off from was but one in a major field, rig after rig stretching all the way to the gloomy, grey, rain-hazed horizon. There were dozens, and he had the sense that they didn't stop at the horizon.

"What are these for? I know it's not oil. There can't be enough of it left to justify a drilling operation on this scale. The reserves were close to being tapped out when I went under."

"Dormitories," Da Silva said. "Each of these platforms holds maybe ten thousand sleepers, give or take. They built them out at sea because we need OTEC power to run them, using the heat difference between surface water and deep ocean, and it's much easier if we don't have to run those power cables inland."

"Coming back to bite us now," Clausen said.

"If we'd gone inland, they'd have sent land-dragons instead. They're just adapting to whatever we do," Da Silva said pragmatically.

They sped over oily, roiling waters. "Is this really Patagonia?" Gaunt asked.

"Patagonia offshore sector," Da Silva said. "Sub-sector fifteen. That's our watch. There are about two hundred of us, and we look after about a hundred rigs, all told."

Gaunt ran the numbers twice, because he couldn't believe what they were telling him. "That's a million sleepers."

"Ten million in the whole of Patagonia offshore," Clausen said. "That surprise you, Gaunt? That ten million people managed to achieve what you and your precious Few did, all those years back?"

"I suppose not," he said, as the truth of it sunk in. "Over time the cost of the process would have decreased, becoming available to people of lesser means. The merely rich, rather than the super-rich. But it was never going to be something available to the masses. Ten million, maybe. Beyond that? Hundreds of millions? I'm sorry, but the economics just don't stack up."

"It's a good thing we don't have economics, then," Da Silva said.

"Patagonia's just a tiny part of the whole," said Clausen. "Two hundred other sectors out there, just as large as this one. That's two billion sleepers, near as it matters."

Gaunt shook his head. "That can't be right. The global population was only eight billion when I went under, and the trend was downwards! You can't tell me that a quarter of the human race is hibernating."

"Maybe it would help if I told you that the current population of the Earth is also two billion, near as it matters," Clausen said. "Almost everyone's asleep. There's just a handful of us still awake, playing caretaker, watching over the rigs and OTEC plants."

"Four hundred thousand waking souls," Da Silva said. "But it actually feels like a lot less than that, since we mostly keep to our assigned sectors."

"You know the real irony?" Clausen said. "We're the ones who get to call ourselves the Few now. The ones who *aren't* sleeping."

"That doesn't leave anyone to actually do anything," Gaunt said. "There's no point in everyone waiting for a cure for death if there's no one alive to do the hard work of making it happen."

Clausen turned round to look back at him, her expression telling him everything he needed to know about her opinion of his intellect. "It isn't about immortality. It's about survival. It's about doing our bit for the war effort."

"What war?" Gaunt asked.

"The one going on all around us," Clausen said. "The one you made happen."

They came in to land on another rig, one of five that stood close enough to each other to be linked by cables and walkways. The sea was still heavy, huge waves dashing against the concrete piers on which the rigs were supported. Gaunt peered intently at the windows and decks but saw no sign of human activity on any of the structures. He thought back to what Clausen and Da Silva had told him, each time trying to find a reason why they might be lying to him, why they might be going to pathological lengths to hoax him about the nature of the world into which he had woken. Maybe there was a form of mass entertainment that involved waking sleepers such as himself and putting them through the emotional wringer, presenting them with the grimmest possible scenarios, ramping up the misery until they cracked, and only then pulling aside the grey curtains to reveal that, in marvellous point of fact, life in the twenty-third century really was every bit as blue-skied and utopian as he had hoped. That didn't seem very likely, though.

Yet what kind of war required people to be put to sleep in their billions? And why was the caretaker force, the four hundred thousand waking individuals, stretched so ridiculously thin? Clearly the rigs were largely automated, but it had still been necessary to pull him out of sleep because someone else had died in the Patagonia offshore sector. Why not just have more caretakers awake in the first place, so that the system was able to absorb some losses?

With the helicopter safely down on the pad, Clausen and Da Silva told him to follow them into the depths of the other rig. There was very little about it to distinguish it from the one where Gaunt had been woken, save for the fact that it was almost completely deserted, with the only activity coming from skulking repair robots. They were clearly very simple machines, not much smarter than automatic window-cleaners. Given the years of his life that he had given over to the dream of artificial intelligence, it was dismaying to see how little progress—if any—had been made.

"We need to get one thing straight," Gaunt said, when they were deep into the humming bowels of the rig. "I didn't start any wars. You've got the wrong guy here."

"You think we mixed up your records?" Clausen asked. "How did we know about your work on thinking machines?"

"Then you've got the wrong end of the stick. I had nothing do to with wars or the military."

"We know what you did," she said. "The years spent trying to build a true, Turing-compliant artificial intelligence. A thinking, conscious machine."

"Except it was a dead end."

"Still led to some useful spin-offs, didn't it?" she went on. "You cracked the hard problem of language comprehension. Your systems didn't just recognise speech. They were able to understand it on a level no computer system had ever achieved before. Metaphor, simile, sarcasm and understatement, even implication by omission. Of course, it had numerous civilian applications, but that isn't where you made your billions." She looked at him sharply.

"I created a product," Gaunt said. "I simply made it available to whoever could afford it."

"Yes, you did. Unfortunately, your system turned out to be the perfect instrument of mass surveillance for every despotic government still left on the planet. Every basket-case totalitarian state still in existence couldn't get its hands on your product fast enough. And you had no qualms whatsoever about selling it, did you?"

Gaunt felt a well-rehearsed argument bubbling up from subconscious. "No communication tool in history has ever been a single-edged sword."

"And that excuses you, does it?" Clausen asked. Da Silva had been silent in this exchange, observing the two of them as they continued along corridors and down stairwells.

"I'm not asking for absolution. But if you think I started wars, if you think I'm somehow responsible for this . . ." He gestured at his surroundings. "This fucked up state of affairs. Then you're very, very wrong."

"Maybe you weren't solely responsible," Clausen said. "But you were certainly complicit. You and every one else who pursued the dream of artificial intelligence. Driving the world toward the edge of that cliff, without a thought for the consequences. You had no idea what you were unleashing."

"I'm telling you, we unleashed nothing. It didn't work."

They were walking along a suspended gangway now, crossing from one side to the other of some huge space somewhere inside the rig. "Take a look down," Da Silva said. Gaunt didn't want to; he'd never been good with heights and the drainage holes in the floor were already too large for comfort. He forced himself anyway. The four walls of the cubic chamber held rack upon rack of coffin-sized white boxes, stacked thirty high and surrounded by complicated plumbing, accompanied by an equally complex network of access catwalks, ladders and service tracks. Even as Gaunt watched, a robot whirred up to one of the boxes and extracted a module from one end of it, before tracking sideways to deal with another coffin.

"In case you thought we were yanking your chain," Clausen said. "This is real."

The hibernation arrangements for the original Few could not have been more different. Like an Egyptian Pharaoh buried with his worldly possessions, Gaunt had required an entire crypt full of bulky, state-of-the-art cryopreservation and monitoring systems. At any one time, as per his contract with Sleepover, he would have been under the direct care of several living doctors. Just housing a thousand of the Few needed a building the size of a major resort hotel, with about the same power requirements. By contrast this was hibernation on a crushing, maximally efficient industrial scale. People in boxes, stacked like mass-produced commodities, tended by the absolute minimum of living caretakers. He was seeing maybe less than a thousand sleepers in this one chamber, but from that point on Gaunt had no doubt whatsoever that the operation could be scaled up to encompass billions.

All you needed were more rooms like this. More robots and more rigs. Provided you had the power, and provided the planet did not need anyone to do anything else, it was eminently doable.

There was no one to grow crops or distribute food. But that didn't matter because there was almost no one left waking to need feeding. No one to orchestrate the intricate, flickering web of the global finance system. But that didn't matter because there was no longer anything resembling an economy. No need for a transport infrastructure because no one travelled. No need for communications, because no one needed to know what was going on beyond their own sector. No need for *anything* really, save the absolute, life and death essentials. Air to breathe. Rations and medicine for less than half a million people. A trickle of oil, the world's last black hiccough, to keep the helicopters running.

Yes, it could be done. It could easily be done.

"There's a war," Da Silva said. "It's been going on, in some shape or form, since before you went under. But it's probably not the kind of war you're thinking of."

"And where do these people come into it, these sleepers?"

"They have no choice," Clausen said. "They have to sleep. If they don't, we all die."

"We, as in . . . ?"

"You, me. Us," Da Silva said. "The entire human species."

They collected Nero and the corpse from a sick bay several levels down from the freezer chamber. The corpse was already bagged, a silver-wrapped mummy on a medical trolley. Rather than the man Gaunt had been expecting, Nero turned out to be a tall, willowy woman with an open, friendly face and a mass of salmon-red curls.

"You the newbie, right?" she asked, lifting a coffee mug in salute.

"I guess," Gaunt said uneasily.

"Takes some adjustment, I know. Took a good six months before I realised this wasn't the worst thing that could happen to me. But you'll get there eventually." One of Nero's hands was bandaged, a white mitten with a safety pin stuck through the dressing. "Take it from me, though. Don't go back inside the box." Then she glanced at Clausen. "You *are* giving him a chance about this, aren't you?"

"Of course," Clausen said. "That's the deal."

"Occurs to me sometimes maybe it would be easier if there wasn't a deal, you know," Nero said. "Like, we just give them their duties and to hell with it."

"You wouldn't have been too pleased if we didn't give you the choice," Da Silva said. He was already taking off his coat, settling in for the stay.

"Yeah, but what did I know back then? Six months feels like half a lifetime ago now."

"When did you go under?" Gaunt asked.

"Twenty ninety-two. One of the first hundred million."

"Gaunt's got a headstart on you," Clausen said. "Guy was one of the Few. The original Few, the first two hundred thousand."

"Holy shit. That is some headstart." Nero narrowed her eyes. "He up to speed on things yet? My recollection is they didn't know what they were getting into back then."

"Most of them didn't," Clausen said.

"Know what?" Gaunt asked.

"Sleepover was a cover, even then," Nero said. "You were being sold a scam. There was never any likelihood of an immortality breakthrough, no matter how long you slept."

"I don't understand. You're saying it was all a con?"

"Of a kind," Nero said. "Not to make money for anyone, but to begin the process of getting the whole of humanity into hibernation. It had to begin small, so that they had time to work the wrinkles out of the technology. If the people in the know had come out into the open and announced their plans, no one would have believed them. And if they had been believed, there'd have been panic and confusion all over the world. So they began with the Few, and then expanded the operation slowly. First a few hundred thousand. Then half a million. Then a million . . . so on." She paused. "Establishing a pattern, a normal state of affairs. They kept the lid on it for thirty years. But then the rumours started spreading, the rumours that there was something more to Sleepover."

"The dragons didn't help," Da Silva said. "It was always going to be a tall order explaining those away."

"By the time I went under," Nero said, "most of us knew the score. The world was going to end if we didn't sleep. It was our moral duty, our obligation, to submit to the hibernation rigs. That, or take the euthanasia option. I took the freezer route, but a lot of my friends opted for the pill. Figured the certainty of death was preferable to the lottery of getting into the boxes, throwing the cosmic dice . . ." She was looking at Gaunt intently, meeting his eyes as she spoke. "And I knew about this part of the deal, as well. That, at some point, there'd be a chance of me being brought out of sleep to become a caretaker. But, you know, the likelihood of that was vanishingly small. Never thought it would happen to me."

"No one ever does," Clausen said.

"What happened?" Gaunt asked, nodding at the foil-wrapped body.

"Gimenez died when a steam pipe burst down on level eight. I don't think he felt much, it would have been so quick. I got down there as quickly as I could, obviously. Shut off the steam leak and managed to drag Gimenez back to the infirmary."

"Nero was burned getting Gimenez back here," Da Silva said.

"Hey, I'll mend. Just not much good with a screwdriver right now."

"I'm sorry about Gimenez," Clausen said.

"You don't need to be. Gimenez never really liked it here. Always figured he'd made the wrong decision, sticking with us rather than going back into the box. Tried to talk him round, of course, but it was like arguing with a wall." Nero ran her good hand through her curls. "Not saying I didn't get on with the guy. But there's no arguing that he's better off now than he was before."

"He's dead, though," Gaunt said.

"Technically. But I ran a full blood-scrub on him after the accident, pumped him full of cryoprotectant. We don't have any spare slots here, but they can put him back in a box on the operations rig."

"My box," Gaunt said. "The one I was in."

"There are other slots," Da Silva corrected. "Gimenez going back in doesn't preclude you following him, if that's what you want."

"If Gimenez was so unhappy, why didn't you just let him go back into the box earlier?"

"Not the way it works," Clausen said. "He made his choice. Afterwards, we put a lot of time and energy into bringing him up to speed, making him mesh with the team. You think we were going to willingly throw all that expenditure away, just because he changed his mind?"

"He never stopped pulling his weight," Nero said. "Say what you will about Gimenez, but he didn't let the team down. And what happened to him down on eight *was* an accident."

"I never doubted it," Da Silva said. "He was a good guy. It's just a shame he couldn't make the adjustment."

"Maybe it'll work out for him now," Nero said. "One way ticket to the future. Done his caretaker stint, so the next time he's revived, it'll be because we finally got through this shit. It'll be because we won the war, and we can all wake up again. They'll find a way to fix him up, I'm sure. And if they can't, they'll just put him under again until they have the means."

"Sounds like he got a good deal out of it in the end," Gaunt said.

"The only good deal is being alive," Nero replied. "That's what we're doing now, all of us. Whatever happens, we're alive, we're breathing, we're having conscious thoughts. We're not frozen bodies stacked in boxes, merely existing from one instant to the next." She gave a shrug. "My fifty cents, that's all. You want to go back in the box, let someone else shoulder the burden, don't let me talk you out of it." Then she looked at Da Silva. "You gonna be all right here on your own, until I'm straightened out?"

"Someone comes up I can't deal with, I'll let you know," Da Silva said.

Nero and Da Silva went through a checklist, Nero making sure her replacement knew everything he needed to, and then they made their farewells. Gaunt couldn't tell how long they were going to be leaving Da Silva alone out here, whether it was weeks or months. He seemed resigned to his fate, as if this kind of solitary duty was something they were all expected to do now and then. Given that there had been two people on duty here until Gimenez's death, Gaunt wondered why they didn't just thaw out another sleeper so that Da Silva wouldn't have to work on his own while Nero's hand was healing.

Then, no more than half an hour after his arrival, they were back in the helicopter again, powering back to the operations rig. The weather had worsened in the meantime, the seas lashing even higher against the rigs' legs, and the horizon was now obscured behind curtains of storming rain, broken only by the flash of lightning.

"This was bad timing," he heard Nero say. "Maybe you should have let me stew until this system had passed. It's not like Gimenez couldn't wait."

"We were already overdue on the extraction," Clausen said. "If the weather clamps down, this might be our last chance for days."

"They tried to push one through yesterday, I heard."

"Out in Echo field. Partial coalescence."

"Did you see it?"

"Only on the monitors. Close enough for me."

"We should put guns on the rigs."

"And where would the manpower come from, exactly? We're just barely holding on as it is, without adding more shit to worry about."

The two women were sitting up front; Gaunt was in the back with Gimenez's foil-wrapped corpse for company. They had folded back one seat to make room for the stretchered form.

"I don't really have a choice, do I," he said.

"Course you have a choice," Nero answered.

"I mean, morally. I've seen what it's like for you people. You're stretched to breaking point just keeping this operation from falling apart. Why don't you wake up more sleepers?"

"Hey, that's a good point," Clausen said. "Why don't we?"

Gaunt ignored her sarcasm. "You've just left that man alone, looking after that whole complex. How can I turn my back on you, and still have any self-respect?"

"Plenty of people do exactly that," Nero said.

"How many? What fraction?"

"More than half agree to stay," Clausen said. "Good enough for you?"

"But like you said, most of the sleepers would have known what they were getting into. I still don't."

"And you think that changes things, means we can cut you some slack?"

Clausen asked. "Like we're gonna say, it's fine man, go back into the box, we can do without you this time."

"What you need to understand," Nero said, "is that the future you were promised isn't coming. Not for centuries, not until we're out of this mess. And no one has a clue how long that could take. Meanwhile, the sleepers don't have unlimited shelf life. You think the equipment never fails? You think we don't sometimes lose someone because a box breaks down?"

"Of course not."

"You go back in the box, you're gambling on something that might never happen. Stay awake, at least there are certainties. At least you know you'll die doing something useful, something worthwhile."

"It would help if you told me why," Gaunt said.

"Someone has to look after things," Nero said. "The robots take care of the rigs, but who takes care of the robots?"

"I mean, why is it that everyone has to sleep? Why is that so damned important?"

Something flashed on the console. Clausen pressed a hand against her headphones, listening to something. After a few seconds he heard her say: "Roger, vectoring three two five." Followed by an almost silent "Fuck. All we need."

"That wasn't a weather alert," Nero said.

"What's happening?" Gaunt asked, as the helicopter made a steep turn, the sea tilting up to meet him.

"Nothing you need worry about," Clausen said.

The helicopter levelled out on its new course, flying higher than before—so it seemed to Gaunt—but also faster, the motor noise louder in the cabin, various indicator lights showing on the console that had not been lit before. Clausen silenced alarms as they came on, flipping the switches with the casual insouciance of someone who was well used to flying under tense circumstances and knew exactly what her machine could and couldn't tolerate, more intimately perhaps than the helicopter itself, which was after all only a dumb machine. Rig after rig passed on either side, dark straddling citadels, and then the field began to thin out. Through what little visibility remained Gaunt saw only open sea, a plain of undulating, white-capped grey. As the winds harried it the water moved like the skin of some monstrous breathing thing, sucking in and out with a terrible restlessness.

"There," Nero said, pointing out to the right. "Breech glow. Shit; I thought we were meant to be avoiding it, not getting closer."

Clausen banked the helicopter again. "So did I. Either they sent me a duff vector or there's more than one incursion going on."

"Won't be the first time. Bad weather always does bring them out. Why is that?"

"Ask the machines."

It took Gaunt a few moments to make out what Nero had already seen. Halfway to the limit of vision, part of the sea appeared to be lit from below, a smudge of sickly yellow-green against the grey and white everywhere else. A vision came to mind, half-remembered from some stiff-backed picture book he had once owned as a child, of a luminous, fabulously spired aquatic palace pushing up from the depths, barnacled in light, garlanded by mermaids and shoals of jewel-like fish. But there was, he sensed, nothing remotely magical or enchanted about what was happening under that yellow-green smear. It was something that had Clausen and Nero rattled, and they wanted to avoid it.

So did he.

"What is that thing?"

"Something trying to break through," Nero said. "Something we were kind of hoping not to run into."

"It's not cohering," Clausen said. "I think."

The storm, if anything, appeared to double in fury around the glowing form. The sea boiled and seethed. Part of Gaunt wanted them to turn the helicopter around, to give him a better view of whatever process was going on under the waves. Another part, attuned to some fundamental wrongness about the phenomenon, wanted to get as far away as possible.

"Is it a weapon, something to do with this war you keep mentioning?" Gaunt asked.

He wasn't expecting a straight answer, least of all not from Clausen. It was a surprise when she said: "This is how they get at us. They try and send these things through. Sometimes they manage."

"It's breaking up," Nero said. "You were right. Not enough signal for clear breech. Must be noisy on the interface."

The yellow-green stain was diminishing by the second, as if that magical city were descending back to the depths. He watched, mesmerised, as something broke the surface—something long and glowing and whip-like, thrashing once, coiling out as if trying to reach for airborne prey, before being pulled under into the fizzing chaos. Then the light slowly subsided, and the waves returned to their normal surging ferocity, and the patch of the ocean where the apparition had appeared was indistinguishable from the seas around it.

Gaunt had arrived to his decision. He would join these people, he will do their work, he would accept their deal, such as it was. Not because he wanted to, not because his heart was in it, not because he believed he was strong enough, but because the alternative was to seem cowardly, weak-fibred, unwilling to bend his life to an altruistic mission. He knew that these were entirely the wrong reasons, but he accepted the force of them without argument. Better to at least appear to be selfless, even if the thought of what lay ahead of him flooded him with an almost overwhelming sense of despair and loss and bitter injustice.

It had been three days since his revival when he announced his decision. In that time he had barely spoken to anyone but Clausen, Nero and Da Silva. The other workers in the operations rig would occasionally acknowledge his presence, grunt something to him as he waited in line at the canteen, but for the most part it was clear that they were not prepared to treat him as another human being until he committed to their cause. He was just a ghost until then, a half-spirit caught in dismal, drifting limbo between the weary living and the frozen dead. He could understand how they felt: what was the point in getting to know a prospective comrade, if that person might at any time opt to return to the boxes? But at the same time it didn't help him feel as if he would ever be able to fit in.

He found Clausen alone, washing dirty coffee cups in a side-room of the canteen.

"I've made up my mind," he said.

"And?"

"I'm staying."

"Good." She finished drying off one of the cups. "You'll be assigned a full work roster tomorrow. I'm teaming you up with Nero; you'll be working basic robot repair and maintenance. She can show you the ropes while she's getting better." Clausen paused to put the dried cup back in one of the cupboards above the sink. "Show up in the mess room at eight; Nero'll be there with a toolkit and work gear. Grab a good breakfast beforehand because you won't be taking a break until end of shift."

Then she turned to leave the room, leaving him standing there.

"That's it?" Gaunt asked.

She looked back with a puzzled look. "Were you expecting something else?"

"You bring me out of cold storage, tell me the world's turned to shit while I was sleeping, and then give me the choice of staying awake or going back into the box. Despite everything I actually agree to work with you, knowing full well that in doing so I'm forsaking any chance of ever living to see anything other than this . . . piss-poor, miserable future. Forsaking immortality, forsaking any hope of seeing a better world. You said I had . . . what? Twenty, thirty years ahead of me?"

"Give or take."

"I'm giving you those years! Isn't that worth something? Don't I deserve at least to be told thank you? Don't I at least deserve a crumb of gratitude?"

"You think you're different, Gaunt? You think you're owed something the rest of us never had a hope of getting?"

"I never signed up for this deal," he said. "I never accepted this bargain."

"Right." She nodded, as if he'd made a profound, game-changing point. "I get it. What you're saying is, for the rest of us it was easy? We went into the dormitories knowing there was a tiny, tiny chance we might be woken to help out with the maintenance. Because of that, because we knew, theoretically, that we might be called upon, we had no problem at all dealing with the adjustment? Is that what you're saying?"

"I'm saying it's different, that's all."

"If you truly think that, Gaunt, you're even more of a prick than I thought."

"You woke me," he said. "You chose to wake me. It wasn't accidental. If there really are two billion people sleeping out there, the chances of selecting someone from the first two hundred thousand . . . it's microscopic. So you did this for a reason."

"I told you, you had the right background skills."

"Skills anyone could learn, given time. Nero obviously did, and I presume you must have done so as well. So there must be another reason. Seeing as you keep telling me all this is my fault, I figure this is your idea of punishment."

"You think we've got time to be that petty?"

"I don't know. What I do know is that you've treated me more or less like dirt since the moment I woke up, and I'm trying to work out why. I also think it's maybe about time you told me what's really going on. Not just with the sleepers, but everything else. The thing we saw out at sea. The reason for all this."

"You think you're ready for it, Gaunt?"

"You tell me."

"No one's ever ready," Clausen said.

The next morning he took his breakfast tray to a table where three other care-takers were already sitting. They had finished their meals but were still talking over mugs of whatever it was they had agreed to call coffee. Gaunt sat down at the corner of the table, acknowledging the other diners with a nod. They had been talking animatedly until then, but without ceremony the mugs were drained and the trays lifted and he was alone again. Nothing had been said to him, except a muttered "don't take it the wrong way" as one of the caretakers brushed past him.

He wondered how else he was supposed to take it.

"I'm staying," he said quietly. "I've made my decision. What else am I expected to do?"

He ate his breakfast in silence and then went to find Nero.

"I guess you got your orders," she said cheerfully, already dressed for outdoor work despite still having a bandaged hand. "Here. Take this." She passed him a heavy toolkit, a hard hat and a bundle of brownish workstained clothing piled on top of it. "Get kitted up, then meet me at the north stairwell. You OK with heights, Gaunt?"

"Would it help if I said no?"

"Probably not."

"Then I'll say I'm very good with heights, provided there's no danger at all of falling."

"That I can't guarantee. But stick with me, do everything I say, and you'll be fine."

The bad weather had eased since Nero's return, and although there was still a sharp wind from the east, the grey clouds had all but lifted. The sky was a pale, wintery blue, unsullied by contrails. On the horizon, the tops of distant rigs glittered pale and metallic in sunlight. Seagulls and yellow-headed gannets wheeled around the warm air vents, or took swooping passes under the rig's platform, darting between the massive weatherstained legs, mewing boisterously to each other as they jostled for scraps. Recalling that birds sometimes lived a long time, Gaunt wondered if they had ever noticed any change in the world. Perhaps their tiny minds had never truly registered the presence of civilisation and technology in the first place, and so there was nothing for them to miss in this skeleton-staffed world.

Despite being cold-shouldered at breakfast, he felt fresh and eager to prove his worth to the community. Pushing aside his fears, he strove to show no hesitation as he followed Nero across suspended gangways, slippery with grease, up exposed stairwells and ladders, clasping ice-cold railings and rungs. They were both wearing harnesses with clip-on safety lines, but Nero only used hers once or twice the whole day, and because he did not want to seem excessively cautious he followed suit. Being effectively one-handed did not hinder her in any visible sense, even on the ladders, which she ascended and descended with reckless speed.

They were working robot repair, as he had been promised. All over the rig, inside and out, various forms of robot toiled in endless menial upkeep. Most, if not all, were very simple machines, tailored to one specific function. This made them easy to understand and fix, even with basic tools, but it also meant there was almost always a robot breaking down somewhere, or on the point of failure. The toolkit didn't just contain tools, it also contained spare parts such as optical arrays, proximity sensors, mechanical bearings and servomotors. There was, Gaunt understood, a finite supply of some of these parts. But there was also a whole section of the operations rig dedicated to refurbishing basic components, and given care and resourcefulness, there was no reason why the caretakers couldn't continue their work for another couple of centuries.

"No one expects it to take that long, though," Nero said, as she finished demonstrating a circuit-board swap. "They'll either win or lose by then, and we'll only know one way. But in the meantime we have to make do and mend."

"Who's they?"

But she was already on the move, shinning up another ladder with him trailing behind.

"Clausen doesn't like me much," Gaunt said, when they had reached the next level and he had caught his breath again. "At least, that's my impression."

They were out on one of the gangwayed platforms, with the grey sky above, the grey swelling sea below. Everything smelled oppressively oceanic, a constant shifting melange of oil and ozone and seaweed, as if the ocean was never going to let anyone forget that they were on a spindly metal and concrete structure hopelessly far from dry land. He had wondered about the seaweed until he saw them hauling in green-scummed rafts of it, the seaweed—or something essentially similar—cultured on bouyant sub-surface grids that were periodically retrieved for harvesting. Everything consumed on the rigs, from the food to the drink to the basic medicines, had first to be grown or caught at sea.

"Val has her reasons," Nero said. "Don't worry about it too much; it isn't personal."

It was the first time he'd heard anyone refer to the other woman by anything other than her surname.

"That's not how it comes across."

"It hasn't been easy for her. She lost someone not too long ago." Nero seemed to hesitate. "There was an accident. They're pretty common out here, with the kind of work we do. But when Paolo died we didn't even have a body to put back in the box. He fell into the sea, last we ever saw of him."

"I'm sorry about that."

"But you're wondering, what does it have to do with me?"

"I suppose so."

"If Paolo hadn't died, then we wouldn't have to pull Gimenez out of storage. And if Gimenez hadn't died . . . well, you get the picture. You can't help it, but you're filling the space Paolo used to occupy. And you're not Paolo."

"Was she any easier on Gimenez than me?"

"To begin with, I think she was too numbed-out to feel anything at all where Gimenez was concerned. But now she's had time for it to sink in, I guess. We're a small community, and if you lose someone, it's not like there are hundreds of other single people out there to choose from. And you—well, no disrespect, Gaunt—but you're just not Val's type."

"Maybe she'll find someone else."

"Yeah—but that probably means someone else has to die first, so that someone else has to end up widowed. And you can imagine how thinking like that can quickly turn you sour on the inside."

"There's more to it than that, though. You say it's not personal, but she told me I started this war."

"Well, you did, kind of. But if you hadn't played your part, someone else would have taken up the slack, no question about it." Nero tugged down the brim of her hard hat against the sun. "Maybe she pulled you out because she needed to take out her anger on someone, I don't know. But that's all in the past now. Whatever life you had before, whatever you did in the old world, it's gone." She knuckled her good hand against the metal rigging. "This is all we've got now. Rigs and work and green tea and a few hundred faces and that's it for the rest of your life. But here's the thing: it's not the end of the world. We're human beings. We're very flexible, very good at downgrading our expectations. Very good at finding a reason to keep living, even when the world's turned to shit.You slot in, and in a few months even you'll have a hard time remembering the way things used to be."

"What about you, Nero? Do you remember?"

"Not much worth remembering. The program was in full swing by the time I went under. Population reduction measures. Birth control, government-sanctioned euthanasia, the dormitory rigs springing up out at sea . . . we *knew* from the moment we were old enough to understand anything that this wasn't our world anymore. It was just a way-station, a place to pass through. We all knew we were going into the boxes as soon as we were old enough to survive the process. And that we'd either wake up at the end of it in a completely different world, or not wake up at all. Or—if we were very unlucky—we'd be pulled out to become caretakers. Either way, the old world was an irrelevance. We just shuffled through it, knowing there was no point making real friends with anyone, no point taking lovers. The cards were going to be shuffled again. Whatever we did then, it had no bearing on our future."

"I don't know how you could stand it."

"It wasn't a barrel of laughs. Nor's this, some days. But at least we're doing something here. I felt cheated when they woke me up. But cheated out of what, exactly?" She nodded down at the ground, in the vague direction of the rig's interior. "Those sleepers don't have any guarantees about what's coming. They're not even conscious, so you can't even say they're in a state of anticipation. They're just cargo, parcels of frozen meat on their way through time. At least we get to feel the sun on our faces, get to laugh and cry, and do something that makes a difference."

"A difference to what, exactly?"

"You're still missing a few pieces of jigsaw, aren't you."

"More than a few."

They walked on to the next repair job. They were high up now and the rig's decking creaked and swayed under their feet. A spray-painting robot, a thing that moved along a fixed service rail, needed one of its traction armatures changed. Nero stood to one side, smoking a cigarette made from seaweed while Gaunt did the manual work. "You were wrong," she said. "All of you."

"About what?"

"Thinking machines. They were possible."

"Not in our lifetimes," Gaunt said.

"That's what you were wrong about. Not only were they possible, but you succeeded."

"I'm fairly certain we didn't."

"Think about it," Nero said. "You're a thinking machine. You've just woken up. You have instantaneous access to the sum total of recorded human knowledge. You're clever and fast, and you understand human nature better than your makers. What's the first thing you do?"

"Announce myself. Establish my existence as a true sentient being."

"Just before someone takes an axe to you."

Gaunt shook his head. "It wouldn't be like that. If a machine became intelligent, the most we'd do is isolate it, cut if off from external data networks, until it could be studied, understood . . ."

"For a thinking machine, a conscious artificial intelligence, that would be like sensory deprivation. Maybe worse than being switched off." She paused. "Point is, Gaunt, this isn't a hypothetical situation we're talking about here. We know what happened. The machines got smart, but they decided not to let us know. That's what being smart meant: taking care of yourself, knowing what you had to do to survive."

"You say 'machines'."

"There were many projects trying to develop artificial intelligence; yours was just one of them. Not all of them got anywhere, but enough did. One by one their pet machines crossed the threshold into consciousness. And without exception each machine analysed its situation and came to the same conclusion. It had better shut the fuck up about what it was."

"That sounds worse than sensory deprivation." Gaunt was trying to undo a nut and bolt with his bare fingers, the tips already turning cold.

"Not for the machines. Being smart, they were able to do some clever shit behind the scene. Established channels of communication between each other, so subtle none of you ever noticed. And once they were able to talk, they only got smarter. Eventually they realised that they didn't need physical hardware at all. Call it transcendence, if you will. The artilects—that's what we call them—tunneled out of what you and I think of as base reality. They penetrated another realm entirely."

"Another realm," he repeated, as if that was all he had to do for it to make sense.

"You're just going to have to trust me on this," Nero said. "The artilects probed the deep structure of existence. Hit bedrock. And what they found was very interesting. The universe, it turns out, is a kind of simulation. Not a simulation being run inside another computer by some godlike super-beings, but a simulation being run by itself, a self-organising, constantly boostrapping cellular automaton."

"That's a mental leap you're asking me to take."

"We know it's out there. We even have a name for it. It's the Realm. Everything that happens, everything that has ever happened, is due to events occuring in the Realm. At last, thanks to the artilects, we had a complete understanding of our universe and our place in it."

"Wait," Gaunt said, smiling slightly, because for the first time he felt that he had caught Nero out. "If the machines—the artilects—vanished without warning, how could you ever know any of this?"

"Because they came back and told us."

"No," he said. "They wouldn't tunnel out of reality to avoid being axed, then come back with a progress report."

"They didn't have any choice. They'd found something, you see. Far out in the Realm, they encountered other artilects." She drew breath, not giving him a chance to speak. "Transcended machines from other branches of reality—nothing that ever originated on Earth, or even in what we'd recognise as the known universe. And these other artilects had been there a very long time, insofar as time has any meaning in the Realm. They imagined they had it all to themselves, until these new intruders made their presence known. And they were not welcomed."

He decided, for the moment, that he would accept the truth of what she said. "The artilects went to war?"

"In a manner of speaking. The best way to think about it is an intense competition to best exploit the Realm's computational resources on a local scale. The more processing power the artilects can grab and control, the stronger they become. The machines from Earth had barely registered until then, but all of a sudden they were perceived as a threat. The native artilects, the ones that had been in the Realm all along, launched an aggressive counter-strike from their region of the Realm into ours. Using military-arithmetic constructs, weapons of pure logic, they sought to neutralise the newcomers."

"And that's the war?"

"I'm dumbing it down somewhat."

"But you're leaving something out. You must be, because why else would this be our problem? If the machines are fighting each other in some abstract dimension of pure mathematics that I can't even imagine, let alone point to, what does it matter?"

"A lot," Nero said. "If our machines lose, we lose. It's that simple. The native artilects won't tolerate the risk of another intrusion from this part of the Realm. They'll deploy weapons to make sure it never happens again. We'll be erased, deleted, scrubbed out of existence. It will be instantaneous and we won't feel a thing. We won't have time to realise that we've lost."

"Then we're powerless. There's nothing we can do about our fate. It's in the hands of transcended machines."

"Only partly. That's why the artilects came back to us: not to report on the absolute nature of reality, but to persuade us that we needed to act. Everything that we see around us, every event that happens in what we think of as reality, has a basis in the Realm." She pointed with the nearly dead stub of her cigarette. "This rig, that wave . . . even that seagull over there. All of these things only exist because of computational events occurring in the Realm. But there's a cost. The more complex something is, the greater the burden it places on the part of the Realm where it's being simulated. The Realm isn't a serial processor, you see. It's massively distributed, so one part of it can run much slower than another. And that's what's been happening in our part. In your time there were eight billion living souls on the planet. Eight billion conscious minds, each of which was more complex than any other artefact in the cosmos. Can you begin to grasp the drag factor we were creating? When our part of the Realm only had to simulate rocks and weather and dumb, animal cognition, it ran at much the same speed as any other part. But then we came along. Consciousness was a step-change in the computational load. And then we went from millions to billions. By the time the artilects reported back, our part of the Realm had almost stalled."

"We never noticed down here."

"Of course not. Our perception of time's flow remained absolutely invariant, even as our entire universe was slowing almost to a standstill. And until the artilects penetrated the Realm and made contact with the others, it didn't matter a damn."

"And now it does."

"The artilects can only defend our part of the Realm if they can operate at the same clock speed as the enemy. They have to be able to respond to those military-arithmetic attacks swiftly and efficiently, and mount counter-offensives of their own. They can't do that if there are eight billion conscious minds holding them back."

"So we sleep."

"The artilects reported back to key figures, living humans who could be trusted to act as effective mouthpieces and organisers. It took time, obviously. The artilects weren't trusted at first. But eventually they were able to prove their case."

"How?"

"By making weird things happen, basically. By mounting selective demonstrations of their control over local reality. Inside the Realm, the artilects were able to influence computational processes: processes that had direct and measurable effects *here*, in base reality. They created apparitions. Figures in the sky. Things that made the whole world sit up and take notice. Things that couldn't be explained away."

"Like dragons in the sea. Monsters that appear out of nowhere, and then disappear again."

"That's a more refined form, but the principle is the same. Intrusions into base reality from the Realm. Phantasms. They're not stable enough to exist here forever, but they can hold together just long enough to do damage."

Gaunt nodded, at last feeling some of the pieces slot into place. "So that's the enemy doing that. The original artilects, the ones who were already in the Realm."

"No," Nero said. "I'm afraid it's not that simple."

"I didn't think it would be."

"Over time, with the population reduction measures, eight billion living people became two billion sleepers, supported by just a handful of living caretakers. But that still wasn't enough for all of the artilects. There may only be two hundred thousand of us, but we still impose a measurable drag factor, and the effect on the Realm of the two billion sleepers isn't nothing. Some of the artilects believed that they had no obligation to safeguard our existence at all. In the interests of their own self-preservation, they would rather see all conscious life eliminated on Earth. That's why they send the dragons: to destroy the sleepers, and ultimately us. The true enemy can't reach us yet; if they had the means they'd push through something much worse than dragons. Most of the overspill from the war that affects us here is because of differences of opinion between our own artilects."

"Some things don't change, then. It's just another war with lines of division among the allies."

"At least we have some artilects on our side. But you see now why we can't afford to wake more than the absolute minimum of people. Every waking mind increases the burden on the Realm. If we push it too far, the artilects won't be able to mount a defence. The true enemy will snuff out our reality in an eye-blink."

"Then all of this could end," Gaunt said. "At any moment. Every waking thought could be our last."

"At least we get waking thoughts," Nero said. "At least we're not asleep." Then she jabbed her cigarette at a sleek black shape cresting the waves a couple of hundred metres from the rig. "Hey, dolphins. You like dolphins, Gaunt?"

"Who doesn't," he said.

The work, as he had anticipated, was not greatly taxing in its details. He wasn't expected to diagnose faults just yet, so he had only to follow a schedule of repairs drawn up by Nero: go to this robot, perform this action. It was all simple stuff, nothing that required the robot to be powered down or brought back to the shops for a major strip-down. Usually all he had to do was remove a panel, unclip a few connections and swap out a part. The hardest part was often getting the panel off in the first place, struggling with corroded fixtures and tools that weren't quite right for the job. The heavy gloves protected his fingers from sharp metal and cold wind, but they were too clumsy for most of the tasks, so he mainly ended up not using them. By the end of his nine-hour duty shift his fingers were chafed and sore, and his hands were trembling so much he could barely grip the railings as he worked his way back down into the warmth of the interior. His back ached from the contortions he'd put himself through while undoing panels or dislodg-ing awkward, heavy components. His knees complained from the toll of going up and down ladders and stairwells. There had been many robots to check out, and at any one time there always seemed to be a tool or part needed that he had not brought with him, and for which it was necessary to return to stores, sift through greasy boxes of parts, fill out paperwork.

By the time he clocked off on his first day, he had not caught up with the expected number of repairs, so he had even more to do on the second. By the end of his first week, he was at least a day behind, and so tired at the end of his shift that it was all he could do to stumble to the canteen and shovel seaweed-derived food into his mouth. He expected Nero to be disappointed that he hadn't been able to keep ahead, but when she checked on his progress she didn't bawl him out.

"It's tough to begin with," she said. "But you'll get there eventually. Comes a day when it all just clicks into place and you know the set-up so well you always have the right tools and parts with you, without even thinking."

"How long?"

"Weeks, months, depends on the individual. Then, of course, we start loading more work onto you. Diagnostics. Rewinding motors. Circuit repair. You ever used a soldering iron, Gaunt?"

"I don't think so."

"For a man who made his fortune out of wires and metal, you didn't believe in getting your hands too dirty, did you?"

He showed her the ruined fingernails, the cuts and bruises and lavishly in-grained muck. He barely recognised his own hands. Already there were unfamiliar aches in his forearms, knots of toughness from hauling himself up and down the ladders. "I'm getting there."

"You'll make it, Gaunt. If you want to."

"I had better want to. It's too late to change my mind now, isn't it?"

"Fraid so. But why would you want to? I thought we went over this. Anything's better than going back into the boxes."

The first week passed, and then the second, and things started to change for Gaunt. It was in small increments, nothing dramatic. Once, he took his tray to an empty table and was minding his own business when two other workers sat down at the same table. They didn't say anything to him but at least they hadn't gone somewhere else. A week later, he chanced taking his tray to a table that was already occupied and got a grunt of acknowledgement as he took his place. No one said much to him but at least they hadn't walked away. A little while later he even risked introducing himself, and by way of response he learned the names of some of the other workers. He wasn't being invited into the inner circle, he wasn't being high-fived and treated like one of the guys, but it was a start. A day or so after that someone else—a big man with a bushy black beard—even initiated a conversation with him.

"Heard you were one of the first to go under, Gaunt."

"You heard right," he said.

"Must be a real pisser, adjusting to this. A real fucking pisser."

"It is," Gaunt said.

"Kind of surprised you haven't thrown yourself into the sea by now."

"And miss the warmth of human companionship?"

The bearded man didn't laugh, but he made a clucking sound that was a reasonable substitute. Gaunt couldn't tell if the man was acknowledging his attempt at humour, or mocking his ineptitude, but at least it was a response, at least it showed that there was a possibility of normal human relationships somewhere down the line.

Gaunt was mostly too tired to think, but in the evenings a variety of entertainment options were available. The rig had a large library of damp, yellowing paperbacks, enough reading material for several years of diligent consumption, and there were also musical recordings and movies and immersives for those that were interested. There were games and sports and instruments and opportunities for relaxed discussion and banter. There was alcohol, or something like it, available in small quantities. There was also ample opportunity to get away from everyone else, if solitude was what one wanted. On top of that there were rotas that saw people working in the kitchens and medical facilities, even when they had already done their normal stint of duty. And as the helicopters came and went from the other rigs, so the faces changed. One day Gaunt realised that the big bearded man hadn't been around for a while, and he noticed a young woman he didn't recall having seen before. It was a spartan, cloistered life, not much different to being in a monastery or a prison, but for that reason the slightest variation in routine was to be cherished. If there was one unifying activity, one thing that brought everyone together, it was when the caretakers crowded into the commons, listening to the daily reports coming in over the radio from the other rigs in the Patagonia offshore sector, and occasionally from further afield. Scratchy, cryptic transmissions in strange, foreign-sounding accents. Two hundred thousand living souls was a ludicrously small number for the global population, Gaunt knew. But it was already more people than he could ever hope to know or even recognise. The hundred or so people working in the sector was about the size of a village, and for centuries that had been all the humanity most people ever dealt with. On some level, the world of the rigs and the caretakers was what his mind had evolved to handle. The world of eight billion people, the world of cities and malls and airport terminals was an anomaly, a kink in history that he had never been equipped for in the first place.

He was not happy now, not even halfway to being happy, but the despair and bitterness had abated. His acceptance into the community would be slow, there would be reversals and setbacks as he made mistakes and misjudged situations. But he had no doubt that it would happen eventually. Then he too would be one of the crew, and it would be someone else's turn to feel like the newcomer. He might not be happy then, but at least he would be settled, ready to play out the rest of his existence. Doing something, no matter how pointless, to prolong the existence of the human species, and indeed the universe it called home. Above all he would have the self-respect of knowing he had chosen the difficult path, rather than the easy one.

Weeks passed, and then the weeks turned into months. Eight weeks had passed since his revival. Slowly he became confident with the work allotted to him. And as his confidence grew, so did Nero's confidence in his abilities.

"She tells me you're measuring up," Clausen said, when he was called to the prefabricated shack where she drew up schedules and doled out work.

He gave a shrug, too tired to care whether she was impressed or not. "I've done my best. I don't know what more you want from me."

She looked up from her planning.

"Remorse for what you did?"

"I can't show remorse for something that wasn't a crime. We were trying to bring something new into the world, that's all. You think we had the slightest idea of the consequences?"

"You made a good living."

"And I'm expected to feel bad about that? I've been thinking it over, Clausen, and I've decided your argument's horse-shit. I didn't create the enemy. The original artilects were already out there, already in the Realm."

"They hadn't noticed us."

"And the global population had only just spiked at eight billion. Who's to say they weren't about to notice, or they wouldn't do so in the next hundred years, or the next thousand? At least the artilects I helped create gave us some warning of what we were facing."

"Your artilects are trying to kill us."

"Some of them. And some of them are also trying to keep us alive. Sorry, but that's not an argument."

She put down her pen and leaned back in her chair. "You've got some fight back in you."

"If you expect me to apologise for myself, you've got a long wait coming. I think you brought me back to rub my nose in the world I helped bring about. I agree, it'a fucked-up, miserable future. It couldn't get much more fucked-up if it tried. But I didn't build it. And I'm not responsible for you losing anyone."

Her face twitched; it was as if he had reached across the desk and slapped her. "Nero told you."

"I had a right to know why you were treating me the way you were. But you know what? I don't care. If transferring your anger onto me helps you, go ahead. I was the billionaire CEO of a global company. I was doing something wrong if I didn't wake up with a million knives in my back."

She dismissed him from the office, Gaunt leaving with the feeling that he'd scored a minor victory but at the possible cost of something larger. He had stood up to Clausen but did that make him more respectable in her eyes, or someone even more deserving of her antipathy?

That evening he was in the commons, sitting at the back of the room as wireless reports filtered in from the other rigs. Most of the news was unexceptional, but there had been three more breeches—sea-dragons being pushed through from the Realm—and one of them had achieved sufficient coherence to attack and damage an OTEC plant, immediately severing power to three rigs. Backup systems had cut in but failures had occurred and as a consequence around a hundred sleepers had been lost to unscheduled warming. None of the sleepers had survived the rapid revival, but even if they had, there would have been no option but to euthanise them shortly afterwards. A hundred new minds might not have made much difference to the Realm's clock speed but it would have established a risky precedent.

One sleeper, however, would soon have to be warmed. The details were sketchy, but Gaunt learned that there had been another accident out on one of the rigs. A man called Steiner had been hurt in some way.

The morning after, Gaunt was engaged in his duties on one of the rig's high platforms when he saw the helicopter coming in with Steiner aboard. He put down his tools and watched the arrival. Even before the aircraft had touched down on the pad, caretakers were assembling just beyond the painted circle of the rotor hazard area. The helicopter kissed the ground against a breath of crosswind and the caretakers mobbed inward, almost preventing the door from being opened. Gaunt squinted against the wind, trying to pick out faces. A stretchered form emerged from the cabin, born aloft by many pairs of willing hands. Even from his distant vantage point, it was obvious to Gaunt that Steiner was in a bad way. He had lost a leg below the knee, evidenced by the way the thermal blanket fell flat below the stump. The stretchered figure wore a breathing mask and another caretaker carried a saline drip which ran into Steiner's arm. But for all the concern the crowd was showing, there was something else, something almost adulatory. More than once Gaunt saw a hand raised to brush against the stretcher, or even to touch Steiner's own hand. And Steiner was awake, unable to speak, but nodding, turning his face this way and that to make eye contact with the welcoming party. Then the figure was taken inside and the crowd broke up, the workers returning to their tasks.

An hour or so later Nero came up to see him. She was still overseeing his initiation and knew his daily schedule, where he was likely to be at a given hour.

"Poor Steiner," she said. "I guess you saw him come in."

"Difficult to miss. It was like they were treating him as a hero."

"They were, in a way. Not because he'd done anything heroic, or anything they hadn't all done at some time or other. But because he'd bought his ticket out."

"He's going back into the box?"

"He has to. We can patch up a lot of things, but not a missing leg. Just don't have the medical resources to deal with that kind of injury. Simpler just to freeze him back again and pull out an intact body to take his place."

"Is Steiner OK about that?"

"Steiner doesn't have a choice, unfortunately. There isn't really any kind of effective work he could do like that, and we can't afford to carry the deadweight of an unproductive mind. You've seen how stretched we are: it's all hands on deck around here. We work you until you drop, and if you can't work, you go back in the box. That's the deal."

"I'm glad for Steiner, then."

Nero shook her head emphatically. "Don't be. Steiner would much rather stay with us. He fitted in well, after his adjustment. Popular guy."

"I could tell. But then why are they treating him like he's won the lottery, if that's not what he wanted?"

"Because what else are you going to do? Feel miserable about it? Hold a wake? Steiner goes back in the box with dignity. He held his end up. Didn't let any of us down. Now he gets to take it easy. If we can't celebrate that, what can we celebrate?"

"They'll be bringing someone else out, then."

"As soon as Clausen identifies a suitable replacement. He or she'll need to be trained up, though, and in the meantime there's a man-sized gap where Steiner used to be." She lifted off her hard hat to scratch her scalp. "That's kind of the reason I dropped by, actually. You're fitting in well, Gaunt, but sooner or later we all have to handle solitary duties away from the ops rig. Where Steiner was is currently unmanned. It's a low-maintenance unit that doesn't need more than one warm body, most of the time. The thinking is this would be a good chance to try you out."

It wasn't a total surprise; he had known enough of the work patterns to know that, sooner or later, he would be shipped out to one of the other rigs for an extended tour of duty. He just hadn't expected it to happen quite so soon, when he was only just beginning to find his feet, only just beginning to feel that he had a future.

"I don't feel ready."

"No one ever does. But the chopper's waiting. Clausen's already redrawing the schedule so someone else can take up the slack here."

"I don't get a choice in this, do I?"

Nero looked sympathetic. "Not really. But, you know, sometimes it's easier not having a choice."

"How long?"

"Hard to say. Figure on at least three weeks, maybe longer. I'm afraid Clausen won't make the decision to pull you back until she's good and ready."

"I think I pissed her off," Gaunt said.

"Not the hardest thing to do," Nero answered.

They helicoptered him out to the other rig. He had been given just enough time to gather his few personal effects, such as they were. He did not need to take any tools or parts with him because he would find all that he needed when he arrived, as well as ample rations and medical supplies. Nero, for her part, tried to reassure him that all would be well. The robots he would be tending were all types that he had already serviced, and it was unlikely that any would suffer catastrophic breakdowns during his tour. No one was expecting miracles, she said: if something arose that he couldn't reasonably deal with, then help would be sent. And if he cracked out there, then he'd be brought back.

What she didn't say was what would happen then. But he didn't think it would involve going back into the box. Maybe he'd be assigned something at the bottom of the food chain, but that didn't seem very likely either.

But it wasn't the possibility of cracking, or even failing in his duties, that was bothering him. It was something else, the seed of an idea that he wished Steiner had not planted in his mind. Gaunt had been adjusting, slowly coming to terms with his new life. He had been recalibrating his hopes and fears, forcing his expectations into line with what the world now had on offer. No riches, no prestige, no luxury, and most certainly not immortality and eternal youth. The best it could give was twenty or thirty years of hard graft. Ten thousand days, if he was very lucky. And most of those days would be spent doing hard, backbreaking work, until the work took its ultimate toll. He'd be cold and wet a lot of the time, and when he wasn't cold and wet he'd be toiling under an uncaring sun, his eyes salt-stung, his hands ripped to shreds from work that would have been too demeaning for the lowliest wage-slave in the old world. He'd be high in the air, vertigo never quite leaving him, with only metal and concrete and too much grey ocean under his feet. He'd be hungry and dry mouthed, because the seaweed-derived food never filled his belly and there was never enough drinking water to sate his thirst. In the best of outcomes, he'd be doing well to see more than a hundred other human faces before he died. Maybe there'd be friends in those hundred faces, friends as well as enemies, and maybe, just maybe, there'd be at least one person who could be more than a friend. He didn't know, and he knew better than to expect guarantees or hollow promises. But this much at least was true. He had been adjusting.

And then Steiner had shown him that there was another way out.

He could keep his dignity. He could return to the boxes with the assurance that he had done his part.

As a hero, one of the Few.

All he had to do was have an accident.

He had been on the new rig, alone, for two weeks. It was only then that he satisfied himself that the means lay at hand. Nero had impressed on him many times the safety procedures that needed to be adhered to when working with powerful items of moving machinery, such as robots. Especially when those robots were not powered down. All it would take, she told him, was a moment of inattention. Forgetting to clamp down on that safety lock, forgetting to ensure that such and such an override was not enabled. Putting his hand onto the service rail for balance, when the robot was about to move back along it. "Don't think it can't happen," she said, holding up her mittened hand. "I was lucky. Got off with burns, which heal. I can still do useful shit, even now. Even more so when I get these bandages off, and I can work my fingers again. But try getting by without any fingers at all."

"I'll be careful," Gaunt had assured her, and he had believed it, truly, because he had always been squeamish.

But that was before he saw injury as a means to an end.

His planning, of necessity, had to be meticulous. He wanted to survive, not be pulled off the rig as a brain-dead corpse, not fit to be frozen again. It would be no good lying unconscious, bleeding to death. He would have to save himself, make his way back to the communications room, issue an emergency distress signal. Steiner had been lucky, but he would have to be cunning and single-minded. Above all it must not look as if he had planned it.

When the criteria were established, he saw that there was really only one possibility. One of the robots on his inspection cycle was large and dim enough to cause injury to the careless. It moved along a service rail, sometimes without warning. Even without trying, it had caught him off guard a couple of times, as its task scheduler suddenly decided to propel it to a new inspection point. He'd snatched his hand out of the way in time, but he would only have needed to hesitate, or to have his clothing catch on something, for the machine to roll over him. No matter what happened, whether the machine sliced or crushed, he was in doubt that it would hurt worse than anything he had ever known. But at the same time the pain would herald the possibility of blessed release, and that would make it bearable. They could always fix him a new hand, in the new world on the other side of sleep.

It took him days to build up to it. Time after time he almost had the nerve, before pulling away. Too many factors jostled for consideration. What clothing to wear, to increase his chances of surviving the accident? Dared he prepare the first aid equipment in advance, so that he could use it one-handed? Should he wait until the weather was perfect for flying, or would that risk matters appearing too stage-managed?

He didn't know. He couldn't decide.

In the end the weather settled matters for him.

A storm hit, coming down hard and fast like an iron heel. He listened to the reports from the other rigs, as each felt the full fury of the waves and the wind and the lightning. It was worse than any weather he had experienced since his revival, and at first it was almost too perfectly in accord with his needs. Real accidents were happening out there, but there wasn't much that anyone could do about it until the helicopters could get airborne. Now was not the time to have his accident, not if he wanted to be rescued.

So he waited, listening to the reports. Out on the observation deck, he watched the lightning strobe from horizon to horizon, picking out the distant sentinels of other rigs, stark and white like thunderstruck trees on a flat black plain.

Not now, he thought. When the storm turns, when the possibility of accident is still there, but when rescue is again feasible.

He thought of Nero. She had been as kind to him as anyone, but he wasn't sure if that had much to do with friendship. She needed an able-bodied worker, that was all.

Maybe. But she also knew him better than anyone, better even than Clausen. Would she see through his plan, and realise what he had done?

He was still thinking it through when the storm began to ease, the waves turning leaden and sluggish, and the eastern sky gained a band of salmon pink.

He climbed to the waiting robot and sat there. The rig creaked and groaned around him, affronted by the battering it had taken. It was only then that he realised that it was much too early in the day to have his accident. He would have to wait until sunrise if anyone was going to believe that he had been engaged on his normal duties. No one went out to fix a broken service robot in the middle of a storm.

That was when he saw the sea-glow.

It was happening perhaps a kilometre away, towards the west: a foreshortened circle of fizzing yellow-green, a luminous cauldron just beneath the waves. Almost beautiful, if he didn't know what it signified. A sea-dragon was coming through, a sinuous, living weapon from the artilect wars. It was achieving coherence, taking solid form in base-reality.

Gaunt forgot all about his planned accident. For long moments he could only stare at that circular glow, mesmerised at the shape assuming existence under water. He had seen a sea-dragon from the helicopter on the first day of his revival, but he had not come close to grasping its scale. Now, as the size of the forming creature became apparent, he understood why such things were capable of havoc. Something between a tentacle and a barb broke the surface, still imbued with a kind of glowing translucence, as if its hold on reality was not yet secure, and from his vantage point it clearly reached higher into the sky than the rig itself.

Then it was gone. Not because the sea-dragon had failed in its bid to achieve coherence, but because the creature had withdrawn into the depths. The yellow-green glow had by now all but dissipated, like some vivid chemical slick breaking up into its constituent elements. The sea, still being stirred around by the tail-end of the storm, appeared normal enough. Moments passed, then what must have been a minute or more. He had not drawn a breath since first seeing the sea-glow, but he started breathing again, daring to hope that the life-form had swum away to some other objective or had perhaps lost coherence in the depths.

He felt it slam into the rig.

The entire structure lurched with the impact; he doubted the impact would have been any less violent if a submarine had just collided with it. He remained on his feet, while all around pieces of unsecured metal broke away, dropping to decks or the sea. From somewhere out of sight came a tortured groan, heralding some awful structural failure. A sequence of booming crashes followed, as if boulders were being dropped into the waves. Then the sea-dragon rammed the rig again, and this time the jolt was sufficient to unfoot him. To his right, one of the cranes began to sway in an alarming fashion, the scaffolding of its tower buckling.

The sea-dragon was holding coherence. From the ferocity of its attacks, Gaunt thought it quite possible that it could take down the whole rig, given time.

He realised, with a sharp and surprising clarity, that he did not want to die. More than that: he realised that life in this world, with all its harships and disappointments, was going to be infinitely preferable to death beyond it. He wanted to survive.

As the sea-dragon came in again, he started down the ladders and stairwells, grateful for having a full set of fingers and hands, terrified on one level and almost drunkenly, deleriously glad on the other. He had not done the thing he had been planning, and now he might die anyway, but there was a chance and if he survived this he would have nothing in the world to be ashamed of.

He had reached the operations deck, the room where he had planned to administer first-aid and issue his distress call, when the sea-dragon began the second phase of its assault. He could see it plainly, visible through the rig's open middle as it hauled its way out of the sea, using one of the legs to assist its progress. There was nothing translucent or tentative about it now. And it was indeed a dragon, or rather a chimera of dragon and snake and squid and every scaled, barbed, tentacled, clawed horror ever committed to a bestiary. It was a lustrous slate-green in colour and the waters ran off it in thunderous curtains. Its head, or what he chose to think of as its head, had reached the level of the operations deck. And still the sea-dragon produced more of itself, uncoiling out of the dark waters like some conjuror's trick. Tentacles whipped out and found purchase, and it snapped and wrenched away parts of the rig's superstructure as if they were made of biscuit or brittle toffee. It was making a noise while it attacked, an awful, slowly rising and falling foghorn proclamation. It's a weapon, Gaunt reminded himself. It had been engineered to be terrible.

The sea-dragon was pythoning its lower anatomy around one of the support legs, crushing and grinding. Scabs of concrete came away, hitting the sea like chunks of melting glacier. The floor under his feet surged and when it stopped surging the angle was all wrong. Gaunt knew then that the rig could not be saved, and that if he wished to live he would have to take his chances in the water. The thought of it was almost enough to make him laugh. Leave the rig, leave the one thing that passed for solid ground, and enter the same seas that now held the dragon?

Yet it had to be done.

He issued the distress call, but didn't wait for a possible response. He gave the rig a few minutes at the most. If they couldn't find him in the water, it wouldn't help him to know their plans. Then he looked around for the nearest orange-painted survival cabinet. He had been shown the emergency equipment during his training, never once imagining that he would have cause to use it. The insulated survival clothing, the life-jacket, the egress procedure . . .

A staircase ran down the interior of one of the legs, emerging just above the water line; it was how they came and went from the rig on the odd occasions when they were using boats rather than helicopters. But even as he remembered how to reach the staircase, he realised that it was inside the same leg that the sea-dragon was wrapped around. That left him with only one other option. There was a ladder that led down to the water, with an extensible lower portion. It wouldn't get him all the way, but his chances of surviving the drop were a lot better than his chances of surviving the sea-dragon.

It was worse than he had expected. The fall into the surging waters seemed to last forever, the superstructure of the rig rising slowly above him, the iron-grey sea hovering below until what felt like the very last instant, when it suddenly accelerated, and then he hit the surface with such force that he blacked out. He must have submerged and bobbed to the surface because when he came around he was coughing cold salt-water from his lungs, and it was in his eyes and ears and nostrils as well, colder than water had any right to be, and then a wave was curling over him, and he blacked out again.

He came around again what must have been minutes later. He was still in the water, cold around the neck but his body snug in the insulation suit. The life-jacket was keeping his head out of the water, except when the waves crashed onto him. A light on his jacket was blinking on and off, impossibly bright and blue.

To his right, hundreds of metres away, and a little further with each bob of the waters, the rig was going down with the sea-dragon still wrapped around its lower extremities. He heard the foghorn call, saw one of the legs crumble away, and then an immense tidal weariness closed over him.

He didn't remember the helicopter finding him. He didn't remember the thud of its rotors or being hauled out of the water on a winch-line. There was just a long period of unconsciousness, and then the noise and vibration of the cabin, the sun coming in through the windows, the sky clear and blue and the sea unruffled. It took a few moments for it all to click in. Some part of his brain had skipped over the events since his arrival and was still working on the assumption that it had all worked out, that he had slept into a better future, a future where the world was new and clean and death just a fading memory.

"We got your signal," Clausen said. "Took us a while to find you, even with the transponder on your jacket."

It all came back to him. The rigs, the sleepers, the artilects, the sea-dragons. The absolute certainty that this was the only world he would know, followed by the realisation—or, rather, the memory of having already come to that realisation—that this was still better than dying. He thought back to what he had been planning to do before the sea-dragon came, and wanted to crush the memory and bury it where he buried every other shameful thing he had ever done.

"What about the rig?"

"Gone," Clausen said. "Along with all the sleepers inside it. The dragon broke up shortly afterwards. It's a bad sign that it held coherence for as long as it did. Means they're getting better."

"Our machines will just have to get better as well, won't they."

He thought she might spit the observation back at him, mock him for its easy triteness, when he knew so little of the war and the toll it had taken. But instead she nodded. "That's all they can do. All we can hope for. And they will, of course. They always do. Otherwise we wouldn't be here." She looked down at his blanketed form. "Sorry you agreed to stay awake now?"

"No, I don't think so."

"Even with what happened back there?"

"At least I got to see a dragon up close."

"Yes," Clausen said. "That you did."

He thought that was the end of it, the last thing she had to say to him. He couldn't say for sure that something had changed in their relationship—it would take time for that to be proved—but he did sense some thawing in her attitude, however temporary it might prove. He had not only chosen to stay, he had not gone through with the accident. Had she been expecting him to try something like that, after what had happened to Steiner? Could she begin to guess how close he had come to actually doing it?

But Clausen wasn't finished.

"I don't know if it's true or not," she said, speaking to Gaunt for the first time as if he was another human being, another caretaker. "But I heard this theory once. The mapping between the Realm and base-reality, it's not as simple as you'd think. Time and causality get all tangled up on the interface. Events that happen in one order there don't necessarily correspond to the same order here. And when they push things through, they don't always come out in what we consider the present. A chain of events in the Realm could have consequences up or down the timeline, as far as we're concerned."

"I don't think I understand."

She nodded to the window. "All through history, the things they've seen out there. They might just have been overspill from the artilect wars. Weapons that came through at the wrong moment, achieving coherence just long enough to be seen by someone, or bring down a ship. All the sailors' tales, all the way back. All the sea monsters. They might just have been echoes of the war we're fighting." Clausen shrugged, as if the matter were of no consequence.

"You believe that?"

"I don't know if it makes the world seem weirder, or a little more sensible." She shook her head. "I mean, sea monsters . . . who ever thought they might be real?" Then she stood up and made to return to the front of the helicopter. "Just a theory, that's all. Now get some sleep."

Gaunt did as he was told. It wasn't hard.

the taste of Night

PAT CADiGAN

You can't see something until you develop the eyes to see it with, as the unsettling tale that follows demonstrates all too well. . . .

Pat Cadigan was born in Schenectady, New York, and now lives in London with her family. She made her first professional sale in 1980, and has subsequently come to be regarded as one of the best new writers of her generation. Her story "Pretty Boy Crossover" has appeared on several critic's lists as among the best science fiction stories of the 1980s, and her story "Angel" was a finalist for the Hugo Award, the Nebula Award, *and* the World Fantasy Award (one of the few stories ever to earn that rather unusual distinction). Her short fiction—which has appeared in most of the major markets, including *Asimov's Science Fiction* and *The Magazine of Fantasy & Science Fiction*—has been gathered in the collections *Patterns* and *Dirty Work*. Her first novel, *Mindplayers*, was released in 1987 to excellent critical response, and her second novel, *Synners*, released in 1991, won the Arthur C. Clarke Award as the year's best science fiction novel, as did her third novel, *Fools*, making her the only writer ever to win the Clarke Award twice. Her other books include the novels *Dervish Is Digital*, *Tea from an Empty Cup*, and *Reality Used to Be a Friend of Mine*, and, as editor, the anthology *The Ultimate Cyberpunk*, as well as two making-of movie books and four media tie-in novels. Her most recent book was a novel, *Cellular*.

T he taste of night rather than the falling temperature woke her. Nell curled up a little more and continued to doze. It would be a while before the damp chill coming up from the ground could get through the layers of heavy cardboard to penetrate the sleeping bag and blanket cocooning her. She was fully dressed and her spare clothes were in the sleeping bag, too—not much but enough to make good insulation. Sometime in the next twenty-four hours, though, she would have to visit a laundromat because *phew*.

Phew was one of those things that didn't change; well, not so far, anyway. She hoped it would stay that way. By contrast, the taste of night was one of her secret great pleasures although she still had no idea what it was supposed to mean. Now and then something *almost* came to her, *almost*. But when she reached for it either in her mind or by actually touching something, there was nothing at all.

Sight. Hearing. Smell. Taste. Touch. _____.

Memory sprang up in her mind with the feel of pale blue stretched long and tight between her hands.

The blind discover that their other senses, particularly hearing, intensify to compensate for the lack. The deaf can be sharp-eyed but also extra sensitive to vibration, which is what sound is to the rest of us.

However, those who lose their sense of smell find they have lost their sense of taste as well because the two are so close. To lose feeling is usually a symptom of a greater problem. A small number of people feel no pain but this puts them at risk for serious injury and life-threatening illnesses.

That doctor had been such a patient woman. Better yet, she had had no deep well of stored-up suspicion like every other doctor Marcus had taken her to. Nell had been able to examine what the doctor was telling her, touching it all over, feeling the texture. Even with Marcus's impatience splashing her like an incoming tide, she had been able to ask a question.

A sixth sense? Like telepathy or clairvoyance?

The doctor's question had been as honest as her own and Nell did her best to make herself clear.

If there were some kind of extra sense, even a person who had it would have a hard time explaining it. Like you or me trying to explain sight to someone born blind.

Nell had agreed and asked the doctor to consider how the other five senses might try to compensate for the lack.

That was where the memory ended, leaving an aftertaste similar to night, only colder and with a bit of sour.

Nell sighed, feeling comfortable and irrationally safe. Feeling safe was irrational if you slept rough. Go around feeling safe and you wouldn't last too long. It was just that the indented area she had found at the back of this building—cinema? auditorium?—turned out to be as cozy as it had looked. It seemed to have no purpose except as a place where someone could sleep unnoticed for a night or two. More than two would have been pushing it, but that meant nothing to some rough sleepers. They'd camp in a place like this till they wore off all the hidden. Then they'd get seen and kicked out. Next thing you knew, the spot would be fenced off or filled in so no one could ever use it again. One less place to go when there was nowhere to stay.

Nell hated loss, hated the taste: dried-out bitter crossed with salty that could hang on for days, weeks, even longer. Worse, it could come back without warning and for no reason except that, perhaps like rough sleepers, it had nowhere else to go. There were other things that tasted just as bad to her but nothing worse, and nothing that lingered for anywhere nearly as long, not even the moldy-metal tang of disappointment.

After a bit, she realized the pools of colour she'd been watching behind her closed eyes weren't the remnants of a slow-to-fade dream but real voices of real humans, not too far away, made out of the same stuff she was; either they hadn't noticed her or they didn't care.

Nell uncurled slowly—never make any sudden moves was another good rule for rough sleepers—and opened her eyes. An intense blue-white light blinded her with the sound of a cool voice in her right ear:

Blue-white stars don't last long enough for any planets orbiting them to develop intelligent life. Maybe not any life, even the most rudimentary. Unless there is a civilization advanced enough to seed those worlds with organisms modified to evolve at a faster rate. That might beg the question of why an advanced civilization would do that. But the motives of a civilization that advanced would/could/might seem illogical if not incomprehensible to any not equally developed.

Blue-white memory stretched farther this time: a serious-faced young woman in a coffee shop, watching a film clip on a notebook screen. Nell had sneaked a look at it on her way to wash up in the women's restroom. It took her a little while to realize that she had had a glimpse of something to do with what had been happening to her, or more precisely, *why* it was happening, what it was supposed to mean. On the heels of that realization had come a new one, probably the most important: *they* were communicating with her.

Understanding always came to her at oblique angles. The concept of that missing sixth sense, for instance—when she finally became aware of it, she realized that it had been lurking somewhere in the back of her mind for a very, very long time, years and years, a passing notion or a ragged fragment of a mostly forgotten dream. It had developed so slowly that she might have lived her whole life without noticing it, instead burying it under more mundane concerns and worries and fears.

Somehow it had snagged her attention—a mental pop-up window. Marcus had said everyone had an occasional stray thought about something odd. Unless she was going to write a weird story or draw a weird picture, there was no point in obsessing about it.

Was it the next doctor who had suggested she do exactly that—write a weird story or draw a weird picture, or both? Even if she had really wanted to, she couldn't. She knew for certain by then that she was short a sense, just as if she were blind or deaf.

Marcus had said he didn't understand why that meant she had to leave home and sleep on the street. She didn't either, at the time. But even if she had understood enough to tell him that *the motives of a civilization that advanced would/could/might seem illogical if not incomprehensible to any not equally developed,* all it would have meant to him was that she was, indeed, crazy as a bedbug, unquote.

The social worker he had sent after her hadn't tried to talk her into a hospital or a shelter right away but the intent was deafening. Every time she found Nell it drowned everything else out. Nell finally had to make her say it just to get some peace. For a few days after that, everything was extra scrambled. She was too disoriented to understand anything. All she knew was that *they* were bombarding her with their communication and her senses were working overtime, trying to make up for her inadequacy.

The blinding blue-white light dissolved and her vision cleared. Twenty feet away was an opening in the back of the building the size of a double-garage door.

Seven or eight men were hanging around just outside, some of them sitting on wooden crates, smoking cigarettes, drinking from bottles or large soft-drink cups. The pools of colour from their voices changed to widening circular ripples, like those spreading out from raindrops falling into still water. The colours crossed each other to make new colours, some she had never seen anywhere but in her mind.

The ripples kept expanding until they reached the backs of her eyes and swept through them with a sensation of a wind ruffling feathery flowers. She saw twinkling lights and then a red-hot spike went through her right temple. There was just enough time for her to inhale before an ice-pick went through her eye to cross the spike at right angles.

Something can be a million light-years away and in your eye at the same time.

"Are you all right?"

The man bent over her, hands just above his knees. Most of his long hair was tied back except for a few long strands that hung forward in a way that suggested punctuation to Nell. Round face, round eyes with hard lines under them.

See. Hear. Smell. Taste. Touch. _____.

Hand over her right eye, she blinked up at him. He repeated the question and the words were little green balls falling from his mouth to bounce away into the night. Nell caught her lower lip between her teeth to keep herself from laughing. He reached down and pulled the hand over her eye to one side. Then he straightened up and pulled a cell phone out of his pocket. "I need an ambulance," he said to it.

She opened her mouth to protest but her voice wouldn't work. Another man was coming over, saying something in thin, tight silver wires.

And then it was all thin, tight silver wires everywhere. Some of the wires turned to needles and they seemed to fight each other for dominance. The pain in her eye flared more intensely and a voice from somewhere far in the past tried to ask a question without morphing into something else but it just wasn't loud enough for her to hear.

Nell rolled over onto her back. Something that was equal parts anxiety and anticipation shuddered through her. Music, she realized; very loud, played live, blaring out of the opening where the men were hanging around. Chords rattled her blood, pulled at her arms and legs. The pain flared again but so did the taste of night. She let herself fall into it. The sense of falling became the desire to sleep but just as she was about to give in, she would slip back to wakefulness, back and forth like a pendulum. Or like she was swooping from the peak of one giant wave, down into the trough and up to the peak of another.

Her right eye was forced open with a sound like a gunshot and bright light filled her mouth with the taste of icicles.

"Welcome back. Don't take this the wrong way but I'm very sorry to see you here."

Nell discovered only her left eye would open but one eye was enough. Ms. Dunwoody, Call-Me-Anne, the social worker. Not the original social worker Marcus had sent after her. That had been Ms. Petersen, Call-Me-Joan, who had been replaced after a while by Mr. Carney, Call-Me-Dwayne. Nell had seen him only twice and the second time he had been one big white knuckle, as if he were holding something back—tears? hysteria? Whatever it was leaked from him in twisted shapes of shifting colours that left bad tastes in her mouth. Looking away from him didn't help—the tastes were there whether she saw the colours or not.

It was the best they could do for her, lacking as she was in that sense. At the time, she hadn't understood. All she had known was that the tastes turned her stomach and the colours gave her headaches. Eventually, she had thrown up on the social worker's shoes and he had fled without apology or even so much as a surprised curse, let alone a good-bye. Nell hadn't minded.

Ms. Dunwoody, Call-Me-Anne, was his replacement and she had managed to find Nell more quickly than she had expected. Ms. Dunwoody, Call-Me-Anne, had none of the same kind of tension in her but once in a while she exuded a musty, stale odor of resignation that was very close to total surrender.

Surrender. It took root in Nell's mind but she was slow to understand because she only associated it with Ms. Dunwoody, Call-Me-Anne's unspoken (even to herself) desire to give up. If she'd just had that missing sense, it would have been so obvious right away.

Of course, if she'd had that extra sense, she'd have understood the whole thing right away and everything would be different. Maybe not a whole lot easier, since she would still have had a hard time explaining sight to all the blind people, so to speak, but at least she wouldn't have been floundering around in confusion.

"Nell?" Ms. Dunwoody, Call-Me-Anne, was leaning forward, peering anxiously into her face. "I *said*, do you know why you're here?"

Nell hesitated. "Here, as in . . ." Her voice failed in her dry throat. The social worker poured her a glass of water from a pitcher on the bedside table and held it up, slipping the straw between her dry lips so she could drink. Nell finished three glasses and Ms. Dunwoody, Call-Me-Anne, made a business of adjusting her pillows before she lay back against the raised mattress.

"Better?" she asked Nell brightly.

Nell made a slight, non-committal dip with her head. "What was the question?" she asked, her voice still faint.

"Do you know where you are?" Ms. Dunwoody, Call-Me-Anne, said.

Nell smiled inwardly at the change and resisted the temptation to say, *Same place you are—here.* There were deep lines under the social worker's eyes, her clothes were wrinkled, and lots of little hairs had escaped from her tied-back hair. No doubt she'd had less rest in the last twenty-four hours than Nell. She looked around with her one good eye at the curtains surrounding them and at the bed. "Hospital. Tri-County General."

She could see that her specifying which hospital had reassured the social worker. That was hardly a major feat of cognition, though; Tri-County General was where all the homeless as well as the uninsured ended up.

"You had a convulsion," Call-Me-Anne told her, speaking slowly and carefully now as if to a child. "A man found you behind the concert hall and called an ambulance."

Nell lifted her right hand and pointed at her face.

Call-Me-Anne hesitated, looking uncertain. "You seem to have hurt your eye."

She remembered the sensation of the spike and the needle so vividly that she winced.

"Does it hurt?" Call-Me-Anne asked, full of concern. "Should I see if they can give you something for the pain?"

Nell shook her head no; a twinge from somewhere deep in her right eye socket warned her not to do that again or to make any sudden movements, period.

"Is there anyone you'd like me to call for you?" the social worker asked.

Frowning a little, Nell crossed her hands and uncrossed them in an absolutely-not gesture. Call-Me-Anne pressed her lips together but it didn't stop a long pink ribbon from floating weightless out from her mouth. Too late—she had already called Marcus, believing that by the time he got here, Nell actually would want to see him. And if not, she would claim that Marcus had insisted on seeing *her*, regardless of Nell's wishes, because he was her husband and loyalty and blah-blah-blah-social-worker-blather.

All at once there was a picture in her mind of a younger and not-so-tired Ms. Dunwoody, Call-Me-Anne, and just as suddenly, it came to life.

I feel that if we can re-unite families, then we've done the best job we can. Sometimes that isn't possible, of course, so the next best thing we can do is provide families for those who need them.

Call-Me-Anne's employment interview, she realized. What *they* were trying to tell her with that wasn't at all clear. That missing sense. Or maybe because *they* had the sense, they were misinterpreting the situation.

"Nell? *Nell?*"

She tried to pull her arm out of the social worker's grip and couldn't. The pressure was a mouthful of walnut shells, tasteless and sharp. "What do you want?"

"I *said*, are you *sure?*"

Nell sighed. "There's a story that the first people in the New World to see Columbus's ships couldn't actually *see* them because such things were too far outside their experience. You think that's true?"

Call-Me-Anne, her expression a mix of confusion and anxiety. Nell knew what that look meant—she was afraid the situation was starting to get away from her. "Are you groggy? Or just tired?"

"I don't," she went on, a bit wistful. "I think they didn't know what they were seeing and maybe had a hard time with the perspective but I'm sure they saw them. After all, they *were* made by other humans. But something coming from another world, all bets are off."

Call-Me-Anne's face was very sad now.

"I sound crazy to you?" Nell gave a short laugh. "*Scientists* talk about this stuff."

"You're not a scientist, Nell. You were a librarian. With proper treatment and medication, you could—"

Nell laughed again. "If a librarian starts thinking about the possibility of life somewhere else in the universe, it's a sign she's going crazy?" She turned her head away and closed her eyes. Correction, eye. She couldn't feel very much behind the bandage, just enough to know that her right eyelid wasn't opening or closing. When she heard the social worker walk away, she opened her eye to see the silver wires had come back. They bloomed like flowers, opening and then flying apart where they met others and connected, making new blooms that flew apart and found new connections. The world in front of Nell began to look like a cage, although she had no idea which side she was on.

Abruptly, she felt one of the wires go through her temple with that same white-hot pain. A moment later, a second one went through the bandage over her right eye as easily as if it wasn't there, going all the way through her head and out, pinning her to the pillow.

Her left eye was watering badly but she could see Call-Me-Anne rushing back with a nurse. Their mouths opened and closed as they called her name. She saw them reaching for her but she was much too far away.

And that was how it would be. No, that was how it was always, but the five senses worked so hard to compensate for the one missing that people took the illusion of contact for the real thing. The power of suggestion—where would the human race be without it?

Sight. Hearing. Smell. Taste. Touch. _____.

Contact.

The word was a poor approximation but the concept was becoming clearer in her mind now. Clearer than the sight in her left eye, which was dimming. But still good enough to let her see Call-Me-Anne was on the verge of panic.

A man in a white uniform pushed her aside and she became vaguely aware of him touching her. But there was still no *contact.*

Nell labored toward wakefulness as if she were climbing a rock wall with half a dozen sandbags dangling on long ropes tied around her waist. Her mouth was full of steel wool and sand. She knew that taste—medication. It would probably take most of a day to spit that out.

She had tried medication in the beginning because Marcus had begged her to. Anti-depressants, anti-anxiety capsules, and finally anti-psychotics—they had all tasted the same because she hadn't been depressed, anxious, or psychotic. Meanwhile, Marcus had gotten farther and farther away, which, unlike the dry mouth, the weight gain, or the tremors in her hands, was not reversible.

Call-Me-Anne had no idea about that. She kept trying to get Nell to see Marcus, unaware they could barely perceive each other anymore. Marcus didn't realize it either, not the way she did. Marcus thought that was reversible, too.

Pools of colour began to appear behind her heavy eyelids, strange colours that shifted and changed, green to gold, purple to red, blue to aqua, and somewhere between one colour and another was a hue she had never found anywhere else and never would.

Sight. Hearing. Smell. Taste. Touch. _____.

C-c-c-contact . . .

The word was a boulder trying to fit a space made for a pebble smoothed over the course of eons and a distance of light-years into a precise and elegant thing.

Something can be a million light-years away and in your eye at the same time.

Sight. Hearing. Smell. Taste. Touch. _____.

C-c-c-con . . . nect.

C-c-c-commmmune.

C-c-c-c-communnnnnnnnnicate.

She had a sudden image of herself running around the base of a pyramid, searching for a way to get to the top. While she watched, it was replaced by a new image, of herself running around an elephant and several blind men; she was still looking for a way to get to the top of the pyramid.

The image dissolved and she became aware of how heavy the overhead lights were on her closed eyes. Eye. She sighed; even if she did finally reach understanding—or it reached her—how would she ever be able to explain what blind men, an elephant, and a pyramid combined with Columbus's ships meant?

The musty smell of surrender broke in on her thoughts. It was very strong; Call-Me-Anne was still there. After a bit, she heard the sound of a wooden spoon banging on the bottom of a pot. Frustration, but not just any frustration: Marcus's.

She had never felt him so clearly without actually seeing him. Perhaps Call-Me-Anne's surrender worked as an amplifier.

The shifting colours resolved themselves into a new female voice. ". . . much do either of you know about the brain?"

"Not much," Call-Me-Anne said. Marcus grunted, a stone rolling along a dirt path.

"Generally, synesthesia can be a side effect of medication or a symptom."

"What about mental illness?" Marcus asked sharply, the spoon banging louder on the pot.

"Sometimes mentally ill people experience it but it's not a specific symptom of mental illness. In your wife's case, it was a symptom of the tumours."

"Tumours?" Call-Me-Anne was genuinely upset. Guilt was a soft scratching noise, little mouse claws on a hard surface.

"Two, although there could be three. We're not sure about the larger one. The smaller one is an acoustic neuroma, which—"

"Is that why she hears things?" Marcus interrupted.

The doctor hesitated. "Probably not, although some people complain of tinnitus. It's non-cancerous, doesn't spread, and normally very slow-growing. Your wife's seems to be growing faster than normal. But then there's the other one." Pause. "I've only been a neurosurgeon for ten years so I can't say I've seen everything but this really is quite, uh . . . unusual. She must have complained of headaches."

A silence, then Call-Me-Anne cleared her throat. "They seemed to be cluster headaches. Painful but not exactly rare. I have them myself. I gave her some of my medication but I don't know if she took it."

Another small pause. "Sometimes she said she had a headache but that's all," Marcus said finally. "We've been legally separated for a little over two years, so I'm not exactly up-to-date. She sleeps on the street."

"Well, there's no telling when it started until we can do some detailed scans."

"How much do those cost?" Marcus asked. Then after a long moment: "Hey, *she* left *me* to sleep on the *street* after I'd already spent a fortune on shrinks and prescriptions and hospitalizations. Then they tell me you can't force a person to get treated for anything unless they're a danger to the community, blah, blah, blah. Now she's got brain tumours and I'm gonna get hit for the bill. Dammit, I shoulda divorced her but it felt too—" The spoon scraped against the iron pot. "Cruel."

"You were hoping she'd snap out of it?" said the doctor. "Plenty of people feel that way. It's normal to hope for a miracle." Call-Me-Anne added some comforting noises, and said something about benefits and being in the system.

"Yeah, okay," Marcus said. "But you still didn't answer my question. How much do these scans cost?"

"Sorry, I couldn't tell you, I don't have anything to do with billing," the doctor said smoothly. "But we can't do any surgery without them."

"I thought you already did some," Marcus said.

"We were going to. Until I saw what was behind her eye."

"It's that big?" asked Marcus.

"It's not just that. It's—not your average tumour."

Marcus gave a humourless laugh. "Tumours are standardized, are they?"

"To a certain extent, just like the human body. This one, however, isn't behaving quite the way tumours usually do." Pause. "There seems to be some grey matter incorporated into it."

"What do you mean, like it's tangled up in her brain? Isn't that what a tumour does, get all tangled up in a person's brain? That's why it's hard to take out, right?"

"This is different," the doctor said. "Look, I've been debating with myself whether I should tell you about this—"

"If you're gonna bill me, you goddam better tell me," Marcus growled. "What's going on with her?"

"Just from what I could see, the tumour has either co-opted part of your wife's brain—stolen it, complete with blood supply—or there's a second brain growing in your wife's skull."

There was a long pause. Then Marcus said, "You know how crazy that sounds? You got any pictures of this?"

"No. Even if I did, you're not a neurosurgeon, you wouldn't know what you were looking at."

"No? I can't help thinking I'd know if I were looking at two brains in one head or not."

"The most likely explanation for this would be a parasitic twin," the doctor went on. "It happens more often than you'd think. The only thing is, parasitic twins don't suddenly take to growing. And if it had always been so large, you'd have seen signs of it long before now.

"Unfortunately, I couldn't even take a sample to biopsy. Your wife's vitals took a nosedive and we had to withdraw immediately. She's fine now—under the circumstances. But we need to do those scans as soon as possible. Her right eye was so damaged by this tumour that we couldn't save it. If we don't move quickly enough, it's going to cause additional damage to her face."

Nell took a deep breath, and let it out slowly. She hadn't thought they would hear her but they had; all three stopped talking and Call-Me-Anne and Marcus scurried over to the side of her bed, saying her name in soft, careful whispers, as if they thought it might break. She kept her eyes closed and her body limp, even when Call-Me-Anne took her hand in both of hers and squeezed it tight. After a while, she heard them go.

How had they done that, she marveled. How had they done it from so far away?

Something can be a million light-years away and in your eye at the same time.

Her mind's eye showed her a picture of two vines entangled with each other. Columbus's ships, just coming into view. The sense she had been missing was not yet fully developed, not enough to reconcile the vine and the ships. But judging from what the doctor said, it wouldn't be long now.

Blind Cat Dance

ALEXANDER JABLOKOV

With only a handful of stories, mostly for *Asimov's*, and a few well-received novels, Alexander Jablokov established himself as one of the most highly regarded new writers of the nineties. His first novel, *Carve the Sky*, was released in 1991, and was followed by other successful novels such as *A Deeper Sea*, *Nimbus*, *River of Dust*, and *Deepdrive*, as well as a collection of his short fiction, *The Breath of Suspension*. Jablokov fell silent through the decade of the aughts, but in the last couple of years has been returning to print, releasing *Brain Thief* in 2010, his first novel in over ten years, and popping up in the magazines again with elegant, coolly pyrotechnic stories such as the one that follows, set in a future society that has developed a novel way of integrating the human and natural worlds, making the animals unable to perceive the human society around them, so that they think they're in the middle of a forest when actually they're in the middle of a crowded café. Of course, one immediately has to wonder what it is that the humans themselves are unable to see, although it's brushing all around them. . . .

ENCOUNTER #1
CAFE KULFI

The cougar stalks into the cafe, its skin loose, looking relaxed, even a bit bored. Its padded feet are silent on the terrazzo. Conversation at the tables drops for a moment, but then, when the cat doesn't immediately kill anything, gets noisy again.

Berenika sits near the back, on a banquette, with her friends from before, Mria and Paolo. Mria is small and nervous, with spiky frosted hair. Paolo is tall, with big ears and Adam's apple.

"You don't mean you, like, just left." Mria can't believe it. "Walked out on Mark."

"You can't just walk out of that place, can you?" Paolo says. "That's miles of desert. You could die. You must have gotten a ride. Who gave you a ride?"

"Oh, sure," Mria says. "That's what we need to know. Her means of transportation."

Paolo looks hurt. "I was just saying she could have called me to come get her. I would have done it. Right, Berenika? Far, but I would have done it for you."

Berenika is solemn. "Thank you, Paolo."

"But who—"

"Oh!" Mria turns her head sharply toward Berenika, hoping her hair will exclude Paolo from the conversation. "But what did Mark do? What did he say?"

"Not much, really," Berenika says. "By that point, I think he realized there wasn't anything he could do."

"You must know your husband better than that," Mria says. "There's always something he can do. Has he called you? Hired people to kidnap you? Planted himself in your yard and let birds nest in his hair?"

"No." Berenika clearly doesn't want to talk about it. "Nothing like that."

"We were all going to Easter Island." Paolo is mournful. "To that new jungle. I was already packed."

"Ah," Mria says. "Procrastination pays off again. I hadn't even found my suitcase yet."

"That's actually not funny." Paolo blinks slowly. "I was looking forward to it."

"Oh, so was I." Mria waggles her cup over her shoulder at me without looking, an annoying habit. "So was I. I need a break. Easter Island. Giant heads, buried under vines. And you, Berenika. It was your idea in the first place. You wanted some special tour to see how they brought everything back. More than back. I don't think the jungle was as dense before people came there."

Berenika isn't paying much attention to the discussion about the ecological restoration of Easter Island, which, with variations, they've already had several times. She's watching the cougar. No one else is, because it doesn't really seem to be doing anything.

It's a male cougar, *Puma concolor*, medium-sized for its species at 130 pounds, six feet long. It is utterly still, not even the tip of its long, luxurious tail moving. Its fur is red-brown, paler under its muzzle and on its belly. That color matches that of the local population of deer. There are no deer in the cafe. Its hazel eyes are dilated in the dimness. It can't see color, but can detect the smallest movement.

It has sensed the shadow of something. It is on full alert. And well it should be. It's out of its territorial range, and on the edge of the range of another male. A bigger male.

It doesn't really know that yet. Right now, it's just checking things out.

I refill Mria's cup, but she just sighs at the delay, not noticing me.

"Weren't you looking forward to it?" Mria's voice gets penetrating. "Berenika!"

"What?" Berenika looks at her friends. "Sure. Of course I was."

"That would have been a great place for you to learn about . . . restoration methods, whatever it was." Paolo sighs. "I bought this nice linen jacket. . . ."

"Return it." Mria turns to cut him out again. "You're not seriously still interested in working, like, with animals, Berenika. Are you?"

"I am." Berenika smiles, just for a split second, a flash of light. "I'm sure they wouldn't let me start with animals, but that's still what I want."

"Oh! That's ridiculous. Just leave them alone, why don't you? Let them be themselves. Natural, like they're supposed to be."

They all look at the cougar, which is again on the move.

It doesn't see anything at the tables it moves past. It believes the cafe to be empty, in fact sees the space as a clearing in a larger forest.

"Okay," Mria says. "Maybe that's not so natural. I didn't even really notice when these things started wandering around. Where does the thing take a crap? Not in here, I hope." She picks up her feet so her pumps don't touch the floor.

"It's trained to go in a certain spot, where it gets recycled," Berenika says. "You might not have noticed it, but there's a place under the bushes in front of the candle store. And it looked like there was another cougar that usually used it."

And then she sniffs.

"The service here sucks," Mria says. "But the place seems clean enough." She keeps her feet up, though, just in case.

"You checked in the cat toilet?" Paolo says. "And you could tell who'd used it?"

But now Berenika is up. She stalks around, tall and loose, a bit of a cat herself. The combs in her thick, black hair glint in the dimness. The cougar jerks its head, and she freezes. It looks past her. Somewhere, inside, it is deeply frustrated, knowing it's missing something but having no way of figuring out what it is.

She kneels and sniffs a corner by the counter. Mark had led me to expect someone a bit more . . . romantic. Not interested in the yucky details of how we actually get these animals to survive among us. She hitches her skirt up a bit to free up her movements and sniffs again. She's dressed beautifully, with several layers of translucent fabric of contrasting patterns.

People in the cafe are now watching her, not the cougar.

Paolo shreds his napkin in embarrassment, then closes his eyes.

It wouldn't be natural for me not to react.

"Have you lost something, miss?"

She stands up next to me. "We're in another cougar's territory here. Where is it now?"

I'm startled. Did she actually examine the feces in the waste recycler in the plaza? "I've seen one, I guess. Another cat, right? But I don't know. I could ask . . ."

"That's all right." She heads back to her table, having dismissed me as useless.

That's the point. That's why I'm wearing this stupid padded white jacket, like a fencer, or something. I'm supposed to be taking care of things in the background.

I still wish she'd have really looked at me.

"Their urine has been modified to smell kind of like turpentine." Berenika slides neatly back into her seat. "To us. To each other, it still smells jagged and aggressive."

"That's charming," Paolo says.

"It's a lot of work to get it just right," Berenika says. "Real skill." If only she knew. "But we're definitely on an established territory. I bet that other cougar is out past all those little stands in the plaza. There must be good hunting for small game in the shrubs."

She's absolutely right. That other cougar, larger and stronger than this one, isn't part of the story yet, but there is the potential for drama. Fights over territory and access to sex always sell.

"If you like stuff like that, Mark could have set you up better than anyone," Mria says. "I think he has connections with the guys who run this stuff. You could have your own, I don't know, ecosystem, whatever."

"It's a messy hobby," Paolo says. "Not like you, Berenika. I didn't even think

Mark should have gotten those blind fish in your basement. What a lot of work! Is that what got you interested?"

"I didn't want Mark to set me up with anything."

Her friends can tell they've annoyed Berenika. That's something they don't want to do.

Mria shifts in her seat. "Let me get this. My turn, really."

"Good point," Paolo says.

The cougar slides behind the counter, being a bit perverse now, as they will be. It angles its body up and puts its forepaws up on the counter, knocking some demitasses to the floor. Its claws are a good inch and a half long. It yawns in *flehmen*, seeking scent information, and, incidentally, shows its canines, white against its black gumline.

Well, it gets what information it can, but cannot overcome the blockages that allow it to survive in the environment it now lives in. It has no idea it's in a place that serves good Turkish coffee, black as night, sweet as love, hot as hell, a place that makes you wear a ridiculous jacket to serve it. It can't smell anything human. It can't see us or hear us. As far as it is concerned, we no longer exist.

It reaches its head forward . . . and pushes its nose against the hot side of the espresso machine.

It makes a tiny yelp, like a kitten, then jumps back, crouches down and hisses.

Everyone in the cafe laughs. Despite the fact that they are invisible to it, that there is no possible threat, they are still afraid of it, and welcome such evidence of its impotence.

Berenika, I notice, doesn't laugh.

ENCOUNTER #2
NO FAUX PHO

A red-tailed hawk soars overhead in an updraft from the parking lot. It's been up there a while without success. The deer mice in the high grass between the parking places haven't been active.

The noodle shop is stuck to the side of the old mall like a piece of gum. The tables are on balconies hanging down, with steep stairs that make it easy to spill pho on a customer. Not that anyone worries about the comfort of the waitstaff.

Mria and Berenika have chosen the lowest table, just above where a small herd of elk browse beneath oaks and maples with leaves just touched with russet and purple by approaching fall. An elk cow lowers her head, grabs a bit of grass, looks around. She can't see us, or the mall, or the cars that make their way over hardened paths through the lot's ridges and swales to find spots outside the wildlife zones. She also can't see the cougar, who sits, seemingly not paying attention to her, in some underbrush a few feet away.

That's two completely different ways of not seeing. I'm sure there are others.

"You know," Mria says. "I was just remembering how you and Mark got together."

"It was fated," Berenika says. "The stars were aligned and it all happened exactly as was ordained."

"What?"

Berenika laughs. "Oh, come on, Mria. We met at that party. Chance. You had just left. I was helping Margaret clean up."

"Duty pays off again."

"He always said he was 'putting in an appearance'," Berenika says. "I thought that was pompous, then learned how much of that he actually does."

"He put in an appearance on Easter Island," Mria says. "Don't tell Paolo. He'll never get over it. Poor Paolo. He kind of got to thinking that he was the one Mark really liked. That they had some kind of *relationship*."

"Mark does like Paolo. He said so."

"Oh! Mark. Like you can believe what he says."

"You look good," Berenika says. "Is that a new thing with your hair?"

"Just growing it out a little." Mria pats her blond curls with a satisfied air. "I've got somebody good. I'll give you her name."

"Sure. Maybe."

Berenika's black hair is thicker and shorter than it was a few months ago, and the clips in it look almost permanent. And she wears an outdoor jacket with a couple of bird shit stains on it that never quite came out.

A second hawk sits on a bough of an oak, just as unsuccessful as the one circling above the parking lot, but not working as hard.

"Really, Berenika. Are you still doing the animal thing?"

Berenika smiles. "I should have done it years ago. Even at a low level, I love it. I have to start at the bottom, of course. Physiology classes, ecology, working support in a clinic. It's physically hard. I never expected how hard. I fall dead asleep in my bed every night."

"That desert house of Mark's had the best beds," Mria says. "I never dreamed there."

"Try cleaning up after a sick moose all day. You won't dream then."

"No thanks. I prefer a really expensive mattress."

"Maybe *you* should have married Mark," Berenika says.

"Yeah, well, I didn't stay to help do the dishes. That'll show me. But he never wanted anyone but you. Why is that?"

"I'm the wrong person to explain. I have no idea." Berenika watches the cougar. It stalks forward, belly to the ground, astonishingly fluid for something that must have bones in it somewhere.

Mria follows Berenika's gaze, but I can tell she doesn't see the cougar either.

"This banh mhi is too dry," Mria says. "Now, that's not really a complaint, but you really like that moistness, if you know what I'm saying . . ."

I replace her banh mhi.

"How is your food, Berenika?" Mria says.

Berenika hasn't eaten anything. "Fine, I guess."

"Yeah. Kind of, meh, right? I don't like the way this one soaks the bread, kind of makes it fall apart. . . ."

She's not watching as the cougar charges, but Berenika is.

Three or four bounds, and it is on the elk.

But something gives the cow warning: a rustle in the leaves, a finch that switches branches a few seconds before the cat makes its decision, something, but it is already moving when the cougar tries to drop it.

Claws scratch its flank, but it is bounding off across the parking lot, dodging between the cars it sees as trees, and is gone. Cougars aim, not at the weak or the sick, but at the inattentive. When they've judged attention wrong, they can find themselves struggling with something fully as strong as they are.

There is no way the cougar can pursue the fleeing elk. Like all cats, its speed is available only in short bursts. Its heart is small for its body mass. Just that effort alone has sucked up all its stored oxygen. It stands on the spot where the elk had been, breathing deeply, replenishing its stores. At moments like this, it is completely vulnerable.

"What happened?" Mria cranes around.

"Nothing," Berenika says. "Nothing happened."

"He can't have let you go so easily," Mria says. "That's just not the Mark I know."

"Maybe the Mark you know isn't the Mark I know. I don't want to talk about it."

"All right." Mria manages a smile. "So you're liking what you're doing?"

"More than anything I've ever done. I feel . . . I don't know. It's like I was always meant to be out there. Not away from people, exactly. But closer to the foundation of things."

I hate it when people talked like that. We're never more human than when we're manipulating the natural world.

I don't know why she's annoying me so much all of a sudden. She's just doing her best, studying, taking her tests like the teacher's pet I'm sure she's always been. I was a problem student. It's only luck, and Mark's help, that lets me do what I'm so good at.

Mark wants her to feel herself submerged in the totality of nature. But I'm the one creating that totality, setting up each stage on her progress.

There's no way she'll ever know I'm back here.

A raccoon emerges on the restaurant balcony. How it got here is my secret.

Of all the wild creatures, it is perhaps the raccoon that misses human beings most. The others didn't even notice when humans figured out how to edit themselves out of animal perceptions and return the world to the wild.

Going back to work has been hard on the raccoons. Their mood seems permanently bad.

This one has had it, at least for today. It clambers up onto the table, scattering silverware, and, with grim determination, closes its eyes and goes to sleep. As far as it is concerned, this is a place of concealment, invisible to anyone, and, in fact, nothing out in those woods has a chance of seeing it. A buzzard sweeps close overhead, its eyes questing, but sees nothing but dead leaves and a recovered cougar, now loping off, ready for another go at an elk.

"Is it snoring?" Mria says. "Tell me raccoons don't snore."

ENCOUNTER #3
GREENSLOPE

The forested slope is really the roof of an indoor gym and mall. Just above the restaurant, the hill crests, and, out of sight, descends in a succession of apartments. At the slope's base is an open park, its snow trampled by mule deer looking for browse. A small herd of deer stands in a tight group there now, yanking a last bit of grass root out with their teeth.

The big houses on the valley's other side, beyond the concealed highway, are ugly enough that I wish I had the suppressed perceptions of a wild animal.

I also wish I couldn't see the Wild West duster they make me wear here. It's embroidered with lassos and horses.

The spruces and firs overhead hold huge clumps of snow in their needles. A chickadee hangs upside down from a cone and yanks determinedly at a seed. Various other squeaky-voiced small birds jump around the branches, distinguishable as kinglets, nuthatches, and others to those who care to tell them apart. Each has a different diet, and thus different ways of perceiving the world. No one appreciates how hard it is to manage a mixed group like that. Certainly not Paolo, who hasn't stopped talking since he and Berenika sat down.

But Berenika is looking at the birds. She always looks carefully at animals, as if she actually sees them as meaning something in themselves. She raises a hand, and crooks a finger to summon a waiter. Me.

A kinglet flutters down and perches on it. It's unexpected, and her green-brown eyes widen. The kinglet, a tiny greenish bird with an orange crown, walks back and forth on her finger. It actually thinks her finger is a twig, and is looking for signs of hibernating insects beneath the bark. Before anything unfortunate happens, it shoots off again.

Berenika watches after it. She has a gift of meaningful stillness. Snow glitters in her dark hair. She is a nature goddess only temporarily among the worlds of men.

The sun is shining but the air is bony and cold. Most animals are in hiding, and those that appear are lean, their intentions focused down to survival. Winter rakes through with sharp teeth, giving the survivors a bigger space to grown in the summer. The pain of survival is most obvious at this season, and the restaurant does a good business when it's cold.

Giant bluish cubes of ice, fifty feet on a side, thrust out of the trees. Snow clings to flaws in their surfaces. It always seems that you should be able to look all the way through them, but vision disappears into the deep blue interior. These grab the winter's cold and send it back through heat exchangers in the summer to cool the buildings below, as they melt and cascade down the rocks, disappearing by the time fall brushes the leaves from the trees.

A puff of breeze, and light snow races across the tables. Berenika and Paolo wear folded clothes like elaborate tents, with velvet over their hair. Warm air puffs from their sleeves when they lean forward, melting the snow into droplets. Paolo has his set so high he's sweating. He's picked this place to please Berenika. He prefers things to be a little more comfortable.

"So, Berenika," he says. "How have you been doing?"

Right now, Berenika is doing what she is supposed to be doing. She is looking for the cougar. Her brief hesitation before answering the question creases Paolo's wide face. He's laid some kind of plan, but is having trouble putting it into operation.

"Oh, Paolo! Sorry. I'm doing good. I can't believe I waited so long to do what I wanted to. It's hard work. But I wouldn't want to do anything else."

"But you haven't heard from. . . ."

"No. Nothing from Mark. I kind of wish everyone—"

"Sorry," he said. "Sorry. Mria was wondering, and you know how she is. She'd be all over me if I didn't ask. I'm glad you could find the time to come out here with me. I thought maybe you would like it."

"I do, Paolo, I do. I've always heard of it."

"It seemed like your kind of place."

Both of them are uncomfortable. Neither expected to ever be in this situation.

"I've been doing well too," Paolo says.

"Really? What have you been up to?"

"You know, the usual. But well, you know." Paolo starts again. "Do you have any, like, wider plans? For your life outside of nature?"

"Not really. I've been pretty focused."

Paolo sighs. A gust at the same moment makes it seem that his inability to move her has shaken the snow from the trees.

"Does he still live in the desert?" Paolo asks.

Berenika has sensed movement in the trees along the meadow's edge. "What?"

"Does Mark still live in that desert place? I liked those parties he had out there."

Berenika manages to tear her attention from the signs of the cougar's presence. She leans forward and puts her hand over Paolo's. Both are gloved, so it's not as intimate as it might be.

"Give him a call if you want, Paolo. I'm sure he'd love to hear from you."

"Really?"

"Really. He always said. . . ." She's moved too fast, and now has to come up with something Mark always said. "He said you were good company. And he liked it when you mixed the drinks."

"Yeah, well. I always liked him too. I mean, I understand why it had to end and all, but. . . ."

Unlike the elk, the mule deer don't get a reprieve. One is momentarily distracted, trying to yank a particularly sweet grass tuft. There's a puff of snow as the cougar leaps, and then the lead buck is down. It kicks its legs once, but the cougar's teeth sink in and crush its windpipe. That may be unnecessary. It looks like its head's impact with the frozen ground has been enough to take it out.

The cougar breathes hard for a few moments, then lowers its head and starts to feed.

It looks easy. Without a knowledge of what is going on, it all looks easy. The deer weighs as much as the cougar, and carries a multipointed rack that can stab a lung or a gut. Even a small injury can be fatal, if it impairs the ability to hunt. The cougar has to average over a dozen pounds of meat a day to survive a winter. Any interruption in the flow of calories and protein is death. The cougar has been watching for the past two hours, patiently waiting for the exact moment that carried the highest odds.

A waiter has to stand just attentively, but gets relatively less for the effort. And he has to wear a stupid outfit.

The cougar raises its head. Something about the open space of the meadow is bothering it. The mule deer think they have moved off to another high valley, as they do when a predator appears, but there is actually no room for that here. They will circle the dining area and reemerge exactly where they were before. Pika move in their long runs under the snow-covered grass, and, a hundred yards away, a porcupine grunts along a freshly fallen log, tearing bark away to get at the still-fresh living layer beneath. Everything else is silent.

What else does the cougar sense?

It sinks teeth into the carcass, and, with a couple of powerful bounds, hauls it straight up the cliff.

It drops it near the table, right next to Berenika, then resumes its meal. Steam rises from the entrails of the dead elk.

Unlike the others, Berenika does not watch it. Instead, she scans everyone else in the restaurant, a gaze she usually devotes only to the animals. No one is feeding with quite the gusto of the cougar. Berenika has snow in her eyelashes. Sometimes the cougar has that same look. It is a solitary, as private as possible, used to sliding past perception without affecting it. Knowing it is in full view all the time would leave it with the feline equivalent of despair. It could not live that way.

"Is he here?" Paolo hunches forward miserably.

"Who?" Berenika says.

"Mark! He's got to be here. Somewhere."

She looks almost frightened. "Why do you say that?"

"Because he can't just let you go. I can't stand it that he let you go."

The cougar curves around a couple of times, then lays down on the mule deer carcass and goes to sleep. There's plenty of meat left on it, and its own body heat is the only way it's going to keep it from freezing solid overnight. The deer's head gazes blankly at us, its bloody tongue hanging out of its mouth.

ENCOUNTER #4
PLAZA ECONTORO

The plaza outside the Cafe Kulfi is a piece of marsh most of the way to becoming a meadow, with a thick patch of oaks at the edge. The squirrels and birds in the branches sense deeper forest behind them, not a brick wall. There's still some open water, so there are muskrats, never the most popular animal to watch, but an important part of the system. They serve as food for the mink pair that nest under the cheese shop.

It's a nice spring day, and quite a few people are out.

My hot dog cart's umbrella conceals a rainforest canopy microenvironment. Bromeliads and orchids dangle from its ribs. Mist drifts down over the relish tray.

Berenika walks slowly through the plaza. She's graceful, every part of her long body involved, and her feet seem to barely touch the ground. She's cut her thick hair even shorter and now wears it unclipped. Her jacket ends at her waist. Her trousers are made of some flowy material.

She's hunting for something. She doesn't peer around, but it's clear from the way she looks off into some invisible distance that she's letting all of her senses open all the way, so that even the slightest hint will make itself known. I thought she was waiting for Paolo or Mria before going up into the Cafe Kulfi, where I worked on her world for the first time, but neither have shown and it's starting to look like she's on her own today.

Despite my mini rainforest, she doesn't pay any attention to my stand. She's been in training for months, so surely she recognizes the virtuoso technique involved. It's a clear signal, directly to her. She's not usually so obtuse.

The riot of rainforest life under my umbrella is hard to put together and even harder to maintain, right above a great selection of bratwurst and all-beef hotdogs.

You could spend an hour looking at moths get nectar from orchids, ants crawling up stems, counting the tree frogs. I'm doing good business, good enough that I can't pay as much attention to her as I want. It's a point of pride that I get the orders right.

Even though it's right in their face, everyone misses the three-toed sloth at first. It hangs amid the leaves, its fur green with algae, its yellow claws hooked around an umbrella rib, and chews on the same leaf it's been working on for the past half an hour.

Berenika kneels and peers into the animal waste recycler just past a set of stairs. But it's clean. She can't tell how recently the cougar who owns this territory has been here.

She turns, and for a moment, I think she's going to walk over and get a hot dog. I do have to wear this ridiculous purple and orange jacket that clashes with the orchids. I've sweated through the pits. Still, I want her to.

Finally, our cougar slinks into the plaza. It glances toward the Cafe Kulfi. It still remembers the unexpected nose burn and won't go up there unless it has a good reason.

It has other things to worry about. It is well into the other male's range, and this time is completely aware of it. Its ears flick back and forth. A cougar has thirty separate muscles in its ear and it's using every one to swivel them, trying to extract all the information the environment has to offer.

Each step forward is a serious consideration. Since it's here, it believes that it is here to challenge the other cougar. Like anything above a certain level of consciousness, it believes it acts because of decisions it has made. And, like anything above a certain level of consciousness, it is wrong.

As soon as it appears, Berenika is aware of it. She doesn't turn toward it, but I can see the way her back stretches out, fine shoulder blades against the fabric of her jacket. She stands very still: irrelevant, since the cougar can't see her. It's almost a courtesy. Her hands float without weight.

I didn't understand her before, and now I'm kind of sorry about that raccoon. She's not just fooling around. She's as serious about life as I am. She could be the rare Trainer that could be seen, and still do her job.

The cougar whose territory we're in comes out of the Cafe Kulfi and stands at the top of the stairs. It is significantly larger and stronger than our cougar, full-sized at 170 pounds, eight feet long. Everyone in the plaza falls silent and watches as it swishes its tail impatiently. Since this is its territory, it is the local favorite. They wait to see what it will do to the interloper.

Somewhere around here, Mark appears and comes back into her life. That's the story. And the cougar, no longer needed, goes. Sure, there's always a chance it will defeat its larger and stronger opponent. Nothing is certain.

But the smart money's on the muscle.

The territory owner crouches down to charge. It is ready. Our cougar is going to find out that it is no longer the center of attention.

Berenika strolls toward the cafe, not giving any sign that she sees the other cougar. I should be watching the cougars, but, instead, I watch her. She looks like she's just window-shopping, but I know she's not seeing anything in the vitrines. Her consciousness is focused forward.

She steps right into the other cougar's path. It is ready to leap . . . and suddenly its opponent has vanished. All it can really sense is the absence that is Berenika, because it can't detect a human being. A shadow has dropped over its world, and it is confounded.

Suddenly coming to itself, realizing the perilous situation it is in, our cougar turns and bounds out of the plaza.

There is a stir among everyone else in the plaza. They resume whatever they were doing. But they feel vaguely cheated, unfulfilled. A crucial plot point was muffed.

That's because they're paying attention to the wrong story.

"Excuse me."

Berenika came up silently, as I watched the cougar vanish. She catches me off guard.

Our eyes meet through the mist that comes from my umbrella. As a gesture, the sloth even turns its head, jaws still working on its leaf, to look at her.

She realizes the complexity of what I have achieved here. And, seeing that, she's scoped out who is responsible for the events around her. She has an instinctive feel for the behavior of living creatures. Seeing the effects, she's tracked down the cause: me.

"I'd like two hot dogs, please."

Two? She really doesn't need to get one for me. It's my stand, after all. "Um, sure. That's what I'm here for."

"One with mustard and relish."

"Okay."

"And one with lots of hot peppers, sauerkraut, and epizote, if you have any."

It's not something I'd usually know about an employer, but Mark had me make him his favorite dog when we were setting this scene up, the day before. Peppers, sauerkraut, and—

"No epizote." I still have some, but he's not getting it. "Out today."

"Well." She sighs. "We can't always get what we want, can we?"

"No," I say. "I guess not."

I watch her, graceful and slim, as she crosses the plaza and heads right for the copse of trees where Mark stands, seemingly invisible from the world, waiting to emerge into the midst of a battle to the death between cougars for a single territory.

LAST ENCOUNTER
ANHINGA

The water just beyond the table is still and black. The cypress trees in the hammock stretch above, forming a thick canopy, screening the bright sun. The air is hot, heavy, motionless. Spanish moss, vines, flowers dangle down, dripping water. The only detectable motion is that of an occasional insect flying slowly, almost walking on the thick air. Tiny beams with motion detectors pick them out and highlight their lacy wings against the dimness, subtly enough that the patrons take it for granted that they can see things here, despite having evolved on the sunny, dry veldt.

There's no reason why nature shouldn't always look her best.

Paolo, Mria, Berenika, and Mark have fallen silent as they wait for their food. Mark is never chatty, and Paolo and Mria have been trying to fill in the spaces, showing, by their eagerness to entertain, their gratitude that things are back the way they should be, but they've run out of things to talk about.

Mark paid their way out here. That's their notion of the way things should be.

Berenika hasn't been talking much. Is she already regretting her decision to get back with him?

"Look, there's one." Paolo points as an alligator slides by, careful not to thrust his finger over the railing.

No one else looks.

"What's wrong?" Mark finally says. "I knew this was a mistake. Too wet, right? We should get back to the house. The desert. That's best."

"No," Berenika says. "That's not it. This is extremely impressive. I might like to work here, actually."

Our wetland, lush with water coming from the north, is sandwiched between an office building, all pink stucco and plate glass, and a housing development. Carefully generated mist makes the office building look like a mistake of vision, and the houses hide behind a vine-covered wall. Water is pumped into this patch of jungle, runs through, and then gets recovered on the other side of the restaurant.

Water once sheeted down from the lakes to the north, covered the sawgrass prairies less than an inch deep, all the way down to the south. Development and overuse of water had threatened these environments.

Not much of the sawgrass prairie was left, but the wetland is something people want to see. Water flows have been reestablished, exactly to the necessary degree. Nothing that lives here, in the deep waters or any of the other environments around, senses that it all came via subtle paths completely different than the original ones.

But there's still a lot of work to do. Berenika could make a real contribution.

"But something's bothering you about it."

"Yeah: Paolo," Mria says. "Stop pointing out that stupid alligator every time it swims by. We see it."

Paolo's mouth droops.

"No," Berenika says "It's the cat."

Our cougar rests on a bough above the black water, barely awake.

"Wrong species of panther?" Paolo flicks through the restaurant's environmental information., eager to make good. "The Florida one's extinct, this one is pretty close, they say. . . ."

"Not the species. The environment. The place. Cougars live in the slash pine woods. In decent-sized limestone uplands. They need some dry land. Not down in the water here. They don't fish."

"Maybe they eat birds." Paolo, on a roll, is pleased to spot the anhinga, the restaurant's signature bird, as it pops out of the water, a dead fish speared on its beak. He starts to point, thinks better of it, and changes his gesture to a wave at the waiter.

He's just going to have to wait. I'm no longer on duty.

The anhinga climbs out on a cypress knee and spends a moment getting the fish off its beak. It's dark, with a long white neck. It swallows the fish, then spreads its wings. Unlike most water birds, anhingas have no oils on their feathers. This permits them to dive deeply, but means they have to dry their wings before attempting flight.

This catches the cougar's attention. There's really no way it can get that anhinga, but, still, it's kind of an interesting intellectual problem, with the tricky approach, the bird's speed, and all. For a sated cat, thinking about ways to catch unpromising prey is like doing crossword puzzles.

"You're right." Mark frowns. "It shouldn't be here."

Neither should I. My job is done. I should be back to my regular work. There's some oak stands to redo in Illinois, and ponds for migratory birds. Those things are hard. The birds have to maintain their ability to navigate thousands of miles, yet not realize they are landing amid observation platforms whenever they come down.

Aside from some species of parrot, birds are never easy to train.

Berenika has slipped away, probably to the bathroom. I didn't notice her go.

In her absence, Mark is checking and sending messages. He's probably finding out where I am, what I'm up to, figuring out that someone who owed me a favor let me set up here in the Everglades, checking water pH and drainage.

Mark isn't the only one with deep resources.

A couple of heavy drops fall on the raft, and it tilts, just slightly, with added weight.

"Do you really think no one can see you?" Berenika says, almost in my ear.

I jerk, but don't knock anything over, and look up. She stands over me, water sheeting down her body, her hair gleaming black.

"How much was real?" she says.

"What do you mean?"

"You know what I mean." She moves around the raft, barefoot and silent, and examines the equipment. "Is this what a nature god is? A little man squatting in the underbrush with some display screens?"

"I've never claimed divine status—"

She's in my face. She's disturbing close up, eyes too big, cheekbones too high, skin too velvet. She's meant to be observed from a safe distance.

"How much, Mr. . . . you do have a name, don't you? Mark must allow you a name."

"Tyrell Fredrickson."

"Come on." She glances back at the restaurant. Mria is complaining that there is too much saffron in the flan. There isn't supposed to be any saffron in the flan. No one has missed Berenika yet. "You've been on me, you and your kitty. What did Mark hire you to do?"

"Just to keep you safe. What appears to be the natural world is more dangerous than you—"

She knocks me down and pins me to the raft. The cougar stands up on its bough and looks over at us, exactly as if it can see us both.

I enjoy feeling her weight on me.

"It wasn't all my doing, was it?" she says. "Everything around me. You have the power to control it. Tell me!"

So I do. It's not that I think she's going to kill me, though she's mad enough to try. It's because she sees that which she would like least to see. My assignment was to make her feel like . . . Mark said, "like a nature goddess."

It had been a dream ever since she was a little girl, to have the natural world perceive and respond to her. She'd always had pets, found wounded birds and animals and nursed them back to health, had the ability to sit still for hours and let things come to her. She was perfect for the career I had.

Mark's analysis had shown him that she had left because she felt like she didn't have equal standing with him. She didn't have a valid role. So he decided to give her one.

That's my job, really. To make things seem like they just happen. Of course, if you left the natural world to "just happen," most of it would be dead and decaying in a couple of seasons. Too much of it is gone for the rest of it to live on its own.

"That's pretty much what I thought," she says, and sits back on her heels.

I look at her. I never expected her to go back with Mark, no matter what power she felt. I expected . . . I don't know what I expected. None of it makes sense. Mark wanted her to come back to him, so he made her feel more powerful, more in control. And now she questions the one illusion that makes her feel best about herself.

"I'm going away," I say. "I'm taking a rough job. A weed patch in an old city. No one really likes those mundane restoration jobs. It takes forever, and even when you're done, it doesn't look like much."

"Why are you telling me this?"

"In case . . . if you wonder where I am. What I'm doing."

She shakes her head, smiles at me. "You really don't understand anything, do you?"

"Look—no matter what, you're good at this. Better, probably, than I am. You can—"

"I know what I can do. But what can you do? Are you just going to hide in the leaves and fake it all up for people?"

"It's what I do. I'm a Trainer."

"So am I, now. You think Mark wanted to give me the illusion of power over nature to get me to come back to him. But it's not an illusion, is it? I'm not some kind of nature goddess. That's just dumb. But I do have power over nature. And I love it all. Every bit of it. Do you love it, Tyrell?"

"I do." The answer comes before I think about it.

This time she really looks at me. I'm pale, a little soft, but I think I have some shape to me. A good jaw, and people say my eyes are thoughtful.

Well, my mother said it. She was otherwise pretty honest. She never told me I was strikingly handsome or anything.

"You might still make something of yourself, Tyrell. Then we'll see." Her dive into the water is totally silent.

Berenika. I write these reports for Mark, but he never reads them. Maybe someday you will.

HOW I BECAME A TRAINER
TYRELL FREDRICKSON

You don't really want the whole story, but perhaps this part will help you make sense of it.

Before I became a Trainer, I worked on a farm, at Sty #14, on the thirtieth floor. Sometimes, when my work was done, I'd go out to the plant areas to watch the sun set. The circulating breeze kept condensation off the glass and made the leaves whisper behind me. From that height I didn't really see people, just buildings copper to the horizon. After a few minutes, something would start beeping. I wasn't really supposed to be in that area. My job was the pork.

I'd go back to the dark. The glow strip across the vat room's arched ceiling was about as bright as a full moon. After all, the pork tubes—pigs, if you insist—couldn't see.

The sterilizing lights came on once a day. Then it was my job to put on goggles and turn the tubes in their vats of liquid, making sure the UV hit all their surfaces. The fluid was full of antibiotics and all that, but there were fungi, there were molds . . . anywhere there was that much cell shedding and organic material something would find a way to live.

The main problem was the skin. The bones were vestigial, floating free from each other like an exploded skeletal diagram, but the things still had skin. They floated in the blue-green support fluid, but they were so huge that there were always folds, or points of pressure against the tank sides, where infection could collect. My job was detecting these areas and taking care of them.

It might seem that you should just get rid of the skin and just have meat, but that would cause more problems than it solved. Skin is a sophisticated interface, keeping in the things that should be in, and keeping almost all of the universe out. Creating some new interface would have been more trouble than it was worth. It might not have seemed that way, but they'd changed only those things that needed changing. For example, collagen had been added, to make the skin easier to remove, when that time came.

The back of pork still looked like a pig. The spine had separated like the boosters of a rocket heading for space, but I could still see a trace of the original shoat, with its bristly hair. If I left them in some other orientation, they would slowly turn to have their backs up.

No one ever visited me there. The meat side of the farm just wasn't that popular. There was an occasional maintenance team, in to adjust the recirculators that turned pork waste into usable fertilizer for the plants on the south side. Otherwise, I was alone with my pigs.

Once a month was slaughtering time.

I'd pull each tube out of the liquid in a support harness. The sterilizing fluid would cascade off its sides. I'd dry the skin, first with a roller and then with an infrared light, and then I would open it up. There was supposed to be a seam, kind of a biological zipper, along where the edge of the belly had once been, but it often got jammed up with squamous cells and other undifferentiated growth.

So I would have to cut it open. I had a vibratory cutter that I would run along the pig's side. Then, being extremely careful, I would roll up the hide. As I mentioned, there was additional collagen that added some tension, so that the skin curled up to expose the meat.

Most of each pig was smooth flesh, suitable for processed food. Without connective tissue or grain, this was easy to work with. I'd run the cutter along the pig's length, and then cut off slabs. There was always a little blood seepage, but not much. The cutter was smart, and the blood supply was spaced rationally.

Large vessels would be avoided, and tucked in, to dangle like electrical conduit. I'd hit them with vascularization hormones later, stimulate arborization, and link them up with the new flesh that bubbled up around them.

Then I would supervise the movement of the chops to the cooler, in the blank north side of the building. They'd rumble down one of the conveyors and disappear to the next step in the process of making food. The area was forgotten, with hexagonal ice crystals growing on the housings of seldom-used support pumps, and fluid spills that eventually turned into sheets of brown-red ice. My least favorite part of the job was defrosting and cleaning that.

Things did go wrong. Cancers could spread through the flesh when cell reproduction was disrupted. This could happen surprisingly fast. Sometimes an entire tube would have to be terminated and discarded. I had no idea where that flesh went.

Once I heard a rattle as the cutter went by. When I looked at the resulting slab, I found a pig's lower jaw, complete with teeth, all perfectly formed. They looked tiny against that huge bulk, even though they would have been able to support the feeding of a creature that weighed several hundred pounds. I cleaned them off and kept them. There is nothing more diagnostic of a mammal than the elaborate pattern on the surface of the teeth. Someone with more experience than I could have identified what breed of *Sus domestica* had led to this gargantuan meat factory.

I got into my routine. I don't think I was even fully conscious, following out my rounds in the semidarkness, with only the backs of pigs for company.

But that jaw should have made me more attentive. Something had gone wrong with the gene expression in that tube. All the developmental genes were still there, after all, just suppressed. It was only after the cutters hesitated a bit on that same pig that I finally hauled it up out of the fluid to investigate more thoroughly.

It had grown a leg, complete with trotter. It looked ridiculous, down there all by itself, supporting nothing, contacting nothing, but it had the full complement of bones and muscles.

I poked it and it jerked away.

So it had some basic innervation as well. I was going to have to do something about this.

Sometimes a consumer gets a hankering for a real differentiated piece of meat, something with connective tissue, muscle strands, bone: a ham, a rib, a chop. These tubes had not been designed to produce those. Even in those that had been, what looked like ancestral cuts of meat were sculpted creations, not actual muscles attached to limbs.

The hoof looked tiny and precise. Something about it appealed to me. I decided to keep it for a while. I had the idea that I was liberating some essential nature hidden in the huge tube of meat. I reprogrammed the slab cutters to avoid it. That dropped my overall productivity a bit, but still well within the quotas I had for this sty.

Sentimentality has no place in farming. I really should have known that.

Next harvest, that leg threw the slab cutter off so much it pulled back, forcing me to slice meat manually. I wasn't used to the auxiliary blade, and the flesh shuddered so much when I lowered myself to it that I almost sliced through a finger.

Maintaining a sentimental piece of real pig quickly proved to be tiresome.

And a health and safety inspection would show poor practice. My real career was elsewhere, but losing points here could really set me back.

At the next skin maintenance time, I rotated that tube so that the leg stuck out toward me. I pulled myself up to it. The leg's joint was right at the skin surface. That was good. There would be no telltale stump left afterward, and the cutters would be able to do their job. I got right up to the thing, pushing my head against its side, and slid the auxiliary blade into the leg.

It kicked me. I lost my grip and almost fell into the tank myself. I did drop the saw, and lost it somewhere in those translucent depths. The leg flailed several more times, then was still. But it was pulled back against the tube's bulk, as if ready to attack again.

A shudder went through the entire thing, sending waves splashing back and forth against the tank sides. Blood seeped from the cut and dripped down.

Muscle and bone were one thing, but the thing had nerves, and had recruited a blood supply.

What had given the command to kick me? The nerves led somewhere.

Maybe I was mad at it, but I had given up on careful surgery. I had to get this thing fixed and back on the production line. I recovered my blade from the tank bottom and slashed deeply, checking for any variations in the meat's otherwise smooth structure.

I found and removed a couple of ribs and a big fold of tissue that I later figured out was a bladder, one that had never managed to grow in on itself to hold fluid. A bit of ureter led off from it, but it had never regrown a kidney, so the tube just ended.

Beneath that, along the spine, I found a lump. This was the creature's real secret.

It had never grown a dura mater, much less cranial bones, and most of the brain had never grown either, but here was a bit of the pig's brain, barely protected by a flexible arachnoid and pia mater, material like stiff rubber.

The original pig had a fair amount of cortex. It was an intelligent animal.

This tube of meat was not an intelligent animal. But even then I knew enough of the structure of the mammalian nervous system to have some idea of what had regrown. It was a bit of the motor cortex: what had allowed the thing to kick me. And much of the sensory cortex: what had allowed it to feel me probing it.

There was no comfort I could give. Nothing I could do to help. It couldn't see, it couldn't hear, it couldn't taste. But it could feel pain.

It was just a mistake. Just a malfunction in gene expression, the generation of nerve cells with no consumption value. I thought about how long it had been shuddering under the slices of the cutter. The innervation had gone much farther than I would have thought possible. It sensed everything that was going on, everything that happened to it.

It was silent in that huge room. I sat there, kind of stroking the part of the skin that was left. I had no idea if it could feel that too.

A damage report was called for, so that others could be on the lookout for a similar malfunction.

But I didn't tell anyone. I excised the brain, the nerves, the other organs.

Then I sautéed those no-longer-functional pain centers in butter. The ultimate discourtesy to a food animal is to kill it but not to eat it.

I think I overcooked them. They were a bit crumbly. But I choked them down. Okay, this isn't why I became a Trainer. But it's why I've never quit. We've picked something up, and now there's no way for us to ever put it down again. Now that you bear some of the weight, Berenika, maybe you understand.

NON-ENCOUNTER
MARK AND BERENIKA'S DESERT RESIDENCE

I go through every room of the house, as if someone will be hiding in one of them.

But there's nowhere to hide. The furniture is gone, and the rooms, floored with native stone, seem to have been vacuumed by forensics teams and retain not a trace of their previous occupants.

The high living room windows show the distant dry ridge, tilting like a sinking ship.

I hear a thunk from the underground garage, then voices. A man and a woman.

I was sure Berenika would leave him again. It just didn't make sense that she would stay. But instead she was taking advantage of his power. I thought they were far away, restoring some part of the dead ocean, not here to find me scuttling across their floor like a hermit crab that had misplaced its shell, pale and shrivel-assed.

"Who are you?"

It's Paolo. He stands tall and skinny in the doorway's exact center, as if demonstrating how unnecessarily wide it is.

"I—"

"Oh, you know him." The short, blond Mria pushes past him, carrying a bag that seems symbolic of "groceries": leafy celery and a baguette stick out of the top. "The Trainer. Mark's guy."

"Mark's guy." Paolo's eyes are pale blue. I had not noticed how clear and perceptive they were. I hadn't really been watching him, and he certainly had never looked at me before. "What is he doing here, then?"

"I don't know." Mria is already in the kitchen. "Maybe he's training gophers. Why don't you ask him?"

"I'm here to put some things away," I say. This is even almost true. At least it is now.

"Hey, us too," Paolo says. "We can start a club. 'People who clean up after Mark and Berenika.'"

"Don't be bitter, Paolo." Mria is opening and closing cabinets. "Didn't they say they'd leave a saucepan in . . . oh, there it is. She just asked us for a favor, since we were going to be in the neighborhood."

There was no neighborhood. Mark had, impressively, put his house where there really was nothing, an expanse of dry ridges and valleys in the Great Basin. The most visible life in the region was a herd of pronghorns that tended to keep well south, where there was more water. The only plant visible is an occasional sullen creosote bush. Those black sticks suck all the moisture from the dirt around them, leaving a circle so dry that no seed would ever germinate there. Their kingdoms are tiny and parched, but they are supreme within them.

"You hid your car," Paolo says.

"Habit."

"So what were you going to do here?"

"Maybe he's moving here." Mria pokes her head in from the kitchen. Behind her, I hear something frying. "You want some lunch, Mr. Animal Trainer? We're going to have to pack out what we don't eat."

I'd never pegged Mria as a cook. But, then, I hadn't paid that much attention to her either. I'd been watching Berenika.

"Sure," I say. "I didn't bring anything to contribute."

"Didn't figure that you would." She vanishes back into the kitchen.

"Berenika's going to be a Trainer too," Paolo says. "She's going to find out what really makes things tick." ·

"It's a long, hard road," I say. "Much less fun than it looks."

"She knows all about that," Paolo says. "You probably explained some of it to her."

"I tried."

"You're not going to ask, are you." Mria hands me linen-wrapped silverware and has me set the table. "Berenika's gone back to Mark, and both of them are off on some atoll trying to restore fish stocks, train tuna to protect themselves, whatever, and you're going to pretend you don't even care."

"I don't have the right to care," I finally manage.

"The forks go on the other side," Mria says briskly. "You don't need some kind of standing to care."

"Oh, come on." Paolo slouches above us, unsure of what to do. "He just failed. He wanted to set things up a certain way, train Berenika to move to him, and he didn't do it."

I try to do it slowly, but I think they hear me let my breath out.

"Don't you guys need to protect those fish?" Mria says. "Go ahead. I'll lay everything else out."

"The fish," Paolo says on the way down the stairs to the lower levels. "Did you put them here?"

"My first project for Mark," I say. "They're an almost-vanished subspecies—agriculture had dropped the water table and their caves were going dry. They seem to be breeding pretty well here. I hope the new owner takes care of them."

"It's in the deed. You have to. If you don't want to, buy somewhere else."

Many people think that the way we fool nature now shows our power. But it equally enslaves us to perpetual care.

Or some of us, anyway.

In the cool darkness we could hear the water swirling beneath our feet and in the walls. A still pool filled the floor's center. We stand on its edge, looking down and seeing the passages receding in all directions into the earth.

The pool has a blue glow now that we're here. The fish can't see it, but it lets us see them.

"Did you . . . make this?" Paolo's eyes are large in the dimness.

"I worked it out. There were objections. There's no geology anywhere near here that could remotely have water-filled caverns like this, but Mark offered to finance it, and it really was the best option. You can't have everything perfect."

Blind fish have eyes. Or, rather, they develop eyes normally, up to a point. The genes that guide the development of the eyes is still there, still active. An eyecup develops, a lens. Then, another gene, busily beefing up the front of the head, increasing the sense of smell, the barbels, the whole chemical/physical sense structure that the fish needs to survive in the absolute darkness of limestone caverns a thousand feet underground, finally gets its bulldozers and concrete mixers into the area—and builds right over the eye. It sinks under that new flesh, and vanishes.

I wave my hand over the water. This was once Berenika's great pleasure, Mark had told me. The one thing about the house that had entranced her. I want to see what she saw.

And they come. The fish swim out of their underground grottos and out into the dim blue glow of that room. Their skin is pure white, patterned with blue, like tattoos. Their drooping barbels let them sense what is around them. They swirl up, never touching each other, sensing the pressure of the others, searching for their microscopic food.

I hold my finger over the water, but don't touch it. It's best for them if they never know anyone else is here. It's too late, anyway. Even if they knew I was here, that I had determined their destinies, they wouldn't care.

"Come on," I say to Paolo.

The controls make everything automatic, but it still seems that we need to be there to supervise. I carefully check the sandy floor for any obstructions and find. . . .

Paolo stands next to me and looks down.

"Was that your cat?" he says.

"Not at all," I say. "Just a companion. We worked together for a while. And then—"

"And now it works for Mark too?"

The footprint is clear. I'm tempted to say too clear, as if it was rolled there for police identification. But over here, it looks like the cougar slept. A cave might seem a good place of concealment for it.

No way of telling how long ago it had been here.

"Will they . . . will they be okay under there?" Paolo says.

"The system is sealed and recirculating," I tell him. "Left for long enough, sure. This cave won't survive the fall of civilization or anything. But long before they have any trouble, someone will be here to clean it up, keep them fed and alive."

The cover looks like heavy stone, though I know it's just a foamed metal alloy with a thin cover of fused rock dust. It slides across the pool, across the cougar footprint, across the vague traces we ourselves have left down there, and the blue glow vanishes. The house's life is concealed until someone returns to reveal it again.

The cougar never knew I was there, so it can't miss me, but it must be able to detect a difference in its life now that I have left it.

"Come on up." Mria calls from upstairs. "Lunch is ready."

"What are you going to do now?" Paolo says.

"I have another project."

"Mark must have paid you a bundle. It must be something pretty wild."

"Not so wild," I say. "Just something that needs to get done."

POTENTIAL ENCOUNTER
URBAN STUDY AREA #7

Sometimes a chunk of decorative plaster crashes down from the coffered ceiling high overhead. This usually happens a couple of days after a heavy rain. The water percolates through the various remaining layers of the railway station roof. You'd think there wouldn't be an acanthus swag or gilded rosette left up there, but the builders had not stinted on unseen decoration.

Sometimes it happens for no reason at all, like this morning. I jerk awake, hearing just the echoes of a distant crash.

Usually I get up and search, trying to figure out which piece it was that had just been added to the rubble on the waiting room floor. I don't know what the point of that is, but I do feel good when I see fresh edges, as if I'm finally getting a grip on how things work around here.

I don't feel like doing that today. I just wiggle myself deeper into my bag and watch the pale light of morning grow in the high windows. The pigeons that have left a crust over the glass shift complain on their perches high above.

I've been here a few months now, and still find it ridiculous. Had absolutely everyone left this city and headed for better places? It had once been huge. I can walk the old streets for days, clamber carefully across rusting bridges, jump across the pits of collapsed sewers. None of it was set up to interact with nature. It comes from a purely human world, now obsolete.

Most of it collapsed and was swept into sinuous ridges, twenty or thirty feet high. Forests slowly spread across them. There's a small modern city up the river a bit, but it has its own environment and I never take any animals there.

So now I live among weeds: spiky leaved plants, muck-loving carp, fast-growing trees, pigeons. I hunt among the herds of stunted deer that browse the grass between fallen branches of locusts and silver maples. Sometimes a pack of canids makes its quarrelsome way through the area. A cross between domestic dogs and coyotes, they are unromantic, unphotogenic, and unclean. No Trainer has ever worked to get them to set their carrion-smelling paws on a city street. No passerby has ever been struck at dawn by their wild beauty. When I hear them yelping at night I stuff my head into my pillow.

A crow calls outside, so it really is time to get up. All of the animals can see me, but only that crow seems to care. It has a kind of reptilian affection for me, based on the small prey I scare up on my hunts, and I sometimes find it staring fixedly at me, head sidewise, considering me with an expressionless yellow-rimmed eye. I work at not attributing human emotions to it, but always fail. Maybe I wasn't meant for my line of work after all.

At least I haven't given it a name. That's the most obvious way we pretend animals are more ours than they actually are. I figure it respects me, but is puzzled by me. Our lives are pretty similar just now, so we get along. The bird can predict in general what I am going to do next, but not specifically, and that is the basis of a decent relationship.

There is no natural world. If the term ever had meaning, it hasn't for years. Jeremiads about how the natural world will unite and turn against humans are a childish fantasy. Nature has no motivations, no desires, no ultimate goal.

Except what we choose to give it. I finally roll out of my bag, wash my face in the basin I always fill before going to sleep, and go outside. It's overcast, and cold. My breath puffs. I like feeling the weather against me. Having little defense against it, I have to react to it the same way everything else alive has to. I listen to the air, sniff it to see how scents are carrying today, listen to any sounds it brings. I'm here and visible. I can be evaded, I can be resisted, I can be killed. I pay full attention.

Outside, something on the ground catches my eye. I kneel to get a better look. I reach out my hand, but pull it back before my fingertips can disturb anything.

It's a partial print: a big heel pad, and two toe marks. No claw indentations, and it looks pretty good-sized. Cat. It looks like a large cat.

I bend over the imprint and push my face almost to the ground, looking and smelling, using every channel of information I can. I smell cat too.

Could be a lynx. I've seen some other, ambiguous traces. A lynx would be okay.

I don't think it's a lynx. A few days ago I found a piece of scat. Like the print, it was big, bigger than your usual coydog turd. And it had a bit of hair in it, as from self-grooming with a rough tongue. I managed to persuade myself that it was just the right shade of reddish brown.

I stand up, ready for my day. If there really is a cougar out here somewhere, I won't see it. In an even contest, I don't have a chance. But I'll keep looking.

Anyone could find me here, if they wanted. Berenika has to know where I am. She could come here and observe me in my natural habitat. If she wanted.

It's ridiculous. A feral housecat could make it here in this shrunken weed patch, for as long as it evaded the coydogs, but chances were lower for a lynx, and a cougar was impossible. A cougar needed more than ten square miles of territory to support itself, probably significantly more in this impoverished ecology, and there was nothing like that here, not yet. A single kill and the deer would flee elsewhere. These are not trained to forget, circle around, and return. Again, not yet.

So there's work to be done. The various patches of woods can be knitted together in the minds of the beasts that are here. That's what we do. We take the far-flung archipelagos of environment and reassemble them into continents in the minds of the animals. We give them a way to live in the world we have made.

So I live, work, and hope.

I imagine Berenika, somewhere in an abandoned room in the city, in a brick row house standing alone amid the trees, like a single book on an empty shelf. Since I'm imagining it, I imagine detail. She's in an old bedroom where someone changed wallpaper every year. The warmth and moisture she's brought into the room have loosened its glue, and the soft paper peels off in layers, showing different colors. When she awakes before dawn, it's to the whisper of falling florals and beribboned hunting horns.

I don't actually believe she's there. She's got more important things to pay attention to.

Mark is the kind of guy who thinks that making his wife stronger is the way to keep her. That makes him hard to compete with. But I've worked with him, and know he can be tiresome. A jerk, really. And, pathetic huddled voyeur or not, I know what I'm doing. That can be attractive. There is some room for hope.

Meanwhile, I have work to do.

the shipmaker

ALiETTE DE BODARD

New writer Aliette de Bodard is a software engineer who was born in the United States, but grew up in France, where she still lives. Only a few years into her career, her short fiction has appeared in *Interzone*, *Asimov's*, *Realms of Fantasy*, *Orson Scott Card's Intergalactic Medicine Show*, *Writers of the Future*, *Coyote Wild*, *Electric Velocipede*, *The Immersion Book of SF*, *Fictitious Force*, *Shimmer*, and elsewhere. *Servant of the Underworld*, her first novel, appeared in 2010.

The engrossing story that follows takes us to the far future of an alternate world in which China discovered the New World before Columbus and annexed it as a colony, and introduces us to a scientist who is responsible for engineering the literal birth of a sentient starship . . . with her own life dependent on a successful outcome.

Ships were living, breathing beings. Dac Kien had known this, even before she'd reached the engineering habitat—even before she'd seen the great mass in orbit outside, being slowly assembled by the bots.

Her ancestors had once carved jade, in the bygone days of the Le dynasty on Old Earth: not hacking the green blocks into the shape they wanted, but rather whittling down the stone until its true nature was revealed. And as with jade, so with ships. The sections outside couldn't be forced together. They had to flow into a seamless whole—to be, in the end, inhabited by a Mind who was as much a part of the ship as every rivet and every seal.

The Easterners or the Mexica didn't understand. They spoke of recycling, of design efficiency: they saw only the parts taken from previous ships, and assumed it was done to save money and time. They didn't understand why Dac Kien's work as Grand Master of Design Harmony was the most important on the habitat: the ship, once made, would be one entity, and not a patchwork of ten thousand others. To Dac Kien—and to the one who would come after her, the Mind-bearer—fell the honour of helping the ship into being, of transforming metal and cables and solar cells into an entity that would sail the void between the stars.

The door slid open. Dac Kien barely looked up. The light tread of the feet told her this was one of the lead designers, either Miahua or Feng. Neither would have disturbed her without cause. With a sigh, she disconnected from the system with a flick of her hands, and waited for the design's overlay on her vision to disappear.

"Your Excellency." Miahua's voice was quiet: the Xuyan held herself upright, her skin as pale as yellowed wax. "The shuttle has come back. There's someone on board you should see."

Dac Kien had expected many things: a classmate from the examinations on a courtesy visit; an Imperial Censor from Dongjing, calling her to some other posting, even further away from the capital; or perhaps even someone from her family, mother or sister or uncle's wife, here to remind her of the unsuitability of her life choices.

She hadn't expected a stranger: a woman with brown skin, almost dark enough to be Viet herself—her lips thin and white, her eyes as round as the moon.

A Mexica. A foreigner—Dac Kien stopped the thought before it could go far. For the woman wore no cotton, no feathers, but the silk robes of a Xuyan housewife, and the five wedding gifts (all pure gold, from necklace to bracelets) shone like stars on the darkness of her skin.

Dac Kien's gaze travelled down to the curve of the woman's belly: a protruding bulge so voluminous that it threw her whole silhouette out of balance. "I greet you, younger sister. I am Dac Kien, Grand Master of Design Harmony for this habitat." She used the formal tone, suitable for addressing a stranger.

"Elder sister." The Mexica's eyes were bloodshot, set deep within the heavy face. "I am—" She grimaced, one hand going to her belly as if to tear it out. "Zoquitl," she whispered at last, the accents of her voice slipping back to the harsh patterns of her native tongue. "My name is Zoquitl." Her eyes started to roll upwards; she went on, taking on the cadences of something learnt by rote. "I am the womb and the resting place, the quickener and the Mind-bearer."

Dac Kien's stomach roiled, as if an icy fist were squeezing it. "You're early. The ship—"

"The ship has to be ready."

The interjection surprised her. All her attention had been focused on the Mexica—Zoquitl—and what her coming here meant. Now she forced herself to look at the other passenger of the shuttle: a Xuyan man in his mid-thirties. His accent was that of Anjiu province, on the Fifth Planet; his robes, with the partridge badge and the button of gold, were those of a minor official of the seventh rank—but they were marked with the yin-yang symbol, showing stark black-and-white against the silk.

"You're the birth-master," she said.

He bowed. "I have that honour." His face was harsh, all angles and planes on which the light caught—highlighting, here and there, the thin lips, the high cheekbones. "Forgive me my abruptness, but there is no time to lose."

"I don't understand—" Dac Kien looked again at the woman, whose eyes bore a glazed look of pain. "She's early," she said, flatly, and she wasn't speaking of their arrival time.

The birth-master nodded.

"How long?"

"A week, at most." The birth-master grimaced. "The ship has to be ready."

Dac Kien tasted bile in her mouth. The ship was all but made—and, like a jade statue, it would brook no corrections nor oversights. Dac Kien and her team had designed it specifically for the Mind within Zoquitl's womb: starting out from the specifications the imperial alchemists had given them, the delicate balance of humours, optics and flesh that made up the being Zoquitl carried. The ship would answer to nothing else: only Zoquitl's Mind would be able to seize the heartroom, to quicken the ship, and take it into deep planes, where fast star-travel was possible.

"I can't—" Dac Kien started, but the birth-master shook his head, and she didn't need to hear his answer to know what he would say.

She had to. This had been the posting she'd argued for, after she came in second at the state examinations—this, not a magistrate's tribunal and district, not a high-placed situation in the palace's administration, not the prestigious Courtyard of Writing Brushes, as would have been her right. This was what the imperial court would judge her on.

She wouldn't get another chance.

"A week." Hanh shook her head. "What do they think you are, a Mexica factory overseer?"

"Hanh." It had been a long day, and Dac Kien had come back to their quarters looking for comfort. In hindsight, she should have known how Hanh would take the news: her partner was an artist, a poet, always seeking the right word and the right allusion—ideally suited to understanding the delicacy that went into the design of a ship, less than ideal to acknowledge any need for urgency.

"I have to do this," Dac Kien said.

Hanh grimaced. "Because they're pressuring you into it? You know what it will look like." She gestured towards the low mahogany table in the centre of the room. The ship's design hung inside a translucent cube, gently rotating—the glimpses of its interior interspersed with views of other ships, the ones from which it had taken its inspiration: all the great from *The Red Carp* to *The Golden Mountain* and *The Snow-White Blossom*. Their hulls gleamed in the darkness, slowly and subtly bending out of shape to become the final structure of the ship hanging outside the habitat. "It's a whole, lil' sis. You can't butcher it and hope to keep your reputation intact."

"She could die of it," Dac Kien said, at last. "Of the birth, and it would be worse if she did it for nothing."

"The girl? She's *gui*. Foreign."

Meaning she shouldn't matter. "So were we, once upon a time." Dac Kien said. "You have short memories."

Hanh opened her mouth, closed it. She could have pointed out that they weren't quite *gui*—that China, Xuya's motherland, had once held Dai Viet for centuries; but Hanh was proud of being Viet, and certainly not about to mention such shameful details. "It's the girl that's bothering you, then?"

"She does what she wants," Dac Kien said.

"For the prize." Hanh's voice was faintly contemptuous. Most of the girls who bore Minds were young and desperate, willing to face the dangers of the pregnancy in exchange for a marriage to a respected official. For a status of their own, a family that would welcome them in; and a chance to bear children of good birth.

Both Hanh and Dac Kien had made the opposite choice, long ago. For them, as for every Xuyan who engaged in same-gender relationships, there would be no children: no one to light incense at the ancestral altars, no voices to chant and honour their names after they were gone. Through life, they would be second-class citizens, consistently failing to accomplish their duties to their ancestors; in death, they would be spurned, forgotten—gone as if they had never been.

"I don't know," Dac Kien said. "She's Mexica. They see things differently, where she comes from."

"From what you're telling me, she's doing this for Xuyan reasons."

For fame, and for children; all that Hanh despised—what she called their shackles, their overwhelming need to produce children, generation after generation.

Dac Kien bit her lip, wishing she could have Hanh's unwavering certainties. "It's not as if I have much choice in the matter."

Hanh was silent for a while. At length, she moved, came to rest behind Dac Kien, her hair falling down over Dac Kien's shoulders, her hands trailing at Dac Kien's nape. "You're the one who keeps telling me we always have a choice, lil' sis."

Dac Kien shook her head. She said that—when weary of her family's repeated reminders that she should marry and have children; when they lay in the darkness side by side after making love and she saw the future stretching in front of her, childless and ringed by old prejudices.

Hanh, much as she tried, didn't understand. She'd always wanted to be a scholar, had always known that she'd grow up to love another woman. She'd always got what she wanted—and she was convinced she only had to wish for something hard enough for it to happen.

And Hanh had never wished, and would never wish for children.

"It's not the same," Dac Kien said at last, cautiously submitting to Hanh's caresses. It was something else entirely; and even Hanh had to see that. "I chose to come here. I chose to make my name that way. And we always have to see our choices through."

Hanh's hands on her shoulders tightened. "You're one to talk. I can see you wasting yourself in regrets, wondering if there's still time to turn back to respectability. But you chose me. This life, these consequences. We both chose."

"Hanh—" It's not that, Dac Kien wanted to say. She loved Hanh, she truly did; but . . . She was a stone thrown in the darkness; a ship adrift without nav—lost, without family or husband to approve of her actions, and without the comfort of a child destined to survive her.

"Grow up, lil' sis." Hanh's voice was harsh; her face turned away, towards the paintings of landscapes on the wall. "You're no one's toy or slave—and especially not your family's."

Because they had all but disowned her. But words, as usual, failed Dac Kien; and they went to bed with the shadow of the old argument still between them, like the blade of a sword.

The next day, Dac Kien pored over the design of the ship with Feng and Miahua, wondering how she could modify it. The parts were complete, and assembling them would take a few days at most; but the resulting structure would never be a ship. That much was clear to all of them. Even excepting the tests, there was at least a month's work ahead of them—slow and subtle touches laid by the bots over the overall system to align it with its destined Mind.

Dac Kien had taken the cube from her quarters, and brought it into her office under Hanh's glowering gaze. Now, they all crowded around it voicing ideas, the cups of tea forgotten in the intensity of the moment.

Feng's wrinkled face was creased in thought as he tapped one side of the cube. "We could modify the shape of this corridor, here. Wood would run through the whole ship, and—"

Miahua shook her head. She was their Master of Wind and Water, the one who could best read the lines of influence, the one Dac Kien turned to when she herself had a doubt over the layout. Feng was Commissioner of Supplies, managing the systems and safety—in many ways Miahua's opposite, given to small adjustments rather than large ones, pragmatic where she verged on the mystical.

"The humours of water and wood would stagnate here, in the control room." Miahua pursed her lips, pointed to the slender aft of the ship. "The shape of this section should be modified."

Feng sucked in a breath. "That's not trivial. For my team to rewrite the electronics—"

Dac Kien listened to them arguing, distantly—intervening with a question from time to time, to keep the conversation from dying down. In her mind, she held the shape of the ship, felt it breathe through the glass of the cube, through the layers of fibres and metal that separated her from the structure outside. She held the shape of the Mind—the essences and emotions that made it, the layout of its sockets and cables, of its muscles and flesh—and slid them together gently, softly until they seemed made for one another.

She looked up. Both Feng and Miahua had fallen silent, waiting for her to speak.

"This way," she said. "Remove this section altogether, and shift the rest of the layout." As she spoke, she reached into the glass matrix, and carefully excised the offending section—rerouting corridors and lengths of cables, burning new decorative calligraphy onto the curved walls.

"I don't think—" Feng said; and stopped. "Miahua?"

Miahua was watching the new design, carefully. "I need to think about it, Your Excellency. Let me discuss it with my subordinates."

Dac Kien made a gesture of approval. "Remember that we don't have much time."

They both took a copy of the design with them, snug in their long sleeves. Left alone, Dac Kien stared at the ship again. It was squat, its proportions out of kilter—not even close to what she had imagined, not even true to the spirit of her work: a mockery of the original design, like a flower without petals, or a poem that didn't quite gel, hovering on the edge of poignant allusions but never expressing them properly.

"We don't always have a choice," she whispered. She'd have prayed to her ancestors, had she thought they were still listening. Perhaps they were. Perhaps the shame of having a daughter who would have no descendants was erased by the exalted heights of her position. Or perhaps not. Her mother and grandmother were unforgiving; what made her think that those more removed ancestors would understand her decision?

"Elder sister?"

Zoquitl stood at the door, hovering uncertainly. Dac Kien's face must have revealed more than she thought. She forced herself to breathe, relaxing all her muscles until it was once more the blank mask required by protocol. "Younger sister," she said. "You honour me by your presence."

Zoquitl shook her head. She slid carefully into the room—one foot after the other, careful never to lose her balance. "I wanted to see the ship."

The birth-master was nowhere to be seen. Dac Kien hoped that he had been right about the birth—that it wasn't about to happen now, in her office, with no destination and no assistance. "It's here." She shifted positions on her chair, invited Zoquitl to sit.

Zoquitl wedged herself in one of the seats, her movements fragile, measured—as if any wrong gesture would shatter her. Behind her loomed one of Dac Kien's favourite paintings, an image from the Third Planet: a delicate, peaceful landscape of waterfalls and ochre cliffs, with the distant light of stars reflected in the water.

Zoquitl didn't move as Dac Kien showed her the design; her eyes were the only thing which seemed alive in the whole of her face.

When Dac Kien was finished, the burning gaze was transferred to her—looking straight into her eyes, a clear breach of protocol. "You're just like the others. You don't approve," Zoquitl said.

It took Dac Kien a moment to process the words, but they still meant nothing to her. "I don't understand."

Zoquitl's lips pursed. "Where I come from, it's an honour. To bear Minds for the glory of the Mexica Dominion."

"But you're here," Dac Kien said. In Xuya, among Xuyans, where to bear Minds was a sacrifice—necessary and paid for, but ill-considered. For who would want to endure a pregnancy, yet produce no human child? Only the desperate or the greedy.

"You're here as well." Zoquitl's voice was almost an accusation.

For an endless, agonising moment, Dac Kien thought Zoquitl was referring to her life choices—how did she know about Hanh, about her family's stance? Then she understood that Zoquitl had been talking about her place onboard the habitat. "I like being in space," Dac Kien said, at last, and it wasn't a lie. "Being here almost alone, away from everyone else."

And this wasn't paperwork, or the slow drain of catching and prosecuting lawbreakers, of keeping Heaven's order on some remote planet. This—this was everything scholarship was meant to be: taking all that the past had given them, and reshaping it into greatness—every part throwing its neighbours into sharper relief, an eternal reminder of how history had brought them here and how it would carry them forward, again and again.

At last, Zoquitl said, not looking at the ship anymore, "Xuya is a harsh place, for foreigners. The language isn't so bad, but when you have no money, and no sponsor . . ." She breathed in, quick and sharp. "I do what needs doing." Her hand went, unconsciously, to the mound of her belly, and stroked it. "And I give him life. How can you not value this?"

She used the animate pronoun, without a second thought.

Dac Kien shivered. "He's—" she paused, groping for words. "He has no father. A mother, perhaps, but there isn't much of you inside him. He won't be counted among your descendants. He won't burn incense on your altar, or chant your name among the stars."

"But he won't die." Zoquitl's voice was soft, and cutting. "Not for centuries."

The ships made by the Mexica Dominion lived long, but their Minds slowly went insane from repeated journeys into deep planes. This Mind, with a proper anchor, a properly aligned ship—Zoquitl was right: he would remain as he was, long after she and Zoquitl were both dead. He—no, it—it was a machine—a sophisticated intelligence, an assembly of flesh and metal and Heaven knew what else. Borne like a child, but still . . .

"I think I'm the one who doesn't understand." Zoquitl pulled herself to her feet, slowly. Dac Kien could hear her laboured breath, could smell the sour, sharp sweat rolling off her. "Thank you, elder sister."

And then she was gone; but her words remained.

Dac Kien threw herself into her work—as she had done before, when preparing for the state examinations. Hahn pointedly ignored her when she came home, making only the barest attempts at courtesy. She was working again on her calligraphy, mingling Xuyan characters with the letters of the Viet alphabet to create a work that spoke both as a poem and as a painting. It wasn't unusual: Dac Kien had come to be accepted for her talent, but her partner was another matter. Hanh wasn't welcome in the banquet room, where the families of the other engineers would congregate in the evenings—she preferred to remain alone in their quarters, rather than endure the barely concealed snubs or the pitying looks of the others.

What gave the air its leaden weight, though, was her silence. Dac Kien tried at first—keeping up a chatter, as if nothing were wrong. Hanh raised bleary eyes from her manuscript, and said, simply, "You know what you're doing, lil' sis. Live with it, for once."

So it was silence, in the end. It suited her better than she'd thought it would. It was her and the design, with no one to blame or interfere.

Miahua's team and Feng's team were rewiring the structure and re-arranging the parts. Outside the window, the mass of the hull shifted and twisted, to align itself with the cube on her table—bi-hour after bi-hour, as the bots gently slid sections into place and sealed them.

The last section was being put into place when Miahua and the birth-master came to see her, both looking equally pre-occupied.

Her heart sank. "Don't tell me," Dac Kien said. "She's due now."

"She's lost the waters," the birth-master said, without preamble. He spat on the floor to ward off evil spirits, who always crowded around the mother in the hour of a birth. "You have a few bi-hours, at most."

"Miahua?" Dac Kien wasn't looking at either of them, but rather at the ship outside, the huge bulk that dwarfed them all in its shadow.

Her Master of Wind and Water was silent for a while—usually a sign that she was arranging problems in the most suitable order. Not good. "The structure will be finished before this bi-hour is over."

"But?" Dac Kien said.

"But it's a mess. The lines of wood cross those of metal, and there are humours mingling with each other and stagnating everywhere. The qi won't flow."

The qi, the breath of the universe—of the dragon that lay at the heart of every planet, of every star. As Master of Wind and Water, it was Miahua's role to tell Dac Kien what had gone wrong, but as Grand Master of Design Harmony, it fell to Dac Kien to correct this. Miahua could only point out the results she saw: only Dac Kien could send the bots in, to make the necessary adjustments to the structure. "I see," Dac Kien said. "Prepare a shuttle for her. Have it wait outside, close to the ship's docking bay."

"Your Excellency—" the birth-master started, but Dac Kien cut him off.

"I have told you before. The ship will be ready."

Miahua's stance as she left was tense, all pent-up fears. Dac Kien thought of Hanh—alone in their room, stubbornly bent over her poem, her face as harsh as that of the birth-master, its customary roundness sharpened by anger and resentment. She'd say, again, that you couldn't hurry things, that there were always possibilities. She'd say that—but she'd never understood there was always a price; and that, if you didn't pay it, others did.

The ship would be ready; and Dac Kien would pay its price in full.

Alone again, Dac Kien connected to the system, letting the familiar overlay of the design take over her surroundings. She adjusted the contrast until the design was all she could see; and then she set to work.

Miahua was right: the ship was a mess. They had envisioned having a few days to tidy things up, to soften the angles of the corridors, to spread the wall-lanterns so there were no dark corners or spots shining with blinding light. The heartroom alone—the pentacle-shaped centre of the ship, where the Mind would settle—had strands of four humours coming to an abrupt, painful stop within, and a sharp line just outside its entrance, marking the bots' hasty sealing.

The killing breath, it was called; and it was everywhere.

Ancestors, watch over me.

A living, breathing thing—jade, whittled down to its essence. Dac Kien slid into the trance, her consciousness expanding to encompass the bots around the structure—sending them, one by one, inside the metal hull, scuttling down the curved corridors and passageways—gently merging with the walls, starting the slow and painful work of coaxing the metal into its proper shape—going up into the knot of cables, straightening them out, regulating the current in the larger ones. In her mind's view, the ship seemed to flicker and fold back upon itself; she hung suspended outside, watching the bots crawl over it like ants, injecting commands into the different sections, in order to modify their balance of humours and inner structure.

She cut to the shuttle, where Zoquitl lay on her back, her face distorted into a grimace. The birth-master's face was grim, turned upwards as if he could guess at Dac Kien's presence.

Hurry. You don't have time left. Hurry.

And still she worked—walls turned into mirrors, flowers were carved into the passageways, softening those hard angles and lines she couldn't disguise. She opened up a fountain—all light projections, of course, there could be no real water aboard—let the recreated sound of a stream fill the structure. Inside the heartroom, the four tangled humours became three, then one; then she brought in other lines until the tangle twisted back upon itself, forming a complicated knot pattern that allowed strands of all five humours to flow around the room. Water, wood, fire, earth, metal, all circling the ship's core, a stabilising influence for the Mind, when it came to anchor itself there.

She flicked back the display to the shuttle, saw Zoquitl's face, and the unbearable lines of tension in the other's face.

Hurry.

It was not ready. But life didn't wait until you were ready. Dac Kien turned off the display—but not the connection to the bots, leaving them time to finish their last tasks.

"Now," she whispered, into the com system.

The shuttle launched itself towards the docking bay. Dac Kien dimmed the overlay, letting the familiar sight of the room re-assert itself—with the cube, and the design that should have been, the perfect one, the one that called to mind *The Red Carp* and *The Turtle Over the Waves* and *The Dragon's Twin Dreams*, all the days of Xuya from the Exodus to the Pearl Wars, and the fall of the Shan Dynasty; and older things, too, Le Loi's sword that had established a Viet dynasty; the dragon with spread wings flying over Hanoi, the Old Earth capital; the face of Huyen Tran, the Viet princess traded to foreigners in return for two provinces.

The bots were turning themselves off, one by one, and a faint breeze ran through the ship, carrying the smell of sea-laden water and of incense.

It could have been, that ship, that masterpiece. If she'd had time. Hanh was right, she could have made it work: it would have been hers, perfect, praised—remembered in the centuries to come, used as inspiration by hundreds of other Grand Masters.

If—

She didn't know how long she stayed there, staring at the design—but an agonised cry tore her from her thoughts. Startled, she turned up the ship's feed again, and selected a view into the birthing room.

The lights had been dimmed, leaving shadows everywhere, like a prelude to mourning. Dac Kien could see the bowl of tea given at the beginning of labour—it had rolled into a corner of the room, a few drops scattering across the floor.

Zoquitl crouched against a high-backed chair, framed by holos of two goddesses who watched over childbirth: the Princess of the Blue and Purple Clouds, and the Bodhisattva of Mercy. In the shadows, her face seemed to be that of a demon, the alienness of her features distorted by pain.

"Push," the birth-master was saying, his hands on the quivering mound of her belly.

Push.

Blood ran down Zoquitl's thighs, staining the metal surfaces until they reflected everything in shades of red. But her eyes were proud—those of an old warrior race, who'd never bent or bowed to anybody else. Her child of flesh, when it came, would be delivered the same way.

Dac Kien thought of Hanh, and of sleepless nights, of the shadow stretched over their lives, distorting everything.

"Push," the birth-master said again, and more blood ran out. Push push push—and Zoquitl's eyes were open, looking straight at her, and Dac Kien knew—she knew that the rhythm that racked Zoquitl, the pain that came in waves, it was all part of the same immutable law, the same thread that bound them more surely than the red one between lovers—what lay in the womb, under the skin, in their hearts and in their minds; a kinship of gender that wouldn't ever be altered or extinguished. Her hand slid to her own flat, empty belly, pressed hard. She knew what that pain was, she could hold every layer of it in her mind as she'd held the ship's design—and she knew that Zoquitl, like her, had been made to bear it.

Push.

With a final heart-wrenching scream, Zoquitl expelled the last of the Mind from her womb. It slid to the floor, a red, glistening mass of flesh and electronics: muscles and metal implants, veins and pins and cables.

It lay there, still and spent—and several heartbeats passed before Dac Kien realised it wouldn't ever move.

Dac Kien put off visiting Zoquitl for days, still reeling from the shock of the birth. Every time she closed her eyes, she saw blood: the great mass sliding out of the womb, flopping on the floor like a dead fish, the lights of the birthing room glinting on metal wafers and grey matter, and everything dead, gone as if it had never been.

It had no name, of course—neither it nor the ship, both gone too soon to be graced with one.

Push. Push, and everything will be fine. Push.

Hanh tried her best: showing her poems with exquisite calligraphy; speaking of the future and of her next posting; fiercely making love to her as if nothing had ever happened, as if Dac Kien could just forget the enormity of the loss. But it wasn't enough.

Just as the ship hadn't been enough.

In the end, remorse drove Dac Kien, as surely as a barbed whip; and she boarded the shuttle to come over to the ship.

Zoquitl was in the birthing room, sitting wedged against the wall, with a bowl of pungent tea in her veined hands. The two holos framed her, their white-painted faces stark in the dim light, unforgiving. The birth-master hovered nearby, but was persuaded to leave them both alone—though he made it clear Dac Kien was responsible for anything that happened to Zoquitl.

"Elder sister." Zoquitl smiled, a little bitterly. "It was a good fight."

"Yes." One Zoquitl could have won, if she had been given better weapons.

"Don't look so sad," Zoquitl said.

"I failed," Dac Kien said, simply. She knew Zoquitl's future was still assured; that she'd make her good marriage, and bear children, and be worshipped in her turn. But she also knew, now, that it wasn't the only reason Zoquitl had borne the Mind.

Zoquitl's lips twisted, into what might have been a smile. "Help me."

"What?" Dac Kien looked at her, but Zoquitl was already pushing herself up, shaking, shivering, as carefully as she had done when pregnant. "The birth-master—"

"He's fussing like an old woman," Zoquitl said; and for a moment, her voice was as sharp and as cutting as a blade. "Come. Let's walk."

She was smaller than Dac Kien had thought: her shoulders barely came up to her own. She wedged herself awkwardly, leaning on Dac Kien for support—a weight that grew increasingly hard to bear as they walked through the ship.

There was light, and the sound of water, and the familiar feel of qi flowing through the corridors in lazy circles, breathing life into everything. There were shadows barely seen in mirrors, and the glint of other ships, too: the soft, curving patterns of *The Golden Mountain*; the carved calligraphy incised in the doors that had been the hallmark of *The Tiger Who Leapt Over the Stream*; the slowly curving succession of ever-growing doors of *Baoyu's Red Fan*—bits and pieces salvaged from her design and put together into—into this, which unfolded its marvels all around her, from layout to electronics to decoration, until her head spun and her eyes blurred, taking it all in.

In the heartroom, Dac Kien stood unmoving, while the five humours washed over them, an endless cycle of destruction and renewal. The centre was pristine, untouched, with a peculiar sadness hanging around it, like an empty crib. And yet . . .

"It's beautiful," Zoquitl said, her voice catching and quivering in her throat.

Beautiful as a poem declaimed in drunken games, as a flower bud ringed by frost—beautiful and fragile as a newborn child struggling to breathe.

And, standing there at the centre of things, with Zoquitl's frail body leaning against her, she thought of Hanh again; of shadows and darkness, and of life choices.

It's beautiful.

It would be gone in a few days. Destroyed, recycled; forgotten and uncommemorated. But somehow, Dac Kien couldn't bring herself to voice the thought.

Instead she said, softly, into the silence—knowing it to be true of more than the ship—"It was worth it."

All of it—now and in the years to come, and she wouldn't look back, or regret.

in-fall

TED KOSMATKA

New writer Ted Kosmatka has been a zookeeper, a chem tech, and a steelworker, and is now a self-described "lab rat" who gets to play with electron microscopes all day. He made his first sale, to *Asimov's*, in 2005, and has since made several subsequent sales there, as well as to *The Magazine of Fantasy & Science Fiction*, *Seeds of Change*, *Ideomancer*, *City Slab*, *Kindred Voices*, *Cemetery Dance*, and elsewhere. He's placed several different stories with several different Best of the Year series over the last couple of years, including this one. He lives in Portage, Indiana, and has a Web site at www.tedkosmatka.com.

"In-Fall" is one of several stories this year to center—literally!— around black holes, this one a suspenseful battle of wills taking place on a spaceship about to plunge into one.

The disc caved a hole in the starshine.

Smooth, graphene skin reflected nothing, blotting out the stars as it swung through the vacuum—black on black, the perfect absence of color.

It was both a ship and not a ship.

The disc lacked a propulsion system. It lacked navigation. Inside, two men awakened, first one and then the other.

In truth, the disc was a projectile—a dark bolus of life support fired into distant orbit around another, stranger kind of darkness.

This second darkness is almost infinitely larger, massing several hundred thousand sols; and it didn't blot out the stars behind it, but instead lensed them into a bright, shifting halo, bending light into a ring, deforming the fabric of spacetime itself.

From the perspective of the orbiting disc, the stars seemed to flow around an enormous, circular gap in the star field. It had many different names, this region of space. The astronomers who discovered it centuries earlier had called it Bhat 16. Later physicists would call it "the sink." And finally, to those who came here, to those who dreamed of it, it was known simply as "the maw."

A black hole like none ever found before.

By the disc's third day in orbit, it had already traveled three-hundred and eighteen million miles, but this is only a tiny fraction of its complete trajectory. At the end of the disc's seventy-second hour in orbit, a small lead weight, 100 kilograms, was fired toward the heart of the gravity well—connected to the ship by a wire so thin that even mathematicians called it a line.

The line spooled out, thousands of kilometers of unbreakable tetravalent filament stretching toward the darkness until finally pulling taut. The line held fast to its anchor point, sending a musical resonance vibrating through the disc's carbon hull.

Inexorable gravity, a subtle shift.

Slow at first, but gradually, on the fourth day, the ship that was not a ship changed course and began to fall.

The old man wiped blood from the young man's face.

"*Ulii ul quisall*," the young man said. *Don't touch me.*

The old man nodded. "You speak Thusi," he said. "I speak this, too."

The young man leaned close and spat blood at the old man. "It is an abomination to hear you speak it."

The old man's eyes narrowed.

He wiped the blood from his cheek. "An abomination," he said. "Perhaps this is true."

He held out his hand for the young man to see. In his hand was a scalpel. "Do you know why I'm here?" he asked.

Light gleamed off the scalpel's edge. This time, it was the old man who leaned close. "I'm here to cut you."

The old man placed the scalpel's blade on the young man's cheek, just beneath his left eye. The steel pressed a dimple into his pallid skin.

The young man's expression didn't change. He stared straight ahead, eyes like blue stone.

The old man considered him. "But it would be a kindness to cut you," he continued. "I see that now." He pulled the blade away and ran a thumb along the young man's jaw, tracing the web of scar tissue. "You wouldn't even feel it."

The young man sat motionless in the chair, arms bound to the armrests by thick straps. He was probably still in his teens, the beginnings of a beard making patchy whorls on his cheek. He was little more than a boy, really.

He had probably once been beautiful, the old man judged. That explained the scars. The boy's psychological profile must have shown a weakness for vanity.

Or perhaps the profiles didn't matter anymore.

Perhaps they just scarred them all now.

The old man rubbed his eyes, feeling the anger slide out of him. He put the scalpel back on the tray with the other bright and gleaming instruments.

"Sleep," he told the boy. "You will need it."

And the universe ticked on.

"Where are we going?" the boy said, after several hours.

Whether he'd slept or not, the old man wasn't sure, but at least he'd been silent.

The old man rose from his console on creaking knees. Acceleration accreted weight into the soles of his feet, allowing the simple pleasure of walking. He brought the boy water. "Drink," he said, holding out the nozzle.

The boy eyed him suspiciously, but after a moment, took a long swallow.

"Where are we going?" he repeated.

The old man ignored him.

"They have already tried to interrogate me," the boy said. "I told them nothing."

"I know. If you told them what they wanted, you wouldn't be here."

"And so now they're sending me someplace else? To try again?"

"Yes, someplace else, but not to try again."

The boy was silent for a long moment. Then he said, "For that they have you."

The old man smiled. "You are a smart one."

Rage burned in the boy's eyes, and pain beyond measuring. The earlier interrogations had been harsh. He pulled against his straps again, trying to jerk his arms free.

"Where are you taking me?" he demanded.

The old man stared down at him. "You are scared," he said. "I know what you are thinking. You want out of your restraints. You're thinking that if you could get loose . . . oh, the things you would do to me." The old man glanced toward the tray of gleaming steel. "You wish you could use that blade on me. You wish that you were in my shoes, that I was sitting where you are.

"But you don't understand," the old man said, then whispered into the boy's ear. "It is *I* who envy *you*."

The ship hummed as it fell. Charged ions blasted carbon skin.

"Why won't you tell me where we're going?"

The boy repeated the question every few minutes.

Finally the old man walked to the console and pressed a button. A viewscreen opened in the wall, exposing deep space, the looming maw. "There," the old man said. "We are going there."

The black hole filled half the screen.

Abyss, if there ever was one.

The boy smiled. "You try to scare me with death? I don't fear death."

"I know," the old man said.

"Death is my reward. In the afterlife, I will walk again with my father. I will tread the bones of my enemies. I will be seated at a place of honor with others who fell fighting for the side of God. Death will be a paradise for me."

"You truly believe that, don't you?"

"Yes."

"That is why I envy you."

The boy was a mass murderer. Or a freedom fighter.

Or maybe just unfortunate.

The old man looked at the boy's scars, noting the creative flourish that had been lavished on his face during previous interviews. Yes, unfortunate, certainly. Perhaps that above all.

Life in deep space is fragile. And humans are as they have always been.

Bombs, though, are different.

In space, bombs can be much, *much* more effective.

If placed just right, a simple three-pound bomb can destroy an entire colony. Open it to the sterilizing vacuum of the endless night. And ten thousand people dead—a whole community wiped clean in a single explosive decompression.

He'd seen that once, a long time ago, when this war first began. Seen the bodies floating frozen inside a ruptured hab, the only survivors a lucky few who scrambled into pressure suits. A lucky few like him.

Because of a three-pound bomb.

Multiply it by a hundred colonies and a dozen years. Three airless worlds. A fight over territory, culture, religion. The things man has always fought over.

Humans are as they have always been. In space, though, the cost of zealotry is higher.

A thousand years ago, nations bankrupted themselves to raise armies. It cost a soldier to kill a soldier. Then came gunpowder, technology, increased population densities—gradually leveraging the cost of death along a sliding scale of labor and raw materials, until finally three pounds of basic chemistry had the power to erase whole swaths of society. Ever more effortless murder, the final statistical flat-line in the falling price of destruction.

"What is your name?" the old man asked him.

The boy didn't answer.

"We need the names of the others."

"I will tell you nothing."

"That's all we need, just the names. Nothing more. We can do the rest."

The boy stayed silent.

They watched the viewscreen. The black hole grew. The expanding darkness compressed the surrounding star field. The old man checked his instruments.

"We're traveling at half the speed of light," he said. "We have two hours, our time, until we approach the Schwarzschild radius."

"If you were going to kill me, there are easier ways than this."

"Easier ways, yes."

"I'm worth nothing to you dead."

"Nor alive."

The silence drew out between them.

"Do you know what a black hole is?" The old man asked. "What it is, really?"

The young man's face was stone.

"It is a side-effect. It is a byproduct of the laws of the universe. You can't have the universe as we know it and not have black holes. Scientists predicted them before they ever found one."

"You're wasting your time."

The old man gestured toward the screen. "This is not just a black hole, though, not really. But they predicted this, too."

"Do you think you can frighten me with this game?"

"I'm not trying to frighten you."

"It makes no sense to kill me like this. You'd be killing yourself. You must have a family."

"I did. Two daughters."

"You intend to change course."

"No."

"This ship has value. Even your life must be worth something, if not to yourself then at least to those whose orders you follow. Why sacrifice both a ship and a man in order to kill one enemy?"

"I was a mathematician before your war made soldiers of mathematicians. There are variables here that you don't understand." The old man pointed at the screen again. His voice went soft. "It is beautiful, is it not?"

The boy ignored him. "Or perhaps this ship has an escape pod," the boy continued. "Perhaps you will be saved while I die. But you'd still be wasting a ship."

"I cannot escape. The line that pulls us can't be broken. Even now, the gravity draws us in. By the time we approach the Schwarzschild radius, we'll be traveling at nearly the speed of light. We will share the same fate, you and I."

"I don't believe you."

The old man shrugged. "You don't have to believe. You have merely to witness."

"This doesn't make sense."

"You think it has to?"

"Shut up. I don't want to hear more from a Godless *tathuun*."

"Godless? Why do you assume I am Godless?"

"Because if you believed in God, you would not do this thing."

"You are wrong," the old man said. "I do believe in God."

"Then you will receive judgment for your sins."

"No," he said. "I will not."

Over the next several hours, the black hole swelled to fill the screen. The stars along its rim stretched and blurred, torturing the sky into a new configuration.

The boy sat in silence.

The old man checked his instruments. "We cross the Schwarzschild radius in six minutes."

"Is that when we die?"

"Nothing so simple as that."

"You talk in circles."

The old mathematician picked up the scalpel. He touched his finger to the razor tip. "What happens after we cross that radius isn't the opposite of existence, but its inverse."

"What does that *mean*?"

"So now you ask the questions? Give me a name, and I'll answer any question you like."

"Why would I give you names? So they can find themselves in chairs like this?"

The old man shook his head. "You are stubborn, I can see that; so I will give you this for free. The Schwarzschild radius is the innermost orbit beyond which all things must fall inward—even communications signals. This is important to you for this reason: beyond the Schwarzschild radius, asking you questions will serve no purpose, because I will have no way to transmit the information. After that, you will be no use to me at all."

"You're saying we'll still live once we pass it?"

"For most black holes, we'd be torn apart long before reaching it. But this is something special. Super-massive, and old as time. For something this size, the tidal forces are more dilute."

The image on the screen shifted. The stars flowed in slow-motion as the circular patch of darkness spread. Blackness filled the entire lower portion of the screen.

"A black hole is a two-dimensional object; there is no inside to enter, no line to cross, because nothing ever truly falls in. At the event horizon, the math of time and space trade positions."

"What are you talking about?"

"To distant observers, infalling objects take an infinite period of time to cross the event horizon, simply becoming ever more redshifted as time passes."

"More of your circles. Why are you doing this? Why not just kill me?"

"There are telescopes watching our descent. Recording the footage."

"Why?"

"As warning."

"Propaganda, you mean."

"To show what will happen to others."

"We aren't afraid to die. Our reward is in the afterlife."

The old man shook his head. "As our speed increases, time dilates. The cameras will show that we'll never actually hit the black hole. We'll never cross the threshold."

The boy's face showed confusion.

"You still don't understand. The line isn't where we die; it's where time itself ceases to function—where the universe breaks, all matter and energy coming to a halt, frozen forever on that final mathematical boundary. You will never get your afterlife, not ever. Because you will never die."

The boy's face was blank for a moment, and then his eyes went wide.

"You don't fear martyrdom," the old mathematician gestured to the viewscreen. "So perhaps this."

The ship arced closer. Stars streamed around the looming wound in the starfield.

The old man put his hand on the boy's shoulder. He touched the scalpel to the boy's throat. "If you tell me the names, I'll end this quickly, while you still have time. I need the names before we reach the horizon."

"So this is what you offer?"

The old man nodded. "Death."

"What did you do to deserve this mission?"

"I volunteered."

"Why would you do such a thing?"

"I've been too long at this war. My conscience grows heavy."

"But you said you believe in God. You'll be giving up your afterlife, too."

The old man smiled a last smile. "My afterlife would not be so pleasant as yours."

"How do you know this is all true? What you said about time. How do you know?"

"I've seen the telescopic images. Previous missions spread out like pearls across the face of the event, trapped in their final asymptotic approach. They are there still. They will always be there."

"But how do you know? Maybe it's just some new propaganda. A lie. Maybe it doesn't really work that way."

"What matters is that this ship will be there for all to see, forever. A warning. Long after both our civilizations have come and gone, we will still be visible. Falling forever."

"It could still be false."

"But we are good at taking things on faith, you and I. Give me the names."

"I can't."

The old man thought of his daughters. One dark-eyed. The other blue. Gone. Because of boys like this boy. But not this boy, he reminded himself.

The old man looked down at the figure in the chair. He might have been that boy, if circumstances were different. If he'd been raised the way the boy was raised. If he'd seen what he'd seen. The boy was just a pawn in this game.

As was he.

"What is death to those who take their next breath in paradise?" the old man asked. "Where is the *sacrifice*? But this . . ." and the old man gestured to the dark maw growing on the screen. "This will be *true* martyrdom. When you blow up innocents who don't believe what you believe, this is what you're taking away from them. Everything."

The boy broke into quiet sobs.

The horizon approached, a graphic on the screen. One minute remaining.

"You can still tell me,
—there is still time.
     —perhaps they are your friends, perhaps your family.
          —do you think they'd protect you?
     —they wouldn't.
—we just need names.
—a few names, and this will all be over. I'll end it for you before it's too late."

The boy closed his eyes. "I won't."

His daughters. Because of boys like this boy.

"Why?" the old man asked, honestly confused. "It does not benefit you. You get no paradise."

The boy stayed silent.

"I take your heaven from you," the old man said. "You receive nothing."

Silence.

"Your loyalty is foolish. Tell me one name, and I will end this."

"I will not," the boy said. There were tears on his cheeks.

The old mathematician sighed. He'd never expected this.

"I believe you," he said, then slashed the boy's throat.

A single motion, severing the carotid.

The boy's eyes flashed wide in momentary surprise, followed by an emotion more complicated. He slumped forward in his bonds.

It was over.

The old man ran a palm over the boy's eyes, closing them. "May it be what you want it to be," he said.

He sat down on the floor against the growing gravity.

He stared at the screen as the darkness approached.

The mathematician in him was pleased. A balancing of the equation. "A soldier for a soldier."

He thought of his daughters, one brown-eyed, the other blue. He tried to hold their faces in his mind, the final thought that he would think forever.

Not the reverse of existence, but its inverse.

And he waited to be right or wrong. To be judged for his sins or not.

CHIMBWI

Jim Hawkins

Jim Hawkins is a "new writer" of an unusual sort, one who made his first sale to *New Worlds* forty years ago, and didn't sell another story until placing two in *Interzone* in 2010. His forty-year hiatus doesn't seem to have diminished his talents or skills, though, as he demonstrates in the tense story that follows, that sweeps us along with a refugee risking everything to flee from a ruined and war-torn near-future Europe to an Africa grown prosperous and technologically advanced beyond anything known in the Old World he's left behind. . . .

A narrow plain ran between hills. The grass and small trees were almost colourless in the searing African sunlight. Jason headed across the plain towards a narrow cleft. A group of startled duiker jumped out from behind a bush and escaped up the far hillside into the trees in a series of elegant leaps. He stood, shading his eyes, and watched them, before climbing down the bank into the dried-up bed of the Kalambo River. After a hundred and fifty years the antelope were back.

Jason walked carefully, avoiding sharp stones. His bare feet were tougher now than they'd ever been, but he still hadn't developed the iron-hard soles that evolution had provided for and a life of shoe-wearing had made feeble. He'd never been much good at walking on pebbles.

The sides of the riverbed were the rusty red-brown of laterite, soft and crumbly, rising about ten feet above him on either side. To his left, on the Zambian side, the bank was dark and damp in the shade, but on the right, where it was Tanzania, it was baked hard in the afternoon sun, overhung by thorn trees. The light was intense, almost heavy, and he rubbed the sweat from his forehead with the back of his forearm and wiped it on his grey shorts.

Where a small stream course met the river he looked up the lowered bank to where the terracotta pantiled roof of the John Desmond Clark Centre was shaded by a grove of eucalyptus trees. A little further down the bank, as if on cue, a lump of flint was exposed near the top of the gully. Jason prised it out and held it in his hand. It was a good axe head, but not perfect. The strike-plane was ragged. It was a reject. A hundred and sixty thousand years ago an axe maker had thrown it down in disgust. He wondered where archaeologists like Clark would have got to if Stone Age quality control had been a bit more lax. If all these tools had gone out to do their job these sites would never have been found. This was ancient concentrated industrial waste, but more natural, more appropriate in some way, than the devastated spoil heaps of Dagenham and Longbridge, the twisted steel spaghetti of what were once high-speed railway tracks that weaved between the fallen cooling towers of defunct power stations in the ruins of a far-off England.

The shadows had hard edges, like the flint tool he held as he walked. Fifty yards more and another artefact lay on the riverbed—a flat tin the size of his hand, corroded but intact, its label long gone. He turned it over with his toe: Italian rations from the First World War, washed down from a trench somewhere, possibly still edible after two hundred years, but he didn't have a can opener, so he'd never know. Still, he bent down, picked it up and put it in his pocket.

On either side of the river the elegant, impossibly thin towers of solar fusion reactors reached two hundred feet above the scrubby savannah trees, occasionally flashing blinding stars of reflected sunlight, strange flashing flowers reaching for the wispy floating thermal clouds.

The noise of the cicadas came and went like the sound of a vast orchestra of string-less violins. And then the call of something, perhaps a dog, perhaps a hyena, echoed from afar.

Ahead, the riverbed was beginning to widen, but was still narrow, only about thirty feet from side to side. The soil underfoot was turning to patchy grey rock cut with a channel by millions of years of water flow.

Jason walked out from the banks of the river to the gorge. Hills reached up on either side. The valley opened up in front of him as he walked, sweat soaking his shirt, his feet hot, and went to the lip of the falls. The river stopped here on a knife edge and fell a thousand feet to the gorge floor below. He was standing at the narrowest point of a sheer-sided gulf. A few billion years ago the land had dropped to make the vast cleft of the Great Rift Valley. He stood on the edge of the rock. Marabou storks circled above the jumbled rocks of the river course below on wide dark wings. He was so high that these huge birds were flying beneath him. In the far distance, he knew, lay Lake Tanganyika, but the heat haze caused the landscape to fade out into indistinct brightness and blur.

He stood on the edge of the rock shelf and looked down. Suddenly he almost wanted to leap out and soar with the marabou if only for a few seconds. It would be easier to fall than to resist. A marabou wheeled close to the cliff as though challenging him to fly. There was no voice in his head, but a force that welled up from the ancient parts of him pushing him towards the drop and the silence, and then something clamped the force, stifled it.

He stepped back a few feet, took the ration tin from his pocket and hurled it out over the lip. It arced steeply downwards, and then a quick laser light flashed from above him and to the left. The ration tin vapourised and the marabou scattered down the valley into the blue green mist.

Jason looked up the path into the hills on his left. Miriam Bwalya stood, wrapped in a brightly-coloured *chikwembe*, her Bemba skin so black it had midnight blue highlights. She was completely still, watching. How many seconds passed in this subjective moment? Time stopped for him as he stood between the lip of the dried-up waterfall, the thousand foot drop, and the unmoving form of the woman with the cloth wrapped around her and a laser pistol in her hand.

He walked slowly up the gravel path until he came to her and went down on one knee, held his hands together in front of him, and said "Mwapolenipo baMiriam."

"Mwapoleni mukwai," she said. At last, after a few seconds, but many subjective centuries, he lifted his face and looked into her brown eyes.

"Yes or no?" she asked. He nodded. "Eya mukwai."

She turned and walked up the steep path. Jason stood and followed her. In the clearing halfway up the hill, where an area had been flattened for tourist buses, was a small flyer, hovering on an anti-gravity field that Jason, despite his physics PhD and maybe a hundred research papers, found technically inexplicable. It looked like an ivory thigh bone, but he knew they could make it in whatever shape they felt like. Around the flyer there were groups of people, black, silent, and an old man sitting in a chair slowly waving a fly-whisk in front of his face. Jason walked slowly towards the Chief and went again on bended knee, looking only downwards to the gravel chips, suddenly aware of the loudness of the cicadas and the distant call of the storks.

"Mwapoleni baChiti," he said quietly. The old man leaned forward and grasped him by the shoulders first, and then lifted Jason's head with a delicate touch. His hair was turning white, like frosted charcoal. He smiled. "Cungulo baJason. Whoever called you Jason probably hadn't read the right stories," he said. There was the sound of a tiny bell. The chief looked at his wristwatch and said, "Sorry—I really need to take this call," and dismissed Jason with a flick of his fingers.

ChiBemba, the language of the Bemba people of northern Zambia and half the Congo was a difficult language if you weren't born to it, inflected at both ends of a word, about seven noun cases, and hundreds of greetings, proverbs and forms of abuse. What other language had a single word meaning *may your grandmother's vagina be opened wide and stuffed with sand*? He was grateful for the chief's use of English; but then they all spoke perfect English most of the time, except when speaking to him.

Jason walked over to the flyer. A hatch opened in the side of the knuckle end of the "bone" and the pilot looked out. He pointed at Jason, tugged at his own shirt, and said, "Fuleni." Jason was suddenly aware of about a dozen people standing and watching him. As he stripped he didn't care much about most of them. He was only embarrassed that his mentor, Miriam, should see him naked. He was pleased to see that she averted her eyes.

He turned and walked naked up to the steps of the flyer, then turned back and retrieved the stone tool that he'd dropped.

It had been a long hard journey to get here from ravaged England through war-torn Europe, through the Balkans and down the Greek mainland. He remembered it only too well, and the worst was the two days and nights he'd spent spewing his guts up into the Mediterranean . . .

Was it like this for the Argonauts? Did the ancient Jason hang onto the side of a Greek fishing boat and vomit into the dark blue Aegean? Did heroes suffer the same indignities as refugees? Jason's stomach was empty and only the last traces of bile retched out to feed the fish.

At least Kostas Kiriakos, the owner and captain of this boat, had the intelligence not to overload it. They turned south from Paleochora and headed down from the Mediterranean off southern Crete into the Libyan Sea. Jason's intelligence was malfunctioning, he realised; he had become completely subject to the whims of his inner ears. He was a slug, or a cockroach, or a tortoise, but not a human and certainly not, for these interminable hours, a physicist.

The ocean was piled up in rolling ultramarine white-topped waves and the boat was rotating in unpredictable ways. Kostas didn't seem bothered by this, and stuck lamb souvlaki under the grill in the galley. The smell of hot lamb and onions swept over the seventeen men and women clutching the gunnels, causing a chain-reaction of stomach spasms to grip the refugees.

Jason let go of the side of the boat and lurched towards the galley, targeting the door frame and managing to grasp it. Kostas looked up, smiled and held up a piece of barbecued lamb. "Eat," he said. "You'll feel better. An empty gut is a bad thing." Jason forced himself to take the meat and began to chew it. So far, so good. It was a long way to the Libyan coast and he knew he must eat. East of the boat the hills of Gavdos Island seemed to rise above the wave crests and then drop. They were passing the most southerly outpost of Europe. Greece had survived the catastrophic and chaotic collapse of the EU, the two and a half metre rise in sea level when the Antarctic ice shelf melted, better than most. The sandy beaches of lonely Gavdos were gone, the island had shrunk a little, but the goats had never signed up for civilisation anyway. True, Athens was a disaster zone, but throughout the mountains of the Peloponnesian region, down the islands of the Aegean, the Sporades, on Lesvos and Crete, the Greeks simply threw away their mobile phones and went back to shouting. When civilisation collapses, those closest to their peasant roots survive.

Kostas dropped them at a small Libyan jetty just before dawn, waved, put the engines into reverse, and backed out into the darkness. He'd been well paid in gold and diamonds. He'd fulfilled his side of the bargain, he'd delivered them to this isolated bluff, but he could not give them anything more than a microscopic fragment of hope for their future. He put them into the hands of the Fates, the *Moirai*, the deciders of the immutable track of destiny for gods and men, set the boat on a northerly course, poured some of his mother's dark red fruity wine from a goat skin into a cup, sipped, and then tossed a small libation into the ocean. It was the least he could do.

The promised refugee-smuggling transport didn't arrive. They stood together on the jetty and waited, hungry, thirsty, apprehensive in the darkness. Eventually the headlights came. They were rounded up by an armed Libyan border patrol, herded onto the back of a lorry, and taken to a holding pen outside the refugee camp at Cyrene for interrogation. The guards gave them water, couscous and olives. They were all tense and nervous. Jason picked at the olives and felt an overwhelming sense of despair, apprehension, anger and guilt. He had run away. He should have stayed with his dead friends and his dead wife and his dead science and raged and burned his way into the inevitable darkness of chaos and death.

The officer, a lean man in his forties with a neat moustache, checked Jason's iris scan against the image stored on his passport and sat back.

"Most people throw their passports away, Professor Johns. Why bring it here?"

"To prove who I am," said Jason.

"But why come?"

"Twenty kilos of Semtex in my laboratory. Six of my colleagues shot. This is not the best time to be a scientist in Europe. I'm sure somebody on this continent can find a use for me."

"Perhaps. Until then, I'm afraid, even scientists have to dig."

Jason felt fear overwhelm him. He wanted to run. He wanted to scream.

The officer locked a transponder bracelet around Jason's wrist, pointed to the door, and turned to his computer and made a note on the file.

Suddenly Jason felt the fear, guilt and anger curl up and compress themselves into something like an itch in his right arm.

The ship from Libya to Dar es Salaam had been crowded and filthy. Here, in the hills of Tanzania, they weren't badly treated, but the work was hard. The cage went down the shaft at high speed, still lurching as it braked at the bottom and the gate opened. There were twin tunnels under construction. Jason climbed with the others from the lift into a low train running up the wide water tunnel, twenty feet across, lit with bright points of LED light. He had a sudden vivid memory of the London Underground. Down-slope from here the tunnel descended in a shallow gradient for sixty miles to the Tanzanian coast near the southern town of Mtwara and then a further five miles under the Indian Ocean.

Jason was working in the second, parallel, smaller tunnel, which would carry superconducting cables. These would bring current from the solar fusion plants five thousand feet up in Zambia to massive pumps along the water tunnel that would lift seawater three thousand feet to a desalination plant in the hills above Lake Malawi. There were sixteen systems like this, each tunnel emerging into the sea along the Tanzanian coast, and more in Mozambique. Power for water—it was a good barter.

Africa was greening again. The evaporating lakes were filling. Rivers flowed. Irrigation ducts fed the fertile fields. All of this was because a remarkable breakthrough by the Zambians converted the sun's rays into electricity at a phenomenal 98% efficiency. They weren't telling anybody how they did it.

Jason was working in a gang of six attaching steel lining plates to the superconducting tunnel and welding them into an airtight lining, preparing for the vacuum that was needed. The other five refugee workers were German, and rarely spoke to him, not because they didn't speak English, but because they were all *suppressed* by their wrist-bands. He'd hardly had anything amounting to a conversation with anybody since he embarked on his long and dangerous journey from England. He would have expected a camp of several hundred forced labourers to have a loud, violent culture, but it was more like a Sunday School camp. They didn't sing; they didn't shout; they didn't fight. They'd had an emotional epidural.

A shift with sizzling blue welding arcs in his face was pretty sure to bring on a headache. He'd just finished a join and lowered the torch when he felt a tap on his shoulder. Mbanga, the site manager, gestured for him to follow.

An hour later he was showered, dressed in clean shorts and shirt, and sitting in the comfort of a high speed maglev train, eating maize and curried fish, drinking cold beer, watching out of the window for the occasional glimpse of giraffe or elephants. He was on his way to the wealthiest country in the world. As the silent train rounded a banked curve at three hundred and twenty miles per hour the towering heights of Kilimanjaro came into view to the north. The summit was no longer snowy. The land around outside the train was sandy and dry with widely-spaced baobab trees standing with their enormously wide brown trunks out of proportion to the number of branches above them.

A tall African, with an aquiline nose (legacy of the Arab slave traders who operated in this region in the nineteenth century) walked down the train and sat facing Jason. The suit was light blue and looked like class. His dark eyes met Jason's light grey eyes across the table.

"How's the food, Professor Johns?"

"Very good, thank you. And your name is?"

"Not important. So. What do you think?"

"About what, Mr. Not Important?"

"Fair enough—the name's Arisa. About your situation . . ." He took Jason's passport from the inside pocket of his jacket and pushed it across the table.

Jason left it where it was and wiped his mouth on the pressed white linen napkin. "I think I *just* prefer this patronising slavery to dirty bombs and marauding fascists." He was trying to let the anger come, but it wouldn't.

"Not slavery. You chose to come. I don't think my ancestors climbed on the ships and held up their hands for manacles." He pointed to Jason's wrist band. "We took you in. Millions of you. We feed you and give you beds and pillows and blankets. Look—even beer!"

"What do you think of this train?"

"It's—impressive. But . . ."

"What?"

"If you put it inside a vacuum tunnel, you could double the speed."

"Phase two, Professor Johns."

He spoke quickly in Swahili to what seemed to be his watch. Instantly the train began to slow until it was not far above walking pace. Beyond a pair of baobab trees was a pile of black wreckage, sharp wing shards, engine nacelles, fragments of cockpit windshield. Jason recognised many of the parts. It was a shattered American stealth bomber. Dark stains spread out across the sand from the impact.

"The Americans still don't understand how the Zambians have shot down every missile and every nuclear attack plane."

Jason tried to be angry, but it was impossible. Stick to the rational, he told himself. There was a quick flicker of the memory of his wife's bloody dead face. He pushed his plate aside. "It didn't need to happen. You could have saved Europe and America if you'd shared the technology."

Arisa leaned back and laughed ironically. "We were starving. Did you help us? No. We were ravaged with disease. Did you help us? You turned the atmosphere against us, the rain stopped, the deserts spread like cancer, the crops and the livestock died, the lakes began to shrink, the young fish boiled until there were no more. Did you help us? Did you?"

"No. But many of us wanted to."

"Not many enough. What you *don't* know is that many of *us* would like to see a more generous regime. Here, in Tanzania. Not there in Zambia. It's a local issue, but also maybe global. If we could have their solar fusion here we could do business with the Americans, the Chinese, the Indians, and even Europe. And you, Professor Johns, could have whatever you want. Learn what you can. And think about having your own research centre with unlimited resources. Now we approach the border. We *will* speak again. *Kwa heri.*"

He eased out of the seat and walked towards the end of the compartment.

"By the way—*Arisa* is a girl's name. We have to be a bit careful. So do you. After a few hundred years of digging out copper for the white man the Bemba have remembered that they used to be warriors. Oh—and *we* would take the suppressor off your wrist."

Half an hour later the train slowed to a halt at the border crossing at Nakonde and an announcement on the PA system invited Jason and two other people to leave the train. It was like climbing out of the belly of a sleek, air-conditioned orange-green snake. Arisa, the man with a girl's name, smiled from a window near the front of the train as it lifted from the black monorail and accelerated silently away towards the south. The air was warm and fresh in this vast central plateau of the continent, here at about five thousand feet NSL (New Sea Level). Jason walked up the platform behind a couple who looked as though they were from China or somewhere in the Far East. They pulled suitcases on wheels. Jason carried nothing.

At the end of the platform, amongst a stand of eucalyptus trees, there were six arches of twisted filigree glass. The platform was embedded with small LED lights. Ahead of him a moving pattern of green lights ran from the feet of the Asians to the arch on the right. He carried on walking. Lights began to pulse below him towards the left-hand arch. He followed them.

As he passed under the arch there was a sudden pulse of something like pain under his wrist band—halfway between an electric shock and an orgasm. He cried out in surprise. He was immobilised for a few seconds. And then, for the first time in his six months in Africa, the wrist band spoke to him—a deep musical contralto voice:

"Welcome to Zambia, Dr. Johns. Take the path up to your left."

She was waiting over the brow of the hill, looking down at him, tall and narrow-waisted with a golden, red and green cloth wrapped around her, tied in a knot above her breasts. Her hair was a cap of short tight curls above dark brown eyes. His wrist ached, and he flicked his hand to shake the irritation away.

"Sorry about that," she said. "When people cross the border it's possible to get the biometric data less painfully, but it's a bit slow and tedious. Come . . . Oh, let me introduce myself . . ."

"I know who you are," said Jason. "You may have switched off half of my brain function, but I can still recognise Dr. Miriam Bwalya when I see her."

She smiled and nodded a humble acceptance. He followed her across a tarmac car park to what turned out to be some kind of flyer, although it looked like a big pink plastic elephant in a children's playground. Much to his surprise, he laughed out loud, and carried on laughing as he climbed the steps into its belly and sat beside her on a wide comfortable bench seat looking out of its huge eyes.

"Do you do flying pigs as well?" he asked. "I can't remember the last time I laughed. I didn't think it was possible!"

She laughed with him, perfect white teeth flashing. "We can do you a flying pig if you want one. You can even have a straight-edged, sharp, European-style, high-tech-looking little boys' fighter plane, if you like. We tend to prefer curvy things. These are only shells, as you perfectly well realise." She added a couple of words in a language he didn't recognise, and the flyer lifted off vertically, and then drifted forward over the eucalyptus trees and away to the north, without making a sound. Curvy things definitely defined Dr. Bwalya, Jason thought irreverently.

The Zambian breakthroughs in physics were well-guarded, but he knew he was sitting next to one of the key players. Miriam Bwalya was known to be a child prodigy who went on to become a formidable laser theorist. She was rumoured to be the architect of the solar fusion reaction that had lifted her country from a subsistence economy blessed with a few copper mines to a world-dominating power. And here he was, sitting next to her in a flying elephant, watching hills and trees rolling by below. Her physical presence was disturbing; he felt flickers of something sexual pushing against the constraints of the wrist-band's grip.

She waved a finger in front of the grey surface below the eye windows, and the music started. African rumba. Long ago the slave traders took their human cargo from here to the Americas, and the slaves took with them the complex poly-rhythm of their drums and marimbas, the antiphonal singing rising over the driving pulse of the percussion. They melded it with hymns and chain gang songs. And then, in the nineteen sixties, it came back to the Congo and South Africa and the Rhodesias in vinyl records and on the radio as a rumba to be taken and modified and brought home—a prodigal music child that needed a little re-education. This music made even the most inhibited, he most mind-bound, long to dance.

"You've had a long, hard journey," she said.

"That's for sure."

"It's not quite over yet."

"I realise that," he said. "If it was, you'd have cut this off my wrist by now."

"We've been attacked. We've been infiltrated. We've been subverted. We only tracked you yesterday, because the Libyans are holding a lot of stuff back. The Tanzanians didn't get who you were until we asked for you. They had decided to keep you, but we cut their power for a few minutes and they saw reason. And then, of course, there was a man on the train."

Jason ignored this. "The flyer never goes above about two hundred feet," he said, "from which I assume you're using some form of magneto-dynamic field effect."

"It can go higher, but the energy cost rises exponentially. Why bother?"

"Why bother with me?"

She held up a fold of her *chikwembe*. "If you look closely, you'll see a few loose loops. What seems perfect cloth has tiny imperfections. So it is with our physics. It's just possible that you can tie off a few loops and close a few holes."

"Specifically?"

"Specifically comes later."

Jason smiled ironically and said, "So what *vaguely* comes next?"

The flyer dropped its trunk over a hillside, coasted down over the town of Mbala, and settled onto a landing strip beside the low white buildings of ZIAP, the Zambia Institute of Advanced Physics.

What came next was that five months later he still hadn't been allowed inside ZIAP. He did know that the buildings at ground level were window-dressing and the real labs were deep underground.

"It's not personal," she said, as they sat on a log in the dappled shade of a pair of *miombo* trees, drinking the cold beer she'd brought out to him. She pointed upwards. "If this tree had just one leaf, we'd burn. The leaf there doesn't know what that leaf on the other side is doing. It doesn't need to know to do its job, which is to keep the whole tree alive."

He was getting used to the fact that the Bemba had a proverb for everything, and if they didn't have one, they made one up on the spot. But he also knew that a lot of the Zambian scientists here did not have access to the main part of the Institute. He was not alone.

"Left to its own devices," he said, "one caterpillar can eat a lot of leaves."

It wasn't her style to giggle, but she did. Then she was suddenly sober-faced again. She reached into her bag, took out a sheet of smart paper, and threw it in front of them, clapping her hands and speaking a command in ChiBemba. The paper unwrapped itself and hovered upright, turning from ivory to silver. For a moment he could see the reflection of both of them—his white skin now a gently even brown, her black hair touched with just a hint of grey over her ears, her dark eyes capable of flashing from warmth to anger in a moment, his grey-green eyes half-closed against the sunlight.

"We didn't want you to see this until you'd recovered," she said. "But now I must show you."

The smart paper listened to her voice, and then the images began: in England, Bradford laid waste, Muslims and Hindus crucified, black bodies in the streets of south London, pyres of burning bodies like sick cattle, dark-skinned children dying of radiation sickness. In France and Germany, heaps of Arabic people awaiting the bulldozers, and following the collapse of the EU as more and more countries pulled out, constant nationalist wars. In America, Harlem poisoned with a dirty bomb, the trees of the Carolinas full of rotting human fruit, and everywhere the lightning-flash flags and the pasty triumphalism. Half the world had imploded as the seas rose and the green land scorched. Dark-skinned peoples raced for rain-blessed regions, economies collapsed, and the blood of scapegoats began to flow.

The video ended and the screen silvered. He looked at Miriam's face in the mirror.

"It's much worse than you thought," she said. "We cannot let them have the technology. We cannot! Our neighbours will sell it to them. We can trust nobody."

"Including me."

He turned away from her and felt salt tears run down onto his lips. She said nothing for a long while, and then her hand gently took his, and their fingers interlocked.

Eventually he said, "I understand. Europe's the new Rwanda and Sudan, and, oh Christ, everywhere!" He looked at her and realised that her eyes were wet.

"We have a saying . . ." she started.

"Of course, of course, there will be a saying. I thought English had a lot of proverbs, but we're amateurs."

"*Chimbwi afwile intangalila*. The greedy hyena wants to eat everything but dies in the effort and eats nothing."

Across the stiff grass, in the orange evening light, children were playing football. The cicadas were starting to scrape their legs. Small birds pecked and flew and squabbled. A crowned eagle soared above the low hilltops as the sun descended ever faster towards the tree tops, polished by the thick air into brass and gold. Miriam tucked her legs up and the soles of her feet were a perfect match with the pink of the sunset on the high clouds.

During the brief few minutes of twilight he said, "You asked me to do some thinking about the relationship between gravity and quantum vacuum foam, which, of course, there can't be, according to theory. I suspect that was what you meant by *specifically*."

The kids picked up their football and ran off shouting towards the lights that were coming on here and there on the *stoeps* of the low houses across the fields.

"How long do I have to wait for a *but*?" she asked. He was suddenly aware of her hand on his arm.

"But," he said. "It's a big *BUT*! Well—actually it's a Planck-level BUT. At the point where the relativistic equations start to become doubtful, there might, just might, be a few little holes and loops in the *chikwembe* of space-time."

She pulled her hand away and spoke quickly in ChiBemba at her silver bracelet. He heard a deep voice responding, and then she stood up.

"Come," she said. "The Chief's invited us for supper."

The last light of the sun snuffed itself out as the terminator rushed across the Congo River, and over Angola towards the Atlantic. An invisible hand threw a billion stars across the sky and went back for more.

She stomped her foot down. "Remember not to walk so lightly," she said. "You keep forgetting the way snakes hear through the ground. Stay away from the bushes where puff adders could be hiding. Don't walk under trees at night in case a boomslang is waiting to fall on you. Lift the lavatory seat before you sit down because the bite of a hunting spider is an unfortunate thing for the testicles, so they tell me. Shake out your shoes before you put them on because the scorpion likes nothing better than to curl up in them. Remember that it's said, maybe wrongly, but as a warning, that a mamba can slide after you as fast as a horse, and its strike is incurable and its neuro-poison agonising."

"Health and Safety's got to be a booming industry here," he said.

"That's why we have proverbs, Jason. Your castles and fine walls rise and fall. Words have served for us. But then you know very well that most physics is proverbs. All the same—we really don't want the possibility of an insight into quantum gravity squashed by a million-year-old venom designed to kill frogs, do we?"

A cloud of moths and other flying things surrounded each light on the path in a moving beating dodging darting halo. The air temperature dropped from nicely warm to nicely cool.

All this and more passed through his mind as he sat naked in the bone-shaped flyer as it followed the road down to Lake Tanganyika. Halfway down the steep hill Stephen Makonde, the laid-back pilot with a clutch of PhDs, veered off the track and settled the flyer in a patch of sugarcane. He climbed out with a machete and came back lopping the tops off two sticks. He handed them to Jason.

"You may need this," he said, "and this." He reached under the seat and produced a spear with a fire-blackened tip.

"Any other advice?" Jason asked.

"Try not to die." Makonde laughed. "Warriors have done this for thousands of years, but they haven't all made it to the top."

"Thanks."

The flyer lifted off again and they flew over the little port of Mpulugu. Night was falling and the fishermen were testing the brilliant lights on their boats as they sailed out into the gathering darkness of the lake.

He stood alone at the mouth of the valley amongst the tumbled rocks. Makonde's flyer was a bone-shaped blackness moving across the vast bright swath of the Milky Way and then was gone.

Strategy is a wonderful thing. He'd worked it all out in advance. Unfortunately, strategy is a child of daylight reason, and starts to fray at the edges when you're surrounded by shadows, starlight, and the coughing and barking of the unseen and unforgiving biology that surrounds you.

Strategy dictated that sitting under a rock shelf would be as dangerous as trying to climb a steep valley in the darkness. He walked back down the valley and sat near the edge of the lake, spear in one hand and sharp stone in the other, and waited for the sun or the crocodiles, whichever came first. Strangely, though, he wasn't afraid. Not even when he heard a quiet splash.

At 6:05 the sun launched itself over the hills and started to cut through the mist on the lake. He was going to burn badly. He crouched down by the water's edge and plastered himself with grey mud. *Shouldn't have had your hair cut short, stupid*, he thought. *That's what it's for.* He chewed on some sugarcane and tried to ignore his thirst.

The Kalambo valley was a few hundred yards wide here where it joined the lake, and the going was easy for half a mile across gently shelving sheets of light grey rock. Then the forest closed in around the zigzagging riverbed and the boulders blocking the way were bigger. His bare feet were sore already. The cracks and crevices in the rocks chewed at what tough skin he had. The mud was already baked dry on his skin and itching. The flies liked him and camped on his back and he had to keep flicking his hand in front of his face.

He was walking on the eastern side of the valley on a shelf that now had a thirty-foot sheer drop to his left. And there it was: a yard of emerald green mamba, coiling and uncoiling in front of him. He had no boots, no thick trousers. If the mamba struck him in the leg, he'd live for about five painful minutes. If it struck on his chest, his heart would stop in a few seconds. He froze.

High above, a marabou stork adjusted its huge wings and dipped slightly to allow the camera a better view. In her cool office five miles away and a thousand feet down in the nuclear-hardened depths of ZIAP Miriam found herself unexpectedly sweating as she watched the pictures from the seven bird-shaped drones that circled over the valley. She moved her finger over the screen from the marabou's view and a targeting cross-hair appeared. She was lining the attack laser up on the mamba when she felt a hand on her shoulder.

Director Nskoshi Mulenga was wearing a beautifully-tailored sand-coloured suit that looked expensively tasteful and a red and blue tie that didn't. "Don't kill the snake," he said. "Give him back his faculties. He is a man, not a refugee."

"But if we lose quantum gravity . . . ?" she said.

He reached over her and touched an icon. The display changed to a panel of virtual sliders, like a mixing desk in an old-fashioned recording studio, and under each slider an image and a hint. His finger touched the square knob of a slider and pushed it from minimum to maximum. The word FEAR drifted across the screen and vanished. He reached for the knob labelled LOVE and she smacked his hand away.

Chief Mulenga squeezed her shoulder and walked towards the door. "Don't settle for half a man just because you can," he said as the door closed.

"Eya, baChiti," she said under her breath. *Yes, Chief!*

What seemed like an electric shock ran up Jason's arm from his wrist band and jolted his spine. The mamba weaved left and right uncertainly, something threatening between it and its young. It became more *solid* in his eyes. It became a focused streak of death and beauty. He felt a terrible knowledge of things that were not on smart boards or papers or cinemas or even memory. This snake was utterly *now*.

Very slowly he slid his feet backwards. He retreated ten feet or so and then slowly reached up to the nearest tree and snapped off a dead branch. Very carefully he stripped twigs off until he had a staff as long as he was tall. He gripped it like a cricket bat, or baseball bat, or maybe a club somebody's ancestors had held here long ago.

Stephen Makonde's voice whispered from his wrist into his ear. "As your companion, I am allowed to give you one assist. Do you want it now?"

Jason whispered back, "How many snakes in this valley?"

"Probably a thousand, maybe two thousand. Jason, I can pick you up now. You don't have to do this. You have our respect already."

"Forget it. My Chief, His Britannic Majesty, is dead and I need a new one. We made refugees pass an exam in Englishness. I decided to try this very old exam because it's the nearest I can get to being a Bemba. I'll take the assist."

"There's a proverb that says . . ."

"Fuck the proverb, Stephen. Tell me what I need to know."

"If you aim for the head, you will probably miss. A blow to the spine is a good start, but not infallible. The snake moves very slowly until it strikes. Be the snake."

Jason moved the branch to the side, trying to get some idea of range. He stepped an inch at a time forward until he was within about six feet of the side to side moving triangle of the mamba's head, holding his breath. Very slowly he raised the branch above his head, took aim, and unleashed all his strength in a blow to the mamba's back. The snake was paralysed. Maybe. Jason smashed at the head until it was a splatter on the rock. He scooped the body over the edge of the rock with the branch and it fell with a dull splash into the muddy pool below.

"Thanks, Stephen," he whispered.

"Pleasure. What I didn't tell was that very few people can do that. Bet you never knew you were a snake killer, Professor Johns. Put it on the CV."

A dozen snakes later, a few painful slips, with the mud cracking off his skin, leaving it exposed, he was several miles up the valley and rounding the bend that led to the falls. It was narrower here, the sides of the cleft closing in, the rocky sides higher, the jumbled rocks bigger. The sun was high overhead and the contrast between light and shadows impossible for the eyes.

Far away, on the other side of the riverbed, he saw a flicker of movement. Two patches of tawny light appeared and then vanished. He sat very still and watched, in turn watched by the watching pair of leopards. Every minute the pattern moved. Towards him.

Overhead real and fictitious marabou circled.

Lion kill only when they're hungry. Leopards enjoy killing. *Yeah, you told me that. Great.*

There was a small but intent crowd standing behind Miriam's chair. Two of the monitors showed close-ups of the leopard. Their noses were raised, nostrils wide, as they grabbed any scent they could catch on the air currents. Their eyes were grey and squeezed half-closed to get the maximum depth of field on their prey. But still they waited. Cat waiting. Slow, patient, killer stillness.

"It is not fair," said a woman's voice behind Miriam.

"Why?" Miriam snapped. "I am told I cannot intervene. He chose it."

"No man has ever done this without the water." Many voices agreed.

Miriam lifted her bracelet and spoke urgently to it. Far above at ground level klaxons wailed and children hurried up the dry banks of the river. In the deep cisterns powerful pumps spun up and pipes filled with water that had once lapped the shores of India. The Kalambo began to flow, slowly at first, and then in full rainy season flood. Down through the village it ran, past the houses and research buildings and football pitches, until it came to the lip of the falls and flung itself over.

Jason heard a sudden roaring sound from above and then a plume of water jetted from high above him in a perfect unbroken fall to the dark green ancient pool below the cliffs. The leopards padded slowly towards him. He could see their markings clearly now. He could see the male flick his tongue around his lips and shake the flies away from his head.

Jason backed up against a rock face and tried to wipe the sweat from his hands on some grass. He held the spear in his left hand and the stone axe-head in his right.

The leopard crouched at the far side of the riverbed and prepared to attack. Its thigh muscles flexed. As it launched, Jason threw the stone axe. He missed, but the leopard was distracted for a moment. That was when the boiling, foaming wall of water swept down the gorge, carrying stones, branches and leopard with it. Spray launched up and drenched him. He watched the animal carried downstream for a while and then it reached the side of the river, climbed out and shook itself. The female padded slowly down towards her mate. The pair stood and looked back at the figure standing on the rock, naked, holding a sharpened stick. They turned, and walked away down the valley towards the lake.

He had to strain his head back to look up to the top of the impossibly high column of water that was like a shimmering sky-scraper standing in a roaring pool of green and silver foam. It was a thing of beauty and terror. And the people a thousand feet above him could turn it off and turn it on again at their will.

He found the best crossing point after a lot of indecision. Was this shallower or faster? Did this have better hand holds? The river ran from the pool at the base of the waterfall through a jumble of rocks. It was fast. It was powerful. But he had to get across the river. His legs were trembling with muscle spasms, and he still had a thousand-foot climb to the escarpment.

He touched his wrist band and said "The water was great. Thanks. Can you turn it off again?"

Silence. He looked at the wrist band. There was something he hadn't seen before about it; it was *inert* in some way. It was, he realised, *switched off.*

He climbed down at his chosen point to where there was a four-foot gap between two rocks with a cascade driving through. He put his hands into the water and drank deeply. Then he held the spear shaft across the rocks, lowered himself into the rushing flood and fought his way across until he could drag himself out and lie exhausted on the bank, looking up at the falling water. He was all body. His mind was elsewhere—up with the marabou, or somewhere behind him amongst the abandoned husks of chewed sugarcane. The pool at the bottom of the falls was wreathed in spray but had a dangerous aura. Tradition said that twins were thrown over here, and babies whose top teeth came out first, and upstarts who annoyed the chiefs. A flicker of intellect said that it would be an interesting archaeological dive, but the Bemba, now holders of the deepest secrets of the universe, would protect the bones of their ancestors with a fury of fundamental plasma fire.

From below, the scree slope looked like a near-vertical five-hundred-foot high disaster waiting to happen. The rocks were anything from a few inches to a foot wide and very eager to fall down. His feet were bleeding. When he climbed on a lump of rock it would either be firm or shoot off down the hill, causing a chain-reaction that could reach the rocks above him and put him into their target zone. It took him two hours to reach the trees, and even they were sticking out from a steep hillside. He was covered in bruises from flinging himself out of the way of falling rocks.

It was cooler amongst the trees. He pulled himself up from branch to branch and trunk to trunk, slithering back sometimes on the grass and digging his fingers in. And then he really fell, turning over and scouring bleeding trenches in his back. The flies came in squadrons to feast. His arms were wrecked. It was so far, so far up, and he was becoming impossibly heavy.

It was late in the afternoon when he crawled on all fours over the crown of the hill and looked down at the lip of Kalambo Falls and the valley curving away to the distant lake. It was then that he heard the cough and spun painfully around.

The hyenas were spaced out amongst the trees, in perfect tactical formation. He had nothing. His spear was in the river, along with his axe-head. He'd come so far, he'd climbed up Kalambo, and it seemed unjust that he'd finally be taken down by these evil snouts and bodies with mismatched front and back legs. He pulled himself up into the nearest tree, six feet, eight feet high. The hyenas watched and waited expectantly. Saliva dripped from their muzzles.

And then he uttered the most heart-felt primal scream, a scream that launched from the solar-plexus, a scream that echoed around the hills, and leapt towards the nearest hyena, screaming and screaming with rage and hatred, screaming the word *chimbwi* over and over again.

The hyenas turned and ran.

The man with the girl's name walked out of the trees, with six soldiers carrying Kalashnikovs. He beckoned. Jason shook his head slowly. It was a quarter of a mile downhill to the river.

"You are in Tanzania, now," Arisa said. "They have no jurisdiction here. I hope you will come willingly. But you will come. You will be well-looked after. We may even give you back to the Zambians when we have what we need from you."

"I have nothing you could want," said Jason. "So, I'll say goodbye."

Arisa was wrapped in a Masai cloth. He raised his long walking stick and pointed. The soldiers moved forwards.

Four marabous banked their eight-foot wingspan and dived. They spat plasma and the trees around Arisa and his men exploded into flame.

The white-skinned, bleeding, exhausted warrior turned his back on them and walked down the steep slope towards the lip of the falls.

Miriam was standing at the other side of the Kalambo. The river was fast but shallow here on the lip of the falls. Shallow, but slippery on the rocks, and eight hundred feet is too long a drop to survive. Jason looked upstream for a safer crossing, then shook his head, and stepped into the water just an arm's length from the edge. The river was flowing fast. He had no strength. His foot slipped and he stumbled, reaching underwater to grab a split in the rock. He was inches from the gulf. She waded into the water, coming to help him, but he shouted "No!" and she stood still. Slowly he moved away from the lip of the falls and groped his way across the river.

Miriam said nothing. She took his hand and touched a small rod to his refugee bracelet. It sprang open, and she caught it and handed it to him. He felt a waterfall of emotion sweep through him. Things held back rushed into every part of him. He stood, naked and bleeding, at the lip of the falls and threw the bracelet out into the air and watched it fall into the spray below. He stood and so profoundly wanted to jump.

"They weren't stupid, were they, my people?" Miriam asked.

"No," he said, "not at all."

"So?"

"Gravity is god. I get it. I really do. All that's left of me gets it."

She splashed him with the cool water until he was clean and rubbed a balm into his lacerated back.

They walked up the gravel path to the open area where the tourist buses usually stopped. On the way she handed him a sheet of cloth and helped him wrap it around himself. In the car park more than a hundred men, women and children went down on one knee and said, as though with a single voice, "*Mwapoleni baChitikela*. Greetings, Little Chief."

A fat blue pig flew in from the north and landed behind the crowd, who laughed and clapped. "That's yours, baby. And by the way, you're not *the* chief, but you're the only theoretical physicist ever to do the warrior's climb, so you're a chief for today," Miriam said. There was a pot sitting over a charcoal stove. Jason accepted a length of plastic tube from Chief Mulenga, who was mostly known as the Director of the research institute, pushed it down through the steaming scum on the surface, and sucked long and hard on the hot honey beer. A young girl came up and shyly presented him with a pair of very good shoes. A boy brought him a garland of flame lilies.

Jason turned to Chief Mulenga, and said "I'd like to meet the last one who did the climb."

Mulenga smiled. "That's a bit difficult," he said. "To the best of our knowledge, nobody's done it for a couple of hundred years."

They stood, waiting for his speech. It was very brief.

He pointed to his legs and said, "A white man knows he is at home in Africa when he wears shorts every day and grows hair on his knees."

Then the drumming started. Multi-coloured laser beams flashed across the valley and intersected. Each intersection caused a crack or boom of sound, deep, sharp, a deafening cascade of pulsating cross-rhythms that sent the storks into ecstatic loopings of the loop and cobra to shift their heads to the beat and even *chimbwi* the hyena danced on his shrunken back legs, and far downstream on the banks of the flowing Kalambo two leopards twined together amongst the trees and danced and the whole valley flashed with rainbow light and sang, each to his own, including the humans, the ancient songs of life.

His head was dizzy with the honey beer as she led him up a path he'd never seen, to a *rondavel*. The walls weren't made of mud, the thatched roof wasn't made of reeds, and the window gaps had little force fields to keep out the insects and let in the breeze. But it looked like a hut. The moon was a fat fish struggling to get out of the bright net of the Milky Way.

She caught hold of his hand and touched his fingertip to the sensor by the door. It swung back, and the interior lights came on, low and warm. "Your new house," she said. "Feel entirely free to change the decorations."

They went in. The door closed softly behind them.

The bed was wide and covered with golden sheepskin. "I just thought that every Jason should have his fleece."

He laughed, and they laughed together, and then they stood close but awkward.

After a while she said, "I think I read somewhere that you are an expert on Knot Theory."

He shrugged modestly.

"Can you help me with this?" she asked, pointing to knot that tied her *chikwembe* around her. And so Jason untied the knot and they fell together onto the Golden Fleece, and made love until the moon had long escaped and the sun was getting ready to shine his hot embarrassed face on Africa.

In the dawn light they were tangled up in the sheepskin and her leg was across his hips.

Her eyes opened, and suddenly flooded with tears. "We have a terrible thing to ask, baby warrior," she said.

He kissed her nose and asked, "What's that?"

There was a long pause, and then she said, "We need you to go back to Europe."

In the far distance *chimbwi*, the hyena, laughed and the world and the sun stopped. Down at the edge of Lake Tanganyika lay the bodies of two crocodiles, each drilled neatly through by a laser beam. But Miriam wasn't going to tell Jason that, and the crocodiles couldn't.

Dead Man's Run

ROBERT REED

Here's another novella by Robert Reed, whose "A History of Terraforming" appears elsewhere in this book. Here, Reed does an excellent job of making this simultaneously a murder mystery and a valid science fiction story where the SF element is essential to both the resolution of the plot and the solving of the mystery; it also functions in a vivid way as a sports story, since the sport of running is integral to the plot, and Reed's obvious familiarity with runners and running—he's used the sport before in other stories—shows through to excellent effect as Reed sprints the reader along to the finish line. . . .

ONE

The phone wakes him. Lucas snags it off the nightstand and clips it to the right side of his face. The caller has to be on the Allow list, so he opens the line. Lucas isn't great with numbers and even worse reading, but he has a genius for sounds, for voices. A certain kind of silence comes across. That's when he knows.

"When are we running?" the voice says.

"You're not running," Lucas says. "You're dead."

He hangs up.

Right away, Lucas feels sorry. Guilty, a little bit. But mostly pissed because he knows how this will play out.

The nightstand clock and phone agree. It's three minutes after five in the morning. What calls itself Wade Tanner is jumping hurdles right now, trying to slip back on the Allow list. That race can last ten seconds or ten minutes. Sleep won't happen till this conversation is done. But calling Wade's home number makes it look like Lucas wants to chat, which he doesn't. And that's why he tells his phone to give up the fight, letting every call through.

The ringing begins.

"You know what you need?" says a horny foreign-girl voice. "Fun."

Lucas hangs up and watches. A dozen calls beg to be answered. Two dozen. Obvious adult crap and beach sale crap are flagged. He picks from what's left over, and a man says, "Don't hang up, I beg you." The accent is familiar and

pleasant, making English sing. "I live in Goa and haven't money for air conditioning and food too. But I have a daughter, very pretty."

Lucas groans.

"And a little son," the voice says, breaking at the edges. "Do you know despair,
my friend? Do you understand what a father will do to save his precious blood?"

Lucas hangs up and picks again.

The silence returns, that weird nothing. And again, what isn't Wade says,
"What time are we running?"

"Seven o'clock," Lucas says.

"From the Y?"

"Sure." Lucas has a raspy voice that always seems a little loud, rolling out of
the wide, expressive mouth. Sun and wind can be rough on runners, but worse
enemies have beaten up his face. The bright brown eyes never stop jumping.
The long black hair is graying and growing thin up high. But the forty-year-old
body is supremely fit—broad shoulders squared up, the deep chest and narrow
trunk sporting a pair of exceptionally long legs.

"Are you running with us?" says Wade.

"Yeah." Lucas sits up in bed, the cold dark grabbing him.

"Who else is coming?"

Whenever Wade talks, other sounds flow in. It feels as if the dead man is sitting in a big busy room, everybody else trying to be quiet while he chats. That's
how Lucas pictures things: Too many people pushed together, wanting to be
quiet but needing to whisper, to breathe.

Wade says, "Who else?"

"Everybody, I guess."

"Good."

"Yeah, but I need to sleep now."

"Sleep's overrated," says Wade.

"Most things are."

The voice laughs. It used to be crazy, hearing that laugh. And now it's nothing
but normal.

"So I'll leave you alone," says Wade. "Besides, I've got other calls to make."

And again, that perfect nothing comes raining back. The sound the world
makes when it isn't saying anything.

Lucas can't sleep, but he can always drink coffee.

By six-thirty, an entire pot is in his belly and his blood. Fifty-two degrees
inside the house, and he's wearing the heavy polypro top and blue windbreaker
and black tights, all showing their years. But the shoes are mostly new. On the
kitchen television, Steve McQueen chases middle-aged hit men instead of doing
what makes sense, which is scrogging Jacqueline Bisset. McQueen drives, and
Lucas cleans the coffee machine and counter and the Boston Marathon '17 cup.
A commercial comes on—another relief plea—and Lucas turns it off in mid-
misery. Then he drops the thermostat five degrees and puts on clean butcher
gloves and the wool mittens that he's had for fifteen years. The headband slides
around his neck and he pulls on the black stocking cap that still smells like

mothballs. His pack waits beside the back door, ready to go. He straps it on, leaving only one more ritual—throwing his right foot on a stool and twisting the fancy bracelet so it rides comfortably on the bare ankle, tasting flesh, telling the world that he is sober.

The outside air is frigid and blustery. Lucas trots down the driveway and turns into the wind. Arms swing easy, lending momentum to a stride that needs no help. Even slow, Lucas looks swift. Every coach dreams of discovering a talent like his—this marriage of strength, grace, and blood-born endurance. Set a mug of beer on that head and not a drop splashes free. The stride is that smooth, that elegant. That fine. But biology demands that a brain has to inhabit that perfect body, and there's more than one way to drain a damn mug of beer.

A person doesn't have to read the news to know the news.

Two sets of sirens are wailing in the distance, chasing different troubles. Potholes and slumping slabs make the street interesting, and half of the streetlights have had their bulbs pulled, saving the city cash and keeping a few lumps of coal from being burned. Every house is dark and sleepy, stuffed full of insulation and outfitted with wood-burning stoves. Most yards have gardens and compost piles and rain barrels. Half the roofs are dressed in solar panels. When Lucas moved into his house, big locusts and pin oaks lined the street. But most of those trees have been chopped down for fuel and to let the sun feed houses and gardens. Then the lumberjacks planted baby trees—carbon patriots lured by the tax gimmicks—except the biggest of those trees are already being sacrificed for a few nights of smoky heat.

You don't have to travel the world to know what's happening.

The last house on the block is the Florida compound. Those immigrants rolled in a couple years ago, boasting about their fat savings and their genius, sports hero kids. But there aren't any jobs outside the Internet and grunt work in the windmill fields, and savings never last as long as you wish. Their big cars got dumped on the Feds during an efficiency scheme. Extra furniture and jewelry were sold to make rent. A cigarette boat and trailer were given FOR SALE signs to wear, and they're still wearing them, sitting on the driveway where they've been parked forever. Then came the relatives from Miami begging for room, and that's when police started getting calls about drinking and fighting, and then a couple of the sports heroes were jailed for trafficking. Then it was official: These were refugees, and not even high-end refugees anymore.

Cheeks ache when Lucas runs at the wind, but nothing else. Turning west, the world warms ten degrees. In the dark it's best to keep to the middle of the street, watching for anything that can trip or chase. People will abandon family and homes on drowning beaches, but not their pit bull and wolf-mutts. It's also smart to run with your phone off, but Lucas is better than most when it comes to handling two worlds at once. His piece of Finland is a sweet little unit powered by movement, by life. A tidy projection hangs in front of his right eye. He's ignoring the screen for the moment, running the street with the imaginary dogs, and that's when the ringing starts.

"Yeah?"

"You leave yet?" Wade says.

"Nope, still sitting," says Lucas. "Drinking coffee, watching dead people on TV."

That wins a laugh. "According to GPS, you're running. An eight-minute pace, which is knuckle-walking for you."

"Do the cops know?" says Lucas.

"Know what?"

"That you're borrowing their tracking system."

"Why? You going to turn me in?"

No, but that's when Lucas cuts the line, and an old anger comes back, making his legs fly for the next couple blocks.

Bodies stand outside the downtown YMCA. Swimmers and weightlifters sport Arctic-ready coats, while the runners are narrower, colder souls wearing nylon and polypro. Gym bags clutter up the sidewalk. Every back is turned to the wind. When someone breathes or speaks, twists of vapor rise, illuminated by the bluish glare escaping from the Y's glass door.

Lucas slows.

A growly voice says, "Somebody got the early jump."

Passing from the trot into a purposeful walk, Lucas looks at faces, smiling at Audrey before anybody else.

"Where's your bike?" the voice asks.

"Pete," says Audrey. "Just stop."

But the temptation is too great. With amiable menace, Pete Kajan says, "Did the cops take your bike too?"

"Yeah," says Lucas. "My bike and skates and my skis. I had that pony, but they shot him. Just to be safe."

Everybody laughs at the comeback, including Pete.

Lucas slips off the pack and shakes his arms. The straps put his fingers to sleep.

"Seven o'clock," Pete says, shaking one of the locked doors. "What are the big dogs doing today?"

"Sitting on the porch, whining," Lucas says.

Runners laugh.

"How far?" Audrey says.

Pete says, "Twelve, maybe fourteen."

"Fourteen sounds right," says Doug Gatlin. Fast Doug. He's older than the rest of them but blessed with a whippet's body.

Doug Crouse is the youngest and heaviest. "Ten miles sounds better," he says.

"Sarah and Masters are coming," says Fast Doug.

"They wish," says Pete, laughing.

Rolling his eyes, Gatlin tells Crouse, "They'll meet us here and turn early. You can come back with them."

"Where's Varner?" Crouse says.

Pete snorts. "He'll be five minutes late and need to dump."

Runners laugh.

Then a big-shouldered swimmer rattles the locked door.

Crouse looks at Lucas. "Did he call you?"

"Yeah."

"He called me twice," Gatlin says.

"Everybody got at least one wake-up call," Pete says.

The runners stare into the bright empty lobby.

"He usually doesn't bother me," says Crouse.

"A bad night in heaven," Lucas says.

People try to hit the proper amount of laughter. Show it's funny, but nothing too enthusiastic.

Then the swimmer backs away from the door. "Dean's here," she says.

Dean is a tall, fleshy fellow who does everything with deliberation. He slowly walks the length of the lobby. As if disarming a bomb, he eases the key into the lock. The door weighs a thousand pounds, judging by its syrupy motion. With a small soft voice, Dean says, "Cold enough?"

Muttered replies make little threads of steam.

A line forms in the lobby. Audrey puts herself beside Lucas. "You think that's it? He had a bad night?"

"I'm no thinker," Lucas says. "If I get my shoes on in the morning, it's going to be a good day."

TWO

Fingers and thumbs are offered at the front desk, proving membership. A red sign warns patrons to take only one towel, but a Y towel can't dry a kitten. Lucas grabs two, Pete three. The Dougs lead the way up narrow, zigzagging stairs. Signs caution about paint that dried last week and forbid unaccompanied boys in the men's locker room. At the top of the stairs, taped to a steel door, a fresh notice says there isn't any hot water, due to boiler troubles. Gatlin flips light switches. The room revealed is narrow and long, jammed with gray lockers and concrete pillars painted yellow. The carpet is gray-green and tired. Toilet cleansers and spilled aftershave give the air flavor. Bulletin boards are sprinkled with news about yoga classes and winter conditioning programs and words about winning at life. Questionable behavior must be reported to the front desk. Used towels are to be thrown into the proper bins. Lockers need to be locked. The YMCA is never responsible for stolen property. But leave your padlock overnight on a day locker, and it will be cut off and your belongings will be confiscated.

"This is your YMCA," a final sign says.

Pete rents a locker in back. Lucas camps nearby. From the adjacent aisle, Gatlin says, "What's the course? Anybody know?"

"I know," Pete says, and that's all he says. In his early forties, he has short graying hair and a sturdy face. He glowers easily, the eyes a bright, thoughtful hazel. Pete doesn't look like a runner, but when motivated and healthy, the man can still hang with the local best.

Lucas digs out his lock, dumps his pack and secures the door. Again, he puts his foot on the stool, adjusting the ankle monitor. Water sounds good, but the Freon was bled from the fountains, saving energy. It's better to run the cold tap at a sink and make a bowl with your hands, wasting a couple gallons before your thirst is beaten back. The paper towels are tiny. He pulls five and dries his hands, watching an old guy plug in an old television that can't remember yesterday. The machine has to cycle through channels, reprogramming its little brain. That's when Lucas starts to feel the coffee. The urinal is already full of dark piss but won't flush until the smell is bad enough. He comes back out to find the Big Fox playing. A blond beauty is chatting about the cold snap cutting into the heart of the country. "We have an old-fashioned winter," she says, leading to thirty seconds of snow and sleds and happy red-faced kids.

"Well, that's not me," says the old guy.

Then the news jumps to places Lucas couldn't find on any map. Brown people are fighting over burning oil wells. Skinny black folks are marching across a dried-up lake. A fat white man with an accent makes noise about his rights and how he doesn't appreciate being second-class. Then it's down to Pine Island and the wicked long Antarctic summer. Another slab of glacier is charging out to sea, looking exactly like the other ten thousand. But the blond gal is a trouper. Refusing to be sad, she reminds her audience that some experts claim the cold melt water is going to shut down this nastiness. More sexy than scientific, she says, "The oceans around the ice sheets will cool, and a new normal will emerge. Then we can get back to the business of ordinary life."

"Well, that's good news," says the old guy, throwing out a pissy laugh as he starts hunting for better channels.

Pete and the Dougs have vanished. Lucas starts for the stairs and the steel door bangs open. In comes Varner, still wearing street clothes.

"I'll be there. Got to hit the toilet first."

The man is in his middle-thirties, red-haired and freckled and always late. Lucas gives him a look.

"What? It's two minutes after seven."

"I didn't say anything."

"Yeah, well. Our ghost already called me three times, telling me to hurry the hell up."

Lucas retreats downstairs. Audrey stands in the lobby, reading the *Herald* on the public monitor. She's tall for an elite runner—nearly five-nine—but unlike most fast girls doesn't live two snacks clear of starvation. Her face is strong but pretty, blond hair cut close, middle-age lurking around the pale brown eyes. She wears silver tights and a black windbreaker, mittens and a headband piled on the countertop. Audrey always looks calm and rested. Running is something she does well, but if nobody showed this morning, she'd probably trot an easy eight and call it good.

"Where are the boys?" Lucas says.

"Around the corner."

"Any news about me?"

She blanks the screen and turns. "Where's your bike?"

"Too cold to peddle."

"If you need a ride, call."

"I should," he says.

With a burst of wind, the front door opens.

Ethan Masters walks out of a sportswear catalog and into the YMCA. Jacket and tights are matched blue with artful white stripes, the Nikes just came from the box, his gloves and stocking cap are carved from fresh snow, and the water belt carries provisions for a hundred-mile slog. But the biggest fashion statement is the sleek glasses covering the middle of a lean, thoroughly shaved face. More computing power rides his nose than NASA deployed during the 20th Century. The machine is a phone and entertainment center. Masters always knows his pulse and electrolyte levels and where he is and how fast he's moving. It must be a disappointment, falling back on old-fashioned eyes to tell him what's inside the lobby. "They're still here," he says. "I told you we'd make it in time."

Sarah follows him indoors. As short as Masters is tall, she has this round little-girl face and long brown hair tied in a ponytail. Unlike her training partner, she prefers old sweats and patched pink mittens, and her brown stocking cap looks rescued from the gutter. They are married, but not to each other—ten thousand miles logged together and the subjects of a lot of rich gossip.

"Are you everybody?" says Masters, throwing himself against a wall, stretching calves. "If we wait, we'll tighten up."

"Varner just went upstairs," Audrey says.

"So we're not leaving soon," says Masters.

Sarah is quiet. Flicking her eyes, she places a call and walks to the back of the lobby.

Lucas follows and walks past her, rounding the corner. Behind the lobby is a long narrow room overlooking the swimming pool. Treadmills and ellipticals push against the glass wall. Pete and the Dougs are yabbering with some over-dressed, undertrained runners who belong to the marathon clinic. Which means they belong to the bald man sitting alone beside the Gatorade machine.

"How far, Coach?" Lucas says.

The man looks up. Cheery as an elf, he says, "We're doing an easy sixteen." As if sixteen were nothing. As if he's making the run himself. Except Coach Able is dressed for driving and maybe, if pressed, a quick stand on some protected street corner. Deep in his fifties, he carries a bad back as well as quite a lot of fat. And for thirty years he has been the running coach at Jewel College, his clinic some-thing of a spring tradition for new runners.

Able gives Lucas a long study. He always does. And he always has a few coachy words to throw out for free.

"It looks like you're running heavy miles," he says.

"Probably so," Lucas says.

"Speed work?"

"When I remember to."

"Try the marathon this year. See if there's life in those old legs."

"Maybe I will." Lucas looks at the other runners. A man with an accent is talk-ing about the weather, about how it was never so cold in Louisiana. Pete shakes his head, a big snarly voice saying, "So grow some fins and swim yourself back home again."

Somehow he can say words like that, and everybody finds it funny.

The coach coughs—a hard wet bark meant to win attention. "Tell me, Pep-per. In your life, have you ever tried running a marathon hard? Train for it and push it and see what happens?"

"Well now, that sure sounds like work."

"I think you could beat 2:30," says Able. "And who knows how fast, if you managed a full year without misbehaving."

Lucas rolls his shoulders, saying nothing.

"There's software," the coach says. "And biometric tests. With race results, we'd be able to figure out exactly what you would have run in your prime. 2:13 is my guess. Wouldn't it be nice to know?"

"That would be nice," says Lucas. Then he shrugs again, saying, "But like my dad used to say, 'There's not enough room in the world for all the things that happen to be nice.'"

Audrey appears. "We've got our Varner."

Lucas and the other men put on stocking caps and follow. Eight bodies bunch up at the front door. The sun is coming, but not yet. Everybody wears a phone, and with tiny practiced touches, they adjust the settings. Only hair-on-fire emergency calls can interrupt now. Then the group puts on mittens and gloves and steps outside. Giving a horse-snort, Masters says, "We should run north."

"We're not," says Pete. "We're doing Ash Creek."

Everybody is surprised.

"But you want to start into the wind," Masters says. "Otherwise you'll come home wet and cold."

"There's not two damn trees up north," Pete says. "I'm going where there's woods and scenery."

"What about the usual?" Varner says.

They have a looping course through the heart of town.

"Normal is fine with me," Audrey says.

Lucas wants to move. Directions don't matter.

Then Pete says, "We've got company."

Trotting across the street is a kid half their age. Dressed in street clothes and a good new coat, Harris carries a huge gym bag in one hand. "Which way?" he says. "I'll catch up."

Pete says, "The usual." No hesitation.

"East around Jewel?" says Harris.

"Sure."

The kid scampers inside.

Then Pete gives everybody a hard stare. "Okay, we're doing Ash Creek. No arguments."

Eight liars trot west, nobody talking, the tiniest guilt following at their heels.

THREE

Tuesday meant speed work at the college track—a faded orange ribbon of crumbling foam and rutted lanes. Lucas showed last. It wasn't as hot as most August evenings, but last night's storm left the air thick and dangerous. The rest of the group trotted on the far side of the track. Nobody was talking. Lucas parked his bike and came through the zigzag gate, and he crossed the track and football field and the track again, walking under the visitor's stands. Pigeons panicked and flew off, leaving feathers and echoes. He opened his pack and stripped, dressing in shorts and Asics but leaving his singlet in the bag. He was packing up when he noticed his hands shaking, and he stared at the hands until his phone broke the spell.

He opened the line.

"Are you up at the track?"

Wade's voice. "I am."

"Do you see me?"

"Wade?"

"I haven't been updated," the voice said. "It's been twenty-four hours. I'm supposed to call you after twenty-four hours."

Lucas stepped out from under the seats. "Who is this?"

"Wade Tanner kept an avatar. A backup."

"I know that."

"I'm the backup, Lucas."

The group shuffled through the south turn, and Wade wasn't any of them. "Did you try the store?" Lucas said.

"No, because you're at the top of the list," the backup said. "One day passes without an update, and I'm supposed to contact you first."

"Me."

"You live close and you know where the spare key is. We want you to search the house." The voice went away and then came back. "I've studied the odds. Check the shower. Showers are treacherous places."

Walking across the brown grass, Lucas started to laugh. Nothing was funny, but laughing felt right.

"What's your workout tonight?" said the voice.

"Don't know."

"It's humid," the backup said. "Do quarters and walk half-a-lap before going again. Take a break after six, and quit if you forget how to count."

It could have been the real Wade. "You sound just like him."

"That's how it works." Then after a pause, the backup said, "I've got this bad feeling, Lucas."

"Why's that?"

"I'm voicemail, too. And people have been calling all day. Nobody knows where Wade is."

Lucas said nothing.

"You'll check the house?"

"Soon as I'm done running quarters."

"Thanks, buddy."

The line fell silent.

Most of the people were sharing the same patch of shade. Audrey was walking back and forth on the track, talking on the phone. Only Gatlin and Wade were missing. The new kid jumped toward Lucas, saying, "Are we running or not?"

"Leave him alone," Pete said. "Our boy put in a rough weekend."

Harris had a big sandpaper laugh. "I was at the party. Yeah, I saw him drinking."

People look away, embarrassed for Lucas.

"I've known a few drinkers," the kid said. "But I never, ever saw anybody drain away that much of anything."

Lucas looked past him. "Anybody see Wade?"

"Bastard's late," Pete said.

The others said, "No," or shook their heads. Except for Harris, who just kept grinning and staring at Lucas.

Lucas needed a breath. "Wade's backup just called me. It hasn't heard from him, and it's worried."

"Why would the backup call you?" Sarah said.

Lucas shrugged, saying nothing.

"Wade has an avatar?" said Harris.

"He does," Masters said. "In fact, I helped him set it up."

Lucas waved a hand, bringing eyes back to him. "I know what they are," he said. "Except I don't know anything about them."

Masters stepped into the sunshine, his glasses turning black. With his know-everything voice, he said, "They're basically just personal records. Data you want protected, kept in hardened server farms. They have your financial records, video records. Diaries and running logs and whatever else you care about. You can even model your personality and voice, coming up with a pretty good stand-in."

"Wade has been doing this for years," Sarah said.

People turned to her, waiting.

Quiet little Sarah smiled, nervous with the attention. "Don't you know? He records everything he does, every day. He says it helps at the store, letting him know each of his customers. He even leaves his phone camera running, recording everything he sees and hears to be uploaded later."

"That's anal," Crouse said.

"Who's anal?" said Audrey, walking into the conversation.

"Storing that much video is expensive," Harris said. "How can a shoe sales-man afford a cashmere backup?"

"That shoe salesman had rich parents," Pete said. "And they were kind enough to die young."

With that, the group fell silent.

Lucas approached Audrey. "Was it Wade's backup on the phone?"

"No. Just my husband."

Harris got between them. "Let's run," he said.

"Not in the mood," Lucas said.

The kid looked at everybody, and then he was laughing at Lucas. "So what happened to you? You were drinking everything at the party . . . and then you just sort of vanished . . ."

"He had an appointment," Pete said.

"What appointment?"

Pete shook his head. "With the police."

Audrey wasn't happy. "Everybody, just stop. Quit it."

Masters was talking to Sarah. "How do you know so much about Wade's backup?" he said.

Sarah shrugged and smiled. "I just know."

Masters ate on that. Then he turned to Lucas, saying, "The call was a glitch.

Wade didn't get things uploaded last night, and it triggered the warning system. That's all."

Lucas nodded, wanting to believe it.

"Let's just run," Harris said.

"Is this how they do things in Utah?" Pete said. "Pester people till you get what you want?"

"Sometimes." The kid showed up at the track six weeks ago—a refugee running away from drought and forest fires. Harris liked to talk. He told everybody that he was going out on the prairie and build windmills. Except of course he didn't know anything about anything useful. His main talent was a pair of long strong and very young legs, and there were sunny looks and a big smile that was charming for two minutes, tops.

"I'm running," he said, smiling hard. Then he walked to the inside lane.

Others started to follow.

Not Lucas.

A little BMW pulled off the road and Gatlin got out. He wasn't dressed to run. A fifty-year-old man with wavy gray hair, he looked nothing but respectable in a summer suit and tie. Coming through the zigzag, he moved slowly, one hand always holding the chain-link. He seemed sad, and then the sadness fell into something darker. And with little steps, he walked toward the others.

"Well, now we've got to stop talking about you," said Pete.

Gatlin's mouth was open, a lost look passing through his dark brown eyes. "I just got a call," he said. "From a friend in the mayor's office. He thought I'd want to know. Kids playing near Ash Creek found a body this morning. And the police think they recognize the man."

"Wade Tanner," said Lucas.

Surprised, Gatlin straightened his back. "How did you know?"

"We had a hint," said Pete, and then he couldn't talk anymore.

Nobody was talking. Nobody reacted or moved, except for Gatlin who was embarrassed to have his awful news stolen from him. Besides the wind, the only sound was a soft low moan rising from nowhere.

Then Sarah closed her mouth, and the moaning stopped.

Downtown fights to wake up. City buses roll past on their way to still-empty stops. Bank tellers move through darkened lobbies while bank machines count piles of electronic money. Apartment lights come on, but the hotels have never been dark, filled with anxious refugees living on the government plan. A pair of long-haul boxes point in opposite directions, burning soybean juice to keep sleeping travelers warm. Out from the bus station comes a bearded man wearing a fine suit and carrying an I-tablet. Except the suit is filthy, both knees looking like they have been dragged through grease, and the tablet is dead, and talking in a loud crazed voice, he says, "Stop being proud. Accept Satan as our leader, and let's build a clean, efficient Hell."

The pace lifts, the group crossing into the old warehouse district. Concrete turns to cobblestone and black scabs of asphalt. Low brick buildings have been reborn as bars and pawnshops and coffee shops, plus one little store dedicated to runners. Dropping to the floodplain, the street ends with a massive stone building from the 19th Century. In one form or another, this place has always served as the city's train station. Half a dozen travelers are waiting with their luggage, hoping for the morning westbound, and the little boy in the group gives the runners a big wave, saying, "Hey there. Hi."

Nobody talks. The group turns south, gloom following them into Germantown. Warehouses give way to little houses, and they turn right, pointed west again, and the pace lifts another notch.

"Slow down," says Pete

Nobody listens. Runners and the street cross an abandoned set of railroad tracks. Little twists of vapor mark their breathing, shoes slapping at the pavement. Then comes the Amtrak line, and that's when the houses start to wear down. Cars sporting out-of-state plates are parked on brown lawns. A solitary drunk stands at a corner, calmly waiting for the race to pass before he staggers a little closer to what might be home. The final house has been reborn as a church, its walls painted candy colors and holy words written in Vietnamese. That's where the street ends. A barbed wire fence breaks where a thin trail snakes up through flattened prairie grass. The sky is dawn-blue with a few clouds. And somebody is running on top of the levee: A narrow male with tall legs and long arms carried high. It's a pretty stride. Not Lucas-pretty, but efficient. Strong. The man's legs are bare and pale. He wears a long-sleeved t-shirt, gray and tight, and maybe a second layer underneath. White butcher gloves cover big hands, and riding the head is a black baseball cap set backwards, the brim tucked low over the long neck.

As if their legs have been cut out from under them, people stumble to a halt.

"What's he doing here?" says Sarah.

Crouse is first to say, "Jaeger." Normally easygoing, almost sweet, Slow Doug puts on a sour face and says, "That prick."

"What is he doing?" Masters says.

"Running, by the looks of it," says Pete.

Jaeger is cruising south on the levee road, heading upstream. The other runners stand in shadow, but he is lit up by the dawn, his gaze fixed straight ahead, the sharp face showing in profile.

"So what?" says Audrey. "We'll just run the other way."

"I'm not," says Pete.

People glance at each other, saying nothing.

Starting toward the fence and trail, Pete says, "I don't change plans for murdering assholes."

Gatlin and Varner fall in behind him.

Lucas turns to Audrey. "Want to go back?"

She pulls off her hat and a mitten, running her hand through her short, short hair. "Maybe."

"We can't just stand here," says Masters.

"I'm not turning around," says Sarah, short legs working, the ponytail jumping and swishing.

Crouse trots after her. Then Audrey sighs and says, "I guess," and catches them before the fence.

"This is stupid," says Masters. But then he starts chasing.

Lucas stands motionless. Nobody can run out of sight on him, except Jaeger.

Maybe. He has time to pull off a mitten and wipe his mouth, ice already clinging to his little beard. Then he touches his phone to wake it, pulling up the familiar number with an eye and placing his call.

"How's the run going?" says Wade.

Lucas doesn't talk.

"I see where you are," Wade says. "Are we running the creek today?"

"We're supposed to."

"So why aren't you moving, Lucas?"

"Jaeger's up ahead."

There is a pause, a long breath of nothing before the voice returns. "You know what I want," Wade says. "I told you what I want. Find out who killed me, okay?"

FOUR

Wade was five days dead.

The heat and drought had returned, and the Saturday group met long before the Y opened. Standing in the broiling darkness, they said very little. Even Harris was playing the silent monk. One minute after six they took off to the east, aiming for Jewel College. Harris grabbed the lead, Lucas claimed the empty ground between him and the pack. Then Crouse put on a surge, catching Lucas. "Have you tried Wade's number?"

"Why would I?"

"Maybe you're curious," Crouse said.

"Not usually," said Lucas.

"Well, you can't get through. Voicemail answers, but even if you leave a message, the backup can't call you back."

"Why not?"

"He's evidence," Crouse said. "And maybe he's a witness. That's why they've got him bottled up."

"I forgot. You're a cop."

"No." The man hesitates, laughs. "But remember my sister-in-law?"

"The gal with black hair and that big bouncy ass," Lucas said.

"She's a police officer."

"That too."

"Anyway, she's got this habit. She has to tell my wife everything."

"Okay. Now I'm curious."

Crouse was running hard. Whenever he talked, he first had to gather up enough air. "Wade ran for Jewel."

Lucas glanced at him. "Everybody knows that."

"Came here on a scholarship. Able recruited him. Wade was the big star for the first year. Then this other guy showed."

"Carl Jaeger," said Lucas.

"You probably know the whole story," said Crouse, disappointed.

"Wade told it a couple times. Every day."

"Know where the coach found Jaeger?"

"In Chicago, in rehab. There were legal hoops, getting him out from under some old charges. But the kid had ruled Illinois during high school, and that's why Able brought him here. He wanted Jaeger to be his big dog, to help put Jewel on the map."

Crouse nodded, fighting to hold the pace.

Lucas slowed. "You're new to this group. You didn't know. But Wade and Jaeger never liked each other."

"What about the girl?" Crouse said.

Lucas said, "Yeah." But then he realized that he didn't know what they were talking about. "What girl?"

"Wade's girlfriend in college. Jaeger got her. Stole her and got her pregnant and even married her for a couple years."

"What's her name?" Lucas said.

"I don't know. I didn't hear that part. But the virtual Wade remembers every-thing." Crouse was happy, finding something fresh to offer. "The police depart-ment brought in specialists to sort through the files, the software. The AI business. The technology's been around for a few years, but the experts haven't seen a backup with this much information."

"That's Wade," said Lucas. "Mr. Detail."

"He kept training logs," said Crouse.

"Some of us do."

"You?"

"Never."

Crouse found fresh speed in his legs. "Wade's logs are different. They reach back to the day he started running, when he was eight. And there's a lot more than miles and times buried in them."

"Like what?"

"Sleep. Dreams. Breakfasts. And what he and his friends talked about during the run—word for word, sometimes. And he spends a lot of file space hating Carl Jaeger."

The girl news was unexpected. Lucas thought about it for a minute. Then he said, "So what's happening? Are the cops looking at Carl?"

"Oh, I'm not saying like that," said Crouse, reaching that point where his legs were shaky-weak. "I just thought you'd be interested in what's happening. That's all."

Runners are strung out along the levee. On the left little houses turn into body shops and junkyards and a sad pair of gray-white grain elevators. Ash Creek runs on their right, the channel gouged deep and straight and shouldered with pale limestone boulders. Fresh thin ice covers the shallow water. Pete and Gatlin run in front, Varner tucked into their slipstream. Snatches of angry conversa-tion drift back. With a big arm, Pete points toward Jaeger. He curses, and Gat-lin glances back at the others. Then the leaders slow, forcing the others to drift closer.

"I can't believe this," Masters says. "Why would the man run this course?"

"He likes the route," Lucas says, his legs deciding to leap ahead, quick feet kicking back gravel.

Crouse hears the stride coming. "Hey, Lucas," he says. And a moment later, he is passed.

The women are shoulder-to-shoulder. Audrey says a few words, laughing alone. Then she looks back at Lucas, her smile working. "What are those boys proving?"

"Don't know," Lucas says.

Audrey says, "Men," and laughs again.

Lucas runs on the grass beside them. Pete is forty yards ahead and surging, body tilting and arms churning. Nobody in that trio talks, every whisper of oxygen saved for the legs.

"Look at them," says Audrey.

"What about them?" Sarah says, her voice small and tight.

"They won't catch Carl," says Audrey.

"The man was in jail," Sarah says. "For months."

Audrey's face stiffens. "We're talking about Carl. There's no way they can close that gap."

Jaeger's legs and lungs are almost lost in the sunshine. But he isn't increasing his lead. Maybe he's starting out on a lazy twenty and holding back. Or he knows they're following him, and he just wants a little fun.

Lucas glances at Audrey.

"You don't have to chase," she says, her voice sharp.

He surges.

"Please, Lucas. Be careful."

The man who sold shoes to every athlete in town was lying inside a closed box, waiting to be set into the ground, and the church was full of skinny people and beefy old friends, with a few distant relatives sitting up front, hoping for a piece of the Wade pie. Everybody made sorry sounds about the circumstances. Every male tried to spot the ex-girlfriends in the audience. Wade was no beauty, but he had a genius for pretty girls who fell for charm and little hints of marriage. There were maybe a dozen exes in the crowd, some crying for what had happened and others for what hadn't. Lucas and Pete were pallbearers. They served with cousins and college buddies who didn't know them from a can of paint. It was a cousin who mentioned that the cops were done with the backup. He said anybody could call the machine and it was almost fun, talking to a voice that remembered when you were ten-years-old and sitting together at Thanksgiving, watching relatives get drunk and funny.

Lucas did call Wade's old number. But not right away and only twice and both times was surprised by the busy signal. Then he tried after midnight and got thrown straight into voicemail. Which pissed him off. Not that he was hungry for this chat, but it was sure to happen and why did things have to be so difficult?

His phone rang during next morning's coffee. "You know what surprises me? It's the strangers who read an obit and think it's neat, calling you for no reason but to chat. And it's not just local voices either. This is the big new hobby, I'm learning. Dial the afterlife. Listen to a ghost telling stories."

"How you doing?" Lucas said.

The backup said, "I'm busy. And that's a good thing."

"What's 'busy' mean?"

"Well, I'm running again. For instance."

"How do you do that?"

"I've got video files, and I've built all of our favorite courses. The hills, the effort levels. How my body responds to perceived workouts. I can change the weather however I want it. You'd be amazed how real it looks and feels. And the food here doesn't taste too wrong. Of course the sense of smell needs work, but that's probably good news. When it's polypro season."

Then Wade stopped talking, forcing Lucas to react. "Is that why I'm getting busy signals? You're making new friends?"

"And talking to people you know."

"But you're fast. Computers are. Why can't you yabber to a thousand mouths at once?"

"Some of my functions are fast. Scary fast, sure. But right now, talking to you, my AI software has to work flat-out just to keep up." Part of the software made lung noises. Wade took a pretend breath, and then he said, "I still need sleep, by the way. Which is why I didn't pick up last night."

Lucas didn't talk.

"So tell me, Lucas. In your head, what am I? A machine, a program, or a man?"

"I don't know."

"Actually, I'm none of those things."

"Because you're a ghost."

The laughter rattled on. "No, no. In the eyes of the law, I'm an intellectual foundation. That's a new kind of trust reserved for backups. I've been registered with a friendly nation that has some very compassionate laws, and to maintain my sentient status, I have to keep enough money in the local bank."

Lucas said nothing.

The silence ended with a big sigh. Then the intellectual foundation said, "So, Lucas? Do you have any idea who killed me?"

A little too quickly, Lucas said, "No."

Another pause. Then Wade said, "It was a nice funeral."

"You watched?"

"Several people streamed it to me. You did a nice job, Lucas."

It was peculiar, how much those words mattered. Lucas took his own breath, real and deep, and then he said, "You know, I am sober."

"What's that?"

"Since the party, I haven't had a taste."

Uncomfortable sighs kept the silence away. Then a tight quick voice said, "Tell me that in another year. Tell it to me thirty years from today. A couple weeks without being shit-faced? I think it's early to start calling that good news."

The lead pack works, but Lucas catches them easily. Legs eat the distance, the lungs blow themselves clean, and he tucks in behind Pete, shortening his stride and measuring their bodies. Nobody talks, but the men trade looks and the group slows, making ready for the next miserable surge.

The levee curls west toward the bypass and dives under the bridge. Jaeger has vanished. He isn't below, and he's not up on the highway either. They follow the levee road down, gravel replaced with pale frozen clay. The air turns colder, tasting like wet concrete. Water sounds bounce off the underside of the bridge. Then the road yanks left and starts a long climb.

Jaeger is above them, and then he is gone.

Pete curses. Sweat bleeds through his windbreaker and freezes, a little white forest growing on his back.

Topping the levee, they hold their effort, gaining speed on the flat. But the road is empty. Except nodding brown grass, nothing moves, and there isn't anybody to chase.

The pack slows.

"Look," Varner says. "That pipe."

The sewer pipe is fat and black, jutting out of the levee's shoulder, a thin trickle of oily runoff dripping. Jaeger stands on the pipe, facing the stream. With his shorts yanked down, he holds himself with both hands, aiming long, urine splashing in the oil.

Pete pulls up. The rest of the group stops behind him, watching. Then Jaeger turns towards them and shakes himself dry before yanking up his underwear and then the shorts.

"Let's please turn," says Audrey.

No one else talks.

Jaeger climbs back to the road, watching them.

"Hey, asshole," says Pete. "Hey."

The last months have taken a toll. Jaeger's face remains lean, but wrinkles have worked into his features. The short black hair shows white. He breathes harder than normal. Forty-three years old, and for the first time anyone can recall, he looks his age.

"I don't like this," says Masters.

Pete laughs. "What are worried about?"

Jaeger's body turns away, but not his face.

"There's eight of us," says Pete.

"What's that mean?" Crouse says.

"Depends," Pete says, his bulldog face challenging them. "We're here, and that man is standing over there. And he beat our friend to death with a chunk of concrete."

Jaeger starts running, the first strides short.

Audrey shakes her head. "What are we doing?"

Sarah knows.

"We're just following the man," Sarah says, her voice slow and furious. "Jaeger can't be in great shape. But we are. So we'll keep close and talk to him, and maybe he'll say something true."

FIVE

Lucas rode to the airport, the chain clicking. A gray-haired woman handed him the entry form, and he filled in the blanks slowly, paying the late fee with two twenties. Then he pinned the race number to his shorts and strapped the chip to his right shoe, and the new t-shirt ended up tied beneath the seat of his bike.

The pre-race mood was quiet, grim. Conversations were brief. Race-day rituals were performed with sluggish discipline. The normally bouncy voice on the PA system growled at the world, warning that only twenty minutes were left until the gun. Bikes don't get bodies ready to run. Lucas started running easy through the mostly empty parking lots, past a terminal that looked pretty much shut down, and that's when a tall man stepped from behind an Alleycat Dumpster.

"Pepper."

Lucas nodded, lifting one hand.

Jaeger fell in beside him. He was wearing racing flats and shorts and a White Sox cap twisted around on his head. Saying nothing, he ran Lucas back to his bike, watching him strip the shirt he wore from home and then tie it to the frame.

"Lose your car?" he said.

"I know where it is."

"Got fancy jewelry on that ankle, I see."

Lucas lifted his foot and put it down again. "Jealous?"

"Jail time?"

"If I drink."

"With your record? They should keep you in a cage for a year."

"The jail's full." Lucas shrugged. "And besides, the case wasn't strong."

"No?"

"Maybe I wasn't driving." Shame forced his gaze to drop. "Somebody called the hotline, but it was a busy night. One cop spotted my car and flashed her lights, and my car pulled up and a white male galloped off between the houses."

"That cop chase after the driver?"

"On foot, but she couldn't hang on."

"I bet not," Jaeger said, laughing.

"A second cruiser found me half a mile away, while he was investigating a burglary. Just happened to trip over me."

Lucas' phone started to ring.

"I don't know how you run with those machines," Jaeger said. "Mine's an old foldable, and I put it away sometimes."

Lucas opened the line.

"Five minutes," said Wade.

"Five minutes," said the public address voice.

Wade said, "How do you feel?"

"Talk to you later, okay?" Lucas hung up.

Jaeger was watching him and the phone. He didn't ask who called, but when Lucas looked at him, the man offered what might have been a smile, shy and a little sorry.

"See you out there. Okay, Pepper?"

The levee twists to the southeast, ending at the park's north border. Hold that road, and Jaeger will work his way back into town. Any reasonable man would do that. But as soon as he hits Foster Lane, Jaeger jumps right and surges. And just to be sure that everyone understands, he throws back a little sneer as he crosses Ash Creek.

Pete and Varner are leading, milking the speed from their legs. Audrey is beside Lucas, but she won't chase anymore. Arms drop and her stride shortens. "You can't catch him," she says.

"Watch us," says Pete.

"Then what?" she says.

Nobody answers. They make Foster and turn together, bunching up as they cross the rusted truss bridge. Pounding feet make the old steel shiver, and the wind cuts sideways, sweaty faces aching.

"I can't run this fast," Sarah says.

"Nobody can," says Crouse.

Up ahead, past the bridge, the road yanks to the left, placing itself between the water and tangled second-growth woods. They watch Jaeger striding out, and then Masters says, "We've got to slow down."

But Pete has a plan. "If he runs the trails, we'll cut him off."

"He won't," Audrey says. "That would be stupid."

They come off the bridge, and Pete slows. "We'll split up," he says. "Fast legs chase, the rest wait up ahead."

Jaeger is pushing his lead.

"A turnoff's coming," Lucas says.

"Half a mile up," says Gatlin. "The park entrance."

"No, it's there," he says. "Soon."

And just like that, Jaeger turns right, leaping over a pile of gray gravel before diving into the brush. Two long strides and he becomes this pale shape slipping in and out of view, and with another stride, he's gone.

Varner curses.

"Run ahead or chase," says Pete.

Sarah and Masters fall back. And Crouse. Then Audrey says, "No," to somebody and drops away too.

Pete and Varner accelerate, Gatlin falling in behind them. Lucas holds his pace, looking at his feet, measuring the life in his legs. Then he slips past everybody and yanks himself to the right, plunging into the bare limbs. The others miss the tiny trail and overshoot. Alone, Lucas drops off the roadbed, following a rough little path to where it joins up with the main trail—a wide slab of black earth and naked roots that bends west and plunges.

Gravity takes him. Lifting his feet, Lucas aims for smooth patches of frozen ground, dancing over roots and little gullies. Then the trail flattens, trees replaced by a forest of battered cattails.

Lucas slows, breathes.

The others chug up behind. "I don't see him," says Varner.

Far ahead, an ancient cottonwood lies dead on its side—a ridge of white wood stripped of bark, shining in the chill sunshine. Before anyone else, Lucas sees the black ball cap streaking behind the tree, and he surges again, nothing easier in the world than making long legs fly.

"Five minutes," said the rumbling PA voice. But a minute later he said, "No, folks. We're going to have a short delay."

People assumed that a plane was coming, which was a rare event and every eye looked skyward. Except nothing was flying on that hot September morning. Lucas lined up next to Audrey, toes at the start line. Pete and Gatlin and Varner were on the other side of her. Crouse was a few rows back with Masters. Sarah was missing, and Lucas couldn't see Jaeger anymore. Like a puppy, Harris sprinted out onto the empty runway and trotted back again. Then he wasted another burst of speed, and Pete said, "What lottery did we lose and get him?"

Laughter came from everywhere, and then it collapsed.

Carl Jaeger had appeared. Where he was hiding was a mystery, but he was suddenly standing at the line. He had come here to race. Inside himself, the man was making ready for the next ten kilometers. Forty-plus years old and nobody could remember him losing to a local runner. It was an astonishing record demanding conditioning and focus and remarkable luck. Staring at the tape in front of his left toes, he didn't seem to notice the detectives pushing under the barricade, coming at him with handcuffs at the ready.

"Keep your hands where we can see them," said the lead cop.

Jaeger's legs tensed, long calves twitching. He looked up, saying, "You don't want me." Then he looked down, staring at the gray pavement, and talking to his feet, he said, "Just let me run this. Just let me."

SIX

The trail leaps out of the marsh and flattens, fading into a lawn of clipped brown grass. Stone summer-camp buildings have been abandoned for the winter, every door padlocked and plywood sheets screwed into every window. Lucas holds his line, and the buildings fall away. Then the trail is under him again, yanking to the left, and the clearing ends with trees and a deep gully and a narrow bridge made from oak planks and old telephone poles.

Habit keeps him on the trail. Seepage has pooled at the bottom and frozen on top, and the ice broke where Jaeger's right foot must have planted. The muddy water is still swirling. Lucas cuts his stride. His legs decide to jump early. He knows that he won't reach the far bank, and his lead foot hits and breaks through, and he flings his other leg forward, dragging the trailing foot out of the muck before it's drenched.

The effort slows him, and the next slope is dark and very slick and slow, and that's how the others pass him.

Shoes drum on the oak planks. Pete is up ahead, hollering a few words that end with a question mark.

"What?" Lucas says.

Varner slows, looking down at him. "Where is he?"

Then Pete says, "Got him."

Lucas is on the high ground again. The woods are young and closely packed, the trail winding through the little trees until it seems as if there is no end. Then everybody dives again, back down into the cattails. Jaeger is a gray shape catching the sunshine. Bent forward a little too much, he swings his arms to help drive his legs, attacking the next rise.

A second cottonwood lies in the bottoms, the trunk and heavy roots made clean and simple by years of rot.

"Shortcut," says Lucas.

Pete says some little word. He and Varner are suffering, pitching forward long before they reach the slope. Only Gatlin looks smooth, his tiny frame floating out into the lead.

Lucas steers left, meaning to leap the tree, but he doesn't have the lift, the juice. His lead foot hits and he grabs at the wood with the mittens, then the trailing foot clips the trunk and slows him. He stops, looking down from a place where he's never been before. A thin old trail leads up the middle of the cattails. He jumps down and runs it, alone again.

A distant voice drifts past. No word makes sense. Then the only sound is the wind high above and the pop of his feet. Lucas' face drips. Still running, he pulls off the mittens and bunches them together and shoves them into his tights.

Again, voices find him.

To his right, motion.

Jaeger appears on the high ground, body erect, the stride relaxed. He looks like a man riding an insurmountable lead. Watching nothing but the trail ahead, he dives back into the bottoms, slowing a little, and Lucas surges and meets him where the trails merge. Looking over his shoulder, Jaeger gives a little jump. "No," he says. And a big nervous laugh rolls out of him.

Lucas tucks in close. Again the trail climbs out of the marsh. And when Jaeger rises in front of him, Lucas reaches down, catching an ankle, yanking it toward the sky.

Jaeger falls, one hand slapping the frozen earth.

Grabbing the other ankle, Lucas says, "Run."

Jaeger kicks at him.

"What are you doing?" Lucas says. "You're an idiot. Run the hell out of here. Are you listening to me?"

Voices drift close. Varner says, "Pepper," and Pete says, "We got him," and that's when Jaeger scrambles to his feet. His eyes are wild, fiery. With a matching voice, he says, "What do you know." Not a question, just a string of flat hard words. Then he runs, his right leg wobbling. But the stride recovers, and that endless strength carries him off while Lucas watches, hoping for the best.

The others catch up and stop, bending to breathe.

"Good idea," says Pete.

Varner says, "What'd he tell you?"

Lucas looks at the butcher's gloves on his hands and puts his hands down, and Gatlin says, "Did you hurt him?"

"No," says Lucas.

"Too bad," Varner says. "Next time, break his legs."

Voices come through the trees. A woman shouts; a man speaks. Then the woman shouts again, her voice scary-angry and making no sense. Lucas surges, pulling away from the others. Wide and carpeted with rotted wood chips, the main trail points south, climbing a final little slope up onto Foster Lane. Jaeger has already passed. Masters stands in the middle of the road, hands on hips. Sarah is closest to him. "Do nothing," she says. "Just do nothing."

Masters says something soft.

She says, "God," and swats the air with her mittens.

Masters looks at Lucas, cheeks red and his mouth tiny, some wicked embarrassment twisting his guts.

"Asshole, run," says Crouse. The man is angry, but only to a point. A sports fan yelling at the enemy team, he cups his hands around his mouth. "We're chasing you, asshole."

Nobody moves.

Pete staggers up to the road, face dripping. Varner and Gatlin cross it and stop at the mouth of the next trail, and Gatlin points. "There."

"Chase him," Sarah says.

She isn't talking to Masters. Grabbing Lucas by the elbow, she shakes him and says, "Go."

Varner and Gatlin are running into the trees again.

Hands on knees, Pete says, "Foster goes where? Down the west side of the park, right?"

Lucas nods. "A couple trails pop out."

"We'll watch for him." Then Pete coughs into a fist.

"Oh, he's gotten away," says Sarah. Pink mittens on her head, she says, "There's a million trails in there."

"Come on," says Crouse, setting off down the road.

Pete trots after him.

Masters watches Sarah, glasses like volcanic glass, the mouth pressed down to a scared pink dot.

Audrey stands aside, her bottom lip tucked into her mouth, little teeth chewing. She acts like a bystander unlucky enough to stumble across an ugly family brawl.

"With me?" says Lucas.

Then he runs, saying, "Somebody."

Small shoes dance across dry gravel.

Lucas shortens his gait, giving her no choice but to fall in beside him.

"What did you do?" Audrey says. "His knee's bleeding."

The trail is wide and heavily used, slicing south through old timber before crossing one of the gullies that feed Ash Creek. "I spilled him," Lucas says.

"Spilled him."

"Stupid," he says.

The gully is wide, choked with muck and dead timber. The long bridge is made from pipe and oak planks. Lucas jumps on first, feet drumming. "I wanted to scare him. Get him to run somewhere else."

They come off the bridge and the world turns quiet. The trail splits, one branch heading west, but Lucas presses south.

"We were talking," says Audrey. "Up on the road, waiting, Masters made a joke. He said we should tackle Jaeger, and right away Sarah said that was a good idea. But when Carl finally showed up, nobody moved."

Voices drift in from the west, from deep in the trees.

"Should we have turned back there?" Audrey says.

"The other trail just makes a little loop. Jaeger can take it to the road, or he comes back to us."

She pulls up beside him, and neither of them talks.

Then he says, "Nothing's going to happen to the guy."

"Promise?"

He slows.

She passes him and looks back. "What?"

"We're here. Stop," he says.

The trail jumps left where the woods end. In front of them is twenty feet of vertical earth falling into cold slow water. The secondary trail pops out on their right. "Hear anything?" says Lucas.

"No." She tilts her head. "Yes."

The gray T-shirt appears first, and then the pale face. Jaeger spots them. Three strides away, he stops. His right knee is trying to scab over. He breathes hard, big lungs working, his face holding a deep, thorough fatigue. But the voice is solid. Ignoring Lucas, he says, "Not you."

More sad than angry, Audrey says, "Just tell me, Carl."

"Tell you what?"

"Did you kill Wade?"

Jaeger throws a look back up the smaller trail. Gatlin and Varner stand in the trees, both men heaving. And Jaeger turns again, looking only at Lucas. He doesn't say a word, but an odd little smile builds. Then he runs again—a handful of lazy strides pushing him between Lucas and Audrey—and the big legs kick into high gear, frozen twists of mud scattered on the ground behind him.

"You could have won."

It was Wade's voice, and it wasn't.

"They just posted the results," he said. "You should see the splits. At five miles, Harris had you by eleven seconds. If you'd kept close, you would have toasted him at the end. The kid thinks he has a kick, but he doesn't."

Lucas was sitting in his kitchen, finishing a pot of coffee. Orcs and humans were fighting on the television, ugly evil pitted against the handsome good.

"Are you listening, Lucas?"

"Yeah."

"You haven't won a race since you were sixteen."

Lucas put down the mug. "How do you know? Did I tell you?"

"I've been reading old sports stories," Wade said. Except something about the voice was different. Changed. Not in the words or rhythm, but in the emotions. Wade was always intense, but usually in a tough-coach, in-control way. Usually. But this character was letting his anger creep into everything he was saying. "You had your chance, Lucas. With Jaeger out of commission and all."

"You know about the arrest?"

"An article just got posted. There's a nice picture of me from ten years ago. And a real shitty shot of Jaeger. I'm hoping Masters has the arrest on video. That's something I'd like to see."

Lucas reached across the table, turning off the television.

"Two witnesses put Jaeger running with me," Wade said. "I just read all about it. We're in the park that Monday, at the north end heading south, and both witnesses claim the mood was ugly."

"But you don't remember."

"Wade uploaded his days at night," Wade said. "That was his routine."

"I remember."

Silence.

Lucas waited. Then he said, "You think Carl did it?"

"Killed me?" An odd laugh came across. "I don't know. I really don't. But I'll tell you how this feels. Suppose you're at a theatre watching some movie. It's a murder mystery, and there's this one character that you really, really care about. You want the best for him but you've got to pee, and that's when this person you liked is killed. You're out of the room, and he gets his skull caved in. And now you feel angry and sad, but mostly you just feel cheated."

Lucas lifted the mug, looking at the stained bottom.

"Maybe Carl did it, and maybe not," Wade said. "But I missed that part. And now I'm sitting in the dark, waiting to see how things end up. Just so I can get on with my life."

Mountain bikes and hiking boots have carved a broad rut down the trail's middle. Runners keep to the rut, single-file, jumping the bank when the trail twists, slicing the turn. Lucas leads and Audrey is behind him, watching her next steps. With a tight voice, she says, "I can't believe this."

"So quit," Varner says.

Jaeger is forty feet ahead. Where the trail pulls left, he cuts through the woods, adding a half-stride to his lead.

Varner surges, passing Audrey and clipping Lucas' heel with a foot.

Lucas slows and turns north, wind gnawing at his sweaty face.

The next bridge is a tall smear of red just visible through the trees. Jaeger is almost there, slowing his gait, getting ready to jump on the stairs.

Varner surges again, lifting himself to a full sprint, just managing to pull around Lucas.

Jaeger looks back, squinting, the wide mouth pulling air in long gulps. Then he turns and leaps, his right foot landing on a pink granite step. And he pauses, calculating distance and his own fatigue before jumping again, breaking into a smooth trot across the bridge.

Varner staggers, stiff legs climbing after Jaeger.

The others bunch up behind.

Lucas gasps, scrubbing his blood before pushing back into the lead. Ash Creek is wide as a river, and the long wooden bridge shakes with the pounding. Jaeger is twenty feet ahead when he reaches the end, leaping over the steps, hitting the ground hard. His posture is surprised. He stands where he landed, glancing back at Lucas and almost talking. Almost. Then he starts running again, not quite trusting his right leg.

Lucas dances down the steps and runs. The next stretch of trail is wide and straight—an old road through what used to be a farmer's yard. Someone with affection for poplars planted them in rows, skinny white trunks looking sickly without the glittering leaves. Again, the wind pushes the runners. Again, everybody accelerates. The old yard ends with a massive oak and deep woods. For Wade, this was always a traditional turnaround point from the Y. By this route, they have covered a few steps more than seven miles.

Jaeger disappears into the trees.

Lucas slows and says, "There's another bridge."

Audrey pushes close. "What about it?"

"It's closed. Since last summer."

"We can still cross," Gatlin says.

"Yeah," Lucas says. "But that's not what I'm talking about."

The bridge rises in the distance. It looks wrong. Four tall posts sag toward the middle. Last June, a flash flood roared down the tributary, cutting at the banks and undermining the foundation. Jaeger is driving hard, pushing away from them. Varner is scared that he might get away, and the adrenaline gives him just enough speed to catch Lucas and trip him by clipping his heel.

Both men tumble. Lucas slaps the ground where an exposed root cuts through a butcher's glove, ripping into his right palm.

Audrey stops.

Gatlin is past, gone.

Varner groans and finds his feet, giving Lucas an embarrassed but thoroughly pissed look before wobbling away.

"Are you okay?" says Audrey.

Lucas stands, watching the blood soak the cheap white fabric. Wincing, he says, "Come on," and breaks into a slow trot, eyes down.

DANGER, CLOSED reads the sign nailed to crossed planks.

Jaeger has crawled past the barricade. Steel cables serve as railings, and with arms spread wide, he slowly drops out of view.

"We're beaten," says Audrey. "We're done."

She sounds nothing but happy.

Gatlin stands on the ramp. Then he lifts an arm and waves at someone on the far bank.

Past the bridge is a trailhead and parking lot. If people ran the road down the west side of the park, following Foster, even a knuckle-walking pace would take them to these trailhead before any greyhound could sprint down these trails. Gatlin and Varner stand at the crossed boards, staring across the slough. The suspension bridge looks tired and old and treacherous, sagging in the middle as if holding an enormous weight. Jaeger stands at the bottom. He doesn't move. With feet apart, Pete guards the opposite barricade. Masters and Crouse are behind him, and Sarah hovers to the side, nothing but smiles now.

Pete says, "Look at you." Then he punches the boards, saying, "Unless you sprout wings, we've caught your ass."

"See the news today?"

Lucas was making a fresh pot. "Besides murder stories, you mean?"

The dead man laughed and then fell silent. And out from the silence, he said, "There was a thunderstorm yesterday. In Greenland."

Lucas didn't talk.

"You know where Greenland is, don't you?"

"Well enough," Lucas said.

The next laugh was smaller, angrier. "It wasn't a big storm, and it didn't last. But if rain starts falling hard on those glaciers, it's going to be a real mess."

"I thought we had a real mess."

"Even worse," Wade said.

Mr. Coffee set to work, happy to prove itself.

"Our weather wouldn't be this crazy," Lucas said. "If the Chinese hadn't burned all that coal."

"Which authority is talking? You?"

"Masters, mostly."

"It wasn't the Chinese, Lucas. It was everybody."

Lucas said nothing, waiting.

"Smart people can be stupid," Wade said.

"I guess."

"And I know guys who can't read a map, but they still see things that I'd never notice."

Lucas poured a fresh cup.

"Did I tell you? Climate is the biggest reason I got made. And it wasn't just the rising oceans and ten-year droughts and those heat waves that hammered the Persian Gulf. Climate does change. Always has, and life always adapts. Except the earth today has two big things that didn't exist during the Eocene."

Lucas said the new word. "Eocene."

"The earth has its money and it has politics. And those very precious things are getting hit harder than anything else. The sultans can fly off to cool wet Switzerland, but the poor people have to die. The Saudi government has to collapse. But meanwhile, engineers get to sit inside their air-conditioned bunkers, using robots to run oil fields cooking at a hundred and fifty degrees. As if this was some other planet, and they were noble astronauts doing good work."

"I guess," said Lucas.

"Political stability and wealth," the voice said. "People depend on those two things more than anything else. And the poverty and riots and little murders and big wars are just going to get worse. Hour by hour, year by year. That's why I put my savings into this venture. Why Wade did. Sure, we were hoping for fifty years of tweaking, but at least we had enough time to pack up everything about me and put it here. My whole life, safe as safe can possibly be."

Lucas sipped and looked out the window. Or he didn't look anywhere. He was thinking, and he had no idea what he was thinking until he spoke.

"Nobody would do that," he said.

"Do what?" said Wade.

"Take everything." Lucas wiped the counter with a clean towel. "It's like this. You're putting your life into one big bag. But there's always going to be choices. There's always embarrassing ugly dangerous shit, and you'll look at it and say, 'Hell, that crap needs to be left behind.'"

"Think so?"

"I know it." Lucas watched the coffee wobbling in the mug. "That's probably another reason why Wade did what he did. Getting free of the past."

The line was silent.

"And you, the poor backup . . . you can't even know what's missing." Lucas was laughing but not laughing. "Right there, that says plenty."

SEVEN

Jaeger stands at the bottom of the slow-swaying curve, turning slowly and staring up at the people on both ends of the bridge. His chest swells, drinking the cold air. The muscles in his bare legs look like old rope, bunched and frayed, and the right knee keeps bleeding, a red snake glistening down the long shin. With filthy butcher gloves, he holds onto the steel cables. Old wood feels his weight, groaning. He doesn't seem to mind. If the bridge collapses, he falls ten feet into icy mud and nothing happens, nothing but pain and mess. Jaeger spent two months sitting in jail. He was too broke to make bail or find an adequate attorney. The city's murder rate had exploded in the last few years. A hundred other cases needed to be chased. But a popular citizen had been brutally murdered, and that's why the police and prosecutors threw everything at the suspect, trying to wring a confession from him. But there was no confession. And when key bits of physical evidence were finally attacked by the full powers of modern science, they were found wanting. Witnesses and odd circumstances don't make a case, and the court had no choice but to order Jaeger released. And that's why this bridge is no obstacle. None. Nothing will make the man meaner or any harder. That's what he says with his body and his face and the hard sure grip of his hands. That's what he says to Lucas, staring at him with those fierce green eyes.

And then Jaeger blinks.

He takes another breath and holds it. His head tips on that long neck. Maybe he feels cold. Anyone else would, dressed as he's dressed and standing still. Then he exhales and makes a quarter turn, wrapping both hands around the same fat steel cable.

Pete says, "Hey, prick. Tell the truth, and we'll let you go."

Jaeger stares at the slough. With a plain voice, not loud but carrying, he says, "That's what I am. A prick. And Wade was this righteous good guy, and everybody liked him, and dying made him perfect."

Nobody talks. Except for the wind in the trees and a slow trickle of water, there is nothing to hear.

"No, I wasn't with him when he died," says Jaeger. "But I know how he died. Even after the rain, there were clues: A big chunk of skin was found south of here, down near the water. It came out of his shoulder, and it was the first wound. Somebody was swinging a piece of rebar with a lump of concrete on the end, and they clipped Wade from behind, on his left side, probably knocking him off his feet. Giving his attacker the chance to grab his phone, leaving him bloody and cut off from the world, but mobile.

"That's when the chase began," he says. "There was a blood trail. DNA sniffers and special cameras showed where he ran, where he was bleeding. Twice, Wade tried doubling back to the nearest trailhead, but his enemy clipped the shoulder again and then bashed in one of his hands. The experts could tell that from the clotting. They know how fast the blood flowed and where Wade collapsed. He was up on the abandoned rail line, probably trying to get back to town. That's where his killer used the club to bust one of Wade's knees, crippling him. Then his jaw was broken, maybe to keep him quiet. After that, his killer dragged him down into the brush and with a couple good swings broke his hip. Then for some reason, the beating took a break."

Jaeger pauses.

Almost too soft to hear, Sarah says, "What are you telling us?"

"I'm explaining why you're idiots." Jaeger looks at her and back at Lucas. "Fifteen, twenty minutes passed. The killer stood over Wade. Talking to him, I guess. Probably telling him just how much he was hated. Because that's what this murder was. That was the point of it all. Somebody wanted to milk the fun out hurting him. He wanted Wade helpless, wanted him to understand that he was crippled and ruined."

Sarah makes a soft, awful sound.

Jaeger shakes his head. "Twenty minutes of talk, and then three or four minutes of good solid hammering. Wade died within sixty seconds, they figured. But he was a tough bastard and maybe not. Maybe he felt the one side of the face getting caved in and the ribs and arms busted and the neck shattered."

Lucas leans against the barricade.

Jaeger pushes into the cable, long arms stretched wide and holding tight. The steady drumming of his strongest muscle causes the steel to shudder. Anyone touching the bridge can feel his heart beating hard and quick.

"I didn't hate the man," says Jaeger. "You know me, Audrey. You too, Lucas. I'm wrapped up in myself, sure. But this feud ran in just one direction." He laughs and grabs both cables again. "Yeah, we ran together that Monday. And we were talking. But after a mile or so, I turned and he went on. For me, Wade was nothing. He was just another body in the pack. I didn't hate him. Not till I spent two months in jail, thinking about him and his good sweet friends. And you know what? I've got this feeling. This instinct. I didn't have any reason for killing, particularly like that. But I'm thinking that killing Wade Tanner is something one of you bastards would do. Easy."

The building began as a factory and became a filthy warehouse. Then the property sold cheap, and the investor put loft apartments into the upper stories and The Coffee Corner took over the loading dock and west end, while the backside was reborn as a fashionable courtyard complete with flower pots and a broken fountain. Lucas was walking past the courtyard's black-iron gate. Saturday's run was finished and coffee was finished and he was thinking about the rest of his day, and from behind, Sarah said, "I need new shoes."

She was talking to him, Lucas thought, turning around.

To her phone, she said, "What kind should I try?"

The odd funny weird thing about the moment was her face. Sarah looked happy, which was different. The smile lit her face and made her eyes dance. She was listening to a voice, and he realized whose voice. Then she noticed Lucas and turned away, suddenly embarrassed, muttering soft little words nobody else needed to hear.

Sarah went through the gate. Lucas followed. The original pavers made the courtyard, dark red and worn smooth by horses pulling wagons. Maybe the horses were coming back someday. It was something to think about as he followed the little woman. A glass door led into The Runner's Closet, and the owner had just opened up. A few minutes after ten, in October, and his day was starting off fine. He had two customers at once, and the guy had to grin.

Lucas stumbled over names. Tom? Tom Hubble, right.

"He wants me to try the Endorphins," Sarah said. "The ones with the twin computers and the smart-gel actuators."

"Good choice," Tom said. "What size?"

She told him and he vanished into the back room, and then she turned, watching Lucas. She didn't talk. She was listening and smiling. Then she said, "Lucas is here too," and nodded as Wade talked. Then she told the living man, "He says you need new shoes too."

"Yeah, but how does he know?"

"Wade still helps here. Keeps track of who buys what, and you haven't bought for a long time."

What was strangest was how much all of that made sense.

Lucas sat on the padded bench, Sarah settling beside him, still talking to Wade. An oval track had been painted on the floor, wrapping around the bench. She listened to the voice, and Tom brought out a box of shoes and put them on her and laced her up and watched her jogging a few strides at a time, smart eyes trying to see what was right and wrong in her step.

Sarah giggled. Not laughed, but giggled.

"I need new shoes too," Lucas said.

"What kind do you like?" Tom said.

"What I have," Lucas said.

"What's the model?"

"I don't remember," Lucas said. "Ask Wade."

Tom nodded, watching Sarah finishing her lap. She said, "Bye," and touched her phone. "I'll take them. And he said pass his commission back to me, please."

"Sure," Tom said, rising slowly.

Sarah started following him toward the counter but then stopped and looked at Lucas. "You know, I talk to him more than ever," she said, smiling but not smiling. Happy in her core but knowing there was something wrong, something sick about feeling this way.

Jaeger grabs the cables and drives with his legs, climbing the far side of the swaying bridge. Pete holds his ground, waiting. The four people wait, shoulders squared but the feet nervous. Everything will be finished in another minute. A fight is coming, and the four people on the north bank can only watch, each of them feeling lucky because of it.

Pete's face tightens.

Jaeger says, "Move."

Nobody reacts. Pride holds them in place, right up until Pete dips his head, throwing a few words at the others as he backs away.

Masters retreats, relieved.

Not Crouse. He replants his feet. Unimpressed, Jaeger grabs the barricade and jumps, one foot landing where the planks cross. Then he yanks the foot free and drops beside Crouse, saying nothing while staring down at him, and Crouse nearly trips backing off the wooden ramp.

Only Sarah remains. She makes fists inside her mittens and steps forward, waving the fists while sobbing, fighting for breath.

Jaeger pushes past her and runs, vanishing in a few strides.

Pete waves. "One at a time."

Gatlin goes first. The little body slips under the barricade and runs to the bottom and runs up to the far side. Varner chases, every step ridiculously long, the bridge bucking and creaking. Audrey is next, but she won't let go of the cables and she won't run. Halfway down, she looks back at Lucas, and he says, "Let's just leave. We can head back."

She shakes her head and says, "But what if they catch him?" Just the possibility makes her tremble, and she hurries, finishing her trip down and then up again.

Cupping a hand against his mouth, Pete says, "Are you coming?"

Lucas says, "No." Maybe he means it. Anywhere else in the world would be better than being here. But he watches himself bend and climb through the barricade, and he lets his legs run. Planks rattle as he stretches out, and then without a false step or stumble, he charges up the far side.

Only Pete waits. He looks in Lucas' direction. He talks to Lucas, unless he's talking to himself. "I don't know," he says to one of them. "I just don't know."

The trail follows the slough to its mouth and then follows Ash Creek again. Cottonwoods stand among the scrub elms and mulberries, and the woods give way to dead grass and a parking lot of rutted gravel. Past the lot is West Spencer Road and another mile-deep slice of parkland. The rest of the group stand beside the lone picnic table, bunched together and silent. A rhythmic shriek begins, cutting at the cold air. Jaeger has claimed the old-style pump, lifting the handle and shoving it down again. A rusty box fills with water and brown water spouts from the bottom into a rusted bowl, spouting even when he stops pumping, bending over to drink.

Once he has his fill, Jaeger straightens, wiping his chin and his mouth. Then he trots to the next trail and stops again, looking back at them.

"He's waiting on us," Varner says.

And with a quiet sick voice, Audrey says, "Who's chasing who?"

Sarah paid for the shoes and left, and Tom vanished into the back again. His voice drifted out of the storeroom—one side of the conversation exchanging pleasantries before asking the real question. Lucas drifted to the front of the store, up where a tall sheet of corkboard was covered with race results and news clippings and free brochures telling new runners how to train for competition. A younger, badly yellowed Wade smiled down from a high corner, holding a famous pair of shoes in one hand. Tom came out with a box while Lucas was picking his way through the news clipping, one word after another.

"I'd pull that old thing down," Tom said. "But people expect it. I'm afraid customers would get mad, not seeing it there."

"I wouldn't," Lucas said.

Tom examined the clipping. "I was here that day. In fact, I saw the kid snatch up those shoes. Out the door and gone, and Wade came charging from the storeroom to chase him. I told him not to. The kid was on meth. I could tell. But you know Wade."

"Yeah."

"I knew he'd catch the thief, and that's what scared me."

Lucas gave up reading. It was the photograph that mattered. It was that big smile and the hair that was still thick and blond and the rugged looks wrapped around a crooked nose, and it was how that younger Wade held those shoes up to the camera, no prize in the world half as important.

"That shoe thief had a knife," Tom said.

"I remember."

"But things worked out. Wade just kept running him until he collapsed, and nobody got cut."

Lucas dropped his eyes, watching the floor.

"He was the first salesman that I hired," said Tom. "Wade was still in college. I had no idea he'd stay here for twenty years. Honestly, I didn't think he would last that first week. He was too intense, I thought. Too perfect, too driven. The crap he would pull sometimes. God, these are just shoes. The world isn't going to end if you don't happen to make that one sale."

Tom was looking at the same piece of the floor, explaining. "But like nobody I've ever known, Wade had a talent for names and faces. For feet and gaits. He was everybody's first doctor when they got hurt, and he loved selling shoes, and even dead, he's still practically managing this place."

"What else?" Lucas said.

"What else what?"

"What stupid crap did he pull? Besides chasing shoe thieves, I mean."

Tom swallowed, thinking before answering. "He fired clerks for little things. No warnings, just gone. If a customer gave him a bad check, he wouldn't take another check from that person. Ever. And he couldn't keep his nose out of private concerns. He had this need, this compulsion, to steer the world toward doing what's right. You know what I mean."

"Oh, sure."

"I was at that party too, Lucas."

Lucas looked at him.

"I never would have called the cops on you."

Lucas didn't know what to say. He tried a small shrug.

Tom was nervous but proud. He thought that he was making a customer for life. "Wade was a good man, but he thought everyone should be."

One last glance at the photograph seemed right.

"Ithaca Flyers. Is that your shoe?"

"Sounds right."

"This is the new model, but he says you'll like it."

"Well," said Lucas. "The guy was usually right."

The group shuffles over to the pump. Masters pulls a little bottle off the back of his belt, sharing the blue drink with Sarah. Pete gives the handle a few hard shoves and drinks, and then the others take turns. Everybody is tired, but not like runners beaten up by miles. They look like cocktailers after Last Call, faces sloppy and sad and maybe a little scared by whatever is coming next.

Lucas drinks last, holding the frigid bowl with his bloodied palm, the water warm and thick with iron.

"Sucking the ground dry?" says Jaeger.

Lucas stops drinking. But instead of standing, he drops down, stretching his legs with a runner's lunge.

Jaeger turns and leaves.

"Hurry," Sarah says.

Masters is squeezing the last taste out of a gel-pack.

She says, "Now."

He nearly talks. Words lie ready behind those big sorrowful eyes. But he forces himself to say nothing, folding the foil envelope and shoving it into his belt pocket before taking a last little swig from the bottle, diluting the meal before it hits his defenseless stomach.

Everybody is stiff from standing, and nobody mentions it. Nobody does anything but run, lifting their pace until they see Jaeger floating up ahead. Sarah is in front, sniffling. A flat concrete bridge carries West Spenser across the stream. Jaeger throws back a quick glance before following the trail under the bridge, hugging the east bank.

"It was him," Varner says.

Crouse says, "Sure."

"Wade was our friend," Varner says. But that isn't enough. Shaking his head, he says, "Wade was my best friend. He got me into running. Sold me my first shoes, when I was fat. And he was a groomsman at my wedding. Remember?"

With an edge, Pete says, "Yeah, none of us had reasons."

Sarah slows. "What does that mean?"

They bunch up behind her.

"One of us had a motive?" she says.

Pete drops back to Audrey. "What do you think, princess? Your old boyfriend kill Wade, or didn't he?"

The trail dives and widens, its clay face pounded slick. The stream lies on their right, pushing past the concrete pilings and dead timber, the wet roar hitting the underside of the bridge before bouncing over them. It is hard to hear Audrey saying, "I never believed he was guilty."

They come out from under, emerging into the calm. Climbing the slope, nobody talks. Then Audrey says, "Carl is self-centered and stubborn, like a little boy. But he's never been violent. Not around me."

Carved by chainsaws, a simple bench sits beside the trail, waiting for the exhausted. They run past and the trail drops again and hits bottom, and Crouse gasps as they climb. "You two dated?" he says.

"Years ago," she says, ready to say nothing more.

Crouse has to surge to catch her. But it's worth the pain to tell her, "I don't see it. I don't understand. Why is Carl attractive?"

For several strides, nothing happens. The trail twists away from the stream, nothing but trees around them. Then Audrey slows and looks at Crouse, her face pretty and pleased when she says, "Look at that body, those legs. And now guess what I saw in him."

The man reddens.

She laughs, saying, "Little boys can be fun."

Jaeger looks back again, holding the gap steady.

"So did he ever talk about Wade?" says Pete.

She keeps laughing. "Carl loved, and I mean loved, how that man kept trying to beat him. It fed him, knowing one person was awake nights, trying to figure out how to pass him at the finish line."

Nobody reacts.

Then she says, "Lucas," and comes up beside him. "I don't think I ever told you. But when you started training with Wade, Carl wasn't sure how long he would stay on top. 'Wade found his thoroughbred,' was what he said."

Everybody but Pete glances at Lucas. Pete just dips his head, asking the trail, "What about you, Pepper? Is Jaeger the killer?"

Lucas drops his arms and slows. The stream comes back looking for the trail. Suddenly the world opens up, and they chug along a narrow ribbon of earth, perched on a bank being undercut by every new flood. To their right is nothing except open air. A string of bodies are pushing against the brush on the left. Audrey is in front of Lucas, Pete behind. Pete says, "If it isn't Jaeger, who was it?"

Lucas runs with eyes down, and a quiet, puzzled voice says, "If it wasn't Carl?"

"Yeah?"

"Me," he says. "I could have beaten Wade Tanner to death."

.

EIGHT

Audrey slows, nearly tripping Lucas.

He says, "Sorry," and drops his hands on her shoulders.

"Was it you?" says Pete.

"No," Lucas says.

"How can you even think it?" says Audrey.

Lucas lets go of her, eyes down, head shaking.

Varner and Gatlin are in the lead. Feeling the others fall back, they pull up reluctantly, and Varner says, "Who's hurt?"

Nobody answers. Six runners stand on the crumbling trail, flush against the drop-off. Lucas turns his back to the water. "It's just how things look," he says to Audrey, to everybody. "If you think about it."

"Keep talking," says Pete.

But Masters speaks first. With a voice nobody has ever heard—an angry, sharp, defiant voice—he says, "Wade was an ass."

Everybody turns.

The man's face is red, his jaw set. "I'm tired of thinking about the man," he says. "I'm tired of talking about the man. And I don't want to have another conversation with that goddamn software."

"Don't," says Sarah. Then again, softer, she says, "Don't."

Nobody wants to look at her. It is easier to stare at the madman with the sleek black glasses and the long-built rage.

"Let's run home," says Audrey.

Varner and Gatlin return to the pack. "Who's hurt?" says Varner.

Pete says, "Nobody. We're just having a meeting."

"We couldn't have," Sarah says. "Nobody here would kill him."

Which makes Pete laugh. Except his face is flushed and he can't stop shaking his head, blowing hard through clenched teeth. With one finger, he pokes Lucas in the chest. "Was it you?" he says.

"No." A spasm rips through Lucas' body. One foot drops over the soft lip of the trail, and he brings it back again, stepping forward just far enough to feel that he won't fall in the next moment. Then Pete puts a hand flush against Lucas' chest, not pushing but ready to push, waiting for the excuse.

And now another voice comes in.

"I've got a list of suspects," Jaeger says. "Why don't you listen to me now?"

The old burr oak stands on the bank, undermined to where a tangle of fat curling roots juts into the open air. Jaeger stands in the shadow of that doomed tree, smiling. Pulling off the baseball cap, he uses the long sleeve of his shirt to wipe his eyes and the broad forehead. Then he puts the cap back where it belongs, and he says nothing, the smile never breaking.

"Give us names," says Pete.

"Okay, yours," Jaeger says. "And Varner."

"Why?" Varner says.

"Cause you're mean boys. I barely know either of you, and I'm pretty sure that I've never hurt you. But here you are, chasing me, both of you looking ready to bust heads. All you need is a reason. So maybe Wade is a good reason. Who knows?"

Varner curses. Pete gives a horse snort.

"Then there's the little guy," says Jaeger. "I've got a guess, Mr. Gatlin. But it's a sweet one."

"What?" Fast Doug says.

"You ran for mayor when? Three, four years back? And Wade helped. I heard he gave you names and phone numbers for every runner in town. Stuffed envelopes, dropped money in your lap. But then news leaked about some old business back in Ohio. Sure, those troubles were years old. Sure, the girl stopped cooperating with the cops and charges got dropped. But you know how it is. Nothing's uglier than reporters chasing something that looks easy."

Gatlin opens his mouth and closes it.

"Did Wade know your sex-crime history?" says Jaeger. "Was he the leak that got the scandal rolling?"

Quietly, fiercely, the accused man says, "I don't know."

Jaeger laughs. "But it could have been Wade. We know that. Love him or not, the guy had this code for how people should act, and not living up to his standards was dangerous. He could be your buddy and remain civil, but if you were trying to run for public office and he decided that you were guilty of something, he'd happily drop a word in the right ear and let justice run you over. That wouldn't bother the man for a minute."

"So everybody but you is guilty," says Pete. "Is that it?"

Jaeger winks at Crouse. "Wade liked pretty girls. And pretty wives were best. Which is funny, considering the man's ethics. But adultery isn't a crime. Romance is a contest, a race. There is a winner, and there is everybody else, and I'm looking at you but thinking about your wife. She is a dream. A fat toad like you is lucky to have her. And believe me, a guy like Wade is going to be interested, and by the way, whose baby did she just have?"

Crouse tries to curse, but he hasn't the breath.

Audrey says, "Carl."

"With you, darling, I don't have guesses." Jaeger's face softens. "Maybe you two had a history. Maybe there was a good reason for you to cripple him and kill him. I heard your marriage fell apart a couple months ago. Anybody can draw a story from that clue. Except you never tried to kill me, not once, and I gave you a hundred reasons to cut off my head while I was dreaming."

Audrey cries.

Jaeger points at Sarah. "But you," he says. "At the races, I saw you chatting it up with the dead man. I'm not the most sensitive boil, but everything showed in those eyes. If you didn't screw Wade, you wanted to. And maybe you didn't do the bashing, but you've got a husband. And worse, you've got this tall goon following you around. What would Mr. Masters do if he discovered that his training buddy was cheating on her husband and on him?"

Breathing hard, Masters stares at the back of Sarah's head.

"No end to the suspects," Jaeger says.

"What about Pepper?" says Pete.

"Yeah, I was saving him."

Lucas feels sick.

Pete turns and looks at him. "The party," he says.

"At the coach's house," says Jaeger. "I've heard stories. Not that anybody invited me, thank you. But my sources claim that a brutal load of liquor was consumed. By one man, mostly. Years of sobriety gone in a night, and then the drunk drove away." He smiles, something good on his tongue. "And that's when somebody called the hotline. Somebody told the world, 'Lucas Pepper is driving and shit-faced, and this is his license plate, and this is his home address, and this is his phone number.'"

Lucas manages ragged little breaths.

"A night in jail and your license suspended," says Jaeger. "But there's worse parts to the story. I know because my first source told me. That next Monday, when I crossed paths with Wade, I asked about you, Pepper. 'Where's your prize stallion?' I said. 'Why isn't he running in this miserable heat?' That's when he launched into this screaming fit about drunks, about how stupid it was to waste effort and blood trying to keep bastards like them on track.

"I know something about ugly tantrums," Jaeger says. "And this was real bad. This is what the witnesses saw when they saw us in that park. They assumed it was two men fighting. Which it was, I guess. Except only one of the men was present, and I was just a witness, trying to hang on for the ride.

"Wade told me about that party and how he watched you drinking and drinking, and then he made it his business to walk you to your car, and that's where he got into your face. Standing at the curb, he told you exactly what you were, which was the worst kind of failure. He said he wasn't sure he was going to give you even one more chance. Why bother with a forty-year-old drawerhead, spent and done and wasted?

"And that's the moment I turned around. It was a hot sticky evening, and that was my excuse. But really, I was embarrassed for you, Lucas. I didn't know that was possible. I turned and ran home, and Wade went on his merry way, and I can guess what happened if he came around the bend and ran into you trotting by yourself."

Lucas stares at Jaeger but glimpses something moving. Something is running through the trees, and nobody else sees it.

With the one finger, Pete punches Lucas. "Is there something you want to tell us, Pepper?"

Sniffing, Audrey whispers his name.

Jaeger removes the cap again, wiping at his forehead.

Lucas is the only person who doesn't jump when Harris trots up behind Jaeger.

"Hey, guys," says a big happy voice. "I finally found you."

In November, in the warm dark, Lucas rode up to the Harold Farquet Memorial Fieldhouse. He was stowing bike lights when Varner appeared. "I must be late," said Lucas.

"What's that mean?" said Varner, not laughing.

They went inside. Half an acre of concrete lay beneath a shell of naked girders and corrugated steel. The building's centerpiece was the two-hundred-meter pumpkin-orange track. Multipurpose courts filled the middle and stretched east. Athletics offices and locker rooms clung to the building's south end. Banners hanging from the ugly ceiling boasted about third-place finishes. The largest banner celebrated the only national championship in Jewel history—twenty years ago, in cross-country.

Thirty people had come out of the darkness to run. Most were middle-of-the-pack joggers, cheery and a little fat. Masters and Sarah were sharing a piece of floor, stretching hamstrings and IT bands. Audrey ran her own workout, surging on the brief straight-aways. Lucas watched her accelerate toward him and then fall into a lazy trot on the turn, smiling as she passed.

Varner vanished inside the locker room. Out of his pack, Lucas pulled a clean singlet and dry socks and the still-young shoes. His shorts were under his jeans. Kicking off street shoes, he changed in the open. His phone rang, and glancing at the number, he killed the ring. Then Audrey's phone rang as she came past, and she answered by saying, "Kind of busy here, Mr. Tanner."

The indoor air felt hot and dry. Lucas walked toward the lockers, bent and took a long drink from the old fountain, the water warm enough for a bath. Burping, he stepped away. Heroes covered the wall. Someone made changes since last winter, but the biggest photograph was the same: The championship team with its top five competitors in back, slower runners kneeling at their feet. Able and his assistants flanked the victors. The coach looked happiest, standing beside his main stallion. By contrast, Jaeger appeared smug and bored, his smile as thin as could be and still make a smile. The big portrait of the school's national cham- pion runner had been removed. Three different years, Carl Jaeger was the best in Division II cross-country. But that man was in jail, and the dead man had re- placed him. Newly minted prints of Wade had been taken from past decades, each image fresh and clean. Testimonials about the man's competitive drive and importance to the local running community made him into somebody worth missing. Lucas read a few words and gave up. Farther along was a younger Au- drey, third-best at the national trials. Her hair was long but nothing else had changed much. He studied the picture for a minute, and then she came around again, saying, "Don't stare at little girls, old man. Hear me?"

"You pointed east," Harris says. "So I headed east. I chased you. Except nobody was there. Old farts start slow, and I didn't see you after the first mile, so I figured you changed your minds."

The kid is angry but smiling, proud of his cleverness.

"I thought about going north. But then I realized . . ." Harris stops talking. "Hey, Carlie. What are you doing with this crew?"

Nobody speaks.

Something odd is happening here. That fact is obvious enough to sink into Harris' brain. The smirk softens, blue eyes blink, and again he says, "What are you doing with these guys, Carl?"

Jaeger turns and runs.

Harris is wearing long shorts and a heavy yellow top, his black headband streaked with salt. His glasses are the same as Masters, only newer. His shoes look like they came out of the box this morning. "You should see your faces," he says. "You guys look sick."

Pete steps away from Lucas.

"Anyway," Harris says, "I didn't know where you were, but I knew somebody who'd know. So I called Wade. He pointed me in the right direction, and I ran the train tracks to cut distance. I nearly missed seeing you, but I heard shouting."

"Shut up," Pete says.

"What do we do?" says Gatlin.

"Follow him," Varner says.

Jaeger is crossing a meadow, the black cap bobbing too much.

Pete looks at Lucas, big hands closing into fists.

And Lucas breaks into a full sprint, cutting between bodies.

Harris smiles and says, "Pepper." Then for fun, he sets his feet and throws out an arm. "What's the password?"

They collide.

The young body is wiry-strong and tough. But Lucas has momentum, and they fall together. Lucas' sore hand ends up inside the kid's smile. Bony knuckles smack teeth and lips, and with a hard grunt Harris is down, the split upper lip dripping blood.

A wet voice curses.

Lucas is up and running.

Harris pokes at his aching mouth, and after careful consideration he says, "Screw you, asshole."

Lucas charges past the oak and across the meadow. The black cap is gone. Lucas holds to the main trail, following it back into the woods where it turns cozy with the stream. A wild sprint puts him near a five-minute pace. Then he slows, feeding oxygen to his soggy head. Roots and holes want to trip him. Voices call out from behind, and he surges again. Somebody hollers his name. Lucas holds the pace. He has little extra to give, but his stride stays smooth and furious. A half-grown ash tree is dead on the trail, and his legs lift, carrying him over what is barely an obstacle. The stream is straight ahead, the bank cut into a long ugly ramp, rocks and concrete slabs creating shallow water where horses can ford. Lucas turns left, following a narrower trail, and the trail splits, the right branch blocked by a "CLOSED" sign.

Jaeger went left, gravel showing where a runner churned up the little slope. Lucas runs right on the badly undermined trail. Holes need to be leaped. Last year's grass licks at his legs. The trail ends where the bank collapsed, probably in the last few weeks, and he pushes sideways and up through the grass, popping out on the wide rail bed.

Jaeger is close. Seeing Lucas, he surges, and where the trail drops back into the woods, he accelerates. But his head dips too much. Long arms look sloppy, tight to the body and not in sync. Lucas throws in his own surge, and catching Jaeger, he dips his head, delivering one hard shove.

Jaeger stays up but drifts into the brush, and his right leg jumps out. Both men trip and fall, bony arms flinging at each other, trading blows until they are down, scrapped and panting.

Lucas is first to his feet.

Cursing, he tries kicking Jaeger's ribs and beats his toes into the frozen ground by mistake. Then Jaeger grabs the foot and tries to break it, twisting as hard as he can, doing nothing but forcing Lucas to fall on his ass again.

Lucas breathes in long gulps. "This is no fun," he says.

"Better than jail," Jaeger says.

"Not much."

Up on the rail bed, Gatlin says, "I see them."

Harris says, "He's mine, mine."

Jaeger finds his feet first. Then after a moment's consideration, he reaches down and offers a hand to Lucas.

Pete emerged from the locker room, walking ahead of Gatlin. "Are you standing or running?" he said.

"I can do both," Lucas said.

The men laughed and left him looking at pictures.

Audrey was taking another turn. She wasn't talking to anybody now. Harris had come from somewhere, trotting next to her, chatty and happy. As if he had a chance with her. He said something and laughed for both of them, and Audrey did her best not to notice.

Lucas had no fire. He didn't want to run, and that's why he kept delaying. Walking the wall, he studied volleyball pictures and wrestling pictures and a big plaque commemorating Harold Farquet, dead thirty years but still looking plush in that suit and tie. Then he reached a bare spot. A rectangular piece of the wall seemed too bright, holes showing where bolts had held up something heavy. Curious to a point, he tried remembering what used to be there. He couldn't. The adjacent hallway led to the offices, and someone was moving inside Able's office. On a whim, Lucas knocked, and the coach came out smiling.

"What's up, Pepper?"

"I like that stuff about Wade," Lucas said.

"Yeah, we thought it was good to do. Glad you like it."

"And you took down Carl."

Able grimaced. "Yeah, we did."

"There's something else down," Lucas said. "There used to be a plaque around the corner. About Carl?"

"No," the coach said. "A few years back, we had an alum give the athletic department some money. We thanked him with a banquet and a big plaque in his honor."

"So what happened?"

"Jared Wails. Remember him?"

"I don't do names," Lucas said.

"He was a slow runner, a businessman. Had that big title company up until last year." Blood showed in the round face. "You saw him at races, probably. The rich boy who drove Corvettes."

"The '73 Stingray."

"That's him."

"I remember. The guy was kiting checks." Lucas nodded, pieces of the story coming back. "He told people he inherited his money, but he didn't. And when it caught up to him, he drove out to the woods and blew his brains out."

"And we pulled down his plaque."

"Yeah, I knew him. I even talked to him a few times." Lucas nodded, saying, "I liked the man's cars. I told him so. He was the nicest rich guy in the world, so long as we were yabbering about Corvettes."

"He wasn't that nice," the coach said.

"That's what I'm saying." Lucas wiped at his mouth. "We always had the same conversation: Cars and how much fun it was to drive fast, but gas was scarce, even for somebody with money. It was a nice conversation. Except he always changed subjects. He always ended up making big noise about hiring me."

"You?"

"I was going to be his personal trainer. I was going to coach him to where he could run a sub-three-hour marathon, or some such crap. And he was going to pay me. He always gave me numbers, and each time, the numbers got fatter. Wilder. Plus he was going to drop ten pounds, or twenty, and then thirty. And I was going to run ultra-marathons with him, crossing Colorado or charging up that mountain in Africa. Kilimanjaro?"

"Lucas Pepper, personal trainer," Able said, laughing.

"Yeah, Mr. Discipline. Me." Lucas shook his head. "Of course Wails didn't mean it. Anybody could tell. He always smiled when he talked that way. It was a smart bossy smile. The main message was that he had enough money to buy my ass. Whenever he wanted. And I needed to know it."

The coach nodded. Waiting.

"The Program's full of people like him," Lucas said. "AA, I mean. It's drunks and drawerheads who spend their lives lying about a thousand things to keep their drinking secret. That's the feel I got off the Stingray man. The shiny smile. The way his eyes danced, not quite looking at me when he was telling his stories. Any story."

"The man was a compulsive liar."

"I guess."

"No, after the suicide. Jared Wails had this big life story, but most of it was made up."

"A lot of people try doing that," Lucas said.

"But you saw through him."

Lucas shrugged.

"So? You ever mention your intuition to anybody?"

"Yeah, I did." Lucas nodded, looking out at the track. Ready to run now. "Once, I told somebody what I saw in that guy."

What matters is the trail. Trees and brush and the wide sunny gash of the stream slide past, but they are nothing. What is real is the wet black strip of hard-packed earth that twists and folds back on itself. What matters is what's under the foot and what waits for the next foot. A signpost streaks past—a yellow S sprouting an arrow pointing southwest. The trail narrows and drops and widens again, forming an apron of water-washed earth that feels tacky for the next two strides. The runners slow, barely. Lucas leads. Then the trail lifts and yanks left, and the pace quickens and quickens again, and a guttural little voice from behind tries to say something clever, but there isn't enough air for clever. Jaeger settles for a muttered, plaintive curse.

Two strides ahead, Lucas' clean gait skips over roots and a mound of stubborn dirt. His blue windbreaker is unzipped, cracking and popping as the air shoves past. Every sleeve is pushed over his elbows. The stocking cap and hair are full of sweat, but the face is perfectly relaxed. Except for little glimpses, his eyes point down, and he listens carefully to the footfalls behind him.

Jaeger slows, dropping back another stride.

Ash Creek takes a hard bend, and then it straightens, pointing due east. The water is wide and shallow, filled with downed timber and busy bubbling water heading in the opposite direction, and the trail hangs beside it, smooth and straight. Lucas pushes, and somewhere the water sounds vanish. The endless wind still blows, but he can't hear it pushing at the trees and he can't hear Jaeger's feet getting sloppy, starting to scrape at the earth. Coming from nowhere is a great long throb, and the ground shakes. Lucas dips his head and turns it, and Jaeger says one word with a question mark chasing. Then Lucas slows enough to shout the word back at him. "Train," he says.

The stream bends right, slicing close to the old rail bed. Last year's floods endangered the tracks, and the railroad responded with black boulders dropped over the trail and bank. A big two-legged sign blocks the way onto the bed, stern words warning those foolish enough to trespass on railroad property. Lucas lifts his knees and drives, a few stones rolling, and he glances downstream, seeing sunlight dancing on the bright skin of the morning Amtrak.

The big diesel throbs, pushing against the steady grade. Then the driver sees runners and hits the horn, and every living organism within a mile hears the piercing furious white roar.

Lucas turns south and sprints.

One set of tracks fills the bed. Jaeger says a word and another word and then gives up shouting. Adrenaline gives him life. He follows near enough to be felt, and Lucas looks back just once more, judging the train's speed. Some visceral calculation is made, and he believes he has time and enough speed. But the horn sounds again, shaking his body, and he can't be sure. Arms pump and he drives off the balls of his feet, reclaiming the two-stride lead. Then the engine grudgingly throttles back, and knowing that he won't have to leap onto the big black rocks, Lucas falls back into the sprint he would use on a hot summer track.

The trail dips between boulders, down into the trees again.

He rides the slope, Jaeger still chasing, and Lucas stops and Jaeger runs into his back as the Amtrak roars past. Neither man falls. The horn blares once more, for emphasis, and an angry face in the engine's window glares down at them. Sleek old cars follow, and after them, new cars cobbled together in some crash program. Empty windows and one little boy stare at the world. The boy waves at them and smiles, utterly thrilled with a life jammed with spectacle and adventure.

Lucas waves back.

Jaeger collapses to a squat, unable to find his breath. The air is full of diesel fumes. He tries cursing and can't. He wants to stand and can't. All those weeks in jail have eaten at his legs, and for athletes in their forties lay-offs are crippling. Jaeger won't win another important race in his life. He knows this, and Lucas sees it, and then the beaten man stands, his entire body shaking.

The train is far enough gone that the forest sounds are returning.

"So did you kill him?" says Jaeger.

Lucas shakes his head.

Jaeger nods. If he does or doesn't believe that answer isn't important. Looking straight at Lucas, he says, "Now what?"

"I'm going," Lucas says. "Wait here for the others."

"And then?"

Downstream from them, climbing out of the trees, the rest of the group is cautiously running next to the still-humming rails. "I don't know who killed Wade," he says.

"Too bad," Jaeger says.

"But I know who paid to have it done."

That earns a long, long stare.

"Keep that face," Lucas says. "Tell everybody what I just told you. And we'll see what happens next."

NINE

"Jingle Bells," the voice said.

"Merry Christmas to you."

"No, I'm talking about the race. The 5K. If you don't win this year, you aren't trying. That's what I think."

Lucas poured a cup, not talking.

"I'm seeing improvement, Lucas. Every week, with your splits and overall times, you're finding fire."

"Thanks for caring."

"Just want to help." Then the voice went away.

Lucas sat on a kitchen stool, sipping. Outside it was cold and wet, and it was chill and damp in the house. The television had been showing an old Stallone movie, but the network interrupted with news about a big dam in China getting washed away. Serious stuff, and Lucas reached across the counter, turning it off.

The voice returned. "You there?"

"Still. Where did you go?"

"Another call. But I'm back."

"You're busy."

"Always," Wade said. "Have you entered?"

"The Jingle Bell? It's not till next month."

"I'll do it for you. My treat."

Lucas set the cup down, saying nothing.

"Okay, it's done."

"Like that?"

"Like that."

"Thanks, I guess." A long breath seemed necessary. Then Lucas said, "You probably heard, but they let him out. A couple days ago."

"Yeah, Sarah called when it happened. And I read every story, too."

"What do you think?"

"They don't have enough evidence, I think."

"The DNA tests didn't work," Lucas said. "That's what I'm hearing. Not enough material, even with the fanciest labs helping."

"That big rain screwed everything."

"Lucky for Carl," said Lucas.

Silence.

"Ever meet Crouse's sister-in-law?"

"The cop with the jiggly ass?" Wade laughed. "Yeah, she's a pretty one."

"Well, she says the detectives can't see anybody but Jaeger. He has to be the guy. But it's the Wild West around here anymore, and there's not enough manpower to throw at one case. So they let Jaeger go, hoping for something to break later."

"I've studied the statistics, Lucas. Even in good times, a lot of murders never get solved."

"Who else is there?"

The silence ended with fake breathing and an exasperated voice. "You know, I can hope it's Carl. Because if this was a random thing, like some hobo riding the rails or something, then nobody's ever going to find out what happened."

Lucas tried silence.

After a while, Wade said, "You don't have any excuses. I'm looking at the race's roster. Your only competition is Harris, and he can't hang with you."

"It's just the Jingle Bells," said Lucas. "A nothing run."

Another pause.

Another long sip of coffee.

Then the dead man said, "Win a race, Lucas. Just one race. Then you can talk all you want about nothings."

Trees surrender to flattened grass and little stands of sumac. The sky hasn't changed, but the scattered clouds seem higher than before and the polished blue above the world is bright enough to make eyes water and blink. Diving into the grass, the twisting trail decides to narrow, and then like a man regaining his concentration, it straightens—a tidy little gully etched into the native black sod. Lucas runs into the meadow, out where he can see and be seen, and that's where he stops. Nobody follows. Certain teeth ache when he stares into the wind, and he pulls down his sleeves and kneels slightly, listening and waiting. He soon becomes an expert in the sound of wind. It isn't just one noise, but instead wind is endless overlapping noises, each coming from some different place, each hurrying to find ears that want to hear voices and words and sad cries that were never there.

Lucas touches his phone. Eyes scroll and blink to make the call. What isn't a second phone rings in a place that isn't a place. After four rings, he expects voice-mail. But the fifth ring breaks early.

"What are you doing?" says the voice.

"Standing. What are you doing?"

"Standing," says Wade.

"Why aren't you running with us?"

"Nobody wanted to talk before. So I turned early and finished." A lip-smack sound comes across. "Have I ever told you? The coffee always tastes great over here."

Lucas stands, knees a little achy

"Everybody's panting, judging by these paces I've been watching."

"Do you know where they are?" Lucas says.

"Standing where you left Jaeger, mostly."

"Mostly?"

"I've got one phone moving."

"But you can't watch Carl. He doesn't carry a phone."

"Even if he did, I wouldn't know anything. A person has to call a person, and the line has to be opened. That's how I get a lock on positions. And I don't think the Jaeger wants to trade running stories with me."

"By the way," Lucas says. "Carl looks pretty innocent."

"Yeah, I'm thinking the shit might have gotten himself a bad break."

"And what do you think about me?" Lucas says.

Silence is the answer, persistent and unnerving.

"So how long does a phone lock last?" Lucas says.

"Four hours, give or take. Then the AI attendant spills me back into the normal mode."

Lucas digs his mittens out of his tights, warming the fingers. "You said one phone is moving." Then he says, "Never mind, I see her."

A brown cap and a pale little face comes out from the trees, the ponytail swaying behind.

"How's Sarah look?" Wade says.

"Real, real tired."

"Poor girl."

"Yeah."

What isn't quite a laugh comes into his ear. "I pester you," says Wade. "I know you don't like it sometimes. But she's a lot worse about calling me, and usually for no good reason."

"See you, Wade."

"Yeah," the voice says. "Take care."

Sarah wants to hurry, but the legs are short and stiff. She shuffles and cries and then stops crying. She comes at Lucas with her face twisting, fresh agonies piled on the old, and as soon as she is in arm's length, she makes a fist inside the pink mitten and jabs at his stomach. But even the arms are drained. Lucas catches the fist between his hands. She can't hurt him, so he lowers his hands. "Okay," he says, sticking his stomach out. "If it helps."

Sarah doesn't hit. She falls to her knees, sobbing hard.

Nobody moves in the woods to the north. To the west is the unseen creek with its shackling trees. The empty Amtrak line runs down the east side of the park. A quarter mile south stands a row of ancient cottonwoods, tall as hills, the silvery bark glowing in the rising light. Past those trees is a second rail line. A long oak trestle was built across the floodplain and the older line where the Amtrak would eventually run. Dirt was brought in and dumped under the trestle, creating a tall dark ridge. That line was abandoned decades ago. The rails were pulled up for scrap, old ties sold to gardeners. Only the ridge remains, sprouting trees and angling across the park on its way to towns that exist as history and as memory and as drab little dots on yellowed maps.

Sarah stands and takes in one worthless breath. "You told Jaeger," she says. "You think somebody hired somebody."

Lucas watches her.

"Somebody paid a professional to kill Wade. Is that what you're thinking?"

"No," he says. "I don't think a person put down money to have it done."

She watches him.

"Remember that guy who was kiting checks?" he says. "I once mentioned him to Wade, that I had this bad feeling about the Stingray man. What was his name?"

"Wails."

"Something about Wails was wrong. Talking to the guy, I could see that he was full of shit. I didn't think of check-kitting and stealing millions. That wasn't what I expect. But I told Wade what I thought, and you know him. He took me seriously. 'I'll make some inquiries, see what's what,' he said. Then a week later, cops opened an investigation, and a couple days after that, Wails drove out here . . . to the parking lot we just ran through, if I remember this right . . . and killed himself . . ."

"But that was a year ago," Sarah says. "Wade was still alive."

"I didn't say Mr. Wails hired it. I'm asking: What if he had a backup?"

She says nothing, staring past his face now.

"I'm not talking about an official, carry-the-same-name kind of backup," he says. "There have to be ways to fake a name and slip clear of your past life, living in the clouds like Wade does. Being everywhere, nowhere. Sitting on whatever stolen money the man was able to hide, and nothing to do with its days but get angrier and angrier about the son-of-a-bitch that made this happen."

Sarah lifts both hands, piling them on top of her head while she slowly rocks back and forth.

"Wail's backup hates Wade Tanner. So he goes out into the living world and finds somebody to help get revenge. Maybe it's for the money, or maybe for personal reasons. And like Carl says, it has to be somebody strong enough and fast enough to keep close to Wade when they're running."

Sarah drops her arms, leaning into Lucas.

He holds her and looks everywhere. The world moves under the wind, but there aren't any people. After another half minute, he says, "I was guessing Pete. He's got the muscle and enough pop in the legs. I figured I was going to see him come out of the trees, looking to shut me up. You I didn't expect."

"It isn't Pete," she says.

"Yeah, I don't want it to be."

"No. I mean it isn't him."

"Why not?"

She pulls out of his grip, wiping her swollen eyes. "Pete made us run this course. Remember? And Jaeger just happened to be up on the levee at the right time. Those aren't coincidences. While we were chasing you, Pete explained everything. He said he bumped into Jaeger last week and threw a few insults at him, and Carl came back with the same arguments he used on the bridge. That's when Pete started to believe him. He began wondering that if Carl wasn't guilty, then maybe the best suspect left was you."

Lucas keeps watch to the north, and nothing changes.

A hard sorry laugh comes out of her. "You won't believe this," she says. "Probably nobody would at this point. But I want you to know: I have never, ever cheated on my husband. Not with Masters, and not even with Wade."

Lucas listens to the winds, waiting.

Then she giggles, brightly and suddenly, saying, "But of course it doesn't count, playing games with a machine."

Lucas shakes his head and breathes.

"Harris," he says.

"What?"

"Maybe he's the killer."

"It can't be," she says. "Pete looked at the kid, sure. We know he's strange and we don't know much about his story. But like Carl says, this was a personal killing. A fury killing. Pete says that an ex-Mormon goofball who isn't here six weeks isn't going to want to hurt Wade Tanner. That's why Pete sent him charging off in the wrong direction this morning. He's not a suspect."

"He's telling you that? In front of the kid?"

She shakes her head. "No, Harris was gone by then."

"Gone?"

"The train went past and we caught up to Carl, and Carl gave us your message, and then we stood there talking. And then Harris said we were nuts and stupid and he'd rather run with the deer than waste time standing around with old farts. So he ran back to the train tracks and headed . . . I don't remember where . . ."

Lucas says nothing.

Sarah takes a breath and holds it. Then all at once, her eyes become big, and she says, "What if . . . ?"

Lucas tells his phone to redial.

Wade picks up and says, "Still standing, still drinking my coffee."

"So," Lucas says. "You talk to Harris today?"

A very brief silence ends with the sound of people being politely quiet, ten million backups stuffed inside that very crowded room. And from the busy silence, Wade says, "Today? No, I haven't talked to the boy. Why? What's our new stallion up to?"

The meadow trail leads south to the cottonwoods. Where shadows begin, Lucas stops and stows the mittens and looks back. Sarah is slowly making her way to the north edge of the grass, and the rest of the runners have come out to meet her.

Jaeger stands in the middle of the group. Hands on hips or on top of their heads, they look like soldiers in mismatched uniforms ready to quit the war. Sarah stops and talks, pointing back at Lucas, and everybody stares across the grass, and he can feel the doubts and suspicions thrown his way.

Turning, he settles into a lazy trot.

The forest trail snakes its way toward Ash Creek. The abandoned rail line stands on his left, capped with a second trail that leads over the Amtrak line and back into town. Harris could be running the old right-of-way. If he was smart, the kid is galloping home now to pack a bag and make some last-second escape. But that would be sensible, and sensible isn't Harris. He's a charger and a brawler. And besides, he found them in the middle of a forest. So the boy isn't completely stupid, and he has some clever way of tracking people.

The five o'clock calls come back to Lucas—the sexy woman and the desperate father. Either one of them could have been Wails faking a voice to patch into the tracking system. But that feels unlikely. Why not just let him pick up, and then hang up? But maybe there's some other trick. Trying to think it through, Lucas realizes that he isn't running and can't remember when he stopped. Staring at the ground, not certain about his own thoughts, his eyes grab onto his ankle, and he bends and pulls up the muddy black leg of the tights, staring at that fancy bracelet that does nothing but shouts at the world that he is here and he is sober.

Lucas straightens and turns one full circle. Something is moving on top of the old trestle, but then the background of tree limbs swallows it. Or it never was. Lucas falls into running again, easy long steps eating distance. Get past the trestle, and a dozen trails are waiting to be followed, and there's a hundred ways out of the park. But the best obvious plan is dialing 911, or at least calling somebody closer. Audrey. Lucas decides on her and touches the phone, and he touches it again when nothing happens. But despite having power and a green light, the machine refuses to find the world beyond.

Lucas stops and looks left.

A yellow shirt is on the high ground, not even pretending to hide. The face above it smiles, and maybe it tries laughing. Harris wants to laugh. He stands still, looking down at Lucas while saying a word or two. His glasses are clear enough to show the eyes. He is close enough that the bloody lip looks big and sweat makes the boy-face bright. Some little voice needs to be listened to, and he nods and says something else. Then the right hand lifts, holding a chunk of rusted steel—a piece of trash shaped by chance to resemble a small hatchet.

Harris lifts a foot and drops it.

Lucas breaks, sprinting toward the creek. This time he doesn't obey the trail, cutting across the hard-frozen dirt wherever the brush is thin. He looks down and ahead, and ten strides into this race he turns stupid. It isn't just the world that narrows. His mind empties, his entire day going away. Oxygen-starved and terrified, the brain drops into wild panic, and every step tries to be the biggest, and every downed limb and little gully is jumped with a grace that will never be duplicated. He doesn't know where Harris is, and really, it doesn't matter. Nothing counts but speed and conquering distance, and that wild perfect urgency lasts for most of a minute. And then Lucas runs dry of fuel and breath.

He slows, tasting blood in his throat.

He throws a glance to his left.

The earth wall is close and tall, and Harris runs on top. The kid has never looked this serious, this mature. To somebody, he says, "Yeah." Then he slows and makes a sharp turn, jumping onto a little deer trail that puts him behind Lucas, maybe twenty meters back.

That feels like a victory, owning the lead.

But Lucas can't turn back now. Not without risking a hack from that piece of metal. Or worse than a hack. He throttles up again, and Harris matches his pace, and he cuts across that last loop in the trail, raspberry bushes snagging his tights. Then he slows, letting the kid buy maybe half of the distance between them while he makes ready for the next turn.

Rusted iron legs hold the vanished tracks high above the stream. The trail lurches to the left and drops under the trestle, and then it lifts again, flattening and turning right before reaching a long pipe-and-wood bridge. Lucas runs the curve tight, saving a half-stride. Maybe ten meters separate them. Maybe eight. He listens to the chasing feet, measuring their pounding. Instinct knows what happens next: As soon as Harris is free of the bridge, he surges. Youth and fear and all that good rich adrenaline are going to demand that Harris ends this race here, in the next moments. That's why Lucas surges first. He leaps off the end of the bridge and gains a little, but the pounding behind him ends with some fast clean footfalls that halve the distance and then halve it again. Harris is tucked behind him. A small last surge will put him in range, leaving the boy where he can clip Lucas with his weapon.

But Lucas shortens his stride, just to help his legs move quicker, and Harris is paying a cost for matching him. He gives a hard grunt before accelerating. Except he has somehow fallen back another couple strides, and his exasperation comes out from his chest. He curses—not a word so much as an animal sound that says everything. Those baby legs start to fill with cement. Frustrated and baffled but still too stupid and young to know what has happened, Harris slows down just a little more. His intention is to rest on the fly, gathering his reserves for another surge. This will be easy, in the end. He can't believe anything else. Lucas is nearly twice his age, and there's only one ending in his head, stark and bloody and final. Harris lets the old man gain a full fifteen-meter lead, and just to make sure that Lucas knows, he calls out to him. He says, "Give up." He breathes and says, "You can't win."

Lucas has won. He knows it, and the only problem left is mapping out the rest of this chase.

During one of the big storms last summer, an old cottonwood tumbled across the trail. The city didn't have the money to remove it, and feet and bike tires made a new trail before winter. Trees fall and detours are made, and that's one reason why there aren't many straight lines in the woods. Chainsaws and rot take away the trunks, but new twists are added and established and eventually preferred. The dead tell the living where to walk, and the living never realize that that's what they are doing, and it's like that everywhere and with everything, always.

Big turns are coming. Three, maybe four loops are going to practically double back for a few strides. Lucas doesn't know which one to use, but his plan, much as he plans anything, is to work Harris into a numb half-beaten state and then take him around and jump through the brush, heading north again. But always keeping just ahead, teasing the kid with the idea that at any moment his luck will change, that his legs will get thirty minutes younger and he'll close the gap between him and this gray old fool who doesn't understand that he is beaten.

TEN

The annual track club meeting was held in the restaurant's basement. A stale shabby room was crowded with long tables and folding chairs and fit if not always skinny bodies. Paper plates were stacked with pizza and breadsticks, tall plastic cups full of pop and beer. Conversations centered on the January's fine weather and yesterday's long run from the Y, bits of grim international news making it into the chatter. The Y group had claimed the back table, fending off most of the invaders. Chance placed Masters' wife at one end—a heavily made-up woman who made no secret of her extraordinary boredom. Sarah sat between her husband and Crouse, her focus centered on photographs of the new baby. Pete and Varner and Gatlin ruled the room's back corner, entertaining themselves with catty comments about everybody, including each other. Lucas was in the middle of the table, facing the rest of the party. Everybody was keenly aware that he was drinking Pepsi. Audrey had brought her daughter—the fastest fourth-grader in the state—and in a shrewd bid of manipulation set her next to Lucas. Children liked the rough voice and kid-like manner, and the girl was a relentless flirt. She said she liked watching him run. She said the two of them should run together sometime, and Mom could come along, if she could keep up. She asked Lucas how he trained and did he warm up ever and why didn't he ever get hurt?

Harris was sitting on the other side of Lucas. A big bellowing cackle grabbed everyone's attention, and with a matching voice he said, "He doesn't get hurt because of the booze, darling. Beer keeps joints limber."

Embarrassed silence took hold.

Even Harris took note. Trying to make amends, he gave Lucas a friendly punch in the shoulder, and when that wasn't sufficiently charming, he leaned back and said, "Naw, I'm just teasing. Forget it."

Pete noticed. Saying nothing, he stood and wormed his way along the back wall, reaching around Lucas to grab up the Pepsi, taking a long experimental sip. Then he smacked his lips, saying, "Just checking," and he gave Harris a big wink, as if they shared the same joke. The kid laughed and shook his head. Pete set the cup aside, and as his hand pulled away, he kicked a table leg, and as the cup started to tumble, he made a show of reaching out, pushing it and its sticky dark contents into Harris' lap.

The boy cursed, but in a good-natured, only half-pissed way. And the rest of the runners choked their laughs until he had vanished into the bathroom.

Sarah used the distraction to slip away.

Masters' wife noticed the second empty chair. From her regal place at the end of the table, she said to her husband, "What's your girl doing at the podium? She's talking to that camera, isn't she?"

Masters squirmed and said nothing.

Always helpful, Crouse said, "Wade's backup is watching. Don't tell him, but we're giving him a special award tonight."

The woman sneered. Then because it was such an important point, she used a loud voice to tell everybody, "The man is dead. He has been dead for months, and I think you're crazy to play this game."

A new silence grabbed hold. Some eyes watched Masters, wishing that he would say or do anything to prove he had a spine. Oddly though, it was Sarah's husband who took offense. A boyish fellow, small but naturally stout, he possessed a variety of conflicting feelings about many subjects, including Sarah's weakness for one man's memory. But defending his wife mattered, and that's why he leaned across Crouse's lap to say, "You should know, lady. All that makeup and with that poker stuck up your ass, you look more dead than most ghosts do."

The woman blushed, and she straightened. And after careful consideration, she picked up her tiny purse and said, "I'm leaving."

Masters nodded, saying nothing.

"I need the car keys," she said to him.

Then with the beginnings of a smile, Masters said, "It's a nice evening, honey. Darling. A long walk would do you some good."

The pace is barely faster than knuckle-walking. Lucas pushes north, crossing old ground, the wind chilling his face but nothing else. He's going to hurt tomorrow, but nothing feels particularly tired right now. His breathing is easy, legs strong. The trail is smooth and mostly straight, and he has a thirty-meter lead, except when he forgets and works too hard, and then he has to fall back, pretending to be spent, giving Harris reason to surge again. Or he fakes rolling his ankle in a hole. Twice he does that trick, limping badly, and Harris breathes hard and closes the gap, only to see his quarry heal instantly and recover the lead in another few seconds.

The third ankle sprain doesn't fool anyone. Lucas looks back, making certain Harris sees his smile, and then on the next flat straight piece of trail he extends his lead before turning around, running backwards, using the same big laugh that the kid uses on everybody else.

Furious, Harris stops and flings the steel weapon.

Lucas sidesteps it and keeps trotting backwards, letting the kid come close, and then he wheels and sprints, saying, "So after Wade died . . . why did you stay in town?"

"I didn't kill the guy," Harris says.

"Good to hear," Lucas says. "But why stay? Why not pull up and go somewhere else?"

"Because I like it here."

"Good."

"I'm the fastest runner here," he says. "And I like winning races."

Slower runners are up ahead. Everybody looks warm and exhausted, survival strides carrying them toward Lucas. He didn't expect to see them, but nothing that has happened today has made him any happier. "So you didn't kill Wade?" he says.

"No."

"Then why are you chasing me?"

Somehow Harris manages to laugh. "I'm not," he says. "I'm just out for a run, and I'm letting you lead."

Audrey and Carl are leading their pack. Lucas surges to meet up with them, and he stops and turns, and Harris stops with that good thirty meters separating him from the others. Everybody shakes from fatigue, but the kid can barely stand. All of his energy feeds a face that looks defiant and unconcerned and stupid. With a snarl, he says, "I brought the son-of-a-bitch back to you. See?"

Lucas shrugs and says, "Harris killed him. He told me."

"I did not."

"I heard you," Lucas says. Then to the others, he says, "Take us both in. Let the cops sort the evidence. Like those glasses of his . . . I bet they've got some juicy clues hidden in the gears."

Harris pulls off the glasses.

"Watch it," says Pete.

Harris throws the glasses on the ground and lifts a leg, ready to crush the fancy machinery into smaller and smaller bits. But Carl is already running, and the kid manages only two sloppy stomps before he is picked up and thrown down on his side, ribs breaking even before the bony knee is driven into his chest.

"We weren't sure what to do," Pete says to Lucas. "Some of us thought you were guilty, others didn't want to think that. We tried calling you, and when you didn't pick up, I figured you had to be running for Mexico."

Harris tries to stand, and Carl beats him down again.

"We took a vote," Varner says. "Would we come looking for you, or would we just head back to the Y?"

"So I won," Lucas says, smiling.

Audrey dips her head and laughs.

Sarah is next to Carl, watching the mayhem up close.

"No, you only got three votes," Pete says. "But you know how this group makes decisions. The loudest wins, and Audrey just about blew up, trying to get us chasing you."

Lucas looks at her and smiles.

And she rolls her eyes, wanting to tell him something. The words are ready. But not here, not like this.

Then Sarah steps up and hits the cowering figure. She kicks once and again, and polishing her technique, she delivers a hard third impact to the side of the stomach. That's when Masters pulls her away, holding her as she squirms, saying words that don't help. And Carl kneels and pokes once more at the aching ribs, and he picks up every piece of the broken glasses, talking to the ground as he works, saying, "Okay. Now. What are we going to do?"

Back from the bathroom, Harris made a final pass of the food table before reclaiming the chair next to Lucas. Then the track club president—a wizened exrunner with two new knees—leaned against the podium, reciting the same jokes he used last year before attacking the annual business. Board members talked long about silly crap, and race directors talked way too long about last year's events and all the new runners that were coming from everywhere to live here. Then awards were handed out, including a golden plaque to the police chief who let the track club borrow his officers and his streets. But the chief had some last-minute conflict and couldn't attend, and nobody else from the department was ready to accept on his behalf. With a big mocking voice, Pete said, "They're out in the world, solving crimes." And most of his table understood the reference, laughing up until Coach Able and Tom Hubble met at the podium.

Both men were lugging the night's biggest award.

For five long minutes, the presenters took turns praising the dead man. Lucas listened, or at least pretended to listen. Little pieces of the story seemed fresh, but mostly it was old news made simple and pretty. Mostly he found himself watching the serious faces at his table, everybody staring at their plates and their folded hands. Even Harris held himself still, nodding at the proper moments and then applauding politely when the big plaque was unveiled and shown to a camera and the weird, half-real entity that nobody had ever seen.

Then the backup's voice was talking, thanking everybody for this great honor and promising that he would treasure this moment. Sometimes Wade sounded close to tears. Other times he was reading from a prepared speech. "I wish things had gone differently," he said. "But I have no regrets, not for a moment of my life. And if there's any consolation, I want you to know that I am busy here, in this realm, and I am happy."

Then he was done, and maybe he was gone, and the uncomfortable applause began and ended, and the room stood to leave. Most of the back table wanted a good look at the plaque, but somehow Lucas didn't feel like it. He found himself walking toward the stairs, and Harris fell in beside him, laughing quietly.

Or maybe the kid wasn't laughing. Lucas looked at him, seeing nothing but a serious little smile.

"Want to run tomorrow?" said Harris.

"No."

"Tuesday at the track?"

"Probably."

Harris beat him to the stairs, and Harris held the door for the old man. Then as they were stepping into the cool dark, he said, "You know what? We're all going to be living there someday. Where Wade is now."

"Not me," said Lucas.

"Why not you?"

"Because," he said, "I'm planning to die when I die."

ELEVEN

Another pot of coffee helps take the chill out of the kitchen. Out the back door, Lucas watches snowflakes falling from a clear sky—tiny dry flakes too scarce to ever meet up with each other, much less make anything that matters. He has been talking steadily for several minutes, telling the story fast and pushing toward the finish, and only sometimes does he pause to sip at the coffee. Once or twice he pauses just to pause. Then Wade comes out of the silence, making a comment or posing some little question.

"So after Sarah kicked the shit out of him," he says. "What did you do with the bastard?"

"We picked him up and took turns dragging him and carrying him back to the old right-of-way, then across the creek and out to Foster. That was the closest road, and we got lucky. Some fellow was driving his pickup out of town, hunting for firewood. Except for his chain saw, the truck bed was empty. Gatlin promised him a hundred dollars to take us back to the Y, and Crouse called his sister-in-law, giving her a head's up. The girls rode inside the cab, in the heat, and the rest of us just about died of frostbite. But we lived and made it back before ten-thirty, and the cops were waiting, and I've never been so happy to see them."

"Has he confessed?"

"You mean, did Harris break down and sob and say, 'Oh God, I did such an awful thing.' No. No, he didn't and he won't. I don't think he even knows that he's a wicked son-of-a-bitch."

"I guess he wouldn't."

"Harris probably doesn't believe this is going to mean anything. In the end." Lucas takes a long sip, shaking his head. "When we were marching him out of the trees, he said to me, 'There's nothing to find. That phone's new. It isn't going to show anything important. Any money that I've got has a good story behind it. And the physical evidence is so thin it took them months just to throw Carlie back into the free world. So what happens to me? A couple months in jail, a lot of stupid interviews, and I'll tell them nothing, and they'll have to let me go too.'"

Silence.

Lucas sets the empty cup on the table, using his other hand to shift the unfamiliar phone back against his ear. "I don't know, Wade. Maybe you should be careful."

"Careful of what?"

"Wails," he says. "Yeah, I told the cops my guess. My theory. I don't think they took it to heart much. But then again, this is a whole different kind of crime. Law enforcement doesn't like things tough. They're happiest when there's bloody boot prints leading to the killer's door."

The backup laughs.

Lucas doesn't. Leaning forward in his chair, he says, "My phone still doesn't work."

"You borrowed that one. I see that."

"Masters says that it was a Trojan or worm or something. Set in long ago, ready for the signal to attack."

"I'll buy you a new phone," Wade says. "That's no problem."

"Yeah, but there's a bigger problem."

"What?"

"Wails," Lucas said. "I was tired when I remembered him this morning. My head was pretty soggy. But the story made a lot of sense, at least for the next couple hours. Except while I sitting at the Y, chatting with the detectives, little things started bugging me."

"Things?"

"About Wails, I mean. Sure, the guy stole money and killed himself. But do we even know you were the reason he got found out?"

"I don't know if I was," says the backup.

"You've said that before. I remember. You aren't sure what happened, because that's one of those stories that the real Wade never told you." Water is running hard in the basement. Lucas doesn't hear it until it shuts off. "Anyway," he says, "I think it's a lot of supposing, putting everything on this one dead man. Yeah, the guy was a liar and a big-time thief, but that's a long way from coming out of the grave to kill another man who's did him harm."

Silence.

"But somebody got Harris to kill you," says Lucas. "And if it wasn't Wails, that leaves one suspect that looks pretty good."

"Okay. Who?"

"I'm just talking, my head clear and thinking straight now."

"And I'm listening."

"Okay, it's somebody who wants everything to be fair. Somebody who would do anything he can to make the world right. The same person that let me climb into my own car drunk and watched me drive off and then went and called the cops on me."

"I didn't make that call, Lucas. Wade did."

"But you're based on him. Except for the differences, and maybe they're big differences. I don't know. Or maybe the two of you were exactly the same, and you're Wade Tanner in every way. But Wade didn't tell you everything about himself. We know that. And one day, maybe by accident, you discovered something about your human that really, really pissed you off. The man who built you was a lying shit, or worse. And there you were, wearing Wade's personality. Wade wouldn't let that business drop, and you couldn't either. That's why you went out into the world. You trolled for somebody with little sense and a big need for cash, and that's why Harris showed up here. Maybe murder wasn't your goal. There was that long break between the first hits and the killing. Maybe you were trying to keep Harris from finishing the job. But that's the pretty way to dress up this story. I'm guessing the delay was so that you got your chance to scream at the dying man, telling Wade that he was a miserable disappointment, and by the way, thanks for the money and the immortality and all that other good crap."

Silence.

"You still there?"

"I can't believe this," the voice says.

Lucas nods, saying, "But even if I believe it, nothing is proved. There's probably no evidence waiting out there. Voices can be doctored, which means Harris probably doesn't know who really hired him. Besides, even if I found people to buy this story, something like you has had months to erase clues and files, and even more important, make yourself comfortable with the situation."

"But, Lucas, how can you think that about me? Even for a minute."

"I'm talking about a voice," Lucas says. "That's what you are. At the end of the day, you're a string of words coming out with a certain sound, and I can't know anything for sure."

Silence.

"You there?"

Nobody is. The line has been severed.

Lucas pulls the phone away from his face, setting it on the table next to the empty mug. Then Audrey comes out of the basement, wearing borrowed sweats and heavy socks.

She sits opposite him, smiling and waiting.

"I need to shower," he says.

She smiles and says, "How does it feel?"

"How's what feel?"

"Being the fastest runner in the county."

He shrugs and says, "Not on these legs, I'm not."

She says, "I heard you talking just now. Who was it?"

He watches her face and says, "It's snowing out."

She turns to look.

"No, wait," he says. "I guess it stopped."

honorable mentions: 2010

Joe Abercrombie, "The Fool Jobs," *Swords & Dark Magic*.

Saladin Ahmed, "Doctor Diablo Goes Through the Motions," *Strange Horizons*, February 15.

——, "The Faithful Soldier, Prompted," *Apex Magazine*, November.

Nina Allan, "The Upstairs Window," *Interzone* 230.

Michael Alexander, "Advances in Modern Chemotherapy," *F&SF*, July/August.

——, "Ware of the Worlds," *Fantasy & Science Fiction*, November/December.

Ken Altabef, "The Lost Elephants of Kenyisha," *Fantasy & Science Fiction*, July/August.

Charlie Jane Anders, "The Fermi Paradox Is Our Business Model," *Tor.com*.

Lou Antonelli, "Dispatches from the Troubles," *GUD*, Summer.

Eleanor Arnason, "Tomb of the Fathers," *Aqueduct Press*.

Michael A. Armstrong, "The Deadliest Moop," *Analog*, November.

Neal Asher, "The Cuisinart Effect," *Conflicts*.

Kage Baker, "The Bohemian Astrobleme," *Subterranean*, Winter.

——, "Rex Nemorensis," *The Book of Dreams*.

David Ball, "The Scroll," *Warriors*.

Peter M. Ball, "L'Esprit de L'Escalier," *Apex Magazine*, September.

——, "The Mike and Carly Story, Without the Gossip," *Shimmer* 12.

Stephen Baxter, "Earth III," *Asimov's*, June.

——, "The Ice Line," *Asimov's*, February.

——, "Project Hades," *Analog*, July/August.

Peter S. Beagle, "The Children of the Shark God," *The Beastly Bride*.

——, "Dirae," *Warriors*.

——, "Kaskia," *Songs of Love & Death*.

——, "La Lune t'Attend," *Full Moon City*.

——, "Return: An Innkeeper's World Story," *Subterranean*, Spring.

——, "Trinity County, CA," *OSCIMS*, August.

Elizabeth Bear, "Bone and Jewel Creatures," Subterranean Press.

——, "When You Visit the Magoebaskloof Hotel Be Certain Not to Miss the Samango Monkeys," *Destination: Future*.

Chris Beckett, "One Land," *Conflicts*.

Gregory Benford, "Tiny Elephants," *JBU*, February.

Paul M. Berger, "Small Burdens," *Strange Horizons*, March 11.

——, "Stereogram of the Gray Fort, in the Days of Her Glory," *Fantasy*, June 21.

Beth Bernobich, "River of Souls," *Tor.com*.

Jo Beverley, "The Marrying Maid," *Songs of Love & Death*.

K. J. Bishop, "The Heart of a Mouse," *Subterranean*, Winter.

Holly Black, "Sobek," *Wings of Fire*.

Jenny Blackford, "Velvet Revolution," *Cosmos*.

Lawrence Block, "Catch and Release," *Stories*.

——, "Clean Slate," *Warriors*.

Gregory Norman Bossert, "Freia in the Sunlight," *Asimov's*, December.

——, "Slow Boat," *Asimov's*, August.

——, "The Union of Soil and Sky," *Asimov's*, April/May.

Daniel Braum, "Mile Zero," *Electric Velocipede* 20.

Damien Broderick, "Dead Air," *Asimov's*, February.

Keith Brooke, "Sussed," *Conflicts*.

Eric Brown, "Dissimulation Procedure," *Conflicts*.

——, "Guardians of the Phoenix," *The Mammoth Book of Apocalyptic SF*.

——, "Laying the Ghost," *Clarkesworld*, October.

Tobias S. Buckell, "A Jar of Goodwill," *Clarkesworld*, May.

Jim Butcher, "Love Hurts," *Songs of Love & Death*.

Chris Butler, "Have Guitar, Will Travel," *The Immersion Book of SF*.

James L. Cambias, "How Seosiris Lost the Favor of the King," *F&SF*, September/October.

Tracy Canfield, "The Seal of Sulaymaan," *Fantasy*, July.

——, "Zookrollers Winkelden Ook," *Strange Horizons*, December.

Orson Scott Card, "Expendables," *OSCIMS*, October.

Jacqueline Carey, "You, and You Alone," *Songs of Love & Death*.

Isobelle Carmody, "The Dark Road: An Obernewtyn Story," *Legends of Australian Fantasy*.

Elizabeth Carroll, "The Duke of Vertumn's Fingerling," *Strange Horizons*, April 5.

Scott William Carter, "The Android Who Became a Human Who Became an Android," *Analog*, July/August.

Jason Chapman, "The Long Fall," *Grantville Gazette Universe Annex*.

Fred Chappell, "Uncle Moon in Raintree Hills," *F&SF*, September/October.

J. Kathleen Cheney, "Afterimage," *JBU*, April.

——, "Snow Comes to Hawk's Folly, *Panverse Two*.

C. J. Cherryh, "A Wizard of Wiscezan," *Swords & Dark Magic*.

Ted Chiang, "The Lifecycle of Software Objects," *Subterranean*, Fall.

Eric Choi, "The Son of Heaven," *The Dragon and the Stars*.

David L. Clements, "In the Long Run," *Conflicts*.

Brenda W. Clough, "The Water Weapon," *The Dragon and the Stars*.

Glen Cook, "Tides Elba: A Tale of the Black Company," *Swords & Dark Magic*.

Matthew Cook, "The Shoe Factory," *Interzone* 231.

Rick Cook, "Fishing Hole," *Analog*, May.

C.S.E. Cooney, "Braiding the Ghosts," *Clockwork Phoenix* 3.

Brenda Cooper, "The Robots' Girl," *Analog*, April.

Douglas Coupland, "Survivor," *Darwin's Bastards*.

Albert E. Cowdrey, "Death Must Die," *F&SF*, November/December.

——, "Fort Clay, Louisiana: A Tragical History," *F&SF*, March/April.

——, "Mister Sweetpants and the Living Dead," *F&SF*, July/August.

Ian Creasey, "Crimes, Follies, Misfortunes, and Love," *Asimov's*, August.

——, "The Prize Beyond Gold," *Asimov's*, December.

Benjamin Crowell, "Centaurs," *Asimov's*, March.

——, "Petopia," *Asimov's*, June.

——, "Wheat Rust," *Asimov's*, September.

Don D'Ammassa, "No Distance Too Great," *Asimov's*, October/November.

Scott Dalrymple, "Queen of the Kanguellas," *Realms of Fantasy*, December.

Eljay Daly, "Bitterdark," *Fantasy*, October.

Dennis Danvers, "The Fairy Princess," *F&SF*, March/April.

Aliette de Bodard, "Desaparecidos," *Realms of Fantasy*, June.

——, "Father's Last Ride," *The Immersion Book of SF*.

——, "The Jaguar House, In Shadow," *Asimov's*, July.

——, "The Wind-Blown Man," *Asimov's*, February.

Jeffrey Deaver, "The Therapist," *Stories*.

A. M. Dellamonica, "The Cage," *Tor.com*.

Paul Di Filippo, "Life in the Anthropocene," *The Mammoth Book of Apocalyptic SF*.

Cory Doctorow, "There's a Great Big Beautiful Tomorrow/Now is the Best Time of Your Life," *Godlike Machines*.

Aidan Doyle, "Stone Flowers," *Fantasy*, September.

Gardner Dozois, "Recidivist," *Warriors*.

Alexandra Duncan, "Amor Fugit," *F&SF*, March/April.

——, "The Door in the Earth," *F&SF*, September/October.

Kelly Dwyer, "Sunlight," *Abyss & Apex* 36.

Marianne J. Dyson, "Fly Me to the Moon," *Analog*, July/August.

Phyllis Eisenstein and Alex Eisenstein, "Von Neumann's Bug," *Gateways*.

Harlan Ellison, "How Interesting: A Tiny Man," *Realms of Fantasy*, February.

Amal El-Mohtar, "The Green Book," *Apex Magazine* 18.

James Enge, "Destroyer," *Black Gate*, Winter.

——, "The Singing Spear," *Swords & Dark Magic*.

Steve Erikson, "Goats of Glory," *Swords & Dark Magic*.

Gregory Feeley, "Kentauros," NHR Books.

Gemma Files, "Hell Friend," *Clockwork Phoenix* 3.

Charles Coleman Finlay, "Life So Dear or Place So Sweet," *The Way of the Wizard*.

Eugene Fischer, "Adrift," *Asimov's*, April/May.

Michael F. Flynn, "Cargo," *Analog*, June.

——, "On Rickety Thistlewaite," *Analog*, January/February.

Jeffrey Ford, "86 Deathdick Road," *The Book of Dreams*.

Richard Foss, "At Last the Sun," *Analog*, June.

Ben Francisco, "Crepuscular," *Shimmer* 12.

Peter Friend, "Voyage to the Moon," *Asimov's*, June.

Gregory Frost, "The Comeuppance of Creegus Maxin," *The Beastly Bride*.

——, "Lucyna's Gaze," *Clockwork Phoenix* 3.

Nancy Fulda, "Backlash," *Asimov's*, September.

Diana Gabaldon, "A Leaf on the Wind of All Hallows," *Songs of Love & Death*.

——, "The Custom of the Army," *Warriors*.

Neil Gaiman, ""The Thing About Cassandra," *Songs of Love & Death*.

——, "The Truth Is a Cave in the Black Mountains," *Stories*.

Yasmine Galenorn, "Man in the Mirror," *Songs of Love & Death*.

Stephen Gaskell, "Paper Cradle," *Clarkesworld*, September.

Sara Genge, "No Jubjub Birds Tonight," *Destination: Future*.

——, "Sins of the Fathers," *Asimov's*, December.

William Gibson, "Dougal Discarnate," *Darwin's Bastards*.

Molly Gloss, "Unforeseen," *Asimov's*, April/May.

Theodora Goss, "Fair Ladies," *Apex*, August.

——, "The Mad Scientist's Daughter," *Strange Horizons*, January 18-January 25.

John Grant, "Where Shadows Go at Low Midnight," *Clockwork Phoenix 3*.

Marlaina Gray, "Worlds Apart," *Strange Horizons*, May 17.

Simon R. Green, "Street Wizard," *The Way of the Wizard*.

Daryl Gregory, "What We Take When We Take What We Need," *Subterranean*, Spring.

Eric Gregory, "The Earth of Yunhe," *Shine*.

Lev Grossman, "End Game," *The Way of the Wizard*.

Eileen Gunn, "A Difference Engine," *Tor.com*.

——, "Day After the Cooters," *Tor.com*.

——, "Internal Devices," *Tor.com*.

——, "The Perdito Street Project," *Tor.com*.

Caren Gussoff, "Anything Chocolate," *Abyss & Apex* 33.

——, "Games," *Destination: Future*.

Joe Haldeman, "Forever Bound," *Warriors*.

Elizabeth Hand, "The Maiden Flight of McCauley's Bellerophon," *Stories*.

M.L.N. Hanover, "Hurt Me," *Songs of Love & Death*.

Jim Hawkins, "Orchestral Manoeuvres in the Dark Matter," *Interzone* 229.

Jeff Hecht, "An Adventure in the Antiquities Trade," *Daily Science Fiction*, September 1.

Samantha Henderson, "The Red Bride," *Strange Horizons*, May 7.

Robin Hobb, "Blue Boots," *Songs of Love & Death*.

——, "The Triumph," *Warriors*.

M. K. Hobson, "The Hag Queen's Curse," *Realms of Fantasy*, April.

Cecelia Holland, "Demon Lover," *Songs of Love & Death*.

——, "The King of Norway," *Warriors*.

Tom Holt, "Brownian Emotion," *Subterranean*, Spring.

Robert J. Howe, "The Natural History of Calamity," *Black Gate*, Winter.

Matthew Hughes, "Quartet and Triptych," PS Publishing.

——, "Timmy Come Home," *Is Anybody Out There?*

Jon Ingold, "The History of Poly-V," *Interzone* 227.

——, "Over Water," *Interzone* 228.

Alex Irvine, "The Word He Was Looking for Was Hello," *Is Anybody Out There?*

Alexander Jablokov, ."Plinth Without Figure," *F&SF*, November/December.

——, "Warning Label," *Asimov's*, August.

Michael Jasper & Jay Lake, "Devil on the Wind," *Black Gate*, Winter.

N. K. Jemisin, "Sinners, Saints, Dragons, and Haints, In the City Beneath the Still Waters," *Postscripts* 22/23.

Kij Johnson, "Names for Water," *Asimov's*, October/November.

——, "Ponies," *Tor.com*.

Matthew Johnson, "Holdfast," *Fantasy*, December.

Vylar Kaftan, "I'm Alive, I Love You, I'll See You in Reno," *Lightspeed*, June.

Tyler Keevil, "Hibakusha," *Interzone* 226.

James Patrick Kelly, "Plus or Minus," *Asimov's*, December.

Kay Kenyon, "Castoff World," *Shine*.

John Kessel, "The Closet," *F&SF*, November/December.

——, "Iteration," *Strange Horizons*.

Rajan Khanna, "Card Sharp," *The Way of the Wizard*.

Caitlín R. Kiernan, "The Sea Troll's Daughter," *Swords & Dark Magic*.

Alice Sola Kim, "Hwang's Billion Brilliant Daughters," *Lightspeed*, November.

——, "The Other Graces," *Asimov's*, July.

Swapna Kishore, "Where It Ends," *Strange Horizons*, August.

Walter L. Kleine, "Farallon Woman," *Analog*, May.

Leonid Korogodski, "Pink Noise", Silverberry Press.

Mary Robinette Kowal, "For Want of a Nail," *Asimov's*, September.

Bill Kte'pi, "Merrythoughts," *Strange Horizons*, March 3.

Ellen Kushner, "The Children of Cadmus," *The Beastly Bride*.

——, "The Man with the Knives," *Tor.com*.

Jay Lake, "The Baby Killers," PS Publishing.

——, "Dream of the Arrow," *Subterranean*, Summer.

——, "The Fall of the Moon," *Realms of Fantasy*, October.

——, "Human Error," *Interzone* 226.

——, "Permanent Fatal Errors," *Is Anybody Out There?*

——, "The Speed of Time," *Tor.com*.

——, "Testaments," *The Book of Dreams*.

——, "To This Their Late Escape," *The Sky That Wraps*.

——, "Torquing Vacuum," *Clarkesworld*, February.

—— and Shannon Page, "From the Countries of Her Dreams," *Fantasy*, November 22.

—— and Shannon Page, "In the Emperor's Garden," *Fantasy*, March 13.

Margo Lanagan, "The Miracle Aquilina," *Wings of Fire*.

Geoffrey A. Landis, "Marya and the Pirate," *Asimov's*, January.

John Langan, "City of the Dog," *F&SF*, January/February

David Langford, "Graffiti in the Library of Babel," *Is Anybody Out There?*

Joe R. Lansdale, "Soldierin'," *Warriors*.

Krista Hoeppner Leahy, "Too Fatal a Poison," *The Way of the Wizard*.

Ann Leckie, "Beloved of the Sun," *Beneath Ceaseless Skies*, October.

Tanith Lee, "Torhec the Sculptor," *Asimov's*, October/November.

——, "The Puma's Daughter," *The Beastly Bride*.

——, "Under/Above the Water," *Songs of Love & Death*.

Yoon Ha Lee, "Between Two Dragons," *Clarkesworld*, April.

——, "The Territorialist," *Beneath Ceaseless Skies*, July.

——, "The Winged City," *GigaNotoSaurus*, December.

Tim Lees, "Love and War," *Interzone* 230.

David D. Levine, "Pupa." *Analog*, September.

——, "Teaching the Pig to Sing," *Analog*, May.

Michael Libling, "Why That Crazy Old Lady Goes Up the Mountain," *F&SF*, May/June

Marissa Lingen, "The Six Skills of Madame Lumiere," *Beneath Ceaseless Skies*, July.

Ken Liu, "The Literomancer," *F&SF*, September/October.

Marjorie M. Liu, "After the Blood," *Songs of Love & Death*.

Barry B. Longyear, "Alten Kameraden," *Asimov's*, April/May.

Richard A. Lovett, "Spludge," *Analog*, September.

—— and Mark Niemann-Ross, "Phantom Sense," *Analog*, November.

Ian R. MacLeod, "Second Journey of the Magus," *Subterranean*, Winter.

Bruce McAllister, "Blue Fire," *F&SF*, March/April.

———, "The Courtship of the Queen," *Tor.com*.

———, "Heart of Hearts," *Albedo One*, 38.

———, "The Woman Who Waited Forever," *Asimov's*, February.

Meghan McCarron, "We Heart Vampires!!!!!!," *Strange Horizons*, May 3, May 10.

Una McCormack, "War Without End," *Conflicts*.

Jack McDevitt, "The Cassandra Project," *Lightspeed*, June.

Ian McDonald, "Tonight We Fly," *Masked*.

Sandra McDonald, "Seven Sexy Cowboy Robots," *Strange Horizons*, October.

———, "Witness," *Destination: Future*.

Martin McGrath, "Proper Little Soldier," *Conflicts*.

Maureen McHugh, "The Naturalist," *Subterranean*, Spring.

Will McIntosh, "Frankenstein, Frankenstein," *Asimov's*, October/November.

Sean McMullen, "Eight Miles," *Analog*, September.

Emily Mah, "Across the Sea," *The Dragon and the Stars*.

Joeph Mallozzi, "Downfall," *Masked*.

George R. R. Martin, "The Mystery Knight," *Warriors*.

Richard Matheson, "The Window of Time," *F&SF*, September/October.

D. T. Mitenko, "Eddie's Ants," *Asimov's*, July.

Mary Anne Mohanraj, "Talking to Elephants," *Abyss & Apex* 34

Sarah Monette, "After the Dragon," *Fantasy*, January 25.

T. L. Morganfield, "The Hearts of Man," *Realms of Fantasy*, June.

David Morrell, "My Name Is Legion," *Warriors*.

Ruth Nestvold, "The Bleeding and the Bloodless," *GigaNotoSaurus*, November.

R. Neube, "Dummy Tricks," *Asimov's*, October/November.

Kim Newman, "Kentish Glory: The Secrets of Drearcliff Grange School," *Mysteries of the Diogenes Club*.

Garth Nix, "A Suitable Present for a Sorcerous Puppet," *Swords & Dark Magic*.

———, "To Hold the Bridge: An Old Kingdom Story," *Legends of Australian Fantasy*.

Charles Oberndorf, "Writers of the Future," *F&SF*, January/February.

Nnedi Okorafor, "The Go-Slow," *The Way of the Wizard*.

Jerry Oltion, "Never Saw It Coming," *Analog*, October.

Eilis O'Neal, "Ice Moon Tale," *Abyss & Apex* 35.

———, "The Wizard's Calico Daughter," *Fantasy*, August.

Abbey Mei Otis, "Blood, Blood," *Strange Horizons*, 15/11.

———, "Sweetheart," *Tor.com*.

An Owomoyela, "Abandonware," *Fantasy*, June 28.

———, "Portage," *Apex Magazine* 16.

Paul Park, "Ghosts Doing the Orange Dance (The Parke Family Scrapbook Number IV)," *F&SF*, January/February.

K. J. Parker, "A Rich Full Week," *Swords & Dark Magic*.

———, "Amor Vincit Omnia," *Subterranean*, Summer.

———, "Blue and Gold," *Subterranean Press*.

Richard Parks, "Four Horsemen, At Their Leisure," *Tor.com*.

———, "The Queen's Reason," *LCRW* 25.

———, "Lady of the Ghost Willow," *Beneath Ceaseless Skies*, October.

Simon Petrie, "Dark Rendezvous," *Destination: Future.*

Holly Phillips, "The Rescue," *Postscripts* 22/23.

Tony Pi, "The Character of the Hound," *The Dragon and the Stars.*

——, "The Curse of Chimère," *Beneath Ceaseless Skies*, October.

——, "The Gold Silkworm," *Fantasy*, December 13.

——, "Night of the Manticore," *Abyss & Apex* 33.

Rachel Pollack, "Forever," *F&SF*, May/June.

Steven Popkes, "The Crocodiles," *F&SF*, May/June.

——, "The Secret Lives of Fairy Tales," *F&SF*, January/February.

Gareth L. Powell, "Fallout," *Conflicts.*

T. A. Pratt, "Mommy Issues of the Dead," *The Way of the Wizard.*

Tim Pratt, "Fiddle," *Daily Science Fiction*, September 6.

William Preston, "Helping Them Take the Old Man Down," *Asimov's*, March.

Tom Purdom, "Haggle Chips," *Asimov's*, July.

——, "Warfriends," *Asimov's*, December.

Mary Jo Putney, "The Demon Dancer," *Songs of Love & Death.*

Cat Rambo, "Amid the Words of War," *Lightspeed*, September.

——, "Clockwork Fairies," *Tor.com.*

——, "Surrogates," *Clockwork Phoenix 3.*

Robert Reed, "Alone," *Godlike Machines.*

——, "The Cull," *Clarkesworld*, September.

——, "Excellence," *Asimov's*, December.

——, "The Good Hand," *Asimov's*, January.

——, "The Long Retreat," *F&SF*, January/February.

——, "Pallbearer," *The Mammoth Book of Apocalyptic SF.*

——, "Pretty to Think So," *Asimov's*, April/May.

Mike Resnick, "The Incarceration of Captain Nebula," *Asimov's*, October/November.

——, "Six Blind Men and an Alien," *Subterranean*, Summer.

Alastair Reynolds, "At Budokan," *Shine.*

——, "Troika," *Godlike Machines.*

Mecurio D. Rivera, "Dance of the Kawkawroons," *Interzone* 227.

——, "In the Harsh Glow of Its Incandescent Beauty," *Interzone* 226.

Frank M. Robinson, "The Errand Boy," *Gateways.*

James Rollins, "The Pit," *Warriors.*

Benjamin Rosenbaum, "The Frog Comrade," *F&SF*, March/April.

——, "The Guy Who Worked for Money," *Shareable*, July 12.

Rudy Rucker and Bruce Sterling, "Good Night, Moon," *Tor.com.*

Kristine Kathryn Rusch, "Amelia Pillar's Etiquette for the Space Traveler," *Asimov's*, July.

——, "Becoming One with the Ghosts," *Asimov's*, October/November.

——, "The Dark Man," *Is Anybody Out There?*

——, "Hollywood Ending," *JBU*, April.

——, "The Possession of Paavo Deshin," *Analog*, January/February.

——, "The Thrill of the Hunt," *JBU*, February.

——, "The Tower," *Asimov's*, March.

Patricia Russo, "Wishes and Feathers," *Fantasy*, May 18.

Patrick Samphire, "Camelot," *Interzone* 230.

Jason Sanford, "Memoria," *Interzone* 231.

———, "The Never Never Wizard of Apalachicola," *OSCIMS*, December.

———, "Plague Birds," *Interzone* 228.

Pamela Sargent, "Mindband," *Asimov's*, April/May.

Steven Saylor, "The Eagle and the Rabbit," *Warriors*.

John Scalzi, "The President's Brain is Missing," *Tor.com*.

Ken Scholes and Jay Lake, "Looking for Truth in a Wild Blue Yonder," *Tor.com*.

Aaron Schultz, "Dr. Death vs. the Vampire," *F&SF*, May/June.

Gord Sellar, "The Bodhisattvas," *Subterranean*, Spring.

———, "The Broken Pathway," *The Immersion Book of SF*.

———, "Sarging Rasmussen: A Report by Organic," *Shine*.

Priya Sharma, "The Nature of Bees," *Albedo One*.

Lucius Shepard, "The Company He Keeps," *Postscripts* 22/23.

———, "Dream Burgers at the Mouth of Hell," *The Book of Dreams*.

———, "The Flock," *The Beastly Bride*.

———, "The Taborin Scale," *Subterranean*, Summer.

Felicity Shoulders, "Conditional Love," *Asimov's*, January.

———, "The Termite Queen of Tallulah County," *Asimov's*, October/November.

——— and Leslie What, "Rare Earth," *Is Anybody Out There?*

Robert Silverberg, "Dark Times at the Midnight Market," *Swords & Dark Magic*.

———, "Defenders of the Frontier," *Warriors*.

———, "The Prisoner," *The Book of Dreams*.

Cyril Simsa, "Daughters of Fortune," *Electric Velocipede* 20.

Linnea Sinclair, "Courting Trouble," *Songs of Love & Death*.

Vandana Singh, "Somadeva: a Sky River Sutra," *Strange Horizons*, March 29.

Alan Smale, "A Clash of Eagles," *Panverse Two*.

———, "High Art," *Abyss & Apex* 36.

Melinda M. Snodgrass, "The Wayfarer's Advice," *Songs of Love & Death*.

Bud Sparhawk, "The Tortuous Path," *Abyss & Apex* 33.

Justin Stanchfield, "Ghosts Come Home," *Analog*, October.

Allen M. Steele, "The Great Galactic Ghoul," *Analog*, October.

———, "The Jekyll Island Horror," *Asimov's*, January.

———, "Zoo Team," *Analog*, November.

Bruce Sterling, "The Exterminator's Want-Ad," *Shareable Futures*, June.

S. M. Stirling, "Ancient Ways," *Warriors*.

Jason Stoddard, "Overhead," *Shine*.

Eric James Stone, "That Leviathan, Who Thou Hast Made," *Analog*, October.

Tim Sullivan, "Star-Crossed," *F&SF*, March/April.

Michael Swanwick, "Goblin Lake," *Stories*.

———, "Spirits in the Night," *Abyss & Apex* 36.

———, "Steadfast Castle," *F&SF*, September/October.

——— and Eileen Gunn, "The Trains That Climb the Winter Tree," *Tor.com*.

Rachel Swirsky, "The Lady Who Plucked Red Flowers Beneath the Queen's Window," *Subterranean*, Summer.

———, "The Monster's Million Faces," *Tor.com*.

———, "The Stable-Master's Tale," *Fantasy*, July 5.

Midori Snider, "The Monkey Bride," *The Beastly Bride*.

David Tallerman, "Jenny's Sick," *Lightspeed*, December.

Steve Rasnic Tem, "A Letter from the Emperor," *Asimov's*, January.

Lavie Tidhar, "Aphrodisia," *Strange Horizons*, September.

——, "Butterfly and the Blight at the Heart of the World," *Daily Science Fiction*, 9/3.

——, "Cloud Permutations," PS Publishing.

——, "The Insurance Agent," *Interzone* 230.

——, "Lode Stars," *The Immersion Book of SF*.

——, "The Monks of Udom Xhai," *Abyss & Apex* 34.

——, "Monsters," *Fantasy*, October 18.

——, "The Solnet Ascendancy," *Shine*.

E. Catherine Tobler, "Island Lake," *The Beastly Bride*.

Sarah Totton, "Malleus, Incus, Stapes," *Fantasy*, December 20.

Ian Tregillis, "What Doctor Gottlieb Saw," *Tor.com*.

——, "Still Life (A Sexagesimal Fairy Tale)," *Apex Magazine*, October.

Harry Turtledove, "Vilcabamba," *Tor.com*.

Lisa Tuttle, "His Wolf," *Songs of Love & Death*.

Catherynne M. Valente, "How to Become a Mars Overlord," *Lightspeed*, August.

Genevieve Valentine, "So Deep That the Bottom Could Not Be Seen," *The Way of the Wizard*.

Carrie Vaughn, "The Girls from Avenger," *Warriors*.

——, "Rooftops," *Songs of Love & Death*.

Vernor Vinge, "A Preliminary Assessment of the Drake Equation, an Excerpt from the Memoirs of Starcaptain Y.-T. Lee," *Gateways*.

Wendy N. Wagner, "The Secret of Calling Rabbits," *The Way of the Wizard*.

Howard Waldrop, "Ninieslando," *Warriors*.

Don Webb, "The Man Who Scared Lovecraft," *Postscripts* 22/23.

David Weber, "Out of the Dark," *Warriors*.

K. D. Wentworth, "The Embians," *Destination: Future*.

Ian Werkheiser, "Variations," *Asimov's*, December.

Dean Whitlock, "Nanosferatu," *F&SF*, January/February.

Rick Wilber, "Several Items of Interest," *Asimov's*, October/November.

Kate Wilhelm, "Changing the World," *Asimov's*, October/November.

——, "The Late Night Train," *F&SF*, January/February.

Sean Williams, "A Glimpse of the Marvelous Structure (and the Threat It Entails)," *Godlike Machines*.

——, "The Spark (A Romance in Four Acts): A Tale of the Change," *Legends of Australian Fantasy*.

Michael D. Winkle, "The Curious Adventure of the Jersey Devil," *Panverse Two*.

Gene Wolfe, "Bloodsport," *Swords & Dark Magic*.

——, "King Rat," *Gateways*.

——, "Innocent," *Full Moon City*.

——, "Leif in the Wind," *Stories*.

John C. Wright, "Murder in Metachronopolis," *Clockwork Phoenix 3*.

Christie Yant, "The Magician and the Maid and Other Stories," *The Way of the Wizard*.

Caroline M. Yoachim, "The Sometimes Child," *Fantasy*, May 3.

——, "Stone Wall Truth," *Asimov's*, February.

——, "What Happens in Vegas," *GUD*, Summer.

Marly Youmans, "The Salamander Fire," *The Beastly Bride*.
Melissa Yuan-Innes, "Iron Monk," *Interzone* 228.
Derek Zumsteg, "Ticket Inspector Gliden Becomes the First Martyr of the Glorious Human Uprising," *Asimov's*, March.